LaVyrle Spencer

THREE COMPLETE NOVELS

THREE COMPLETE NOVELS

LaVyrle Spencer

MORNING GLORY
VOWS
THE GAMBLE

G. P. PUTNAM'S SONS   NEW YORK

G. P. Putnam's Sons
Publishers Since 1838
200 Madison Avenue
New York, NY 10016

Library of Congress Cataloging-in-Publication Data
Spencer, LaVyrle.
[Selections. 1994]
Three complete novels / LaVyrle Spencer.
p.   cm.
Contents: Morning glory—Vows—The gamble.
I. Title.   II. Title: 3 complete novels.
PS3569.P4534A6 1994   93-32684-CIP
813'.54—dc20
ISBN 0-399-13923-0

Printed in the United States of America
1   2   3   4   5   6   7   8   9   10

CONTENTS

MORNING GLORY

Prologue

❦

1917

The train pulled into Whitney, Georgia, on a leaden afternoon in November. Clouds churned and the first droplets of rain pelted like thick batter onto the black leather roof of a waiting carriage. Both of its windows were covered with black. As the train clanged to a stop, one shade was stealthily lifted aside and a single eyeball peered through the slit.

"She's here," a woman's voice hissed. "Go!"

The carriage door opened and a man stepped out. He, like the carriage, was garbed in black—suit, shoes and flat-brimmed hat worn level with the earth. He glanced neither right nor left but strode purposefully to the train steps as a young woman emerged with a baby in her arms.

"Hello, Papa," she said uncertainly, offering a wavering smile.

"Bring your bastard and come with me." He turned her roughly by an elbow and marched her back to the carriage without looking at her or the infant.

The curtained door was thrown open the instant they reached it. The young woman lurched back protectively, drawing the baby against her shoulder. Her soft hazel eyes met the hard green ones above her, framed by a black bonnet and mourning dress.

"Mama . . ."

"Get in!"

"Mama, I—"

"Get in before every soul in this town sees our shame!"

The man gave his daughter a nudge. She stumbled into the carriage, scarcely able to see through her tears. He followed quickly and grasped the reins, which were threaded through a peekhole, yielding only a murky light.

"Hurry, Albert," the woman ordered, sitting stiff as a grave marker, staring straight ahead.

He whipped the horses into a trot.

"Mama, it's a girl. Don't you want to see her?"

"See her?" The woman's mouth pursed as she continued staring straight ahead. "I'll have to, won't I, for the rest of my life, while people whisper about the devil's work you've brought to our doorstep."

The young woman clutched the child tighter. It whimpered, then as a jarring crash of thunder boomed, began crying lustily.

"Shut it up, do you hear!"

"Her name is Eleanor, Mama and—"

"Shut it up before everyone on the street hears!"

But the baby howled the entire distance from the depot, along the town square and the main road leading to the south edge of town, past a row of houses to a frame one surrounded by a picket fence with morning glories climbing its front stoop. The carriage turned in, crossed a deep front yard and pulled up near the back door. The mother and child were herded inside by the black-garbed woman and immediately a dark green shade was snapped down to cover a window, followed by another and another until every window in the house was shrouded.

The new mother was never seen leaving the house again nor were the shades ever lifted.

Chapter 1

❦

AUGUST 1941

The noon whistle blew and the saws stopped whining. Will Parker stepped back, lifted his sweat-soaked hat and wiped his forehead with a sleeve. The other millhands did the same, retreating toward the shade with voluble complaints about the heat or what kind of sandwiches their wives had packed in their lunch pails.

Will Parker had learned well not to complain. The heat hadn't affected him yet, and he had neither wife nor lunch pail. What he had were three stolen apples from somebody's backyard tree—green, they were, so green he figured he'd suffer later—and a quart of buttermilk he'd found in an unguarded well.

The men sat in the shade of the mill yard, their backs against the scaly loblolly pines, palavering while they ate. But Will Parker sat apart from the others; he was no mingler, not anymore.

"Lord a-mighty, but it's hot," a man named Elroy Moody complained, swabbing his wrinkled red neck with a wrinkled red hanky.

"And dusty," added the one called Blaylock. He hacked twice and spit into the pine needles. "Got enough sawdust in my lungs to stuff a mattress."

The foreman, Harley Overmire, performing his usual noon ritual stripped to the waist, dipped his head under the pump and came up roaring to draw attention to himself. Overmire was a sawed-off runt with a broad pug nose, tiny ears and a short neck. He had a head full of close-cropped dark hair that coiled like watchsprings and refused to stop growing at his neckline. Instead, it merely made the concession of thinning before continuing downward, giving him the hirsute appearance of an ape when he went shirtless. And Overmire loved to go shirtless. As if his excessive girth and body hair made up for his diminutive height, he exposed them whenever the opportunity arose.

Drying himself with his shirt, Overmire sauntered across the yard to join the men. He opened his lunch pail, folded back the top of his sandwich and muttered, "Sonofabitch, she forgot the mustard again." He slapped the sandwich together in disgust. "How many times I got to tell that woman it's pork plain and mustard on beef!"

"You got to train 'er, Harley," Blaylock teased. "Slap 'er upside the head one time."

"Train her, hell. We been married seventeen years. You'd think she'd know by now I want mustard on my beef." With his heel he ground the sandwich into the dry needles and cursed again.

"Here, have one o' mine," Blaylock obliged. "Bologna and cheese today."

Will Parker bit into the bitter apple, felt the saliva spurt so sharply it stung his jaws. He kept his eyes off Overmire's beef sandwich and Blaylock's spare bologna and cheese, forcing himself to think of something else.

The neatly mowed backyard where he'd ransacked the well. Pretty pink flowers blooming in a white enamel kettle sitting on a tree stump by the back door. The sound of a baby crying from inside the house. A clothesline with white sheets and white diapers and white dishtowels and enough blue denim britches that one pair wouldn't be missed, and a matching number of blue cambric shirts from which he'd nobly taken the one with a hole in the elbow. And a rainbow of towels, from which he'd selected green because somewhere in the recesses of his memory was a woman with green eyes who'd once been kind to him, making him forever prefer green over all other colors.

The green towel was wet now, wrapped around the Ball jar. He folded it aside, unscrewed the zinc lid, drank and forced himself not to grimace. The buttermilk was sickeningly sweet; even the wet towel hadn't managed to keep it cool.

With his head tilted back against the bole of the pine tree, Parker saw Overmire watching him with beady mustardseed eyes while stretching to his feet. The jar came down slowly. Equally as slowly, Parker backhanded his lips. Overmire strutted over and stopped beside Will's outstretched feet, his own widespread, firmly planted, his beefy fists akimbo.

Four days Will Parker had been here, only four this time, but he knew the look on the foreman's face as if the words had already been spoken.

"Parker?" Overmire said it loud, loud enough so all the others could hear.

Will went stiff, slow-motion like, bringing his back away from the tree and setting the fruit jar down by feel.

The foreman pushed back his straw hat, let his forehead wrinkle so all the men could see how there was nothing else he could do. "Thought you said you was from Dallas."

Will knew when to keep his mouth shut. He wiped all expression from his face and lifted his eyes to Overmire's, chewing a piece of sour apple.

"You sayin' that's where you're from?"

Will rolled to one buttock as if to rise. Overmire planted a boot on his crotch and pushed. Hard. "I'm talkin' to you, boy!" he snapped, then let his eyes rove over his underlings to make sure none of them missed this.

Parker flattened both palms against the earth at the sudden jolt of pain. "I been there," he answered stoically.

"Been in Huntsville, too, haven't you, boy?"

The strangling sense of subjugation rose like bile in Parker's throat. Familiar. Degrading. He felt the eyes of the men measuring him above their half-formed, prepotent grins. But he'd learned not to talk back to that tone of superiority, and especially not to the word "boy." He felt the cold sweat break out on his chest, the sense of helplessness at the term calculated to make one man look small, another powerful. With Overmire's boot exerting pressure, Will repressed the awful need to give vent to the loathing he felt, sealing himself in the cocoon of pretended indifference.

"They only put the tough ones in there, ain't that right, Parker?" Overmire pushed harder but Will refused to wince. Instead, he clamped a hand on the ankle, forcing the dusty boot aside. Without removing his eyes from the foreman, Will rose, picked up his battered Stetson, whacked it on his thigh and settled the brim low over his eyes.

Overmire chuckled, crossed his burly arms, and fixed the ex-convict with his beady eyes. "Word came down you killed a woman in a Texas whorehouse and you're fresh out for it. I don't think we want your kind around here where we got wives and daughters, do we fellows?" He let his eyes flick to the men briefly.

The fellows had quit rummaging through their lunch pails.

"Well, you got anything to say for yourself, boy?"

Will swallowed, felt the apple skin hitting bottom. "No, sir, except I got three and a half days' pay comin'."

"Three," Overmire corrected. "We don't count no half days around here."

Will worked a piece of apple peel between his front teeth. His jaw protruded and Harley Overmire balled his fists, getting ready. But Will only stared silently from beneath the brim of his sorry-looking cowboy hat. He didn't need to lower his eyes from Overmire's face to know what his fists looked like.

"Three," Will agreed quietly. But he hurled his apple core out beneath the pines with a fierceness that made the men start their rummaging again. Then he scooped up his towel-wrapped jar and followed Overmire into the office.

When he came back out the men were huddled around the time board. He passed among them, sealed within a bubble of dispassion, folding his nine dollars into his breast pocket, staring straight ahead, avoiding their self-righteous expressions.

"Hey, Parker," one of them called when he'd passed. "You might try the Widow Dinsmore's place. She's so hard up she'd probably even settle for a jailbird like you, ain't that right, boys?"

Jeering laughter followed, then a second voice. "Woman like that who'll put her card up in a sawmill's bound to take anything she can git."

And finally, a third voice. "You shoulda stepped a little harder on his balls, Harley, so the women around here could sleep better nights."

Will headed off through the pines. But when he saw the remains of someone's sandwich, left amid the pine needles for the birds, hunger overcame pride. He picked it up between two fingers as if it were a cigarette, and turned with a forced looseness.

"Anybody mind if I eat this?"

"Hell, no," called Overmire. "It's on me."

More laughter followed, then, "Listen, Parker, y'all give crazy Elly Dinsmore a try. No tellin' but what the two of you might hit it off right nice together. Her advertisin' for a man and you fresh outa the pen. Could be there's more'n a piece o' bread in it for y'!"

Will swung away and started walking. But he balled the bread into a hard knot and flung it back into the pine needles. Stalking away, he shut out the pain and transported himself to a place he'd never seen, where smiles were plentiful, and plates full, and people nice to one another. He no longer believed such a place existed, yet he escaped to it more and more often. When it had served its purpose he returned to reality—a dusty pine forest somewhere in northwest Georgia and a strange road ahead.

What now? he thought. Same old bullshit wherever he went. There was no such thing as serving your time; it was never over. Aw, what the hell did he care? He had no ties in this miserable jerkwater burg. Who ever heard of Whitney, Georgia, anyway? It was nothing but a flyspeck on the map and he could as easily move on as stay.

But a mile up the road he passed the same neatly tended farm where he'd stolen the buttermilk, towel and clothes; a sweet yearning pulled at his insides. A woman stood on the back porch, shaking a rug. Her hair was hidden by a dishtowel, knotted at the front. She was young and pretty and wore a pink apron, and the smell of something baking drifted out and made Will's stomach rumble. She raised a hand and waved and he hid the towel on his left side, smitten with guilt. He had a wrenching urge to walk up the drive, hand her her belongings and apologize. But he reckoned he'd scare the hell out of her if he did. And besides, he could use the towel, and probably the jar, too, if he walked on to the next town. The clothes on his back were the only ones he had.

He left the farm behind, trudging northward on a gravel road the color of fresh rust. The smell of the pines was inviting, and the look of them, all green and crisp against the red clay earth. There were so many rivers here, fast-flowing streams in a hurry to get to the sea. He'd even seen some waterfalls where the waters rushed out of the Blue Ridge foothills toward the coastal plain to the south. And orchards everywhere—peach, apple, quince and pear. Lord, what it must look like when those fruit trees bloomed. Soft pink clouds, and fragrant, too. Will had discovered within himself a deep need to experience the softer things in life since he'd gotten out of that hard place. Things he'd never noticed before—the beginning bloom on the cheek of a peach, the sun caught on a droplet of dew in a spiderweb, a pink apron on a woman with her hair tied in a clean white dishtowel.

He reached the edge of Whitney, scarcely more than a widening in the pines, a mere slip of a town dozing in the afternoon sun with little more moving than the flies about the tips of the chicory blossoms. He passed an ice house on the outskirts, a tiny railroad depot painted the color of a turnip, a wooden platform stacked with empty chicken crates, the smell of their former occupants rejuvenated by the hot sun. There was a deserted house overgrown with morning glory vines behind a seedy picket fence, then a row of occupied houses, some of red brick, others of Savannah gray, but all with verandas and rocking chairs out front, telling how many people lived in each. He came to a school building closed for the summer, and finally a town square typical of most in the south, dominated by a Baptist church and the town hall, with other businesses scattered around, interspersed by vacant lots—a drugstore, grocery, cafe, hardware, a blacksmith shop in front of which stood a brand-new gas pump topped by a white glass eagle.

He stopped before the office of the town newspaper, absently gazing at his reflection in the window. He fingered the few precious bills in his pocket, turned and glanced across the square at Vickery's Cafe, pulled his hat brim down lower and strode in that direction.

The square held a patch of green grass and a bandstand wreathed by black iron benches. In the cool splash of shade beneath an enormous magnolia tree two old men sat, whittling. They glanced up as he passed. One of them nodded, spat, then returned to his whittling.

The screen door on Vickery's Cafe had a wide red and white tin band advertising Coca-Cola. The metal was warm beneath Will's hands and the door spring sang out as he entered the place. He paused a moment to let his eyes adjust to the dimness. At a long counter, two men turned, regarded him indolently without removing their elbows from beside their coffee cups. A buxom young woman ambled the length of the counter and drawled, "Howdy. What can I do for y', honey?"

Will trained his eyes on her face to keep them off the row of plates behind the counter where cherry and apple pie winked an invitation.

"Wondered if you got a local paper I could look at."

She smiled dryly and cocked one thin-plucked eyebrow, glanced at the lump of wet green terrycloth he held against his thigh, then reached beneath the counter to dig one out. Will knew perfectly well she'd seen him pause before the newspaper office across the street, then walk over here instead.

"Much obliged," he said as he took it.

She propped the heel of one hand on a round hip and ran her eyes over the length of him while chewing gum lazily, making it snap.

"You new around these parts?"

"Yes, ma'am."

"You the new one out at the sawmill?"

Will had to force his hands not to grip the folded paper. All he wanted was to read it and get the hell out of here. But the two at the counter were still staring over their shoulders. He felt their speculative gazes and gave the waitress a curt nod.

"Be okay if I set down a spell and look at this?"

"Sure thing, help yourself. Can I get ya a cup of coffee or anything?"

"No, ma'am, I'll just . . ." With the paper he gestured toward the row of high-backed booths, turned and folded his lanky frame into one of them. From the corner of his eye he saw the waitress produce a compact and begin to paint her lips. He buried his face in the *Whitney Register.* Headlines about the war in Europe; disclosure of a secret meeting between President Roosevelt and Prime Minister Churchill, who'd drafted something called the Atlantic Charter; Joe DiMaggio playing another in his long string of safe-hit games; *Citizen Kane,* starring Orson Welles, showing at someplace called The Gem; the announcement of a garden party coming up on Monday; an advertisement for automobile repair beside another for harness repair; the funeral announcement of someone named Idamae Dell Randolph, born 1879 in Burnt Corn, Alabama, died in the home of her daughter, Elsie Randolph Blythe on August 8, 1941. The want ads were simple enough to locate in the eight-page edition: a roving lawyer would be in town the first and third Mondays of each month and could be found in Room 6 of the Town Hall; someone had a good used daybed for sale; someone wanted a husband . . .

A husband?

Will's eyes backtracked and read the whole ad, the same one she'd tacked up on the time board at the mill.

> WANTED—A HUSBAND. Need healthy
> man of any age willing to work a
> spread and share the place. See E.
> Dinsmore, top of Rock Creek Road.

A healthy man of any age? No wonder the millhands called her crazy.

His eyes moved on: somebody had homemade rag rugs for sale; a nearby town needed a dentist and a mercantile establishment an accountant.

But nobody needed a drifter fresh out of Huntsville State Penitentiary who'd picked fruit and ridden freights and wrangled cattle and drifted half the length of this country in his day.

He read E. Dinsmore's ad again.

Need healthy man of any age willing to work a spread and share the place.

His eyes narrowed beneath the deep shadow of his hat brim while he studied the words. Now what the hell kind of woman would advertise for a man? But then what the hell kind of man would consider applying?

The pair of locals had twisted around on their stools and were overtly staring. The waitress leaned on the counter, gabbing with them, her eyes flashing often to Will. He eased from the booth and she sauntered to meet him at the glass cigar counter up front. He handed her the paper, curled a hand around his hat brim without actually dipping it.

"Much obliged."

"Anytime. It's the least I can do for a new neighbor. The name's Lula." She extended a limp hand with talons polished the same vermilion shade as her lips. Will assessed the hand and the come-hither jut of her hip, the unmistakable message some women can't help emanating. Her bleached hair was piled high and tumbled onto her forehead in a studied imitation of Hollywood's newest cheesecake, Betty Grable.

At last Will extended his own hand in a brief handshake accompanied by an even briefer nod. But he didn't offer his name.

"Could you tell me how to find Rock Creek Road?"

"Rock Creek Road?"

Again he gave a curt nod.

The men snickered. The smile fell from Lula's sultry mouth.

"Down past the sawmill, first road south of there, then the first road left offa that."

He stepped back, touched his hat and said, "Much obliged," before walking out.

"Well," Lula huffed, watching him walk past the window. "If he ain't a surly one."

"Didn't fall for your smile now either, did he, Lula?"

"What smile you talkin' about, you dumb redneck? I didn't give him no smile!" She moved along the counter, slapping at it with a wet rag.

"Thought y' had a live one there, eh, Lula?" Orlan Nettles leaned over the counter and squeezed her buttock.

"Damn you, Orlan, git your hands off!" she squawked, twisting free and swatting his wrist with the wet rag.

Orlan eased back onto the stool, his eyebrows mounting his forehead. "Hoo-ee! Would y' look at that now, Jack." Jack Quigley turned droll eyes on the pair. "I never knew old Lula to slap away a man's hand before, have you, Jack?"

"You got a right filthy mouth, Orlan Nettles!" Lula yelped.

Orlan grinned lazily, lifted his coffee cup and watched her over the brim. "Now what do you suppose that feller's doing up Rock Creek Road, Jack?"

Jack at last showed some sign of life as he drawled, "Could be he's goin' up to check out the Widow Dinsmore."

"Could be. Can't figger what else he'd of found in that newspaper, can you, Lula?"

"How should I know what he's doin' up Rock Creek Road? Wouldn't open his mouth enough to give a person his name."

Orlan loudly swallowed the last of his coffee. "Yup!" With the back of a hand he smeared the wetness from the corners of his mouth over the rest of it. "Reckon he went on up to check out Eleanor Dinsmore."

"That crazy old coot?" Lula spat. "Why, if he did, he'll be back down in one all-fire hurry."

"Don't you just wish, Lula . . . don't you just wish?" Orlan chuckled, bowed his legs and backed off the stool, then dropped a nickel on the counter.

Lula scraped up her tip, dropped it into her pocket and dumped his coffee cup into a sink beneath the counter. "Go on, git out o' here, you two. Ain't givin' me no business anyway, sittin' there soppin' up coffee."

"C'mon, Jack, what say we sashay up to the lumber mill, do a little snoopin' around, see what we can find out."

Lula glared at him, refusing to break down and ask him to come back and tell her what he learned about the tall, handsome stranger. The town was small enough that it wouldn't take her long to find out on her own.

By the time he found the Dinsmore place it was evening. He used his green towel to wash in a creek before going up, then hung it on a tree limb and set the fruit jar carefully beneath it. The road—if you could call it that—was steep, rocky and full of washouts. Reaching the top, he found himself sweating again but figured it really didn't matter; she wouldn't take him anyway.

He left the road and approached through the woods, standing hidden in the trees, studying the place. It was a mess: chicken dung, piles of rusting machinery, a goat chewing his cud on a back stoop that looked ready to drop off the house, outbuildings peeling, shingles curled, tools left out in the weather, a sagging clothesline with a chipped enamel kettle hanging from one pole, remnants of a weedy garden.

Will Parker felt as if he fit right in.

He stepped into the clearing and waited; it didn't take too long.

A woman appeared in the doorway of the house, one child on her hip, another burrowing into her skirts with a thumb in its mouth. She was barefoot, her skirt faded, its hem sagging to the right, her blouse the color of muddy water, her entire appearance as shabby as her place.

"What can I do for you?" she called. Her voice sounded flat, wary.

"I'm lookin' for the Dinsmore place."

"You found it."

"I come about the ad."

She hitched the baby higher onto her hip. "The ad?" she repeated, squinting for a closer look.

"The one about the husband." He moved no closer, but stayed where he was at the edge of the clearing.

Eleanor Dinsmore kept a safe distance, unable to make out much of him. He wore a curled cowboy hat pulled low over his eyes, stood with his weight—what there was of it—on one bony hip with his thumbs hitched in his back pockets. She made out scuffed cowboy boots, a worn blue cambric shirt with sweat-stained armpits and faded jeans several inches too short for his lanky legs. There was nothing to do, she guessed, but go on out there and take a look at him. Wouldn't matter anyhow. He wouldn't stay.

He watched as she picked her way around the goat, down the steps and across the clearing, never taking her eyes off him, that young one still riding her hip, the other one tagging close—barefoot, too. She came slow, ignoring a chicken that squawked and flapped out of her path.

When she stood no more than ten feet before him she let the baby slip down and stand by himself, braced against her knee.

"You applying?" she asked smilelessly.

His eyes dropped to her stomach. She was pregnant as hell.

She watched, waiting for him to turn heel and run. Instead, his eyes returned to her face. At least she thought they did from the slight lifting of his hat brim.

"I reckon I am." He stood absolutely still, not a nerve flinching.

"I'm the one placed the ad," she told him, so there'd be no question.

"Figured you were."

"There's three of us . . . nearly four."

"Figured there were."

"The place needs work."

She waited, but he didn't say he figured it did, didn't even glance sideways at all the junk in the yard.

"You still interested?" she asked.

She'd never seen anyone could stand so still. "I reckon so." His britches were so loose she expected them to drop over his hipbones any second. His gut was hollow. But he had wiry arms, the kind that look as strong relaxed as flexed, with veins standing out in the hollows where the flesh was palest. He might be thin, but he wasn't puny. He'd be a worker.

"Then take your hat off so's I can see you one time."

Will Parker wasn't fond of removing his hat. When he'd been released from prison his hat and boots were the only things they'd returned to him. The Stetson was oily, misshapen, but an old friend. Without it he felt naked.

Still, he answered politely, "Yes, ma'am."

Once the hat was off he stood without fidgeting, letting her get a gander at his face. It was long and lean, like the rest of him, with brown eyes that looked as if he worked hard to keep the expression out of them. Same with his voice; it was respectful but flat. He didn't smile, but his mouth was good, had a nice shape to the upper lip with two definite peaks, which she liked. His hair was a dirty blond, the color of a collie, shaggy at the back and around his ears. The front was plastered against his brow from his hatband. "You could use a haircut," was all she said.

"Yes, ma'am."

He put his hat back on and it hid his eyes again, while from beneath its shadow he took in the woman's worn cotton clothes, the sleeves rolled to the elbow, the soiled skirt where her belly was fullest. Her face might have been pretty, but looked old before its time. Maybe it was just the hair, flying around like goose grass from whatever moored it at the back of her neck. He took her for thirty, maybe, but thought if she ever smiled it might take five years off her.

"I'm Eleanor Dinsmore . . . Mrs. Glendon Dinsmore."

"Will Parker," he returned, curling a hand around his hat brim, then catching his thumb in a back pocket again.

She knew right off he was a man of few words; that'd suit her just fine. Even when she gave him the chance he didn't ask questions like most men would. So she went on asking them herself.

"You been around here long?"

"Four days."

"Four days where?"

"Been workin' at the sawmill."

"Workin' for Overmire?"

Will nodded.

"He's no good. You're better off workin' here." She glanced in a semicircle and went on: "I been here all my life, in Whitney."

She didn't sigh, but she didn't need to. He heard the weariness in her words as she scanned the dismal yard. Her eyes returned to him and she rested one knobby hand on her stomach. When she spoke again her voice held a hint of puzzlement. "Mister, I've had that ad up at the sawmill for over three months now and you're the first one fool enough to come up that hill and check it out. I know what this place is. I know what I am. Down below they call me crazy." Her head jutted forward. "Did you know that?"

"Yes, ma'am," he answered quietly.

Her face registered surprise, then she chuckled. "Honest, ain't you? Well, I'm just wondering why you ain't run yet, is all."

He crossed his arms and shifted his weight to the opposite hip. She had the shoe on the wrong foot. Once she found out about his record he'd be marching down that road faster than a roach when the light comes on. Telling her was as good as putting a shotgun in her hands. But she was bound to find out eventually; might as well get it over with.

"Maybe you should be the one runnin'."

"Why's that?"

Will Parker looked her square in the eyes. "I done time in prison. You might's well know it, right off."

He expected quick signs of withdrawal. Instead Eleanor Dinsmore pursed her mouth and said in an ornery tone, "I says to take that hat off so's I can see what kind of man I'm talkin' to here."

He took it off slowly, revealing a countenance wiped clean of all emotion.

"What'd they put you in there for?" She could tell by the nervous tap of his hat brim on his thigh that he wanted to put it back on. It pleased her that he didn't.

"They say I killed a woman in a Texas whorehouse."

His answer stunned her, but she could be as poker-faced as he. "Did you?" she shot back, watching his unflinching eyes. The control. The expressionlessness. He swallowed once and his Adam's apple bobbed.

"Yes, ma'am."

She submerged another jolt of surprise and asked, "Did you have good reason?"

"I thought so at the time."

Point-blank, she asked, "Well, Will Parker, you plan on doing that to me?"

The question caught Will by surprise and tipped up the corners of his lips. "No, ma'am," he answered quietly.

She stared hard into his eyes, came two steps closer and decided he didn't look like a killer, nor act like one. He was sure no liar, and he had a workingman's arms and wasn't going to gab her head off. It was good enough for her.

"Okay, then, you can come on up to the house. They say I'm crazy anyway, might's well give 'em something to back it up." She picked up the baby, herded the toddler along by the back of his head and led the way toward the house. The toddler peeked around to see if Will was following; the baby stared over its mother's shoulder; but the mother herself turned her back as if to say, do what you will, Will Parker.

She walked like a pelican, swaying with each step in an ungainly fashion. Her hair was dull, her shoulders round and her hips wide.

The house was a tacky thing, atilt in several directions at once. It looked to have been built in stages, each addition blown slightly off level by the prevailing wind of the moment. The main body listed northeast, an ell west and the stoop east. The windows were off square, there were tin patches on the roof, and the porch steps were rotting.

But inside it smelled of fresh bread.

Will's eyes found it, cooling on the kitchen cupboard beneath a dishtowel. He had to force his attention back to Eleanor Dinsmore when she put the baby in a high chair and offered, "How about a cup of coffee?"

He nodded silently, venturing no further than the rag rug at the kitchen door. His eyes followed as she fetched two cracked cups and filled them from a white enamel pot on the iron cookstove while the blond child hid in her skirts, hindering her footsteps.

"Leave off now, Donald Wade, so I can get Mr. Parker his coffee." The child clung, sucking his thumb until at last she reached down to pick him up. "This here is Donald Wade," she said. "He's kind of shy. Hasn't seen many strangers in his life."

Will remained by the door. "Howdy, Donald Wade," he said, nodding. Donald Wade buried his face in his mother's neck while she sat down on a scarred wooden chair at a table covered with red flowered oilcloth.

"You gonna stand by that door all night?" she inquired.

"No, ma'am." He approached the table cautiously, pulled out a chair and sat well away from Eleanor Dinsmore, his hat again pulled low over his eyes. She waited, but he only took a pull on his hot coffee, saying nothing, eyes flickering occasionally to her and the boy and something behind her.

"I guess you're wondering about me," she said at last. She smoothed the back of Donald Wade's shirt with a palm, waiting for questions that didn't come. The room carried only the sound of the baby slapping his hand on the wooden tray of the high chair. She rose and fetched a dry biscuit and laid it on the tray. The baby gurgled, took it in a fat fist and began gumming it. She stood behind him and regarded Will while repeatedly brushing the child's feathery hair back from his forehead. She wished Will would look at her, would take that hat off so they could get started. Donald Wade had followed her, was again clinging to her skirts. Still feathering the baby's hair, she found Donald Wade's head with her free hand. Standing so, she said what needed saying.

"The baby's name is Thomas. He's near a year and a half old. Donald Wade here, he's going on four. This one's going to be born just shy of Christmas, close as I can reckon. Their daddy's name was Glendon."

Will Parker's eyes were drawn to her stomach as she rested a hand on it. He thought about how maybe there was more than one kind of prison.

"Where's their daddy?" he inquired, lifting his eyes to her face.

She nodded westward. "Out in the orchard. I buried him out there."

"I thought—" But he stopped.

"You got a strange way of not sayin' things, Mr. Parker. How's a body supposed to make up a mind when you keep closed up so?" Will studied her, finding it hard to let loose after five years, and especially when she stood with her children at guard. "Go on, then, say it," Eleanor Dinsmore prodded.

"I thought maybe your man run off. So many of 'em are doin' that since the depression."

"I wouldn't be lookin' for no husband then, would I?"

His glance dropped guiltily to his coffee cup. "I reckon not."

"And anyway, Glendon woulda never dreamed of runnin' off. He didn't have to. He was so full of dreams he wasn't here anyways. Always miles away dreamin' about this and that. The two of us together, we had lots of dreams once." The way she looked at him, Will knew she harbored dreams no longer.

"How long's he been dead?"

"Oh, don't you worry none, the baby is his."

Will colored. "I didn't mean that."

"Course you did. I watched your eyes when you first come up here. He's been dead since April. It was his dreams killed him. This time it was the bees and his honey. He thought he'd get rich real fast making honey out in the orchard, but the bees they started swarmin' and he was in too much of a hurry to use good sense. I told him to shoot the branch down with a shotgun, but he wouldn't listen. He went out on a branch, and sure enough, it broke, and so did he. He never would listen to me much." A faraway look came into her eyes. Will watched the way her hands lingered in the baby's hair.

"Some men are like that." The words felt strange on Will's lips. Comfort—either getting it or giving it—was foreign to him.

"We sure were happy, though. He had a way about him." Her expression as she spoke made Will sure it had once been Glendon Dinsmore's hair through which she'd run her fingers that way. She acted as if she'd forgotten Will was in the room. He couldn't quit watching her hands. It was another of those soft things that got him deep in the gut—the sight of her leafing through the baby's airy hair while the child continued with its biscuit and made gurgling sounds. He wondered if anyone had ever done that to him, maybe sometime long before he had memory, but he had no conscious recollection of ever being touched that way.

Eleanor Dinsmore drew herself back to the present to find Will Parker's eyes on her hands.

"So, what're your thoughts, Mr. Parker?"

He glanced up, refocused his eyes. "It don't matter about the kids."

"Don't matter?"

"I mean, I don't mind that you've got them. Your ad didn't say."

"You like kids then?" she asked hopefully.

"I don't know. Never been around 'em much. Yours seem nice enough."

She smiled at her boys and gave each a love pat. "They can be a joy." He couldn't help wondering at her reasoning, for she looked tired and worn beyond her years, having the near-three she did. "Just make sure, Mr. Parker," she added, " 'cause three's a lot. I won't have you layin' a hand on them when they're troublesome. They're Glendon's boys and he woulda never dreamed of layin' a hand on them."

Just what did she take him for? He felt himself blush. But what else was she supposed to think after what he'd revealed out there in the yard?

"You got my word."

She believed him. Maybe because of the way his eyes lingered on Baby Thomas's hair. She liked his eyes, and they had a way of turning soft when they'd light on the boys. But the boys weren't the only consideration.

"It's got to be said," she went on. "I loved Glendon somethin' fierce. It takes some time to get over a man like that. I wouldn't be lookin' for a man 'less I had to. But winter's comin', and the baby, too. I was in a fix, Mr. Parker. You understand, don't you?"

Will nodded solemnly, noting the absence of self-pity in her voice.

"Another thing." She concentrated on Thomas's hair, stroking it differently, distractedly, her cheeks turning pink. "Having three babies under four years old, well—don't get me wrong—I love 'em something fierce, but I wouldn't want any more. Three's plenty to suit me."

Lord a-mighty, the thought hadn't crossed his mind. She was almost as sorry-looking as her place, and pregnant to boot. He needed a dry bed, but preferably not one with her in it.

When she glanced up, Will Parker glanced down. "Ma'am . . ." His voice croaked. He cleared his throat and tried again. "Ma'am, I didn't come up here lookin' for . . ." He swallowed, glanced up, then sharply down. "I need a place is all. I'm tired of movin'."

"You moved a lot, have you?"

"I been movin' since I remember."

"Where'd you start from?"

"Start from?" He met her eyes, puzzled.

"You mean you don't remember?"

"Texas someplace."

"That's all you know?"

"Yes, ma'am."

"Maybe you're lucky," she commented.

Though he shot her a glance, the remark went unexplained. She merely added, "I started from right down there in Whitney. Never moved farther than from the town to the top of this hill. I reckon you've been around, though."

He nodded silently. Again, she found herself pleased by his brusqueness, his lack of curiosity. She thought she could get along quite well with a man like him.

"So you're lookin' for a dry bed and a full plate is all."

"Yes, ma'am."

She studied him a moment, the way he sat on the edge of his chair, taking nothing for granted, the way he kept his hat brim pulled low as if protecting any secret she might read in his eyes. Well, everybody had secrets. Let him keep his and she'd keep hers. But she sure as shootin' wasn't going to strike up an agreement with a man whose eyes she hadn't even seen in the clear light. And besides, suppose *he* didn't want *her.*

He was a vagrant ex-con; she poor, pregnant and unpretty. Who was the bigger loser?

"Mr. Parker, this house ain't much, but I'd appreciate it if you'd take your hat off when you're in it."

He reached up slowly and removed the hat. She lit the kerosene lantern and pushed it aside so they need not look around it.

For long moments they studied each other.

His lips were chapped and his cheeks gaunt, but his eyes were true brown. Brown as pecans, with blunt black lashes and a pair of creases between well-shaped brows. He had a nice knife-straight nose—some might even call it handsome—and a fine mouth. But so sour all the time. Well, maybe she could make it smile. He was quiet-spoken—she liked that. And those arms might be skinny, but they'd done their share of work. That, above all, mattered. If there was one thing a man would have to do around here it was work.

She decided he'd do.

She had fine-textured skin, strong bones and features that, if taken one by one, weren't actually displeasing. Her cheekbones were slightly too prominent, her upper lip a little too thin, and her hair unkempt. But it was honey-brown, and he wondered if with a washing it might not turn honeyer. He shifted his study to her eyes and saw for the first time: they were green. A green-eyed woman who touched her babies like every baby deserved to be touched.

He decided she'd do.

"I wanted you to see what you'd be gettin'," she told him. "Not much."

Will Parker wasn't one for fancy words, but this much he could say: "That's for me to decide."

She didn't fluster or blush, only pushed herself out of the chair and offered, "I'll get you more coffee, Mr. Parker."

She refilled both their cups, then rejoined him. He wrapped both hands around the hot cup and watched the lamplight play on the surface of the black liquid. "How come you're not afraid of me?"

"Maybe I am."

His glance lifted. "Not so it shows."

"A person doesn't always let it show."

He had to know. "Are you?"

In the lanternlight they studied each other again. All was quiet but for Donald Wade's bare toes bumping a rung of the chair and the baby sucking his gooey fingers.

"What if I said I was?"

"Then I'd walk back down the road the way I came."

"You want to do that?"

He wasn't used to being allowed to speak his mind. Prison had taught him the road to the least troubles was to keep his mouth shut. It felt strange, being granted the freedom to say what he would.

"No, I don't reckon so."

"You wanna stay up here with the whole bunch of them down there thinking I'm crazy?"

"Are you?" He hadn't meant to ask such a thing, but she had a way of making a man talk.

"Maybe a little. This here what I'm doing seems crazy to me. Doesn't it to you?"

"Well . . ."

She sensed that he was too kind to say yes.

At that moment a pain grabbed Will's gut—the green apples catching up with him—but he wished it away, telling himself it was only nerves. Applying for a job as a husband wasn't exactly an everyday occurrence.

"You could spend the night," she offered, "look the place over in the morning when the light is up. See what you think." She paused, then added, "Out in the barn."

"Yes, ma'am." The pain wrenched him again, higher up this time, and he winced.

She thought it was because of what she'd said, but it'd take some time before she'd trust him in the house nights. And besides, she might be crazy, but she wasn't loose.

"Nights are plenty warm. I'll make you a shakedown out there."

He nodded silently, fingering the brim of his hat as if anxious to put it back on.

She told her older son, "Go fetch Daddy's pillow, Donald Wade." The little boy hugged her shyly, staring at Will. She reached for his hand. "Come along, we'll get it together."

Will watched them leave, hand in hand, and felt an ache in his gut that had nothing to do with green apples.

When Eleanor returned to the kitchen, Will Parker was gone. Thomas was still in his high chair, discontented now that his biscuit was gone. She experienced a curious stab of disappointment—he'd run away.

Well, what did you expect?

Then, from outside she heard the sound of retching. The sun had gone behind the pines, taking its light with it. Eleanor stepped onto the sagging back stoop and heard him vomiting. "You stay inside, Donald Wade." She pushed the boy back and closed the screen door. Though he started crying, she ignored him and walked to the top of the rotting steps.

"Mr. Parker, are you sick?" She didn't want any sickly man.

He straightened with an effort, his back to her. "No, ma'am."

"But you're throwing up."

He gulped a refreshing lungful of night air, threw back his head and dried his forehead with a sleeve. "I'm all right now. It's just those green apples."

"What green apples?"

"I ate green apples for lunch."

"A grown man should have more sense!" she retorted.

"Sense didn't enter into it, ma'am. I was hungry."

She stood in the semidark, hugging Glendon Dinsmore's pillow against her swollen stomach, watching and listening as another spasm hit Will Parker and he doubled over. But there was nothing more inside him to come up. She left the pillow on the porch rail and crossed the beaten earth to stand behind his slim, stooping form. He braced both hands on his knees, trying to catch his breath. His vertebrae stood out like stepping-stones. She reached out a hand as if to lay it on his back, but thought better of it and crossed her arms tightly beneath her breasts.

He straightened, muscle by muscle, and blew out a shaky breath.

"Why didn't you say something?" she asked.

"I thought it'd pass."

"You had no supper, then?"

He didn't answer.

"No dinner either?"

Again he remained silent.

"Where did you get them apples?"

"I stole them off somebody's tree. A pretty little place down along the main road between here and the sawmill with pink flowers on a tree stump."

"Tom Marsh's place. And good people, too. Well, that'll teach you a lesson." She turned back toward the steps. "Come on back in the house and I'll fix you something."

"That's not necessary, ma'am. I'm not—"

Her voice became sharper. "Get back in the house, Will Parker, before your foolish pride pushes your ribs right through your thin skin!"

Will rubbed his sore stomach and watched her mount the porch steps, treading near the edges where the boards were still good. The screen door whacked shut behind her. Inside Donald Wade stopped crying. Outside, night peepers started. He glanced over his shoulder. The shadows lent a velvet richness to the dusky clearing, disguising its rusted junk and dung and weeds. But he remembered how sorry it had looked by daylight. And what a wreck the house was. And how worn and lackluster Eleanor Dinsmore looked. And how she'd made it clear she didn't want any jailbird sleeping in her house. He asked himself what the hell he was doing as he followed her inside.

Chapter 2

She left him sitting in the kitchen while she put the boys to bed. He sat eyeing the room. The cabinets consisted of open shelves displaying cookpots and dishes beneath a workbench crudely covered with cracked linoleum. Between the nails that held it on, chunks were missing. The sink was old, chipped and stained, with a single short pipe to drop the runoff into a slop pail underneath. There was no pump. Instead, a dipper handle protruded from a white enamel water pail beneath which the linoleum held a sunburst of cracks. The floor was covered with linoleum of a different pattern, but it showed more black backing than green ivy design. The ceiling needed washing. It was gray with soot above the woodstove. Apparently someone had had dreams of resurfacing the walls but had gotten only as far as tearing off the old plaster on a wall and a half, leaving the wooden slats

showing like the bones of a skeleton. Will found it surprising that a room so ramshackle could smell so good.

His eyes moved to the bread and he forced himself to sit and wait.

When Eleanor Dinsmore returned to the kitchen he made sure his hat was on
the tabletop instead of on his head. With an effort he rose from the rung-back
chair, bolstering his stomach with one arm.

"No need to get up. You rest while I get something started."

He let his weight drop back while she opened a wooden trapdoor in the floor
and disappeared down a set of crude, steep steps. Her hand reappeared, setting a
covered kettle on the floor, then she emerged, climbing clumsily.

When she reached for the ring on the trapdoor he was waiting to lower it for
her. Her startled look told Will she wasn't used to men doing it for her. It had
been a long time, too, since he'd performed courtesies for a woman, but he found
it impossible to watch a pregnant one struggling up a cellar hatch without offering
a hand.

For a moment neither of them knew what to say.

Finally she glanced away, offering, "I appreciate it, Mr. Parker." And when he'd
lowered the trapdoor behind her, "Never had a man openin' and closin' doors for
me. Glendon, he never learnt how. Makes me feel a little foolish. Anyway, I
thought I told you to set. Your belly's bound to be hurtin' after you brought them
apples up for another look."

He grinned at her homey turn of speech and returned to the chair, watching as
she added wood to the stove and put the kettle on to heat.

"I'm sorry about what happened out there in the yard. I guess it embarrassed
you."

"It's a purely natural act, Mr. Parker." She stirred the contents of the pot. "Besides, I don't embarrass easy." She set the spoon down and gave him a wry smile.
"And leastways, you did it *before* you tasted my cooking."

She gave him a cajoling grin and got one of his rare ones in return. He tried
to recall if he'd ever known a woman with a sense of humor, but none came to
mind. He watched her move around in an ungainly, swaying way, placing a hand
to her roundness when she reached or stooped. He wondered if she really was
crazy, if he was, too. Bad enough taking a strange woman for a wife. Worse taking
one who was pregnant. What the hell did he know about pregnant women? Only
that in his time he might have left a few of them behind.

"You'd probably feel better if you washed up some," she suggested.

In his usual fashion, he neither moved nor replied.

"There's the basin." She gestured, then turned away, busying herself. He threw
a longing glance at the basin, the soap, the white towel and washcloth hanging on
nails at the front of the sink.

After a minute she turned and asked, "What's the matter? Stomach hurt too bad
to get up?"

"No, ma'am." He wasn't accustomed to freedom yet, didn't believe it fully. It
felt as if anything he reached for would be snatched away. In prison a man learned
early to take nothing for granted. Not even the most basic creature comforts. This
was *her* house, *her* soap, *her* water. She couldn't possibly understand what prizes
they seemed to a man fresh out.

"Well, what is it?" she demanded impatiently.

"Nothing."

"Then help yourself to the teakettle and washbasin."

He stretched to his feet, but moved cautiously. He crossed behind her and found
a clean white washbasin in the sink, and on the nail, the clean white towel and

washcloth. So white. Whiter than anything he remembered. In prison the wash-cloths had been puce green and had grown musty smelling long before clean ones were issued.

Eleanor peered over her shoulder as he filled the washbasin, then dipped his hands into the cold water. "Don't you want it warmed up?" He glanced back over his shoulder. His eyes, when they weren't carefully blank, were questioning and uncertain.

"Yes, ma'am," he answered. But when he'd shaken off his hands and turned he made no move toward the teakettle. She plucked it off the stove and poured the warm water for him, then turned her back, pretending to go back to work. But she glanced surreptitiously over her shoulder, confounded by his strange hesitancy. He flattened both palms against the bottom of the basin and leaned forward with his head hung low. There he stood, stiff-armed, as if transfixed. What in the world was he doing? She tipped sideways and peeked around him—his eyes were closed, his lips open. At last he scooped water to his face and gave a small shudder. Lord a-mercy, so that was it! Understanding swamped her. She felt a surge of heat flush her body, a queer sympathetic thrill, a gripping about her heart.

"How long has it been?" she asked quietly.

His head came up but he neither turned nor spoke. Water dripped from his face and hands into the basin.

"How long since you had warm water?" she insisted in the kindest tone she could manage.

"A long time."

"How long?"

He didn't want her pity. "Five years."

"You were in prison five years?"

"Yes, ma'am." He buried his face in the towel—it smelled of homemade lye soap and fresh air, and he took his time savoring its softness and scent.

"You mean the water's cold in there?"

He hung up the towel without answering. The water had been cold all his life—creeks and lakes and horse troughs. And often he dried himself with his shirt, or on a lucky day, the sun.

"How long you been out?"

"Couple of months."

"How long since you ate a decent meal?"

Still silent, he closed two buttons on his shirt, staring out a filmy window above the sink.

"Mr. Parker, I asked you a question."

On a crude shelf to his left a small round mirror reflected her image. What he saw mostly was obstinacy.

"A while," he replied flatly while their mirrored eyes locked.

Eleanor realized he was a man who'd accept a challenge more readily than charity, so she carefully wiped all sympathy from her voice. "I should think," she admonished, stepping close behind him, holding his gaze in the mirror, "a man that's been roughing it might need a touch of soap." She reached around him, picked up a bar of Ivory and plopped it into his hand, then rested her own on her hips. "You're not in prison anymore, Mr. Parker. Soap is free for the taking here, and there's always warm water. Only thing I ask is that when you're through you spill it out and rinse the basin."

Staring at her in the mirror, he felt as if an immense weight had lifted from his chest. She stood in the pose of a fighter, daring him to defy her. But beneath her stern façade, he sensed a generous spirit. "Yes, ma'am," he returned quietly. And this time before leaning over the welcome warm water, he shrugged out of his shirt.

Holy Moses, was he thin. From behind she eyed his ribs. They stuck out like a kite frame in a strong wind. He began spreading soapsuds with his hands— chest, arms, neck and as far around his trunk as he could reach. He bent forward, and her eyes were drawn down his tan back to where a white band of skin appeared above the line of grayed elastic on his underwear.

She had never seen any man but Glendon wash up. Grandpa was the only other male she'd ever lived with and he certainly hadn't bared himself to any female. Staring at Will Parker while he performed his ablutions, Eleanor suddenly realized she was watching a very personal thing, and turned away guiltily.

"Washcloth's for you—use it." She left the room to give him privacy.

She returned several minutes later to find him shiny faced, buttoning up his shirt. "Got this." She held up a yellow toothbrush. "It was Glendon's, but I'll clean it with soda if you don't mind using it secondhand."

He did, but ran his tongue over his teeth and nodded. She fetched a cup, spooned in soda and filled it with boiling water from the teakettle. "Person oughta have a toothbrush," she declared, stirring with Glendon Dinsmore's.

She handed it to Will along with a can of toothpowder, then stood and watched while he dumped some in his palm.

Will didn't like being watched. He'd been watched for five years and now that he was out he ought to be able to do his private business without feeling somebody's eyes on him. But even with his back turned, he felt her scrutiny all the while he used her husband's toothbrush, savoring the toothpowder that was so sweet he wanted to swallow it instead of spitting it out. When he finished, she ordered, "Well, set yourself down at the table."

She served him vegetable soup, hot and fragrant, thick with okra and tomato and beef. His hands rested beside the bowl while he fought the compulsion to gobble it like an animal. His stomach seemed to roll over and beg, but he hesitated, savoring not only the smell but the anticipation, and the fact that he was allowed as much time as he wanted—no bells would ring, no guards would prod.

"Go ahead . . . eat."

It was different, being told by her instead of the guards. Her motives were strictly friendly. Her eyes followed his head as he dipped the spoon and lifted it to his lips.

It was the best soup he'd ever tasted.

"I asked how long since your last meal. You gonna tell me or not?"

His glance flickered up briefly. "A couple of days."

"A couple of days!"

"I stopped in a restaurant in town to read the want ads but there was a waitress there I didn't particularly care for, so I moved on without eating."

"Lula Peak. She's a good one to avoid, all right. She been chasin' men since she was tall enough to sniff 'em. So you been eating green apples a coupla days, have you?"

He shrugged, but his glance darted briefly to the bread behind her.

"There's no disgrace in admitting you've gone hungry, you know."

But there was. To Will Parker there was. Just emerging from the jaws of the depression, America was still overrun with tramps, worthless vagrants who'd deserted their families and rode the flatcars aimlessly, begging for handouts at random doorsteps. During the past two months he'd seen—even ridden with— dozens of them. But he'd never been able to bring himself to beg. Steal, yes, but only in the most dire straits.

She watched him eat, watched his eyes remain downcast nearly all the time. Each time they flicked up they seemed drawn to something behind her. She twisted in her chair to see what it was. The bread. How stupid of her. "Why didn't you say you wanted some fresh bread?" she chided as she rose to get it.

But he'd been schooled well to ask for nothing. In prison, asking meant being jeered at or baited like an animal and being made to perform hideous acts that made a man as base as his jailers. To ask was to put power into the sadistic hands of those who already wielded enough of it to dehumanize any who chose to cross them.

But no woman with three fresh loaves could comprehend a thing like that. He submerged the ugly memories as he watched her waddle to the cabinet top and fetch a knife from a crock filled with upended utensils. She scooped up a loaf against her hip and returned to the table to slice off a generous width. His mouth watered. His nostrils dilated. His eyes riveted upon the white slice curling softly from the blade.

She stabbed it with the tip of the knife and picked it up. "You want it?"

Oh, God, not again. His hungry eyes flew to her face, taking on the look of a cornered animal. Against his will, the memory was rekindled, of Weeks, the prison guard, with his slitty, amphibian eyes and his teeth bared in a travesty of a smile, his unctuous voice with its perverted laughter. "You want it, Parker? Then howl like a dog." And he'd howled like a dog.

"You want it?" Eleanor Dinsmore repeated, softer this time, snapping Will back from the past to the present.

"Yes, ma'am," he uttered, feeling the familiar knot of helplessness lodge in his throat.

"Then all you got to do is say so. Remember that." She dropped the bread beside his soup bowl. "This ain't jail, Mr. Parker. The bread ain't gonna disappear and nobody's gonna smack your hand if you reach for it. But around here you might have to ask for things. I'm no mind reader, you know."

He felt the tension drain from him, but he held his shoulders stiff, wondering what to make of Eleanor Dinsmore, so dictatorial and unsympathetic at times, so dreamy and vague at others. It was only the painful memories that had transported him—she wasn't Weeks, and she wouldn't make him pay for picking up the food.

The bread was soft, warm, the greatest gift he'd ever received. His eyes closed as he chewed his first bite.

They flew open again when she grunted, "Humph!"

Puzzled, he watched her turn her back and move across the room to fetch a crock full of the most beautiful lemon-bright butter in the world. She came back and held it just beyond his reach.

"Say it."

He swallowed. His shoulders stiffened and the wary look returned to his face. His voice came reluctantly. "I'd like some o' that butter."

"It's yours." Unceremoniously she clapped it down, then herself, across from him. "And it didn't hurt you one little bit to ask for it, did it?" She brushed off her fingers and admonished, "Around here you ask, 'cause things are in such a mess it's the only way you'll find it most of the time. Well, go ahead, butter your bread and eat."

His hands followed orders while his emotions took additional moments to readjust to her quicksilver mood changes. As he bent over his soup, she warned, "Watch you don't overdo it. Best if you eat slow till your stomach gets used to decent food again."

He wanted to tell her it was good, better than good, the best he remembered.

He wanted to tell her there was no butter in prison, the bread there was coarse and dry and certainly never warm. He wanted to tell her he didn't remember the last time he'd been invited to sit at somebody's kitchen table. He wanted to tell her what it meant to him to sit at hers. But compliments were as foreign to him as crocks of butter, so he ate his bread and soup in silence.

While he ate she brought out her crocheting and sat working on something soft and fuzzy and pink. Her wedding ring—still on her left hand—flashed in the lanternlight in rhythm with the hook. Her hands were nimble, but work-worn, and the skin looked like hide. It appeared all the tougher when contrasted against the fine pink yarn as she payed it out from one calloused finger.

"What you watchin'?"

He glanced up guiltily.

She adjusted the yarn and smiled. The smile transformed her face. "Never seen a woman crochet before?"

"No, ma'am."

"Makin' a shawl for the baby. This here's a shell design." She spread it out on her knee. "Pretty, ain't it?"

"Yes, ma'am." Once again he was assaulted by yearning, a sense of things missed, a desire to reach out and touch that soft pink thing she was creating. Rub it between his fingers as if it were a woman's hair.

"I'm makin' it in pink cause I'd sure like a girl this time. A girl'd be nice for the boys, don't you think?"

What did he know about babies—girls, boys, either one? Nothing except they scared him to death. And girls? He'd never found girls to be especially nice except maybe when they were older, when a man was sinking his body into them. Then, for a few minutes, while they stopped harping or threatening or tormenting, maybe they were nice.

Mrs. Dinsmore's silver hook flashed on. "Baby'll be needing a warm blanket. This old house gets plenty cold in the winter. Glendon, he always meant to fix it up and seal up the cracks and such, but he never got around to it."

His eyes lifted to the walls with the missing plaster.

"Maybe I could seal up the cracks for you."

She glanced up and smiled, unrolling more slack from the basket on the floor. "Maybe you could, Mr. Parker. That'd sure be nice. Glendon, he meant well, but somehow there was always something new he was going to try."

No matter what her mood, when she spoke the name *Glendon* a softness crept into her voice, a smile, too, whether there was one on her face or not. Will supposed there'd never been a woman in the world who'd looked so sentimental when speaking his name.

"Would you like some more soup, Mr. Parker? A little might be okay."

He ate until his stomach felt hard as a baseball. Then he sat back, rubbed it and sighed.

"You sure can pack it away." She tucked her piece of handiwork into the basket and stood up to clear the table.

He watched her move across the kitchen, thinking if he lived to be two hundred he'd never forget this meal, nor how nice it had felt to sit and watch her work fine pink yarn into a shell design and believe that tomorrow when he woke up, he might not have to move on.

She carried Glendon Dinsmore's pillow and quilt and led the way to the barn. He found himself again performing uncustomary courtesies, carrying the lantern, opening the screen door, letting her walk first through the littered yard.

The moon had risen. It rode the eastern trees like an orange pumpkin bobbing on dark water. The chickens were roosting—somewhere in the junk, undoubtedly. He wondered how she ever found eggs.

"I tell you what, Mr. Parker," she told him as they walked through the moonlight, "tomorrow morning when you look the place over you might decide it's not such a good idea to stay. I sure wouldn't hold you to it, no matter what you said when you first come up here."

He watched her waddle along in front of him, hugging her husband's patchwork quilt against her stomach.

"Same goes for you, Mrs. Dinsmore."

Just before they reached the barn she warned, "Be careful, there's a pile of junk here."

A pile? That was a laugh. She sidestepped something made of black spiked iron and opened the barn door. Its unoiled hinges squeaked. Inside there were no animals, but his nose told him there had been.

"Guess this barn could do with a little cleaning," she noted while he raised the lantern over his head and surveyed the circle of light.

"I can do that tomorrow."

"I'd be grateful. So would Madam."

"Madam?"

"My mule. This way." She led him to a wall-mounted ladder. "You'll sleep up there."

She would have begun climbing but he grabbed her arm. "Better let me go first. That ladder doesn't look too dependable."

He slipped the lantern over his arm and started up. When his foot took the third rung it splintered and dumped him flush against the wall, where he dangled like a puppet with a broken string.

"Mr. Parker!" she shrieked, grabbing his thighs while he pedaled for a toehold.

"Get back!"

She leaped back and held her breath as the lanternlight swung wildly. At last he found a solid rung, but tested the rest before putting his weight on each. She pressed a hand to her heart, watching him climb until he safely reached the loft with his elbows. "Lord, you gave me a fright. Be careful."

His head disappeared into the dark square above, then the lantern went up with him, gilding the underside of his hat brim. Only when he stood on solid planking did he look back down. "You're a fine one to talk. If I would've come down I'd have taken you right with me."

"I reckon this old ladder's about as rickety as everything else around here."

"I can fix it tomorrow, too." He raised the lantern and checked the loft. "There's hay." He disappeared and she listened to his footsteps thud overhead.

"I'm sorry about the smell in here," she called.

"It's not as bad up here. This'll be fine."

"I would've cleaned it if I'd known I'd be havin' overnight company."

"Don't worry. I slept in much worse in my day."

He reappeared, knelt, and set the lantern at his knee. "Can you toss up the bedding?"

The pillow went up perfectly. The quilt took three tries. By the third, he was grinning. "Ain't got much for muscles, have you?"

It was the first lighthearted thing he'd said. She stood with her fists on her hips, gazing up at him while he held the patchwork quilt. It might not be so bad having him around if he'd lighten up this way more often.

"Oh, ain't I? I got those up there, didn't I?"

"Just barely."

The grin softened his face. The cockiness sharpened hers. For the first time they began to feel comfortable with each other.

He flopped to his belly and hung over the edge of the hatch. "Here, you take the lantern."

"Don't be silly. I been walkin' in this barnyard since before you owned that thing you call a cowboy hat."

"What's wrong with my cowboy hat?"

"Looks like it's been through a war."

"It's my own. It and my boots." He waggled the lantern. "Here, take it."

So that was why he kept that sorry-looking thing on his head all the time.

"Take it yourself," she said, and disappeared from sight. He knelt on his haunches and listened for her footsteps, but she was barefoot.

"Mrs. Dinsmore?" he called.

"Yes, Mr. Parker?" she called from the opposite end of the barn.

"You mind my asking how old you are?"

"Be twenty-five on November tenth. How about you?"

"Thirty or so."

Silence, while she digested his answer. "Or so?"

"Somebody left me on the steps of an orphanage when I was little." Will hadn't told that to many people in his life. He waited uncertainly for her reaction.

"You mean you don't know when your birthday is?"

"Well . . . no."

The barn grew silent. Outside a whippoorwill called and the frogs sang discordantly. Eleanor paused with her hand on the latch. Will knelt, gripping his thighs.

"We'll have to pick you out a birthday if you decide to stay. A man should have a birthday."

Will smiled, imagining it.

"G'night, Mr. Parker."

"G'night, Mrs. Dinsmore." He heard the barn door squeak open and called again, "Mrs. Dinsmore?"

The squeaking stopped. "What?"

Five seconds of silence, then, "Much obliged for the supper. You're a good cook." His heart thumped gladly after the words were out. It hadn't been so hard after all.

In the dark below she smiled. It had been good to see a man at her table again.

She made her way to the house, prepared for bed and eased into it with a sigh. As she straightened, a faint cramp caught her low across the stomach. She cradled it, rolling to her side. She had chopped wood today, though she knew she shouldn't have. But Glendon had scarcely managed to get the day-to-day tasks done, let alone stockpiling for tomorrow. The seasoned wood needed splitting, and next year's supply should be cut so it could start to dry. Besides the wood, there was always water to carry. So much. And there'd be more when the new baby came and she'd have two of them in diapers.

She stretched out on her back and rested a wrist on her forehead, picturing the veins along the inside of Will Parker's arms, the cluster of wiry muscles. She remembered how hard his legs had been when she'd touched them as he hung on the ladder.

Stay, Will Parker. Please stay.

In the hayloft, Will sank his head into a pillow made of real feathers and stretched out on a soft handmade quilt. His belly was full, his teeth were clean, his skin smelled of soap. And somewhere out there was a mule, and beehives and chickens and a house with possibilities. A place where a man could make a go of it with a little hard work. Hell, hard work came easy.

Just give me a chance, Eleanor Dinsmore, and I'll show you.

He remembered her standing barefoot in the yard with her two boys, her stomach round as a watermelon, eyeing him warily. He remembered the detached look on her face when she'd questioned him and the momentary flash of shock when he told her about Huntsville. She was probably mulling it over right now, having second thoughts about keeping a jailbird around. And by morning she'd have decided he was too much of a risk. But in the morning he'd show her. First thing, before she had a chance to put him off the place he'd show her he intended to earn his keep.

Chapter 3

Lula Peak lived in the tiny bungalow on Pecan Street where she'd grown up. While her mother was alive the furnishings had been adequate, if old. Now, however, the kitchen sported a spanking new Frigidaire electric refrigerator, a bathroom with hot and cold running water and in the living room a new Philco radio.

At eight o'clock that night the Philco and Lula were both tuned to Atlanta, both blasting out "Oh, Johnny, Oh." Dressed in a slinky red-orange wrapper, Lula tilted toward the bathroom mirror, scavenging with the tips of a tweezer for any wayward hair with the audacity to be growing beyond the periphery of her pencil-thin eyebrows.

Oh Johnny, oh, Johnny, how you can love . . .

She stopped her fruitless search and ran her palms up her silkcovered arms as she'd seen Betty Grable do in the movies.

Oh, Johnny, oh, Johnny, heaven's above . . .

She made a moue at her reflection in the mirror, then shimmied and dipped her knees, letting her palms brush the sides of her breasts. The satin rubbed seductively over her nipples and they popped up like balloons taking air. Lula loved getting hot, either by herself or with someone else—didn't matter which. But to really cool down, she needed a man. Lula always needed a man, and Whitney didn't have enough of them. When Lula itched, she needed scratching. And Lula itched all the time.

She plucked up a bottle of Evening in Paris cologne and spun twice while dabbing it on, watching her face flash across the bathroom mirror. After a third spin she balanced one high-heeled foot on the toilet seat, then touched some of the cologne to the thick thatch of blond hair revealed by the gaping gown. She dropped the foot to the floor, then ran her hand down her belly while giving the mirror a sultry kiss, leaving the imprint of vermilion lipstick on the cold glass.

"Lula, what the hell's goin' on in here?" Harley Overmire bellowed from her living room. "Music's so goddamn loud any bum coulda walked in here and you wouldnt'a even known it."

"Harley-honey, is that you?" The music suddenly dimmed and Lula came flying out of the bathroom, pouting. "Harley, turn that back up! That's my favorite song!" She darted to the Philco—a flash of white limbs and flaming silk—and cranked it up.

Oh, Johnny, oh, Johnny, oh . . .

Harley immediately turned it down. "Lula-honey, I didn't come over here to get my eardrums broke."

"Oh, yeah? Then what did you come for, Harleykins?"

Lula turned the radio to a thunderous volume.

Oh, Johnny . . .

She swung toward him, her expression sultry as she pressed the sides of her ample breasts, accentuating the deep cleavage as she stalked him and slipped one white leg through the break in the garish satin wrapper. Her painted lips pouted voluptuously as she sidled close and rubbed herself against him, straddling one of his thighs.

Harley's eyes became hooded, his lips dropped open with lascivious expectation as he lifted his knee against her.

"Ooh-hoo-hoo, Lula-baby, sugar-pie, you sure know how t' do it to a man."

"You bet I do, kiddo, and you'd like it right now, wouldn't you?"

He gripped her hips with both hands. "I'm here, ain't I, baby?"

She took his hands and transferred them to her breasts. "Feel that? I got gumdrops just thinkin' about you. Wanna know what else happened when I thought about you, Harleykins?"

"Yeah," Harley growled, low and lusty, manipulating her pelvis. "What?"

They ground against each other in earnest. Harley's root had sprung up like a mushroom after two weeks of rain. She grasped his neck and put her lips to his ear and whispered something coarse, for good measure.

He laughed gutturally and said, "Oh, yeah? Let's see," then reached for the thatch of blond hair and slipped a finger inside her.

"Ooh-hoo-hoo, Lula-baby, you need your damper turned down, and how."

She unbuttoned his shirt and pushed it off till it hung from his waist, all the while riding his hand, which was braced against his thigh. She looped both arms around his neck, nipped his ear, licked the inside of it and suggested, "What I need is one of them new electric fans that turns back and forth. I seen one down in a hardware store in Atlanta last time I visited my sister Junie." She eased down and ran her lips across his chest, then splayed her hands on the black curly hair. "Mmm . . . I love my men hairy. Gets me itchin' somethin' awful."

Harley was nearly at the bursting point already. "Honey, I ain't made of money, you know."

She bit his nipple, then tugged it until he yelped and jerked back, nursing it. She gazed into his eyes, her face feigning innocence as she gyrated against him. "I bet your wife's got one o' them electric fans already, hasn't she, Harley?"

"Come on, Lula, let's go to bed. I'm hurtin', honey."

"What about that fan?"

"Maybe next payday."

She pouted her vermilion lips and ran one finger down her damp cleavage. "Next payday's too late. Why, it's been so hot, I just can't hardly sleep nights at all." She wiped her collected sweat beneath his nose.

"Lula, be reasonable. I already give you that Frigidaire and the Philco and had that closet made into a bathroom for you. I had to do some fancy explainin' to Mae about where the extra money went."

Abruptly she gave him a shove and flounced away from him, throwing her hands in the air. "Mae, Mae, Mae! I swear that's all I hear from you, Harley Overmire! Well, if you won't get me that electric fan, I know somebody who will. Why, just today Orlan Nettles was in the cafe and all I'da had to do was crook my little finger and it woulda been him here tonight instead of you. I'll bet you five dollars Orlan never did it the way I had in mind to do it with you tonight."

"You thought of a new way?" Harley was pure miserable by this time.

With her back turned, she inspected her painted nails. "It was a good one, too."

The music on the Philco had changed to "Paper Doll." It continued blasting as he came up behind her and clamped his teeth on her neck, reached around front and started convincing her again. But Lula had coercion down to an art. She dipped her knees and got the most out of Harley's strokes, but she could remain unyielding till she got what she wanted, and it was always more than just an orgasm. If she was going to live the rest of her life in this little jerkwater town, she'd live it in luxury, by God. The fan and the bathroom and the Philco were just the beginning. She intended to have a Ford, and a carpeted front room and an R.C.A. Victor phonograph before this was over.

Behind her, Harley was breathing like a winded horse. What he had inside his pants felt like it belonged to a horse, too. She reached back to help Harley make his decision.

He groaned against her neck and said, "Okay, Lula-honey, I'll get you the fan."

"Tomorrow, Harleykins?" she purred.

"Tomorrow. I'll think of somethin' I got to run down to Atlanta for."

Lula didn't expect something for nothing. The change in her was immediate and inspired. She swung around and began removing Harley's clothes, licking his chest, fondling him while backing him toward the kitchen.

"What's your favorite kind of sandwich, Harleykins?"

He stumbled over a pantleg and laughed. "Roast beef and mustard."

"Mmm ... roast beef and mustard. You like mustard, do you, Harley?" She knew he liked mustard. She knew everything about Harley Overmire and used every scrap of knowledge to best advantage.

"Damn right, and Mae, she's always forgettin' to put it on."

"That's the trouble with Mae," Lula purred, pushing his boxer shorts to the floor. "Mae doesn't know what a man likes. But I do." Harley chuckled, thinking he'd get Lula the biggest damn fan in the city of Atlanta. "And where should a man eat his roast beef and mustard sandwich, Harleykins?" She stroked him till he felt hard and pulsing as a jackhammer.

"At the kitchen table?" *Oh, merciful heavens,* he thought. *This is gonna be good.*

"That's right, honey-lamb. I got cold roast beef in my new Frigidaire, just waitin' for you, and all the mustard you want, and I'm gonna serve 'em both to you on the kitchen table, and afterwards you and me're gonna climb in that beautiful new bathtub and run some of that luscious hot water from my brand-new water heater, and we're gonna put some Dreft in there and get lost in the bubbles, and everytime you open your lunch pail up at the mill and see a roast beef sandwich without mustard, you're gonna remember who it is that treats you right—aren't you, Harleykins?"

They spent forty minutes on the kitchen table, and the things Lula did with that mustard would have sold millions of bottles, had the manufacturer had the ingenuity to suggest such uses.

Later, in Lula's shiny new porcelain tub, she ran her bare toes up Harley's hairy chest. His eyes were closed and his beefy arms rested on the wide edge.

"Harley?"

"Hm?"

"A stranger came into the cafe today."

"Hm." He sounded disinterested.

Two minutes passed in silence while Lula patiently rested with her eyes closed. She was bright enough to know that if she asked, she'd arouse his suspicion. But if Harley thought he alone could scratch her itch, he was sadly mistaken.

"Don't get many strangers through here," she murmured in due time, as if half asleep.

Harley lifted his head. "Tall guy? Wiry? Wearin' a battered cowboy hat?"

"Yeah, that's the one," she replied dreamily, following with a throaty chuckle. "Hey, Harley, how come you always know everything before I can tell you?"

He chortled and laid his head back. "You got to get up pretty early in the mornin' to put one over on old Harley."

"He just read the paper and moved on."

"Prob'ly lookin' at the want ads. I fired him from the mill today."

"What'd he do wrong?"

"Done five years in Huntsville State Pen for killin' a whore in some whorehouse down there."

Lula's foot hit the water with a splash as she sat bolt upright. "My God, Harley, he didn't!" Her blood ran fast at the mere idea of being in the same room with a man like that. "Lord, we women won't be safe on the streets."

"That's what I told him. Parker, I said, we don't want your kind around here. Pick up your pay and git."

So his name was Parker.

"Good for you, Harley." She lay back and stroked his genitals with her heel. Beneath the bubbly water they were sleek. She began growing aroused again, touching Harley, but picturing the tall, tacit cowboy who'd said so little and had hidden beneath the brim of his hat. Still waters, she thought, and felt her heart begin to race. Going to bed with a man like that would be the ultimate excitement; she imagined it in vivid detail—the danger, the challenge, the sexual drive behind a man who'd been cut off from women for five years. Lord a-mighty, it would be one she'd never forget.

"Bet I know somethin' you don't know, Harley." She let her toes climb his chest like an inchworm.

"What?"

"He went up to see crazy Elly Dinsmore about that ad she run."

"What!" The water slopped over the edge of the tub as Overmire shot up.

"I know damn well he did 'cause first he asked to see the paper, then he sat and read it, then he asked how to find Rock Creek Road, and when I told him he headed off in that direction. What else would he be goin' up there for?"

Overmire roared with laughter and fell back in the water. "Wait'll I tell the boys about this. Jesus, will they laugh. Crazy Elly Dinsmore ... ha, ha, ha!"

"She really is crazy, isn't she?"

"As a bedbug. Advertisin' for a husband. Christ."

"Course, what could you expect after she was locked up in that house all her life?" Lula shivered.

"I went to school with her mother, you know. Course, that was before she dropped her whelp and they locked her up."

"You did?" Lula sat up and reached over the edge of the tub for a towel. She stood and began drying herself. Harley did the same.

"She stared at the wall a lot, and drew pictures all the time. Once she drew a picture of a naked man on a windowshade. The teacher didn't know it was there and when she pulled it down the class went crazy. Course, they never proved it was Lottie See drew it, but she was always drawin', and who else'd be crazy enough to do a thing like that?"

Harley stepped from the tub and began drying his legs. Suddenly he stopped and stared at the hairless insides of his thighs. "Damn it all, Lula, how'm I gonna explain these mustard stains to Mae?"

Lula explored the evidence, giggled and turned to the mirror, tightening one of the combs that held her upsweep. "Tell her you got the yellow jaundice."

Harley guffawed and slapped her fanny. "Hey, Lula, you're all right, kid." Abruptly he sobered. "You're sure tonight was okay to do it—I mean, you couldn't get pregnant or anything, could you?"

Lula grew piqued. "You're a little late askin', aren't you, Harley?"

"Jesus, Lula, I depend on you to tell me if I need to use anything."

She dabbed Evening in Paris behind her ears, between her thighs. "How dumb do you think I am, Harley?" She capped the bottle and slammed it down. He was always asking the same question, as if she were too ignorant to use a calendar. She'd answered it scores of times, but it always left her feeling empty and angry. So, she wasn't his wife. So, she couldn't have his babies. Who'd want 'em? She'd seen his kids and they were stubby, ugly little brats that looked like bug-eyed monkeys. If she was ever going to have a kid, it sure as hell wouldn't be his. It'd be somebody's like that Parker's, somebody who'd give her handsome, brown-eyed darlings that other women would envy.

The thought of it gripped her with a sense of urgency. She was thirty-six already and no marriage prospects in sight. She'd live the rest of her life in this stinking little dump where she'd probably die, just like her mother had. And when she got so old Harley didn't want to do it on the kitchen table anymore—or couldn't, for that matter—he'd retire to his rocking chair on the front veranda with his precious, boring Mae. And all those homely little monkeys of his would turn out *more* homely little monkeys and old Grampa Harley'd be happy as a tick on a fat sheep.

And she—Lula—would be here alone. Aging. Going to fat. Eating beef and mustard sandwiches by herself.

Well, not if she could help it, Lula vowed. Not if she could by God help it.

Chapter 4

Eleanor awakened to a pink sunrise creeping over the sill and the sound of an ax. She peeked across her pillow at the alarm clock. Six-thirty. He was chopping wood at six-thirty?

Barefoot, she crept to the kitchen window and stood back, studying him and the woodpile. How long had he been up? Already he'd split a stack waist-high. He had tossed his shirt and hat aside. Dressed only in jeans and cowboy boots, he looked as meaty as a scarecrow. He swung the ax and she watched, fascinated in spite of herself by the hollow belly, the taut arms, the flexing chest. He'd done some splitting in his time and went at it with measured consistency, regulating his energy for maximum endurance—balancing a log on the stump, standing back, cracking it dead center and cleaving it with two whacks. He balanced another piece and—whack! whack!—firewood.

She closed her eyes—lordy, don't let him leave—and rested a hand on her roundness, recalling her own clumsiness at the task, the amount of effort it had taken, the length of time.

She opened the back door and stepped onto the porch. "You're sure up with the chickens, Mr. Parker."

Will let the ax fall and swung around. "Mornin', Mrs. Dinsmore."

"Mornin' yourself. Can't say the sound of that ax ain't welcome around here."

She stood on the stoop in a white, ankle-length nightgown that exaggerated her pregnancy. Her hair hung loose to her shoulders, her feet were bare, and from this distance she looked younger and happier than she had last night. For a moment Will Parker imagined he was Glendon Dinsmore, he really belonged here, she was his woman and the babies inside the house, inside her, were his. The brief fantasy was sparked not by Eleanor Dinsmore but by things Will Parker had managed to miss in his life. Suddenly he realized he'd been staring and became self-conscious. Leaning on the ax, he reached for his shirt and hat.

"Would you mind bringin' in an armload of that wood so I can get a fire started?" she called.

"No, ma'am, don't mind at all."

"Just dump it in the woodbox."

"Yes, ma'am."

The screen door slammed and she disappeared.

He hated to stop splitting wood even long enough to carry it into the house. In prison he'd worked in the laundry, smelling the stink of other men's sweat rising from the steaming water as he tended the clothes in a hot, close room where no sunlight reached. To stand in the morning sun while the dew was still thick, sharing the lavender circle of sky with dozens of birds that flitted from countless gourd birdhouses hung about the place—ahh, this was sheer heaven. And gripping an ax handle, feeling its weight slice through the air, the resistance as it struck wood, the thud of a piece falling to the earth—now that was freedom. And the smell—clean, sharp and on his knuckle a touch of pungent sap—he couldn't get enough of it. Nor of using his muscles again, stretching them to the limit. He had grown soft in prison, soft and white and somehow emasculated by doing women's work.

If the sound of the ax was welcome to Mrs. Dinsmore, the feel of it was emancipation to Will Parker.

He knelt and loaded his arm with wood—good, sharp, biting edges that creased his skin where his sleeve was rolled back; grainy flat pieces that clacked together and echoed across the clearing. He piled it high until it reached his chin, then higher until he couldn't see over it, testing himself again. This was man's work. Honest. Satisfying. He grunted as he stood with the enormous load.

At the screen door he knocked.

She came running, scolding, "What in heaven's name're you knockin' for?"

"Brought your wood, ma'am."

"I can see that. But there's no need to knock." She pushed the screen door open. "And y' got to learn that around here y' can't stand on that rotting old porch floor with a load so heavy. It's likely t' take you right through."

"I made sure I walked near the edge." He felt with the toe of his boot, stepped up and crossed the kitchen to clatter the wood into the woodbox. Brushing off his arms, Will turned. "That oughta keep you for—" His words fell away.

Eleanor Dinsmore stood behind him, dressed in a clean yellow smock and matching skirt, brushing her hair into a tail. Her chin rested on her chest, and a checkered ribbon was clamped in her teeth. How long had it been since he'd seen a woman putting up her hair in the morning? Her elbows—pointed toward the ceiling—appeared graceful. They lifted the hem of her smock, revealing a crescent of white within the cutout of her skirt. She snatched the ribbon from her teeth and bound the hair high and tight. Lifting her head, she caught him gawking.

"What're you staring at?"

"Nothing." Guiltily, he lurched for the door, feeling his face heat.

"Mr. Parker?"

"Ma'am?" He stopped, refusing to turn and let her see him blushing.

"I'll need a little kindling. Would you mind breaking off a few smaller pieces?" He nodded and left.

Will had been unprepared for his reaction to Mrs. Dinsmore. It wasn't *her*— hell, it could have been any woman and his reaction would probably have been the same. Women were soft, curvy things, and he'd been without them for a long, long time. What man wouldn't want to watch? As he knelt to tap kindling off a chunk of oak, he recalled the checkered ribbon trailing from her teeth, the white flash of underwear beneath her smock, and his own quick blush.

What the hell's the matter with you, Parker? The woman's five months pregnant, and plain as a round rock. Get that kindling back in there, and find somethin' else to think about.

She'd scolded him once for knocking, but returning with the kindling, he paused again. Even before prison, there had been few doors open to Will Parker, and—fresh out—he was too accustomed to locks and bars to open a woman's screen and walk right in.

Instead of knocking, he announced, "Got your kindling."

She glanced up from the bacon she was slicing and called, "Put it right in the stove."

He not only put it in the stove, he built the fire. Such a simple job, but a pleasure. In all his life, he'd never owned a stove. It had been years since he'd had the right to one, even one owned by somebody else. He took care laying the kindling, striking the match, watching the sticks flare. Savoring. Taking as much time as he pleased, realizing time was no longer controlled by someone else. When the kindling had a hearty start, he added a thick log, and though it was a warm morning, extended his palms toward the heat.

Building a fire in a stove was just another morning chore to Eleanor. Watching him enjoy the job made her wonder about the life he'd lived, the comforts he hadn't had. She wondered what was going through his mind as he stared at the flames. Whatever it was, she'd probably never know.

He turned from the stove reluctantly, dusting his hands on his thighs. "Anything else?"

"You could fill that water pail for me."

From behind he scanned her yellow outfit—yellow as a buttercup—and the tail of hair bound by the checkered ribbon. She had donned an apron styled like a pinafore, tied loosely at the back. Studying the bow in the shallows of her spine, he experienced again the wrenching sense of home that had been denied him all his life, and along with it a queer reluctance to approach her. But the water pail was at her elbow, and deliberately stepping close to a woman—any woman—since doing time for killing one made him constantly expect her to leap aside in fright. He made a wide berth around her and, reaching, muttered, " 'Scuse me, ma'am."

She glanced up and smiled. " 'Preciate your buildin' the fire, Mr. Parker," she offered, then returned to her slicing.

Crossing the room with the water pail, he felt better than he had in years. At the door, he stopped. "I was wonderin', ma'am . . ."

With the knife in the bacon she looked back over her shoulder.

"You milk that goat out there?" He thumbed toward the yard.

"No. I milk the cow."

"You have a cow?"

"Herbert. She's probably down by the barn by now."

"Herbert?" A corner of his mouth quirked.

She shrugged while humor lit her face. "Don't ask me how the name got on her. She's always been Herbert and that's what she answers to."

"I could milk"—his grin spread—"Herbert for you if you tell me where to find another pail."

She completed the slice and wiped her hands on her apron, fixing a teasing grin on her mouth. "Well, my, my . . ." she drawled. "Is that a smile I see threatenin' the man's face?"

He allowed it to remain as they openly regarded one another, finding that the morning had brought changes they each liked. Seconds passed before they were smitten by self-consciousness. He glanced away. She turned to fetch him a galvanized pail.

"There's a milk stool standin' against the south side o' the barn."

"I'll find it."

The screen door slammed and she crossed to it, calling, "Oh, Mr. Parker?"

He pivoted in the path. "Ma'am?"

She studied him through the screen.

He had a pair of the nicest lips she'd ever seen, and they were downright pretty when they smiled.

"After breakfast I'm gonna cut that hair for you."

The grin mellowed and reached his eyes. "Yes, ma'am," he said softly with a touch on his hat brim.

As he turned downyard with the pail swinging at his side, he wondered when he'd been happier, when life had looked more promising. *She was going to keep him!*

Herbert turned out to be a friendly cuss with big brown eyes and a brown and white hide. She and the goat seemed to be pals, exchanging a hello of noses. The mule was out behind the barn, too, with its eyes half closed, facing the wall. Will chose to milk the cow outside instead of in the smelly barn. He tied her to a fencepost, stripped off his shirt and hunkered on the stool while the heat of the sun pelted his back. It seemed he couldn't soak up enough of it to make up for the five years' dearth. Beside him the goat watched, chewing its cud. The cow chewed too—loud, grinding beats. Comfortable. In time Will's milking matched the rhythm of Herbert's jaws. It was soothing—the warm bovine flesh against his forehead, the warmer sun, the homely sound, and the heat building up the length of his arms. In time his muscles burned—satisfying, honest heat generated by his own body toiling as a body ought. He increased his speed to test his mettle.

While he worked, the hens came out of their night roosts, one by one, clucking throatily, walking as if on sharp stones, exploring the grass for snails. He eyed the yard, imagining it clean. He eyed the chickens, imagining them penned. He eyed the woodpile imagining it chopped, ranked and filed. There was one hell of a lot to do, but the challenge fired him with eagerness.

A mother cat showed up with three taffy-colored kittens, a trio of clowning puffballs with tails straight as pokers. The mother curled against Will's ankle and he paused to scratch her.

"What's your name, missus?" She stood on her hind legs, braced her forefeet on his thigh, begging. Her fur was soft and warm as she jutted against his fingers. "You feedin' those three, huh? Need a little help?" He found a sardine can inside the doorway of the barn and filled it, then watched the four of them eat, one of the babies with a foot in the can. He chuckled . . . and the sound of his own laughter was so foreign to his ears it made his heart hammer. He tilted his head back and squinted at the sky, letting freedom and happiness overcome him. He chuckled again, feeling the wondrous thrust of the sound against his throat. How long since he'd heard it? How long?

When he delivered the milk to the house he smelled bacon frying from twenty feet down the yard. His stomach growled and he paused with his hand raised to knock on the screen door.

Inside the kitchen, Eleanor lifted her head and their gazes caught.

He dropped the hand and opened the door, taking the risk and finding it easy, after all.

"Met the animals," he announced, setting the pail on the cupboard. "Mule's a little stuck-up, compared to the others."

"Well, bless my soul," Eleanor remarked. "A regular speech."

He backed off, rubbing his hands on his thighs self-consciously. "I'm not much for small talk."

"I've noticed. Still, you might try it out on the boys."

The pair was up, dressed in wrinkled pajamas. The older one looked up from where he was entertaining the young one on the floor with five wooden spools. He stared at Will.

"Howdy, Donald Wade," Will ventured, feeling awkward and uncertain.

Donald Wade stuck his finger in his mouth and poked his cheek out.

"Say good morning, Donald Wade," his mother prompted.

Instead Donald Wade pointed a stubby finger at his brother and blurted out, "That's Baby Thomas."

Baby Thomas drooled down the front of his pajamas, stared at Will and clacked two spools together. To the best of Will's recollection he had never spoken to a person so young. He felt foolish waiting for an answer and didn't know what to do with his hands. So he stacked three spools in a tower. Baby Thomas knocked them over, giggled and clapped. Will looked up and found Eleanor watching him, stirring something on the stove.

"I laid out Glendon's razor for you, and his mug and brush. You're welcome to use them."

He rose to his feet, glanced at the shaving equipment, then at her. But already she'd turned to her cooking, giving him a measure of privacy. He'd been shaving with a straightedge and no soap, hacking his skin all to hell; the mug and brush would be as welcome as the hot water, but he paused before moving toward them.

He'd just have to get used to it: they were going to share this kitchen every morning. He'd have to wash and shave and she'd have to comb her hair and cook breakfast and tend her babies. There were bound to be times when he'd have to brush close by her. And she hadn't jumped away so far, had she?

"Excuse me," he said at her shoulder. She glanced at the mug and shifted over without missing a beat in stirring the grits, letting him reach around her for the teakettle.

"You sleep all right last night?"

"Yes, ma'am."

He filled the cup and the washbasin, whipped up a froth of shaving bubbles and lathered his face, back to back with her.

"How do you like your eggs?"

"Cooked."

"Cooked?" She spun around and their eyes met in the mirror.

"Yes, ma'am." He tilted his head and scraped beneath his left jaw.

"You mean you're in the habit of eating 'em raw?"

"I been known to."

"You mean straight out of some farmer's hen house?"

He shaved away, avoiding her eyes. She burst out laughing, drawing his reflected glance once again. She laughed long, unrestrainedly, resting an arm on her stomach, until his eyes—black as walnuts above the white shaving soap—took on a hint of amusement.

"You think it's funny?" He rinsed the razor.

She sobered with an effort. "I'm sorry."

She sounded anything but sorry, but he found her amusement did pleasant things to her face. Outlining a sideburn, he said, "Farmers tend to blame it on the foxes, so nobody comes lookin'."

She studied him a while, wondering how many miles he'd drifted, how many hen houses he'd raided, how long it would take him to lose that distance he maintained so carefully. For the moment she'd created a crack in it, but inside he was rolled up like a possum.

She found herself enjoying the smell of shaving soap in the house again. His face emerged, one scrape at a time, the face she'd be looking at across her table for years to come, should he decide to stay. She was surprised to find herself fascinated by it, by the shape of his jaw, the clean line of his nose, the thinness of his cheeks, the darkness of his eyes. When he glanced up and found her still studying him, she spun back toward the stove.

"Fried soft, hard or scrambled?"

His hands fell still at the question. In prison they were always scrambled and tasted like damp newspaper. My God—to be given a choice.

"Fried soft."

"Soft it'll be."

While he washed up and combed his hair, he listened to the spatter as the eggs hit the pan, a sound he'd seldom heard, living in bunkhouses and boxcars as he had for much of his free life. Sounds. In his life he'd heard a lot of rumbling wheels and other men snoring. Clanging bars, male voices, washing machines.

Behind him the boys jabbered and giggled, and the wooden spools clattered to the floor. The stovelids clanged. The ashes collapsed. A log thudded. The teakettle hissed. A mother said, "Time for breakfast, boys. Jump up on your chairs now."

The smells in this kitchen were enough to make a man drown in his own saliva. In prison the two prevailing smells were those of disinfectant and urine, and food there seemed to have as little smell as it did taste.

When they sat down to breakfast, Will openly stared at the wealth of food on his plate: three eggs—three!—done to a turn. Grits, bacon, hot black coffee and toast with boysenberry jam.

She saw his hesitation, saw him rest his hands on his thighs as if afraid to reach out again.

"Eat," she ordered, then began chopping up an egg for Baby Thomas.

As he had last night, Will ate in a state of disbelief at his good fortune. He was half done before realizing she was only picking at a piece of dry toast. His fork-hand paused.

"What's the matter?" she inquired, "Somethin' cooked wrong?"

"No. No! It's . . . why, it's the best breakfast I ever had in my life, but where's yours?"

"Food don't agree with me this early in the morning."

He couldn't imagine anyone not eating if food was plentiful. Had she given him her share, too?

"But—"

"Women get that way when they're expectin'," she explained.

"Oh." His eyes dropped to her belly, then quickly aside.

Why, I swear, she thought. *That man's blushin'!* For whatever reason, the thought pleased her.

After breakfast she sat him on a chair in the middle of the kitchen and tied a dishtowel around him, backward. Her first touch sent shivers down his calves. He listened to the scissors snip, felt the comb scrape his skull and closed his eyes to savor each movement of her knuckles against his head. He shuddered and let his hands go limp on his thighs, covered by the dishtowel.

She saw his eyes drop closed.

"Feel good?" she asked.

They flew open again. "Yes, ma'am."

"No need to stiffen up." She nudged his shoulder gently. "Just relax."

After that, she worked in silence, letting him absorb the pleasure undisturbed.

His eyelids slid closed again and he drifted beneath the first gentle woman's touch he'd experienced in over six years. She brushed the tip of his ear, the back of his neck, and he was lulled into his private, soft place. Lord, lord . . . it was good . . .

When the haircut was done she had to wake him.

"Hm?" He lifted his head, then jerked awake, dismayed at finding he'd dozed. "Oh . . . I must've—"

"All done." She whisked the dishtowel off and he rose to peer into the tiny round mirror next to the sink. The hair was slightly longer above his right ear than above his left, but overall the haircut was a great improvement over the close shearing he'd received in prison.

"Looks good, ma'am," he offered, touching a sideburn with his knuckles. He looked back over his shoulder. "Thank you. And for breakfast, too."

Whenever he thanked her she brushed it off as if she'd done nothing. Sweeping the floor, she didn't look up. "You got a healthy head of hair there, Mr. Parker. Glendon's was thin and fine. Always cut his, too." She waddled to the side of the room for a dustpan. "Enjoyed doin' it again. Enjoyed the smell of the shavin' soap around the house again, too."

She had? He thought he'd been the only one to enjoy those things. Or perhaps she was being kind to put him at ease. He found himself wanting to return the favor.

"I can do that," he offered as she bent to collect his streaky brown hair from the floor.

"It's as good as done. Wouldn't mind, however, if you took over the chore of feeding the pigs."

She straightened and their eyes met. In hers he saw uncertainty. It was the first thing she'd asked him to do, and not too pleasant. But what was unpleasant to one man was freedom to Will Parker. She'd fed him, lent him her husband's razor, shared her fire and her table and had put him to sleep with a comb and scissors. His lips opened and a voice inside urged, *Say it, Parker. You afraid she'll think you ain't much of man if you do?*

"That haircut was the best thing I've felt for a long time."

She understood perfectly. She, too, had spent so much of her life in a loveless, touchless world. Odd, how a statement so simple formed a sympathetic bond.

"Well, I'm glad."

"In prison—"

Her eyes swept back to his. "In prison, what?"

He shouldn't have started, but she had a way about her that loosened his jaws, made him want to trust her with the secrets that hurt most. "In prison they use these buzzy little clippers and they cut off most of your hair so you feel—" He glanced away, reluctant to complete the thought, after all.

"You feel what?" she encouraged.

He studied his own hair lying on the dustpan, remembering. "Naked."

Neither of them moved. Sensing how hard it had been for him to admit such a thing, she wanted to reach out and touch his arm. But before she could, he took the dustpan and dumped it in the stove.

"I'll see after the pigs," he said, ending the moment of closeness.

Donald Wade agreed to show Will where the pigs were, and Eleanor sent them out with a half-pail of milk and orders to feed it to them.

"To the pigs!" Will exclaimed, aghast. He'd gone hungry most of his life and she fed fresh milk to the pigs?

"Herbert gives more than we can use, and the milk truck can't get in here, what with the driveway all washed out. Anyway, I don't want no town people nosing around the place. Feed it to the pigs."

It broke Will's heart to carry the milk out of the house.

Donald Wade led the way, though Will could have found the pigpen with his nose alone. Crossing the yard, he took a better look at the driveway. It was sorry, all right. But Mrs. Dinsmore had a mule, and if there was a mule there must be implements to hitch to it. And if there were no implements, he'd shovel by hand. He needed the driveway passable to get the junk hauled out of here. Already he was assessing that junk not as waste but as scrap metal. Scrap metal would soon bring top dollar with America turning out war supplies for England. The woman was sitting on top of a gold mine and didn't even know it.

Not only was the driveway sad; the yard in broad daylight was pitiful. Dilapidated buildings that looked as if a swift kick would send them over. Those with a few good years left were sorely in need of paint. The corncrib was filled with junk instead of corn—barrels, crates, rolls of rusty barbed wire, stacks of warped lumber. Will couldn't tell what kept the door of the chicken coop from falling off. The smell, as they passed, was horrendous. No wonder the chickens roosted in the junkpiles. He passed stacks of machinery parts, empty paint cans—though he couldn't figure out where the paint might have been used. The goat's nest seemed to be in an abandoned truck with the cushion stuffing chewed away. Lord, thought Will, there was enough work here to keep a man going twenty-four hours a day for a solid year.

Bobbing along beside him, Donald Wade interrupted his thoughts.

"There." The boy pointed at the structure that looked like a tobacco-drying shed.

"There what?"

"That's where the pig mash is." He led the way into a building crammed with everything from soup to nuts, only this time, usable stuff. Obviously Dinsmore had done more than collect junk. Barterer? Horse trader? The paint cans in here were full. The rolls of barbed wire, new. Furniture, tools, saddles, a newspaper press, egg crates, pulley belts, canepoles, the fender of a Model-A, a dress form, a barrel full of pistons, Easter baskets, a boiler, cowbells, moonshine jugs, bedsprings . . . and who knew what else was buried in the close-packed building.

Donald Wade pointed to a gunnysack sitting on the dirt floor with a rusty coffee can beside it. "Two." He held up three fingers and had to fold one down manually.

"Two?"

"Mama, she mixes two with the milk."

Will hunkered beside Donald Wade, opened the sack and smiled as the boy continued to hold down the finger. "You wanna scoop 'em for me?"

Donald Wade nodded so hard his hair flopped. He filled the can but couldn't manage to pull it from the deep sack. Will reached in to help. The mash fell into the milk with a sharp, grainy smell. When the second scoop was dumped, Donald Wade found a piece of lath in a corner.

"You stir with this."

Will began stirring. Donald Wade stood with his hands inside the bib of his overalls, watching. At length he volunteered, "I can stir good."

Will grinned secretly. "You can?"

Donald Wade made his hair flop again.

"Well, good thing, 'cause I was needin' a rest."

Even with both hands knotted hard around the lath, Donald Wade needed help from Will. The man's smile broke free as the boy clamped his teeth over his bottom lip and maneuvered the stick with flimsy arms. Will's arms fit nice around the small shoulders as he knelt behind the boy and the two of them together mixed the mash.

"You help your mama do this every day?"

"Prett-near. She gets tired. Mostly I pick eggs."

"Where?"

"Everywhere."

"Everywhere?"

"Around the yard. I know where the chickens like it best. I c'n show you."

"They give many eggs?"

Donald Wade shrugged.

"She sell 'em?"

"Yup."

"In town?"

"Down on the road. She just leaves 'em there and people leave the money in a can. She don't like goin' to town."

"How come?"

Donald Wade shrugged again.

"She got any friends?"

"Just my pa. But he died."

"Yeah, I know. And I'm sure sorry about that, Donald Wade."

"Know what Baby Thomas did once?"

"What?"

"He ate a worm."

Until that moment Will hadn't realized that to a four-year-old the eating of a worm was more important than the death of a father. He chuckled and ruffled the boy's hair. It felt as soft as it looked.

I could get to like this one a lot, he thought.

With the hogs fed, they stopped to rinse the bucket at the pump. Beneath it was a wide mudhole with not even a board thrown across it to keep the mud from splattering.

Naturally, Donald Wade got his boots coated. When they returned to the house his mother scolded, "You git, child, and scrape them soles before you come in here!"

Will put in, "It's my fault, ma'am. I took him down by the pump."

"You did? Oh, well . . ." Immediately she hid her pique, then glanced across the property. When she spoke, her voice held a quiet despondency. "Things are a real fright around here, I know. But I guess you can see that for yourself."

Will sealed his lips, tugged his hat brim clear down to his eyebrows, slipped his hands flat inside his backside pockets and scanned the property expressionlessly. Eleanor peeked at him from the corner of her eye. Her heart beat out a warning. *He'll run now. He'll sure as shootin' run after getting an eyeful of the place in broad daylight.*

But again he saw the possibilities. And nothing on the good green earth could make him turn his back on this place unless he was asked to. Gazing across the yard, all he said, in his low-key voice was, "Reckon the pens could use a little cleanin'."

Chapter 5

They went for a walk when the midmorning sun had lifted well above the trees—a green and gold day smelling of deep summer. Will had never walked with a woman and her children before. It held a strange, unexpected appeal. He noticed her way with the children, how she carried Baby Thomas on one hip with his heel flattening her smock. How, as they set off from the porch, she reached back for Donald Wade, inviting, "Come on, honey, you lead the way," and helped him off the last step. How she watched him gallop ahead, smiling after him as if she'd never before seen his flopping yellow hair, his baggy striped overalls. How she locked her hands beneath Thomas's backside, leaned from the waist, took a deep pull of the clear air and said to the sky, "My, if this day ain't a blessin'." How she called ahead, "Careful o' that wire in the grass there, Donald Wade!" How she plucked a leaf and handed it to Thomas, then let him touch her nose with it and pretended it tickled her and made the young one giggle.

Watching, Will became entranced. Lord, she was some mother. Always kind voiced. Always finding the good in things. Always concerned about her boys. Always making them feel important. Nobody had ever made Will feel important, only in the way.

He studied her covertly, noting more clearly the bulk of her belly, outlined by the baby's leg. Donald Wade had said she gets tired. Recalling the boy's words, Will considered offering to carry the baby, but he felt out of his depth around Thomas. He'd be no good at getting his nose tickled or making chitchat. Besides, she might not cotton to a stranger like him handling Glendon Dinsmore's boys.

They went around to the back of the house where the dishtowel flapped on a line strung between teetering clothespoles that had been shimmed up by crude wood braces. Beyond these were more junkpiles before the woods began—pines, oaks, hickories and more. Sparrows flitted from tree to tree ahead, and Eleanor followed with her finger, telling the boys, "See? Chipping sparrows." A brown thrasher swept past and perched on a dead limb. Again she pointed it out and named it. The sun glinted off the boys' blond heads and painted their mother's dress an even brighter hue. They walked along a faint double path worn by wheels some time ago. Sometimes Donald Wade skipped, swinging his arms widely. The younger one tipped his head back and looked at the sky, his hand resting on his mother's shoulder. They were so happy! Will hadn't come up against many happy people in his day. It was arresting.

A short distance from the house they came upon an east-facing hill covered by regular rows of squat fruit trees.

"This here's the orchard," Eleanor announced, gazing over its length and breadth.

"Big," Will observed.

"And you ain't seen half of it. These here are peach. Down yonder is a whole string of apples and pears . . . and oranges, too. Glendon had this idea to try orange trees, but they never did much." She smiled wistfully. "Too far north for them."

Will stepped off the path and inspected a cluster of fruit. "Could have used a little spraying."

"I know." Unconsciously she stroked the baby's back. "Glendon planned to do that, but he died in April and never got the chance."

This far south the trees should have been sprayed long before April, Will thought, but refrained from saying so. They moved on.

"How old are these trees?"

"I don't know exactly. Glendon's daddy planted most of them when he was still alive. All except the oranges, like I said. There's apples, too, just about every kind imaginable, but I never learned their names. Glendon's daddy, he knew a lot about them, but he died before I married Glendon. He was a junker, too, just like Glendon. Went to auction sales and traded stuff with anybody that came along. No reason to any of it, it seemed." Abruptly, she inquired, "You ever tasted quince? Those there are quince."

"Sour as rhubarb."

"Make a luscious pie, though."

"I wouldn't know about that, ma'am."

"Bet you'd like to try one, wouldn't you?"

He gave her a sideward glance. "Reckon I would."

"Could use a little fat on them bones, Mr. Parker."

He leveled his eyes on the quince trees and tugged his hat brim so low it cut off his view of the horizon. Thankfully, she changed the subject.

"So where'd you eat 'em, then?"

"California."

"California?" She peered up at him with her head cocked. "You been there?"

"Picked fruit there one summer when I was a kid."

"You see any movie stars?"

"Movie stars?" He wouldn't have guessed she'd know much about movie stars. "No." He glanced at her. "You ever seen any?"

She laughed. "Now where would I see movie stars when I never even seen a movie?"

"Never?"

She shook her head. "Heard about 'em from the kids in school, though."

He wished he could promise to take her sometime, but where would he get the money for movies? And even if he had it, there was no theater in Whitney. Besides, she avoided the town.

"In California, the movie stars are only in Hollywood, and it gets cold in parts where there are mountains. And the ocean's dirty. It stinks."

She could see she had her work cut out for her if she was to get that pessimism out of him. "You always so jolly?"

He would have tugged his hat brim lower, but if he did he'd be unable to see where he was walking. "Well, California isn't like what you think."

"You know, I can't say I'd mind if you'd smile a little more often."

He tossed her a sullen glance. "About what?"

"Maybe, Mr. Parker, you got to find that out for yourself." She let the baby slip from her hip. "Lord, Thomas, if you ain't gettin' heavier than a guilty conscience, I don't know. Come on, take Mommy's hand and I'll show you somethin'."

She showed him things Will would have missed: a branch shaped like a dog's paw—"A man could whittle forever and not make anything prettier," she declared. A place where something tiny had nested in the grass and left a collection of empty seed pods—"If I was a mouse, I'd love livin' right here in this pretty-smellin' orchard, wouldn't you?" A green katydid camouflaged upon a greener blade of grass—"Y' got to look close to see he's makin' the sound with his wings." And in the adjacent woods a magnolia tree with a deep bowl, head-high, where its branches met, and within that bowl, a second tree taken root: a sturdy little oak growing straight and healthy.

"How'd it get there?" Donald Wade asked.

"How d' you think?"

"I dunno."

She squatted beside the boys, gazing up at piggyback trees. "Well, there was this wise old owl lived in these woods, and one evenin' at dusk he came by and I ast him the same thing. I says to him, how'd that li'l old oak tree get t' growin' in that magnolia?" She grinned at Donald Wade. "Know what he told me?"

"Uh-uh." Donald Wade stared at his mother, mystified. She dropped to her rump and sat like an Indian, stripping bark from a stick with her thumbnail as she went on.

"Well, he said there was two squirrels lived here, years ago. One of 'em was a hard worker, spent every day totin' acorns into that little pocket in the tree up there." She pointed with the stick. "The other squirrel, well, he was lazy. Laid on his back on that limb over there" —she pointed again, to a nearby pine—"and made a pillow out of his tail and crossed his legs and watched the busy squirrel gettin' ready for winter. He waited until there was so many nuts they was about to start spillin' over the edge. Then when the hardworking squirrel went off to look for one last nut, the lazy one scrambled up there and ate and ate and ate, until he'd ate every last one of 'em. He was so full he sat on the limb and let out a burp so almighty powerful it knocked him off backwards." She drew a deep breath, braced her hands on her knees and burped loudly, then flopped back, arms outflung. Will smiled. Donald Wade giggled. Baby Thomas squealed.

"But it wasn't so funny, after all," she continued, gazing at the sky.

Donald Wade sobered and leaned over her to look straight down into her face. "Why not?"

"Because on his way down, he cracked his head on a limb and killed himself deader'n a mackerel."

Donald Wade smacked himself in the head and fell backward, sprawled on the grass beside Eleanor, his eyelids closed but twitching. She rolled up and took Thomas into her lap. "Now when the busy little squirrel come back with that one last nut between his teeth, he climbed up and saw that all his acorns were gone. He opened his mouth to cry and the last acorn he brung up, why, it fell into the nest beneath the nutshells the greedy squirrel had left." Donald Wade, too, sat up, his interest in the story aroused once again. "He knew he couldn't stay here for the winter, 'cause he'd already gathered up all the nuts for miles around. So he left his cozy nest and didn't come back till he was old. So old it was hard for him to climb up and down the oak trees like he used to. But he remembered the little nest in the magnolia where it had been warm and dry and safe, and he climbed up there to see it again, just for old times' sake. And what do you think he found?"

"The oak tree growin' there?" the older boy ventured.

"That's right." She finger-combed Donald Wade's hair off his brow. "A sturdy little oak with enough acorns that the old squirrel never had to run up and down a tree again, 'cause they was growin' all around his head, right there in his warm, cozy nest."

Donald Wade popped up. "Tell me another one!"

"Uh-uh. Got to go on, show Mr. Parker the rest of the place." She pushed to her feet and reached for Thomas's hand. "Come on, boys. Donald Wade, you take Thomas's other hand. Come on, Mr. Parker," she said over her shoulder. "Day's movin' on."

Will lagged behind, watching them saunter up the lane, three abreast, holding hands. The rear of her skirt was wrinkled from the damp grass, but she cared not a whit. She was busy pointing out birds, laughing softly, talking to the boys in her singsong Southern fashion. He felt a catch in his heart for the mother he'd never known, the hand he'd never held, the make-believe tales he'd never been told. For a moment he pretended he'd had one like Eleanor Dinsmore. Every kid should have one like her. *Maybe, Mr. Parker, you got to find that out for yourself.* Her words echoed through his mind as they moved on, and Will found himself glancing back over his shoulder at the oak tree growing out of the magnolia, realizing fully what a rare thing it was.

In time they came to a double flank of beehives, grayed, weathered and untended, dotting the edge of the orchard. He searched his mind for any knowledge of bees, but found none. He saw the hives as a potential source of income, but she gave them wide berth and he recalled that her husband had died tending the bees, was buried somewhere out here in the orchard. But he saw no grave and she pointed none out. In spite of the way Dinsmore had died, Will felt himself drawn to the hives, to the few insects that droned around them, and to the scent of the fruit—wormy or whole—as it warmed beneath the eleven o'clock sun. He wondered about the man who'd been here before him, a man who maintained nothing, finished nothing and apparently never worried about either. How could a man let things run to ruin that way? How could a man lucky enough to own things—so many things—care so little about their condition? Will could count in ten seconds the number of things he'd ever owned: a horse, a saddle, clothing, a razor. Lengthening his stride to catch up with Eleanor Dinsmore, he wondered if she were as hopeless a dreamer as her husband had been.

They came to a pecan grove that looked promising, hanging thick with immature nuts, and in the lane over the next hill a tractor, which blocked their way.

"What's this?" Will's eyes lit up.

"Glendon's old Steel Mule," she explained while Will made a slow circuit around the rusting hulk. "This was where she stopped running, so this is where he left 'er." It was an old Bates Model G, but of what vintage Will couldn't be sure—'26 or '27, maybe. At the front it had two wide-set steel wheels, and on each side at the rear three wheels of telescoping size surrounded by tracks with lugs. The lugs were chewed, in some places missing. He glanced at the engine and doubted it would ever make a sound again.

"I know a little about engines, but I think this one's shot for good."

They moved on, reaching the far end of the property, turning back toward the house on another path. They passed stubbled fields and patches of woods, eventually topping a rise where Will stopped dead, pushed back his hat and gaped. "Holy smokes," he muttered. Below lay a veritable graveyard of iron stoves, rusting in grass tall enough to bend in the wind.

"A bunch of 'em, huh?" Eleanor stopped beside him. "Seemed like he'd haul another one home every week. I said to him, 'Glendon, what're you going to do with all them old stoves when everybody these days is changin' to gas and kerosene?' But he just kept hauling 'em in here whenever he heard of someone changin' over."

There had to be five hundred of them, as bright orange as the road to Whitney.

"Holy smokes," Will repeated, lifting his hat and scratching his head, imagining the chore of hauling them out again.

She glanced at his profile, clearly defined against the blue sky, with the hat pushed back beyond his hairline. Did she dare tell him about the rest? Might as well, she decided. He'd find out eventually anyway. "Wait'll you see the cars."

Will turned her way. After all he'd seen, nothing would be a surprise. "Cars?"

"Wrecks, every one of 'em. Worse'n the Steel Mule."

Hands on hips, he studied the stoves a long moment. At length he sighed, tugged down his hat brim and said, "Well, let's get it over with."

The cars lay immediately behind the band of woods surrounding the outbuildings—they'd come nearly full circle around the place—and created a clutter of gaping doors and sagging roofs in the long weeds. They approached the windowless wreck of an old 1928 Whippet. Wild honeysuckle climbed over its wire wheels and along the front bumper. On the near runningboard a bird had made its nest against the lee of the back fender.

"Can I drive it?" Donald Wade asked eagerly.

"Sure can. Wanna take Baby Thomas with you?"

"Come on, Thomas." Donald Wade took his brother's hand, plowed through the grass and helped Thomas board. The two clambered up and sat side by side, bouncing on the tattered seat. Donald Wade pumped the steering wheel left and right, making engine noises with his tongue. When Eleanor and Will approached, he whipped the wheel even more vigorously. Imitating his brother, Thomas stuck out his tongue and blew, sending specks of saliva flying onto a cobweb strung across the faded black paint of the dashboard.

Eleanor stood beside the open door and laughed. The more she laughed, the more the boys bounced and blew. The more they bounced and blew, the more animatedly Donald Wade worked the steering wheel.

She crossed her arms on the window opening, bent forward and propped her chin on a wrist. "Where y'all goin', fellers?"

"Atlanta!" squealed Donald Wade.

" 'Lanta!" parroted Thomas.

"Atlanta?" teased their mother. "What y'all think y're gonna do clear over there?"

"Don' know." Donald Wade drove hell-bent for leather, the old wheel spinning in his freckled hands.

"Care to give a pretty lady a ride?"

"Can't stop—goin' too fast!"

"Hows 'bout if I just jump on the runnin' board while you whiz by?"

"Okee-dokee, lady!"

"Ouch!" Eleanor jumped back and grabbed her foot. "You run over my toe, young feller!"

"Eeeeech!" Donald Wade's stubby foot slammed the brake pedal to the floor as he came to a screeching halt. "Git in, lady."

Eleanor acted affronted. She put her nose in the air and turned away. "Don't reckon I care to, now you run over my toes that way. Reckon I'll find myself somebody drives less reckless than you. But you might ask Mr. Parker here if he needs a lift to town. He's been walkin' some and he's probably plum tuckered, ain't you, Mr. Parker?" She squinted up at him with a crooked smile.

Will had never played such games before. He felt conspicuous and unimaginative, while they all watched him, waiting for a reply. He frantically searched his mind and came up with a sudden stroke of genius. "Next time, boys." He lifted one scuffed boot above the grass. "Just got this here new pair of boots and I gottta get 'em broke in before the dance Saturday night."

"Okee-dokee, mister. *Bbvvrr-n-n-n!*" More spit accompanied the engine noise, and more laughter from Eleanor Dinsmore. She and Will stood in the dappled light from a wide oak, in grass and honeysuckle to their knees, and Will felt himself becoming a child again, experiencing delights he hadn't known the first time around. The day was warm and smelled green, and for the moment there seemed no need to rush or plan, to wish or regret. It was enough to watch two blond tykes drivin' down to Atlanta in a 1928 Whippet.

Eleanor's laughter faded, but her smile remained as she studied Will. He leaned against the side of the car with his weight on one foot, arms crossed loosely over his chest. The sunlight lit the tip of his nose. On his lips was a genuine smile. "Well, now, would you lookit there," she said softly.

He glanced up and found her studying his mouth. So she'd done it; she'd made him smile. It felt as revitalizing as a full belly, and he neither dimmed nor hid it, but rained it on Eleanor Dinsmore.

"Feels good, don't it?" she asked quietly.

His brown eyes softened as they appreciated her green ones. "Yes, ma'am," he replied quietly.

Smiling up at him, noting the pleasure in his eyes, Eleanor thrilled at the realization that she and the boys had succeeded in putting it there. Heaven's sake, what a smile did to Will Parker's face—eyes hooked down at the corners, lids lowered to half-mast, lips softened, the emotionlessness gone. *I could get along with this man quite easy, now I know I can get him to smile.*

His smile traveled from her mouth to her rounded stomach, a tarrying trip. She remained unflinching under his steady regard, wondering what he was thinking. "For life" was a long time. Let him look, let him decide. She'd do the same. She had never cared one way or the other about how people looked. But Will Parker, relaxed and smiling, made a fetching sight, no question about it. Only after the thought struck did she grow uneasy beneath his perusal. His gaze lifted and meeting hers, made Eleanor blush inside.

"You know, Mrs. Dinsmore—"

Thomas's scream interrupted. Will glanced over his shoulder. "What the—"

Donald Wade screamed—pained and panicked.

Will snapped around and shouted, "Jesus Christ, get them out of there!" He lunged toward the car and hauled Donald Wade out by one arm. "Run! Get away from here! Bees!" Half a dozen of them buzzed around Will's head. One stung him on the neck, another on the wrist, as he reached for a yowling Thomas. By the time he withdrew from the car, the insects swarmed everywhere. Ignoring the stings that fell on him, he swatted the bees off Thomas with his cowboy hat. Eleanor and Donald Wade took off at a run, but just as Will caught up to them Donald Wade tipped over, face first, screaming. Will scooped him up and kept running. His legs were longer than Eleanor's and he soon outdistanced her. Halting uncertainly, he turned back. Behind him, she struggled along at an awkward gait, supporting her stomach with one hand, fanning the air about her head with the other. The bees had thickened and set up an angry hum.

"Mrs. Dinsmore!" he called.

"Take them and run!" Eleanor hollered. "Don't wait for me!"

Will saw the terror in her eyes and paused in indecision.

"Go!" she screamed.

One landed on Thomas's arm. He screamed and began thrashing wildly on Will's arm. Will turned and barreled up the lane, with the boys bellowing and bouncing. When he'd outrun the swarm, he paused, panting, and spun just in time to see Eleanor stumble and go down on her face. His heart seemed to jump into his mouth. He dropped the boys in the middle of the lane and ordered, "Wait here!" Then he was pounding back to her, ignoring the howls behind him. He ran harder than ever before in his life, toward the woman who rolled over slowly and pushed herself up. On one hip she sat, eyes closed, rocking, clutching her stomach. *Oh, Jesus, sonfoabitch, Christalmighty*—Will prayed in the only way he knew how—*don't let her be hurt!* He skidded to a halt on one knee, reaching for her.

"Mrs. Dinsmore . . ." he panted.

Her eyes opened. "The boys—are the boys all right?"

"Mostly scared." He took off his hat and flapped angrily at two buzzing bees that hovered about her head. "Git out of here, you sons a bitches!" From up the path the screams continued. Will threw an uncertain glance at the boys, then at Eleanor, fighting panic. He took her by the arms and forced her back. "Lay down here a minute. The bees are gone."

"But the boys—"

"The boys got a few bites, but let 'em howl for a minute. Here now, you lay back like I said." She stopped resisting and wilted to the earth. He stuffed his hat under her. "Here, you put your head on this."

She rested but small pains arced through her abdomen.

"You hurt anything when you fell?" Will asked anxiously, kneeling beside her, wondering what he was supposed to do if she started losing the baby out here in the middle of this weed patch. He watched her stomach lifting and falling in panting beats, wondered if he should touch it, test it. But for what? He sat on one heel, hands resting uncertainly on his thighs.

"I'm okay. Please . . . would you just see after the boys?"

"But you're—"

"I'll just lay here a while. You take the boys up to the well and plaster some mud on their bee stings quick as you can. It'll cut the swelling."

"But I can't just leave you here."

"Yes, you can! Now do as I say, Will Parker! Them bee stings could kill Thomas if he got enough of them, and I already lost their daddy to the bees—don't you understand!" Her eyes filled with tears and Will reluctantly got to his feet. He glanced toward the pair, still sitting abjectly in the middle of the lane, bawling their heads off. He glanced at their mother and pointed authoritatively at her nose.

"Don't you move until I get back." Then he was off at a run again. A moment later he rescued the two squalling boys and trotted on.

"Maa-maaaaw! I want my maa-maaw!" Donald Wade had several welts on his face and hands. One ear was scarlet and puffed. He ground his fists into his eyes.

"Your mama can't run as fast as I can. Hang on and we'll put somethin' cool on them bites."

Baby Thomas was running from all ports and had bites all over, including a mean-looking cluster on his neck. They'd already begun swelling. At the thought of what could happen, should they be swelling as much on the inside as they were on the out, Will made his legs pump harder. He tried to think rationally, to remember if he'd seen where Mrs. Dinsmore kept her bread knife. A picture of the long silver blade flashed through his mind and he imagined having to slip it into Baby Thomas's windpipe, through that soft, pink baby skin. His stomach tumbled at the thought. He wasn't sure he could do it. *Goddammit, don't let this kid choke, you hear me!*

Don't think of it, Parker, just keep runnin'! As long as he's screaming like a banshee he ain't strangling.

Baby Thomas yowled all the way back to the yard. Will hit the mud patch by the pump doing seven miles an hour. His left foot flew west, his right east, and a moment later he landed on his seat with a splat. There he sat with two bawling boys. A bubble formed in Baby Thomas's right nostril. Tears rolled down Donald Wade's cheeks, wetting the bee stings. Will reached up and pulled Donald Wade's fist down.

"Here, don't rub 'em." He sat in the cold, slimy mud and started dabbing it on both boys at once. Thomas fought him tooth and nail, jerking his head back, pushing at Will's hands. But in time the visible welts were covered. The howling subsided to jerky sobs, then the jerky sobs to breathy chuffs of wonder as it dawned on the boys that they were sitting beneath the pump, being plastered with mud. Will unhooked Donald Wade's suspenders, turned his bib down and his shirt up. He treated several stings on his back and belly, then removed the baby's shirt and did likewise.

"They got you, all right," Will confirmed, examining for any he might have missed.

"Are they all right?"

Will's chin snapped up at the sound of Eleanor's voice. She stood at the edge of the puddle, holding his flattened hat in her hand. "I thought I told you to stay put till I could get back to you."

"Are they all right?" she repeated.

"I think so. Are you?"

"I think so."

"Mama . . ." The baby reached toward her, but Will held him in place.

"You sit here a minute, sport. You'll get your mama all muddy."

Suddenly Eleanor's face crinkled and a chuckle began deep in her throat. Will shot her a glare.

"What you laughin' at?"

"Oh, mercy, if you could see the picture you three make." She covered her mouth and doubled forward, laughing. "It just struck me."

Sudden anger boiled up in Will. How dare she stand there cackling when he'd just had five good years scared out of him! When his heart was knocking so hard his temples hurt! When he sat with the mud oozing up through his only pair of jeans! And all because of her and her boys!

"There ain't a damn thing funny, so stop your crowin'!" He planted both boys on their feet as if they were spades and he was done shoveling. Clumsily he extracted himself from the mud and stood bowlegged, like a toddler with full diapers. All the while she giggled behind her hand. Giggled, for chrissake, when she could be standing there at this very minute having a miscarriage!

He got madder. His head jutted forward. "You crazy, woman?"

"I reckon I am," she managed through her laughter. "Leastways, they all say so, don't they?"

Her good humor only intensified his choler. Incensed, he pointed. "You git up to the house and—and—" But he didn't know what to advise. Hell, what was he, a midwife?

"I'm going, Mr. Parker, I'm going," Eleanor returned jauntily. She punched out the dome of his hat and plopped it on her own head, where it fell past her ears. "But how could I pass by without noticing you sitting there in the mud?" She reached down for Baby Thomas and Will barked, "I'll take care of them! Just get up there and see to yourself!"

She turned away, chuckling, and waddled up the path.

Damn woman didn't have the sense God gave a box of rocks if she didn't realize she should be flat on her back, resting, after the fall she'd taken. It'd take some getting used to, living with a single-minded woman who laughed at him every chance she got. And didn't she know what a scare she gave him? Now that it was over, his knees felt like a pair of rotting tomatoes. That, too, made him mad. Getting watery-kneed over somebody else's woman, and a stranger to boot! None too gently, he called after her, "How long does this mud have to be on 'em?"

From up the path she called, "Ten minutes or so should do it. I'll fix somethin' to help the itching." She dropped his hat on the porch step and disappeared inside.

Will removed the boys' shoes and let them play in the mud. He himself felt twenty pounds heavier with so much goo hanging off his backside. Now and then he glanced at the house, but she stayed inside. He didn't know if he wanted her to come out or not. Confounded woman, standing there laughing at him while he was trying to calm down her howling kids. And nobody wore his hat. Nobody!

At the house, Eleanor set to work smashing plantain leaves with a mortar and pestle. You really don't know a person till you see him mad. So now she'd seen Will Parker mad, and even riled he was pretty mellow—a good sign. What a sight he'd made, sitting in that mudhole with his dark eyes snapping. If he stayed, years from now they'd laugh about it.

She looked up and saw a sight that made her hands fall still. "Well, would y' look at that," she murmured to herself. Will Parker came stalking toward the house with her two naked sons on his arms. Their rumps looked pink and plump against Parker's hard brown arms, their hands fragile on his wiry shoulders. He had a long-legged stride, but moved as if hurry were a stranger to him. His head was bare, his shirt unbuttoned with the tails flapping, and he scowled deeply. What a sight to see her boys with a man again. Strangers scared them, but in less than a day they had taken to Will Parker. And in the same length of time she'd seen all she needed to be convinced he'd do all right at daddyin', whether the boys were his own or not. He'd be gentle with them. And caring.

She watched from the shadows of the kitchen as he approached the house and paused uncertainly at the foot of the porch steps. She stepped out, noting that his pants and shirttails were dripping.

"Y'all washed in that cold well water?"

"Thought you'd be laying down." His voice still hinted at displeasure.

"I had a pang or two but there's nothin' serious wrong."

"Shouldn't you see a doctor or something?"

"Doctor," she scoffed. "What do I need with a doctor?"

"I could walk to town, see if we could get one out here."

"Town ain't got no use for me, I ain't got no use for it. I'll get along just fine."

Lord a-mercy, she was five months pregnant and she hadn't seen a doctor? His eyes dropped to the dish she held. "What's that?"

"Crushed plantain leaves for the bites. But we better dry the boys off first. You mind doin' one while I do the other?"

She was gone inside the house before Will could reply. A moment later she returned with two towels, tossed one to Will and sat on the bottom step with the other. While she dried Donald Wade, Will found himself balancing on the balls of his feet with Thomas between his knees. Another first, he thought, awkwardly drawing the child closer. Thomas was pink and gleaming and his little pecker stuck out like a barricade at a railroad crossing. He stared straight into Will's eyes, silent. Will grinned. "Got to dry you off, short stuff," he ventured quietly. This time he didn't feel as ignorant, talking to the little guy. Thomas didn't yowl or fight him, so he figured he was doing all right. He soon learned that babies do little in the way of helping at bath time. Chiefly, Thomas stared, with his lower lip hanging. He had to have his arms lifted, his fingers separated, his body turned this way and that. Will dried all the cracks and crannies, going easy where the bites were worst. Thomas's neck was so small and fragile-looking. His skin was soft and he smelled better than any human being Will had ever been near. Unexpected pleasure stole over the man.

He glanced up and discovered Eleanor watching him.

"How you doin'?" She smiled lazily.

"Not bad."

"First time?"

"Yes, ma'am."

"Never had any o' your own?"

"No, ma'am."

"Never married?"

"No, ma'am."

They fell silent, rubbing down the boys. The mellowness inspired by the task spilled over in Will and softened his annoyance with the woman.

"You scared the hell out of me, you know, falling like that."

"Scared the hell out of myself." Her lazy smile continued.

"Didn't mean to bark at you that way."

"It's all right. I understand." After a pause, she added, "Reckon you're a little shivery in those wet britches yourself."

"They'll dry."

Thomas stood complacently between Will's knees, and Will had no warning until he felt something warming the cold denim on his inner thigh. He glanced down, yelped and leaped to his feet. Baby Thomas unconcernedly bowed his legs and continued relieving himself in a splattering yellow arc.

"Mercy, Thomas, look what you've done!" Eleanor pushed Donald Wade aside and came up off the step. "Oh, mercy, Mr. Parker, I'm sorry." She dropped a self-conscious glance to Will's thigh. "Baby Thomas, he ain't trained yet, you see, and sometimes—well, sometimes—" She fumbled to a stop and turned pink. "I'm awful sorry."

Will stood with feet widespread, surveying the damage. "Like you said, they were wet anyway."

"I'd be happy to wash them for you, and I'll get you something of Glendon's to wear till they're dry," she offered.

He lifted his head and their eyes met. Hers were dismayed, his bemused. A smile began tugging at one corner of his mouth, a smile as slow as his walk, climbing one cheek until an attractive crescent dented it. He snickered. Inside him the laughter built until it erupted. And as Eleanor's chagrin turned to relief, she joined him.

They stood in the sun laughing together for the first time, with the naked children gazing up at them.

When it ended a subtle change had transpired. Their smiles remained while possibilities drifted through their minds.

"So," he said at length, "is this how you initiate all the men who come up here to answer your ad?" he teased drolly.

"You never know what to expect when you got two this little."

"I'll remember that next time."

"I'll get them clothes of Glendon's and you can take a pail of warm water to the barn."

"Appreciate it, ma'am."

For the moment neither of them moved. They stood rooted by surprise and curiosity, now that they'd seen each other in a new light. Her face radiated more than the reflection of her yellow dress. He thought about reaching up and touching it, thought about what her skin might feel like—maybe soft like Donald Wade's and warm beneath the sun. Instead, he bent to retrieve his hat from the step and settled it on his head. From the safety of its shadow he told her, "I've decided to stay, if you still want me."

"I do," she said directly.

The thrill shot straight to his vitals. For as long as he could remember, nobody had wanted Will Parker. Standing in the sun with one foot on her porch steps and her bare children at his feet, he vowed he'd do his best by her or die trying. "And as far as marrying goes, we'll put that off till you feel comfortable. And if it's never, well, fine. I'll be happy in the barn. How's that?"

"Fine," she agreed, flashing him a brief, nervous smile. He wondered if her insides were stirring like his. He might never have known had she not at that very moment dropped her gaze and fussily checked the hair at the back of her neck.

Well, I'll be damned, Will thought. *I'll be ding-dong double damned.*

Chapter 6

That first week Will Parker was there Eleanor hardly saw him except at meal-times. He worked. And worked and worked. Sunup to sunrise, he never stopped. Their first morning had established a routine which they kept by tacit agreement. Will chopped wood, carried it in and made a fire, then filled the water pail and left to do the milking, giving her privacy in the kitchen. She'd be dressed by the time he returned, and would start breakfast while he washed up and shaved. After they'd eaten, he fed the pigs, then disappeared to do whatever tasks he'd set for himself that day.

The first two things he did were to make a slatted wooden grid for beneath the pump and to fix the ladder to his hayloft. He cleaned the barn better than Eleanor ever recalled seeing it—cobwebs, windows and all—hauled the manure out to the orchard and spread the gutters with lime. Next he attacked the hen house, mucking it out completely, fixing some of the broken roosts, putting new screen on the door and the windows, then sinking posts to make an adjacent pen for the chickens. When it was done, he announced that he could use a little help herding the birds inside. They spent an amusing hour trying to do so. At least, Eleanor found it amusing. Will found it exasperating. He flapped his cowboy hat and cursed when a stubborn hen refused to go where he wanted her to. Eleanor made clucking noises and coaxed the hens with corn. Sometimes she imitated their strut and made up tales about how the hens came to walk that way, the most inventive one about a stubborn black cricket that refused to slither down a hen's throat after it was swallowed. Chickens weren't Will's favorite animal. Goddamn stupid clucks is what he called them. But by the time they got the last one into the hen house, Eleanor had teased a reluctant smile out of him.

Will got along well with the mule, though. Her name was Madam, and Will liked her the moment he saw her wide hairy nose poking around the barn door while he was doing the evening milking. Madam smelled no better than the barn, so as soon as it was clean, Will decided she should be, too. He tethered her by the well and washed her down with Ivory Snow, scrubbing her with a brush and rinsing her with a bucket and rag.

"What the devil are you doing down there?" Eleanor called from the porch.

"Giving Madam a bath."

"What in blazes for?"

"She needs one."

Eleanor had never heard of an animal being scrubbed with Ivory Snow! But it was the durndest thing—Glendon had never been able to do a thing with that stubborn old cuss, but after her bath, Madam did anything Will wanted her to. She followed him around like a trained puppy. Sometimes Eleanor would catch Will looking into Madam's eye and whispering to her, as if the two of them shared secrets.

One evening Will surprised everyone by showing up at the back porch with Madam on a hackamore.

"What's this?" Eleanor stepped to the door, followed by Donald Wade and Baby Thomas.

Will grinned and hoped he wasn't about to make a fool of himself. "Madam and me . . . well, we're goin' to Atlanta and we'll take any passengers who want to come along."

"Atlanta!" Eleanor panicked. Atlanta was forty miles away. What did he want in Atlanta? Then she saw the grin on his lips.

"She said she wanted to see a Claudette Colbert movie," Will explained.

Suddenly Eleanor understood. She released a peal of laughter while Will rubbed Madam's nose. Foolery wasn't easy for him—it was apparent—so she appreciated it all the more. She stood in the doorway with a hand on Donald Wade's head, inquiring, "Anybody want a ride on Madam?" Then, to Will, "You sure she's safe?"

"As a lamb."

From the porch Eleanor watched as Will led the smiling boys around the yard on Madam's back, that back so broad their legs protruded parallel with the earth. Donald Wade rode behind Thomas with his arms folded around the baby's stomach. Surprisingly, Baby Thomas wasn't frightened. He clutched Madam's mane and gurgled in delight.

In the days following that ride, Donald Wade took to trailing after Will just as Madam did. He pitched a fit if Eleanor said, no, it was time for a nap, or no, Will would be doing something that might be dangerous. Nearly always, though, Will would interject, "Let the boy come. He's no trouble."

One morning while she was mixing up a spice cake the pair showed up at the back porch with saws, nails and lumber.

"What're you two up to now?" Eleanor asked, stepping to the screen door, stirring, a bowl against her stomach.

"Will and me are gonna fix the porch floor!" Donald Wade announced proudly. "Ain't we, Will?"

"Sure are, short stuff." Will glanced up at Eleanor. "I could use a piece of wool rag if you got one."

She fetched the rag, then watched while Will patiently sat on the step and showed Donald Wade how to clean a rusty sawblade with steel wool and oil and a piece of soft wool. The saw, she noticed, was miniature. Where he'd found it she didn't know, but it became Donald Wade's. Will had another larger one he'd cleaned and sharpened days ago. When the smaller saw was clean, Will clamped the blade between his knees, took a metal file from his back pocket and showed Donald Wade how a blade is sharpened.

"You ready now?" he asked the boy.

"Yup."

"Then let's get started."

Donald Wade was nothing but a nuisance, getting in Will's way most of the time. But Will's patience with the boy was inexhaustible. He set him up with his own piece of wood on the milking stool, showed him how to anchor it with a knee and get started, then set to work himself, sawing lumber to replace the porch floor. When Donald Wade's saw refused to comply, Will interrupted his work and curled himself over the boy, gripping his small hand, pumping it until a piece of wood fell free. Eleanor felt her heart expand as Donald Wade giggled and looked up with hero-worship in his eyes. "We done it, Will!"

"Yup. Sure did. Now come over here and hand me a few nails."

The nails, Eleanor noticed, were rusty, and the wood slightly warped. But within hours he had the porch looking sturdy again. They christened it by sitting on the new steps in the sun and eating spice cake topped with Herbert's whipped cream.

"You know"—Eleanor smiled at Will—"I sure like the sound of the hammer and saw around the place again."

"And I like the smell of spice cake bakin' while I work."

The following day they painted the entire porch—floor in brick red, and posts in white.

At the "New Porch Party" she served gingerbread and whipped cream. He ate enough for two men and she loved watching him. He put away three pieces, then rubbed his stomach and sighed. "That was mighty good gingerbread, ma'am." He never failed to show appreciation, though never wordily. "Fine dinner, ma'am," or "Much obliged for supper, ma'am." But his thanks made her efforts seem worthwhile and filled her with a sense of accomplishment she'd never known before.

He loved his sweets and couldn't seem to get enough of them. One day when she hadn't fixed dessert he looked let-down, but made no remarks. An hour after the noon meal she found a bucket of ripe quince sitting on the porch step.

The pie—she'd forgotten. She smiled at his reminder and glanced across the yard. He was nowhere to be seen as she picked up the bucket and headed inside and began to mix up a piecrust.

For Will Parker those first couple of weeks at Eleanor Dinsmore's place were unadulterated heaven. The work—why, hell—the work was a privilege, the idea that he could choose what he wanted to do each day. He could cut wood, patch porch floors, clean barns or wash mules. Anything he chose, and nobody said, "Boy, you supposed to be here? Boy, who tol' you to do that?" Madam was a pleasurable animal, reminded him of the days when he'd done wrangling and had had a horse of his own. He flat liked everything about Madam, from the hairs on her lumpy nose to her long, curved eyelashes. And at night now, he brought her into the barn and made his own bed beside her in one of the box stalls that were cleaned and smelled of sweet grass.

Then came morning, every one better than the last. Morning and Donald Wade trailing along, providing company and doting on every word Will said. The boy was turning out to be a real surprise. Some of the things that kid came up with! One day when he was holding the hammer for Will while Will stretched wire around the chicken pen, he stared at an orange hen and asked pensively, "Hey, Will, how come chickens ain't got lips?" Another day he and Will were digging through a bunch of junk, searching for hinges in a dark tool shed when a suspicious odor began tainting the air around them. Donald Wade straightened abruptly and said, "Oh-oh! One of us farted, didn't we?"

But Donald Wade was more than merely amusing. He was curious, bright, and worshiped the shadow Will cast. Will's little sidekick, following everywhere—"I'll help, Will!"—getting his head in the way, standing on the screwdriver, dropping the nails in the grass. But Will wouldn't have changed a minute of it. He found he liked teaching the boy. He learned how by watching Eleanor. Only Will taught different things. Men's things. The names of the tools, the proper way to hold them, how to put a rivet through leather, how to brace a screen door and make it stronger, how to trim a mule's hoof.

The work and Donald Wade were only part of what made his days blissful. The food—God, the food. All he had to do was walk up to the house and take it, cut a piece of spice cake from a pan or butter a bun. What he liked best was taking something sweet outside and eating it as he ambled back toward some half-finished project of his choice. Quince pie—damn, but that woman could make quince pie, could make anything, actually. But she had quince pie down to an art.

He was gaining weight. Already the waistband on his own jeans was tight, and it felt good to work in Glendon Dinsmore's roomy overalls. Odd, how she volunteered anything at all of her husband's without seeming to resent Will's using it— toothbrush, razor, clothes, even dropping the hems of the pants to accommodate Will's longer legs.

But his gratitude was extended for far more than creature comforts. She'd offered him trust, had given him pride again, and enthusiasm at the break of each new day. She'd shared her children who'd brought a new dimension of happiness into his life. She'd brought back his smile.

There was nothing he couldn't accomplish. Nothing he wouldn't try. He wanted to do it all at once.

As the days passed, the improvements he'd made began tallying up. The yard looked better, and the back porch. The eggs were easy to find since the hens were confined to the hen house and, slowly but surely, the woodpile was changing contours. As the place grew neater, so did Eleanor Dinsmore. She wore shoes and anklets now, and a clean apron and dress every morning with a bright hair ribbon to match. She washed her hair twice a week, and he'd been right about it. Clean, it took on a honey glow.

Sometimes when they'd meet in the kitchen, he'd look at her a second time and think, *You look pretty this morning, Mrs. Dinsmore.* But he could never say it, lest she think he was after something more than creature comforts. Truth to tell, it had been a long, long time, but always in the back of his mind lingered the fact that he'd spent time in prison, and what for. Because of it, he kept a careful distance.

Besides, he had a lot more to do before he'd proved he was worth keeping. He wanted to finish the plastering, give the house a coat of paint, improve the road, get rid of the junk cars, make the orchard produce again, and the bees . . . The list seemed endless. But Will soon realized he didn't know how to do all that.

"Has Whitney got a library?" he asked one day in early September.

Eleanor glanced up from the collar she was turning. "In the town hall. Why?"

"I need to learn about apples and bees."

Will sensed her defiance even before she spoke.

"Bees?"

He fixed his eyes on her and let them speak for him. He'd learned by now it was the best way to deal with her when they disagreed.

"You know about libraries—how to use 'em, I mean?"

"In prison I read all I could. They had a library there."

"Oh." It was one of the rare times he'd mentioned prison, but he didn't elaborate. Instead, he went on questioning. "Did your husband have one of those veiled hats, and things to tend bees with?" He didn't know a lot, but he knew he'd need certain equipment.

"Somewhere."

"Think you could look around for me? See if you can find 'em?"

Fear flashed through her, followed quickly by obstinacy. "I don't want you messin' with those bees."

"I won't mess with 'em till I know what I'm doing."

"No!"

He didn't want to argue with her, and he understood her fear of the bees. But it made no sense to let the hives sit empty when honey could bring in cold, hard cash. The best way to soften her might be by being soft himself.

"I'd appreciate it if you'd look for them," he told her kindly, then pushed back from the dinner table and reached for his hat. "I'll be walkin' into town this afternoon to the library. If you'd like I can take whatever eggs you got and try to sell them there."

He took a bucket of warm water and the shaving gear down to the barn and came back half an hour later all spiffed up in his own freshly laundered jeans and shirt. When they met in the kitchen, her mouth still looked stubborn.

"I'm leaving now. How about those eggs?"

She refused to speak to him, but thumbed at the five dozen eggs sitting on the porch in a slatted wooden crate.

They were going to be heavy, but let him carry them, she thought stubbornly. If he wanted to go sellin' eggs to the creeps in town, and learning about bees, and getting all money-hungry, let him carry them!

She pretended not to watch him heft the crate, but her curiosity was aroused when he set it back down and disappeared around the back of the house. A minute later he returned pulling Donald Wade's wooden wagon. He loaded the egg crate on board only to discover the handle was too short for his tall frame. She watched, gratified when with his first steps his heels hooked on the front of the wagon. Five minutes later—still stubbornly silent—she watched him pull the wagon down the road by a length of stiff wire twisted to the handle.

Go on, then! Run to town and listen to every word they say! And come back with coins jingling in your pocket! And read up on bees and apples and anything else you want! But don't expect me to make it easy on you!

Gladys Beasley sat behind a pulpit-shaped desk, tamping the tops of the library cards in their recessed bin. They were already flat as a stove lid, but she tamped them anyway. And aligned the rubber stamp with the seam in the varnished wood. And centered her ink pen on its concave rest. And adjusted her nameplate— Gladys Beasley, Head Librarian—on the high desk ledge. And picked up a stack of magazines and centered her chair in the kneehole. Fussily. Unnecessarily.

Order was the greatest force in Gladys Beasley's life. Order and regimentation. She had run the Carnegie Municipal Library of Whitney, Georgia, for forty-one years, ever since Mr. Carnegie himself had made its erection possible with an endowment to the town. Miss Beasley had ordered the initial titles even before the shelves themselves were installed, and had been working in the hallowed building ever since. During those forty-one years she had sent more than one feckless assistant home in tears over a failure to align the spine of a book with the edge of a shelf.

She walked like a Hessian soldier, in brisk, no-nonsense steps on practical, black Cuban-heeled oxfords to which the shoemaker had added a special rubber heel which buffered her footfalls on the hardwood floors of her domain. If there was one thing that ired Gladys worse than slipshod shelving, it was cleats! Anyone who wore them in *her* library and expected to be allowed inside again had better choose different shoes next time!

She launched herself toward the magazine rack, imposing breasts carried like heavy artillery, her trunk held erect by the most expensive elastic and coutil girdle the Sears Roebuck catalogue had to offer—the one tactfully recommended for those "with excess flesh at the diaphragm." Her jersey dress—white squiggles on a background the color of something already digested—hung straight as a stovepipe from her bulbous hips to her club-shaped calves and made not so much as a rustle when she moved.

She replaced three *Saturday Evening Post* magazines, tamped the stack, aligned it with the edge of the shelf and marched along the row of tall fanlight windows, checking the wooden ribbing between the panes to be sure Levander Sprague, the custodian, hadn't shirked. Levander was getting old. His eyesight wasn't what it used to be, and lately she'd had to upbraid him for his careless dusting. Satisfied today, however, she returned to her duties at the central desk, located smack in front of double maple doors—closed—that led to wide interior steps at the bottom of which were the main doors of the building.

Overdue notices—bah!—there should be no such thing. Anyone who couldn't return a book on time should simply be disallowed the privilege of using the library again. That would put an end to the need for overdue notices, but quick. Gladys's mouth was puckered so tightly it all but disappeared as she penned addresses on the penny postcards.

She heard footfalls mounting the interior steps. A brass knob turned and a stranger stepped in, a tall, spare man dressed like a cowboy. He paused, letting his eyes scan the room, the desk, and her, then silently nodded and tipped his hat.

Gladys's prim mouth relaxed as she returned the nod. The genteel art of hat doffing had become nearly obsolete—what was the world coming to?

He took a long time perusing the place before moving. When he did, there were no cleats. He went directly, quietly, to the card catalogue, slid out the *B*'s, flipped through the cards and studied them for some time. He closed the drawer soundlessly, then scanned the sunlit room before moving between the oak tables to nonfiction. There were library patrons who, ill at ease when alone in the vast room with Miss Beasley, found it necessary to whistle softly through their teeth while scanning the shelves. He didn't. He selected a book from the 600's—Practical Science—moved on to select another and brought them straight to the checkout desk.

"Good afternoon," Gladys greeted in a discreet whisper.

"Afternoon, ma'am." Will touched his hat brim and followed her lead, speaking quietly.

"I see you found what you were looking for."

"Yes, ma'am. I'd like to check these out."

"Do you have a card?"

"No, ma'am, but I'd like to get one."

She moved with military precision, yanking a drawer open, finding a blank card, snapping it on the desktop off the edge of a tidily trimmed fingernail. The nail was virgin, Will was sure, never stained by polish. She closed the drawer with her girded torso, all the while holding her lips as if they were the mounting for a five-karat diamond. When she moved, her head snapped left and right, fanning the air with a smell resembling carnations and cloves. The light from one of the big windows glanced off her rimless glasses and caught the rows of uniform silver-blue ringlets between which the warp and woof of her skull shone pink. She dipped a pen in ink, then held it poised above the card.

"Name?"

"Will Parker."

"Parker, Will," she transposed aloud while entering the information on the first blank.

"And you're a resident of Whitney, are you?"

"Yes, ma'am."

"Address?"

"Ahh . . ." He rubbed his nose with a knuckle. "Rock Creek Road."

She glanced up with eyes as exacting as calipers, then wrote again while informing him, "I'll need some form of identification to verify your residency."

When he neither spoke nor moved, her head snapped up. "Anything will do. Even a letter with a canceled postmark showing your mailing address."

"I don't have anything."

"Nothing?"

"I haven't lived there long."

She set down her pen with a long-suffering air. "Well, Mr. Parker, I'm sure you understand, I cannot simply loan books to anyone who walks in here unless I can be assured they're residents. This is a municipal library. By its very meaning, the word *municipal* dictates who shall use this facility. *Of a town,* it means, thus this library is maintained *by* the residents of Whitney, *for* the residents of Whitney. I wouldn't be a very responsible librarian if I didn't demand some identification now, would I?" She carefully placed the card aside, then crossed her hands on the desktop, giving the distinct impression that she was displeased at having her time and her card wasted.

She expected him to argue, as most did at such an impasse. Instead, he backed up a step, pulled his hat brim low and studied her silently for several seconds. Then, without a word, he nodded, scooped the books against his hip and returned to the nonfiction side where he settled himself on one of the hard oak armchairs in a strong shaft of sunlight, opened a book and began reading.

There were several criteria by which Gladys Beasley judged her library patrons. Cleats, vocal volume, nondisruptiveness and respect for books and furniture. Mr. Parker passed on all counts. She'd rarely seen anyone read more intently, with less fidgeting. He moved only to turn a page and occasionally to follow along with his finger, closing his eyes as if committing a passage to memory. Furthermore, he neither slouched nor abused the opposite chair by using it as a footstool. He sat with his hat brim pulled low, elbows on the table, knees lolling but boots on the floor. The book lay flat on the table where it belonged, instead of torqued against his belly, which was exceedingly hard on spines. Neither did he lick his finger before turning the page—filthy, germ-spreading habit!

Normally, if people came in and asked for a paper and pencil, Miss Beasley gave them a tongue-lashing instead, about responsibility and planning ahead. But Will Parker's deportment and concentration raised within her regret for having had to deny him a borrower's card. So she bent her own standard.

"I thought perhaps you might need these," she whispered, placing a pencil and paper at his elbow.

Will's head snapped up. His shoulders straightened. "Much obliged, ma'am."

She folded her hands over her portly belly. "Ah, you're reading about bees."

"And apples. Yes, ma'am."

"For what purpose, Mr. Parker?"

"I'd like to raise 'em."

She cocked one eyebrow and thought a moment. "I might have some pamphlets in the back from the extension office that would help."

"Maybe next time, ma'am. I got all I can handle here today."

She offered a tight smile and left him to his studies, trailing a scent strong enough to eat through concrete.

It was mid-afternoon. The only things moving in town were the flies on the ice cream scoop. Lula Peak was bored to distraction. She sat on the end stool in an empty Vickery's Cafe, grateful when even her brassiere strap slipped down and she had to reach inside her black and white uniform to pull it up. God, this town was going to turn her into a cadaver before she even kicked the bucket! She could die of boredom right here on the barstool and the supper customers would come in and say, "Evenin', Lula, I'll have the usual," and not even realize she was a goner until thirty minutes later when their blue plate specials hadn't arrived.

Lula yawned, leaving her hand inside her uniform, absently rubbing her shoulder. Being a sensual person, Lula liked touching herself. Sure as hell nobody else around this miserable godforsaken town knew how to do it right. Harley, that dumb ass, didn't know the first thing about finesse when he touched a woman. Finesse. Lula liked the word. She'd just read it in an article on how to better yourself. Yeah, finesse, that's what Lula needed, a man with a little finesse, a *better* man in the sack than Harley-Dumb-Ass-Overmire.

Lula suppressed a yawn, stretched her arms wide and thrust her ribs out, swiveling idly toward the window. Suddenly she rocketed from the stool.

Christ, it was him, walking along the street pulling a kid's wagon. She ran her eyes speculatively over his lanky form, concentrating on his narrow hips and swaying pelvis as he ambled along the town square and nodded at Norris and Nat McCready, those two decrepit old bachelor brothers who spent their dotage whittling on the benches across the street. Lula hustled to the screen door and posed behind it. *Look over here, Parker, it's better than them two boring old turds.*

But he moved on without glancing toward Vickery's. Lula grabbed a broom and stepped into the sun, making an ill-disguised pretense of sweeping the sidewalk while watching his flat posterior continue around the square. He left the wagon in the shade of the town hall steps and went inside.

So did Lula. Back into Vickery's to thrust the broom aside and glance impatiently at the clock. Two-thirty. She drummed her long orange nails across the countertop, plunked herself onto the end stool and waited for five minutes. Agitated. Peeved. Nobody was going to come in here for anything more than a glass of iced tea and she knew it. Not until at least five-thirty. Old Man Vickery would be madder than Cooter Brown if he found out she'd slipped away and left the place untended. But she could tell him she'd run over to the library for a magazine and hadn't been gone a minute.

Deciding, she twisted off the stool and flung off her three-pointed apron. The matching headpiece followed as she whipped out her compact. A dash of fresh blaze orange on her lips, a check of the seams in her silk stockings and she was out the door.

Gladys Beasley looked up as the door opened a second time that afternoon. Her mouth puckered and her chin tripled.

"Afternoon, Mizz Beasley," Lula chirped, her voice ringing off the twelve-foot ceiling.

"Shh! Read the sign!"

Lula glanced at the sign on the front of Miss Beasley's desk: SILENCE IS GOLDEN. "Oh, sorry," she whispered, covering her mouth and giggling. She glanced around—ceiling, walls, windows—as if she'd never seen the place before, which wasn't far from the truth. Lula was the kind of woman who read *True Confessions,* and Gladys didn't stoop to using the taxpayers' money for smut like that. Lula stepped farther inside.

Cleats!

"Shh!"

"Oh, sorry. I'll tiptoe."

Will Parker glanced up, scanned Lula disinterestedly and resumed his reading.

The library was U-shaped, wrapped around the entry steps. Miss Beasley's desk, backed by her private workroom, separated the huge room into two distinct parts. To the right was fiction. To the left nonfiction. Lula had never been on the left where Parker sat now. Remembering about finesse, she moved to the right first, drifting along the shelves, glancing up, then down, as if examining the titles for something interesting. She removed a book bound in emerald green—the exact shade of a dress she'd been eyeing over at Cartersville in the Federated Store. Classy color that'd look swell with her new Tropical Flame nail polish—she spread her hands on the book cover and tipped her head approvingly. She'd have to think up something good to entice Harley to buy that little number for her. She stuck the book back in its slot and moved to another. Melville. Hey, she'd heard of this guy! Must've done something swell. But the spine was too wide and the printing too small, so she rammed it back on the shelf and looked further.

Lula *finessed* her way through a full ten minutes of fiction before finally tip-toeing past Miss Beasley to the other side. She twiddled two fingers as she passed, then clamped her hands at the base of her spine, thrusting her breasts into bold relief.

Gladys tightened her buttocks and followed where Lula had been, pushing in a total of eleven books she'd left beetling over the edges of the shelves.

Lula found the left side arranged much as the right, a spacious room with fan-light windows facing the street. Bookshelves filled the space between the windows and the floor, and covered the remaining three walls. The entire center of the room was taken up by sturdy oak tables and chairs. Lula sidled around the perimeter of the room without so much as peeking at Will. She grazed one fingertip along the edge of a shelf, then sucked it with studied provocativeness. She turned a corner, eased on to where a bank of shelves ran perpendicular to the wall and moved between them, putting herself in profile to Will, should he care to turn his head and see. She clasped her hands at the base of her spine, creating her best silhouette, watching askance to see if he'd glance over. After several minutes, when he hadn't, she grabbed a biography of Beethoven and, while turning its pages, eyed Will discreetly.

God, was he good looking. And that cowboy hat did things to her insides, the way he wore it low, shadowing his eyes in the glare of the afternoon sun. *Still waters,* she thought, taken by the way he sat with one finger under a page, so unmoving she wished she were a fly so she could land on his nose. What a nose. Long instead of pug like *some* she knew. Nice mouth, too. Ooo, would she like to get into that.

He leaned forward to write something and she ran her eyes all over him, down his tapered chest and slim hips to the cowboy boots beneath the table, back up to his crotch. He dropped his pencil and sat back, giving her a clearer profile shot of it.

Lula felt the old itch begin.

He sat there reading his book the way all the "brains" used to read in school while Lula thought about bettering herself. When she could stand it no longer she took Beethoven over and dropped it on the table across from him.

"This seat taken?" she drawled, inverting her wrists, leaning on the tabletop so that her breast buttons strained. His chin rose slowly. As the brim of the cowboy hat lifted, she got a load of deep brown eyes with lashes as long as spaghetti, and a mouth that old Lula had plenty of plans for.

"No, ma'am," he answered quietly. Without moving more than his head, he returned to his reading.

"Mind if I sit here?"

"Go ahead." His attention remained on the book.

"Watcha studyin'?"

"Bees."

"Hey, how about that! I'm studyin' *B*'s, too." She held up her book. "Beethoven." In school she'd liked music, so she pronounced it correctly. "He wrote music, back when guys wore wigs and stuff, you know?"

Again Will refused to glance up. "Yeah, I know."

"Well . . ." The chair screeched as Lula pulled it out. She flounced down, crossed her legs, opened the book and flapped its pages in rhythm with her wagging calf. "So. Haven't seen y' around. Where y' been keepin' yourself?"

He perused her noncommittally, wondering if he should bother to answer. Mercy, she was one hard-looking woman. She had so much hair piled onto her forehead it looked as if she could use a neck brace. Her mouth was painted the color of a chili pepper and she wore too much rouge, too high on her cheeks, in too precise a pattern. She overlapped her wrists on the table edge and rested her breasts on them. They jutted, giving him a clearer shot of cleavage. It pleased Will to let her know he didn't want any.

"Up at Mrs. Dinsmore's place."

"Crazy Elly's? My, my. How is she?" When Will declined to answer, she leaned closer and inquired, "You know why they call her crazy, don't you? Did she tell you?" Against his will, he became curious, but it would seem like an offense against Mrs. Dinsmore to encourage Lula, so he remained silent. Lula, however, needed no encouragement. "They locked her in that house when she was a baby and pulled all the shades down and didn't let her out until the law forced 'em to—to go to school—and then they only turned her loose six hours a day and locked her up again, nights." She sat back smugly. "Ah, so you didn't know." Lula smiled knowingly. "Well, ask her about it sometime. Ask her if she didn't live in that deserted house down by school. You know—the one with the picket fence around it and the bats flyin' in the attic window?" Lula leaned closer and added conspiratorially, "If I were you, I wouldn't hang around up there at her place any longer than I had to. Give you a bad reputation, if you know what I mean. I mean, that woman ain't wrapped too tight." Lula sat back as if in a chaise, letting her eyelids droop, toying absently with the cover of Beethoven, lifting it, letting it drop with soft repeated *plops*. "I know it's tough being new around town. I mean, you must be bored as hell if you have to spend your time in a place like this." Lula's eyes made a quick swerve around the bookshelves, then came back to him. "But if you need somebody to show y' around, I'd be happy to." Beneath the table her toe stroked Will's calf. "I got me a little bungalow just four houses off the town square on Pecan Street—"

"Excuse me, ma'am," Will interrupted, rising. "Got some eggs out in the sun that need selling. I'd better see to 'em."

Lula smirked, watching him move to the bookshelves. He'd got the message. Oh, he'd got it all right—loud and clear. She'd seen him jump when her foot touched his leg. She watched him slip one book into place, then squat down to replace the other. Before he could escape, she sidled into the aisle behind him, trapping him between the two tiers of shelves. When he rose to his feet and turned, she was gratified by his quick blush. "If you're interested in my offer, I work most days at Vickery's. I'm off at eight, though." She slipped one finger between his shirt buttons and ran it up and down, across hair and hard skin. Putting on her best kewpie doll face, Lula whispered, "See y' round, Parker."

As she swung away, exaggeratedly waggling her hips, Will glanced across the sunlit room to find the librarian's censoring eyes taking in the whole scene. Her attention immediately snapped elsewhere, but even from this distance Will saw how tightly her lips pursed. He felt shaky inside, almost violated. Women like Lula were a clear path to trouble. There was a time when he'd have taken her up on the offer and enjoyed every minute of it. But not anymore. Now all he wanted was to be left to live his life in peace, and that peace meant Eleanor Dinsmore's place. He suddenly felt a deep need to get back there.

Lula was gone, cleats clicking, by the time Will reached the main desk.

"Much obliged for the use of the paper and pencil, ma'am."

Gladys Beasley's head snapped up. The distaste was ripe on her face. "You're welcome."

Will was cut to the quick by her silent rebuff. A man didn't have to make a move on a hot-blooded woman like that, all he had to do was be in the same pigeonhole with her. Especially—Will supposed—if he'd done time for killing a whore in a Texas whorehouse and people around town knew it.

He rolled his notes into a cylinder and stood his ground. "I was wonderin', ma'am—"

"Yes?" she snapped, lifting her head sharply, her mouth no larger than a keyhole.

"I got a job. I'm workin' as a hired hand for Mrs. Glendon Dinsmore. If she'd come in here and tell you I work for her, would that be enough to get me a library card?"

"She won't come in."

"She won't?"

"I don't believe so. Since she married she's chosen to live as a recluse. I'm sorry, I can't bend the rules." She picked up her pen, made a check on a list, then relented. "However, depending upon how long you've been working for her, and how long you intend to stay, if she would verify your employment in writing, I should think that would be enough proof of residency."

Will Parker flashed a relieved smile, hooked one thumb in his hind pocket and backed off boyishly, melting the ice from Gladys Beasley's heart. "I'll make sure she writes it. Much obliged, ma'am." He headed for the door, then stopped and swung back. "Oh. How late you open?"

"Until eight o'clock weekdays, five Saturdays, and of course, we're closed Sundays."

He tipped his hat again and promised, "I'll be back."

As he turned the doorknob she called, "Oh, Mr. Parker?"

"Ma'am?"

"How is Eleanor?"

Will sensed that this inquiry was wholly different from Lula's. He stood at the door, adjusting his impression of Gladys Beasley. "She's fine, ma'am. Five months pregnant for the third time, but healthy and happy, I think."

"For the third time. My. I remember her as a child, coming in with Miss Buttry's fifth grade class—or was it Miss Natwick's sixth? She always seemed a bright child. Bright and inquisitive. Greet her for me, if you will."

It was the first truly friendly gesture Will had experienced since coming to Whitney. It erased all the sour taste left by Lula and made him feel suddenly warm inside.

"I'll do that. Thanks, Mrs. Beasley."

"Miss Beasley."

"Miss Beasley. Oh, by the way. I got a few dozen eggs I'd like to sell. Where should I try?"

Exactly what it was, Gladys didn't know—perhaps the way he'd assumed she had a husband, or the way he'd rejected the advances of that bleached whore, Lula, or perhaps nothing more than the way his smile had transformed his face at the news that he could have a library card after all. For whatever reason, Gladys found herself answering, "I could use a dozen myself, Mr. Parker."

"You could? Well . . . well, fine!" Again he flashed a smile.

"The rest you might take to Purdy's General, right across the square."

"Purdy's. Good. Well, let me go out and— Oh—" His thumb came out of the pocket, his hand hung loosely at his hip. "I just remembered. They're all in one crate."

"Put them in this." She handed him a small cardboard filing box.

He accepted it, nodded silently and went out. When he returned, she asked, "How much will that be?" She rummaged through a black coin purse and didn't look up until realizing he hadn't answered. "How much, Mr. Parker?"

"Well, I don't rightly know."

"You don't?"

"No, ma'am. They're Mrs. Dinsmore's eggs and these're the first I've sold for her."

"I believe the current price is twenty-four cents a dozen. I'll give you twenty-five, since I'm sure they're fresher than those at Calvin Purdy's store, and since they're hand delivered." She handed him a quarter, which he was reluctant to accept, knowing it was higher than the market value. "Well, here, take it! And next week, if you have more, I'll take another dozen."

He took the coin and nodded. "Thank you, ma'am. 'Preciate it and I know Mrs. Dinsmore will, too. I'll be sure to tell her you said hello."

When he was gone Gladys Beasley snapped her black coin purse shut, but held it a moment, studying the door. Now *that* was a nice young man. She didn't know why, but she liked him. Well, yes she did know why. She fancied herself an astute judge of character, particularly when it came to inquiring minds. His was apparent by his familiarity with the card catalogue, his ability to locate what he wanted without her assistance and his total absorption in his study, to say nothing of his eagerness to own a borrower's card.

And, too, he was willing to go back out to Rock Creek Road and work for Eleanor Dinsmore even after the pernicious twaddle spewed by Lula Peak. Gladys had heard enough to know what that harlot was trying to do—how could anyone have missed it in this echoing vault of a building? And more power to Will Parker for turning his back on that hussy. Gladys had never been able to understand what people got out of spreading destructive gossip. Poor Eleanor had never been given a fair shake by the people of this town, to say nothing of her own family. Her grandmother, Lottie McCallaster, had always been eccentric, a religious fanatic who attended every tent revival within fifty miles of Whitney. She was said to have fallen to her knees and rolled in the throes of her religious conviction, and it was well known she got baptized every time a traveling salvation man called for sinners to become washed in the Blood. She'd finally nabbed herself a self-proclaimed man of God, a fire-and-brimstone preacher named Albert See who'd married her, gotten her in a family way, installed her in a house at the edge of town and gone on circuit, leaving her to raise her daughter, Chloe, chiefly alone.

Chloe had been a silent wraith of a girl, with eyes as large as horse chestnuts, dominated by Lottie, subjected to her fanaticism. How a girl like that, who was scarcely ever out of her mother's scrutiny, had managed to get pregnant remained a mystery. Yet she had. And afterward, Lottie had never shown her face again, nor allowed Chloe to, or the child, Eleanor, until the truant officer had forced them to let her out to attend school, threatening to have the child legally removed to a foster home unless they complied.

What the town librarian remembered best about Eleanor as a child was her awe of the spacious library, and of her freedom to move through it without reprimand, and how she would stand in the generous fanlight windows with the sun pouring in, absorbing it as if she could never get enough. And who could blame her—poor thing?

Gladys Beasley wasn't an overly imaginative woman, but even so, she shuddered at the thought of what life must have been like for the poor bastard child, Eleanor, living in that house behind the green shades, like one buried alive.

She'd almost be willing to give Will Parker a borrower's card on the strength of his befriending Eleanor alone, now that she knew of it. And when she marched back to nonfiction and found a biography of Beethoven lying on a table, but "Bees" and "Apples" tucked flush in their slots, she knew she'd judged Will Parker correctly.

Chapter 7

Calvin Purdy bought the eggs at twenty-four cents a dozen. The money belonged to Mrs. Dinsmore, but Will had nine dollars of his own buttoned safely into his breast pocket. He touched it—hard and reassuring behind the blue chambray—and thought of taking something to her. Just because people called her crazy and she wasn't. Just because she'd been locked inside some house most of her life. And because they'd had words before he left. But what should he take? She wasn't the perfume type. And anyway, perfume seemed too personal. He'd heard that men bought ribbons for ladies, but he'd feel silly walking up to Purdy and asking him to cut a length of yellow silk ribbon to match her yellow maternity dress. Candy? Food made Eleanor sick. She pecked like a sparrow, hardly ate a thing.

In the end he chose a small figurine of a bluebird, gaily painted. She liked birds, and there wasn't much around her house in the way of decorations. The bluebird cost him twenty-nine cents, and he spent an additional dime on two chocolate bars for the boys. Pocketing his change, he felt a keen exhilaration to get home.

On his way out of town he passed the house with the tilting picket fence surrounding it like the decaying ribs of a dead animal. He stopped to stare, involuntarily fascinated by the derelict appearance of the place, the grass choking the front steps, the rangy morning glories tangling around the doorknob and up a rickety trellis on the front stoop. Tattered green shades covered the windows, their bottoms shredded into ribbons. Gazing at them, he shivered, yet was tempted to investigate closer, to peek inside. But the shades seemed to warn him away.

They'd locked her in? And pulled down the shades? A woman like Eleanor, who loved birds and katydids and the sky and the orchard? Again Will shivered and hurried on with his cargo of two chocolate bars and a glass bluebird, wishing he could have bought her more. It was a curious feeling for a man to whom gift-giving was foreign. The exchange of gifts implied that a person had both friends and money, but Will had seldom known both at once. Though he'd often imagined how exciting it would be to get gifts, he'd never expected this exhilaration at giving them. But now that he knew about Eleanor Dinsmore's past, he felt provoked by a great impatience to make reparation for the kindness she'd been robbed of as a child.

Would she still be peeved at him? An unexpected ripple of disquiet swept through him at the thought. He stalked along, studying the ground. The wagon rattled behind him. How do a man and woman learn to make up their differences? At thirty years old, Will didn't know, but it suddenly became vital that he learn. Always before, if a woman harassed him, he moved on. This was different, Eleanor Dinsmore was different. She was a good mother, a fine woman who'd been locked in a house and called crazy, and if he didn't tell her she wasn't, who would?

Eleanor had been miserable ever since Will left. She'd been churlish and snappy with him and he'd been gone nearly three hours on a trip that should have taken only half that time and she was sure he wasn't coming back. *It's your own fault, Elly. You can't treat a free man that way and expect him to come back for more.*

She put supper on to cook and looked out the back door every three minutes. No Will. She put on a clean dress and combed her hair, twisting it tight and neat on her head. She studied her wide, disturbed eyes in the small mirror on the kitchen shelf, thinking of his face trimmed with shaving lather. *He ain't comin' back, fool. He's ten miles in the other direction by now and how you gonna like choppin' that wood in the morning? And how you gonna like mealtimes lookin' at his empty chair? And talkin' to nobody but the boys?* Closing her eyes, she wrapped her fists around one another and pressed them to her mouth. *I need you, Parker. Please come back.*

As Will hurried up the rutted driveway he heard his own heart drumming in his ears. Reaching the edge of the clearing, his footsteps faltered: she was waiting on the porch. Waiting for him, Will Parker. Dressed in her yellow outfit with her hair freshly combed, the boys romping at her ankles and the smell of supper drifting clear across the yard. She raised a hand and waved. "What took you so long? I was worried."

Not only waiting, but worried. A burst of elation ricocheted through his body as he smiled and stretched his stride.

"Studying takes time."

"Will!" Donald Wade came running. "Hey, Will!" He collided with Will's knees and clung, head back and hair hanging, making the welcome complete. Will roughed the boy's silky hair.

"Hi, short stuff. How's things around here?"

"Everything's peachy." He fell into step beside Will, helping to pull the wagon. "What'd you do while I was gone?"

"Mama made me take a nap." Donald Wade made a distasteful face.

"A nap, huh?" Reaching the bottom of the porch steps, Will dropped the wagon handle and lifted his eyes to the woman above him. "Did she take one with you?"

"No. She took a bath in the washtub."

"Donald Wade, you hush now, you hear?" Eleanor chided, her cheeks turning suspiciously bright. Then, to Will, "How'd you do?"

"Did good." He handed her the money. "Miss Beasley at the library took one dozen eggs for twenty-five cents, and I sold the rest to Calvin Purdy for twenty-four cents a dozen. It's all there, a dollar twenty-one. Miss Beasley said to tell you hello."

"She did?" Eleanor's palm hung in midair, the money forgotten.

"Said she remembers you comin' in with Miss Buttry's fifth grade class or Miss Natwick's sixth."

"Well, imagine that." Her smile was all amazement and wide eyes. "Who'd have thought she'd remember me?"

"She did, though."

"I never even thought she knew my name."

Will grinned. "Don't think there's much that woman doesn't know."

Eleanor laughed, remembering the librarian.

"I'll bet it was pretty in the library, wasn't it?"

"Sure was. Bright." Will gestured in the air. "With big windows, rounded at the top. Smelled good, too."

"Did you get your card?"

"Couldn't. Not without you. Miss Beasley says you'll have to verify that I work for you."

"You mean go in there?" The animation left Elly's face and her voice quieted. "Oh, I don't think I could do that."

Yesterday he'd have asked why. Today he only replied, "You can write a note. She said that'd be okay and I can bring it next time I go in. Have to go in next week again. Miss Beasley said she'll want another dozen eggs."

"She did?" Eleanor's elation returned as quickly as it had fled.

"That's right. And, you know, I was thinking." Will tipped his hat brim back, hooked one boot on the bottom step and braced a hand on the knee. "If you were to pack the extra cream in pint jars I think I could sell it, too. Make a little extra."

She couldn't resist teasing, "You gonna turn into one of those men who loves money, Mr. Parker?"

He knew full well there was more than teasing behind the remark—there was her very real aversion to town. A recluse, Miss Beasley had called her. Was she really? To the point of avoiding contact with people even if it meant making money? She hadn't even bothered to count what he'd handed her. He supposed this was something they'd have to work out eventually. "No, ma'am." He withdrew his boot from the step. "It's just that I don't see any sense in losing the opportunity to make it."

Donald Wade spotted the brown paper bag and tugged Will's sleeve. "Hey, Will, what you got in there?"

Will reluctantly pulled his attention from Eleanor and went down on one knee beside the wagon, an arm around the boy's waist. "Well, what do you think?" Donald Wade shrugged, his eyes fixed on the sack. "Maybe you better look inside and see." Donald Wade's hazel eyes gleamed with excitement as he peeked into the bag, reached and withdrew the two candy bars.

"Candy," he breathed, awed.

"Chocolate." Will crossed his elbows on his knee, smiling. "One for you, one for your little brother."

"Chocolate." Donald Wade repeated, then to his mother, "Lookit, Mama, Will brung us chocolate!"

Her appreciative eyes sought Will's and he felt as if someone had just tied a half-hitch around his heart. "Now wasn't that thoughtful. Say thank you to Mr. Parker, Donald Wade."

"Thanks, Will!"

With an effort, Will dropped his attention to the boy. "You peel one for Thomas now, all right?"

Grinning, he watched the boys settle side by side on the step and begin to make brown rings around their mouths.

"I appreciate your thinkin' of them, Mr. Parker."

He slowly stretched to his feet and looked up into her face. Her lips were tipped up softly. Her hair was drawn back in a thick tied-down braid the color of autumn grain. Her eyes were green as jade. How could anybody lock her in a house?

"Boys got to have a little candy now and then. Brought something for you, too."

"For me?" She spread a hand on her chest.

He extended an arm with the sack caught between two fingers. "It isn't much."

"Why, whatever—" Elly excitedly plunged her hand inside, wasting not a second on foolish dissembling. Withdrawing the figurine, she held it at shoulder level. "Oh myyy . . . oh, Mr. Parker." She covered her mouth and blinked hard. "Oh, myyyy." She held the bluebird at arm's length and caught her breath. "Why, it's beautiful."

"I had a little money of my own," he clarified, since she hadn't bothered to count the egg money and he didn't want her thinking he'd spent any of hers. He could tell by her expression the thought hadn't entered her mind. She smiled into the bluebird's painted eye, her own shining with delight. "A bluebird . . . imagine that." She pressed it to her heart and beamed at Will. "How did you know I like birds?"

He knew. He knew.

He stood watching her, feeling ready to burst with gratification as she examined the bird from every angle. "I just love it." She flashed him another warm smile. "It's the nicest present I ever got. Thank you."

He nodded.

"See, boys?" She squatted to show them. "Mr. Parker brought me a bluebird. Isn't it about the prettiest thing you ever saw? Now where should we put it? I was thinkin' on the kitchen table. No, maybe on my nightstand—why, it would look good just about anyplace, wouldn't it? Come in and help me decide. You too, Mr. Parker."

She bustled inside, so excited she forgot to hold the screen door open for Thomas to scramble inside. Will plucked him off the step and got chocolate on his shirt, but what was a little chocolate to a man so happy? He stood just inside the kitchen doorway with the baby on his arm, watching Eleanor try the bird everywhere—on the table, on the cupboard, beside the cookie jar. "Where should we put it, Donald Wade?" Always, she made the boy feel important. And now Will, too.

"On the windowsill, so all the other birds will see it and come close."

"Mmm . . . on the windowsill." She pinched her lower lip and considered the sills—east, south and west. The kitchen jutted off the main body of the building, a room with ample brightness. "Why of course. Now why didn't I think of that?" She placed the bluebird on a west sill, overlooking the backyard, where the clothespoles had been repaired and now stood straight and sturdy. She leaned back, clapped once and pressed her folded hands against her chin. "Oh, yes, it's exactly what this place needed!"

It needed a lot more than a cheap glass figurine, but as Eleanor danced across the room and squeezed Will's arm, he felt as if he'd just bought her a collector's piece.

*   *   *

If Will had been eager to make improvements around the place before his trip to town, afterward he worked even harder, fired by the zeal to atone for a past which was none of his making. He spent hours wondering about the people who'd locked her in that house behind the green shades. And how long she'd been there, and why. And about the man who'd taken her away from it, the one she said she still loved. And how long it might take for that love to begin fading.

It was during those days that Will became aware of things he'd never noticed before: how she hadn't hung a curtain on a window; how she paused to worship the sun whenever she stepped outside; how she never failed to find praise for the day—be it rain or shine—something to marvel over; and at night, when Will stepped out of the barn to relieve himself, no matter what the hour . . . her bedroom light was always burning. It wasn't until he'd seen it several times that he realized she wasn't up checking on the boys, but sleeping with it on.

Why had her family done it to her?

But if anyone respected a person's right to privacy it was Will. He needn't know the answers to accept the fact that he was no longer laboring only to have a roof over his head, but to please her.

He mended the road—oiled the harness and hitched Madam to a heavy steel road scraper shaped like a giant grain shovel, with handles like a wheelbarrow, an ungainly thing to work with. But with Madam pulling and Will pushing, directing the straight steel cutting edge into the earth, they tackled the arduous task. They shaved off the high spots, filled in the washouts, rolled boulders off to the sides and grubbed out erupted roots.

Donald Wade became Will's constant companion. He'd take a seat on a bank or a branch, watching, listening, learning. Sometimes Will gave him a shovel and let him root around throwing small rocks off to the side, then praised him for his fledgling efforts as he'd heard Eleanor do.

One day Donald Wade observed, "My daddy, he didn't work much. Not like you."

"What did he do, then?"

"He puttered. That's what Mama called it."

"Puttered, huh?" Will mulled this over a moment and asked, "He treated your Mama nice though, didn't he?"

"I guess so. She liked him." After a moment's pause, Donald Wade added, "But he din't buy her bluebirds."

While Will considered this, Donald Wade voiced another surprising question.

"Are you my daddy now?"

"No, Donald Wade, I'm sorry to say I'm not."

"You gonna be?"

Will had no answer. The answer depended on Eleanor Dinsmore.

She came twice a day—morning and afternoon—pulling Baby Thomas and a jug of cool raspberry nectar in the wagon. And they'd all sit together beneath the shade of her favorite sourwood tree and relish the treat while she pointed out the birds she knew. She seemed to know them all—doves and hawks and warblers and finches. And trees, too—the sourwood itself, the tulip poplar, redbud, basswood and willow, so many more varieties than Will had realized were there. She knew the small plants, too—the gallberry and snow vine, the sumac and crownbeard and one with a lovely name, summer farewell, which brought a winsome tilt to her lips and made him study those lips more closely than the summer farewell.

Those minutes spent resting beneath the sourwood tree were some of the finest of Will's life.

"My," she would say, "this is gonna be some road." And it would be all the charge Will needed to return to the scraper and push harder than before.

The day the road was done Will whispered his thanks into Madam's ear, fed her a gold carrot from the garden and gave her a bath as a treat. After supper, he and Eleanor took the boys for a wagon ride down the freshly-bladed earth that rose firm into the trees before dripping to link their house with the county road below.

"It's a beautiful road, Will," she praised, and he smiled in quiet satisfaction.

The next day he tightened up a wagon, replaced two boards on its bed, hitched up Madam and took his first load of junk to the Whitney dump. He took, too, a note from Eleanor, and Miss Beasley's eggs, plus several dozen more and five pints of cream, one which never made it farther than the library.

"Cream!" Miss Beasley exclaimed. "Why, I've had the worst craving for strawberry shortcake lately and what's strawberry shortcake without whipped cream?" She chuckled and got out her black snap-top coin purse.

And though Will checked out his first books with his own library card, just before he left she remembered, "Oh, I *did* find some pamphlets on beekeeping while I was sorting in the back room. You need not return these." She produced a mustard-yellow envelope bearing his name and laid it on the desk. "They're put out by the county extension office . . . *every five years,* mind you, when the bee is the only creature on God's green earth that hasn't changed its habits or its habitat since before man walked upright! But when the new pamphlets come in, the old ones get thrown—useful or not!" She blustered on, busying her hands, carefully avoiding Will's eyes. "Why, I've got a good mind to write to my county commissioner about such outright waste of the taxpayers' money!"

Will was charmed.

"Thank you, Miss Beasley."

Still she wouldn't look at him. "No need to thank me for something that would've gone to waste anyway."

But he saw beyond her smokescreen to the woman who had difficulty befriending men and his heart warmed more.

"I'll see you next week."

She looked up only when his hand gripped the brass knob, but even from a distance he noted the two spots of color in her cheeks.

Smiling to himself, Will loped down the library steps with his stack of books on one hip and the yellow envelope slapping his thigh.

"Myyy, myyy . . . if it isn't Mr. Parker."

Will came up short at the sight of Lula Peak, two steps below, smiling at him with come-hither eyes. She wore her usual Betty Grable foreknot, lipstick the color of a blood clot, and stood with one hip permanently jutted to hold her hand.

"Afternoon, ma'am." He tried to move around her but she sidestepped adroitly.

"What's your hurry?" She chewed gum as gracefully as an alligator gnawing raw meat.

"Got cream in the wagon that shouldn't be sitting in the sun."

She smoothed the hair up the back of her head, then, raising her chin, skimmed three fingertips down the V of her uniform. "Lawzy . . . it's a hot one all right." Standing one step below Will, Lula was nearly nose to navel with him. Her eyes roved lazily down his shirt and jeans to the envelope on which Miss Beasley had written his name. "So it's Will, is it?" she drawled. Her eyes took their time climbing back up, lingering where they would. "Will Parker," she drawled, and touched his belt buckle with the tip of one scarlet nail. "Nice name . . . Will." It took control for him to resist leaping back from her touch, but he stood his ground politely while she tipped her head and waggled her shoulders. "So, Will Parker, why don't you stop in at the cafe and I'll fix you a ni-i-ice glass of iced tea. Taste good on a hot one like this, mmm?"

For one horrified moment he thought she might run that nail straight down his crotch. He jumped before she could. "Don't think I'll have time, ma'am." This time she let him pass. "Got things to do." He felt her eyes following as he climbed the wagon wheel, took the reins and drove around the town square to Purdy's.

That woman was trouble with a capital T, and he didn't want any. Not of it or of her. He made sure he avoided glancing across the square while he entered the store.

Purdy bought the cream and the eggs and said, "Fine, anytime you got fresh, just bring 'em in. I got no trouble getting rid of fresh."

Lula was gone when Will came out of the store, but her kewpie doll act left him feeling dirty and anxious to get back home.

Eleanor and the boys were waiting under their favorite sourwood tree this time. Will gravitated toward them like a compass needle toward the North Pole. Here was where he belonged, here with this unadorned woman whose simplicity made Lula look brassy, whose wholesomeness made Lula look brazen. He found it hard to believe that in his younger days he'd have chosen a woman like *that* over one like this.

She stood, brushing off the back of her skirt as he drew up and reined in Madam.

"You're back."

"Yup."

They smiled at each other and a moment of subtle appreciation fluttered between them. She boosted the boys up onto the wagon seat and he transferred them into the back, swinging them high and making them giggle. "You sit down back there now so you don't tumble off." They scrambled to follow orders and Will leaned to extend a helping hand to their mother. He clasped her palm and for the space of two heartbeats neither of them moved. She poised with one foot on a wagon cleat, her green eyes caught in his brown. Abruptly she clambered up and sat down, as if the moment had not happened.

He thought about it during the days that followed, while he continued improving the place, scrubbing walls and ceilings, finishing the plastering and painting walls that appeared to never have seen paint before. He put doors on the bottom kitchen cabinets and built new ones for above. He bartered a used kitchen sink for a piece of linoleum (both at a premium and growing scarcer) with which he covered the new cabinet top. The linoleum was yellow, streaked, like sun leaching through daisy petals: yellow, which seemed to suit Eleanor best and set off her green eyes.

She grew rounder and moved more slowly. Day after day he watched her hauling dishpans and slop buckets out to slew in the yard. She washed diapers for only one now, but soon there'd be two. He dug a cesspool and ran a drainpipe from underneath the sink, eliminating the need for carrying out dishpans.

She was radiant with thanks and rushed to dump a first basin of water down the drain and rejoice when it magically disappeared by itself. She said it didn't matter that he hadn't been able to find enough linoleum for the floor, too. The room was brighter and cleaner than it had ever been before.

He was disappointed about the linoleum for the floor. He wanted the room perfect for her, but linoleum and bathtubs and so many other commodities were getting harder and harder to come by with factories of all kinds converting to the production of war supplies. In prison Will had read the newspaper daily but now he caught up with world events only when he went to the library. Still, he was aware of the rumblings in Europe and wondered how long America could supply England and France with planes and tanks without getting into the fighting herself. He shuddered at the thought, even as he took his first load of scrap metal to town and got a dollar per hundredweight for Glendon Dinsmore's "junk."

There was talk of America actively joining the war, though America Firsters—among them the Lone Eagle, Charles Lindbergh—spoke out against the U.S. drift toward it. But Roosevelt was beefing up America's defenses. The draft was already in force, and Will was of age, healthy and single. Eleanor remained blissfully ignorant of the state of the world beyond the end of their driveway.

Then one day Will unearthed a radio in one of the sheds. It took some doing to find a battery for it—batteries, too, were being gobbled up by England to keep walkie-talkies operable. But again he bartered with a spare can of paint, only to find that even when the battery was installed, the radio still refused to work. Miss Beasley found a book that told him how to fix it.

The particular hour he coaxed it back to life, "Ma Perkins" was on the air on the blue network. The boys were having their afternoon nap and Eleanor was ironing. As the staticky program filled the kitchen, her eyes lit up like the amber tube behind the RCA Victor grille.

"How 'bout that—it works!" Will said, amazed.

"Shh!" She pulled up a chair while Will knelt on the floor and together they listened to the latest adventure of the widow who managed a lumberyard in Rushville Center, U.S.A., where she lived, by the golden rule, with her three kids, John, Evey and Fay. Anybody who loved their kids as much as Ma Perkins was all right with Eleanor, and Will could see Ma had gained a faithful listener.

That evening they all hovered close to the magical box while Will and Eleanor watched the boys' eyes alight at the sound of "The Lone Ranger" and Tonto, his faithful Indian friend, whom he called *kemo sabe*.

After that, Donald Wade never walked; he galloped. He whinnied, shied, made hoof sounds with his tongue and hobbled "Silver" at the door each time he came in. Will playfully called him *kemo sabe* one day, and after that Donald Wade tried their patience by calling everybody else *kemo sabe* a hundred times a day.

The radio brought more than fantasy. It brought reality in the form of Edward R. Murrow and the news. Each evening during supper Will tuned it in. Murrow's grave voice with its distinctive pause, would fill the kitchen: "This . . . is London." In the background could be heard the scream of German bombers, the wail of air raid sirens and the thunder of antiaircraft fire. But Will thought he was the only one in the kitchen who truly believed they were real.

Though Elly refused to discuss it, the war was coming, and when it did his number might be called. He pushed himself harder.

He put up next year's wood, scraped the old linoleum off the kitchen floor, sanded and varnished it, and began fantasizing about installing a bathroom—if he could come up with the fixtures.

And in secret, he read about bees.

They held, for him, an undeniable fascination. He spent hours observing the hives from a distance, those hives he'd at first believed abandoned by the insects but were not. He knew better now. The appearance of only a few bees at the hive opening meant nothing, because most of them were either inside waiting on the queen or out in the fields gathering pollen, nectar and water.

He read more, learned more—that the worker bees carried pollen in their back legs; that they needed saltwater daily to drink; that the honey was made in stackable frames called supers which the beekeeper added to the tops of the hives as the lower ones filled; that the bees ate their own honey to survive the winter; that during summer, the heaviest production time, if the laden supers weren't removed the honey grew so heavy it sometimes crowded the bees out and they swarmed.

Experimentally, he filled a single pan with saltwater one day. The next day it was empty, so he knew the hives were active. He watched the workers leaving with their back legs thin and returning with their pollen sacks filled. Will knew he was right without even opening the hives to see inside. Glendon Dinsmore had died in April. If no supers had been added since then, the bees could swarm anytime. If none had been taken since then, they were laden with honey. A lot of honey, and Will Parker wanted to sell it.

The subject hadn't come up again between himself and Eleanor. Neither had she produced any veiled hat or smoker, so he decided to go it without them. Every book and pamphlet advised that the first step toward becoming a beekeeper was to find out if you are bee-immune.

So Will did. One warm day in late October he followed instructions minutely: took a fresh bath to wash any scent of Madam from his body, raided Eleanor's mint patch, rubbed his skin and trousers with crushed leaves, folded his collar up, his sleeves down, tied string around his trouser cuffs and went out to the derelict Whippet to find out what the bees thought of Will Parker.

Reaching the car, he felt his palms begin to sweat. He dried them on his thighs and eased closer, reciting silently, Move slow . . . bees don't like abrupt movement.

He inched toward the car . . . into the front seat . . . gripped the wheel . . . and sat with his heart in his throat.

It didn't take long. They came from behind him, first one, then another, and in no time at all what seemed like the whole damn colony! He forced himself to sit motionless while one landed in his hair and walked through it, buzzing, the rest still in flight about his face. Another lighted on his hand. He waited for it to drill him, but instead the old boy investigated the brown hair on Will's wrist, strolled to his knuckles and buzzed away, disinterested.

Well, I'll be damned.

When he told Eleanor about it, she made up for the stings the bees had foregone.

"You did what!"

She spun from the cupboard with her hands on her hips, her eyes fiery with anger.

"I went out and sat in the Whippet to see if I was bee-immune."

"Without even a veiled hat!"

"I figured you never found one."

"Because I didn't want you out there!"

"But I told you, I rubbed mint on myself first and washed the smell of Madam off me."

"Madam! What in the sam hell has she got to do with it?"

"Bees hate the smell of animals, especially horses and dogs. It gets 'em mad."

"But you could have been stung. Bad!" She was livid.

"The book says a beekeeper's got to expect to get stung now and then. It comes with the job. But after a while you get so you hardly notice it."

"Oh, swell!" She flung up a hand disparagingly. "And that's supposed to make me feel good?"

"Well, I figured since I read it in the pamphlet it must be the right way to start. And the book—"

"The book!" She scoffed. "Don't tell me about books. Did you wear gloves?"

"No. I wanted to find out—"

"And you didn't take the smoker either!"

"I would have if you'd have given it to me."

"Don't you blame me for your own stupidity, Will Parker! That was a damn-fool thing to do and you know it!"

She was so upset she couldn't countenance him any longer. She spun back to the cake she'd been making, grabbed an egg and cracked it against the lip of the bowl with enough force to annihilate the shell.

"Damn! Now see what you've done!"

"Well, if I'd have known you were gonna get mad—"

"I'm not mad!" She fished out a smashed shell and flung it aside vehemently.

"You're not mad," he repeated dryly.

"No, I'm not!"

"Then what are you hollering about?"

"I'm not hollering!" she hollered and rounded on him again. "I just don't know what gets into men's heads sometimes, that's all! Why, Donald Wade would've had more sense than to go out there into a beehive with no more protection than a smear of *mint!*"

"I didn't get bit though, did I?" he inquired smugly.

She glared at him, cheeks mottled, mouth pursed, and finally swung away, too frustrated to confront him any longer. "Go on." The order came out low and sizzling. "Git out of my kitchen." She slammed another egg against the bowl, smashing it to smithereens.

He stood five feet away, arms crossed, one shoulder braced indolently against the front room doorway, admiring her angry pink face, the spunky chin, the bounce of her breasts as she whipped the batter. "You know, for someone who's not mad, you're sure makin' a hell of a mess out of those eggshells."

The next thing he knew, an egg came flying through the air and hit him smack in the middle of the forehead.

"Elly, wh—what the hell—"

He bent forward while yolk ran down his nose and white dangled from his chin, dripping onto his boots.

"You think it's so funny, go stick your head in a beehive and let them clean it off for you!" She stabbed a finger at the door. "Well, git, I said! Git out of my kitchen!"

He turned to follow orders but even before he reached the door, he was laughing. The first bubble rippled up as he reached the screen door, the second as he jogged down the steps, scraping the slime from his face. By the time he hit the yard he was hooting full-bore.

"Git!"

He shook his head like a dog after a swim and cackled merrily. Behind him the screen door opened and he spun just in time to form a mitt for the next egg she let fly. It burst in his palms, against his hip.

He jigged backward, chortling. "Whooo—ee! Look out, Joe DiMaggio!"

"Damn you, Parker!"

"Ha! Ha! Ha!"

All the way to the well he laughed, and kept it up while he inspected his shirt, stripped it off and rinsed it and himself beneath the pump. He was still chuckling as he hung it on a fencepost to dry.

Then the truth struck him and he became silent as if plunged underwater.

She cares!

It caught him like an uppercut on the chin, snapped him erect to stare at the house.

She cares about you, Parker! And you care about her!

His heart began pounding as he stood motionless in the sun with water streaming down his face and chest. *Care about her? Admit it, Parker, you love her.* He scraped a hand down his face, shook it off and continued staring, coming to grips with the fact that he was in love with a woman who had just fired an egg at him, a woman seven months pregnant with another's man's baby, a woman he had scarcely touched, never kissed and never desired carnally.

Until now.

He began moving toward the house in long, unhurried strides, feeling the awesome thump of his pulse in his breast and temples, wondering what to say when he reached her.

She was already on her knees with a bucket and rag when he opened the screen door and let it thud quietly behind him. She went on scrubbing, riveting her attention on the floor. The boys were napping, the radio silent. He stood across the room, watching, wondering, waiting.

Go on, then. Lift her to her feet and see if you were right, Parker.

He moved to stand over her, but she toiled stubbornly, her entire body rocking as she scrubbed with triple the energy required for a simple egg.

"Eleanor?"

He'd never called her by her first name before and it doubled his awareness of her as a woman, and hers of him as a man.

"Go away."

"Eleanor"—spoken softer this time while he gripped her arm as if to tug her up. Her head snapped back, revealing green eyes glimmering with unshed tears.

She was angry, so angry. And the tender tone of his voice added to it, though she didn't completely understand why. She dashed away the infuriating tears and looked up the considerable length of him, to his bare, wet chest, his attractive face still moist with well water, his hair standing in rills. His eyes appeared troubled, the lashes spiky with moisture. His skin was brown from a long summer's shirtless labor, and he had filled out until he looked like a lean, fit animal. The sight of him sent a thrill through her vitals. He was all the things that Glendon hadn't been—honed, hard and handsome. But what man who looked like that would welcome the affections of a plain, crazy woman seven months pregnant, shaped like a watermelon?

Eleanor dropped her chin. He tipped it up with one finger and gave her face a disarming perusal before letting a grin tip the corner of his mouth. "You got one hell of an arm, you know that?"

She jerked her chin away and felt his charm seep through her limbs, but nothing in her life had led her to believe she could attract a man like him so she assumed he was only having fun with her. "It's not funny, Will."

Standing above her, he felt disappointment spear him deeply. He dropped to a squat, his gaze falling on her hands, which rested idly over the edge of a white enamel bucket. "No, it's not," he replied quietly. "I think we'd better talk about this."

"There's nothing to talk about."

"Isn't there?"

She suddenly made an L of her arms and dropped her face against her knuckles. "Don't cry."

"I'm n—not." Whatever was wrong with her? She never cried, and it was embarrassing to do so before Will Parker for absolutely no good reason at all.

He waited, but she continued sobbing softly, her stomach bobbing. "Don't . . ." he whispered, pained.

She threw back her head, rubbed the tears aside and sniffed. "Pregnant women cry sometimes, that's all."

"I'm sorry I laughed."

"I know, and I'm sorry I threw that egg." She dried her face roughly with her apron. "But, Will, you got to understand about the bees."

"No, *you've* got to understand about the bees."

"But, Will—"

He held up both palms. "Now wait a minute before you say anything. I'm not going to lie to you. I *have* been in the orchard . . . a lot. But I'm not him, Eleanor, I'm not Glendon. I'm a careful man and I'm not going to get hurt."

"How do you know that?"

"All right, I don't. But you just can't go through life shying away from things you're scared are going to happen. Chances are they never will anyway." He suddenly dropped both knees to the floor and rested his hands on his thighs, leaning forward earnestly. "Elly, there are bees all over the place. And honey out there, too, a lot of it. I want to gather it and sell it."

"But—"

"Now wait a minute, let me finish. You haven't heard it all." He drew a deep breath and plunged on. "I'll need your help. Not with the hives—I'll take care of that part so you don't have to go near them. But with the extracting and bottling."

She glanced away. "For money, I suppose."

"Well, why not?"

She snapped her gaze back to him, spreading her palms. "But I don't care about money."

"Well, maybe I do. If not for myself, for this place, for you and the kids. I mean, there are things I'd like to do around here. I've thought about putting in electricity . . . and a bathroom maybe. With the new baby coming, I thought you'd want those things, too. And what about the baby—where you gonna get the money to pay the doctor?"

"I told you before, I don't need any doctors."

"Maybe you didn't the day the boys got stung—we were lucky that day—but you'll need one when the baby is born."

"I'm not having any doctor," she declared stubbornly.

"But that's ridiculous! Who's going to help you when the time comes?"

She squared her chin and looked him dead in the eye. "I was hopin' you would."

"Me?" Will's eyebrows shot up and his head jutted forward. "But I don't know the first damn thing about it."

"There's nothing to it," she hurried on. "I'll tell you everything you need to know beforehand. About all you'd have to do is tie the—"

"Now, wait a minute!" He leaped to his feet, holding up both palms like a traffic cop.

Riveting her eyes on him, she got clumsily to her feet. "You're scared, aren't you?"

He stuffed his hands into his back pockets, gripping his buttocks. A pair of creases appeared between his eyebrows. "Damn right I'm scared. And it doesn't make a bit of sense, not when there's a qualified doctor down there in town who can do it."

"I told you once, the town's got no use for me, I got no use for it."

"But that's cr—" He stopped himself short.

"Crazy?" She finished for him.

"I didn't mean to say that." Damn his thoughtless tongue. "It's risky. All kinds of things could happen. Why, it could be born with the cord wrapped around its neck, or breech—what if that happened?"

"It won't. I had two that come out with no trouble at all. All you'd have to do—"

"No!" He put six feet of space between them before facing her again, scowling. "I'm no midwife, goddammit!"

It was the first time Elly had seen him truly angry and she wasn't sure how to handle him. They faced off, as motionless as chess pieces, their color high and their mouths set while Eleanor felt uncertainty creeping in. She needed him, but he didn't seem to understand that. She was afraid, but couldn't let it show. And if what she was about to say backfired, she'd be the sorriest woman in Gordon County.

"Well, then, maybe you'd better collect your things and move on."

A shaft of dread speared through him. So much for love. How many times in his life had he been through this? *Sorry, boy, but we won't be needin' you any-more. Wish we could keep you on, boy, but—* No matter how hard he worked to prove himself, the end was always inevitable. He should have grown used to it by now. But it hurt, goddammit. It hurt! And she was being unreasonable to expect this of him.

He pulled in a deep, shaky breath and felt his stomach quiver. "Can't we talk about this, Elly?"

She loved the sound of her name rolling off his tongue. But she wasn't keeping him around as an ornament. If he was going to stay he had to understand why. Obstinately she knelt and returned to her scrubbing. "I can do it alone. I don't need you."

No, nobody ever had. He'd thought this once maybe it'd turn out different. But he was as dispensable to Eleanor Dinsmore as he'd been to everyone from his mother on down to the state of Texas. He could give up and simply walk away from this place, away from her, but whether she loved him or not, he was happy here, happier than he ever remembered being, happy and comfortable and busy and achieving. And that was worth fighting for.

He swallowed his pride, crossed the half-scrubbed floor and squatted beside her, resting both elbows on his knees. "I don't want to go . . . but I didn't hire on here to deliver babies," he argued quietly, reasonably. "I mean, it's"—he swallowed—"it's a little personal, wouldn't you say?"

"I guess that would bother you," she returned tightly, continuing to scrub, moving to a new patch of floor to avoid his eyes.

He considered long and hard, fixing his attention on the top of her head. "Yes . . . yes it would."

"Glendon did it . . . twice."

"That was different. He was your husband."

Still scrubbing, she said, "You could be, too."

A shaft of hot surprise sizzled through his veins. But what if he'd misunderstood? Weighing her words, he balanced on the balls of his feet, watching her rock above the scrub rag as the wet spot spread. Her cheeks grew flushed as she clarified, "I mean, I've been thinking, and it's okay with me if we went ahead and got married now. I think we'd get along all right, and the boys like you a lot and

you're real good with them, and . . . and I really don't throw eggs very often."
Still she wouldn't look up.

He contained a smile while his heartbeat clattered. "Is that what you want?"
"I guess."

Then look at me. Let me see it in your eyes.

But when she finally glanced up he saw only embarrassment at having asked.
So . . . she was not in love, only in a bind . . . and he was convenient. But, after
all, he'd known that from the first time he'd walked in here, hadn't he?

The silence remained tense. He stretched to his feet and crossed to a window,
looked out at the backyard he'd cleaned, the clothespoles he'd sturdied, thinking
of how much more he wanted to do for her. "You know, Eleanor, it's silly for us
to do this just because you put up some ad in the sawmill and just because I answered it. That isn't reason enough for two people to tie up for life, is it?"

"Don't you want to?"

He glanced over his shoulder to find her watching him with face ablaze.

"Do you?"

I'm pregnant and unbright and unpretty, she thought.

I'm an ex-con woman-killer, he thought.

And neither of them spoke what was in their hearts.

At length, he glanced out at the yard again. "It seems to me there should be
some . . . some feeling between people or something." It was his turn to flush, but
he kept it hidden from her.

"I like you fine, Will. Don't you like me?"

She might have been discussing which new rake to select, so emotionless was
her tone.

"Yeah," he said throatily, after a moment. "I like you fine."

"Then I think we ought to do it."

Just like that—no harp music swelling out of the heavens, no kissing beneath
the stars. Only Elly, seven months pregnant, struggling to her feet and drying her
hands on her apron. And Will standing six feet clear of her, staring in the opposite
direction. The way they'd laid it out made it sound as exciting as President Roosevelt's Lend-Lease Program. Well, enough was enough. Before Will agreed, he
was going to know exactly what he was getting into here. Resolutely he turned to
face her.

"You mind my asking something?"

"Ask."

"Where would I sleep?"

"Where would you want to sleep?"

He really wasn't sure. Sleeping with her would be tough, lying beside her pregnant body and not touching it. But sleeping in the barn was mighty lonely. He decided to give away no more or less than necessary. "The nights are getting pretty
cool out in that barn."

"The only place in here is where Glendon slept, you know."

"I know." After an extended silence, "So?"

"You'd be my husband."

"Yeah," he said expressionlessly, realizing she wasn't too thrilled at the prospect.

"I . . . I sleep with the light on."

"I know."

Her eyebrows lifted. "You do?"

"I've been up at night and seen it."

"It'd probably keep you awake."

What was she doing arguing against it when the idea made her have to fight for breath?

He thought long and hard before trusting her enough to reveal a crack in his defenses. "In prison it was never completely dark either."

He noted a softening in her expression and wondered if someday he could trust her with the rest of his vulnerabilities.

"Well, in that case . . ." The silence welled around them while they tried to think of what to say or do next. Had this been a regular proposal with the expected emotions on both sides, the moment would undoubtedly have been intimate. Because it wasn't, the strain multiplied.

"Well . . ." He rubbed his nose and chuckled nervously.

"Yes . . . well." She spread her hands, then linked them beneath her swollen belly.

"I don't know how a person goes about getting married."

"We do it at the courthouse in Calhoun. We can get the license right there, too."

"You want to drive in tomorrow, then?"

"Tomorrow'd be fine."

"What time?"

"We'd better start early. We'll have to take a wagon, 'cause the boys'll be with us. And as you know, Madam's pretty slow."

"Nine o'clock then?"

"Nine should be fine."

For a moment they studied each other, realizing to what they'd just agreed. How awkward. How incredible. Self-consciousness struck them simultaneously. He reached up to pull his hat brim down, only to discover he'd left his hat hanging on the fencepost. So he hooked a thumb in his hind pocket and backed up a step.

"Well . . . I got work to finish." His thumb jabbed the air above his shoulder.

"So do I."

He backed up two more steps, wondering what she'd do if he switched directions and kissed her. But in the end he followed his own advice and left without trying.

Chapter 8

Falling into bed that night, Eleanor lay wide-awake, thinking of the day past, the day to come, the years ahead. Would she and Will live peaceably or fight often? Fighting was something new to her. In the years she'd been married to Glendon, they'd never fought—perhaps because Glendon was just too lazy.

In the place where she'd grown up there was no fighting either. And no laughter. Instead, there had been tension, never-ending tension. From her earliest memories it was there, always hovering like a monster threatening to swoop down and scoop her up with its black wings. It was there in the way Grandmother carried herself, as if to let her shoulders wilt would displease the Lord. It was there in her mother's careful attempts to walk quietly, carry out orders without complaint, and never meet Grandmother's eyes. But it was greatest when Grandfather came home. Then the praying would intensify. Then the "purifying" would begin.

Eleanor would kneel on the hard parlor floor, as ordered, while Grandfather raised his hands toward the ceiling and, with his scraggly gray beard trembling and his eyes rolled back in his head, would call down forgiveness from God. Beside her, Grandmother would moan and carry on like a dog having fits, then start talking gibberish as her body trembled. And Mother—the sinner—would squeeze her eyes shut and interlace her fingers so tightly the knuckles turned white, and rock pitifully on her knees while her lips moved silently. And she, Eleanor—the child of shame—would lower her forehead to her folded hands and peek out with one eye at the spectacle, wondering what it was she and her mother had done.

It seemed impossible that Mother could have done anything bad. Mother was meek as a violet, hardly ever spoke at all, except when Grandfather demanded that she pray aloud and ask forgiveness for her depravity. What was depravity? the child, Eleanor, wondered. And why was she a child of shame?

While Eleanor was small Mother sometimes talked to her, quietly, in the privacy of the bedroom they shared. But as time went on, Mother grew more tacit and withdrawn. She worked hard— Grandmother saw to that. She did all the gardening, while Grandmother pulled back the edge of the shade and stood sentinel. If anyone passed on the road, Grandmother would hasten to the back door and hiss through a crack, "Ssst! Get in here, Chloe!" until in time, Chloe no longer waited for the order, but scuttled inside at the first glimpse of anyone approaching.

Three were allowed near, only three, and these out of necessity: the milkman, who left his bottles on the back step; the Raleigh man from whom they bought their pantry stock; and an old man named Dinsmore who delivered ice for their icebox until his son, Glendon, took over. If anyone else knocked on their door— the school principal, an occasional tramp looking for a free meal, the census taker—they saw no more than a front shade being bent stealthily from inside.

Eventually the truant officer began coming, pounding on the door authoritatively, demanding that it be opened. Did they have a child in there? If so, she had to attend school: it was the law.

Grandmother would stand well away from the drawn shades, her face a deadly mask, and whisper, "Silence, Eleanor, don't say a word!"

Then one time the truant officer came when Grandfather was home. This time he shouted, "Albert See? We know you have a child in there who's school age. If you don't open this door I'll get a court order that'll give me the right to break it down and take her! You want me to do that, See?"

And so Eleanor's schooldays began. But they were painful for the colorless child already a year older and a head taller than the others in her first grade class. The other children treated her like the oddity she was—a gawky, silent eccentric who was ignorant of the most basic games, didn't know how to function in a group, and stared at everything and everybody with big green eyes. She was hesitant at everything and when she occasionally showed moments of glee, jumping and clapping at some amusement, she did so with disquieting abruptness, then fell still as if someone had turned off her switch. When teachers tried to be kind, she backed away as if threatened. When children snickered, she stuck out her tongue at them. And the children snickered with cruel regularity.

School, to Eleanor, seemed like exchanging one prison for another. So she began playing hooky. The first time she did it she feared God would find out and tell Grandmother. But when He didn't, she tried it again, spending the day in the woods and fields, discovering the wonder of true freedom at last. She knew well how to sit still and silent—in that house behind the green shades she did a lot of that—and for the first time, it reaped rewards. The creatures learned to trust her, to go about their daily routine as if she were one of them—snakes and spiders and squirrels and birds. Most of all the birds. To Eleanor, those wonderful creatures, the only ones not restrained to earth, had the greatest freedom of all.

She began studying them. When Miss Buttry's fifth grade class went to the library Eleanor found an Audubon book with colored plates and descriptions of birds' habitats, nests, eggs and voices. In the wilds, she began identifying them: the ruby-crowned kinglet, a spirited bundle of elfin music; the cedar waxwings, who appeared in flocks, seemed always affectionate and sometimes got drunk on overripe fruit; the blue jay, pompous and arrogant, but even more beautiful than the meek cardinals and tanagers.

She brought crumbs in her pockets and laid them in a circle around her, then sat as still as her friend, the barred owl, until a purple finch came and perched in a nearby pine bough, serenading with its mellifluous warble. In time it descended to a lower branch where it cocked its head to study her. She outwaited the finch until eventually he advanced and ate her bread. She found the finch a second day—she was convinced it was the same bird—and yet a third, and when she'd learned to imitate its call, summoned it as effortlessly as other children whistled up their dog. Then one day she stood like the Statue of Liberty, the crumbs in her palm, and the finch perched on her hand to eat.

At school shortly thereafter, a group of children were exchanging boasts. A little girl with black pigtails and an overbite said, "I can do thirty-seven cartwheels without getting dizzy." Another, with the fattest belly in class, boasted, "I can eat fourteen pancakes at one time!" A third, the most notorious liar in class, claimed, "My daddy is going on a safari hunt to Africa next year and he's taking me with him."

Eleanor edged close to their exclusive circle and offered timidly, "I can call the birds and make them eat off my hand."

They gaped at her as if she were lunatic, then tittered and closed their ranks once again. After that the taunts were whispered loudly enough so they wouldn't fail to reach her ears—Crazy Elly See, talks to birds and lives in that house with the shades pulled down, she and her batty mother and her battier grandma and grandpa.

It was during one of her truancies from school that she first spoke to Glendon Dinsmore. She was late heading home and came bursting from the woods, clattering down a steep embankment, sending rocks tumbling to the road below, startling a mule which brayed and sidestepped, nearly overturning Dinsmore's wagon.

"Whoa!" he barked, while the animal nearly splintered the singletree with a powerful kick. When he'd gotten the beast under control, he took off his dusty felt hat and whacked it on the wagon seat in agitation. "Lord a-mighty, girl, what you mean by stormin' outa the woods that way!"

"I'm in a hurry. Gotta get home before the schoolkids walk by."

"Well, you scared poor Madam out of her last-year's hair! You ought to be more careful around animals."

"Sorry," she replied, mollified.

"Aww . . ." He thumped his hat back on and seemed to mellow. "Guess you didn't stop to think. But you be more careful next time, you hear?" He glanced speculatively at the woods, then back at her. "So you're playin' hooky, huh?"

When she didn't answer, his look grew shrewder and he thrust his head forward. "Hey, don't I know you?"

She crossed her arms behind her back, rocked left to right twice. "You used to deliver ice to our house when I was little."

"I did?" She nodded while he scratched his temple, pushing the hat askew. "What's your name again?"

"Elly See."

"Elly See ..." He paused to recall. "Why, of course. I remember now. And mine's Glendon Dinsmore."

"I know."

"You know?" He gave a crooked smile of surprise. "Well, how about that? Don't come to your house no more, though."

Elly scuffed the dirt with her toe. "I know. Grampa bought an electric refrigerator so we wouldn't have to have ice delivered no more. They don't like people comin' in."

"Oh ... so ... I wondered." He motioned along the road with a thumb and offered, "I'm goin' your way. Can I give you a lift?"

She shook her head, clasping her hands more tightly behind her back, making her dress front appear as if she'd tucked two acorns inside. He was a grown-up man by now, a good seventeen, eighteen years old, she figured. If Grandma saw her coming home in his wagon she'd end up doing hours on her knees.

"Well, why not? Madam don't mind pullin' two."

"I'd get in trouble. I'm s'posed to come straight home from school and I ain't supposed to talk to strangers."

"Well, I wouldn't want to get you in trouble. You come up this way often?"

She studied him warily. "Just ... sometimes."

"What you do up there in the woods?"

"I study birds." As an afterthought, she added, "For school, you know?"

He raised his chin and nodded wisely, as if to say, Ah, I see.

"Birds is nice," he offered, then picked up the reins. "Well, maybe I'll run into you again someday, but I better not keep you now. So long, Elly."

She watched him drive away, mystified. He was the first person in her twelve-year experience who'd ever treated her as if she weren't either crazy or a child of shame. She thought about him during prayers after that, to take her mind off her aching knees. He was a rather scruffy-looking fellow, dressed in overalls and thick boots, with only enough beard to make him look prickly. But she didn't care about his looks, only that he treated her as if she weren't some oddity.

The next time she escaped to the woods she found a spot high above the rocky bank behind a juniper bush where she could watch the road and remain hidden. From her secret perch she waited for him to reappear. When he didn't, she was surprised to find herself disappointed. She watched for three days before giving up, never fully understanding what she'd expected had he come along the road as before. Talk, she supposed. It had felt good to simply talk to someone.

Nearly a full year passed before she ran into him again. It was autumn but warm, a day of bright leaves and dusky sky. Elly was stalking bobwhites, the little lords of the fencerows whose voices she loved. Unable to flush any along the fenceline, she headed into the woods to search in heavier cover where they roosted in bevies on the ground, facing outward. She was calling in a clear whistle: *quoi-lee, quoi-lee,* when she flushed not a quail from the sumac bushes, but Glendon Dinsmore from over the next hill. She stopped in her tracks and watched him approach, cradling a gun in one arm. He raised the other, waved, and called, "Hey, Elly!"

She stood sober, awaiting his arrival. Stopping in front of her, he repeated, "Hey, Elly."

"Hey, Glendon," she returned.

"How you doin'?"

"Doin' all right, I reckon."

They stood for a moment in a void. She appraised him smilelessly, while he appeared pleased at having run into her. He looked exactly as he had last time: same overalls, same scruffy beard, same dusty hat. Finally he shifted his stance, rubbed his nose and inquired, "So, how's them birds of yours?"

"What birds?" Her birds were her business, nobody else's.

"You said you was studyin' birds. What you learnin'?"

He'd remembered for a whole year that she studied birds? Elly softened. "I'm tryin' to call the bobwhites outa hiding."

"You can *call* 'em? Golly." He sounded impressed, unlike the girls at school.

"Sometimes. Sometimes it don't work. What you doin' with that there gun?"

"Huntin'."

"Huntin'! You mean you shoot critters?"

"Deer, I do."

"I couldn't never shoot no critter."

"My daddy and me, we eat the deer."

"Well, I hope you don't get one."

He reared back and laughed, one brief hoot, then said, "Girlie, you're somethin'. I 'membered, you was somethin'. So, did you see any bobwhites?"

"Nope. Not yet. You see any deer?"

"Nope, not yet."

"I seen one, but I won't tell you where. I see him almost every day."

"You come out here every day?"

"Pret' near."

"Me too, during huntin' season."

She pondered that momentarily, but any suggestion of meeting again seemed ludicrous. After all, she was only thirteen and he was five years older.

Frightened by the mere thought, she spun away abruptly. "I gotta go." She trotted off.

"Hey, Elly, wait!"

"What?"

She halted twenty feet away, facing him.

"Maybe I'll see y' out here sometime. I mean, well, huntin' season's on a couple more weeks."

"Maybe." She studied him in silence, then repeated, "I gotta go. If I ain't home by five after four they make me pray an extra half hour."

Again she spun and ran as fast as her legs would carry her, amazed by his friendliness and the fact that he seemed to care not a whit about her craziness. After all, he'd been inside that house; he knew where she came from, knew her people. Yet he wanted to be her friend.

She went back to the same spot the next day but hid where he couldn't see her. She watched him approach over the same hill, the gun again on one arm, a fat cloth sack in his other. He sat down beneath a tree, laid the gun across his lap and the sack at his hip. He pushed back his dusty hat, fished a corncob pipe from his bib, filled it from a drawstring sack and lit it with a wooden match. She thought she had never in her life seen anyone so content.

He smoked the entire pipe, his lumpy boots crossed, one arm resting over his stomach. When he knocked the dottle from his pipe and ground it dead with his boot, she grew panicky. In a minute he would leave!

She stepped out of hiding and stood still, waiting for him to spot her. When he did, his face lit in a smile.

"Well, howdy!"

"Howdy yourself."

"Fine day, id'n't it?"

One day was pretty much like the next to her. She squinted at the sky and remained silent.

"Brought you somethin'," he said, getting to his feet.

"For me?" Her eyes grew suspicious. Where she came from nobody did anything nice for anybody.

"For your birds." He leaned down and picked up the fat sack tied with twine. She stared at it, speechless.

"How's your bird studyin' comin'?"

"Oh . . . fine. Just fine."

"Last year you was studyin' them for school. What you doin' it for this year?"

"Just for fun. I like birds."

"Me too." He set the sack near her toes. "What grade you in?"

"Seventh."

"You like it?"

"Not as much as last year. Last year I had Miss Natwick."

"I had her, too. Didn't care much for school, though. I dropped out after eighth. Took the ice route then and help my daddy around the place." He gestured with his head. "Me and him, we live back there, up on Rock Creek Road."

She glanced that direction but her eyes dropped quickly to the sack lying on the forest floor.

"What's in it?"

"Corn."

The shy blue grosbeaks might like corn. Maybe with it she could get closer to them. She should thank him, but she'd never learned how. Instead she gave him the second-best thing, a tidbit of her precious knowledge of birds.

"The orioles are my favorite. They don't eat corn, though. Only bugs and grapes. The grosbeaks, though, they'll prob'ly love it."

He nodded, and she saw that her reply was all the thanks he needed. He asked more questions about school and she told him she studied the birds sometimes in library books. Sometimes she brought those books to the woods. Other times she came with only a tablet and crayons and drew pictures which she took back to the library to identify the birds.

Out at his place, he told her, he'd put up gourds for birdhouses.

"Gourds?"

"The birds love 'em. Just drill 'em a hole and they move right in."

"How big of a hole?"

"Depends on the size o' the bird. And the gourd."

In time he pulled out a watch and said, "It's goin' on four. You best be gittin'."

She got only as far as the deadfall beyond the nearby hill before dropping to her knees and untying the twine with trembling fingers. She stared into the sack and her heart raced. She plunged her hands into the dry golden kernels and ran them through her fingers. Excitement was something new for Elly. She'd never before had something to look forward to.

The next day he didn't show up. But near the sumac bushes where they'd met twice before he left three lumpy green and yellow striped gourds, each drilled with a different-sized hole and equipped with a wire by which to hang it.

A gift. He had given her another gift!

All of the hunting season passed before she saw him again on the last day. He sauntered over the hill with his shotgun and she stood waiting in plain sight, straight as a needle, a flat, unattractive girl whose eyes appeared darker than they really were in her pale, freckled face. She neither smiled nor quavered, but invited him straight-out, "Wanna see where I hung the gourds?" Never in her life had Elly placed that much trust in anyone.

They met often after that. He was easy to be with, for he understood the woods and its creatures as she did, and whenever they walked through it he kept a respectable distance, walking with his thumbs in his rear overall pockets, slightly bent.

She showed him the orioles, and the blue grosbeaks, and the indigo buntings. And together they watched the birds who came to take up residence in the three striped gourds—two families of sparrows and, in the spring, a lone bluebird. Only after they'd been meeting for many months did she lift a palmful of corn and show him how she could call the birds and entice them to eat from her hand.

The following year, when she was fourteen, she met him one day with a glum expression on her face. They sat on a fallen log, watching the cavity in a nearby tree where an opossum was nesting.

"I can't see you no more, Glendon."

"Why's that?"

"Because I'm sick. I'm prob'ly gonna die."

Alarmed, he turned toward her. "Die? What's wrong?"

"I don't know, but it's bad."

"Well . . . did they take you to the doctor?"

"Don't have to. I'm already bleedin'—what could he do?"

"Bleeding?"

She nodded, tight-lipped, resigned, eyes fixed on the opossum hole.

His eyes made one furtive sweep down her dress front, where the acorns had grown to the size of plums.

"You tell your mother about it?"

She shook her head. "Wouldn't do any good. She's tetched. It's like she don't even know I'm there anymore."

"How 'bout your grandma?"

"I'm scared to tell her."

"Why?"

Elly's eyes dropped. "Because."

"Because why?"

She shrugged abjectly, sensing vaguely that this had something to do with being a child of shame.

"You bleedin' from your girl-place?" he asked. She nodded silently and blushed. "They didn't tell you, did they?"

"Tell me what?" She flicked him one glance that quickly shied away.

"All females do that. If they don't, they can't have babies."

Her head snapped around and he shifted his attention to the sun peeking around the trunk of an old live-oak tree. "They shoulda told you so you'da known to expect it. Now you go on home and tell your grandma about it and she'll tell you what to do."

But Eleanor didn't. She accepted Glendon's word that it was something natural.

When it happened at regular intervals, she began keeping track of the length of time between the spells, in order to be prepared.

When she was fifteen she asked him what a child of shame meant.

"Why?"

"Because that's what I am. They tell me all the time."

"They tell you!" His face grew taut and he picked up a stick, snapped it into four pieces and flung them away. "It's nothin'," he said fiercely.

"It's somethin' wicked, isn't it?"

"Now how could that be? You ain't wicked, are you?"

"I disobey them and run away from school."

"That don't make you a child of shame."

"Then what does?" When he remained silent, she appealed, "You're my friend, Glendon. If you won't tell me, who will?"

He sat on the forest floor with both elbows hooked over his knees, staring at the broken stick.

"All right, I'll tell you. Remember when we saw the quails mating? Remember what happened when the male got on top of the female?" He gave her a quick glance and she nodded. "That's how humans mate, too, but they're only supposed to do it if they're married. If they do it when they're not, and they get a baby, people like your grandma call it a child of shame."

"Then I am one."

"No, you ain't."

"But if—"

"No, you ain't! Now that's the last I wanna hear of it!"

"But I ain't got no daddy."

"And it ain't your fault neither, is it? So whose shame is it?"

She suddenly understood the cleansings, and why her mother was called the sinner. But who was her daddy? Would she ever know?

"Glendon?"

"What?"

"Am I a bastard?" She'd heard the word whispered behind her back at school.

"Elly, you got to learn not to worry about things that ain't important. What's important is you're a good person inside."

They sat silently for a long time, listening to a flock of sparrows twittering in the buckthorn bushes where the gourds hung. Eleanor raised her eyes to the swatches of blue sky visible between the branches overhead.

"You ever wish somebody would die, Glendon?"

He considered soberly before answering. "No, guess I haven't."

"Sometimes I wish my grandparents would die so my mother and me wouldn't have to pray no more and I could pull up the shades in the house and let Mother outside. A person who's good inside wouldn't wish such a thing, I don't think."

He reached out and laid a consoling hand on her shoulder. It was the first time he'd ever touched her deliberately.

Eleanor got her wish the year she turned sixteen. Albert See died while on circuit . . . in the bed of a woman named Mathilde King. Mathilde King, it turned out, was black and gave her favors only for money.

Elly reported his death to Glendon with no show of grief. When he touched her cheek she said, "It's all right, Glendon. He was the real sinner."

The shock and shame of the circumstances surrounding her husband's death rendered Lottie See incapable of facing even her daughter and granddaughter thereafter. She lived less than a year, most of that year spent sitting in a hard, spindle-backed chair facing one corner of the front parlor where the green shades had been sealed to the edges of the window casings with tape. She no longer spoke except to pray, or force Chloe to repent, but simply sat staring at the wall until one day her head slumped over and her hands dropped to her sides.

When Elly reported her grandmother's death to Glendon there were again no tears or mourning. He took her hand and held it while they sat silently on a log, listening to the woodlife around them.

"People like them . . . they're probably happier dead," he said. "They had no notion of what happiness is."

Elly stared straight ahead. " I can see you whenever I want from now on. Mother won't stop me, and I'll be quittin' school to stay home and take care of her."

Eleanor removed the tape from the shades, but when she pulled them up Chloe screeched and huddled, protecting her head as if from a blow. Her manic fright no longer held any connection to reality. The death of her parents, instead of freeing Chloe, cast her deeper into her world of madness. She could do nothing for herself, so her care was left to Eleanor, who fed and clothed her and saw to her daily needs.

When Elly was eighteen Glendon's father died. His grief was a sharp contrast to Elly's own lack of emotions upon the deaths of her grandparents. They met in the woods and he cried pitifully. She opened her arms and held him for the first time. "Aw, Glendon, don't cry . . . don't cry." But secretly she thought it beautiful that anyone could cry for the death of a parent. She cradled him against her breast, and when his weeping stopped, he expunged his residual grief within her virgin body. For Elly it was an act not of carnal, but of spiritual love. She no longer prayed, nor would she, ever again. But to comfort one so bereaved in such a manner was a prayer more meaningful than any she'd ever been forced to say on her knees in that house of shadow.

When it was over, she lay on her back, studying the pale gold sky through the tender new shoots of spring buds, and said, "I don't want no children of shame, Glendon."

He held her hand tightly. "You won't have. You'll marry me, won't you, Elly?"

"I can't. I have to take care of my mother."

"You could take care of her just as good at my house, couldn't you? And it's gonna be awful lonely there. Why, we could take care of her together. I wouldn't mind having her live with us—and she remembers me, doesn't she? From when I used to deliver ice to your house?"

"I never told her about you, Glendon. She wouldn't understand anyway. She's crazy, don't you see? Scared of the daylight. She never goes out of our house anymore, and I'm afraid if I tried to take her out she'd just plain die of fright."

But Chloe died anyway, within a year of her parents, peacefully, in her sleep. The day she was buried, Elly packed her few meager possessions, closed the door on all those drawn shades, boarded Glendon's wagon and never looked back. They drove to Calhoun, picked up a wedding license at the courthouse and were married within the hour. Their wedding was not so much the consummation of a courtship as a natural extension of two lonely lives that were less lonely when combined. Their married life was much the same: companionship, but no great passion.

And now Elly was marrying again, in a similar way, for similar reasons. She lay in her bed, thinking about tomorrow, a lump in her throat. How was it crazy Elly

See never ended up making a marriage that was more than a commonsense agreement? She had feelings too—hurts, wishes, wants like anybody else. Had they been sealed inside her so long that they'd become dried up by all the years she'd been forced into submission and silence in that darkened house? Nobody had taught her a woman's ways with a man. Loving the boys was easy, but letting a man know how you felt about him was another thing.

Why couldn't she have said, Will, I'm scared you'll get hurt out there with the bees? Instead she'd thrown an egg. An egg, for mercy sake, when he'd done so much for her and only wanted to do more. Tears of mortification stung her eyes and she covered them with an arm, remembering. Something strange had happened when he went away laughing instead of angry. Something strange in the pit of her stomach. It was still there when he returned to the house for supper, a feeling she hadn't had before, not even with Glendon. A highness, sort of. A pushing against the bottom of her heart, a tightness in the throat.

It came again, strong and insistent as she pictured Will, all lank and lean and so different from Glendon. Shaved every morning, washed three times a day and put on clean britches each sunrise. Made her more dirty laundry in one week than Glendon had made in a month. But she didn't mind. Not at all. Sometimes, ironing his clothes, she'd think of him in them, and the feeling would come again. A tumble in her stomach, a rise in her blood.

When he had come into the kitchen earlier, and had taken her arm, naked-chested, dark-skinned and still wet from washing at the well, she'd felt almost lightheaded from it. Crazy Elly, wishing Will Parker would kiss her. For a minute she'd thought he might, but he hadn't after all, and common sense told her why. 'Cause she was pregnant, plain and dumb.

She curled into a ball on the bed, miserable, because tomorrow was her wedding and she'd been the one who'd had to do the asking.

Chapter 9

On his wedding day Will awakened excited. He had a secret. Something he'd been working on for two weeks and had finished by lanternlight last night at two A.M. Stepping from the barn, he checked the sky—dull as tarnished silver, promising a gloomy, damp day. Women, he supposed, liked sun on their wedding days, but his surprise should cheer her up. He knew exactly when and how he'd present it to her, not until it was time to leave.

They met in the kitchen, feeling uncomfortable and anxious with each other. An odd start to a wedding day with the bride dressed in a blue chenille house robe and the groom in yesterday's overalls. Their first glances were quick and guarded.

"Mornin'."

"Mornin'."

He brought in two pails of bathwater, set them on the stove and began building a fire.

"I suppose you were hopin' for sun," he said with his back to her.

"It would've been nice."

Smiling to himself, thinking again of his secret, he offered, "Maybe it'll break up by the time we leave."

"It don't hardly look like it, and I don't know what I'll do with the boys if it rains. If it does, should we wait till tomorrow?"

He glanced back over his shoulder. "You want to?"

Their eyes met briefly. "No."

Her answer made him smile inside as he headed for the chores. But at breakfast time the tension escalated. It was, after all, their wedding day, and at its end they'd be sharing a bed. But something more was bothering Will. He put off approaching the subject until the meal ended and Elly pushed back her chair as if to begin clearing the table.

"Elly . . . I . . ." He stammered to a stop, drying his palms on his thighs.

"What is it?" She paused, holding two plates.

He wasn't a money-hungry man, but he suddenly understood greed with disarming clarity. He pressed his hands hard against his thighs and blurted out, "I don't know if I got enough money for a license."

"There's the egg money and what you got for selling the scrap metal."

"That's yours."

"Don't be silly. What will it matter after today?"

"A man should buy the license," he insisted, "and a ring."

"Oh . . . a ring." Her hands were in plain sight as she stood beside the table, holding the dirty dishes. He glanced at her left hand and she felt stupid for not having thought to take off her wedding band and leave it in her bureau drawer. "Well . . ." The word dwindled into silence while she pondered and came up with one possible solution. "I . . . I could use the same one."

His face set stubbornly as he rose, pulled his hat on low and lunged across the room toward the sink. "That wouldn't be right."

She watched him gather soap, towels and bathwater and head for the door, pride stiffening his shoulders and adding force to his footsteps.

"What does it matter, Will?"

"It wouldn't be right," he repeated, opening the back door. Half out, he turned back. "What time you wanna leave?"

"I have to get me and the boys ready to go and the dishes washed. And I suppose I should pack some sandwiches."

"An hour?"

"Well . . ."

"An hour and a half?"

"That should be fine."

"I'll pick you up here. You wait in the house for me."

He felt like a fool. Some courtship. Some wedding morning. But he had exactly eight dollars and sixty-one cents to his name, and gold rings cost a damn sight more than that. It wasn't only the ring. It was everything missing in the morning. Touches, smiles, yearning.

Kisses. Shouldn't a bride and groom have trouble restraining themselves at a time like this? That's how he always imagined it would be. Instead they'd scarcely glanced at each other, had discussed the weather and Will Parker's financially embarrassed state.

In the barn he scrubbed his hide with a vengeance, combed his hair and donned freshly laundered clothes: jeans, white shirt, jean jacket, freshly oiled boots and his deformed cowboy hat, brushed for the occasion. Hardly suitable wedding apparel, but the best he could do. Outside thunder rumbled in the distance. Well, at least she didn't have to worry about rain. He had that much to offer his bride this morning, though much of his earlier elation over the surprise had vanished.

In the house Eleanor was on her knees, searching for Donald Wade's shoe under the bed while upon it he and Thomas imitated Madam, kicking and braying.

"Now settle down, boys. We don't want to keep Will waitin'."

"Are we really goin' for a ride in the big wagon?"

"I said so, didn't I?" She caught a foot and started forcing the brown high-top shoe on. "Clear into Calhoun. But when we get to the courthouse you got to be good. Little boys got to be like mice in the corner during weddings, y' understand?"

"But what's weddings, Mama?"

"Why, I told you, honey, me and Will are gettin' married."

"But what's married?"

"Married is—" She paused thoughtfully, wondering exactly what this marriage would be. "Married is when two people say they want to live with each other for the rest of their lives. That's what me and Will are gonna do."

"Oh."

"That's all right with you, ain't it?"

Donald Wade flashed a smile and nodded vigorously. "I like Will."

"And Will likes you, too. And you too, punkin." She touched Thomas's nose. "Nothin's gonna change after we're married, 'cept . . ." The boys waited with their eyes on their mother. " 'Cept y' know how sometimes I let you come in with me at night—well, from now on there won't be no room 'cause Will's gonna be sleepin' with me."

"He is?"

"Aha."

"Can't we even come in when it thunders and lightnin's?"

She pictured them four abreast beneath the quilts and wondered how Will would adjust to the demands of fatherhood. "Well, maybe when it thunders and lightnin's." Thunder rumbled at that moment and Eleanor frowned at the window. "Come on. Will should be comin' any minute." Distractedly she added, "Lord, I got a feelin' we're gonna be soaked before we get to any courthouse."

She helped the boys into jackets, donned her own coat and had just picked up the red sandwich tin from the kitchen cupboard when the thunder growled again, long and steady. She turned, glanced toward the door and cocked her head. Or was it thunder? Too unbroken, too high-pitched and drawing closer. She moved toward the back door just as Donald Wade opened it and a rusty Model A Ford rolled into the clearing with Will at the wheel.

"Glory be," Eleanor breathed.

"It's Will! He gots a car!" Donald Wade tore off at a dead run, slamming the screen, yelling, "Where'd you get it, Will? We gonna ride in it?"

Will pulled up at the foot of the path and stepped out in his coarse wedding attire. Standing with a hand draped over the top of the car door, he ignored Donald Wade in favor of Eleanor, who came onto the porch in his favorite yellow dress covered by a short brown coat that wouldn't close over her stomach. Her hair was pulled back in a neat tail and her face glowed with surprise.

"Well, you ain't got a ring," he called, "but you got a jitney to ride to your wedding in. Come on."

With the sandwich tin in one hand and Baby Thomas on her free arm, she left the porch. "Where did you get it?" she asked, moving toward Will like a sleep-walker, picking up speed as she neared.

He let a grin quirk one corner of his mouth. "Out in the field. Been working on it whenever I could sneak in an hour here and there."

"You mean it's one of the old junkers?"

"Well . . . not exactly one." With a touch at the back of his hat brim he tilted it well forward, his eyes following as she reached the Ford and circled it with a look of admiration on her face. "More like eight or ten of the junkers, a little bit of this one and a little bit of that one, held together with baling twine and Bazooka, but I think it'll get us there and back all right."

She came full circle and smiled up into his face. "Will Parker, is there anything you can't do?"

He relieved her of the red sandwich tin and handed it to Donald Wade, then plucked Thomas from her arms. "I know a little about engines," he replied modestly, though inside he glowed. With so few words she'd restored his exhilaration. "Get in."

"It's actually running!" She laughed and clambered under the wheel to the far side while the idling engine shimmied the car seat.

"Of course it's running. And we won't have to worry about any rain. Here, take the young 'un." He handed Thomas inside, then swung Donald Wade onto the seat and followed, folding himself behind the wheel. Donald Wade stood on the seat, wedging himself as tightly against Will as possible. He laid a proprietary hand on Will's wide shoulder. "We ridin' to town in *this?*"

"That's right, *kemo sabe.*" Will put the car in gear. "Hang on." As they rolled away, the children giggled and Eleanor clutched the seat. Pleased, Will observed their expressions from the corner of his eye.

"But where did you get gasoline?"

"Only got enough to get us to town. Found it in the tanks out there and strained the rust out of it with a rag."

"And you fixed this all by yourself?"

"There were plenty of junkers to take parts from."

"But where'd you learn how?"

"Worked in a filling station in El Paso one time. Fellow there taught me a little about mechanics."

They turned around in a farmyard which was far neater than it had been two months ago. They motored down a driveway which two months ago had been unusable. They traveled in a car that two weeks ago had been a collection of scrap metal. Will couldn't help feeling proud. The boys were entranced. Eleanor's smile was as broad as a melon slice as she steadied Thomas on her knees.

"Like it?"

She turned shining eyes toward Will. "Oh, it's a grand surprise. And my first time, too."

"You mean you never rode in a car before?" he asked, disbelievingly.

"Never. Glendon never got around to fixing any of 'em up. But I rode on his steel mule one time, down the orchard track and back." She shot him a sportive grin. "The noise like to shake m' teeth outa my skull, though."

They laughed and the day lost its bleakness. Their smiles brought a gladness missing till now. While their gazes lingered longer than intended, the fact struck: they were chugging off to the courthouse to get married. Married. Husband and wife forever. Had they been alone, Will might have said something appropriate to the occasion, but Donald Wade moved, cutting off his view of Eleanor.

"We done good on the driveway huh, Will?" The boy cupped Will's jaw, forcing his direct attention.

"We sure did, short stuff." He ruffled Donald Wade's hair. "But I got to watch the road."

Yes, they'd done good. Guiding the wheel of the Model T, Will felt as he had the day he'd bought the candy bars and bluebird—heated and good inside, expansive and optimistic. In a few hours they would be his "family." Putting pleasure on their faces put pleasure on his own. And it suddenly didn't matter so much that he had no gold ring to offer Eleanor.

Her elation dimmed, however, as they approached Whitney. When they passed the house with the drawn shades she stared straight ahead, refusing to glance at the place. Her lips formed a grim line and her hands tightened on Thomas's hips.

Will wanted to say, I know about that house, Eleanor. It don't matter to me. But a glance at her stiff pose made him bite back the words.

"Got to stop at the filling station," he mentioned, to distract her. "It'll only take a minute."

The man at the station cast overt, speculative glances at Eleanor, but she stared straight ahead like one walking through a graveyard at midnight. The attendant gave Will the twice-over, too, and said, "Nasty weather brewin', looks like."

Will only glanced at the sky.

"Feller'd be happy to have a car on a day like this," the attendant tried again while his eyes darted to Eleanor.

"Yup," Will replied.

"Goin' far?" the man inquired, obviously less interested in pumping gas than in gawking at Eleanor and trying to puzzle out who Will might be and why they were together.

"Nope," Will answered.

"Goin' up Calhoun way?"

Will gave the man a protracted stare, then let his eyes wander to the gas pump. "Five gallons comin' up."

"Oh!" The pump clicked off, Will paid 83 cents and returned to the car, leaving the attendant unenlightened.

When they were on their way again and had left Whitney behind, Eleanor relaxed.

"Someone you know?" Will inquired.

"I know 'em all and they all know me. I seen him gawkin'."

"Prob'ly 'cause you're lookin' right pretty this mornin'."

His words did the trick. She turned a wide-eyed look his way and her ears turned pink. Cheeks, too, before she transferred her attention to the view ahead.

"You don't need to make up pretty words just 'cause it's my weddin' day."

"Wasn't makin' 'em up."

And somehow he felt better, having spoken his mind and given her a touch of what a bride deserves on her wedding day. Better yet, he'd made her forget the house with the picket fence and the gawking gas station attendant.

The ride took them through some of the prettiest country Will had ever seen—rolling hills and gurgling creeks, thick stands of pine and oaks just beginning to turn a faint yellow. Outside, the mist put a sheen on each leaf and rock and turned the roads a vibrant, glistening orange. Wet tree trunks appeared coal black against the pearl-gray sky. The road curved and looped, the elevation constantly dropping until they rounded a bend and saw Calhoun nestled below.

Situated in a long narrow valley, the lowest spot between Chattanooga and Atlanta, the town stretched out along the tracks of the L & N Railroad, which had spawned its growth. U.S. 41 became Wall Street, the main street of town. It paralleled the tracks and carried travelers into a business section that had taken on the same rangy shape as the steel rails themselves. The streets were old, wide, built in the days when mule and wagon had been the chief mode of transportation. Now there were more Chevrolets than mules, more Fords than wagons, and, as in Whitney, blacksmith shops doubling as filling stations.

"You know Calhoun?" Will inquired as they passed a row of neat brick houses on the outskirts.

"Know where the courthouse is. Straight ahead on Wall Street."

"Is there a five-and-dime somewhere?"

"A five-and-dime?" Eleanor flashed him a puzzled look but he watched the road beyond the radiator cap. "What do you want with a five-and-dime?"

"I'm gonna buy you a ring." He'd decided it somewhere between the compliment and Calhoun.

"What's a five-and-dime, Mommy?" Donald Wade interrupted.

Eleanor ignored him. "Oh, Will, you don't have—"

"I'm gonna buy you a ring, I said, then you can take his off."

His insistence sent a flare to her cheeks and she stared at his stubborn jaw until the warmth spread down to her heart. She turned away and said meekly, "I already did."

Will shot a glance at her left hand, still resting on the baby's hip. It was true— the ring was gone. On the steering wheel his grip relaxed.

Donald Wade patted his mother's arm, demanding, "What's a five-and-dime, Mommy?"

"It's a store that sells trinkets and things."

"Trinkets? Can we go there?"

"I reckon that's where Will's takin' us first." Her eyes wandered to the driver and found him watching her. Their gazes locked, fascinated.

"Oh-boy!" Donald Wade knelt on the seat, balancing himself against the dashboard, staring at the town with unbridled fascination. "What's that, Mommy?" He pointed. She didn't hear and he whapped her arm four times. "Mommy, what's that?"

"Better answer the boy," Will advised quietly, and turned his attention back to the street, releasing her to do the same.

"A water tower."

Baby Thomas repeated, *"Wa-doo tow-woo."*

"What's that?" Donald Wade asked.

"A popcorn wagon."

"Pop-cone," the baby echoed.

"They sell it?"

"Yes, son."

"Goll-eee! Can we git some?"

"Not today, dear. We got to hurry."

He watched the wagon until it disappeared behind them and Will mentally tallied up the remainder of his money. Only six bucks, seventy-eight cents, and he had to buy a ring and a license yet.

"What's that?"

"A theater."

"What's a theater?"

"A place where they show movies."

"What's a movie?"

"Well, it's sort of a picture story that moves on a big screen."

"Can we see it?"

"No, honey. It costs money."

The marquee said *Border Vigilantes,* and Will noted how both Donald Wade's and Eleanor's eyes lingered on it as they passed. Six measly bucks and seventy-eight measly cents. What he wouldn't do for full pockets right now.

Just then he spotted what he was looking for, a brick-fronted building with a sign announcing, WISTER'S VARIETY—HOUSEWARES, TOYS & SUNDRIES.

He parked the car and reached for Donald Wade. "Come on, *kemo sabe,* I'll show you a five-and-dime."

Inside, they walked the aisles on creaking wood floors between six rows of pure enchantment. Donald Wade and Thomas pointed at everything and squirmed to get down and touch—toy cars and trucks and tractors made of brightly painted metal; rubber balls of gay reds and yellows; marbles in woven sacks; bubble gum and candy; six-shooters and holsters and cowboy hats like Will's.

"I want one!" Donald Wade demanded. "I want a hat like Will's!"

"Hat," parroted Thomas.

"Maybe next time," Will replied, his heart breaking. At that moment the only thing he wanted worse than a ring for Eleanor was enough cash to buy two black cardboard cowboy hats.

They came to the costume jewelry and stopped. The display was dusty, spread on rose taffeta between glass dividers. There were identification bracelets; baby necklaces shaped like tiny gold crosses; little girls' birthday sets—rings, bracelets and necklaces—all dipped in gold paint, set with brightly colored glass gems; women's earrings of assorted shapes and colors; and beside them, on a blue velvet card, a sign that said, "Friendship Rings—19¢."

Will studied the cheap things, stung at having to offer his bride a wedding band that would surely turn her finger green before a week was up. But he had little choice. He set Donald Wade down. "You take Thomas's hand and don't let him touch anything, all right?"

The boys headed back toward the toys, leaving Will and Eleanor standing self-consciously side by side. He slipped his hands into his hind pockets and stared at the fake-silver rings with their machine-stamped lattice designs covered with crudely formed roses. He reached for one, plucked it from the card and studied it glumly.

"I never cared much before whether I had money or not, but today I wish my name was Rockerfeller."

"I'm glad it ain't, 'cause then I wouldn't be marrying you."

He looked down into her eyes—eyes as green as the fake peridots in the August birth rings—and it struck Will that she was one of the kindest persons he'd ever met. How like her to try to make him feel good at a moment like this. "It'll probably turn your finger green."

"It don't matter, Will," she said softly. "I shouldn't have offered to use my old one again. It was thoughtless of me."

"I'd give you gold if I could, Eleanor. I want you to know that."

"Oh, Will . . ." She reached out and covered his hand consolingly as he went on.

"And I'd take them two to the movies, and afterwards maybe buy 'em an ice cream cone at the drugstore, or popcorn at that popcorn wagon like they begged for."

"I brought the egg and cream money, Will. We could still do that."

His gaze shifted to the ring. "I'm the one that should be payin', don't you see?"

She released his hand and took the ring to try it on. "You got to learn not to be so proud, Will. Let's see if it fits." The ring was too big, so she chose another.

The second one fit and she spread her fingers in the air before them, as proud as if she wore a glittering diamond.

"Looks fine, doesn't it?" She wiggled the ring finger. "And I *do* like roses."

"It looks cheap."

"Don't you dare say that about my weddin' ring, Will Parker," she scolded him with mock haughtiness, slipping it off and depositing it in his palm. "The sooner you pay for it the sooner we can get on down to the courthouse and speak our words."

She turned away blithely, but he caught her arm and spun her around.

"Eleanor, I . . ." He looked into her eyes and didn't know what to say. A lump of appreciation clotted his throat. The value of the ring honestly made no difference to her.

She cocked her head. "What?"

"You never complain about anything, do you?"

It was subtle praise, but no poetry could have pleased her more.

"We got a lot to be thankful for, Will Parker. Come on." Her smile flashed as she grabbed his hand. "Let's go get married."

They found the Gordon County courthouse with no trouble, a red brick Victorian edifice on a crest of land framed by sidewalks, green grass and azalea bushes. Will carried Donald Wade; Eleanor, Thomas as they ascended a bank of steps and crossed the lawn, gazing up at the rounded turret on the right, and on the left, a square cenotaph to General Charles Haney Nelson. It sat sturdily on thick brick arches culminating in a pointed clock tower that overlooked the chimneyed roof. The mist was cold on their uplifted faces, then disappeared as they mounted the second set of steps beneath the arches and entered a marble-floored hall that smelled of cigar smoke.

"This way." Eleanor's voice rang through the empty hall, though she spoke quietly. Turning right, she led Will to the office of the Ordinary of the Court.

Inside, at an oak desk beyond a spindled rail, a thin, middle-aged woman—her nameplate read Reatha Stickner—stopped typing and tipped her head down to peer over rimless octagonal spectacles.

"May I help you?" She had a cheerless, authoritarian voice. It echoed in the barren, curtainless room.

"Yes, ma'am," Will replied, stopping just inside the door. "We'd like to get a marriage license."

The woman's sharp gaze brushed from Donald Wade to Baby Thomas to Eleanor's stomach, then back to Will. He firmly grasped Eleanor's elbow and ushered her toward the breast-high counter. The woman pushed away from her desk and shuffled toward them with an extreme limp that dipped one shoulder and left one foot dragging. They met on opposite sides of the barrier and Reatha Stickner fished inside the neck of her dress to pull up an underwear strap that had slipped down while she walked.

"Are you residents of Georgia?" From beneath the counter she drew a black-bound book the size of a tea tray and clapped it down between them without glancing up again.

"I am," Eleanor spoke up. "I live in Whitney."

"Whitney. And how long have you lived there?" The black cover slapped open, revealing forms separated by carbons.

"All my life."

"I'll need proof of residency."

Will thought, *Oh no, not again.* But Eleanor surprised him by depositing

Thomas on the high counter and producing a folded paper from her coat pocket. "Got my first wedding license here. You gave it to me, so it should be okay."

The woman examined Eleanor minutely, without a change of expression—pursed lips, haughty eyebrows—then turned her attention to the license while Thomas reached for a stamp pad. Eleanor grabbed his hand and held it while he objected vocally and struggled to pull it free.

"Don't touch," she whispered, but of course, he grew stubborn and insisted, louder than before. Will set Donald Wade on the floor and plucked the baby off the counter to hold him. Donald Wade immediately tried to climb Will's leg, complaining, "I can't see. Lift me up." The boy's fingertips curled over the countertop and he tried to climb it with his feet. Will gave him a yank to straighten him up. "Be good," he ordered, bending momentarily. Donald Wade wilted against the counter, pouting.

Reatha Stickner cast a disapproving glance at the faces visible above her counter, then moved away to fetch a pen and inkholder. She had to adjust her strap again before writing in the wide book.

"Eleanor Dinsmore—middle name?"

"I ain't got one."

Though the clerk refused to lift her eyes, the pen twitched in her fingers. "Same address?"

"Yes . . ." Imitating Will, Eleanor added belatedly, ". . . ma'am."

"And are there any encumbrances against you getting married?"

Eleanor fixed a blank look on the woman's spectacles. Reatha Stickner glanced up impatiently and said, "Well?"

Eleanor turned to Will for help.

Will felt his hackles rise and spoke sharply. "She's not married and she's not a Nazi. What other encumbrances are there?"

Everything was silent for three seconds while the stern-faced clerk fixed Will with a disapproving glare. Finally, she cleared her throat, dipped her pen and loftily returned her attention to the application blank. "And how about you? Are *you* a Nazi?" It was asked without a hint of humor while she gave the impression that she might have looked up but for the fact that the person she was serving wasn't worthy.

"No, ma'am. Just an ex-convict." Will felt a deep thrill of satisfaction as her head snapped up and a white line appeared around her lips. He reached casually into his shirt pocket for his release papers. "Think you have to see these."

Her strap fell down and had to be hitched up again as she accepted Will's papers. She examined them at length, gave him another sour glance and wrote on the application.

"Parker, William Lee. Address?"

"Same as hers."

The clerk's eyes, magnified by her glasses, rolled up for another lengthy visual castigation. In the silence Donald Wade's footsteps could be heard climbing the desk wall as he hung on it and gazed at the door, upside-down.

Will thought, *Go to it, Donald Wade!*

Primly, the woman wrote on, taking the information from Will's papers. "How long have you been at this address?" she asked, while her pen scratched loudly.

"Two months."

Her eyes flickered to Eleanor's bulbous stomach, the thin band of yellow showing behind the brown coat. Her chin drew in, creating two folds beneath it. She applied her official signature, and ordered coldly, "That'll be two dollars."

Will stifled a sigh of relief and dug the money from his breast pocket. The clerk dipped below the counter, came up with an official rubber stamp and with curt motions stamped the license, tore it out, slapped the book closed—fap! sktch! whp!—and brandished the paper across the counter.

Stone-faced, but seething, Will accepted it and tipped his hat. "Much obliged, ma'am. Now, who marries us?"

Her eyes drifted over his blue denim work clothes, then dropped to the rubber stamp. "Judge Murdoch."

"Murdoch." When she looked up, Will gave her a cool nod. "We'll find him."

Acidly she hurried to inform them, "He has a full docket this morning. You should have made arrangements in advance."

Will settled Baby Thomas more comfortably on his arm, peeled Donald Wade off the counter, headed him toward the door, then clasped Eleanor's elbow and guided her from the office without acknowledging Reatha Stickner's high-handed order. His grip was biting and his footsteps unnaturally lengthy. In the corridor, he grated, "Goddamn old biddy. I wanted to slap her when she looked at you like that. What right's she got to look down her nose at you!"

"It don't matter, Will. I'm used to it. But what about the judge? What if he's too busy?"

"We'll wait."

"But she said he—"

"We'll wait, I said!" His footsteps pounded harder. "How long can it take him to mutter a few words and sign a paper?" Coming up short, he stopped Eleanor. "Just a minute." He stuck his head inside an open doorway and asked, "Where do we find Judge Murdoch?"

"Second floor, halfway down the hall, the double doors on your left."

With the same stubborn determination, Will herded them to the second floor, through the double doors, where they found themselves in a courtroom presently in session. They stood uncertainly in the aisle between two flanks of benches while voices from up front reverberated beneath the vaulted ceiling. An officer in a tan uniform left his station beside the doors. "You'll have to be seated if you want to stay," he whispered.

Will turned, ready to do mortal injury to anyone who got uppity with them again. But the man was no more than twenty-five, had a pleasant face and polite manner. "We want the judge to marry us but we don't have an appointment."

"Step outside," the deputy invited, opening one of the doors and holding it while they filed into the hall. Joining them, he checked his watch. "He's got a pretty full day, but you can wait outside his chambers if you want. See if he can squeeze you in."

"We'll do that. Appreciate it if you'd head us in the right direction," Will returned tightly.

"Right this way." He led them to the end of the hall and pointed to a narrower corridor leading off at a right angle. "I have to stay in the courtoom, but you'll find it easily. His name is above the door. Just have a seat on the bench across from it."

Neither Will nor Eleanor owned a watch. They sat on an eight-foot wooden bench, staring at a maple door for what seemed hours. They read and reread the brass plaque above it: ALDON P. MURDOCH, DISTRICT COURT JUDGE. The boys tired of climbing over the curved arms of the bench and grew fractious. Donald Wade badgered, "Mommy, let's *go-o-o.*" Thomas started whining and flailing his feet against the seat. Finally he fell asleep, sprawled on the bench with his head in Eleanor's lap, leaving Will to keep Donald Wade occupied.

The door opened and two men bustled out, talking animatedly. Will jumped to his feet and raised a finger, but the pair marched away, deep in discussion, without sparing a glance for the four on the bench.

The wait continued; Eleanor got a backache and had to find the bathroom. Thomas woke up with an ugly disposition and Donald Wade whined that he was hungry. When Eleanor returned, Will ran to the car for their sandwiches. They were sitting on the bench eating them, trying to convince Baby Thomas to give up crying and try a bite, when one of the two men returned.

This time he stopped voluntarily. "Got a cranky one there, huh?" He smiled indulgently at Thomas.

"Judge Murdoch?" Will leaped to his feet, whipping his hat from his head.

"That's right." He was gray-haired, rotund and had a jowls like a bloodhound. But though he wore the air of a busy man, he seemed approachable. "I'm Will Parker. And this is Eleanor Dinsmore. We were wondering if you'd have time to marry us today."

Murdoch extended a hand. "Parker." He nodded to Eleanor. "Miss Dinsmore." He gave each of the boys a grandfatherly glance, then assessed Eleanor thoughtfully. "You were here when I left for lunch, weren't you?"

"Yessir," she answered.

"How long before that?"

"I don't know, sir, we ain't got no watch."

The judge shot a cuff and checked his own. "Court reconvenes in ten minutes."

Eleanor rushed on. "We ain't got no phone either, or we'd've called to make an appointment. We just drove up from Whitney, thinkin' it'd be all right."

Again the judge smiled at the boys, then at the sandwich in Eleanor's hand. "Looks like you brought your witnesses with you."

"Yessir . . . I mean, no sir. These are my boys. That's Donald Wade . . . and this here is Baby Thomas."

The judge leaned down and extended a hand. "How do you do, Donald Wade." The youngster glanced up uncertainly at Will and waited for his nod before hesitantly giving his hand to the judge. Murdoch performed the handshake with gravity and a half-smile. Next he offered Thomas a wink and a chuckle. "You boys have had a long enough morning. How would you like a jelly bean?"

Donald Wade inquired, "What's a jelly bean?"

"Well, come into my office and I'll show you."

Again Donald Wade looked to Will for guidance.

"Go ahead."

To the adults, Judge Murdoch advised, "I think I can squeeze you in. It won't be fancy, but it'll be legal. Step inside."

It was a crowded room with a single north window and more books than Will had ever seen anywhere except in the Whitney library. He glanced around, his hat forgotten against his thigh, while the judge gave his attention first to the boys. "Come around here." He moved behind a cluttered desk and from a lower drawer extracted a cigar box labeled "Havana Jewels." The boys peered inside as he opened it and announced, "Jelly beans." Without objection they allowed the district court judge to set them side-by-side on his chair and roll it close to the desk, where he placed the cigar box on an open law book. "I keep them hidden because I don't want my wife to catch me eating them." He patted his portly stomach. "She says I eat too many of them." As the boys reached for the candy, he warned with a twinkle in his eye, "Now be sure you save some for me."

From a coat tree he took a black robe, inquiring of Will, "Do you have a license?"

"Yessir."

A door opened on his left and the same young deputy who'd directed Will and Eleanor to the judge's chambers stuck his head inside. "One o'clock, your honor."

"Come in here, Darwin, and close the door."

"Pardon me, sir, but we're runnin' a little late."

"So we are. They won't go anyplace, not until I say they can."

As the young man followed orders, the judge buttoned his robe and performed introductions. "Darwin Ewell, this is Eleanor Dinsmore and Will Parker. They're going to be married and we'll need you to act as witness."

The deputy shook their hands, wearing a pleasant smile. "Pleasure, sir ... ma'am."

The judge indicated the boys. "And the two with the jelly beans are Donald Wade and Baby Thomas."

Darwin laughed as he observed the pair selecting another color from the cigar box, paying no attention to the others in the room. In moments the judge stood before Will and Eleanor, examining their license, then placing it on the desk behind him and crossing his hands over his mounded stomach.

"I've got books I could read from," he informed them with a benevolent expression on his face, "but they always sound a little stilted and formal to me so I prefer to do this my own way. The books always manage to miss some of the most important things. Like do you know each other well enough to believe what you're doing is the right thing?"

Taken by surprise at the unorthodox beginning, Will was a little slow to reply. He glanced at Eleanor first, then back at the judge.

"Yessir."

"Yessir," Eleanor repeated.

"How long have you known each other?"

Each waited for the other to answer. Finally Will did. "Two months."

"Two months ..." The judge seemed to ponder, then added, "I knew my wife exactly three and a half weeks before I proposed to her. We've been married thirty-two years—happily, I might add. Do you love each other?"

This time they stared straight at the judge. Both of them turned slightly pink.

"Yessir," came Will's answer.

"Yessir," Eleanor's echoed, more softly. Will's heart thundered, while he wondered if it was true.

"Good ... good. Now the times when I want you to remember that are the times when you'll be at cross purposes—and nobody who remains married for thirty-two, or fifty-two or even *two* years can avoid them. But disagreements can become arguments, then battles, then wars, unless you learn to compromise. It's the wars you'll have to avoid, and you do that by remembering what you've just told me. That you love each other. All right?" He waited.

"Yessir," they replied in unison.

"Compromise is the cornerstone of marriage. Can you work things out and reach compromises instead of giving way to anger?"

"Yessir."

"Yessir." Eleanor's eyes couldn't quite meet the judge's as she remembered the egg running down Will's face. Then honesty got the best of her and she added, "I'll try real hard."

The judge smiled, then nodded approvingly. "And you'll work hard for Eleanor, Will?"

"Yessir, I already do."

"And will you provide a good home for Will, Eleanor?"

"Yessir, I already do."

To the judge's credit, he didn't bat an eye.

"I take it the children are yours by a former marriage, is that right?"

She nodded.

"And the one you're expecting—that makes three." He turned his attention to Will. "Three children is a grave responsibility to take on, and in the future there may be more. Do you accept responsibility for them, along with that of being a husband and provider for Eleanor?"

"Yessir."

"You're both young yet. In your lives you may meet others who attract you. When that happens, I exhort you to recall this day and what your feelings were for each other as you stood before me, to remember your vows of fidelity and remain true to one another. Would that be hard for you?"

Will thought of Lula. "No, it wouldn't."

Eleanor thought of the jeers she'd received from boys in school and how Will was the only one since Glendon who'd treated her kindly. "No, not at all."

"Then, let's seal it with a promise—to love each other, to remain true to each other, to provide love and material care for each other and for all the children entrusted to you, to work hard for one another, practice patience, forgiveness and understanding, and treat each other with respect and dignity for the rest of your lives. Do you so promise, William Lee Parker?"

"I do."

"And do you so promise, Eleanor Dinsmore?"

"I do."

"Are there rings?"

"Yessir." Will found the dime-store ring in his breast pocket. "Just one."

The judge seemed unsurprised by its obvious cheapness. "Put it on her finger now and join right hands."

Will reached for Eleanor's hand and slid the ring partially over her knuckle. Their eyes met briefly, then skittered downward as he held her hand loosely. Judge Murdoch continued, "Let this ring be a symbol of your constancy and devotion. Let it remind you, William, who gives it, and you, Eleanor, who wears it, that from this day until you're parted by death you will remain forever one, inseparable. Now, by the power invested in me by the sovereign state of Georgia, I pronounce you husband and wife."

It had been so quick, so undramatic. It didn't feel done. And if done, not real. Will and Eleanor stood before the judge like a pair of tree stumps.

"Is that it?" Will inquired.

Judge Murdoch smiled. "All but the kiss." Then he twisted around to sign the marriage certificate on the desk behind him.

The pair stared at Murdoch's shoulders but didn't move. On the chair the boys munched jelly beans. From the courtroom came the murmur of voices. On the stiff paper the pen scratched while Deputy Ewell watched expectantly.

The judge dropped his pen and turned back to find the newlyweds standing stiffly, shoulder to shoulder.

"Well . . ." he prompted.

Their faces bright with color, Will and Eleanor turned toward each other. She lifted her face self-consciously and he looked down likewise.

"My court is waiting," Judge Murdoch admonished softly.

With his heart racing, Will placed his hands lightly on Eleanor's arms and bent to touch her lips briefly. They were warm and open, as if in surprise. He got a glimpse of her eyes at close range—also open, as his own were. Then he straightened, ending the uncomfortable moment as they faced the judge self-consciously.

"Congratulations, Mr. Parker." Judge Murdoch pumped Will's hand. "Mrs. Parker." And Eleanor's. As he pronounced her new name Eleanor's discomfort intensified. Heat climbed her body and her cheeks burned hotter.

Judge Murdoch handed the marriage certificate to Will. "I wish you many years of happiness, and now I'd better get back to my courtroom before they start beating on my door." He turned toward it in a flurry of black robes and paused with a hand on the knob. "You have a fine pair of boys there—so long, boys!" With one last wave, he disappeared. Darwin Ewell, also due back in court, wished them luck and hastily ushered them out.

It had taken less than five minutes from the time they'd entered the judge's chambers until they found themselves in the hall again, united for life. The judge's whirlwind pace left them both feeling disoriented but scarcely married. It had been startlingly unceremonious; they hadn't even been aware that the first questions were part of the judge's unorthodox rite. It had ended much the same—no pomp, no pageantry, only a simple pronunciation beneath clasped hands, and—bango!—back in the hall. If it hadn't been for the kiss, they might not believe a marriage had taken place at all.

"Well," Will said breathlessly with a mystified laugh. "That was that."

Eleanor's perplexed gaze remained on the closed door. "I guess it was. But . . . so quick."

"Quick, but legal."

"Yes . . . but . . ." She lifted dubious eyes to Will and thrust her head forward. "But do you *feel* married?"

Unexpectedly, he laughed. "Not exactly. But we must be. He called you Mrs. Parker."

She lifted her left hand and gazed at it disbelievingly. "So I am. Mrs. Will Parker."

The belated impact struck them full force. *Mr. and Mrs. Will Parker.* They absorbed the fact with all its attendant implications while their eyes were drawn to one another as if by polaric force. He thought about kissing her again, the way he wanted to. And she wondered what it would be like. But neither of them dared. In time they realized how long they'd been staring. Eleanor grew flustered and let her gaze drop. Will chuckled and scratched his nose.

"I think we should celebrate," he announced.

"How?" she asked, reaching down for Baby Thomas. Will nudged her aside and hoisted Thomas onto his arm.

"Well, if my arithmetic is right, I still have five dollars and fifty-nine cents. I think we should take the boys to the movie."

Excitement splashed across Eleanor's face. "Really?"

Donald Wade began jumping up and down, clapping. "Yeah! Yeah! The movie! Take us to the movie, Mommy, pleeeease!" He clutched Eleanor's hand.

Will took Eleanor's free elbow, guiding her down the hall. "I don't know, Donald Wade," he teased, turning a crooked grin on his wife's eager face. "It looks to me like we might have some trouble convincing your mama."

Then Mr. and Mrs. William Lee Parker—and family—left the courthouse smiling.

Chapter 10

The smell of popcorn greeted them in the theater lobby. With eyes wide and fascinated, the boys stared up at the red and white popcorn machine, then appealed to their mother. "Mama, can we have some?" Will's heart melted. He was reaching into his shirt pocket before Eleanor could frame a refusal. Inside the dimly lit auditorium, Donald Wade and Thomas sat on their knees, munching, until the screen lit up with *Previews of Coming Attractions*. When scenes from *Gone With the Wind* radiated overhead, their hands and jaws seemed to stop functioning. So did Eleanor's. Will eyed her askance as myriad reactions flashed across her face—amazement, awe, rapture.

"Oh, Will," she breathed. "Oh, Will, look!"

Sometimes he did. But he found the study of their faces—especially hers—far more fascinating as they were transported for the first time into the world of celluloid make-believe.

"Oh, Will, look at that dress!"

His attention wavered briefly to the billowing, hoop-skirted garment, then returned to his wife's face, realizing something new about her: she was a woman whose head could be turned by finery. He would not have guessed so from the ordinary way she dressed. But her eyes shone and her lips looked as if they were about to speak to the images on the screen.

The color film disappeared and a newsreel came on in black and white: goose-stepping German soldiers, bombs, mortar shells, the battlefront in Russia, wounded soldiers—an abrupt plunge from fantasy to reality.

Will watched the screen with rapt interest, wondering how long America could possibly stay out of the war, wondering how long he himself could stay out of it if the inevitable happened. He had a family now; his welfare suddenly mattered fiercely, whereas it never had before. It was a shock to him to realize this.

As the newsreel ended he turned and caught Eleanor watching him above the boys' heads. The gaiety had disappeared from her eyes, replaced by a troubled frown. Obviously the grim reality of war had finally imposed itself upon her. He felt a stab of remorse for having been the one to expose her to it, the one who'd brought her here to have her sunny illusions shattered. He wanted to reach above the pair of blond heads and touch her eyelids, say to her, close your eyes for a moment and go back to pretending it isn't happening. Be the happy recluse you were.

But just as he could not ignore the battles in Europe, and America's ever-increasing support for England and France, neither must she. She couldn't remain an ostrich forever, not when she was married to a man of prime age for induction, one with a prison record who was sure to be one of the first called up.

The newsreel ended and the main feature began.

Border Vigilantes turned out to be a Hopalong Cassidy movie, and the boys' reaction made it well worth the six bits Will had laid out. He himself enjoyed the show, and Eleanor's elation returned. But the boys—oh, those two little boys. What a sight they made with their entranced faces lifted to the silver screen while the masked rider fought for law and justice on his white steed, Topper. Donald Wade's mouth hung open when Topper galloped into view for the first time and reared up majestically, his silver-haired rider flourishing a black hat like Will's own. Baby Thomas pointed and stared with owl-eyes, his mouth forming a tight O. Then he squealed and clapped and had to be shushed. Eleanor's expression shifted from one of rapt wonder to childlike delight as the scenes rolled on.

Hopalong got the lady in the end, and when he kissed her Will glanced over at his new wife. As if she felt his survey, she turned again. Their profiles, illuminated by fluttering light, appeared as half-moons in the dark theater while their own first kiss came back afresh, and they were reminded of the night ahead. In that brief moment feelings of anxiety somersaulted through them. Then the finale music swelled, Hopalong rode off into the sunset and the boys set up an exciting babbling.

"Is it all done? Where did Hopalong go? Can we come again, Will, can we, huh?"

In the car there was no talk between Will and Eleanor as there'd been that morning. Baby Thomas slept curled on her lap. Donald Wade—wearing Will's hat—pressed himself against Will's shoulder and exuberated over the wonders of Hopalong and Topper. Though Will answered, his thoughts projected to the night ahead. Bedtime. He cast occasional covert glances at Eleanor but she stared straight ahead and he wondered if she was thinking about the same thing as he.

At home, Will tended the evening chores automatically, his mind on the bedroom he'd never seen, their first kiss today, how guarded they'd been with each other, the night ahead, a real bed and a woman to share it. But a pregnant woman, pregnant enough to eliminate the possibilities of any conjugal commerce. He wondered what a woman as pregnant as Elly looked like naked and his body felt taut with a combination of chagrin at the thought of possibly seeing her that way, and the idea of lying beside her all night long without touching her.

Had he imagined a wedding day, ever, it wouldn't have been like this—himself in blue jeans, the bride seven months pregnant, a dime-store ring, five minutes in a judge's chamber and a Hopalong Cassidy movie with two rambunctious boys. But the unlikely events of the day weren't over yet.

Supper—due to their late return—was scarcely a wedding feast. Scrambled eggs, green beans and side pork. Donald Wade bawled when Eleanor refused to let him wear Will's hat at the table. Baby Thomas spit out his green beans on Eleanor's yellow dress, and when she scolded him he swatted his tumbler of milk across the room. Eleanor, her skirt soaked, leaped up and slapped his hand. Thomas howled like a fire siren while Will sat by helplessly, realizing that family life had some surprises in store for him. Eleanor went off to fetch a basin and a rag, leaving him to ponder the probability that if this wedding day seemed a letdown to an unsentimental fool like him, it must seem a sore disappointment to her. She returned to the fiasco at the table but he wouldn't let her get down on her hands and knees in her pretty yellow dress, especially when she had to struggle these days to get up and down.

"Here, I'll do that." He took the pail from her hand, trying to imagine what it must be like to carry a bride across the threshold of a honeymoon suite on the twentieth floor of the Ritz Hotel. He wished he could do that for her. Instead he could only offer, "You go take care of your dress."

She lifted her face and he saw in her green eyes the same misgivings he had, the same strain, intensified by the boys' uncharacteristic naughtiness on this night when it was the last thing they needed. He was touched more deeply by the fact that she was near tears.

"Thank you, Will."

"Go." He turned her toward the bedroom and gave her a gentle shove.

Funny how one bit of cooperation led to another. A half hour later he found himself beside her, drying dishes, and a half hour after that, helping her get the boys ready for bed.

The pair had had a tiring day and they surrendered to their pillows with remarkable docility. While she tucked them in he wandered the room collecting their discarded clothes, small items that smelled of spilled milk and first trips to town, popcorn and broomstick cowboys. From beside a scarred chest of drawers Will watched Eleanor kiss them goodnight, smiling at the scene. Two pajama-clad boys with faces scrubbed shiny being reassured by their mother that they were loved in spite of their recent misbehavior. She had changed into a worn smock of faded brown that bellied out as she leaned over Donald Wade, kissed his mouth, his cheek; touched his nose with her own and murmured something for his ears only. And next, Baby Thomas, over the side of the crib, kissing him, toppling him into a tired heap, then brushing his hair back while he clasped a favorite blanket and stuck a thumb in his mouth.

Resting an elbow on the dresser top, Will smiled softly. Again came the yearning for things missed, but watching was almost as good as taking part. In those moments, his love for Eleanor swelled, became something more than the love of a husband for a wife. She became the mother he'd never known, the boys became himself—safe, secure, cared for.

With a pang of awe he realized he would be part of this tableau every night. He could wash freckled faces, stuff arms into pajama sleeves, collect dirty clothes and hover over their affectionate goodnights. Vicariously he might recapture a portion of what he'd missed.

The ritual ended. Eleanor lifted the side of the crib and waggled two fingers at Donald Wade. Abruptly he sat up and demanded, "I wanna kiss Will goodnight."

Will's elbow came off the dresser and his face registered surprise. Eleanor turned and met his gaze across the lamplit room.

She noted his hesitation but saw beyond it to the stronger tug of anticipation. "Donald Wade wants to kiss you," she reiterated.

"Me?" He felt like an interloper though his chest tightened expectantly. Donald Wade lifted his arms. Will glanced again at Eleanor, chuckled, scratched his chin and crossed the room, feeling awkward and out of place. He sat on the edge of the bed and the boy's arms clasped his neck without restraint. The small mouth— moist and smelling faintly of milk—pressed Will's briefly. It was so unexpected, so . . . so . . . genuine. He'd never kissed a child goodnight before, had never guessed how it got to your insides and warmed you from there, out.

"Night, Will."

"Night, *kemo sabe.*"

"I'm Hopalong."

Will laughed. "Oh, my mistake. I shoulda checked to see which horse was tied at the hitchin' rail outside."

When Will rose from Donald Wades' bed, Baby Thomas was no longer lying down. He was standing at the rail of his crib with his mouth plump and his eyes unblinking, watching. Baby Thomas ... who'd taken longer to warm to Will. Baby Thomas ... who still intimidated the grown man at times. Baby Thomas ... who imitated everything his older brother did. His kiss was hugless, but his tiny mouth warm and moist when Will bent to touch it.

Lord a-mighty, he'd never have guessed how a pair of goodnight kisses could make a man feel. Wanted. Loved.

" 'Night, Thomas."

Thomas stared at him with big hazel eyes.

"Say goodnight to Will," his mother prompted softly.

"G'night, Wiw."

Never before had Thomas spoken Will's name. The distorted pronunciation went straight to the thin man's heart as he watched Eleanor settle him down a second time before joining Will in the doorway.

They stood a moment, shoulder to shoulder, studying the children. A closeness stole over them, binding them with an accord that washed away the many shortcomings of this day, leaving them with a faith in better things to come.

Leaving the boys' door ajar, they stepped into the front room. It was dark but for the trailing light from the boys' lantern and another on the kitchen table.

Will ran a hand through his hair, draped it around his neck and smiled at the floor. After a moment his chest lifted with a pleasured chuckle.

"I never did that before."

"I know."

He searched for a way to express the fullness in his heart. But there was no way. To an orphan turned drifter, a drifter turned prisoner, a prisoner turned hired hand, a hired hand turned stand-in daddy, there was no way to express what the last five minutes had meant to him. Will could only waggle his head in wonder. "That's somethin', isn't it?"

She understood. His surprise and wonder said it all. He had never expected the right to her children to come along with the right to her house. Yet she recognized his growing affection for them, saw clearly what kind of father he could be— gentle, patient, the kind who'd take none of the small pleasures for granted.

"Yes, it is."

He dropped his hand and lifted his head. A soft smile curved his lips. "I really like those two, you know?"

"Even after the way they acted at supper?"

"Oh, that—that was nothin'. They'd had a big day. I reckon their springs were still twangin'."

She smiled.

He did, too, briefly before sobering. "I want you to know I'll do right by them."

Her voice softened. "Oh, Will ... I know that."

"Well," he went on almost sheepishly, "they're pretty special."

"I think so, too."

Their gazes met momentarily. They searched for something to say, something to do. But it was bedtime; there was only one thing to do. Yet both of them were reluctant to suggest it. In the kitchen the radio was playing "Chattanooga Choo Choo." The strains came through the lighted doorway into the shadows where they paused uncertainly. Across from the boys' room, their own bedroom door stood open, an oblique shadow waiting to take them in. Beyond it waited uncertainty and self-consciousness.

Eleanor fiddled with her hands, searching for a subject to put off bedtime. "Thank you for the movie, Will. The boys will never forget it and neither will I."

"I enjoyed it, too."

End of subject.

"I liked the popcorn, too," she added hurriedly.

"So did I."

End of subject, again.

This time Will found a diversion—the boys' clothes, still balled in his hands. "Oh, here!" He thrust them into hers. "Forgot I still had 'em." He rammed his hands into his pockets.

Looking down at Thomas's milk-streaked shirt, she said, "Thanks for helping me get them ready for bed."

"Thanks for letting me."

A quick exchanged glance, two nervous smiles, then silence again, immense and overpowering, while they stood close and studied the collection of clothes in her hands. It was her house, her bedroom— Will felt like a guest waiting to be invited to stay the night, but still she made no mention of retiring. He heard his own pulse drumming in his ears and felt as if he were wearing somebody else's collar, one size too small. Somebody had to break the ice.

"Are you tired?" he asked.

"No!" she replied, too quickly, too wide-eyed. Then, dropping her head, "Well . . . yes, I am a little."

"I guess I'll step out back then."

When he was gone, her shoulders wilted, she closed her eyes and pressed her burning cheeks into the stale-smelling clothes. *Silly woman. What's there to be skittish about? He's going to share your mattress and your quilts—so what?*

She freed her hair, washed her face and got ready for bed in record time. By the time she heard him reenter the kitchen she was safely dressed in a white muslin nightgown with the quilts tucked to her armpits. She lay stiffly, listening to the sounds of him washing up for bed. He turned off the radio, checked the fire, replaced a stovelid. Then all remained quiet but for the beat of her own pulse in her ears and the tick of the windup alarm clock beside the bed. Minutes passed before she heard his footsteps cross the front room and pause. She stared at the doorway, imagining him gathering courage while her own heart throbbed like the engine of Glendon's old Steel Mule the time she'd ridden it.

Will paused outside the bedroom doorway, fortifying himself with a deep breath. He crossed the threshold to find Eleanor lying on her back in a proper, white, long-sleeved nightie. Her brown hair lay free against the white pillow and her hands were crossed over the high mound formed by her stomach beneath the quilts. Though her expression was carefully bland, her cheeks wore two blots of pink, as if some seraph had winged in and placed a rose petal upon each. "Come in, Will."

He swept a slow glance across the room—curtainless window, homemade rag rug, hand-tied quilt, iron bedstead painted white, a closet door ajar, a bedside table and kerosene lamp, a tall bureau with a dresser scarf and a picture of a man with large ears and a receding hairline.

"I've never seen this room before."

"It's not much."

"It's warm and clean." He advanced two steps only, forcing his eyes to range further until they were drawn, against his will, back to the picture.

"Is that Glendon?"

"Yes."

He crossed to the bureau, picked up the framed photo and held it, surprised at the man's age and lack of physical attractiveness. A rather beaked nose and a bony, hollow-eyed face with narrow lips. "He was some older than you."

"Five years."

Will studied the picture in silence, thinking the man looked much older.

"He wasn't much of a looker. But he was a good man."

"I'm sure he was." A good man. Unlike himself, who had broken the laws of both God and man. Could a woman forget such transgressions? Will set the picture down.

Eleanor asked, "Would it bother you if I left the picture there—so the boy's don't forget him?"

"No, not at all." Was it a reminder that Glendon Dinsmore still held a special place in her heart? That though Will Parker might share her sheets tonight, he had no right to expect to share anything else—ever? He faced the wall while pulling his shirttails out, wanting to impose nothing upon her, not even glimpses of his bare skin.

She watched him unbutton his shirt, shrug it off, hang it on the closet doorknob. Her fascination came as a surprise. There were moles on his back, and firm, tan skin. He was tapered as a turnip from shoulder to waist, and his arms had filled out considerably in the two months he'd been here. Though she felt like a window-peeper, she continued gaping. He unbuckled his belt and her eyes dropped to his hips—thin, probably even bony inside his jeans. When he sat down the mattress sagged, sending her heart aflutter—even so slight a sharing of the bed felt intimate, after having it to herself for over half a year. He hoisted a foot, removed a cowboy boot and set it aside, followed by its mate. Standing, he dropped his jeans to the floor, then stretched into bed with one fluid motion, giving no more than a flash of thighs textured with dark hair and an old pair of Glendon's shorts before the quilt covered him and he stretched out beside her with his arms behind his head.

They stared at the ceiling, lying like matched bookends, making sure not so much as the hair on their arms brushed, listening to the tick of the clock, which seemed to report like rifle shots.

"You can turn down the lantern some. It doesn't need to be that bright."

He rolled and reached, tugging the bedclothes. "How's that?" He peered back over his outstretched arm while the light dimmed to pale umber, enhancing the shadows.

"Fine."

Again he stretched flat. The silence beat about their ears. Neither of them risked any of the settling motions usually accompanying the first minutes in bed. Instead they lay with hands folded primly over quilts, trying to adjust to the idea of sharing a sleeping space, dredging up subjects of conversation, discarding them, tensing instead of relaxing.

Presently, he chuckled.

"What?" She peeked at him askance. When his face turned her way she fastened her gaze on the ceiling.

"This is weird."

"I know."

"We gonna lay in this bed every night and pretend the other one isn't there?"

She blew out a long breath and let her eyes shift over to him. He was right. It was a relief, simply acknowledging that there was another person in the bed. "I wasn't looking forward to this. I thought it'd be awkward, you know?"

"It was. It is," he admitted for both of them.

"I been jumpy as a flea since suppertime."

"Since morning, you mean. Hardest thing I ever did was to open that door and walk into the kitchen this morning."

"You mean you were nervous, too?"

"Didn't it show?"

"Some, but I thought I was worse that way than you."

They mulled silently for some time before Will remarked, "A pretty strange wedding day, huh?"

"Well, I guess that was to be expected."

"Sorry about the judge and the kiss—you know."

"It wasn't so bad. We lived through it, didn't we?"

"Yeah, we lived through it." He crossed his hands behind his head and contemplated the ceiling, presenting her with a hairy armpit that smelled of Ivory soap.

"I'm sorry about the lantern. It'll keep you awake, won't it?"

"Maybe for a while, but it doesn't matter. If you hadn't slept in a real bed for as long as me, you wouldn't complain about a lantern either." He lowered one hand and ran it across the coarse, clean sheet which smelled of lye soap and fresh air. "This is a real treat, you know. Real sheets. Pillow cases. Everything."

No reply entered Eleanor's mind, so she lay in silence, adjusting to the feeling of his nearness and scent. Outside a whippoorwill sang and from the boys' room came the sound of the crib rattling as Thomas turned over.

"Eleanor?"

"Hm?"

"Could I ask you something?"

"Course."

"You afraid of the dark?"

She took her time answering. "Not afraid exactly . . . well, I don't know. Maybe." She thought a moment. "Yeah, maybe. I been sleepin' with the lantern on so long I don't know anymore."

Will turned his head to study her profile. "Why?"

Her eyes met his, and she thought about her fanatic grandparents, her mother, all those years behind the green shades. But to talk about it would make her seem eccentric in his eyes, and she didn't want to be. Neither did she want to ruin her wedding day with painful memories. "Does it matter?"

He studied her green eyes minutely, wishing she'd confide in him, tell him the facts behind Lula's gossip. But whatever secrets she held, he wouldn't hear them tonight. "Then tell me about Glendon."

"Glendon? You want to talk about him . . . tonight?"

"If you do."

She considered for some time before asking, "What do you want to know?"

"Anything you want to tell. Where did you meet him?"

Studying the dim circle of light on the ceiling, she launched into her recollection. "Glendon delivered ice to our house when I was a little girl. We lived in town then, my mother and my grandparents and me. Grandpa was a preacher man, used to go out on circuit for weeks at a time." She peered at Will from the corner of her eye, gave a quirk of a smile. "Fire and brimstone, you know. Voice like a cyclone throwing dirt against the house." She told him what she chose, winnowing out any hints of her painfully lonely youth, the truth about her family, the bad memories from school. Of Glendon she spoke more frankly, telling about their meetings in the woods when she was still a girl, and of their shared respect for wild creatures. "The first present he ever brought me was a sack of corn for the birds, and from then on we were friends. I married him when I was nineteen and I been livin' here ever since," she finished.

At the end of her recital, Will felt disappointed. He'd learned nothing of the house in town nor why she had been locked in it, none of the secrets of Eleanor

Dinsmore Parker. The truth seemed strange: she was his wife, yet he knew less about her than he knew of some of the whores he'd frequented in his day. Above all, he wanted to know about that house so that he could assure her it made no difference to him. Given time, she might tell him more, but for now he respected her right to privacy. He, too, had secret hurts too painful to reveal yet.

"Now your turn," she said.

"My turn?"

"Tell me about you. Where you lived when you were a boy, how you ended up here."

He began with sterile facts. "I lived mostly in Texas but there were so many towns I couldn't name 'em all. Sometimes in orphanages, sometimes people would take me in. I was born down around Austin, they tell me, but I don't remember it till I grew up and went back there one time when I was doing some rodeoing."

"What *do* you remember?"

"First memories, you mean?"

"Yes."

Will thought carefully. It came back slowly, painfully. "Spilling a bowl of food, breakfast cereal, I think, and getting whupped so hard I forgot about being hungry."

"Oh, Will . . ."

"I got whupped a lot. All except for one place. I lived there for a half a year, maybe . . . it's hard to remember exactly. And I've never been able to remember their names, but the woman used to read me books. She had this one with a real sad story I just loved called *A Dog of Flanders,* and there were drawings of a boy and this dog of his, and I used to think, Wow, it must be something to have a dog of your own. A dog would always be there, you know?" Will mused a moment, then cleared his throat and went on. "Well, anyway, this woman, the thing I remember about her most is she had green eyes, the prettiest green eyes this side of the Pecos, and you know what?"

"What?" Elly turned her face up to him.

Smiling down, he told her, "The first time I walked into this house that was what I liked best about you. Your green eyes. They reminded me of hers, and she was always kind. And she was the only one who made me think books were okay."

For a moment they gazed at each other until their feelings came close to surfacing, then Elly said, "Tell me more."

"The last place I lived was with a family named Tryce on a ranch down near a dump called Cistern. The old man's watch came up missing and I figured soon as I heard what was up that they'd pin the blame on me, so I lit out before he could whup me. I was fourteen and I made up my mind as long as I stayed on the move they couldn't stick me in any more schools where all the kids with ma's and pa's looked at me like I was a four-day-old pork chop left in somebody's pocket. I caught a freight and headed for Arizona and I been on the road ever since. Except for prison and here."

"Fourteen. But that's so young."

"Not when you start out like I did."

She studied his profile, the dark eyes riveted on the ceiling, the crisp, straight nose, the unsmiling lips. Softly, she asked, "Were you lonely?" His Adam's apple slid up, then down. For a moment he didn't answer, but when he did, he turned to face her.

"Yeah. Were you?"

Nobody had ever asked her before. Had he been anyone from town, she could not have admitted it, but it felt remarkably good to answer, "Yeah."

Their gazes held as both recognized a first fallen barrier.

"But you had a family."

"A family, but no friends. I'll bet you had friends."

"Friends? Naww." Then, after thoughtful consideration, "Well, one maybe."

"Who?"

He tipped an eyebrow her way. "You sure you wanna hear this?"

"I'm sure. Who?"

He never talked about Josh. Not to anyone. And the story would lead to a conclusion that might make Eleanor Parker rethink her decision to invite him into her bed. But for the first time, Will found he wanted it off his chest.

"His name was Josh," he began. "Josh Sanderson. We worked together on a ranch down near a place called Dime Box, Texas. Near Austin." Will chuckled. "Dime Box was somethin'. It was like ... well, maybe like watchin' the black and white movie after seeing the previews in color. A sorry little dump. Everything kind of dead, or waitin' to die. The people, the cattle, the sagebrush. And nothing to do there on your night off. Nothing." Will paused, his brow smooth while his thoughts ranged back in time.

"So what'd you do?"

He shot her one quick glance. "This ain't much of a subject for a wedding night, Eleanor."

"Most wives already know this kind of stuff about their husbands by their wedding night. Tell me—what'd you do?"

As if settling in for a long talk, he rolled his pillow into a ball, crooked his head against it, lifted one knee and linked his fingers over his belly. "All right, you asked, I'll tell you. We used to go down to La Grange to the whorehouse there. Saturday nights. Take a bath and get all duded up and take our money into town and blow damn near all of it on booze and floozies. Me, I wasn't fussy. Take anyone that was free. But Josh got to liking this one named Honey Rossiter." He shook his head disbelievingly. "Honey—can you believe that? She swore it was her given name but I never believed her. Josh did, though. Hell, Josh'd believe anything that woman told him. And he wouldn't hear anything bad about Honey. Got real pissed off if I said a word against her. He had it bad for her, that's a fact.

"She was tall—eighteen hands, we used to joke—and had this head full of hair the color of a palomino, hung clear down to her rump. It was some hair all right, curly but coarse as a horse's mane, the kind a man could really sink his hands into. Josh used to talk about it, laying in his bunk at night—Honey and her honey hair. Then pretty soon he started talking about marrying her. Josh, I says, she's a whore. Why would you want to marry a whore? Josh, he got real upset when I said that. He was so crazy over her he couldn't tell truth from lies.

"She was like ..." He rested a wrist on the updrawn knee, absently toying with a piece of green yarn on the quilt. " ... well, like an actress in a picture show— played at being whatever a man needed. She'd change herself to suit the man, and when she was with Josh she acted like he was the only man for her. Trouble is, Josh started believing it.

"Then one night we came there and when Josh asked for Honey the old harlot who ran the place says Honey's been spoken for for the next two hours. Who else would he like?

"Well, Josh never wanted anybody else, not after Honey. He waited. But by the time she come back down he was so steamed his lid was rattlin' and he was ready to blow. She comes saunterin' into the Leisure Room—that's what they called the bar where the men waited on the women—and Lord a-mighty, you never heard such a squall as when Josh jumped her about who she was spendin' *two hours* with while he was left downstairs coolin' his heels.

"She says to him, You don't own me, Josh Sanderson, and he says, Yeah, well, I'd like to. Then he pulls a ring out of his pocket and says he'd come there that night intendin' to ask her to marry him."

Will shook his head. "She laughed in his face. Said she'd have to be crazy to marry a no-count saddle bum who'd probably keep her pregnant nine months out of twelve and expect her to take care of a houseful of his squallin' brats. Said she had a life of luxury, spendin' a few hours on her back each night and wearing silk and feathers and eatin' oysters and steak anytime she wanted 'em.

"Well, Josh went wild. Told her he loved her and she wasn't gonna screw anybody else—never. She was gonna leave with him—*now!* He made a grab for her and out of nowhere she pulls this little gun—Christ, I never knew the girls there even carried 'em. But there it was, pointed right at Josh's eye and I reached for a bottle of Old Star whiskey and let her have it. Hell, I didn't think. I just . . . well, I just beaned her. She went down like a tree, toppled sideways and cracked her head on a chair and laid there in a puddle of broken glass and blended whiskey and hardly even bled, she died so fast. I don't know if it was the bottle or the chair that killed her, but it didn't matter to the law. They had me behind bars in less than half an hour.

"I figured things'd come out all right—after all, I was defending Josh. If I hadn't clunked her, she'd have shot Josh smack through his left eye. But what I didn't figure was how serious he was about marrying her, how broke up he was when she died.

"He . . ." Will closed his eyes against the painful memory. Eleanor sat up, watching his face closely.

"He what?" she encouraged softly.

Will opened his eyes and fixed them on the ceiling. "He testified against me. Told this sob story about how he was gonna make an honest woman out of Honey Rossiter, take her away from her lousy life in that whorehouse and give her a home and respectability. And the jury fell for it. I did five years for savin' my *friend's* life." Will ran a hand through his hair and sighed. For seconds he stared at the ceiling, then rolled to a sitting position with arms loosely linked around his knees. "Some friend."

Eleanor studied the moles on his back, wanting to reach out and touch, comfort. Like him, she'd had only one friend. But hers had turned out loyal. She could imagine how deep her own hurt would have gone had Glendon betrayed her.

"I'm sorry, Will."

He threw his head aside as if to look back at her, but didn't. Instead his gaze dropped to his loosely linked wrists. "Aw, what the hell. It was a long time ago."

"But it still hurts, I can tell."

He flopped back, ran both hands through his hair and clasped them behind his head.

"How'd we get on a subject like that anyway. Let's talk about something else."

The mood had grown somber, and as they lay side by side Eleanor could think of little except Will's sad, friendless youth. She had always thought herself the loneliest soul on earth, but . . . poor Will. Poor, poor Will. Now he had her at least, and the boys. But how long would it last if the war came?

"Is the war really like that, Will . . . like they showed in the movies?"

"I guess so."

"You think we're gonna be in it, don't you?"

"I don't know. But if not, why is the President drafting men for the military?"

"If we were, would you have to go?"

"If I got drafted, yes."

Her mouth formed an oh, but the word never made it past her lips. The possibility pressed upon her, bringing with it a startling dread. Startling because she hadn't guessed she'd feel so possessive about this man once he was her husband. The fact that he was made a tremendous difference. The black and white pictures from the newsreel flashed through her memory, followed by the colored ones of the War between the States. What an awful thing, war. She supposed, in the days when Grandpa had been alive, they would have prayed that America stay out of it. Instead, she closed her eyes and forced the grim pictures aside to make way for those of the beautiful ladies in their enormous silk skirts, and the men in their top hats, and Hopalong waving his white hat . . . and Donald Wade in Will's black one . . . and eventually when she rode the thin line between sleep and wakefulness, Will himself riding Topper, waving his hat at her from the end of the driveway . . .

Minutes later, Will turned to say, Let's not worry about it until the time comes. But he found she had fallen asleep, flat on her back, lips parted, hands crossed demurely beneath her breasts. He watched her breathe, a strand of hair on her shoulder catching the light with each beat. His gaze drifted down to her stomach, back up to her breasts, soft and unsculptured beneath her nightgown. He thought about how good it would feel to roll her onto her side, curl up behind her with his arms where hers were now and fall asleep with his face against her back. But what would she think if she awakened and found him that way? He would have to be on guard, even asleep.

His eyes wandered once more to her stomach.

It moved!

The quilts shifted as if a sleeping cat had changed positions underneath. But she slept soundly, as still as a mummy. The baby? Babies moved . . . *that much?* Cautiously, he braced up on one elbow until he sat over her, studying the movements at close range. Boy or girl? It shifted again and he smiled. Whatever it was, it was rambunctious; he couldn't believe all that commotion didn't wake her up. He resisted the urge to turn the quilts back for a better look, the even greater one to rest a hand on her and feel what he was watching. Either—of course—was out of the question.

He lay back down to worry that he'd agreed to deliver that baby. God, what had he been thinking? He'd kill it for sure with his big, clumsy hands.

Don't think about it, Will.

He closed his eyes and concentrated instead on the goodnight kisses of Donald Wade and Baby Thomas. He recalled their childish voices wishing him goodnight, especially Thomas—" 'Night, Wiw . . ." He tried to wipe his mind clean of all thought so sleep would come. But the light shone through his eyelids, urging them open once again.

Eleanor flipped onto her side, facing him. He studied her eyelashes lying like fans against her cheeks, the palm of her left hand resting near his chin with the friendship ring peeking through her relaxed fingers. He let his eyes roam over the button placket of her nightgown, the quilt that had slipped down to her waist, the white cloth covering her breasts. He reached out carefully—very carefully—and took the fabric of her sleeve in his fingers, rubbing it as a greedy man rubs two coins together. Then he withdrew his hand, flipped over in the opposite direction and tried to forget the light was on.

Chapter 11

In the morning Eleanor opened her eyes to the back of Will Parker's head. His hair was flattened into a pinwheel, giving a clear view of his white skull underneath. She smiled. The intimacies of marriage. She watched each breath lift his shoulder blades, studied his back with its distinctive triangle of moles, the hindside of one ear, the pattern of the hairline at his nape, the ridges of his vertebrae disappearing beneath the covers just above his waist. His skin was so much darker than Glendon's, so much barer; Glendon always slept in an undershirt. Will's skin looked seasoned, whereas Glendon's had been doughy.

The object of her study snuffled and rolled onto his back. His eyeballs moved behind closed lids, but he slept on, his face exposed to the sun. It turned him all gold and brown and put glints of color in his pale hair like those in a finch's wing. His beard grew fast, much faster than Glendon's, and there was more hair on his arms and chest. Studying it gave her an unexpected jolt of reaction, down low.

She slammed her eyes closed only to realize that he smelled different from Glendon. No smell she could name, only the distinctive one given him by Nature—warm male hide and hair and breath—as different from Glendon's as that of an apple from an orange. Her eyes opened stealthily, halfway, as if such caution would prevent him from waking. Through nearly closed eyelids she admired him, letting the sunlight shatter on her lash tips and diffuse over his image as if he were sprinkled with sequins. A handsome, well-built man. The whores in La Grange probably fought over him.

Again the queer radiant disturbance intensified low in her belly as she lay with her knees only inches from his hip, his unfamiliar man-smell permeating her bedclothes, his warmth and bulk taking up half the sleeping space. It was a shock to find herself susceptible to fleshly thoughts when she'd thought pregnancy made her immune.

Another disturbing consideration struck. Suppose he had studied her as intimately as she now studied him. She tried to recall falling asleep but couldn't. They'd been talking—that was the last she remembered. Had she been lying on her back? Facing him? She glanced at the table; the lantern still hissed. He had left it on, could have lain awake for hours after she'd dropped off, taking an upclose tally of her shortcomings. Studying his becoming face, she became all too aware of how she suffered by comparison. Her hair was dirt brown, plain, her eyelashes thin and stubby, her fingers wide-knuckled, her stomach popping, her breasts mammoth. Sometimes she snored. Had she snored last night while he watched and listened?

She rolled toward her edge of the bed, thinking, just forget he's back there and go about dressing as if it were any other day.

At her first movement Will came awake as if she'd set off a firecracker. He glanced at her back, the alarm clock, then sat up and reached for his pants, all in one motion.

They dressed facing opposite walls, and only when the final buttons were closed did they peer over their shoulders at each other.

"Mornin'," she offered self-consciously.

"Mornin'."

"Sleep okay?"

"Fine. Did I crowd you?"

"Not that I remember. Did I crowd you?"

"No."

"You always wake up that quick?"

"It's nearly eight. Herbert's gonna bust." He sat down on the edge of the bed and yanked his boots on. A moment later he was stalking out the door, stuffing in his shirttails.

When he was gone, she dropped onto the bed and sighed with relief. They'd done it! Gone to bed, slept together, gotten up and dressed without once making physical contact, and without him seeing her ugly, bloated body.

She sat moments longer staring despondently at the mopboard.

Well, that's what you wanted, wasn't it?

Yes!

Then why are you sitting here moping?

I'm not moping!

Oh?

Well, I'm not!

But you're thinking about when the judge ordered him to kiss you.

Well, what's wrong with that?

Nothing. Nothing at all.

Leave me alone.

Silence. For minutes and minutes only obedient silence hummed inside her head.

If you wanted him to kiss you goodnight, you should've just leaned over and done it yourself.

I didn't *want* him to kiss me goodnight.

Oh, sorry. I thought that's why you were moping.

I wasn't moping.

But she was, and she knew it.

At midmorning that day, with breakfast eaten and his routine chores done, Will returned to the house to find the veiled hat, hive tool and smoker on the back-porch steps. He grinned. So . . . no more egg grenades. Going inside to thank her, he almost regretted the loss.

The house was empty, on the table, a note: *Gone to pick pecans with the boys.* He took the stub of a pencil, scrawled across the bottom, "Thanks for the wedding gift!" and hit for the mint patch.

Their first twenty-four hours as husband and wife seemed to set the tone for the days that followed. They lived together amicably if not intimately, helping one another in small ways, adapting, sharing a mutual enjoyment of the children and their uncomplicated family life. From the first they accommodated each other—as with the beekeeping gear—so there were no more bursts of anger. Life was peaceful.

Though the sudden appearance of the hive tool, hat and smoker was never mentioned between them, it signaled the true beginning of Will's work with the bees. He sensed that Eleanor would rather not know when he was out in the orchard, so he kept the equipment in an outbuilding when it was not in use, and retrieved it without telling her. Only when he returned to the house with the honeycomb frames did she know he'd been among the bees.

He learned to respect them. There was a calm about the orchard that seeped into him each time he passed there, a serenity not only among the insects, but within himself for the necessity of having to move slowly while among them. But as slowly as he moved, it was inevitable that he should eventually get stung. The first time it happened he jumped, swatted and yowled, "Ouch!" For his efforts he received three additional stings. He learned, in time, not to jump and most certainly not to swat, forcing the stinger farther into his skin. But more importantly, he learned to recognize the variations in the sounds of the bees—from the squeaky piping of the contented workers as they moved about their business on humming gauze wings to the altogether different "quacking" occasionally set up by a single provoked bee, warning him to anticipate the sting and be ready to fend it off. He came to recognize the feel of bee feet digging into his body hair for a good grip, and to pluck the insect away gently before the grip became a sting. He learned that bees are soothed by the sound of human whistling, that their least favorite color is red and their most favorite, blue.

So it was a happy man who walked among the peach trees, whistling, dressed all in blue, a veiled hat protecting his face. He could never get used to the clumsiness of gloves, so worked barehanded, scraping at the hard, varnishlike propolis with which the bees sealed every minute crack between the supers. Inside the smoker, which was little more than a spouted tin can with an attached bellows, he lit a smudge of oiled burlap. Several puffs into the open hive subdued the bees, enabling him to remove the comb cases without danger. These he transported back to the house, where he carefully scraped the wax caps off the comb with a knife heated above a kerosene lantern. The first time Eleanor saw him doing so she opened the porch door and stepped outside, shrugging into a sweater, carrying a knife. "You'll need a little help with that," she said flatly, without casting him a glance. But she sat down on the opposite side of the lantern and showed him that it wasn't the first time she'd scraped wax. Nor was it the first time she'd extracted, nor rendered, when it came time to do those jobs.

The extracting—pulling the honey from the combs—was done in a fifty-gallon drum equipped with a crank that spun the combs and forced the honey out by centrifugal force. From a spigot at the bottom the honey was drained—littered with fragments of comb and wax—then heated and strained before the wax was allowed to separate to the top and be skimmed off. The two products were then packed separately for sale.

There was much Will didn't know, particularly about the rendering process, knowledge that could be learned only by experience. Eleanor taught him—albeit grudgingly most of the time, but she taught him just the same.

"How do we clean up this mess?" Will inquired of the sticky drum with its honey-coated paddles and spigot.

"We don't. The bees do," she replied.

"The bees?"

"Bees eat honey. Just leave it outside in the sun and they'll find it."

Sure enough, any honey-coated tool left outside soon became cleaner than if it had been steamed.

Will knew perfectly well she saw the occasional welts on his skin, but she made no comments about them and soon his body built up a natural immunity until the bee stings scarcely reacted. When he came in with a load of comb, she tacitly went into the cellar for fruit jars, washed and scalded them, then lent a hand processing and bottling the honey.

Those honey days were a time of acquaintance for Will and Eleanor. As with their first night in bed when they'd lain so still, growing accustomed to lying side by side, working with the honey lent them proximity and time to adjust to the fact that they were bound for life. Sometimes, while scraping wax or holding a funnel, Will would look up and find himself being studied. The same was true for Eleanor. There would follow quick mutual smiles and a sense of growing acceptance, each for the other.

At night in bed, they talked. He, of the bees. She of the birds. Never of the birds and bees.

"Did you know a male worker bee has thirteen thousand eyes?"

"Did you know the flycatcher makes his nest out of discarded snakeskin?"

"There are nurses in a bee colony and all they do is take care of the nymphs."

"Most birds sing, but the titmouse is the only one who can actually whisper."

"Did you know the bees' favorite color is blue?"

"And the hummingbird is the only bird that can fly backwards?"

These discussions sometimes led to insights into each other. One night Will spoke of the worker bees. "Did you know they work so hard during their lifetime that they actually work themselves to death?"

"No . . ." she replied disbelievingly.

"It's true. They wear down their wings till they're so frayed they can't fly anymore. Then they just die." His expression turned troubled. "That's sad, isn't it?"

Eleanor studied her husband in a new light and found she liked what she saw. He lay in the dim lanternlight, contemplating the ceiling, saddened by the plight of the worker bees. How could a woman remain aloof to a man who cared about such things? Moved, she reached out to console, grazing the underside of his upraised arm.

His glance shot down to her and their gazes caught for several interminable seconds, then her fingers withdrew.

On a night shortly thereafter Will came up with another amazing apian phenomenon. "Did you know the workers practice something called flower fidelity? It means each bee gathers nectar and pollen from only one species of flower."

"Oh, you're making that up!" Her head twisted to face his profile.

"I am not. I read about it in one of the books Miss Beasley gave me. Flower fidelity."

"Really?"

"Really."

He lay as he did every night during their talks—on his back with his hands behind his head. Silent, she regarded him, digesting this new snippet of information. At length she squared her head on the pillow and fixed her attention on the pale glow overhead. "I guess that's not so unusual. Some birds practice fidelity, too. To each other. The eagles, the Canadian geese—they mate for life."

"Interesting."

"Mm-hmm."

"I've never seen an eagle," Will mused.

"Eagles are . . ." Eleanor gestured ceilingward—"Majestic."—then let her hands settle to her stomach again. A smile tipped her lips. "When I was a girl I used to see a golden eagle in a huge dead tree down in the swamp near Cotton Creek. If I were a bird, I'd want to be an eagle."

"Why?" Will turned to study her.

"Because of something I read once."

"What?"

"Oh ... nothing." She twined her fingers and looked down her chest at them.

"Tell me." He sensed her reluctance but kept his gaze steady, unrelenting. After some time she sent Will a quick peek.

"Promise you won't laugh?"

"I promise."

For several seconds she concentrated on aligning her thumbnails precisely, then finally quoted shyly.

> *"He clasps the crag with crooked hands;*
> *Close to the sun in lonely lands,*
> *Ring'd with the azure world, he stands.*
>
> *The wrinkled sea beneath him crawls;*
> *He watches from his mountain walls,*
> *And like a thunderbolt he falls."*

She paused before adding, "Somebody named Tennyson wrote that."

In that moment Will saw a new facet of his wife. Fragile. Impressionable. Touched by poets' words, articulate combinations of words such as she herself never used.

"It's beautiful," he said softly.

Her thumbnails clicked together as she vacillated between the wish to hide her feelings and reveal more. The latter won as she swallowed and added softly, "Nobody laughs at eagles."

Oh, Elly, Elly, who hurt you so bad? And what would it take to make you forget it? Will rolled to face her and braced his jaw on a fist. But she wouldn't turn, and her cheeks burned brightly.

"Did somebody laugh at you?" His voice was deep with caring. A tear plumped in the corner of her eye. Understanding her chagrin at its arrival, Will pretended not to notice. He waited motionlessly for her answer, studying the ridge of her nose, the outline of her compressed lips. When she spoke it was an evasion.

"For a long time I didn't know what azure meant."

He watched as her throat contracted and the florid spots in her cheeks stood out like pennies on an open palm. His hand burned to touch her—her chin maybe, turn it to face him so she would see that he cared and would never ridicule her. He wanted to take her close, cradle her head and rub her shoulder and say, "Tell me ... tell me what it is that hurts so bad, then we'll work at getting you over it." But every time he considered touching her his insecurities reared up to confront and confine him. Woman killer, jailbird, she'll jump and yelp if you touch her. On the first day you were warned to keep your distance.

So he stayed on his own side of the bed with one wrist riveted to his hip, the other folded beneath an ear. But what he couldn't relay by touch he put into his expressive voice.

"Elly?" It came out softly, the abbreviated name falling from his lips as an endearment. Their gazes collided, her green eyes still luminous with unshed tears, his brown ones filled with understanding. "Nobody's laughing now."

Suddenly everything in her yearned toward him.

Touch me, she thought, *like nobody ever did before, like I touch the boys when they feel bad. Make it not important that I'm plain and unpretty and more preg-*

nant than I wish I was right now. You're the man, Will—don't you see? A man's got to reach first.

But he couldn't. Not first.

Touch me, he thought, *my arm, my hand, a finger. Let me know it's all right for me to have these feelings for you. Nobody's cared enough to touch me for years and years. But you've got to reach first, don't you see? Because of how you felt about him, and what I am, what I did, what we agreed to the first day I came here.*

In the end, neither of them moved. She lay with her hands atop her swollen stomach, her heart hammering frantically, afraid of rejection, ridicule, the things she had been seasoned by life to expect.

He lay feeling unlovable due to his spotty past and the fact that no woman including his own mother had found him worth the effort, so why should Elly?

And so they talked and gazed during those lanternlit nights of acquaintance— crazy Eleanor and her ex-con husband—learning respect for each other, wondering when and if that first seeking might happen, each hesitant to reach out for what they both needed.

The honey was all bottled. The hives received fresh coats of white paint, their bases—as suggested in print—a variety of colors to guide the workers back from their forays. When Will left the orchard for the last time, the hives held enough honey to feed the bees through the winter.

He packed away the extractor in an outbuilding until the spring honey run began and announced that night at supper, "I'll be going to town tomorrow to sell the honey. If there's anything you need, make a list."

She asked for only two things: white flannel to make diapers and a roll of cotton batting.

The following day when Will stepped through the library doors, Gladys Beasley was immersed in lecturing a cluster of schoolchildren on the why and wherefore of the card catalogue. With her back to Will, she looked like a dirigible on legs. Packed into a bile-green jersey dress, wearing club-heeled shoes and the same cap of precise blue ringlets against a skull of baby pink, she gestured with her head and spoke in her inimitable pedantic voice.

"The Dewey Decimal System was named after an American librarian named Melvil Dewey over seventy years ago. James," she digressed, "quit picking your nose. If it needs attention, please ask to be dismissed to the lavatory. And in the future please see to it that you bring your handkerchief with you to school. Under the Dewey Decimal System books are divided into ten groups . . ." The lecture continued as if the remonstration had not interrupted.

Meanwhile, Will stood with an elbow braced on the checkout desk, waiting, enjoying. A little girl pirouetted on her heels—left, right—gazing at the overhead lights as if they were comets. A red-headed boy scratched his private rear quarters. Another girl balanced on one foot, holding the opposite ankle as high against her buttock as she could force it. Since coming to live with Elly and the boys Will had grown to appreciate children for their naturalness.

". . . any subject at all. If you'll follow me, children, we'll begin with the one hundreds." As Miss Beasley turned to herd stragglers, she caught sight of Will lounging against the desk. Involuntarily her face brightened and she touched her heart. Realizing what she'd done, she dropped and clasped her hand and recovered her customary prim expression. But it was too late—she was already blushing.

Will straightened and tipped his hat, pleasantly shocked by her telling reaction, warmed more than he'd have thought possible by the idea of such an unlikely woman getting flustered over him. He'd been doing everything in his power to get his wife to react that way but he'd certainly never expected it here.

"Excuse me, children." Miss Beasley touched two heads in passing. "You may explore through the one hundreds and the two hundreds." As she approached Will the tinge of pink on her cheeks became unmistakable and he grew more amazed.

"Mornin', Miss Beasley."

"Good morning, Mr. Parker."

"Busy today," he observed, glancing at the children.

"Yes. Mrs. Gardner's second grade."

"Brought you something." He held out a pint jar of honey.

"Why, Mr. Parker!" she exclaimed, touching her chest again.

"From our own hives, rendered this week."

She accepted the jar, lifting it to the light. "My, how clear and pale."

"Lots of sourwood out our way. Sourwood honey's light like that. Takes on a little color from the tupelo, though."

She drew in her chin and gave him a pleased pout. "You *did* do your homework, didn't you?"

He crossed his arms and planted his feet firmly apart, smiling down at her from the shadow of his hat brim. "I wanted to thank you for the pamphlets and books. I couldn't've done it without them."

She held the jar in both hands and blinked up at him. "Thank *you,* Mr. Parker. And please thank Mrs. Dinsmore for me, too."

"Ah . . ." Will rubbed the underside of his nose. "She's not Mrs. Dinsmore anymore, ma'am. She's Mrs. Parker now."

"Oh." Surprise and deflation colored the single word.

"We got married up at Calhoun the end of October."

"Oh." Miss Beasley quickly collected herself. "Then congratulations are in order, aren't they?"

"Well, thank you, Miss Beasley." He shifted his feet uneasily. "Ma'am, I don't want to keep you from the kids, but I got honey to sell and not much time. I mean, there's a lot to do out at the place before—" Again he shifted uneasily. "Well, you see, I'm wantin' to put in an electric generator and a bathroom for Eleanor. I was wondering if you'd see what you got for books on electricity and plumbing. If you could pick 'em out, I'll stop back for 'em in an hour or so when I get rid of the honey."

"Electricity and plumbing. Certainly."

"Much obliged." He smiled, doffed his hat and moved toward the door. But he swung back with designed offhandedness. "Oh, and while you're at it, if you could find any books about birthing, you could add them to the stack."

"Birthing?"

"Yes, ma'am."

"Birthing what?"

Will felt himself color and shrugged, feigning nonchalance. "Oh . . . ah . . . horses, cows . . ." He gestured vaguely. "You know." His glance wandered nervously before flicking back to her. "Humans, too, if you run across anything. Never read anything about that. Might be interesting."

He felt transparent beneath her acute scrutiny. But she set the jar in the place of honor beside her nameplate and advised in her usual caustic voice, "Your books will be ready in one hour, Mr. Parker. And thank you again for the honey."

Calvin Purdy bought half the honey and, after some dickering, took four more jars in exchange for ten yards of white flannel and a bat of cotton. At the filling station Will bartered two more pints of honey for a tankful of gasoline—it had been on his mind to keep the tank full from now until the baby came, just in case. While the gas was being pumped he lowered his brows and ruminated on Vickery's Cafe, down at the corner. Biscuits and gravy in the morning; biscuits and *honey* in the evening, he'd guess. But to make a sale he'd probably have to face Lula Peak again, and there was no telling where she might decide to run her scarlet claw this time. He scratched his chest and glanced away in distaste. The honey wouldn't spoil.

With a full tank of gas, he motored around the square to the library again. Mrs. Gardner's second grade was gone, leaving silence and an empty library.

"Hello?" he called.

Miss Beasley came out of the back room, dabbing her mouth with a flowered handkerchief.

"Am I interrupting your lunch?"

"Actually, yes. You've caught me sampling your honey on my muffin. Delicious. Absolutely delicious."

He smiled and nodded. "The bees did most of the work." She chuckled tightly, as if laughter were illegal. But he could see how pleased she was over his gift. On the surface she wasn't a very likable woman—militant, uncompromising—probably hadn't many friends. Perhaps that was why he was drawn to her, because he'd never had many either. Her lips were surrounded by more than their fair share of baby-fine, colorless hair. A tiny droplet of honey clung to one on her top lip. Had he liked her less, he might have let it go unmentioned. As it was, he pointed briefly—"You missed something"—then hooked his thumb on his back pocket.

"Oh! ... Oh, thank you." Fussily she mopped her mouth but managed to miss what she was after.

"Here." He reached. "May I?" Taking her hand, hanky and all, he guided it to the proper spot.

It was one of the most decidedly personal touches Miss Beasley had ever experienced. Men were put off by her, always had been, especially in college, where she'd proved herself vastly more intelligent than any who might have taken an interest. The men in Whitney were either married or too stupid to suit her. Though she had accepted her spinsterhood long ago, it startled Gladys to find a man who—given other circumstances, other times—might have suited nicely in both temperament and intellect. When Will Parker touched her, Gladys Beasley forgot she was shaped like a herring barrel and old enough to be his grandmother. Her old maid's heart flopped like a fresh-caught bream.

The touch was brief and not untoward. Quickly, almost shyly, he backed off and let his thumb find his rear pocket again. When Gladys lowered the handkerchief she was decidedly rattled, but he graciously pretended not to notice.

"So. Did you find anything for me?" he inquired.

She produced a stack of five books, some with slips of paper marking selected spots. Curious, he tried to read the titles upside down as she stamped each card. But she was very efficient with her *Open, stamp, slap! Open, stamp, slap!* He hadn't made out one title before she pushed the pile his way with his card placed neatly on top.

"Much obliged, Miss Beasley."

"That's my job, Mr. Parker."

His smile spread slowly, formed only halfway before he touched his hat brim and slipped the books to his hip. "Much obliged anyway. See you next week."

Next week, she thought, and her heart raced. Fussily she tamped the tops of the recessed cards to cover her uncharacteristic flutteriness.

She had chosen for him *The Plumber's Handbook, The ABC's of Electricity, Edison's Invention, Animal Husbandry for the Common Farmer,* and another entitled *New Era Domestic Science.*

That night after supper while Eleanor shelled pecans at the kitchen table, Will sat at a right angle to her, turning pages. He spent an informative half hour spot-reading in three of the books, then picked up the fourth—*New Era Domestic Science.* It covered a range of subjects, some vital, others—to Will—silly. He smiled in amusement at such subjects as "How to Choose a House Boy," "How to Clean a Flatiron by Rubbing on Salt." There was a recipe for "Meat Jelly," another for fried tomatoes, then dozens of others; a discourse on insomnia, entitled, "The Science of Sleep"; a tip about cleansing the interior of your teakettle by boiling an oyster shell in it. His finger stopped shuffling when he arrived at "A Chapter for Young Women." His eyes scanned ahead, then retreated to an essay on "Choosing a Husband." As he began reading, he slumped lower and lower in his chair until his spine was bowed, the book rested against the edge of the table and an index finger covered his grin.

You now need the advice of your parents more than ever before, the essay advised, *for the young man will be attracted by you and you will be attracted by him. This is natural. If you make a mistake it may wreck your whole life. Take your mother into your confidence. There are some rules that are safe to follow in this matter. Never have anything to do with a young man who is "sowing his wild oats," or who has sown them.*

Will absently rubbed his lip and peeked at Eleanor, but she was busy with the nutcracker.

Never marry a man to reform him. Leave those who need reforming severely alone. There are men who do not drink and yet who are more dangerous to you than drunkards. A man who sows his wild oats or is morally lax may be afflicted with diseases that can be given to an innocent and pure wife and thus entail upon her life-long suffering. Marriage is a lottery. You may draw a prize, or your life may be made miserable. Tell your parents if you are attracted toward a young man so that they may find out if he is a man of good character and pure in heart and life. It is so much better to remain single than to make an unfortunate marriage.

He wondered how many ignorant virgins had read this stuff and ended up more confused than ever about the facts of life.

His speculative gaze wandered to Elly. She dropped a pecan into the bowl and his eyes followed. Her stomach had grown so full it barely left room for the bowl on her knees. Her breasts seemed to have doubled in size in the last three months. Had she been a virgin when she married Glendon Dinsmore? Had Glendon "sowed wild oats" like Will Parker had? Had Elly consulted her parents and had they checked out Dinsmore's character and found him pure in heart and life—unlike her second husband?

She picked another pecan clean and raised the last morsel to her mouth. Will's eyes again followed and he absently stroked his lips. One thing about Elly—she sure hadn't married to reform him. If he had reformed it was because of her acceptance, rather than the lack of it.

He turned a page to a section in which Miss Beasley had left a marker. "How to Conceive and Bear Healthy Children." All right, he thought, secretly amused, tell me how.

The one main reason for the establishment of marriage was for the bearing and rearing of children. Nature has provided for man and woman the organs for this purpose and they are wonderfully constructed.

End of enlightenment. Will swallowed another chortle and his finger continued hiding the grin. He couldn't help picturing Miss Beasley reading this, wondering what her reaction had been.

From his delight over the construction of human organs the author had skipped directly to a passel of ludicrous advice on conception: *If the parents are drunk at the time the child is conceived they cannot expect healthy offspring, either physically or mentally. If the parents dislike each other they will transmit something of that disposition to their offspring. If either one or both of the parents are much worried at the time of conception the child will be the sufferer.*

Without warning Will burst out laughing.

Eleanor looked up. "What's so funny?"

"Listen to this . . ." He straightened in his chair, laid the book flat on the table and read the last passage aloud.

Eleanor gazed at him unblinkingly, her hands poised around a pecan in the jaws of the nutcracker. "I thought you were reading about electricity."

He sobered instantly. "Oh, I am. I mean, I . . . I was."

She reached across the table and, with the nose of the nutcracker, tipped the book up.

"New Era Domestic Science?"

"Well, I . . . it . . ." He felt his cheeks warming and randomly flipped the pages. They fell open to a diagram of a homemade telephone. "I was thinking about making one of these." He turned the book and showed her.

She glanced at the diagram, then skeptically at him before the pecan shell cracked and fell into her palm. "And just who did you think we'd call on it?"

"Oh, I don't know. You never can tell."

He hid his discomposure by delving into the book again.

After you become pregnant you owe it to yourself, your husband and especially your unborn young one to see that it comes into the world endowed with everything that a true, good, and devoted mother can possibly give it, both physically and mentally. To this end, keep yourself well and happy. Eat only such foods as are easily digested and that will keep your bowels regular. Read only such books as will tend to make you happier and better. Choose the company of those whom you feel will lift you up. Gossips will not do this so do not listen to croakers who are so ready to converse with you at this time.

Such capricious advice went on and on, but Will's amusement died when he found what he'd been looking for: "Preparations for Labor." It began with a list of recommended articles to have on hand:

> 5 basins
> 1 two-quart fountain syringe
> 15 yards unsterilized gauze
> 6 sanitary bed pads; or,
> 2 pounds cotton batting for making same
> 1 piece rubber sheeting, size 1 by 2 yards
> 4 ounces permanganate of potash
> 8 ounces oxalic acid
> 4 ounces boric acid
> 1 tube green soap
> 1 tube Vaseline

100 Bernay's bichloride tablets
8 ounces alcohol
2 drams ergotol
1 nail brush
2 pounds absorbent cotton

My God, they'd need all that? Will began to panic.

The opening instructions read, *The nurse should prepare enough bed and perineal pads, sterilizing them a week before, along with towels, diapers, ½ pound absorbent cotton and some cotton pledgets.*

Nurse? Who had a nurse? And enough? What was enough? And what did perineal mean? And what were pledgets? He couldn't even understand this, much less afford it! Pale now, he turned the page only to have his disillusionment doubled. Phrases jumped out and grabbed him by the nerve-endings.

Cramp-like pains in the lower abdomen . . . rupturing membranes . . . watery discharge . . . a marked desire to go to stool . . . bulging of the pelvic floor . . . tearing of the perineal flesh . . . temple bones engaged in the vulva . . . proper manipulation to expel the afterbirth . . . stout clean thread . . . sever immediately . . . exception being when child is nearly dead or does not breathe properly . . .

He slammed the book shut and leaped to his feet, pale as seafoam.

"Will?"

He stared out a window, knees locked, cracking his knuckles, feeling his pulse thud hard in his gut.

"I can't do it."

"Do what?"

Fear lodged in his throat like a hunk of dry bread. He gulped, but it stayed. "I wasn't reading about electricity. I was reading about delivering babies."

"Oh . . . that."

"Yes, that." He swung to face her. "Elly, we've never talked about it since the night we agreed to get married. But I know you expect me to help you, and I just plain don't know if I can."

She rested her hands in the bowl and looked up at him expressionlessly. "Then I'll do it alone, Will. I'm pretty sure I can."

"Alone!" he barked, lurching for the book, agitatedly flapping pages until he found the right one. "Listen to this—'The cord is usually tied before being cut, the exception being when the child is nearly dead and does not breathe properly. In such a case it is best to leave the cord untied so that it may bleed a little and aid in establishing respiration.' " He dropped the book and scowled at her. "Suppose the baby died. How do you think I'd feel? And how am I supposed to know what's proper breathing and what isn't? And there's more—all this stuff we're supposed to have on hand. Why, hell, some of it I don't even know what it is! And it talks about you tearing, and maybe hemorrhaging. Elly, *please* let me get a doctor when the time comes. I got the car filled with gas so I can run into town quick and get him."

Calmly she set the bowl aside, rose and closed the book. "*I* know what we'll need, Will." Unflinchingly she met his worried brown eyes. "And I'll have it all ready. You shouldn't be reading that stuff, 'cause it just scares you, is all."

"But it says—"

"I know what it says. But having a baby is a natural act. Why, the Indian women squatted in the woods and did it all alone, then walked back into the fields and started hoeing corn as soon as it was over."

"You're no Indian," he argued intensely.

"But I'm strong. And healthy. And if it comes down to it, happy, too. Seems to me that's as important as anything else, isn't it? Happy people got something to fight for."

Her calm reasoning punctured his anger with surprising suddenness. When it had disappeared, one fact had impressed him: she'd said she was happy. They stood near, so near he could have touched her by merely lifting a hand, could have curled his fingers around her neck, rested his palms on her cheeks and asked, Are you, Elly? Are you really? For he wanted to hear it again, the evidence that for the first time in his life, he seemed to be doing something right.

But she dropped her chin and turned to retrieve the bowl of nuts and carry them to the cupboard. "Not everyone can stand the sight of blood, and I'll grant you there's blood when a baby comes."

"It's not that. I told you, it's the risks."

She turned to face him and said realistically, "We got no money for a doctor, Will."

"We could get up enough. I could take another load of scrap metal in. And there's the cream money, and the eggs, and now the honey. Even pecans. Purdy'll buy the pecans. I know he will."

She began shaking her head before he finished. "You just rest easy. Let me do the worrying about the baby. It'll turn out fine."

But how could he not worry?

In the days that followed he watched her moving about the place with increasing slowness. Her burden began to ride lower, her ankles swelled, her breasts widened. And each day brought him closer to the day of delivery.

November tenth brought a temporary distraction from his worries. It was Eleanor's birthday—Will hadn't forgotten. He awakened to find her still asleep, facing him. He rolled onto his stomach and curled the pillow beneath his neck to indulge himself in a close study of her. Pale brows and gold-tipped lashes, parted lips and pleasing nose. One ear peeking through a coil of loose hair and one knee updrawn beneath the covers. He watched her breathe, watched her hand twitch once, twice. She came awake by degrees, unconsciously smacking her lips, rubbing her nose and finally opening sleepy eyes.

"Mornin', lazybones," he teased.

"Mmm . . ." She closed her eyes and nestled, half on her belly. "Mornin'."

"Happy birthday."

Her eyes opened but she lay unmoving, absorbing the words while a lazy smile dawned across her face.

"You remembered."

"Absolutely. Twenty-five."

"Twenty-five. A quarter of a century."

"Makes you sound older than you look."

"Oh, Will, the things you say."

"I was watching you wake up. Looked pretty good to me."

She covered her face with the sheet and he smiled against his pillow.

"You got time to bake a cake today?"

She lowered the sheet to her nose. "I guess, but why?"

"Then bake one. I'd do it, but I don't know how."

"Why?"

Instead of answering, he threw back the covers and sprang up. Standing beside the bed with his elbows lifted, he executed a mighty, twisting stretch. She watched with unconcealed interest—the flexing muscles, the taut skin, the moles, the long legs dusted with black hair. Legs planted wide, he shivered and bent acutely to the left, the right, then snapped over to pick up his clothes and begin dressing. It was engrossing, watching a man donning his clothes. Men did it so much less fussily than women.

"You gonna answer me?" she insisted.

Facing away from her, he smiled. "For your birthday party."

"My birthday party!" She sat up. "Hey, come back here!"

But he was gone, buttoning his shirt, grinning.

It was a toss-up who had to work harder to conceal his impatience that day— Will, who'd had the plan in his head for weeks, Eleanor, whose eyes shone all the while she baked her own cake but who refused to ask when this party was supposed to happen, or Donald Wade, who asked at least a dozen times that morning, "How long now, Will?"

Will had planned to wait until after supper, but the cake was ready at noon, and by late afternoon Donald Wade's patience had been stretched to the limit. When Will went to the house for a cup of coffee, Donald Wade tapped his knee and whispered for the hundredth time, "Now, Will . . . pleeeease?"

Will relented. "All right, *kemo sabe*. You and Thomas go get the stuff."

The stuff turned out to be two objects crudely wrapped in wrinkled white butcher's paper, drawn together with twine. The boys each carried one, brought them proudly and deposited them beside Eleanor's coffee cup.

"Presents?" She crossed her hands on her chest. "For me?"

Donald Wade nodded hard enough to loosen the wax in his ears.

"Me 'n' Will and Thomas made 'em."

"You *made* them!"

"One of 'em," Will corrected, pulling Thomas onto his lap while Donald Wade pressed against his mother's chair.

"This one." Donald Wade pushed the weightier package into her hands. "Open it first." His eyes fixed on her hands while she fumbled with the twine, pretending difficulty in getting it untied. "This dang ole thing is givin' me fits!" she exclaimed. "Lord, Donald Wade, help me." Donald Wade reached eagerly and helped her yank the bow and push the paper down, revealing a ball of suet, meshed by twine and rolled in wheat.

"It's for your birds!" he announced excitedly.

"For my birds. Oh, myyy . . ." Eyes shining, she held it aloft by a loop of twine. "Won't they love it?"

"You can hang it up and everything!"

"I see that."

"Will, he got the stuff and we put the fat through the grinder and I helped him turn the crank and me 'n' Thomas stuck the seeds on. See?"

"I see. Why, I s'pect it's the prettiest suet ball I ever seen. Oh, thank you so much, darlin' . . ." She gave Donald Wade a tight hug, then leaned over to hold the baby's chin and smack him soundly on the lips. "You too, Thomas. I didn't know you were so clever."

"Open the other one," Donald Wade demanded, stuffing it into her hands.

"Two presents—my goodness gracious."

"This one's from Will."

"From Will . . ." Her delighted eyes met her husband's while her fingers sought the ties on the scroll-shaped package. Though his insides were jumping with impatience, Will forced himself to sit easy in the kitchen chair, an arm propped on the table edge with a finger hooked in a coffee cup.

Opening the gift, Eleanor gazed at him. With an ankle braced on a knee his leg formed a triangle. Thomas was draped through it. It suddenly occurred to Eleanor that she wouldn't trade Will for ten Hopalong Cassidys. "He's somethin', isn't he? Always givin' me presents."

"Hurry, Mama!"

"Oh . . . o' course." She turned her attention to opening the gift. Inside was a three-piece doily set—an oval and two crescents—of fine linen, all hemstitched and border stamped, ready for crochet hook and embroidery needle.

Eleanor's heart swelled and words failed her. "Oh, Will . . ." She hid her trembling lips behind the fine, crisp linen. Her eyes stung.

"The sign called it a Madiera dresser set. I knew you liked to crochet."

"Oh, Will . . ." Gazing at him, her eyes shimmered. "You do the nicest things." She stretched a hand across the table, palm-up.

Placing his hand in hers, Will felt his pulse leap.

"Thank you, dear."

He had never thought of himself as dear. The word sent a shaft of elation from his heart clear down to the seat of his chair. Their fingers tightened and for a moment they forgot about gifts and cakes and pregnancies and pasts and the two little boys who looked on impatiently.

"We got to have the cake now, Mama," Donald Wade interrupted, and the moment of closeness receded. But everything was intensified after that, tingly, electric. As Eleanor moved about the kitchen, whipping cream, slicing chocolate cake, serving it, she felt Will's eyes moving with her, following, questing. And she found herself hesitant to look at him.

Back at the table, she handed him his plate and he took it without touching so much as her fingertip. She sensed his distance as a cautious thing, an almost unwillingness to believe. And she understood, for in her craziest moments she'd never have believed anything as crazy as this could happen. Her heart thundered at merely being in the same room with him. And a sharp pain had settled between her shoulder blades. And she found it hard to draw a full breath.

"I'll take Baby Thomas." She tried to sound casual.

"He can stay on my lap. You enjoy your cake."

They ate, afraid to look at each other, afraid they had somehow misread, afraid they wouldn't know what to do when the plates were empty.

Before they were, Donald Wade looked out the window and pointed with his fork. "Who's that?"

Will looked and leaped to his feet. "Lord a-mighty!"

Eleanor dropped her fork and said, "What's she doing here?"

Before Will could conjure a guess, Gladys Beasley mounted the porch steps and knocked on the door.

Will opened it for her. "Miss Beasley, what a surprise."

"Good afternoon, Mr. Parker."

"Come in."

He had the feeling she would have, whether invited or not. He poked his head outside. "Did you *walk* clear out here from town?"

"I don't own an automobile. I didn't see any other way."

Surprised, Will ushered her inside and turned to perform introductions. But Gladys took the matter out of his hands.

"Hello, Eleanor. My, haven't you grown up."

"Hello, Miss Beasley." Eleanor stood behind a chair, nervously fingered her apron edge as if preparing to curtsy.

"And these are your sons, I suppose."

"Yes, ma'am. Donald Wade and Baby Thomas."

"And another one on the way. My, aren't you a lucky child."

"Yes'm," Eleanor answered dutifully, her eyes flashing to Will's. *What does she want?*

He hadn't an inkling and could only shrug. But he understood Eleanor's panic. How long had it been since she'd engaged in polite conversation with anyone from town? In all likelihood Miss Beasley was the first outsider Eleanor had ever allowed in this house.

"I understand congratulations are in order, too, on your marriage to Mr. Parker."

Again Eleanor's eyes flashed to Will, then she colored and dropped her gaze to the chair, running a thumbnail along its backrest.

Miss Beasley glanced at the table. "It appears I've interrupted your meal. I'm—"

"No, no," Will interjected. "We were just having cake."

Donald Wade, who never spoke to strangers, inexplicably chose to speak to this one. "It's Mama's birthday. Will and me and Baby Thomas was givin' her a party."

"Won't you sit down and have some?" Eleanor invited.

Will could scarcely believe his ears, but the next moment Miss Beasley settled her hard-packed bulk in one of the chairs and was served a piece of chocolate cake and whipped cream. Though Will hadn't actually missed having outsiders around, he found their absence unhealthy. If there was ever the perfect person to draw Eleanor out of her reclusiveness, it was Miss Beasley. Not exactly the gayest person, but fair-minded to a fault, and not at all the sort to dredge up painful past history.

Miss Beasley accepted a cup of coffee, laced it heavily with cream and sugar, sampled the cake and pursed her hairy lips. "Mmmm . . . quite delectable," she proclaimed. "Quite as delectable as the honey you sent, Eleanor. I must say I'm not accustomed to receiving gifts from my library patrons. Thank you."

Donald Wade piped up. "Wanna see the ones we give Mama today?"

Miss Beasley deferentially set down her fork and focused full attention on the child. "By all means."

Donald Wade scrambled around the table, found the suet ball and brought it to the librarian couched in his hand. "This here's for her birds. Me'n Will and Baby Thomas made it all ourselfs."

"You made it . . . mmm." She examined it minutely. "Now aren't you clever. And a homemade gift is certainly one from the heart—the best kind, just like the honey your mother and Mr. Parker gave me. You're a lucky child." She patted him on the head in the way of an adult unused to palavering socially with children. "They're teaching you the things that matter most."

"And this here . . ." Donald Wade, excited at having someone new on whom to shower his enthusiasm, reached next for the doilies. "These're from Will. He bought 'em with the honey money and Mama she can embroidry on 'em."

Again Miss Beasley gave the items due attention. "Ah, your mother is lucky, too, isn't she?"

It suddenly struck Donald Wade that the broad-beamed woman was a stranger, yet she seemed to know his mother. He looked up at Miss Beasley with wide, unblinking eyes. "How do you know 'er?"

"She used to come into my library when she was a girl not much bigger than you. Occasionally I was her teacher, you might say."

Donald Wade blinked. "Oh." Then he inquired, "What's a lie-bree?"

"A library? Why, one of the most wonderful places in the world. Filled with books of all kinds. Picture books, storybooks, books for everyone. You must come and visit it sometime, too. Ask Mr. Parker to bring you. I'll show you a book about a boy who looks quite a bit like you, actually, named *Timothy Totter's Tatters.* Mmmm ..." Leaning back, she tapped an index finger on her lips and examined Donald Wade as if a decision hung in the balance. "Yes, I should say Timothy Totter is just the book for a boy ... what? Five years old?"

Donald Wade made his hair bounce, nodding.

"Do you have a dog, Donald Wade?"

Mystified, he wagged his head slowly.

"You don't? Well, Timothy Totter does. And his name is Tatters. When you come, I'll introduce you to both Timothy and Tatters. And now, if you'll excuse me, I must speak to Mr. Parker a moment."

Miss Beasley could not have chosen a gentler method of bringing Eleanor around to the idea of bumping up against the outside world again. If there was an ideal way to reach Eleanor it was through her children. By the time Miss Beasley's interchange with Donald Wade ended, Eleanor was sitting, looking less as if she was preparing to bolt. Miss Beasley told her, "That's the best chocolate cake I've ever had. I wouldn't mind having the recipe," then turned to Will without pause. "I've come bearing some sad news. Levander Sprague, who has cleaned my library for the past twenty-six years, dropped dead of a heart attack night before last."

"Oh ... I'm sorry." He'd never heard of Levander Sprague. Why in the world had she brought the news clear out here?

"Mr. Sprague shall be sorely missed. However, he lived a long and fruitful life, and he leaves behind nine strapping boys to see their mother through her last years. I, however, am left without a custodian. The job pays twenty-five dollars a week. Would you like it, Mr. Parker?"

Will's face flattened with surprise. His glance shot to Elly, then back to the librarian, as she hastened on. "Six nights a week, after the library closes. Caring for the floors, dusting the furniture, burning the trash, stoking the furnace in the winters, occasionally carrying boxes of books to the basement, building additional shelves when we need them."

"Well ..." Will's amazement modified into a crooked smile as he chuckled and ran a hand down the back of his head. "That's quite an offer, Miss Beasley."

"I thought about offering it to one of Mr. Sprague's sons, but quite frankly, I'd rather have you. You have a certain respect for the library that I like. And I heard that you were summarily dismissed from the sawmill, which irritated my sense of fair play."

Will was too surprised to be offended. His mind raced. What would Elly say? And should he be gone evenings when she was so close to due? But twenty-five dollars a week—every week—and his days still free!

"When would you want me to start?"

"Immediately. Tomorrow. Today if possible."

"Today ... well, I ... I'd have to think it over," he replied, realizing Elly ought to have a say.

"Very well. I'll wait outside."

Wait outside? But he needed time to feel Elly out. He should have guessed that Miss Beasley would tolerate no shilly-shallying. He was already scratching his jaw in consternation as the door closed. At the same moment Eleanor arose stiffly from her chair and began clearing away the cake plates.

"Elly?" he asked.

She wouldn't look at him. "You take it, Will. I can see you want to."

"But you don't want me to, right?"

"Don't be silly."

"I could buy fixtures for a bathroom and I'd still have days free to put it in for you."

"I said, take it."

"But you don't like me hangin' around town, do you?"

She set the dishes in the dishpan and did an about-face. "My feelings for town are mine. I got no right to keep you from it, if that's what you want."

"But Miss Beasley's fair. She never put you down for anything, did she?"

"Take it."

"And what about when the baby starts coming?"

"A woman has plenty of warning."

"You're sure?"

She nodded, though he could see that it cost her dearly to let him go.

He crossed the room in four strides, grasped her jaw and planted a quick, hard kiss on her cheek. "Thank you, honey." Then he slammed out the door.

Honey? When he was gone she placed her palms where his had been. She was probably the most unhoney female within fifty miles, but the word had warmed her cheeks and tightened her chest. Before the thrill subsided, Will came slamming back inside.

"Elly? I'm giving Miss Beasley a ride back to town and she'll show me around the library, then I'll probably sweep up for her before I come back. Don't wait supper for me."

"All right."

He was half out the door before he changed his mind and returned to her side. "Will you be all right?"

"Fine."

Looking up into his eager face, she bit back all her misgivings. He'd never know from her how badly she wanted him here from now until the baby came. Or how she feared having him working in town where everyone called her crazy, where prettier and brighter women were bound to make him take a second look at what he'd married and regret it.

But how could she hold him back when he could scarcely stand still for excitement?

"I'll be fine," she repeated.

He squeezed her arm and was gone.

Chapter 12

Will took the car, in deference to Miss Beasley. On the way into town they spoke of the boys, the birthday, and finally of Elly.

"She's a stubborn woman, Miss Beasley. You might as well know, the reason I asked for that book on human birthing was because she refuses to have a doctor. She wants me to deliver the baby."

"And will you?"

"Reckon I'll have to. If I don't she'll do it alone. That's how stubborn she is."

"And you're scared."

"Damn right, I'm scared!" Will suddenly remembered himself. "Oh, sorry, ma'am—I mean, well, who wouldn't be?"

"I'm not blaming you, Mr. Parker. But apparently her other two were born at home, weren't they?"

"Yes."

"Without complications."

"Now you sound like her."

He told her about the book and how it had scared him. She told him about going off to college and how it had scared her, but how the experience had made her a stronger person. He told her about the boys and how awkward he'd felt around them at first. She told him she too had felt awkward around them today. He told her how scared Elly was of the bees and how he himself loved working with them. She told him how she loved working among the books and that in time Elly would come to see he was cautious and industrious, but he must be patient with her. He asked her what kind of man Glendon Dinsmore had been and she answered, as different from you as air is from earth. He asked which he was, air or earth? She laughed and said, "That's what I like about you—you really don't know."

They talked all the way to town—argued some—and neither of them considered what a queer combination they made—Will, with his prison record and slapdash education, Miss Beasley with her estimable position and college degree. Will with his long history of drifting, Miss Beasley with her long one of permanence. He with his family of near-three, she an old maid. Both had been lonely in their own way. Will, because of his orphaned past, Gladys because of her superior intellect. He was a man who rarely confided, she a woman in whom people rarely confided. He felt lucky to have her as a sounding board and she felt flattered to be chosen as such.

Diametric opposites, they found in each other the perfect conversational complement, and by the time they reached town their mutual respect was cemented.

The library was closed that afternoon in memory of Levander Sprague, who'd worked there nearly a third of his life. It was a cloudy day, but inside the building was warm and bright. Entering, Will looked at the place through new eyes—gleaming wood, towering windows and flawless order. How incredible that he could work in such a place.

Miss Beasley walked him through, explained his duties, showed him the janitor's supplies, the furnace, asked that he arrive each day five minutes before closing so she could give him any special instructions, then extended a key.

"For me?" He stared as if it were her great-grandfather's gold watch.

"You'll be locking up when you leave each night."

The key. My God, she was willing to trust him with the key. In all his life he'd had no place. Now he had a house *and* a library he could walk into anytime he chose.

Staring at the cool metal in his palm, he told her quietly, "Miss Beasley, this library is public property. Some folks around here might object to your giving the key to an ex-con."

She puffed out her chest until her bosom jutted, and locked her wrists beneath it. "Just let them try, Mr. Parker. I'd welcome the war." She reached down and closed his fingers over the key. "And I'd win it."

Without a doubt, she was right. In his palm the brass warmed while a smile lifted one corner of his lips and spread to the other. Some poor damn fool could have had her behind him all his life and had passed up the opportunity, he thought. This town had to be filled with some mighty stupid men.

She left him, then, went home to spend the remainder of her rare day off. He walked through the silent rooms in wonder, realizing there'd be no supervisor, foreman or guard; he could do things his way, at his own pace. He liked the silence, the smell, the spaciousness and purpose of the place. It seemed to represent a facet of life he'd missed. Stationary people came here, secure ones. From now on he'd be one of them—leaving his comfortable home and coming here to work each day, picking up a paycheck each week, knowing he'd do the same next week and the next and the next. Brimming with feelings he could find no other way to express, he pressed both hands flat on one of the study tables—solid, functional, necessary, as he'd be now. Good wood, good hard oak in a table built to last. He'd last, too, at this job because he'd found in Miss Beasley a person who judged a man for what he was, not what he had been. He stood at one of the enormous fan-light windows and looked out on the street below. *Levander Sprague, wherever you are, thank you.*

The janitor's room smelled of lemon oil and sweeping compound. Will loved it and the idea that it was his own domain. Gathering supplies, he went eagerly into the public area and upended chairs and swept the hardwood floors with an oiled rag-tail mop. He dusted the windowsills, the furniture, the top of Miss Beasley's neat desk, emptied the wastebasket, burned the papers in the incinerator and felt as if he'd just been elected governor.

At six-thirty, he headed home.

Home.

The word had never held such promise. She was waiting there, the woman who'd called him dear. The one whose cheek he'd kissed. The one whose bed he shared. At the thought of returning to her, visions filled his head—of walking into her arms, feeling her hands close over his shoulders, burying his face in her neck. Of being held as if he mattered.

He felt different now that he had a job. Bolder, worthier. Perhaps tonight he'd kiss her and to hell with the consequences.

The kitchen was empty when he arrived, but his supper waited in a pie tin on the reservoir lid. The birthday cake sat in the middle of the cleared table. From the boys' room came a spill of light and the murmur of voices. He carried his plate and fork to the doorway and found Elly sitting beneath the covers in Donald Wade's bed, an arm around each of the boys.

" . . . took a scamper 'round that hen house a-yowlin' at that fox fit to kill, and when he—" She glanced up. "Oh . . . Will . . . . hi." Her face registered pleasure. "I was tellin' the boys a bedtime story."

"Don't stop."

Their eyes held for several electric beats while her color heightened and she tucked a stray hair behind one ear. Finally, she continued her tale. He lounged against the doorframe, eating his leftover hash and black-eyed peas, listening and chuckling while she entertained the boys with a sprightly story peopled with furry critters. When the tale ended she gave each of her sons a kiss, then edged off the bed and held out her hands for Thomas.

Will pushed off the doorway. "You shouldn't be lifting him. Here, hold this." He handed her his plate and swung Thomas up, transferring him to the crib. There followed the ritual goodnight kisses, then they left the boys' door ajar and ambled toward the kitchen.

"So, how was it at the library?"

"Do you know what she did?" he asked, amazed.

"What?"

"She gave me the key. Feature that. Me with a key to anything."

Eleanor was touched, not only by his astonishment, but by Miss Beasley's trust in him. He rinsed his dish and described his duties while she settled into a rocker and pressed one of the Madeira doilies into an emroidery hoop. He dragged a kitchen chair near, sipped a cup of coffee and watched her fingers create colored flowers where only blue ink had been. They talked quietly, calm on the surface but with an underlying tension simmering as the clock inched closer to bedtime.

When it arrived, Will arched and stretched while Eleanor tucked her handiwork away. They made their trips outside, battened down the house for the night and retired to their room to undress, back to back, as had become their habit. When he had stripped to his underwear, Will turned to glance over his shoulder and caught a glimpse of her naked back and the side of one breast as she threw a white nightgown over her head.

Dear. The memory of the simple word gripped him with all its attendant possibilities. Had she meant it? Was he really dear to someone for the first time in his life?

He sat on the edge of the bed and wound the alarm clock, waiting for the feel of her weight dipping the mattress before he settled back and lowered the lantern wick.

They lay memorizing the ceiling while memories of the day returned—a birthday gift, an endearment, a handclasp, a parting kiss—none very remarkable on the surface. The remarkable was happening within.

They lay flat, quivering inside, disciplining themselves into motionlessness. From the corner of her eye she glimpsed his bare chest, the looming elbows, the hands folded behind his head. From the corner of his eye he saw her pregnant girth and her high-buttoned nightie with the quilts covering her to the ribs. Beneath her hands she felt her own heartbeat driving up through the quilt. On the back of his skull he felt the accelerated rhythm of his pulse.

The minutes dragged on. Neither moved. Neither spoke. Both worried.

One kiss—is that so hard?

Just a kiss—please.

But what if she pushes you away?

What is there for him in a woman so pregnant she can scarcely waddle?

What woman wants a man with so many tramps under his bridge?

What man wants to roll up against someone else's baby?

But most of them were paid, Elly, all of them meaningless.

Yes, it's Glendon's baby, but he never made me feel like this.

I'm unworthy.

I'm undesirable.

I'm unlovable.

I'm lonely.

Turn to her, he thought.

Turn to him, she thought.

The lantern wick sputtered. The flame twisted, distorting the impression of the chimney rim on the ceiling. The mattress seemed to tremble with their uncertainties. And when it seemed the very air would sizzle with heat lightning, they spoke simultaneously.

"Will?"

"Elly?"

Their heads turned and their eyes met.

"What?"

A pause. Then, "I ... I forgot what I was going to say."

Ten seconds of beating silence before she said softly, "Me too."

They stared at each other, feeling as if they were choking, each afraid ... each desperate ...

Then all of his past, all of her shortcomings, billowed up in a conflagration and exploded as might some distant star.

Her lips parted in unconscious invitation. His shoulder came off the bed and he rolled toward her, slowly enough to give her time to skitter if she would.

Instead her lips shaped his name. "Will ..." But it escaped without a sound as he bent above her and touched her mouth with his own.

No passionate kiss, this, but a touch fraught with insecurities. Tentative. Uncertain. A mingling of breath more than of skin. A thousand questions encapsulated in the tremulous brushing of two timid mouths while their hearts thundered, their souls sought.

He lifted ... looked ... into eyes the color of acceptance, deep-sea green in the shadow of his head. She, too, studied his eyes at close range ... brown, vulnerable eyes which he'd hidden so often beneath the brim of a battered hat. She saw the doubts that had accompanied him to this brink and marveled that someone so good, so inwardly and outwardly beautiful, should have harbored them when she was the one ... she. Plain and pregnant Elly See, the brunt of laughter and pointed fingers. But in his eyes she saw no laughter, only a deep mystification to match her own.

He kissed her again ... lightly ... lightly ... the brush of a jaconet wing upon a petal while her fingertips brushed his chest.

And at long, long last the loneliness of Will Parker's life stopped hurting. He thought her name over and over—Elly ... Elly—a benediction, as the kiss deepened, firmer, fuller, but still with a certain reserve—two people schooled to reject the possibility of miracles now forced to change their beliefs.

His hand closed over her arm and hers flattened on the silken hairs of his chest, but he remained a space apart as he urged her lips open with his own, bringing the first touch of tongues—warm, wet and still atremble. Hearts that had hammered with uncertainty did so now in exultation. They searched for and found a more intimate fit, enhanced by the sway and nod of heads that built the kiss into something more than either had expected. Sweet sweet commingling, bringing more than the rush of blood and the thrust of hearts, bringing too, the assurance that Will and Eleanor were to one another beings of great moment.

He hovered above her, bearing his weight on both elbows, afraid of hurting her. But she bade him come. Nearer ... heavier ... to the spot where her heart lifted toward his. And he rested upon her breasts, gingerly at first, until her acquiescence seemed unmistakable.

For long wondrous minutes they sated themselves with what both had known too little of before Will broke away, looked down into her face to find the same expression of wonder he himself was feeling. They stared—renewed—then wrapped each other tight and rocked because kissing hardly seemed an adequate expression of all they felt.

In time he hauled them safely to their sides, pressing his face to her throat, folding himself like a jackknife around her protruding stomach.

"Elly ... Elly ... I was so scared."

"So was I."

"I thought you'd turn me away."

"But that's what I thought you'd do."

He pulled back to see her face. "Why would I do that?"

"Because I'm not very pretty. And I'm pregnant and awkward."

He cradled her cheek tenderly. "No . . . no. You're a beautiful person. I saw that the first morning I was here."

She held the back of his hand and hid her eyes in its palm. These things were easier to admit behind closed eyes. "And I'm not very bright, and maybe I'm crazy. You knew all that."

He made her lift her chin and look at him. "But I killed a woman. And I've been in prison and in whorehouses. You knew that."

"That was a long time ago."

"Most people never forget."

"I thought because it was Glendon's baby inside me you wouldn't want to touch me."

"What does that have to do with anything?"

Her heart seemed too small to contain such joy. "Oh, Will."

He asked, "Could I touch it once? Your stomach? I never touched a woman who was pregnant."

She felt warm and shy but nodded.

His hands molded the sides of her stomach as if it were a bouquet of crushable flowers. "It's hard . . . you're hard. I thought it'd be soft. Oh God, Elly, you feel so good."

"So do you." She touched his hair, thick and springy and smelling of his unmistakable individual scent. "I've missed this."

He closed his eyes and gave her license. If he lived to be a thousand he'd never get enough of the feeling of her hands in his hair.

In time he let his eyes drift open and they lay for minutes, gazing, taking their fill. She of his incredible eyes and jumbled hair. He of her softly swollen lips and green, green eyes. He found himself unreasonably jealous of her early years with Glendon Dinsmore. "Do you still think of him?"

"I haven't for weeks."

"I thought you still loved him."

She drew courage and repeated his words. "What does that have to do with anything? Do you think I'll love this baby any less, just because two others came before it?"

He braced up on an elbow, stared at her and swallowed. He felt as if a great fist had closed around his chest. When he spoke the words sounded pinched. "Elly, nobody ever—" Abashed, he couldn't go on.

"Nobody ever loved you before?" She tenderly cupped his cheek. "Well, I do."

His eyes slid closed and he turned his mouth hard into her palm, clasping it to his face. "Nobody. Ever," he reiterated. "Not in my whole life. No mother, no woman, no man."

"Well, your life ain't even half over yet, Will Parker. The second half's gonna be much better'n the first, I promise."

"Oh, Elly . . ." Above all the things he'd missed, this had left the greatest void. Just once in his life he wanted to hear it, the way he'd dreamed of hearing it during five long years in a cell, and all the lonely years he had drifted, and all through childhood while he watched other children—the lucky ones—pass the orphanage and gawk from the security of their parents' carriages and cars. "Could you say it once," he entreated, "like they say people do?"

Her heart beat like the wings of an eagle, taking her soaring as she spoke the words. "I love you, Will Parker."

The sting hit his eyelids and he hung his head because nobody had prepared him for this, nobody had said, When it happens you'll be resurrected. All that you were you will not be. All that you weren't, you are. He lunged against her, burying his face above her breasts, holding fast. "Oh, God, . . ." he groaned. "Oh, God."

She held his head as if he were a child awakening from a bad dream.

"I love you," she whispered against his hair, feeling her own tears build.

"Oh, Elly, I love you, too," he uttered in a broken voice, "but I was so afraid nobody could love me. I thought maybe I was unlovable."

"Oh no, Will . . . no . . . not you." His bittersweet words filled her with the deep wish to heal, left her throat aching as she curled around him, held his head protectively and felt him breathe against her breasts. She threaded her hands through his hair and felt him grow still with pleasure. She raked her nails over his skull in long, slow sweeps . . . time . . . and time . . . and time again, lifting his scent, memorizing it, impressing it forever in her senses. His hair was thick, coarse, the color of dry grass. It had grown since she'd cut it, became shaggy at the neck where she brushed it up from his nape, then smoothed it before beginning another long, sensuous stroke at the crown of his head. He shivered and made a sound of gratification, deep in his throat.

His whole life he'd longed for someone to touch him this way, to touch the boy in him as well as the man, to soothe, reassure. The feel of her fingers in his hair brought back a measure of all he'd missed. He was parched earth, she fresh rain. He, a waiting vessel, she rich wine. And in those moments of closeness she filled him, filled all the lacks endowed him by his shiftless, loner's life, becoming at once all the things he'd needed—mother, father, friend, wife, and lover.

When he felt sated he lifted his head as if drunk with pleasure.

"I used to watch you touch the boys that way. I wanted to say, Touch me, too, like you touch them. Nobody ever did that to me before, Elly."

"I'll do it anytime you like. Wash your hair, comb it, rub your back, hold your hand—"

His mouth stopped her words. It seemed risky to accept too much in this first, grand rush. He kissed her with gratitude changing swiftly to the lushness of fresh-sprung love. He braced higher and pushed her softly into the pillow, letting his hand rove over her neck and shoulder, suckling her mouth, spreading his fingers on her face, resting a thumb so near it almost became part of the kiss. His body beckoned to join more fully in this union. Realizing this was impossible, he broke the kiss but spanned her throat with his hand. Her pulsebeat matched the quickness of his own.

"You know how long I've loved you?"

"How long?"

"Since the day you threw the egg at me."

"All that time and you never said anything. Oh, Will . . ."

A swift slew of possessiveness hit him. He claimed her mouth again, washing its interior with his tongue, holding her arms locked hard around his neck. He bit her lips. She bit back. He lifted a knee and pressed it high and hard between her legs. She opened them and squeezed his thigh. He circled her immense waist and held her as if forever.

"Tell me again." he demanded insatiably.

"What?" she teased.

"You know. Tell me."

"I love you."

"Once more. I got to hear it more."

"I love you."

"Will you get tired of me asking you to say it?"

"You won't have to ask."

"Neither will you. I love you." Another kiss—a hard, short stamp of possession, then a question filled with boyish impatience. "When did you know?"

"I don't know. It just came upon me."

"When we got married?"

"No."

"When we bottled the honey?"

"Maybe."

"Well, sure's heck not when you threw that egg."

She chuckled. "But I noticed your bare chest for the first time that day and I liked it."

"My chest?"

"Aha."

"You liked my chest before you liked me?"

"When you were washing, down by the well."

"Touch it." Jubilantly he flattened her hand against it. "Touch me anyplace. God, do you know how long it's been since a woman touched me?"

"Will . . ." she chided timidly.

"Are you shy? Don't be shy. I thought I was, too, but all of a sudden it seems like we got so much time to make up for. Touch me. No, wait. Get up. First I gotta see you." He piled onto his knees and pulled her up to kneel before him, holding her hands out from her sides. "Mercy, are you a pretty sight. Let me look at you." Her chin dropped shyly and he lifted it, pressed the tousled hair back from her temples, then fluffed it with his fingertips and arranged it on her collarbones. "You mean I don't have to sneak anymore when I want to look at you? You got the greenest eyes. Green is my favorite color, but you knew that."

She folded her hands between her knees, quite overcome by this exuberant, demonstrative Will.

"I used to think if I was ever lucky enough to have a woman of my own, she'd have to have green eyes. Now here you are. You and your green eyes . . . and your pink cheeks . . . and your pretty little mouth . . ." With his thumbs he touched its corners and let his hands trail down to her shoulders, to her upper arms where they stopped. "Elly," he whispered, "don't move." He slipped his palms to the sides of her breasts and held them lightly while the blood rushed to her cheeks and she searched for a safe place to rest her gaze. The dim light shifted on the folds of her nightgown as he cupped a breast in each hand, his palms too narrow to contain their prenatal fullness. Gently, he reshaped and lifted, then released them to glide one hand down the fullest part of her belly. There it rested, fingers splayed. He watched the hand, soon joined by the other to smooth the cloth toward her hips where he held it taut, disclosing the impression of her distended navel. Bending, he kissed her. There. On the stomach she'd thought ugly enough to put him off.

"Will." She found his chin and attempted to lift it. "I'm fat as a pumpkin. How can you kiss me there?"

He straightened. "You're not fat, you're only pregnant. And if I'm going to deliver that baby I'd better get to know him."

"I thought I married a shy, quiet man."

"I thought so too."

He smiled for the length of three glad heartbeats, then laughed. And wondered if life would ever again be this good. And decided surely tomorrow and tomorrow and tomorrow it could only get better.

* * *

He was right. He'd never imagined happiness such as he knew in the days and nights that followed. To roll over in sleep and draw her back against him and drift off again in a cocoon of bliss. Or better yet, to roll the other way and feel her follow, then press close behind him. To feel her hand circle his waist, her feet beneath his, her breath on his back. To awaken and find her lying with an elbow beneath her cheek, studying him. To kiss her then in the buttery light of early morning and know that he could do so anytime. To leave her with a goodbye kiss and return anxious. To step into the kitchen and find her working at the sink, glancing shyly over her shoulder then down at her hands until he crossed the room and slipped both hands into her apron pockets and rested his chin on her shoulder. To kiss—over her shoulder—awaiting the exquisite moment when she'd turn and loop her arms up in a welcoming embrace. To eat cake from her fork, braid her hair, refill her coffee cup, watch her embroider. To lean over the sink and shiver while she washed his hair, then wilt on a kitchen chair while she dried, combed and cut it, and sometimes kissed his ear, and sometimes teased him when he dropped off and she had to awaken him with a kiss on the mouth. To walk down the driveway holding hands, pulling the boys in the wagon.

Only one thing disturbed him during those serene days. Lula Peak. It hadn't taken her long to get the news that Will was the custodian at the library. One evening within a week of his starting she walked in the back door and found Will in the storeroom gluing a loose chair rung. "Hey, sugar, where y' been keepin' yourself?"

Will jumped and swung around, startled by her voice.

"Library's closed, ma'am."

"Well now, I know that. So's the cafe, 'cause I just shut off the light. Thought I'd sashay on over and congratulate you on your new job." She leaned against the doorframe, one arm crossing her waist, the other hand dangling near the white V of her uniform collar. "That's the neighborly thing to do, i'nt it?"

" 'Preciate it, ma'am. Now if you'll excuse me, I got work to do."

He squatted again, turning his back, minding the chair. She moved into the windowless room and stood behind him with her knee against his back. "You thought any more about what I said, sugar?" She kneaded the side of his neck. "Man like you makes a girl lay awake nights. Figured maybe you lay awake, too, what with that wife o' yours bein' pregnant. No sense in both of us losin' sleep now, is there?"

He spun to his feet, took her by the shoulders and pushed her back.

"I ain't lookin' for trouble, I told you once before." He stuffed his hands in his pockets, feeling soiled from touching her. "I'm a happily married man, Miss Peak. Now I'm afraid I'll have to ask you to leave, 'cause I got work to do."

She let her eyes meander over him, from forehead to hips and back up. "You're blushin', sugar, you know that? Must mean you're hot . . . let's see." She reached to touch his face but he grabbed her wrist and held it away, squeezing hard.

"Dammit, Lula, I said leave off!"

Her eyes took fire, radiating excitement. "Well, that's an improvement. At least we're on a first-name basis."

"I don't want you comin' here again."

"Some men don't know what they want." Like a cobra she struck, biting his knuckles and retreating in one flashing movement.

"Ouch, goddammit!" He nursed the hand and already saw blood.

"What's it take, Parker, huh?" she challenged from the doorway, shoulders thrown back, hands on hips, eyes glinting with demonic glee. "I know things that crazy wife of yours never dreamed of. You think about it." She turned and ran.

He felt violated. And angry. And guilty. And powerless because she was a woman and he couldn't level her with his fists as he had the men who'd tried to seduce him in prison. That night, returning to Elly, he held his feelings inside, afraid to tell her about Lula, afraid to jeopardize their new burgeoning closeness.

At the library he had always locked the front door. After Lula's intrusion he locked the back, too. But she cornered him one night when he took the trash out to burn in the incinerator behind the building, slipping up behind him in the dark and touching him before he was aware of her presence. He shoved her harder this time, knocking her against the incinerator, cursing, raising his fist but halting himself just in time.

"Do it," she goaded. "Do it, Parker," and he realized she was sick, driven by some twisted need that scared him.

"Keep outa my way, Lula," he growled, picked up his trash can and ran.

He tried to put the incident from his mind, but found himself looking over his shoulder every time he stepped out the library door, every time he locked it at the end of the night. He grew closer to Elly, appreciated her more, soothed himself with her goodness.

Nights, when he'd return home, she'd awaken and stretch and watch him shuck off his outerwear and slip in beside her. And her arms would open and they'd lay kissing and murmuring until the hour grew wee and the moon began its descent. Though they were husband and wife, their embraces remained chaste. Sometimes he caressed her breast, but as her time grew closer she'd flinch and he was smitten by a wave of guilt.

"Elly, honey, I'm sorry, Did I hurt you?"

"They're always a little tender, late like this."

After that he kissed and held her, but no more. She always wore her long white nightie and he knew she was shy about exposing her distorted body. Though he was tempted to do more, he never pushed, but settled for kissing and lying with their limbs entwined, their hands safely removed from intimate territory.

Until one night in early December when he'd found a note from Lula on the back door as he left work. It was graphic, obscene, suggesting how she might thrill him when he finally broke down and accepted her invitation. That night he had a dream. He was walking through a dry wash in Texas. It was high noon and so hot the earth burned through the soles of his boots. His mouth felt parched and a dull ache bowed his shoulders. He labored up a rocky ridge, panting and tired, then halted in surprise at the sight beyond the crest. A layer of sky might have dropped from overhead, so brilliant was the valley below. Filled with Texas blue-bonnets, it seemed to reflect the hard cobalt blue of the bowl overhead. A ribbon of sparkling water bisected the field as he wallowed through it in flowers as deep as a man's boot tops. He knelt to drink, swashing his face and neck, dampening his collar and leather vest. He cupped his hand again, and as he knelt, sipping, a pair of feet waded into view beneath his nose. A gauzy yellow skirt floated on top of the water. He looked up into eyes as black as Apache tears, and hair to match.

"Hola, Weel—jew been lookin' for me?" It was Carmelita, one of the women from the whorehouse in La Grange. She had Mexican blood, enough to make her skin dusky and her lips a ripe plum red.

He pushed himself onto his haunches and backhanded his mouth slowly, eyeing her as she caught her hands on both hips and rocked seductively. Her feet were widespread, thighs silhouetted through the yellow gauze skirt. She reached down and lazily wet her arms, bending forward until her breasts hung pendulously within the peasant-style blouse.

" 'Ey, Weell Parker, wot jew lookin' at, eh?" She straightened, still with legs spraddled, and wrung out her skirt, enticing him with a glimpse of bare skin and black pubic hair underneath. She laughed throatily and wallowed to the bank. Standing ankle-deep, she began washing his face with the wet skirt. He reached beneath it and gripped her bare hips. Immediately she shoved him away, scuttled backward into the swifter water, laughing throatily. "Jew want Carmelita . . . come and get hur." He was stripping off his vest before the words cleared her lips. Down to bare skin, he shucked, then plunged into the cold, rippling creek. She shrieked and ran, but he caught and spun her, took her down and himself, too, into the purling water that turned her clothes transparent. He bit her nipple through the wet gauze and she shrieked again, laughing, then squiggled away, fighting against the current while stripping off her dress and flinging it back in his face. He plunged after her, scraping the clinging gauze off his head, and tackled her as she scrambled up the bank, kissing her voluptuously while her wet black hair got between their tongues. His finger was inside her before their ripples disappeared downstream, and she bucked up lustily, chuckling in a rich contralto. They rolled wildly, collecting sand on their backs. When they stopped, breathless, she was on top, urging him with practiced hips.

"Jew like, eh, hombre?" She growled low in her throat and took him in hand with little gentleness and less pause. Firmly stroking him, she let her eyes flash wickedly. "Jew will like this even more." She dove down without invitation, opened her mouth and narrowed his world to a thin corridor where carnality was all that mattered.

"Will . . . wake up, Will!"

Disoriented, he opened his eyes to find himself not in a field of Texas bluebonnets but in an iron bed; with a face dampened not by creekwater but by his own sweat; not with Carmelita, but with Elly. His body was swelled like a cactus in a March rain and his hand was inside Elly's cotton underwear, in her pregnant body.

Startled, she looked back over her shoulder. He held himself rigid, too near climax to risk even the faintest movement.

"I was dreaming," he managed in a raspy voice.

"You awake now?"

"Yes." He withdrew his hand and rolled onto his back, covering his eyes with a wrist. "Sorry," he mumbled.

"What were you dreaming?"

"Nothin'."

"Of me?"

Afraid of hurting her feelings, he remained silent, damning Lula, and the dream, and his own body for needing release. "Elly, you scared to let me touch you?"

"You touch me all the time."

"Not there."

Silence . . . then, "I don't want you to see me. Pregnant women aren't so pretty to look at."

"Who told you that?"

"They just aren't."

"I'll see you when the baby is born."

"Not for long. And afterwards I won't look like this."

He moved his wrist and stared at the ceiling, thinking, *It isn't natural, two people lying beside each other, married all this time and never touching deliberately.* "I'm gonna turn off the lamp, Elly."

No reply, so he reached over and lowered the wick. In the unaccustomed darkness they lay in the strong scent of kerosene smoke.

"Come here." He reached, closed his hand over her arm and pulled gently. "It's time for this, don't you think?"

"Will, I like it when you kiss me and hold me, but I can't do any more."

"I know." He found her hips and rolled her to face him. "But I'm dying every night, wondering. Aren't you? I'll be gentle as anything you ever felt." He pulled her nightgown up and laid both hands on her. "I want you to know somethin', Elly." He kissed her mouth, breathed on her, felt his heart drumming everywhere, everywhere. "I wish this baby was mine."

He explored her skin as if it were braille, leaving no further secrets. "Ah, Elly ... Elly ..." he murmured throatily. Then he found her hand and placed it upon himself and his breathing became a battle for air. He shuddered and ejaculated in her hand. Swiftly. Afterward he felt healed and renewed and reached for her again, to repay her in kind. But she pushed his hand away, sighed and curled close against him.

He lay holding her while emotions came to cleanse him. He thought of thanking her, but considered himself inarticulate in a moment too precious to jade with words. So he enfolded her, rubbed her back, her spine, her hair, pressing her even closer at intervals when his sense of fulfillment cried for expression.

Outside a solitary woodcock called, rising on whistling wings. The wind rested, stilling the tree tips. Off in the distance a barred owl called, like the bark of a dog at first, then, as if questioning, *Who-looks-for-you? Who looks for you?*

Inside, entwined, Will and Elly drifted to sleep.

And neither of them thought to turn the light back on.

Chapter 13

Elly went into labor near noon of December fourth. She'd had a low backache all morning, then a bloody show, and by dinnertime her first two distinguishable contractions had come, fifteen minutes apart. The second hit hard enough to perch her on the edge of a chair, trying to catch her breath for the better part of a minute. When it ended she braced her back and rose awkwardly, then waddled into the front room.

Will was working on the bathroom, sitting crosslegged on the floor, whistling. He had cut a doorway through the front-room wall and sectioned off an end of the porch, which already had a window installed and the pipes jutting up from the crawl space underneath. With his first check he had proudly purchased bathroom fixtures—used, though neither Will nor Elly cared in their excitement over the prospect of having such a room. The sink and stool were stored elsewhere, but the tub was in place, standing inside the skeletal walls which, too, awaited finishing after the pipework was done.

Elly paused in the bathroom doorway, watching Will, listening to him whistle "In My Adobe Hacienda," which they'd been hearing on the radio lately. Wielding a pipe wrench, he faced the far wall. His cowboy hat sat at a jaunty angle on the back of his head. Sawdust coated its brim, and the back of his blue shirt was smudged with dirt from lying on his back in the crawl space. She smiled as he hit several sour notes.

He gave the wrench a last mighty tug that interrupted his song, then set it down with a clatter and tested the pipe junction with his fingers, picking up the tune again, softly, through his teeth. He got to one knee and picked up a copper elbow joint, bending forward while figuring the height at which it should adjoin the pipe connections on the tub.

"Hey, you," she greeted amiably, wearing an appreciative smile.

He twisted at the waist and sent her an answering grin. "Hiya, doll."

She laughed and leaned against the doorframe. "Some doll, shaped like a bloated horse."

"C'm'ere." He fell to his seat, legs outstretched, leaning against a wall stud and reaching out one dirty hand. They grinned at each other silently for a long moment. "Over here." He patted his lap.

She boosted off the doorframe and picked her way through tools and pipes scattered upon the floor to stand above him.

"Right here." He patted his lap again as she turned sideways.

"No, not that way—this way." He grabbed her ankle and planted it beyond his far hip, grinning suggestively. "Come on down here."

"Will . . . the boys," she whispered, throwing a cautious glance over her shoulder at the doorway.

"So what?" Gripping her hands he forced her to straddle him with her skirt bunched up to midthigh.

"But they might come in."

"So they find me kissing their mother. Be good for 'em." He linked his wrists behind her waist and settled her paunch against his belly while she crossed her arms behind his neck.

"Will Parker . . ." She smiled into his upraised face. "You're the crazy one, not me."

"Damn right, woman. Crazy for you." He lifted his mouth for a long, involved kiss—lips, tongues, and plenty of head motion. It was something new for Eleanor, necking in the middle of the day. With Glendon there had been restraint during daylight hours, perhaps even less than restraint, for the idea of an interlude like this never entered their heads. But with Will . . . oh, her Will. He was insatiable. She couldn't carry a stack of clean laundry through his vicinity without being waylaid, and pleasantly so. He was a devilishly good kisser. She'd never before given much consideration to the quality of kisses. But straddling Will's lap, with his mouth wide, sucking gently on hers, with his silky tongue stroking everything reachable within her mouth, she appreciated his skill. He didn't simply kiss. He lavished, then lingered, then drew away by slow degrees, as if he would never tire of her. Sometimes he murmured wordlessly, often nuzzled, making parting as sweet as joining had been.

The kiss ended with all due reluctance, and with Will's nose buried in her collar, his hat fallen to the floor.

"My hands are dirty or you know where they'd be, don't you?"

Eyes closed, face tilted up, she held his head and lightly raked his skull the way he loved. "Where?"

He closed his teeth on her collarbone, chuckled and teased, "In the kitchen, building a sandwich. I'm starved."

She laughed and pushed away in mock rebuff. "You're always starved. What do you think I came in here for?"

"To call me for dinner?" He leaned back and grinned into her happy green eyes. "What else?"

"And instead you pinned me to the floor and wasted all this time when I could've been eating?"

"Who wants to eat when you can neck?"

He feigned disgust and reached for his hat, plunking it on his head. "Here I am, minding my own business, puttin' in a bathroom, when out of nowhere this woman jumps me. I mean, I got my wrench out and I'm connectin' pipe and not botherin' a livin' soul when—"

"Hey, Will?" she interrupted teasingly. "Guess what."

"What?"

"Dinner's ready."

"Well, it's about time." He tried to rise, but she remained on his lap.

"Guess what else."

"I dunno."

"My labor's started."

His face flattened as if she'd struck him across the Adam's apple with the pipe wrench.

"Elly. Oh, my God, you shouldn't be sitting here. Lord, did I hurt you, pulling you down? Can you get up?"

She chuckled at his overzealous reaction. "It's all right. I'm between pains. And sitting here took my mind off 'em."

"Elly, are you sure? I mean, is it really time?"

"I'm sure."

"But how can it be? It's only December fourth."

"I said December, didn't I?"

"Yeah, but—well, December's a long month!" His brow furrowed as he carefully boosted her up and followed. "I mean, I thought it'd be later. I thought I'd have time to finish the bathroom so it'd be ready when the baby came."

"It's a funny thing about babies." She held his dirty hands and lifted a reassuring smile. "They don't wait for things to get done. They just come whenever they feel like it. Now listen, I got some things to get ready, so if you'd fix the boys' plates and your own it'd sure be a help."

Will became a bundle of nerves. She shouldn't have found it amusing, but couldn't help smiling covertly. He balked at being out of her sight, even for the short time it took him to settle the kids at the table with their plates. Instead of filling a plate for himself he followed her to the bedroom, where he found her stripping the bed.

"What're you doing?"

"Getting the bed ready."

"Well, *I can do that!*" he reprimanded sharply, clumping inside.

"So can I. Will, please . . . listen." She dropped the corner of the quilt and clasped his wrist. "It's best if I move around, all right? It could be hours yet."

He elbowed her aside and began jerking the soiled bedclothes off the mattress. "I don't see how you could've just sat there on the bathroom floor letting me make jokes while it was already started."

"So what else should I do?"

"Well, I don't know, but Jesus, Elly, there I was, pulling at your ankles, making you sit on me." She moved as if to resume her chore, and he erupted. "I said I'll fix the bed! Just tell me what you want on it."

She told him: old newspapers against the mattress, covered by absorbent cotton flannel sheets folded into thick pads, and finally the muslin sheet. No blankets at all. It looked so stark and foreboding, the sight of it scared him worse than ever. But while he stood staring she had a new surprise in store for him.

"I want you to go down to the barn and get a pair of tugs."

"Tugs?" His unblinking eyes grew round.

"Tug straps. From Madam's harness."

"What for?"

"And you might as well start carrying water. Fill the boiler and the reservoir and the teakettle. We need to have both warm and cold on hand. Now go."

"What for? What d'you need those tug straps for?"

"Will . . . please," she said with forced patience.

He raced down to the barn, cursing himself for not getting the running water in before this, for not hooking the water heater up to the wind generator, for not realizing babies sometimes come early. He tore the spare harness from the wall and fumbled with the leather, removing the tugs. Less than three minutes later he panted to a halt at the bedroom door to find her poised on the edge of a hard wooden chair, back arched, eyes closed, her hands gripping the edge of the seat.

"Elly!" He dropped the tugs and fell to one knee before her.

"It's all right," she managed, breathless, her eyelids still closed. "It's going away now."

He touched her kneecaps, quaking with fear. "Elly, I'm sorry I shouted before. I didn't mean to. I was just scared."

"It's all right, Will." The pain eased as she opened her eyes and slowly sank back in the chair. "Now listen to me. I want you to take that harness and lay it out flat on the porch floor and scrub it hard with a brush and that yellow soap. On both sides. Scrub good around the buckles and even in the buckle holes. And scrub your hands and fingernails at the same time. Then bring the tugs inside and boil them in the dishpan. While they're boiling in one pan, I want you to boil the scissors and two lengths of hard string in a separate one. You'll find them in the kitchen in a cup next to the sugar bowl. Then as soon as the water is hot, bring some in here, and the yellow soap so I can take a bath."

"All right, Elly," he answered meekly, rising, backing away doubtfully.

"And put the boys down for a nap as soon as they're finished eating."

He followed her instructions minutely, rushing from task to task, afraid something would happen while he wasn't at her side. When he brought the empty washtub into the bedroom he found her drawing fresh white baby clothing from the bureau drawer—a tiny flannel kimono, a receiving blanket, an undershirt, a diaper. He stood and watched as she lovingly catalogued each item and placed it on a stack. Next came the pink shawl she'd crocheted herself, and a pair of incredibly small booties to match. She turned and found him watching.

Her smile was so peaceful, so unafraid, it brought a measure of ease to him. "I just know it's going to be a girl," she said.

"I'd like that, too."

He watched as Elly got the laundry basket from behind the bedroom door, emptied it of dirty clothes and prepared it with a white pad, followed by rubber and cotton sheets. Then came the pink shelldesigned shawl and lastly a white flannel receiving blanket. "There." She smiled down at the basket with the same pride a queen might have exhibited over a golden cradle lined with swansdown.

He set the washtub down without dropping his eyes from her, stepped around it and touched her tenderly, below one jaw. "Rest now while I bring the water."

She looked into his eyes and told him, "I'm awful glad you're here, Will."

"So am I."

It wasn't strictly true. He'd rather be in the car on his way to fetch the doctor, but it was too late for discussing that. He filled her washtub and went to the kitchen to clean up the lunch dishes. Returning to the bedroom minutes later, he found Elly standing in the washtub, covered with soap. She stood at half-profile to him, presenting a view of her back and the side of one breast. He'd never seen her naked before. Not out of bed. The sight stirred him deeply. She was misproportioned, bulky, but the reason for it lent her a different feminine beauty from any he'd ever witnessed. She passed the cloth down her stomach, between her thighs, cleansing the route for the awaited one, and he stood watch, unabashed, without a thought of turning away. Suddenly she was seized by a new pain and dropped into a half-crouch. Her fist closed around the washcloth, sending lather plopping into the water. Will moved as if propelled by black powder, across the room to slide an arm around her slick body, supporting her through the brunt of it. When it began ebbing, he eased her lower until she rested on the edge of the tub, panting.

He felt helpless and distraught, wanting to do more, *needing* to do more than simply comfort. He wished he could bear the next pain himself.

When it was over, she wilted. "That was a strong one. They're comin' faster this time than when Thomas was born."

"Here. Kneel down."

She knelt and he rinsed her back, arms, breasts, relieved to be doing something concrete. He held her hand as she stepped over the rim of the tub, then dried her back.

"Thank you, Will. I can finish." While he carried the tub away she dressed in a clean white nightgown and beneath the bed found a white cloth sack from which she drew several large folded dried leaves. Taking them, she followed Will to the kitchen. She stood a moment, watching him spill her bathwater at the sink. With the dipper he rinsed the tub, then mopped it with a rag. Only then did he turn and find her standing behind him, watching.

"Should you be out here?"

"You mustn't worry so, Will. Please. For me?"

"That's not an easy order."

"I know." She could see on his face how difficult it was for him to remain stalwart, and loved him for his valiant effort. "But now I need to talk to you about what to expect, what to do."

"I know it all." He set the tub down. "I read it in the book so many times that it might as well be branded on my arm. But reading it and doing it are two different things."

She moved close to him and touched his hand. "You'll do fine, Will." Calmly she found a kettle into which she put the leaves, covering them with water from the teakettle. She set them to simmer on the rear of the range.

Will watched, feeling his stomach tensing more each minute. "What's that?"

"Comfrey."

He was almost afraid to ask. It took two tries before his throat released the sound. "What for?"

"Afterwards, if I tear, you got to make a poultice of it and put it on me. It'll draw the skin back together and help it heal. But you got to remember—don't waste no time on me till you seen to the baby, understand?"

If she tears. The words shook him afresh. It took an effort for Will to concentrate on the remainder of her instructions.

"Only use the sterilized rags I laid on the dresser. Everything else you need is there too. Scissors, strings, pledgets, alcohol and gauze for the baby's cord, and Vaseline for under the cotton when you bandage her. You'll do that after you give her a bath. Make sure you keep enough warm water for that, and a tubful of cold for the sheets, 'cause you'll have to change them when it's over. When you give her a bath don't use the yellow soap, but the glycerine. Make sure you hold her head all the time—soon as it comes out of me, and while you're waiting for the rest of her body to be born, and when you give her a bath, too. But, Will, you got to remember, through it all, the baby comes first. The most important thing is to get her breathing, then bathed and dressed and warm so she doesn't get chilled."

"I know, I know!" he replied impatiently, wishing she wouldn't talk about it. He'd read the birth attendant's instructions until he could recite them verbatim. It was the very images they conjured that rattled him.

Quietly she said, "Now walk with me."

"Walk?"

"It'll bring it on faster."

If he could choose, he'd postpone it indefinitely. The thought brought a spear of guilt for her plight, and he did as bid. He had never felt as protective as during the following two hours while they strolled the length of the small rooms, back and forth, stopping only for each new contraction. She was intrepid; to be less himself would have made him a burden rather than a support. So he held her hand in the crook of his arm and accompanied her as if they were out for a sojourn on the town green at the height of the season. He teased when she needed brightening. And soothed when she needed support. And talked when she needed talking. And learned what a pledget was when he saw a stack of carefully formed rectangular cotton pads bound in gauze.

At half past two the boys woke up and he dressed them in their warm jackets and sent them out to play, hoping fervently they'd stay out till sunrise.

Shortly past three Elly announced quietly, "I think I'd like to lay down now. Bring the tug straps, dear." In the bedroom, with a sigh she rolled onto the clean white sheet and ordered, "Tie them to the footrail as far apart as my knees."

His stomach lurched, his salivary glands seemed to kick into overtime and his hands felt clumsy. When the leather straps were knotted, leaving ample leads and loops for her legs, they appeared like trappings in a medieval torture chamber. He found them hideous as he waited for her next contraction. When it hit, it seemed to hit them both. With acute shock, Will felt the sympathetic pain rip through his groin and down his thighs just as it did down Elly's. It was a hard one, and long, lasting nearly a minute, markedly advanced from those before.

When it ended, she rested, panting, then whispered, "Wash your hands again, Will, and trim your nails. It won't be long now."

Trim his nails? This time he didn't ask why. He feared he knew. In case trouble developed and he had to help from the inside.

He scrubbed his knuckles until they stung, and snipped his nails to the quick with the sterilized scissor, fighting down panic. Oh God, why hadn't he gone against her wishes and driven into town for the doctor the minute she'd had her first pain? What if the cord was wrapped around the baby's neck? What if Elly hemorrhaged? What if the boys came in in the middle of it?

As if his very thought conjured them, the pair clattered into the kitchen, calling for their mother.

Will went out to waylay them, soiling his sterilized hands as he stopped Donald Wade and Thomas with a hand on each chest as they charged for the closed bedroom door.

"Hold up there, buckaroos!" He went down on one knee and gathered them close.

"We got to show Mama somethin'!" Donald Wade held a bird's nest.

"Your mama's resting."

"But, look what we found!" Donald Wade strained toward the door but Will tightened his arm.

"You remember when your mama told you about how that baby was gonna come out someday in the basket?" They stopped struggling and gazed at Will with innocent curiosity. "Well, the baby's gonna be born pretty soon, and your mother's not gonna feel so good while it's happening, but the same was true when you guys were born, so don't be scared, okay?" He gently squeezed their necks. "Now, I want you to be good boys. Donald Wade, you get some cookies and take your brother outside, and don't come back in till I call you, all right?"

"But—"

"Now listen, I ain't got time to argue, 'cause your mama needs me. But if you do like I say I'll take you to the movie house one day soon. Deal?" Donald Wade vacillated, glancing from Will toward the bedroom door.

"To Hopalong Cassidy?"

"You bet. Go on now," Will gave them each a little shove toward the kitchen and the cookie jar. As soon as they were safely outside, he rescrubbed his hands, jogged back to the bedroom, closed the door with his boot and pushed it tight with a shoulder.

"The boys—I bribed them with a trip to the movie house and sent them outside with a handful of cookies. How're you?" He moved to the side of the bed and sat on the hard wooden chair.

"I hurt." She chuckled and cradled her stomach.

He reached as if to brush Elly's brow.

"Don't touch me, Will. You mustn't."

Reluctantly he withdrew his cleansed hand to sit in misery, waiting, feeling useless.

The next pain lifted her midsection off the mattress and brought Will from his chair to lean over her, watching her face contort as her knees parted and she reached up to grip the iron rails above her head. When she held her breath, he held his. When she grimaced, he grimaced. When she bared her teeth, he bared his. The sixty seconds during her contraction felt longer than his stint in prison.

At its end, she opened her dazed eyes and rolled her head to look at him. "It's t–time, W–Will," she managed. "Wash me with alcohol n–now, and h–help me find the t–tugs."

His hands trembled as he moved to the foot of the bed, folded back her nightgown and stared. Oh, Lord. Lord o' mercy, how she must hurt. She was swollen, distended, distorted beyond anything he'd imagined. He could actually see the bulge caused by the baby's head just above the apex of her legs. Her genitals appeared inflamed, as if bee-stung, and they were seeping, staining the bedclothes a dim pink. He gulped, but came from his stupor when she reared up and a great gush of transparent fluid flowed from her body, wetting a wide circle on the sheet. The sight of it galvanized him into action. He knew what it was, knew it meant the baby was pressing low, preparing for its arrival into the world.

Suddenly his purpose here became crystal clear, and as it dawned all Will's fears disappeared. His stomach grew calm. His hands grew steady. The jitters fled, chased away by the realization that he was needed by both the baby and its mother. But they needed him competent.

With a pad of cotton he generously swabbed her stomach, thighs and genitals with alcohol. It stung his own fingers where he'd broken the cuticles with the scrub brush, but he scarcely noticed. For good measure, he swabbed the tug straps before gently lifting her heels and slipping the leather loops snug behind her knees. Then he placed an additional clean folded flannel sheet beneath her.

"W–W–Will," she panted as another contraction began.

"Yes, love," he answered quietly, but stood at his post, eyes riveted on her constricting belly, watching it slowly begin to arch, watching her dilation grow with the pain.

"W–W–*Wiiiiill!*" It tore from her as a rasping cry while the contraction built and peaked. He placed his palms beneath her thighs and helped her through it, feeling her muscles tighten as she lifted. Only when she relaxed did he raise his eyes to her face. Beads of sweat stood on her brow. The fine strands of hair at her hairline were damp and darkened to the color of aged cornsilk. Her lips looked dry and cracked. She wet them with her tongue while he thought of the jar of Vaseline he dared not touch. Before her lips had dried, another pain arrived and with it the sight of the baby's dark scalp.

"I see her!" Will cried. "Come on, darlin', once more and she'll be here!"

He waited with his hands spread in welcome, chancing not so much as a glance away from the dark hair now clearly visible. Elly's womb arched, her legs tightened on the straps, her hands on the iron rails. A ragged scream rent the air and Will learned what perineum meant as he watched Elly's tear. But he had no time to dwell on it, for at the same moment the baby's head slipped through—facing backward, as promised, facedown and slippery in his waiting hands. Then, as if by some miracle, it turned to the side, following the normal course of events, and he cradled it on his palm, tiny and sleek and red.

"Her head is out, darlin'. Oh, God, she has dark eyebrows." The distorted face was frighteningly dark and marked from the rigors of birth, but the warning in the book stood Will in good stead as he told himself it was to be expected; the child would not choke from the perineum drawn tightly about its neck. *Don't panic! Don't try to pull her out!* "Easy there, now, little one," he murmured to the baby. "I got to clean your mouth out." As if Nature knew exactly what she was doing, she allowed just enough time for Elly to rest and for Will to run his finger into the baby's mouth and clear it before Elly bore down and the baby's lower shoulder appeared, followed by the upper, then, in one grand release, the full birth happened. Into Will's waiting hands spilled a creature with a dark face, connected to its mother by a thin, crimped lifeline. Slippery and wet she came, filling his heart with a wild thrum of excitement, his face with a wide beam of wonder.

"She's here, Elly, she's born! And you were right. She's a girl. And . . . oh . . . lord, smaller than my hands." Even as he spoke, he rested his precious cargo on Elly's stomach while she panted in the brief natural respite following full birth. Releasing her grip on the headrail, Elly reached down to touch the baby's head, lifting her own with an effort and smiling wearily. As her head fell back she laughed and tears leaked down her temples.

"Is she pretty?"

"She's the sorriest mess I ever seen." He laughed in relief. Until Elly was hit by an aftershock and grunted, straining until her face shook and turned purple. He laid the baby down and tried to help Elly through the second wave of pushing pains. But the afterbirth refused to come. She fell back, panting, near exhaustion, her eyelids quivering. Another pushing pain produced the same results, and Will swallowed the lump of fear in his throat, doing what he knew he must do. He rested one hand in the soft hollow of her stomach, fitting its heel at the top of her womb and manipulating it to create a man-made contraction. She moaned and mindlessly tried to push his hand away. He forced from his mind the fact that he must hurt her to help her. His eyes smarted. He cleared them on his shoulder and vowed he'd never make her pregnant. He reached inside her tender flesh, loosening the afterbirth while kneading her soft stomach. Suddenly he felt a change as her own body took over. Her abdomen contracted and beneath his ministration the afterbirth pulled loose inside, dropping low to create a slight swelling beneath her matted hair. "Come on, Elly-honey, one more push and you can rest." From some hidden source she found the strength for another mighty effort that brought a last gush as her body delivered the afterbirth, severing her completely from the life she'd supported for nine months.

Will's shoulders drooped. He closed his eyes, sucked in a great lungful of air, dried his brow on a sleeve and praised simply, "Good, honey. It's all done. Hang on now." His hands were remarkably calm as he tied the first string an inch and a half from the baby's body, leaving only enough space between it and the second stricture for the scissor to do its work. The silver blades met and the deed was done. The baby was on her own.

Breathe! Breathe! Breathe!

The word resounded through Will's mind as he picked up the baby and watched it fold into a fetal position within his hands. Through his memory skittered the various directions for shocking a newborn into drawing its first breath. A smart smack. Cold water. Artificial respiration. But to do any of them to 'a creature so tiny seemed sadistic. Come on, girl, *breathe! ... Breathe!* Fifteen seconds sped by, then thirty. *Don't make me use that cold water. And I'd rather cut off my own hand than slap you.* He heard the boys come in and call from the other side of the door. They scarcely registered. His heart raced. Desperation clawed at him. He gave the baby a shake. *Breathe, dammit, breathe!* Panicking now, he tossed her a foot in the air and caught her as she dropped. A second after she hit his hands her mouth opened, she hiccuped, started flailing with all fours and began bawling in the puniest voice imaginable. It came in undulations—wauu, wauu, wauu— accompanied by a comical face with pinched mouth, flattened nose and the beat of her tiny fists against the air. It was a soft cry, but healthy and wonderfully vexed at being treated so roughly during her first minute in the outside world.

Will looked down into the bloody face, heard the welcome complaint and laughed. In relief. In celebration. He kissed the miniature nose and said, "Way to go, girl. That's what we wanted to hear." Then, to his wife, "She's breathing, and beautiful and looks as normal as a one-dollar bill." Abruptly his mood sobered. "Elly, you're shivering." During the minute he'd concentrated on his duty, she'd been gripped by natural chills. She lay now shuddering, her exposed limbs damp, the bedding beneath her soaked. Lord, a man needed six hands at a time like this.

"I'll be all right," Elly assured him. "Take care of her first."

It was hard to do, but he had little choice, given the fact that Elly's directive agreed with those he'd memorized. So far things had gone in perfect, natural order. He'd proceed by the book and hope their luck held. But he paused long enough to lay the baby down and gently remove Elly's legs from the tug straps, lower them and cover her. He brushed a light kiss on her dry lips, and whispered, "I'll be back as soon as I get her bathed. You be okay?"

She nodded weakly and closed her eyes.

He crooked the baby in one arm, opened the door with the other and found Donald Wade and Thomas on the other side, holding hands and crying pitifully.

"We heard Mama scream."

"She's better now—look." Will knelt. The sight of the red, squawling baby stopped their crying with amusing suddenness. "You got a baby sister." Donald

Wade's mouth dropped open. The tears hung on Baby Thomas's sooty lashes. Neither of them spoke a word. "She just got here."

As one, they resumed bawling.

"I wanna see Mamaaaa!"

"Maamaaa!"

"She's fine—see?" Will held the door open a crack and let them peek inside for reassurance. All they saw was their mother lying at rest with her eyes closed. Will closed the door. "Shh. She's restin' now, but we'll all go in later and see her, soon as we get the baby a bath. Come on now, you might have to help me."

They followed as if mesmerized. "In the real bathtub?"

"No, the real one ain't ready yet."

"In the sink?"

"Yep."

They screeched chairs across the kitchen floor and stood one on either side of Will as he lowered their sister into a dishpan of warm water. Her crying stopped immediately. Cradled in Will's long hands, she stretched, opened dark eyes and peered at the world for the first time. Thomas reached out a tentative finger as if to test her for realness.

"Uh-uh. Mustn't touch her yet." Thomas withdrew the finger and gazed up at Will respectfully.

"Where'd she come from?" asked Donald Wade.

"From inside your mother."

Donald Wade looked skeptical. "She din't neither."

Will laughed and gently swished the baby through the water.

"She sure did. Been curled up inside her like a little butterfly inside a cocoon. You seen a cocoon, haven't you?" Of course they had. With a mother like theirs, the boys had been watching cocoons since they were old enough to say the word. "If a butterfly can come out of a cocoon, why can't a little sister come out of a mother?"

Because neither could answer, they believed.

Then Donald Wade remarked, "She ain't got no wink!"

"She's a girl. Girls don't have winks."

Donald Wade stared at his sister's pink skin. He looked up at Will. "She gonna get one?"

"Nope."

Donald Wade scratched his head, then pointed. "What's that?"

"It's gonna be her belly button."

"Oh." And after some thought, "Don't look like mine."

"It will."

"What's her name?"

"You'll have to ask your mother that."

The baby hiccuped and the boys laughed, then stood by watchfully while Will washed her with glycerine soap. He spread it over the pulsing scalp, down the spindly legs, between tiny toes and miniature fingers that had to be forced open. So fragile, so perfect. He had never felt skin so soft, never handled anything so delicate. Within the length of time it took to bathe her for the first time the tiny being had worked her way so deeply into Will's heart she'd never lose her place there. No matter that she wasn't his own. In his heart she was. He'd delivered her! He'd forced her to breathe her first breath, given her her first bath! A man couldn't have a heart this full and care about whose seed had spawned the life that was bringing this bursting sense of fulfillment to him. This little girl would have a father in Will Parker, and she'd know the love of two parents.

He laid her on a soft towel, cleaned her face and ears and dried all the nooks and crannies, experiencing a growing ebullience that put a soft smile on his face. She grew chilled and began crying in chuffy, hiccuping spurts.

"Hey there, darlin', the worst is over," Will murmured. "Get y' warm in a minute." He surprised himself by delighting in this first monologue to the infant. A person couldn't *not* talk to somethin' sweet as this, he realized.

Will carefully tended her cord, applying alcohol, and a cotton bandage, then Vaseline against her stomach before tying the bandage down and diapering her for the first time. She recoiled like a spring every time he tried to maneuver his hand into position for pinning. The boys giggled. She retracted her arms while he tried to feed them into her tiny undershirt and kimono. The boys giggled some more. When Will reached for one pink bootie, Donald Wade was proudly waiting to hand it to him.

"Thanks, *kemo sabe,*" Will said, and tied the booty on a skinny ankle. Thomas was waiting to hand him the other.

"Thanks, Thomas," he said, roughing the boy's hair.

When the baby was ready to present to her mother, Will picked her up carefully. "Now your mother wants to see her, and in about fifteen minutes or so she'll want to see you, so you both wash your hands and comb your hair and wait in your room. I'll call you when she's ready, okay?"

Pausing before the closed bedroom door, Will studied the baby who stared at him with unfocused eyes. She lay still, silent, her fists closed like rosebuds, her hair fine as cobwebs. He shut his eyes and kissed her forehead. She smelled better than anything else in the world. Better than sizzling bacon. Better than baking bread. Better than fresh air.

"You're somethin' precious," he whispered, feeling his heart swell with love so unexpected it made his eyes sting. "I think you'n me are gonna git along just fine."

Then he nudged the bedroom door open, stepped inside and closed it with his back.

Elly lay slumbering. She looked haggard and exhausted.

"Elly-honey?"

She opened her eyes and saw him standing with the baby in his arms, his shirt damp in spots, the sleeves rolled to the elbow, his hair messy and a soft smile on his lips.

"Will," she breathed, smiling, holding out an arm.

"Here she is. And more presentable now." He placed the bundle in Elly's arm and watched her tuck the blanket away from the baby's chin for a better look. Within him sprang a wellspring of emotion. Love for the woman, welcome for the baby, and in a corner of his soul, the lonely plaint of a man who would always wonder if his own mother had ever held him that way, smiled at him with such sweetness, explored his face with a fingertip and kissed his forehead with the reverence that brought a choking sensation as he looked on.

Probably not. He knelt beside the bed and folded aside the opposite edge of the soft flannel receiving blanket. Probably not. But he'd make up for it by watching Elly lavish this precious one with the love he'd never known.

"Oh, Will, isn't she pretty?"

"She sure is. Just like you."

Elly lifted her gaze and let it drop as the baby's fist closed around her little finger. "Oh, I'm not pretty, Will."

"I always thought you were."

The baby's other hand took Will's finger. Linked by her, the man and wife shared an interlude of closeness. Reluctantly, Will ended it.

"I'd better tend to you now, don't you think? Get you washed, and in some clean clothes."

Elly regretfully relinquished the baby, and Will laid her in the basket. Kneeling beside it on one knee, he adjusted the pink shawl around her tiny form, touched her hair with a fingertip and murmured, "Sleep now, precious one."

He rose to find Elly's eyes on him and experienced a brief stab of self-consciousness. He was a man who'd had to learn how to talk to the boys, who'd taken weeks to feel comfortable with them. Yet here he was, after less than an hour, murmuring soft things to the baby girl who couldn't even understand. His thumbs went to his rear pockets in the unconscious gesture that said Will Parker was out of his depth.

"I put her on her stomach like you said." Deep love softened Elly's smile while he stood fidgeting. "I—I'll get your bathwater and—and be right back," he sputtered.

"I love you, Will," she said. She knew the look well, the pacified one that overcame him when things got too perfect for him to contain. She knew the stance, the thumbs-in-the-pocket, still-as-a-shadow suppression that said things were working inside him, good things he sometimes failed yet to believe. That was when she wanted him close enough to touch.

"Come here first." He approached but stood a safe distance, as if touching the bed would damage her. "Here, beside me."

He sat gingerly on the edge of the mattress and she had to reach up and pull him down before she could give the hug she knew he needed.

"You done good, Will. You done so good."

"I'll hurt you, Elly, layin' on you this way."

"Never."

Suddenly they were hugging fiercely. He turned his face against her ear. "Jesus, she's so beautiful."

"I know. It's a miracle, ain't it?"

"I never knew I'd feel that way when I held her the first time. It didn't matter that she wasn't mine. It was as if she really was."

"I know. You can love her all you want, Will, and we'll pretend that she is. A year from now she'll be callin' you Daddy."

He squeezed his eyes shut and pressed his mouth to Elly's temple, then forced himself to sit up. "I best get that warm water now, little mother. The boys are waitin' to come in and see you."

With a soft cloth and the baby's soap, he sponged Elly's tired limbs and sore flesh. Of the comfrey he fashioned a poultice, laid it on her torn skin and secured it with a cotton pledget and her plain cotton undergarments. He helped her don a clean white brassiere, clasping it for her before holding a fresh nightgown and watching her slip it on. He changed the bed and lifted Elly back into it before carrying out the soiled sheets to soak and finally going to fetch the boys, who'd waited in their rooms with the mysterious docility lent to children by solemn occasions.

"Ready?"

They nodded silently. Will hid a smile: Donald Wade had combed his own and Thomas's hair, slicking it down with water until both heads looked flat as wheat in a cyclone.

"Your mother's waiting."

They paused inside their mother's bedroom door, holding Will's hands, glancing up at him questioningly.

"Go on then, but don't bounce on the bed."

They perched one on each side of Elly, studying her as if she'd turned into a character from one of her own fables, someone magical and shining.

"Hi," she said, taking their hands.

They stared as if mute.

"Did you see your li'l sister?"

"We hepped Wiw give her a baff."

"And we helped him dress 'er."

"I know. Will told me. He said you both done good." They smiled, proud. "Would you like to see her again?"

They nodded like horses making a harness jingle. Elly told Will, "Bring her here, honey."

She was asleep. When he laid her in the crook of Elly's arm her fist went to her mouth and she sucked hard enough to make noise. The boys laughed and Will knelt beside the bed, leaning forward on his elbows. For minutes they all studied the baby while awe stole their voices.

At last Elly asked, "What should we name her?" She glanced up. "You know a pretty name, Will?" But his mind went blank. "How 'bout you, Donald Wade, what do you wanna call her?"

Donald Wade had no more notion that Will.

"You got a name, Thomas?"

Of course he didn't. She'd asked him out of courtesy, so he wouldn't feel left out. Touching the baby's hair with a knuckle, Elly said, "I been thinkin' about Lizzy. What you all think o' that?"

"Lizzy?" Donald Wade scrunched up his nose.

"Lizzy the lizard?" Thomas put in.

They all laughed. "Now, where'd you get that?"

Donald Wade reminded her, "From the story you told us about how the lizard got bumps."

"Oh . . ." She continued fondling the fine black hair on the baby's head. "No, this one'll just be Lizzy. Elizabeth Parker, I think."

Will's eyes shot to Elly's. "Parker?"

"Well, you delivered her, didn't you? Man deserves some credit for a thing like that."

Lord, in a minute he was gonna burst. This woman would give him everything. Everything, before she was through! He reached for the baby's head and stroked her temple with the back of a finger. *Lizzy,* he thought. *Lizzy P. You'n me gonna be buddies, darlin'.* He stretched one hand to Elly's hair, and circled Donald Wade's rump with his free arm and touched Thomas's leg, on the far side of Elly. And he smiled at Lizzy P. and thought, *Heaven's got nothin' on being the husband of Eleanor Dinsmore.*

Chapter 14

Will's smile announced the news to Miss Beasley even before his words. "She had a girl."

"And *you* delivered her."

He shrugged and quirked his head at an angle. "It wasn't so hard after all."

"Don't be so humble, Mr. Parker. *I* would collapse in fright if I had to deliver a baby. It went all right?"

"Perfect. Started yesterday around noon and ended around three-thirty. Her name's Lizzy."

"Lizzy. Very fetching."

"Lizzy P."

"Lizzy P." She cocked an eyebrow.

"Yes'm." He fairly twitched with excitement, a rare thing.

"And what is the P for?"

"Parker. Feature that—she named that little girl after me. After a no-count drifter who doesn't even know where he got that name. Wait'll you see her, Miss Beasley, she's got hair black as coal and fingernails so small you can hardly find 'em. I never saw a baby up close before! She's incredible."

Miss Beasley beamed, hiding a swift pang of regret for the child she'd never had, the husband who'd never rejoiced over it.

"You must congratulate Eleanor for me and tell her I'll expect Lizzy to begin visiting the library no later than her fifth birthday. You cannot get a child interested in books too early."

"I'll tell 'er, Miss Beasley."

Those were special days and nights, immediately after the baby's birth—Will awakening to the sound of Lizzy tuning up in the basket, rising with Elly to turn her over and talk soft nonsense to her. The two of them together, laughing when the cold air hit the baby's skin and her face puckered in preparation for the adorable soft sobbing that hadn't yet grown to be an irritation. And each morning, Will cooking breakfast for the boys, delivering Elly a tray and a kiss, then giving Lizzy P. her bath before washing diapers and hanging them out to dry. He changed Lizzy's diaper whenever Elly didn't beat him to it. He dusted the house and put the bluebird on her bedside table. He sterilized the rubber nipples and prepared the watered-down milk and got the bottles ready during the days before Elly's milk came in. He prepared supper and got the boys all fed and changed into pajamas before kissing them and Elly and Lizzy goodbye and heading into town.

But afterward was best. After the long day when he'd return and there'd be lazy minutes lying in bed with the baby between Elly and him while they watched her sleep, or hiccup, or cross her eyes or suck her fist. And they'd dream about her future and theirs, and look into each other's eyes and wonder if there'd be another like her, one of their own.

They had three such glorious days before the bombs fell.

On Sunday "Ma Trent" wasn't on, but Elly was lying in bed listening to the Columbia Broadcast System while the New York Philharmonic tuned up for Symphony #1 by somebody called Shostakovich when John Daly's voice announced, "The Japanese have attacked Pearl Harbor!"

At first Elly didn't fully understand. Then the tension in Daly's voice struck home and she sat up abruptly. "Will! Come quick!"

Thinking something was amiss with her or the baby, he came on the run. "What's wrong?"

"They bombed us!"

"Who?"

"The Japanese—listen!"

They listened, like all the rest of America, for the remainder of the day and evening. They heard of the sinking of five U.S. battleships on a peaceful Hawaiian island, of the destruction of 140 American aircraft and the loss of over 2,000 American lives. They heard the voice of Kate Smith singing "God Bless America" and the national army band playing the "Star-Spangled Banner." They heard of blackout alerts along the western seaboard, where a Japanese invasion was feared and where thousands rushed to volunteer for the armed forces. There were amazing stories of men rising from restaurant tables, leaving unfinished plates, walking to the closest recruiting office to find the line of volunteers—within an hour of the first radio reports—already eight city blocks long.

In Whitney, Georgia—a short plane ride from another vulnerable shore—Will and Elly turned out the lights early and went to bed wondering what the next day would bring.

It brought the voice of President Roosevelt.

"Yesterday, December 7, 1941—a date which will live in infamy—the United States of America was suddenly and deliberately attacked by naval and air forces of the Empire of Japan. In addition, American ships have been reported torpedoed on the high seas between San Francisco and Honolulu.

"Yesterday the Japanese Government also launched an attack against Malaya.

"Last night Japanese forces attacked Hong Kong.

"Last night Japanese forces attacked Guam.

"Last night Japanese forces attacked the Philippine Islands.

"Last night the Japanese attacked Wake Island.

"This morning the Japanese attacked Midway Island. . . . Hostilities exist. There is no blinking at the fact that our people, our territory, and our interests are in grave danger.

"With confidence in our armed forces—with the unbounded determination of our people—we will gain the inevitable triumph—so help us God.

"I ask that the Congress declare that since the unprovoked and dastardly attack by Japan on Sunday, December seventh, a state of war has existed between the United States and the Japanese Empire."

Will and Elly stared at the radio. At each other.

Not now, she thought. *Not now, when everything just got right.*

So this is it, he thought. *I'll go just like hundreds of others are going.*

He was surprised to find himself fired with some of the same outrage as that conflagrating through the rest of America: for the first time Will felt the righteousness of President Roosevelt's "Four Freedoms" because for the first time he enjoyed them all. And being a family man made them the more dear.

In bed that night he lay awake and thoughtful. Elly lay tense. After a long silence she rolled to him and held him possessively.

"Will you have to go?"

"Shh."

"But you're a father now. How could they take a father with a brand-new baby and two others to see after?"

"I'm thirty. I'm registered. The draft law says twenty-one to thirty-five."

"Maybe they won't call you up."

"We'll worry about it when the time comes."

Minutes later, when they'd lain clutching hands in the silence, he told her, "I'm gonna get that generator goin' for you, and fix up a refrigerator and an electric washer and make sure everything's in perfect shape around the place."

She gripped his hand and rolled her face against his arm. "No, Will . . . no."

At one in the morning, when Lizzy woke up hungry, Will asked Elly to leave the lamp on. In the pale amber lantern glow he lay on his side and watched her nurse the baby, watched the small white fists push the blue-tinged breast, watched the pocket-gopher cheeks bulge and flatten as they drew sustenance, watched Elly's fingers shape a stand-up curl on Lizzy's delicate head.

He thought of all he had to live for. All he had to fight for. It was only a matter of making Elly and the kids secure before he left.

The radio was never off after that. Day by day they heard of an unprepared America at war. In Washington, D.C., soldiers took up posts at key government centers, wearing World War I helmets and carrying ancient Springfield rifles, while on December eighth Japanese bombers struck two U.S. airfields in the Philippines and on the tenth Japanese forces began to land on Luzon.

At first it all seemed remote to Elly, but Will brought the newspapers home from the library and studied the Japanese movement on tiny maps which brought the war closer. He worked in the town hall where recruiters were already posted twelve hours a day. Billboards out front and in the vestibule entreated, DEFEND YOUR COUNTRY—ENLIST NOW—U.S. ARMY. Across America it continued. The outrage. The bristling. The growing American frenzy to "join up."

Will found himself in a frenzy of his own—to get things done.

He finished the wind generator and hooked it to the radio because their batteries were nearly worn out and new ones unobtainable. Since the wind generator wouldn't create enough electricity to power larger appliances, he installed a gasoline-driven motor on an old hand-operated agitator washing machine and fashioned a homemade water heater fueled by kerosene. It stood beside the tub like a gangly monster with a drooping snout. The day he filled the bathtub for the first time they celebrated. The boys took the first baths, followed by Elly and finally by Will himself. But there was no denying that the elation they'd expected upon using the tub for the first time was tempered by the unspoken realization of why Will was hurrying to get so much done around the place.

Miss Beasley came to call when Lizzy was ten days old, surprising everyone. She brought a sweater and bootee set for the baby and *Timothy Totter's Tatters* for the boys—not the library copy but a brand-new one they could keep. They were awed by a stranger bringing them a gift and by the book itself and the idea that it belonged to them. Miss Beasley got them set up studying the pictures with a promise to read the book aloud as soon as she'd visited with their mother.

"So you're up and about again," she said to Eleanor.

"Yes. Will spoils me silly, though."

"A woman deserves a little spoiling occasionally." Without the slightest hint of warmth in her voice she dictated, "Now, I should very much like to see that young one of yours."

"Oh . . . of course. Come, she's in our bedroom."

Elly led the way and Will followed, standing back with his hands in his rear pockets while Miss Beasley leaned over the laundry basket and inspected the sleeping face. She crossed her hands over her stomach, stepped back and declared, "You have a beautiful child there, Eleanor."

"Thank you, Miss Beasley. She's a good sleeper, too."

"A blessing, I'm sure."

"Yes'm, she is."

To Will's surprise, Miss Beasley informed Elly, "Mr. Parker was quite, quite pleased that you named the child after him."

"He was?" Elly peeked over her shoulder at Will, who smiled and shrugged.

"He most certainly was."

Silence fell, strained, before Elly thought to offer, "Got some fresh gingerbread and hot coffee if you'd like."

"I'm quite partial to gingerbread, thank you."

They all trooped back to the kitchen and Will watched Elly nervously serve the sweet and coffee and perch on the edge of her chair like a bird ready to take wing. Given a choice, she would probably have forgone this entire visit, but nobody turned Miss Beasley out of the house, not even out of the bedroom when she came to call. Will studied the librarian covertly, but she rarely glanced his way. The entire get-together was being carried out with the same pedantic formality with which Miss Beasley conducted a library tour for the children. It struck him that she was no more comfortable being here than Elly was having her. So why had she come? Duty only, because he worked for her?

Eventually the talk turned to the war and how it was spawning the most fierce patriotism in memorable history. "They're signing up as if it was a free-ice-cream line," Miss Beasley said. "Five more today from Whitney alone. James Burcham, Milford Dubois, Voncile Potts and two of the Sprague boys. Poor Esther Sprague—first a husband and now two sons. Rumor has it that Harley Overmire received a draft notice, too." Miss Beasley didn't gloat, but Will had the impression she wanted to.

"I've been worried about Will maybe having to go," Eleanor confided.

"So have I. But a man will do what he must, and so will a woman, when the time comes."

Was this, then, why she'd come, to prepare Elly because she already guessed his decision was made? To ease into Elly's confidence because she knew Elly would need a friend when he was gone? Will's heart warmed toward the plump woman who ate gingerbread with impeccable manners while a tiny dot of whipped cream rested on the fine hair of her upper lip.

In that moment he loved her and realized leaving her would make his going more difficult. Yet leave them he would, for it had already become understood that to be of military age and not join up was to be physically or mentally impaired, or the subject of suspicion and innuendo about one's condition and courage.

Right after Christmas, Will decided. He'd wait until then to talk to a recruiter and to tell Elly. They deserved *one* Christmas together anyway.

He threw himself into holiday plans, wanting all the traditional trappings—the food, the tree, the gifts, the celebration—in case he never had the chance again. He made a scooter for the boys and bought them Holloway suckers, Cracker

Jacks, Bunte's Tango bars and Captain Marvel comic books. For Elly he bought something frivolous—the popular Chinese Checker game. It took two to play Chinese Checkers, but he bought it anyway as a portent of hope for his return.

December 22 brought news that a large Japanese landing had been staged just north of Manila. On Christmas Eve came news of another, just south of that city, which was in danger of falling to the enemy.

After that Elly and Will made a pact to leave the radio off for the remainder of the holiday and concentrate on the boys' enthusiasm.

But she knew. Somehow, she knew.

Filling the stockings, Elly looked up and watched Will drop in a handful of roasted peanuts, nearly as excited as if the stocking were his instead of Thomas's. She felt a stinging at the back of her nose and went to him before any telltale evidence formed in her eyes. She laid her cheek against his chest and said, "I love you, Will."

He toyed with her hair as she stood lightly against him. "I love you, too."

Don't go, she didn't say.

I have to, he didn't reply.

And in moments they returned to filling the stockings.

For Will, Christmas morning was bittersweet, watching the boys' eyes light up at the sight of the scooter, laughing while they dug into their stockings, holding them—still in their pajamas—on his lap while they sampled the candy and ogled the comic books. These were firsts for Will. He lived them vicariously with Donald Wade and Thomas as he himself never had as a boy.

Elly gave him a mail-order shirt which he wore while they played Chinese Checkers and the boys rode their scooters across the living room and kitchen floor.

For dinner they had no traditional turkey. Will had offered to take Glendon's old double-bore shotgun and try his hand at bagging one, but Elly would hear none of it.

"One of my birds? You want to shoot one of my wild turkeys, Will Parker? I should say not. We'll have pork." And they did.

Pork and cornbread stuffing and fried okra and quince pie with Miss Beasley as their guest.

Miss Beasley, who had celebrated so many wretched Christmases alone that she glowed like a neon light when Will came to pick her up in the auto. Miss Beasley, who had actually *excited* Elly about having an outsider at her table for a meal. Miss Beasley, who brought gifts: for Elly a beautiful seven-piece china tea set decorated with yellow birds and clover on a background of tan luster; for Will a pair of capeskin gloves; for the boys a pair of glass and Pyralin automobiles filled with colorful soft cream candies shaped like elephants, horns, guns and turtles, and a new book, *'Twas the Night Before Christmas,* which she read to them after dinner.

Christmas, 1941 . . . over too soon.

When Will returned Miss Beasley to her brick bungalow on Durbin Street, he wore his new gloves and walked her to the door.

"I want to thank you for all the gifts you brought."

"Nonsense, Mr. Parker. It is I who should be thanking you."

"These gloves're . . ." He smacked them together and rubbed them appreciatively. "Why, they're just . . . heck, I don't even know what to say. Nobody ever gave me anything so fine before. I felt awful 'cause we didn't give you anything."

"Didn't *give* me anything? Mr. Parker, do you know how many Christmases I've spent alone since my mother passed away? Twenty-three. Perhaps an intelligent man like you can figure out exactly what it is you and Eleanor gave me today."

She often said things like that, calling him an intelligent man. Things no other person had ever said to Will, things that made him feel good about himself. Looking into her fuzzy face, he clearly understood what today had meant to her, though her expression would never show it. She remained as persimonny-mouthed as ever. He wondered what she'd do if he leaned over and kissed her. Probably cuff him upside the head.

"Elly, she didn't know what to make of that tea set. I never saw her eyes grow so big."

"You know what to make of it though, don't you?"

He studied her eyes for a long moment. They both knew; that when he was gone Elly would need a friend. Someone to have tea with perhaps.

"Yes, ma'am, I reckon I do," Will answered softly. Then he put his gloved hands on Miss Beasley's arms and did what his heart dictated: he placed an affectionate kiss on her cheek.

She didn't cuff him.

She turned the color of a gooseberry and blinked rapidly three times, then scuttled into the house, forgetting to bid him goodbye.

Within five weeks after Pearl Harbor Bell Aircraft built a huge new bomber factory in Marietta. The last civilian auto rolled off the assembly lines in Detroit, and Japan had seized Malaya and the Dutch East Indies, cutting off ninety percent of America's rubber supply. National Price Administrator Leon Henderson was pictured in every newspaper in America pedaling his "Victory bicycle" as a stand-in for the automobile. The wealthy deserted their St. Simons Island mansions as German submarines began patrolling the coast, and the people of Georgia organized the Georgia State Guard, a citizens' army composed of those too young, too old, or too unfit for the draft, who set about preparing coastal defenses for an anticipated German invasion. Georgia convicts were conscripted and put to work round the clock to improve seashore approaches and build bridges over which the homegrown army would defend their state.

And up at the mill one day Harley Overmire set his jaw, shut his eyes and ran his trigger finger through a buzz saw.

The news had a curious effect on Will. It galvanized his intentions. He decided suddenly that not only would he join up, but he'd join the toughest branch—the Marines—so that when he came back cowards like Overmire could never look down on him or his again. It seemed almost fated that the very day he made his decision the draft board made it irreversible. The letter began with the infamous word that had already taken thousands of men from their homes and families:

"GREETINGS . . ."

Will opened the draft notice alone, down by the mailbox, read the words and shut his eyes, breathing deep. He gazed at the Georgia sky, blue and sunny. He walked at a snail's pace up the red clay road and sat for five minutes beneath their favorite sourwood tree, listening to the redbirds, the winter quiet. He'd rather do anything than tell Elly. Rather *go* than tell her he had to.

She was nursing the baby when he returned to the house, lying diagonally on the bed. He stopped in the doorway and studied her, impressing the image in his memory for bleaker days—a woman in a faded print dress with the buttons freed, her hair in a loose tan braid, one arm crooked beneath her ear, the infant at her breast. A lump formed in Will's throat as he knelt beside the bed and laid the backside of a finger on Lizzy's pumping cheek, then skimmed it over her delicate skin. He leaned on his elbows close to Elly's head, his gaze still resting on the nursing infant.

Don't tell her yet.

"She's growin', isn't she?" he murmured.

"Mm-hmm."

"How long will you nurse her?"

"Till she gets teeth."

"When will that be?"

"Oh, when she's about seven, eight months."

I wanted to be here to see every new tooth.

His knuckle moved from the baby's cheek to his wife's breast.

"This is my favorite way to find you when I come in. I could watch this till the grass grew right up over the porch step and into the house and never get tired of it."

She rolled her head to study him, but his eyes followed his finger, which glided over her full breast.

"And I reckon I'd never get tired of you watchin', Will," she told him softly.

Elly, Elly, I don't wanna go but I got to.

Contemplating mortality made a man say things he otherwise would hold inside. "I wondered so many times if my mother ever held me, if she nursed me, if she was sorry to give me up. I wonder every time I watch you with Lizzy."

"Oh, Will . . ." She touched his cheek tenderly.

At that moment his feelings for her were convoluted and he struggled to understand them. She was his wife, not his mother, yet he loved her as if she were both. For some ungraspable reason he thought she had a right to know that before he left. "Sometimes I think I halfway wanted to marry you 'cause you were such a good mother and I never had one. I know that sounds strange, but I . . . well, I just wanted to tell you."

"I know, Will."

His head lifted and their eyes met at last. "You know?"

Her thumb brushed his lower lip. "Reckon I knew all the time. I figured it out when I washed your hair the first time. But I knew it wasn't the only reason. I figured that out, too."

He stretched to kiss her, his shoulder pocketing Lizzy's head while the sound of her suckling and swallowing continued. He would never forget this moment, the smell of the baby and the woman, the warmth of the one against his shoulder, the other beneath his hand, which rested on her warm hair. When the kiss ended he stared into Elly's green eyes while his thumb idled on the part in her hair. Slowly he collapsed to rest facedown against the mattress, still embracing them both.

"Will, what's wrong?"

He swallowed, his face flattened into the bedding, which smelled of them and of baby powder.

"You picked up the mail, didn't you?"

His thumb wagged across her skull. Tears stung his eyes but he pinched them inside. No man cried, not these days. They marched off to war triumphant.

"I was thinkin'," she continued chokily, "maybe I'll make a quince pie for supper. I know how you like your quince pie."

He thought of prison mess halls and soldiers' rations and Elly's quince pie with a lattice crust, and worked hard to keep his breath steady. *How long? How long?* The baby stopped suckling and heaved a delicate, broken sigh. Will pictured her milky mouth falling gently from Elly's skin and turned his temple to the mattress. Opening his eyes, he saw Elly's nipple at close range, almost violet in hue, still puckered while Lizzy's moist lips occasionally sucked from an inch away.

"I promised the boys I'd take 'em to a movie one day. I got to be sure to do that."

"They'd like that."

Silence settled, growing oppressive. "Can I come along?" she asked.

"Movie wouldn't be no fun without you."

They both smiled sadly. When the smiles faded they listened to each other breathe, absorbing the nearness and dearness of each other, storing memories against lorn days.

"I have to teach you to drive the car," he said at length.

"And I got to give you that birthday party I promised."

They lay in silence a long time before Elly uttered a desolate throaty sound, reached up and gripped the back of Will's jacket. Burying her face in the bedding, she held him so and grieved.

Later he showed her the letter and while she read it told her, "I'm volunteering for the Marines, Elly."

"The Marines! But why?"

"Because I can be a good one. Because I already had the training my whole life long. Because bastards like Overmire are cuttin' off their trigger fingers and I want to make sure his kind can never make degrading remarks about me or you again."

"But I don't care what Harley Overmire says about us."

"I do."

Her expression soured as the hurt set in: he'd made such a decision without consulting her, to jeopardize the life she now valued more than her own. "And I don't have anything to say about it, whether you go to the Army or the Marines?"

His face closed over, much as it had beneath his cowboy hat during his first days here. "No, ma'am."

He had nine days, nine bittersweet days during which they never spoke the word war. Nine days during which Elly remained cool, hurt. He took the family to the movie, as promised—Bud Abbott and Lou Costello. The boys laughed while Will took Eleanor's unresponsive hand and held it as both of them tried to forget the newsreel which showed scenes of the Pearl Harbor attack and other actions in the Pacific that had occurred since America had entered the war.

He taught Elly to drive the car but couldn't get her to promise she'd use it to go into town in case of an emergency. Even while practicing, she refused to leave their own land. In other days, under other circumstances, the lessons might have been a source of amusement, but with both of them counting down the hours, laughter was at a premium.

He put up more cordwood, wondering how many months she'd be alone, how long the supply would last, what she'd do when it was gone.

She gave him a birthday party on January 29, three days before he was due to leave. Miss Beasley came, and they used the new china tea set, but the occasion held an undertone of gloom, this arbitrary day of celebration for a man who'd never celebrated his birth before, celebrating it now because it might be his last chance.

Then came his last night at the library. Miss Beasley was waiting when he arrived for work and gave Will his last paycheck with as much warmth as General MacArthur issuing an order. "Your job will be waiting when you get back, Mr. Parker." No matter what her feelings for Will, she'd never used his familiar name. It wouldn't have seemed right to either of them.

He stared at the check while his throat tightened. "Thank you, Miss Beasley."

"I thought, if it's all right with you, I'd come down to the train station to see you off tomorrow."

He forced a smile, meeting her eyes. "That'd be nice, ma'am. I'm not sure Elly will make it."

"She still refuses to come to town?"

"Yes, ma'am," he replied quietly.

"Oh, that child!" Miss Beasley grasped her hands and began pacing in agitation. "At times I'd like to sit her down for a stern lecture."

"It wouldn't do any good, ma'am."

"Does she think she can hide in that woods forever?"

"Looks that way." Will studied the floor. "Ma'am, there's somethin' I got to ask you. Somethin' I been wonderin' for a long time." He scratched the end of his nose and looked anywhere but at her. "That day when that woman Lula was in here, I know you heard what she said to me about Elly, about how her family locked her in that house on the edge of town and that's why everybody calls her crazy. Is it true?"

"You mean she's never told you?"

Lifting his gaze, Will slowly wagged his head.

Miss Beasley considered at length, then ordered, "Sit down, Mr. Parker."

They sat on opposite sides of a study table amid the smell of wax and oil and books. Outside, plodding hooves sounded on the street, merchants closed their shops and went home for supper, an auto rumbled past and faded while Miss Beasley considered Will's question.

"Why hasn't she told you?"

"I don't rightly know, ma'am. It must bother her to talk about it. She's got touchy feelin's."

"It should be her place to tell you."

"I know that, ma'am, but if she hasn't yet I doubt she will tonight, and I'd sure like to know before I leave."

Miss Beasley debated silently, staring Will full in the face. Her lips pursed, relaxed, then pursed again. "Very well, I'll tell you." She twined her fingers and rested them on the tabletop with the air of a judge resting a gavel.

"Her mother was a local girl who became pregnant out of wedlock and was sent away by her parents to have the child. Eleanor was the result of that pregnancy. When she was born, Chloe See—that was her mother—brought her back here to Whitney. On the train, the story goes. They were picked up at the depot by Eleanor's grandparents and whisked off in a carriage with the black shades securely drawn, and taken to their house—the same one that still stands on the outskirts of town. Lottie See, Eleanor's grandmother, pulled down the shades and never pulled them up again.

"Albert See and his wife were queer people, to say the least. He was a circuit preacher, so it was understandably difficult for them to accept Chloe's illegitimate child. But they went beyond the bounds of reason by keeping their daughter a virtual prisoner in that house until the day she died. People say she went crazy in there and Eleanor watched it happen. Naturally, they thought the same thing of poor Eleanor, living all those years with the rest of that eccentric bunch.

"They might have kept Eleanor locked up forever, but the law forced them to let her out to go to school. That's of course when I first met her, when she came here to the library with her classes.

"The children were merciless to Eleanor, you yourself know *how* cruel after what that—that painted hussy Lula Peak spewed out to you in this very building."

Miss Beasley tucked her chin back severely, creating bifolds beneath it. "With lit-tle more provocation I would have slapped that woman's face that day. She's a—a—" Miss Beasley puffed up and turned red, then forcibly squelched her choler. "If I were to express my true feeling for Lula Peak it would make me a twattler no better than she, so I'll restrain myself. Now where was I?

"Oh, yes—Eleanor. She wasn't gregarious like the rest of the children. She didn't know how to blend, having come out of the home life she did. She was dreamy and stared a lot. So the children called her crazy. How she endured those days I don't know. But she was—underneath her dreaminess—intelligent and re-silient, apparently. She made out all right.

"This is all heresay, mind you, but the story goes that Albert See had a mistress somewhere. A black mistress in whose bed he died. The shame of it finally tipped his wife over the edge, and she became as tetched as her own daughter, hiding in that house, speaking to no one, mumbling prayers. All of Eleanor's family died within three years, but it was their deaths that finally freed her.

"How she knew Glendon Dinsmore, I can only guess. He delivered ice, you know, so I suppose he was one of the few people ever allowed into that house. Albert See died in 1933, his wife in '34 and his daughter in '35. The women died right in that house that had become their prison. It wasn't a week after Chloe's death that Eleanor married Glendon and moved to the place where you live now. Her grandparents' house has sat vacant all these years. Unfortunately, it keeps people's memories alive. I sometimes think it would be better for Eleanor if it had been torn down."

So now he knew. He sat digesting it, damning people he'd never known, won-dering at cruelties too bizarre to comprehend.

"Thank you for telling me, Miss Beasley."

"Understand, I would not have if it weren't for this . . . this damned war."

In all the time he'd known her she'd never spoken an unladylike word. Her doing so now created an intimacy of sorts, an unspoken understanding that his leaving would break not one but two hearts. He reached across the table and took her hands, squeezing hard.

"You've been good to us. I'll never forget that."

She allowed her hands to be held for several wrenching seconds, then withdrew them and rose staunchly, affecting a stern voice to cover her emotionalism.

"Now get out of here. Go home to your wife. A library's no place to be spend-ing your last night at home."

"But, my check . . . I mean, you paid me for today and I didn't do my work."

"Haven't you learned after all this time that I don't like to be crossed, Mr. Parker? When I say get, I mean get."

He let a grin climb his cheek, tugged at the brim of his hat and replied, "Yes, ma'am."

He reached home in time to help Elly put the boys to bed. Last times. Last times. *I'm comin' home, boys, I'm by-God comin' back home 'cause you need me and I need you and I love doin' this too much to give it up forever.*

Without discussing it, Will and Elly closed the boys' bedroom door for the first time ever. They stood in the front room much as they had on their wedding night, tense and uncertain because she had been remote and cool toward him throughout their last precious days together and now their final night had come and they'd never made love.

Sand seemed to be falling through an hourglass.

He hooked his thumbs in his back pockets and stared at the back of Elly's head, at the nape of her neck bisected by one thick braid, fuzzy at the edges. He wanted so badly to do this right, the way this woman deserved.

"I like your hair in a braid," he began uncertainly, lifting it, feeling inept at this business of courting a wife. Had she been some harlot he'd have known the procedure, but he supposed it must be different when you cared this much.

Abruptly she spun and threw her arms around his neck. "Oh, Will, I'm sorry I've been so mean to you."

"You haven't been mean."

"Yes, I have, but I've been so scared."

"I know. So have I." He rocked her, arms doubled around her back, and dropped his nose to her neck. She smelled of homey things—supper and starched cotton and milk and babies. Ah, how he loved the smell of this woman. He straightened and held her cheeks, the drawn hair at her temples. "What do you say we take a bath together? I always wanted to do that."

"I have too."

"Why didn't you ever say so before?"

"I didn't know if people did that."

He catalogued her features, branding each in his memory, then replied softly, "I reckon they do, Elly."

"All right, Will." Her hands trailed down, catching one of his as she turned and led the way to the bathroom. Inside, he lit a lantern on a shoulder-high shelf while she knelt to place the plug in the tub and turn on the taps. He closed and locked the door, then leaned against it, watching her.

"Put in some Dreft," he said. "I never took a bath in bubbles."

Her head lifted sharply. He leaned against the door, freeing his cuff buttons, marveling that they could be shy after he had delivered her baby, washed her, cared for her. But sex was different.

She reached for the cardboard box which was wedged between the copper pipes and the end of the clawfoot tub. When the bubbles were rising, she stood, turned her back to Will and began unbuttoning her dress. He pushed away from the door and captured her shoulders, swinging her to face him.

"Let me, Elly. I never have before, but I'm gonna have the memory—just one time." Her dress was faded green, a housedress as ordinary as quack grass, with buttons running from throat to belly. He took over the task of freeing them, then pushed the garment off and let it fall to the floor. Without hesitation he lowered her half-slip, then held her hand and ordered, "Sit down." While she perched on the closed lid of the stool, he went down on his knee, removed her scuffed brown oxfords, her anklets, then stood and drew her to her feet, reached beneath her arms and unclasped her bra. Before it hit the floor he was skinning her last remaining garment down her legs.

He stood for a long moment, holding both her hands, letting his eyes drift over her—weighty breasts, enlarged nipples, rounded stomach and pale skin. Had he the power, he would not have changed one inch of her contour. It spoke of motherhood, the babies she'd had, the one she was nursing. He wished it had been his babies that had shaped her this way, but had it been so, he couldn't have loved her more. "I want to remember you this way."

"You're a sentimental fool, Will. I'm—"

"Shh. You're perfect, Elly . . . perfect."

She would never get used to his adoring her. Her eyes dropped shyly while beside them the water rumbled and the bubbles rose in a fragrant white cloud.

"Who's going to undress me?" he teased, wanting other memories to carry away. He tipped up her chin. "Elly?"

"Your wife," she answered quietly and did what she'd never done with Glendon, what Will had to teach her a man liked. Shirt, T-shirt, boots, socks and jeans. And the last piece of clothing, which hooked on something on its way down.

They stood a foot apart, heartbeats falling like hammerblows in the steamy room, studying each other's eyes while anticipation painted their cheeks shining pink. His head dipped, her face lifted and they kissed lingeringly, letting their bodies brush, swaying left and right, experiencing a hint of textures. Straightening, he slid his hands to her armpits, ordering, "Hang on," as he boosted her up. With her legs and arms wrapped around him, Will stepped into the tub. When he sat, the water rose to their elbows. She reached beneath his arms to turn off the taps, and when she would have backed up he clamped and held her there.

"Where you goin'?" he whispered near her lips.

"No place . . ." she breathed, closing the distance.

The first was a soft kiss—suspended anticipation. Two mouths, two tongues, sampling before the glut. With Eleanor's legs still looped about Will's waist, their intimacy below the water made mockery of their guardedness above. Still they played at the kiss, letting it laze as it would—crossed mouths, brushing lips, teasing tongues, then a lackadaisical repeat at a new angle. A nudge, a parting, a search of eyes, a sinking together once more.

She pressed her warm, wet palms to his back and he settled her breasts against his chest. She was smooth, he rough. She soft, he hard. The difference intensified the kiss. Eagerness fired it and he clasped her close, running hands and arms over her soapy skin above and below the water—sleek, warm wife's skin so different from his own. He acquainted himself with her flaring hips, narrowing waist, firm back and bulging breasts that ruched tightly at his touch.

The water lapped her breasts as she reached down to cup bubbles over his shoulders until his skin turned to satin beneath her hands. Her fingertips found the three moles on his back, three slick beads which she read as braille. Her palms skimmed his ribs, arms, shoulder blades, learning each dip and furl, each shift of muscle as his hands moved likewise over her.

With her legs she clung, compressing him, herself, so nearly joined that they could not tell her heat from his.

"It'll be all right tonight, won't it, Elly?"

"Yes . . . yes."

"Will it hurt you?"

"Shh . . ." She muffled his question with her kiss.

He pulled back. "I don't want to hurt you."

"Then come back to me alive."

Neither of them had voiced it before. Desperation now became part of their embrace while urgency moved their hands to fondle, explore, stroke. They drew deep breaths, holding momentarily still, the better to absorb the moment, the memory.

". . . ohhh . . ." she breathed, and her head dropped back until her braid touched the water.

He uttered a throaty approval, licked the underside of her chin and kissed what he could reach of her breasts. She was limp with acquiescence and he bade his time, pleasuring her, being pleasured, watching her eyelids flicker open, then close, her lips grow lax, her tongue tip appear as she drifted in a mindless torpor. In time she began moving, stirring the water until it lapped against his chest. Her caresses kept rhythm and he set his teeth, then arched like a strung bow.

The water became quicksilver. Tomorrow became an illusion. Here and now became the imperative.

"Oh, Elly, I wanted to do this so long ago."

"Why didn't you?"

"I was waiting for you to say it was all right."

"It would've been all right two weeks ago."

"Why didn't you say something?"

"I don't know . . . I was scared. Shy."

"Maybe I was, too. Let's not be shy."

"I never did things like this with Glendon."

"I can show you more."

She hid her face against his neck.

"Can I wash you?" he asked.

"You want to?"

"I want to be in you. That's what I want."

"That's what I want, too, so hurry."

They shared the soap. They shared each other. They got to their knees and forsook washcloths in favor of hands. They lathered and kissed, sleek as seals, and twined together and murmured sweet sentiments and adored with hands and tongues. And when the compulsion was magnified to a welcome ache, he grasped her wet arms and pushed her back, freeing his lips. "Let's go to bed."

They stood in the steamy bathroom, impatiently wielding towels, caring little about dry or wet, watching each other, grabbing a quick kiss, laughing excitedly— tense, aroused, ready. He plucked his jeans from the floor and found in a pocket a prophylactic.

"What's that?"

He closed it in his palm and looked at her. "I don't want to get you pregnant again. You got all you'll be able to handle with no man around the place."

"You won't need that."

"I don't want to leave you with another one, Elly."

She stepped across his wet towel, took the packet from his hand and laid it on the high shelf.

"Women don't get pregnant when they're nursing, didn't you know that, Will?"

By an arm she tried to lead him from the room, but he balked. "Are you sure?"

"I'm sure. Come."

He took the lantern and they tiptoed into their own bedroom. In it she turned, placed a finger over her lips and mouthed, "Shh." Each one taking an end of the basket, they moved Lizzy out into the front room for the night.

When their door was closed they turned to each other. Their pulses seemed to do a stutter step, but neither of them moved. Alone . . . suddenly hesitant. Until she took the first step and they came together swiftly, kissing and clinging, reminded again of the hourglass shifting its sand. So little time . . . so much love . . .

Impatiently he hooked her beneath her knees and carried her to the bed, whispering, "Pull down the covers." Riding in his arms, she dragged the spread and blanket over the foot of the bed. On knee and elbows he took her down, dropping across her with their mouths already joined in a frenzied kiss, tongues reaching deep, arms and legs taking possession. It was untamed, that prelude, all lust and anticipation drawn to its maximum. Twist and roll, thrust and rut. Sexual greed such as neither had experienced until now.

When it stopped, it stopped abruptly, he above, she below, their breaths gusty, labored.

"Do you need anything . . . to make it easier?" The baby's Vaseline was on the bureau. He'd studied it dozens of times while imagining this moment.

"I need you, Will . . . nothing else."

Her kiss silenced him as she hooked his neck with an arm and brought him down.

"I want to make it good for you, Green Eyes."

He knew how. He'd been taught by the best in a place called La Grange, Texas. He touched her—deep, shallow—with hands and tongue until she bent like a willow in the wind.

As he eased into her body she closed her eyes and saw him as he'd looked that first night, standing on the edge of the clearing, lean and hungry, wary and secretive, hiding beneath his hat—hiding his feelings, his loneliness, his needs.

She closed her eyes and opened her body, offering solace and love to equal his own. It hurt after all, but she hid it well, grasping his head and pulling it down for a deep kiss within which she disguised a soft moan. But soon the moan was dictated by pleasure instead of pain. He took her to the tallest tip of a tree, where she poised—a graceful bird at last, trembled upon the brink of flight, then soared for the first time. Becoming one with the sky, she called his name, twisting, lifting, reborn.

And when her cataclysm had passed, she opened her eyes and watched him follow the way she'd come, watched his gold-beaten hair tapping his forehead, the muscles in his arms standing out like formations in stone, beads of sweat dotting his brow.

He quivered, groaned and pressed deep, arching. He uttered her name, but the sound was trapped by his clenched jaw. When he shuddered in release, she found it glorious to witness, a blessing to receive. She held his shoulders and felt his deep tremors and thought it more beautiful than the flight of an eagle.

When it was over he fell to his side, draping a limp arm on her ribs, waiting for his breathing to slow. Eyes closed, he laughed once, satisfied, replete, then rolled her close, held her in a powerless caress with their damp skins touching.

He rolled his head tiredly and let his eyes caress her. "You all right, Elly?"

She smiled and touched his chin. "Shh . . . I'm holdin' it in."

"What?"

"Everything. All the feelin's you give me."

"Aw, Elly . . ."

He kissed her forehead and she spoke against his chin. "I had three babies, Will—three of 'em—but I never had this. I didn't know nothin' about this." She clutched him close. "Now I find out about it on our last night. Oh, Will, why did we waste two weeks?"

He had no answer, could only hold her and stroke her hair.

"Will, I felt like I always wished I could feel—like I was flying at last. How come that never happened with Glendon?" She braced up on an elbow to look him in the face.

She was such an unspoiled thing, innocent like no woman he'd ever known. "Maybe 'cause you were married to a good man who never visited a whorehouse."

"You're a good man, Will, don't you say different. And if that's what you learned there, I'm glad you went." She drew up the covers while he smiled at her unexpectedness: shy one minute, earthy the next. He gathered his wife close and found reason to be glad. It had been a circuitous route that had led him to her. Without La Grange, without Josh, without prison, he'd never have ended up in Georgia. He'd never have married Elly. But he didn't want to dwell on it tonight.

"Elly-honey, you mind if we don't talk about that for a while? I wanna talk about . . . about the flowers you're gonna plant for next summer, and how you're gonna pick the quince and how the boys're gonna help you shell pecans and—"

"You're gonna be back before that, Will. I just know you will."

"Maybe."

Through the hourglass the sand spilled faster. She rested her cheek and hand on his chest, against his strong, sure heartbeat, praying it would never be stopped by a bullet.

"I'll write to you." More sand . . . more heartbeats . . . and two throats tightening.

"And I'll write to you."

"I'll remember this night forever, and how wonderful it was."

"I'll remember . . ." He tipped her head back to look into her glistening eyes. "I'll remember a lot of things." Beneath the covers he found her breast and tenderly took it in hand. "I'll remember that day you threw the egg at me. That was the day I realized I was falling in love with you. I'll remember you slicing bacon in the morning, and leaning on the door of the Whippet while the boys pretended they were driving up to Atlanta. And that first morning, you tying your hair up in a tail with a yellow ribbon. And whippin' up a cake, holding the bowl against your belly. And the way you looked sitting in the boys' bed when I come home from work, telling 'em a bedtime story. And you-all waiting beneath the sourwood tree when I come driving back from town. Ah, that one's gonna be the best. Did I ever tell you how much I liked sittin' under that sourwood tree with you?" He kissed her forehead and made her eyes sting.

"Oh, Will . . ." She clasped him and blinked hard. "You got to come back so we can do it again. All those things. This summer . . . promise?"

He rolled against her and looked into her eyes. "If I make a promise, you got to make one, too."

"Wh–what?" She sniffled.

"That you'll go to town, take the boys out. You got to go, Elly, don't you see? Donald Wade, he'll be seven next year and he'll be starting school. But if you—"

"I can teach him what he—"

"You listen to me, now. They got to get out. Take 'em to the library and get books for 'em so when they're old enough for school they'll know what to expect. You want 'em to grow up less ignorant than me and you, don't you? Look how little we went to school and how hard we have to fight for everything. Give 'em a chance to be smarter and better than us. Take 'em in and get 'em used to town, and people—and—and surviving. 'Cause that's what life's all about, Elly, surviving. And you—you go in and keep selling the eggs and milk to Purdy. You buy Dreft instead of making that homemade soap. It's too hard on you, Elly, to do all that. The Marines'll be sending my checks to you, so you'll have the money. But you put half in War Bonds and spend the other half, you hear? Buy good shoes for the boys and whatever Lizzy needs. And you hire somebody to do whatever needs doin' around the place. And if I'm not back by the time the honey runs, you hire somebody to open the hives and sell the honey. It'll bring good money with sugar being scarce."

"But, Will—"

"You listen now, Elly, 'cause I haven't got a whole lot of time to convince you. Miss Beasley, she'll be your friend. You're gonna need a friend, and she's fair and honest and smart. If you need help you go to her and she'll help you or find somebody else who will. Promise, Elly?"

He held her lightly by the throat. Beneath his palm he felt her swallow.

"I promise," she whispered.

He forced a grin, made it teasing, the way he knew she needed right now. "You got your fingers crossed under them covers, missus?"

"N–no," she choked, releasing a laugh that was half sob.

"All right. Now listen." He wiped her cheek dry and said what needed saying. "I got to tell you this before I go. It might not've been fair of me to ask Miss Beasley, but I did, and she told me about how your mama she never was married, and how your family locked you up in that house when you were a little girl, and all the rest of it. Elly, how come you never told me?"

Her gaze dropped to his chest.

He lifted her chin with a finger. "You're as good as any of them down there—better. And don't you forget it, Mrs. Parker. You're bright, and you got a pair of real bright boys, too, you hear me? You got to go down into that town and show 'em."

He could see she was on the verge of big tears. "Aw, Elly, honey . . ." He wrapped her close and rocked her. "This war is gonna change things. Women're gonna have to do for themselves a lot more. And for you, facing town might be part of it. Just remember what I said. You're good as any of them down there. Now I got to ask you something, all right?" Once more he pressed her away and studied her eyes. "Do you own that house?"

"The one in town?"

"Yes. Where you used to live."

"Yes. But I ain't goin' in it."

"You don't have to. Just remember, though, if an emergency comes up and you need big money for anything, you can sell that place. Miss Beasley'll be able to help you. Will you do that if something goes wrong and I don't come home?"

"You're comin' home, Will, you *are!*"

"I'm gonna try, darlin'. A man with this much waitin' for him's got plenty to fight for, don't you think?"

They held each other and willed that it should be so. That when Lizzy took her first step he'd be there with his arms outstretched, waiting to catch her. When summertime came and the honey was running he'd be there to see after the bees. And when autumn came and the sourwood tree changed to scarlet he'd be there to join them beneath it.

"I love you, Elly. More'n you'll ever know. Nobody ever was as good to me as you. You got to remember one thing always. How happy you made me. When I ain't here and you get low, you think about what I said, how happy you made me, feedin' me quince pies and giving me three little babies to love, and making me feel like I'm somebody special. And remember how much I loved you, only you, the only one in my whole entire life, Eleanor Parker."

"Will . . . Will . . . oh, God . . ."

They tried to kiss but couldn't; their tears got in the way, filling their throats and thickening their tongues. They clung, legs braided, arms pulling as if to protect each other from tomorrow's separation.

But it would come. And it would take him and leave her and nothing they could do or say would prevent the sand from running out.

Chapter 15

They said goodbye under the sourwood tree. Donald Wade coasted down with one knee in the wagon; Thomas rode the scooter. Will and Elly followed, he with his few possessions in a brown paper bag and she carrying Lizzy P.

When they stopped beneath the outspread branches, his wrist rested on her shoulder. Instead of looking at her, he squinted at the sky.

"Well . . . got a good day for it. Can almost feel spring comin'."

"Not a cloud in that sky."

Why were they talking weather when there were a dozen more urgent feelings tumbling through their hearts?

"Donald Wade said just yesterday he seen a nest with some speckled eggs in it."

Will put his palm on Donald Wade's hair. "That right, *kemo sabe?"*

"Three of 'em, down by the Steel Mule."

"You didn't touch 'em, did you?"

Donald Wade wagged his head hard. "Uh-uhhh! Mama said."

Will went down on one knee and set his sack in the wagon. "Come here. You too, Thomas." Thomas dropped the scooter and both boys stood close while Will looped his arms around their waists. "You always do what your mama says, all right? I'm countin' on you to be good boys."

They both nodded solemnly, aware that Will's leaving was of import but too young to understand why.

"How long'll you be gone, Will?"

"Oh, a while, I reckon."

"But how *long?"* Donald Wade insisted.

Will carefully kept his eyes from Elly.

"Till them Japs're killed, I reckon."

"You gonna get a real gun, Will?"

He drew Donald Wade against his thigh. "Tell you what—I'll tell you all about it when I get back. Now you be a good boy and help your mother with Lizzy P. and Thomas, okay?"

" 'Kay." His voice lacked its usual vibrancy as Will's leave-taking became real. They kissed. Hard and hearty while the back of Will's nose stung.

" 'Bye, *kemo sabe."*

" 'Bye, Will."

" 'Bye, sprout."

" 'Bye, Wiw." Another soft mouth, another hard hug and Will clasped them both, closing his eyes.

"I love you two little twerps—an awful lot."

"I love you, Will."

"I wuv you, Wiw."

He got quickly to his feet, afraid of what would happen if he didn't.

"I want to hold Lizzy P. one time, all right?" He reached for the baby, held her upright with her feet at his chest. She peeked out from beneath a home-knit cap and a warm flannel quilt. When he put his nose to her cheek she smelled of a fresh bath and powdering. "I'm comin' back, Lizzy P., you sweet, sweet thing. Got to see them teeth you'll be sproutin' and see you ride the schoolbus to town." He made it brief—a nuzzle and a kiss—because it was too painful. "Here, Donald Wade, you hold your sister in the wagon, son."

When Lizzy P. was settled in her brother's lap, Will turned to Elly and took her by both hands. She was crying quietly. No sobbing, only the tears rolling down her pale cheeks.

"You keep them quince ready, missus, 'cause you never can tell when I'm gonna come traipsin' into this yard hungry as a spring bear."

Though the tears continued streaming, she lifted her chin high and affected a discommoded attitude. "Always were a peck o'trouble, Will Parker, you 'n' that sweet tooth of yours."

The tears he'd contained so well could be hidden no longer. They glimmered on his eyelids as he and Elly lunged together in a fierce, possessive hug. He dropped his head and she lifted on tiptoe, each seizing the other while their false gaity dissolved.

"Oh, Elly . . . Jesus."

"You come back to me, Will Parker, you hear?"

"I will, I will, I promise I will. You're the first thing I ever had to come back *to*. How could I not come back to you?"

They kissed, feeling cheated out of so much they hadn't had time for.

"Send me your picture soon as it's taken, in them fancy soldiers' clothes."

"I will. And remember what I said . . ." He held her face in both hands, looking into her precious green eyes. "You're as good as anybody in town. Take the boys in, and go to Miss Beasley if you need anything."

She nodded, biting her lips, then pulled him close, grasping the back of his denim jacket in her fists.

"I love you s–so m–much," she choked.

"I love you, too."

They kissed again, tongues reaching, arms clasping, tears falling while somewhere a train rolled toward Whitney to bear Will away. He forced his wife from his arms and ordered shakily, "Now get Lizzy P. and the boys and y'all sit under the sourwood tree. I wanna see you there when I go 'round the bend. 'Bye, boys. Be good."

He picked up his brown paper bag and watched Elly reach for the baby, swinging away before she'd straightened, striking off down the driveway, blinking to clear his vision, dashing a hard denim cuff against his eyes. He didn't turn until the last possible moment, when he knew the bend would hide them from his sight. He drew a deep breath . . . pivoted . . . and the picture branded itself upon his heart.

They were clustered beneath the sourwood tree, the boys pressed close to their mother as they sat on the sere grass of late winter. Blue overalls, brown boots, curled toes, thick woolen jackets . . . a green and pink quilt, a tiny face pointed in his direction . . . a faded blue housedress, a short brown coat, bare legs, brown oxfords, anklets, a long sandy braid. The boys were waving. Donald Wade was crying. Thomas was calling " 'Bye, Wiw! 'Bye, Wiw!" Elly held the baby high against her cheek, manipulating Lizzy's tiny hand and her own in a final wave.

Oh, God . . . God . . .

Will raised his free hand and forced himself to turn, stalk away.

Think about coming back, he recited like a litany. *Think about how lucky you are you got them four waitin' under a sourwood tree. Think about how pretty that little place is you're leaving, and what it's gonna be like to see those boys come runnin' when you walk back up this road, and what it'll be like to hold Elly again and know you won't have to let her go, and how you're gonna smile when Lizzy P. calls you daddy for the first time, and how you're gonna have one of your own someday just like her, and you and Elly'll watch all four of 'em grow up and get married and get grandbabies and bring 'em back home on Sundays and you'll show 'em the old sourwood tree and tell 'em all how you marched off to war and left their grandmama and mama and daddies sittin' under it wavin' you goodbye.*

By the time he reached Tom Marsh's place, he was calmer. He stood at the edge of their property, looking up at the neat white house, the empty clothesline in the backyard, the stump where the kettle held only dirt, no petunias. A new white picket fence surrounded the yard; he opened the gate, clicked it shut behind him and approached the house with his eyes fixed on it. A shaggy yellow dog came off the porch, barking and sniffing his calves, a half-grown pup, more inquisitive than threatening.

"Hey, girl . . ." Will bent and scratched her neck. "Where's your folks, huh?"

When he straightened, a woman had opened the door and stepped onto the back stoop. The same young woman as before, dressed in a trim red dress with a white mandarin collar, shrugging into a white sweater.

"Hello!" she called.

Will approached slowly and removed his hat. "Mrs. Marsh?"

"That's right."

"My name's Will Parker. I live up on Rock Creek Road. Eleanor Dinsmore's my wife."

She came down two steps and extended her hand. She was a pretty woman, thin and leggy, with bouncing black curls, cheek rouge and lipstick that made her look sweet, not hard like Lula Peak. "I've seen you pass on the road several times."

"Yes, ma'am. I work at the library for Miss Beasley. I mean, I did. I'm . . ." He gestured toward town with his hat. "I'm on my way to Parris Island."

"The Marine camp?"

"Yes, ma'am."

"You got drafted?"

"Yes, ma'am."

"So did my husband. He'll be leavin' at the end of the week."

"I'm sorry, ma'am. I mean . . . well, it's a heck of a thing, this war."

"Yes, it is. I have a brother, seventeen. He quit school and enlisted in the Navy already. Mama and Daddy just couldn't keep him at home."

"Seventeen . . . that's young."

"Yes . . . I worry about him so." A brief silence passed before she inquired, "Is there something I can do for you, Mr. Parker?"

"No, ma'am. Somethin' I had to do for you before I leave." Holding the paper sack against his stomach, Will reached in, pulled out a quart jar of honey and handed it to her. "A few months back I stole a quart jar full of buttermilk from your well. This here is it. Buttermilk's gone, of course, but that's our own honey—we keep bees at our place." Next came the towel. "Stole this green towel off your clothesline, too, and a set of your husband's clothes, but I'm afraid they're about worn out—"

"Well, I declare," she breathed, accepting the honey.

"—or I'd've returned them, too. I was hard up then, but that's no excuse. I just wanted to apologize, Mrs. Marsh. It's been on my mind a long time, is all, and it bothered me, stealin' from good people—Elly, she says you're good people." He backed away, pointing at the jar. "So there. Honey's not much, but—well—it's—" He donned his hat and rolled the top of the sack down tightly, still backing away. "My apologies, ma'am, and I sure hope your husband makes it back from this war."

"Just a minute, Mr. Parker!" He paused near the gate and she hurried down the walk.

"Give me a minute to let this sink in—nobody's ever—well, if this isn't the darndest thing." She chuckled as if in surprise. "I always wondered where those clothes went."

Will turned red to the ears while she seemed pleasantly amused.

"I got no excuse, ma'am, but I'm sorry. I'll rest easier now that I got it off my chest."

"Thank you for the honey. It'll come in handy with sugar being so dear."

"It's nothin'."

"It'll more than pay for those old clothes of Tom's."

"I hope so, ma'am." He pushed the gate open and the pup tried to slip through. She leaned down and grabbed its collar as Will closed the gate between them.

"I'm impressed by your honesty, Mr. Parker," she offered, rising.

He chuckled self-consciously and dropped his gaze to the gate while absently fingering one of its pointed slats.

"I appreciated the buttermilk and jeans at the time."

They studied each other, strangers caught in the backlash of war, considering the possibilities of death and loss, amazed that those possibilities could so swiftly create a tie between them. She reached out her hand once more and he took it in a prolonged handclasp.

"I hope to see you passing on the road again—soon."

"Thank you, Mrs. Marsh. If I do I'll give a holler and a hello."

"You do that."

He dropped her hand. "Well, . . . goodbye."

"God bless you."

He tipped his hat and headed for the road. Several paces away he turned back. She was dipping her finger into the honey. As she stuck it in her mouth she looked up and found him watching, grinning.

"It's delicious." She smiled broadly.

"I was just thinkin', ma'am. You asked if there was anything you could do and maybe there is."

"Anything for a soldier."

"My wife, Elly—she's got a new baby just two months old plus two others, and she doesn't get out much. If you should get—well, I mean, if you needed a friend, or someplace to go visit, I know you got kids of your own and maybe y'all'd like to walk up to our place and say hey sometime. Kids could maybe play together, you two ladies could have tea. Seein' as how your husband'll be gone, too."

Her pretty face puckered in thought. "Eleanor . . . Elly—your wife was Elly See, wasn't she?"

"That's right, ma'am. But what they say about her ain't true. She's a fine person, and brighter than some who spread rumors about her."

Mrs. Marsh recapped the quart jar, held it as a bride holds a bouquet and replied, "Then I'll want to thank her for the excellent honey, won't I?"

He smiled, gladdened, and thought how Mrs. Marsh's prettiness went deeper than skin and hair and cheek rouge.

"Enjoy that honey," he said by way of farewell.

She raised a hand and waved. "Come back."

As he turned away they both hoped fervently they'd meet again, felt a vague sense of deprivation, as if they might have been friends had they met when there was more time to explore the possibility.

The railroad station seemed to be the busiest building in town these days. Two young recruits—one white, one black—already waited with their tickets in hand, surrounded by their families on separate sides of the depot. A troop of Girl Scouts in uniform broke into two factions—the black girls to present the black recruit with a small white box, the white girls to do the same for the white recruit. A contingent of local DAR ladies waited for the train with juice and cookies for any war-bound men who might need a snack. A thin young man in a baggy suit and felt hat interrupted the family goodbye of the white recruit to get a last-minute interview for the local paper. A black minister with springy white curls rushed in to add his farewell to those of the black family.

And Miss Beasley was there, too, dressed in her usual puce coat, club shoes and a hideous black straw hat shaped like a soup kettle with netting. In her left hand she held a black purse, in her right a book.

"So Eleanor didn't come," she began before Will even reached her.

"No, ma'am. I said goodbye to her and the kids on our own road, where I want to remember them."

Miss Beasley shook a finger beneath his nose. "Now you stop talking so fatalistically, do you hear? I'll have none of it, Mr. Parker!"

"Yes, ma'am," Will replied meekly, warmed immediately by her stern demeanor.

"I have decided to give your job to a high school student, Franklin Gilmore, with the express understanding that it is a temporary arrangement until you return. Is that understood?" She gave the impression that she'd *get* any Japanese soldier who dared fire a bullet at Will Parker.

"Yes, ma'am."

"Good. Then take this and put it with your things. It's a book of poems by the masters, and I want your assurance that you'll read and reread it."

"Poems . . . well . . ."

"A man, it is said, can live three days without water but not one without poetry."

He accepted the book, looked down at it with a full heart.

"Thank you."

"No thanks are necessary. Only the promise that you'll read it."

"I promise."

"I can see your dubiousness. Undoubtedly you've never thought of yourself as a poetic man, but I've heard you talking about the bees and the boys and the boughs—they have been your poetry. This shall stand in lieu of them . . . until your return."

He gripped the book in both hands as if swearing upon it. "Until my return."

"So be it. Now . . ." She paused as if putting aside one subject before attacking another. "Do you have money for your fare?"

It was a question a mother might have asked, and it went straight to Will's heart. "The draft board sent me a ticket."

"Ah, of course. And decent meals while you travel?"

"Yes, ma'am. Besides, Elly packed me some sandwiches and a piece of quince pie." He hefted his bag.

"Why, of course. How silly of me to ask."

They paused, trying to think of something to fill the awful void which seemed impacted with hidden emotions.

"I told her to come to you if she needs help with anything. She don't have nobody else, so I hope that's okay."

"No sense in getting maudlin, Mr. Parker. I'd be insulted if she didn't. I shall write to you and keep you informed of the goings-on about the library and town."

" 'Preciate it, ma'am. And I'll write back, tell you 'bout all them Japs and Jerries I get."

The train steamed in on a billow of smoke and noise. They were at once relieved and sorry it had finally arrived. He touched her arm and moved toward the silver car with the black and white families and the Girl Scouts and the DAR ladies and the local reporter, all who politely nodded and called Miss Beasley by name.

The sun still shone in an azure sky pocked with bundles of clouds a shade darker than the smoke spouting from the locomotive. A flock of pigeons dropped down in a flurry of wings to settle on the baggage dray. The black family kissed their boy goodbye. The white family kissed theirs. The conductor said, *"Boooooard!"* but Will Parker and Gladys Beasley stood uncertainly before one another—a portly old woman in an ugly black hat and a rangy young man in a battered felt one. They looked at their feet, their hands, her purse handle, his brown paper bag. And finally at each other.

"I shall miss you," she said, and for once her sternness was gone, the dry-pudding lines relaxed about her mouth.

"In my whole life I never had anybody to miss—now I got so many. Elly, the kids and you. I'm a lucky man."

"If I were a sentimental woman I might say, if I had a son, and all that."

"Booooard!"

"I imagine conductors these days get hoarse calling that word," she ventured, and suddenly they pitched together, his book pressed against her back, her purse thumping his hindside. Immersed in her spicy scent, he closed his eyes a moment, thinking of how grateful he was that she'd come into his life.

"If you get yourself killed I shall never forgive you, Mr. Parker."

"I know. Neither will I. Take care of yourself and I'll see you when I get back."

They lurched apart, searched each other's faces—hers pruned to keep her from breaking down, his wearing a soft grin—then he kissed her swiftly on the mouth and spun for the steps of the waiting car.

Chapter 16

FEB. 26, 1942

Dear Elly,

I'm at Parris Island and the trip down wasnt bad. I had to change trains in Atlanta, and made it into Yemassee in late afternoon. Met there by marine corp recruit bus and rode it thirty mi. to the base, which is just outside Buford an ugly town I was glad I dint live in. Crossed a bridge and traveled thru a big marsh to get here. Yellow grass and birds by the hundruds you would love to see em. Met by our drill sergeant a big mean bull name of Twitchum and he right away starts laying it to us. He roars like a sonuvabee and says how we got to start and end everything we say with sir, like—sir request permission to speak sir—and he makes a couple recruits crinj and feel dumb and theres a few farm boys here from Iowa and Dakota who never saw anything but the back end of a horse, and they're pretty big-eyed I dont know why they came to the marines but some think the armys the worst and would rather take the sea instead thinking to keep away from the front maybe. Them farmboys looked ready to jump the fence but Ive seen all kinds in prison, so boot camp's nothing new. Twitchum he likes to make those farmboys scart. Kept em up till all hours making them learn how to make up a bed before they could sleep in it cause their mamas allways made theres up at home so they never lurnd how. Me I had five years of making up my own and plenty worse to pay if it wasn't done right than around here. Twitchum he comes by and gives everybody the old eagle eye and he sees my bed done up good and stops with his nose so close to mine I could smell his snot and he says to me (testing me, see)—what's your name boy and I says sir-Parker-William-Lee-sir, and he says to me—northerner or southerner? But Ive seen his kind before and Ive seen how he looks at those yankee farmboys and enjoys making them squirm and how he takes digs at the black boys and makes them squirm too so I says to him—sir-westerner-sir. He thinks about it a hen's blink and barks—Bunk patrol every morning at 0-500 hours, Parker. You dont teach them farmboys how to do womens work and its your ass! So I reckon I got me a duty already. How about that. Miss Beasley gave me a fare-well book of poems and I gave her a kiss she din't seem to mind They issued us our fatigues and blankets and toilet artikles and marched us in here to our barracks and half of em are laying here snivveling for home I reckon. Me I know theres worse places than this cause I been there. But I sure miss you green eyes and those babies and our bed. I ate the sandwiches and the pie on the train and they tasted real good and I probly never told you before but you make the best quince pie of anything. Lites out theyre saying so I have to end here and I'm sorry if this aint so clear my writing never was good cause I hated school and dint go much less they made me.

Your loving husband
Will

Feb. 26, 1942
Dear Will,

I never wrote no letter before I don't know how but its time I lurn don't you think. We ate supper without you but the boys were frack fracshus (sorry I ain't got no eraser) and I had trouble looking at your chair I kep wonderin where you were and if you had got there yet and if they fed you and give you a warm bed and all them things. And did miss Beasley come to the stashion like she said she would I can't spell nor think clear on paper but feelings are a diffurnt thing and them I got aplenty I miss you so already Will and you been gone only today

This took me near an hour and it dont seem like much for so long but tomorr I'll write more.

With love
Eleanor

Feb. 28, 1942
Dear Will,

Your letter came and Parris Island sounds just awful I cried because I felt so bad for you like you are being brave on my account when you say it aint so bad there. I did *not* cry for myself this time but I feel bad for you being there I hope you are okay that Twitchum sounds like a regular satan and I read plenty about him in my time . . .

Parris Is., So. Carolina
28 Feb. 1942
Dear Elly,

. . . I'm sending you my application for war bonds and insurance. Be sure to keep them in a safe place . . .

March 1, 1942
Dear Will,

I thot sure I'd get another letter from you Are you okay? Everyday when the mail comes I run down there and see if theres a letter in the box but there was only that one. Are you sure you are okay? . . .

Parris Is., So. Carolina
2 March 1942
Dear Eleanor,

I sure miss you green eyes and I would of writen before but they dont give us time we're up at 0430 hours (that's 4:30 in civvy time) and Twitchum wakes us up by kicking a shit can (that's a trash can) down the squad bay and we hit the deck running. They give us each exactly three minuts in the latrine to shower and shave and you know what else if we got to and he's in there barking like a mad dog all the time and the rest of the day its go go go till 0900 hours and then we get one hour of free time but it aint free cuz Twitchum comes in and makes us do drill or polish his boondockers (that's boots here). So no time for writing till now.

I been what they called processed so I got no hair left kiddo and I look ugly as a coot with mange but it saves time in the morning and you don't want no picture of anything this ugly. Anyways, they have'nt offered for us to get any pictures taken yet so maybe later. Also they fixed my teeth and gave me 7 shots in different places, four you-know-where. Ouch! Those needles could be a little sharper. In bed at night I think of you and the kids and your good cooking but the chow here ain't as bad as I expected, better than in prison I can tell you. I don't . . .

Ran out of time—mailing this on the run

Love,
W

4 March 1942
Dear Elly,

Your letter came in yesterdays mail call after I already sent mine the day before and I told you why I had not written. Dont worry about me I'm doing fine Twitchum lays off me but I see him watching close in case I make a mistak don't worry I ain't gonna make any I'm gonna act like his trained monkey. I sure do miss you and the kids and I suppose Lizzy P is growing. I have read your letters til the edges are getting raggy but don't you worry about me I'm just a little lonesome is all. They feed me good here and when your bellys full you can put up with near anything. Don't worry about me tho I'm just fine. Things here are speeding up. Today we got issued our .30 caliber rifles and bayonets and we have to memorize the model numbers—1903 & 1905. Every day I go to physical training, bayonet training and a class on military history who ever would've thought I'd be back in school again at my age but I am and next week we start first aid classes and articles-of-war classes and of course there is always close-order drill for hours and hours every day. They say all that marching teaches discipline and thats important in a military organization but now I reckon I know why they call this *boot* camp cause these boots sure get a workout ever day. Theres sure all kinds here Elly—course I was with all kinds in Huntsville too but heres diffrent cause your closer to them all the time. Some of them stink so bad we all got to go to hygiene lessons and lots of them can't read so they go to reading classes The blacks got their own barracks and we got ours but everybodys got a buddy it seems. Mine's this lanky redhead from Kentucky named Otis Luttrell. We get along good cause neither one of us likes to talk much . . .

March 13, 1942,
Dear Mr. Parker,

By now you are becoming acclimated to Marine life while we at home slowly become acclimated to the idea of our country being at war. We here in town are being propagandized more and more now that America is actively in it. It seems there's a new sign each week encouraging us to do our part, the latest one a picture of Uncle Sam shushing us, saying, "A slip of the lip can sink a ship." It seems incredible to believe there could be spies working among us in a place as small as Whitney.

Every organization from the Boy Scouts to the Jane Austen Society is sponsoring a scrap drive these days. To my chagrin they have even taken the Civil War cannon from the Town Square to be melted down as scrap iron. I raised a formal objection with the Town Council—after all, posterity must also be served—but of course their attitude was one of righteous patriotism, thus I was overridden.

Norris and Nat MacReady have volunteered to organize a Civil Patrol and be air raid wardens. They patrol each night to make sure everyone is in off the streets by ten and all blackouts are observed. Frankly, after all the years they have spent whittling on that bench across the street I thought they had grown into it!

I am making it a Saturday ritual to go out to visit Eleanor immediately after closing, since the days are longer now. Also it helps that we get an extra hour since "War Time" has gone into effect to save on electricity. Your wife and I always have a pleasant visit and a game or two of Chinese checkers. I take the boys books which occupy them while I'm there. They are looking healthy and robust, and Elizabeth is content and growing weekly.

I have put in a little Victory Garden but I fear I am not blessed with a green thumb like Eleanor. But I shall struggle on with it and perhaps get a tomato or two. Eleanor has volunteered to teach me to put up vegetables. I didn't want to hurt the poor child's feelings, but I'm afraid I've been behind a desk too long to be handy with colanders and sieves. Still, I shall try.

The butcher shop is acting as a collection depot for wastefats. The billboard there claims one pound of fat contains enough glycerine to make a pound of black powder, so we are all saving our bacon drippings for that cause.

Yet another new billboard has been posted in the town square right beside the MacReadys' bench. On it is listed the names of all the local boys who have joined up. Your name is listed on the right column between Okon, Robert Merle, United States Navy, and Sprague, Neal J., United States Army. Thankfully none have a star behind them yet.

Franklin Gilmore is working out fine at the library although he occasionally shirks when it comes to dusting the top shelves which he thinks I never check.

I hope this finds you well and tolerating the rigors of military life with a minimum of discomforts. I shall look forward to hearing from you only if you may spare the time, which I'm given to understand is at a minimum during basic training.

My best to you,
Gladys Beasley

Mar. 15, 1942
Dear Will,
You'll never guess who come over here today That pretty young Lydia Marsh from down the town road. Come up the road while I was planting my *victory garden*—ha! I been planting garden since I was old enough to hoe and all of a sudden they call it by some name so the town people will plant one too but thats neither here nor there. Mrs. Marsh she come to buy honey said she heard we had it for sale but she brung her two kids a girl four name Sally and a boy two name Lonn and the boys got along with them just fine and they were playin in the yard so I offered Mrs. Marsh tea and she stayed a bit and what a nice woman . . .

20 March 1942
Dear Miss Beasley,
Thank you for your letter and it sure was full of news I didnt know all that was going on back home Elly must not go to town cause she don't tell me about it. I read some of the poems and they were intresting My favorite was When a Man Turns Homeward by Daniel Whitehead Hicky. I picture it would be like that when I can come back home to Elly and the kids and we will close the door and leave the world like a kitten outside . . .

25 March 1942
Dear Elly,
This has probly been the worst day since I left home. The whole company is pretty upset the whole base really. You probly heard about it on the radio how this lieut. Calvin Murphree had a platoon out on bivouac and sent them under the barbed wire on their bellies while he was strafing (that means shooting shells over their heads) and he went berzerk and started shooting to kill and he killed one private named Kenser or Kunzor or something like that and wounded two others before somebody stopped him. A man expects to get shot at when he reaches the front but not in boot camp by your own officers. Oh God Elly I miss you so much tonight green eyes. I got out my book of poems from Miss Beasley and read my favorite one to make me feel better. It's about a man coming home through the moonfall and a woman is waiting with a candle. Only four weeks and one day and basic will be over and I should get leave and be able to come home . . .

March 25, 1942
Dear Will,
Everything is good here except for how much I miss you. Miss Beasley she comes every Saturday after work when the library closes early. She brought me

a spelling book and is helping me work on my writing so my letters are better. We play Chinese checkers and guess what else she has done. She has started the milk truck coming out here to pick up our milk and the price is up to 11¢ a quart and 30¢ for a pound of butter and eggs up to 30¢ a dozen too and the driver takes them all for me . . .

27 March 1942
Dear Elly,
   I shouldn't have written that last letter when I was in such a rotten mood. I dont want you worrying about me you got enough to worry about with the boys and anyway I'm better now and things are going along fine. Did good on my first aid class test but I drew KP this week and I dont care for that much. Rifle practice every day and you know its a funny thing about some of those backwoods boys that cant read and write they can take apart a rifle and put it together in the dark. Me and Red (that's what I call my buddy Otis) do good on that too . . .

March 29, 1942
Dear Will,
   I wonder what your doing tonight. I been listening to the radio and they been playing The White Cliffs of Dover and I wonder if you'll be shipped to England . . .

11 April 1942
Dear Elly,
   It's a good thing we get to send these letters for free I never thought I'd write so many letters in my whole life as I wrote since I been here. I got a one-day pass and Red and me went with a bunch who caught the recruit bus in to Buford and we went to a movie. It was Suspicion starring Cary Grant and Joan Fontaine and afterwards just about everybody got drunk and tried to pick up local girls but me. Only 19 days and I should be able to come home . . .

April 14, 1942
Dear Will,
   I just don't know how the days could go any slower. I keep thinking about when you get here and how it will be. How long will you be able to stay? Will you take the train again? I got a surprise for you but I won't tell you till you get here. The boys got a calendar and they drew a big yellow star on the day you get off, and they put a big x on every day just before bedtime . . .

19 April 1942
   Only six more days, green eyes! . . .

April 19, 1942
Dear Will,
   How many quince pies you want? . . .

21 April 1942
Dear Elly,
   I don't know how to tell you this because I know it's gonna break your heart. I'd rather do anything than tell you this sugar but we just got orders and it looks like we are not gonna get our weeks leave like we expected. Instead we're being assigned to the New River Marine Base at New River, North Carolina and we leave direcly from here next Thursday. They won't tell us why we don't get leave but

theres plenty of grumbling and a few already went AWOL soon as they got the news. Now honey I don't want you to worry about me, I'm doing fine. I just hope you and the kids are too and that you'll understand and keep your spirits up . . .

April 23, 1942
Dearest Will,
    I tried real hard not to cry because I know your the one whos doing the hard part and I held off till bedtime after your letter came but then I just couldn't hold the tears in any more . . .

3 May 1942
Dear Elly,
    Well, I'm here at the new barracks and you can send my mail to PFC William Lee Parker, 1st Raider Bn., 1st Marines, New River Marine Base, New River, North Carolina. I got my gold stripe and had to pay Bilinski a buck to sew it on for me cause I'm so clumsy with a needle. Bilinski is this Polish butcher from Detroit who's in my outfit and always out to make a buck. So we call him Buck Bilinski. Me and Red got bunks side by side this time and I'm sure glad we din't get separated . . .

May 6, 1942
Dear Will,
    Miss Beasley and I looked at a map and found New River and now I imagine you up there where the map shows that river poking into the land beside the ocean . . .

14 May 1942
Dear Elly,
    I'm sorry I haven't written for so long but they've really been keeping us busy the whole outfit is wondering what they intend to do with us and when but it seems like soon and it seems like it'll be the real thing whenever we leave here because they got us in intensive combat training, even close hand-to-hand combat. I made up my combat pack so many times I could do it in the dark with my fingers glued together. Theres five kinds and we got to know what to put into each kind. The full field transport packs got everything in it down to the marching pack thats only got the bare essentials. They got us in the water a lot in little rubber rafts. Me and Red were talking the other day and supposing why they're drilling us so hard and whatever it is, we think its gonna be big . . .

May 17, 1942
Dear Will,
    I know I ought to be brave but I get scared when I think about you going to the front. Your the kind of man who belongs in a orchard keeping bees and I think back to how I worried about you doing that and now compared to what you might have to do how foolish it seems that I worried about the bees. Oh my darling Will how I wish you could be here cause the honey is running and I wish I could see you out there in the orchard beneath the trees filling the water pans and taking off your hat to wipe your forehead on your sleeve . . .

4 June 1942
Dear Elly,
    We're under orders now for sure but they arent saying for where. All they say is we got to be ready to ship out when word comes down . . .

Chapter 17

"Good morning. Carnegie Municipal Library."

"Hello, Miss Beasley?"

"Yes."

"It's Will."

"Oh, my goodness, Will—Mr. Parker, are you all right?"

"I'm just fine but I'm in kind of a hurry. Listen, I'm sorry to call you at work but I couldn't think of any other way to get word to Elly. And I have to ask you to do me the biggest favor of my life. Could you possibly go out there or pay somebody else to get word to her? We just found out we ship out Sunday and we got forty-eight hours' leave but if I take a train clear down there I'll have to turn around and come right back. Tell her I want her to take the train and meet me in Augusta. It's the only thing I can figure out is if we meet halfway. Tell her I'll be leaving here on the next train and I'll wait at the train depot—oh, Jesus, I don't even know how big it is. Well, just tell her I'll wait near the women's rest room, that way she'll know where to look for me. Could you do that for me, Miss Beasley?"

"She'll have the message within the hour, I promise. Would you like to call back for her answer?"

"I haven't got time. My train leaves in forty-five minutes."

"There's more than one way to skin a cat, isn't there, Mr. Parker?"

"What?"

"If this doesn't get her off that place, nothing will."

Will laughed appreciatively. "I hadn't thought of that. Just tell her I love her and I'll be waiting."

"She shall get the message succinctly."

"Thank you, Miss Beasley."

"Oh, don't be foolish, Mr. Parker."

"Hey, Miss Beasley?"

"Yes?"

"I love you, too."

There followed a pause, then, "Mr. Bell didn't invent this instrument so Marines could use it to flirt with women old enough to be their mothers! And in case you hadn't heard, there's a war on. Phone lines are to be kept free as much as possible."

Again Will laughed. " 'Bye, sweetheart."

"Oh, bosh!" At her end, a blushing Gladys Beasley hung up the telephone.

Elly had ridden on a train only once before but she'd been too young to remember. Had someone told her four months ago that she'd be buying a ticket and heading clear across Georgia by herself she'd have laughed and called them a fool. Had someone told her she'd be doing it with a nursing baby and changing trains in Atlanta, heading for a city she'd never seen, a railroad depot she didn't know, she'd have asked who the crazy one was supposed to be.

Before he'd left, Will had said women will have to do more for themselves, and here she was, sitting in a rocking, rumbling railroad car surrounded by uniforms and dresses with shoulder pads, and noise and too little space and what appeared to be a weeks' worth of squashed cigarette butts on the floor. Trains grossly overbooked passengers these days, so people were standing, sitting in aisles and crowded three and four into a bank of seats meant for only two. But because she was traveling with a baby, people had been kind. And because Lizzy P. had been fractious they'd been helpful. A woman with bright-red lipstick, bright-red high-heeled shoes and a red and white tropical print dress offered to hold Lizzy for a while. The soldier accompanying the woman took off his dog tags and twirled them in the air to entertain the baby. In the foursome of seats across the aisle eight soldiers were playing poker. Everyone smoked. The air in the car was the color of washwater but not nearly as transparent. Lizzy grew tired of the dog tags and began crying again, grinding her fists into her eyes, then twisting and reaching for Elly. When the woman in the tropical dress figured out that the baby was hungry but Elly nursed, she whispered to her young lieutenant and in no time at all he'd rounded up a porter who cleared out a pullman unit and ushered Elly to it, giving her thirty minutes of privacy to feed Lizzy and change her diaper.

The Atlanta train depot was as crowded as steerage, a melee of people, all rushing, shouldering, bumping, kissing, crying. The loudspeaker and rumbling trains scared Lizzy and she bawled for the entire forty-minute layover until Elly herself was close to tears. Her arms ached from battling the bucking child. Her head ached from the noise. Her shoulder blades ached from tension. Frightening questions kept hammering the inside of her skull: what would she do if she got to Augusta and Will wasn't there? And where would they sleep? And what would they do with Lizzy?

The final leg of the trip was on an older train, so dirty Elly was afraid Lizzy would catch something, so crowded she felt like a hen being crated off to market, so noisy Lizzy couldn't sleep, no matter how tired she was. In a single seat a woman slept on a man's lap, their heads clunking together in rhythm with the wheels rolling over the uneven seams in the rails. A group of soldiers were singing "Paper Doll" while one of them strummed a guitar discordantly. They had sung it so many times Elly wanted to put a foot through the guitar. Men with loud voices told stories about boot camp, interspersing them with curse words and simulated sounds of machine-gun fire. In another part of the car the inevitable poker game created sporadic cheers and bursts of howling. In the seat next to Elly a fat woman with a mustache and an open mouth slept, snoring. A female with a shrill laugh used it too often. Periodically the conductor fought his way through and bellowed out the name of the next town. Somebody smelled like used garlic. The cigarette smoke was suffocating. Lizzy kept bawling. Elly kept wanting to. But, looking around, she realized she was no different from hundreds of others temporarily misplaced by the war, many of them hurrying to a brief, frantic, final meeting with someone they loved, as she was.

She wiped Lizzy's dripping nose and thought, *I'm coming, Will, I'm coming.*

The train terminal of Augusta, servicing the traffic to and from countless military bases, was worse than any so far. Debarking, Elly felt lost in a sea of humanity. With Grandfather See's suitcase in one hand and the baby in the other, she struggled up a set of steps, swept along like flotsam at high tide, not knowing if she was heading in the right direction but having little choice.

Somebody bumped her shoulder and the suitcase fell. As Elly bent to retrieve it, Lizzy slipped down and somebody bumped them from behind, nearly knocking them to the floor. "Oops, sorry!" The private in the army green helped Elly up, snapped the suitcase and handed it to her. She thanked him, gave Lizzy a bounce to get her balanced and moved on with the crush toward what she hoped was the main body of the terminal. Overhead, a nasal, monotone voice announced as if echoing down a culvert, "The five-ten to Columbia, Charlotte, Raleigh, Richmond and Washington, D.C., is now boarding at gate three." She had vague impressions of passing a newspaper stand, a restaurant, a cigarette stand, a shoeshine boy, queues of faceless people waiting to buy tickets, a pair of nuns who smiled at Lizzy, and so many military uniforms that she wondered who was out there fighting the war.

Then she saw a swinging door that said "men" and a moment later its twin, swinging shut, adding "Wo—"

Women.

She stopped and reread the entire word to make sure, spun around, and there he was, already hurrying toward her.

"Elly!" He smiled, waved. "Elly!"

"Will!" She dropped her suitcase and waved back, jumping twice, her heart drumming crazily, her eyes already filling. He zigzagged closer, moving people aside. Another moment and he reached her.

"Elly-honey—oh, God, you came!" He lifted her clean off the floor, kissing her open-mouthed, with Lizzy squashed between them. Is-it-really-you-I-missed-you-so-I-love-you-oh-God-it's-been-so-long . . .

The floor shook as trains rumbled, the air was a cacophony of voices, the room a melange of motion, while Will and Elly shared a lusty kiss, timeless and prolonged, with tongues swirling and arms clinging and the salt of Elly's tears flavoring their reunion.

Then Lizzy started squirming and they broke apart, laughing, suddenly aware that they'd been crushing her.

"Lizzy P., oh, sugar, you're here too . . . let me look at you . . ." Will took her from Elly and held her aloft, smiling up at her apple cheeks and eyes whose lashes and irises were much darker than last time he'd seen them. With so many new distractions Lizzy didn't know whether to fret or laugh. "Lizzy P., you sweet thing, look at how fat you're getting." He kissed her soundly, set her on his arm and said, "Hello, sweet thing."

"I'm sorry, Will, I had to bring—"

Will's mouth stopped Elly's explanation. The second kiss began jubilant, became sensual, then commandeering with full complement of tongue and lips while Lizzy squirmed on his arm but went ignored. He grasped the back of Elly's head and told her without words what she could expect when they were alone. When the kiss ended, he pulled back while they studied each other's faces.

She found him stunning in his crisp uniform and garrison cap, so incredibly handsome she felt as if she'd stepped into a fantasy.

He found her thinner, prettier, her face trimmed with a pale touch of makeup, the first he'd ever seen her wear.

"God," he whispered, "I can't believe you're here. I was so scared you wouldn't come."

"I might not have if it wasn't for Miss Beasley. She made me."

He laughed and kissed her again briefly, then held her hand and backed up a step, scanning her length. "Where'd you get the dress?" It, too, was stylish: yellow with black military-type trim and buttons, padded at the shoulder, trim at the hip and flaring to a short hem that revealed her legs from the knee down. And she was wearing sling-back high heels with a cutaway toe!

Elly's gaze dropped self-consciously. "I made it for when you were supposed to come home the last time. Remember, I said I had a surprise for you?"

He gave a slow whistle and stole a phrase from radio's Captain Marvel. "Shazaam!"

Elly colored becomingly, touched a button at her waist and glanced up shyly into Will's handsome face. It was odd—she was almost afraid to stare at him too much, as if doing so might jeopardize her right to someone so dignified-looking, so attractive. "Lydia Marsh lent me her pattern and I ordered the cloth and shoes from the catalogue."

He was so impressed he didn't know on what to comment first, the fact that she'd made a friend or the updated change in her looks. Her hair was twisted high and away from her face the way the women in the munitions factories often wore theirs beneath safety scarves. One soft wave dipped low over the side of her forehead; her eyebrows had been slightly plucked and her lips painted pale pink.

"And makeup, too," he said approvingly.

"Lydia thought I ought to try it. She showed me how."

"Honey, you look so pretty you take my breath away."

"So do you." She took a full draught of him in his dress greens: wool blouse and crisply creased trousers, gleaming shoes, khaki shirt and tie and the Sam Browne belt running from his right shoulder to his left waist; the shining Marine Corps emblem—eagle, glove and anchor—centered above the leather bill of his garrison cap, which gave him the look of some important stranger. He had put on weight, was thicker at the shoulders and chest, but it definitely became him. The sight of her husband in the hard, tailored suit made Elly's heart swell with pride.

In a soft, teasing voice she asked, "Where is my cowboy?"

"Gone, ma'am." Will replied with banked pride. "He's a soldier now."

"You look like somebody who'd guard a door at the White House."

He chuckled and she requested, "Let me see that hair they cut off."

"Aww, you don't wanna see that."

"Yes, I do, Private First Class Parker." She playfully flicked the single gold chevron on his sleeve.

"All right—you asked for it."

He removed the garrison cap and she couldn't withhold a gulp of regret at the sight of his skull showing through the mere sprinkling of hair remaining on his head. Gone was the thick pelt she'd often washed and cut and combed. *The Marines ought to hire a new barber,* she thought. Why, she could do better with her plain kitchen scissors. But she searched for something heartening to say.

"I don't think I ever saw your ears before, Will. You got fine ears, and even without no hair you're still pretty to me."

"And you're a pretty li'l liar, Mrs. Parker." Laughing, he replaced the hat, stole another kiss, picked up her suitcase and his duffel in a single hand. "Hang on," he ordered. "I don't want to lose you in this mob. Lizzy P. is a surprise. How you doin', Lizzy-girl? You tired, babe?" He kissed her forehead while she whimpered softly and rubbed her eyes. "How was she on the train?"

"Terrible."

"Sorry for the quick orders. But on a *forty-eight* I didn't have time to think about arrangements for the kids. To tell you the truth, I wouldn't have cared if you had to bring 'em all, as long as I got to see you. Where are the boys?"

"At Lydia Marsh's. They kicked up a fuss when they found out I was comin' to see you, but it was bad enough havin' to bring this one. I had to though, 'cause she's still nursing."

"I realized that after I'd hung up. I made it awful hard for you, didn't I? How long ago did she eat?"

"Around three."

"And how 'bout you—are you hungry?"

"No. Yes." She glanced at the neon light over the door of the coffee shop as they passed it. "Well, sort of." She hugged his arm. "I mean, I don't want to waste time in any restaurant and I don't know how much longer Lizzy will hold out."

He led her outside into the humid summer late-afternoon. "I got us a room at the Oglethorpe. What do you say we pick up some hamburgers and take 'em back there?" They stood at the curb, their eyes exchanging mixed messages of hunger and impatience.

"Fine," she forced herself to answer.

"It's eight blocks or so. You think you can walk it in those shoes?"

"A real hotel?"

"That's right, green eyes. For tonight, a real hotel."

Privacy.

They stood gazing at each other while a taxi honked and car doors slammed. His heart leaped. Hers answered. They wanted to kiss but refrained, postponing any further intimacies until time and place allowed them full savor.

"On second thought," she murmured, "I wouldn't mind forgetting about the hamburgers."

"You should eat something, and drink some milk, too—for Lizzy."

"Do I have to?"

"It won't take long." He smiled and led the way along the sidewalk.

Twenty-five minutes later they entered their room behind a "bellgirl" instead of a "bellboy." The young woman was friendly, hospitable and wore a red pillbox hat. While Will set their brown paper sack of hamburgers on the dresser, Elly stood by the door, taking in her surroundings. The bellgirl laid their suitcases on the bed, opened a window and pointed out the adjoining bath with its black and white hexagonal marble tile, claw-foot tub and pedestal lavatory. The bedroom itself was small, done in deep green with touches of maroon and peach. The floor was lined with a bound rug, the windows decorated with frond-patterned drapes, fronted by two overstuffed chairs and a table. The focal point of the room was a wooden bed covered with a peach chenille spread and a bedside stand bearing a lamp shaped like a maroon ocean wave.

Will politely allowed the bellgirl to do her job and show it all, suppressing the urge to shove her out the door and lock it behind her.

Finally he tipped her and the moment the door closed he turned to Elly for a kiss. Scarcely had their lips touched when Lizzy complained, forcing them to consider her first.

"Will she settle down?"

"I hope so. She's dead tired."

Their gazes met. *How long? A half hour? An hour? I want you now.*

"What're we gonna do with her, Will? I mean, where will she sleep?"

He scanned the room and suggested, "How about the chairs?" In four long strides he reached the pair of overstuffed armchairs and turned them seat-to-seat, creating a perfect crib, soft and safe with the arms and seats butted.

"This would work, wouldn't it?"

She was so relieved her smile broke easily. "It'll be perfect."

He flashed her a return smile and moved toward the suitcase. "You get her wet stuff off and I'll find her clean clothes."

While Will dug through the suitcase, Elly laid the baby on the bed and began changing her clothes for nighttime. Lizzy rubbed her eyes and whimpered.

"She's beat, poor thing," Will said, sitting down beside Lizzy, bracing on an elbow, watching, enjoying. In minutes she was changed into clean diapers and a lightweight kimono.

"Keep your eye on her a minute, okay?" Elly plunked Lizzy on Will's arm and turned away. Talking sweet nothings to the baby, he watched Elly remove her yellow dress, hang it in the closet, then turn, barefoot, dressed in a white half-slip and bra.

For a moment their gazes locked and all was still but for Lizzy's soft whimpering and the clamoring of their two hearts. Will's eyes dropped, lingered on the bare band of skin between the two white garments while Elly's traced the length of his dark, flattering uniform. When their eyes met again his breathing had accelerated and her cheeks had taken on an added glow.

"God, you look good," he breathed in a tight, reedy voice.

"So do you," she whispered.

She reached behind herself, released the hook on her bra and removed it, all the while holding him captive with her eyes. Her breasts were heavy, the nipples wide and florid, radiating faint blue lines. She stood unmoving, framed by the bathroom doorway, learning the exquisite pleasure of letting another study her body through the eyes of love. How different she felt about herself now than in the days after she'd first met him. Love, she had discovered, left her with no desire to hide.

She watched Will swallow. His nostrils dilated and his breathing grew noticeably rushed. Though Lizzy still fretted, Elly crossed the room slowly and rested a knee on the mattress, bending over Will for one lingering kiss. He reached up and brushed her pendulous breast with a knuckle, nudged her lips away and whispered, "Hurry."

She sat on one of the overstuffed chairs with Lizzy in the crook of her arm. Will rolled onto his belly, crossed his wrists beneath his chin and observed as his wife looked down, took a nipple between two fingers and guided it to the baby's open mouth. His eyes became dark as onyx, his body aroused as he imbibed the image, both maternal and sexual. When he could bear it no longer he rose to prowl the room, striving to keep his eyes off her. He laid his hat upside down on the dresser, removed his wool blouse and hung it in the closet, opened the bag of food, peered inside and took out one hamburger wrapped in waxed paper. "You want one while you feed her?"

She accepted the hamburger and began eating it while he found the glass bottle of milk, removed the cardboard stopper, searched out a glass in the bathroom, filled it and set it on the table beside her. When he neared, her head swiveled, following his every movement. Her eyes lifted and lingered on his face, allowing him to witness how her impatience had grown to the same gnawing insistence as his own.

But the baby had to come first. Reluctantly he turned away.

She watched minutely, becoming aroused by the nuances of motion peculiar to him and no other man. He removed his tie, folded it neatly beside his hat, freed his cuff buttons and rolled his sleeves back to midarm. Watching him move about the room, performing mundane tasks, she became awed that such simple movements could stir her, make her feel carnal in a way she never had before. She welcomed the feeling, eager for the moment when she could loose it upon him.

He stacked both bed pillows and sat against them, with one foot outstretched, the other on the floor. The pose accentuated the masculinity already underscored by the uniform—the brilliant shine on his brown dress shoes, the sharp crease along his trousers, the fine press on his collar. She remembered him in scuffed cowboy boots, faded jeans hanging from lean hips, a crinkled shirt with sweat-stained arms. It struck her that the change in his clothing made him appear not only masculine and clean, but important and intelligent, and that this aspect of his appearance affected her as much as any other. It caught her in the hollow between her breasts like a sharp blow, made her heart leap and her blood sing. He reached into his breast pocket, removed a pack of Lucky Strikes and methodically tapped one against his thumbnail. Next he produced a book of matches, lit up and sat idly smoking, studying Elly through the rising skein of gray. She became mesmerized by the sight of his well-kept hands with the cigarette held deep between his fingers while he closed and opened the matchbook between drags, all the time watching her with his eyelids at half-mast.

"When did you start smoking?"

"A while ago."

"You never told me in your letters."

"I didn't think you'd like it. Everybody does it. They even give us free cigarettes in our K-rations. Besides, it calms the nerves."

"It makes you seem like a stranger to me."

"If you don't like it I'll—"

"No. No, I didn't mean that. It's just ... I haven't seen you for so long and when I do you're wearing clothes like you never had before, and a haircut that makes you look different, and you've got new habits."

He inhaled deeply, expelled the smoke through his nostrils. "Inside I haven't changed though."

"Yes, you have. You're prouder." When he made no reply, she added, "So am I. Me and Lydia we talked about it. At first I told her how I hated having you go, but she said that I oughta be proud you're wearing a uniform. And now that I've seen you in it, I am."

"You know something, Elly?" She waited while he twirled the cigarette coal against a glass ashtray, rubbing ashes off. At last he looked up. "These're the nicest clothes I ever owned."

His remark made her understand as she never had before the extent of his early deprivation, and that in the Marines he was like everybody else, no longer the odd man out.

"When I saw you at the station—well, it was a funny thing. All the while I was on the train I pictured you like you looked back home, and me too. But then I saw you and—well, something happened—here." She touched her heart. "This crazy knocking, you know? I mean, I wanted you to be the same, but I was glad you weren't. Those clothes ..." Her eyes flicked over his length. "I can't believe how you look in those clothes."

He smiled crookedly and kept his eyes steady on hers, but somehow she knew they wanted to rove. "The same thing happened when I saw you. Just sitting there in that chair, you make it happen all over again."

They studied each other while Lizzy suckled. Will's eyes fell to Elly's naked breast and he drew deeply on the cigarette.

"Aren't you going to eat your hamburger?" she asked.

"I'm not very hungry right now. How's yours?"

"It's delicious." But she had laid the sandwich aside, half-eaten, and they both realized why. She took a drink of milk. A droplet of condensation fell from the cool glass onto Lizzy's cheek and she awakened with a start, releasing Elly's nipple with a snap, her face and fists rebelling against the sudden interruption.

"Shh . . ." Elly soothed, and transferred her to the right breast.

Will's eyes homed in on the abandoned one with its wet, distended tip. Abruptly he swung off the bed, crushed out his cigarette and disappeared inside the bathroom. Elly dropped her head back, closed her eyes, and felt herself growing ready for him.

Oh, Lizzy P., hurry and finish, darlin'.

Inside the bathroom the water ran, a glass clinked, then silence . . . tense silence before Will appeared once more in the doorway, staring at her, wiping his hands on a white towel. He tossed the towel aside, skinned off his outer shirt and stood in a T-shirt that rode his muscles as closely as a skiff rides the sea.

When he spoke his voice was low, on the edge of control. "I want you like I never wanted a woman before in my life. You know that, Elly?"

"Come here, Will," she whispered.

He flung his shirt aside and moved behind her chair, stretching a hand over her naked shoulder, his fingers trailing over her breast. He dropped his head and she tipped hers to give him access to the side of her throat. She lifted her free arm, looped it around his head, feeling the unfamiliar stiffness of his bristly hair. His skin smelled of unfamiliar soap as his hand slipped over the unoccupied breast.

Her eyes drifted closed. "How much time do we have?"

"I have to report back at 1800 hours tomorrow."

"What time is that?"

"Six P.M. I catch a train at two-thirty. Lizzy's done eating. Can't we put her down now?"

She smiled at Will upside down and asked, "Is it always like this for you?"

"Like what?" he asked, his voice soft and gruff.

"Like you're gonna die if you have to wait another minute?"

The hand on her breast closed . . . lifted . . . molded. A thumb ran across its hardened tip.

"Yes, since the day I stood at the well with egg on my face and fell in love with you. Get up."

She rose and watched Will hurriedly push the chairs back together, counting seconds as he spread them with a quilt. When she bent to lay Lizzy down, his hand rode her naked shoulder. She straightened and they stood on opposite sides of the chairs, staring at each other, anticipating, suffering one last self-imposed hiatus that only made their blood beat stronger. He reached out a hand and she laid hers in it, feelings pouring already between their linked fingers.

His grip tightened, drawing her along the length of the makeshift crib while their eyes clung, dark with intent.

When they met it was lush and impatient, two bodies starved for one another, two tongues parched by months apart. It was love and lust complementing each other to the fullest. It was impact and immediacy following one upon the other, a fast hard seeking to touch all, taste all, even before their clothing was removed.

"Oh, Elly . . . I missed you." His hands skimmed low, drew her in.

"Our bed was so lonesome without you, Will." She ran her hands over his trousers, reaching for his buckle.

Their clothing fell like furled sails. Murmuring, they fell to the bed.

"Let me see you." He pulled back, let his hands and eyes travel over her, kissing where he would.

She fell back with arms upthrown, becoming the chalice from which he sipped. Likewise, she tasted him, and their timidity fled, chased by the distant acknowledgment of last chances.

Joined at last, they fit exquisitely.

They spun a web of wonder and trembled upon it, suspended in the sweet awaited union of hearts and bodies. They locked out the specters of death and war, those unpretentious intruders, and steeped themselves in each other, accepting gratification as their mortal due.

"I love you," they reiterated again and again in hoarse whispers. "I love you."

It was the sustenance they would take with them when they left this room.

The sun was setting somewhere on a horizon they could not see. A bell buoy chimed in the distance. The smell of humid salt-air drifted in the window. An arm, wilted and weighty, lay across Elly's shoulder, a knee across her thigh.

She hooked his lower lip with a finger, let it flip back up. He grinned tiredly, but his eyes remained closed.

"Hey, Will?"

"Hm?"

"Am I ever glad I came clear across Georgia on them dirty trains."

His eyes opened. "So'm I."

Their grins faded and they gazed at each other, replete. "I missed you so much, Will."

"I missed you, too, green eyes."

"Sometimes I'd turn around and look at the woodpile and expect to see you chopping wood there."

"I will be again—soon."

The reminder took them too close to tomorrow, so they withdrew into now, touching, whispering, kissing, loving being lovers. They lay brow to brow and trailed fingers up and down, fit knees and feet in places that accommodated as if made for the purpose. When they had rested they ignited one another again, and savored their second lovemaking at a more sedate pace, watching each other's faces as pleasure once more leached their bodies.

In time, when they had spoken of home and necessary things—the temperamental wind generator, the fall butchering, the gold mine of used auto parts—he lit another cigarette and lay with his shoulder pillowing her cheek.

She stared at the sheet draped over his toes and took the plunge she'd been dreading. "Where they sendin' you, Will?"

He took a deep, slow drag before answering. "I don't know."

"You mean they haven't told you yet?"

"There's scuttlebutt about the South Pacific but nobody knows where, not even the base commander. The CO's keep using the word 'spearhead'—and you know what that means."

"No, what?"

He reached for an ashtray, laid it on his stomach and tapped it with the cigarette. "It means we'd lead an attack."

"Attack?"

"Invasion, Elly."

"Invasion?" She lifted her head to search his eyes. "Of what?"

He didn't want to talk about it and, in truth, knew nothing. "Who knows? The Japs are all over the Pacific, controlling most of it. If they're sending us there we could end up anyplace from Wake to Australia."

"But how can they send you someplace and not even tell you where you're going?"

"Surprise is part of military strategy. If that's how they plan it we follow orders, that's all."

She digested that for long minutes, while his heart beat steadily beneath her ear. At length she asked quietly, "Are you scared, Will?"

He touched her hair. "Course I'm scared." He considered and added, "At times. Other times I remind myself that I'm part of the best-trained military unit in the history of the world. If I got to fight, I'd rather do it with the Marines than anybody else. And I want you to remember that when you get worried about me after I'm gone. In the Marines it's everybody for the group. Nobody thinks of himself first. Instead, everybody thinks of the group, so you always got that reassurance behind you. And every Marine is trained to take over the next higher position if his CO is injured in battle, so the company's always got a leader, the squad's always got a leader. That's what I have to concentrate on when I start gettin' the willies about maybe being shipped to the Pacific, and that's what you got to concentrate on, too."

She tried, but images of bayonets and guns got in the way.

He saw the images, too, the ones from the movie theater in the black and white newsreel. "Hey, come on, sweetheart." He crushed out his cigarette and gathered her close, rubbed her naked spine. "Let's talk about something else."

They did. They talked about the boys. And Miss Beasley. And Lydia Marsh. And the way Will had filled out. And the way Elly had learned to apply makeup and fix her hair. When dark had fallen they took a bath together, touching and teasing, giggling behind the closed bathroom door. They made love against it and ate the cold hamburgers and he talked about the food at the base and taught her all the "leatherneck lingo" he'd learned in the galley. She laughed at canned milk called armored heifer; eggs, cackleberries; pancakes, collision mats; tapioca, fish eyes; and spinach, Popeye. Around midnight they made love on the maroon rug with its green leaf design. Sometimes they laughed—perhaps a little desperately as they felt the hours slipping away. He told her about his buddy, Otis Luttrell, the carrottop fellow from Kentucky, and how they were hoping they'd ship out together. He said Otis was engaged to a pretty young woman named Cleo who worked in a grenade factory in Lexington, and that he'd never had a friend he liked as much as Otis.

The night sped by and they sat on the windowsill, watching the distant darkness where they knew ships rested at anchor. But all was pitch black, blacked out lest some German submarine be slipping through the East Coast defenses.

The war was there . . . happening . . . no matter how they tried to block it out. It was there, coloring each thought, each touch, each fleeting heartbeat they shared.

Toward dawn they slept, against their wills, touching even in slumber, then roused again to hoard each wakeful moment like misers counting pennies.

When Lizzy awakened shortly before seven they brought her into bed with them and Will lay on his side, head braced on a hand, watching once more the sight he'd never grow tired of. After the feeding he said he wanted to give Lizzy her bath. Elly watched, wistful and yearny while Will knelt beside the deep tub and took joy in caring for the baby. He did it all, dried and diapered her and dressed her in clean rompers, then lay on the bed playing with her and laughing at her gurgling baby-talk and teddy-bear poses. But often his eyes would lift to Elly's, on the other side of the baby, and the unspoken sorrow would be rife between them.

They ate in their room and remained in it until a different bellgirl came to inquire if they were staying a second day. They packed their meager bags and stood in the doorway, looking back at the room that had provided a haven for the past eighteen hours. They turned to each other and tried to look brave, but their last kiss in private was one of trembling lips and despairing thoughts.

They took to the streets of Augusta, ambling along the hot pavement until they found a park with a deserted bandstand surrounded by iron benches. They sat on one and spread a blanket on the grass where they settled Lizzy to play with Will's dog tags. They looked at the trees, the clear blue Georgia sky, the child at their feet—but most often at each other. Occasionally they kissed, but lightly, with their eyes open, as if to close out the sight of the other for even a moment was unthinkable. More often they touched—his hand lightly grazing her shoulder blade or her palm resting on his thigh while he toyed with the friendship ring which had, indeed, turned her finger green.

"When I come back I'm gonna buy you a real gold wedding ring."

"I don't want a real gold wedding ring. I want the one I wore the day I married you."

Their eyes met—sad eyes no longer denying what lay ahead.

"I love you, green eyes. Don't forget that."

"I love you, too, soldier boy."

"I'll try to write often but . . . well, you know."

"I'll write every day, I promise."

"They're gonna censor everything, so you still might not know where I am, even if I tell you."

"It won't matter. Long as I know you're safe."

Another extended gaze ended when he rested his forehead upon hers. They sat thus, fingers loosely entwined, for minutes. Somewhere in the park a pair of herring gulls screeched. Out on the water a steam whistle sounded. From nearer came the clink-clink of Lizzy flailing the chain and dog tags. And over all rested the smell of purple petunias blossoming at the foot of a tiny fountain.

Will felt his throat fill, swallowed and told his wife, "It's time to go."

She suddenly radiated false brightness. "Oh . . . course it is . . . why, we better get Daddy to that station, hadn't we, Lizzy?"

He carried the baby and she carried their bags until they stood again in the noisy, crowded depot where they faced each other and suddenly found themselves tongue-tied. Lizzy became fascinated with a button on his blouse, trying to pull it off with a chubby hand.

"The two-thirty for Columbia, Raleigh, Washington and Philadelphia now boarding at gate three!"

"That's me."

"You got your ticket?" Elly asked.

"Yes, ma'am."

Their eyes met and he circled the slope of her neck with his free hand, squeezing hard.

"Give the boys a kiss from me and give 'em those chocolate bars."

"I w–will. And send me your address as soon as th–they—" She couldn't go on, afraid of releasing the choking sobs that filled her chest.

He nodded, his face doleful.

"Last call for Columbia, Raleigh—"

Her eyes were streaming, his filled to glittering.

"Oh, Will . . ."

"Elly . . ."

They hugged awkwardly, with the baby between them. "Come back to me."

"You damn right I will."

Their kiss was a terrible thing—goodbye, keep low, keep safe—with tongues thickened by the need to cry.

A whistle wailed. *"Booooard!"* The train lumbered to life.

He tore his mouth away, thrust the baby into her hands and ran, leaped and boarded the rolling car, turning at the last possible moment to catch a blurry glimpse of Elly and Lizzy waving from amid a crowd of strangers in a dirty train depot in a hot Georgia town.

Eleanor Parker no longer prayed, so perhaps it was more imprecation than prayer when she choked against her fist, "Damn it, k–keep him safe, you hear?"

Chapter 18

18 JUNE 1942

Dear Elly,

What a crazy life this is. Yesterday I was with you and today I'm on a train heading for San Francisco. Red is with me but he isn't as much company as you. Ive just been thinking over and over about how wunderfull it was being with you and how much I love you and how glad I am that we had that one day together it was like being in heaven green eyes . . .

June 18, 1942
Dear Will,

I'm writing this cuz I just got to. My hearts so full and feels like its gonna spill over less I tell you how I feel about our night in Augusta. I don't know when this will get to you cause I don't know where to send it but feelings are feelings and mine will be just as true even if you read this a month from now. (I'll save it and send it when you send me your address.) You know Will when I first met you I said I still loved Glendon and I thought I did. Glendon was the first real nice person that ever come into my life. He treated me like I was put on this earth for something besides repenting and being poked fun at. He was a real good man Glendon was and at the time when I was married to him I was real happy for the first time in my life so I thought that meant I loved him somethin fearful. And I did love him don't get me wrong but when Glendon and me did private things together it was never like it is with me and you. I never told you before but the first time Glendon and me ever did it was in the woods and we did it cause his daddy died and he was greevin. I remember how I layed there on my back lookin up at the green branches and thought about the sound of this one bird that kept calling and calling off in the distance, and I wondered what it was and much later I found out it was a common snipe doing his flight call which is this mournful whistle that lifts up & up & up with each beat. Its funny now to think back on how my mind was always on other things when Glendon and me got private. He and me begot three children and that ought to mean we were as close in spirit as a man and woman can get but Will I had two nights being close with you and they are the two nights that showed me what love really is. The flight call of the snipe was the farthest thing from my mind when you and me were making love Will. I can't quit thinking about it and how I got to feeling just looking at you before you even got undressed. I watch you move around taking off your tie and your jacket and I feel like heat lightnin is going thru my insides Will. I says to myself nobody moves like him. Nobody unbuttons his cuffs like him. Nobody's got eyes as pretty as him. Nobody's luckier than me.

I went back and read what I wrote and it still don't seem to say it like I feel but telling what love is like is a lot like telling what the call of a bird is like. You hear it and you reckoniz it and its in yourself so strong you think for sure you can repeat it for someone else. But you can't. I just wanted you to know though that I love you different from what I loved Glendon. They say everybody goes through life searching for the other half of hisself and I know now you're the other half of me cause when I'm with you I feel hoel . . .

July 16, 1942
Dear Mr. Parker,

Eleanor shared your last letter with me and together she and I have looked at the atlas and tried to imagine exactly where you are. I have taken her books about the Pacific Islands so that she can see what the flora and fauna are like there, also the weather and the ocean itself.

Things are changing here. The town seems quite deserted. Not only are our young men gone, the young women are leaving, too. The latest billboard pictures a woman and the slogan, "What job is mine on the Victory line?" So many are leaving to find jobs at Lockheed in Marietta, the shipyards in Mobile and at Packard and Chrysler up north, making engines and fuselages and landing gear. When I was young there were few choices given to a woman who did not marry. Teaching, becoming a domestic, or a librarian. Even female nurses were frowned upon then. Today the women are driving city buses, using acetylene torches and running cranes. I cannot help but wonder what will happen when the Allies are victorious and all you men come home. Rest assured, *your* job will be waiting.

Everything is getting scarce here. Canned fruit (thank heavens I live in Georgia where it will soon be fresh on the vine), tar (the roads are abysmal), sugar (which I miss most of all), bobby pins (the women are shearing their hair until they look like recruits in basic training), cloth (Washington has issued a directive that for the duration of the war men's suits shall be manufactured without cuffs, pleats and patch pockets), can openers (thank heavens I own one). Even meat and cars. One only chuckles at the mention of a new car nowadays. Yesterday's paper reported that Mr. Edsel Ford is unable to get a new car of his own until a Detroit rationing board can consider his application. Isn't that unbelievable when his family has manufactured *thirty million* automobiles!

If there is one thing this war does it is to equalize.

Things at the library are much as when you left except that since you joined up Lula Peak doesn't come around any more *to better herself.* Forgive me my face-tiousness but Lula, as you know, is a sore spot. I fear I may lose Franklin Gilmore, who is talking about not going back to high school for his senior year but enlisting instead. Fewer books are being manufactured what with so many of the lumber companies supplying wood for packing crates instead of paper. But one title is being printed in greater numbers than any other, The Red Cross First Aid Manual, which is the bestselling book ever.

I still go to see Eleanor and the children each Saturday but have been unable to convince her to come into town. However, she has developed a friendship with Mrs. Marsh and speaks of her fondly. I am taking it upon myself to send the grade school principal out to your place to see that Donald Wade is enrolled in first grade, come September. I shall not tell Eleanor I sent him and I would prefer if you did not tell her either. Donald Wade is a bright lad and is already reading at first grade level. He can recite verbatim the announcements of many radio shows and is quite a little singer, which you may not know. He and Thomas sang for me the last time I was there, the Cream of Wheat song from "Let's Pretend." It was amusing but I praised them heartily and told Donald Wade that when he is in school he will be singing every day and took it upon myself to teach him one which I remember from when I was a child.

> *October gave a party*
> *The leaves by hundreds came*
> *The ashes, oaks and maples*
> *And leaves of every name*
> *The sunshine spread a carpet*
> *And everything was grand*
> *Miss Weather led the dancing*
> *Professor Wind the band.*

I believe, however, that Eleanor liked the song as much as Donald Wade, she who takes time to explore and appreciate the wonders of the woods and all its creatures. She sang it along with Donald Wade and hummed it while clearing away our tea things. She is well but misses you greatly.

And with this I must end. I shall not dwell on good luck wishes which seem so paltry in light of where you are and the service you are providing for those of us who keep lights in our windows. I shall simply say, you are in my prayers nightly.

Affectionately,
Gladys Beasley

23 June, 1942
Somewhere on the Pacific Ocean
Dear Elly,

Well I'm on a ship green eyes but that's about all I'm allowed to tell you not the name of it or our destination, which none of us have been told yet. We all got ideas though, judging from the direction we're traveling. We rode the train to San Francisco and embarked here 21 June and life aboard a troop transport ain't so bad. The navy is playing host so we got the soft life for a while and can cork off. Chow is good, all fresh meat and vegtubles and spuds and the navy does KP. About all we do is attend classes on Japanese intelligence and do calesthenics on the deck every day but tomorrow they say we're gonna have a field day which means we got to clean our bunk area top to bottom. Mine's in the forward hold, starboard, which is good. Not much engine noise and pretty smooth sailing. Red's got the sack just below mine they're like canvas cots. We play a lot of poker and a lot of the guys read comic books and trade them. Some of them read paper books and everybody talks about his sweetheart back home I don't talk about you tho except to Red cause he's my buddy and he dont go blabbin everything a man says. I didnt tell him the personal stuff about in Augusta but I told him about the time you threw the egg at me and he laughed hisself sick. He wants to meet you when this damn war is over. Well here's my address till I let you know different— Pfc. William Lee Parker, 1st Raider Bn., 1st Marines, So. Pacific. I'll probly write every day till we get to wherever they're sending us cuz there's plenty of time on this ship. I told you before how we call our rifles our sweethearts but when I write it now it means you. I love you sweetheart.

Your Will

June 28, 1942
Dearest Will,

This waiting is awful because I don't know where you are and there's no way to tell when I'll find out . . .

22 July, 1942
Somewhere in the South Pacific
Dear Elly,

We're anchored offshore again and where we are is the last Navy post office and we're on definite orders. Tomorrow we sail for the last time and this is it. So tonight is our last night for writing letters and when we give em to our unit postal clerk for mailing we don't know when we'll get a chance to write again. We been told now where we're goin' and why but I can't tell you sweetheart. All I can tell you is I'll be riding on a sub tomorrow. I just want you to know that everybody's calm here. It's funny, it don't seem like we're going into battle except everybody's talking quieter tonight and polishing their rifles even though they're already shining like the north star. I can tell you this much and hope they don't cross it off. Where we are there ain't no north star. Instead we see the southern cross which we have all learned to find in the night sky. I'm laying in my sack thinking of you and the kids and smoking a Lucky Strike and trying to think of all the things that are in my heart that ought to be said in this letter. But all I do is get a lump in my throat and think to myself god damn it Parker your goin back home, you hear? Elly what you did for me in the last year is more than anybody did for me in my whole life. I love you so much Elly that it hurts inside way deep down in my gut when I even think about it. You gave me a home and a family and love and a place to come back to and when I say thank you it sounds so damn small and not nearly as powerful as what I feel in my heart. I looked in Miss Beasley's book of poems to try to find one that says what I'm feeling but there ain't even words in there that'll do it. You just gotta know green eyes that youre the best thing that ever came along in my whole life and no ocean and no war is ever gonna change that. Now I got to go cause I'm getting to feel a little blue and lonesome but dont you worry about me cuz like I said before I'm with the best outfit there is. Just remember how much I love you and that I'm coming home when this thing is over.

All my love,
Will

August 1, 1942
Dear Will,

I got what I think is your last letter you wrote from on the ship and I got to feeling so blue I had to take a walk with the kids in the orchard to keep from breaking down. It's so awful not knowing where you are or if you're safe ...

August 4, 1942
Dear Will,
   It's a big day today cause Lizzy P is 8 months old and I'm weaning her. My breasts are so full of milk they feel like they're ready to bust ...

August 10, 1942
Dear Will,
   Miss Beasley brought the newspapers and the headlines are big today. I always get scared when I see the letters two inches high ... this time about a big battle in the Solomons and all the damage to our ships and I'm so scared you were on one of them ...

August 11, 1942
Dear Will,
   ... They just don't tell us much here except to say the offensive continues with "considerable enemy resistance encountered." It is only Monday but Miss Beasley came out again cause she believes like I do that youre someplace out there in the middle of that awful mess in the Solomons where the Japs are claiming they sank 22 ships and damaged 6 more ...

August 18, 1942
Dear Will,
   ... you can't imagine how hard it is to read the war news in the papers and still not know anything ...

20 Aug 1942
Somewhere in the Pacific
Dearest Elly,
   I'm alive and unhurt but I been in battle now so I know how it feels to kill another human being. You just have to keep telling yourself that he's the enemy and thinking about when you get home how good things will be. I'm sitting here in a foxhole thinking about the back porch steps and that day I washed the boys at the well and we dried them off together. I'd give anything for a bath. Where I am it never stops raining. There's palm trees and a lot of yellowish grass stretching from the beach to the jungle. I can't say I like the jungle much but it does have things to eat. We were cut off from supplies for quite awhile and I want to tell you it was a sickening feeling when we looked out at the water and saw our ships gone. I drank so much coconut milk its coming out of my ears, which by the way got some kind of fungus growing in them. Between that and mosquito bites and rain it's a pretty hellish place here but I don't want you to worry because today our fighter planes got in. I wish you could've heard us cheer when they swung over and landed. It was the most beautifull sight Ive ever seen. Not only did they bring fresh supplies but they said the mail can go out. We never know if it'll reach you though, but if this does kiss those babies for me and tell Miss Beasley I had to leave my book of poems behind but I tore out the page with my favorite one and I carry it in my field pack. Reading it and your letters is about the only thing that keeps me going ...

September 4, 1942
Dear Will,
 ... well, Donald Wade went off on the schoolbus for the first time today ...

Oct. 3, 1942
Dearest Will,
 ... The boys taught Lizzy P. to say daddy today ...

Oct. 4, 1942
Dearest Will,
 Your letter finally reached me, the first one from the battle zone. Oh Will I'm so worried about your ears I wish I could drop some warmed sweet oil in them for you and wash your hair and comb it the way you used to like for me to do. Miss Beasley and I think we figured out for sure where you are and we think it's Guadalcanal and it scares me to death to think of you there cause I know the fighting has been terrible there and its Japanese territory ...

WESTERN UNION

REGRET TO INFORM YOU YOUR HUSBAND WAS SERIOUSLY
WOUNDED IN ACTION 25 OCT IN SOLOMON ISLANDS. UNTIL
NEW ADDRESS IS RECEIVED MAIL FOR HIM QUOTE
CORPORAL WILLIAM L. PARKER 37 773 785
HOSPITALIZED CENTRAL POSTAL DIRECTORY APOO640 CARE
POSTMASTER NEW YORK NY UNQUOTE NEW ADDRESS AND
FURTHER INFORMATION FOLLOW DIRECT FROM HOSPITAL J
A ULIO THE ADJT GENERAL 7:10 A.M.

Nov. 1, 1942
Dear Will,
 I'm so worried. Oh Will I got a telegram and they said you were seriously wounded but nothing else—not where you are or how you are or anything ...

Nov. 2, 1942
Dear Will,
 I didn't sleep a wink last night just laid awake crying and wondering if you're still alive or if you have lost an arm or a leg or your beautiful brown eyes ...

Nov. 3, 1942
Dear Will,
 ... Sometimes I get so upset because all anybody will tell you is Somewhere In The South Pacific but Miss Beasley pointed out an article about Mrs. Roosevelt visiting the troops overseas and even it started "Somewhere In England," so I guess if it's good enough for the president's wife it'll have to be good enough for me but I'm worried sick about you ...

November 4, 1942
Dear Will,
 It just struck me that the telegram said corporal so you got promoted! I shucked off my drears and turned my thoughts positive cause thats the only thing to do. You're alive I know it I won't give up hope and I'll write every single day whether I hear from you or not ...

4193 US Navy Hosp. Plant
APO 515
New York, NY
Dear <u>Mrs. Parker,</u>
I am pleased to inform you that on <u>1 Nov 1942</u> your <u>husband, Corp. William L.</u>
<u>Parker, 37 773 785, was making normal improvement.</u> Diagnosis <u>wound left thigh.</u>

Thomas M. Simpson
1st Lieut. M.A.O. Registrar

4193 US Navy Hosp. Plant
APO 515
New York, NY
Dear <u>Mrs. Parker,</u>
I am pleased to inform you that on <u>6 Nov 1942</u> your <u>husband, Corp. William L.</u>
<u>Parker, 37 773 785, was evacuated to zone of noncombat and underwent surgery</u>
<u>on wound, left thigh. Is making normal improvement.</u>

Virgil A. Saylor, 1st Lt.,
MAC Registrar

U.S. War Department
Official Business
20 Nov 1942
Dear Mrs. Parker,

As commanding officer of your husband, Corporal William L. Parker who was injured in action 1 Nov 1942 on the Island of Guadalcanal I felt it imperative to reassure you that his condition is no longer life threatening and that eventual recovery can be fully expected. On 6 November he was transferred by air to the Navy hospital at Melbourne, Australia where he underwent successful surgery and awaits transfer to the United States.

Corporal Parker is a credit to his company and to the United States Marines. He fought well and without complaint. On 14 Sept 1942, while engaging the enemy in action on Guadalcanal, Corporal Parker displayed conspicuous gallantry in attempting to rescue Private Otis D. Luttrell by dragging him to a foxhole under heavy enemy fire. On 25 October Corporal Parker again proved himself a leader by singlehandedly knocking out a Japanese dugout emplacement which was holding up our advance. The enemy hole-up was situated in a cave made inaccessible by severe enemy fire from inside. Corporal Parker voluntarily crawled to the cave from its blind side, attempted to knock a hole in the roof and when unable to do so, attempted to kick the rocks away at the foot of the cave. Four times he threw hand grenades inside only to have them promptly returned by the Japanese. Next Corporal Parker tried holding the grenades for three seconds before delivering them. When these were also returned, Parker reportedly "got mad" and made a dynamite bomb which he thrust into the breach killing eight Japanese soldiers but receiving injuries to himself from an enemy fragmentation grenade which simultaneously detonated at the mouth of the cave.

Because of Corporal Parker's determination and bravery the 1st Raider Bn. won a decisive victory over the Japanese at the mouth of the Ilu River, rendering them a loss of 12 tanks and some 600 troops in the 1st Marine sector.

It is with pride and pleasure that for heroism above and beyond the call of duty I am recommending to the Commander in Chief of the United States Armed Forces that Corporal William L. Parker, USMC 1st Raider Battalion, be awarded the medal of valor of the Order of the Purple Heart.

Yours truly,
Col. Merritt A. Edson
Commander, 1st Marine Raiders
USMC

Balboa Naval Hospital
San Diego, California
Dear <u>Mrs. Parker,</u>
I am pleased to inform you that on <u>6 Dec 1942</u> your <u>husband, Corp. William L. Parker, 37 773 785, was transferred to Balboa Naval Hospital, San Diego U.S.A. for further medical treatment.</u>

Balboa Naval Hospital
San Diego
7 Dec. 1942
Dear Elly,

I'm home again and you don't need to worry any more. A Red Cross nurse is writing this for me because the doc won't let me sit up yet. I finally got all your letters. They caught up with me in a hospital in Melbourne. Elly honey it was so good to read all those words from you, all about Donald Wade going to school and Lizzy P. saying her first words and how they taught her to say Daddy. I wish I was there with you all now but it looks like that'll be a while yet. My leg isn't so good but at least I've still got it and it might be stiff but I'll be able to walk, they say. The docs here say I'm still carrying a piece of metal in my left leg and I may have to have surgery again. But what the heck, at least I'm alive.

I'm sorry they didn't tell you more right after I got hit so you wouldnt have worried so much. I would have done so myself but I guess I wasn't in much shape for writing. But don't you worry now. I'm okay and I mean it.

By now you know I got hit by a Jap grenade while I was trying to flush eight of them out of a holeup near the airfield on the Canal which it's okay now to tell you where I was, on Guadalcanal. The Canal was rough and we lost a lot there but we set them back and the airstrip is ours now. If we hadn't the Pacific would still be theirs and I'm damn proud of what we did. I might as well tell you now my buddy Red didn't make it and thats all I can say about it at the moment because its hard for me to think about it. So as I was saying it doesn't seem much to put up with a few chunks of steel in your leg. But I have to confess I never was so glad to see anything as I was to see Old Glory waving over the Navy Hospital on good old American soil when I debarked here. Damn, Elly, I wish I could see you but this leg will have to mend first so I'll be here a while but I'll sure be looking for your letters. It seems like since I joined the Marines I've lived for mail call. Now that I'm in one place your letters will get to me so write often, okay green eyes? Please don't worry about me. Now that I'm back things'll be just fine. Kiss the kids for me and tell Miss Beasley to write, too.

All my love,
Will

Dec. 9, 1942
Dear Will,
   Oh Will your home at last. Your letter just came and I cryed when I read it I was so happy. They won't send you back will they? Is your leg healing any better? I'm so worried about it and what you must be going through with the operations and the pain. If you weren't so far away I'd come to you again like I did in Augusta, but I just don't see how I can come clear to California. But would't it be something if we could be together for Christmas? . . .

24 Dec. 1942
Dear Elly,
   The nurses strung colored lights across the foot of our beds but looking at them gives me that choky feeling again. I'm layin here thinking of last Christmas eve when you and me filled the stockings for the boys. I want to be home so bad.

Jan 29, 1943
Dear Will,
   Happy birthday . . .

5 Feb. 1943
Dear Elly,
   They got me up on crutches today . . .

Chapter 19

Calvin Purdy dropped Will at the end of his driveway.
   "Thanks a million, Mr. Purdy."
   "No thanks necessary, Will, not from a GI. You sure you don't want me to take you the rest o' the way on up't the house?"
   "No, sir, I was always partial to this little stretch of woods. Sounds good to walk through the quiet alone, if you know what I mean."
   "Sure do, son. Ain't no place prettier'n Georgia in May. You need any help with them crutches?"
   "No, sir. I can manage." Leading with both feet, Will worked his way out of Calvin Purdy's '31 Chevrolet while Purdy retrieved Will's duffel bag and brought it around, then laced it over Will's shoulder.
   "Be more'n happy to take your duffel up," Purdy repeated accommodatingly.
   " 'Preciate it, Mr. Purdy, but I kinda wanted to surprise Elly."
   "You mean she doesn't know you're comin'?"
   "Not yet."
   "We-e-e-ll, then I understand why you want to go up alone . . . Corporal Parker." Grinning, Purdy extended his hand and gripped Will's tightly. "Anytime I can give you a lift or be of any he'p, just holler. And welcome home."

After Purdy pulled away, Will stood for a moment, listening to the silence. No cannonade in the distance, no bullets *thupping* into the earth beside him, no mosquitos buzzing, no men screaming. All was silence, blessed May silence. The woods were in deep leaf, heavy green weighting down the branches. Beside the road a patch of wild chicory created a cloud of blue stars. Nearby a clump of wild clover startled, livid in the heat of its summer blush. Some creature had feasted on a smilax vine, spreading a scent like root beer in the air. A yellow warbler did a flight dance, landed on a branch and sang its seven clear, sweet notes, eyeing Will with head atilt.

Home again.

He moved up the driveway beneath the arch of branches that allowed the azure sky entry. He tipped his head and admired it, marveling that he need not cock an ear for the sound of distant engines, nor squint an eye in an effort to identify a wing shape or a rising red sun painted on a fuselage.

Forget it, Parker, you're home now.

The driveway was soft, the air warm, his crutches poked holes in the red earth. They must've had rain recently. Rain. He'd never much cared for rain, not in his early life when he'd lived mostly in the open, certainly not on the Canal, where the damned rain was ceaseless, where it filled foxholes, turned tent camps to fetid quagmires, rotted the soles off sturdy leather boots and fostered mosquitos, malaria and a host of creeping fungi that grew between toes, inside ears and anyplace two skin surfaces touched.

I said, forget it, Parker!

The odd thing was, though he'd been Stateside for six months he still couldn't acclimate to it. He still scanned the skies. Still listened for stealthy movement behind him. Still expected the telltale clack of two bamboo stalks rubbing. Still flinched at sudden noises. He closed his eyes and breathed deep. The air here had no mildewy smell, instead it held a tang of wild tansy which seemed familiar and welcoming and very native. During his drifting years whenever he'd caught a cold he'd brewed himself a cup of tansy tea, and once when he'd gashed his hand on a piece of rusty barbed wire he'd made a compress of it that cured the infection.

Walking up his own road amid the smells of tansy and smilax, he let the fact sink in: he was home for good.

At the sourwood tree he stopped, let his canvas duffel bag slip down and lowered his left foot to the ground. Real, solid ground, a little moist maybe, but American. Safe. Ground he'd shaped himself with a mule named Madam while a little boy sat and watched, and the boy's mother brought red nectar and a baby brother down the lane in a faded red wagon.

He resisted the urge to drop his crutches and ease onto the bank where the grass was green-rich and wild columbine blossomed. Instead, he shouldered his bag and moved westward toward the opening in the trees where the clearing lay.

Reaching it, he paused in surprise. During his stretch in the South Pacific, when he'd pictured home, he often saw it as it had first been, a motley collection of scrap iron and chicken dung beside a teetering house patched with tin. What he saw today made him hold his breath and stand stone still in wonder.

Flowers! Everywhere, flowers . . . and all of them blue! Gay, uncivilized blossoms, clambering unchecked without a hint of order or precision. How like his Elly to sow wildly and let rain and sun—Will smiled—and all those years of chicken manure do the rest. He scanned the clearing. Blue—Lord a-mercy, he'd never seen so much blue! Flowers of every shade and tint of blue that nature had ever produced. He knew them all from his study of the bees.

Nearest the house tall Persian blue phlox bordered the porch, thick and high and tufted, giving way to Canterbury bells that bled from deepest royal purple to a pale violet-pink. At their feet began a rich spread of heliotrope in coiled blue-violet sprays. Against the east wall of the chicken house a clematis climbed a trellis of strings. There, too, began a carpet of long-stemmed cornflowers, as deep and true as the sky, continuing along the adjacent chicken-yard fence in a wall of royal color. At the shady border beneath the trees, pale violets began, giving way to deep-hued forget-me-nots which ranged in the open sun, meeting a spread of blue vervain. On the opposite side of the yard a wooden wagon wheel had been painted white and stood as a backdrop for a stand of regal larkspur which covered the blue spectrum from purple to indigo to palest Dresden. Before them, much shorter and more delicate, a patch of flax-flowers waved in the breeze on fernlike stems. Somewhere in the conglomeration purple petunias bloomed. Will could smell them as he moved up the path, which was bordered by fuzzy ageratum. Where that path led around the back of the house a new pergola stood, laden with morning glories, their bells lifted to heaven. Birds darted everywhere, a chirping cacophony. A ruby-throated hummingbird at the morning glories. Wrens lambasting him with music from the low branch of a crabapple tree, and appropriately enough, a pair of bluebirds near one of the gourds. Spotting them, he smiled, recalling Donald Wade placing the bluebird figurine on the windowsill for just this reason. Well, they had their bluebirds now.

And bees ... everywhere, bees, gathering nectar and pollen from the sea of color they loved best, humming, lifting on gauzy wings to move to the next blossom and join their wing-music to that of the birds.

Only as he neared the house did Will find a ruddy splash. Several feet off the last porch step stood a washtub, painted white, bulging with cinnamon pinks so thick they cascaded over the sides—crimson and heliotrope and coral and rose—so fragrant they made his head light. On the porch steps lay a cluster of them, crushed, wilted. He picked them up, held them, smelled them, glanced around the clearing before depositing them where they'd been, carefully, as if they were the trappings of a religious ceremony.

He raised his eyes to the screen door, mounted the steps and opened the screen, expecting any moment to hear Elly or the kids call, "Who's there?"

The kitchen was empty.

"Elly?" he called, letting his duffel bag slip from his shoulder.

In the answering silence wands of sunlight angled across the scrubbed floor and climbed the mopboard. The room smelled good, of bread and spice. On the table was a crocheted doily and a thick white crockery pitcher filled with a sampling of flowers from the yard; on the windowsill, the bluebird figurine. The room was neat, orderly, clean. His eyes moved to the cupboard where a white enamel cake pan was covered with a dishtowel. He lifted a corner of the cloth—bars, unfrosted, half-gone. He tucked a pinch into his mouth, then poked his head into the front room.

"Elly?"

Silence. Summer afternoon silence, stretching into Will's very soul.

Their bedroom was empty. He stood in the doorway imbibing familiarities—the Madeira lace dresser set, a slipper-shaped dish holding bobby- and hair-pins, a stack of freshly folded diapers ... the bed. It was not, he discovered, disappointing to arrive to an empty house. He'd had so little time alone. These minutes, reacclimating, seeped within his bones in a wholly healing way.

Neither was anyone in the boys' room. The crib, he noted, had been moved in here.

Back in the kitchen he cut an enormous square of the moist golden bars and took a bite—honey, pecans, cloves and cinnamon. Mmmm ... delicious. He anchored the remaining piece in his teeth and stumped to the door, then outside.

"Elly?" he bellowed from the top of the steps, pausing, listening. "Elllleeeee?"

From beyond the barn a mule brayed as if objecting to being awakened. Madam. He headed that way, found the beast but no Elly. He checked the chicken coop—it was clean; the storage sheds—their doors were all closed; the vegetable garden, it was empty; and finally the backyard, passing under the pergola with its bonnet of morning glories. Nobody at the clothesline either.

With all these flowers and the warm temperatures, undoubtedly the honey would be running. He'd walk down the orchard to see, to pass the time reacquainting himself with the bees while waiting for Elly.

The earth wore a mantle of heavy grass but he made his way easily with the crutches, following the overgrown double-trail compacted long ago by Glendon Dinsmore's Steel Mule. Everything was as he remembered, the hickories and oaks as green as watermelon rind, the katydids fiddling away in the tall redtop grass, the dead branch shaped like a dog's paw, and, farther along, the magnolia with the oak growing from its crotch. He topped a small rise and there lay the orchard on the opposite hill, steeping in the warm May sun, smelling faintly of other years' fermented fruit and the flowering weeds and wildings that bordered the trees and surrounding woods. He let his eyes wander appreciatively over the squat trees— peach, apple, pear and quince, marching around the east-sloping hill as if in formation. And along the south edge, the hives, rimmed in red and blue and yellow and green, as he'd painted them. And halfway down ... a ... a woman? Will's head jutted. Was it? In a veiled hat and trousers? Filling the saltwater pans? Naw, it couldn't be! But it was! A woman, working in fat yellow farmer gloves that met the cuffs of one of his old blue chambray shirts whose collar was buttoned tightly and turned up around her jaws. Toting two buckets in the boys' wagon. Bending to dip the water with a tin dipper and pour it into the low, flat pans. A woman— *his wife*—tending the bees!

He smiled and felt a surge of love strong enough to end the war, could it have been harnessed and channeled. Jubilantly, he raised a hand and waved. *"Elly?"*

She straightened, looked, looked harder, lifted the veil up, shaded her eyes ... and finally the shock hit.

"Will!" She dropped the dipper and ran. Flat-out, arms and feet churning like steel drivers. "Will!" The hat bounced off and fell but she ran on, waving a yellow glove. "Will, Will!"

He gripped his crutches and stumped toward her, fast, hard, reaching, his body swinging like a Sunday morning steeple bell. Smiling. Feeling his heart clubbing. His eyes stinging. Watching Elly race toward him while the boys spilled out of the woods and ran, too, taking up the call, "Will's home! Will! Will!"

They met beside a rangy apple tree with a force great enough to send one crutch to the ground and Will, too, had she not been there to clasp him. Arms, mouths, souls combined once again while bees droned a reunion song and the sun poured down upon a soldier's hat lying on the verdant ground. Tongues and tears, and two bodies yearning together amid a rush of kisses—deep, hurried, unbelieving kisses. They clung, choked with emotion, burying their faces, smelling one another—Velvo shaving cream and crushed cinnamon pinks—joined mouths and tongues to taste each other once more. And for them the war was over.

The boys came pelting—"Will! Will!"—and Lizzy P. toddled out of the woods crying, left behind.

"Kemo sabe! Sprout!" Will bent stiffly to hug them against his legs, circling them both in his arms, kissing their hot, freckled faces, clasping them close, smell-

ing them, too—sweaty little boys who'd been playing in the sun long and hard. Elly warned, "Careful for Will's leg," but the hugging continued in quartet, with her arms around Will even as he greeted the boys, everybody kissing, laughing, teetering, while down the lane Lizzy stood in the sun, rubbing her eyes and wailing.

"Why didn't you tell us you were comin'?"

"I wanted to surprise you."

Elly wiped her eyes on the thick gloves, then yanked them off. "Oh, lorzy, what am I doin' with them still on?"

"Come here." He snagged her waist, kissed her again amid the scrambling boys, who still had him shackled and were peppering him with news and questions: "Are you stayin' home? . . . We got kittens . . . Wow, is this your uniform? . . . I got vacation . . . Did you kill any Japs? . . . Hey, Will, Will . . . guess what . . ."

For the moment both Elly and Will were oblivious to the pair. "Oh, Will . . ." Her eyes shone with joy, straight into his. "I can't believe you're back. How is your leg?" She suddenly remembered. "Here, boys, back off and let Will sit. Can you sit on the grass—is it okay?"

"It's okay." He lowered himself stiffly and breathed in a great gulp of orchard air.

Down the lane Lizzy continued bawling. Donald Wade tried on Will's garrison cap, which covered his eyebrows and ears. "Wow!" he crowed. "Lookit me! I'm a Marine!"

"Lemme!" Thomas reached. "I wanna wear it!"

"No, it's mine!"

"Ain't neither—I get it, too!"

"Boys, go get your sister and bring her here."

They dashed off like puppies after a ball, Donald Wade in the lead, wearing the hat, Thomas in pursuit.

Elly sat on her knees beside Will, her arms locked around his neck. "You look so good, all tan and pretty."

"Pretty!" He laughed and rubbed her hip.

"Well, prettier'n me in these durn britches and your old shirt." They couldn't quit touching each other, looking at each other.

"You look good to me—good enough to eat."

He tasted her jaw, nipping playfully. She giggled and hunched a shoulder. The giggling subsided when their gazes met, leading to another kiss, this one soft, unhurried, unsexual. A solemnization. When it ended he breathed the scent of her with his eyes still closed.

"Elly . . ." he prayed, in thanksgiving.

She rested her hands on his chest and gave the moment its due.

At length they roused from their absorption with one another and he asked, "So, what're you doing out here?"

"Tendin' your bees."

"So I see. How long's this been goin' on?"

"Since you been gone."

"Why didn't you tell me in your letters?"

" 'Cause I wanted to surprise you, too!"

There were a thousand things he wanted to say, as a poet might say them. But he was an ordinary man, neither glib nor eloquent. He could only tell her, quietly, "You're some woman, you know that?"

She smiled and touched his hair—it was long again, streaky yellow, bending toward his face just enough to please her. She rested her elbows on his shoulders and wrapped both arms around his head and simply held him, bringing to him again the scent of crushed cinnamon pinks from her skin. He buried his nose in her neck.

"Mercy, you smell good. Like you been rollin' in flowers."

She laughed. "I have. I didn't like the mint, but your pamphlets said cinnamon pinks worked just as good so I smeared myself with them. Guess what, Will?" Exhilarated, she backed up to see his face, leaving her arms twined about his neck.

"What?"

"The honey is runnin'."

He let his eyelids droop, let his lips soften suggestively and closed both hands upon her breasts, hidden between them. "Y' damned right it is, darlin'. Wanna feel?"

Her blood rushed, her heart pounded and she felt a glorious spill deep within.

"More than anything," she whispered, nudging his lips, but the children were near so he sat back with his hands flattened against the hot grass while she angled her head, tasted him shallow and deep. He opened his mouth and remained unmoving as her tongue played upon his in a series of teasing plunders. He returned the favor, washing her sweet mouth with wet kisses, sucking her lower lip.

"What you guys doin'?" Donald Wade stood beside them, holding Lizzy P. on his hip while Thomas approached, wearing Will's hat.

Leaving her arms across Will's collarbones, Elly squinted over her shoulder. "Kissin'. Better get used to it, 'cause there's gonna be a lot of it goin' on around here." Unrattled, she dropped down beside her man on the grass, raising her hands for the baby. "C'm 'ere, sugar. Come see daddy. Well, goodness gracious, all those tears—did you think we all run off and left you?" Chuckling, she brought the baby's cheek against her own, then set her down and began cleaning up Lizzy's tearful face while the little girl trained a watchful stare on Will. The boys plopped down, doing the things that big brothers do. Thomas took Lizzy's palm and bounced it. "Hi, Lizzy." Donald Wade brought his eyes down to the level of hers and talked brightly. "This's Will, Lizzy. Can you say, *Daddy?* Say, *Daddy,* Lizzy." Then, to Will, "She only talks when she wants to."

Lizzy didn't say Daddy, or Will. Instead, when he took her, she pushed against his chest, straining and twisting back for Elly, beginning to cry again. In the end he was forced to relinquish her until she grew used to him again.

"The orchard looks good. Did you have the trees sprayed?"

"Didn't *have* 'em sprayed, I did it myself."

"And the yard, why that's the prettiest thing I've seen in years. You do all that?"

"Yup. Me'n the boys."

"Mama let me put seeds in the holes!" piped up Thomas.

"Good boy. Who built the archway for the morning glories?"

"Mama."

Elly added, "Me'n Donald Wade, didn't we, honey?"

"Yeah! An' I pounded the nails and everything!"

Will put on a proper show of enthusiasm. "You did! Well, good for you."

"Mama said you'd like it."

"And I do, too. Walked into the yard and figured I was in the wrong place."

"Did you really?"

Will laughed and pressed Donald Wade's nose flat with the tip of a finger.

They all fell quiet, listening to the drone of bees and the wind's breath in the trees around them. "You can stay now, can't you?" Elly asked quietly.

"Yes. Medical discharge."

Keeping one arm around Lizzy's hip, she found Will's fingers in the grass behind them and braided them with her own. "That's good," she said simply, running a hand down Lizzy's hot hair while her eyes remained on her husband's face, tanned to a hickory brown, compellingly handsome above the tight collar and tie of his uniform. "You're a hero, Will. I'm so proud of you."

His lips twisted and he chuckled self-consciously. "Well, I don't know about that."

"Where's your Purple Heart?"

"Back at the house in my duffel bag."

"It should be right here." She lay a hand flat against his lapel, then slipped it underneath because she found within herself the constant need to touch him. She felt his heartbeat, strong and healthy against her fingertips, and recalled the hundreds of images she'd suffered, of bullets drilling him, spilling his blood on some distant jungle floor. Her precious, dear Will. "Miss Beasley told the newspaper about it and they put an article in. Now everybody knows Will Parker is a hero."

His look grew pensive, fixed on a distant hive. "Everybody in that war is a hero. They oughta give a Purple Heart to every GI out there."

"Did you shoot anybody, Will?" Donald Wade inquired.

"Now, Donald Wade, you mustn't—"

"Yes, I did, son, and it's a pretty awful thing."

"But they were bad guys, weren't they?"

Will's haunted gaze fixed on Elly, but instead of her he saw a foxhole and in it six inches of water and his buddy, Red, and a bomb whistling down out of the sky turning everything before him scarlet.

"Now, Donald Wade, Will just got back and you're pepperin' him with questions already."

"No, it's okay, Elly." To the child he said, "They were people, just like you and me."

"Oh."

Donald Wade grew solemn, contemplating the fact. Elly rose from her knees and said, "I have to finish filling the water pans. It won't take me long."

She kissed Will's left eyebrow, drew on her farmer gloves and left the children with Will while she headed back to work, turning once to study her husband again, trying to grasp the fact that he was back for good.

"I love you!" she called from beside a gnarled pear tree.

"I love you, too!"

She smiled and spun away.

The children examined Will's uniform—buttons, chevrons, pins. Lizzy grew less cautious, toddling around in the grass. The sun beat down and Will removed his blouse, laid it aside and stretched out supine, shutting his eyes against the brightness. But the sun on his closed eyelids became scarlet. Blood scarlet. And he saw it happen all over again—Red, scrambling on his belly across a stretch of kunai grass beside the Matanikau River, suddenly freezing in the open while from the opposite shore enemy .25 calibers cracked like oxwhips, submachine guns thundered, and a ranging grenade launcher sent its deadly missiles closer and closer. And there lay poor Red, stretched flat with no cover, facedown, shaking, biting the grass, halted by an unholy terror such as a lucky Marine never knows. Will saw himself scrambling back out amid the strafing, heard the bullets' deceptively soft sigh as they sailed over his head, the dull thud as they struck behind him, left, right. The earth rained dirt upward as a grenade hit fifteen feet away. "Christ, man, you gotta get outta here!" Red lay unmoving, unable. Will felt again his own panic, the surge of adrenaline as he grabbed Red and hauled him backward through mud and tufts of uprooted grass into a foxhole with six inches of muddy water—"Stay here, buddy. I'm going to get them sonsabitches!"—then going over the top again, teeth clenched, crawling on his elbows while the tip of his bayonet swung left and right. Then, overhead, the planes wheeling out of nowhere, the warning whistle, dropping, and behind him, Red, in the foxhole where the bomb fell.

Will shuddered, opened his eyes wide, sat up. Beside him the children still played. At the hive openings bees landed with their gatherings. Elly was returning with the wagon in tow, the two empty metal buckets clanging like glockenspiels as the wheels bumped over the rough turf. He blinked away the memory and watched his wife come on in her masculine apparel. *Don't think about Red, think about Elly.* He watched until her shadow slipped across his lap, then raised a hand and requested quietly, "Come here," and when she fell to her knees, held her. Just held her. And hoped she'd be enough to heal him.

Their lovemaking that night was golden.

But when it was over Elly sensed Will's withdrawal from more than her body.

"What's wrong?"

"Hm?"

"What's wrong?"

"Nothing."

"Your leg hurt?"

"Not bad."

She didn't believe him, but he wasn't a complainer, never had been. He reached for his Lucky Strikes, lit one and lay smoking in the dark. She watched the red coal brighten, listened to him inhale.

"You want to talk about it?"

"About what?"

"Anything—your leg . . . the war. I think you purposely kept the bad stuff out of your letters for my sake. Maybe you wanna talk about it now."

The red arc of the cigarette going to his mouth created a barrier more palpable than barbed wire.

"What's the sense in talking about it? I went to war, not an ice cream social. I knew that when I joined up."

She felt shut out and hurt. She had to give him time to open up, but tonight wouldn't be the night, that was certain. So she searched for subjects to bring him close again.

"I'll bet Miss Beasley was surprised when she saw you."

He chuckled. "Yeah."

"Did she show you the scrapbook of newspaper clippings she kept about all the action in the South Pacific?"

"No, she didn't mention that."

"She clipped articles only about the areas where she thought you might be fighting."

He chuckled soundlessly.

"You know what?"

"Hm?"

"I think she's sweet on you."

"Oh, come on, she's old enough to be my grandma."

"Grandmas got feelings, too."

"Lord."

"And you know what else? I think you kind of feel the same."

He felt himself blush in the dark, recalling times when he'd purposely charmed the librarian. "Elly, you're crazy."

"Yeah, I know, but it's perfectly okay with me. After all, you never had a grandma, and if you wanna love her a little bit it don't take nothin' away from me."

He tamped out his cigarette, drew her against his side and kissed the top of her head. "You're some woman, Elly."

"Yeah, I know."

He pulled back and looked down into her face, forgetting momentarily the haunting visions that sprang into his mind uninvited. He laughed, then Elly snuggled her cheek against his chest once more, and went on distracting him. "Anyway, Miss Beasley was wonderful while you were gone, Will. I don't know what I would've done without her—and Lydia, too. Lydia and I got to be such good friends. And you know what? I never really had a friend before." She mused before continuing. "We could talk about anything ... " She ruffled the hair on his chest and added, "I'd like to have her and the kids out sometime so you can get to know her better. Would that be all right with you, Will?"

She waited, but he didn't answer.

"Will?"

Silence.

"Will?"

"What?"

"Haven't you been listening?"

He removed his arm and reached for another cigarette. She'd lost him again.

There was no doubt about it, Will was different. Not only the limp, but the lapses. They happened often in the days that followed, lengthy silences when he became preoccupied with thoughts he refused to share. An exchange would become a monologue and Elly would turn to find his eyes fixed on the middle distance, his thoughts troubled, miles away. There were other changes, too. At night, insomnia. Often she'd awaken to find him sitting up, smoking in the dark. Sometimes he dreamed and talked in his sleep, swore, called out and thrashed. But when she'd awaken him and encourage, "What is it, Will? Tell me," he'd only reply, "Nothing. Just a dream." Afterward he'd cling to her until sleep reclaimed him and his palms would be damp even after they finally fell open.

He needed time alone. Often he went down to the orchard to ruminate, to sit watching the hives and work through whatever was haunting him.

The smallest sounds set him off. Lizzy knocked her milk glass off the high chair one day and he rocketed from his chair, exploded and left the house without finishing his meal. He returned thirty minutes later, apologetic, hugging and kissing Lizzy as if he'd struck her, bringing by way of apology a simple homemade toy called a bull-roarer which he'd made himself.

He spent a full hour with the three children that afternoon, out in the yard, spinning the simple wooden blade on the end of the long string until it whirled and made a sound like an engine revving up. And, as always, after being with the children, he seemed calmer.

Until the night they had a thunderstorm at three A.M. An immense clap of thunder shook the house, and Will sprang up, yelling as if to be heard above shelling, "Red! Jesus Christ, R-e-e-e-e-e-d!"

"Will, what is it?"

"Elly, oh God, hold me!"

Again, she became his lifeline, but though he trembled violently and sweated as if with a tropical fever, he held his horrors inside.

Physically, he continued healing. Within a week after his return he was restless to walk without crutches, and within a month, he followed his inclination. He loved the bathtub, took long epsom salts soaks that hastened the healing, and always eagerly accepted Elly's offers to scrub his back. Though he'd been ordered by Navy doctors to have checkups biweekly, he shunned the order and took over tending the bees even before he discarded the crutches, and went back to his library job in his sixth week home, without consulting a medic. His hours there were the same as before, leaving his days free, so he painted and posted a sign at the bottom of their driveway—USED AUTO PARTS & TIRES—and went into the junk business, which brought in a surprising amount of steady money. Coupled with his library salary, government disability check and the profit from the sale of eggs, milk and honey, which was constantly in demand now that sugar was heavily rationed, it brought their income up to a level previously unheard of in either Will's or Elly's life.

The money was, for the most part, saved, for even though Will still dreamed of buying Elly luxuries, the production of most domestic commodities had been halted long ago by the War Production Board. Necessities—clothing, food, household goods—were strictly rationed, at Purdy's store, their point values posted on the shelves beside the prices. The same at the gas station, though Will and Elly were classified as farmers, so given more gas rationing coupons than they needed.

The one place they could enjoy their money was at the theater in Calhoun. They went every Saturday night, though Will refused to go if a war movie was showing.

Then one day a letter arrived from Lexington, Kentucky. The return address said Cleo Atkins. Elly left it propped up in the middle of the kitchen table and when Will came in, pointed to it.

"Somethin' for you," she said simply, turning away.

"Oh . . ." He picked it up, read the return address and repeated, quieter, "Oh."

After a full minute of silence she turned to face him. "Aren't you going to open it?"

"Sure." But he didn't, only stood rubbing his thumb over the writing, staring at it.

"Why don't you take it down to the orchard and open it, Will?"

He looked up with pain in his deep, dark eyes, swallowed and said in a thick voice, "Yeah, I think I'll do that."

When he was gone, Elly sat down heavily on a kitchen chair and covered her face with her hand, grieving for him, for the death of his friend whom he couldn't forget. She remembered long ago how he'd told her of the only other friend he'd ever had, the one who'd betrayed him and had testified against him. How alone he must feel now, as if every time he reached out toward another man, that friendship was snatched away. Before the war she would not have guessed the value of a friend. But now she had two—Miss Beasley and Lydia. So she knew Will's pain at losing his buddy.

She gave him half an hour before going out to find him. He was sitting beneath an aged, gnarled apple tree heavy with unripe fruit, the letter on the ground at his hip. Knees up, arms crossed, head lowered, he was the picture of dejection. She approached silently on the soft grass and dropped to her knees, putting her palms on his forearms, her face against his shoulder. In ragged sobs, he wept. She moved her hands to his heaving back and held him lovingly while he purged himself. At last he railed, "Jesus, Elly, I k–killed him. I d–dragged him back to that f–foxhole

and left him th–there and the n–next thing I knew a b–bomb hit it d–dead center
and I t–t–turned around and s–saw his r–red h–hair flyin' in ch–chunks and—"

"Shh . . ."

"And I was screamin, Red! . . . *Re-e-e-d!*" He lifted his face and screamed it
to a silent sky, screamed it so long and loud the veins stood out like marble carv-
ings along his temples, up his neck and above his clenched fists.

"You didn't kill him, you were trying to save him."

Rage replaced his grief. *"I killed my best friend and they gave me a fucking
Purple Heart for it!"*

She could have argued that the Purple Heart was justly earned, in a different
battle, but she could see this was no time for reasoning. He needed to voice his
rage, work it out like pus from a festering wound. So she rubbed his shoulders,
swallowed her own tears and offered the silent abeyance she knew he needed.

"Now his fianceé writes—God, how he loved her—and says, It's okay, Corporal
Parker, you mustn't blame yourself." He dropped his head onto his arms again.
"Well, doesn't she see I got to blame myself? He was always talkin' about how
the four of us were g–gonna meet after the w–war and we'd maybe buy a car and
go on v–vacation someplace together, maybe up in the Smoky Mountains where
it's–it's c–cool in the s–summer and him and me c–could go–go f–fish—" He
turned and threw himself into Elly's arms, propelled by the force of anguish. He
clasped her, burrowing, accepting her consolation at last. She held him, rocked
him, let his tears wet her dress. "Aw, Elly—Elly—g–goddamn the war."

She held his head as if he were no older than Lizzy, closed her eyes and grieved
with him, for him, and became once again the mother/wife he would always need
her to be.

. In time his breathing grew steadier, his embrace eased. "Red was a good
friend."

"Tell me about him."

"You want to read the letter?"

"No. I read enough letters when you were gone. You tell me."

He did. Calmly this time, what it had *really* been like on the Canal. About the
misery, the fear, the deaths and the carnage. About the "Last Supper" on board
The Argonaut, steak and eggs in unlimited supply to fill a man's gut before he hit
the beach expecting to have it shot out; about boarding a rubber raft in a pounding
surf that roared so loud in the limber holes of the sub that no man could be heard
above it; about that bobbing ride over deadly coral that threatened to slash the
rubber boats and drown every man even before they reached the Japanese-infested
shore; about arriving wet and staying so for the next three months; about watching
your fleet chased off by the enemy, leaving you cut off from supplies indefinitely;
about charging into a grass hut with your finger cocked and watching human beings fly backwards and drop with the surprise still on their faces; about learning
what three species of ants are edible while you lay on your belly for two days
with a sniper waiting in a tree, and the ants beneath your nose become your dinner; about the Battle of Bloody Ridge; about watching men lie in torment for days
while flies laid eggs in their wounds; about eating coconuts until you wished the
malaria would get you before the trots did; about the twitch of a human body even
after it's dead. And finally, about Red, the Red he'd loved. The live Red, not the
dead one.

And when Will had purged himself, when he felt drained and exhausted, Elly
took his hand and they walked home together through the late-afternoon sun,
through the orchard, through the flower-trimmed pergola, to begin the thankless
job of forgetting.

Chapter 20

The war had been hard on Lula. It deprived her of everything she cared most about: nylon stockings, chocolate ice cream—and men. Especially men. The best ones, the healthy, young, virile ones were gone. Only shits like Harley were left, so what choice did she have but to keep on getting what she needed from the big ape? But she couldn't even blackmail him anymore. In the first place there was no gas to drive to Atlanta and window-shop the way she used to—who could go *anywhere* on three measly gallons a week!—and even if she could, there was nothing in the stores worth blackmailing for. That damn Roosevelt had control of everything—no cars, no bobby pins, no hair dryers. And *nothing,* absolutely *nothing* chocolate! It was beyond Lula why every GI in Europe got so many Hershey bars they were giving them away when folks back home had to do without! She'd put up with a lot, but it took the cake when Roosevelt handed down the order dictating what flavors of ice cream could be made! How the hell did he expect a restaurant to stay in business without chocolate ice cream? And without coffee?

Lula rested a foot on the toilet lid and spread brown leg makeup from toes to thigh, riled afresh by having to do without nylons. How the hell many parachutes did they need anyway? Well, never let it be said that Lula didn't look her best, no matter what inconveniences she had to put up with. When the makeup was applied, she carefully drew a black line up the back of her leg with a "seam pencil." Dressed in bra and panties, she scooted into her bedroom, leaped onto the high bed and turned her back to the dresser mirror to check the results.

Straight as a shot of Four Feathers blended, right from the bottle!

From her closet she chose the sexiest dress she owned, orange and white jersey with enormous shoulder pads, a diamond cutout above the breast, bared knees and nice, clingy hips. One more time she'd try it, just once, and if she didn't get results this time, the high and mighty Will Parker could cut holes in his pockets and play with himself for all she cared. After all, a woman had pride.

She squirmed into the dress, tugging it over her head, then returned to the bathroom to comb out her pincurls and fashion her hair into its usual whisked-up foreknot of curls. At least she had wave-set; the curls were hard as metal springs and bounced against her forehead gratifyingly.

All zipped, made-up and perfumed, she patted her hair, posed before the mirror with hands akimbo and calves pressed close, like Betty Grable, practiced her kittenish moue, bared her teeth to check for lipstick smudges, and decided the man'd have to be out of his mind to choose Crazy Elly See over *this!*

She licked her teeth, breathed into her cupped palm, smelled her breath and dug in her purse for a packet of Sen-Sen. Damn Wrigley's right along with Roosevelt, for supplying the entire U.S. military service with free gum for the duration of the war while people out here who were willing to pay for it had to suck this rotten Sen-Sen!

But her breath was sweet, her legs sexy and her cleavage showing as she set out to bag her prey. Hot diddly, that man set her to itchin' worse than ever! An ex-Marine now with a Purple Heart—imagine that!—with a bit of a hitch still detectable in his walk. It only made him more appealing to Lula.

She'd seen him from the window of the restaurant the day in May when he returned from the war, and she'd nearly drowned in her own saliva watching him limp up those library steps to see that old biddy, Mizz Beasley. Before he'd reached the door Lula had pressed her pubis against the backside of the counter for a little relief, and it hadn't changed since. By August she was still watching the square incessantly for mere glimpses of him, and when he wasn't in town all she had to do was think of him to get the old juices flowing. Lord, the way he'd looked in that uniform, with those crutches, and that tan, and those sultry eyes beneath the visor of his Marine dress cap. He was the best piece of flesh this town had to offer, and Lula'd have him, by God, or wrinkle up trying!

The back door of the library was unlocked. She turned the knob soundlessly. Inside, a radio played softly and a dim fog of light showed at the far end of the narrow back hall. On tiptoe Lula crept its length, paused at the end to peer into the poorly lit main room of the library. He had only one light on, and the blackout curtains drawn. A stroke of luck—privacy!

He was working with his back to her, squatting down on one knee, peering up at the underside of a table with a screwdriver in his hand, whistling along with "I Had the Craziest Dream." Lula silently slipped off her shoes, left them beside the checkout desk and crossed the room on catfeet.

Stopping close behind him, she could smell his hair tonic. It set her nostrils quivering and her private muscles twitching. As usual, Lula followed the instincts of her body, not her brain. She didn't stop to figure that you don't blind-side a jumpy ex-Marine who's fought on Guadalcanal, whose reaction time is quick, whose instincts are deadly and who's been trained in the art of survival. He looked good, he smelled good, and he was going to feel good, she thought, as with a feminine, gliding motion she moved in and began slipping her hands around his trunk.

His elbow flew back and rammed her in the gut. He lurched to his feet, spun, knocked her off-kilter, landed a deadly blow on the side of her neck and slammed her to the floor, where she slid six feet before coming to a stop wrapped around the leg of a table.

"What the hell are you doing in here!" he exploded.

Lula couldn't talk, not with the breath knocked from her.

"Get up and get out of here!"

I can't, she tried to say, but her jaws flapped soundlessly. She curled up and hugged her stomach.

War had taught Will that life was too precious to squander in any way, even a few precious moments spent with people you didn't like. He stomped over and jerked Lula roughly to her feet. "What you got to learn, Lula, is that I'm a happily married man and I don't want what you're sellin'. So get out and leave me alone!"

Doubled over, she stumbled several steps. "You . . . hit . . . me . . . you bastard!" she managed between gulps.

He had her by the hair so fast he nearly left her leg makeup on the floor.

"Don't you ever call me that!" he warned from behind clenched teeth.

"Bastard, put me down!" she screamed as he held her aloft.

Instead he raised her higher. "Whore!"

"Bastard!"

"Whore!"

"Owww! Put me down!"

He opened his hand and she fell like a piece of wet laundry.

"Git out and never come sniffin' around me again, you hear? I had enough of your kind when I was too damn dumb to know the difference! Now I got a good woman, a *good* one, you hear?" He picked her up by the front of the dress, slammed her to her feet and nudged her roughly from behind—nine times—all the way to the back door, snatching up her shoes on the way. He fired the shoes like two orange grenades into the alley, pushed her outside and offered in parting, "If you're in heat, Lula, go yowl beneath somebody else's window!"

The door slammed and the lock clicked.

Lula glared at it and hollered, "Goddamn you, you peckerhead! Just who do you think you're knockin' around!" She kicked the door viciously and sprained her big toe. Clutching it, she screamed louder, "Peckerhead! Asshole! Toad-suckin' Marine! Your dick prob'ly wouldn't fill my left ear anyway!"

With tears and black mascara streaking her face, Lula hobbled down the steps, retrieved her shoes and limped away.

She arrived back home enraged and marched straight to the telephone.

"Seven-J-ring-two!" she yelled, then waited impatiently with the black candle-stick mouthpiece tapping against her chest, the earpiece pressed above her orange flamingo-feather earring.

After two rings she heard, "H'llo?"

"Harley, this is Lula."

"Lula," he whispered warily, "I told you never to call me at home."

"I don't give a large rat's ass what you told me, Harley, so shut up and listen! I got me a hard-on that's bigger'n any you ever had and I need you to do somethin' about it, so don't say yes or no, just get in your goddamn truck and be at my house in fifteen minutes or I'll be on my bike so fast I'll leave a trail like a cyclone. And when I'm done payin' your precious Mae a little social call she won't be left wonderin' what them yellow stains on your belly was from, *com-prend-ay?* Now move, Harley!"

She slammed the receiver into the prongs and nearly loosened the table legs whacking the telephone down.

Harley had little choice. The older he got the less he needed Lula. But she was dumb and ornery enough to louse things up real good between him and Mae, and he had no intention of losing Mae over a two-bit whore. No sirree. When he retired from that mill with his pockets full after this lucrative war made him rich, he intended to have Mae to bring him iced tea on the porch and his boys to go fishing with and the girls—well, hell, girls weren't much use, but they were entertaining. The oldest one was sixteen already. Another couple years and she could be married, having his grandchildren. The thought held a curious appeal for Harley. Damn Lula, she could louse it up good if she started flappin' her trap.

When he opened her door he was already yelling.

"Lula, you got no brains or what? Where the hell are you, Lula?"

Lula was sprawled on the bed, wearing her orange high heels and her orange flamingo-feather earrings and a few black and blue marks from Will Parker's hands. An ingot of incense burned on the bedside table and her lacy underpants were draped over the lampshade to cut the light.

"Lula, what the hell you mean, callin' me up and givin' me orders like I was some—"

Harley rounded her doorway and stopped yelling as if a guillotine had dropped across his tongue. Lula was touching herself with one hand, reaching toward him with the other . . .

* * *

Two months later, on a bleak day in October, Harley got another call from Lula, this time at the mill.

"Harley, it's me."

"Jesus, what's the matter with you, callin' me here! You want the whole damn world to know about us?"

"I gotta see you."

"I'm working a shift and a half today."

"I gotta see you, I said! I got somethin' important to tell you."

"I can't tonight, maybe Thurs—"

"Tonight, or I'll blurt it out on this phone with Edna Mae Simms rubbering in down at central right now—you there, Edna Mae? You gettin' all of this?"

"All right, all right!"

"Eight-fifteen, my place."

"I don't get off till—"

The phone clicked dead in Harley's hands.

When he arrived at Lula's house she was dressed in a black sheeny dressing gown patterned with cerise orchids the size of cymbals. Her hair was neatly up-swept and she wore high-heeled shoes to match the orchids. They reminded Harley of one time when his mother had made him eat beets and he'd vomited afterward. Lula opened the door and closed it behind Harley with a sober snap, then turned to face him with her hands on her hips.

"Well, I'm knocked up, Harley, and it's yours. I wanna know what you're gonna do about it."

Harley looked like a bazooka had just been fired three inches from his ear. For a moment he was too stunned to speak. Lula sauntered into the parlor, chin lowered while she pressed a bobby pin into its holding place high on her head.

Bug-eyed, breathless, Harley stammered, "Kn–knocked up?"

"Yup, all yours and mine, Harleykins." She patted her stomach and flashed a sarcastic smile. "Bun in the oven."

"B–but I ain't seen you for two months, Lula!"

"Exactly, and if you'll remember, you didn't use any rubber."

"How could I when I didn't have any! Goddamn rubbers're gettin' as scarce as tires these days. It's a wonder Roosevelt hasn't got the Boy Scouts out collectin' used ones like they collect everything else!" Harley dropped to the sofa and raked a hand through his hair, muttering, "Pregnant . . . Christ."

Lula braced a stiff arm on the back of an overstuffed chair, drumming paradiddles with her hot-pink nails.

"Oughta be here about next May."

"You seen a doctor already?"

"Yup. Went to Calhoun today."

Harley jumped to his feet and paced. "Dammit, Lula, why didn't you tell me you could've got pregnant that night! This is your fault, not mine!"

Lula came to life like a kicked cobra. "My fault! Why you cheap, sniveling penny-pincher, don't you blame this on me! You've always been a great one to hump first and ask second. And I know why! 'Cause all you think of is money-money-money! Up there at the mill haulin' it in hand over fist puttin' up government contracts at time and a half overtime, and too cheap to go to the drugstore and spend a quarter! Well, don't you point fingers at me, Harley Overmire! All you'da had to do that night was take ten seconds to put one on, but no, you had to leap on me like some tomcat sniffin' pussy!"

"Now you just wait a minute, Lula. I come in here and you were sprawled out like a tomato sandwich waitin' for salt and pepper and you expect *me* to back off and *think!* You could've shut your legs for just a minute, you know!"

"Me, me, always me!" Lula yowled. "You been layin' me for six years and how many times you ever thought about it before? Huh? Answer me that, Harley! I'm always the one got to think about it—well, I get sick of it! Just once I'd like you to do the thinkin' and treat me like the lady I am and take a little time first, instead of jumpin' on me and ruttin' like a boar!"

"A boar! So now I'm a boar!"

"Don't change the subject, Harley. I said I wanna know what you're gonna do about it and I want an answer!"

"Answer—hell, where'm I supposed to get an answer?"

Lula had done some reconsidering and had come to the conclusion that Harley Overmire was better than nothing. Besides, he wasn't really so bad in bed. And at least her kid would have an old man. Lula curled four fingers and studied her nail polish for chips while suggesting, "You could leave Mae and marry me."

"Leave Mae!"

Lula's nonchalance disappeared abruptly and her mouth grew sullen. "Well, what's she to you anyway—you never even do it with her. You told me so yourself!"

"She's the mother of my children, Lula."

"Oh." Lula tapped her chest. "And what am I?"

Harley couldn't think up a fast answer.

"What am I, huh, Harley? There's one of yours breedin' in me right now, but since Mae is the mother of your children, maybe she'd like to add it to her collection, huh? How about that? How about I pay Mae a call and just happen to mention, Oh by the way, Mae, I'll have another little monkey-faced brat to add to your brood next summer. How about that, Harley? Would that suit you?"

"Lula, be reasonable—"

"Be reasonable! Be reasonable, he says, when *I'm* the one faced with disgrace and he's off rockin' on his front veranda with Mae and his *legitimate* brats. Be reasonable? I'll give you reasonable, Harley. How's this for reasonable? Two months. Two months and I'll be starting to show, and by that time I want one of two things. Either your name on a wedding license beside mine so I'll know my kid'll be provided for for the rest of his life, or ten thousand dollars in the bank, in my name, Lula Peak."

"Ten thousand dollars!"

Turning to a bevel-edged mirror on the living room wall, Lula opened her lips and edged each corner with the side of a finger. She patted her varnished topknot and added as if in afterthought, "Or I could still offer it to Mae to raise and my worries'd be over." She swung to face Harley in a shimmer of black and cerise. "Oh, well . . ." She flipped her palms up. "I never cared much for monkey-faced brats anyway."

It was not a good autumn for Harley Overmire. Lula wouldn't leave off him. He earned good money at the mill—sure—but it'd be a cold day in hell before he'd hand over ten thousand dollars to a slut like her. And she'd almost torn his face off when he'd suggested looking for a doctor to get rid of it. But worst of all, she was beginning to pester him at home, calling him in the middle of the night, at breakfast time, asking for some trumped-up name if Mae happened to answer.

She showed up at the mill one night when he was getting off at nine o'clock, just to remind him he had only four weeks left to come up with the money or the marriage. When another week passed without any progress toward a solution, she actually called Mae, giving her correct name, and told him about it afterward.

"I talked to Mae today."

"You *what?*"

"I talked to Mae today. I called her up and said I was collecting for the Red Cross and wondered if she had any donations for Care packages. She said she had buttons and soap and tablets and pencils, and that I could come over there and pick them up anytime, so I did."

"You didn't!"

"Oh, but I did! I went right over and walked up to your front door and knocked and Mae answered and we had a pleasant little chat."

"Goddammit, Lula—"

Lula's expression turned serpentine. "You see how easy it is, Harley?"

Harley developed an ulcer. The stomach pains intensified one night when he came home and looked through the mail to find Lula had brazenly directed the doctor in Calhoun to send his bill directly to Harley's house. When Mae asked what the bill was for, he told her somebody had been hurt at the mill and the bill had come to the house accidentally.

But Lula's harassment continued daily. Harley began to detest her, wondering what he'd ever seen in her in the first place. She was hard and shallow and stump-dumb to boot. To think he'd actually jeopardized his marriage over a pussy like that.

At work Harley was distracted. At home, jumpy. Everyplace else, wary. The damn woman would show up anywhere, saying anything, doing any rash thing she took a mind to do.

The corker was when she stopped his oldest boy, Ned, coming home from school one day and talked him into Vickery's to give him a free ice cream cone. Afterward, she had the gall to tell Harley what she'd done and add in a sultry voice while fussing with the ugly yellow hair of hers, "You haven't been around much, Harley. And that boy of yours is gettin' better lookin' by the day. Losin' his monkey face and growin' tall. How old is he now, Harley? Fourteen? Fifteen maybe?"

The threat was clear as that varnish she spread on her pincurls and it was the last straw. When she started in on the kids, it was time to put a stop to Lula Peak.

Harley planned it out carefully in his mind. The gift he'd left under Lula's Christmas tree would shut her up temporarily, but he'd do it right after the holiday.

It'd work. He knew Lula and what Lula craved worse than anything, and it'd work. He hadn't been deaf, dumb and blind these last couple years. The men at the mill made ribald jokes about how Lula stalked Parker, how she ogled him out the window of the restaurant and even pursued him outright at the library. But word had it Parker had never given her a tumble, so Lula'd still be itchin' to get at him.

Parker. Even the name galled Harley yet. Parker and his goddamn Purple Heart. Parker, the town hero while people sneered at Harley Overmire behind his back and accused him of cutting off his finger on purpose to avoid the draft. Not one of them could even guess what kind of courage it took to run your finger through a sawblade! And besides, *somebody* had to stay behind and make crates for all those rifles and ammo.

So you think you're a hero, eh, Parker? Hobbling into town on those crutches and parading around the square in your fancy uniform so everybody'll fall on their knees and wave banners. Well, I didn't like you the first time I clapped eyes on you, whore-killer, and I don't like you any better now. It might not've worked when I tried to run you out of town the first time, but this time it will. And it'll be the law that'll do it for me.

It took Harley three nights of scouting the library trash cans in the back alley before finding the perfect garrote: a piece of discarded shop rag filled with easily identifiable dust and lemon cleaning oil.

Once it was in his possession, Harley prepared the note carefully, selecting oversize individual words and letters from newspapers which he glued perpendicular to the typesetting on an ordinary sheet of want ads from the *Atlanta Constitution*. No stationery to identify, no fingerprints left on the greasy newsprint.

MEET ME BACK DOOR LIBRARY 11 O'CLOCK TUESDAY NIGHT. W.P.

He mailed it in a used envelope from his electricity bill, addressing it by cutting away the old address with a razor blade and fitting a newsprint address in its place.

When Lula got the note in the mail she tore it in quarters and swore like a long-shoreman. *Fat chance, Parker, after you knocked me around and called me a whore! Go cut holes in your pockets!*

But Lula was Lula. Undeniably hot-blooded. The longer she thought about Will Parker, the hotter she got. Big bad boy. Big tough Marine. All shoulders and legs and sulk. She loved that sulkiness and the brooding silences, too. But she'd had a taste of his temper, and if he flared like that in the middle of a good piece of sex—oooo-ee! That'd be one to remember! And another thing she'd learned—men with long earlobes usually had peckers to match, and Parker's earlobes weren't exactly miniature.

By nine o'clock Tuesday night, Lula was taping together the torn note. By nine-thirty she felt like a piece of itchweed was stuck in her pants. By ten o'clock she was in a tub full of bubbles, getting ready.

Harley Overmire hunkered in the cold December drizzle, cursing it. One thing was lucky though: the blackout was still in effect in the coastal states. No streetlights. No window lights. Nobody on the streets after ten unless they had a permit.

Come on, Lula, come on. I'm cold and damp and I wanna get home to bed.

The rear door of the library was eight feet above his head, giving onto a set of high concrete steps with an iron handrail. He'd heard Parker lock the door and leave well over half an hour ago, had sat as still as a sniper in a tree, listening to Parker's footsteps scrape down the steps, to the sound of his car starting and driving away without lights on.

Now Harley hunkered in his black rubber jacket and old fedora hat, feeling the rain seep into a tear on his shoulder. He hugged himself with crossed arms, feeling the cold concrete pressed against his back, and listened to the rain drip from the library eaves onto the alley below. In his fist the oily dustrag formed a hard knot. Something solid to hold on to.

When he heard Lula's footsteps his heart hammered like that of a coon before a pack. High heels—click . . . click . . . click . . . probably toeless, because she stepped in a puddle and cursed. He waited till she'd reached the third step, then quickly slithered around the base of the steps and up behind her.

He'd planned to do it swift, clean, anonymously. But the damn rag was old and rotten and tore and she struggled free, turned and saw his face.

"Harley . . . don't . . . pl—"

And he was forced to finish the job with his hands.

He hadn't planned to see the shock and horror on her face. Or the grotesqueness of the throes of death. But no blackout was total enough to hide it. And Lula struggled, fought longer and harder than he'd have thought a woman of her size could.

When she finally succumbed, Harley staggered down the steps and threw up against the north wall of the library.

Chapter 21

On a day in late December, Elly was working in the kitchen when she looked up and saw Reece Goodloe pull into the yard in a dusty black Plymouth with adjustable spotlights and the official word SHERIFF on the door. He'd held office for as long as Elly could remember, since before he'd come knocking on the door of Albert See's house, forcing him to let his granddaughter go to school.

Reece had grown fat over the years. His stomach bobbed like a water balloon as he hitched up his pants on his way up the walk. His hair was thin, his face florid, his nostrils as big as a pair of hoofprints in the mud. In spite of his unattractiveness, Elly liked him: he'd been the one responsible for breaking her out of that house.

"Mornin', Mr. Goodloe," she greeted from the porch, shrugging into a homemade sweater.

"Mornin', Mizz Parker. You have a nice Christmas?"

"Yessir. And you?"

"A fine Christmas, yes we did." Goodloe scanned the clearing, the gardens neatly cleared for the winter, the junk piles gone. Things sure looked different around here since Glendon Dinsmore died.

"Your place looks good."

"Why, thank you. Will done most of it."

Goodloe took his time gazing around before he inquired, "Is he here, Mizz Parker?"

"He's down yonder in the shed, painting up some supers for the hives, getting everything ready for spring."

Goodloe rested a boot on the bottom step. "You mind fetchin' him, Mizz Parker?"

Elly frowned. "Somethin' wrong, Sheriff?"

"I just need to talk to him about a little matter come up in town last night."

"Oh . . . well . . . well, sure." She brightened with an effort. "I'll get him."

On her way through the yard Elly felt the first ominous lump form in her belly. What did he want with Will? Some sheriffing business, she was sure. His homesy chitchat was too obvious to be anything but a cover for an official call. But what? By the time she reached the open shed door, her misgivings showed plainly on her face.

"Will?"

With paintbrush in hand, Will straightened and turned, his pleasure unmistakable. "Missed me, did ya?"

"Will, the sheriff is here lookin' for you."

His grin faded, then flattened. "About what?"

"I don't know. He wants you to come to the house."

Will went stone still for ten full seconds, then carefully laid the paintbrush across the top of the can, picked up a rag and dampened it with turpentine. "Let's go." Wiping his hands, he followed her.

With each step Elly felt the lump grow bigger, the apprehension build. "What could he want, Will?"

"I don't know. But we'll find out, I reckon."

Let it be nothing, she entreated silently, let it be a carburetor for that dusty black Plymouth, or maybe Will's got his road sign on county property or they need to borrow the library chairs for a dance. Let it be somethin' silly.

She glanced at Will. He walked unhurried but unhesitant, his face revealing nothing. It wore his don't-let-'em-know-what-you're-thinking expression, which worried Elly more than a frown.

Sheriff Goodloe was waiting beside the Plymouth, with his arms crossed over his potbelly, leaning on the front fender. Will stopped before him, wiping his hands on the rag. "Mornin', Sheriff."

Goodloe nodded and boosted off the car. "Parker."

"Somethin' I can do for you?"

"A few questions."

"Somethin' wrong?"

Goodloe chose not to answer. "You work at the library last night?"

"Yessir."

"You close it up, as usual?"

"Yessir."

"What time?"

"Ten o'clock."

"What'd you do then?"

"Came home and went to bed, why?"

Goodloe glanced at Elly. "You were home then, Mizz Parker?"

"Of course I was. We got a family, Sheriff. What's this all about, anyway?"

Goodloe ignored their questions and uncrossed his arms, firming his stance before firing his next question at Will. "You know a woman named Lula Peak?"

Will felt the anxiety begin at the backs of his knees and crawl upward—sharp needles of creeping heat. Hiding his worry, he tucked the rag into his hind pocket. "Know who she is. Wouldn't exactly say I know her, no."

"You see her last night?"

"No."

"She didn't come in the library?"

"Nobody comes in the library when I'm there. It's after hours."

"She never came there . . . after hours?"

Will's lips compressed and a muscle ticked in his jaw, but he stared squarely at Goodloe. "A couple of times she did."

Elly glanced sharply at Will. *A couple times?* Her stomach seemed to lift to her throat while the sheriff repeated the words like an obscene litany.

"A couple o'times—when was that?"

Will crossed his arms and stood spraddle-footed. "A while ago."

"Could you be more specific?"

"A couple of times before I went in the service, once since I come home. Back in August or so."

"You invited her there?"

Again Will's jaw hardened and bulged, but he exercised firm control, answering quietly, "No, sir."

"Then what was she doing there?"

Will was fully aware of Elly staring at him, dumbfounded. His voice softened with self-consciousness. "I think you can prob'ly guess, bein' a man."

"It's not my job to guess, Parker. My job is to ask questions and get answers. What was Lula Peak doing at the library in August after hours?"

Will turned his gaze directly into his wife's shocked eyes while answering, "Lookin' to get laid, I guess."

"Will . . ." she admonished breathily, her eyes rounded in dismay.

Having expected circumvention, the sheriff was momentarily nonplussed by Will's bluntness. "Well . . ." He ran a hand around the back of his neck, wondering where to go from here. "So you admit it?"

Will pulled his eyes from Elly to answer, "I admit I knew that's what she was after, not that she got it. Hell, everybody in Whitney knows what she's like. That woman prowls like a she-cat and doesn't make any effort to hide it."

"She . . . prowled after you, did she?"

Will swallowed and took his time answering. The words came out low and reluctant. "I guess you'd call it that."

"Will," Elly repeated in dull surprise. "You never told me that." Her insides felt hot and shaky.

Again he turned his brown eyes directly on her, armed only with the truth. " 'Cause it meant nothin'. Ask Miss Beasley if I ever gave that woman any truck. She'll tell you I didn't."

The sheriff interjected, "Miss Beasley saw Lula . . . shall we say, ah . . . pursuin' you?"

Will's gaze snapped back to the uniformed man. "Am I bein' accused of somethin', Sheriff? 'Cause if I am I got a right to know. And if that woman's made any charges against me, they're a damn lie. I never laid a hand on her."

"According to the record, you did a stretch in Huntsville for manslaughter—that right?"

The sick feeling began to crawl up Will's innards but outwardly he remained stoic. "That's right. I did my time and I got out on full parole."

"For killing a known prostitute."

Will fit the edges of his teeth together and said nothing.

"You'll excuse me, ma'am," The sheriff quirked an eyebrow at Elly. "But there's no way to avoid these questions." Then, to Will, "Have you ever had sexual intercourse with Lula Peak?"

Will repressed his seething anger to answer, "No."

"Did you know she was four months pregnant?"

"No."

"The child she was expecting is not yours?"

"No!"

The sheriff reached into his car and came up with a cellophane packet. "You ever seen this before?"

Standing stiffly, Will let his glance drop, examined the contents of the transparent packet without touching it. "Looks like a dustrag from the library."

"You read the newspaper regular-like, do you?"

"Newspaper. What's the newspaper—"

"Just answer the question."

"Every night when I take a break at the library. Sometimes I bring 'em home when the library's done with 'em."

"Which one you read most often?"

"What the hell—"

"Which one, Parker?"

Will grew aggravated and temper colored his face. "I don't know. Hell ..."

"The New York Times?"

"No."

"What then?"

"What is this, Goodloe?"

"Just answer."

"All right! The *Atlanta Constitution,* I guess."

"When's the last time you saw Lula Peak?"

"I don't remember."

"Well, try."

"Earlier this week ... no, it was last week, Wednesday maybe, Tuesday— Christ, I don't remember, but it was when I drove in to work, she was locking up Vickery's when I went past on my way to the library."

"And you haven't seen her since last week, Tuesday or Wednesday?"

"No."

"But you admit you went to your job as usual last night and left for home around ten P.M.?"

"Not *around.* At. I always leave exactly at ten."

Goodloe squared his stance, giving himself a clear shot of both Will's and Elly's faces. "Lula Peak was strangled last night on the rear steps of the library. The coroner puts the time of death at somewhere between nine and midnight."

The news hit Will like a fist in the solar plexus. Within seconds he went from hot to icy, red to white. *No, not me, not this time. I paid for my crime. Goddammit, leave me alone. Leave me and my family in peace.* While the tumult of sick fear built within him, he stood unmoving, wary of reacting the wrong way lest he be misread. His stomach trembled. His palms turned damp, his throat dry. In that quick black flash of time while the sheriff threw out his bombshell, a montage of impressions wafted through Will's head, of the things he valued most— Elly, the kids, the life they'd built, the good home, the financial stability, the future, the happiness. At the thought of losing them, and unjustly, despair threatened. *Aw, Jesus, what does a man have to do to win ... ever?* He was struck by the irony of having fought and survived that miserable war only to come home to this. He thought of all else he'd survived—being orphaned, the years of lone drifting, the time in prison, the hungry days afterward, the taunts, the jeers. For what? Rage and despair slewed through him, bringing the unholy wish to sink his fist into something hard, batter something, curse the uncaring fates who time after time turned thumbs down on Will Parker.

But none of what he felt or thought showed on his face. Dry-throated, expressionless, he asked flatly, "And you think I did it?"

The sheriff produced a second cellophane packet matching the first, this one bearing the pieces of newsprint with the cryptic message. "I got some pretty convincing evidence, Parker, starting with this right here."

Will's eyes dropped to the incriminating note, then lifted again to Goodloe before he slowly reached to take the packet and read it. A rush of hatred poured through him. For Lula Peak, who just wouldn't take no for an answer. For the person who did her in and pinned the blame on him. For this potbellied vigilante who was too stupid to reason beyond the end of his horsey nostrils.

"A man'd have to be pretty damn dumb to leave a message that clear and expect to get away with it."

Elly had been listening with growing dread, standing like one mesmerized by the sight of a venomous snake slithering closer and closer. When Will began handing the packet to Goodloe she intercepted it. "Let me see that."

MEET ME BACK DOOR LIBRARY 11 O'CLOCK TUESDAY NIGHT. W.P. While she stood reading it the kitchen door opened and Thomas called from the porch, "Mama, Lizzy wet her pants again!"

Elly heard nothing beyond the frantic thumping of her own heart, saw nothing beyond the note and the initials, W.P. Terror rushed through her. *Oh, God, no. Not Will, not my Will.*

"Mama! Come and change Lizzy's pants!"

She fixed her thumbs over the edge of the cellophane simply for something to hang on to, something to steady her careening world. From the recent past she heard again Will's voice admitting things that she wished now she had never heard . . . *We used to go down to La Grange to the whorehouse there . . . Me, I wasn't fussy, take any one that was free . . . I picked up a bottle . . . She went down like a tree and hardly even bled, she died so fast . . .*

For a moment Elly closed her eyes, gulping, unable to swallow the lump of fear that suddenly congealed in her throat. Was it possible? Could he have done it again? She opened her eyes and stared at her thumbs; they felt weighty and thrice their size as shock controlled her system.

Will watched the reactions claim his wife. He watched her struggle for control, watched her momentarily lose and regain it. When she lifted her eyes they were like two dull stones in a face like bleached linen.

"Will . . . ?"

Though she spoke only his name, the single word was like a rusty blade in his heart.

Oh, Elly, Elly, not you, too. They could all think whatever they wanted, but she was his wife, the woman he loved, the one who'd given him reason to change, to fight, to live, to plan, to make something better of himself. She thought him *capable* of a thing like this?

After a life filled with disappointments, Will Parker should have been inured to them. But nothing—nothing had ever reduced him like this moment. He stood before her vanquished, wishing that he had been in that foxhole with Red, wishing he'd never walked into this clearing and met the woman before him and been given false hope.

On the porch a door slammed and Thomas called, "Mama, what's wrong?"

Elly didn't hear him. "W–Will?" she whispered again, her eyes wide, her throat hot and tight.

Aggrieved, he turned away.

The sheriff reached to the back of his belt for a pair of handcuffs and spoke authoritatively. "William Parker, it's my duty to inform you that you're under arrest for the murder of Lula Peak."

The awful reality hit Elly full force. Tears squirted into her wide, frightened eyes, and she pressed a fist to her lips. It was all happening so fast! The sheriff, the accusation, the handcuffs. The sight of them sent another sickening bolt through Elly.

At that moment Thomas eased up behind his mother. "Mama, what's the sheriff doing here?"

She could only stand gaping, unable to answer.

But Will knew all about hurtful childhood memories and wanted none for Thomas. As the sheriff pulled his left arm back and snapped the cuff on, Will ordered quietly, "Thomas, you go see after Lizzy P., son." He stood woodenly, waiting for the second metallic click, cringing inside, thinking, *Dammit, Goodloe, at least you could wait till the boy goes back in the house!*

But Thomas had seen too many cowboy movies to misinterpret what was happening. "Mama, is he takin' Will to jail?"

Taking Will to jail? Elly suddenly came out of her stupor, incensed. "You can't just . . . just take him!"

"He'll be in the county jail in Calhoun until bail is set."

"But what about—"

"He might need a jacket, ma'am."

A jacket? She could scarcely think beyond the frantic churning in her head that ordered, Stop him somehow! Stop him! But she didn't know how, didn't know her rights or Will's. Tears slid down Elly's cheeks as she stood by dumbly.

"Mama . . ." Thomas began crying, too. He ran to Will, clutched at his waist. "Will, don't go."

The sheriff pried the boy off. "Now, young man, you'd best go in the house."

Thomas swung on him, pummeling with both fists. "You can't take Will! I won't let you! Git away from him!"

"Take him in the house, Mizz Parker," the sheriff ordered in an undertone.

Thomas fought like a dervish, swinging, fending off their efforts to calm or remove him.

"Get in the car, Parker."

"Just a minute, sheriff, please . . ." Will went down on one knee and Thomas threw himself on the man's sturdy neck.

"Will . . . Will . . . he can't take you, can he? You're a good guy, like Hopalong."

Will swallowed and turned entreating eyes up to Goodloe. "Take the cuffs off for a minute—please." Goodloe drew in a deep, unsteady breath and glanced at Elly sheepishly. At his hesitation, Will's anger erupted. "I'm not runnin' anyplace, Goodloe, and you know it!" The sheriff's distraught gaze fell to the boy sobbing against Will's neck and he followed his gut instincts, freeing one of Will's wrists. Will's arms curled around Thomas, the metal cuff dangling down the boy's narrow back. Closing his eyes, Will clutched the small body and spoke softly against Thomas's hair. "Yeah, you're right, short stuff. I'm a good guy, like Hopalong. Now you remember that, okay? And just remember I love you. And when Donald Wade gets home from school tell him I love him, too, okay?"

He pushed Thomas back, wiped the child's streaming face with the knuckles of his uncuffed hand. "Now you be good and go in the house, and help your mother take care of Lizzy. You do that for old Will, all right?"

Thomas nodded meekly, studying the ground at Will's knee. Will turned him around and gave him a push on his backside. "Now, go on."

Thomas ran around his mother, sobbing, and a moment later the screen door slammed. Elly watched Will stretch to his feet, his image a blur beyond her streaming eyes. With a wooden face he willingly put both hands behind himself and allowed the sheriff to snap the cuffs in place once more.

"Will—oh, Will—what—oh, God . . ." Elly moved at last, but her speech and motion patterns had turned jerky. She cast her gaze around like a demented thing, reaching out a hand, pacing like a wild animal the first time it's caged, as if not fully comprehending its inability to change a situation. "Sheriff . . ." She touched his sleeve but he ignored her plea, tending his prisoner. Abruptly she veered to her husband. "Will . . ." She grasped him, clutching the back of his shirt, her wet cheek pressed to his dry one. "Will—they can't t–take you!"

Unbending he stared straight ahead, and ordered coldly, "Let's go."

"No, wait!" Elly cried, overwrought, turning beetlelike from one man to the other, "Sheriff—couldn't you—what's going to happen to him—wait—I'll get his jacket . . ." Belatedly she ran to the house, not knowing what else to do, returned panicked, to find both men already in the Plymouth. She tried the back door but it was locked, the windows up.

"Will!" she cried, pressing the jacket to the glass, already realizing what had caused his cold indifference, already repentant, needing to do something to show she'd been hasty and had reacted without conscious thought. "Here—here I b–brought your jacket! Please, take it!" But he wouldn't look at her as she pressed the denim against the glass.

The sheriff said, "Here, I'll take it," and hauled it in through his window and handed her, in exchange, the paint rag on which Will had earlier wiped his hands. "Best thing you can do, Mizz Parker, is get a lawyer." He put the car in gear.

"But I don't know no lawyers!"

"Then he'll get a public defender."

"But when can I see him?" she called as the Plymouth began to move.

"When you get a lawyer!"

The car pulled away, leaving Elly in a swirl of exhaust with her hand reaching entreatingly.

"Will!" she cried after the departing vehicle. She watched it carry him away, his head visible through the rear window. She twisted her fingers into the smelly rag and covered her mouth with it, hunched forward, breathing its turpentine fumes, fighting panic, staring aghast at the empty driveway.

The jail was in a stone building styled much like a Victorian house, situated just behind the courthouse where Will had gotten married. He held himself aloof from emotion during the booking procedure, the frisking, the walk down the echoing corridor, the cold metallic clang of the iron door.

He lay in his cell facing a gray wall, smelling the fetid odors of old urine and pine-scented disinfectant, on a stale-smelling pillow and a stained mattress, with ink on his fingertips and his belt confiscated and dullness in his eyes and the familiarity of his surroundings consciously shut out. He thought about hunkering in a ball but had no will to do so. He thought about crying but lacked the heart. He thought about asking for food, but hunger mattered little when life mattered not at all. His life had lost value in the moment when his wife looked at him with doubt in her eyes.

He thought about fighting the charges—but for what? He was tired of fighting, so damned tired. It seemed he'd been fighting his whole life, especially the last two years—for Elly, for a living, for respect, for his country, for his own dignity. And just when he'd gained them all, a single questioning stare had undone him. Again. When would he learn? When would he stop thinking he could ever matter to anyone the way some people mattered to him? Fool. Ass. Stupid *bastard!* He absorbed the word, with all its significance, rubbed it in like salt in a wound, willfully multiplying his hurt for some obscure reason he did not understand. Because he was unlovable after all, because his entire life had proved him so and it seemed the unlovable ones like himself were put on this world to accumulate all the hurts that the lucky, the loved, magically missed. She couldn't love him or she'd have jumped to his defense as thoughtlessly as Thomas had. Why? Why? What did he lack? What more must he prove? *Bastard,* Parker! When you gonna grow up and realize that you're alone in this world? Nobody fought for you when you were born, nobody'll fight for you now, so give up. Lay here in the stink of other men's piss and realize you're a loser. Forever.

In a clearing before a house on Rock Creek Road Eleanor Parker watched the law haul her husband off to jail and knew a terror greater than the fear of her own death, a desperation sharper than physical pain, and self-reproach more overpowering than the rantings of her own fire-and-brimstone grandfather.

She knew before the car disappeared into the trees that she had made one of the gravest mistakes in her life. It had lasted only a matter of seconds, but that's all it had taken to turn Will icy. She had seen and felt his withdrawal like a cold slap in the face. And it was entirely her fault. She could well imagine what he was suffering as he rode to town with his hands shackled: desolation and despair, all because of her.

Well, blast it, she was no saint nor seraph! So she'd reacted in shock. Who in tarnation wouldn't? Will Parker could no more kill Lula Peak than he could Lizzy P., and Elly knew it.

The fire-and-brimstone blood of Albert See suddenly leaped in her veins where it had been slogging since her birth, waiting a chance to flow hot for a cause. And what a cause—the love of her man. She'd spent too long finding it, had been too happy enjoying it, had changed too beneficially under its influence to lose it, and him, now.

So she straightened her spine, cursed roundly and turned her terror into energy, her despair into determination and her self-reproach into a promise.

I'll get you out of there, Will. And by the time I'm done you'll know that what you saw in my eyes for that piddly instant didn't mean nothing. It was human. I am human. So I made a mistake. Now watch me unmake it!

"Thomas, get your jacket!" Elly shouted, slamming into the house with yard-long strides. "And three extra diapers for Lizzy P. And run down in the cellar and fetch up six jars of honey—no, eight, just in case! We're goin' to town!"

She grabbed ration coupons, a peach crate for the honey, a tin of oatmeal cookies, a jar of leftover soup, Lizzy (wet pants and all), a skeleton key, and a pillow to help her see over the steering wheel. Within five minutes that wheel was shuddering in her hands, which were white-knuckled with fright. But fright wouldn't stop Elly now.

She had driven only a few times before, and those around the yard and down the orchard lane. She nearly broke three necks shifting for the first time, felt certain she'd kill herself and her two young ones before she reached the end of the driveway. But she reached it just fine and made a wide right turn, missed the far ditch and corrected her course without mishap. Sweat oozed from her pores, but she gripped the wheel harder and *drove!* She did it for Will, and for herself, and for the kids who loved Will better than popcorn or movie shows or Hopalong Cassidy. She did it because Lula Peak was a lying, laying, no-good whore, and a woman like that shouldn't have the power to drive a wedge between a husband and wife who'd spent damn near two years showing each other what they meant to one another. She did it because someplace in Whitney was a scum-suckin' skunk who'd done Lula in and wasn't going to get by with pinning the blame on *her* man! Nossir! Not if she had to drive this damned car clear to Washington, D.C., to see justice done.

She dropped Thomas, Lizzy P., the cookies and the soup at Lydia's house with only a terse explanation: "They've arrested Will for the murder of Lula Peak and

I'm goin' to hire a lawyer!" She drove at fifty bone-rattling miles an hour the rest
of the way into town, past the square and out to the schoolhouse on the south side,
where she flattened ten yards of grass before coming to a stop with the left front
tire crushing a newly planted rosebush that the second-grade teacher, Miss Natalie
Pruitt, had brought from her mother's garden to beautify the stark schoolground.
Elly left word that Donald Wade was to get off the bus at Lydia Marsh's place,
then backtracked to the library and accidentally drove the car up onto the sidewalk, parking. There it stayed, blocking pedestrians, while she ran inside and told
the news to Miss Beasley.

"That piss-ant Reece Goodloe come out to the house and arrested Will for killing Lula Peak. Will you help me find a lawyer?"

What followed proved that if one woman in love can move mountains, two can
turn tides. Miss Beasley outright plucked the books from the hands of two patrons,
ordering, "The library's closing, you'll have to leave." Her coat flew out behind
her like a flag in high wind as she followed Elly to the door, already advising.

"He should have the best."

"Just tell me who."

"We'd need to get to Calhoun somehow."

"I drove to Whitney, I can drive to Calhoun."

Miss Beasley suffered a moment's pause when she observed the Model A with
its radiator cap twelve inches from the brick wall. The town constable came running down the sidewalk at that moment, shaking his fist over his head. "Who in
the sam hell parked that thing up there!"

Miss Beasley poked ten fingers in his chest and pushed him back. "Shut up, Mr.
Harrington, and get out of our way or I'll tell your wife how you ogle the naked
aborigines in the back issues of *National Geographic* every Thursday afternoon
when she thinks you're downstairs checking the Ten Most Wanted posters. Get in,
Eleanor. We've wasted enough time." When both women were in the car, bumping back down the curb, Miss Beasley craned around and advised in her usual unruffled, demogogic tone, "Careful for Norris and Nat, Eleanor, they do a great
service for this town, you know." Down the curb they went, across the street and
up the opposite curb, nearly shearing the pair of octogenarians off their whittling
bench before Elly gained control and put the car in first. Miss Beasley's breasts
whupped in the air like a spaniel's ears as the car jerked forward, sped around a
corner at twenty miles an hour and came to a lurching halt beside the White Eagle
gas pump on the adjacent side of the square. Four ration coupons later Elly and
Miss Beasley were on their way to Calhoun.

"Mr. Parker is innocent, of course," Miss Beasley stated unequivocally.

"Of course. But that woman came to the library chasin' him, didn't she? That's
gonna look bad for him."

"Hmph! I got a thing or two to tell your lawyer about that!"

"Which lawyer we gettin'?"

"There *is* only one if you want to win. Robert Collins. He has a reputation for
winning, and has had since the spring he was nineteen and brought in the wild turkey with the biggest spear and the longest beard taken that season. He hung them
on the contest board at Haverty's drugstore beside two dozen others entered by the
oldest and most experienced hunters in Whitney. As I recall, they'd given Robert
short shrift, smiling out the sides of their mouths at the idea that a mere boy could
outdo any one of them—big talkers, those turkey hunters, always practicing their
disgusting gobbles when a girl walked by on the street, then laughing when she
jumped half out of her skin. Well, Robert won that year—the prize, as I recall, being a twelve-gauge shotgun donated by the local merchants—and he's been win-

ning ever since. At Dartmouth where he graduated top in his class. Two years later when he took on an unpopular case and won restitution for a young black boy who lost his legs when he was pushed into the paddlewheel of a gristmill where he worked, by the owner of the mill. The owner was white, and needless to say, an unbiased jury was hard to find. But Robert found one, and made a name for himself. After that he prosecuted a woman from Red Bud who killed her own son with a garden hoe to keep him from marrying a girl who wasn't Baptist. Of course, Robert had every Baptist in the county writing him poison pen letters declaring that he was maligning the entire religious sect. The church deacons were on his back, even his own minister—Robert is Baptist himself—because as it turned out, the murderess was a fervent churchgoer who'd almost single-handedly bulldozed the community into scraping up funds for a new stone church after a tornado blew the clapboard one down. A *do-goodah,*" Miss Beasley added disparagingly. "You know the type." She paused for a brief breath and continued intoning, "In any event, Robert prosecuted her case and won, and ever since, he's been known as a man who won't knuckle under to social pressures, a defender of underdogs. An honorable man, Robert Collins."

Elly recognized him immediately. He was the one who'd come out of chambers in intense conversation with Judge Murdoch on Elly's wedding day. But she had little opportunity to nurse the memory before becoming distracted by the surprising opening exchange between the lawyer and Miss Beasley.

"Beasley, my secretary said, and I asked myself could it be Gladys Beasley?" He crossed the crowded, cluttered anteroom in an unhurried shuffle, extending a skinny hand.

"It could be and is. Hello, Robert."

Clasping her hand in both of his, he chuckled, showing yellowed teeth edged with gold in a wrinkled elf's face surrounded by springy hair the color of old cobwebs. "Forever formal, aren't you? The only girl in school who called me Robert instead of Bob. Are you still stamping books at the Carnegie Library?"

"I am. Are you still shooting turkeys on the Red Bone Ridge?"

Again he laughed, tipping back, still clasping her hand. "I am. Bagged a twenty-one-pound tom my last time out."

"With an eleven-inch beard, no doubt, and an inch-long spur, which you hung on the drugstore wall to put the old-timers in their places."

Once more his laughter punctuated their exchange. "With a memory like that you'd have made a good lawyer."

"I left that to you though, didn't I, because girls were not encouraged to take up law in those days."

"Now, Gladys, don't tell me you still hold a grudge because I was asked to give the valedictory speech?"

"Not at all. The best man won." Abruptly she grew serious. "Enough byplay, Robert. I've brought you a client, vastly in need of your expert services. I should take it as a personal favor if you'd help her, or more precisely, her husband. This is Eleanor Parker. Eleanor, meet Robert Collins."

Meeting his handshake with one of her own, Elly inquired, "You got a wife, Mr. Collins?"

"No, I don't, not anymore. She died a few years back."

"Oh. Well, then this is for you."

"For me," he repeated, pleased, accepting the quart of honey, holding it high.

"And there's more where that came from, plus milk and pork and chickens and eggs for the duration of this war and without rationing coupons, to go along with whatever money you need to clear Will's name."

He laughed again, examining the honey. "Might this be construed as bribery, do you think, Gladys?"

"Construe it any way you like, but try it on a bran muffin. It's indescribable."

He turned, carrying the honey into his messy office, inviting, "Come in, both of you, and close the door so we can talk. Mizz Parker, as for my fee, we'll get to that later after I decide whether or not I can take the case."

Seated in his office, Elly quickly assured Robert Collins, "Oh, I got money, Mr. Collins, never fear. And I know where I can get more."

"From me," put in Miss Beasley.

Elly's head snapped around. "From you!" she repeated, surprised.

"We're digressing, Eleanor, on Robert's valuable time," returned Miss Beasley didactically, "We'll discuss it later. Alone."

It didn't take fifteen minutes for Robert Collins to ascertain the few facts known by the women and inform them that he'd be at the jail as soon as possible to talk to Will and make his decision about defending him.

Before that hour was up, Elly herself was standing in Sheriff Goodloe's office with another jar of honey in her hand. He was deep in conversation with his deputy but looked up as she entered. Straightening, he began, "Now, Elly, I told you at your house you can't see him till you got a lawyer."

She set the jar of honey on his desk. "I came to apologize." She looked him soberly in the eyes. "About an hour ago I called you a piss-ant when actually I've always had a fair deal of respect for you. I always meant to thank you for gettin' me out of that house I grew up in, but this's the first chance I got." She gestured toward the honey. "That's for that. It's got nothin' to do with Will, but I want to see him."

"Elly, I told you—"

"I know what you told me, but I thought about what kind of laws they are that let you lock up a person without letting him explain to people what really happened. I know all about being locked up like that. It ain't fair, Mr. Goodloe, and you know it. You're a fair man. You were the only person ever stood up for me when they kept me in that house and let the whole town think I was crazy because of it. Well, I ain't. The crazy ones are the ones who make laws that keep a wife from seeing her husband when he's in the pit of despair, which is what my Will is right now. I'm not askin' you to open his door or put us in a private room. I'm not even askin' you to leave us alone. All I'm askin' is what's fair."

Goodloe glanced from her to the honey. He plopped tiredly into his chair and ran his hands over his face in frustation. "Now, dang it, Elly, I got regulations—"

"Aw, let her talk to him," the deputy interrupted, fixing a slight smile on Elly. "What's it gonna hurt?" Sheriff Goodloe swung a glance at the younger man, who shrugged and added, "She's right and you know it. It's not fair." Then, to Elly's surprise, the younger man came forward, extending a hand. "Remember me? Jimmy Ray Hess. We were in fifth grade together. Speaking of fair, I'm one of those who used to call you names, and if you can apologize, so can I."

Astounded, she shook his hand.

"Jimmy Ray Hess," she repeated in wonder. "Well, I'll be."

"That's right." He proudly thumbed the star on his shirt. "Deputy sheriff of Gordon County now." In friendly fashion he swung back to his superior. "What d'you say, Reece—can she see him?"

Reece Goodloe succumbed and flapped a hand. "Aw, hell, sometimes I wonder who's the boss around here. All right, take her in."

The deputy beamed and led the way from the office. "Come along, Elly, I'll show you the way."

Walking along beside Jimmy Ray, Elly felt her faith in mankind restored. She counted those who'd helped her today—Lydia, Miss Beasley, Robert Collins, and now Jimmy Ray Hess.

"Why are you doing this, Jimmy Ray?" she asked.

"Your husband—he was a Marine, wasn't he?"

"That's right—First Raiders."

Jimmy Ray flashed her a crooked grin oozing with latent pride. "Gunnery Sergeant Jimmy Ray Hess, Charlie Company, First Marines, at your service, ma'am." Giving her a smart salute, he opened the last door leading into the jail. "Third on the left," he advised, then closed the door, leaving her alone in the corridor fronting a long row of cells.

She had never been in a jail before. It was dank and dismal. It echoed and smelled bad. It dampened the spirits momentarily lifted by Jimmy Ray Hess.

Even before she reached Will her heart hurt. When she saw him, curled on his cot with his back to the bars, it was like looking at herself on her knees in that place, praying forgiveness for something she didn't do.

"Hello, Will," she said quietly.

Startled, he glanced over his shoulder, carefully schooling all reaction, then faced the wall again. "I thought they weren't gonna let you in here."

Elly felt as if her heart would break. "That what you wanted?" When he refused to answer, she added, "Reckon I know why."

Will swallowed and stared at the wall, feeling a clot of emotion fill his throat. "Go on, get out of here. I don't want you to see me in here."

"Neither do I, but now that I have, I got some questions need asking."

Coldly he said to the wall, "Yeah, like did I kill that bitch. Was I carrying on with her." He laughed mirthlessly, then threw over his shoulder: "Well, you can just go on wondering, because if that's all the faith you have in me, I don't need your kind of wife."

Remorse spread its hot charges through Elly. With it came sudden, stinging tears. "Why didn't you tell me about her, Will, back when it happened, when she came to the library? If you had, it wouldn't've been such a surprise to me today."

Abruptly he swung to his feet and confronted her with fists balled and veins standing out sharply on his throat. "I shouldn't have to tell you I *didn't* do things! You should know by what I *do do* what kind of man I am! But all you had to hear was one word from that sheriff to think I was guilty, didn't you? I saw it in your eyes, Elly, so don't deny it."

"I won't," she whispered, ashamed, while he took up a frenzied pacing, driving a hand through his streaked yellow hair.

"Christ, you're my wife! Do you know what it did to me when you looked at me that way, like I was some—some murderer?"

She had never seen him angry before, nor so desolate. More than anything she wanted to touch him, reassure him, but he paced back and forth between the side walls like a penned animal, well out of reach. She closed her hand over a black iron bar. "Will, I'm sorry. But I'm human, ain't I? I make mistakes like anybody else. But I came here to unmake 'em and to tell you I'm sorry it crossed my mind you coulda done it 'cause it didn't take me three minutes after they took you away to realize you couldn't of. Not you—not my Will."

Coming to an abrupt halt, Will pinned her with damning brown eyes. His hair stood disheveled. His fists were still knotted as he and Elly faced off, doing silent battle while he fought the urge to rush across the cell and touch her, crush her hands beneath his on the iron bars, draw from her the sustenance he needed to face the night, and tomorrow, and whatever fight lay ahead. But the hurt within him was still too engulfing. So he returned in a cold, bitter voice, "Yeah, well, you were three minutes too late, Elly, cause I don't care what you think anymore." It was a lie which hurt him as badly as it hurt her. He saw the shock riffle across her face and steeled himself against rushing to her with an apology, taking her face between his hands and kissing her between the bars that separated them.

"You don't mean that, Will," she whispered through trembling lips.

"Don't I?" he shot back, telling himself to disregard the tears that made her wide green eyes look bright as dew-kissed grass. "I'll leave you to go home and wonder, just like I laid here and wondered if *you* meant it!"

For several inescapable seconds, while their hearts thundered, they stared at each other, hurting, loving, fearful. Then she swallowed and dropped her hand from the bar, stepped back and spoke levelly. "All right, Will, I'll leave if that's what you want. But first just answer me one question. Who do you think killed her?"

"I don't know." He stood like a ramrod, too stubborn to take the one step necessary to end this self-imposed hell. *Don't go, I didn't mean it, I don't know why I said it . . . oh, God, Elly, I love you so much.*

"If you wanna see me, tell Jimmy Ray Hess. He'll get word to me."

Only when she was gone did he relent. Tears came as he spun to the wall, pressing fists and forearms high against it, burying his thumb knuckles hard in his eyesockets. *Elly, Elly—don't believe me! I care so much what you think of me that I'd rather be dead than have you see me in this place.*

Miss Beasley had obligingly waited in the car. Returning to it, Elly looked pale and shaken.

"What is it, Eleanor?"

Elly stared woodenly out the windshield. "I did Will wrong," she answered dully.

"Did him wrong? Why, whatever are you talking about?"

"When the sheriff came out to our place and said Lula Peak was dead. You see, it crossed my mind for just a minute that Will might have done it. I didn't say so, but I didn't have to. Will saw it in my face, and now he won't talk to me." Elly tightened her lips to keep her chin from shaking.

"Won't talk to you, but—"

"Oh, he yelled some, got it off his chest how much I hurt him. But he stayed clear across the cell and wouldn't take my hand or smile or anything. He said it didn't matter to him anymore what I th–think." She covered her eyes and dropped her head.

Miss Beasley grew incensed at Will's callousness and took Elly's shoulder.

"Now you listen here, young woman. You didn't do anything that any normal human being wouldn't have done."

"But I should've trusted him better!"

"So you experienced a moment of doubt. Any woman would have done the same."

"But you didn't!"

"Don't be an imbecile, Eleanor. Of course I did."

Surprise brought Elly's head up. Though her eyes were streaming, she swiped at them with a sleeve. "You did?"

"Well, of course I did," Gladys lied. "Who wouldn't? Half of this town will. It means we shall only have to fight harder to prove they're wrong."

Miss Beasley's staunchness suddenly put starch in Elly's spine. She sniffed and mopped her eyes. "That durn husband of mine wouldn't even tell me if he suspected anybody." With the return of control, Elly began rationalizing. "Who could've done it, Miss Beasley? I got to find out somehow. That's the only way I know to get Will back. Who should I start with?"

"How about Norris and Nat? They've been sitting on that park bench for years, watching Lula Peak point her bodice at anything in pants that came along the sidewalk. I'm sure they'd know down to the exact second how long it took her to follow Mr. Parker into the library every time he brought me eggs, and also how long it took her to come back out looking like a singed cat."

"They would?"

"Of course they would."

Elly digested the idea, then had one of her own. "And they're in charge of the town guard, aren't they?"

Miss Beasley's face lit with excitement. "Prowling around town at night, listening for airplane engines, looking through binoculars and checking blackout curtains."

Elly tossed her a hopeful glance, tinged with anticipation. "And chasing curfew violators off the streets?"

"Exactly!"

Elly started the engine. "Let's go."

They found Norris and Nat MacReady soaking up the late afternoon sun on their usual bench in the square. Each received a quart jar of pure gold Georgia honey in exchange for which they gladly revealed the startling details of an overheard conversation behind the library one night last January. They had been together so long they might have had a single brain at work between them, for what one began, the other finished.

"Norris and I," Nat said, "were walking along Comfort Street and had turned up the alley behind the library—where the podocarpus bushes grow by the incinerator—"

"—when a high-heeled shoe sailed out and clunked me on the shoulder. Nat can testify to the fact—"

" 'Cause he had a purple bruise there for well over four weeks."

"Now, Nat," chided Norris, "you might be stretching it a bit. I don't think it was over three."

Nat bristled. "Three! Your memory is failing, boy. It was there a full four, 'cause if you'll recall, I commented on it the day we—"

"Gentlemen, gentlemen!" interrupted Miss Beasley. "The conversation you overheard."

"Oh, that. Well, first the shoe flew—"

"Then we heard young Parker beller loud enough to wake the entire town—"

" 'If you're in heat, Lula, go yowl beneath somebody else's window!' That's exactly what he said, wasn't it, Nat?"

"Sure was. Then the door slams and Miss Lula—"

"—madder than Cooter Brown—pounds on it and calls young Parker a name that you ladies are free to read from our logbook if you like but one that—"

"*Logbook?*"

"That's right. But neither Norris nor myself would care to repeat it, would we, Norris?"

"Most certainly not, not in the company of ladies. Tell 'em what happened next, Nat."

"Well, then Miss Lula yelled that young Will's—ahem—" Nat cleared his throat while searching for a genteel euphemism. But it was Norris who came up with it.

"—his, ahh, *male part*"—the words were whispered—"probably wouldn't fit into Lula's ear anyway."

Almost simultaneously, Miss Beasley and Elly demanded, "Did you tell this to the sheriff?"

"The sheriff didn't ask. Did he, Norris?"

"No, he didn't."

Which gave Elly the idea about running an ad in the newspaper. After all, running an ad had brought results before. Why wouldn't it again? But Miss Beasley's ankles were swollen, so Elly took her home before returning to the *Whitney Register* office to rid herself of another quart of honey as payment for the ad which stated simply that E. Parker, top of Rock Creed Road, would pay a reward for any information leading to the dropping of charges against her husband, William L. Parker, in the Lula Peak murder case. To her amazement, the editor, Michael Hanley, didn't bat an eye, only thanked her for the honey and wished her luck, ending, "That's a fine young man you married there, Mizz Parker. Went off and fought like a man instead of runnin' his finger through a buzzsaw like some in this town."

Which sparked the memory of Harley Overmire's long-ago antagonism toward Will and made Elly wonder briefly if it were worth mentioning to either Reece Goodloe or Robert Collins. But she hadn't time to dwell on it, for from the newspaper office Elly proceeded directly to the office of Pride Real Estate, where she unceremoniously slapped a heavy nickel skeleton key on the counter, followed by yet another quart of honey and announced to Hazel Pride, "I want to list some property." Hazel Pride's husband was fighting "somewhere in the south of France" and had left her to manage the paper while he was gone. She had typeset every word about Will Parker's heroism and his Purple Heart, so greeted Elly affably and said it was a shame about Mr. Parker, and if there was anything Hazel could do, just let her know. After all, Will Parker was a veteran with a Purple Heart, and no veteran who'd been through so much should be treated the way he'd been. Would Eleanor care to ride in Hazel's car out to the house?

Elly declined, following Hazel in her own car through the chill of a late-winter afternoon. The morning glory vines were dry and leafless around the front door, woven into a thick mesh of neglected growth. The grass was the color of twine. The two cars flattened it while pulling around to the back door.

Of all the things Elly had done that day, none was as difficult as entering that dreary house with Hazel Pride, walking into the murky shadows behind those hated green shades, past the spot in the front parlor where she'd prayed, past the corner where her grandmother had died on a hard kitchen chair, past the bedroom where her mother had gone slowly insane, smelling the dry bat droppings from the attic, mixed with dust and mildew and bad memories. It was hard, but Elly did it. Not just because she needed the money to pay Robert Collins but because she'd come so far in one day she figured she might as well go the rest of the way. Also, she knew it would please Will.

In the parlor she snapped up the shades, one after the other, letting them whirl and flap on their surprisingly tensile springs. The sunset poured in, revealing nothing more frightening than dust motes swimming through the stale air of an abandoned house with mouse leavings on the linoleum floor.

"Two thousand, three hundred," Hazel Pride announced, tapping her tablet. "Top listing price, considering the work that would be necessary to make the place livable again."

Twenty-three hundred dollars would more than pay Collins' bill, Elly figured, and leave extra for the rewards she hoped to pay. She insisted on signing the paper there, inside the house, so that when she walked out she'd be free of it forever.

And she was. As she climbed back into Will's car and drove through the hub-high grass of the deep twilit yard to the road, she felt relieved, absolved.

She thought about the day, the fears she had put to rout simply by attacking them head-on. She had driven a car clear to Calhoun for the first time, had confronted a town that seemed no longer intimidating but supportive, had set into motion the machinery of justice and had shed the ghosts of her past.

She was tired. So tired she wanted to pull the car into the next field-access road and drop off till morning.

But Will was still in jail and every minute there must seem like a year to him. So she drove clear back to Calhoun to find Sheriff Goodloe, give him hell about his slipshod methods of investigation and put him onto Norris and Nat MacReady's logbook. She forgot, however, to mention Harley Overmire.

Chapter 22

Will lay on his bunk in a cocoon of misery. From up the corridor came the chiming reverberations of a metal door opening and closing. He remained inert, staring at the wall. Footsteps came closer. One pair, two pair. Leather shoes on concrete, a familiar sound, too familiar.

"Parker?" It was the voice of Deputy Hess. "Your lawyer's here."

Will started. "My *lawyer?*" His head came off the pillow and he craned his neck around.

With young Hess stood an older man with flyaway gray hair and tanned skin; slightly stooped, dressed in a brown suit and a rumpled white shirt with a tie knotted at half-mast. "Your wife came to see me, asked me to come have a talk with you."

Will swung onto the edge of his bunk. "My wife?"

"And Gladys Beasley." The guard unlocked the door and the lawyer ambled inside, extending a hand. "Name's Bob Collins." He waited, peering at Will with gray eyes that appeared perennially amused, as if accustomed to introducing himself to surprised inmates.

"Will Parker." Rising, accepting the handshake, Will thought, *She not only came to Calhoun, she hired a lawyer, too?*

But what kind of lawyer? His suit looked as if it had been washed in a washing machine; his shirt looked as if it hadn't. His hair stood on end like a dandelion gone to seed, an occasional tuft lifted above the rest as if ready to fly at the smallest puff of wind. He was not only disheveled, but moved with a tired slowness that made Will wonder if he'd suddenly rusted up halfway onto his chair. There he hung, backside pointed in the right direction while Will counted the seconds—one, two, three—and finally the old duffer sat, expelling a breath and clasping one bony knee with an equally bony hand. When he finally spoke, his jocular tone of voice was one suited to a speech honoring the outgoing president of the lady's horticultural society. "I went to school with Gladys Beasley. There was a question for a while about which of us would be named valedictorian. It was always my opinion they should have named two that year." He chuckled as if to himself, resting a finger along his jaw. "Gladys Beasley, after all these years—can you beat that?" He glanced up with a hint of devilment in his eyes. "She was a damned fine-lookin' woman. And smart, too. Only one in the whole class who could discuss anything more intelligent than the length of hems and the height of heels. Used to scare the daylights out of me, she was so bright. Always wanted to ask her on a date, can't really say why I never did."

Will sat befuddled, wondering why Gladys Beasley would recommend a creaky old fart like this. In his dotage, smelling like the inside of a mummy's wrappings, and with a wandering, maundering mind. Will wondered if he might be better off defending himself.

But just when Will's opinions crystallized, Collins threw him a curveball.

"So, Will Parker, did you kill Lula Peak or not?"

Will fixed his brown eyes on Collins' faded gray ones and replied unequivocally, "No, sir."

Collins nodded thrice almost imperceptibly, studied Will silently for a full fifteen seconds before asking, "You got any idea who did?"

"Nossir."

Again came the lengthy silence that gave the impression rusty machinery needed oiling inside Collins' scruffy head. But when he spoke, Will was somehow relieved. "Then we have work to do. The arraignment is set for tomorrow."

Collins took the case, promising to apply pressure to every possible quarter in an effort to get it through the courts fast. He was very good, he said, at applying pressure. Will didn't believe him. Yet in spite of his constant half-rumpled appearance and his surface slowness—he had a habit of tugging an earlobe, crossing his arms and pausing as if confused—he was bright, thorough, and totally unimpressed with the prosecution's case. Furthermore, he was convinced that he could gain a jury's sympathy by implying that the law had pounced on Will primarily because of his prison record when it was his war record they ought to bear in mind. He gave little credence to the note bearing Will's initials, even believed it might prove helpful since it would take one all-fired gullible fool to believe it wasn't a plant.

The arraignment was quick and predictable: the court refused bail due to Will's past record. But, true to his word, Collins arranged for a grand jury hearing within a week. Witnesses willing to testify for Will began piling up, but, as is the case with grand juries, the accused was not allowed counsel in the hearing room, thus the Solicitor General's evidence weighed more heavily than it would when rebutted: the grand jury handed down a true bill.

Disappointment crushed Will. He was removed from the hearing room through the back halls which led directly to the jail, so he had no chance to learn if Elly was waiting somewhere in the courthouse for word about the jury's decision. He had foolishly hoped for a glimpse of her, had fantasized about her approaching him with hands outstretched, saying, It's all right, Will, let's forgive and forget and put it behind us.

Instead he returned to his dismal cell to waste away more of his life, to wonder what would happen to him next, and if the shambling old attorney sent to him by Elly and Miss Beasley was senile after all. The confined space seemed suddenly claustrophobic, so he sat sideways on his bunk, his back pressed to the cold concrete blocks, and stared straight through the bars—the longest view—and thought of Texas, broad and flat, with wind blowing through the pungent sage, with an immense blue sky that turned hot pink and purple and yellow at sunset, with Indian paintbrush setting the plains afire just before the sun sank and stars appeared like gems on blue satin.

But imagination could rescue him only temporarily. In time he rolled onto his side and shut his eyes, swallowing hard. He'd lost again, and he hadn't seen Elly. God, how he needed to see her, how he'd banked on it. He didn't know which hurt worse, the fact that she hadn't been there, or that he'd lost the first round in court. But he'd hurt her so badly he'd been afraid to send word through Deputy Hess, afraid he didn't deserve her anymore, afraid that even if he called, she wouldn't come.

But she showed up even as he lay on his bunk, dejected.

"You got a visitor, Parker," announced Hess, opening the door. "Your wife. Follow me."

So she *had* been here all the time, waiting for word. His heart started klunking and he flew from his bunk. "Just a minute, Hess!" He dipped before the mirror and dragged a comb through his hair, four swift strokes. The mirror reflected his cheeks flushed with expectancy before he turned and hurried after Hess.

The visitors' room was a long, empty expanse totally devoid of trim. It held a bare window, a table and three chairs much like those in the Carnegie library. When Will entered, Elly was already seated at the table, wearing something new and yellow, clutching a purse on her lap. Hess motioned Will toward her, then took his place beside the door, crossing his arms as if planted for the duration.

Slipping into the chair opposite Elly's, Will wondered if she could feel the floor tremble from his thudding heart.

For a full ten seconds they stared.

"Hello, Will," Elly greeted with a sad smile in her eyes.

"Hello."

Their words, though softly spoken, echoed clearly through the room.

Will's palms were sweating and his neck felt hot as he drank in the sight of her and suppressed the awful need to reach for her hands across the table.

"I'm sorry about the grand jury decision. I thought . . . well, I hoped you'd be home today."

"So did I. But Collins warned me not to get my hopes up, especially when he couldn't be in there to tell our side of it."

"It don't seem fair, Will. I mean, how can they keep your lawyer out of the hearing room?"

"Collins says that's how the law works, and our chance will come when we go to trial by traverse jury."

"Traverse jury?" Her brow wrinkled.

"The big one, the one that lets us tell our side."

"Oh."

The thought of it shook them both as they gazed at each other, wishing futile wishes, regretting the harsh words of their last meeting. Elly kept a two-handed grip on her purse while Will dried his palms on his thighs.

"Elly, I . . ." *Tell her you're sorry, fool.* But Hess stood guard, listening to every word, and apologizing was hard enough in private. The thought of baring his heart before an audience seemed to paralyze Will's tongue. So instead he told Elly, "I like Collins. He's a good one, I think. Thanks for hiring him."

"Don't be silly. Did you think I wouldn't hire a lawyer for my own husband?"

The words pressed up against Will's throat, and Hess or no Hess, he had to speak them. "I didn't know what to think after the way I talked to you last time."

Elly's eyes skittered aside. "I'd already hired him before I saw you."

"Oh." Will felt justly stung. His hands, only moments ago sweating, grew suddenly icy. *So what'd you expect, Parker, after the way you talked to her?* Again came the aching desire to ask her forgiveness, followed by the godawful fear that she wouldn't warm again, and if that happened, he'd have no reason to fight his way out of here. So he sat in misery, with his heart painfully clamoring and a lump in his throat that felt the size of a baseball.

"You okay?" Elly inquired, letting her glance waver back to him. "They feedin' you okay in here?"

Will swallowed the lump and managed to sound normal. "Pretty good. The sheriff's wife's got the cooking contract."

"Well . . . you look good." She flashed a nervous smile.

Silence again, made more awkward by the passing minutes and the fact that they spoke of everything except what was paramount on their minds.

"How did you get here?" He found himself obsessed with an irrational greed to know everything she'd done and thought since he'd been in here, to fill in the blanks of the time he was forced to forfeit. Life had grown so precious to him since she'd become part of it that he felt doubly robbed of his freedom.

"Oh, I caught a ride," she said evasively.

Distractedly, Elly scratched at the clasp of her purse and they both studied her hands until their eyes seemed to burn. Finally she opened the purse and told him quietly, "I know you told me not to come, Will, but I had to bring these presents from the kids." From the purse she withdrew two scrolled papers and handed them across the table.

"Wait!" Hess ordered sharply and leaped forward to confiscate them.

Elly glanced up, injured. "It's only greetings from the kids."

He examined them, rerolled them and handed them back, then returned to his post beside the door.

Again Elly offered the papers. "Here, Will."

He unrolled them to find a crude color-crayon drawing of flowers and stick people, and the message *I love you, Will* faithfully duplicated in nearly indecipherable printing, followed by their names: Donald Wade and Thomas. Will had never had to work so hard to keep tears from springing.

"Gosh," he remarked thickly, eyes downcast for fear she'd read how closely he treaded the borderline of control.

"They miss you," she whispered plaintively, thinking, *And I miss you. I ache without you. Home is terrible, work is pointless, living hurts.*

But she was afraid to say it, afraid of being rebuffed again.

"I miss 'em, too." Will's chin remained flattened to his chest. "How are they?"

"They're fine. They're at Lydia's house today, all three of 'em. Donald Wade, he gets off the schoolbus there. He loves it at Lydia's. Him and Sally're buildin' a fort."

Will cleared his throat and looked up, his heart still tripping in double-time, wishing futilely that she need not see him in this place that so reduced a man's self-respect, wishing for the hundredth time that he hadn't said what he had the last time he saw her, needing terribly to know if she, like the children, still loved him. *Tell her you're sorry, Parker! Just lay it out there and this misery will be over!*

He opened his lips to apologize but she spoke first. "Miss Beasley says Mr. Collins is the best."

"I trust her judgment." He cleared his throat and sat up straighter. "But I don't know where we're gonna get the money to pay him, Elly."

"Don't you worry about that. The honey run was good and we got money in the bank, and Miss Beasley's offered to help."

"She has?"

Elly nodded. "But I don't aim to take her up on it unless we have to."

"That's probably wise," he added.

Again came the oppressive silence and the swelling compulsion to touch fingertips. But he was afraid to reach and she was afraid Hess would jump all over her again, so neither of them moved.

"Well, listen." She lifted her face and smiled a big jack-o-lantern smile, as false as if it had been carved in a pumpkin by a knife. "I have to go 'cause I been leaving the kids at Lydia's an awful lot lately and I don't want to start takin' her for granted."

Panic swamped Will. He hadn't done any of the things he'd intended—he hadn't touched her, apologized, complimented her on her pretty new dress, told her he loved her, said any of the things crowding his heart. But it was probably best to let her off the hook. No matter what Collins said, the cards were stacked against him. He was a born loser. Innocent or not, he was bound to lose this trial, too, and when he did they'd lock him up for good. They did that on a second murder conviction, he knew. And no woman should have to wait for a man who'd be sixty—or seventy—when he got out. If he got out.

Elly edged forward on her chair.

"Well ..." She rose uncertainly, still with a two-fisted grip on her small black purse. He didn't remember her ever carrying a purse before; it made him feel as if he'd been incarcerated for nine years instead of nine days, as if she were changing subtly while he wasn't there to see.

He, too, stood, tightening the roll of paper with both hands to keep from reaching out for her. "Thanks for coming, Elly. Say hi to the kids and tell the boys thanks for these pictures."

"I will."

"Kiss Lizzy P. for me."

"I w—" The word broke in half. Her chin began trembling and she forcibly tensed it.

They stared at each other until their eyes burned and their heartbeats hurt.

"Elly ..." he whispered, and reached.

Their hands clung, flattening the scroll of paper—a tense, forlorn message of all that had not been said.

Tears glimmered on her lower eyelids. "I got to g—go, Will," she whispered and slowly pulled free. She backed up a step and he saw her chest began to heave as if she were already sobbing internally.

Desperate, he swung away and strode toward the door. "I'm ready, Hess!" The words resounded in the bare room as Will left Elly to shed her tears unobserved.

She didn't come back again. But Miss Beasley did, the next day, with her mouth puckered like a two-day-old pudding and a look of stern reproof on her face.

"So, what have you done to that child?" she demanded before Will even touched his chair.

"What?" His eyes widened in surprise.

"What have you done to Eleanor? She came to my house crying her heart out last night and said you don't love her anymore."

"It's best if she believes that."

"Bullwhacky!" The word resounded from the walls, taking Will aback. He sat in silence while Miss Beasley raged on. "She's your wife, Mr. Parker! How dare you treat her like some passing acquaintance!"

"If you came here to give me hell, you can—"

"That's precisely why I came here, you young upstart! And don't speak to me in that tone of voice!"

Will let his weight drop to the chair and sat back in an insolent sprawl. "Y' know, you're just what I needed today, Miss Beasley."

"What you need, young man, is a good dressing down, and you're going to get it. Whatever you said to that young woman to put her in that state was untenable. If there was ever a time when you need to stand by her, this is it."

"Me stand by her!" Will stiffened and splayed two hands on his chest. "Ask her about standing by me!"

"Oh, I suppose you're sitting in here sulking because she had to take ten seconds to digest Reece Goodloe's accusation before coming to grips with it."

"Digest! She did more than digest!" He pointed toward Whitney. "She thought I *did* it! She actually thought I killed Lula Peak!"

"Oh, she did, did she? Then why is she running ads in the Whitney and Calhoun newspapers offering rewards for any information leading to your acquittal? Why has she single-handedly rounded up a dozen witnesses to testify on your behalf? Why has she learned how to drive a car and refused—"

"Drive a car!"

"—my financial help and run all over Gordon County passing out honey to make people forget all the nasty things they said about her years ago and badgering Sheriff Goodloe to find the real killer? And why has she contacted Hazel Pride and taken her into that deserted house that no woman who's suffered as Eleanor has should ever have to enter again?"

Will finally got a word in edgewise. "Who's Hazel Pride?"

"Our local realtor, that's who. Eleanor has put her grandfather's house up for sale to pay your lawyer's fee, to see that you get the best defense a man can possibly get in this state. But to do it she had to face that house, and a town full of despicable . . . *horses' posteriors* who don't deserve to be groveled to. But grovel she did, and she did it for you, Mr. Parker! Because she loves you so much she would face anything in this world for you. And you pay her back by withholding your forgiveness for a reaction that would have been as natural to you had she been the one with the prison record who was being accused again." Miss Beasley collected herself and sat back self-righteously. "Perhaps I was mistaken about what kind of person you are."

Will was so dazed, he commented on the most incidental fact.

"She told me she caught a ride to Calhoun."

"Caught a ride—hmph! She drives that deplorable automobile you stuck together with spit and baling twine, and if she doesn't kill herself before this is over it'll be a miracle. She nearly killed Nat and Norris, to say nothing of the buildings she's bumped into and the sidewalks she's scaled. Why, a person's rosebushes aren't even safe on the front lawn anymore! She's scared to death of that thing, but she grips the wheel and drives, mind you! Clear up to Calhoun, sometimes twice a day, only to come home believing that you don't love her anymore. Well, shame on you, Mr. Parker!" Miss Beasley shook her finger at Will as if he were six years old. "Now I want you to consider how you've hurt her instead of sitting in here thinking only of yourself. And the next time she comes to visit you, you make amends!"

Like the grand jury, Miss Beasley offered Will no chance to rebut. She sailed out as gustily as she'd sailed in, leaving him feeling as if he'd just taken a ride on a tornado.

Back in his cell, Will experienced a curious reaction, a minute exhilaration. Elly . . . driving the car? Elly . . . rounding up witnesses? Elly . . . going into that *house?*

For him!

It struck him fully what Miss Beasley had set out to do, and in her own inimitable way, she'd done it: made him realize how much Elly loved him. She must, to face all those apprehensions, all those fears that had held her prisoner on Rock Creek Road for years, that had held her aloof from the townspeople, denying that she needed anybody.

In the wake of Miss Beasley's visit, Will's torpor disappeared, replaced by restlessness and a thrill of hope. He paced his cell, cracking his knuckles, wondering what witnesses Elly had found, smiling at the idea of her sweetening them up with honey. God, what a woman! He paced . . . and pondered . . . and thanked his lucky stars for both Elly and Gladys Beasley.

Within an hour after the departure of the latter, Will made a decision.

"Hess!" He bellowed. "Hess, get in here!" He clattered his dinner fork against the bars. "Hess, I want you to get a message to my wife!"

"Hold your horses, Parker!" came a voice from the distance.

"Hurry up, Hess!"

"I'm comin', I'm comin'!" The deputy appeared down the corridor. "What is it?"

"Can the sheriff drive out to my place and get word to Elly that I want to see her?"

"I guess so."

"Well, get him on the radio and tell him I'd appreciate it if he'd do it soon as possible."

"Will do." Hess turned away but stopped and flashed a crooked grin over his shoulder. "Miss Beasley can sure chew ass, can't she?"

"Whew!" Will replied, running a hand through his hair. "Can she ever! Tell you the truth, I was glad to be safe behind these bars."

Hess laughed, took two steps and turned back. "Everybody's talkin' about it. I'm surprised you didn't know."

"Know what?"

"About your wife drivin' that car like there was no rubber rationing, runnin' all over drummin' up witnesses for you, just like Miss Beasley said. You know, Elly and me went to school together and I was one of 'em who called her crazy. But people are sayin' now she's outwitting the Solicitor General. Drivin' *him* crazy, wonderin' what she and Collins will unearth in court!"

Will's heart began to thunder with excitement.

"Could you tell Collins I want to see him, too?"

"Could if he wasn't out of town."

"Out of town. Where?"

"I don't know. That wife of yours has got him runnin' like a fox in front of a pack of hounds, checkin' leads. I do know one thing, though." ·

"What?"

"He got your trial on the docket for the first week in February."

"So fast?"

"Don't underestimate that old bird, especially not when he's got your wife workin' with him." Hess sauntered away, stopped and grinned back at Will. "There's a joke goin' around, only it's not really a joke at all, it's—" Hess scratched his head. "Well, you might say it's a sprinklin' of respect that's about fifteen years late in comin'. Folks're sayin', 'Look out, here comes Elly Parker with her honey!' " Turning away, Hess added, "Nobody's sure if she really gave a quart of it to Judge Murdoch or not, but word's out he's the one who married you two and he's also the one scheduled to preside at your trial." With a last chuckle drifting down the corridor as he opened the far door, Hess added, "I'll get word to your wife, Parker." Then the far door slammed.

Chapter 23

Elly didn't come back again. But she sent a brand-new Calcutta cloth suit and a striped tie and white shirt with cuff links and Will's military dress shoes all spit-polished for him to wear the day of his trial. And a note: *We're gonna win Will. Love, Elly.*

He dressed early, taking great care with his hair, wishing it were shorter above the ears, returning to the mirror time and again to run his fingertips over his shaved jaw, to tighten the knot in his tie, adjust his cuffs, unbutton and rebutton his jacket. At the thought of seeing her again a wedge of expectation tightened deep within him. He paced, cracked his knuckles, checked his reflection once more. Again he ran his knuckles over the hair above his ears, worried that it didn't look trim enough—not for a jury, but for her.

Staring at his own eyes, he thought of hers. *Hang on, green eyes, don't give up on me yet. I'm not the horse's ass I've been acting like lately. After we've won this thing I'll show you.*

Elly, too, had taken great care dressing. Yellow. It had to be yellow, her color of affirmation. The color of sunlight and freedom. She'd made a tailored suit in gabardine as pale as whipped butter, its shoulders built up, its pocket flaps buttoned down. She, too, returned apprehensively to check her reflection in the mirror: she'd had her hair sheared so that when she appeared in public Will would have no cause to feel ashamed. Staring at her shaped eyebrows and coral lips, she saw a woman as sleek and modish as the pictures on the coffee table at Erma's Beauty Nook. *Just wait, Will, when this is over we're gonna be the happiest two people on the face of the earth.*

Sitting in the courtroom waiting, she kept her eyes fixed on the door by which she knew he'd enter.

When he did their eyes met and their hearts leaped. She had never seen him in a civilian suit before. He looked stunning, his hair combed with hair oil that made it appear darker than usual, his tie crisp, his dark face a sharp contrast to the white shirt collar.

He lifted his eyes as he entered and his collar felt suddenly tight. He knew she'd wear yellow. He knew it! As if to point it out, the nine A.M. sun had seen fit to slash through a high window and fall directly across her. God, how he loved her, wanted to be free for her, with her. As he moved across the varnished floor their gazes remained locked. Her hair, what had she done to her hair? She'd had most of it cut off! It was sheared up high on the neck and above the ears, with a side part and a fluffy top. It brought her cheekbones into prominence in a wholly attractive way. He wanted to go to her, tell her how pretty she looked, thank her for the suit and the note and tell her he loved her, too. But Jimmy Ray Hess was at his side, so he could only walk and gawk. She smiled and discreetly waggled two fingers. The sun seemed to turn its warming rays on him. He felt a great rush much like that he'd experienced in the Augusta train station when he'd seen her approaching through the crowd. He smiled in reply.

The woman to Elly's left nudged her and leaned over to say something. For the first time he noticed it was Lydia Marsh. And on Elly's right sat Miss Beasley, stern-faced and sober as ever. Her eyes caught Will's and he nodded, his heart in his throat.

She gave a barely perceptible nod and a tight moue, releasing him to breathe again.

Friends. True friends. Gratitude swamped him but again he had no way to convey it but to nod to Lydia, too, and cast a last lingering gaze over Elly as he reached the defense table and turned his back on them.

Collins was already there, dressed like a dotty museum curator in crinkled puce wool, smelly yellowed cotton, and a silk tie decorated with ... pink flamingos! When the handcuffs were removed, Collins rose and shook Will's hand.

"Things are looking good. I see you've got a cheering section."

"I don't want my wife on the stand, Collins, remember that."

"Only if necessary, I told you."

"No! They'll tear her apart. They'll dredge up all that stuff about her being crazy. You can put me on but not her."

"That *won't* be necessary. You'll see."

"Where were you yesterday? I sent word I wanted to see you."

"Pipe down and have a chair, Parker. I've been out saving your hide, chasing down witnesses your wife dug up."

"You mean it's true? She's been—"

"All rise, please," the bailiff called dryly. "The Gordon County Court is now in session, the honorable Aldon P. Murdoch presiding."

Will gaped as Murdoch entered, garbed in black, but he resisted the urge to glance over his shoulder to see Elly's reaction. Murdoch's eyes scanned the courtroom, paused on Will and moved on. Though his expression was inscrutable, Will had one thought: by whatever miracle, he'd been delivered into the hands of a fair man. The conviction stemmed from the picture of two little boys in a swivel chair sharing a cigar box of jelly beans.

"All be seated, please," ordered Murdoch.

Seating himself, Will leaned toward Collins and whispered, "She didn't really bribe him, did she?"

A pair of half-glasses hung on Collins' porous nose. He peered over them at the papers he was withdrawing from a scuffed briefcase. "Are you kidding? He's unimpressible. He'd've had charges brought against her so fast it would've spun her honey."

The trial began.

Opening statements were given by both attorneys. Collins' was delivered in a slow drawl that gave the impression he hadn't had enough sleep the previous night.

Solicitor General Edward Slocum's was delivered with fire and flourish.

He was half Collins' age and nearly twice his height. In a neat blue serge suit, freshly laundered shirt and crisp tie, he made Bob Collins look dowdy by comparison. With his ringing baritone voice and upright stature, he made Collins look ready for the boneyard. Slocum's eyes were black, intense, direct, and the wave standing along the top of his dark head gave the appearance of a cocky rooster who dared anyone in his roost to cluck without his approval. Vocally eloquent and physically imposing, Slocum promised, through undisputable evidence, to show the jury beyond a glimmer of a doubt that Will Parker had cold-bloodedly, and with malice aforethought, murdered Lula Peak.

Listening to the two men, Will couldn't help but think that if he were a member of the jury, he'd believe anything Slocum said and would wonder if the attorney for the defense was as senile as he appeared.

"The prosecution calls Sheriff Reece Goodloe."

While questioning his witness, Slocum stood foursquare to him, often with his feet widespread, knees locked. He knew how to use his eyes, to pierce the witness as if each answer were a fulcrum on which the outcome of the trial hinged, then to pass them over the jury at the appropriate moment to inculcate upon them the most incriminating portions of the testimony.

From Sheriff Goodloe the jury learned of Will's criminal record, the existence of the torn dustcloth and a note bearing the accused's initials, and his own admission that he often read the *Atlanta Constitution.*

When Bob Collins shuffled to his feet, half the people in the courtroom suppressed a grunt of help. He spent so much time pondering each question that the jury shifted restlessly. When he finally drew it forth, their shoulders seemed to sag with relief. His eyes avoided everything in the room except the floor and the toes of his scuffed brown oxfords. His mouth wore a half-smile, as if he knew an amusing secret which he would, in his own good time, share with them.

His cross-examination of Sheriff Goodloe revealed that Will Parker had served his time in prison, been a model prisoner and been released with a full parole. It also revealed that Sheriff Goodloe himself read the *Atlanta Constitution* daily.

From a gaunt, bespectacled woman named Barbara Murphy, who identified herself as a typesetter for the *Atlanta Constitution,* came unassailable verification that the note was cut from a copy or copies of that newspaper. Upon cross-examination Miss Murphy revealed that the circulation of the newspaper was 143,261 and that it was conceivable that since Calhoun was one of 158 counties in the state, roughly nine hundred copies of the *Atlanta Constitution* flooded into it daily.

From a tired-looking elderly county coroner named Elliot Mobridge the jury learned the time and cause of death and that Lula Peak was carrying a four-month-old fetus when she died. Cross-examination established that there was no way to determine who had sired a four-month-old fetus of a dead woman.

From a brusque female medical examiner who identified herself as Leslie McCooms came the fact that remnants of dust and lemon oil matching those on the torn dustcloth had been found on Lula Peak's neck, along with bruises caused by human hands—probably a man's.

Defense counsel released the witness without questions, reserving the right to cross-examine her later.

From Gladys Beasley, long-standing lioness of estimable repute, came the concession that the dustcloth and lemon oil (exhibit A) could possibly have come from the Carnegie Municipal Library of Whitney, where Will Parker was employed and on duty the night of Lula Peak's murder. Miss Beasley admitted, too, that the library did indeed carry two subscriptions to the *Atlanta Constitution* and she had given Will Parker permission to take home one of the two copies when it was three days old or more.

It was all testimony that Will had expected, yet he felt shaken at how incriminating it sounded when stated by witnesses under oath, from a hard wooden chair on a raised platform beside the judge's dais.

But the tide subtly turned when Robert Collins cross-examined Miss Beasley.

"Did Lula Peak ever visit the library when Will Parker was there?"

"She most certainly did."

"And did she speak to Mr. Parker?"

"Yes."

"How do you know?"

"I could hear their conversation plainly from the checkout desk. The library is U-shaped, with the desk situated in the crossbar so that I can see and often hear everything that's going on. The ceilings are high and everything echoes."

"When did you hear the first such conversation between Peak and Parker?"

"On September second, 1941."

"How can you be sure of that date?"

"Because Mr. Parker asked for a borrower's card and I began to fill one out before realizing he had not established residency in Whitney. The card was filled out in ink, thus I couldn't erase and reuse it for another patron. Abiding by the motto, *Waste not, want not,* I filed Mr. Parker's card in a separate place to reuse when he came back in with proof of residency, as I was sure he would. He still uses that original card, with the date of September second crossed off."

Miss Beasley presented Will's borrower's card, which was entered as exhibit B.

"So," Collins went on, "on the day of September second, you overheard a conversation between Lula Peak and William Parker. Would you repeat that conversation, to the best of your recollection?"

Miss Beasley, prim and well-packed and indubitably accurate, repeated verbatim what she had overheard that first day when Lula sat down across from Will and stuck her foot between his thighs, when she trapped him between the shelves and attempted to seduce him, when she vindictively accused his wife of being crazy from the time Elly was a child, a time when Miss Beasley herself remembered Eleanor See as a bright, inquisitive student with a talent for drawing. She told of Will's polite but hasty exit on that day and others when Lula followed him into the library under the pretext of "bettering herself" with books which she never bothered to check out.

Listening to her testimony, Will sat tense. After the dressing down she'd given him he'd feared her antipathy on the witness stand. He should have known better. He had no better friend than Gladys Beasley. When she was excused she marched past his chair with her typical drill sergeant bearing, without a glance in his direction, but he knew beyond a doubt that her faith in him was unassailable.

Miss Beasley was the prosecution's last witness. Then it was Collins' turn.

He spent thirty seconds boosting himself from his chair, sixty gazing out over the gallery and fifteen removing his glasses. He chuckled, nodded at his toes and called, "Defense calls Mrs. Lydia Marsh."

Lydia Marsh, looking pretty as a madonna with her coal black hair and pale blue dress spoke her oath and stated that she was a housewife and mother of two whose husband was fighting "somewhere in Italy." A careful observer might have seen the almost imperceptible approval in the softening of the jurors' mouths and the relaxing of their hands over their stomachs. Certainly Robert Collins saw and set out to capitalize on the sense of patriotism running rife through every American in that jurors' box.

"How long have you known Will Parker, Mrs. Marsh?"

The questions were routine until Collins asked Lydia to relate a story about what happened the day Will Parker left for Parris Island to be inducted into the United States Marines.

"He came by the house," Lydia recalled, "and called from down by the gate. He acted slightly nervous and maybe a little embarrassed—"

"Objection, your honor. Witness is drawing a conclusion."

"Sustained."

When Lydia Marsh continued it was with the avid determination to paint things accurately. "Mr. Parker refused to meet my eyes at first, and he wiped his hands nervously on his thighs. When I went down to wish him goodbye, he gave me a green towel and a fruit jar full of honey. He told me he'd stolen them from me nearly a year and a half before, when he was down and out and had no money. At the time he stole the fruit jar it had been filled with buttermilk—he'd taken it from our well. And the green towel he'd taken from the clothesline along with a set of my husband's clothes, which had, of course, been worn out long before that day. He apologized and said it had bothered him all that time, stealing from us, and before he went off to war, he wanted to make it right. So he was bringing me the honey, which was all he had to repay us with."

"Because he thought he might not get the chance again? He feared he might die in the war?"

"He didn't say that—no. He wasn't that kind. He was the kind who knew he had to fight and went to do it without complaint, just like my own husband did."

"And more recently, Mrs. Marsh, since William Parker's return from the Pacific, have you been aware of any marital discord between him and his wife?"

"Quite the opposite. They're extremely happy. I believe I would have known if he'd had any reason to seek the company of a woman like Lula Peak."

"And what makes you believe he didn't?"

Lydia's eyes swerved to Elly's and took on a glow. "Because Elly—Mrs. Parker, that is—recently confided in me that she's expecting their first baby."

The shock hit Will as if he'd been poleaxed. He twisted around in his chair and his eyes collided with Elly's. He half-rose, but his attorney pressed him down gently. A rush of joy warmed his face as his glance swept down to his wife's stomach, then lifted once more to her blushing cheeks. *Is it true, Elly?* The words went unsaid but everyone in the courtroom sensed them with their hearts instead of their ears. And every person present saw Elly's answering smile and the merest nod of her head. They watched Will's dazzling, jubilant hosanna of a smile. And twelve out of twelve in the jury who were mothers and fathers felt their heart-strings tugged.

A murmur spread through the gallery and was silenced only when Collins excused the witness and announced the reading by the bailiff of Will Parker's military record into evidence. The bailiff, a small, effeminate man with a high voice, read from a file with eyebrows raised in approval. The records of the United States Marine Corps characterized William L. Parker as a tough recruit who knew how to follow orders and command men, thus earning him the honor of being named squad leader in basic training and in combat, and promotion to the rank of corporal before his medical discharge in May of 1943. Also on record was a citation from Colonel Merrit A. Edson, Commander of the First Marine Raiders, commending Will's bravery in battle and delineating the courageous acts that had won him the Purple Heart in what by now the war correspondents had dubbed "the bloodiest battle of the Coral Sea, the Battle of Bloody Ridge."

The courtroom was respectfully silent when the bailiff closed his file. Collins had the jury in his hand and he knew it. He'd gotten them with respectability, honesty and military valor. Now he'd get them with a bit of levity.

"Defense calls Nat MacReady to the stand."

Nat left his place beside Norris and hustled forward. Though his shoulders were stooped, he walked with amazing agility for one of his age. Nat looked spiffy, dressed in the woolen blouse of his World War I army uniform with its tarnished gold stars and lieutenant's stripes. It was obvious at a glance that Nat was proud to be called upon to help justice prevail. When asked if he would tell the truth, the whole truth and nothing but, he replied, "You bet your boots, sonny."

Judge Murdoch scowled but allowed the chuckles from the gallery as Nat, eager-eyed, seated himself on the edge of his chair.

"State your name."

"Nathaniel MacReady."

"And your occupation."

"I'm a retired businessman. Ran the icehouse out south of town since I was twenty-six, along with my brother, Norris."

"What town is that?"

"Why, Whitney, of course."

"You've lived there all your life, have you?"

"I most certainly have. All except for them fourteen months back in '17 and '18 when Uncle Sam give me a free trip to Europe."

Titters of appreciation sounded. Collins stood back and let the uniform speak for itself; not a soul in the place could mistake Nat's pride in wearing it again.

"So you've been retired now for how many years?"

"Fifteen years."

"Fifteen years . . ." Collins scratched his head and studied the floor. "You must get a little bored after fifteen years of doing nothing."

"Doing nothing! Why, sonny, I'll have you know my brother and I organized the Civilian Guard, and we're out there every night enforcing the curfew and watching for Japanese planes, aren't we, Norris?"

"We sure are," Norris answered from the gallery to another ripple of laughter that had to be silenced by Murdoch's gavel.

"Defense counsel will instruct his witness to direct his responses to the court and not the gallery," Murdoch ordered.

"Yes, your honor," replied Collins meekly before scratching his head again and waiting for the room to still. "Now before we get into your duties as a volunteer guard, I wonder if you'd take a look at something for me." From his baggy pocket Collins withdrew a small wooden carving and handed it to Nat. "Did you make this?"

Nat took it, replying, "Looks like mine." Turning it bottom-side up, he examined it myopically and added, "Yup, it is. Got my initials on the bottom."

"Tell the court what it is."

"It's a wood carving of a wild turkey. Where'd you get it?"

"At the drugstore in Whitney. Paid twenty-nine cents for it off their souvenir counter."

"Did you tell Haverty to mark it in his books so I get credit?"

The judged rapped his gavel.

"I certainly did, Mr. MacReady," Collins answered to the accompaniment of soft laughter from the spectators, then rushed on before drawing further wrath from the sober-faced Murdoch. "And where did you make it?"

"In the square."

"What square?"

"Why, the Town Square in Whitney. That's where me and my brother spend most days, on the bench under the magnolia tree."

"Whittling?"

"Naturally, whittling. Show me an old man with idle hands and I'll show you the subject of next year's obituary."

"And while you whittle, you see a lot of what goes on around the square, is that right?"

Nat scratched his temple. "Well, I guess you could say we don't miss much, do we, Norris?" He chuckled, raising a matching sound from those in the room who knew precisely how little the pair missed.

This time Norris smiled and restrained himself from replying.

Collins took out a pocket knife and began cleaning his nails as if the following question were of little consequence. "Have you ever seen Lula Peak coming and going around the square?"

"Pret' near every day. She was a waitress at Vickery's, you know, and our bench sets right there where we got a clear shot of it and the library and pretty much everything that moves around that square."

"So over the years you saw a lot of Lula Peak's comings and goings?"

"You bet."

"Did you ever see her coming and going with any men?"

Nat burst out laughing and slapped his knee. "Hoo! Hoo! That's a good one, isn't it, Norris!" The whole courtroom burst into laughter.

The judge interjected, "Answer the question, Mr. MacReady."

"She come and go with more men than the Pacific fleet!"

Laughter burst forth and Murdoch had to sound his gavel again.

"Tell us about some you saw her with," Collins prompted.

"How far back?"

"As far back as you can remember."

"Well . . ." Nat scratched his chin, dropped his gaze to the tip of his brown high-top shoe. "Let's see now, that goes back quite a ways. She always did like the men. Guess I can't rightly say which one I saw her with first, but somewhere along when she was just barely old enough to grow body hair there was that dusky-skinned carnie who ran the ferris wheel during Whitney Days. Might've been back in '24—"

"Twenty-five," Norris interrupted from the floor.

Slocum leaped to his feet—"Objection!" just as the judge rapped his gavel. "Lula Peak is not on trial here!" put in the Solicitor General. "William Parker is!"

Collins pointed out calmly, "Your honor, the reputation of the deceased is of utmost importance here. My intent is to establish that because of her promiscuity, Lula Peak might have gotten pregnant by any one of a dozen men she's been known to have consorted with."

"By implying her fetus was sired in 1925?" retorted Slocum irately. "Your honor, this line of questioning is ludicrous!"

"I'm attempting to show a sexual pattern in the deceased's life, your honor, if you'll allow me."

The objection was overruled, but with a warning to Collins to control his witness's penchant for speaking to the gallery and soliciting answers from them.

"Did you ever see Lula Peak coming and going with Will Parker?"

"I seen her try. Whoo—ee, that little gal sure did try, starting with the first day he come into town and went in there where she was workin'."

"In there, meaning in Vickery's Cafe."

"Yessir. And every day after that when she saw him come to town and cross the square, she'd make sure she was out front sweeping, and when he didn't pay her any mind, she'd follow him wherever he went."

"Such as . . ." encouraged Collins.

"Well, such as the library when he came in to borrow books or to sell milk and eggs to Miss Beasley. It wouldn't take Lula two minutes before she took off her apron and hotfooted it after young Parker. I'm an old man, Mr. Collins, but I'm not too old to recognize a woman in heat, nor one that's been refused by a man—"

"Objection!"

"—and when Lula came spittin' out of that library—"

"Objection!"

"—she didn't have no matted fur that I could see—"

"Objection!"

It took a full minute for the din to die down. Though the judge ordered Nat's opinions stricken from the record, Collins knew they could not be stricken from the minds of the jury. Lula Peak was a slut and before he was done they'd all recognize the fact and indict her instead of Will Parker.

"Mr. MacReady," Collins explained quietly, "you understand we have to deal with facts here, only facts, not opinions."

"Sure—sure enough."

"Facts, Mr. MacReady. Now, do you know for a fact that Lula Peak had licentious affairs with more than one man around Whitney?"

"Yes, sir. At least if Orlan Nettles can be believed. He told me once he nabbed her underneath the grandstand at the ballpark during the seventh-inning stretch of the game between the Whitney Hornets and the Grove City Tigers."

"Nabbed her. Could you be more specific?"

"Well, I could except there's ladies present."

"Was *nabbed* the word Orlan himself used?"

"No, sir."

"What word did he use?"

Nat blushed and turned to the judge. "Do I have to say it, your honor?"

"You're under oath, Mr. MacReady."

"All right, then—screwed, your honor. Orlan said he screwed Lula Peak underneath the grandstand at Skeets Hollow Park during the seventh-inning stretch of a game between the Whitney Hornets and the Grove City Tigers."

In the rear gallery a gasp was heard from Alma Nettles, Orlan's wife. Collins noted the eyes of the jurors swerve her way and waited until he'd regained their full attention.

"How long ago did he claim to do this?"

"It was the night the Hornets won seven to six in the top of the ninth when Willie Pounds caught a grounder stretched out on his belly and threw a scorcher into home for the last out. Norris and me never miss a game, and we keep the scorecards, don't we, Norris?" Norris nodded as Nat handed Collins a scrap of white paper. "Here it is, last summer, July eleventh, though I don't know why it was necessary to bring this. Half the men in Whitney know the date 'cause Orlan he told a whole bunch of us about it, didn't he, Norris?"

"Strike that last question." Judge Murdoch ordered as the weeping Alma was escorted from the room in the arms of a solicitous matron.

Above the murmurs from the gallery, Collins inquired of Nat, "Did you ever *see* Lula Peak with a man, under . . . shall we say, a compromising position?"

"Yessir, there was an engineer on the L and N Railroad who used to lay over at Miss Bernadette Werm's boardinghouse. I'm not sure of his name, but he had a bushy red beard and a tattoo of a serpent on his arm—Miss Werm would remember his name. Anyway, I caught 'em one day, in the act you might say, down by Oak Creek where I was fishin'. Naked as jaybirds they were, and when I come upon 'em, Lula she throws back her head and laughs and says to me, 'Don't look so shocked, Mr. MacReady. Why don't y'all come and join us?' "

From the gallery came a chorus of shocked female *ohhs*.

"Just for clarification, Mr. MacReady, when you say they were in the act, you mean in the act of copulation?"

"Yes, sir, I do."

Collins took an inordinate amount of time extracting a wrinkled handkerchief from his pocket, blowing his nose, letting the last bit of testimony sink into every brain that mattered and many that didn't. Finally he pocketed his hanky and approached the witness again.

"Now, let's go back again, if we may, to your very important job as a member of the Civilian Patrol. When you've been on patrol at night during recent months and weeks, is it true that you've repeatedly seen one particular car parked behind Lula Peak's house?"

"Yessir."

"Do you know whose car it is?"

"Yessir, it's Harley Overmire's. Black Ford licence number PV628. He parks it behind the juniper bushes in the alley. I've seen it there a lot, couple nights a week anyway, during the past year. Also seen Harley goin' to Lula Peak's house sometimes in the middle of the day when she ain't workin'. Parks his car on the square, goes in the restaurant as if he's havin' lunch and hits out the back door and takes the alley to her house, which is just around the corner."

"And you've seen Lula Peak with someone else lately."

"Yessir, I have, and truth to tell, I hate to say it in public. Nobody wants to hurt a boy that age, but he's probably too young to realize—"

"Just tell us what you've seen, Mr. MacReady," Collins interrupted.

"Harley's young son, Ned."

"That's Harley Overmire's son, Ned Overmire?"

"Yes, sir."

"Tell us how old you'd guess Ned Overmire is."

"Oh, I'd say fourteen or so. Not over fifteen, that's for sure. He's in the ninth grade anyway, I know that cause my niece, Delwyn Jean Potts is his teacher this year."

"And have you seen Lula Peak with Ned Overmire?"

"Yessir. Right in front of Vickery's. She was sweepin' again—she always sweeps when she wants to ... well ... you know ... latch herself a man, you might say. Anyhow, young Ned comes along the sidewalk one day a couple weeks ago and she stops him like I've seen her stop dozens of others, stickin' that long fingernail of hers into his shirtfront and tickling his chest. She said it was hot, he should come on inside and she'd give him some free ice cream. I could hear it plain as day—heck, I think she wanted me to hear it. She always sort of taunted me, too, after that time I found her with that railroad man. Ice cream— humph!"

"And did the boy follow her inside?"

"He did. Thank heavens he came out again in just a couple minutes with a strawberry ice cream cone and Lula follows him to the door and calls after him, 'Come back now, hear?' "

"And did he?"

"Not that I saw, no."

"Well, thank the lord for that," muttered Collins, drawing a rap from the gavel but the approval of the jury for his reaction.

"But you're sure about Lula having sexual encounters with these others you've named."

"Yessir."

"And to the best of your knowledge, did Lula Peak ever succeed in drawing the attention of Will Parker?"

"No, sir, she never did, not that I knew about, no."

"Your witness."

Slocum's attempt to discredit Nat MacReady as senile, hard of hearing or short of sight proved futile. MacReady had an intimidating memory, and embellished his recollections with anecdotes that were so obviously real that his cross-examination proved more advantageous for the defense than for the prosecution.

When Nat stepped down from the witness stand, Collins stood to announce, "Defense calls Norris MacReady."

Norris stepped up, wearing, like his brother, his scratchy World War I uniform with the collar fitting loosely around his wrinkled throat. His high forehead shone from a recent scrubbing, setting off the liver spots like brown polka dots. Slocum squeezed his lips and cursed beneath his hand, then ran a hand through his hair, wrecking his rooster comb.

"State your name."

"Norris MacReady."

"Occupation?"

"I retired from the icehouse the same year as Nat."

There followed a series of questions regarding the establishment of the Whitney Civilian Town Guard and its function before Collins got down to the meatier inquiries.

"On the night of August 17, 1943, while making a curfew check, did you overhear a conversation at the back door of the Carnegie Municipal Library of Whitney?"

"I did."

"Would you tell us about it, please."

Norris's eyes widened and he glanced from the attorney to the judge. "Do you think I ought to repeat it just like Lula said it?"

The judge answered, "Exactly as you heard it, yes."

"Well, all right, judge . . . but the ladies in the courtroom ain't gonna like it."

"You're under oath, Mr. MacReady."

"Very well . . ." As a gentleman of the old order, Norris hesitated. Then he asked another question, "You think it'd be okay if I read it instead?"

Slocum leaped to his feet, spouting objections.

"Allow me, your honor, to establish the allowability of the reading material," Collins interjected quickly.

"Objection overruled, but establish it with a single question, is that understood, Mr. Collins?"

"It is." Collins turned to Norris. "From what would you like to read?"

"Why, from our log. Nat and me, we keep a log faithfully, don't we, Nat?"

"We sure do," answered Nat from the gallery.

Nobody raised an objection this time. The place was as still as outer space.

"You keep a log while you're on patrol?" Collins prompted.

"Oh, we got to. The government says. Got to record every plane sighting and every person who breaks curfew. This war is different than the Great War. In that one we never had to worry about spies in our own backyard like we have to this time, that's why we got to keep such close records."

"You may read your entry for August seventeenth, Mr. MacReady."

From an inside pocket of his uniform Norris withdrew a green-covered book with worn edges. He settled a pair of wire-rimmed spectacles over his nose, taking long moments to hook the springy bows behind his ears. Then he tipped back his head, licked a finger and turned pages so slowly that titters began in the room before he finally found the correct spot.

" 'August 17, 1943,' " he began in a crackly voice, then cleared his throat. " 'Nat and me went on patrol at nine. All quiet except for Carl and Julie Draith returning from bridge game at the Nelsons' house next door. Ten o'clock—coming up along Comfort Street heard someone entering back door of library. I stayed at the edge of the building while Norris reconnoitered behind the hedge to see who it was. Norris signaled me over and we waited. Less than 5 minutes later the door flew open and a high-heeled shoe came flying out and hit Nat on the shoulder causing a purple lump to form later. Big fight going on between Will Parker and Lula Peak. Parker pushes her out the back door of library and yells, "If you're in heat Lula go yowl beneath somebody else's window." He slams the door in her face and she bangs it with her fist a few times and calls him a goddamn peckerhead and an asshole and a toad-sucking Marine. Then she screams (loud enough to wake the dead) "Your dick probably wouldn't fill my left ear anyway." Such language for a woman.' "

Norris blushed. Nat blushed. Will blushed. Elly blushed. Collins politely took the MacReady's logbook and entered it as exhibit C before turning his witness over for cross-examination.

This time Slocum used his head and excused Norris without further questions. Throughout the courtroom a restlessness had begun. Murmurs sounded continuously from the gallery and spectators edged forward on their seats as Collins called his next witness.

"Defense calls Dr. Justin Kendall."

Kendall strode down the center aisle, an imposing man of well over six feet, wearing a sharply tailored suit of brown serge, his receding hairline framing a polished forehead that looked as if he'd just scrubbed it with a surgical brush, and his frameless glasses giving him the appearance of a scholar. His fingers were long and clean as they pointed toward heaven while he repeated the oath. Collins was already firing questions as Kendall tugged at his trouser creases and took the witness chair.

"State your name and occupation, please."

"Justin Ferris Kendall, medical doctor."

"You practice medicine here in Calhoun, is that correct?"

"It is."

"And did you recently examine the deceased, Lula Peak?"

"Yessir, on October twentieth last year."

"And did you at the time confirm that she was approximately two months pregnant?"

"I did."

"Two months after Will Parker was heard telling her that if she was in heat she should go yowl beneath somebody else's window, you diagnosed her as two months pregnant?"

"Yessir."

"And do you employ a registered nurse named Miriam Gaultier who also acts as your receptionist?"

"I do."

"Thank you. Your witness."

Slocum obviously couldn't divine a reason for this line of questioning and glanced around, confused by the abrupt turnover of the defense's witness.

He half-rose from his chair and replied, "No questions, your honor."

"Defense calls Miriam Gaultier to the stand."

Heads turned as a thin gray wisp of a woman passed through the spindled gate, smiling hello to Dr. Kendall, who held it open for her.

"State your name and occupation, please."

"Miriam Gaultier. I'm a nurse and receptionist for Dr. Justin Kendall."

"You've just heard Dr. Kendall testify that he was visited by the deceased, Lula Peak, on October twentieth last year. Were you working at the doctor's office that day?"

"Yes, I was."

"And did you talk with Lula Peak?"

"Yes, I did."

"And what was the gist of that conversation?"

"I asked Miss Peak for her mailing address for billing purposes."

"Did she give it to you?"

"No, sir, she didn't."

"Why not?"

"Because she advised me to send the bill to Harley Overmire, of Whitney, Georgia."

Nobody heard Collins turn the witness over to Solicitor General Slocum, but they could hear the sweat ooze from Harley Overmire's pores as the prosecution cross-examined Miriam Gaultier in the silent room.

"Was Miss Peak's bill ever paid, Mrs. Gaultier?"

"Yes, it was."

"Can you, beyond a shadow of a doubt, state that it was not paid by Miss Peak herself?"

"Well ..."

"Beyond a shadow of a doubt, Mrs. Gaultier," Slocum reiterated, skewering her with his dark eyes.

"It was paid in cash."

"In person?"

"No, it was mailed in."

"Thank you, you may step down."

"But it was sent in an envelope from—"

"You may step down, Mrs. Gaultier!"

"—the electric company, as if whoever sent it—"

Clakk! Clakk! Murdoch rapped his gavel. "That will be all, Mrs. Gaultier!"

Things were going even better than Collins had hoped for. He hurriedly called his next witness while the tide was rolling in the right direction.

"Defense recalls Leslie McCooms."

The medical examiner was reminded that she was still under oath and Collins made his point without histrionics.

"When you examined the body of Lula Peak you found that her death had not been caused by the dustrag as first believed, but by human hands, probably a man's. Is this true?"

"Yes."

"Tell me, Miss McCooms, how many fingerprints were found on Lula Peak's neck?"

"Nine."

"And which fingerprint was missing?"

"The one from the index finger of the right hand."

"Thank you—your witness."

Will felt hope swell his chest, climb his arms and infuse his head. With one hand balled around the other, he pressed his thumb knuckles to his lips and warned himself, it's not through yet. But he couldn't resist turning to glimpse Elly over his shoulder. Her face was pink with excitement. She made a fist and thumped it against her heart, causing his own to bang with intensified hope.

Slocum took his turn, overtly agitated.

"Is it true, Miss McCooms, that it's possible for a victim to be strangled by someone with ten good fingers, leaving less than ten fingerprints?"

"Yes, it is."

"Thank you. You're excused."

Will's brief hope extinguished but he had little time to grow despondent. The surprising Collins kept a brisk pace, recognizing the value of concentrated shock.

"Defense calls Harley Overmire."

Overmire, looking like a scared, hairy ape, puffed up the center aisle, stuffed into a light blue suit with sleeves six inches too long for his stubby arms, sleeves that nearly concealed his hands.

The bailiff held out his Bible and ordered, "Raise your right hand, please."

Harley's face was pale as a full moon. Beads of sweat stood out on his upper lip and two discs of dampness darkened the armpits of his suit.

"Raise your right hand, please," the bailiff repeated.

Harley had no choice but to do as ordered. Haltingly he lifted his arm, and as he did so his sleeve slipped down. Every eye in the room fixed upon that meaty hand, silhouetted against the white plastered wall of the courtroom, with its index finger missing.

"Do you swear to tell the truth, the whole truth and nothing but the truth, so help you God?"

Harley's voice sounded like the squeak of a mouse when the trap trips.

"I do."

The bailiff droned his questions while Collins scanned the eyes of the jurors, finding every one fixed upon Overmire's trembling, four-fingered hand.

"State your name and occupation, please."

"Harley Overmire, superintendent at the Whitney Sawmill."

"You may be seated."

Collins pretended to read over his notes for a full thirty seconds while Harley quickly sat and hid his right hand at his side. The air felt electric, charged with opinion. Collins let the voltage build while glancing pointedly over the tops of his half-glasses at Harley's hidden hand, the infamous hand that had already gained him a countywide reputation as a military shirker. Collins removed his glasses, stretched to his feet as if his rheumatism was acting up and approached the witness stand. Putting a finger to his chin, he paused thoughtfully, then turned back toward his table as if he'd forgotten something. Halfway there, he did an about-face and stood silently studying Overmire. The courtroom was so silent a spider could have been heard spinning its web. Collins scanned every face in the jury before resting his gaze on its chairman. In a voice rich with innuendo, he said, "No questions."

It was four-twenty P.M. Stomachs were rumbling but not a person thought about supper. Neither did Judge Murdoch check his watch. Instead, he called for closing summations.

They were, to Collins' delight, anticlimactic. Exactly as he would have it. A hungry jury, a judge and gallery in thrall, and a witness sweating on the sidelines.

The jury filed out leaving behind something unheard of: motionlessness.

As if everyone in the room knew the wait would be brief, they all stayed. Including Judge Murdoch. Reverently silent, too warm, hungry, but unwilling to miss the sound of the first returning footstep.

It came in exactly seven minutes.

Twelve pairs of shoes clattered across the raised wooden platform where twelve chairs waited. When the shuffle of bodies stilled, a question vaulted from the high ceiling.

"Ladies and gentlemen of the jury, have you reached your verdict?"

"We have, your honor."

"Would you give it to the bailiff, please?"

The bailiff accepted it, handed it to Murdoch, who opened the small white paper, silently read it, then handed it back to the jury chairman.

"You may read your verdict to the court."

Elly's hands clutched those of Lydia and Miss Beasley. Will stopped breathing.

"We, the jury, find the defendant, William Lee Parker, not guilty."

Pandemonium broke loose. Will spun. Elly clapped her hands over her mouth and started crying. Miss Beasley and Lydia tried to hug her. Collins tried to congratulate him. But they had a single thought: to reach each other. Through the crowd they lunged while hands patted their shoulders but went unheeded. Voices offered congratulations but went unheard. Smiles followed but they saw only each other . . . Will . . . and Elly. In the middle of the throng they collided and clung. They kissed, hard and hasty. They buried their faces in the coves of one another, harboring, holding.

"Elly . . . oh, God . . ."

"Will . . . my darling Will . . ."

He heard her sob.

She heard him swallow.

With eyes sealed tightly, they rocked, smelled each other, felt each other, shutting out all else.

"I love you," he managed with his mouth pressed against her ear. "I never stopped."

"I know that." She kissed his jaw.

"And I'm so damn sorry."

"I know that, too." She laughed but the sound was broken by a sob.

People bumped against them. A reporter called Will's name. Witnesses waited to congratulate them.

"Don't go away," Will's voice boomed at Elly's ear before he tucked her securely beneath his arm. She wrapped her arms around him and pressed close while he performed the rituals expected of him.

He shook Collins' hand and got a firm clap on the back.

"Well, young fellow, it's been a pleasure all the way."

Will laughed. "Maybe for you."

"There was never a doubt in my mind that you'd win."

"We'd win, you mean."

Collins put his free hand on Elly's shoulder, including her. "Yes, I guess you're right. We." He chuckled and added, "Anytime you want a job, young woman, I know a good half dozen lawyers who'd pay you handsome money to ply your wiles on behalf of their clients. You've got a nose and a knack."

Elly laughed and lifted her cheek from Will's lapel long enough to look up into his happy brown eyes.

"Sorry, Mr. Collins, but I got a job, and I wouldn't trade it for the world."

Will kissed her nose and the three of them shared a hearty pileup of hands that passed for a shake until it was interrupted by Lydia Marsh, who caught Elly around the neck. "Oh, Elly, I'm so happy for you." They pressed cheeks. "You, too, Will." On tiptoe she reached up to offer him an impetuous hug.

His heart felt full to bursting. "I don't know how to thank you, Mrs. Marsh."

She shook her head, battling tears, unable to express her fondness in any way but to touch his cheek, then kiss Elly and promise, "I'll see you both soon," before she slipped away.

A second reporter called, "Mr. Parker, may I have a minute?" But there were Nat and Norris MacReady, smiling like liver-spotted bookends, standing proud in their military uniforms which smelled of mothballs.

"Nat . . . Norris . . ." Will gave them each a hand-pump and a bluff squeeze on the neck. "Was I glad to have you two on my side! What can I say? Without you it might've gone the other way."

"Anything for a veteran," Nat replied.

"Say you'll keep a supply of that honey comin'," Norris put in.

While they laughed Mrs. Gaultier and Dr. Kendall brushed past, touching Will's shoulders, smiling.

"Congratulations, Mr. Parker."

The reporter snapped a picture while Will shook their hands and thanked them.

Feeling as if he was caught in a millrace, Will was forced to give himself over to strangers and friends alike while the reporters continued firing questions.

"Mr. Parker, is it true that you were once fired from the mill by Harley Overmire?"

"Yes."

"Because of your prison record?"

"Yes."

"Is it true he cut his finger off to avoid the draft?"

"I really couldn't speculate on that. Listen, it's been a long day and—"

He tried to ease toward the door but the well-meaning crowd swarmed like gnats around a damp brow.

"Mr. Parker . . ."

"Congratulations, Will . . ."

"Eleanor, you too . . ."

"Congratulations, young man, you don't know me but I'm—"

"Hey, Mr. Parker, can I have your autograph?" (This from a youth in a baseball cap.)

"Nice goin', Will . . ."

"Elly, we're so happy for you both."

"Congratulations, Parker, you and the missus come by the cafe and have a free meal on me . . ."

Will had no wish to be the center act of a three-ring circus, but these were his fellow townspeople, welcoming him and Elly into their fold at last. He accepted their handshakes, returned their smiles and acted duly appreciative. Until he simply had to escape and be alone with Elly. In response to someone's humorous banter he squeezed Elly tighter, tipped her till one of her feet left the ground and pressed a kiss to her temple, whispering, "Let's get out of here." She hugged his waist as they turned toward the door.

And there stood Miss Beasley, patiently waiting her turn.

The reporter hounded Will and Elly as they moved toward the librarian. "Mr. Parker, Mrs. Parker, could either of you make a comment on the arrest of Harley Overmire?"

They ignored the question.

Miss Beasley was dressed in drab bile green and held her purse handle over the wrists crossed militantly beneath her superfluous breasts. Will propelled Elly forward until the two of them stood within two feet of Miss Beasley. Only then did he release his wife.

A male voice intruded. "Mr. Parker, I'm from the *Atlanta Constitution.* Could you—"

Elly ran interference for him. "He's busy right now. Why don't you wait outside?"

Yes, Will was busy. Fighting a losing battle against deep, swamping emotions as he stepped close to Gladys Beasley and folded her in his arms, hooked his chin on her tight blue curls and held her firmly, choking in the scent of carnations but loving every second of it.

Unbelievably, she returned the caress, planting her palms on his back.

"You gave me one hell of a scare, you know that?" Will's voice was gruff with emotion.

"You needed it, you stubborn thing."

"I know. But I thought I'd lost you and Elly too."

"Oh, bosh, Mr. Parker. You'll have to do more than act like a complete fool to lose either one of us."

He chuckled, the sound reluctantly escaping his taut throat. They rocked for several seconds.

"Thank you," he whispered and kissed her ear.

She patted his hard back, her purse rapping his hip, then blinked forcefully, pulled away and donned her didactic façade again. "I'll expect you back at work next Monday, as usual."

With his hands resting on her shoulders, Will's attractive brown eyes fell to her face. A crooked smile lifted a corner of his mouth. "Yes, ma'am," he drawled.

Collins interrupted.

"You gonna hold that woman all day or let somebody else have a crack at her?"

Surprised, Will stepped back. "She's all yours."

"Well, good, because I thought I might take her over to my house and feed her a little brandy—see what develops. What do you say, Gladys?" Miss Beasley was already blushing as Collins commandeered her. "You know, when we were in high school I always wanted to ask you on a date, but you were so smart you scared the hell out of me. Do you remember when—"

His voice faded as he marshaled her toward the door. Elly slipped her arm through Will's and together they watched the pair leave.

"Looks like Miss Beasley's got herself an admirer at last."

"Two of them." Elly grinned up at him.

He covered her hand, squeezed it tightly against his arm and let his eyes linger in hers. "Three."

"Mr. Parker, I'm from the *Atlanta Constitution*—"

On tiptoe, Elly whispered in Will's ear, "Answer him, please, so we can get rid of him. I'll wait in the car."

"No, you don't!" He tightened his hold. "You're staying right here with me."

They weathered the questions together, begrudging every moment that kept them from privacy but learning that a warrant had already been issued for the arrest of Harley Overmire and he was already in custody. When asked to comment, Will only replied, "He'll need a good lawyer and I know a damned fine one I could recommend."

It was nearing dusk when Elly and Will escaped to their car at last. The sun glowed low along the rough stone building they left behind, lighting it to a pale copper. On the grounds of the courthouse the camellias were in full bloom, though the branches of the ash trees were bare, casting long thin shadows along the hood of their ramshackle automobile which sported a wrinkled front bumper and one blue fender on a black body.

When Elly headed for the passenger side, Will tugged her in the opposite direction. "You drive," he ordered.

"Me!"

"I hear you learned how."

"I don't know if Miss Beasley would agree with that."

He glanced at the bumper and the fender. "Banged 'er up a little, did you?"

"A little."

"Who put the new fender on?"

"Me'n Donald Wade."

Will regarded his wife with glowing eyes. "You're some woman, you know that, Mrs. Parker?"

A glow kindled deep within Elly. "Since I met you," she answered quietly.

They let their eyes linger for another devout moment before he ordered, "Get in. Show me what you learned."

He clambered in the passenger side and left her no choice. When the engine was revved she clutched the wheel, manhandled the stubborn shift, took a deep breath—"Okay . . . here goes"—and promptly drove onto the sidewalk, hitting the brakes in a panic, jouncing them till their heads hit the roof and rebounded toward the windshield.

"Dammit, Will, I'm scared to death of this thing!" She socked the steering wheel. "It never goes where I want it to!"

He laughed, rubbing the crown of his head. "It brought you to Calhoun to hire a lawyer, didn't it?"

She felt herself blush, wanting to appear competent and prove how worldly she'd become in his absence. "Don't tease me, Will, not when this—this piece of junk is acting up."

His voice softened and lost its teasing note. "And it brought you to Calhoun to visit your husband."

Their eyes met—sober, yearning eyes. His hand took hers from the wheel, his thumb rubbed her knuckles.

"Elly—is it true? Are you pregnant?"

She nodded, a trembling smile tilting her lips. "We're gonna have us a baby, Will. Yours and mine this time."

Words eluded him. Emotion clotted his throat. He reached for the back of her neck and her belly, placing a hand on each, drawing her across the seat to rest his lips against her forehead. She closed her eyes and put both hands over his widespread right hand, covering the life within her body.

"A baby," he breathed at last. "Imagine that."

She pulled away to see his eyes. For infinite seconds they gazed, then suddenly both laughed.

"A baby!" he cheered.

"Yes, a baby!" She took his head in both hands and ruffled his hair. "With shaggy blond hair and big brown eyes and a beautiful mouth like yours." She kissed it and his lips opened to taste her, possess her, gratify her. His hand moved on her stomach, slid lower and made her shiver.

Against her lips he said, "When this one's born you'll have a doctor."

"All right, Will," she answered meekly.

He deepened his kiss and his caress until she was forced to remind him, "Will, there are still people going by."

Drawing a tortured breath he released her and said, "Maybe I'd better drive after all. We'll get there faster." The door slammed behind him and he jogged around the hood while she slid over. As he put the car in reverse he warned, "Hang on to that young one. We don't want to shake her loose." He backed down the curb, bouncing them a second time, while Elly clutched her stomach and they both laughed.

They drove around the courthouse square and out onto Highway 53, headed southeast. Behind them the sun sank lower. Before them the road climbed out of the valley, lifting them through rolling woodland that soon would burgeon with green. Will rolled down the window and breathed deep of the fresh winter air. He locked his elbows, caught the wheel with his thumbs and thrust his wrists forward, tasting freedom, drinking it like one parched.

Free. And loved. And soon to be a father. And befriended. And accepted—even admired—by a town that sprang to his defense. And all because of one woman.

It overwhelmed Will. *She* overwhelmed him.

Abruptly he pulled off the highway, bumped along a field access and pulled up behind a clump of leafless willows. In one motion he killed the engine and turned to his wife.

"Come here, green eyes," he whispered, loosening the knot of his tie. Like heat lightning she moved into his embrace. Their lips and breasts met and their tongues, cautious no longer, made reckless sweeps. Crushed together, they healed.

He broke away to hold her head and gaze into her eyes. "I missed you so damn much."

"Not as much as I missed you."

"You cut your hair." He scraped it back with both hands, freeing her face for his adoring gaze.

"So I'd look up-to-date for you."

He scanned her countenance, hairline to chin, and wondered aloud, "What did I ever do to deserve you?"

"Don't thank me, Will, I—"

He cut her off with a kiss. As it lengthened they grew breathless, feeling the bond strengthen between them. At last he freed his mouth. "I know everything you did. I know about the honey, and the ads, and the witnesses you found, and the car you had to learn to drive and the town you had to face. But the house, Elly. My God, you faced that house, didn't you?"

"What else could I do, Will? I had to prove to you that it wasn't true what you saw on my face the day you were arrested. I never meant it, Will ... I ..." She began crying. He caught her tears with his lips, moving across her face as if taking sustenance.

"You didn't have to prove anything to me. I was scared and stubborn and I acted like a fool, just like Miss Beasley said. When you came to visit me the first time I was hurt, and I—I wanted to hurt you back. But I didn't mean what I said, Elly, honest I didn't." He kissed her eyes, murmuring softly, "I didn't mean it, Elly, I'm sorry."

"I know, Will, I know."

Again he held her face, searching her pale eyes. "And when you came the second time, I kept telling myself to apologize but Hess was there listening, so I talked about stupid things instead. Men can be such fools."

"It doesn't matter now, Will, it doesn't—"

"I love you." He held her possessively.

"I love you, too."

When they'd held each other a while he said, "Let's go home."

Home. They pictured it, felt it beckon.

He took a lock of her short brown hair between his fingers, rubbing it. "To the kids, and our own house, and our own bed. I've missed it."

She touched his throat and said, "Let's go."

They drove on home through the purple twilight, through the brown Georgia hills, past cataracts and piney woods and through a quiet town with a library and a magnolia tree and a square where an empty bench awaited two old men and the sunshine. Past a house whose picket fence and morning glories and green shades were gone, replaced by a mowed yard, scraped siding and gleaming windows reflecting a newly risen moon. As they passed it, Elly snuggled close to Will, an arm around his shoulders, her free hand on his thigh.

He turned his head to watch her eyes follow the place as the car pulled abreast of it, then past.

She felt his gaze and lifted her smile to him.

You all right? his eyes asked.

I'm all right, hers answered.

He kissed her nose and linked his fingers with those hanging over his left shoulder.

Content, they continued through the night, to a steep, rocky road that led them past a sourwood tree, into a clearing where blue flowers would soon tap against a skewed white house. Where three children slept—soon to be four. Where a bed waited . . . and forever waited . . . and the bees would soon make the honey run again.

VOWS

Author's Note

The readers familiar with the Sheridan and Buffalo areas will find that I took liberties with the history of their towns. Actually, Sheridan's Main Street would not have been as built up as I've depicted, nor would the town have had Victorian homes as fine as the ones I've sketched; they were not built until around the turn of the century. In 1888 Munkers & Mathers didn't own their hardware store yet, and, of course, the Mint Saloon hadn't been built, either. But some landmarks call to be included, so forgive me for bending the calendar to suit my story.

L. S.

Chapter 1

WYOMING TERRITORY 1888

Tom Jeffcoat shifted his rump on the hard wagon seat, blinked twice, and peered northward. From beneath the brim of a dusty brown Stetson, he squinted until the blurred outline of a town came into focus. A thrill shot through his belly—Sheridan, Wyoming, at last! And with any luck at all, a bath, a real bed, and a decent, hot supper, his first in eighteen days.

He clucked to the team and they picked up speed.

From several miles out the town appeared as no more than a mole on the jaw of the broad, fertile valley, but the setting proved as beautiful as promised in the ad. Basking in lush bluegrass, it nestled where the eastern face of the Big Horns met the wide Goose Creek Valley in which Big and Little Goose creeks merged. The paths of the streams were clearly marked by a meandering line of diamond willows and cottonwoods, the latter in seed now in early June, dropping their cotton tufts like a white flotilla onto the waters.

But the mountains themselves provided the grandeur; snow-capped, blue girded, they rose like knuckles on a tight fist, holding back the harsher Rockies to the west. Those mountains had become protective old friends, ever off Jeffcoat's left shoulder on his long journey up from Rock Springs. Already he loved them: the Big Horns, majestic giants clothed—up high—in the blue-black of Rocky Mountain cedars, fading at the foothills into every conceivable shade of green. Those foothills billowed like a giant ruffled skirt and in their velvet folds nestled his new home: Sheridan.

"West of worry," the ad had boasted, "with no heat, no dust, no wind, and where the nights are always cool."

Well, we'll see.

As he neared the town, individual buildings took shape, then a street—no, streets, by God!—a grid of them, laid out straight and wide and already named on wooden signs—Perkins, Whitney, Burkitt, Works, Loucks, and the widest artery, Main, by which he entered. Deeper in the heart of town the creeks themselves snaked together, breaking the streets into short, oblique avenues. Off on the side streets he saw houses, mostly of frame or peeled-log construction, with high pitched roofs to shed snow. Many of the plots were surrounded by lines of demarcation: picket fences, hitching posts, outbuildings at rear property lines, newly planted vegetable gardens, and hedgerows of flowers. Entering the business district, he slowed his horses to an easy walk, perusing his surroundings. There must have been fifty buildings, and boardwalks old enough to have become weathered but not warped, and a goodly number of established businesses: a hotel, butcher shop, barber shop, drug store, law office, several stores, a newspaper office; and the inevitable saloons that catered to the cowboys driving cattle up the Bozeman

Trail, up which he himself had just come. There were the Star, the Mint, and one called the Silver Spur, beside which a corral held a half dozen wild elk. Several cowboys were using them for roping practice, and the sound of the men's laughter and the animals' bawling brought a smile to Jeffcoat's lips.

Farther along he passed other signs of progress; a building with its double doors thrown wide, revealing a side-stroke fire pump with its brass fittings gleaming; a house bearing a doctor's shingle—L. D. STEELE, PHYSICIAN; a school—settlers were bound to come faster with a school; and a harness and shoe shop, of which Jeffcoat took particular notice.

Eventually he came to a creek—bridgeless—swelled with spring runoff, where a lanky man in baggy pants and knee-high boots filled his water wagon with a bucket on the end of a long pole. Painted on the side of the tin drum was the advertisement: *Fresh Water Delivered Daily, 25¢ a barrel, 5 barrels for $1.00, Andrew Dehart's Sparkling Water Service.*

"H'lo, there!" Jeffcoat called, reining in.

The man paused and turned. "Hello!" He had a bushy beard and a great hook nose, which he blew—without benefit of a handkerchief—into the grass, leaning first left, then right.

"Which creek is this then, Big Goose or Little Goose?"

"Big Goose. Around here we just call it Goose. You new in town?"

"Yessir. Been here five minutes."

"Well, howdy! Andrew Dehart's the name." He nodded at the announcement on the side of his water wagon.

"Tom Jeffcoat's mine."

"You need water, I'm the man to see. You stayin'?"

"Yessir. That's the plan."

"Got lodging?"

"Not yet."

"Well you passed the only hotel, the Windsor, back that-a-way. And Ed Walcott runs the livery. Turn left on Grinnell." He pointed.

"Thank you, Mr. Dehart."

Dehart waved him off and turned back to his work, calling, "New blood's always welcome around here!"

The creek seemed to mark the end of the major business section. Beyond it lay mostly houses, so Jeffcoat reversed direction and headed back the way he'd come.

He found Grinnell without any problem and a huge unpainted barn of a building with a tent-shaped roof, gaping double doors, and a prominent white-and-black sign up high above the hay port: WALCOTT'S LIVERY, HORSES BOARDED & BEDDED, RIGS FOR RENT. He turned up Grinnell to have a look.

In a corral on the near side of the building a half dozen healthy-looking horses stood dozing in the two o'clock sun, their nose hairs touching the wall. On the far side was a deserted horseshoe pit overhung by a line of lopsided cottonwoods, which spilled a patch of shade onto the street over the far hitching rail. The barn itself was an immense, open-ended building constructed of vertical weatherbeaten boards and sliding double doors that stood open on both ends.

Choosing the shady hitching rail on the right over the sunny one on the left, Jeffcoat passed the open door, glimpsing inside the silhouette of a man framed clearly in the open-ended building, working over a horse's foot.

His competition.

He pulled up in the shade, wrapped the reins around the brake handle, pushed to his feet, and, with fists to ears, twisted at the waist. His hide felt stiff as whangleather. Letting out a great gust of air, he vaulted over the side. At the great south door of the livery barn he paused, peering inside. It was like a railroad tunnel, dark and cool within, bright at both ends. At the far end the fellow still worked, facing the opposite door, couching the hoof of a huge liver chestnut stallion in his lap.

As Jeffcoat approached, he took stock of both the horse and the man. The stallion was snip nosed, broad chested, and tall. The man—upon closer perusal—turned out to be no man at all, but a skinny boy, no bigger than a good strip of trap bait, dressed in worn blue britches, a faded red shirt, black suspenders, an ankle-length leather apron, and a floppy brown wool cap with a button on its crown.

At Jeffcoat's approach, the chestnut nickered, dropped his forefoot, and belly-bumped the lad, knocking his cap askew.

"Blast you, Sergeant, you ring-boned hunk o' gleet! Hold still!" The boy cuffed the horse on the shoulder and centered his cap with a jerk. "You do that one more time and I'll leave you to take care of your miserable quarter crack by yourself!" He clapped a hand around the horse's off fore cannon, forced it into his lap, and resumed wielding the hoofpick.

Jeffcoat smiled; the animal outweighed the youth by a good thousand pounds. But young as he was the kid knew what he was doing. Quarter crack was nothing to fool around with.

"You in charge around here, young fellow?"

Emily Walcott dropped Sergeant's hoof and spun around indignantly. She let her eyes scan with deliberate distaste a swarthy young man who could use a shave and some sleeves on his shirt: someone had torn them off at the shoulder. She gave his bare arms, dusty britches, and whiskered face a singeing once-over before replying sardonically, "Yes, *ma'am,* I sure am."

Jeffcoat grabbed for his hat. "Oh ... my mistake. I thought—"

"Never mind what you thought! I can do without hearing it again. And don't bother doffing your hat after *that*!"

She was thin as a whipsnake and about as shapely, seventeen or thereabouts, all blue eyes and indrawn lips and two cheeks flaring with indignation. Never having seen a woman in britches before, Jeffcoat stood nonplussed.

"I beg your pardon, ma'am."

"It's miss, and don't bother begging my pardon." She threw aside the hoofpick. "What can I do for you?"

"I've got a hungry team outside that needs putting up."

Sergeant chose that moment to stretch his neck, pluck off Miss Walcott's cap, and begin chewing it.

"Blast your hide, Sergeant, give me that!" She yanked it from his teeth, dried it on the seat of her pants, and examined it crossly while her black hair drooped in scraggles, half held to her skull by combs. "Now look what you've done, dammit. You put holes in it!"

Jeffcoat worked hard to hide a grin. "You ought to tie him off with two clip ropes instead of just one so he can't get by with that."

Emily eyed him maliciously while hooking the hat on her head, cramming her hair up inside it and cocking it toward her left ear so the short bill angled over her black, angry eyebrows. With the cap on, and covered to the collarbones by the dirty leather apron, she looked more like a boy than ever.

"Thank you, I'll remember that," she answered sarcastically, heading for the street, the apron thwapping her calves with each long step. "What do you want, stable 'em only? That'll be a buck a night, including hay. Dessert is extra. Two bits for an extra pail of oats. Curry 'em down'll be another two bits. Stable 'em outside in the corral you can save a dime." She reached the team and turned, but Jeffcoat hadn't followed. "Hey, mister," she bellowed, "I got work to do!" She hooked two dirty hands on her hips, fingers impatiently tapping the hard leather apron. "Where do you want 'em? Inside or out?" When no answer came she poked her head around the door, then bawled, "Hey, what do you think you're doing?" and steamed back inside with fists swinging at her sides like bell clappers.

"This is no quarter crack, it's a sand crack." He was examining Sergeant's forefoot, for all the world as if he owned the place. "He'll need a three-quarter shoe or maybe even a copper plate to put pressure on the frog and wall if you want to keep him from going lame permanently. Or maybe a rivet might do."

"I'll see after my own horses, thank you," she returned acidly, untying Sergeant's single snap line and leading him into a stall. *Who the Sam Hill did he think he was, coming in here giving her advice? Some dirty cowpoke without so much as sleeves on his shirt, busting into somebody else's livery barn and spouting off like a geyser when she knew everything there was to know about the care of hooves. Everything!*

But Emily Walcott burned with indignation because she knew the stranger was right—she should have used two snap lines, but she'd been in too big a hurry.

She granted the stranger not so much as a flicking glance as she marched from the stall and left him behind. "We stable horses here. We feed 'em, and curry 'em, and water 'em, and outfit 'em, and rent out rigs. But we *don't* let tinhorn hostlers work out their apprenticeships on our stock!"

To Emily's chagrin, as she stormed past him, the man burst out laughing. She swung around with murder in her glare and the corners of her mouth looking as if they were attached to her shoes. "Mister, I don't have time to waste on you. Your horses, maybe, if you speak up fast. Now what'll it be, inside or out? Hay or oats?"

"Tinhorn hostler?" he managed, still chortling.

"All right, have it your way." Obstinately, she changed directions, heading toward an open hatch to the hayloft, passing him with a venomous expression on her face. "Sorry, we're all full up," she advised dryly. "You can try down at Rock Springs. It's a few miles that way." She thumbed southwest. Rock Springs was 350 miles, and it had just taken him eighteen days to cover them. Up the ladder she went, until her ascent was stopped by a hand grabbing her beat-up, stretched-out, horsey-smelling cowboy boot.

"Hey, wait a minute!"

The boot came off in Jeffcoat's hand.

Surprised as much as she, he stood gaping at her bare foot with its dirty ankle and flecks of hay pressed onto the skin, thinking this was the most bizarre introduction he'd ever had to one of the opposite sex. Where he came from, ladies wore gingham dressed with ten-gallon petticoats, and starched white aprons instead of leather ones, and leghorn hats instead of boys' knockabouts, and dainty buttoned shoes instead of dung-crusted cowboy boots. And stockings . . . wispy lisle stockings that no gentleman ever saw. But there he stood, staring at her bare foot.

"Oh, I . . . I beg your pardon, miss, I'm so sorry."

He watched her descend and turn stiffly, presenting a face as brilliant as an Au-gust sunset.

"Has anyone ever told you that you're a rude, infernal pain in the hindside?" She grabbed the boot, overturned an enamel bucket, and dropped onto it to pull the boot back on. Before she managed to do so, he snatched it from her hand and went down on one knee to do the honors.

"Allow me, miss. And to answer your question, yes, my mother and my grandmother and my fiancée and my teachers. All my life I've seemed to irritate women, but I could never understand why. You know, I've never done this before, have you?" He held the boot at the ready.

She felt her whole body flush, from her dirty bare toes clear up to her brother's cap. She grabbed the boot and yanked it on herself.

Watching, he grinned and answered belatedly, "Oats, please, and stable them inside and curry them, too. Do I pay in advance?"

"We're full up, I said!" Leaping to her feet, she fled him in a swirl of wrath and climbed to the loft. "Take your business elsewhere!"

He peered up after her, seeing nothing but rafters and dust motes.

"I'm sorry, ma'am. Really I am."

A pitchforkful of hay landed on his head. He doubled forward, blowing and snorting. "Hey, watch it!" Overhead her footsteps clunked as she dragged her boots across the floorboards. Another forkful of hay appeared and he backed off, calling, "Can I leave the horses or not?"

"No!"

"But this is the only livery barn in town!"

"We're full up, I said!"

"You are not!"

"We are, too!"

"If it's about your bare foot, I said I was sorry. Now come down here so I can give you some money."

"I said, we're full up! Now get out!"

From the other end of the barn, Edwin Walcott listened to the exchange with growing interest. He stood surveying the stranger with hay on his hat and shoulders, watched another load come raining down through the hatch, heard his daughter's obvious lie, and decided it was time to step in.

"What's going on here?"

Silence fell, broken only by a blacksmith's hammer from down the street.

Jeffcoat spun around to find a stocky man framed in the doorway standing with hands akimbo, his meaty arms and hairy chest showing beneath the uprolled sleeves and open collar of a faded red flannel shirt. His black britches were tucked into calf-high boots, and striped suspenders emphasized his muscular girth. He had tumbled black hair flecked with gray, a full black mustache, blue eyes, and a mouth reminiscent of the girl's.

"Something I can do for you, Mister—?"

Jeffcoat brushed off his shoulders and whacked his hat on his thigh. Stepping forward, he extended a hand. "Tom Jeffcoat's the name, and yessir, there is. I'd like to leave my horses for a few days if I could."

"Edwin Walcott's mine. Is there some reason why I shouldn't let you?"

"No, sir, none that I know of."

"What's this about you and my daughter's bare foot?"

"She was climbing up the ladder and I accidentally pulled her boot off, trying to stop her."

"Emily!" Walcott cocked his head toward the haymow. "Is that true?"

Beyond her father's range of vision, Emily buried the fork tines in the hay, wishing she could bury herself in it and stay till Tom Jeffcoat disappeared from the face of the earth.

"Emily?" her father repeated, more demandingly.

"Yes!" she delivered in an ornery bellow.

"He try anything else you want to tell me about?"

She kicked a lump of hay, sending it flying, but refused to answer.

"Emily?"

Mortified, she stared at the hay, her mouth cinched tighter than a seaman's knot, working her hands about the smooth pitchfork handle as if applying liniment to a horse's leg. At last she clomped to the hay hatch. Planting her feet wide and ramming the pitchfork tines into the pine floor, she met her father's upturned gaze.

"He came in here and started spouting off about the horses and how I should've cross-tied Sergeant, and taking the liberty of examining his hoof and offering advice on how to take care of it. He made me mad, that's all."

"So you turned his business away?"

Pride held her silent.

"I didn't mean any disrespect," Jeffcoat interrupted, placatingly. "But I'll admit, I was teasing her, and I made the mistake of thinking she was a boy when I walked in. It seemed to set her off, sir."

Turning away, Walcott bit his inner lip to keep from smiling. "Come into the office. We'll do business there. How many days will you be leaving your team here?"

Instead of following immediately, Jeffcoat stepped beneath the ladder and raised his eyes to the girl who glared down from above. "A week for sure, maybe more." He knew beyond a doubt that she'd like nothing better than to fire that pitchfork at his head. But she stood with both hands gripping its handle, staring him down with silent venom.

"Good afternoon, Miss Walcott," he offered quietly, and with a doffing of his hat, followed her father.

Walcott led him through a door into a lean-to attached to the east side of the barn, a small room with a bumpy concrete floor and four small-paned windows, two facing the street and two the empty lot. At sunrise the office would be bright but now in midafternoon it was cool and shadowed. It held a scarred desk with the rolltop missing, its pigeonholes overflowing with papers above a dusty top littered with bridle rings, snaffle bits, horseshoe nails, tack hammers, horse liniment, and a white dinner plate with a few green beans and a dried breadcrust stuck in a streak of hardening gravy. The desk chair was tilted on its casters and worn bare of varnish on its back and arms. Against the north wall slumped a metal daybed, its exposed springs covered with a homemade mattress made of stuffed burlap, topped by a multicolored rag rug where a taffy-colored cat slept. To the right of the door sat a small potbellied stove. The walls were hung with an assortment of oddities: beaver traps; stage schedules; patent-medicine trade cards; an advertisement for Buffalo Bill Cody's Wild West Show; a collection of oxbow keys; last summer's schedule for the Philadelphia Professional Baseball Club; and an ancient pendulum clock, ticking slow. The office smelled of onion gravy, aromatic liniment, grain, and hemp—the latter presumably exuding from a lineup of plump burlap bags propped against the wall to the left of the door.

"It's understandable why my daughter would be a little touchy over being criticized about the horses," Walcott commented, dropping onto the chair and rolling it toward his desk. It bumped over the rough floor like an unsprung wagon over frozen ruts. "She's been around 'em all her life and she's corresponding with a man from Cleveland, name of Barnum, who's teaching her veterinary medicine."

"Veterinary medicine—a girl?"

"There are a lot of animals out here. She's putting it to good use."

"You mean she's studying by mail?" Jeffcoat inquired with wonder.

"That's right," Walcott confirmed, reaching for a receipt book and a pen. "It comes pretty regular now, five times a week most weeks, by horseback. Here you go." Walcott swiveled around and handed Jeffcoat a receipt made out for two bays with white markings and a doublebox wagon, green with red trim. A careful man, Walcott, one who'd never be accused of horse theft, keeping records as he did.

"You mind my asking what you're doing in town, Mr. Jeffcoat?"

Pocketing the receipt, Jeffcoat answered, "Not at all. A man named J. D. Loucks placed an advertisement in the Springfield newspaper about this town and what it had to offer an enterprising young man. It sounded like a place I'd like to live, so I took the train to Rock Springs, outfitted there, and drove the rest of the way by wagon; and here I am."

"And here you are . . . to do what?"

"I intend to set up a business and make my home here as soon as I buy some land to do it on."

"Well"—the older man chuckled quietly—"J. D. Loucks'll be more than happy to sell you as many lots as you want, and this town can use more young people. What's your line of work?"

Jeffcoat hesitated a beat before replying, "I do some blacksmithing. Taught by my father in Springfield."

"Would that be Missouri or Illinois?"

"Missouri."

"Missouri, eh? Well then, he shod plenty that came through this territory on their way up the Oregon Trail, didn't he?"

"Yessir, he did."

"This town's already got one smithy, you know."

"So I see. I drove the streets before stopping here."

Edwin rose and led the way to the team still waiting outside. "But I'll tell you something that's no secret to anyone in Sheridan. Old Pinnick could do better work and more of it. Spends more time at the Mint Saloon than at his forge, and if he'd've shod Sergeant right in the first place we wouldn't be doctoring him now."

"Pinnick, huh?"

"That's the name of your competition: Walter Pinnick. Too lazy to put a sign out above his smithy that says so. Instead he just lets the sound of his hammer bring in the customers . . . when it's ringing." Outside in the sun Walcott paused to cock his head and listen, and—sure enough—the ringing of earlier was absent. "Old Pinnick must've got a touch of the *dry throat,*" he ended with a sarcastic drawl, then moved on toward the team.

Jeffcoat cogitated momentarily before deciding it was best to be straightforward with this man.

"I want to be honest with you, sir. I've been around horses all my life, too, and I plan to do a little more than smithing. The truth is, I plan to open a livery stable."

Walcott paused with his hand on a bridle, and turned to look back at the younger man. The wind seemed to catch in his throat before he let it escape with a soft whistle.

"Well . . ." he said, letting his chin drop. For a moment he mulled, then chuckled and looked up. "You kind of took me by surprise there, young man."

"I think, from what I've seen and read, that there's business enough in this town for two of us. Lots of Texas cowboys either trailing herds through here, or starting their own small ranches in the vicinity, aren't there? And immigrants coming, too, now that the land has been thrown open for homesteading. A valley like this is bound to attract them. Hell, it's ninety-five miles wide, to say nothing of the sheep-ranching land in the hills up there. I think Loucks is right. This town is going to be the center of commerce, and soon."

Again Walcott chuckled wryly. "Well, let's hope so. So far it looks like the center of commerce around here is Buffalo, but we're growing." He turned toward the horses. "You plan to leave the wagon, too?"

"If I could."

"I'll pull it around back by the horseshoe pits. From the looks of this load you plan to get busy building right away."

"Soon as I buy that plot."

"You'll find Loucks's place up on Smith Street. Ask anybody, they'll point it out."

"Thank you, Mr. Walcott."

"Call me Edwin. It's a small town. We mostly go by first names."

Jeffcoat extended a hand, relieved that the man had taken the news so graciously.

"I appreciate your help, Edwin, and you can call me Tom."

"All right, Tom. I'm not sure whether to wish you good luck or not."

They laughed, parting; and Jeffcoat removed his carpetbag from his wagon, raised a hand in farewell, and advised, "The horses' names are Liza and Rex."

Watching Tom Jeffcoat move off, Edwin felt a brief stab of envy. Young—no more than twenty-five—and adventurous, far flying, with his whole life before him and choices still to be made in a territory where young people were granted the right to make those choices for themselves. It had been different when he was in his twenties. Then a man's future was often dictated—as his had been—by stern, dominating parents who planned his life with the best of intentions, but without consulting him. They'd planned it all, from how he would earn a livelihood right down to the woman he would marry, and he'd been a dutiful, obedient son. He'd become a hostler like his father, and had married one Miss Josephine Borley, to whom he was still respectfully wed. But there was another whom he'd never forgotten.

It had been twenty-two years but he thought of her still. Fannie. With her bright eyes and blustery spirit. Fannie, Josephine's cousin, as different from Josie as ash is from coals. Fannie, who instead of asking *why,* always asked *why not.* Fannie, who at age seventeen had fought for women's suffrage, ridden astride, and secretly smoked a cigar with him, then demanded, "Kiss me and tell me if I taste like smoke." Fannie, from whom he'd run soon after his marriage, because remaining near her would have proven dangerous. Fannie, who'd inherited her parents' wealth after their deaths and had used it to travel and experience things that most women would have found outlandish, even improper. Fannie, whose latest letter reported in her usual breezy fashion that she'd purchased a Monarch bicycle and had joined the Ladies' North Shore Bicycling Club, which was planning a four-day outing from Malden to Gloucester, Massachusetts, with overnight layovers at Pavilion and Essex House, briefer stops at Marblehead Neck and Nahant, and such attractions as a picnic lunch on the rocks at Pigeon Cove and visits to Rafe's Chasm and Norman's Woe.

Fannie, outrageous Fannie—what did she look like now? Was she happy? Did she love anyone? She'd filled her life with the uncommon, the progressive, the liberal, but never with a husband. Why? In twenty-two years, had there been anyone special? Her letters never included any mention of men beyond the most casual description of her social activities. But Edwin had never stopped wondering if there was one special man, and he never would.

It was because of his memories of Fannie, he knew, that he'd never resisted any of Emily's outrageous wishes. Emily was so much like the Fannie he remembered that he loved her unconditionally and had always secretly hoped she might turn out like Fannie—part rebel, part sprite, but all woman. When his daughter began tagging along to the livery stable, asking to help with the horses, Edwin had laughingly allowed it. When she narrowed a pair of his pants and began wearing them around the barn, he made no comment. When she read in the newspaper of Dr. Barnum's correspondence course on veterinary medicine and asked permission to apply, he had obligingly paid for it.

Because his own life had been indubitably dulled by parents who'd forced their will on him, he had, as a young father, vowed he'd never do the same to his children.

And now Emily was eighteen, and quite, quite like the Fannie of old—single-minded, wearing britches, taking up masculine interests, an upstart in the eyes of many.

Returning to her after the departure of Tom Jeffcoat, Edwin found Emily much mollified. She was waiting in the corridor between the box stalls with two feed boxes already filled and four snap lines in her hand as he led Jeffcoat's horses inside and stopped before her.

"Oh, Papa. I'm sorry." She walked against him and hugged his chest with the ease of one accustomed to doing so often. With reins in both hands, Edwin could only drop his cheek affectionately against her scratchy wool cap.

"No harm done. We got his business anyway."

She stepped back and looked into her father's face, finding the forgiving grin she'd expected.

"He did make me angry though, calling me *young fellow.* Do I look like a young fellow to you?"

"Mmm . . ." With a half smile on his face he assessed her cap, apron, and boots. "Now that you mention it . . ."

She tried to hold back a smile, but it won in the end. "Honestly, Papa, sometimes I don't know why I love you so." She gave him an affectionate mock punch, then sobered. "How's Mother?"

"Resting. There's no need for you to hurry back. Help me take care of the horses first." He understood that she preferred the work at the livery barn to the nursing and housework at home and tried not to burden her unfairly with domestic tasks that seemed never-ending as the ailing Josephine grew less and less able to cope with them. He sensed his daughter's unconscious relief as she eagerly took a pair of reins, looked up into the mare's brown eyes, and asked, "What's her name?"

"Liza."

"And his?"

"Rex."

"Come on, Liza, let's get you undressed and rubbed down."

They worked together amiably, securing the horses in the center of the corridor, removing their harnesses, cleaning their coats with dandy brushes, raising the fecund scent of horse sweat. While she stroked Liza's warm, damp hide, Emily inquired, "How long will these two be staying?"

"A week . . . maybe more."

"While he does what?" She refused to speak Jeffcoat's name, though she'd clearly overheard it.

"Buys himself a lot and puts up a building."

Emily's hand stopped moving. "A building?"

"He's a blacksmith. He's here to set up a business."

"A blacksmith!"

"That's right, so try to get along with him if you can. We'll probably be using his services in the future if he turns out to be even a quarter as sober as Pinnick."

She started brushing again, with more elbow grease than necessary. Edwin glanced at his daughter's face to find it darkened with a scowl as she wielded the dandy brush, then tossed it aside in favor of a curry comb. Guessing her reaction to the rest of his news, Edwin added carefully, "That's not all."

Emily's head snapped up and their gazes met.

"What else?"

"He plans to do his smithing in his own livery barn."

Her mouth dropped open. "He what!"

"You heard me right."

"Oh, Papa . . ." Her dropping note held true sympathy. With all he had to worry about, must there be more? Mama ill and everybody trying to do double shifts at home and here. And now this! She'd like to take J. D. Loucks *and* his advertisement *and* Mister Tom Jeffcoat and drop them off the edge of a butte!

"At least he was honest about it," Edwin observed.

"What else could he be when he's going to build something as big as a livery barn?"

"It's a free country, and for all we know he might be right. There might be enough business here for two."

"Where does he plan to build?" she asked belligerently.

"Your guess is as good as mine."

But they both knew. J. D. Loucks could sell him whatever lot he wanted. The town was his. He'd bought it seven years ago, staked it out on a forty-acre plot, drawn up a plat on a piece of brown wrapping paper from his store, prepared a petition for incorporation, and was granted such a year later by the Wyoming Territorial Assembly. He got himself chosen as mayor, named the town after his Civil War commander, General Philip H. Sheridan, and went to work enticing young blood to settle there.

It was a rancher's town. Loucks had made it so, recognizing the value of the valley's rich grassland and anticipating a prosperous future brought by the drovers herding cattle up the Bozeman Corridor from the depleted grasslands of Texas. The town had everything: vast tracts of sub-bituminous coal within a few miles, meandering Goose Creeks tracing irregular dark green lines across it, the second-lowest average wind velocity in the United States, and thousands of adjacent acres of Indian lands thrown open to the public domain now that the Indian Wars were over.

The tempting ads Loucks had placed in eastern newspapers bore speedy results. Naturally, the lots along Main Street had sold first; already Main was filled with businesses, from the Windsor Hotel at the south end to the creek at the north. It was the side streets such as Grinnell on which lots were still available.

"Well, he'd better stay away from here!" Emily Walcott seethed, turning Jeffcoat's horse into a stall. "I don't want to be bumping into him any more than I have to."

As it turned out, she bumped into him less than an hour later. She was heading home to check on her mother as Jeffcoat and J. D. Loucks came rolling down the street in Loucks's fine Peerless buggy, obviously on a tour of the town. She came up short in the middle of the boardwalk as Loucks, with his flowing white beard, drove past behind his matched grays. Emily glared, tight-lipped, at the man beside him. He must have gone to the hotel and mucked off. The whiskers were gone, and his frock coat had sleeves, and his string tie looked proper enough against a clean white shirtfront. But his grin made her fists ball.

Jeffcoat touched his hat brim and nodded while Emily felt the color soar to her cheeks. His eyes remained fixed on her until the carriage drew abreast and passed. Only then did she resume her angry stride, wishing she had fired the pitchfork at him when she'd had the chance.

Chapter 2

❦

The home of Emily Walcott was unlike the other homes she knew. It was always messy; meals were never ready on time; sometimes they ran out of clean laundry; and the lamp chimneys were in constant need of polishing. It hadn't always been that way. When Mother was healthy, back when they lived in Philadelphia, their house had been cheery and well maintained. Suppers were ready on time, laundry hung on the line every Monday morning and was ironed on Tuesday. Wednesday meant mending. Thursday odd jobs, Friday bread baking, and Saturday cleaning.

Then Mother had started ailing and all that had changed. At the beginning they hadn't thought much of her fatigue. In fact, they'd all laughed and teased her the first time they'd come home to find her napping when dinner should have been on the table. Her illness had advanced insidiously, and months passed while none of them attributed her weight loss to anything out of the ordinary. She'd always, since bearing her two children, been plump. As the pounds disappeared and she took on a trimmer, younger shape, Papa had looked pleased and sometimes teased her and made her blush. But then the coughing started and his teasing changed to concern.

"You must see a doctor, Josephine," he'd insisted.

"It's nothing, Edwin, really," Mother had countered. "Just old age creeping up on me."

But that had been only two years ago, when she was thirty-eight. Thirty-eight, yet she had begun withering away before their eyes. Her cough grew harsh and frequent and left her increasingly weaker while her family stood by feeling helpless.

Then Papa had read the article about the successful Philadelphia hatter, John B. Stetson. Stetson had been a young man when the doctors told him he had lung trouble and gave him but a few months to live. Deciding there was only one way to prove their prognosis wrong, young Stetson had made up his mind that he must get away from the crowded, smoke-clogged city and out into the open; he'd struck out for the Far West, which at that time meant Missouri. Yet he'd continued even farther, all the way to Pike's Peak, tramping much of the way on foot, sleeping in the open, taking the weather as it came. In spite of the hardships of the trail and of the year he spent as a placer-miner in the high Rockies, his health made a remarkable improvement. He's returned to Philadelphia with a mere hundred dollars in diggings, but with the most robust health he'd ever enjoyed. Strapping and strong, John B. Stetson had credited the West with giving him back his health.

With the hundred dollars he'd built a hatting empire. And with his eternal gratitude for the restoration of his good health, he'd schooled and cared for others, becoming a stickler for fresh air and sunshine, flooding his factories with both. He'd been too busy to go to a doctor, so when the need arose, his physician came to him in his own office. Stetson next began bringing into his office any of his employees needing treatment. This idea, like all of his ideas, was enlarged upon. When his own physician's services were outgrown, specialists in various lines were called in. A day came when Stetson realized that if he wanted to escape the parade of doctors and employees now marching through his office, he must make other arrangements.

So he'd built a hospital, magnanimously refusing to confine its relief to his employees only, but making its benefits free to all.

It was there that Edwin Walcott took his wife after reading the article, hoping to find a possible cure for her consumption. The fates had smiled upon them both that day, for while waiting in an anteroom, they had met the great John B. himself. It was impossible to meet and discourse with the man and go away unencouraged. Hale and fit, he made a convincing case for clean living, and credited his cure to that single year of fresh air, pure water, and sunshine.

"Go west!" he'd advised Josephine Walcott. "Go west where the climate is salubrious, where mountain streams are pure as crystal, and the high altitudes purify and strengthen your lungs by making them work harder. Build your house facing south and east, give it plenty of windows, and open them daily. Nightly, too."

And so they had come. They'd built their house facing not only north and east, but west, too, and had given it all the windows John B. Stetson recommended. They had added a wraparound porch where Josephine could take the air and sunshine in long drafts, and from which she could watch the sun rise over the Powder River pampas and set behind the majestic Big Horns.

But what had cured John B. Stetson had failed to cure Josephine Walcott. In the eighteen months they'd been here she had only grown weaker. Her body, once portly and Rubenesque, had dissipated to a mere ninety-five pounds. Her cough had become so constant it no longer awakened her children at night. And recently, bloodstained handkerchiefs had begun appearing in the dirty laundry.

It was the laundry that concerned Emily as she returned home that June afternoon.

Climbing the wide porch steps, she glanced over her left shoulder at the sun, wondering if there was time enough for things to dry before dusk.

She entered the parlor and paused despondently, glancing around. Dust. Everywhere dust. And bric-a-brac enough to dizzy a person. Papa had prospered as a Philadelphia liveryman and in spite of Mother's debilitated condition she wanted everyone in Sheridan to know of his success. Being a modern Victorian matron, she displayed the proof in her parlor, as had her friends in Philadelphia, adapting to the modern decorating principle that *more was better.*

Though the room had been designed by Papa to give an impression of space, Mother had done everything to fill it, insisting not only on bringing her piano but on placing it in the popular way with its back to the room instead of to the wall, thereby enabling her to "dress" it. Festooned with a drapery of swagged multicolored China silk edged with gimp and cordball fringe, the huge upright formed the nucleus of the monstrosity Mother called a parlor. Against the piano was shoved a backless divan; upon it was displayed an assortment of fans and framed photographs; beside it a jardiniere of peacock feathers. She had insisted on leaving behind not one item of her life's collection of litter, and had stuffed the room with an eye-boggling clutter of umbrellas, plaster busts, wicker rockers, cushions, coat racks, china cabinets, scarves, piecrust tables, clocks, and gimcracks. The floor was covered with fillings, then Oriental rugs, and then the easychairs hidden by embroidered cushions and Turkish tidies. The lovely bay window, which Papa had installed to let in plenty of light, was nearly obscured by hanging ferns and tassled draperies.

Perusing it all, Emily sighed. Often she wished Papa would insist on clearing it out and leaving only a wicker chaise and a table or two, but she knew her mother's illness prevailed upon him to let her have her way.

For Mother was dying.

They all knew it but nobody said so. If she wanted her fringed piano cover and gimcracks around her while she did, who in this family would deny her?

Emily collapsed onto the ugly rolled divan, dropped her crossed arms and head onto her knees, and gave in to the depression that hung over this house.

Oh, Mother, please get well. We need you. Papa needs you. He's so lonely and lost, even though he tries to hide it. He's probably worried sick right now about what will happen with another livery stable starting up right under his nose. He'd never let on to me, but he would to you if you were strong.

And Frankie—he's only twelve and he needs so much mothering yet. Who'll give it to him if you die? Me, when I still need mothering myself? I need it at this very moment. I wish I could run to you and talk about my fears for Papa, and my hopes of becoming a veterinarian, which I want more than anything I can ever remember, and about Charles and my uncertainties regarding him. I need to know if what I feel is strong enough or if there should be more. Because he's warned me—he's going to ask me again, soon; and what should I say this time?

With her face buried in her arms, Emily thought of Charles. Plain, good, hardworking Charles who had been her playmate since childhood, who'd been so devastated by the news of her leaving Philadelphia that he'd made the monumental decision to come along with her family to the Wyoming Territory and make his start in the world.

Charles, whom she was so grateful to have at first, living in a new place where there were few other young people her age. Charles, who was becoming insistent about setting a date for their wedding when she wanted instead to learn veterinary medicine first. Charles, to whom she felt betrothed even before she was.

She sighed, pushed herself up, and went to the kitchen. By virtue of necessity, it was the only room in the house devoid of extraneous decor. It had the best range money could buy, and a real granite sink with an indoor pump. A washroom was located at the back with a coal oil heater, a washing machine with metal gears and an easy-to-manipulate hand agitator, and real wooden wringers with a convenient hand crank.

Emily took a look at it and turned away in disgust, wishing she could be at the livery barn cleaning stalls.

Instead, she went upstairs to check on her mother.

The house was rich by Sheridan standards, not only because Papa doted on his ailing wife, but also because Charles Bliss was a carpenter and had brought along his talent and his blueprints—a great relief to Mother, who'd been so afraid she'd have to live in a peeled-log hut with mice and insects. Instead, she'd been built an elegant frame house of two full stories with large airy rooms, long windows, and an impressive entry hall with an open stairway and spooled railings.

Mounting that stairway, Emily turned at the top and paused in the doorway of her parents' bedroom—a spacious room with a second doorway giving onto a small railed roof facing south. Papa had insisted that Charles include the veranda so Mother could step out and enjoy fresh air and sunshine whenever she felt the need. But Mother hardly used the veranda anymore. Its door stood open now, throwing sunshine across the varnished floor of the room where she lay upon the immense sleigh-design bed in which Emily and Frankie had been born. Upon that bed, Mother looked frailer than ever.

She had been handsome once, her hair thick and glossy, a rich bay color. She had worn it with as much pomp as she'd worn her bustles, the rich dark skeins twisted up tightly into an impressive figure-eight knot that thrust out in back even as her generous bust had thrust forward in front. Now her hair was lustreless, lying in a limp braid, and her bust nearly nonexistent. She wore a faded silk bed jacket instead of the crisp sateens and malines she once had donned. Her skin had taken on an alarming number of wrinkles and had become flaccid on her frame.

While Emily studied her sleeping mother, Josephine coughed, covering her mouth with the ever-present hanky, a function that had become as involuntary as the cough itself.

Emily's sad eyes moved to the cot against the side window where her father had taken to sleeping in recent months so as not to disturb his wife—reasoning over which Emily often wondered, since it was most certainly Mother's coughing that disturbed Papa.

She stood for a moment, wondering things a proper Victorian young lady ought not wonder, things about mothers and fathers and shared beds and when—if ever—that sharing ceased to matter. She had never seen Papa touch Mother in any but the most decorous manner. Even when he came into this room, if she—Emily—were there, and Mother was having a bad day, he never kissed her, but only touched her forehead or her hand briefly. Yet he loved her unquestionably. Emily knew he did. After all, she and Frankie were living proof, weren't they? And Papa was so sad since Mother's illness had worsened. Once, in the middle of the night, Emily had discovered him sitting on the front porch with tears running down his face reflecting the moonlight. She had crept back inside without his ever suspecting that she'd discovered his secret grief.

If a man loved a woman, did he display it in the respectful way Papa displayed it to Mother, or by touching her as Charles had recently begun touching Emily? How had Mother reacted the first time Papa had touched her so? And had he done it before they were married? Emily had difficulty imagining her mother allowing such intimacies even when she'd been healthy, for there was an air of propriety about Josephine Walcott that seemed to shun such possibilities.

How disrespectful to be thinking such thoughts in the doorway of her parents' bedroom when her mother lay ill and dying, and her father faced not only that sad truth but a business crisis as well.

"Emily?"

"Oh, Mother, I'm sorry. Did I wake you?" Emily moved to the bedside, taking her mother's frail hand. Josephine smiled, closed her eyes, and rolled her head weakly. They all knew she rarely slept soundly anymore but existed in a state of quasi-sleep as tiring as a day of manual labor might be for a healthy person. She opened her eyes and tapped the bedding at her hip. More and more often lately she used motions to convey her messages, saving every possible breath.

"No," Emily replied. "I'm dirty. I've been helping Papa in the barn. And besides, I have some things to do downstairs. Can I get you anything?"

Josephine answered with a desultory wag of her head.

"If I can, just ring the bell." A small brass handbell had rolled down along the ridge of bedding below Josephine's knee, and Emily retrieved it and put it near her palm.

"Thank—" A spasm of coughing interrupted and Emily escaped the room, feeling guilty for having brought it on and for preferring even washing clothes to watching her mother suffer.

It took the better part of an hour to heat the water, and a lot of knuckle-work to remove the bloodstains. Emily was still at it when Frankie came home with two black spotted trout gill-strung on a forked stick.

"Look what I got, Emily!"

He was the prettiest boy Emily had ever seen—she'd often said Frankie got the looks in their family—with long-lashed blue eyes, twin dimples, a beautiful mouth, and a head of dark hair that was going to make plenty of female fingers itch to touch it within a very few years. Once he'd lost the last of his baby teeth, he'd grown a set of the most remarkably large and perfect ones. They never failed to startle Emily, for though they were the only part of him that had attained their mature size, they brought with them the promise of complete maturity in the very near future. His limbs were stretching already, and if the length of his toes was any indication, Frankie would soon gain the height of their mother, who topped Papa by a good two inches.

Emily felt bad for Frankie. He was still only twelve, but with Mother so sick, the last of his boyhood was being robbed of the happy abandon he deserved. It wasn't fair; but then this trial wasn't fair to any of them, least of all Mother, was it? They had to pitch in and handle the housework the best they could, like it or not. So Emily steeled herself against the appeal she knew was forthcoming as she admired Frankie's catch.

"Mmm . . . nice fish. Who's going to clean them?"

"Me and Earl. Where's Papa?"

"Still at the livery."

"I gotta go show him!"

"Wait a minute!"

"But Earl's waiting!" Frankie halted impatiently, his face skewing as he realized his mistake in stopping by the kitchen.

"You promised to be home by three to help me."

"I didn't have any watch."

"You can see the sun, can't you?"

"I couldn't." His eyes widened to best advantage. "Honestly, I couldn't, Emily! We were down by the big cottonwoods in the empty lot behind Stroth's place and I couldn't see the sun behind the trees!"

She pitied the poor girl who tried to tie this one down. Dressed in a straw hat, wearing neither shirt nor shoes beneath his overalls, with his wide eyes shining and his lips open in feigned innocence, Frankie presented a charming picture, one Emily had difficulty resisting. Still, she tried.

"Here." She released the agitator lever on the washing machine. "Your turn. My arm is ready to fall off."

"But I want to take my fish uptown and show Papa. And besides, Earl's waiting, and soon as we show Papa we're gonna come straight back here and clean these so you can fry them for supper. Please, Emily . . . *pleeeease?*"

She let him go because when she was twelve she had not had to wash clothes at four o'clock on a warm summer afternoon. Without his help, the washing took longer than she'd planned, and she was just finishing up when Papa came home for supper. True to his word, Frankie had cleaned the trout, and tonight he and

Papa took over the cooking while Emily put the washroom in order and stacked the wet laundry to wait till morning.

Papa's cooking left room for improvement. The potatoes were mushy; the trout was a little too brown; the coffee boiled over; and the biscuits stuck to the pan. But worst of all, Mother was absent from the table. Edwin took a tray up to her but returned to catch Emily's eye across the room and give a sad shake of his head. The empty chair cast a pall over the meal, as usual, but Emily tried to brighten it.

"From now on, I'll do the cooking and you can clean up the washroom," she chided.

"We'll do as we've been doing," Edwin returned. "We'll get along just fine."

But when his eyes met those of his daughter she caught a momentary hint of despair such as she'd witnessed in his private midnight session on the porch. As quickly as it appeared, Edwin hid it and lurched to his feet, reaching for dishes to carry to the sink.

"We'd better clean up. Charles said he'd be stopping by later tonight."

Charles stopped by most nights. He had a house of his own, but it was undeniably lonely for him living in it by himself. It was natural for him to want to be with the Walcotts, having known them all his life, and having come to Wyoming at the same time as they. Since their relocation in Sheridan he had come to be a dear friend to Edwin in spite of the difference in their ages. And Mama had always shown a distinct affection for him, having known him since he was a boy. Charles, she often reiterated, came from a staunch religious upbringing, knew the value of hard work, and would someday make a dedicated husband for Emily. As for Frankie—well, Frankie absolutely idolized Charles.

Charles arrived in time to help wipe dishes. Whenever he arrived lately, it seemed there was something he could help with, and he always did so gladly. Emily had grown tired of hearing her father say, "That Charles, he sure knows what work is." Of course Charles knew what work was—didn't they all?

After dishes Frankie talked Charles into a game of dominoes. They all retired to the parlor where the two set up their pieces while Emily watched and Edwin smoked a last pipe before going upstairs to read to his wife.

"I suppose you met the new man in town," Charles said to nobody in particular.

"We've got his horses at the livery," Edwin responded.

"What new man?" Frankie inquired.

"His name is Jeffcoat. Tom Jeffcoat," Charles answered, placing a five on a five.

"So you've met him, too?" Edwin inquired,.

"Yes. Loucks sent him over, told him I was a carpenter."

"He wants to hire you, of course," Edwin ventured.

Charles glanced up. His eyes met Edwin's, and Emily witnessed the ambivalence in his glance.

"Yes, he does."

"Well, if his money is green, you'd better say yes."

"Do you know what he's building, Edwin?"

"A livery stable, he tells me."

"He *told* you?"

"As Emily pointed out, it'd be hard to hide a livery stable once it starts going up."

"Emily met him, too?" Charles's eyes veered to her as she leaned over Frankie's shoulder, studying his domino selection.

"I'm sorry to say I did," she replied coolly, without once raising her eyes to Charles's.

"Oh?"

She picked up one of Frankie's dominoes and played it while answering. "First he called me 'young fellow,' then tried to give me advice about how to take care of Sergeant's cracked hoof. I didn't appreciate either one."

Edwin chuckled, holding the pipestem at the corner of his mouth. "I can vouch for that. She was whetting the edge of her tongue on him when I walked in and saved a week's worth of business she had just sent packing."

"Papa!" Emily spouted irritably. "You don't have to tell everything!"

"Emily did that?" Frankie put in, losing interest in the game, grinning with wonder at his sister.

"Now, Emily, we have no secrets from Charles."

Which, in Emily's opinion, was one of the reasons she couldn't generate any romantic gust for him. It felt as if she'd already lived with him for the last two years, he was here so much. She gave up playing Frankie's dominoes and plopped down on the divan.

"I hope you spit in his eye, Charles!" she said pugnaciously.

"Now, Emily, be sensible. How could Charles do that?" her father chided.

"*I* did it, didn't I?" she challenged.

To Emily's surprise Charles said, "As a matter of fact, I rather liked him."

"Liked him!" Emily exclaimed. "Charles, how could you!"

"Emily, you seem to forget Charles has a business to run!" Edwin's tone grew sharper, then mellowed as he turned to Charles. "Whatever she says, you know I wouldn't hold it against you if you worked for Jeffcoat."

"He wants to see my blueprint collection, too. After the livery barn he intends to put up a house."

"So he said. And it could mean a tidy profit for you, Charles."

"Maybe so, but I don't like working for your competition."

Edwin took a puff on his pipe, found it dead, fished a horseshoe nail from his shirt pocket, and began scraping out the dottle into an ashtray. "Charles, I'm not your father," he began after a thoughtful silence, "but I think I know what he'd say if he were here to advise you at this moment. He'd say this is one of those occasions where you have to be a businessman first and a friend second. As for me, I'll respect you as much for making a prudent business decision as I will for being loyal, so tell Jeffcoat yes. It's what you came here for, isn't it? Because you thought the town would prosper, and you, too, along with it? Well, you can't do that by turning down paying customers."

Charles turned his gray eyes to Frankie. "Frankie, what do you say?"

"I don't care if Papa doesn't care."

"Emily?" He lifted his eyes to her and she had difficulty separating her distaste for Jeffcoat from the realization that Papa was probably right. Was she the only one in the place aggravated by the entire situation? Well, she hadn't their magnanimity, and she wouldn't pretend she did! With a flash of annoyance, she shot from her chair toward the front door. "Oh, I don't care!" she called back. "Do what you want!" A moment later the front screen door slammed.

Emily's peevishness put an end to the games in the parlor. Charles rose and said, "I'll go out and talk to her."

Edwin said, "Frankie, make sure you bury those fish guts before you go to bed." He went up to spend the remainder of the evening with his wife.

The porch wrapped around three sides of the house. Charles found Emily on the west arm, sitting on a wicker settee, facing the Big Horns and the paling peach sky.

She heard Charles's footsteps approach but continued leaning her head against the wall as he perched on the edge of the settee beside her, making the wicker snap. He joined his hands loosely between his knees and studied them.

"You're upset with me," he said quietly.

"I'm upset with life, Charles, not with you."

"With me too, I can tell."

She relented and rolled her head his way, studying him. She had grown up in an era when most men wore facial hair, yet she would never grow accustomed to it on Charles. His sandy brown mustache and beard were thick and neatly sculptured, yet she missed the clean, strong lines it hid. He had a fine jaw and a good chin, too attractive to hide beneath all that nap. The beard and mustache made him look older than he really was. Why would a man of twenty-one want to look like one approaching thirty? She stifled the critical thoughts and studied his eyes— intelligent gray eyes watching her now with the hurt carefully concealed.

"No," she assured him more softly, "not with you. With all the work, and the worry about Mother, and now this new man coming to town and competing with Papa. It's all very upsetting." She turned her gaze back to the Big Horns and sighed before going on. "And sometimes I miss Philadelphia so badly I think I'll simply die."

"I know. Sometimes I do, too."

They watched the sky take on a blue tint and eventually Charles inquired, "What do you miss most?"

"Oh ..." She missed so many things—at that moment she could not choose one. "The skating parties and the round of visiting on New Year's Day and the summertime picnics. All the things we used to do with our friends. Here all we do is work and sleep, then work again and sleep again. There's no ... no gaiety, no social life."

Charles remained silent. Finally, he said, "I miss it a lot, too."

"What do *you* miss most?"

"My family."

"Oh, Charles ..." She felt tactless for having asked when she knew how lonely she herself would feel if she were suddenly two thousand miles away from Papa and Mother and Frankie. "But we're here for you anytime you need us," she added, because it was true. Because she could not imagine her home without Charles there most evenings and Sundays. Too late she saw the appeal in his eye and knew he would reach for her hand. When he did, she felt no more excitement than she had when she was six and he was nine and he had squired her down a Philadelphia street with their mothers behind them pushing perambulators.

"I have an idea," Charles said, suddenly brightening. "You're missing the picnics in Philadelphia, so why don't we plan one?"

"Just the two of us?"

"Why not?"

"Oh, Charles ..." She retrieved her hand and dropped her head against the wall. "I barely have time to do the washing and ironing and fix suppers and take my turn with Mother."

"There's Sunday."

"The cooking doesn't stop for Sundays."

"Surely you can find a couple of hours. How about this Sunday? I'll bring the food. And we'll take your father's little black shay for two and drive up into the foothills and drink sarsaparilla and stretch out in the sun like a couple of lazy lizards." In his earnestness he captured both of her hands. "What do you say, Emily?"

To get away for even an afternoon sounded so wonderful that she couldn't resist. "Oh, all right. But I won't be able to leave until the others are fed."

Elated, Charles kissed her hands—two grazing touches meant to keep the mood gay. But when his head lifted, he gripped her fingers more tightly and the expression in his eyes intensified.

Oh no, don't spoil it, Charles, she thought.

"Emily," he appealed softly while lifting one of her hands again to his lips. The sky had darkened to midnight blue and nobody was around to see what happened in the shadow of the deep porch as he took her arms and drew her close, dropping his mouth over hers. She acquiesced, but at the touch of his warm lips and prickly mustache she thought, Why must I have known you all my life? Why can you not be some mysterious stranger who galloped into town and gave me a second look that rocked me off my feet? Why is the scent of wood shavings on your skin and of tonic on your hair too familiar to be exciting? Why must I love you in the same way I love Frankie?

When the kiss ended her heart was plunking along as restfully as if she'd just awakened and stretched from a long nap.

"Charles, I must go in now," she said.

"No, not yet," he whispered, holding her arms.

She dropped her chin so he wouldn't kiss her again. "Yes . . . please, Charles."

"Why do you always pull away?"

"Because it isn't proper."

He drew an unsteady breath and released her. "Very well . . . but I'll plan on Sunday then."

He walked her to the door and she felt his reluctance to leave, to return to his empty house. It brought to Emily a nagging sense of guilt for being unable to conjure up the feelings he wanted of her, for being unable to fill the void left by his family, even for finding disfavor with his mustache and beard when other women, she was sure, found them most appealing.

She knew when he paused and turned to her that he wanted to kiss her again, but she slipped inside before he could.

"Good night, Charles," she said through the screen door.

"Good night, Emily." He stood studying her, banking his disappointment. "I'll win you over yet, you know."

As she watched him cross the porch she had the deflating feeling was was right.

Upstairs, Edwin was reading to Josephine from *Forty Liars and Other Lies* by Edgar Wilson Nye, but he knew her mind was far from Nye's humorous depictions of the West.

". . . leading a string of paint ponies along an arroyo where—"

"Edwin?" she interrupted, staring at the ceiling.

He lowered the book and studied her anxiously. "Yes, dear?"

"What are we going to do?" she whispered.

"Do?" He set the book aside and left his cot to sit on the edge of the big bed.

"Yes. What are we going to do from now until I die?"

"Oh, Josie, don't—"

She gestured to silence him. "We both know it, Edwin, and we must make plans."

"We don't know it." He took her pale, frail fingers and squeezed them. "Look at what happened to Stetson."

"I've been here well over a year already and by now I know I won't be as lucky as Stet—" She broke into a spasm of coughing that bent her and made her quiver like a divining rod. He bolstered her back and leaned close. "Don't talk anymore, Josie. Save your breath . . . please."

The racking cough continued for a full two minutes before she fell back, exhausted. He brushed the hair away from her sweating brow and studied her gaunt face, his own weighted with despair at being unable to help her in any way.

"Rest, Josie."

"No," she mouthed, grasping his hand to keep him near. "Listen to me, Edwin." She struggled to control her breathing, taking deep drafts of air, building her reserve for the words ahead. "I'm not going to get downstairs again and we both know it. I scarcely have the strength to feed myself—how will I ever handle house chores ag—again?" Another cough interrupted momentarily, then she went through the struggle again, recouping her strength before finally continuing: "It isn't fair to expect the children to do my part and care for me, too."

"They don't mind, and neither do I. We're getting along just f—"

She squeezed his hand weakly. Her sunken eyes rested on his, begging for his indulgence. "Emily is eighteen. We've put too great a load on her. She'd rather . . ." Josephine stopped again for breath. "She'd rather work at the livery stable with you and she needs more time to study if she's to complete the course from Dr. Barnum. Is it fair of us to expect her to be housekeeper and nurse, too?"

He had no answer. He sat stroking her blue-white hand, staring at it while regret filled his throat.

"I believe," Josephine added, "that Charles has asked her to marry him and she turned him down because of me."

He couldn't deny it; he was certain that what his wife said was true, though Emily had never admitted it to either of them.

"She's a good girl, Edwin, devoted to us. She'll help you in the livery stable and me in this house until Charles grows tired of waiting and asks someone else."

"That will never happen."

"Perhaps not. But suppose she wanted to say yes right now—don't you see that she should be caring for her own house . . . her own children, instead of Frankie and you and me?"

Despondent, Edwin had no answer.

"Edwin, look at me."

He did, his face long with sorrow.

"I am going to die, Edwin," she whispered, "but it may take . . . some time yet. And it will not be easy . . . on any of you, least of all Emily. She should have . . . the right to say yes to Charles, don't you see? And Frankie still needs a woman's strong hand, and this house should be cared for . . . and meals cooked properly, and you . . . should not have to take turns hanging laundry and frying fish . . . so I have written to Fannie and asked her to come."

A bolt of fire seemed to shoot through Edwin's vitals. "Fannie?" He blinked and his spine straightened. "You mean your cousin, Fannie?"

"Do you know any other?"

He sprang from the side of the bed to face the veranda door and hide his heating face. "But she has a life of her own."

"She has no life at all; surely you can read between the lines of her letters."

"On the contrary, Fannie has so many interests and . . . and friends, she . . . why, she . . ." Edwin stammered to a halt, feeling his blood continue to rush at the mere mention of the woman's name.

Behind him Josephine said softly, "I need her, Edwin. This family needs her."

He spun and retorted, "No, I won't have Fannie!"

For a moment Josephine stared at him while he felt foolish and transparent, by turns. All these years he'd hidden the truth from her and he would not risk her learning it now when she had so much else to suffer. He forcibly calmed himself and softened his voice. "I won't have Fannie put in the position of having to say yes, just because you're family. And you know she would do just that, in a minute."

"I'm afraid it's too late, Edwin . . . she's already agreed."

Shock drained the blood from his face. His fingertips felt cold and his chest tight.

"Her letter arrived today." Josephine extended a folded piece of stationery. He stared at it as if it were alive. After a long silence he reluctantly moved toward it.

Josephine watched the color return to his face as he read Fannie's reply. She saw him carefully attempt to mask his feelings, but his ears and cheeks turned brilliant red and his Adam's apple bobbed. Watching, she hid the regret begotten by years of marriage to a man who had never loved her. *Edwin, my gallant and noble husband, you will never know how hard I tried to make you happy. Perhaps at last I've found a way.*

When he'd finished reading, he folded the letter and returned it to her, unable to hide the reproof in his eyes and voice. "You should have consulted me first, Josephine." He only called her Josephine when he was inordinately upset. The rest of the time it was Josie.

"Yes, I know."

"Why didn't you?"

"For exactly the reason you're displaying."

He slipped his hands into his rear pockets, afraid she would see them trembling. "She's a city woman. It's not fair to ask her to come out here to the middle of nowhere. The children and I can handle it. Or perhaps I could hire someone."

"Who?"

They both knew women were scarce out here in cowboy country. Those of eligible age remained single very briefly before taking on their own husband and house. He would find no one in Sheridan willing to hire on as nurse and housekeeper.

"Edwin, come . . . sit by me."

Reluctantly he did, studying the floor morosely. She touched his knee—a rare intimacy—and took his hand. "Grant me this . . . please. Set the children free of the burdens I've brought them . . . and yourself, too. When Fannie comes, make her feel welcome. I think she needs us as badly as we need her."

"Fannie has never needed anyone."

"Hasn't she?"

Edwin felt a tangle of emotions: fear as great as any he'd ever known, matched by unbounded exhilaration at the thought of seeing Fannie again; pique with Josie for putting him in this ungodly position; relief that she had at last found an answer to their domestic turmoil; a sense of encroaching duplicity, for surely he would practice it from the very moment Fannie Cooper set foot in this house; resolution that, no matter what, he would never desecrate his marriage vows.

"Where do you intend to put her?"

"In with Emily."

Edwin sat silent for a long time, still adjusting to the shock, trying to imagine himself lying in this room on his cot night after night with Fannie across the hall. There was nothing he could do; she was already en route, even as he sat with his stomach quaking and his leg muscles tense. She would arrive by stagecoach within the week and he would pick her up at the hotel and pretend he had not kept her memory glowing in his heart for twenty-two years.

"Of course I'll be cordial to her, you know that. It's just—"

Their eyes locked and exchanged a silent acknowledgment. Fannie's coming represented so much more than the arrival of help. It represented the first in a series of final steps. Always until now they had lived with the delusion that one day soon Josephine would awaken and feel revived enough to take up her duties again. That life would return to normal. Upon Fannie's arrival they would lay that idea to rest with the same darkening finality as the knowledge that this woman—this wife and mother—would herself be laid to rest in the foreseeable future.

Edwin felt his throat tighten and his eyes sting. He doubled forward, covering Josie's frail torso with his sturdy one, slipping his hands between her and the stacked pillows. He rested his cheek upon her temple but dared not press his weight upon her. She felt like a stranger, bony and wasted. Odd how he could experience such deep sorrow at the difference in her emaciated body when he'd taken so little pleasure in it while it was plump and healthy. Perhaps it was that, too, which he mourned.

Dear Josie, I promise my fidelity till the end—that much I can give you.

She held him and pinched her eyes closed against the pain of losing him to Fannie, wondering why she had never been able to welcome his embrace this effortlessly during her hale years.

Dearest Edwin, she'll give you the kind of love I was never able to give—I'm sure of it.

Chapter 3

Emily was in the tack room at the livery stable the following day when Tarsy Fields came flying in like a kite with a broken string. "Emily, have you *seen him yet!* He's absolutely *gorgeous!*" Tarsy was given to flamboyant gestures, exaggeration, and general excess of enthusiasm over anything she liked.

"Seen who?"

"Why, Mr. Jeffcoat, of course! Tom Jeffcoat—don't tell me you haven't *heard* of him!"

"Oh, him." Emily made a distasteful face and turned away, continuing her preparation of a linseed-meal poultice for Sergeant's foot.

"Did he bring his horse in here?"

"We're the only livery in town, aren't we?"

"So you *did* see him! And probably met him, too. Oh, Emily, you're *soooo* lucky. I only passed him on the boardwalk as he was coming out of the hotel, and I didn't get a chance to talk to him or meet him, but I went inside and found out his name from Mr. Helstrom. Tom Jeffcoat—what a name! Isn't he absolutely *daz-*

zling?" Tarsy clasped her hands, straightened her arms, and gazed at the rafters in a surfeit of ecstasy.

Dazzling? Tom Jeffcoat? The man with no sleeves and no manners? The know-it-all bounder who was setting out to ruin her father's business?

"I hadn't noticed," Emily replied sourly, spreading the thick yellow paste on a white rag.

"Hadn't noticed!" Tarsy shrieked, throwing herself against the workbench at Emily's elbow, bending at the waist to gush in Emily's face. "Hadn't noticed those . . . those bulging arms! And that face! And those eyes! Emily, my *grandmother* would have noticed, and she's got cataracts. Mercy sakes, those lashes . . . those limpid pools . . . those drooping lids . . . why, when he looked at me I went absolutely limp." Tarsy affected a swoon, falling forward across the workbench like a dying ballerina, overturning a bottle of carbolic acid with an outflung hand.

"Tarsy, would you mind going limp somewhere else?" Emily righted the bottle. "And how could you notice all that when you only passed him on the street?"

"A girl's *got* to notice things like that if she doesn't want to live her life as an old maid. Honestly, Emily, don't tell me you didn't notice how good-looking he is."

Emily picked up the poultice and headed for the main part of the barn with Tarsy at her heels, still rhapsodizing.

"I'll bet he's got fifty eyelashes for every one of Jerome's. And when he smiles he gets a dimple in his left cheek. And his lips—oh, Emily." Tarsy appeared about to be laid low by another near-collapse, then popped out of it to demand, "Tell me everything you know about him. Everything! Which horse is his? What's he doing here? Where did he come from? Is he staying?" Tarsy folded her hands along her chest, squeezed her eyelids closed, and lifted her face. "Oh, please, God, let him stay!"

Entering Sergeant's stall, Emily said, "You're wasting your time, Tarsy. He's engaged."

"Engaged!" Tarsy wailed. "Are you sure?"

Squatting to strap the poultice to Sergeant's foot, Emily added, "He mentioned a fiancée."

"Oh, horse puckey!" the blonde pouted, stamping her foot. "Now I *will* end up an old maid!"

Though Tarsy was Emily's best friend, there were times when Emily thought the girl hadn't a brain in her head. She was an inveterate flirt, constantly vocalizing her fear of being an old maid when there was about as little chance of that happening as of Sergeant strapping this poultice on himself. But Tarsy was fond of agonizing over the possibility, sitting on Emily's porch swing or in her bedroom, or coming here to the livery stable and flinging her body about as if in near-despair, waxing melodramatic about how lonely life would be at fifty when she was a childless, gray-haired spinster living alone sewing gloves. It wasn't Tarsy's fault she was born needing constant compliments in order to be happy. Or that she'd been endowed with a bent toward melodrama. Emily found both traits amusing and irritating, by turns, especially in light of Tarsy's ability to charm men. For Tarsy, too, had fifty eyelashes for every one of Jerome Berryman's, and poor Jerome was smitten with each one of hers, as were several other local swains. She had reams of bouncing blond hair, a beautiful heart-shaped face highlighted by her abundantly fringed brown eyes, tiny bones, and a nearly nonexistent waist that drew second glances like a field of blooming buckwheat draws honeybees.

But, as always, she wanted one more bee.

"Emily, tell me about him anyway, *pleeze.*"

"I don't know much except that he's staying and I'm not too happy about it. He's already seen Loucks about buying property and he intends to build a livery stable and go into competition with Papa."

Tarsy came out of her self-absorption long enough to cover her lips in dismay. "Oh, dear."

"Yes. Oh, dear."

"Whatever is your papa going to do?"

"What can we do? It's a free country, he says."

"You mean he isn't upset?"

"*I'm* the one who's upset!" Emily finished doctoring Sergeant, stood, and wiped her hands agitatedly. "Papa's got enough to worry about with Mama getting worse. And now this." She related what had transpired the previous day, ending, "So if you hear where he intends to put up his livery stable, I'd appreciate your letting us know."

But before the day was out Emily learned for herself. She was in the office studying, sitting Indian-fashion on the cot with her shoulders curled against the wall, one hand on the sleeping cat and a book in her lap, when Jeffcoat himself appeared in the doorway.

She glanced up and her eyes iced over.

"Oh, it's you."

"Good afternoon, Miss Walcott." He surveyed her unladylike pose while she defiantly refused to alter it on his behalf. A grin unbalanced his mouth as he tipped his hat, and she cursed Tarsy for being right: he did have a dimple in his left cheek and his eyelashes were devilishly thick and long, and he had a disarmingly attractive mouth. And dressed in the same shirt with the missing sleeves, his bulging biceps were as conspicuous as the spine of the Big Horns. But she sensed a cockiness in his unconventional attire, a flaunting of masculinity to which a gentleman would not stoop: his tall black boots led to high-waisted black britches with bright red suspenders that looked quite superfluous on pants that tight. But above all he flaunted those muscular arms, framed by the threads of blue chambray where the sleeve had been chewed off at the armhole. Oh, and didn't he know how to pose the whole collection to best advantage, standing with feet widespread, hands hooked at his waist, as if to say, take a look, lady.

"What do you want?" she demanded rudely.

"My horses. I'll need them for a few hours."

Emily flopped her book facedown, sending the cat bounding away. She bounced off the cot and strode for the door at full steam, refusing to excuse herself as she forced Jeffcoat to jump back or be flattened. He jumped. Then whistled as if singed and ambled farther into the empty office to glance amusedly at the cover of her book. *The Science of Veterinary Medicine* by R. C. Barnum. The amusement left his face, replaced by interest as he turned the volume over, cocked his head, and perused the header on the open page: "Diseases of the Generative Organs of Both the Horse and Mare." His eyes wandered across the cot, across the rag rug, which still held a depression from her rump, to a sheaf of papers that had been at her knee. With a single finger he pivoted them and saw what appeared to be a prepared quiz. He read: *What is the most common cause of barrenness in mares and what is its treatment?*

Beneath it she had filled in the answer: *An acid secretion of the genital organs or a retention of the afterbirth. The most common treatment is with yeast as follows: Mix 2 heaping tsp. of yeast into a pint of boiled water, keep warm for 5 or*

6 hours. Flush affected parts first with warm water, then inject with yeast. Animal should be mated from 2–6 hours after treatment.

His eyebrows rose. So the little smart-mouth knew her stuff!

A hand reached around and snatched the papers from under his nose. "This is a private office!"

He neither flinched nor blustered but turned loosely to watch her bury the papers beneath a ledger on the littered desk. She was dressed once again in britches and the wool cap, but this time the leather apron was absent and he saw that he'd been mistaken; she did have breasts after all, plum sized and minimized by a perfectly atrocious open-collared boy's shirt the color of horse dung. He made sure his survey of her breasts was completed before she whipped around to confront him with her fists akimbo.

"You're a nosy, rude man, Mr. Jeffcoat!"

"And your parents could have taught you a few manners, Miss Walcott."

"I don't appreciate people sticking their noses into my personal business, and you've done it twice now! I'll thank you not to do it again!"

For a moment he considered making some comment on her mode of dress, compliment her on how the hue of the shirt did wonders for her complexion, just to nettle her. Actually, she looked quite fetching with her feet spraddled, her fists bunched, and her blue eyes bright and angry. It was a curiosity to find a woman so feisty and outspoken in an age when the ideal female was purported to be one of dulcet voice and retiring comportment. She possessed neither, and it fascinated him. But in the end Jeffcoat decided he might need the use of her veterinary medicine book sometime, so he decided to soothe the waters.

"I'm sorry, Miss Walcott."

"If you want your horses, follow me. I don't see any reason why I should get them both out while you dally in here reading other people's mail." She strode for the door, calling back, "What do you want them hitched to, your own wagon?"

"Are all the women in this town as friendly as you?" he called, following.

"I said what do you want them hitched to?"

"Nothing. Just harness 'em and I'll drive 'em out."

She returned, hands on hips, to advise him with an air of long-suffering, "I don't *just harness* them, you help me."

"So what am I paying you for?"

"You want your horses or not, Jeffcoat?"

Taking a lead rope, she tossed him another, pushed aside a pole barrier to a stall, and nodded toward an adjacent one. "Liza's in there. Get her."

Bossy young thing, he thought, grabbing the rope on the fly. But before he could say so she disappeared and he dropped the pole from Liza's stall and stepped inside. "Hiya, girl." He gave Liza a critical look-over, rubbing her withers and shoulders. She'd been brushed down as ordered; her hide was smooth and flat. Miss Britches might have the tongue of an adder but she knew how to put away a horse.

"Liza looks good," he offered, backing the horse into the corridor where Emily was already waiting with Rex. "I can tell you spent plenty of time brushing her."

For his efforts he received a scowl that said clearly, only an idiot abuses good horseflesh. With the snap lines secured, she turned away haughtily, leading the way to the rear of the barn where carriages and wagons were stored. Inside a separate tack room the equipage hung on wooden pegs. They took his gear down together—she sullen, he amused—and carried it to the main aisle where they began in silence to harness Rex and Liza. When the job was done, she headed for the office, offering not a word of farewell.

"I'll have them back tonight," he called, "but you can charge me for the full day."

"You can bet your shabby shirt I will!" she returned without a backward glance, and disappeared into her lair.

He glanced down at his bare arms, grinned, and thought, all right, so we're even, young fellow.

Inside the office, sitting cross-legged again with the book on her lap, Emily found her concentration shattered. Her stomach was jumping and her tongue ached from being pressed so tensely to the roof of her mouth. Damn his insufferable hide! When she tried to read, his criticism seemed to superimpose itself upon the words in the book. Infernal, distasteful man! She heard him cluck to the team, heard their hooves clop across the hard dirt floor and move up the street. When the sound disappeared she sat with her head against the wall and her eyes closed, agitated as no man had managed to make her before. Where was he taking the horses without the wagon? And how dare he criticize her papa, whom he didn't even know! His own manners left plenty to be desired!

Twenty minutes later she'd managed to refocus her attentions on her studies when a screech distracted her. She cocked her head and listened—it sounded like metal on stones. *Metal on stones?* Suspicion dawned and she tore outside, halted at the wide double doors, and gaped at the jarring sight of Jeffcoat leveling a lot not a hundred feet down the street on the opposite side. He had rented Loucks's steel grader, a monstrous affair painted parsley green that kept the town's streets bladed during summer and plowed in winter, and made Loucks some fairly decent rental money with each lot he sold. The implement had a long-nosed frame upon which the metal blade was tilted by a pair of upright wheels and attached cables. Jeffcoat stood between the wheels on a railed metal platform driving his team like some misplaced Roman gladiator.

Emily was marching toward him the moment her outrage blossomed.

"Just what do you think you're doing, Jeffcoat!" she bellowed, approaching him as the rig moved away from her, rolling dirt to one side.

He glanced over his shoulder and smiled, but kept the team moving. "Leveling my land, Miss Walcott!"

"In a pig's eye!" She stomped along off his right flank while he rode three feet above her.

"No, in J. D. Loucks's grader!"

It was a toss-up who screeched louder, the rocks or Emily. "How dare you pick this spot right on top of my father's!"

"It was for sale."

"So were twenty others on the outskirts of town where we wouldn't have to look at you!"

"This's prime land. Close to the business section. It's a much better buy than the ones out there."

He reached the far edge of his site and brought the team about, heading back toward Emily.

"What'd you pay for it?" she shouted.

"Now who's sticking their nose into other people's business, Miss Walcott?" While he spoke he concentrated on adjusting the two huge metal wheels. His muscles stood out in ridges as the cables groaned and the blade tilted to the proper angle. When he drove past Emily the blade sent a furl of soil cascading across her ankles.

She jumped over it and roared, "How much!"

"Three dollars and fifty cents for the first lot and fifty cents each for the other three."

"Other three! You mean you bought four?"

"Two for my business. Two for my home. Good price." He grinned down at her while she stalked along beside him, shouting above the screech of steel on stone.

"I'll buy them all from you for double what you paid."

"Oh, I'd have to get more than double. After all, this one's already been improved."

"Jeffcoat, stop that blasted team this minute so I can talk to you!"

"Whoa!" The team halted and into the sudden silence he said, "Yes, Miss Walcott," flipped the reins around a flywheel, and bounced down beside her. "At your service, Miss Walcott."

His choice of words, drawled through his insufferable grin, made her agonizingly aware that she was dressed in her brother's gnawed-up cap and britches. She scowled menacingly. "This town is only big enough for one livery stable and you know it!"

"I'm sorry, Miss Walcott, but I disagree. It's spreading faster than gossip." He wiped his brow on a forearm, tugged off a pair of dirty leather gloves, and flapped them toward the north end of Main Street. "Just look at the building going on. Yesterday when I rode through I counted four houses and two businesses under construction, and by my count the town's got two harnessmakers. If there's business enough for two harnessmakers, there's business enough for two stables. And a school already up, and I hear tell the next thing's going to be a church. That sounds like a town with a future to me. I'm sorry if I have to run your father a little competition, but I'm not out to ruin him, I assure you."

"And what about Charles? You've already talked to Charles!"

"Charles?"

"Charles Bliss. You intend to hire him to help you put up your buildings!"

"You have some objection to that, too?"

She objected to everything this man had precipitated in the last twenty-four hours. She objected to his brazenness. To his choice of lots. To his grin and his sweaty smell and his tight trousers, and his cocky good looks, and his stupid unnecessary suspenders and the way he set Tarsy in a dither, and the fact that he tore the sleeves off his shirts, and the more distressing fact that both she and her father would have to look at his damned livery stable out the office window of their own for the rest of their lives!

She decided to tell him so.

"I object, Mr. Jeffcoat, to everything you do and are!" She thrust her nose so close to his that she could see herself reflected in his black pupils. "And particularly to your putting Charles into a position where he must choose loyalties. He's been a friend of our family since we were both knee high."

For the first time she saw the spark of anger in Jeffcoat's cobalt blue eyes. His jaw took on the same tense bulge as his biceps, and his voice had a hard edge. "I've traveled over a thousand miles, left my family and everyone I hold dear, ridden into this backwoods cow town with honorable intentions, honest money, and a strong back. I've bought land and hired a carpenter and I plan to take up my trade in peaceable fashion and become a permanent, law-abiding citizen of Sheridan. So, what do they send me as a welcoming committee but a sassy-mouthed young whelp who needs to have her mouth washed out with soap and be shown what a petticoat is! Understand this, Miss Britches . . ." Nose to nose, he backed her up as he spoke. "I'm getting mighty damned tired of you raising objections to my every move! I'm not only tired of your orneriness, I'm in a hurry to get my place raised, and I don't intend to take any more sass from an impertinent young tomboy like you. Now, I'll thank you, Miss Walcott, to get off my property!"

He pulled on his gloves and swung away, leaving her red-faced and speechless. With a deft leap he mounted the railed platform of the grader, took the reins, and shouted, "Hey, giddap, there!"

And with that their enmity was sealed.

The following day was Sunday. Church services were held in Coffeen Hall, the only building in town with enough adult-sized chairs to accommodate the worshipers from mixed denominations who congregated and were led in prayer by Reverend Vasseler, who'd recently arrived from New York to organize an Episcopal congregation. His voice was mellifluous, his message inspired; thus he'd already attracted an impressive number of families to his fold. The hall was crowded when Reverend Vasseler began the service by leading the gathering with the hymn, "All Praise, All Glory Now We Sing." Standing between Charles and her father, Emily sang in a doubtful soprano. Halfway through the song she felt eyes probing and turned to find Tom Jeffcoat in an aisle seat at the rear, singing and watching her. She snapped her mouth shut and stared at him for a full ten seconds.

"*. . . worship now our heav'nly king . . .*"

He sang without benefit of a hymnal, belting out the notes robustly, startling her. She had been prepared to see him as the Devil incarnate, but finding him singing hymns at her own church service cast him in quite the opposite light. She snapped her attention to the front and vowed not to give him so much as another glance.

The hymn ended and they sat. Reverend Vasseler gave a short sermon on the Good Samaritan, then announced that J. D. Loucks had donated a lot on East Loucks Street for the building of a real church. Smiles and murmurs accompanied a general scanning of the room as members of the congregation picked out Loucks and beamed approval. The minister appealed to all the men to do their fair share. He outlined a building plan by which the structure would be up and roofed by midsummer, and totally completed by autumn. Joseph Zollinski had volunteered to organize the volunteer building crew, and Charles Bliss to oversee the work, and all the men present were to see either one of them after the service to volunteer at least a day of their time.

When the service ended Charles stayed to organize volunteers while Emily left the hall on her father's arm. Halfway to the door, Emily was caught by Tarsy, who grabbed her arm and whispered breathlessly, "He's here!"

"I know."

"Introduce us."

"*I will not!*"

"Oh, Emily . . . pleeeeze!"

"If you want to meet him go introduce yourself, but don't expect me to. Not after yesterday!"

"But, Emily, he's absolutely the most luscious creature I've—"

"Well, good morning, Tarsy," Edwin interrupted.

"Oh, good morning, Mr. Walcott. I was just saying to Emily that the neighborly thing to do is to welcome newcomers to the town, wouldn't you say?"

Edwin smiled. "I would."

"So would you mind introducing me to Mr. Jeffcoat?"

Edwin was familiar with Tarsy's flighty ways and thought little of her suggestion. He was too congenial a person to snub anybody—even his competitor. Outside in the sunlight of the fair June morning Edwin guided Tarsy to Jeffcoat while Emily hung back, pretending disinterest in the entire episode, excusing herself by saying she'd wait near the door for Charles.

But she kept one eye on the introductions.

"Mr. Jeffcoat, hold up there!" called Edwin.

Jeffcoat turned in mid-stride and smiled congenially. "Ah, good morning, Edwin."

"You look like a man in a hurry."

"I've got a building to put up. I'm afraid I can't waste a day like this, whether it's the Lord's day or not." He cocked his head at the faultless blue sky.

Edwin did likewise. "Can't say I blame you. It is a fine day."

"Yessir, it is."

"I'd like you to meet my daughter's friend, Miss Tarsy Fields."

Jeffcoat transferred his attention to the pretty blonde. "Miss Fields."

"Mr. Jeffcoat." She bobbed and flashed her most dazzling smile. "I'm positively delighted to meet you."

Jeffcoat had been around enough women to recognize eager interest when it stood pent up before him. She was curvier, prettier, and more polite than Emily Walcott, who stood by the door, feigning indifference. He extended his hand and, when Miss Fields's was in it, gave her face the lingering attention such beauty deserved, and her fingers enough pressure to suggest reciprocal interest.

"I must confess," Tarsy admitted, "I asked Mr. Walcott to introduce us."

Jeffcoat laughed and held her hand longer than strictly polite. "I'm glad you did. I believe we passed each other in front of the hotel yesterday, didn't we? You were wearing a peach-colored dress."

Tarsy's pleasure doubled. She touched her collarbone and opened her lips in the beguiling way she often practiced in the mirror.

Jeffcoat smiled down into her stunning brown eyes with stunners of his own and refrained from allowing them to pass lower. But he was fully aware of her flattering rose frock and how it endowed each of her estimable assets.

"And you, I believe, were wearing a shirt without sleeves."

He laughed with a flash of straight, white teeth. "I find it's cooler that way."

In the silence that followed, while they allowed their eyes to tarry and tally, Jeffcoat recognized her for exactly what she was: a flirt looking for a husband. Well, he was willing to oblige with the flirting. But when it came to matrimony, he was admittedly aisle-shy, and with good reason.

"I hear you're a liveryman, Mr. Jeffcoat," Tarsy ventured.

"Yes, I am." His gaze drifted to Walcott, still at Tarsy's elbow, and on to Emily. He caught her watching, but immediately she snapped her attention away.

"And a blacksmith," Edwin added.

"My goodness, a blacksmith, too. How enterprising of you. But you must promise not to interfere with Mr. Walcott's business." Tarsy took Edwin's arm and smiled up at him, wrinkling her nose attractively. "After all, he was here first." Again she shifted her smile to the younger man. "My father is the local barber, so I'm sure you'll meet him soon. Until you do, I thought it only neighborly to extend a welcome on behalf of our family, and let you know that if there's anything we can do to help you get settled, we'd be delighted."

"That's most gracious of you."

"You must stop by the barbershop and introduce yourself. Papa knows everything about this town. Anything you need to know, just ask him."

"I'll do that."

"Well, I'm sure we'll meet again soon." She extended her gloved hand.

"I hope so," he said charmingly, accepting it with another lingering squeeze.

She sent him a parting smile warm enough to sprout daisies in the dead of winter and he responded with a flirtatious grin while speaking to Edwin.

"Thank you for stopping me, Edwin. You've definitely made it a memorable morning."

As they parted, Jeffcoat again found Emily Walcott watching. Perversely, he gave her a nod and tipped his hat. She offered not so much as a blink, but stared at him as if he were made of window glass. She was wearing a dress this morning, but nothing so pretty or colorful as Tarsy Fields's; a hat, too—a flat little specimen nearly as unattractive as the boy's wool cap had been. She had hair as black as his own, but it was hitched up into some sort of utilitarian twist that said very clearly she hadn't time for female fussing. She was long-waisted, slim, and, as always, sour-faced.

To Jeffcoat's surprise, she suddenly smiled. Not at him but at Charles Bliss, who stepped out of Coffeen Hall and took her hand—not her elbow, her hand—winning a full-fledged smile that Jeffcoat would have sworn her incapable of giving. Even a stranger could see it was unpracticed, unaffected. No batting lashes, no syrupy posturing such as Tarsy Fields put on. Jeffcoat observed the interchange with interest.

"We can go now," he heard Bliss say, turning Emily in his direction. "I'm sorry it took so long."

"I didn't mind waiting, and anyway, Papa was busy visiting. Oh, I'm so glad it's sunny, Charles, aren't you?"

"I ordered it for you," he said, and they laughed as they headed for the street.

"Good morning, Tom," Charles greeted, in passing.

"Hello, Charles. Miss Walcott."

She nodded silently and her eyes turned glacial. They moved past and Charles called back, raising a hand, "See you tomorrow morning, bright and early."

"Yessir, bright and early," replied Jeffcoat. He overheard Charles ask Emily, "What time should I pick you up?"

And her reply, "Give me an hour and a half so I can . . ."

Their voices faded and Jeffcoat heard no more. Looking after them as they moved away with their heads close together, he thought wryly, well, well, so the tomboy has a beau.

The tomboy had more than a beau. Charles Bliss was a devoted servant who would have done anything for her. He had first fallen in love with her when they were ten and thirteen years old but had waited to declare it until she was sixteen and had brought him the news that her family was moving to Wyoming.

"If you're going, I'm going," Charles had declared unequivocally.

"But, Charles—"

"Because I'm going to marry you when you're old enough."

"M—marry me?"

"Of course. Didn't you know that?"

Maybe she always had, for she'd stared at him, then laughed, and they'd hugged for the first time and she'd told him how very, very happy she was that he was coming. And she had remained happy, until earlier this year when she'd turned eighteen and he'd proposed seriously for the first time. He'd asked her twice since, and she was becoming guilt-ridden from refusing so often. Yet Charles had become a habit that was hard to break.

When he came at noon to pick her up for their picnic she found herself more than anxious to get away with him. He gave a sharp, shrill whistle of announcement as he jogged across the front yard, and slammed inside without knocking. "Hey, Emily, you ready? Oh, hello, everybody!"

Edwin and Frankie were both in the kitchen. Frankie ducked a mock punch, then collared Charles from behind. Charles bent forward with the boy on his back, and spun around twice before dumping his burden off.

"Where you two going?" Frankie wanted to know, hanging on to Charles's arms.

"That'd be telling."

"Can I go?"

"Nope, not this time." Charles made a fist and pressed it dead center on Frankie's forehead, fending him off affectionately. "We're taking the shay for two."

"Aww, gee ... come on, Charles."

"Nope. This time it's just Emily and me."

Edwin inquired, "Is everything all right at the stable?"

"Yup. I left the back door open. Nobody's around." Charles rambled in and out of their livery stable as he did in and out of their house, and, naturally, any time he had need of a rig there was no thought of charging him. "How's Mrs. Walcott doing today?"

"A little tired, I'm afraid, and somewhat forlorn. She misses going to church with us."

"Tell her Emily and I will bring her some wildflowers if we find any. Are you ready, Emily?"

Emily removed an apron and hung it behind the pantry door. "Are you sure there's nothing I can bring?"

"It's supposed to be your day off. Just turn your cuffs down and follow me. I've got everything in the rig."

It was a perfect day for an outing—clear, warm, and windless. The Big Horns appeared as multiple tiers of blue rising to greet the sky along a clear, undulating horizon line. They headed southwest into the foothills, toward Red Grade Springs, following Little Goose Creek until they left the valley to begin climbing. Ahead, the jagged top of Black Tooth Mountain appeared and disappeared as they paralleled draws and rounded the bases of rolling green hills. They startled a herd of white-rumped antelopes and watched them spring away across a green rise. They disturbed a jackrabbit who bounded off on oversized feet to disappear into a clump of sage. They reached the vast forests where the pinery crews had cleared great open tracts and cut skidding roads. The smell was spicy, the road quiet with its bed of needles. At Hurlburn Creek they forded, rounded a curve, and broke into the open above an uplands meadow where the creek looped around nearly upon itself. In the center of the loop, Charles brought the team to a halt.

The sylvan spot, so perfect, so peaceful, brought Emily immediately to her feet. She stood in the buggy, shaded her eyes, and gazed about in rapture.

"Oh, Charles, however did you find it?"

"I was up here last week buying lumber."

"Oh, it's beautiful."

"It's called Curlew Hill."

"Curlew Hill," she repeated, then fell silent to appreciate the scene before her.

The creek rushed out of the mountains, purling over rocks that shone like silver coins, smoothed by years of liquid motion. The water made a tight horseshoe bend enclosing a field of thick bluegrass that gave way to tufts of feathery sheep fescue nearer the water. In certain places the creek was outlined by balsam poplars, their new olive-yellow leaves filling the air with a sweet resinous scent. Huddling beneath them were thickets of wild gooseberry and hawthorn blooming in clusters of pink. In the distance a dense patch of golden banner spread across the meadow in a mass of yellow, following summer up to the tree line.

"Oh, look." Emily pointed. "Yellow peas." She called the wildflowers by their common name. "After we've eaten we must walk out and pick some. They're Mother's favorites."

Charles dropped off the wagon into grass a foot high, and Emily followed. From the storage box beneath the seat he drew a hamper and blanket, which, when spread, remained aloft on the sturdy green stems of grass. On hands and knees they flattened it, laughing, then settled cross-legged in their warm nest. Charles opened the hamper, displaying each item with a flourish. "Smoked sausage! Cheese! Rye bread! Pickled beets! Tinned peaches! And iced tea!" He set the fruit jar down and admitted, "It's not fried chicken and apple pie, but we bachelors eat pretty simple."

"It's a feast when you don't have to cook it."

They ate the plain food while a tattler called in tinkling notes from its hidden spot at the stream's edge, and overhead a sparrow hawk hunted, drifting on an updraft, cocking his head at them. Nearby an electric-blue bottlefly buzzed. The sun was beatific, captured in their bowl like warm yellow tea in a cup.

Their stomachs filled, Emily and Charles grew heavy with thought.

"Charles?"

There were things Emily needed to talk about, painful things that somehow seemed approachable out here where the sun and grass and flowers and birdsong made the formidable seem less dire.

"Hmm?"

For moments she was silent, toying with two breadcrumbs caught in a fold of her skirt. She lifted her eyes to the distant yellow flowers and told him quietly, "My mother is going to die."

Charles changed his mind about the bite of bread he'd been about to take and laid it aside. "I guessed as much."

"Nobody's ever said it in so many words, but we all know. She's already begun coughing blood."

He reached across the picnic hamper and took her hand. "I'm sorry, Emily."

"It . . . it felt good to say it at last." To no one but Charles would she have been able. With no one but Charles would she have allowed her tears to show.

"Yes, I know."

"Poor Papa." She turned her hand over and twined her fingers with Charles's because he understood her devastation as no one else. Again she lifted her eyes to his. "I think it's hardest on Papa. I've seen him crying on the porch at night when he thinks everybody else is asleep."

"Oh, Emily." Charles squeezed her hand tighter.

Suddenly she forced a bright expression. "But guess what?"

"What?"

"We're going to have a houseguest."

"Who?" Charles released her hand and laid his plate in the hamper.

"Mother's cousin Fannie, whom she hasn't seen since the year she and Papa got married. She was due in today. Papa is probably picking her up at the stage depot right now."

"Fannie of the outrageous letters?"

Emily laughed. "The same. I'm curious to meet her. She's always seemed so worldly, so . . . so unfettered by convention. Papa says she certainly is—he knows her, too, of course, since they all grew up in Massachusetts. After all these years of outlandish letters I'm not sure what to expect. But she's coming to take care of Mother."

"Good. That'll take the pressure off you."

"Charles, can I tell you something?"

"Anything."

She pleated and repleated the fabric of her skirt as if reluctant to divulge her thought. "Sometimes I feel guilty because I tried very hard to take over Mother's chores, but I . . . well, I don't care much for cooking and cleaning. I'd much rather be with the horses." She abandoned the pleating and turned sharply away from Charles, displeased with herself. "Oh, that sounds so self-indulgent, and I don't want to be that way. Really, I don't."

"Emily." He took her shoulders and pivoted her around to face him. "You'll like housework better when the house is your own."

She stared into his familiar eyes and answered frankly, "I doubt it, Charles."

Disappointment touched his face, then he swallowed and asked in a pained voice, "Why do you fight it so? How many more times will I have to ask?"

"Oh, Charles . . ." She shrugged free of his touch and placed her plate in the hamper.

"No, don't avoid the issue again." He set the hamper aside and moved closer to her, face to face, hip to hip. "I want to marry you, Emily."

"You want to marry a woman who's just admitted she hates housework?" She forced a chuckle, unable to meet his gaze. "What kind of wife would I make?"

"You're the only one I've ever wanted." He took her by both arms. "The only one," he repeated softly.

At his words her eyes lifted. "I know, Charles, but with Mother ill I don't think—"

"You've just said Fannie is coming to take care of her, so why must we wait? Emily, I love you so . . ." His caresses became more insistent. "I rattle around in that great big house of mine wishing you were in it with me. I built it for you, don't you know that?"

She did know, and it added to her sense of obligation.

"I want you in it . . . and our children," he pleaded in a low, throaty voice, transferring his hands to her shoulders, rubbing his thumbs over her collarbones.

"Our children?" she repeated, feeling a shaft of panic at the thought. Taking care of a stableful of horses she could handle, but she felt totally unprepared for motherhood. Another thought came and a blush warmed her chest and rose to her cheeks. She tried to imagine herself begetting children with Charles but could not. He was too much like a brother for it to be seemly.

"I want children, Emily, don't you?"

"Right now I want a certificate of veterinarian medicine much more than I want children."

"All right—a year, two years. How long will it take you to get it? We'll wait to get married until you've finished your course. But in the meantime, we'll announce that we're betrothed. Please say yes, Emily." As he lowered his face toward hers he repeated in a whisper, "Please . . ." Their mouths touched as he drew her close, raised one knee, and lay her in the crook of his lap. She felt her breast flatten against his chest, and his arms slip to her back. His hands spread upon it and began moving. His elbow brushed the side of her breast and sent a spear of reaction to its tip. Goose bumps shivered up her nape, which he circled with his fingers. She rested a palm on his breast and felt his heart ramming against it, and wondered—if she waited long enough, would the same thing happen to her own?

Then Charles did the most unexpected thing. He opened his lips and touched her with his tongue, holding absolutely still everywhere else, waiting for her reaction. The warm wet contact sent a jolt of fire to her extremities. He rode his tongue along the seam of her lips, wetting them as if to dissolve some invisible stitches holding them sealed. She forgot about the prickliness of his mustache as he touched her teeth, drew wider circles, inscribing upon her a message that seemed shocking. Yet her virgin body hearkened to it. Curiously, timidly, her tongue reached out to touch him, too. She felt the difference in him immediately. He shuddered, and expelled a great gust of breath against her cheek, and held her hard against him while their tongues tasted each other for the first time and increased their ardor in a great, grand rush.

This, then, was the forbidden, the reason for all the veiled warnings, a thing only husbands and wives were supposed to do. His head began moving, his mouth opened wider, and his hands caressed her waist, her spine. She allowed it, partook, because it was the first time and she had not expected such an immediate response. Phrases from the Bible crossed her mind—sins of the flesh, lust—now she understood. His hand began moving toward her breast and she quickly drew back.

"No, Charles . . . stop."

His eyes glittered, his cheeks blazed; a lock of hair had fallen on his forehead.

"I love you, Emily," he uttered through strident breaths.

"But this is forbidden. We must not do it till we're married."

Surprise wiped his face clean of passion and replaced it with elation. "Then you'll do it? Oh, Emily, you really mean it?" He embraced her fiercely, rocked and hugged her till the breath whooshed from her lungs. "You've made me the happiest man on earth!" He was ecstatic. "And I'll make you the happiest woman."

So she had agreed. Or had she? Perhaps it had been an intentional slip of the tongue, a way to agree without having to agree. Whatever her intention, wrapped in Charles's arms Emily knew there was no reneging. How could she say to this glad man, No, Charles, I didn't mean it that way? And must she not love him to have allowed such a kiss, and to have experienced such a forbidden thrill? And wasn't it almost predestined that she marry him? And to whom else in the world could she talk as she could to Charles? And with whom could she trust her tears? If that wasn't love, what was?

But rocking in his arms she opened her eyes to a blue sky and a hawk still circling and felt again a ricochet of panic. *What am I doing, hawk?* She squeezed her eyes closed and willed away her apprehension. *Oh, don't be silly, who else would you ever marry but Charles?*

He kissed her once more, jubilant, then cupped her face and looked into her eyes with adoration so palpable she felt small for her misgivings.

"I love you so much, Emily, so very, very much."

What else could she say? "I love you too, Charles." And it was true, she told herself, *it was!*

He placed a light, reverent kiss on her lips, then rested his fingertips on her jaws and looked into her eyes. "I've dreamed of this day for years. I've been dead certain for so long. I even told your father when I was thirteen that I wanted to marry you some day; did he ever tell you that?"

"No." She laughed, but it felt forced.

"Well, I did." He, too, chuckled at the memory, then his face took on a satisfied expression. "Your mother and father are going to be so pleased."

That much she knew indubitably and it was a great reassurance. "Yes, they will."

"Let's go home and tell them."

"All right."

They packed up their picnic gear and made a quick trip across the meadow for golden banner before heading home. Charles chattered all the way, already making plans. Emily held the flowers and replied to his exuberant questions. But long before they reached town she realized she'd been squeezing the flower stems so tightly they'd wilted and stained her palm green.

Chapter 4

Fannie Cooper was due to arrive on the 3:00 P.M. stage from Buffalo, thirty miles to the south. Emily had promised to be back by three but at ten minutes before the hour she hadn't returned. Frankie was gone fishing and Edwin tried his best to appear unruffled as he fetched a clean bed jacket for Josie and helped her rebraid her hair.

"You'd better go, Edwin," Josie said.

He pulled his watch from his vest pocket, needlessly flipped open the cover—he already knew the exact time—and agreed, "Yes, I'd better. When those children get back here they're going to get a good talking-to."

"Now, Edwin, you know Fannie isn't one to s . . . stand on formalities. She would rather have them off enjoying themselves than pay . . . paying duty calls on their o . . . old-maid cousin."

He pocketed the watch, patted Josie's shoulder, and asked, "You're sure you'll be all right?"

"Yes. Just help me into b . . . bed, then you must hur . . . hurry."

It had been months since he'd seen Josie this excited about anything. It robbed her of breath. Leaning over her, Edwin smiled as he lifted the coverlets to her hips. "If the stage is on time I should have her back here in twenty minutes. Now you rest so you'll have plenty of strength to visit with her."

She nodded, settling back on the pillows stiffly as if to keep her hair undisturbed. He smiled into her eyes and squeezed her hand before turning to leave.

"Edwin?" She spoke anxiously.

"Yes, dear?"

When he turned, she was reaching out a hand. He put his in it and received a squeeze. "I'm so happy Fan . . . nie is coming."

He bent and touched his lips to her fingers. "So am I."

Once free of the room he paused at the top of the steps, took a deep breath, and, with eyes closed, pressed both palms against his diaphragm. *So am I.* Did he mean it? Yes. Lord help him, yes. He took the steps at a jog, like a twenty-year old.

Downstairs he sidetracked into the dining room, where the mahogany sideboard contained the only mirror on the main floor. It was built in at rib height, separating the upper glass from the lower dresser. He ducked down to check his appearance in the beveled glass. His cheeks were flushed, his eyes too bright, his breath fast and shallow. Damn, had Josie noticed? This was insanity, trying to fool her. Why, Fannie wasn't even here yet and his hands were shaking as if with chills. Abruptly he made two tight fists, but it helped little, so he pressed their butts against the sharp dresser edge and locked his elbows, feeling his heart sledge until it seemed it would rattle the dishes above his head.

His intentions had been good: to have the children with him when he went to collect Fannie, to avoid at all costs their being alone. But it hadn't worked out that way. *Emily, I was relying on you! Where the devil are you? You promised you'd be back by now!*

Only his thumping heart answered.

He checked his reflection once more, happy it was Sunday, and that he'd been able to leave on his worsted suit after church and hadn't had to worry about how it would look if he changed clothes in the middle of a work day. He reworked his black four-in-hand tie, tugged at his lapels, and ran a hand over the graying hair at his temples. *Will she be gray, too? Will I look old to her? Are her hands shaking like mine and her heart pounding as she rides toward me? When our eyes meet for the first time will we see breathlessness and blushes in each other, or will we be lucky and see nothing?*

What do you think, Edwin, when your hands are already sweating and your heart is galloping like the leader of a stampede?

He dried his palms on his jacket tails, then spread them wide, studying their backs and their palms. Great, wide, callused hams that had been a young man's hands—soft and narrow and unmarked—when they'd first held Fannie. Hands with three chipped nails, ingrained dirt, and scars meted out by years of hard work; two crooked fingers on the left upon which a horse had stepped; a scar on the back of the right from a run-in with barbed wire; and the ever-present rim of black beneath his nails that he was unable to clear, no matter how hard he scrubbed. He hurried to the kitchen, pumped a basinful of water, and scrubbed them again, but to no avail. All he had done was make himself late for the stage.

Grabbing his black bowler off the hat-tree in the parlor he took the porch steps at a trot. Within half a block he was winded and had to slow down lest he arrive at the stage depot panting.

The Rock Creek Stage—better known as the Jurkey—pulled in at the hotel at the same time as Edwin. It stopped amid a billow of dust, the clatter of sixteen hooves, and the roaring of Jake McGiver, an ex-bullwhacker who'd miraculously made it through the Indian Wars and last year's blizzards with neither arrow wound nor frostbite. "Whoa, you sons-o'-bitches," Jack bawled, hauling back on the reins, "before I make saddlebags out o' your mangy, flea-bit hides! Whoa, I said!"

And before the dust had settled, Fannie was peering up at McGiver from an open window, laughing, holding onto her mile-high hat. "Such language, Mr. McGiver! And such driving! Are you sure my bicycle is still on board?"

"Indeed it is, ma'am. Safe and sound!"

McGiver clambered onto the roof to begin untying both the bicycle and the baggage while Fannie opened the door.

Edwin hurried forward and was waiting when she bent to negotiate the small opening.

"Hello, Fannie."

She looked up and her mirthful face sobered. He thought he saw her breath catch, but immediately she brought back the wide smile and stepped down. "Edwin. My dear Edwin, you're really here."

He took her gloved hand and helped her down to find himself heartily hugged in the middle of Main Street. "How good it is to see you," she said at his ear, quickly backing away and studying him while continuing to squeeze both his hands. "My, you look wonderful. I worried that you might have gotten fat or bald, but you look superb."

So did she. Smiling, as he always pictured her, her hair faded from its earlier vibrant red to a soft peach color but still with its unruly natural curl that looked as if it were put in with tongs. It was—he knew—part of her own natural sizzle. Her hazel eyes had crow's-feet at the corners but more merriment and sparkle than a gypsy dance. She had retained the tiny waist of her teen years but her breast was fuller. The spare cut of her copper-colored traveling suit pointed out the fact, and Edwin felt a swell of pride that neither had she gotten fat nor lost her teeth or her inimitable spirit.

"I've wondered about you, too, but you're just as I remember you. Ahh, Fannie, what has it been? Twenty years?"

"Twenty-two." He knew as well as she but had intentionally miscalculated for the benefit of those looking on. When he would have pulled free she held him anchored with a two-handed grip, as if she had no notion it was as improper as the hug had been. "Imagine that, Edwin, we're middle-aged."

He chuckled and released himself under the pretext of having to close the stage door. "Middle-aged and riding bicycles, are we?"

"Bicycle—oh, my goodness, that's right!" She swung around and looked up, shading her eyes with one hand. "Be careful with that, Mr. McGiver! It's probably the only one for three hundred miles around."

McGiver's head appeared above their heads. "Here it comes, all in one piece!"

She reached up as if to take it herself, asking no help from Edwin.

He suddenly jumped. "Here, let me!"

"I've lived without a man's help for forty years. I'm perfectly capable."

"I'm sure you are, Fannie"—he had to move her bodily aside—"but I'll help just the same."

The contraption was passed into his hands and dropped to the ground with a thud. "Good Lord, Fannie, you can't mean to say you actually ride this thing. Why, it's heavier than a cannon!"

"Of course I ride it. And you will, too, as soon as I can teach you. You'll love it, Edwin. Keeps the legs firm and the blood healthy, and it's great for the lungs. There's nothing like it. I wonder if we could get Josie on it. Might do her wonders. Did I tell you about the trip to Gloucester?"

"Yes, in your last letter." Edwin found himself smiling already. She hadn't changed at all. Unpredictable and unconventional, and spirited as no other woman he'd ever known. He had grown so accustomed to Josie's weakness that Fannie's robust independence was startling. While he stood examining the bicycle she reached up as if to take the luggage Mr. McGiver was handing down.

Again Edwin had to interrupt. "*I'll* help Mr. McGiver with your luggage. You hold the bicycle!"

"All right, if you insist. But don't get bossy with me, Edwin, or we shan't get along at all. I'm not used to taking orders from men, you know."

As he reached up for the first dusty bag, he glanced over his shoulder to find her smirking like a leprechaun. The first bag was followed by a second, third, fourth and fifth. When her luggage sat in a circle at their feet he pushed back his bowler and, with his hands on his hips, scanned the collection of grips and trunks. "Good Lord, Fannie, all this?"

She arched one of her strawberry-blond eyebrows. "Why, of course, all that. A woman can't traipse out into the middle of no-man's-land with nothing more than the clothes on her back. Who knows *when* I'll get to a proper toggery again. And even if I did, I doubt that out here I could even *find* a pair of knickerbockers."

"Knickerbockers?"

"Kneepants. For riding the bicycle. Whatever would I do with all these bustles and petticoats in those wheels? Why, they'd get tangled in the spokes and I'd break every bone in my body. And I value my bones very highly, Edwin." She held out one arm and assessed it fondly. "They're still very serviceable bones. How are your bones, Edwin?"

He laughed and replied, "I can see Emily is going to love you. Let's get these off the street."

"Emily—I can't wait to meet her." While he transferred her baggage to the boardwalk, Fannie chattered. "What's she like? Is she dark like you? Did she get Josephine's seriousness? I hope not. Josie was always too serious for her own good. I told her so from the time we were ten years old. There's so much in life about which we *must* be serious that I simply cannot abide being so when it's not necessary, don't you agree, Edwin? Tell me about Emily."

"I can't do Emily justice with words. You'll just have to meet her. I'm sorry she's not here. Both of the children assured me they would be, but Frankie is gone fishing and must have lost track of time, which he does quite frequently, and Emily went off on a picnic with Charles. They're not back yet."

"Charles Bliss?"

"Yes."

"Ah, the young man in her life. I feel as if I've met them both, I've heard so much about them in Josephine's letters. Do you think they'll be married, Edwin?"

"I don't know. If so, they haven't told us yet."

"Do you like him as much as Josie claims you do?"

"The whole family likes him. You will, too."

"I'll reserve my opinions till I've met him, if you please. I'm not a woman whose judgments can be dictated."

"Of course," Edwin replied with a crooked smirk. Her quicksilver spunkiness was only one of the attributes to which his parents had objected years ago. Thank heaven she hadn't lost it. She could scold and praise in the same breath, inquire and preach, sympathize and rejoice without breaking rhythm. Life with her would have been a ride on an eccentric wheel instead of a walk on a treadmill.

"I'm afraid I wasn't expecting you to have so much baggage. If you'll wait here I'll go over to the livery and get a wagon for it. It'll only take me—"

"I wouldn't dream of waiting here. I'll come along. You can give me a tour of your place."

He threw a cautious glance along the street, but it was Sunday, people were at home resting. The only ones about seemed to be the stage driver and a pair of cowboys lounging on the hotel step. He reminded himself Fannie was a relative. It was only his own apprehensions leading him to believe people would peek through their lace curtains and raise eyebrows.

"All right. It's only three blocks. Can you make it in those?" He gestured toward her shoes, which sported two-inch heels shaped like rope cleats.

She pulled up her skirt, revealing that her shoe tops were made of golden-brown silk vesting, which shimmered in the sun. "Of course I can make it. What a silly question, Edwin. Which way?" Her skirts fell and she captured his arm, striding in a strong, long step that made her skirts sound like flapping sails. He was struck anew by her vitality and lack of guile. Obviously, she was a woman to whom conventionalities came second to naturalness. Everything she did seemed natural, from her strong, loud laugh to her almost masculine stride to her unaffected hold on his arm. She seemed unaware that the side of her breast brushed his sleeve as they moved along Main Street toward Grinnell.

"How was your trip?"

"Ach! Ghastly!" she shot back, and while she amused him with tales of jarred bones and Jake McGiver's ribald language Edwin nearly managed to forget about the proximity of her breast.

They rounded the corner and approached the livery barn. The town seemed as sleepy as the horses who stood on three feet to the west of the building. Edwin rolled back the broad front doors, which hung on a steel track. He opened them to their limits so that anyone passing could freely look inside and see that the only thing happening was an innocent tour of the facilities.

Inside all was quiet, different on Sunday when little commerce was about. A slice of sun fell across the dirt floor, but inside it was cool, shadowed, redolent of horses and hay. Fannie walked ahead, straight up the aisle between the stalls, looking left and right while Edwin stayed in the sun shaft and watched her. When she reached the far end she took it upon herself to roll open one of the north doors three feet and look out back. He watched her silhouette, stark black against the bright rectangle as she leaned over and poked her head out, looking up at the doorsill, then turned. She bracketed her mouth with both hands. When she called, her voice sounded distant and resonant through the giant barn.

"Edwiiiiiiiiiiiiin!"—as if she were atop an Alp.

He smiled, cupped his mouth, and returned, "Fannieeeeeee?"

"You have a great place heeeeere!"

"Thank youuuuuuuuu!"

"Where did you get all these buggieeeees?"

"In Rockforrrrrrrrrd."

"Where's thaaaaaaat?"

"West of Cheyeeeeeeene."

"Are you riiiiiiiich?"

Edwin dropped his hands and burst out laughing. *Fannie, darling Fannie, I will play hell resisting you.* He slowly walked the length of the barn and stopped before her, studying her for a long moment before answering quietly, "I've done all right. I've built Josie a fine house with two stories and plenty of windows."

Fannie sobered. "How is she, Edwin? How is she, really?"

For the first time their eyes met with all pretense stripped away and he saw that she cared deeply, still, not only about him but about her cousin.

"She's dying, Fannie."

Fannie moved to him so swiftly he had no chance to evade her. "Oh, Edwin, I'm so sorry." She captured his two hands, folded them between her own, and rested her lips against the tips of his longest fingers. For moments she stood just so, absorbing the truth. Drawing back, she gazed into his eyes with a determination so palpable he could not look away. "I promise you I'll do everything in my power to make it easier on both of you. As long as it takes ... whatever it takes ... do you understand?"

He could not answer, for his heart seemed to have expanded and filled his throat, where it clamored at her touch. She was near enough that he could smell the dust in her clothing, the scent of her hair, of her skin; could feel her breath upon their aligned hands while a sunprick of light touched her somber hazel eyes.

"Because I have never stopped loving either one of you," she added, and stepped back so abruptly he was left with his hands folded in midair. "Now show me your stable quickly so I can go see my cousin."

He did so in a tangle of emotions, her words shimmering along his nerve endings. Whatever it takes . . . do you understand? He feared that he did understand, but in the next instant her mercurial mood change made him wonder if he was right. As he showed her the office, which he had neatened for her arrival, and the stalls, which he'd cleaned, and the stock, which he'd curried, she was as breezy as she'd been while calling messages across the barn; as if her quieter, startling words had never been spoken. When the brief tour ended she stood motionless, watching him hitch a horse to a wagon. She did not try to disguise her keen study of him under any pretense of studying the interior of the barn but stood arrow straight with her hands pressed down along her skirts. Not so much as a muscle moved, save those with which she breathed. He moved about, completing his chore, avoiding her glance, feeling as he thought a piece of fruit must feel as it ripens on a tree—warm inside, pressing out, out against its own skin, expanding. She might have been the sun, ripening him.

It was her way. She was an observer, a listener, an imbiber. When they were young she had hauled him by the hand into her mother's side yard one night and said, "Shh! Edwin, listen! I believe I can hear the apples growing." And after a moment: "They grow by starlight, instead of by sunlight, you know."

"Fannie, don't be silly," he'd said.

"I'm not silly. It's true. I'll show you tomorrow."

The next day she had cut an apple in half cross-wise and shown him the star inside, formed by the seeds. "See? Starlight," she'd chided, and made a believer of him.

Perhaps now she was cataloging the changes in him. Whatever her thoughts, he grew uneasy while her eyes followed him as he moved around Gunpowder, a pure black gelding, whom he was hitching to the buckboard.

"Do your children know?"

Neither of them had spoken for so long he'd lost the train of conversation. For one startled moment he thought she meant about them—did his children know about himself and Fannie, twenty-two years ago?

"The children?" He stood with the gelding between them, his hands on the animal's broad, curved back.

"Yes, do they know she's dying?"

He released his breath with superb control so she could not guess his thoughts. "I believe Emily has guessed. Frankie's too young to dwell on it much."

"I want one thing understood. There'll be no talk of death as long as I'm in your house. She's alive, and as long as she is we must do her the honor of enhancing that life in whatever ways possible."

Their eyes met over the horse's back, carrying another unspoken vow of honor. Nothing had changed for either of them, but this was as close as they must come to saying it. Still, they plucked from the afternoon this one ripe moment to look truly into each other's eyes, to accept the creases added to their skin by the years, the paleness of her hair, the brush of silver in his; and to pledge silently never to allow their naked feelings to show like this again.

"You have my word, Fannie," he said quietly.

The sound of an approaching wagon interrupted as Emily and Charles pulled into the open doorway.

Emily spoke before Charles drew the rig to a halt. "Oh, she's here!" Emily bounced down and went straight to Fannie. "Hello, Fannie, I'm Emily."

"Well, of course you are. I'd have picked you out in a crowd of strangers." The mercurial Fannie was capable of shifting moods as the situation demanded and chattered gaily, "Edwin, she's the spitting image of you with those blue eyes and black hair. But the mouth I think is Josie's." Holding Emily's hands, she added, "My goodness, child, you're lovely. You got the best of both parents, I'd say."

Emily had never considered herself lovely, by anybody's yardstick. The compliment went straight to her heart and brought a moment of self-consciousness as she searched for a graceful response.

"Unfortunately, I didn't get Mother's domestic skills, so the entire family is overjoyed to see you here."

They all laughed and Emily turned to her father. "I'm sorry we're late, Papa. We went a little farther than I expected."

"No harm done."

"Fannie, you haven't met Charles." He had drawn up beside them and stepped from the rig. "Charles, this is Mother's cousin, Fannie Cooper. This is Charles Bliss."

"Charles . . . quite as I pictured you." She took stock of his neatly trimmed beard and gray eyes.

"How do you do, Miss Cooper."

"Now that's the *last* time I want to be called 'Miss Cooper.' I'm Fannie. Just Fannie." They, too, exchanged handclasps. "You realize, of course, that I know at what age you learned to walk on stilts and what kind of a student you were and what an excellent carpenter you are."

Charles laughed, readily charmed. "From Mrs. Walcott's letters, of course."

"Of course. And speaking of which, I've written one of my own telling her when to expect me and I'm not there, am I?"

Edwin spoke up. "Fannie and I were just leaving to collect her baggage and go on up to the house. Will you be coming along?"

"As soon as we put Pinky up and check Sergeant's foot. How is it, Papa?"

His startled expression turned momentarily sheepish. "I haven't looked. I was . . . well, I was giving Fannie a tour."

"I'll do it. You two go on and we'll be right along."

When Edwin tried to help Fannie clamber onto the buckboard, she brushed his hand aside and declared, "I'm limber as a willow switch, Edwin. Just help yourself up."

Emily watched them leave with an admiring glow in her eyes. "Isn't she wonderful, Charles?"

"She is. I don't know what I expected but in spite of her letters I pictured her more like your mother."

"She's as different from Mother as snow is from rain."

It was true. Edwin felt it even more sharply than his daughter. When Fannie saw his house from the outside she tipped her head back to glimpse the roof peak where a web of wheel-shaped gingerbread trim highlighted the fish-scale siding. "Why, Edwin, it's beautiful. Charles built this?"

"Charles and I. With a little fetching and carrying from Frankie and a surprising amount of help from Emily."

"Absolutely beautiful. I never knew you were so talented." It was more than Josie had ever said, for she'd taken the house as her due, and any appreciation she might have felt was eclipsed by her relief in not having to live in a dreary hovel.

"I built the wraparound porch so Josie could sit outside and face the sun at any

time of day. And upstairs, there . . ." He pointed to the white-railed balcony contrasted against the black shingles. "A small veranda off our bedroom so she could
step outside anytime she wanted."

Fannie, who had never owned a house of her own, thought, lucky, lucky Josie.

Edwin took Fannie in past the front parlor. Though her eyes scanned the clutter,
she made no comment.

"Josie is upstairs." He motioned her ahead of him and watched her bustle
bounce and her long copper skirttail glide ahead of his boots as he followed with
two grips. "The first door on your left," he directed.

Inside, Josephine waited with excited eyes, her hands extended. "Fannie . . .
dear Fannie. You're here at last."

"Joey."

Fannie rushed to the bed and they hugged.

"That awful name. I haven't . . . heard it for twenty years." Josephine lost her
breath on a flurry of choked laughter.

"How your parents hated it when I called you that."

They parted and took stock of one another. Josephine said, "You look elegant."

Fannie retorted, "Dusty and battered from that Jurkey ride, more likely, but I
enjoyed Mr. McGiver immensely. And you look thin. Edwin said you've been
having a bad time of it." She laid a hand on her cousin's cheek. "Well, I'm going
to pamper you silly, just watch and see. UP to a point. I've actually learned how
to cook—imagine that. But I can*not* make pudding without scorching it, so don't
expect any. I'm fair at meat and vegetables, however, and devilishly good with
shellfish, but wherever will we get shellfish out here in the mountains? Then
there's bread . . . hmm . . ." Fanny gave her attention to tugging off her gloves. "I
fear my bread is rather glutinous, but edible. Just barely. I'm always in too much
of a rush to let it rise properly. You wouldn't happen to have a bakery in this
town, would you?"

"I'm afraid not."

"Well, no worry. I can make biscuits light as swansdown. I know that's hard to
believe after the way my mother threw her hands up in despair when she was trying to teach me my way around a kitchen." Fannie bounced off the bed and toured
the bedroom, glancing at the dark, handsome furniture, batting not a lash at the
spare cot. "Light as swansdown, I swear. Shall I bake you some for supper?"

"That would be wonderful."

"And when I put them before you, you'd better eat!" Fannie pointed at her
cousin's nose. "Because I've brought along my bicycle and I fully intend to get
you strong enough to ride on it."

"Your bicycle! But, Fannie, I can't ri . . . ride a bicycle."

"Why ever not?"

"Because . . ." Josephine spread her hands. "I'm a . . . a consumptive."

"Well, if *that* isn't the frailest excuse I've ever heard, I don't know what is! All
that means is that you've got weak lungs. You want to make them strong, you get
on that set of wheels and make them work harder. Have you ever seen a blacksmith with puny arms? I should say not. So what can be so different about lungs?
It'll be the best thing for you, to get out in the fresh mountain air and rebuild your
strength."

Looking on, Edwin thought there hadn't been so much merry chatter in this
bedroom since it had been built. Fannie's gaiety was infectious; already Josie's
face wore a dim hint of pink, her eyes were happy, her lips smiling. Perhaps he
tended to mollycoddle her and in doing so, encouraged her to feel worse.

The young people arrived; they'd picked up Frankie somewhere along the way and from below came his voice as he led the trio up the steps. "Hey, everybody, there's a bicycle downstairs!"

He burst into the bedroom, followed by Emily and Charles.

"It's mine," Fannie announced.

Edwin stopped his son's headlong charge into the room. "Frankie, I want you to meet your cousin Fannie. Fannie, this is our son Frank, who smells a little fishy right now, if my nose doesn't deceive me."

Fannie extended her hand nonetheless. "I'm pleased to meet you, Master Frank. How long would you guess your legs are?" She leaned back to take a visual measure. "They'd have to be—oh, say, a good twenty-four inches for you to ride the bicycle with any ease at all."

"Ride it? Me? Honest?"

"Honest." Fannie held up a palm as if taking an oath and charmed yet another member of the Walcott family.

Emily could not take her eyes off Fannie. She was a dazzling creature, the same age as Mother, yet years younger in action, temperament, and interest. Her voice was animated, her movements energetic. She had a contumacious look about her—that kinky apricot hair, perhaps, frizzing about her face like lantern-lit steam around a newborn colt—that made her seem untrammeled by the gravity that made most women dull and uninteresting. Her eyes constantly shone with interest and her hands never remained still when she talked. She was worldly: she rode bicycles and had traveled alone clear from Massachusetts, and had boated under sail to a place called Nantucket where she gigged for clams; and she had attended the opera, had seen Emma Abbott and Brignoli starring in *The Bohemian Girl,* and had had her fortune told by a palm reader named Cassandra. The list went on and on—tales from her letters that Emily had been absorbing ever since she was old enough to read. How incredible to think such a worldling was here, and would stay, would sleep in Emily's own bed where they could talk in the dark after the lanterns were extinguished. Already the house seemed transformed by her presence. Gaiety came with her, a carnival atmosphere that had been so badly needed. Mother, too, had fallen under Fannie's spell. She had forgotten her illness for the moment; it was plain on her face. And Papa stood back with his arms crossed, smiling, relieved at last of a portion of his worries. For bringing all this to the Walcott family within an hour of her arrival, Emily loved Fannie already.

Just then Papa boosted himself away from the chiffonier and said, "Speaking of bicycles, I'd best get Fannie's in the shed and bring her trunks up, too. Charles, perhaps you could give me a hand."

"Just a minute, sir . . ." Charles stopped Edwin with a hand on his arm.

"Sir?" Edwin's eyebrows elevated and amusement quirked his mouth. "Charles, since when do you call me *sir?*"

"It seemed appropriate today. I thought as long as we're all together, and Mrs. Walcott is feeling so well, and Fanny's just arrived and the mood is festive, I might as well add to it." He took Emily's hand and drew her against his side. "I want you all to know that I've asked Emily to be my wife and she's accepted . . . at last."

Myriad reactions broke through Emily: a sinking sense of finality now that the announcement was made, contraposed by gladness at the pleased look on her mother's and father's faces, and amusement at Frankie's reaction.

"Yippee! It's about time." Everyone in the room laughed and exchanged hugs. Josephine wiped a tear from her eye, and Papa clapped Charles on the arm and pumped his hand and gave him a solid thump on the back. Fannie kissed Charles's cheek and in the middle of it all someone knocked on the door downstairs.

"Emileee?" It was Tarsy, calling to be heard above the happy voices. "Can I come in?"

Emily went to the top of the stairs and shouted, "Come in, Tarsy, we're up here!"

Tarsy appeared below, excited, as usual. "Is she here?"

"Yes."

"I couldn't wait to meet her!" She started up the steps. "Are all those bags outside hers?"

"Every one. And she's exactly like her letters."

Another devotee fell under Fannie's spell the moment introductions were performed. "But, of course," said Fannie, "Emily's friend, the barber's daughter, the girl with the prettiest hair in town. I've already been told to expect to see a lot of you around here." She laid a touch on Tarsy's golden curls, and gave the proper amount of attention before turning the focus back toward the recent announcement. "But you haven't heard Emily and Charles's news, have you?"

"What?" Tarsy turned to her friend with a blank, receptive expression.

"Charles has asked me to marry him and I've accepted."

Tarsy reacted as she did to all excitement: giddily. She threw herself on Emily with nearly enough force to break bones, and went into raptures of *oohs* and gushes of felicitations; and overtook Charles next, kissing his cheek and exclaiming she knew they'd be *sooooo* happy and she was positively *green* with envy (which wasn't true, Emily knew); then threw her attention back to Fannie with amusing abruptness.

"Tell me all about your ride on the stagecoach."

Fannie told, and Tarsy stayed for supper, which turned out to be a picnic on Josephine's bed, at Fannie's insistence. She declared Joey was simply not to be left at the height of this celebration while the others went downstairs. They would bring the festivities to her.

So Papa and Fannie and Frankie sat on the big bed while Emily, Charles, and Tarsy took Papa's cot and balanced their plates on their knees. They all supped on creamed peas over Fannie's swansdown biscuits and Frankie's latest catch, fried to the texture of a bootheel, for which Fannie laughingly refused to apologize: "The biscuits are perfection itself. The rest I'll get better at in time." And afterward Emily announced they'd all draw straws to see who'd help with dishes. Frankie lost and his mouth grew sulky. Fannie scolded, "Better get used to it, lad, because I intend to draw straws every night and you'll have to expect to draw the short one occasionally. Now let's get going and leave your father and mother a little time to themselves."

Charles said he had an early day tomorrow and bid them good night, kissing Emily briefly on the mouth when she saw him out to the porch. But she was too impatient to linger long with Charles. Fannie was in the kitchen, and where Fannie was, Emily wanted to be.

The girls let Frankie off the hook and said they'd do dishes tonight because Tarsy was nowhere near ready to go home and leave Fannie's magical presence. Though Fannie had good intentions of doing a share of the cleanup work she somehow never got her hands wet. They were occupied instead gesturing and illustrating as she told enchanting tales of attending Tony Pastor's Vaudeville Emporium, where the dancers twirled umbrellas and sang "While Strolling through the Park One Day." She sang the song in a clear-pitched voice and performed a dance around the kitchen table, twirling the stove poker as if it were an umbrella, filling the girls' heads with vivid pictures.

Fannie seemed to recall that she was here to do dishes, wiped one, then forgot to wipe another as she launched into the intriguing account of her recently acquired passion for archery. She illustrated by stepping on one corner of the dish towel, stretching the diagonal corner high, and drawing back on it as if seating an arrow and taking aim. When the arrow hit its mark on the kitchen stovepipe she snapped the towel around her neck as if it were a fur collar and declared she had, to date, participated in three tournaments, the last of which won her a loving cup and a kiss on the hand from an Austrian prince. And as soon as she got back East, where more and more sidewalks were being laid, she intended to buy herself a pair of the astonishing things called roller skates and give them a try.

Fannie seemed amazed when she realized the dishes were all put away.

"Gracious, I didn't do a one!"

"We don't care," Tarsy said. "Tell us more."

They trailed upstairs where the stories continued as Fannie began unpacking a trunk, winning a series of near-swoons from Tarsy as she pulled out dress after dress, more glamorous than anything Sheridan had ever seen.

"The last time I wore this one, I swore I never would again." Fannie held up a dress with lace rosettes running diagonally from breast to hip. "We were playing parlor games and it gave me away."

"Parlor games?" Tarsy's eyes danced with interest.

"They're the rage back East."

"What kind?"

"Oh, many different kinds. There's whist and dominoes and hangman. And of course, the men-and-women kind."

"Men-and-women kind?"

Fanny laughed enchantingly and collapsed on the side of the bed with the dress heedlessly smashed onto her lap. "I'm afraid I shouldn't have brought them up. They can be quite naughty at times."

Tarsy bent forward, insisting, "Tell us!"

Fannie seemed to consider, then folded the dress with the rosettes and crossed her hands on it. "Very well, but it wouldn't be a good idea if your parents found out about them, particularly Joey. She never approved of levity, and most certainly not this sort!"

Agog, Tarsy wiggled closer. "We won't tell, will we, Emily? What kind of games?"

"Well, there's Poor Pussy and Musical Potatoes, for laughs, and Alice, Where Art Thou, in which the suspense gets hairsplitting. And then when the night gets older and everyone is feeling . . . well, freer, shall we say, there's the Blind Postman, and French Blind Man's Buff. That's the one we were playing the night this dress gave me away."

Fannie gave a provocative sideward glance and a mincing grin. Tarsy fell forward in a melodramatic show of impatience. "But what were you *doing?*"

"Well, you see, one player is blinded—he has a scarf tied over his eyes, naturally—*but* . . ." Fannie paused effectively. "His hands are tied behind his back."

Tarsy gasped and waved her hands beside her cheeks as if she'd just taken a bite of something too hot. Emily barely kept her eyes from rolling.

Fannie went on: "The others position themselves around the room and the blind man is only permitted to walk backwards. The others tease and buff him by pulling at his clothes or tickling his face with a feather. When he finally succeeds in seizing someone, the blind man has to guess who it is. If he guesses right, the prisoner must pay a forfeit."

"What's a forfeit?"

"Oh, forfeits are the most fun."

"But what *are* they?"

"Whatever the blind man decides. Sometimes the prisoner must become the blind man, sometimes if everyone's in a silly mood he must imitate an animal, and sometimes . . . if it's one of the opposite sex, she must pay a kiss."

Emily found herself startled by the very idea. Kissing was an intimate thing; she could not imagine doing it in a parlor with a roomful of people looking on. But Tarsy flung herself backwards and groaned ecstatically, fantasizing. She gazed at the ceiling, one foot dangling over the edge of the mattress. "I'd give anything to go to a party like that. We *never* have parties. It's dull as liver around here."

"We could have one—not that kind, of course. It wouldn't be proper. But it certainly seems that Emily's betrothal deserves a formal announcement. We could invite all your young friends, and certainly Edwin and Joey will want to ring out the news to *their* friends and business acquaintances. Why don't we plan one?"

Tarsy sprang up and grabbed Emily, nearly toppling her off the bed. "Of course, Emily! It's the perfect idea. I'll help. I'll come over and . . . and . . . well, anything at all. Say yes, Em . . . pleeeeease!"

"We could have it next Saturday night," Fannie suggested. "That would give you a full week to get the word out."

"Well . . . it . . . I . . ." The idea became suddenly exciting to Emily. She imagined how Papa would enjoy having people in the house again, and how proper it would be for both him and Charles to invite those with whom they did business. And Tarsy was right, this town was dull as liver, hadn't she just said as much to Charles? But suddenly Emily's expression became a warning signal and she pointed straight at Tarsy. "No kissing games though, do you understand?"

"Oh, perfectly," Tarsy agreed breezily. "Right, Fannie?"

"Oh, none!" Fannie seconded.

The two of them had only met today and Emily had heard every word they'd said to one another. Yet she couldn't shake the uneasy feeling that they were wordlessly conspiring.

Chapter 5

On Monday morning, Tom Jeffcoat awakened in his room at the Windsor Hotel and lay staring at the ceiling, thinking of Julia. Julia March, with her heart-shaped face and almond eyes, her caramel-blond hair and dainty hands. Julia March, who'd worn his betrothal brooch for more than half a year. Julia March, who had thrown him over for another.

His eyes slammed shut.

When would the memory stop stinging?

Not today. Certainly not today when it was only 5:30 A.M. and she was on his mind already.

It's done with. Get that through your head!

Throwing the covers back, he leapt from bed and skinned on his britches, letting the suspenders dangle at his sides. Snatching the white porcelain pitcher from the washstand, he stepped barefoot into the hall and helped himself to a generous slough of hot water from a covered tin container waiting on a trivet.

Hell, the Windsor wasn't so bad. It was clean, the food was decent, and the water hot when promised. Besides, he wouldn't be here long. He fully intended to have his own house up before the snow flew.

But what about then? Would it be any less lonely? Would he miss his family any less? Would he miss Julia any less?

Julia's practically on her way up the aisle. Put her from your mind.

But it was impossible. Being alone so much gave him plenty of time for thinking, and Julia filled his thoughts day and night. Even now as he washed from the waist up he studied himself in the mirror, wondering what it was that she'd found preferable about Hanson. The blond hair? The brown eyes? The beard? The money? Well, he wasn't blond, his eyes were blue, he didn't like beards, and he sure as hell wasn't rich. He was so *un*rich he'd had to borrow money from his grandmother to come here. But he'd pay her back and make something of himself in this town. He'd show Julia! He might even become rich as a lord, and when he was, he wouldn't share a penny of his money with any woman alive. Women! Who needed the mercenary, fickle bitches?

He poured hot water into his shaving mug, worked up a lather, and lifted the brush toward his face. But he paused uncertainly, running four fingertips over his scratchy jaw, wondering if he should let the beard grow. Was it true? Did women really like them? Why, even that mouthy Walcott tomboy preferred a man with a beard. But he'd tried one before and found it hot, dangerous around the forge, and prickly when the hair grew in a tight curve and got long enough to poke him in the underside of his chin. Resolutely he lathered and scraped his face clean, then observed his bare-chested reflection with a critical eye. *Too dark. Too much hair on the chest. The wrong color eyes. Eyelashes too short. The dent in the left cheek ridiculously lopsided without a matching one on the right.*

Suddenly he threw down the towel and released a disdainful snort.

Jeffcoat, what the hell are you doing? You never gave a damn before about how you measured up to other men.

But the fact remained: being spurned by a woman undermined a man's self-regard.

In the hotel dining room he ate an immense breakfast of steak and eggs, then headed toward Grinnell Street to get his wagon, dreading the idea of running into Emily Walcott in his present state of mind. If that damned little snot was there she'd better button her lip this time or he'd wrap that leather apron over her head and slip a horseshoe around her neck.

She wasn't. Edwin was. A likable man, Edwin Walcott, affable even at seven A.M.

"I hear you're meeting Charles this morning and going up to the Pinery after lumber."

"That's right."

Edwin smiled smugly. "Well, you'll be spending the day in the company of a happy man."

He offered no more, but minutes later when Jeffcoat pulled up before Charles's house, Bliss jogged out with a smile on his face. "Good morning!" he called.

"Morning," Tom replied.

"A wonderful morning!" exclaimed his companion.

It was, in fact, drearier than a Quaker wardrobe.

"You look happy."

"I am!" Charles bounded aboard.

"Any special reason?"

As the wagon began rolling Charles slapped both knees, then gripped them firmly. "The fact is, I'm getting married."

"Married!"

"Oh, not for a year or more, but she's finally said yes."

"Who?"

"Emily Walcott."

"Em—" Jeffcoat's eyes bugged out and his head jutted forward. "Emily Walcott!"

"That's right."

"You mean the Emily Walcott with the britches and the leather apron?"

"That's right."

Jeffcoat rolled his eyes and muttered, "Jesus."

"What does that mean . . . Jesus?"

"Well, I mean . . . she's . . ." Tom gestured vaguely.

"She's what?"

"She's a shrew!"

"'A shrew . . .'" Surprisingly, Charles laughed. "She's a little spunky, but she's no shrew. She's bright and she cares about people, she's a hard worker—"

"And she wears suspenders."

"Is that all you can think of, is what a girl wears?"

"You mean it doesn't matter to you?"

"Not at all."

Tom found that magnanimous. "You know, I like you, Bliss, but I still feel like I ought to offer condolences instead of congratulations."

Amiably, Charles replied. "And I'm damned if I know why I don't knock you off that wagon seat."

"I'm sorry, but that girl and I get along like a pair of cats in a sack."

The two assessed each other, realizing they'd been wholly honest in a way that friends—even friends of long standing—can rarely be. It felt good.

Suddenly they both laughed, then Tom angled his new friend a half grin and challenged, "All right, tell me about her. Try to change my mind."

Charles did so gladly. "In spite of what you think of her, Emily's a wonderful girl. Our families were friends back in Philadelphia, so I've known her all my life. I decided when I was thirteen that I wanted to marry her. Matter of fact, I told Edwin so then, but he wisely advised me to put off asking her for a while." They both chuckled. "I asked her the first time about a year ago, and it took four proposals to get her to say yes."

"Four!" Jeffcoat raised one eyebrow. "Maybe you should have stopped while you were ahead."

"And maybe I'll knock you off that wagon seat yet." Charles playfully tried to do so. He punched Tom soundly on the arm, rocking him sideways.

"Well, *four!* My God, man, I'd have gone where I was welcome long before that."

Charles turned serious again. "Emily had things she wanted to do first. She's taking a correspondence course in veterinary medicine but she ought to finish that sometime next summer."

"I know. Edwin told me. And I made the mistake of peeking at her papers the first time I walked into the livery office. As usual, she lit into me. If I remember right, *that time* she called me rude and nosy." His inflection made it clear the altercation was only one of many.

Charles had no sympathy. "Good for her. You probably deserved it."

They laughed again, then fell into companionable silence.

Odd, Jeffcoat thought, how you could meet some people and feel an instant aversion, meet others and feel like an empty spot inside you is about to be filled. That's how Bliss made him feel.

"Listen"—Charles interrupted Tom's thoughts—"I know Emily wasn't exactly cordial to you when you came into town, but—"

"Cordial? She ordered me out. She came over to my lot and stomped along beside the grader and called me names."

"I'm sorry, Tom, but she's got a lot on her mind. She's really devoted to her father, and she spends nearly as much time in the livery stable as he does. It's natural that she'd be defensive about it. But it isn't just the livery stable. Things around her house are pretty grim right now. You see, her mother is dying of consumption."

A faint thread of remorse spiraled through Jeffcoat. Consumption was incurable, and not pretty to watch, especially near the end. For the first time, Jeffcoat softened toward the tomboy. "I'm sorry," he said. "I didn't know."

"Of course you didn't. It's getting bad now. I have a feeling Mrs. Walcott is failing fast. It was another reason I wanted Emily to finally say yes to me. Because I think her mother will die a little more peacefully knowing Emily will be safely married to me."

"The Walcotts were happy about the news then?"

"Oh, yes, and Fannie, too. I haven't told you about Fannie." He explained about Mrs. Walcott's cousin having arrived from Massachusetts to help out the family. "Fannie is remarkable," he ended. "Wait till you meet her."

"I probably won't. Not as long as she lives in your fiancée's house."

"Oh, yes you will. Somehow we'll all be friends. I know we will."

They rode in thoughtful silence for some time before Tom inquired, "How old are you?"

"Twenty-one."

"Twenty-one!" Tom straightened and studied Bliss's profile. "Is that all?" He looked older; undoubtedly it was the beard. And he certainly acted older. "You know, in some ways I envy you. Only twenty-one and already you know what you want out of life. I mean, you left your family and came out here to settle. You have your trade, and a home, and you've picked out a woman." Tom ruminated momentarily, studying the tip of a mountain ridge shrouded in haze. "I'm twenty-six and mostly I know what I *don't* want."

"For instance?"

Tom dropped a sideward glance at Bliss. "Well, a woman for starters."

"Every man wants a woman."

"Maybe I should say a wife, then."

"You don't *want* to get married?" Charles sounded astonished.

A cynical expression settled on Tom's face as he spoke. "A year ago I became engaged to a woman, a woman I'd known for years. Next Saturday she's going to marry another man. You'll pardon me if I don't think too highly of the fairer sex right now."

Charles looked appropriately sympathetic and breathed, "Damn, that's tough."

In a hard voice Jeffcoat observed, "Women are fickle."

"Not all of them."

"You're besotted right now; naturally you'd say that."

"Well, Emily isn't."

"I thought the same about Julia." Jeffcoat gave a rueful chuckle, staring straight ahead. "I thought I had her signed, sealed, and delivered until she walked into the blacksmith shop one afternoon and announced that she was breaking our engagement to marry a banker named Jonas Hanson, a man fifteen years older than her."

"A banker?"

"You guessed it. Inherited money . . . lots of inherited money."

Charles digested the news, eyeing Tom covertly while Tom stared pensively at the horses' rumps. For a while neither of them spoke, then Tom sighed heavily and leaned back. "Well, I guess it was better that I found out beforehand."

"That's why you came here then? To get away from Julia?"

Tom glanced at Charles and forced a lazy grin. "I wasn't sure I wouldn't break into her bedroom one night and toss old moneybags onto the floor and jump into bed in his place."

Bliss laughed and scratched his bearded cheek, admitting, "To tell you the truth, I've spent some time lately thinking about bedrooms myself."

Surprised, Jeffcoat peered askance at his new friend. How could a man get spoony over a girl who dressed like a blacksmith, smelled like horses, and wanted to be a veterinarian? Curiosity prompted his next question.

"Does *she?*"

Bliss glanced at him calmly. "Does she what?"

"Think about bedrooms?"

"Unfortunately, no. Did your Julia?"

"Sometimes I think she was tempted but I never got beyond her corset stays."

"Emily doesn't wear a corset."

"I'm not surprised. Course, she wouldn't need one with that stiff leather apron."

They laughed together yet again, then rode for some minutes in silence. At length Tom commented, "If this isn't the damnedest conversation. I had friends back in Springfield I couldn't talk this easy with, friends I'd known for years."

"I know what you mean. I never talked about things like this with anyone. As a matter of fact, I'm not sure a gentleman should."

"Maybe not, but here we are, and I don't know about you, but I've always considered myself a gentleman."

"Me, too," Charles agreed.

They rode in silence for several minutes before Charles added dubiously, "But do you feel a little guilty for talking behind the girls' backs?"

"I probably would if I were still engaged to Julia. Do you?"

Charles studied the clouds and said, "Well, let's put it this way . . . I wouldn't want Emily to find out what I said. But on the other hand, it feels good to know other men go through the same thing when they're engaged."

"Don't worry. She'll never find out from me. If you want to know the truth, that woman of yours scares me a little. She's a regular hellcat and I don't want to tangle with her any more than I have to. But one thing's for sure—life should never be dull with a woman like that."

When they reached the Pinery, Charles introduced Tom as "my new friend, Tom Jeffcoat," and indeed it became true. Throughout the remainder of that day, and those that followed, while the two men worked side by side, the spontaneity between them began to grow into a strong bond of friendship.

Right from the first, Charles did all he could to smooth the way for Jeffcoat in the new town, amid new people. At the Pinery he joshed the owner, Andrew Stubbs, and his son, Mick, into giving Tom a more than fair price on his lumber. In town he took him personally into J. D. Loucks's store and introduced him to the locals while Tom bought nails. Together they began constructing the framework of Tom's livery barn, and when the skeleton walls and roof joists lay stretched out on the earth, Charles took a walk down Main Street and came back with nine hearty townsmen to help raise them. He brought Will Haberkorn, the local butcher, and his son, Patrick, both still wearing their stained white aprons. With the Haberkorns came Sherman Fields, Tarsy's father, a congenial and dapper man with center-parted hair and a waxed handlebar mustache. There were Pervis Berryman and his son, Jerome, who bought and sold hides, and made boots and trunks. Charles also brought the stocky Polish cabinetmaker, Joseph Zollinski, whom Tom recognized from church. J. D. Loucks came with the hotel owner, Helstrom, who said to his tenant, "You support me, I support you." And Edwin Walcott, in a true show of welcome, walked over from across the street. Charles introduced Tom to those he hadn't already met and arranged a fast, sincere welcome in the form of the wall-raising.

Loucks had brought new rope from his store, and within minutes after the group convened, muscles strained in the June sun. By the end of the day the skeleton of the building stood silhouetted against the evening sky.

"I don't know how to thank you," Tom told Charles when everyone else had gone and they were left together, gazing up at the sharp angles of the roof.

"Friends don't need thanks," Charles replied simply.

But Tom clapped his friend's shoulder just the same. "This friend does."

As they began picking up their tools Charles said, "Fannie insists on throwing an engagement party for Emily and me this Saturday night. It might be just what you need to forget about that wedding back East. Will you come?"

Tom considered declining, in deference to Miss Walcott. But nights got long and lonely, and he was anxious to socialize with the young people he'd met, many of whom would be his future customers. More importantly, it was Charles's party, too, and Charles was his friend. He *wanted* to go, whether it was to the tomboy's house, or not.

He put a wry twist on his lips and inquired, "Will Tarsy Fields be there?"

Charles shot him a man-to-man grin. "Oh, Tarsy, is it?"

Tom turned his attention to closing a nail keg for the night. "Sometimes a man gets a message from a girl the minute they meet. I think I got one from Tarsy."

"She's easy on the eye."

"I thought so."

"And entertaining."

"She seems to be."

"And empty-headed as that nail keg is going to be when we're done building this barn."

Jeffcoat laughed freely, slapped Bliss on the shoulder, and declared robustly, "Damn, but I like you, Bliss!"

"Enough to come on Saturday night?"

"Of course," Tom agreed, hoping he and Emily Walcott could remain civil to one another.

The following day Tom and Charles began enclosing the roof and sides of the livery barn, but the next day they gave to the church, which was in a similar stage of development. It was that, more than anything, which earned Tom Jeffcoat the full approval of the town's matrons. With a building of his own only half-done, they gossiped on the boardwalks, that young man gave his full day to help erect the new church. Now, *there* was an example for their young boys to follow!

One young boy took to following everything that was going on at the new lot on Grinnell Street. Frankie Walcott showed up the first morning, drawn by his idol Charles, only to find before day's end that he had *two* idols. They put him to work, and he worked willingly, carrying, measuring, even hammering. When they went to church to offer their day's labor, Frankie went along. When Frankie went along, so did his fat friend Earl Rausch. Earl had an unmanageable sweet tooth and spent much of his time filching doughnuts and cookies sent along with the workers by their wives. But Earl's idol was Frankie, and what Frankie did, Earl did. He brought the men drinks in the dipper and ran errands and straightened bent nails. When the town matrons learned that Frankie and Earl had volunteered their time to help at the church, they signed up their own sons to do likewise.

Frankie Walcott was having the time of his life. Things had never been so lively around Sheridan. All day long he could be with Charles and the new guy, Tom. He liked Tom. Tom grinned a lot, and teased, and his livery barn was *really* going to be something.

At suppertime he chattered constantly about the building going up on Grinnell Street.

"Tom brought windows clear from Rock Springs—twenty-four of 'em! And he's gonna put in a floor made of real bricks! He already ordered 'em down in Buffalo!"

Emily refused to glance up or to acknowledge Frankie's exuberance.

"But guess what else he brought? This ... this thing. This turntable, and he's gonna put it in the middle of the floor so it'll turn the wagons around and head 'em back out the door just as easy as *I* can turn around. He brought it clear from Springfield on the train and from Rock Springs to here on his wagon. Tom says back East all the roundhouses have turntables and he says they use 'em to turn the trains around."

"Why, that's the silliest thing I ever heard of!" spouted Emily, unable to hold her tongue any longer. "Back East where it's crowded they need turntables. Out here in the wide open spaces it's nothing but a waste."

"Well, I don't think so. I think he's smart to think of it, and Tom says as soon as it's in Earl and me can ride on it."

Emily jumped to her feet. "Tom says! Tom says!" She reached for two empty serving bowls and plucked them off the table. "Honestly, Frank, I get so tired of you talking about that man. Surely there are other things happening around this town besides that infernal building of his!"

Fannie's speculative gaze followed Emily as the younger woman whisked to the granite sink, clunked down the bowls, and began agitatedly pumping water. Fannie calmly rested her spoon in her sauce dish and remarked, "He sounds enterprising."

"He's rude and outspoken!" Emily exclaimed, pumping harder.

"He is not!" Frankie retorted. "He's just as nice as Charles, and Charles likes him, too. Ask him if he don't!"

"I'll ask nothing about him!" shot back Emily, glaring over her shoulder at her brother. "Not when he's competing with Papa!"

Fannie chose the moment to inform her niece, "Charles has invited him to your party tomorrow night."

Emily spun around so fast water sprayed from her fingertips. "He what!"

"He invited Mr. Jeffcoat to your betrothal party tomorrow night. And Mr. Jeffcoat accepted."

"Why didn't you tell me!"

Fannie ate a spoonful of applesauce and replied negligently. "Oh, I thought I did."

"I won't have him here!"

"Now, Emily—" put in Edwin.

"I won't, Papa! Not when he's down there at this very minute, building a . . . a *livery stable!*"

"But Charles has invited him, and it's Charles's party, too. The two of them seem to have become quite good friends already."

Emily appealed to her cousin. "Do something, Fannie."

"Very well." Fannie arose calmly, carrying her dirty dishes to the sink. "I'll ride my bicycle down there tomorrow and tell him he's not invited to the party after all. I'll explain that there simply isn't room in the parlor for the number who've accepted so we'll have to cut it down. I'm sure he'll understand. Charles will, too. Shall we draw straws now to see who helps with dishes?"

"Fannie, wait."

Fannie paused in mid-motion, lifting innocent eyes to her young cousin. "Is there something else you want me to tell him?"

Emily wilted onto a chair and sat sulkily, her hands dangling between her knees.

"Let him come," she grumbled bad-naturedly.

Fannie stepped before Emily and straightened several strands of her black hair, stretching them back from her forehead as if measuring out embroidery skeins. When she spoke her voice held a quiet note of reasonableness. "He plans to live here for a good long time. You'll be—shall we say—contemporaries. The two of you will be thrown together on both social and business occasions many times in the years to come. You're very young, dearling. Young and stubborn. You haven't learned yet that life necessitates many compromises. But believe me, you'll feel better if you make up your mind to greet him civilly and make him feel welcome. If your father can, and Charles can, you can, too. Now what do you say?"

Emily lifted indignant eyes. "He called me a tomboy."

Fannie cupped the younger woman's chin in her palm. "Ah, so that's the reason for this stubborn lip. Well, we shall just have to show him that you're not, won't we?"

Emily stared at Fannie, her chin still stubborn. "I don't want to show him anything."

"Not even that a tomboy can magically be transformed into a lady?"

Fannie could see she had fired Emily's interest. Before losing it, she swung on Frankie. "And you, young man . . ." She leveled him with a warning stare. "Not one word about this conversation to anyone, do you hear?"

Everyone in the room knew Frankie wanted to run down to Grinnell Street and spout what he'd heard. But nobody crossed Fannie.

"Yes, ma'am," Frankie mumbled, disappointed.

Fannie's curiosity had been understandably piqued. What was he like, this man who raised Emily's ire so? Fannie had watched her young cousin all week long, and every time Tom Jeffcoat's name was mentioned she grew irascible. But her cheeks also got pink and she refused to meet anybody's eyes. Such a reaction for a man she hated?

On Saturday morning when the breakfast oatmeal had been set to simmer, Fannie wheeled her bicycle from the backyard shed and took a ride. It was early—6:30. Behind, she left a sleeping house, but from somewhere across town came the sound of hammering. Sheridan was small and Edwin lived a mere five blocks from Main Street and only six from his livery stable on Grinnell. As she turned down Grinnell the sun roosted on the brim of the eastern plain like a flaming orange. Against it loomed the outline of the new livery building, with its roof already enclosed. She passed Edwin's place on her left. One of his horses whickered a soft greeting. Her bicycle wheels grated softly on the sandy street while the breeze unfurled strands of her loosely upswept hair and ruffled the folds of her scratchy woolen knickers against her legs. Somewhere in the distance a rooster crowed, and the sound of Jeffcoat's hammer cracked like an oxwhip as it reverberated off the valley walls.

She was happy as she'd never been in her life. She was living in Edwin's house, sharing his life, growing acquainted with his children, passing his stable and greeting his horses. She was cooking his meals and pouring his morning coffee and rolling the used napkin that had brushed his lips, and washing and ironing the clothes that had touched his skin. If there was the slightest chance that Emily was planning to do these things for a man named Bliss when she ought to be doing them for one named Jeffcoat, Fannie was making it her business to find out before it was too late.

She pulled up beside the livery barn, sat astraddle the bicycle, shaded her eyes, and peered at the figure high above, nailing shingles in place.

"Mr. Jeffcoat?"

The hammering ceased and he turned to look over his shoulder. "Well . . . good morning!"

She liked how he said it, with a half turn and a nudge of his hat, setting it farther back on his head. The roof was steep; he had a rope tied about his waist, threaded over the ridgepole to the opposite side. He balanced, hunkered, with his boot caught on a temporary rung he'd nailed to the sharp slant below him.

"I'm Fannie Cooper!"

"I thought so. Wait a minute." He descended the roof like a mountain climber, kicking into thin air, falling in breathtaking sweeps, slipping down the rope until he reached the ladder leaning against the building. Down it he came, agilely, while she watched and admired his grace and form and his outlandish mode of dress—the britches too tight, the suspenders red, and the shirt devoid of sleeves. Before he reached her he'd pulled off a leather glove and extended a hand.

"Hello, Fannie, I'm Tom Jeffcoat."

"I know."

"You're Emily Walcott's cousin."

"Yes, after a fashion. Second cousin, to be exact. And you're Edwin's competition."

He smiled. "I didn't mean to be."

She liked his answer. She liked his dimple. She liked him. Fannie Cooper was not a typical Victorian woman who postured and pretended indifference to men. When she met one of whom she approved she felt justified in manifesting that approval in whatever way struck her fancy. Sometimes by flirting, sometimes by complimenting, often by parrying words as she did now.

"Yet you seem to be an early bird . . . out after the worm perhaps?"

Again he laughed—a masculine motion—tipping back from the waist and releasing his enjoyment to the morning sky. "Shouldn't you be making comfits and straining fruit juices for tonight?"

"I'm not serving comfits, I'm serving finger sandwiches. And for a betrothal party it's entirely proper to serve spiked punch so don't get cheeky with me, Mr. Jeffcoat."

"I didn't mean to get cheeky." Drawing the glove back on he made a shallow, flirtatious bow. "I apologize."

She perused him. She perused the great roof, half-shingled, "The barn is coming along nicely. You've ordered bricks for the floor."

"Yes."

"And you've brought twenty-four windows."

"My goodness, word spreads."

"Frankie spreads it quite effectively."

"Ah, Frankie. I like that boy."

"Your livery barn is going to be quite something. Emily is jealous."

His face gave no clue to his feelings. It contained an easy smile that changed not in the least as he divulged, "Emily wishes I were on a windjammer with a broken mainmast, rounding Cape Horn. I try not to aggravate her."

"You've also brought a turntable for the carriages, I hear."

"Yes."

"Why?"

"A curiosity, nothing more. A whim. As a boy, I liked the train yards—the turntables in particular. An engineer once gave me a ride on one. I've wanted to own one ever since."

"Are you an impetuous man, then, Mr. Jeffcoat?"

"I don't know. I never thought about it one way or the other. Are you an impetuous woman, Miss Cooper?"

"Most assuredly."

"I thought so by your bicycle and your . . ." He leaned back from the waist and scanned her legs. "What are they called?"

"Knickerbockers. Do you like them? Don't answer that! They're convenient in any case, and there are women who wear what suits them whether the men like it or not."

"So I've learned since I got to Sheridan."

She gave a smile with an abrupt start and finish, then mercurially shifted subjects. "Do you dance, Mr. Jeffcoat?"

"As little as possible."

She laughed and advised, "Well, get ready. There will be dancing tonight, among other distractions. We're all happy you're coming. Now, I must get back for breakfast. Observe my technique in getting this contraption rolling, and don't take it lightly. Starting and stopping are the hardest parts. It took me three weeks to learn how to start without falling on my face and I'm rather proud of it." She gave the bicycle a push and hopped on with perfect balance. Pedaling away, she called without turning back, "I'm pleased to meet you, Mr. Jeffcoat."

"And I you, Miss Cooper."

"Then call me Fannie!"

"Then call me Tom!" He smiled, watching her roll up the street.

It was a hectic day but Fannie had things under control. She spoke with Josephine about the parlor and its overcrowded condition and suggested that they place the piano against the wall and clear out some of the clutter to give the young people space for dancing. Josephine agreed. But she would have agreed to anything; she was happier than she'd been in months, for she, too, had been put to work and it felt so refreshing to be useful again. She sat on a chair in the sun on the upper veranda, polishing silver.

Downstairs, dust flew. Tarsy had come to help, as promised. She made sandwich filling while Frankie polished the stair rungs, carried the ferns into the yard, and beat the rugs. Emily packed away bric-a-brac and Fannie found places to hide the heavy furniture draperies, scarves, Turkish tidies, peacock feathers, and plaster busts. They washed the windows and lamp chimneys and pushed the piano's sounding board against the wall where it belonged. They mopped the floor, left it bare, and relegated the offensive pieces of furniture to the porch, returning to the room only enough chairs and tables to give it balance and grace. An excess of chairs, claimed Fanny, only encouraged guests to sit on their duffs instead of dancing and making merry. The fewer chairs, the better!

Frankie washed the piano keys, Tarsy polished the punch bowl, Emily hung the clean lace curtains (leaving the heavy, tassled draperies folded away), and Fannie selectively chose small items to be scattered sparsely about the room.

When it was finished the four of them stood staring at it in its fresh, bright state, and Fannie clapped once, declaring, "This calls for a celebration. A musical celebration!" Abruptly she plunked onto the claw-foot piano stool, swiveled to face the keys, and performed a rousing rendition of "The Blue-Tailed Fly."

The piano notes drifted upstairs, through Josephine's bedroom and out the open door to the veranda where Josie smiled and stopped polishing. She dropped her head against the back of the chair and closed her eyes, unconsciously tapping a half-polished spoon against her knee in rhythm with the music.

When she opened her eyes, Edwin was coming home along the street below. It was halfway between dinner and supper, and she felt a stir of gladness to see him arriving at the uncustomary time. She waved and he waved back, flashing a smile up to her. She watched him cross the yard and disappear onto the porch below while the music continued, and Fannie's voice came along with it.

". . . the devil take the blue-tail fly. Jimmy crack corn and I don't care . . ."

Downstairs, Edwin stepped into his front parlor to find it transformed. Sunlight cascaded through white lace curtains, lighting the polished floor to the color of deep tea. The furniture had been thinned, and uncovered, and was complemented by only a few figurines and knicknacks and a single feathery fern beside the bay window. The piano, with its back against the wall and its top swept clean of all but an oil lamp and their family pictures, rang out while Tarsy clapped and his children laughingly danced an untutored, reckless polka.

Fannie sat at the piano, pounding the ivory keys and singing gustily. Her head was covered with a white dish towel, knotted top-center where sprigs of peachy-colored frizz stuck out. Her apron and skirts were hiked up to her knees, showing black high-topped shoes, which thumped the foot pedals powerfully enough to set the oil lamp rocking. She saw Edwin's entry reflected in the polished wood of the piano front, and turned a glimpse over her shoulders, continuing to sing and play full force.

"That horse he run, he jump, he pitch, he throw my master in de ditch . . ."

When she reached the chorus, the children chimed in, and Edwin stood laughing.

"Sing, Edwin!" Fannie ordered, interrupting herself only for that second before jumping back into the song.

He added his inexpert tenor, and the five of them together made enough racket to shake the soot out of the kitchen stovepipe. Still dancing, Emily tripped over Frankie's feet. They giggled, caught their balance, then continued thumping their way around the room with as much grace as a pair of lumberjacks.

During the final chorus, Fannie raised her face to the ceiling and bellowed. *"Are you singing, Joey?"*

In that instant Edwin felt a burst of renewed love for Fannie.

He made it upstairs—two at a time—before the final chorus died and found Josie, indeed, singing softly to herself on the veranda in the sun, with a smile on her face.

Sensing him behind her, she stopped and smiled self-consciously over her shoulder.

"Edwin, you're home early."

"I left a note on the door at the livery. I thought they might need my help downstairs, but it doesn't look like it." He stepped onto the veranda and went down on one knee beside her chair, squeezing her hand, which still held the polishing rag and spoon. "Oh, Josie, it's so wonderful to hear you singing."

"I feel so much better, Edwin." Her smile reiterated her words. "I think I can go downstairs tonight . . . for a while anyway, and greet Emily's guests."

"That's wonderful, Josie . . ." He squeezed her hand again. "Just wonderful." Looking into her eyes he recalled their own betrothal party. How he had despaired, and how he'd hidden it. But their life hadn't been so bad after all. They'd had twenty good healthy years before she'd grown ill, and from those years had come two beautiful children, and a lovely house, and a deep respect for one another. And if their relationship had not been as intimate or demonstrative as he'd hoped, perhaps it was partly his fault. He should have admired her more, complimented, wooed, touched. Because he hadn't, he did so now.

"You look very lovely sitting here in the sun." He took the spoon from her hand and fitted his palm to hers, entwining their fingers. "I'm so glad I came home early."

She blushed and dropped her eyes. But her glance lifted in surprise when he turned his head and kissed her palm. With her free hand she tenderly touched his bearded cheek.

"Dear Edwin," she said fondly.

Downstairs the piano stopped and laughing voices drifted off to the kitchen. For a while, both Edwin and Josephine were happier than they had been in years.

Chapter 6

With two hours to spare before the guests began arriving, the house was in perfect order. The finger sandwiches were sliced, the cakes frosted, and the brandy punch mixed. Tarsy had gone home to change clothes; Josephine, her hair freshly washed, was resting; in the kitchen, Edwin was combing Frankie's hair and giving him strict orders about allowing Earl no more than two sandwiches before getting him out of the house and over to Earl's, where the boys would spend the night.

Upstairs in the west bedroom Fannie was having a grand time creating a mess, strewing dresses from her trunks like a rainbow across Emily's bed and rocker.

"Green?" She whisked a silky frock against Emily's front. It was pale as seafoam and trimmed with bugle beads. Emily scarcely got a glimpse of it before it was gone. "No, no, it does nothing for your coloring." Fannie tossed it onto the pile, while Emily's eyes followed it longingly.

Next Fannie plucked up a splash of yellow. "Ah . . . saffron. Saffron will set off your hair." She plastered the dress to Emily, gripped her shoulders, and whirled her to face the mirror.

Emily found the yellow even more inviting than the green. "Oh, it's beautiful."

"It's good ... still ... mmm ..." Fannie lay a finger beside her mouth and studied Emily thoughtfully. "No, I think not. Not tonight. We'll save it for another time." The becoming yellow dress went flying while Emily disappointedly watched it hit the bed and slide to the floor in a puddle of material. "Tonight it's got to be the absolute perfect frock ... mmm ..." Fanny tapped her lips, perused the jumble on the bed, and abruptly spun toward the closet. "I've got it!" She fell to her knees and dragged out another trunk, thumped the lid back, and scavenged through it like a dog disinterring a bone.

"Pink!" Kneeling, Fannie held it high—a dress as true hued as a wild rose. "The perfect color for you." She stood and whacked it against her knees, then whisked the rustly creation against Emily's front. "Would you look at how that girl can wear pink! I never could. I don't know why I bought this thing. It makes me look like a giant freckle. But you, with your black hair and dark complexion ..." Even wrinkled, the dress was stunning, with a dropped neckline bordered by embroidered tea roses, wondrous bouffant elbow-length sleeves and a matching pouff at the spine. When it shifted, it spoke—a sibilant whisper telling of Eastern soirees where such frocks were customary. The dress was more beautiful than anything Emily had ever owned, but as she gazed wistfully at her reflection she was forced to admit, "I'd feel conspicuous in something this eye-catching."

"Nonsense!" Fannie retorted.

"I've never had a dress this pretty. Besides, Mother says a lady should wear subdued colors."

"And I always told her, Joey, you're old before your time." Conspiratorially, Fannie added, "Let your mother choose all the subdued colors she wants for herself, but this is your party. You may wear whatever you choose. Now what do you think?"

Emily gazed at the strawberry-pink confection, trying to imagine herself wearing it downstairs in the parlor as the guests arrived. She could well imagine Tarsy wearing such a dress—Tarsy with her blond curls, pouting mouth, pretty face, and undeniably voluptuous figure. But herself? Her hair might be dark, but it had not been curled since she was old enough to say no to sleeping in rags. And her face? It was too long and dark-skinned, and her eyebrows were as straight and unattractive as heel marks on a floor. Her eyes and nose, she guessed, were passable, but her mouth was less than ordinary, and her teeth overlapped on top, which had always made her self-conscious when she smiled. No, her face and body were much better suited to britches and suspenders than to rose-colored frocks with bouffant sleeves.

"I think it's a little too feminine for me."

Fannie caught Emily's eye in the mirror. "You wanted to make Mr. Jeffcoat eat his words, didn't you?"

"Him! I don't give a rip what Mr. Jeffcoat thinks."

Fannie whisked the dress into the air and brushed at the wrinkles with her hand. "I don't believe you. I think you would love to appear downstairs in this creation and knock his eyeballs out. Now, what do you say?"

Emily reconsidered. If it worked, it would be better than spitting in Tom Jeffcoat's eye, and she had never been one to resist a challenge.

"All right. I'll do it ... if you're sure you don't mind."

"Heavens, don't be silly! I'll never wear it again."

"But it's all wrinkles. How will we—"

"Leave that to me." Fannie flipped the dress over her shoulder and went off to shout over the banister, "Edwin, I'll need some fuel ... kerosene, preferably! Coal oil if that's all you have." A moment later she stuck her head back into Emily's bedroom. "Brush your hair, light the lantern, and heat the curling tongs. I'll be right back." Again she disappeared, trailing a call. "Edwiiiiin?"

Within minutes she returned with Edwin in tow. From the depths of a trunk she produced a hunk of steel she introduced as a steamer. She held it while Edwin filled it with coal oil and water, and when it was lit and hissing, she put him to work steaming his daughter's dress while Fannie herself took over the curling tongs and arranged Emily's hair.

Submitting to her cousin, Emily watched her transformation while Papa, happy and humming, exclaimed as the wrinkles fell out of the pink satin; Mother came from across the hall dressed in a fine midnight blue serge dress, with her hair neatly coiled, and sat on the rocking chair to watch. Clamping a tress of hair in the hot tongs, Fannie described the newest hairdos from the East—crimps or waves, which would Emily prefer?

Emily chose crimps, and when the hairdo was done, piled atop her head like a dark puffy nest, she stared at herself disbelievingly, with her heart jumping in excitement. Standing behind Emily, inspecting her handiwork in the mirror, Fannie yelled, "Frankie, where are you?"

Frankie appeared in the doorway behind them. "What?"

"Go downstairs and pick a sprig of impatiens and bring them here—and don't ask me what they are. Those tiny pink flowers beside the front door!"

When he returned, and when the delicate blossoms were nestled in the misty-looking curls above Emily's left ear, Frankie stood back with big eyes and open lips, exclaiming in astonishment, "Wowwww, Emily, do you ever look pretty!"

At eight P.M. she stood before the dining room mirror *feeling* pretty, yes—but conspicuous. She dipped down to peer at her reflection and glimpsed her flushed cheeks. Goodness! It was a little breathtaking to see one's self in pink and crimps for the first time. She touched her chest—so much of it was bare—and stared.

She had never spared time for feminizing herself; she'd had no reason. Most girls primped and preened to attract the attentions of men, but she'd had Charles's attention forever. Staring at her reflection, she felt a sting of guilt, for it was not only Charles she wanted to impress tonight, but Tom Jeffcoat—that jackal who'd called her a tomboy. What pleasure she'd take in making him eat his words. All the while Fannie had been fussing over her Emily had gloated, imagining it.

But now, peering in the dining room mirror with her stomach trembling, she feared she'd be the one who felt awkward, instead of him. Fannie had powdered her face and chest with a light dusting of flour, and had tinted her cheeks by wetting swatches of red crepe paper, then rubbing them lightly on her skin. "Lick your lips," Fannie had ordered. "Now clamp them hard over the paper." Again . . . magic! But it was very uncertain magic, for a mere touch of the tongue removed it. Staring at her pink lips, Emily scolded herself silently: So help me, if you lick them before Jeffcoat arrives, you deserve every name he's called you!

"Emily?"

Emily jumped and spun around.

"Oh, Charles, I didn't hear you come in."

He stared as if he'd never seen her before. His cheeks became pink and his mouth dropped open, but not a word came out.

Emily laughed nervously. "Well, gracious, Charles, you act as if you don't recognize me."

"Emily?" Astonished and pleased, he let out the single word while moving slowly toward her, as if permission might possibly be required. "What have you done to yourself?"

She glanced down and plucked at her voluminous skirts, making them rustle like dry leaves. "Fannie did it."

He took her hands and held her at arm's length, turning them both in a half-circle. "Aren't I the lucky one? The prettiest girl in town."

"Oh, Charles, I'm not either, so stop your fibbing."

"That dress . . . and your hair . . . I never saw your hair so pretty before."

She felt herself blushing profusely.

Holding her hands, Charles let his eyes drift down over her floured chest and her corseted waist. She grew even more uneasy under his obviously delighted regard. "Oh, Emily, you look beautiful," he said softly, dipping his head as if to kiss her.

She feinted neatly aside. "Fannie colored my lips with crepe paper, but it comes off easily. I wouldn't want you looking marked." Though Charles politely straightened, he continued holding her hands and studying her with ardent eyes the way other men often studied Tarsy. Again Emily felt a pant of guilt. After all, it was fifteen minutes before their engagement party, and her fiancé wanted nothing more than an innocent stolen kiss. Yet she put him off, more concerned about keeping her lip coloring intact so she could make an impression on Tom Jeffcoat. She assuaged her guilt by telling herself that when she was married to Charles she would kiss him any time he wanted, and would make up for all the times she'd coyly withdrawn.

The guests began arriving, and Charles and Emily went to join the family in the parlor, where Mama had insisted upon having a receiving line. Edwin had carried and seated Josephine in the bay window, where he stood between her and Fannie, introducing the latter to each new arrival, and announcing Charley and Emily's engagement with great alacrity. The house filled fast with businessmen and their wives, neighbors, fellow church members, owners of outlying ranches, Reverend Vasseler, Earl Rausch and his parents, Mr. and Mrs. Loucks. There were young people, too, all acquaintances of Emily's and Charles's—Jerome Berryman, Patrick Haberkorn, Mick Stubbs; and girls who'd come with their parents—Ardis Corbeil, Mary Ess, Lybee Ryker, Tilda Awk.

When Tarsy arrived she left her parents at the door and rushed directly to Emily. "Oh, Emily, you look stunning, is he here yet?"

"Thank you and no, he's not."

"Does my hair look all right? Do you think I should have worn my lavender dress? I didn't think my mother and father would *ever* get ready! I almost wore a hole in the rug, waiting for them. Poke me if you see him come in when I'm not looking. Fannie says there's going to be dancing later on. Oh, I hope he'll ask me!"

Emily found herself aggravated by Tarsy's gushing over the wonders of the mighty Jeffcoat, and further annoyed by the realization that she herself was unable to stop her own fixation with the front door. By 8:30 he still had not walked through it. Her lips felt stiff from smiling without rubbing them together. Though she was thirsty and tense, and though Charles had brought her a cup of punch, she would not touch the cup to her lips. Her ribs itched from the corset Fannie had forced her into, but she was afraid to scratch for fear he'd walk in and catch her at it.

That swine was thirty minutes late!

So help me, Jeffcoat, if you don't come after all this I'll make you suffer just like I'm suffering!

He arrived at 8:45.

Emily had intended to have Charles at her side, and a line of guests moving past them. She'd intended to give Tom Jeffcoat the full two seconds' worth of attention he deserved before scattering her courtesy to the others waiting in line. She'd intended to show him how little he mattered, so little that she need not even be caustic with him any longer.

But as it turned out, by 8:45 the receiving line had already broken up, Charles was in the dining room with his back to her, the guests were mingling, and she stood in the middle of the room alone. Tom Jeffcoat's eyes found her immediately.

For several uncomfortable seconds they took measure of one another, then he began moving across the room toward her. She felt an unwelcome panic and the absurd pounding of her heart—hard enough, she feared, to shake the flour off her chest. *Please, God, don't let it fall off!*

She watched him approach, feeling trapped and frantic, tricked by some unkind fortune who'd painted him more attractive than she wanted him to be, who'd given him a preference for clean-shavenness and blessed him with beautiful black hair, startlingly handsome blue eyes, a full, attractive mouth, and an easy saunter. She damned Tarsy for pointing it all out, and Charles for abandoning her when she needed him, and her own stupid heart, which refused to stop knocking in her chest. She noted, as if distanced from herself, that his suit was faintly wrinkled, his boots by contrast shiny and new, and that Tarsy had appeared in the dining room archway and was staring at him like a drooling basset hound. But his eyes remained riveted upon Emily as he crossed the room.

By the time he reached her, she felt as if she were choking. He stopped before her, so tall she had to raise her chin to meet his eyes.

"Good evening, Miss Walcott," he said in a painfully polite voice.

"Good evening, Mr. Jeffcoat."

He let his eyes whisk down and up once, without lingering anywhere, but when they returned to hers he wore a faint grin, which she longed to slap from his face.

"Thank you for inviting me." But they both knew she hadn't invited him; Charles had. "I understand congratulations are in order. Charles told me about your engagement."

"Yes," she replied, glancing away from his eyes, which, though holding a surface politeness, seemed to be laughing at her. "We've known each other forever. It was only a matter of time before we named a date."

"So Charles tells me. A year from now, is it?"

"Give or take a month or two." She was, after all, no good at guile; her responses came out brusque and cool.

"A pleasant time of year for a wedding," he observed conversationally, proving himself much better than she at observing the amenities. Her tongue seemed to be bonded to the top of her mouth as she stared at anything in the room but Tom Jeffcoat. After several beats of silence, he added, "Charles is . . . ecstatic."

His pause injected the remark with dubious undertones, and she felt herself coloring. "Help yourself to punch and sandwiches anytime you want, Mr. Jeffcoat. I'd best talk to some of the other guests." But when she moved he caught her lightly by an arm.

"Are you forgetting? I haven't met your mother yet."

He hadn't said a word about her appearance. *Not one word!* And damn him for making her lose her composure. She dropped her glance to the hand that sent an unwarranted sizzle up her arm, then pierced him with a haughty look. "You're wrinkling my sleeve, Mr. Jeffcoat."

"I apologize." He dropped her elbow immediately, and ordered, "Introduce me to your mother, Miss Walcott."

"Certainly." She spun to find that her mother had been watching them all the while, and for a heartbeat she froze. When Jeffcoat touched her politely on the back she shot forward. "Mother, this is Charles's friend, Tom Jeffcoat. You remember, Papa was talking about him during supper the other night?"

"Mr. Jeffcoat ..." Queenlike, Josephine presented her frail hand. "Edwin's competitor."

He bowed over it graciously. "Fellow businessman, I hope. If I didn't think there was enough business in Sheridan for both of us I'd have settled someplace else."

"Let us hope you're right. Of course, any friend of Charles's and Emily's is welcome in our home."

"Thank you, Mrs. Walcott. It's a beautiful house." He glanced around. "I can't wait to have my own."

"Charles and Edwin built it, of course."

"Charles will be building mine, too, as soon as the barn is done."

"What's this we hear about a turntable in your barn?"

He laughed. "Oh, Charles has been talking?"

"Mostly Frankie."

"Ah, Frankie, our young apprentice ..." He chuckled fondly. "The turntable is a whim, Mrs. Walcott, nothing more than a whim."

Fannie sailed up on the tail end of the comment. "What's a whim? Hello, Tom."

He turned and let his hands be captured. "Hello, Fannie."

"You two have met?" inquired Emily, surprised.

"Yes, this morning." Fannie slipped her arm through Tom's as if they were old friends while he smiled down at her upraised face.

"She was out for a bicycle ride and stopped by my place to introduce herself."

"I'm so glad you've come. Have you talked to Charles yet?"

"No, I was just heading over."

"Oh, and here's Tarsy. Tarsy, you've met Tom already, haven't you?" Tarsy's hand shot out fast enough to create a draft. He bowed over it gallantly.

"Miss Fields, how nice to see you again. You're looking lovely tonight."

"Why don't you take him over and see that he gets a cup of punch?" Fannie suggested to the blonde.

Tarsy appropriated Tom's arm and gave him a 150-candlepower smile while leading him away, chiding, "Shame on you for being late. I was about to give up hope."

Emily steamed, watching them move off toward Charles. *Miss Fields, you're looking lovely tonight!* Wasn't he just *oozing* charm?

She watched all night while men and women alike succumbed to it. He moved among the houseful of guests with singular effortlessness, comfortable meeting strangers, quick to pick up conversational threads, to win slaps on the back from the men and charming smiles from the ladies.

Reverend Vasseler shook his hand heartily and thanked him for getting the young boys to help at the church. The young boys themselves followed him, avid-eyed, and asked when his turntable would be ready. The mothers with unmarried daughters invited him to dinner. The ranchers with stock for sale invited him to look over their horseflesh. Fannie made plans to teach him how to ride her bicycle. Charles spent more time with him than with his bride-to-be. And Tarsy clung to his arm like a barnacle.

Meanwhile, Emily had one of the most miserable evenings of her life.

When the punch bowl was half-empty and the first wave of socializing past, Fannie called upon Edwin to make a betrothal toast. He filled Josephine's glass and his own, handed drinks to Charles and Emily, and stood in the bay window with his arm around his daughter.

"Before the evening gets away from us," he addressed his guests, "Emily's mother and I want you all to know how happy we are over the announcement of Emily's engagement. We've known Charles here since . . ." He turned to glance affectionately at his future son-in-law. "How long has it been, Charles?" He turned back to his guests. "Well, since he was wiping his nose on his shirtsleeve, anyway." Everyone laughed.

"For those of you who may not know it, his parents were our dear friends back in Philadelphia, friends we still miss, and we wish they could be here with us tonight." He cleared his throat and went on. "Well, for years Charles and Emily have been running in and out of our house together. I think we've fed him as many meals as we've fed our own two. I seem to recall back around the time they were waist-high or so she stole his pet frog and left it in a cricket box until it was flat and hard as a silver dollar, and Charles—if memory serves—beat her up and gave her a black eye."

After another ripple of mirth Edwin continued: "But they worked it all out and, believe it or not, Charles came to me when he was just about eye level to my chin and announced very seriously . . ." Edwin paused to study the contents of his wineglass. " 'Mr. Walcott.' " He lifted his face like an orator. " 'I want you to know that I'm going to marry Emily as soon as we're old enough.' I remember trying hard not to laugh." Edwin turned toward Charles with a rubicund glow on his cheeks. "Good heavens, Charles, do you realize your voice hadn't decided yet at that point whether it wanted to be bass or soprano?" After more laughter Edwin grew serious.

"Well, it was good news then and it's good news now. Sometimes it's hard to believe our little Emily is all grown up. But Emily, honey . . ." He squeezed her shoulders and gazed adoringly into her face. "A year from now when we make a toast to the bride and groom, you know you'll have your mother's and my blessings. We already think of Charles as our son." Edwin raised his glass, inviting his guests to follow suit. "To Charles and Emily . . . and their future happiness."

"Hear, hear!"

"To Charles and Emily!"

Salutations filled the room. Edwin kissed Emily's right temple and Charles kissed her left. Josephine reached up from her chair and took Emily's hand. As she leaned down to kiss her mother's cheek Emily felt small for having been so sulky all night long and promised herself she would throw herself into the spirit of the party for the remainder of the evening. As she straightened she saw Tom Jeffcoat studying her. He raised his glass in a silent salute and emptied it, watching her over the rim of his glass.

The brandy in her stomach felt as if it had been touched by a match. Confused, she turned her attention to Charles.

"I'm warm, Charles. Could we step outside for a few minutes?"

But out on the porch she discovered that Charles had imbibed enough brandy to make him distinctly amorous. He took her around the corner of the porch, flattened her against the wall, and removed all traces of Fanny's handiwork from her lips, then tried to do the same with the flour on her chest. But she caught his hand and ordered, "No, Charles. Anyone could come out."

He caught her head in both hands, kissing her insistently, passionately, and she realized her mistake in coming outside with him, dressed in Fannie's dress, when he'd been drinking. In the end, she had to snap at him. "Charles, I said no!"

For a moment he glared at her, frustrated, looking as if he wanted to either shake her or drag her off the porch, away from the window lights, and make their engagement official with far more than a paltry kiss. She watched him gather composure until finally he stepped back and drew a shaky breath. "You're right. You go back in and I'll follow in a minute."

When she reentered the parlor her cheeks were flushed and she had lost the impatiens from her hair. Father was carrying Mother upstairs, Fannie was playing the piano, and Tom Jeffcoat was watching the doorway with rapt absorption.

Their eyes met and she felt again a flash of attraction for him, felt as if he could divine everything that had transpired on the porch. Were her lips puffy? Did the path of Charles's hand show? Did she look as kissed clean and defloured as she felt?

Well, it was no business of Tom Jeffcoat's what she did with her fiancé. She lifted her chin and turned away.

Though she avoided him for the remainder of the evening, she knew where he was each moment, whom he talked with, how many times he laughed with Tarsy, and how many times with Charles. She knew, too, exactly how many times he studied with Charles's new fiancée in her borrowed pink dress when he thought she wasn't aware.

Shortly before midnight Fannie sat down at the piano and struck into the melifluent strains of Strauss's *Blue Danube* and called everyone to dance. The married couples did, but the young people held back, the males declaring they didn't know how, the females wishing the men would learn. Fannie leapt from the piano stool and scolded, "Nonsense! Anyone can dance. We'll have a lesson!" She made everyone form a circle, experienced dancers interspersed with novices, and taught them the steps of the waltz, singing all the while, *Da da da da dum . . . Dum-dum! Dum-dum!* Guiding the unbroken ring of feet first forward, then back, first left, then right, she made everyone vocalize the familiar Viennese waltz. *Da da da da dum . . . Dum-dum! Dum-dum!* And while they sang and waltzed she chose a partner and drew him into the center—Patrick Haberkorn, who blushed and moved clumsily, but gave in to Fannie good-naturedly.

"Just keep singing," she instructed in Patrick's ear, "and forget about your feet except to pretend they're leading mine instead of following them." When Patrick was moving reasonably smoothly she danced him to Tilda Awk and negotiated the transition of partners. One after another she took the young men and showed them how fun dancing could be. When she had trained the feet of Tom Jeffcoat she turned him over to Tarsy Fields. When she'd done the same for Charles, she paired him off with Emily. And when all were matched and only Edwin remained, she opened her arms to him and became his partner, hiding the fact that her heart swelled at being in his arms at last, and that her laugh was only a facade for the intense love she felt. Edwin obliged, sweeping her around the parlor as together they sang *Da da da da dum . . . dumdum!*

Less than a minute they danced before Fannie reluctantly left him and slid back onto the piano stool and called out, "Change partners!"

Shuffling and confusion ensued, and when it settled Emily found herself in her father's arms. He was smiling and smart-stepping as he led her.

"Are you having a good time, honey?"

"Yes, Papa. Are you?"

"The best."

"I didn't know you could dance."

"I haven't done it in years. Your mother never cared to."

"Do you think we're keeping her awake?"

"Of course. But she told me she would enjoy listening."

"I think she had a good time tonight."

"I know she did."

"She seemed stronger, and her cheeks were actually pink."

"It's Fannie. Fannie is a miracle worker."

"I know. I'm so happy she's here.",

"So am I."

"Change partners!"

"Oops!" Papa said. "Here you go."

Emily whirled around and found herself with Pervis Berryman, short and broad as a washtub, but a surprisingly agile dancer. He congratulated her on her engagement and said the party was just what this town needed and wasn't it good to see the young people dancing this way?

"Change partners!"

Pervis turned her over to Tarsy's father, whose hair was parted down the middle and slicked flat with pomade. He smelled like his barber shop—slightly soapy, slightly perfumed—and his waxed mustache twitched when he talked. He, too, congratulated her on her engagement, told her she was getting a hell of a good man, and told her that Tarsy was so excited about the party tonight she'd asked permission to have one of her own next Saturday.

"Change partners!"

Emily twirled around and found herself in the arms of Tom Jeffcoat.

"Hiya, tomboy," he said, grinning.

"You insufferable wretch," she returned pleasantly.

"Ha-ha-ha!" He laughed at the ceiling.

"I'll get even with you yet."

"For what? I've been on my best behavior tonight, haven't I?"

"I don't think you know what good behavior is."

"Now, Emily, don't start fights. I promised Charles I'd do my best to get along with you."

"You and I will never get along, and you know it perfectly well. You also know that if it weren't for Charles you wouldn't be in this house right now."

"Do you practice being mouthy or does it just come naturally?"

"Do you practice insulting women or does it just come naturally?"

"Hostesses are supposed to be polite to their guests."

"I am. To *my* guests."

"You know, Charles and I get along remarkably well. I have a feeling he and I are destined to be friends. If you're going to marry him, don't you think we should try to grin and bear each other—for his sake?"

"You already grin more than I can bear."

"But we'll be bumping into each other at occasions like this for . . . well, who knows how long?"

It was essentially what Fannie had said, but he need not know that.

Jeffcoat went on. "Take for instance next Saturday night. Tarsy is planning another party and we'll probably end up dancing together again."

"I hope not. You're a terrible dancer."

"Tarsy doesn't think so."

"Get off my toes, Mr. Jeffcoat. Tarsy Fields has never danced before in her life. How would she know?"

"You've never danced before either, so how would you know?"

"Look . . ." She pulled back and flattened her skirt with one hand. "You've undoubtedly scuffed the toe of Fannie's shoe."

He glanced down briefly, then resumed dancing. "Fannie? So that's where you got the clothes."

"Not that you noticed."

"Did you want me to?"

"You're the one who called *me* a tomboy!"

"After you called me shabby. I dress the way I do because it's the most sensible when I work."

"So do I."

Their eyes met and each gave the other a begrudging point.

"So what do you say, should we call a truce? For Charles's sake?"

She shrugged and glanced aside indifferently.

"He tells me you're going to be a veterinarian."

"Yes, I am."

"Those were some of your papers I saw at the livery stable that day?"

"I was studying."

"You think you're strong enough?"

"Strong enough?" She tossed him a puzzled glance.

"To treat farm animals. It can take a surprising amount of strength."

"Sometimes a smaller hand and a thinner arm can be an advantage. Have you ever pulled a calf?"

"No, only foals."

"Then you know."

Yes, he did. And he understood her reasoning.

"So you know a lot about animals."

"I suppose I do."

He glanced around. "Out of all the ranchers here, who would you say raises the best horseflesh?"

She was surprised that he'd ask her opinion but his face was serious as he scanned the guests. She, too, took their measure. "It's hard to say. Wyoming's climate produces some of the finest horses in America. We have one hundred and fifty different grasses in this state and each one is better than the next for grazing. The cold winters, the clear water, and the pure air give our horses stamina and good lungs. The army buys most of their horses here."

"I know that. But who would you buy from?"

Before she could answer, Fannie called, "Change partners!"

They stopped dancing abruptly and withdrew from each other to stand uncertainly, realizing they'd embarked upon their first civil exchange and that it hadn't hurt one bit.

"I'll think about it," she said.

"Fine. And think about who I ought to buy hay from, too. I'll need advice if I'm going to make it here."

Again she felt stunned that he'd seek it from her. But he was offering an olive branch for Charles's sake, and the least she could do was accept it.

"Hay's not so touchy. Anybody."

He nodded as if accepting her word.

A new partner waited, but as Emily turned to him, Jeffcoat grabbed her arm and twirled her back to face him. Grinning into her eyes, he said in an undertone, "Thanks for the dance, tomboy."

He stood too near, his lopsided smile six inches from her eyebrow, and she could smell the faint scent of his flesh, warm from dancing, and see clearly the grain of his skin on his clean-shaven chin, the single dimple in his left cheek, the edges of his teeth, the humor in his eyes. She felt something stir between them and wondered in a brief flash how it would feel to be flattened against the porch wall and kissed clean by him instead of Charles.

The insanity lasted a mere second before she pulled free and quipped, "You'd better brush up for next week. My toes are wrecked."

For the remainder of the night they politely avoided each other, while Fannie taught everyone to dance the varsovienne—a cross between the polka and the mazurka. Emily stuck to Charles and Tom to Tarsy. Before the evening broke up Tarsy spread the word that her party would be at the same time next week at her house and all the young people were invited. When it was time to wish their guests good night, Emily and Charles stood at the door side by side, accepting parting wishes. Charles got a handshake from Tom while Emily got a hug from Tarsy, who whispered into her ear, "He's walking me home! I'll tell you about it tomorrow!"

When Charles was gone, Emily helped Fannie and Papa clean up the house and wondered if Tom Jeffcoat was pushing Tarsy against her porch wall and if Tarsy was enjoying it.

Silly question! Tarsy probably had *him* pushed against the porch wall!

She wondered about kissing and why some girls enjoyed it and others didn't. She thought about herself earlier tonight with Charles, and how she'd felt almost reviled by his groping. She was engaged to him now, and if Tarsy were any authority, it was supposed to be enjoyable, even desirable.

Maybe there was something wrong with her.

She went upstairs five minutes before Fannie and sat in the lamplight worrying about it. Should a girl prefer working in a stable to kissing her intended? Surely not. Yet it was true—sometimes when Charles kissed her, when she gave in to him out of a sense of sheer obligation, she thought of other things—the horses, pitching hay, riding across an open field with her hair blowing like the mane of the animal beneath her.

Dejectedly Emily removed the pink dress and hung it up, took down her hair and brushed it, thoughtfully studying her reflection in her mirror. She touched her lips, then closed her eyes and skimmed her fingertips over her own chest, pretending it was Charles. When he was her husband he would touch her not only here, but in other places, in other ways. Her eyes flew open and met their mirrored images, chagrined. She'd seen horses mating and it was a graceless, embarrassing thing. However could she do that with Charles?

Worrying, she donned her nightdress and slipped into bed, listening to the murmur of Papa and Fannie as they came up the stairs and said good night in the hall. Then Fannie came in and closed the door, unhooked her dress, untied her corset, and brushed her hair, humming.

Oh, to be like Fannie. To whisk through life worrying about nothing, single and happy to be, pursuing whatever flight of fancy beckoned. Fannie would have the answers, Emily was certain.

When the wick was lowered and the bedsprings quiet, Emily stared at the black ceiling with a lump in her throat.

"Fannie?" she whispered at last.

"Hm?" Fannie murmured over her shoulder.

"Thank you for the party."

"You're welcome, dearling. Did you have a good time?"

"Yes . . . and no."

"No?" Fannie rolled over and touched Emily's shoulder. "What's wrong, Emily?"

Emily took a full minute summoning her courage before enquiring, "Fannie, can I ask you something?"

"Of course."

"It's something personal."

"It usually is when girls whisper in the dark."

"It's about kissing."

"Ah, kissing."

"I'd ask Mother, but she's . . . well, you know Mother."

"Yes, I do. I wouldn't ask her either, if she were my mother."

"Have you ever kissed a man?"

Fannie laughed softly, rolled to her back, and snuggled more deeply into her pillow. "I love kissing men. I've kissed several."

"Do they all kiss the same?"

"Not at all. A kiss, dearling, is like a snowflake—no two are alike. There are brief ones, long ones, timid ones, bold ones, teasing ones and serious ones, dry ones and wet ones—"

"Wet ones, yes. Those are the ones. They're . . . I . . . Charles . . . what I mean to say is . . ."

"They're heavenly, aren't they?" mused Fannie.

"Are they?" Emily returned doubtfully.

"You mean you don't think so?"

"Well, sometimes. But other times I feel like . . . well, like it's not allowed. Like I'm doing something wrong."

"You don't get heady or impatient?"

"Once I did . . . rather. It was the day Charles proposed. But I've known him so long sometimes he seems more like a brother to me, and who wants to kiss their brother?"

All grew quiet while the two lay in private thought.

Finally Emily spoke. "Fannie?"

"Hm?"

"Have you ever been in love?"

Silence again until, across the hall, Josephine coughed and another occupant of the house rolled over in his bed.

"Deeply."

"How does it feel?"

"It hurts." The pillowslip rustled as Emily turned her head sharply to study Fannie in the dark. But before she could ask any more questions, Fannie ordered gently, "Go to sleep now, dearling, it's late."

Chapter 7

The following day was Sunday, and Tarsy was waiting to pounce on Emily outside Coffeen Hall even before church services began. She grabbed Emily's arm and pulled her aside without so much as a greeting.

"Emily, wait till I tell you! You won't believe it! But there isn't time now. Tell Charles you're walking home with me and I'll tell you everything then!"

As it turned out, Tarsy was walked home by Tom Jeffcoat, but she found Emily later that afternoon at the livery stable.

"Em, are you here?" she called.

"I'm up here!" Emily answered from the hay loft.

Tarsy crossed to the foot of the ladder and peered up. "What are you doing up there?"

Emily's head appeared overhead. "Studying. Come on up."

"I can't climb that ladder in my dress."

"Sure you can. I'm wearing mine. Just hike it up around your waist."

"But, Emily—"

"It's nice up here. This is one of my favorite places, especially on Sunday when nobody's around. Come on."

Tarsy hitched up her skirts and made the climb. The immense arrow-shaped grain door was open, letting a swash of sunlight set the hay alight. Swallows flew in and out, nesting in the rafters, and beyond the open door lay a panoramic view of the town, the southerly opening into the valley and the blue Big Horns to the southwest. Tarsy noticed none of it. She collapsed and fell back supine, stretching and losing her eyes.

"Oh, I'm so tired," she breathed.

Emily sat nearby, watching a battalion of dust motes lift, smelling the scent of stirred hay. "It was a late night," she said.

"But I had such a good time. Thank you, Emily." Tarsy opened her eyes to the swallows and the rafters, stretched out a tress of her hair, and murmured dreamily, "I think I'm in love."

Emily threw the girl a jaundiced glance. "With Tom Jeffcoat?"

"Mmm . . . who else?"

"That was fast."

"He's wonderful." Tarsy gave a self-satisfied smile and wound the lock of hair around a finger to her scalp. "He walked me home last night and we sat on the porch steps talking until nearly three o'clock. He told me everything about himself . . . everything!" Tarsy's exhaustion seemed to vanish in a blink and she popped up with bright-eyed exuberance. "He's twenty-six years old and he lived in Springfield, Missouri, all his life with his mother, father, one brother, and three sisters who still live there. He borrowed the money to come here and set himself up in business from his grandma. But he says he plans to pay her back within five years and he knows he can do it because he's sure the town will grow and he's not afraid of hard work. But listen to this!" Sitting cross-legged, Tarsy leaned forward avidly. "A year ago he got engaged to a woman named Julia March, but after nine months she threw him over for a rich banker named James or Jones or something like that, and yesterday, back in Springfield, it was her wedding day. Imagine that! All the while he was dancing and putting on a happy front at your party, he was really hiding a broken heart because it was his ex-fiancée's wedding night. He seemed so sad when he was telling me about it, and then he put his arms around me and held me and rested his chin on the top of my head and pretty soon he kissed me."

What was it like? The question popped into Emily's mind before she could block it out, and Tarsy answered it unwittingly.

"Oh, Emileeeee . . ." She sighed and fell backwards in the hay as if bedazed. "It was heavenly. It was like sliding down a rainbow. It was like angels dancing on my lips. It was—"

"You've only known him a week."

Tarsy's eyes opened. "What difference does that make? I'm smitten. And he's so much more grown up than Jerome. When Jerome kisses me nothing happens. And Jerome's lips are hard. Tom's are soft. And he opened them, and I thought I'd absolute *die* of ecstasy."

Emily felt a flash of irritation. It had never been like that for her with Charles. Sliding down a rainbow? How absurd. And how imprudent of Tarsy to reveal such private details to anyone. What the girl did with Jeffcoat should have been held in strictest confidence. It made Emily uncomfortable, listening, as if she'd hidden and watched the episode undetected.

After the day in the hayloft, every time Emily saw Tom Jeffcoat she remembered Tarsy's rapturous account and, picturing it, speculated about what *his* reaction had been. By choice she would have avoided him, but he walked past several times a day on his way to and from his own livery stable. Often as not, Charles was with him, since the two ate many of their meals together at the hotel and worked daily, side by side on Jeffcoat's building. Sometimes Charles would drop in at Walcott's Livery just to say hello or to let Emily know if he'd be coming to the house in the evening, and Jeffcoat would stand in the background, never intruding, but always making her wholly aware of his presence. While she and Charles talked he'd lean against a beam chewing a piece of hay with his hat pushed back and one thumb in the waist of his indecently tight pants. As the two left Jeffcoat would nod politely and speak for the first time: "Good day, Miss Walcott," to which she'd reply flatly without glancing at him. Why he should irritate her so keenly, she didn't understand, yet he did. His very presence in her father's stable made her want to plant a boot in his backside and send him flying!

She avoided his livery stable assiduously, even when Charles was there working. Sometimes she would stand at the great open grain door of her own and listen to their hammers, watching the building near completion and wish a bolt of lightning would flash down out of heaven and level the place.

And sometimes she'd stand there and wonder if his lips were really soft.

On the Friday afternoon following her party she was alone in the office, memorizing ointment recipes with her feet propped on the desk and her back to the door, when a voice spoke behind her.

"Hiya, tomboy."

She catapulted from the chair as if propelled by black powder. Her book clapped to the floor as she spun. There, lounging in the doorway, grinning crookedly, stood the rat, Jeffcoat.

"A little jumpy, aren't you?"

"What are *you* doing here?" she glowered.

"Is that any way to greet a friend?" He peeled himself from the doorframe, swiped up the book, and handed it to her. "Here. You dropped something."

His lips—damn them!—did look like something angels might dance on. She grabbed the book rudely and slammed it on the desk. "What do you want?"

"Can we talk?"

"About what?"

Without answering, he sauntered toward the cot where the caramel cat slept in its customary place, scooped it up, and stood with his back to Emily, nose to nose with the creature while it hung from his thumbs. "You've got some kind of life, critter. Every time I come in here you're curled up sleeping. What's your name, huh?"

"Taffy," Emily replied indignantly. "Is that what you came to find out, the name of my cat?"

Jeffcoat threw a half grin over his shoulder, then returned his attention to the cat. "Taffy," he repeated, scratching it beneath the chin. In his own good time, he dropped to the cot, still cradling the feline and making it purr. "I need to buy stock for my livery stable," he announced, with his eyes still on the cat. "Will you help me?"

"Me!" Surprise set Emily back on her chair. "Why me?"

At last Jeffcoat looked at her. "Because Charles says you know horses better than most men do."

"Doesn't it strike you as a little presumptuous, Mr. Jeffcoat—"

"Tom."

"—to ask me to help you set up your business when I don't want it here in the first place?"

"Maybe. But you've lived here longer than I have, you know the ranchers—who's honest, who's not, who's got the best horses, where they live. I'd appreciate your help."

She drew in a breath and held it, preparing a tirade. Instead the lungful came out with an unexpected chug of laughter. "You know, you amaze me."

"What's so amazing?"

"Your temerity."

He blew on the cat's face and suggested, "We could go this afternoon maybe. Or Monday." The cat sneezed and shook its head. Jeffcoat chuckled, then shifted his regard to Emily. "I need to pin down a good dozen horses, and find a rancher who'll contract to sell me hay. By the end of next week I'll have the turntable in place, but I haven't got horses *or* wagons yet. What do you say, will you help?"

For a moment she was tempted. He would, after all, open his doors for business and there was no way she could stop him. Also, his friendship with Charles seemed cemented; it would be hard on Charles if she, as his wife, continued discouraging it.

But while she was considering, her eyes dropped to Jeffcoat's lips and out of nowhere came Tarsy's description of kissing him.

"Sorry, Jeffcoat." She leapt to her feet and headed to the door. "You'll have to find somebody else. I'm busy."

Naturally, Charles heard that she'd refused to help his friend, and that evening he chided gently, "You know, you could be a little nicer to him. It's tough on him being alone out here."

"I dislike him. Why should I help him?"

"Because it's the neighborly thing to do."

"He claims he's been around horses all his life. Let him find his own."

The following morning Emily was cleaning stalls when she heard a wagon approach and tie up outside. Footsteps hurried toward her father's office and a moment later she heard two men talking. Momentarily, Edwin came out to find her.

"Emily?"

"I'm back here, Papa."

He stopped at the stall opening followed by a shorter man with a worried face. "Well, little doctor." Edwin smiled indulgently at his daughter. "You wanted a chance to practice, this is it. You know August, don't you?"

"Hello, Mr. Jagush."

August Jagush was a stocky Pole, fresh from the Old Country. His face was round, ruddy and mustaschioed, and his hands as wide as soup plates. He wore a red plaid shirt buttoned to the throat, and on his head a flat-billed wool cap brought from Poland. Jagush removed the cap and bowed servilely.

"*Ja*, hullo, miss," he said with a heavy accent.

Edwin acted as spokesman. "August has a brood sow who's ready to farrow but she's been trying for over sixteen hours and nothing's happened. He's afraid the pigs will die and maybe the sow, too, if something doesn't happen soon. Will you go out there and have a look?"

"Of course." Emily was already hurrying across the stable. The baby pigs—she knew—could survive in the birth canal a maximum of another two hours, and it might take her most of that to reach Jagush's place. "I'll need to saddle a horse and get my bag."

"I'll saddle Sagebrush for you," Edwin offered.

Jagush said, "The missus she sends a list, so I go to Loucks's first before I head back."

"Have you got some beer out at your place?" Emily asked, shouting from the office.

"Beer? *ja,* what *Polak* don't have beer?"

"Good. I'll need some."

If she waited for Jagush, precious minutes would be wasted. The animal was doubtless in pain and Emily found herself unwilling to prolong its suffering any longer than necessary. "If it's all right with you, Mr. Jagush, I won't wait for you. I know where you live."

"*Ja,* you hurry, miss," he agreed.

Jagush lived—it occurred to Emily—on the road out to the Lucky L ranch. Tom Jeffcoat wanted to buy horses. And Charles was haranguing her to help him. And Cal Liberty had a reputation for raising healthy hearty American saddlehorses and for being too proud of his stock to sell any inferior animals. Emily made a snap decision.

"Papa?" she called.

"What?"

"Saddle Gunpowder, too. I'm taking Jeffcoat along with me."

Her stomach danced with excitement. At last, a real call. Few ranchers had asked for her help. They instinctively doubted her ability since she was a woman, and since she hadn't fully earned her certificate from Barnum yet. Even when she did, it would not be the equivalent of a degree from a college of veterinary medicine. Those colleges were all back East or she'd be attending one right now. But she cared about animals and had what Papa had always called a natural instinct for helping them. It would take time before the bigger ranchers would trust her.

In the meantime, she'd help the smaller farmers like Jagush whenever possible, and wait for her reputation to grow.

In the office she opened a black leather satchel and took stock of her instruments: pincers, twitch, probang, and hopples; forceps in two sizes; balling iron and a balling gun; a pair of curved scissors, hand clippers, a clinch cutter; funnel and rubber tubing; a blacksmith's hoof knife; and an assortment of ordinary tools—a steel chisel, a pair of pliers, and a claw hammer. Yes, everything was there. And the bottles and vials too, neatly lining the sides of the case, each buckled into place by a leather band.

Satisfied, she snapped the bag closed, wrapped it in a black rubber apron, and went to tie it behind her saddle and mount up.

"Wish me luck, Papa," she called, taking Gunpowder's reins from Edwin.

"Bring 'em in alive, honey!" he called as she touched heel to Sage's flanks and took off at a canter through the double-wide door.

Thirty seconds later she reined in at the great north door of Jeffcoat's livery stable leading the spare black gelding.

"Jeffcoat?" she shouted. Inside, the syncopated beats of two hammers stopped. "Jeffcoat, you in there?" She peered into the depths of the building, which she'd never come near before. It was bigger than her father's and promised to be much more serviceable, with its brick floor, loft *steps* instead of a ladder, half-doors on the stalls, and the capstan for the turntable already in place. The windows were seated, the sliding door hung, pushed wide now to light both ends of the building. The stalls along the left were nearly complete, and from one, halfway down, Jeffcoat emerged. Even in silhouette she could tell it was he instead of Charles by the outline of his cowboy hat and the length of his legs.

"That you, tomboy?" he called.

"It's me. You wanna look at horseflesh or not?"

"Hey, Charles!" Tom threw down a hammer. "Can you work without me for a couple hours? Somebody's here who says she'll take me out shopping for horses."

Charles appeared behind Tom and walked with him the length of the building. "Emily, this is a surprise." He stopped beside Sagebrush, pulling off his work gloves, smiling up at her. "Why don't you come in and see the building? It's really shaping up."

"Sorry, I don't have time. I'm on my way out to August Jagush's to look at one of his brood sows that's having trouble farrowing."

"You're taking Tom out *there?*" Charles asked, surprised.

"No, out to the Lucky L after I'm done—it's close by and I figure Cal Liberty will treat him fairly. If you're coming, Jeffcoat, hurry up."

"You sure you don't mind, Charles?" Jeffcoat paused to ask.

"Not at all. Get going."

As Jeffcoat took the reins from Emily and mounted up, Charles squeezed her calf and said quietly, "Thanks, Emily. He's been worried about getting those horses."

"I'll see you tonight," she replied, giving Sagebrush both heels. Tom's stirrups needed lengthening, but Emily took off at a trot leaving him leaning sideways in the saddle.

"Hey, wait a minute."

"You can catch up!" she called without slowing.

While Charles volunteered to adjust the stirrups Tom glanced after his friend's fiancée and inquired, "Is she always this ornery?"

"She'll get used to you. Give her time."

"She's got the temperament of a wounded buffalo. Hell, I don't even know this horse's name."

"Gunpowder."

"Gunpowder, huh?" And to the horse: "Well, you'd better have some in you because we've got some catching-up to do." When the stirrups were adjusted Tom said, "Thanks, Charles. I'll see you here when I get back if it's early enough. Otherwise, at Tarsy's."

He took off at a canter, scowling at the rider ahead. She rode prettier than most women walked, with a natural roll and balance, her back straight, the reins in one hand, the other resting on a thigh. She wore her brother's cap again but she sat her saddle so perfectly it didn't even bounce. As Jeffcoat came up on her left flank he noted the sleek fit of the trousers over her thigh, her intent stare at the horizon, her taut lips. There was no warmth in her today at all, only spunk and determination. Yet she fascinated him.

"Hey, slow up there. You'll get that horse lathered."

"He can take it. Can you?"

"All right, sister, they're your horses."

They rode in silence for nearly an hour and a half. He let her control their pace, slowing to a walk when she slowed, cantering when she cantered. She spoke only once, when they were turning into the driveway at their destination. "This is no country to raise pigs in but Jagush is Polish and the Polish eat pork. He'd have been better off to bring lambs out here when he homesteaded."

A short pudgy woman in a *babushka* came from an outbuilding the moment they arrived. Her face was round as a pumpkin and contorted with worry. "She is down here!" Mrs. Jagush called, gesturing toward the crude log barn. "Hurry."

Dismounting, Emily told Jeffcoat, "You can wait here if you want. It'll smell a lot fresher."

"You might need some help."

"Suit yourself. Just don't get sick on me." Turning sideways in the saddle, she slid to the ground, landed lightly, and let Tom tie both horses to a fence post while she retrieved her pack from behind the saddle. They walked to the barn together, met by Mrs. Jagush, whose creased face spoke of long hours of anxiety.

"Tank you for comink. My Tina she is not so good."

No, her Tina wasn't. The sow lay on her side, shaking violently from fever. It appeared she had gathered straw and arranged a nest, sensing her time was at hand. But she'd been lying in it, probably thrashing, for the better part of a day and at some point her water broke and soiled the bed, which was flattened now into a dish shape. Emily donned her rubber apron, and disregarding the condition of the pen, dropped to her knees and touched the sow's belly, which was bright red instead of its usual pale pink. Her ears, too, were scarlet: a sure sign of trouble. "Not feeling so good, huh, Tina?" She spoke quietly, then informed Mrs. Jagush, "I'll need to wash my hands. And your husband said you have beer in the house. Could you bring me about a quart?"

"*Ja.*"

"And lard, a half cup should do."

When Mrs. Jagush went away, Jeffcoat inquired, "Beer?"

"It's not for me, it's for Tina. Pigs love beer and it calms them. Hand me that pitchfork, so I can get her up."

Jeffcoat obliged, then watched while she slipped the tines beneath the pig and gently rocked them against the floor. Pricked, but unhurt, the sow grunted to her feet.

"Pigs are very maleable. They get up and down naturally all through the birthing anyway, so nudging her up won't hurt her a bit. Good gal," Emily praised, rubbing the sow's back when she was on her feet.

She spoke to the pig with more warmth than she offered most people, Jeffcoat observed. But her concern for the animal had loosened her tongue and she explained to him, "Pigs give birth on two sides, did you know that? First they lay down and bear half the litter on one side, then they get up and clean them before flopping over onto the other side and do the same thing again. Nobody has an explanation why."

Mrs. Jagush returned with the supplies—a white basin, lard, and the beer in a wrinkled tin kettle. When the latter was placed before Tina, she reacted like a true sow, slurped the kettle dry, then fell to her side with a snort.

Emily washed her hands first with plain soap and water, then in a carbolic acid solution, and when they were dry, systematically went on to carbonize the lard and lubricate her right hand.

Jeffcoat watched with growing admiration. Having been around animals his whole life he'd heard plenty of stories of carelessness, and knew that more animals died from infection caused by unsanitary hands than of the natural complications of birthing.

Emily greased her skin well past the wrist, then met his eyes for the first time since entering the barn.

"If you want to help you can hold her head." Without words he took up his station at Tina's head.

"All right, Tina." Emily kept her voice low and soothing while dropping to her knees. "Let's see if we can give you some help."

Jeffcoat observed with added deference as she grasped the pig's tail, made a dart of her fingertips, and forced them into the animal. There could be no more repugnant job in all of animal husbandry, yet she performed it with single-minded purpose. The sow's muscles were tight and not easily breached; had they been otherwise, the baby pigs would undoubtedly have been born already and sucking. Emily set her jaw, stiffened her wrist, and performed the task with an alacrity most men would have found difficult to muster. Her hand disappeared to the wrist, then farther. Her eyes were fixed, her concentration centered deep within the animal. Groping blindly, she bit her lower lip, then whispered, "There you are." When she withdrew the first baby pig the stench hit like a fetid explosion, rolling Tom's stomach with such suddenness he found himself swallowing back his gorge. Emily whipped her face sharply aside, sucked in a quick breath against her shoulder, then turned back to check the piglet.

"It's dead," she reported, "Take it away or she'll try to eat it." Mrs. Jagush hurried over with a shovel and took the fetus away. Emily buried her face against her shoulder to momentarily muffle the stench while she refilled her lungs.

Coming up, she said, "Hang on. Here we go again."

She pulled out five of them and the miasma seemed to grow worse with each one. Tom found his nose flattened against his shoulder more often then not, and he wondered why anybody, much less a woman, would *choose* an occupation like this. After the sixth dead pig was pulled, he said, "Why don't you take a break and grab some fresh air?"

"When I've got them all," she answered stoically, taking no more relief than a quick breath against her own sleeve. In time it, too, grew soiled, dampened by her sweat, fouled in spots by animal offal and excretions. The stench became noxious as the straw grew wet and rank, but she knelt in it without complaint. Toward the end she gagged, but staunchly forced herself to finish the job.

The last few fetuses were carried away by August, who'd arrived from town in time to watch them being delivered dead.

Finally Emily told Tom, "That was the last one. Come on, now we can take a break."

They hurried outside into the clean air and sunshine, fell against the barn wall and sucked in great gulps of breath, closed their eyes and let their heads drop back in relief.

When he could speak again, Tom whispered, "Jesus."

"The worst is over. Thanks for helping."

For minutes they shared the gift of clean air while the Jagushes buried the nine baby pigs. At length, Tom rolled his head to study Emily's profile, her nose raised to the sun, her mouth open, drawing in the freshness.

"Do you do this often?"

She rolled her face toward him and produced a weary, self-satisfied grin. "First time with pigs."

His respect for her grew immensely. There were compliments he might have offered. They crossed his mind in ribbons of praising words. But in the end he simply grinned and said softly, "Y' did good, tomboy."

To his surprise, she replied, "Thanks, blacksmith, you didn't do so bad yourself. Now what do you say we wash our hands before we finish up?"

"There's more?" he asked, dismayed.

"More."

He boosted himself away from the wall. "Lead the way, Doc."

They washed at the well in the yard, and when they'd finished, returned to the barn, where Emily mixed up a solution of tincture of aconite and fed it to Tina to reduce her fever, then prepared a carbolic acid wash to clean out the sow's womb. From her bag Emily produced a rubber hose with a funnel attached to one end.

"Would you mind holding this?" she asked Tom, handing him the funnel.

He found he minded less and less, for watching her was not only an education, it was becoming enjoyable. She had dropped all her veneer of iciness and had become a strong, resolute person who, captivated by her work, had forgotten her antagonism toward Tom Jeffcoat. He could not help admiring again her tolerance and nervelessness as she inserted the hose into Tina, ordered, "Lift the funnel higher," and poured the wash into it. They stood close in the smelly barn, listening to the liquid gurgle as gravity took it down slowly. What they'd been through bound them with a curious, earthy intimacy. Repugnant, at times, yes, but fascinating, as birth always is. They had time now to think back over the past hour and the changes it had wrought in their respect for one another. She filled the funnel again and while they stood waiting for it to empty, their eyes met. Tom flashed a smile—an uncertain, disquieted smile. And Emily returned it. Not the tired grin she'd given without thought as they'd leaned back exhaustedly against the barn wall. This was a genuine, willing smile. Though she dropped her glance the moment she realized what she'd done, the exchange toppled a barrier. Realizing it, too, Tom thought, be careful, Jeffcoat, this tomboy could grow on you.

When the job was done and the instruments washed, he followed her outside where she stood in the late afternoon sun, instructing Mr. and Mrs. Jagush.

"Don't breed her every time she comes into heat. If you do she'll be weak and so will her babies. Give her a rest between times and start feeding her extract of black haw, no more than one ounce each day, mixed with her water. You can get it at the drug store and it'll help prevent abortions. Any questions?"

"*Ja,*" replied August, "how much do this cost me?"

She smiled and tied her pack onto her saddle. "Would one baby pig be too much? If the next brood lives, I'll take one at weaning time and raise him in the corral at the livery stable."

"One baby pig you will get, young missy, and I tank you for comink to help Tina. The missus, she was plenty upset this mornink, wasn't you, missus?"

Mrs. Jagush nodded and smiled, clasping her hands in gratitude. "God bless you, missy. You're a good girl."

Emily and Tom mounted up and waved to the two standing shoulder to shoulder in the driveway.

The road beyond the Jagush place angled northwest and as they took it the sun already shone on their left shoulders. Tom pulled out a pocket watch and snapped it open. "It's already four o'clock and Tarsy's party starts at seven. Maybe you'd rather put off introducing me to Liberty until another time."

"Tarsy's party is going to be silly anyway. I'd rather go to Liberty's than play parlor games."

"Oh, we're going to play parlor games, are we?"

"Fannie put ideas into her head. Musical chairs and charades and who knows what else."

"Seems to me you could stand a little merrymaking after an afternoon like you just put in."

She tossed him a sidelong glance laced with the hint of a smile. "Given a choice between looking at horses and playing parlor games, I'll take the horses every time."

Though he secretly agreed, Tom felt obliged to remind her, "Charles is looking forward to it."

"I know. So I'll go, but he'll find his way to Tarsy's himself if I'm a little late. Come on, let's ride."

With a touch of her heels she sent Sagebrush into an easy canter and Tom followed suit on Gunpowder. Cantering just off her left flank, he studied what he could see of her profile: her stubborn jaw; the full lower lip—jutting slightly as she concentrated on the road ahead; her black eyelashes and the cap angled over her left ear; the single hand holding the reins; her breasts, firm and unbouncing as her spine curved into each rise and fall of the broad back beneath her. His eyes lingered upon her breasts longer than was prudent, and with some shock he realized what he'd been thinking.

Whoa, there, Jeffcoat, just by God, whoa!

He glanced away and concentrated on the scenery instead.

They were in true ranching country where the uncertain horizon changed with each curve in the road. It was a landscape of gulch and rolling hill, sun-baked plateau and cloud-freshened valley. The hillsides were splotched with clusters of chartreuse aspens and darker strings of cottonwoods where busy streams brattled down from the great top country above timberline. Up there, snow still clung, startlingly white against the purple peaks. At lower altitudes additional seams of white appeared: gypsum interbedded with red chugwater rock giving the impression of smears of snow. Aromatic sage thrived everywhere in clumps of downy silver-green, trimmed with yellow blooms that spread their turpentinelike scent through the summer air. In the distance, sheep corrals tumbled like spilled matchsticks down the faces of green hills. So much green—bluegrass, wheatgrass and redtop, all lush and verdant.

In the distance they saw a sheepherder's wagon, tucked beneath a greasewood tree, and a tiny dark dot—a herder watching them from a nearby hillside, where he sat surrounded by his dun-colored herd and two black moving spots—his dogs.

To Tom's surprise, Emily reined in, stood in the stirrups, waved, and bugled, "Halloooo!" They sat still, listening to her call echo and reecho across the valley. The herder stood as the sound reached him. He cupped his mouth. Seconds later his greeting came back: the distinctive Basque yell, "Ye-ye-ye-ye-ye!", undulating across the valley like a shrill coyote yip.

"Who is he?" Tom inquired.

"I don't know. Just a Basque. They live year round in those little wagons with their herds. In the spring they take the sheep up the mountain, and in the fall they bring them back down. The most they ever own is their wagon, a rifle, and a couple of sheep dogs. I've always thought they must have such terribly lonely lives."

As they rode on, Tom puzzled over Emily Walcott. Was it her real self he was seeing today, at last? If so, he was beginning to like it. Animals and Basques warmed a response in her. He wondered what else did.

Once again he forced his thoughts into safer paths. Scanning the hills, he commented, "I hadn't expected so much green."

"Enjoy it while it lasts. By mid-July it'll all be yellow."

"When will winter start?"

She cocked her head and glanced at a distant white-topped peak. "The old-timers have a saying—that in Wyoming winter never ends, that when summer's coming down the mountain it meets winter going back up."

"What? No autumn?"

"Oh we have autumn, all right. Autumn's my favorite. Wait till you see these cottonwood in late September. Papa calls them 'the Midas gift' because they look like hoards of gold coins."

They topped a rise just then and below lay the Lucky L Ranch, spread out across an irregular-shaped valley on Horseshoe Mountain. The Little Tongue River ran through it and its perimeter was clearly defined by the black wall of pine and spruce, which gave it a protected look. Before they'd traveled half the length of the driveway, Jeffcoat realized the Lucky L was more than lucky, it was prosperous. The buildings were painted, the fences in repair, and the stock they passed looked impressively healthy. The house and outbuildings had a planned look, laid out in pleasing geometric relationship to one another. The barns, granaries, and bunkhouse were painted white with black trim, but the house was built of native sandstone. It had two stories, with thick roofbeams extended beneath the eaves, a deep, full-width front porch, and a great fieldstone chimney. Elms surrounded the house on three sides and the outbuildings flanked it, right and left.

Before the house a line of hitching posts waited, each topped by a steed's head of black iron, gripping a brass ring in its teeth.

"Looks like Liberty does all right for himself," Jeffcoat observed, dismounting.

"He sells horses to the army. The army not only pays top dollar, they create a constant demand. If the army thinks Lucky L horses are good enough, I do, too."

Emily led the way to the house, whose door was answered by a short, round woman in a white mobcap and apron. "Mr. Liberty is down behind C Barn." She pointed. "It's that one over there."

The first thing Jeffcoat noticed about Cal Liberty was not his impressive barrel-chested stature, or his expensive, freshly brushed Stetson trimmed with a leather band studded with turquoise set in silver, but the way he treated Emily Walcott—as if she were a ghost he could see through. Liberty immediately shook hands with Tom but ignored the hand that Emily offered. Upon learning that Tom was there to buy horses the rancher invited him over to the next barn, where his foreman was working, but he suggested Emily go to the house to have coffee with his wife.

Emily bristled and opened her mouth to retort, but Jeffcoat cut her off. "Miss Walcott is here to help me choose the horses."

"Oh." Liberty spared her a brief, derogatory glance. "Well, I guess she can come along then."

As they followed Liberty, Tom felt Emily sizzle with indignation. He squeezed her elbow and dropped her a pointed glance that ordered, Shut up, tomboy, just this once? To his relief, she only puckered her mouth and glared at the back of Liberty's head. Tom did likewise, thinking, You pompous ass, you should have seen her an hour ago pulling dead pigs.

They found Liberty's foreman, a seasoned cowboy with skin like beef jerky and hands as hard as saddle leather. His eyes were pale as jade, his legs bowed like a wishbone, and when he smiled the plug of tobacco in his cheek gave him the appearance of a pocket gopher.

"This's Trout Wills," Liberty announced. "Trout, meet Tom Jeffcoat."

Tom shook Trout's hand.

"Jeffcoat wants to look at—"

"And this is Miss Emily Walcott," interrupted Tom.

Trout tipped his hat. "Miss Walcott, how-do."

Liberty picked up where he'd left off, turning a shoulder to cut Emily out. "Jeffcoat wants to look at some horses. See what you can fix him up with."

Though Trout followed orders, Liberty stayed close by, watching. After the rancher's cool dismissal of Emily, Tom took perverse pleasure in allowing her every opportunity to display her knowledge of horseflesh. By some unspoken agreement they'd decided to take Liberty down a notch.

When the cavvy of horses milled before them, Tom asked, loud and clear, "What do you think, Emily?"

They both ignored Liberty, who lounged at a nearby fence. Tom watched as Emily singled out a two-year-old mare, won its confidence, and began a minute inspection. Tom stood back, impressed himself as she went through an entire half dozen animals with educated thoroughness. On each one she checked to make sure the skin was soft and supple, the hairs of the coat lying flat and sleek, the eyes bright, the bearing alert. She checked the membranes of the nostrils to be sure they were a pale salmon pink, felt each crest for possible soreness, each tendon for bursal enlargements, pulled back lips to inspect molars and tushes, picked up feet to examine the condition of the frogs, and even checked pulse rates beneath jaws.

While she was checking that of a healthy-looking sorrel, Tom stood close and inquired in an undertone, "What should it be?"

"From thirty-six to forty. He's right in there."

When one of the horses lifted its tail and dropped a few yellow nuggets, instead of jumping back as most women would, Emily nudged the droppings with her boot and commented, "Good ... not too soft, not too hard, just the way they're supposed to be." When another urinated she watched the proceedings, unfazed, and approved of the urine's color and the lack of strong odor.

"As a lot, they're healthy," she told Tom, adding, "but I was more concerned with their internal health. Anybody who's been around horses as long as you have knows what makes a sound one and which ones are light of bone. You can look them over yourself for conformation."

She stood back and took her turn at studying him as he went through the herd, sizing them up for conformation. She watched each move he made, recognizing what he was searching for: ample width between the eyes; eyes with little white showing; long, arched necks; well-developed shoulders; broad knees tapering front to back; flat shinbones and fetlocks angling at forty-five degrees. He disqualified one for its bell-shaped feet, winning a glance of approval from Emily, then singled out another for its thick cannon bones. Bridle-leading it, he checked its leg and foot action, and led it back to Emily.

"This one's a beauty."

She gave the big buckskin a hand-check and a perusal, then called to Liberty, "What's his name?"

"Buck." It was the first word he'd spoken directly to Emily.

She turned Jeffcoat aside and advised in an undertone, "You're right, he's beautiful, but let Liberty's foreman tack and ride him first. Just because he's beautiful doesn't mean he's manageable. And with a name like Buck ... well, it might be because of his color, but there's no sense taking chances. If anyone gets flattened against the fence or thrown, better the foreman than you."

Jeffcoat smiled and bowed to her wisdom.

Buck turned out to be a real gentleman. He stood docilely while Trout tacked him, then performed with absolute manners while being ridden. When Jeffcoat himself mounted and took Buck through his paces, Emily watched, once more impressed. He wisely walked Buck first instead of sending him into an immediate canter, as a greenhorn might have. He patiently circled, bent, halted, walked on, assessing the horse's reaction to the bit and the strange rider.

When he nudged Buck into a trot Emily watched him master the awkward juggling gait with unusual grace. At trot most women looked like corn being popped, most men like eager children reaching into a candy jar. Jeffcoat rode it rising, perfectly balanced, his hands steady, his loins relaxed, body inclined slightly forward, not just tipped from the hips. Emily's father had taught her to ride, had pointed out how few people could perform the trot gracefully, and that fewer still rode it on the correct diagonal.

Jeffcoat did it all effortlessly.

Equally as effortlessly he kicked Buck into a canter, changed rein to make certain the stallion performed correctly on either lead, and finally set him into a gallop. When Jeffcoat wheeled and stretched out, galloping back to her, he made an impressive sight, with leathers properly shortened, his weight out of the saddle carried on the insides of his thighs and knees, lifting on the balls of his feet.

Damn you, Jeffcoat, you look like you might have been born in that saddle, and the sight of you there does things to my insides.

When he reined in, his touch was light; already he'd learned that much about Buck. He dropped to the ground before the dust had settled, smiled, and told Emily, "This one'll be mine."

She couldn't resist teasing, "Don't you know, Mr. Jeffcoat, that a wise horseman never lets his heart be captured by the first animal he tests?"

"Unless it's the right one," he returned, smiling back.

She relented by patting Buck on his broad forehead. "He's a good choice."

Tom told Liberty, "This one's sold. I'll need four others for riding."

"Three should do," interrupted Emily, quietly.

"Three?"

"You'll find that around here you'll be renting out rigs mostly, to land agents taking immigrant families out to pick out their eighty acres for preemption. You'll need a few who are saddle-broke, sure, but most of your stock should be wagon-trained."

Again Jeffcoat bowed to her judgment, and the selection went on until his four saddlehorses were chosen and the deal made. The horses for the rigs would have to wait until another day, as it was getting late and they'd have to head back or get caught by dark.

"Pleasure doing business with you, Mr. Liberty. I'll be back sometime next week." Tom extended a hand. When Liberty had shaken it he found another waiting.

"You've got basically good sound stock," Emily approved, holding her hand poised where it could not be avoided.

"Thank you. What did you say your name is again?"

"Emily Walcott. I'm Edwin Walcott's daughter and I'm studying to be a veterinarian. That black pointed bay you call Gambler has what appears to be a touch of thoroughpin on his rear off hock that might be worth watching. My guess is he probably had a small sprain that you might not even have known about. It's no cause for worry, but if I were you I'd treat it with equal parts of spirits of camphor and tincture of iodine, and if it should ever grow to where pressure on one side makes it bulge on the opposite side, it should be drained and trussed. In that case, I'll be happy to come out and do it for you. You can find me at my father's livery stable most days. Good-bye, Mr. Liberty."

She and Jeffcoat mounted up and trotted their horses down the driveway feeling smug and amused. When they got beyond earshot, he released a whoop of laughter.

"Did you see the expression on his face!"

She laughed too. "I know I was showing off, but I couldn't resist."

"He deserved it, the pompous ass."

"I should be used to it. I'm a woman, and women, after all, are better at blacking stoves and punching down bread dough, aren't they?"

"I doubt that Liberty thinks so anymore."

She cast her companion an appreciative sidelong glance. "Thanks, Jeffcoat. It was fun."

"Yes, it was. The whole afternoon."

They rode on for some time in companionable silence, adjusting to it with some lingering astonishment after their turbulent beginning. It was a beautiful time of day, nearly sundown, conducive to amity. Behind them a flaming orange ball rested half-submerged below the tip of the mountain. Before them their mounted shadows stretched into distorted caricatures that slipped across the roadside grasses. They flushed a great flock of crows who flapped their way upmountain. At a narrow creek they startled a heron who winged his way to some distant rookery. They passed a spot where blossoming fireweed spread a great sheet of color, its bright pink flowers turned gilt by the flaming sun behind them. And farther along they turned in passing to study a picket-pin gopher sitting motionless atop his mound, as straight as his own shadow. From a roadside fence a meadowlark trilled and overhead the goshawks came out, calling their haunting flight song.

And the peace of evening settled within the two riders.

They listened to the squeak of shifting saddles, the three-time waltz rhythm of cantering hooves, the steady rush and pull of the horses' breath. They felt the east cool their fronts and the west warm their backs and realized they were enjoying each other's presence far more than advisable ... riding ... riding ... a mere horse's width apart ... eyes correctly ahead ... digesting the mellowing turn their relationship had taken in a single day. Something indefinable had happened. Well, perhaps not indefinable—inadmissible, rather—something startling and compelling and very much forbidden. They rode on, each of them battling the urge to turn and study, to confirm with an exchange of glances that the other was feeling it, too—

this newfound confederacy, this inadvisable, insidious fascination. To feel it was one thing; to allow it to show was another.

They rode on, downhill all the way, toward a party they would both be attending, and a dance they might conceivably end up sharing, and an attraction that should never have begun, schooling themselves to remain outwardly aloof while both of them thought of Charles Bliss—his friend, and her intended.

Chapter 8

They were both late to Tarsy's party. By the time Tom walked through the door, the hostess was in a state of near-panic, thinking he wasn't coming.

"Where have you *been?*" Tarsy flew across the room and grabbed his arm hard enough to cause black-and-blue marks.

"At the Lucky L Ranch, buying horses."

"I know *that*. Charles told me. But you're so late."

"We just got back half an hour ago." He scanned the room but Emily hadn't arrived yet.

"We've been waiting for you so we could start the games."

Tarsy commandeered Tom across a parlor filled with many of the same faces he'd met last week, but this time the older generation hadn't been invited. The group appeared to be all young and single. In the adjoining dining room they'd gathered around the table where they talked and laughed and drank punch. Charles was there but when Tom tried to veer over and talk to him Tarsy dragged him away. "Oh, you and that Charles! You see him every day at work, isn't that enough?" She raised her voice and beckoned everyone into the parlor. "Come on, everybody, we can start the games now! Everybody in here!" Tarsy began arranging chairs in a circle.

Tom slipped away to get himself a cup of punch and met Charles in the dining room archway.

"How did it go?" Charles inquired.

"I got a good start—four riding horses."

"And you actually made it back with no mortal wounds?" Grinning, Charles pretended to inspect Tom for damage, front and back. "No broken bones?"

"She was the epitome of politeness. We got along remarkably well."

"I'll know by one glance at her face when she walks through that door."

"Sorry I made her late. Mmm . . . who spiked the punch?"

"Probably Tarsy herself, the little wildcat."

Tom glanced around the two rooms. "No parents around, either?"

"No. I think Tarsy has designs on you and having parents around would be against her better interests. They're out for the evening, playing whist. I think we're being summoned . . . for the second time."

They went to join the others. While Tarsy began explaining the game, Emily arrived—a transformed Emily. Tom took one look at her and felt an involuntary force field build within himself. She'd spent less than an hour converting from tomboy to woman, but the transition was complete. Her hair was twisted high onto her head like an egg in a nest, with loose wisps rimming her face. She wore an astonishing dress of mauve, the rich hue of a spring hyacinth. It was as proper, feminine, and concealing as anything Queen Victoria herself might wear, with its high, banded neck, tucked, tight top, form-fitting long sleeves, and a hip ruffle dropping in a bouncing cascade over her rump. Ivory lace trimmed the garment in such a way that it drew a man's eye to strategic places. Over it she'd thrown a large, fringed shawl, caught carelessly over one shoulder and the opposite elbow. Where was the girl who'd pulled dead pigs all afternoon? And assessed horse-flesh? And ridden several hours on horseback? She was gone, and in her place a woman whose appearance momentarily knocked the breath from Tom Jeffcoat.

He watched her eyes seek and find Charles and telegraph him a private hello, watched his best friend cross the parlor to touch her shoulders and take her shawl while he himself felt the sting of jealousy. Charles rested a hand just above her rear flounce and said something that made her release a short huff of laughter. She replied and they both glanced Tom's way. The amusement fell from her face as if she'd run up against a barbed-wire fence. Immediately she glanced away and Tom raised his punch cup to his lips, realizing Charles observed.

Tarsy called across the parlor. "Oh, Emily, you're here at last. Hurry and take a chair so we can start the game."

Emily and Charles sat across from Tom while he attempted to forget they were there.

He shifted his attention to Tarsy. Tarsy was giddy with excitement, announcing a game called Squeak, Piggy, Squeak. She had placed the chairs in a circle facing inward and when everyone was seated, stood in the center, ordering, "Everyone has to pick a number between one and a hundred to see who's first."

"To do what?" someone asked.

"You'll see. Now pick."

The winning number was chosen by Ardis Corbeil, a tall, freckled redhead who blushed as she reluctantly got to her feet in the center of the circle.

"What do I have to do?"

"You'll see. Now turn around." Tarsy produced a folded scarf.

"You're not going to blindfold me, are you?"

"Well, of course I'm going to blindfold you. Then I'll spin you around a few times and give you a cushion, and the cushion is the only thing you can touch anybody with. The first person you touch, you have to sit on his lap and say 'Squeak, piggy, squeak.' Then he has to squeak and you have to guess who he is."

"That's all?"

"That's all."

Snickers began around the room while Ardis allowed herself to be blindfolded and spun around. Tarsy spun her until the poor girl could scarcely tell up from down.

Muted laughter and whispers tittered through the room. "Shh! No talking or she'll know where you are! Are you dizzy yet, Ardis?"

Poor Ardis was more than dizzy; she reeled and groped and nearly toppled over when released. Tarsy steadied her. "Now, here's your cushion, and remember, no hands! You get three squeaks to guess whose lap you're on, and if you guess right, it's that person's turn to be blindfolded, otherwise you have to pay a forfeit. All right now?"

From beneath the blindfold came Ardis's uncertain nod.

The room quieted of all but smothered snickers. Tipped forward at the waist, Ardis shuffled and stumbled three steps, leading with the cushion.

TT-tt.

"Shh!" Tarsy slipped into a chair and the room grew silent.

Ardis scuffed forward with the cushion extended in both hands, sliding her soles cautiously across the floor. The cushion bumped Mick Stubbs in the face. He drew back and compressed his lips to keep from laughing outright. Ardis patted the cushion up his head, down his shoulder to his chest, and finally to his knees.

Some of the girls blushed and clapped their hands over their mouths.

Tom glanced at Emily and found her watching him. They sat like islands of stillness in the jollity around them while everyone else's attention was riveted on the game. How long? A second? Five seconds? Long enough for Tom Jeffcoat to realize that what he'd sensed happening between them this afternoon had not been a figment of his imagination. She was feeling it, too, and was doing her best to submerge it. He had been in love once before and recognized the warning signs. Fascination. Watchfulness. The urge to touch.

Beside her, Charles laughed, and she glanced aside with forced nonchalance. Tom, too, returned his attention to the game in progress.

Ardis was perched on Mick's knees and his face was red with suppressed laughter.

"Squeak, piggy, squeak," Ardis ordered.

Mick tried, but his squeak sounded more like a snort.

Everybody snickered.

"Shh!"

"Squeak, piggy, squeak!"

This time Mick managed a high-pitched vocal rendition that brought laughter erupting all around. Ardis still failed to identify him.

"Squeak, piggy, squeak!"

Mick's third try was a masterpiece—high, shrill, porcine. Unfortunately for Mick, at its end the entire roomful of people was hooting so loud that he lost control himself, giving away his identity.

"It's Mick Stubbs!" Ardis shrieked, yanking off her blindfold. "I knew it! Now you have to wear this thing!"

Mick Stubbs weighed a good 215 pounds. He had a bushy brown beard, and arms as thick as most men's thighs. He made a hilarious sight being blindfolded, twirled, and groping his way onto the lap of Martin Emerson, another bearded guest. It was impossible not to get caught up in the hilarity of the evening as the game proceeded. Everybody loved it. Martin Emerson groped his way to Tarsy, and Tarsy groped her way to Tilda Awk, and Tilda Awk groped her way to Tom Jeffcoat, and Tom groped his way to Patrick Haberkorn; and along the way Tom found himself laughing as hard as the others. He knew the moment Emily, too, began enjoying herself. He saw her resistance to the game melt when the humor grew infectious. He saw her first smile, heard her first laughter, admired her face wreathed in gayness, a facet of her he'd observed too few times. Emily, smiling, was a sight to behold. But always, beside her was Charles. Charles, to whom she was betrothed.

After "Squeak, Piggy, Squeak," everybody voted to pause and refresh their punch cups.

Tarsy monopolized Tom during the break, and he turned his attentions to her gladly, relieved to have them diverted from Emily Walcott. Tarsy was a pretty girl, amusing, and very lively. He made up his mind the best thing he could do for himself was to enjoy her and forget about this afternoon, and the becoming arrangement of Emily Walcott's hair, and how pretty she looked in the mauve dress, and the glances they'd exchanged across a crowded room.

"Tom, come here! I have to talk to you!" Excited, Tarsy tugged him aside and lowered her voice secretively. "Will you do something with me?"

"Maybe." He grinned down flirtatiously into her brown eyes, sipping his drink. "Depends on what it is."

"Will you be first with me on the next game?"

"Depends on what it is."

"It's Poor Pussy."

His grin idled on her eager face. He knew the game. It was filled with innuendo and a certain amount of touching, and he sensed in an instant her underlying reason for introducing it. "And who's the poor pussy, you or me?"

"I am. All you have to do is sit on a chair and try to stay sober while I do my best to make you laugh."

He took another sip of brandy punch, enjoying her avid brown eyes and thinking, what better way to show everyone—Charles included—that Tarsy was the one who sparked his interest?

"All right."

Tarsy giggled and hauled him by an arm into the parlor to resume the fun. "Come on, everybody, we're going to play a new game. Poor Pussy!"

Tarsy's guests returned eagerly, their party mood enhanced by the brandy and the success of the first game. When everyone was seated, once more in a circle, Tarsy explained, "The object of Poor Pussy is for two people to try not to laugh. I'm going to be a cat, and I'll choose anyone I want to play to. The only word I can say is 'meow,' and whoever I say it to is only allowed to say, 'poor pussy.' Three times is all we can speak. If either one of us laughs we have to pay a forfeit of the other one's choice, all right?"

Tarsy's guests murmured approval and settled into their chairs for more amusement.

"Of course," Tarsy added, "all of you can talk all you want—you can prod and tease and offer any suggestions that come to mind. Here we go."

Poor Pussy was so ridiculously simple, it succeeded for its sheer absurdity. Tarsy dropped to her hands and knees and affected a kittenish pout that began everyone laughing immediately. She arched her back and sidled up to several knees before finally adopting a supplicating posture at Tom Jeffcoat's feet. She batted her eyelashes up at him and gave a pitiful *"Meoooow."* The observers chuckled as Tom sat cross-armed and consoled, "Poor pussy."

From Tom's left, Patrick Haberkorn nudged his elbow and teased, "You can do better than that, Jeffcoat. Stroke her fur a little!"

Unable to speak, lest he end up being the one owing a forfeit, Tom looked her over as if with piqued interest, tilting his head to one side.

Tarsy tried again with a doleful, feline, *"Meeeeeeowwwwww."* She made a winning cat, preening herself against Tom's knee and putting on an appealing pout.

"Poor pussy looks like she's starved for attention," Haberkorn improvised.

Tom reached down and petted Tarsy's head, then scratched her beneath the chin, running his fingertips down her throat. "Pooooor pussy," he sympathized. He was in no danger of laughing, but the dimple in his cheek deepened and his mouth took on a half grin as he teased her overtly.

The others got into the spirit of the game and strengthened their efforts to get either of the pair to laugh.

"Who let that mangy cat in here!"

"Hey, pussy, where's your sandbox?"

Tarsy was in the midst of meowing and rubbing her ear against Tom's pant leg when Charles called, "Anybody got a mouse to feed her?" and Tarsy collapsed in merriment, followed by everyone else in the room. Tarsy knelt on the floor, head hanging, too overcome with mirth to get to her feet, having too much fun to try. Tom caught her arm and drew them both to their feet, enjoying himself immensely. "All right everybody, you heard Tarsy. She has to pay me a forfeit."

Yes, yes, a forfeit. Everyone in the room recognized a budding romance when they saw one.

In the center of the circle Tom kept Tarsy's elbow while perusing her with mock lasciviousness. "What'll it be, puss?" he asked, to everyone's amusement.

Two suggestions were thrown at Tom simultaneously.

"Make her spend the night on the back-porch step."

"Make her take a bath—cat-style!"

Tom knew perfectly well what Tarsy was hoping for. His eyes dropped to her lips—pretty lips, full and pink and slightly parted. A kiss would certainly seal within the minds of everyone here which way the wind blew for Tom Jeffcoat. But this was Tarsy's party: if she wanted to start risqué forfeits, she'd have to instigate them herself.

"Bring her a saucer of milk," he ordered, still holding her arm while her flush grew becoming.

Somebody brought a saucer of milk and set it on the floor. Tarsy promised in an undertone, "I'll get even with you, Tom Jeffcoat. You can't escape me forever." With a flourish of skirts, she gamely dropped onto hands and knees to pay her forfeit.

She made a provocative sight, kneeling bustle-up, lapping milk from the edge of the saucer, as provocative a sight as she'd made rubbing her breast against his knee. Watching her, Tom laughed with the rest, but when she'd been in the ignominious position for a mere fifteen seconds he relented and hauled her to her feet. "Poor pussy is excused," he said for all to hear. Then privately to Tarsy, ". . . for the time being."

Not a soul in the room doubted that there was a genuine spark of interest between the two.

Emily Walcott watched the entire farce with a queer tightness in her chest and a strange, forbidden heaviness in her stomach. It had been highly suggestive. Sometimes she'd tried not to laugh, but had been unable. Sometimes she'd felt embarrassed, but could not drag her eyes away.

What would her parents say? Mother, in particular.

She and every girl in the room had been raised upon rigid, Victorian mores. Blatant flirtatiousness was strictly forbidden and physical contact with the opposite sex was limited to a brief touch of hands in greeting or holding an escort's elbow when walking. Yet these games encouraged a good deal of tactile and vocal innuendo.

She wondered if the other girls felt as she did, drawn and repelled at once, flushed and uncomfortable. Was it the subtle naughtiness of the games themselves or was it Tom Jeffcoat? Watching Tarsy rub against his trouser legs, Emily had felt an insidious stirring inside. When he'd petted Tarsy's hair and run his fingers down her throat Emily had experienced a startling rush of excitement. And something more. Prurience, she was sure, which made these games indecent. Yet she'd been unable to turn away. Not even when Tom had gazed into Tarsy's eyes and employed his flirtatious grin had she turned away. She'd stared, galvanized by a bewildering jolt of jealousy while everyone in the room expected him to demand a kiss as a forfeit. Then he'd called for the saucer of milk and she'd released her breath carefully, hoping Charles wasn't watching her.

Whatever had Tarsy started here?

Tarsy knew precisely what she had started, and she'd done it consciously. At the end of the evening she asked Tom Jeffcoat to stay after the others had gone, to help her push the furniture back into place.

It was a convenient ruse, Tom knew, but he was a red-blooded American male with a little brandy coursing through his veins, and Tarsy was a tempting young lady whose admiration wasn't exactly unwelcome. Furthermore, Miss Emily Walcott was off limits and he'd been too aware of her all night long.

When the punch bowl was carried to the kitchen, the chairs put back in place, and all but one lamp wick lowered, he decided to take advantage of Miss Tarsy Fields's thinly veiled invitation. She had walked him slowly to the door and was reaching for his jacket, which hung on the newel post.

"Come here," he ordered quietly, catching her around the waist and swinging her against him. "Now I'll take the rest of my forfeit."

She forgot about his jacket as he tipped his head and kissed her, chastely at first, then with growing intimacy. He invited her to open her lips and she did. He brushed his tongue across hers and she responded. He ran his hands up her back and she did likewise up his.

He found, to his enjoyment, that it stirred him. Lifting his head slowly he let her read it in his eyes. "I think you've been planning that all night," he told her.

"And you haven't?"

He laughed and ran the backs of his fingers along her jaw. His lips softened into a speculative crook as he continued caressing her jaw, letting his gaze rove from her eyes to her mouth and back again. "I wonder what it is you want from me."

"To have fun. Innocent fun. That's all."

"That's all?"

She took another kiss, in lieu of anything more she might want. She had lush lips and knew instinctively how to use them to best advantage. When she pulled away Tom's lips were wet and he found himself pleasantly aroused.

"You're looking for a husband, aren't you?" he inquired pleasantly.

"Am I?"

"I think so. But I'm not him, Tarsy. I might enjoy kissing you and being your partner for parlor games, and letting you rub against my pant leg, but I'm not in the market for a wife. You'd best know that from the start."

"How honorable of you to forewarn me, Mr. Jeffcoat."

"And how tempting you are, Miss Fields."

"Then is there anything wrong with"—she shrugged—"enjoying each other a little?"

He kissed her once more, lingeringly, resting a hand at the side of her breast, delving deep with his tongue. Their mouths parted reluctantly.

"Mmm . . . you do that so well," she murmured.

"So do you. Have you had much practice?"

"Some. Have you?"

"Some. Shall we have another go at it?"

"Mmm . . . please."

The next "go" was wetter, more promiscuous. When his hand strayed to her breast she drew back discreetly—a woman who knew how to leave a man with something to anticipate. "Perhaps we'd better say good night now."

He found himself mildly amused but scarcely heartbroken. She was a pleasant diversion, nothing more, and as long as they both understood it, he was willing to dive as deep or shallow as she'd allow.

"All right." Unhurriedly he reached for his jacket. "Thank you for a truly amusing party. I think everyone agreed it was an unqualified success."

"It was, wasn't it?"

"I think you've really started something with these parlor games. The men loved them."

"So did the girls, though they don't think they should admit it. Even Emily, who's as prudish as they come, and Ardis, who's decided to have the next party. Will you be there next week?"

"Of course. I wouldn't miss it."

"Even if it's you who has to pay the forfeit?"

"Forfeits can be fun."

They laughed and she smoothed his lapel. On her porch they shared one last, lingering good-night kiss, but in the middle of it he found himself wondering if Charles was doing the same thing with Emily right now, and if so, how obliging she was.

He caught only glimpses of her that week. He chose his carriage horses without her aid, and signed a hay contract with a rancher named Claude McKenzie, who said he'd be cutting his crop by mid-July. He talked with the local harnessmaker, Jason Ess, about the harnesses he'd need. Ess told him Munkers & Mathers Hardware down in Buffalo handled new Bain wagons, and he made the thirty-mile trip to place an order.

Emily, Charles said, had been called out twice that week: to diagnose and treat a cow whose paunch was bound up by a hairball, and to extract a decayed tooth from a horse. In both cases she'd been paid in hard cash and was elated to have earned her first money as a veterinarian.

Frankie came by and said his sister had been trying to ride Fannie's bicycle and had fallen and knocked the wind from herself and gotten so angry she climbed back on, fell a second time, and scraped a patch of skin off her hand and another from her forehead.

"You should've heard her cuss!" Frankie exclaimed. "I never knew girls could cuss like that!"

Tom smiled and thought about her for the remainder of the day.

On Saturday night she showed up at Ardis Corbeil's house sporting a pair of strawberry-red scabs, one just below her hairline and another on her nose. Tom was near the door when the two of them walked in. He offered Charles a congenial hello, but glanced down at Emily and made the mistake of chuckling.

"What are you laughing at!" she snapped, scowling at him.

"Your battle scars."

"Well, at least I tried riding it! If you think it's so easy, you try!"

"I told Fannie I'd love to."

Charles put in, "The subject of the bicycle is a touchy one right now."

Smiling, Tom tipped a shallow bow of apology. "I'm sorry I brought it up, Miss Walcott."

"I'll *bet* you are!" She turned and stalked away.

"Mercy, she really doesn't take teasing well, does she?"

"Especially from you, I'm afraid."

The crowd played a new game that night called "Guessing Blind Man" and what Tom had feared, happened: when it was his turn, he was blindfolded, surrounded by a ring of seated players, and ended up on the lap of Emily Walcott.

Something told him immediately it was she. The reaction of the others, perhaps. To his left he heard a soft "Oh-oh!", then "Shh!"

Everyone in the room knew that from the moment Tom Jeffcoat had come to town Emily Walcott had considered him her archenemy. She would as soon bury him as look at him. Yes, she'd helped him buy horses, but she'd done it begrudgingly, at Charles's request. Even tonight, at the door, she'd snapped at Jeffcoat the moment she'd stepped into the house.

Now here he sat, blindfolded, on her lap, surrounded by titters.

The rules of the game were simple: he had a free pair of hands and three tries to guess who she was.

The tittering stopped. The silence grew pregnant and Tom imagined Charles looking on. The games were getting more and more daring. There was no cushion in use this time, and if his hand groped in the wrong place, no telling what it might touch. Emily sat stone still, scarcely breathing. Someone snickered. Someone else whispered. Beneath him he felt the contact with her slim knees but he let them bear his full weight—anything to make this look as if he were continuing to nettle her for his own amusement. Behind his blindfold he pictured her cheeks, burning with embarrassment, her breath indrawn, her shoulders stiff.

He reached . . . and found her right hand gripping the edge of the chair seat. For a moment they engaged in a silent tug-of-war, but he won and lifted the hand by its wrist, much smaller than the circle of his fingers.

The game gave him license to do what he might never get a chance to do again and he'd do it, by god, with Charles watching, and satisfy his curiosity. Those looking on would see only what they'd been seeing all along—a teasing man having his fun with a woman who could scarcely tolerate him.

Still holding her wrist, he explored with his free hand each long, thin finger, each nail clipped veterinarian-short; callouses (surprising) at the base of her palm, then the palm itself, working it over mortar-and-pestle fashion. Sure enough: a scab—undoubtedly caused by her fall from the bicycle. He felt an acute forbidden thrill.

"Ah, tough hands. Could it be Charles Bliss?"

Everyone roared while Tom concealed his own disturbing reaction beneath a veneer of teasing. He lifted his right hand and found her cheek. She stiffened and drew back sharply. His hand pursued, examining everything but the two scabs he knew were there—one silky eyebrow; one eye, forcing it to close; a soft temple where a pulse drummed crazily; a velvety earlobe.

He leaned close and sniffed: lemon verbena . . . a surprise.

"Mmm . . . you don't smell like Charles."

More laughter as he examined her gauzy hair and the curls outlining her face.

"Charles, if it's you, you've done something new with your hair."

Laughter intensified as he touched Emily's cheek—hot, hot, afire with self-consciousness—and finally her mouth, which opened, emitting a faint gasp. She jerked back so sharply he imagined her head bowed over the back of the chair. When he'd discomfited her to the degree that he was certain everyone in the room knew he was doing it intentionally, he touched her scabbed nose and forehead.

"Is it you, tomboy?" he asked, loud and clear, then bellowed, "Emily Walcott!" leaping from her lap and ripping the blindfold from his eyes.

She had ripened like an August tomato and was staring at her skirt as if trying to suppress tears of mortification.

Tom swung toward Charles. "No offense intended, Charles."

"Of course not, it's all in fun," Charles replied.

Emily's expression turned mutinous and Tom knew he must do something to alleviate the tension. So, there before all her friends he bent swiftly and dropped a kiss on her cheek. "You're a good sport, Walcott," he declared.

She shot up from her chair and skewered him with a feral glare, planted her hands on her hips and came at him with slow, insidious intent while their ring of friends laughed at their antics. Tom retreated behind Charles's chair, extending his palms as if to stave her off. "Charles, help me! Tell your woman to back off!"

Charles joined the parody, pretending to subdue Emily, who strained toward Jeffcoat, warning, "Next time, hostler, I'll dump you on the floor!"

Though Emily had drawn upon feigned vitriol to escape having her incipient feelings for Tom detected, the incident had been unnerving. Not nearly so unnerving as one that happened later in the evening, however.

It was bound to happen sooner or later: Tarsy insisted on playing French Postman. The rules of the game needed no explanation for Emily to guess that its outcome would be kissing. She herself escaped being sent a "letter," but before the game was over, Tarsy sent one to Tom, and when it was delivered, Emily watched with derelict fascination as the two of them stood in the middle of the room and kissed as she had never observed anyone kissing before, with Tom's hands running freely over Tarsy's back, and their mouths open—wide! For a good half minute! A lump formed in Emily's throat as she watched. Hot tentacles of unwanted jealousy and undeniable prurience painted blotches on her neck. Even before the game ended she vowed she would never attend one of these parties again.

To Tom, kissing Tarsy had been nothing but a false show, a convenient opportunity to further divert memories from how he'd made free with Emily Walcott.

For that was the encounter that had rocked him.

Just a game to some, but to him it had been the first feel of her skin, the first scent of her hair, and a telltale gasp that she'd been unable to control when he'd touched her lips. Whatever outward appearance Emily Walcott maintained, she was far from indifferent to him, and the knowledge put a tension around his chest that refused to go away.

During the days that followed, while he worked beside Charles, Tom pretended casual disinterest or amusement whenever her name was mentioned. But at bedtime he fell onto his pillow to stare at the ceiling and ponder his dilemma: he was falling in love with Emily Walcott.

He dreamed up an excuse to avoid the next party, spending instead a miserable night at the Mint Saloon, listening to veiled slurs from his competitor, Walter Pinnick, who sat with a group of his drunken henchmen and blubbered about his failing business. Next he went to the Silver Spur where he played a few hands of poker with a handful of weatherbeaten ranch hands. But they were a poor substitute for the company of his friends who were gathered across town.

The following week he and Charles completed work on his livery barn and Charles suggested, "You should have a party in the loft before McKenzie delivers the hay."

"Me?"

"Why not you? It's the perfect place. Plenty of room."

Tom shook his head. "No, I don't think so."

"A dance, maybe, and invite the local merchants and their wives—a grand opening, if you will. It wouldn't be bad for business, you know."

Upon further consideration, the idea took on merit. A dance. What trouble could he get into at a dance, especially with the older generation around? Hell, he wouldn't even have to dance with Emily Walcott, and Charles was right—it would be a wonderful goodwill gesture from the newest businessman in town. He'd need a band and refreshments, a few lanterns, little more.

He found a fiddler who sometimes played at the Mint, and the fiddler knew a harmonica player, and the harmonica player knew a guitar player, and in no time at all, Tom had his band. They said they'd play for free beer, so on a Saturday night in mid-July the whole town turned out to christen Jeffcoat's Livery Stable.

Josephine insisted that Edwin take Fannie. "She's been in the house too much. She needs to get out and so do you."

"But—"

"Edwin, I won't take no for an answer, and you know how she loves dancing."

"I can't take her to a—"

"You can and you shall," Josephine stated with quiet authority.

He did.

They walked uptown together: Charles and Emily, Edwin and Fannie, through a molten summer sunset, through a windless violet evening, the older couple without touching, except for Fannie's skirts brushing Edwin's ankle like an intimate whisper. He felt young again, released, strolling along beside the woman who was vital and healthy and whose desirability had in no way diminished over the years. If anything, it had grown. He allowed this admission to surface while keeping his gaze locked on his daughter's back. If things had turned out differently Emily might have been theirs—his and Fannie's.

"Oh, Edwin," Fannie declared, when they were halfway to their destination, "I'm so incredibly happy."

Who but Fannie would be happy with this impossible situation?

"You always are."

Their gazes met and hers held a question: Shall I feel guilty because Josephine has shared you with me for the evening, or shall I make the most of it?

They made the most of it. They danced the waltz and the varsovienne, the Turkish trot and the reel. Their hands learned the feel of one another—his as it lay on her waist, hers as it rested on his shoulder. They accepted these touches as a gift.

They grew warm and drank beer to cool off. They laughed. They talked. They conversed and danced with others, distancing themselves to covertly admire one another from room's width. They learned that they could be happy with this and no more.

Tom hadn't intended to ask Emily to dance. He'd brought Tarsy, and Tarsy was enough to wear out any man on the dance floor. He danced with others, too, from his new circle of friends—Ardis and Tilda, Mary Ess, Lybee Ryker; the list had grown. And with many of their mothers, and, of course, with Fannie, who was sought as a partner by every man in the place, regardless of his age.

Fannie brought it about, what Tom had been determined to avoid. She was waltzing with him, chattering about Frankie's capacity for molasses cookies, when Edwin danced past with his daughter.

"Oh, Edwin, could I talk to you?" Fannie heralded, swinging out of Tom's arms. "I wonder if one of us shouldn't go home and check on Joey."

While they carried on a brief conversation Emily and Tom stood by, trying not to look at each other. At length, Fannie touched their arms and said, "Excuse me, Tom, you don't mind finishing this one with Emily, do you?"

And so it happened. Tom and Emily were left facing each other on a crowded dance floor. She wouldn't look at him. He couldn't help himself from looking at her. He saw the telltale hint of pink creeping up her cheeks and decided it was best to keep the mood convivial.

"I guess we're stuck with each other." He grinned and opened his arms. "I can bear it if you can."

They moved toward each other gingerly and began waltzing, maintaining a careful distance but bound by unmerciful memories of the last evening they'd spent together.

His fingertips learning the textures of her face.

His hands and tongue on Tarsy.

"I wasn't sure you'd come," he said, meeting the eyes of Charles, who watched from the edge of the floor.

"Papa and Fannie and Charles wouldn't have missed it."

"So you got roped into it."

"You might say that."

"You're still angry about that silly game." He turned his back to Charles and glanced down at her compressed lips as she stared over his shoulder. "I'm sorry if it embarrassed you." His glance slipped lower, to her chest, tinted by a charming if unladylike vee of sunburned skin shaped like the neck opening of her brother's shirt. There, again, he detected a blush behind a peppering of freckles.

"Could we talk about something else, please?"

"Certainly. Any subject you like."

"You have a fine barn," she offered dutifully.

"I picked out the rest of my horses last week. I can get them any time."

With the subject of horses she was comfortable; she risked meeting his eyes. "From Liberty?"

"Yes. One mare is in foal." She relaxed further as Tom continued with her favorite subject. "And I went down to Buffalo and ordered carriages and wagons from Munkers and Mathers. I'll get them as soon as my hay is delivered."

"Bains?"

"Yup."

"They're good, sturdy wagons. Good axles. They'll last you. What brand of carriages?"

"Studebakers."

"Studebakers ... good."

"I thought I'd need the best, what with these damned washboard roads out here—where there are roads. I ordered my hay from McKenzie, too. As soon as it comes I'll be open for business."

They danced on in a more comfortable silence after the interpersonal talk, still careful not to stray too close.

"So what have you been doing?" he inquired, implying casual disinterest when actually he was avid to know everything that had affected her life since they'd seen each other.

"Not much."

"Charles tells me you removed a hairball and a rotten tooth. Got paid for it, too."

"I removed the tooth, not the hairball. That I took care of with epsom salts and a little raw linseed oil. Distasteful but effective."

"But you *did* get paid."

He watched her face for signs of satisfaction and found them as she answered, "Yes."

"I guess that makes you a real doc now, huh?"

"Not really. Not until spring."

Silence again while they moved to the music, still separated by a body's width, searching for a new distraction. At length she remarked, "Charles says you've picked out blueprints for your house."

"I have."

"Two stories and an L-shaped porch."

"It seems to be the going thing. Tarsy says everybody's got a porch these days."

Their gazes collided and they danced in a web of confused feelings.

You're building it for her?

The tension between them became palpable.

Hoping to remind them both of their obligations, Emily commented, "Charles will do a good job for you. He does everything well."

"Yes," Tom replied, "I imagine he does."

Somewhere a harmonica wailed and a fiddle scraped, but neither of them heard. Their feet continued shuffling while they grew lost in one another's eyes.

Stop looking at me like that.

You stop looking at me like that.

This was impossible, dangerous.

The tension built until Emily felt a sharp pain between her shoulder blades and she lost her will to keep the conversation impersonal. "You didn't come to the party last week," she lamented in a breathy voice.

"No, I . . . I worked on the barn." It was an obvious lie.

"After dark?"

"I used a lantern."

"Oh."

At that moment someone bumped Emily, throwing her against Tom. Her breasts hit his chest and his arms tightened for the briefest moment. But it took no longer for their hearts to race out of control. She jumped back and began prattling to cover her discomposure. "I never did care much for dancing, I mean some girls were born to ride horses and some were born to dance but I don't think many of them were born to do both but just put me on a saddle and watch—"

"Emily!" Tom caught her hand and squeezed it mercilessly. "Enough! Charles is watching."

Her inane chatter stopped mid-word.

They stood before one another feeling helpless beneath the grip of a growing attraction neither of them had sought or wanted. When she had regained some semblance of poise he said sensibly, "Thank you for the dance," then turned her by an arm and delivered her back to Charles.

Chapter 9

Later that night, Emily lay beside a sleeping Fannie, recreating Tom Jeffcoat in thought—gestures and expressions that became disconcertingly attractive in the deep of night. His blue, teasing eyes. His disarming sense of humor. His lips, crooking up to make light of something that felt heavy and treacherous within her. She wrapped herself in both arms and coiled into a ball facing away from Fanny.

I scarcely know him. But it didn't matter.

He's Papa's competition. But noble about it.

He's Tarsy beau. It carried little weight.

He's Charles' friend.

Ah, that one stopped her every time.

What kind of woman would drive a wedge between friends?

Stay away from me, Tom Jeffcoat. Just stay away!

He did. Religiously. For two full weeks while his livery stable opened up for business. And while the framework of his house went up. And while word came back to Emily that he was seeing Tarsy with growing regularity. And while Emily thought, good, be with Tarsy—it's best that way. And while Jerome Berryman hosted a party which Tom again avoided. And while Charles grew more randy and began pressuring Emily to advance the date of their wedding. And while full summer stole over the valley and parched it to a sere yellow, bringing daytime temperatures in the high eighties. The heat made work in a livery barn less enjoyable than at any other time of year. Flies abounded, skin itched from the slightest contact with chaff, and the horses tended to get collar galls from sweating beneath their harnesses.

One morning Edwin took Sergeant across the street to have him shod and in the late afternoon asked Emily to go get him.

Her head snapped up and her heart leapt to her throat. She blurted out the first excuse that came to mind. "I'm busy."

"Busy? Doing what, scratching that cat?"

"Well, I . . . I was studying." His impatient glance fell to her hip where a book rested, facedown.

It was a beastly hot day and her father was fractious, not only from the heat. Mother was worse again, someone had returned a landau with a rip in the seat, and he'd had a set-to with Frankie over cleaning the corral. When Emily balked at collecting Sergeant, Edwin displayed a rare fit of temper.

"All right!" He threw down a bucket with a clang. "I'll go get the damn horse myself!"

He stomped out of the office and Emily shot after him, calling, "Papa, wait!"

He brought himself up short, heaved a deep sigh, and turned to her, the picture of forced patience. "It's been a long day, Emily."

"I know. I'm sorry. Of course I'll go get Sergeant."

"Thanks, honey." He kissed her forehead and left her standing in the great south doorway with doubts amassing as she pondered Jeffcoat's place of business a half block away. In all the time it was going up, and since it had been open for business, she had never been in it alone with him, and now she knew why. She stepped outside and hesitated, telling her pulse to calm, concentrating on the newly painted sign above his door: JEFFCOAT'S LIVERY STABLE—HORSES BOARDED & SHOD, RIGS FOR RENT. A new pair of hitching rails stood out front, their posts of freshly peeled pine shining white in the sun. The line of windows along the west side of his building reflected the blue sky, and in one the afternoon sun formed a blinding golden blaze. In a corral on the near side of the building his new string of horses stood dozing with their tails twitching desultorily at flies.

So, go get Sergeant. Two minutes and you can be in and out.

She drew a deep breath, blew it out slowly, and headed down the street, unconsciously stepping to the rhythmic beat of a hammer on steel.

At his open door she stopped. The sound came from inside: *pang-pang-pang*. Sergeant stood at the opposite end of the building, cross-tied near the smithy door. She walked toward the stallion, skirting the wooden turntable in the center of the wide corridor without removing her eyes from the far doorway.

Pang-pang-pang! It rang through the building, shimmered off the beams overhead and skimmed along the brick floor, as if repeating the rhythm of her heart.

Pang-pang-pang!

She approached Sergeant silently and gave him an affectionate if distracted scratch, whispering, "Hi, boy, how y' doin'?" The hammering stopped. She waited for Jeffcoat to appear, but when he didn't she stepped to the smithy door and peered inside.

The room was hot as hell itself, and very dark, but for the ruddy glow from the forge, which was set in the opposite wall: a waist-high fireplace of brick, with an arched top and deep, deep hearth, ringed with tools—hammers, tongs, chisels, and punches—hung neatly on the surrounding brick skirt. To the right stood a crude wooden table scattered with more tools, to the left a slake trough, and in the center of the room a scarred steel anvil, mounted on a pyramid of thick wooden slabs. Above the forge hung a double-chambered bellows with its tube feeding the fire. Working the bellows, with his back to the door, stood Jeffcoat.

The man she'd been avoiding.

His left hand pumped rhythmically, sending up a steady hiss and a soft thump from the accordion-pleated leather; his right held a long bar of iron, black at one end, glowing at the other, nearly as red as the coals themselves. He worked barehanded, bare-armed, wearing the familiar blue shirt, shorn of sleeves, and over it a soot-smudged leather apron.

He stood foursquare to the forge, his silhouette framed dead-center in the glowing arch, limned by the scarlet radiance of the coals, which brightened as the current of forced air hit them. A roar lifted up the chimney. The sound buffeted Emily's ears, and as the fireglow intensified it seemed to expand Jeffcoat's periphery. Sparks flew from the coals and landed at his feet, unheeded. The acrid odor of smoke mingled with that of heated iron—a singeing, bitter perfume.

Seeing him at his labor for the first time, her perception of him again changed. He became permanent; he was here to stay. Tens and tens of times in her life she would step to this door and find him standing just so, working. Would the sight make her breath catch every time?

She watched him move—each motion enlarged by his hovering vermilion halo. He flipped the iron bar over—it chimed like a brass bell against the brick hearth— and watched it heat. When it glowed a yellowish-white he reached out for a chisel, cut it, and picked it up with a pair of heavy tongs.

He turned to the anvil.

And found her watching from the doorway.

They stood as still as shadows, remaining motionless for so long that the perfect yellow-whiteness of the hot iron began to fade to ochre. He came to his senses first and said, "Well, hello."

"I came to get Sergeant," she announced uneasily.

"He's not quite ready." Jeffcoat lifted the hot iron in explanation. "One more shoe."

"Oh."

Silence again while the bar cooled even more.

"You can wait if you want. It shouldn't take long."

"Do you mind?"

"Not at all."

He turned back to the forge to reheat the bar and she moved farther inside, across a crunching layer of cinders that covered the floor, stopping with the tool table between herself and Jeffcoat. She studied his profile keenly, somehow feeling safe doing so in the darkness of the room. He wore a red bandana tied around his brow. Above it, his hair fell onto his forehead in damp tangles; below it, sweat painted gleaming tracks down his temples. Radiant red light lit the hair on his arms, and that which showed above the bib of his apron. She studied him until it became necessary to invent a distraction. Lifting her eyes to the dark thick-beamed ceiling and shadowed walls, she scanned them as a hunter might the sky.

"Did you run out of windows?" she inquired.

He glanced at her and grinned, then returned his attention to the forge. "Did you come to give me a hard time again?"

"No. I'm curious, that's all."

He turned the bar over and made more music. "You know as well as I do why blacksmiths work in the dark. It helps them gauge how hot the metal is." He brandished the bar, which was brightening to white again. "Color, you see?"

"Oh." And after a moment's silence: "Shouldn't you wear gloves?"

"I caught a cinder down one one time, so now I work without them."

Glancing down, she scuffed a boot against the cinders. "Your floor could use sweeping."

"You *did* come to pester me."

"No. I only came to get Sergeant, honest. Papa sent me."

He considered her askance for a long stretch, then shifted his gaze to his work and decided to enlighten her further. "The cinders keep the floor cool in the summer and warm in the winter."

"This is cool?" She spread her hands in the torpid air.

"As cool as it gets. You can wait outside if you want."

But she waited where she was, watching another bead of sweat trail down Tom Jeffcoat's jaw. He shrugged and caught it with a shoulder. His face held absolutely no shadow, and his eyes looked like two red coals themselves, so intense was the heat from the forge. Yet he pumped the bellows regularly and stood in the blast of heat as if it were little more than a warm chinook wind drifting over the Big Horns.

Time and again she glanced away, but her eyes had a will of their own. She didn't want to find him handsome, but there was no arguing the fact. Or masculine, but he was. Or any of the thousand indefinable things that drew her to him, but she was drawn just the same, against her will.

"It's ready now," he informed her.

The iron bar glowed once more the near-white hue of a full moon. He picked it up with tongs and swung about, selecting a hammer and setting to work at the anvil, battering the metal with singing, ringing blows.

She loved the sound—to the farmer it meant shares being mended; to the wheelwright, rims being formed; but to her it meant horses being cared for. It filled the room, it filled her head—smith's music in the steady repeating note she'd been hearing in the distance all her life.

Pang-pang-pang!

She watched him make it; a maestro in his own right, this man who raised her pulsebeat each time she saw him.

His muscles stood out as he wielded the hammer, changing the shape of the iron, wrapping it beat by beat around the pointed end of the anvil. The music paused. With the tongs he lifted the horseshoe, assessed it, returned it to the anvil and began again the measured staccato strikes. Each blow resounded in the pit of her stomach and fragmented to her extremities.

"I'm using a three-quarter shoe," he shouted above the ringing. "And a copper plate, too, on that off fore. It should keep that sand crack from coming back."

She was reminded of the first day she'd first seen him and how angry he'd made her. If only she could recapture some of that anger now. Instead, she watched his skin gleam in the fireglow and thought how warm it must be. She watched sweat bead in the corner of his eye and thought how salty it must be. She watched his chest flex and thought how hard it must be.

She distracted herself by picking up the conversation. "We took him back to Pinnick and said to reshoe him, but he only did a remove instead of a replace."

"He's a queer little man, that Pinnick. Came in here drunk one day and stood staring at me and weaving on his feet. When I asked if I could help him he muttered something I couldn't hear and stumbled back out again."

"Think nothing of it. He's always drunk, which will work in your favor, I'm sure. You'll get plenty of shoeing business."

He headed for the door, taking the hot shoe along. "Come on. I'll show you what I've done."

In the corridor a blessedly cool draft sailed door-to-door. Surrounded by the mingled scents of new wood, and hot iron and horse, Emily crouched beside Jeffcoat, catching, too, a faint whiff of his sweat as he lifted Sergeant's off forefoot to his lap. Sizing the shoe, he pointed out, "I've put the copper plate on the side, and the longer shoe will give added protection to the wall. This hoof will be like new by the next shoeing. Maybe even before then—in four weeks, I'd say."

"Good," she replied, studying his dirty arm only inches from her own.

The shoe was slightly wide. He took it back inside while she waited in the cool corridor, watching as he gave it several deft raps, then returned to lift Sergeant's hoof again. This time the shoe fit as if it had been cast in a sand mold. He took it back into the shop and she watched from the doorway as he picked up a punch and drove holes in the horseshoe on the flat end of the anvil.

Lifting the shoe, whistling softly through his teeth, he checked the holes against the light of the coals. "There, that should do."

Stepping to his left, he plunged the hot shoe into the slake trough. It sizzled and steamed while he glanced back over his shoulder.

"Grab a handful of clenches from that table, will you?" He gestured with his head.

"Oh . . . oh, sure."

She picked up the nails while he found a square-headed hammer and together they returned to Sergeant. She stood, looking down on his head while he assumed the pose as familiar to her as any a man could assume, thinking how different it looked when he did it. She studied the curve of his spine, the wet blue streak down the center of his shirt, the taut britches belling out infinitesimally at the waist.

He swung on the balls of his feet and caught her staring.

"Nails," he requested, holding out a palm.

"Oh, here!" She dropped four into his hand but he held them without moving. Their eyes locked and fascination multiplied until the air between them seemed to burn like that above his forge.

Abruptly he swung back to work. "So how was the party last week?"

"All right, I guess." She had changed her mind and gone in hopes of seeing him there.

"Charles enjoyed it."

She had gotten caught and had to kiss Charles during French Postman.

"It was silly. I don't like playing those games."

"He does." Tom centered a nail and rapped it in while she stood beside him blushing, unable to think up a reply.

"Did everybody come?" he inquired.

"Everybody but you and Tarsy."

He finished the last nail and straightened, letting the hoof clack to the floor. "Oh, she and I were painting the sign that night." He gestured toward the door with the hammer.

"Ah. Yes. It looks nice."

Their eyes met and parted discreetly. "Well . . . I'd better clip those clenches." He got the proper tool and spent several minutes nipping the ends of the protruding nails from all four hooves while Emily glanced around his barn at the fresh-milled lumber and cobwebless windows, reminding herself that he and Charles had done all this, and while doing it, had become friends.

Tom finished the nails and asked, "Want to lead them toward me and I'll see how the new shoes look?"

He squatted near the smithy door while she led Sergeant away, then back to him, feeling his eyes on her own feet as much as on the horse's. When she approached, he stretched to his feet and scratched Sergeant's nose. "Feels good, huh, Sergeant?" To Emily he added, "I should see him at trot and gallop to make sure they're perfectly flat."

"Pinnick's never in his life taken the time to check things like that."

"That's the way I was taught."

"By your father?"

"Yes."

"He was a farrier?" She glanced into Jeffcoat's clear blue eyes.

"Both my father and my grandfather were." While he spoke he removed his red headband and swabbed his face and neck, then stuck it in a hind pocket. "The bellows and the anvil were his, my grandfather's. My grandmother insisted that I take them when I came out here. For luck, she said." They both raised their eyes to the horseshoe above the smithy door.

"Don't you know you're supposed to hang it heels up so the good luck will get caught inside?"

"Not if you're a blacksmith." He looked down at her. "We're the only ones allowed to hang it heels down, so the luck will run out on our anvil."

Their eyes caught and held. The shoeing was done. She could ride Sergeant out the door any time, and they both knew it. So they dreamed up conversation to keep her here.

"You're superstitious," she observed.

"No more than the next man. But horseshoes are my business. People expect to see them up there."

She glanced up at the horseshoe again and he watched the curve of her throat come into view. He dropped his eyes to the line of her breasts flattened at the tips where her red suspenders crossed them, her thumbs hooked into their brass clasps at the waist of Frankie's britches. He found her as attractive in boy's wear as he did in a mauve gown. He'd never met a more unpretentious woman, nor one who shared as many of the same interests as he. Suddenly he wanted her to see all of his realm, to understand his joy in it, because only another livery owner could appreciate what all this meant.

"Emily, the night of my party you wouldn't look at a damn thing in here except the loft. I'd like you to see the rest. Would you like a little tour?"

She knew it would be wisest to get out of here with all due haste, but she couldn't resist the appeal in his voice.

"All right." In deference to Charles, she added, "But I can't stay long. Fannie will have supper ready soon."

"It'll only take five minutes. Wait a minute." He ducked into the shop and leaned over the slake trough, swabbing off his face and arms with the wet bandana. From the doorway she watched the masculine procedure with a growing lump in her stomach.

"Sorry," he offered sheepishly, straightening and turning to find her watching. "Sometimes I smell worse than my horses." He draped the wet bandana over the warm bricks, dried his palms on the rear of his britches, and said, "Well, we might as well begin in here. Come in." He waited until she stood at his elbow. "The bellows were made in Germany in 1798. They'll last all of my lifetime and longer. The anvil is the one my father learned on, from his father, then taught me on. The one I'll probably teach my sons on." He gave it an affectionate slap and rubbed his hand over the scarred iron. "I know every mark on it. When I left Missouri my mother sent me off with four loaves of her homemade bread for the road. Don't get me wrong—I loved it, but eventually I ate them up. This, though . . ." He gazed down at the anvil, his hand lingering upon it with great affection. ". . . the marks from their hammers will never disappear. When I get to missing them it helps to remember that."

It was an odd, passionless moment in which to recognize that she had fallen in love with him, but it happened to Emily in that instant while she met Tom Jeffcoat's eyes, while he let her see the soul inside the body, and admitted how he longed for his family and how he valued his birthright. It struck her with the force of a blow—*Pang-pang!*—I love him.

She turned away, afraid he'd read it in her eyes. The heat of the room pressed hard upon her flesh, joining the heat from within, an awesome heat spawned by the sudden, jolting admission.

"The slake trough I made myself," Tom continued, "and the base for the anvil—out of railroad ties—and the tool bench. The bricks came from the brickyards in Buffalo." He gestured her ahead of him through the doorway. They walked the length of the barn separated by a full six feet of space while Emily applied herself to the view of box stalls, windows, tack room, and office, when all she wanted was to look at him, at the face of the love she'd only now discovered.

They stopped at the foot of the loft stairs while his monologue continued. "I sleep up there now. No sense paying for a hotel room if I don't have to. It's plenty warm this time of year, and Charles says the house will be finished well before cold weather sets in."

She glanced up the steps, caught the sweet scent of new hay, and pictured herself climbing these stairs some night. Denying the possibility, she turned away.

"You haven't shown me your turntable."

"My turntable. Ah . . ." He laughed and raised one eyebrow. "My folly?"

"Is it?"

They sauntered back to the center of the barn. "The children don't think so. They come in and beg for rides on it."

Stopping on opposite sides of the wooden circle, Tom nudged it with a foot while Emily watched it turn. It scarcely made a sound, rolling on ball bearings.

"So smooth," she commented.

"Folly or not, it comes in damned handy when I want to turn a wagon around. Want to try it?"

Her chin lifted and she gazed at him with a feeling of imminent disaster thrumming through her veins. Ignoring it, she answered, "Why not?"

He halted the turntable and she stepped on. He set it in motion with the toe of a boot and she lifted her face, watching the ceiling beams spin slowly, distracted by the knowledge that he watched her as she circled. The faint tremble of the ball bearings shimmied up her legs to her stomach. She came around and passed him—once, twice—with her face to the rafters. But on the third pass she gave up and dropped her eyes to his as she came around the last half circle.

She reached him and his boot hit the turntable, stopping it.

They stood transfixed, with their pulses drumming crazily, fighting the compulsions that had had them on edge ever since he'd seen her standing silently in the smithy door, watching him. At his hips his fists opened once, then closed. Her lips dropped open but no sound came out. They stood together in a whorl of uncertainty, two people unspeakably tempted.

"Emily . . ." he said in a constricted voice.

"I have to go!" She tried to shoot past him but he reached and caught her forearm.

"You haven't seen the horses." It was not why he'd detained her and they both knew it.

"I have to go."

"No . . . wait." His hand burned on her arm, a poor substitute for the touches they wanted to share.

"Let me go," she pleaded in a whisper, raising her eyes to him at last.

He swallowed once thickly and asked in a tight voice, "What are we going to do?"

"Nothing," she replied flatly, jerking her arm free.

"You're angry."

"I'm not angry!" But she was, not at him, at the hopelessness of this situation.

"Well, what do you expect me to do?" he reasoned. "Charles is my friend. He's out there right now, building my house while I stand here thinking about—"

"Don't you think I know that!" Her eyes blazed into his.

"I've intentionally stayed away from the parties," he argued as if in self-defense.

"I know."

"And I've been seeing a lot of Tarsy, but she's—"

"Don't say it. Just . . . please, Tom, don't say any more. She's my friend, too."

They gazed at each other helplessly, each of them breathing as if they'd just sprinted over a finish line. Finally he stepped back and said, "You're right. You'd better go."

But now that he'd released her, she couldn't. She had taken no more than two steps away from him before she stopped in the middle of the corridor and dropped her forehead into her hands. She neither cried nor spoke, but her dejected pose spoke more clearly than tears or words.

He stood behind her, clinging to control by a thin thread. When he could stand it no longer he spun away and stood back to back with her, picturing her behind him.

It was Emily who broke the silence. "I don't suppose you'll be coming to Tilda's party tomorrow night."

"No, I don't think I'd better."

"No, it's ... I ..." She stammered to a halt and admitted, "I don't want to go, either."

"Go," he ordered sensibly, "with Charles."

"Yes, I must." They thought of Charles again, still back to back, staring at opposite walls.

"I'm getting a lot of pressure from Tarsy to go. I've invited her to dinner instead at the hotel."

"Oh."

He felt as if his chest were being crushed, and finally, in desperation, he turned around to study her slumped shoulders, her wool cap, the nape of her neck, the suspenders pressing her tan shirt against her shoulders. How the hell had this happened? He loved her. She was Charles's woman and he loved her.

"This is terrible ... this is dishonorable," he whispered.

"I know."

When another minute had passed without producing any solutions, Tom repeated, "You'd better go."

Without another word she grasped Sergeant's bridle, swung onto his back, and slapped the reins, shouting, "Heeaww!" By the time she hit the double doorway she was galloping hell-bent for redemption, on an escape route from Tom Jeffcoat and the unpardonable turmoil he had caused in her life.

In the weeks that followed she learned there was no escaping. The turmoil was with her day and night. Days, while she worked within a thirty-second walk of Tom Jeffcoat. Nights, while he infiltrated her dreams.

Such crazy, improbable dreams.

In one he was riding Fannie's bicycle and fell, knocking the wind out of himself. She stood beside him laughing. Then suddenly he was bleeding and she fell to her knees in the middle of Main Street and began tearing bandages from her mother's favorite linen tablecloth. She awakened, thrashing, working at the bedsheets as if to rip them in strips.

In another dream—the one Emily had with the most disturbing frequency—she was dressed in a strange mixture of clothing: Frankie's cap and Mama's bed jacket and Fannie's knickerbockers. She walked down a strange street, barefooted. At the bottom of a hill the roadbed turned into a fetid quagmire of pig dung, and as she slogged through it, Tom stood on the tip of the new church roof with his arms crossed over his chest, laughing at her. She became incensed and tried to fly up to the steeple and tell him so, but she was mired deep and her arms refused to lift her.

In another, they were playing French Postman and he kissed her, which was absurd, because though she continued attending the local parties at Charles's insistence, Tom continued staying away, often as not with Tarsy.

Yet the dream persisted. One night, lying restless and troubled beside Fannie, Emily decided to confide in her.

"Fannie? Are you asleep?"

"No."

Across the hall Mama coughed, then the house became silent while Emily formulated questions and worked up the courage to voice them.

"Fannie, what would you think of an engaged woman who dreams of somebody besides her fiancé?"

"Another man, you mean?"

"Yes."

Fannie sat up. "Gracious, this is serious."

"No, it's not. It's just . . . just dumb dreams. But I have them so often, and they bother me."

"Tell me about them."

Emily did, omitting Tom's name, while Fannie settled herself against the headboard as if for a lengthy talk. She described the two nightmares, and asked, "What do you think they mean?"

"Goodness, I have no idea."

Emily gathered her courage and admitted, "There's another one."

"Mmmm . . ."

"I dream that we're playing French Postman and he's kissing me."

Fannie said simply, "Oh, my."

"And I like it."

"Oh my oh my."

Emily sat up and punched the blanket in self-disgust. "I feel so guilty, Fannie!"

"Why feel guilty? Unless, of course, there's a reason."

"You mean have I actually kissed him? No, of course not! He's never even touched me. As a matter of fact there have been times when I'm not even sure he likes me." After pondering silently for a minute Emily asked, "Fannie, why do you suppose I never dream of Charles?"

"Probably because you see him so much that you don't have to."

"Probably."

After a moment of thoughtful silence Fannie asked, "This man you dream about—are you attracted to him?"

"Fannie, I'm engaged to Charles!"

"That's not what I asked."

"I can't . . . he . . . when we . . ." Emily stammered to a halt.

"You are."

Emily's silence was as good as an admission.

"So what *has* happened between you and your dream man?"

"He's not my dream man."

"All right, this man who doesn't like you sometimes. What happened?"

"Nothing. We've looked at each other, that's all."

"Looked? All this guilt over a few innocent looks?"

"And we played your damned game once—Guessing Blind Man. He was wearing the blindfold and he sat on my lap and he . . . he touched my face . . . and my hair . . . it was awful. I wanted to die on the spot."

"Why?"

"Because Charles was right there watching!"

"What did Charles say?"

"Nothing. He thinks those games are purely innocent."

"Oh, Emily . . ." With a sigh Fannie folded Emily in her arms and held her close, drawing the girl's head to her shoulder and petting her hair. "You're so like your mother."

"Well . . . isn't that good?"

"To a point, yes. But you must try to laugh more, to take life as it comes. What harm is there in a kissing game?"

"It's embarrassing."

Fannie's response, rather than soothing Emily, only added fuel to her misgivings. "Then I fear, you poor misguided dear, that you simply haven't kissed the right one."

In late August Tom received a letter from Julia:

Dear Thomas,

I have been very troubled by what I did to you. It seems the only way to appease my conscience is to write to you and apologize. On my wedding morning I cried. I awakened and looked out my window at the streets where you and I walked so many times, and thought of you so far away, and I remembered the look on your face the day I told you of my plans to marry. I'm so sorry if I hurt you, Tom. I did not mean to. My abrupt termination of our engagement was unpardonable of me, I know. But, Tom, I am so happy with Jonas, and I wanted you to know. I made the right choice, for me, for both of us. Because I am so happy, I wish for you the same kind of happiness. It is my dearest hope that you will find it with a woman who will cherish you as you deserve. When you find her, please don't be pessimistic because of my ill treatment of you. I should not like to believe myself responsible for any cynicism you might harbor toward women. Connubial life is rich and rewarding. I wish it for you, too, perhaps the more so since Jonas and I have learned that we are expecting our first child next March. I hope this finds you content and flourishing in your new environs. I think of you often and with the deepest affection.

Julia.

He read the letter on the boardwalk outside Loucks's store. When he finished it he found himself amazed at how little sentiment it engendered for Julia. There was a time when the sight of her handwriting alone would have made his heart leap. It came as somewhat of a shock to realize that she no longer had the power to hurt him.

But her letter made him homesick. The mention of the street where they'd walked brought back other vivid images of his hometown and family. He was sick of eating in a hotel, of sleeping in a loft, of working fourteen hours a day, first in the livery stable, then on his house. Sometimes, weary from hours of plastering, when he'd walk·back to the livery barn for the night, he'd stare at the early lanternlight in the homes he passed and feel utterly dismal.

So he began spending more time with Tarsy.

Had there been any other girl in Sheridan who interested him, he would have wooed her. But other than Emily Walcott, Tarsy was the only one, and it was natural that the longer they saw one another, the freer they became with each other. In time they found themselves treading a dangerous line between discretion and disaster.

Frustrated by the fact as much as Tom, Tarsy finally had to talk to somebody about it and sought out Emily. She came to the Walcott home after supper on a dreary, misty evening in late September. Charles and Edwin were playing a game of backgammon. Frankie answered the door and took Tarsy back to the kitchen where Emily was helping Fannie with the dishes.

"Emily, can I talk to you?"

"Tarsy—" One look told Emily something was amiss. She laid down her dish towel immediately. "What's wrong?"

"Could we go upstairs to your room?"

Unsuspectingly, Emily obliged.

Upstairs in the lamplight Tarsy removed her wool coat and poked around Emily's room as if reluctant to reveal what was troubling her, now that she had Emily's ear. At the dresser she picked up a brush and absently ran a thumb over the bristles. Discarding it, she chose a comb and ran it once down the back of her hair, which was caught in a black bow and cascaded to her shoulders.

Emily studied her, waiting patiently for whatever it was Tarsy had come here to say. She was slim and pretty, dressed in a white blouse and red plaid skirt, easily the prettiest girl in Sheridan. It often crossed Emily's mind that it was no wonder Tom found himself attracted to Tarsy. They'd been seeing a lot of each other lately, Emily knew, and the effect upon Tarsy had been noticeable.

She had changed over the summer. The giddy, giggly girl was gone, replaced by a level-headed young woman who no longer flung herself across beds or flopped into haystacks, gushing.

Ironically, the change had endeared Tarsy to Emily much more than ever before.

Emily went to her now and turned her around by the arms. "Tarsy, what is it?"

Tarsy raised distressed brown eyes. "It's Tom," she admitted quietly. She spoke his name differently than in the past, with respect now.

"Oh." Emily's hands slid from Tarsy's sleeves.

Tarsy caught one before it could slip away. "I know you don't like him, Emily, but I . . . I don't have anyone else I'd trust with this. I think I love him, Em."

There it was: the confidence. Another load for Emily to carry. Had Tarsy only pretended to swoon as she had a few months ago, it wouldn't have been so tragic. But she was absolutely earnest.

"You love him?"

"Oh, I know, I've said it before. I've mooned around like a star-struck little girl and I've flung myself down in the hayloft and drooled and acted like a perfect ninny over him. But it's different now. It's the real thing." Tarsy pressed a fist beneath her left breast and spoke with alarming sincerity. "It's here, in the deepest part of me, and it's so big I can scarcely carry it around anymore. But I'm afraid to tell him because if he found out, he'd stop seeing me." Tarsy dropped to the edge of Emily's bed and sat disconsolately, staring at the floor. Her hands lay calmly in her lap instead of flapping about melodramatically as they once had.

"You see," she continued, "he told me quite a while ago that he suspected I was looking for a husband. But he made it clear that he was not in the market for marriage. I knew that all along, even when I began to let him kiss me. At first that was all we did, but then we kept on seeing each other and now . . . well, it's only natural that—" Tarsy rose abruptly and walked to the window where she stood staring out at a misty rain. "Oh, Emily, you must think I'm terrible."

"Tarsy, have you and Tom . . ." Emily couldn't think of a discreet way to ask the question. Terrified, she waited for an answer.

Tarsy followed a raindrop with one finger and said levelly, "No, not yet." She turned, fully composed, and returned to sit at Emily's side. "But I'm so tempted, Em. We've come so close."

The girls' eyes met, and in Tarsy's was honesty and culpability such as Emily had never expected to see there. To Emily's chagrin, her friend's eyes flooded with tears and she covered her face with her hands. "It's a sin. I know it's a sin. And it's dangerous, but what do you do when you love someone so much that it no longer seems wrong?"

"I don't know," Emily replied simply, abashed at the turn in the conversation.

"But you're engaged, Emily; you and Charles are together as much as Tom and I are. What do you do when you start feeling that way?"

Was it insight or naïveté that prompted Tarsy to believe love smote everyone in the same way, that it struck mindless passion into a woman simply because she had agreed to marry a man? To Emily's great and growing dismay, Charles had never incited those feelings in her. Indeed, she had come closer to them with Tom Jeffcoat than with her own fiancé.

Which only added to the irony of the situation.

"I don't know what to say, Tarsy."

"There's more. Something even worse," Tarsy admitted. "Sometimes I think about letting it happen and trapping him."

"Don't say that!" Emily exclaimed, horrified. "That's foolish!"

"But it's true. If I got pregnant with his baby he'd have to marry me and sometimes I almost believe the disgrace would be worth it."

"Oh, Tarsy, no." Emily gave in to her own aching heart and held Tarsy with an affection she'd never felt before. How many times had she called this girl a silly twit, and scoffed at her flightiness? Now it was gone and Emily wanted it back, wanted their girlhood back because womanhood was too hurtful and dismaying. "Promise me you'll never do that. Promise. It could ruin your lives forever, and it would be so unfair to him."

Tarsy hid her face against Emily's shoulder and cried. "Oh, Emily, what am I going to do? He loves somebody else."

Panic struck Emily. Panic and guilt. Her face turned red as she held Tarsy tightly, lest she lift her eyes and see.

But Tarsy went on. "It's that woman he was engaged to. He still loves her."

"Well, maybe he does. It's only been a few months since she broke their engagement. It takes time to get over a thing like that. He'll come to see that you're . . . well, that you've grown up, that you're ready for marriage." In an effort to cheer her further, Emily added. "And you're just about the prettiest thing this dumpy little town has ever seen. Why, he'd be a real fool not to see that."

She lifted Tarsy's trembling chin. At first Tarsy resisted being cajoled, but finally gave a sheepish snuffle of laughter. "Oh, *I'm* the fool." She dashed tears from her face with the back of her hand. "I know I am. Just a . . . a silly fool, saying I'd do a thing like that. I never would, you know that, Em, don't you?"

"Of course, I do. Here." Emily found a handkerchief in her bureau drawer and handed it to Tarsy, waiting while she mopped her face and blew her nose. When she had, Tarsy absently wrapped the edge of the hanky over her thumbs and sat staring at it.

"But, Emily . . ." she said plaintively, lifting sad eyes, "I do love him."

Emily dropped to her knees before Tarsy and covered the girl's hands. "I know."

The new, adult Tarsy tried bravely to control the tears that were dangerously close to brimming over again. "Oh, Emily, why does it have to hurt so bad?"

Neither of them knew the answer, nor did they suspect that the hurt would intensify in the weeks that followed.

Chapter 10

There were times when Fannie asked herself why she'd come. Watching someone die was not easy. In recent days the consolation of being near Edwin could not compensate for the pain of dealing with Joey. Poor, failing Joey. She could not lie, nor could she sit, for to recline meant to cough and to sit erect took strength she didn't possess. So she spent her days and nights angled against the pillows, hacking away what little strength she'd garnered from her fitful naps.

Caring for her took a staunchness Fannie had not anticipated. The bedroom stank now, for the coughing had grown so violent it brought on simultaneous incontinence, and no matter how often Fannie changed the sheets, the smell of stale urine persisted. Blood, too, Fannie discovered, had a sickening smell, not only when freshly spilled but when soaking in a tub of lye water.

Fannie's hands burned: every day was washday now, and though Emily helped often, the bulk of the chore fell to Fannie. She disregarded her own minor irritation, which seemed petty compared to the raw bedsores on Joey's elbows. Joey had become a living skeleton, shrunken to a mere ninety pounds, so gaunt there were times Fannie was forced to stifle a gasp when entering the room. Her cousin's hair was nearly too thin to braid, showing pink skull between the limp skeins. The skin over her cheekbones looked like dry corn husks and bruised at the lightest touch. Any physical contact caused her pain; she'd even had to remove her wedding ring from her knobby finger because it felt, she said, like an iron shackle. Wherever she was touched by helping hands, those hands left blue bruises.

She coughed again and Fannie slipped a hand behind the pillows, holding Josephine straighter. The blood came—brilliant carmine against the clean white cotton rags they substituted for handkerchiefs, which were too small to be adequate anymore. They rode it out together, and when the spasm ended, Josephine sank back depleted. Fannie gently released her, touching her hair—the only thing touchable without causing more pain.

"There, Joey, rest now . . ." Trying to compose soothing words had become as great a drain upon Fannie as witnessing Josephine's pain. *Dear God, either take her or produce a miracle.*

"I've got some things to hang on the line. Will you be all right?" Josephine lifted a finger, too weak to nod. "I won't be gone long," whispered Fannie.

She hung the last sheet and returned to the kitchen to hear the coughing resume overhead. Closing her eyes, she dropped her forehead against the cool, varnished doorsill.

That's how Emily found her.

"Fannie?"

Fannie straightened with a snap. "Oh, Emily." Under the guise of picking up the laundry basket she swiped away her telltale tears. "I didn't hear you come in."

"Mother is worse?"

"She's had a bad afternoon. A lot of coughing, and her bedsores are so terrible. Is there anything in your medicine bag that might help her? The poor thing is suffering so."

"I'll see what I can come up with. What about you? You don't look so perky yourself."

"Oh, bosh. Me?" Fannie manufactured an air of blitheness. "Why, you know me . . . I'm like a cat, always land right side up."

But Emily had seen the glint of tears and the dejection. She had seen, in recent days, how tired and care-worn Fannie looked. She crossed the room and took the laundry basket from Fannie's hands. "You need to get away from here for a couple of hours. Leave this, and whatever isn't finished. Comb your hair and put on your knickerbockers and take a ride on your bicycle. Don't come back until you smell supper cooking, and that's an order."

Fannie closed her eyes, composed her emotions, pressed a hand against her diaphragm, and blew out a steadying puff of air. "Thank you, dearling. I'll do exactly that, and gratefully."

She took fifteen minutes to strip off her dress and wash away the stench of sickness, which seemed to pervade her own skin and clothing lately. In a starched white shirtwaist, a trim nutmeg-colored jacket, and matching knickerbockers, with her peachy hair twisted like a cinnamon bun atop her head, she took her bicycle from the shed.

Sweet heavens, it was good to be outside! She lifted her face to the sky and sucked deep. October, and the heavens as blue as a trout's side, the air like tonic, and all around the cottonwoods turning to a king's ransom—gold against blue. Striking out, she reveled in her freedom and wiped concerns from her mind. In the distance the hills rose like the sides of a golden teacup, but along Little Goose Creek the grassy banks still wore Irish green ruddled by splashes of sumac, the earliest foliage to blush. How good to be strong, healthy, robust, out in the open, nosing the wind. Fannie balanced on her bicycle seat and pedaled harder, feeling the breeze catch her hair and drag it like thick, rough fingers. Up the hill southwest of town, down a long grade where rocks made her grip the handlebars tightly to keep from keeling over—pedaling, pedaling, pushing her limits, feeling her tensile muscles tauten and heat, and loving every minute of it, simply because she was firm and hale and able to exert herself to such limits. She stopped at a creek whose name she did not know, and watched it ripple, catch the sky, and toss it back in sequin flashes. She abandoned her bicycle and lay in the grass, pressing her shoulder blades to the earth and imbibing its permanence, letting the sun bake her face. She opened her bodice and let it bathe her chest. She listened to a redwinged blackbird churr in a clump of sedge across the water and knelt to answer, scaring it away. She drank from the stream, rebuttoned her shirtwaist, and returned to town.

Straight down Grinnell Street to Walcott's Livery Stable.

She rode right in, down the aisle dividing the building, and stopped beside a wheelbarrow full of fresh straw outside a stall Edwin was lining. He turned in surprise as she dropped the bicycle on its side.

"Edwin, don't ask any questions, please. I simply need this today." She walked into the stall and straight into his arms.

"Fannie?" Taken by surprise, he stood becalmed, a pitchfork dangling from one fist.

She clasped his trunk and turned her face against his chest. "Dear heavens, you smell good."

"Fannie, what is it?"

"Would you hold me, Edwin? Very hard, and very still for only two or three minutes? That should be enough."

The pitchfork handle thumped against the wooden divider and Edwin's arms tightened around her shoulders.

Edwin had had no time to fortify himself. One moment he'd been forking hay, the next she had stepped against him, fragrant and supple, smelling of crushed grass and fresh air and the herbs she packed among her woolens. From her skull lifted the faint scent of warmth, as if she'd ridden hard. He rested his nose against her sunrise-colored hair and breathed deeply, spread his hands across her back and memorized its contours.

"Mmmmm ... yes," she murmured, nuzzling his shirt, catching the unadulterated scent of man, sweat, and horse, sweetened by the newly strewn hay that filled the stall. "Edwin, I apologize. I simply needed this."

"It's all right, Fannie ... shhh."

They pressed close, rubbing each other's backs—healthy resilient flesh, thought Edwin, such as he had not held in years.

"You feel so good," she whispered.

"You do, too."

"Hard and strong and good."

Edwin's heartbeat seemed to fill his throat. Incredible—he was touching her at last, holding her—the thing he had imagined doing ever since she came, for years before she came. How typical of Fannie to surprise him this way when he least expected it, to walk against him and surround him as if this were her natural place.

"Why today?" he asked, disbelievingly.

"Because I wasn't sure I could go on without it."

"You too, Fannie?"

She nodded, bumping his chin. "You smell of life and vitality."

"I smell worse than that. I've been cleaning stalls."

"Don't! Don't pull away! I'm not through yet."

He closed his eyes and smiled against her hair, feeling it catch in his beard, steeping himself in her unexpected nearness, pulling in deep drafts of her herbal scent. He leaned back to watch her eyes while his hands skimmed her sides, caught her waist—like notches in a fiddle, that waist, dainty and curved. He girded her ribs, rode his thumbs in the depression just below them, wanting to touch her breasts but refraining, because these simply acknowledgments were heaven in themselves. How long had it been since he'd caressed a woman this way? He'd lost track of the years. It might have been as long ago as the last time he'd held Fannie. Josie had always resisted open petting. Whatever sexual—even affectionate—contact they'd shared had happened in the dark of night, discreetly, according to her code of mores. He drew Fannie close once again. Ah, how good, how natural it felt to lay hands on a woman in broad daylight, to drop his face to her hair and draw her hips flush to his. He spread his hands and ran them up till his thumbs touched her armpits, fingers splaying behind, as if she were a nut he might crack open and savor. She shuddered palpably and made an enraptured sound against his throat. When he pushed back to see her face a strand of her pale melon-colored hair caught on his shirt button, tethering them together. Their gazes met, filled with love so certain, so ingrained, it could no longer be denied.

"Forgive me, Fannie, but I must," Edwin uttered softly, and claimed her lips and breasts at once, urging her near with his huge, work-stained hands wrapped around those soft mounds, lowering his head to taste her waiting mouth. They were not children as they'd been when he'd first touched and kissed her. What they did, they did with full acknowledgment of its import and significance. They kissed as two who had paid long and hard for the right, tongue upon tongue, mouths open and pliant, while he reshaped her breasts from below and stroked their tips with his thumbs. He backed her against the rough board wall, sending the pitchfork clattering to the floor as he leaned against her, fully aroused and unwilling to hide it. She was all he remembered, sensuous and passionate and inventive with her mouth. She drew upon his tongue and lips, tasting him shallow and deep with deft swirls of her agile tongue, then with eager lips. The kiss didn't end, it pacified, scattered to other areas—necks, shoulders, throats, ears.

"Fannie, I never forgot . . . never." His words were longing whispers.

"Neither did I."

"We should have been together all these years."

"In my heart we were."

"Oh Fannie, Fannie, my dear, sweet Fan—" Her mouth severed the word, anxious and open beneath his. They kissed with the urgency of time lost—sweet, agitated kisses punctuated by wordless sounds and the ardent pressure of their bodies, as if by holding hard enough they might wipe out the long lapse they'd suffered.

When they paused, panting, he told her, "I'd forgotten how it feels. Do you know how long it's been since I've done anything like this?"

"Shh . . . nothing about her, not ever. This is dishonorable enough."

He gripped her head, held it as a priest holds a chalice, and drank her—Fannie of the bright hair and insatiable spirit and crushed-grass scent. He cherished her—Fannie of the memories and warmth and dew-kissed days of youth. How had he sustained through all these years without her? Why had he ever tried?

He lifted his head and delved into her eyes. "The dishonor was mine in giving you up. What a fool I was."

"You did what you thought you must do."

His thumbs stroked her cheeks. "I love you, Fannie. I've always loved you."

"And I love you, Edwin. I never stopped either."

"You knew it when I married Josie, didn't you? You knew I loved you."

"Of course I did, just as you knew what I felt."

"Why didn't you try to stop me?"

"Would it have done any good?"

"I don't know." His eyes were pained, his voice regretful. "I don't know."

"Your parents exerted very strong wills. So did hers."

"Isn't it strange then, that when I told them Josie and I were leaving Massachusetts they put up no argument? Almost as if they recognized our leaving as a penance they had to pay for manipulating our lives. I knew it was the only way my marriage would survive—I couldn't live near you and not have you. I'd have broken my vows within the year, I'm sure. My precious Fannie . . ." He took her in his arms again—a tender repossession. "I love you so much. Will you come up to the loft with me and let me make love to you?"

"No, Edwin." In typical Fannie fashion, she remained content in his arms, even while refusing.

"Haven't we wasted enough of our lives?" Holding her head, he showered her face with kisses, leaving her skin damp. "When we were seventeen we should have damned the consequences and become lovers like we wanted to. Those consequences couldn't have been any worse than the ones we paid. Please, Fannie . . . let's not prolong the mistake."

She caught his hands and hauled them down, folded them between her own beneath her chin. Her eyelids closed and trembled while emotions tumbled through her aroused body.

"Enough, Edwin. We must stop. You're a married man."

"Married to the wrong woman."

"But married just the same. And I would never do that to Joey. I love her, too."

"Then why did you come here?" he demanded in near-anger.

She would not be harassed by his understandable frustration. Calmly she flattened his hand upon her thrusting heart. "Feel what you've done to me. My blood is coursing. Inside I'm quivering, and I feel very much alive, with a reason to go on. I took this much of you because I felt Joey would have approved. For now it's enough." She refolded his hands between her own, kissed the tips of his longest fingers, and sought his eyes. "I am restored and so are you. But we would suffer within ourselves if we betrayed Joey. You know that as well as I, Edwin. Now I must go back to the house."

He searched her eyes, feeling his momentary irritation fade. "Fannie, when will we—"

"Silence," she ordered softly, covering his lips with a finger. She brushed the width of his mouth lovingly, letting her eyes follow the path of her fingertip. "We are human, Edwin. What we feel for one another cannot always be held in abeyance. Sometimes, when we are bleak and in need, we may find ourselves seeking one another, as I sought you today. But we will not speak of eventualities, nor will we consign ourselves to deceitful *tête-à-têtes*. It would only compound our guilt." Her voice lowered to whisper, "Now I must go. Please let me."

She backed away, reaching out, sliding her hands down his wrists, knuckles, and finally from his fingertips.

"I think of you in bed at night, though," she whispered as she slipped away. "Fannie . . ."

She turned to her bicycle and mounted while she still possessed a thimbleful of honor.

During those days while Josephine suffered her final decline, Tom Jeffcoat worked hard to complete the interior of his house. On a night in mid-autumn, after fifteen hours of nonstop work, he dropped his plastering hawk and trowel, braced his spine with two fists, and bowed backwards. Above his head hung a hissing coal-oil lantern that sent shadows arching across his half-plastered kitchen wall. He'd wanted to get the room done tonight—usually he worked till ten o'clock—but his back ached and the shakedown at the stable sounded irresistible.

He scanned the room, its windows set, its floor covered with canvas drop cloths, wondering what woman might reign over it some day. A disconcerting picture of Emily Walcott appeared, standing where the range would be. Ha. Emily Walcott probably didn't know which end of a spoon to stir with. Hadn't Charles confided that she wasn't very good around the kitchen? In spite of the fact, her image remained while Tom stared, glassy-eyed with fatigue.

Go home, Jeffcoat, before you drop off your feet.

He squatted to scrape the hawk clean, so tired it took an effort to push himself back up. Yawning, he shrugged into a faded flannel jacket, picked up the bucket of dirty tools, and extinguished the lantern. Indigo shadows fell across the room as he paused a moment to reconsider.

It'll probably be Tarsy Fields you'll share this house with. She's about the best this town has to offer.

Outside, a near-full harvest moon poured milky light over the streets, paling rooftops and promising frost by morning. He glanced at the Big Horns. Already their tips were covered with snow at the higher altitudes, glowing almost purple in the moonlight. Turning his collar up, he headed in the opposite direction, toward Grinnell Street. The town was already bundling up for winter. He passed gardens where housewives had cleared all but an occasional pumpkin or a row of carrots left to sweeten in the first frosts. Foundations were ballasted with straw, whose scent mingled with that of freshly rooted soil spiced by old tomato vines and vestiges of gardeners' fires, which marked the end of the harvest season. He wondered what kind of a gardener Tarsy would make. Out here, where tinned goods came by oxcart and cost a modest fortune, housewives had no choice but putting by foods for the winter. Somehow he couldn't imagine her on her knees, weeding. Canning? The picture seemed ludicrous. Bearing children? Not the satin-and-curls Tarsy.

How about Emily Walcott?

The thought of Emily Walcott rattled him, but she persisted in his thoughts almost daily, probably because Charles talked about her so much. Perhaps she disliked domestics, but he could easily feature her bearing children. A woman who could go through anything as unpleasant as the scene at Jagush's could certainly go through childbirth intrepidly.

So Charles was lucky on that score. So what?

Shake her off, Jeffcoat.

Shake her off? She never was on!

Oh no?

She's engaged to Charles.

Tell that to your heart the next time it quakes when she walks into a room.

So, my heart quakes a little, so what?

You'd like to marry her yourself.

The tomboy?

Why have you been picturing her in your kitchen, and having babies? And don't delude yourself that it's Charles Bliss's babies you picture her having.

He was exhausted, that's why his mind kept wandering off on these improbable tangents. Whatever he thought he felt for Emily Walcott would pass. It had to, because there was no other solution. He ambled along, loose-jointed from weariness, the pail thumping his knee, sending out a muffled chime.

He turned onto Grinnell Street, came abreast of Edwin's livery stable ... and halted abruptly.

Why was a light burning in Edwin's place at this time of night? Edwin closed up at six o'clock every night—the same as he did—and never came back after dark. And why was the light so faint, as if filtering to the office window from the main body of the barn?

Horse thieves?

Jeffcoat's hair prickled. He slipped alongside the building, flattened his shoulders against the wall, and silently set down his pail. The rolling door stood open no wider than a man's chest. He edged toward it, listening. Silence. Not even a snuffling horse, so no stranger intruded along the stalls. Holding his breath, he peered around the edge of the door into the murky depths of the building. The main barn was black. The light came from the office itself, but so pale it scarcely lit the door rim. If it were Edwin inside, he'd have the wick up. Did Edwin leave his cash here at night, somewhere among the clutter in that ancient desk?

Jeffcoat sucked in his breath and wedged through the door. A sound came from the office—jerky, nasal breathing, followed by the shuffle of paper. He tiptoed along the wall, feeling with his hands, until they touched something smooth and wooden: a pitchfork handle. Silently he slid his hands down to identify the cold, deadly tines. Gripping the fork, warrior fashion, he tiptoed to one side of the office door, tensed to spring.

"Edwin, is that you?" he called.

The breathing and shuffling stopped.

"Who's in there!" he demanded.

Nobody answered.

His chest constricted and his scalp tingled, but he gripped the pitchfork and sprang into the room like a Zambian warrior, roaring, *"Raaaahhh!"*

The only person in the office was Emily Walcott.

She flattened herself against the back of the desk chair, white-faced and terrified, while he landed with the weapon leveled, knees cocked.

"Emily!" he exclaimed, dropping his arm. "What are you doing here?" But he could see what she was doing here: crying ... in private. Her eyes were swollen and tears continued rolling down her face, even as she gaped in shock.

"What are *you* doing here?"

"I thought you were a horse thief, or somebody rifling the desk for money. Edwin never comes back after six." He set the pitchfork against the wall and turned back to her, distressed at the tears trailing down her wet cheeks. How dismal she looked, in a pumpkin-colored dress with dark blotches dotting her bodice, giving evidence that she'd been weeping for some time. She swiveled to face the pigeonholes, covertly scraping a knuckle beneath each eye.

"Well, it's just me, so you can go," she informed him through a plugged nose.

"You're crying."

"Not for long. I'm all right. You can go, I said."

Her tears were a surprise. He hadn't taken her for a woman easily unstrung, or himself for the kind who'd be rattled by it. But his heart was quaking.

He kept his tone intentionally humoring. "It's too late now, I already caught you at it. So you might as well talk."

She shook her head stubbornly, but dropped her mouth against a handkerchief while her shoulders shook. He stared at her dress, buttoned up the back, drawn tight across her shoulder blades, at the prim white collar and the disheveled black hairs on her nape. He fought the inclination to spin the chair around and pull her into his arms, hold her fast, and let her cry against him. Instead he asked, "Do you want me to go get Charles?"

She shook her head vehemently but continued sobbing into the hanky, her elbows splayed on the desktop.

He stood, disarmed, wondering what to do while she doubled forward, burying her face in an arm, sobbing so hard her ribs lifted. He felt his own chest tighten and a lump form in his throat. What should he do? Mercy, what should he do? He watched until he felt like bawling himself, then dropped to a squat, swinging her chair to face him. "Hey," he urged gently, "turn around here." Her skirt brushed his knees but she refused to lift her face from the hanky, abashed at breaking down before him. "You can talk to me, you know."

She shook her head fervidly, releasing a series of muffled sobs. "Just g—go away. I don't w—want you to see me like this."

"Emily, what is it? Something with Charles?"

She shook her head till a hairpin fell, bouncing off his knee to the floor.

He picked it up and folded it tightly into his palm while studying the part in her hair, only inches from his nose. "Me? Did I do something again?"

Another passionate shake.

"Your little brother? Tarsy? Your father? What?"

"It's my mother." The words, distorted by the handkerchief and her plugged nose, sounded like *by buther.* Her devastated eyes appeared above the limp white cotton, which she pressed against her nose. "Oh Tom"—*Tob,* he heard—"it's so hard to watch her die."

A bolt of emotion slammed through him at her pitiful plea and her unconscious and distorted use of his name. It took a superhuman effort to hunker before her and not reach, not touch.

"She's worse?"

Emily nodded, dropping her gaze while gustily blowing her nose. When she finally rested her hands in her lap, her nose was red and raw. "I took care of her today while Fannie went off b—by herself for a wh—while," she explained choppily, the words broken by residual sobs. "Poor F—Fannie, she's with her all day long. I guess I never r—realized before what a terrible task we gave her, seeing after Mother during these last weeks. But today Fannie asked me if I could—could—" Emily paused, battling a fresh onslaught of emotion. "Could find something to help her bedsores, and I—" Trying her utmost to complete her recital without another breakdown, Emily lifted brimming eyes to the top of the doorway. "I saw . . . them."

She blinked: her eyes remained shut while she pulled in an immense breath, then opened them once more and struggled on. "Fannie gives Mother her baths and changes her clothes and her bedding. I hadn't realized how b—bad her bedsores were till today. And she's so . . . s—skinny . . . there's n—nothing left of her. She c—can't even turn over by herself. P—Papa has to do it for her. But wherever he touches her it leaves a bl—black-and-blue mark." Her tears built again, in spite of her valiant effort to contain them.

On his knees before her, Tom watched helplessly as she again wept brokenly into her hands, her entire frame shaking. *Damn you, Charles, where are you? She needs you!* His heart swelled while he watched, torn and miserable. *Aw, tomboy, don't cry . . . don't cry.*

But she did, torturously, trying to hold the sound within, only to have it escape her throat as a faint, pitiful mewling. He felt the pressure in his own throat and knew he must either touch her or shatter.

"Emily, hush, now . . . here . . ." Still kneeling, he drew her to him, and she came limply, sliding off the chair without resistance. He folded her tenderly in his arms and held her, kneeling on the bumpy concrete floor of the cluttered little office. She wept on jerkily, limp against him, her arms resting loosely up his back while her sobs beat against his chest.

"Oh, Toooom . . ." she wailed dismally.

He cupped her head and drew her face hard against his throat, while her tears seeped through his shirtfront and wet his skin. She wept to near-exhaustion, then rested weakly against him.

He dropped his cheek against her hair, wishing he were wise and clever with words and could voice the consolation he felt in his heart. Instead he could only cradle her and offer silence.

In time her breathing evened and she managed to offer chokily, "I'm sorry."

"Don't be sorry," he chided gently. "If you didn't love her you wouldn't feel so grieved."

He felt her breasts heave in a great shaky sigh as she dried the last of her tears, still lying with her cheek on his chest, showing little inclination to leave. He fixed his gaze on a yellowed calendar hanging above the desk and lightly stroked the back of her neck.

Minutes passed with each of them dwelling upon private thoughts. At last Emily asked tiredly, "Why can't she just die, Tom?"

He heard both guilt and sincerity in her question and understood how painful it must have been for her to ask it. He rubbed her back and kissed her hair. "I don't know, Emily."

For long moments they abided so, pressed close together, joined by her grief and his distress at being unable to deliver her from it. In a voice soft with understanding he gave her the only ease he knew. "But you mustn't feel guilty for wishing she would," he said.

He knew by her stillness that the words had been what she'd needed: an absolution.

Her weeping had ended minutes ago, but they stole more precious time until—as one—they realized they had remained in each other's arms too long. At some point while she rested against him they had crossed the fine line between desolation and yearning.

He drew back, pressing her away by both arms, letting his hands linger, then dropping them reluctantly to his sides. He watched her cheeks heat and read in her blush the thousand shamefaced wishes she, too, had allowed to flee through her mind. But Charles materialized in spirit, and Emily stared at a button on Tom's flannel jacket while he studied her averted face and sat back on his heels to put more distance between them.

"So . . ." he managed shakily, the word trembling between them like a shot bird waiting to plummet. "Are you feeling better now?"

She nodded and glanced up cautiously. "Yes."

He studied her, shaken and uncertain. If she were to move—the subtlest shift—she would be in his embrace again, and this time he'd give her far more than consolation. For a moment he watched temptation dull her eyes, but he produced a tight laugh and a dubious grin. "Well, at least we got you to stop crying."

She covered her cheeks and gingerly touched her lower eyelids. "I probably look awful."

"Yeah, pretty awful," he offered with a false chuckle, watching her test her upper eyelids, which looked bruised and swollen.

"Oh, my eyes hurt," she admitted, dropping her hands and letting him see.

They were indeed swollen and red, and her hair was rubbed from its knot, her cheeks blotchy, and her lips swollen; but he wanted to kiss them and her poor red-rimmed eyes, and her throat and her breast, and say, forget Charles, forget Tarsy, forget your mother and let me make you happy.

Instead he got a grip on his inclinations and took her hands, drawing her to her feet, then stepping back. "So . . . can I walk you home?"

Her eyes said yes, but her voice said, "No, I came down here to get some lanolin for Mother's bedsores." She gestured toward the muddle of papers and the open book on the desk where both of them knew perfectly well she kept no lanolin. "I . . . I have to look for it, so you go on."

He glanced from the desk to her. "You're sure you'll be all right?"

"Yes, thank you. I'll be fine."

The room seemed combustible with suppressed emotions while neither of them moved.

"Well, good night, then."

"Good night."

I should have kissed you when I had the chance.

As he backed toward the door her words stopped him again. "Tom . . . thank you. I needed somebody very badly tonight."

He nodded, gulped, and stalked out before he could dishonor himself and her and Charles.

Chapter 11

October passed and Tom took up residence in his house. It was livable, but bare. The walls were clean and white but begged for wallpaper and pictures, the things a woman was so much more adept at choosing than a man. The windows, with the exception of those in the one bedroom Tom used, remained unadorned. Since he spent most of his time in other places, the livability of his home, for the moment, mattered little. He had an iron bed, a heater stove for the parlor, a cookstove for the kitchen, and one overstuffed chair. Besides these few purchased furnishings he made do with a few empty nail kegs, a crude homemade table, two long benches, and a woodbox. From Loucks he had bought necessities only: bedding, lanterns, wash basin, a water pail, dipper, teakettle, frying pan, and coffeepot. He stored his few groceries—eggs, coffee, and lard—on the kitchen floor in an empty wooden crate from rifle shells.

The first time Tarsy came in, she glanced around and her face flattened in disappointment. "You mean this is *all* you're going to put in here?"

"For now. I'll get more when the oxcarts start moving again in the spring."

"But this kitchen. It's . . . it's bare and awful."

"It needs a woman's touch, I'll grant you that. But it serves my needs. I'm at the livery barn most of the time anyway."

"But you don't even have dishes! What do you eat on?"

"I eat most of my meals at the hotel. Sometimes I fry an egg here for breakfast, but eggs aren't much good without bread. Do you know anybody I could buy bread from?" Tarsy, he could see, was dismayed by his Spartan furnishings.

On a Saturday night in late November he was sitting in his only chair with his stocking feet resting on a nail keg, feeling somewhat dismayed himself. The place felt dismal. He had closed the parlor and stairwell doors, so the kitchen was warm, but too silent and stark with the curtainless windows black as slates and the ghostly white walls broken only by the stovepipe in one corner. If he were at the stable he'd be polishing tack. If he were at home in Springfield, in his mother's kitchen, he'd be prowling for food. If he were with his friends he'd be at a house party, but he'd begged off again, because Emily would be there with Charles. Tarsy had badgered and begged him to change his mind, then stormed off declaring, "All right, then, stay home! But don't expect me to!" So here he sat, staring at the red toes of his gray socks, listening to the silence and wondering how to fill his evening, thinking about Emily Walcott and how the two of them had been avoiding each other for weeks.

Charles had questioned him about why he never came to the parties anymore and he'd concocted the excuse that Tarsy was becoming too possessive and he wasn't sure what he wanted to do about her, which wasn't far from the truth. She was displaying a sudden, alarming nesting instinct. She'd even started baking him bread (heavy and coarse as horse feed, though he thanked and praised her first attempts at domesticity) and showing up at his door uninvited in the evenings; and dropping hints about how she'd love to live anywhere but with her parents; and asking Tom conversationally if he ever wanted to have a family.

He let his head fall back against the overstuffed chair and closed his eyes, wishing he loved Tarsy. But not once had he felt for her the swell of protectiveness and yearning that had overcome him the day Emily Walcott had cried and confided in him. He wondered how Emily was holding up. He knew from Charles that Mrs. Walcott was worse than ever, clinging to life though Dr. Steele had declared weeks ago there was nothing more he could do for her.

In his silent house Tom rolled his face toward the window, wishing he were with Emily and the others. It was a skating party tonight, the first of the year down on Little Goose Creek, and afterwards the group would move to Mary Ess's house for hot punch and cookies . . . and undoubtedly those damned parlor games. No, best he'd stayed away, after all.

In his pensive state, Tom failed to register the first sounds. He heard only the snap of the fire and his own gloomy monologue. Then it came again, a distant clanging, growing louder, accompanied by shouts and hallooing. He listened closer. What the hell was going on out there? It sounded like a gold prospector's pack mule rolling down a mountainside, only it was coming toward his house. He heard his name being called—"Heyyyy, Jeffcoat!"—and left his chair. "Company coming, Jeffcoat! Yoo-hoo, Tommy boy, open up!" More clanging accompanied by laughter, the commotion now seemingly circling his house. Next came the sound of horses' hooves.

At the front window he cupped an eye and peered out into the winter night. What the Sam Hill? A team and wagon were drawn right up to his front porch steps and people milled everywhere! Footsteps thumped on the hollow porch floor and a face peered back at him with crossed eyes: Tarsy. And beside her Patrick Haberkorn, then Lybee Ryker, then a whole chorus of merrymakers, shouting and rapping on the glass. "Hey, Jeffcoat, open the door!"

He threw it open, stood with his hands on his hips, grinning. They were all supposed to be at a skating party.

"What the hell are you fools up to?"

"Shivareeeeeee!"

Lybee Ryker shook silverware inside a covered pot as if it were corn popping. Mick Stubbs banged a frying pan with a wooden spoon, and Tarsy led the pack playing a pair of kettle covers as if they were cymbals. They were all there, all his friends, making such a clatter it seemed as if it would shake the moon from the sky. They left tracks in the snowy yard, clear around his house. Someone's dog had followed, and its barking joined the din. Tom stood on the front porch, laughing and feeling his heart warm, watching their faces flash past in the light from the open door behind him. She was there, too—Emily—though she hung back in the shadows when they all gathered, breathless and excited at the foot of the porch steps.

Overwhelmed, Tom searched for words. "Well, hell, I don't know what to say."

"Say nothing. Just step aside and let us get this stuff inside!"

They filed past him and deposited pots and pans and cutlery on his plank table. Tarsy wrinkled her nose just beneath his and gave a smug, self-satisfied smile as she carried a white bundle inside. "Look out if you don't want to get your toes stepped on."

"Is this your doing, Miss Fields?" He raised an eyebrow, secretly pleased.

"Might be," she said, twitching her skirttails as she passed. "With a little help from Charles."

Charles was busy on the wagon, sliding things to the rear for unloading.

"Bliss, you underhanded scoundrel, is that you out there?"

"I'm busy, you can call me names later!"

"Jerome, Ardis . . . hello." Tom's head swung as he caught glimpses of housewares and spindle chairs being carried past. Cheery voices, warm smiles, and everywhere motion. And somewhere in the middle of it, a much more subdued "Hello, Emily."

And her equally subdued "Hello, Tom," as she moved past him into his kitchen.

Someone kissed his jaw—Tarsy, going back out.

Someone bumped his arm—Martin Emerson heading back in on the lead end of a beautiful hide trunk with Jerome Berryman at the other end.

"Oh, you people, this is too much," Tom said.

But the parade lasted a good five minutes—in and out—with Charles supervising the unloading, until finally, with the help of all the men present, he unloaded a piece of furniture as wide as three men and taller than their heads.

"Charles, good God, what have you done?"

The piece was too heavy to allow Charles more than a few grunted words as he lifted it. "Just ... step aside ... Jeffcoat ... or you'll get ... plowed ov—"

They set it against the south kitchen wall between two long, narrow windows, a beautifully crafted breakfront-server of bird's-eye maple, hand rubbed to the smoothness of an old ax handle. It sported two wide drawers and matching doors below, a wide serving counter at waist level, two more doors and a plate shelf above. Into each of the four doors had been carved shafts of wheat curling up to circle a centered brass handle. Many hours of loving care had gone into the meticulous crafting of the piece.

Tom stood touching it, staggered. "Lord, Charles ... I don't know what to say."

Someone closed the outside door. Though the kitchen was filled with young people, it had grown silent as Charles brushed a haze of condensation off the top of the piece then backed off, removing his gloves. "I thought it'd make the place feel more like home."

Gratitude and an undeniable font of love welled up in Tom Jeffcoat as he closed a hand over his friend's shoulder. "It's beautiful, Charles ... it's ..." It was more than beautiful. It was a heartful. He embraced Charles hard, with a sincere clap on the back. "Thank you, Charles."

Charles chuckled self-consciously and they backed apart—eyes meeting for an awkward moment—then laughed. And when they laughed, the others followed suit, bringing relief from the emotional moment.

Tom turned to the other offerings. "And, Jerome ... you made me a trunk?"

"The old man and me."

Jerome Berryman's gift was almost as surprising as Charles's—a beautiful cowhide trunk with wooden hardware and brass hasp, made in his father's leather shop. Tom inspected it minutely and gave Jerome, too, an affectionate thank-you and slap on the back. "Tell your father thank you, too."

"Open it."

Inside was a motley collection: a boot scraper, a cornbread pan, a pair of dented tin kettles, a collection of clean, washed rags tied in a bundle.

"What's this?"

"Rags."

"Rags?" Tom held them aloft by their twine binding.

"Ma says everybody needs rags around a house."

A burst of laughter began a new round of commotion: the women used some of the rags to wipe melted snow off the kitchen floor while others began unpacking an amazing variety of housewares. Curtains, which one contingent hung while another began lining the pantry shelves with butcher paper. The men opened jugs of homemade beer; someone found glasses in the rummage; someone else opened the parlor door and built a fire in the small heater stove; the Fields's gramophone was wound up and a tube put on, filling the house with music; someone unearthed a reflectorized wall lantern and mounted it on the parlor wall; two of the men returned from taking Edwin's rig back to the livery stable and got scolded for stamping snow off their feet; Lybee Ryker produced a braided rag rug for in front of the door; Tarsy untinned sandwiches. And through it all, Tom unpacked his bounty.

What they hadn't made they'd acquired by raiding their homes. The result was a collection of oddments from spoon holders to spigot jars, some useful, some useless. The women found places for everything as he unpacked: four chipped enamel plates in white, edged with blue; some wrinkled metal flatware; a grater; a wooden potato masher; dishtowels; fruit jars of home-canned vegetables and jellies; three scarred spindle chairs of assorted styles; a dented copper cuspidor; a small square parlor table with one cracked leg; a horsehair sieve; antimacassars; pillowcases; a comb pocket for the wall; a cracked mirror; a hair receiver.

"A *hair receiver?*" Tom covered his head as if to hold his hair on. "Lord, I hope not!"

Everyone laughed as Tarsy came over and ruffled his thick black mane. "No danger yet."

He squeezed her waist and gave her a private smirk. "Pretty sneaky, aren't you?" he teased in an undertone, his eyes crinkling at the corners.

"Having fun?"

"Remind me to thank you later."

One of the last things he unwrapped was a beautiful hand-pieced quilt. The women drew closer, oohing. All except Emily.

"It's from Fannie," she announced quietly, keeping the same distance she'd been maintaining all evening.

Tom met her gaze directly for the first time since the party had moved inside. "She made it?"

"Yes, she did."

"It's very nice. Tell her I said thank you, will you?"

Emily nodded.

Looking on, Charles mistook their careful distance for chilliness and—ever eager to promote amity between the two he loved most—moved to take Emily's hand. "Want to see the house?" he asked. "I'll show it to you."

She flashed him a quick, distracted smile. "Of course."

With Charles she walked through Tom's house, the house the two men had built together: up the stairs with a turn at the landing, through three second-story bedrooms, each with its own closet, and with charming gabled windows jutting from the angled ceilings but without so much as a stick of furniture. Charles could not have been prouder were the house his own. He described each feature enthusiastically, holding the lantern aloft, leading Emily by the hand. In the third bedroom they paused, glancing in a full circle at the new floor, freshly milled and fragrant of wood smell, at the attractive ceiling line, the long, slim windows, bare as the day they were installed. The lantern flooded them with a ring of light. Against the black night their reflections shone clearly in the shiny window glass. They both caught sight of their reflection at the same instant; then Charles tightened his hand around Emily's and bent as if to kiss her.

Dipping, she slipped free.

"Is something wrong?" he asked, masking his disappointment.

She turned away. "No."

"You're awfully quiet tonight."

"It's nothing. I'm worried about Mother, that's all."

It wasn't all. It was Tom Jeffcoat; and this house where he expected to live with a wife someday; and his eyes, which had avoided hers all evening; and the memory of the last time she was with him, crying against his collar, wrapped in his arms, feeling secure and comforted.

"That's not all," Charles insisted, moving close behind her, squeezing her arm. "But how can I understand if you won't tell me?"

She groped and came up with a plausible reply. "It's these bare windows, Charles. Anybody could look in and see us."

"So, what if they did? We're engaged to be married. Engaged couples are supposed to kiss now and then."

She had no further justification for avoiding Charles and turned, lifting apologetic eyes. "I'm sorry, Charles."

His expression appeared hurt.

"I am, too."

He had lowered his arm. The lanternlight lit his face from below, making of his eyes great dark shadows. "Do you know what I think is really bothering you?" She stared at him without answer as he continued, "I think it's Tom."

She felt a hot lump burst in her chest and spread tentacles of guilt to her face. "Tom?"

"Whenever you're around him you change. Either you snub him or cut him. Tonight you've hardly spoken to him, yet this party is in his honor. He's my best friend, Emily, and I feel like I'm caught in the middle of a tug-of-war between you two. Can't you try to be his friend for my sake?"

"I'm sorry, Charles," she replied meekly, feeling the color mount her cheeks, dropping her gaze guiltily.

"You haven't even said one nice thing about the house. You know, I spent most of my summer building it, and I'm pretty proud of it myself."

"I know." She stood before him with the crestfallen expression of a chastised child.

"Then act as if you can at least tolerate him." He lifted her chin with a finger and studied her eyes, as shadowed as his own. "All I want is a little harmony between you two."

"I'll try," she whispered.

He kissed her, there before the naked windows, with the lamplight spotlighting them in the center of the vacant room: a light resting of his lips against hers while holding her chin up; then a second, briefer kiss: all is forgiven.

"Now let me show you the rest," he whispered, and led the way from the room, holding her hand. As they moved on, he explained how the rafters were mortised, pointed out double-hung windows, the fit of the doors, the smoothness of the upstairs handrail, the safe, shallow drop of each riser and the extra width of the stairs. At the bottom of them they turned left instead of right and Emily found herself in Tom Jeffcoat's bedroom.

His bed—of white iron with acorn knots where the bars intersected—stood in a corner flanked by a window on either wall. Instead of a spread the blankets were flung up flat over a single pillow, which looked forlorn on the double width. On a nearby nail keg stood on oil lantern and at its base lay a single black hairpin. Catching sight of it, Emily felt her heart take a leap. Her hand flew to her nape as if the pin had only now fallen. *What was it doing beside his bed?* But Charles had eyes only for the house itself, and she lowered her hand unobtrusively. He pointed out the double astragal moldings on the doors while her gaze drifted over the windows, temporarily curtained with flannel sheets nailed to the tops of the frames. With the exception of the hairpin, the room looked as austere as a monk's cell.

"We put a closet in every room," Charles was saying. "I wish I'd thought of it when I built my house." When she turned, he had opened Tom's closet door, revealing a few garments hanging in a largely unused space. She recognized the black dress suit he wore on Sundays and the faded flannel shirt that had absorbed her tears the last time she'd seen him. On a hook at the rear hung one of his tattered blue shirts with the sleeves torn off, and on the floor lay a carpetbag with an underwear leg trailing from it. Braced in one corner was his rifle. The closet smelled like him—of horses and worn clothing and man.

She could not have felt more discomfited had she walked in on Tom Jeffcoat during his bath.

"We put rosettes on all the corners." Charles pointed to the woodwork above their heads. "And extra wide mopboards . . . beaded. This house is built to last."

"It's very nice, Charles," she replied dutifully. And it was. But she wanted to get out of this bedroom . . . fast.

The lower level of the house could be walked in a circle. Parlor into kitchen, kitchen into a walkthrough, which served as a pantry and housed the foot of the stairway, through the pantry into Tom's bedroom, and through a second bedroom door leading back to the parlor again. Entering that room, Emily breathed a sigh of relief. The gramophone crackled out a tinny song and dancing had begun. Tarsy and Tilda Awk were hanging the quilt for display, stretching it across one corner by slamming its corners into the tops of the sliding windows. Tom's kitchen benches had been carried in and a group sat on them, laughing, hanging spoons from their noses. Others were visiting. Tom Jeffcoat stood in the kitchen doorway, drinking a glass of beer, watching Emily and Charles enter from his bedroom. Emily's eyes locked with his as he swigged, then wrist-wiped his mouth. She was first to turn away. She pivoted to join the group on the benches but Charles caught her hand and propelled her straight across the room to another doorway beside Tom, opening it to reveal one last closet. "We even put one in here." It was absolutely empty.

"Ah," Emily said, sticking her head in, aware of Tom standing two feet away, watching.

"Oh, Tom, you have closets!" Mary Ess exclaimed, rushing over to poke her head inside, too. "Lucky you!"

Mary crowded right into the closet while Charles drew Emily out by an elbow. Turning to Tom, aware of the emotional undertow between him and Emily, Charles said, "She likes your house."

Emily gave Jeffcoat a flat glance. "I like your house," she repeated dutifully, then sidled past him into the kitchen to find something to drink.

The party grew livelier. The gramophone got louder and the dancing got faster. Emily consumed three glasses of beer and began genuinely enjoying herself, neither ignoring nor singling out Tom. She danced the varsovienne and grew pleasantly warm. Between dances, she stopped trying to push Charles's arm from around her waist. Once she glanced across the room to find Tom standing with one wrist draped over Tarsy's shoulders, drawing her against his hip. As if he felt her eyes, he looked over and their gazes locked. He raised his glass and took a drink, watching her all the while. Charles's arm rested around her waist; Tom's rested around Tarsy's shoulder. Emily experienced an irrational flash of jealousy, and again proved the first to glance away.

Someone opened a new jug of homemade beer, stronger than the first. Spirits levitated and humor grew infectious. The men dragged the new trunk into the parlor and stuffed Mick Stubbs into it, declaring the only way he could be freed was if a lady would kiss him. Tilda Awk volunteered and raised a chorus of ballyhooing and wolf whistles when she did so in the middle of the room, standing in the trunk with Mick; then the men playfully tried to close the trunk lid over both of them, which, naturally, didn't work. Tilda and Tarsy got giggly and secreted themselves in the corner behind Fannie's quilt, whispering. Minutes later they flounced out and dragged the rest of the girls behind the quilt, divulging a new game plan.

"We're going to have a toe social!"

A toe social?" Ardis Corbeil whispered, wide-eyed. "What's a toe social?"

Tilda and Tarsy rolled their eyes and giggled. "My mother told me about it," Tilda said. "And if she could do it, why can't I?"

"But what is it?"

It turned out to be another ridiculous game, and very risqué. The women would strip from the knees down, hike up their skirts, and stand behind the quilt revealing their naked feet and calves while the men would try to guess whom they belonged to.

"And if they guess, what then?"

"A forfeit!"

"What forfeit?"

It was Mary Ess's idea: five minutes in that empty closet . . . with the door closed . . . in pairs.

"I won't do it!" declared Emily. But the girls were giddy with excitement and chastised, "Oh, don't be such a wet blanket, Emily. It's only a game."

"But what if I end up with somebody besides Charles?"

"Sing songs," Mary suggested flippantly.

When the men heard the rules of the game they let out roaring yells of anticipation, stuck their fingers in their teeth and whistled shrilly, began punching each other's arms, then murmuring secretly among themselves and breaking into bursts of conspiratorial laughter. Emily's eyes met Charles's and she could see clearly that *he* wouldn't mind spending five minutes in a closet with her. She found her objections overridden and herself swept along as the game proceeded. The men were sent out of the room while the girls sat down to remove shoes, strip off stockings, and pull up their woolen underwear. All the while Emily sat on the floor she tried frantically to remember if Charles had ever seen her feet bare. When they were children, a long time ago, wading together in the brook while their families picnicked. Would he remember what they looked like? Oh, please Charles, remember! You must remember!

The floor was cold, despite the heater stove in the opposite corner. She stood with the other girls, barefoot, on Tom Jeffcoat's freshly laid hard oak floor and took her place in the lineup behind the quilt like some mindless sheep, afraid to walk out of the party as she wanted to, afraid Charles wouldn't recognize her feet and Tom Jeffcoat would.

Mary Ess called, "All right, you can come in now!" The men filed back in, wordlessly. On the opposite side of the quilt they cleared their throats nervously. Emily stood wedged between Tarsy and Ardis, staring at the quilt, three inches from her nose, staring at Fannie's careful coral stitches binding patches of her old dresses and her father's old shirts, feeling as if her stomach had risen to her throat, wondering what in the devil she was doing here, coerced into a game she had no desire to play. The men's shifting stopped, the room grew silent, ripe with tension.

The girls held up their skirts and felt their faces heat. Some crossed their toes shyly. None of them would look at one another. What would happen if their mothers found out about this?

The forbiddenness held them in thrall.

Emily Walcott prayed Charles would choose first . . . and right.

To her horror, she heard Jerome Berryman suggest, "It's your party, Tom, and it's your house. Even your quilt. You want to go first?"

"All right," Tom agreed.

Emily's fists formed knots in the folds of her hip-high skirts. A cold draft sifted across the floor and seemed to turn her toes to ice. Through her mind raced the picture of Tom Jeffcoat holding her boot and kneeling to help put it back on, the first day she'd ever laid eyes on him. It had been horrible then. It was worse now. Had she been standing before him stripped naked she could not have felt more exposed. Why had she ever let herself get sucked into this stupid game? To prove she wasn't a wet blanket? To prove she wasn't a prude? Well, what was wrong with being a prude? There was a lot to be said for prudery! She found this distasteful and prurient and wished she'd had the courage to say so!

But it was too late.

Tom Jeffcoat moved along the line of bare toes slowly, assessingly, coming to a halt before Emily. She squeezed her eyes shut and felt as if her entire body were puffing with each heartbeat. He moved on to the end of the line and she breathed easier. But he was back in a minute, striking panic into her heart. She glanced down. There were the tips of his black boots an inch away from her bare toes.

"Emily Walcott," he said clearly and covered her distinctive longest second toe with the tip of his boot.

She closed her eyes and thought, no, I cannot do this.

"Is it you, Emily?" he asked, and she dropped her skirts as if they were guillotines. She stood staring at the quilt, unable to move, with her stomach tipping and her cheeks ablaze. Tarsy gave her a nudge. "Get going and don't scratch his eyes out." Then, closer to Emily's ear: "I'm quite partial to his eyes!"

Emily ducked around the side of the curtain with her face glowing like a cranberry aspic. She could not—would not!—look at Tom Jeffcoat.

"I think we have to add a new rule," Patrick Haberkorn jested. "You both have to come out of the closet *alive.*"

Everyone laughed except Emily. She sent a silent appeal to Charles, but he called, "Don't hurt him, Em, he's my best friend!" Again her friends laughed while she simply wanted to liquefy and drain away through the cracks between the floorboards.

"Miss Walcott ..." Jeffcoat invited with a slight bow, gesturing toward the open closet door as if it were nothing more out of the ordinary than a waiting carriage. "After you."

Like a martyr to the stake, Emily walked stiffly into the closet. The door closed behind her and she stood smothered by darkness so absolute it momentarily dizzied her, confined with Tom, close enough to smell him. She swallowed an imprecation, sensing him at her shoulder, unruffled, while she felt as if her breath were driven from her lungs by repeated blows. She reached out, touched the cold, flat plaster, ran her hand to the corner and moved toward it, as far from him as she could get. Turning her shoulders against the right wall, she slid down.

He followed suit against the left.

Silence. Mocking silence.

She hugged her knees, curling her bare toes against the new, smooth floor.

She had never been so scared in her life, not even the time when she was four and believed there was a wolf under her bed after her mother had told her the story about her grandfather being chased by wolves when he was a boy.

She heard Jeffcoat pull in a deep breath.

"Are you mad at me for getting you in here?" he asked, just above a whisper.

"Yes."

"I thought so."

"I don't want to talk."

"All right."

Silence again, thicker than before, while she drew her knees to her chest and felt as if she might explode. It was like being twenty feet underwater and out of air—fright and pressure and her heart banging hard enough to burst her eardrums.

"This is a stupid game!" she hissed.

"I agree."

"Then why did you pick me!"

"I don't know."

Anger sluiced through her, rich and revitalizing, replacing some of her fear. Until he admitted, reluctantly, "Yes, I do."

Her nostrils pinched and her shoulder blades threatened to dent his new plastered wall. "Jeffcoat, I warn you . . ." She put out a fending hand and touched black space.

He let the suggestion hover until the walls seemed to shrink. Then he ordered in a voice low and rife with intent, "Come here, tomboy."

"No!"

His hand closed over her bare left ankle.

She recoiled and cracked her skull against the wall.

"No!"

"Why not?"

"Let go!"

"We've both been wondering. It might be our only chance to find out."

The anger left her voice, replaced by pleading. "Tom, don't! Oh God, please don't." Frantically, she tried to pry his hand off her ankle, but he pulled relentlessly until she felt herself sliding across the closet floor, still bent at the knee and hip.

"If you put up too much of a fight they might guess what's really going on in here."

She stopped struggling . . . with everything except breath. It fought its way up her throat and caught on the lump of foreboding that had risen from her chest.

Outside, someone banged on the door, teasing. Emily jumped but Jeffcoat remained unyielding. His hand slid up her calf and came to rest behind her knee. She sat as still as a monument while his other hand searched the dark, found her cheek, then slipped around her nape, pulling, pulling, while she stiffened against it.

"I'm scared, too, tomboy, but I mean, by God, to find out. Now come here."

His mouth missed hers by an inch. He corrected his course, trailing warm breath while she sat unbending, holding her own breath keeping her lips stiff as frozen persimmons. His first kiss was cautious, a mere resting of his lips on hers. When she remained rigid he backed up—by the feel of his breath she knew he was still dangerously close—then went at it again, scarcely separating his lips to impart a hint of dampness. "Don't," she pleaded softly, plaintively.

But he went on as if she hadn't spoken, kissing her compellingly, angling his head, lightly swashing her lips with his tongue, thawing them. "Come on, tomboy, take a stab at it," he encouraged, and took her head in both hands, resting his thumbs beside her unwilling mouth and drawing circles as if to reshape it, rubbing his tongue across her lips persuasively.

She swallowed once, with her lips still closed, her heart thundering with an avalanche of forbidden feelings. He was very persistent, very poised, drawing wet figure eights upon her mouth—lightly, lightly—his breath warming her cheek until her own could no longer be contained. It came out in a rush, accompanied by a shudder, and her willpower disappeared like frost from a sun-kissed windowpane. Wilting against him, she lifted her arms and returned his embrace. When she opened her lips his tongue swept inside them at once, hot and inquisitive, inciting hers to do the same. Explorers, they circled, stroked, delved . . . abashed by their mutual, swift excitement.

It grew too intense, too fast.

They broke apart, hearts hammering and breaths pelting while he rested his lips against the bridge of her nose.

"Emily . . ." he whispered, and tipped her head back, found her lips again impatiently, as if unwilling to waste one moment of this stolen time. No darkness was dense enough to disguise her acquiescence; none complete enough to hide her pliancy as she drooped against him like table linen slipping to the floor and opened her soft, willing mouth to his.

The kiss began with full accord, then ripened with eagerness. A swell of impatience rushed up from Emily's toes, finding her unprepared for its impact. It brought heat and deep quivers and the awful need to press her breasts against him. Yet they could not be pressed firmly enough to ease the sudden ache of arousal. He fed it, kissing her full-mouthed, drawing her across his lap, moving his head to seal their fit just right.

And, oh, it was right. Her mouth seemed designed for his. She coiled around his trunk, drawing her knees up to buffet his ribs, crooking one arm over his shoulder, the other around his side.

His wide hand folded around her upraised elbow and rode it tight and smooth down to her armpit and to her breast. She shuddered, then lay motionless, steeping in new sensations. Her bodice fit snugly, enhancing the feeling of his whole hand cupping her, his thumb searching out the warmest, hardest spot. Deep within she felt a glorious spill and drew her knees up tighter while his hand brought a sweet, impelling ache to her breast.

He freed a slim breadth of space between their mouths and whispered, "How much time do you think we have?"

"I don't know."

Their rejoining was greedy: a revelation. She had never kissed so before, not with this abandon, as if to do so were an imperative. She had never given her breasts for fondling, as if to resist were unthinkable. He was more than she had expected, facile, warm-mouthed, her perfect complement.

Reality nagged: the closed door . . . the ticking clock . . . Charles . . . Tarsy . . . the possibility of being discovered.

A little longer . . . only a little . . .

Tom dragged his mouth from Emily's, lightly bit her lips, her chin, and her breast, through her tight bodice, as if to take away as much as possible when leaving this black cubicle. She hadn't a thought of pushing him away; each of his advances felt integral, undeniably necessary. He kissed her mouth again, fondling her breast while a hard knot formed in her belly, woman-low.

She was kissing him heedlessly when he clasped her arms and roughly pushed her back. "Emily, we'd better stop."

She felt flushed and swollen all over. Prudence took an effort. She still saw nothing but unrelieved blackness, but in it she heard his strident breathing.

"He's going to know," she whispered shakily.

"Then sit back where you were." He pressed her against her own wall and slid back to his. She drew her knees up to her clubbing heart while Tom let one leg stretch flat, hoping to appear natural when the door opened. But she realized they were about to be given away.

"I'll be blushing."

"Then tell him I kissed you and I'll apologize to him and say it was the beer."

"I can't tell him that!"

"Then slap me." A swift motion, and suddenly he was on all fours before her, groping for her hand, kissing it fast before putting it on his rough cheek. "Quick! Haul off and give it to me good so it'll leave a mark."

"Oh, Tom, I can't—"

"Quick! Now!"

"But—"

"Now!"

She slapped him so hard he plunked backward and yowled, "Ouch!" just as the door flew open. He looked up into the inquisitive faces of Tarsy, Charles, and the others. Emily's face was buried in her arms, but Tom had the presence of mind to spring immediately from the closet into the light where the stinging shape of her slap glowed on his cheek. Nursing it, he growled, "That's what comes of trying to make friends with your competitors." Clumping away without offering a hand to help Emily up, he groused to Charles, "You can *have* her, Bliss!"

Emily was no good at duplicity; she had to get out of Tom's house immediately or give herself away. She begged off with an early-morning veterinary call and Charles left with her within minutes after the episode in the closet.

Once out in the cold night she could breathe again but her voice sounded strained, even to her own ears.

"Charles, I don't want to go to any more of those parties."

"But they're only innocent fun."

"I hate them!"

"I think it's Tom Jeffcoat you hate."

"Charles, he kissed me in that closet. He kissed me!"

"I know. He apologized to me for it, and said he'd had a couple too many beers."

"Don't you *care?*" she demanded exasperatedly.

"Care?" He took her arm and stopped her in the middle of the street. "Emily, it was just a game. A silly game. I thought if you two spent five minutes in that dark closet you might come out laughing at yourselves and the way you've been acting ever since he got to town, setting sparks off one another."

Oh, they'd set sparks off one another, all right, but Charles was too trusting to see it. To him it had been just a game, but to Emily it had been much more. It had been a threat and a thrill and a myriad of forbidden feelings so new they left her stunned.

By the time they reached her home she was not only shaken, but angry.

"What kind of a man lets his best friend kiss his fiancée and laughs it off?"

"This kind." Charles grabbed her arm, spun her against himself, and kissed her as forcefully as Tom had. Releasing her, he said throatily, "I love you, Emily, in spite of the fact that you can't treat my best friend civilly."

Minutes later Emily slipped into bed beside Fannie and lay like a fresh-hewn plank, staring up at the ceiling with the quilt edge coiled in both fists beneath her chin. She closed her eyes and saw what she had seen in the closet: nothing. Only blackness, which heightened all her other senses. She had felt him, tasted him, smelled him. Oh, his smell!

She released the quilt and pressed both palms to her nose and sucked in any lingering trace of him that might remain on her skin. Even now on her palms, she recognized it. It was no scent and all scent—clothing, hair, hay, leather, and man in potpourri. Funny, she could not remember what Charles smelled like. But Tom . . .

She rolled to her belly, cupping her breasts in an effort to stop them from aching.

He touched you here and you came alive.
Only because it was dark and forbidden.
It was what you've wanted since that day on the turntable.
No.
And the night he found you crying.
No.
Yes.
*I never intended to kiss him. Not even when I walked into that closet. I only
wanted to prove I was no prude.*
And you did, didn't you?
I never meant to cheat Charles.
*You didn't cheat Charles. You only found out what was lacking between the two
of you.*

The terrifying thought kept Emily awake most of the night.

Chapter 12

The following morning Emily awakened as she had slept—troubled. When she
was troubled she wanted to be in only one place: with the animals. She dressed
in woolen britches, jacket, and bobcap and slipped from the house before anyone
else was up. A new snow had begun falling, brittle and icy. Flat-footed, she skated
through it, head hanging, hands buried in her rib pockets.

Inside, the stable was warm, pleasant. Familiarities soothed—the fecund smell,
the morning routine, the greetings of the horses, who turned their great heads as
she spoke inanities and bumped past their broad bellies while feeding and watering them.

Edwin came at his usual time.

"Up early," he observed.

"Yes," she replied spiritlessly, avoiding his gaze.

"Got the chores done already."

"Yes."

"Anything wrong?"

"Oh, Papa . . ." She went into his arms, closed her eyes, and gulped at the lump
of apprehension in her throat. "I love you."

He drew back and held her by both arms. "Do you want to talk to your old
papa about it?"

She gazed into his caring eyes, tempted. But maybe she had blown last night
out of proportion. Maybe it was nothing more than a kiss in a closet, a silly game
already forgotten by Tom Jeffcoat. Though her father's invitation was sincere, in
the end she shook her head.

To his credit, Edwin asked no questions. He left Emily to herself and stayed out
of the office, where she holed up with her books. But *The People's Home Library*
lay between her elbows as she stared unseeingly at the overflowing pigeonholes

of the scarred desk, her thumbs pressed against her chin . . . thinking . . . thinking . . . tangled with emotions.

A murky dawn had scarcely grayed the windows when the inset door opened and Tom Jeffcoat marched into the office in lengthy strides, a man with an objective. He spun Emily's chair and pulled her from it straight into his arms.

"Tom, I've—"

He stopped her protest with a kiss. Unapologetically. Blatantly. Without hiding in anyone's closet.

Stunned, she forgot to resist, but stood in his arms letting him kiss her until the feelings of last night rose afresh within her. In time common sense prevailed and she arched away, pushing at the thick sleeves of her sheepskin jacket.

"Tom, my fath—"

"I know." He cut her off again, bending her backward like a strung bow until he felt her remit, then drawing her up with their mouths locked. He kissed her as he had last night—tongue and lips and enough wetness to wash away logic. He caught her unfortified, spreading his taste into her mouth with a straightforward appeal she could not withstand.

By the time they parted to search one another's eyes, her resistance had evaporated.

Out of the gray murk of dawning complications splashed a golden moment of thoughtlessness, while they immersed themselves in one another—young, unchary, and greedy. His tongue came strong against hers, and she opened to him gladly, tasting him as one learning to appreciate a new flavor. The flavor was intrinsically "Tom Jeffcoat," as individual as the flecks of color in his blue eyes. He had shaved, smelled of soap and cold air and old sheepskin—not new smells, only a combination individualized by him.

The kiss changed tone, became a grazing exploration of softness and swimming heads while passing minutes brought a new sortie of heart thrusts within them both. They parted, gazing deep again, introducing a tardy question of willingness before coming together again with more fervid intentions. Her arms took him hard around the neck, crossing upon his thick, standing collar; his doubled around her back, fingers spread like starfish along her ribs.

They imbibed the myriad textures of one another—wet tongues, silky inner lips, smooth teeth—as they had not last night with the threat of discovery but a footstep beyond a closet door.

She thought his name—Tom . . . Thomas—and felt the wondrous upheaval of desire blur the edges of discretion.

He thought of her as he always had—tomboy . . . the one I least suspected would ever light such a fire in me.

His palms rode her back, full width and breadth, over crossed suspenders and her brother's rough shirt and the waistband of woolen britches, then slid up to her shoulder blades in search of a safe place to moor. They hooked her shoulders from behind while he struggled for control.

When the kiss ended they studied each other at close range. Amazed. Quite unprepared for the swift response each had triggered in the other.

"I didn't sleep much," he divulged in a sandpapery voice.

"Neither did I."

"This is going to be complicated."

She drew a shaky breath and fought to be sensible. "You take a lot for granted, Tom Jeffcoat."

"No," he answered simply, admitting what she would not. "I waited a long time for the attraction to die, but it didn't. What was I supposed to do?"

"I don't know. I'm still a little stunned." She laughed disbelievingly.

"Do you think I'm not?"

When he would have kissed her again she retreated. "My father ..." She glanced toward the door and put distance between herself and Tom, but he breached it, taking her elbow, pursuing as if compelled by some uncontrollable force.

"Last night when you couldn't sleep, what did you think about?" he wanted to know.

She wagged her head in earnest appeal, backing away. "Don't make me say it."

"I will, before we're through. I'll make you say everything you think and feel for me." She backed into something solid and he closed in, bending to her even as his body came flush against hers. She lifted on tiptoe and embraced him. They kissed hard and wide-mouthed, propelled by the incredible attraction from which they both still reeled.

In the middle of the kiss, Edwin entered the office. "Emily, do you know where—" His words died.

Tom swung about, his lips still wet, one hand trailing at the small of Emily's back.

"Well ..." Edwin cleared his throat, glancing from one to the other. "I hadn't thought about knocking on my own office door."

"Edwin," Tom said gravely, in greeting. The single word held neither excuse nor apology, but outright acknowledgment. He remained as he was, with his arm around Emily while her father's eyes skipped between the two of them.

"So this is what was bothering you this morning, Emily."

"Papa, we ..." There was little excusable about the scene so she gave up trying.

Tom spoke calmly, filling the void. "Emily and I have some things to discuss. I'd appreciate it if you didn't mention this to anyone, especially to Charles, until we have a little time to sort out a few things. Will you excuse us, Edwin?"

Edwin looked incredulous and distempered by turns; first at being politely excused from his own office; second at leaving his daughter in the arms of someone other than Charles. After ten seconds of silent chafing, he turned and left. Tom glanced at Emily and found her red to the hairline, overly chagrined.

"You shouldn't have come here," she said. "Now Papa knows."

"I'm sorry, Emily."

"No, you're not. You faced him without the least shame."

"Shame! I'm not ashamed! What did you expect me to do, pretend it wasn't happening? I'm not fifteen anymore and neither are you. Whatever needs facing we'll face."

"I repeat, you take a lot for granted. What about me? What if I don't want people to know?"

He gripped her shoulders firmly. "Emily, we need to talk, but not here where anybody might walk in. Can you meet me tonight?"

"No. Charles is coming to dinner tonight."

"Afterwards?"

"He never leaves until ten."

"So meet me after ten. At my livery barn or the house or anywhere you say. What about down by the creek, right out in the open if you'll feel safer. All we'll do is talk."

She drew free of his touch, for it beckoned as nothing she had ever experienced.

"I can't. Please don't ask me."

"Don't tell me you're going to pretend this never happened! Jesus, Emily, be honest with yourself. We didn't just pop off a couple of kisses in a closet and go away unaffected. Something is happening here, isn't it?"

"I don't know! It's too sudden, too ... too ..." Her eyes pleaded for understanding.

"Too what?"

"I don't know. Dishonest. Dangerous. And doesn't it bother you, about Charles?"

"How can you ask such a thing? Of course it bothers me. My stomach is in knots right now, but that doesn't mean I'll turn away from it. I need to know your feelings and to come to grips with some of my own, but we need some time. Meet me, Emily, tonight after ten."

"I don't think so."

"I'll wait for you down by the creek where the boys always fish in the summer, near the big cottonwoods behind Stroth's place. I'll be there till eleven." Moving close, he took her head in both hands, covering her ears and the sides of her red bobcap, resting his thumbs beside her mouth. "And try to stop looking as if you've just broken every one of the Ten Commandments. You really haven't done anything wrong, you know." He landed a light kiss on her lips and left.

She felt as if she'd done plenty wrong—all that day and into the evening, while she made up a lie about the veterinary call that had never existed, when Charles asked how it had gone. While they ate roast beef and vegetables and gravy; and played cribbage with Fannie and Frankie; and while she avoided her father's eyes, and breathed a sigh of relief when he went upstairs to sit with Mother instead of joining in the game; and while Charles kissed her good night and left at quarter to ten. And afterwards, as she told Fannie she'd put away the cards and the coffee cups, and suggested Fannie just go on up to bed.

The house grew still. Emily stood at the window facing the creek and Stroth's place, imagining Tom there kicking at the snow, peering into the shadows, waiting for her. She could walk to the cottonwoods in less than ten minutes, but what then? More illicit kissing? More forbidden caresses? More guilt?

It was undignified. And Charles deserved better. It was the kind of thing done by women of questionable reputation.

So she told herself all the while she exchanged button-top shoes for cowboy boots, slipped a hip-length coat over her full-skirted dress, and tugged on her old red bobcap, jamming her hair beneath its ribbing.

This is wrong.

I cannot stop it.

You can, but you won't.

That's right. I can, but I won't.

Papa always did call you willful.

Papa already knows, and he said nothing.

That's rationalizing, Emily, and you know it! He's waiting for you to explain yourself.

How can I explain what I don't understand?

She tiptoed through the parlor and slipped outside, soundlessly. The day's sleet had turned to snow—fluffy as eiderdown. It fell yet, in a path straight as a plumb line through the windless night, building up level on every surface it touched. Beneath it, the icy layer crunched with each of Emily's footsteps. Upon it her skirts swept with a sound like an uninterrupted sigh. The moon hid. The sky hugged close, lit from within itself by the thick white dapples it shed. Here and there a window created a gold ingot, but most were dark in a silent, deserted world.

She came to Stroth's place, cut around his house and along his woodpile with its frosting of white, past a forlorn grindstone left out in the weather, beyond his outbuildings to an open meadow where footsteps marked someone's recent passing. She followed them, placing her own within his—long strides, longer than her natural ones—feeling an uncustomary delight in merely walking where he had gone. Ahead, the cottonwoods created shadowless shapes against the white night. They looked warm, blanketed. From beside them a form separated itself—tall, capped in black, standing still as a pedestal, waiting.

Emily stopped, detailing the euphoria brought about by his presence. It was novel and acute in its magnitude. She didn't recall ever feeling it at the appearance of Charles, nor exalting in something so mundane as following the footsteps he had made in the snow. She was a sensible girl who thought it wholly sensible to marry Charles. But sense was a stranger as she approached Tom Jeffcoat.

Behind him the creek ran, open yet, making night music that joined the sigh of her skirts as she continued toward him. With an arm's length to go, she stopped.

"Hello," he said quietly, reaching out two gloved hands.

"Hello," she said, giving him her fat-mittened ones.

"I'm glad you came. I didn't think you would." He wore a black Stetson that had kept the snow off his collar, but the shoulders of his sheepskin jacket were dusted with white.

"Have you been here long?"

"An hour or so." It was only 10:30. She could not help being pleased.

"You must be freezing."

"My toes . . . a little. It doesn't matter. Can I kiss you?"

She chuckled in surprise. "You're asking this time?"

"I promised we'd only talk. But I want to kiss you."

"If you didn't, I'd be disappointed."

They came together easily, no rush, not clutching, only a tipping of his hat brim and a lifting of her chin, their covered hands scarcely crushing the snowflakes on each other's clothing. To Emily it was more devastating that the frantic clutches she'd shared with him before. Three times she'd kissed him since their physical awareness of one another had taken hold, and each had been different. The first time, in the closet, fear had stopped up her throat. This morning in the office surprise had numbed her at his first appearance. But this was different, full agreement, no hurry. When their mouths parted she remained beneath the shelter of his hat brim, where their breaths mingled as ribbons of white in the cold air.

"I thought of you all day," he told her simply.

"I thought of you, too . . . and of Charles, and Tarsy and my father. I had a very bad day."

"So did I. Did your father say anything after I left?"

"No. But he watched me like an eagle all day long. I'm sure he's trying to figure out exactly what's going on between us."

"What is?"

She backed up a step, resting her mittens on his shearling collar, looking up into his shadowed face. "I don't know," she admitted. "Do you?"

"No . . . not for sure."

In silence they studied each other, evaluating, doubting and considering by turns, because it was so sudden, so unexpected.

"There are so many things I want to know about you," Tom said. "I feel as if I only met you, since we stopped fighting, I mean. Hell, I'm not making any sense."

"Yes you are. I know what you mean. At the beginning we only antagonized each other."

"Didn't we, though?"

They enjoyed a moment of silence, touching lightly through thick, warm clothes, then Tom asked quietly, "How long have you known Charles?"

"All my life. Since my first memories."

"Do you love him?"

"Yes."

"You say that without a qualm."

"Because it's true. I've always loved him—who wouldn't love Charles? Even you love him, don't you?"

"Yes, I'm afraid I do. I've never had a friend like him." Plagued, he rested his hands on her shoulders and studied a point beyond. After moments he shook his head. "Can you beat him? Building that beautiful piece of furniture for my house? He'd done more than anybody else in this town to make me feel welcome."

"Certainly more than I ever did."

"That's what's so unbelievable about this whole thing. You, Emily Walcott, the tomboy—I mean, hell, you hadn't even gotten over resenting me before this . . . this *thing* hit me like an avalanche. I still wanted to throttle you, even when I started thinking about kissing you. It doesn't make any sense. I wasn't even over Julia yet!" He touched her cheek with a gloved finger. "Remember that day on the turntable when we almost kissed?"

"Did we almost kiss that day?"

"You know damned well we did. We were pumping like bellows at a full roar. It was only the thought of Charles that stopped us."

"Charles *and* Tarsy. We can't disregard Tarsy."

"No, unfortunately Tarsy won't let herself be disregarded."

Emily laughed briefly, then sobered. "She does love you, you know. And unless I miss my guess there's probably . . ." She dropped her gaze, discomfited. ". . . well, *more* between you and Tarsy than there is between Charles and me."

"Emily, I'm not going to lie to you. Tarsy and I have been close, in some ways. When I came here I was lonely. I spent a lot of time alone, and between Charles and Tarsy, I've had two good friendships to sustain me. But Tarsy is . . . temporary. She always was, and she understood that. It's Charles who's the permanent fixture between us, and I hate like hell to be sneaking around behind his back."

"I hate it, too."

"So . . ."

"So?"

"We could end it right here and Charles would never be the wiser."

"It would be the honorable thing to do."

But they hadn't the forbearance to stop touching, even as they discussed it.

"Is that what you want to do?"

"I . . ." She swallowed, miserable.

"It isn't, is it?"

Reluctantly, she wagged her head, averting her gaze.

He took her arms and pulled her close to his chest. "Emily, come to the house."

"I'm afraid."

"Nothing will happen, I promise. Just talk. Just for an hour, please?"

"No."

"You might have a little pity on me. My toes really are freezing, after all."

It was a convenient excuse and they both knew it. But neither wanted to part, and nothing had been settled. The frustration had only mounted.

"All right. But only for a half hour or so. Fannie sleeps with me, so she knows I'm gone. I'll tell her I went for a walk in the new snow but a half hour is all I can stay."

They walked back without touching, she along the trail they'd both made, he at her side stamping a new one through Stroth's backyard, along the deserted streets, and into the door through which Charles Bliss had brought his heartwarming housewarming gift little more than twenty-four hours ago.

The kitchen was as black as the inside of a whiskey keg. Stepping in, Emily paused and heard Tom close the door behind them. "There's no fire in the parlor stove, only in here. This way." He nudged her and she followed, touching his sleeve for guidance across the unfamiliar space, around the table to the overstuffed chair pulled up before the kitchen stove, which radiated welcome heat.

"Sit down," he directed. "I'll put some more wood in."

He lifted the stove lid, found the poker, and stirred the embers, lighting the ceiling to a glowing red. He added a log and sparks lifted with subtle pops, then a new flame glowed, and he replaced the stove lid, leaving them in darkness. "You can see through the kitchen curtains and I haven't got shades yet," he explained, adjusting the bottom vent. "Best not light a lamp." He tugged off his gloves, shrugged from his jacket, and tossed it into the darkness, where it hit a bench and slid to the floor. He dropped onto a nail keg and began removing his boots. Two clunks sounded as he set them near the stove, then only silence and a faint hiss threading from the finger-sized airholes at the base of the firebox.

They sat side by side, Tom doubled forward, resting elbows on knees, Emily perched on the edge of her chair. For minutes all was silent. The fire took hold and Tom set a stove lid aside, giving them a glimmering light by which to see each other's faces.

At last he said, "I've been trying to talk myself out of this."

"I know. Me, too."

"I tell myself I really don't even know you, but the hard part is how can I get to if I can't come calling out in the open?"

"What do you want to know?"

"Everything. What were you like as a child? Did you have the whooping cough? Do you like beets? Does wool make your skin itch?" Like a typical smitten man, he felt impatient to catch up with the part of her life that had gone before. "I don't know—everything."

She smiled and accommodated him. "I was inquisitive and willful, I had whooping cough, I can tolerate beets, and the only thing that ever made my skin itch was poison ivy. Mother had to put mittens on my hands in the middle of summer to keep me from scratching it. I was . . . nine years old, I think. There—now you know everything."

They laughed and felt better.

"Is there anything you want to know about me?" he inquired, admiring the pale glow of her face.

"Yes. What was my hairpin doing beside your bed last night?"

Their gazes caught and locked. Silence for several powerful heartbeats before he said, "I think you can figure it out."

"You really ought not leave things like that lying around where your best friend might see them."

"Did he say anything?"

"No. I don't think he noticed. He was too busy pointing out the merits of the house. By the way, I do like your house very much."

"Thank you."

They had exchanged so many double-edged remarks it took some acclimating to get used to the sincere ones. The mood grew heavy and she searched for another question to alleviate the pressure growing in her chest.

"Is your real name Tom or Thomas?"

"Thomas. But the only one who ever called me that was my maternal grandmother."

"Thomas. It has ... stature. Is she still alive, your grandmother?"

"Very much so. All four of my grandparents are alive."

"You miss them?"

"Yes."

"And your ... the woman you were supposed to marry, you miss her, too?"

"Julia? Sometimes. I knew her a long time, just like you've known Charles. Naturally you miss someone like that."

"Naturally." She pondered how she would miss Charles if he suddenly were gone, and found to her distress she would miss him considerably.

"I got a letter from Julia though, and she's very happy. She's married and expecting a child."

"Charles wants children. Right away."

"Yes, he's told me."

"I don't."

"He told me that, too."

"He did?" she asked, surprised.

Casting her a sidelong glance, Tom remained silent.

"So you know more about me than you first let on."

He expanded his lungs and shrugged, forcibly relaxing his shoulders. "Would you mind, Emily, if we didn't talk about Charles anymore? Are your toes cold? Do you want to take your boots off?"

"No, I'm fine."

"Your mittens?"

"No, I'm ... they're ..." She lifted and dropped her hands, clasping them in her lap as if snug wraps could arm her against incipient feelings.

When Tom continued studying her without comment, she grew uneasy and looked away, staring at the golden circle of light on the stovetop. He sat hunched forward, chin hooked between thumbs and forefingers, watching her silently. After some time he rose from the keg and walked off into the shadows behind her.

He stood at the window, staring out, at odds with his conscience. What did one friend owe another? What did a man owe himself? He turned his head to study the dark bulk of the breakfront at his left. He had touched the smooth top dozens of times in the few hours it had been here, touched it and agonized. He did not touch it now, but kept his hands in his pockets.

He turned to study the dim outline of Emily, her bobcap taking on a halo like a rising orange moon, hair winging out below it on either side, creating a bouquet of lightpricks, her shoulders bowed forward as she perched on the chair like a sparrow ready for flight.

Charles, he thought, his heart hammering wildly, *forgive me.*

He moved around her chair and stood directly before her, gazing down at the top of her head, at her mittened hands pinched between her knees. She refused to look up. Dropping to one knee, he gently drew her hands free and removed her mittens, laying them aside; next her boots, first one, then the other, twisting on his haunches to set them beside his own beneath the reservoir. Pivoting on one knee, he reached for her coat buttons, freed them one by one, then pushed the garment from her shoulders. Last, he dragged the hat from her head, leaving her hair standing out in staticky rays. Only then did she lift her beleaguered eyes to his.

"Stop me if I'm wrong," he whispered and, fitting her to his breast, kissed her. There was no bland hello this time, but instant demand, open mouths and seeking tongues. And hands maintaining a shaky propriety, holding fast to the safest places—shoulders, backs. In time he petted her hair, flattening it with the whole of one hand, shaping that hand to her warm skull. He kissed her throat, her chin, her mouth again, until breath became precious and desire weighted their limbs. He bracketed her breasts, kneaded them with the heels of his hands, then did the same with her hips, cradling them with firm pressure.

"Oh," she might have said, but he imprisoned the word within her throat, and made of it an impassioned murmur. She touched his head all over—temples, skull, neck, jaws, and throat, learning each new texture as if imparting it to memory.

His arms slipped beneath her knees, around her back . . . lifting . . . carrying her across the dimly lit kitchen—a scrape on the floor as he jarred a bench, stepped around it, turned her feet aside to negotiate the doorways of the pantry and his bedroom.

The bedsprings chimed as he lowered her and followed, dropping his full length upon her. Braced on his elbows, he toyed with her hair and breathed on her mouth, letting her adapt to his motionless weight and the advent of imprudence. Dropping his head, he invited her one step further, delivering moist kisses across her lips and chin, along her nose, until she followed like a birdling for its food, drawing him down to halt his sojourn. Their kisses grew rugged and wet. Reactions exploded and temperance fled. They pressed close, lifting knees, rolling, twining in damp skirts and petticoats. He stroked her breast . . . both breasts . . . explored their shape with his fingertips and the heels of his hands, and with his mouth through taut cotton. He buried his face between them and breathed against her, heating her skin and her blood while she cradled his head and gave herself over to sensuality. He slid back up, found her open mouth again, and moved his hips in cadence, a mere rhythmic tipping at first, to the counterpoint of his tongue stroking hers. Prone upon her, he dragged his hands down her ribs and hips, slipped them against the quilt and held her fast from behind, curling his fingers into the folds of her skirt and her flesh. His body flashed against hers with unmitigated desire in each upbeat. She closed her eyes and took the ride with him to the brink of hell.

"Tom . . . stop . . ."

He stilled, dropped his face into the lea of her shoulder, and lay upon her, panting.

"This is a sin," she whispered.

He expelled a ragged breath, rolled to his back, dropped one arm across his eyes and the other across his groin.

She rolled away and sat up, but he grabbed her wrist. "Stay. A minute . . . please." She curled toward him, pressing her knees and forehead against his side. For minutes they lay linked by the three contact points, descending like dandelion seeds on a still day. When his pulse had settled he said, "You don't do these things with Charles, do you?"

"No."

"Then why do you do them with me?"

"I don't know. If you're blaming me—"

"I'm not." Again he held her from leaving. "I'm trying to be honest. I think maybe we're falling in love with each other. What do you think?"

She had known the possibility existed the day she toured his barn, but when faced with the words was afraid to say them; they were so absolute and could bring such tumult into so many lives. "This is not the supreme test, I don't think. This is only lust. I've loved Charles for so long—I know I love him, but it's because of years and years of familiarity. Everybody I know married people they'd known a long, long time—my parents, their parents, even my friend's parents. I never thought love happened this fast."

"I never though so, either. I was like the other people you know, in love and engaged to a girl I'd known for years. But she had the honesty to break away when she realized she loved someone else. At first I was bitter about it, but now I'm beginning to see what strength it took for her to admit that her feelings had changed."

The longer Tom spoke the more she wished him silent, for she foresaw great hurt ahead for many should this wellspring between them be what he believed.

"Emily?" He found her hand and held it loosely, stroking it with his thumb while lying in thought for a long time. Finally he went on. "It's not just lust. Not for me. It's things I admire about you—your dedication to your work, and to your family, and to Charles, even. I respect you for not wanting to tread on Charles's feelings, and for not wanting me to tread on Tarsy's . . . and your affection for the animals and your sympathy for your mother and the way you do battle to keep me honorable. Those things count as much as any others. And you're . . . different. Every other woman I know dresses in petticoats and aprons." He rolled toward her and laid a hand on her waist. "I like your independence—britches and veterinary medicine and all. It makes you unique. And I like the color of your hair . . ." He touched it. "And your eyes." He kissed one. "And the way you kiss and the way you smell and the way you look . . . and I like this . . ." He found her hand and placed it on his throat where a strong pulse drummed. "What you do to me inside. If it is lust, all right, that's part of it. But I want you . . . I had to say it, just once."

"Hush." She covered his lips. "I'm so frightened and you don't help at all."

"Tell me," he whispered, closing his eyes, kissing her fingertips.

"I can't."

"Why not?"

"Because I'm still promised to him. Because a betrothal is a kind of vow, and I made that vow to him when I accepted his proposal of marriage. And besides . . . what if this is momentary?"

"Does it feel momentary to you?"

"You ask me for answers I can't give."

"Then why did you meet me tonight?"

"I couldn't seem to help myself."

"So what should I do tomorrow, and the day after that and the day after that?"

"Do?"

"I'm the man. Men pursue."

"But to what end?"

Ah, that was the question—to what end? Neither knew the answer. To mention marriage would, after a mere twenty-four-hour liaison, be precipitous. And anything less would be, as she said, iniquitous. No honorable man would expect a woman to settle for that. Yet to go on deceiving Charles was unthinkable.

Emotionally weary, Emily pulled herself to the side of the bed and sat in a jumble of skirts, holding her head, coiled forward in misery, pressing her elbows against her belly.

Tom sat up, too, equally as heavy-hearted, studying the back of her head, wondering why it had to be she he had tumbled for. In time he lifted a hand and began absently straightening strands of her mussed hair because he could think of nothing else to offer.

"Emily, these feelings aren't going to go away."

She shook her head vehemently, still covering her face.

"They aren't," he repeated.

Abruptly she rose. "I have to go." He stayed behind, staring at the dark floor, listening to her sniffling, donning her outerwear in the kitchen. He felt like hell. He felt like a traitor. With a sigh he rose and went out to her, stood in the dim stovelight watching her button her coat. He followed her silently to the door and stood behind her while she faced it without touching the knob. He touched her shoulder and she spun around, flinging her arms around his neck, gripping him with quiet desperation.

"I'm sorry," he whispered against her bobcap, holding the back of her head as if she were a child he carried through a storm. "I'm sorry, tomboy."

She held her sobs until she was down his porch steps and halfway across his yard, going at a dead run.

Chapter 13

Edwin arose at six the following morning. Outside, the sky was still black above an unbroken blanket of new snow. Stepping out the back door, he breathed deep, pulling in the fragrance of a fresh world after the cloying odor of Josie's sickroom. There were times when he entered it that the gorge rose in his throat, times when he lay in his cot thinking he would suffocate, times when he stood silently in the doorway, watching her suffer, and thought of the nostrums in his daughter's veterinary case: opium, aconite, tannic acid, lead—if administered in large enough doses, any one of them could bring a merciful end to his wife's suffering.

Edwin moved off the step, dropped his chin, and watched his boots lift snow as he walked to the privy.

Would you do that to your own wife? Could you?

I don't know.

If you did, you'd never be sure whether you did it to put her out of her misery or to end your waiting for Fannie.

Worries, worries. Frankie had become a worry, too. He refused to enter the sickroom or to talk to his mother. She had grown so pitifully emaciated that the boy found himself unable to accept the change in her. Frankie seemed to be denying that his mother was dying.

And now this thing with Emily and Tom Jeffcoat—something else to worry about.

Returning to the kitchen, Edwin found Fannie already up, filling the coffeepot, dressed in a blue plaid housedress and a long white bibbed apron. Most mornings Emily arose at the same time as they and was here in the kitchen creating a welcome buffer over breakfast. Not so today. They were alone in the room, with the stovepipe snapping and the lamplight sealed inside by the long shades, still drawn from the night before.

"Good morning," Fannie greeted.

"Good morning."

Edwin closed the door and stripped off his jacket, revealing black suspenders over the top of his woolen underwear.

"Where's Emily?"

"Still sleeping."

He poured water into the basin, began washing his face and hands while listening to Fannie set the coffeepot on the stove, then get out a frying pan. When he straightened, drawing the towel down his face, he found her standing at the stove watching him, a slab of bacon in one hand, a butcher knife in the other, forgotten. For moments neither of them moved. When they did, it felt as natural as receiving falling snowflakes upon a lifted face; they stepped to one another and kissed— good morning, plain and simple, as if they were man and wife.

They parted and smiled into each other's eyes while his hands continued drying on the towel.

"Have I ever told you how much I love finding you here in my kitchen when I walk in?"

"Have I ever told you how much I love to watch you washing at the sink?"

He hung the towel on a peg and she began slicing the bacon on a board.

He combed his hair and she dropped the meat into the pan, sending up a sizzle.

"How many eggs do you want?"

"Three."

"How many slices of toast?"

"Four." So much like man and wife.

She searched out three eggs and the toasting racks and a plump loaf of bread while he went to find a clean shirt, and brought it back to the kitchen to don. Standing just inside the doorway, he watched her turning the bacon while he flipped down his suspenders, slipped his arms into the starched cotton, and slowly began buttoning it.

"I meant it, Fannie," he said quietly.

"Meant what?"

"That I love having you here, baking my bread, keeping my house, washing my clothes." He stuffed his tails into his pants and snapped the suspenders into place. "Nothing's ever felt so right."

She came to him and ran her fingers beneath one suspender, straightening a twist.

"For me either." Their eyes met, caring and momentarily happy. They kissed again, in a room filled with the scent of toasting bread and boiling coffee. When the kiss ended, they hugged, with her nose pressed against the clean starchy scent of his shirt, which she had happily laundered for him; and with his nose nestled in her hair, which smelled faintly of bacon, which he gladly provided for her.

"God, I love you, Fannie," he whispered, holding her by both arms, gazing into her eyes. "Thank you for being here. I couldn't have made it through these days without you."

"I love you, too, Edwin. It seems fitting that we should go through this together, don't you think?"

"No. I want to spare you, yet I can't bear the thought of sending you away. Fannie, I want to confess something to you, because once I confess it I know I'll never do it."

"Do what, dearest?"

"I've thought of taking something from Emily's bag—laudanum, maybe—and ending Josephine's life for her."

Tears glistened in Fannie's eyes. "And I've watched her shrivel away, fighting for breath . . . and I've thought of putting a pillow over her face and ending her painful struggle."

"You have?"

"Of course. No human being with a dram of compassion could help but consider it."

"Oh, Fannie . . ." He hooked an arm around her neck and rested his chin on her head, feeling better, less depraved, knowing she'd thought of it, too.

"It's terrible, thinking such things, isn't it?"

"I've felt so guilty. But poor Josie. Nobody should have to suffer like that."

For a moment she absorbed his strength, then patted his back as if punctuating the end of a statement.

"I know. Now sit down, Edwin, and let's not talk of it again."

While they ate, dawn came, paling the shades at the windows to the color of weak tea, bringing the faraway barking of dogs across town. Often Edwin and Fannie gazed at each other. Throughout the meal they felt the false connubial closeness brought about by the sharing of mundane morning routine. Once he reached across the table to touch her hand. Twice she rose to refill his coffee cup. Returning the second time, she kissed the crown of his head.

He caught her hand against his collarbone, brushed his beard along her palm. "Fannie, I have to talk to you about something else. I need your advice."

"What is it, Edwin?"

She sat down at a right angle to him, their hands joined at the table corner.

Holding her gaze, he told her, "I walked into the livery office yesterday and found Emily kissing Tom Jeffcoat."

Fannie's expression remained unsurprised as she sat back and hooked a finger in her coffee cup. "So, now you know."

"Meaning you have?"

"I've suspected."

"For how long?"

"Since the first time I saw the two of them together. I've only been waiting for Emily to admit it to herself."

"But why didn't you tell me?"

"It wasn't my place to voice suspicions."

"They didn't even act jumpy when I walked in. Jeffcoat calmly asked me to excuse them!"

"And what did you do?"

"Why, I left. What else could I do?"

"And so you want to know if you should give her a lecture on the sacredness of betrothal promises, is that it?"

"I . . ." Edwin's mouth hung open while memories gushed back, of being talked out of marrying the woman he loved by his well-meaning parents.

Fannie rose and aimlessly trod the kitchen, sipping coffee. "She went out last night after the rest of us were in bed, and didn't get back till quite late."

"Oh God . . ."

"Why do you say 'oh God,' Edwin, as if it were come calamity?"

"Because it is."

"Now you sound like your own parents."

"Heaven help me, I know." Covering his face with both hands, Edwin pressed his elbows to the tabletop. She gave him time to worry it through. Finally his eyes appeared, troubled. "But Charles is already like a son to me. He has been his whole life."

"And undoubtedly they said the same thing to you about Joey."

Cupping his hands before his mouth, he studied Fannie while she went on. "I cannot speak for Joey, nor can I guess what you might have felt, but I can tell you what it was like for me. On your wedding day—oh, that day, that dolorous, grief-laden day—I didn't know how to contain my desolation. I wanted to weep, but I couldn't. I wanted to run, but that wasn't allowed. Propriety demanded that I be there . . . to watch the destruction of my happiness. I don't ever remember a sorrow so deep. I felt . . ." She studied her cup, circling its rim with a fingertip, then lifted sad eyes to Edwin. ". . . hapless. I could not function, didn't want to, couldn't project a future without an incentive to live. And you were my incentive. So I went into my father's barn with the intention of hanging myself." She gave a soft, rueful laugh, dropping her gaze to the cup again. "What a ludicrous sight I must have made, Edwin. I . . ." She glanced up sheepishly. "I didn't know how to tie the knot."

"Fannie—"

"No, Edwin." She held up a palm. "Stay there. Let me finish this." She moved to the stove and refilled her cup, stationing herself a goodly distance from him. "I thought about drowning, but it was winter—where could I do it? Poison? I could hardly go to the apothecary and ask for some Paris green, could I? And barring that, I didn't know where to find any. So I lived." She drew a deep breath and set down her cup as if it were too heavy for her. "No, that isn't quite accurate. I existed. Day to day, hour to hour, wondering what to do with my pitiful life." She gazed out the window. "You moved away—I didn't know why."

"Because I wanted you more than I wanted my own wife."

She went on as if he hadn't spoken. "Then Joey's letters began coming. Letters filled with the day-by-day inconsequentialities of married life—the banalities for which I pined. She became pregnant and Emily was born. I wanted Emily to be mine—mine and yours—and I knew that you'd been right to leave, for if you hadn't, I would have borne your child gladly, wed or not.

"Then four years or so after you left I met a man, a married man, the safest kind, I thought . . . the kind who made no promises, presented no expectations. I wrote to you and Joey about him—Ingrahm, was his name, Nathaniel Ingrahm. He was a curator at the museum whose cause I espoused at the time—preservation of the dying art of scrimshanding, or some such vital concern. In those days I was only beginning to take up a long line of vital concerns because I had none of my own." Fannie's thoughts wandered momentarily before she straightened her shoulders and turned toward Edwin. "At any rate, I had a sexual liaison with Nathaniel Ingrahm, chiefly because I wanted to find out what I had missed with you, and I was beginning to see that the chances of my finding a suitable husband were remote. You see, I rejected every prospect when he didn't seem to measure up to you. You were my standard, Edwin . . . you still are."

She drew a staunch breath, coupled her palms, and paced, focusing her attention on the walls, the windows, anything but him. "Within a year I became pregnant with his child. You may recall when I wrote and told you I was recuperating from what my mother referred to as summer muse, some sort of stomach malady that was circulating at the time. That's what I told her I had, but my . . . my *summer muse* was the aborting of the child I wanted by no other man than you. I drank bluing . . . and it . . . it worked."

He sat stunned, pained, wishing futilely that he could change the past, wanting to go to her, embrace her, but held away by her stern posture and evasive eyes.

"Nathaniel Ingrahm never knew." She studied her knit fingers and crossed thumbs. "I gave up my scrimshanding cause and embraced another . . . and another. And there were other men, of course, several—all human beings need love, or whatever substitutes for it—but I was careful. I had learned a trick with a copper coin that prevented conception. You're shocked, Edwin, I can tell. I need not be looking at you to sense your shock."

"Fannie . . ." he breathed, leaving his chair. "My God, I never knew."

"I have done some wicked things in the name of love, Edwin. Unforgivable things."

Reaching her, he gripped her arms. Their sorrowful eyes locked. He drew her to his breast, holding her protectively, cupping her head. "I'm so sorry." He closed his eyes and swallowed, his throat pressed to her hair.

"I didn't tell you to wrest pity from you. I told you so you'd see that you must not chastise Emily. You must let her choose freely, Edwin . . . please." She drew back and appealed with her eyes. "Edwin, I love your children simply because they are yours. I want their happiness because in their happiness they bring the same to you. Edwin, dearest . . ." She took his face in her hands, resting her thumbs at the junction of beard and cheek. "Please don't duplicate your parents' mistake."

When he kissed her his soul felt broken. Tears clogged his throat. He clung to her, aggrieved by the mistakes both of them had made, by the lorn years that had brought them only half-happiness at the best of times, sheer desolation at the worst. Their tongues joined in the testimony—this was meet and fitting, this was how it should have been had they been wiser, more defiant, truer to themselves.

While they embraced they were unaware of the stockinged footsteps of Emily coming down the stairs.

She entered the room and halted in shock. "Papa!"

Edwin and Fannie twisted apart, their hands lagging upon one another. "Emily . . ."

For tense seconds the room remained silent while the trio stood as if paralyzed. Emily's dismayed eyes flashed from Edwin to Fannie and back again. When she spoke her voice was reedy with accusation.

"Papa, how could you do such a thing!" She glared at Fannie. "And *you!* Our *friend!*"

"Emily, hold your voice down," Edwin ordered.

"And with Mama right upstairs!" Tears sprang to Emily's eyes as she whispered fiercely.

"Emily, I'm sorry you discovered us, but please don't judge what you can't begin to understand." He stepped toward her but she jumped back and pierced him with a look of icy reprehension.

"I understand enough. My mother taught me right from wrong, and I'm not a child, Papa, nor am I stupid!"

"We've done nothing wrong, and furthermore, I don't have to answer to you, girl." He pointed a finger. "I'm your father!"

"Then act like one! Show some respect for the dying and for the rest of your family." Her face flamed with rage. "What if it had been Frankie who came downstairs just now? What would he think? He can scarcely accept Mother's illness as it is!"

"He might have offered us a chance to explain."

"There is no explanation. You're despicable—both of you!" Angry and distressed, Emily ran from the room.

"Emily!"

When Edwin would have followed her, Fannie restrained him with a touch on his arm. "Not now, Edwin. She's too upset. Let her go."

The front door slammed. "But she thinks you and I are carrying on here in this house."

"Aren't we?" Fannie asked sadly.

"No!" he glowered. "We've done nothing to be ashamed of."

"Then why did we jump apart?"

"But she didn't give us a chance to explain."

"And if she had, what would you have said? That you and I are excused because we've loved each other since before you married her mother? The mother who is, as Emily had to remind us, dying upstairs? Would you tell her that, Edwin, and open up a Pandora's box of questions? Or do you think she would calmly accept your explanation and say, 'Very well then, Papa, you may carry on with Cousin Fannie'? Edwin, be realistic." With gentle hands she bracketed his bearded face while his expression remained stubbornly defensive. "She would blame you all the more for not having loved her mother as you pretended. And she would be justified. All her life she's seen you and Joey as paragons of virtue, inviolate in your union. She's had a tremendous shock this morning and we must give her time to adjust to it. We must think very clearly about whether *we* are justified in explaining our past to her. The proper thing for us to do might very well be to let her believe the worst about you and me."

"But, dammit, Fannie, I've honored my vows; I've never so much as touched you in this house before today."

"Yes, Edwin . . . before today." She dropped her hands from his face and stepped away. "Do you remember that day last June when I came here, when we were at the livery stable? I made a vow of my own that day, and I have broken it—whether in the flesh or in my imagination, it is broken just the same. A thousand times I have lain with you since I've been beneath this roof, in my wishes."

"But, Fannie, she doesn't understand that I want to marry you, that I will when it's possible."

"And we may have created an obstruction to that possibility this morning, had you considered that?"

"Emily is eighteen years old, a full-grown woman. And just yesterday I caught her in a similar situation. Did I point fingers?"

"She's not married, Edwin. You are."

He glared at her though his true anger was turned toward himself. She waited patiently for him to realize this, and knew the precise moment at which he did. Releasing a breath and running a hand through his hair, he asked contritely, "So what do we do?"

"For the time being, nothing. She'll let us know when she's ready for either apologies or explanations."

Emily strode through the frigid morning with indignation turning to bitterness. What her father had done to Mother, he'd done to her and Frankie, too. Her father—her shining idol, the one she'd loved unconditionally because he was all good, and honorable. In her entire life she'd never known him to consciously hurt another. Her father had betrayed them all.

It hurt even worse because he had been the gentle one, the understanding one, the one she had always turned to as a buffer against the harshness she often found in Mother. Well, at least Mother was no hypocrite! Mother lived what she taught.

Mother . . . poor, undeserving Mother . . . dying bravely upstairs while downstairs Papa profaned their marriage vows with his live-in harlot!

And that harlot—her friend, the one in whom she'd confided, the one she'd admired and trusted with her deepest secrets. Some friend! A Judas, after all.

Betrayal hurt. No, it stung. It brought a sense of stultifying powerlessness. Emily reached the livery stable with tears stubbornly dammed behind the floodgates she refused to lower.

She saddled Sagebrush and rode, hell-bent, until her legs ached and the horse's hide steamed. West. Toward the foothills, across frozen streams, through thickets of frosty sage, across unbroken snow, past startled rabbits and chipmunks and pines laden with new white, down coulees, up ridges, into a serene morning in which she created the only contradiction: a distraught human pushing a dumb animal who could only obey.

She rode until her eyelids felt frozen open and her exposed skin, afire. Until her lips felt cracked and her legs, hot and cramped. Only when the horse reared and whinnied at the crest of a knoll did Emily realize she was abusing the animal. Sagebrush tossed his head till lather flew and Emily reined in at last, slumping, letting her eyes close, feeling despair overwhelm her. She sat for minutes, listening to the animal pant, then slid from the saddle and stood at his jaw, still fighting her own emotions. Sage's hide was warm and damp and pungent with horse smell, but she needed something familiar right now. She dropped her forehead against his great powerful neck, clamping her jaw, gulping back sobs.

I need somebody. God ... somebody ...

Hot from his run, Sagebrush shook his head, forcing Emily to retreat; not even the horse cared, she thought unreasonably.

Flatfooted, she dropped to a squat, arms extended over her knees like a sheepherder rolling a cigarette, stubbornly determined not to cry. Her face burned. Her eyes burned. Her lungs burned. Everything burned—her father's betrayal, Fannie's betrayal, her mother's ceaseless suffering, her own betrayal to Charles. Life was one big burning hell.

She dropped her face between her knees and doubled her arms across the back of her head while she wept.

God, I'm no better than my father.

She returned to the stable for lack of choice. Sagebrush was sheeny, patchy with sweat, like the surface of a pond in an intermittent wind. He was thirsty and tired and hungry and eager for his familiar stall. Where else could she go but to her father's livery stable?

Edwin was there alone, applying a fresh coat of parsley-green paint to a doublebox wagon. The paintbrush paused in midair when Emily led Sagebrush inside and continued toward the stalls without a glance in Edwin's direction.

She watered the horse, removed and wiped down the saddle, brushed his warm chestnut hide until it cooled, caparisoned and stabled him. Passing her father again on her way to mix feed she felt his eyes follow, though he uttered not a word. She stared at the far end of the corridor as if Edwin no longer existed, striding mannishly with a wad of misery in her throat.

God, how she'd loved him.

Returning with a half bucket of grain, she blamed her stinging eyes on the paint fumes, which were thick in the closed building. Again Edward's gaze followed. Again she stared straight on, sensing his remorse and hurt, unwilling to accept it.

When Sage was fed she headed back toward the office, passing her father a fourth time, maintaining the same silent defiance as before.

"Emily!"

Her feet stopped but her eyes remained riveted on the great rolling door twenty feet away.

"I'm sorry," Edwin offered quietly.

She compressed her lips to keep them from trembling.

"Go to hell," she said, stone-faced, and walked on in a cocoon of pain.

She moved through that day with as much life as a door swung by the whim of the wind. She crossed paths with her father—it was inevitable—and spoke to him when necessary. But her voice was glacial and her eyes relentlessly evasive. When he asked if she wanted to go home for noon dinner first she replied, "I'm not eating." When he returned from his own dinner and set a plate of sausage and fried potatoes at her elbow, she cast it a disparaging glance and returned her attention to her needle and whipcord without offering so much as a thank-you. When he saw her leaving shortly after 2:00 P.M. he called, "Emily, are you going home?" His voice sounded lonely, echoing down the shaft of the long building. With grim satisfaction she answered him with only the roll and thump of the closing door.

Outside, ten feet from the building, she met Tom Jeffcoat, heading in.

"Emily, could I—"

"Leave me alone," she ordered heartlessly and left him staring at her back.

At home there was Fannie to face. Emily gave her the same treatment she'd given her father—gazed through her as if she were of no more substance than a cloud. Minutes later Fannie came to the doorway of their shared bedroom and said, "I'll be washing some bedding in the morning. If you have anything that needs doing up, just leave it in the hall."

For the first time Emily met Fannie's eyes—a fierce glare. "I'll do Mother's bedding!" she spat, shouldering past the older woman without touching her, crossing the hall to her mother's room where she closed Fannie out with a firm click of the latch.

She spent the afternoon at a task she detested: crocheting. She was wholly inept with a hook and thread, but worked on a doily as penance and atonement, staying at her mother's bedside until Papa came home from work and looked in.

"How is she?" he inquired, entering the room.

Emily leaned forward and touched Josephine's hand, ignoring Edwin. "It's nearly suppertime. I'll bring your tray up soon, all right, Mother?"

Josephine opened her eyes and nodded weakly. Emily slipped from the room without waiting to observe her mother's pathetic smile shift to Edwin.

When supper was ready Emily ordered in a tone that would brook no refusal, "Frankie, come. You've scarcely seen mother in over two weeks. Bring your plate up while I feed her. She'll be so happy to see you."

Frankie dutifully followed but sat on Papa's cot, picking at his food, staring at his knees instead of at the skeleton on the master bed. When he asked to be excused, looking pale and guilty, Emily let him go, but ordered him to help with dishes because she was going to stay and read to Mother.

A half hour later Edwin's footsteps sounded on the stairs and Emily quickly shut the book and kissed her mother, escaping to her own room, leaving Edwin standing in the upstairs hall, following her with baleful eyes.

By mid-evening she had reached a major decision, the correct one, she was sure. No matter what Papa and Fannie did to Mama, she would send her to her grave happy about one thing.

Emily donned a clean lavender dress, coiled her hair in a perfect ladylike figure eight, and went to Charles's house to announce that she was ready to set the date for their wedding.

Charles's smile was the full sun after an eclipse. "Oh, Em . . ." With a joyous lunge he picked her up and spun her, giving a whoop of laughter. His ecstatic reaction reaffirmed that Emily was doing the correct thing. Swinging around in his arms, she swallowed the lump in her throat and thought, I won't be like Papa, I won't!

Beaming, Charles set her down. "When?"

She smiled because she'd made him happy at last, and he deserved so much happiness. "Next week?"

"Next week!"

"Or as soon as Reverend Vasseler can perform the service. I want us to be married before Mother dies. It will make her very happy."

Charles's smile faded. "But what about your veterinary certificate?"

"I've decided to give it up. What will I ever do with it anyway? I'll be your wife, taking care of your house and your children. I was crazy to think I could go gallivanting around the country pulling calves anyway. I'll have all I can do to keep the socks white."

Charles frowned. "Emily, what's wrong?"

"Wrong? Why, nothing. I've just come to my senses, that's all."

"No . . ." He backed off, holding her gingerly by the elbows, studying her minutely. "Something's wrong."

"The only thing that's wrong is that time is moving too quickly, and Mother is nearly . . ." She swallowed hard. "I want this very badly, Charles, before Mother dies."

"But it takes time to plan a wedding."

"Not this one. We'll be married in Mother's bedroom so she can hear us exchange vows. Would that be all right with you?"

"You don't want a church wedding?"

"I'm not exactly the lacy kind, am I?" Tom Jeffcoat had never ceased calling her tomboy. "Besides, it would save work and trouble. I . . . I really don't want to ask Fannie to prepare all that food and . . . and . . . well, you know how much fussing weddings can be if you let them."

"And how many guests were you intending to have then, none?"

"Just . . . well, just Tarsy for my attendant."

"And just Tom for mine?"

"Tom . . ." She could not meet Charles's eyes while speaking of Tom Jeffcoat. "Well . . . yes, if that's who you choose."

"Who else would I choose?"

"Nobody. I mean, Tarsy and Tom are . . . are fine. The ceremony will only be a few minutes long anyway."

"Have you talked to Fannie about this?"

"Fannie's got nothing to do with it. It's my decision!"

"Have you talked to your father?"

"Charles!" She bristled. "For somebody who's been lathering at the bit to get a date set you certainly don't act too excited."

"I would if I hadn't known you since you were cutting teeth. You're upset about something and I want to know what it is."

She stood before him with the answer burning deep, compelled to lie to keep from hurting him as she'd been hurt. "If you love me, Charles, please do what I ask. I want this for Mother and I don't think we have much time."

He studied her gravely for a full fifteen seconds before dropping his hands and stepping back. "Very well. If you'll answer me one question."

"Ask it."

"Do you love me, Emily?"

His question seemed to resound in the pit of her stomach. And if her answer revealed only the partial truth, her motives were purely honorable.

"Yes," she answered, and caught the nearly imperceptible relaxing of his shoulders.

She did love him, she did! As she'd said to his best friend, who could help but love Charles?

Her reassurance had brought back his enthusiasm. "Should we go tell them?"

"I already did . . . at supper," Emily lied.

"Oh." The flat word reflected his disappointment and she felt guilty for depriving him of the joy of making the announcement. But if the two of them went now to break the news together her displeasure with Papa and Fannie would be clearly evident, not only to Charles but to Mother. "Things aren't exactly bright and cheerful around our house, Charles, with Mother being so bad. I thought . . . well, I thought it might be easier if I simply told them."

"That's . . . that's fine," Charles said doubtfully. "I just thought maybe . . ." His words trailed off.

She took his hand. "I'm sorry, Charles. The whole thing should have been more festive, shouldn't it?"

He shrugged off his disappointment and forced a grin. "Aw, what the heck—it's our lives together that count, not what kind of wedding ceremony we have. And anyway, your parents have known this was coming for years, haven't they? I made sure they did."

He kissed her happily, his bride-to-be, and lightly caressed her breasts, conveying wordlessly how he would treasure and love her. She felt his tongue in her mouth and answered with her own, putting last night from her mind, assuring herself, *You'll get used to the beard in time. You'll get used to his hands on you.*

But she was the first to break away. "Should we talk to Reverend Vasseler tomorrow?"

"Yes."

"Morning or afternoon?"

"Morning. Then I can talk to Tom and you can talk to Tarsy in the afternoon. Oh, Emily . . ." He clasped her close. "I'm so happy."

"So am I . . . but Charles, I have to go now."

She walked home feeling despondent. Where was the sense of eagerness she had expected after making the commitment? At home the emptiness seemed to expand as she hung up her coat and walked through the silent rooms downstairs. *This is not how it should feel. This moment should be splendid, a sharing of the news, a falling into arms, a rejoicing with those you love and who love you.*

She plodded upstairs and stopped in the light shining into the hall from her parents' bedroom, glanced inside, and paused in distaste. All three of them were there, Mother on the bed, Papa on the cot, and Fannie in a side chair. It twisted Emily's vitals, the hypocrisy of the scene. Not even for Mother's benefit could she smile at the other two as she entered the room.

She sat beside Josephine, turning her back on Edwin and Fannie, and took her mother's hand.

"I thought you'd like to know—Charles and I are going to talk to Reverend Vasseler tomorrow morning. We'll be getting married as soon as he can perform the service . . . right here in your room. Would you like that, Mother?"

"Why, Emily . . ." Josie's voice was a weak whisper, but her eyes showed a faint spark of approval.

"I knew you'd be pleased."

"But . . ."

"No questions now. They only make you cough. It's what I want, and what Charles wants, too. We'll talk more about it tomorrow."

Rising from the bed, Emily caught a furtive exchange of glances between Fannie and her father. When their glances lifted to her, nobody moved. *Papa, Papa. I wanted this moment to be so different. I had always pictured it with smiles and hugs.* But Emily held herself aloof, heart-sore.

Fannie alone recovered and rose quickly to act out the expected felicitations for Joey's benefit. "Congratulations, dearling . . ." When she put her arms around Emily and touched the girl's cheek with her own, Emily stiffened. Fannie stepped back and chided with false blitheness, "Edwin, for heaven's sake, have you nothing to say?"

Emily forced herself to stand in place while he rose from the cot and moved toward her with his contrite eyes asking forgiveness and permission. Waiting, her heart pounded with love and remorse. His lips touched her cheek with enough genuine affection to melt the hardest of hearts. "Congratulations, honey."

She stood like a newel post, resisting his endearment, his touch, the awful love she could not help feeling for him.

"I have to go tell Frankie," she mumbled, and escaped, leaving a roaring silence in the room behind her.

Frankie was fast asleep. She sat on his bed and jostled him. "Hey, brub, wake up, huh?" Somehow tonight she needed to use the childish nickname from her youth.

He burrowed into his pillow and grunted.

"Hey, come on, Frankie, wake up, huh? I've got something to tell you." *Please wake up. I need somebody so badly.*

"Get lost . . ."

She leaned close and whispered, "I'm going to marry Charles, probably before the week is out. Just thought you'd want to know.

He raised his face from the pillow and squinted over one shoulder. "Well, why couldn't you tell me tomorrow! Criminy, did you have to wake me up!" Face first he hit the mattress and pulled the pillow over his tousled head.

Frankie, I needed you, to hug, to get excited with. Don't you understand? Of course, he didn't. He was simply a disgruntled little boy disturbed from his sleep. He knew nothing of the turmoil within his sister. Dejected, she went to her own room to find Fannie already there, preparing for bed.

When the door opened Fannie looked up from her seat at the dressing table where she sat removing hairpins from her hair. It was easier for Emily to remain frigid to Fannie than to Papa: she had not loved her an entire lifetime. Too, Fannie was the intruder, doubtless the one most to blame. In that tense moment while their eyes clashed, she saw the caring in Fannie's, but turned, rebuffing it, closing the door, going about her bedtime routine with insular disregard.

It was unsettling, undressing in the same room with someone for whom you felt such enmity. Neither of them spoke as they donned their nighties, turned back the coverlets, extinguished the lantern, and crawled beneath the covers, back to back, hugging their edges of the bed.

Through Emily's mind glimmered memories of the times she had confided in Fannie, times like this when they'd lain in the dark, friends growing dearer to one another with each passing day. But Fannie no longer felt dear. She had abused the hospitality of this house and had proven herself a two-faced friend to Mama, and for that Emily despised her.

Emily had been lying carefully motionless for a full ten minutes before Fannie spoke quietly into the darkness.

"Emily, you're wrong."

"Shut up! I don't want to hear your excuses any more than I want to share my bed with you!"

Fannie closed her eyes and felt tears burn inside. She crossed her wrists beneath her breasts and pressed hard, cradling the hurt tightly, as a mother might cradle a found child. Emily had misunderstood her meaning; she had not meant, Emily, you're wrong about your father and me, but, you're wrong to jump into marriage this way.

Oh, Emily . . . dearling . . . can't you see you're marrying Charles for all the wrong reasons?

But faced with Emily's cold rejection, Fannie let the earnest warning wither in her throat.

Chapter 14

It had been a frustrating thirty-six hours for Tom Jeffcoat. If he had it to do over again he'd use his head and keep no less than two axe handles between himself and Emily Walcott.

At his anvil he beat a piece of hot metal as if it were his own head, which, he conceded, was about as dense as iron and needed some sense whupped into it.

You had to kiss her, didn't you, Jeffcoat? You had to go groping around in that damned dark closet and putting your hands where they didn't belong. You had to find out. Well, now you did, and what did it get you but miserable? Walking around here feeling like a cat gagging on a hairball. It's that woman who's stuck in your throat, and you can't swallow her and you can't cough her up. So just what in almighty hell are you going to do about it?

He beat the iron until the percussions rippled up his arms and jarred his joints. The iron grew too cool to shape but he kept beating anyway.

Emily Walcott. What was a man supposed to make of her? There were times when he wanted to throttle her. That temper—Christ, where did she get it? She seemed to stride through life in a perpetual state of defiance. Over what? She had nothing to defy!

But he admired her guts and her drive. She had more of both than most men.

He tried to imagine taking her back to Springfield and introducing her as his wife—his wife?—the one in the boy's cap and britches, the one who didn't want babies but would rather treat sick animals for a while. Wouldn't his mother pop her sockets? Especially after Julia, the perfect, proper, pregnant Julia. And his father would pull him aside by one arm and say, Son, are you sure you know what you're doing?

The answer was no. Ever since he'd laid lips on her in that closet he hadn't known what he was doing. Standing here beating a piece of cold iron like a fool. With a throaty curse he flung down his hammer and stood staring, brooding, missing her, wanting her.

She came, she met me, she lay with me and kissed me. And there were feelings between us. Not just heat, but feelings. Then the next time I tried to see her it was "Leave me alone!"

Frustrated, he drove eight fingers through his hair and roamed the confines of his smithy, picking up tools, casting them aside.

So what did you expect her to do, fling her arms around you and kiss you in the middle of Grinnell Street when she's engaged to Charles?

Emily Walcott was no dallier, he knew that. She wasn't toying with him as some women would. If he were to be honest with himself he'd admit that she was just plain scared. Scared of the emotional rush that had caught them both by surprise. Of the intensity. Of the eventualities that hung in the balance and the number of people who could get hurt if they pursued their feelings.

And what about you? You're not?

With a weary gust of breath he dropped to a low stool, shoulders slumped, arms hooking his widespread knees. He pulled her hairpin from his skirt pocket, rubbed it between his fingertips . . . again . . . and again . . . and again, staring, remembering her in a myriad of poses: glancing up across the crowded dance floor . . . cupping her mouth to shout the shrill Basque yell . . . riding toward him on the turntable. He heard again her voice coming to him in a close black closet, pleading, "Tom, don't. Oh God, please don't," because even before they'd kissed she recognized as well as he the fascination that had been smouldering beneath their surface antipathy. The memory of that first kiss brought memories of others—in Edwin's office, in a fresh snow, on his bed.

He covered his face with both hands.

All right, so I'm scared, too. Of hurting Charles. Of being hurt myself. Of making a wrong choice or missing the right one. He lifted his head and stared at the glowing orange forge.

The question is, do you love her?

God help me; yes.

Then hadn't you better tell her without beating around the bush?

And then what?

Do you want to marry her?

He swallowed, but the hairball still stuck.

Then hadn't you better tell her that, too?

While he sat with the thought ripe on his mind, footsteps sounded on the floor of the main corridor. Somebody gave the turntable a nudge in passing and made it rumble softly. Seconds later, Charles appeared in the smithy doorway.

"You won't get much work done that way!" he accused, grinning.

Tom grinned back, struggling with torn loyalties, happy to see Charles while wishing he'd never met the man.

"Yeah, well, neither will you." Pushing off both knees, Tom rose from the squatty stool. "What're you doing hanging around here in the middle of the day? Haven't you got some nails to pound?"

Charles stepped forward, stationed himself just inside the doorway, and smiled broadly. "I came to invite you to my wedding."

"Your w—"

"Friday afternoon at one o'clock."

Tom nearly fell back onto the stool. "Friday? You mean *this* Friday?"

"Yup."

"But that's day after tomorrow!"

"I know." Charles clapped his palms and rubbed them. "The stubborn wench finally said yes."

Tom's hairball seemed to inflate to twice its former size. "But ... so soon ..."

Charles respectfully dampened his exuberance and moved farther into the room. "It's because of her mother. Mrs. Walcott's really bad now. Emily thinks she hasn't got long to live, so she wants us to be married right away. Just a small service, right in Mrs. Walcott's bedroom so she can see it." Charles's happiness effervesced again and he beamed at Tom. "Can you believe it, Tom? Emily's actually impatient!"

Or running, thought Tom. "I thought she wanted to get her veterinary certificate first."

"She said she's giving it up." Charles's smile broadened. "Said she'll be too busy raising my babies to have time for anything else."

Night before last she told me she wasn't ready for babies yet.

"Well ... I'll be damned." Trying to disguise his shock, Tom paced, running a hand through his hair. "That's ... well, that's ... congratulations ..." He flashed a doubtful scowl, as he would have before he'd fallin in love with Emily. "I think."

Charles laughed and slapped Tom's shoulder.

"I think you like her more than you let on."

"She's all right, I guess. Just a little mouthy."

"I'm glad you're finally coming around because I've got a favor to ask you."

"Ask away."

"I want you to stand up for me at the wedding."

The hairball threatened to break loose and pull his stomach up with it. *Stand up for him? And remain silent when Vasseler asked if anyone knew of any reason for this couple not to be married? And pass Charles the ring to slip on her finger? And kiss her on the cheek afterwards and wish her a life of happiness with another man?*

Sweet Savior, he couldn't do it!

Hot seemed to turn to cold on his face. Thank God for the dimness in the room. He blinked, gulped, and offered Charles his hand.

"Of course I will."

Charles covered Tom's knuckles with a rough palm. "Good. And Tarsy will stand up for Em. She's over there asking her right now, at any rate. Can't see why she'd say no any more than you would." Charles squeezed extra hard on Tom's hand. His voice roughened with sincerity. "I'm so damned happy, man, you can't know how happy I am."

Tom didn't know where to hide. Afraid the forge would illuminate the underlying dismay in his face, he crooked an elbow and caught Charles around the neck, hauling him close. "Stay that way, Charles. You stay that way forever 'cause you deserve it."

Charles thumped him on the back.

They stepped apart. "Well ..." Tom ran a knuckle beneath his nose, sniffed sheepishly, and stuffed his hands into his hip pockets. "This is getting to be a damned sappy conversation."

They laughed together, self-consciously.

"Yeah, and I've got some nails to pound."

"And I've got an angle-iron to make."

"So?"

"So, get the hell out of here."

"All right . . . I'm gone!"

When he was and Tom remained alone in the smithy, the reaction set in, a gut panic, as if a constrictor were preparing him for dinner.

She's going to do it! The damn fool woman thinks that'll solve everything, to hurry and seal those vows so she'll be safe from her own feelings. Don't tell me that's not why she's doing this!

So are you going to stop her or what?

I'm sure as hell going to try.

Some friend you are.

Goddamn it, leave me alone!

He loaded up a wagon with manure from the paddock—the only likely red herring he could dream up on the spur of the moment—and hitched up Liza and Rex to haul it away. He went smack down Main Street to the corner of Burkitt, where he could look up the hill and see her leave Tarsy's house. Whether she crossed the street to head home or came toward town, he'd catch her either way.

"Whoa," he called, reining in with the horses nosing the intersection. As slowly as prudent, he clambered down and circled the team, checking their feet. He lifted Liza's off fore and examined the shoe, the frog, running a thumb over it, glancing surreptitiously up the hill. The shoe fit fine. The frog was clean. He dropped Liza's foot and checked one of Rex's, then dipped betwee the team's heads and led them forward a step at a time, searching for a nonexistent limp.

Another glance up the hill—not a soul in sight.

He straightened a tug strap, a breech—neither of which needed it—squinted again up Burkitt Street Hill, and there she was, in a brown coat and plaid skirt, crossing Burkitt, heading home. It was a blindingly bright day, the snow almost painful to the eyes beneath an unhampered two o'clock sun. Against the backdrop of white she appeared as stark as an ink spot on a fresh blotter.

He trotted around and boarded, drove up the hill, took a right on Jefferson, and stayed well behind her, watching her skirts flare with each step, feeling his pulse do irrational things at the mere sight of her, with one hand across her chest, chin dropped, pinning the crossed ends of her red scarf to her throat. She walked as she did most things—briskly, with spare efficiency. She'd make some hell of a housewife, whether she knew it or not. She'd run a home and family with the same commitment she gave the stable, the animals. Because that's how she was. He knew it as surely as he knew he wanted the house and family to be his.

When she was a full block from Tarsy's, he came up behind her.

"H'lo, Emily."

She spun as if he'd stuck a gun in her ribs. Her frantic eyes snapped up to his and the arm holding her scarf tightened against her chest.

"You're looking a little pale," he observed somberly.

"I told you to leave me alone." She executed an abrupt about-face and marched on while he followed, off her right shoulder, keeping the team to a sedate walk.

"Yeah, I heard."

"Then, do it."

He considered it . . . for perhaps a quarter of a second.

"Charles just came by with the news." She strode on determinedly, her skirt whipping with each purposeful step. "You'll pardon me if I don't congratulate you," he added dryly.

"Go away."

"Like hell I will. I'm here to stay, tomboy, so you might as well get used to it. What did Tarsy say?"

"She said yes."

"So you expect the two of us to stand up there in front of the Lord and Reverend Vasseler and give our blessings?"

"That wasn't my idea."

"Oh, that's comforting."

"Would you please find someone else to follow? The whole town can see us."

"Come for a ride with me."

She cut him a withering glance. "On your manure wagon."

"Say the word and I'll be back with a cutter before you can reach home."

She stopped and fixed him with a look of long-suffering. "I'm going to marry him, don't you understand that?"

"Yes, I do. But do you? You're running scared, Emily."

"I'm doing the sensible thing." She walked on in less of a rush, as if resigned. He let the horses fall several feet behind, watching her run away from him, from her feelings, from the undeniable truth. When he could see she was determined to outrun him, he reined to a stop and let her get a good fifteen feet away before finally calling, "Hey, Emily, I forgot to tell you something." He waited, but she neither paused nor turned. Though they were flanked by houses on both sides of the street, he stood up on the wagon and shouted, *"I love you!"*

She spun about, her face radiating bald surprise. The town idiot could have detected the magnetism between them as they faced each other across a snow bright afternoon, she fifteen feet up the street, he standing behind a halted team on a manure wagon. More quietly he added, "I suppose you should know that before you marry him."

She gaped at him, stunned, her lips dropped open. "I forgot something else, too. I'd like to marry you." He let the words settle for several heartbeats before sitting down, flicking the reins, and leaving her standing on the edge of Jefferson Street with her breath still trapped in her throat, one mittened hand pressed to her heart and her face pink as a melon.

She spent the day at home, the evening with Charles; Tom knew it and chafed, but could only keep his distance. At his own house that night he paced and worried, wearing a path from window to window in the hope of seeing her coming across his yard. But the yard remained empty, and he became panicky. At midnight he went to bed and lay awake formulating bizarre plans for waylaying her, most of which were too absurd to implement. By two A.M he'd decided this was a desperate situation, and desperate situations required desperate measures. Judging by the time either she or Edwin opened their livery stable, they roused around six A.M. each morning.

He was waiting in her backyard at 5:30.

It was December, and cold, so cold his nostrils kept freezing shut. He turned up the collar of his heavy sheepskin jacket, covered his bare ears with gloved hands, and propped a shoulder against the back of a shed, peering around its corner, watching the path that led from the kitchen door. His own bootprints appeared enormous and obvious, leading off the compacted path to his hiding spot, but the sky was still inky, the moon low and thin on the western horizon. What's more, anyone coming outside would likely be in too much of a hurry to be inspecting the snow for strange footprints.

Up in the mountains a coyote howled, followed by a chorus of *yip-yip-yaps*. Up at the house a door closed and hasty footsteps squeaked on the hard-beaten path with a sound like leather beneath a shifting rider. Tom peeked around the corner. It was Edwin hurrying head-down toward the privy. When the door closed behind him, Tom slipped to the far side of the shed to wait. He watched the moon slip behind the mountains, heard Edwin return to the house, and a minute later someone else come out. When the person got halfway down the path he peered around his corner, making out a short female form and pale hair: Fannie.

Her stay in the privy was brief. When she'd gone back inside the morning felt infinitely colder. God, he'd never shivered so hard. The temperature always dropped before dawn; today it seemed to have plummeted a good twenty degrees. He blew his nose and felt as if his fingers would never thaw after replacing his gloves. His nostrils stuck together again and he skewed his nose to free them. Arms crossed, he stamped his feet and pulled his chin low inside his top button.

Maybe Emily had come out already and he'd missed her. Or maybe she was sleeping late. This was a stupid idea anyway. He should go home and leave her in peace. Maybe she really loved Charles and he'd be doing the right thing.

But he was a man in gut-love, so he stayed.

A full quarter of an hour later Emily appeared. Dawn hovered in the wings, and by its murky light he watched her all the way from the house: taking careful running steps in footwear that made no sound at all, holding her coat lapped closed over her nightgown. Head down and arms crossed, she hurried, her hair creating a black waterfall over her cheeks and shoulders.

Well before she reached his end of the path Tom had stolen around the far side of the building to wait. But when she opened the privy door and stepped out, he was standing foursquare in the middle of the path, feet planted wide, gloved hands pressed together like a ball and socket.

"Good morning."

She straightened in surprise. "Tom!"

"I need to talk to you."

"Are you crazy! It's six o'clock in the morning!" She gripped her coat tightly against her throat.

"I could hardly do it at six o'clock last night, could I?"

"But it's freezing out here!"

"I know. I've been here awhile waiting for you. I was beginning to think you'd never come out."

"I can't talk to you here. I'm . . ." She glanced at the ground. "My feet . . . I'm in my slipper and nighty. And the sky will be getting light pretty soon. Anyone could see us."

"Emily, goddammit, I don't care! You're going to marry the wrong man tomorrow and I don't have a hell of a lot of time to talk you out of it!" In three enormous steps he reached her and scooped her into his arms.

"Thomas Jeffcoat, you put me down!"

"Quit kicking and listen to me." He hauled her behind the shed, pressed his spine against the cold wall, and slid to a squat, burying himself in snow to his hips. "Put your feet in here. Lord God, girl, haven't you got more sense than to come outside in these flimsy things?" Her slippers were knit of black carpet yarn. Wrapping her nightgown around them he doubled her on his lap and lassoed her with both arms, then looked up into her face, which was higher than his.

"Emily, you don't leave a fellow much spare time. I wouldn't have done this if I'd had any other choice. But I told you, the man pursues, so I'm pursuing in the only way I know how, crazy as it may be."

"Crazy will scarcely cover it. That was a terrible thing you did to me yesterday on the street."

"It made you stop and think though, didn't it?"

"But you just don't . . . don't pull up beside a girl in your manure wagon and ask her to marry you!"

"I know, that's why I came back to ask again."

"Behind the toilet this time!"

"The toilet's over there; this is the shed." He gestured with his head.

"Thomas Jeffcoat, you're a lunatic."

"I'm in love. So I came to ask you again—will you marry me?"

"No."

"Do you love me?"

"How can you ask me such a thing when my wedding is set for tomorrow!" Exasperated, she struggled to free herself but he tightened his hold around her shoulders, pinning both her arms and knees.

"Don't answer my question with a question! Do you love me?"

"That has no bearing on my promise to—"

"Do you?" he demanded roughly, clasping her neck with one thick-gloved hand, forcing her to turn her face to his.

"I desire you. I don't know if it's the same th—"

He slammed her mouth down to his, kissed her hard, infusing the kiss with all the love and desperation and frustration he felt. When he released her his breathing was harsh, his eyes earnest. "I desire you, too—I won't deny it—so much that I'd like to lay you down here in the snow. But it's more than that. I walk around my empty house and imgine you in it with me. I want you at my breakfast table whether you can fry eggs or not. We can eat burned toast for all I care—hell, I'll even do the burning, but I want you there, Emily. And at the livery barn—you're so damned good with horses. Can't you see us walking down there every day and working together? What a pair we'd make at that business!

"And what about your studies? Charles told me you're going to give them up to have babies, right after you told me that you don't want babies yet. That's not right, Emily. And I don't want babies either, not any sooner than you do. For a while I want it to be you and me, running around in that big house in our underwear. I don't know how we'll manage that, seeing as how all this desire will be cropping up all the time, but we can try. Emily . . ." This time he inveighed more tenderly. "I love you. I don't want to lose you."

Folded like an *N* she sat in his arms and allowed herself to be convinced, let his cold nose nuzzle her warm cheek and his welcome lips bias her own. She forgot her imminent wedding. She forgot the cold. She forgot to object. She opened her mouth and kissed him back—an inadvisable, ample kiss leading to nothing but further confusion, yet she partook of him with the relish of one soon to be denied. He tasted as she remembered, smelled and felt alarmingly familiar—a tempting combination of wet and soft, pliable and hard. As his tongue slewed hers, nerve bursts of heat warmed her deepest parts. Her head listed, swayed, but the kiss remained unbroken as she freed a trapped hand and rested it on his face. His cheek was warm, bristled yet with a night's growth; his jaw hard; his collar warm and furry. Tipped back, his head pressed the shed wall, and she slipped her hand there to pillow it from the hard, icy surface.

With tongues dancing, they wooed disaster, letting their feelings build. His hands shifted—one to a slim shoulder, one to a round buttock, where her heavy coat hem gave way to lighter cotton. It slipped between the two garments . . . glove over nightgown . . . thick over thin . . . leather over cotton . . . drawing patterns on her firm flesh while he pretended the hand was bare. When their heartbeats and breathing grew taxed, they ended a kiss out of common frustration.

"Oh, Emily . . ." He whispered, tortured.

"Why didn't you ask me earlier?" she despaired, closing her eyes.

"Because I didn't know until I kissed you."

"Then why didn't you kiss me earlier?"

"You know the reasons—Charles, Tarsy . . . even Julia. I thought I was through with women for a long, long time. I was afraid of being hurt again. Now this hurts even worse. Emily, please . . . you have to marry me." He lifted his face but she avoided further kisses.

"Thomas . . . please, the answer is still no."

"But why?"

Heartsore, she looked into his eyes and decided to tell him the truth, and in telling to remind herself as well. "I'm going to tell you something that I trust you'll never repeat. I'm telling you because it seems the only fair thing to do." She drew a shaky breath and began. "The morning after I went to your house I walked into our kitchen and found my father kissing Fannie. I mean, *really kissing.* You can't guess what it was like, Tom. I felt . . . sick and betrayed . . . and angrier than I ever remember being. For myself, and for my brother, but mostly for Mother, who doesn't deserve all the unhappiness and pain that life is throwing at her right now. It isn't enough that she's in constant pain and dying at such a young age. Her husband is carrying on right under her nose! Right under her own roof!

"It made me take a second look at myself, at what I was doing to Charles."

"But your father is—"

"I won't be like him, Tom, I won't! Charles is a fine and admirable person who doesn't deserve to be deceived by his fiancée and his best friend. Just listen to that—*his fiancée and his best friend.* That's what we are, you know. When we're together we tend to forget that."

"So you're marrying Charles to atone for your father's sins? Is that what you're saying?"

It sounded too much like the truth, and she had no reply.

"What about how we feel?" Tom insisted.

"What I feel might very well be panic, which I think every bride feels at the last minute before getting married. But I can't cope with one more crisis right now. The past three days have been terrible. When I walk into Mother's room, I feel guilty. When I look at Charles, I feel guilty. I see you and I feel confused. Papa and Fannie make me so disgusted I can scarcely tolerate being in the same house with them. What I crave is peace and I think I'll have that with Charles. I'm going to marry him and move into his house and start living my own life. That's what I'm going to do."

"You're going to disregard what you feel for me? What we feel for each other?"

"Emileee?" It was Fannie calling from the house.

Behind the shed, Tom and Emily tensed, holding their breaths.

"Emily, are you all right out there?"

"Don't answer her." Tom gripped Emily's wrists, holding her still while their hearts clamored.

"I have to go in," she whispered, straining to rise.

"Wait!"

"Let me up! She's coming!"

Fannie's voice came again through the crisp morning. *"Emily?"*

Emily raised her voice and called, "I'm fine. I'll be in in a minute!" Struggling to rise, gracelessly disentangling themselves, Emily half fell off Tom's lap. Her ankles and one wrist sank into the icy snow. It fell into her slipper tops in cold, wet clumps. It climbed her cuffs and chilled her wrists. It clung to the bottom of Tom's jacket and burned a frigid ring where it melted on his hindside. Embroiled in emotions, neither of them noticed. He gripped her wrist, straining to hold her while she strained to flee.

"Don't do it, Emily."

"I have to."

"Then don't expect me to stand there and witness it! I'll be *damned* if I will, whether I told Charles I would or not!"

"I have to go in."

"You're so damn blind!"

"Let me go . . . please."

"Emily . . ."

"Goodbye, Thomas."

She ran as if a prairie fire were at her heels.

Josephine Walcott lay at death's door, but she wasn't dead yet. Quite the contrary. During the last twenty-four hours her condition had undergone a peculiar turnabout. She had coughed less, felt stronger, and her perceptions had grown uncommonly keen—as she'd heard was often the case during one's last hours—keen enough to ascertain that something was radically wrong in this house.

Emily had grown icy and brusque with Fannie and Edwin. Edwin walked as if on cinders. And Charles hadn't come to announce his own wedding plans. Most peculiar, yet understandable in light of recent outbursts that had filtered up from below.

Josephine awakened well before dawn on the day preceding Emily's wedding and listened to the sounds of the family coming to life. Doors opening and closing, stove lids chiming, the pump gurgling, bacon frying, muffled voices.

From below came the sound of Fannie, speaking quietly to Edwin.

Then Edwin's deeper reply.

Then Fannie again, outside, calling Emily's name worriedly. Twice. Three times.

What on earth?

The fire roared up the stovepipe as if from too much draft, the back door slammed shut, and Edwin inquired, "Emily, are you all right?"

Emily's voice, brusque and rude, came up clearly from below: "Don't set breakfast for me. I'll eat with Mother," followed by her slippered steps pounding up the stairs at breakneck pace.

Fifteen minutes later she appeared with Josephine's breakfast tray, brought it in, and closed the door that during the day had remained steadfastly open until two days ago when Emily had peremptorily begun closing it.

"Good morning, Mother."

Josephine caught Emily's hand as it deposited the tray on the bed. She gave her daughter a smile and reached up to lay her knuckles against Emily's red cheek.

"Are you ill?" Josephine inquired in a whisper.

"Ill? No, I'm . . . I'm fine."

"I heard Fannie calling you. Your cheek is cold."

"I was outside. It's only ten degrees this morning."

"And so red."

Emily busied herself with the breakfast trappings, avoiding Josephine's eyes. "Oatmeal and bacon and eggs this morning. Here, let me pull your pillow up. I hope you're hungry again. It's so heartening to see you eat like you did yesterday." She rambled on—superfluous chatter clearly amplifying her edginess. Her hands flew nervously from one thing to the next—sugar, cream, salt, pepper—superabundant efficiency further underscoring her jumpiness. "I thought I'd clean your room today and wash your hair. I think we can manage it with some oilcloth over the edge of the mattress while you lie across the bed—would you like that? And press your favorite bed jacket and my own blue dress. And, of course, I've got to wash my hair, too, and pack my things to take to Charles's house, and—"

"Emily, what's wrong?"

"Wrong?" Emily's wide eyes contained a hint of terror.

"You needn't protect me from everything," Josephine whispered. "I'm still very much alive and I want to be part of this family again."

Josephine watched her daughter struggle with some hidden turmoil. For a moment she thought Emily would relent and confide, but in the end Emily shot to her feet, turning away, hiding any secrets her eyes might divulge. "Oh, Mother, you've never stopped being a part of my family, you know that. But please don't worry about me. It's nothing."

Yet Emily scarcely ate any breakfast, and when Edwin stepped in before leaving for the livery barn she coldly snubbed him, turning to the bureau and fussing with things on its top, offering not even her usual good-bye.

Soon after Edwin left Fannie appeared, offering to clean the room, but Emily alooftly informed her that she'd do it herself and that she'd also take care of getting her mother ready for tomorrow. The tension in the room was palpable as Fannie looked across the foot of the bed at Emily, then resignedly turned toward the door.

"Fannie!" Emily snapped.

"Yes?" Fannie turned back.

"It won't be necessary for you to prepare a wedding feast, in case you were thinking about it. When the service is over Charles and I will be going directly to his house."

Emily spent the day as she'd spent the preceding one, lavishing time on her mother, doing all the chores she'd outlined for the day. But as it progressed her busyness came to contain an almost frenetic quality. Distressed, Josephine observed and worried.

It was late in the afternoon before the hair washing began. It turned out to be an awkward process, but by its very awkwardness and the reversal of their roles, it brought mother and daughter closer than they had been in years.

When Josephine was again sitting, with the pillows bolstering her back, Emily combed her hair slowly and said, "It won't take long to dry."

"No, it won't . . ." Josephine said sadly, "not anymore."

The words went straight to Emily's heart. Less than a year ago Mother's hair had been dark, thick, and glossy, her greatest asset, her pride. Now it lay in thin strings, faded to the color of beeswax, with her pink skull showing in spots. Josephine herself had lopped the hair off at collar length to make its care easier during her illness. Her semibaldness seemed a final insult to the deteriorating body of the once-robust woman.

Josephine sensed Emily's sadness and lifted her eyes to find her daughter indeed forlorn.

"Emily, dear, listen to me." She took Emily's hand in both of hers and held it, comb and all, while speaking in a whisper to keep from coughing. "It doesn't matter what my hair looks like now. It doesn't matter that your father sleeps on a spare cot, and that he must see me looking more and more like an old dried apple. None of it matters. What matters is that your father and I have lived together for twenty-two years without ever losing the immense respect we hold for one another."

With downcast eyes Emily stared at her mother's withered hand, the fingers too thin to show a mark where her wedding band had been.

"You've been very troubled the last few days, and I believe I know what's brought it on. I appreciate your loyalty, but perhaps it's been misplaced." Josephine's thumb brushed across Emily's bare ring finger. "I *am* sick, Emily, but I'm not blind or deaf. I've seen your sudden aversion to your father and Fannie, and I've heard things . . . through the floor. Things that my ears were not meant to hear, perhaps." With a sigh Josephine fell silent, studying her daughter's dejected expression.

"We've never been particularly close, have we, Emily? Perhaps that's my fault." She continued holding Emily's hand, a familiarity she had never promoted in eighteen years of mothering. It felt unnatural, even now, but she forced it, admitting her own maternal shortcomings. "But you were always so taken by your father, trailing after him, imitating him. I can see that you're hurting terribly each time you shun him . . . and Fannie, too. You have become very close to Fannie, haven't you?"

Emily swallowed, refusing to lift her eyes. Two spots of color rose in her cheeks.

"I think it's time you were told some things. They may not be pleasant for you to hear, but I trust you to understand. You're a mature young woman, about to embark on marriage yourself. If you're old enough for that you're old enough to understand how it is with your father and me."

Emily's troubled blue eyes lifted. "Mama, I—"

"Shh. I tire so easily, and I must whisper. Please listen." Oddly enough, though Josephine had not spoken this long or this uninterruptedly in months, she neither flagged nor coughed, but went on as if some all-caring benefactor had lent her the strength to speak when she most needed it.

"Your father and I grew up much as you and Charles have, knowing each other from childhood. Our parents told us when we were fourteen years old that they had agreed upon a marriage convenant, which they expected the two of us to honor. It had nothing to do with the joining of lands, or of business, which has often made me wonder why they wanted so badly for Edwin and me to marry. Perhaps only because they were friends and knew what kind of children they had turned out—honest Christian children who would grow up to be honest Christian parents, and into whom the Fourth Commandment had been drilled.

"Our betrothal became official when we were sixteen—the same spring that Fannie came home from two years of studying abroad. Her parents threw a party right after she got back, and I recall the night clearly. It was April and the lilacs were blooming. Fannie wore ivory—she always looked stunning in ivory, with that blazing orange hair of hers—rather like a holiday candle, I always thought. I guess I realized from that first night that your father had eyes for Fannie. They danced a quadrille, and I recall them spinning with their arms linked, studying each other with flushed faces and smiling the way I'd never had Edwin smile at me. I suspect he took her outside and kissed her later in the herb garden because I could smell crushed basil on his clothes when he returned.

"I knew after that that I should free him from his betrothal vow, but I was not the most marriageable girl in Boston, nor the prettiest. I could not flirt like Fannie, or . . . or kiss in the herb garden . . . or carry on idle banter the way young swains like a girl to do. But more importantly, I had been raised to believe I must honor the wishes of my father and mother."

Josephine drew a sigh and fell back, fixing her eyes on the ceiling. "Unfortunately, so had Edwin. I knew that he was falling in love with Fannie, and I saw the strain it put on him. But I suspect his parents put him out of mind of breaking off our betrothal. So when the time came, he dutifully married me.

"I want you to understand, Emily . . ." Josephine still held her daughter's hand loosely on the coverlet. "Our marriage has not been intolerable . . . not even bad, but neither has it been the splendid thing it might have been had we shared the feelings that your father and Fannie did. We understood the limitations of our love. Call it respect, that's a truer word, for I always knew that the one Edwin truly loved was Fannie. Oh, he hid it well, and he never guessed that I suspected. But I knew the reason we left Massachusetts was to put distance between the two of them, to put temptation out of his reach. And though she always addressed her letters to me, I knew they were meant to let Edwin know how she was and where she was, and that she never forgot him.

"Did you know, Emily, that I brought Fannie here against your father's will?"

Emily's startled eyes lifted to her mother's as the older woman continued. "He was very angry when I told him she was coming. He shouted at me, one of the few times ever, and said, no, he absolutely wouldn't have Fannie here, which, of course, only confirmed my suspicions—that the memory of her had not dulled over the years, that he still cared deeply for her. But I had taken the choice out of his hands by withholding the news about Fannie's coming until she was already underway."

Josephine smiled at their linked hands, her own thin and transparent as bone china, Emily's strong and marked from hard work. "You think me a little tetched, perhaps, to throw them together like that?" Her whisper suddenly gained vehemence as she gripped Emily's hand hard. "Oh, Emily, look at Fannie, just look at her. She's as different from me as sea is from earth. She's vivacious and spirited, laughing and gay while I'm helplessly staid and Victorian. I've never been like Fannie, never been the things your father really needed. He should have had her all these years, yet he remained loyal to me and honored the vows we made. He should have had the warmth and affection and the demonstrativeness of a woman like her, but instead he settled for me. And now she's here, and unless I miss my guess you discovered them—what? Kissing? Embracing? Is that it?"

From Emily's downcast eyes Josephine knew she'd guessed right.

"Well, perhaps they've earned the right."

"How can you say that, Mother?" Tears glistened in Emily's eyes as she lifted her head. "He's still your husband!"

Josephine released Emily's hand and studied the ceiling again. "This is very hard for me to say." Moments passed before she went on. "I . . . I cannot say I ever relished the marriage act, and I cannot help but wonder if it wasn't because simple respect for your father wasn't quite enough for me either."

In eighteen years Emily had never heard her mother speak of anything remotely bordering on the carnal. Hearing it now made Emily—as well as Josephine— distinctly uncomfortable. Endless seconds ticked by while they struggled with their private embarrassment, then Josephine added, "I only wanted you to know it wasn't all your father's fault."

Their glances met, then strayed to impersonal objects in the room before Josephine found herself able to continue. "Another thing I want you to remember—in all the time Fannie has been here she has never distressed me, never once hinted that I'd done her a grave wrong by marrying the man she should have had. She has been the soul of benevolence—good, kind, and patient. And honorable to the teeth, I'm sure of it. She has made my dying days more bearable, Emily, just by being here."

The shock of hearing her mother predict her own death brought a denial from Emily. "Mother, you're not dying, don't say that!"

"Yes, I am, dear. And soon, I'm stronger today, but it won't last. And when I'm gone I want you prepared. Oh, you'll mourn me, but please, Emily, not for long. And, please, dear, you must give Edwin and Fannie the right to their happiness. If I can, surely you can. When he marries her, and I'm sure he will—he *must!*—you must be as benevolent to Fannie as she's been to me. And your father—well, surely you can imagine the anguish he's suffered, being married to the wrong woman all his life. Doesn't he deserve *some* happiness?"

"Oh, Mother . . ." Dropping to her knees, Emily fell across her mother's bed with tears streaming from her eyes. Josephine was not a woman often disposed to tears. Had she been, perhaps she could have made her husband happier. Dry-eyed, she studied the ceiling while touching the head of her weeping daughter.

"And what about you?" she inquired. "Are you ready to tell me about you and Charles . . . and this Mr. Jeffcoat?"

Startled, Emily's head shot up, her tearful eyes wide.

"You know?"

"Your father told me."

"He did?"

"Of course he did. What do you think we do up here in this room every evening? He tells me about his day, and you are a very important part of all his days."

Josephine's last disclosure had effectively stopped Emily's tears. Running a knuckle beneath each eye she said, "Papa was very upset when he found Tom and me kissing, wasn't he?"

"Yes. But now you should be able to understand why. He was—is—very concerned about you, just as I am. We love Charles very much. But I don't believe either one of us wants you to make the same mistake we did."

Crestfallen, Emily doubled forward and rested her cheek against the back of Josephine's hand. "Oh, Mother, what should I do?"

Josephine took her time answering, weighing her words. "I can't tell you, and I wouldn't presume to, not anymore. You're a very impulsive young woman, Emily. You close doors with the same vehemence with which you open them, just as you did to your father and Fannie. It's still closed—you see?" She turned to glance at the bedroom door. "The only advice I can give is to open the door—open all your doors. It's the only way you can see where you're going."

"Are you saying I shouldn't marry Charles?"

"Not at all. You seem to be the one who's questioning it."

Leaning across her mother's bed, Emily admitted it was true: she was questioning it, had been since her feelings for Tom had surfaced.

Tom.

Charles.

So great a decision to make in so little time.

Realizing the girl would have to make that decision for herself, Josie sent her on her way to do it. "And now I'm very tired, dear. I think I'd like to rest a while." She sighed and let her eyes close. "Please tell Fannie to wake me when your father comes home for dinner so I can eat with them."

Chapter 15

Tiptoeing from her mother's room, Emily left the door open behind her. She stood in the hall staring at the wallpaper for several minutes. Fannie and Papa . . . since before he'd married Mother? How young had they been? Not much older than she was now. And Mother, resisting Papa's advances much as she, Emily, often resisted Charles's? The admission seemed too incredible to reconstruct. Yet Mother had intimated that carnal urgings should not be disregarded in making a decision about whom to marry.

Dazed, Emily navigated herself to her own room and dropped anchor on the foot of the bed. So many parallels, too many to ignore. She stared at the window ledge behind the lace curtains, imagining a love powerful enough to withstand more than twenty-two years, unrequited; a respect immense enough to withstand the same twenty-two years under a mantle of silent misgivings. How difficult for both Mother and Father. Yet they had persevered, given their children a foundation as secure as any religion or creed, for in all her life Emily had never suspected a rift in their devotion to one another.

And Fannie, the lorn one, how empty her life must have been. Beneath her veneer of gaiety, how much heartbreak must be hidden.

Charles would be like Fannie—lorn and empty and heartbroken—should Emily reverse her decision to marry him. But he would not remain cordial through the years as Fannie had with Mother and Father. He would be hurt and angry and would make it impossible for all three of them, herself and Tom and Charles, to live in a town this small without future bitterness.

The afternoon aged; blue shadows stained the snow-covered window ledge. Downstairs the oven door squeaked as Fannie opened and closed it. Emily checked the time: 4:30. In less than twenty-one hours she was scheduled to stand beside Mother's bed and join her life to Charles's. Irreversibly.

Could she do it?

More to the point, could she *not* do it?

She tried to imagine herself, when Charles came tonight, telling him, I've made a mistake, Charles, it's Tom I love, Tom I want to marry.

She crossed her arms and doubled forward, experiencing a real stab of pain. She had let them go on too long, her daunted feelings about Charles. How could she, at this eleventh hour, make such a decision?

Five o'clock came—full dark now, near winter solstice; five-thirty and Mother woke up across the hall; quarter to six and Papa came home, stamping his boots, washing his hands, asking where everybody was. Frankie banged in, fresh from sliding with Earl and the boys. The smell of roasting chicken drifted upstairs.

Emily rose and smoothed her skirt, moving about her dark bedroom, delaying the inevitable. She could not avoid them forever. In the hall a faint light drifted up from below. She stood at the top of the stairs gathering courage to take the first step. All the way downstairs she imagined facing Papa and Fannie to find them changed somehow, now that they had been redeemed by Mother's words. But when she entered the kitchen she found them looking the same as ever—Papa in his work clothes with underwear showing at the neck and wrists, reading the weekly newspaper, and Fannie in a long apron with her pale peach hair slightly ascatter, working at the stove. They looked much like any ordinary husband and wife, and Frankie—setting silverware on the table—might well have been their son. With a start, Emily realized it could have been true. Frankie might have been their son and she their daughter. The thought brought Emily a sharp feeling of inconstancy on Mother's behalf, yet Josephine was probably right: Fannie and Papa would someday be husband and wife.

Sensing that he was being studied, Edwin lowered the paper just as Fannie turned, and the two of them caught Emily watching them from the doorway. The room held the same sense of imminence that had predominated since she had discovered them in it kissing.

"Well." Edwin snapped his newspaper flat. "How is your mother? I was just heading up."

"She's better." Emily answered in the kindest tone she'd used with him since that discovery.

"Good . . . good." Silence reeled itself out, uncomfortably lengthy. Finally Edwin spoke again. "I took the liberty of inviting Charles to supper tonight. I thought it might be appropriate since you won't be having a wedding dinner with us tomorrow."

"Oh . . . fine."

Edwin glanced at Fannie while gauging the reason for Emily's sudden docility. "Fannie's made roast chicken—your favorite."

"Yes, I . . . thank you, Fannie. But Mother asked me to tell you she'd like the three of you to eat together in her room."

"If she's feeling strong enough," Edwin suggested, "maybe I could carry her down and we could all eat together just this once."

Frankie had been staring at all three of them and piped up, "What's the matter with you, anyway? You're standing there gawkin' like a bunch of hoot-owls!"

His observation at last jarred the tension. Emily moved into the room, ordering her brother, "Get the glasses and napkins on for Fannie while I help her mash potatoes."

What a meal, what an evening, what a phantasmal set of circumstances. Charles arrived, jovial and excited. Edwin carried his wife downstairs. Fannie served them all a delectable dinner and they ate as if nothing were amiss. But the tension within Emily felt as if it would cut off her air supply.

She tried—oh how she tried—to find within herself the wherewithal to deal honestly with Charles. But he was so happy, so eager, so amorous when they stepped onto the porch to say good-night.

He kissed her roundly, caressed her as if holding himself on a precipice.

"Tomorrow night at this time," he whispered ardently, "you'll be my wife." He kissed her again and shuddered deeply, breaking the contact to speak throatily at her ear. "Oh, Emily, I love you so."

She opened her lips and began unsteadily, "Charles . . . I . . ."

But he kissed her again, interrupting her confession, and in the end she could not find the means to annihilate him.

When he was gone, she roamed the confines of her room with desperation forming a great knot in her breast and dampening the palms of her hands. Knowing she would be unable to sleep, she went for solace to the animals at the stable, only to discover there another plea from Tom, this one tacked to the outer door where anyone might have found it—a white envelope bearing her name, telling her clearly how desperate he was.

She took it into the office and sat on the creaky, lopsided chair with her heart racing as she withdrew a rich, deeply embossed postcard bearing a swag of rose in shades of mauve and wine and pink, held aloft at the corners by bluebirds from whose beaks bows and ribbons fluttered. In the center of the card more roses and ribbons formed a beautiful floral heart, below which the verse was inscribed in stylized gilt letters pressed deeply into the cardboard:

> *My hand is lonely for your clasping dear*
> *My ear is tired waiting-for your call*
> *I need your help, your laugh to cheer:*
> *Heart, soul, and senses need you, one and all.*

Below the verse he had written, *I love you, please marry me.*

Had Charles sent it, Emily would have been less shattered. But coming from a man like Tom—the one who had ceaselessly teased, aggravated, and called her tomboy—the impassioned plea pierced her heart like an arrow from Cupid's own bow.

She pressed her lips to his signature, closed her eyes, and despaired, loving him, needing him much as the verse on the card had sketched—with heart, soul, and senses. But the clock was ticking off the hours toward her wedding with another, and here she sat, fainthearted and frightened, with tears raining down her face.

There would be times in later life when Emily would study her husband across a lamplit room, feel a surge of love, and be freshly convinced that her mother's last act of mercy was to die that night.

Papa came to break the news, in the predawn hours, sitting on the edge of Emily's bed, shaking her out of a brief and tardy sleep. "Emily, dear, wake up."

"What? . . . mmm . . ."

"Emily, dear . . ."

She sat up with her head pounding from lack of sleep, her eyes gritty and swollen. "Papa? Is something wrong?"

"I'm afraid so, Emily."

He had brought a lantern. She peered through its glare and saw tear tracks gilding Papa's cheeks. She knew the truth even before he spoke the words.

"It's your mother . . . she's gone."

"No!"

He nodded, sorrowfully.

"Oh, Papa."

"She's gone," he repeated quietly.

"But she felt so good yesterday."

"I know."

"Oh, Papa," she cried again, rising on her knees on the bed to clasp and cling to him—her first touch since she had condemned him for loving another. She felt his body quake with inheld sobs, though he made not a sound. She spread her hands on his shoulders, inexplicably saddened because he had loved Mama after all. In his own fashion, he had loved her.

"Papa," she whispered brokenly, "don't cry. She's an angel already, I'm sure."

He didn't cry. But when he straightened, Emily saw in his red-rimmed eyes an emotion far more difficult to bear than grief. She saw regret. Wordlessly he squeezed Emily's hands and rose from the bed, waiting while she got up, too, and moved ahead of him to the room across the hall.

There, in the lanternlight, which was already losing intensity as the sun stole up, Fannie sat on the edge of Josephine's bed, tearless, gently smoothing the brittle white hair back from the pale, wrinkled brow of her dead cousin. Across the white sheets and pillowcases, across Josephine's white nightgown and skin and hair a splattered bloodflow had dried and darkened to a rufous brown.

"Ohhh . . ." The mournful syllable escaped Emily as she drifted to the side of the bed opposite Fannie and, kneeling, pressed her hands to the mattress cautiously, as if the form lying upon it could yet be disturbed. "Mother . . ." she whispered as tears slipped quietly down her cheeks.

Having lived with the certainty of her death lent little ease at its coming. It had reached in and snatched her from those who, unsuspecting, took yesterday's turnabout for a healthy sign. They mourned together: Fannie touching Josephine's hand; Emily kneeling opposite, rubbing her mother's sleeve; Edwin standing behind her. While they lamented, Fannie continued smoothing back Josephine's sparse white hair, murmuring, "Rest, dearling . . . rest."

They thought of her in those first despairing moments, not as she was but as she had been, in haler times when her hair was black and her arms plump, her eyes avid and her limbs quick.

"Were you with her, Papa?" Emily asked solemnly.

"No. I found her when I woke up."

"Didn't she cough?"

"Yes, I seem to remember that she did. But I didn't quite wake up."

Again they fell silent, groping to accept the fact that Josephine was truly dead and nothing any of them might have done could have prevented her death.

"Papa, what about Frankie?"

"Yes, we have to wake Frankie."

But neither of them moved. Only Fannie, who knew what must be done to spare a boy only twelve years old. She fetched a basin of water and with a soft cloth tenderly swabbed the mouth and neck of Edwin's dead wife, his children's mother, then found a clean white sheet and spread it over the soiled bedding, hiding the dried brown stains. When the task was done, she straightened, studying Josephine lovingly. Fannie's own nightgown was wrinkled, her feet bare, and her disorderly hair defied all rules of gravity. But she exuded an undeniable air of decorum as she said quietly, "Now go get Frank, Edwin."

Emily went with her father, carrying a lantern and clasping Edwin's hand. Beside Frankie's bed they paused, studying the sleeping boy, reluctant to awaken him with the dread news, bolstering each other during these brimming minutes of heavyheartedness.

At last Edwin sat down and lined Frankie's pretty cheek with his big work-widened hand. "Son?" The word caught in his throat. Emily gripped her father's shoulder and reached beyond it to do her part.

"Frankie?" she entreated softly. "Wake up, Frankie."

When he did, blinking and rubbing his eyes, Emily took the burden from Edwin and said the words herself. "I'm afraid we have some sad news this morning."

Frankie awakened with unusual suddenness, gazing at his father and sister clear-eyed as he rarely was on an ordinary morning. "Mother's dead, isn't she?"

"Yes, son, she is," Edwin intoned.

Frankie was young enough that he remained untrammeled by the stultifying rules of Victorian mourning. He spoke what he felt, without monitoring either the words or his honest reaction. "I'm glad. She didn't like coughing all the time and being so sick and skinny."

He went with them, stood dutifully beside his mother's bed, gulping, staring, then spinning from the room to do his crying in private. The others remained, exchanging uncertain glances, wishing they could run from duty, too. But there were people to inform, a body to be laid out, a wedding to be canceled, a coffin to be built.

The survivors of Josephine Walcott had no precedent to guide them through the hours that lay ahead. They stood momentarily vacuous, wondering what propriety demanded first.

Edwin took the initiative.

"I'll have to go feed the horses, and hang a sign on the livery door until we can get the black wreaths made. Emily, would you see to it that Frankie gets over to Earl's house when he's calmed down? Maybe Mrs. Rausch would let Earl stay home from school today to keep Frankie company. I'll stop by the schoolhouse and let Miss Shaney know, and I'll go by Charles's, too—that is, unless you'd prefer to tell him yourself, Emily."

"No," she replied, already realizing who'd need her most. "I'll stay here with Fannie."

"As for the laying out . . ." Edwin glanced somberly toward the corpse. "Wait until I get back."

But the moment he'd left, Fannie armed herself in a mantle of efficiency. Picking up the basin and heading briskly for the door, she countered. "A husband should be spared this cross. I'll see to it myself."

As Fannie passed Emily, the younger woman reached out as if to touch her shoulder. But she withdrew the hand indecisively and called instead, "Fannie?"

In the doorway, Fannie turned. Their eyes met and both women realized that the last time they had spoken Emily's heart had been filled with enmity. Her expression held none now, only a ravaged, remorseful gratefulness for Fannie's presence. When she spoke, her voice held a plea for forgiveness. "I'll help . . . it's the daughter's place to help."

"She was your mother and this won't be pleasant. Wouldn't you rather remember her as she was?"

"I will. I'll always remember her with dark hair and heavy arms, but I have to help, don't you see?"

Tears brightened Fannie's eyes and her voice held both understanding and love, as she answered, "Yes, of course, dear. We'll do it together, as soon as Frankie is out of the house."

When Fannie had gone downstairs Emily stood in Frankie's doorway, thrust against her will into a maternal role for which she felt unprepared. Her brother lay facing the wall, as if he'd been thrown onto his bed. She entered and sat behind him, rubbing his back and shoulders. He had calmed somewhat, though an occasional residual sob plucked his breath away.

"Frankie?"

No answer.

"She's happier, just like you said."

Again no answer for long minutes. Then, finally, through a plugged nose, "I know. But now I haven't got no mother."

"You have Papa and me . . . and Fannie."

"But none of you are my mother."

"No, we're not. But we'll help however we can. Now Papa says he wants you to go to Earl's today and spend the day with him. You want me to walk you over there?" He was twelve years old, yet neither of them found the question silly today.

Staring at the corner, Frankie replied colorlessly, "I guess so."

When they were dressed, they walked to Earl's house holding hands. They had not held hands since Frankie had turned seven and given up that sissy stuff, and not since Emily's world had begun revolving around more important matters like her studies and her engagement and growing up. But they walked to Earl's house holding hands.

At the livery stable, Edwin fed the horses and hung a sign on the door: *Closed due to death in the family*. Next, he trudged to Charles's house. When Charles opened the door Edwin told him point-blank: "It's bad news, son. Mrs. Walcott is gone."

Though the unfortunate timing was not mentioned, it was uppermost in both of their minds. Charles masked his disappointment and gripped Edwin's hand hard, drawing him inside. "Oh, Edwin, I'm so sorry." They stood for seconds in silence, still linked by the unbroken handclasp. Finally Charles said, "I'd like to make her coffin if you'd let me, Edwin. I'd like to do that last thing for her."

Their eyes met in mutual affection and regret, and Edwin broke down fully for the first time, clasping the younger man, weeping sorely against his taller shoulder.

"She was a g—good woman but she was never v—very happy. I couldn't make her happy, Charles. I n—never c—could make her happy."

"Aw, Edwin, she was happy, I know she was. She had a good marriage and two fine children. It was just her suffering in the last years, and you did what you could about that. You brought her out here and cared for her. You did all you could."

In spite of Charles's consolation, Edwin's tears continued for minutes. At last he regained composure and stepped back, drying his eyes on a sleeve, hanging his head. To the floor he said, "No sir, when a man lives his whole life with a woman he knows whether or not she's happy, and Josie wasn't. Not very often." Edwin fished a handkerchief from his pocket, cleared his nose, and admitted against the linen, "I didn't do that in front of the women, Charles. Forgive me."

"Aw, Edwin, don't be foolish."

"You're like a son to me, you know that, boy, don't you?"

Charles gulped back emotions of his own. "Yes, sir, I do, and you're like a father to me. I'm sorry . . . awfully sorry."

Edwin sighed, feeling better since his cry. "And I'm damned sorry about your wedding being put off—and not a word of complaint out of you, though you certainly have the right." Edwin squeezed Charles's shoulder affectionately. "You go ahead, you make her coffin and thank you."

"I've got some fine cedar. She'll have the best, Edwin."

Edwin nodded and prepared to leave. When he reached the door Charles inquired, "How is Emily taking it?"

"She's bearing up as well as can be expected, but you know how good Josie felt yesterday—it was a shock to all of us after that."

Charles nodded and reached for his jacket, too. "Well, I'd best get over to see Reverend Vasseler, tell him we won't be needing him today."

But as Edwin left, Charles made up an excuse to stay behind. Alone, he dropped onto a hard kitchen chair and sat lifelessly, his shoulders bowed by disappointment. One thought ran through his mind time and again. *Bless her departed soul, Lord, but when am I ever going to get to marry the woman I love?*

* * *

When Emily returned from walking Frankie to Earl's house, Fannie had the kitchen table extended full length, covered with a freshly scrubbed oilcloth. Emily stared at it in horrified fascination while slowly removing her coat. She lifted her gaze to find Fannie with her hair painfully neat, her apron fresh from the bureau drawer, all starchy peaks and pressed planes, her expression grave and respectful.

"I can do it alone, truly I can, but you'd have to help me carry her down."

"No, Fannie. It'll be easier together. All of it."

They carried Josephine downstairs, sharing an unspoken horror at the indignity suffered by the woman who had lived her life with unfailing decorum—being toted downstairs like some ungainly piece of furniture. If only a band of angels might appear and deposit her with stately grace upon the kitchen table.

But the only angels on duty were Fannie and Emily.

They laid Josephine—ignominiously bent—on the table, and Fannie ordered, "Go around. We must straighten her. Press here and here." But Josephine had died as she'd lived the last few months—sitting up, angled at the hip. Hours had passed, cooling the rigidifying her corpse, rendering the women's attempts at flattening her futile.

"Leave!" ordered Fannie abruptly.

"Leave? But what are you going to do?"

"Leave, I said! Outside, where you can't hear!"

"Hear? But I—"

"Dammit, girl, why do you think this is called the laying out?" Fannie's voice slashed. "Now go! And don't come back until I call!"

It struck Emily what Fannie must do and she blanched, gulped, and ran from the room, out into the sweet clean snow, beneath the great bowl of sun-washed sky, into air pure as dew. Nausea threatened and she doubled forward, braced at the knees, gulping drafts of air. Her stomach keeled and reflex tears spurt into her eyes. *She is breaking my mother's bones!*

She covered her ears as if the brittle sound could reach her through the walls, dropped to her knees in the snow and wept, fledging a part of her youth in a single moment of realization as harsh as any life could mete out. *My mother, who gave me life, who nursed and nurtured me and combed my hair and bathed me and walked me to school and made me eat the foods I disliked. My mother is having her bones broken!*

Soon Fannie approached and gently touched Emily's shoulder. "Come, Emily. The rest won't be so hard." Bolstering the younger woman, the older one walked her inside to the table where the form of Josephine now lay supine, a measure of its dignity restored.

What—if anything—Fannie had used to break the bones remained a mystery, for Emily hadn't the fortitude to ask, nor did Fannie volunteer the information.

They worked together, washing the pale body with its withered skin, then clothing it in Josephine's best black silk dress with a white collar of punched organdy. The dress lay slack upon the shrunken form, so Fannie added padding, inside Josephine's undergarments. At her throat she pinned Josephine's favorite cameo brooch.

Meanwhile, Emily washed the blood from her mother's hair and combed it up in an effort to cover the near-bald spot at the back of her head.

"Her hair was always her pride and joy," Emily recollected sadly.

"How I envied Joey her hair," added Fannie. "On her wedding day she wore it in a pompadour held up by combs trimmed with pearls. My, it was dramatic."

"You were there, then, the day she married Papa?"

"Oh, yes. Oh my, of course, yes, I was there. They made a handsome couple."

"I've seen their daguerreotype."

"Yes, of course. So you know she had an enviable mane of hair. When we were children we would make clover rings to wear as garlands. The flowers always looked so striking on her black hair and so sickly against mine. So one day your mother had the idea to dye mine dark like hers." Fannie chuckled nostalgically. "Heavenly days, the trouble we got into. I said, 'We can't dye my hair, Joey, what will we use?' And she said, 'Why can't we use the same thing Mother uses to dye cotton?' So we sneaked into her mother's pantry and found the recipe for black dye and got what we needed—some of it I believe we stole."

"My mother—stealing?" Emily's eyes widened in amazement.

Again Fannie chuckled. "Yes, your mother, stealing. Potash and lime, as I remember, from one of our father's backyard sheds."

"But she was always so . . . so . . ."

"So obedient?"

"Yes."

"She got into her share of mischief, just like all the rest of us."

Emily found herself transfixed by Fannie's tale, which was revealing a new and unexpected side of the rigidly strict mother she had known all her life. "Tell me about the dye," Emily encouraged as she lit a lantern and began heating curling tongs to tend to her mother's hair.

"Well, we stripped sumac bark and boiled it up with potash and something else—what was it again? Copperas, I think. Yes, copperas. Where we got that I don't remember, but what a vile black liquor it made. And when it was brewed it stank so bad I'm not sure how I ever got up the courage to stick my head into it. As I recall, your mother egged me on when I suggested that perhaps red hair wasn't so bad after all. She said, Did I want to spend my whole life looking like a pink rat, and of course I didn't. So we dyed me black as crape, and fixed the color quite indelibly with lime water. Oh, it was a tremendous success!"

"And then our mothers saw it," Fannie ended on an ominous note.

"What happened?"

"As I recall, neither one of us sat down for days, and I spent weeks wearing a bandana tied around my head, pulled clear down to my eyebrows, because we'd not only dyed my hair, but my forehead and ears as well, and I looked as if I was coming down with leprosy!" Fannie shook her head fondly. "Heavens, I'd forgotten all about that."

The reminiscence had served its intended purpose: it had made the two women forget their aversion to the task at hand. While Emily curled Josephine's hair and Fannie buffed her fingernails, they did so as lovingly as handmaidens working over a bride.

"She's very pale," Fannie observed almost as if Josephine were alive. "Do you think she would like it if we put a touch of color on her cheeks?"

Emily studied her mother's still face. "Yes, I think she would."

Fannie opened a quart jar of raspberry sauce and painted Josie's cheeks with the juice. When the stain had set she washed them clean again and said to the dead woman, "There, dear, you look much, much better. I know what store you always set by your appearance." To Emily she added, "Not too curly now. She always detested the frizzed look."

"Only enough to sweep it away from her face like she always wore it."

"Yes, exactly."

When they had combed Josie's hair, when her hands lay manicured at her sides, and her shoes were on and tied and her clothing plump, they stood on either side of the kitchen table, looking down at her with a measure of ease restored to their hearts.

"There, Mother," Emily said quietly. "You look fine."

"Edwin will be pleased, I think."

At the winsome tone of Fannie's voice Emily looked up. She had never taken time to consider how difficult the last half year must have been for Fannie, loving both Mother and Papa as she did. And she *had* loved Mama; this morning had made that indelibly clear. Studying Fannie, she saw not a woman who had loved another's husband, but one who had selflessly eased a family's burdens during the last six months. Fannie was all the things she'd always been: understanding, strong, cheerful, good. She had come into a home weighted with cares and lightened those cares daily, not only by her good deeds, but by her indefatigable spirit. And who had there been to lighten Fannie's spirit when she needed it? Only Papa. And now, Emily herself.

"Mother told me about you and Papa," Emily admitted gently. "She wanted me to know before she died."

Fannie studied Josephine's berry-stained cheeks for a long moment before speaking. "If I could have loved him less, I would have. It was a great cross for her to bear all her life."

"Fannie . . ." Emily swallowed. "Forgive me?"

Fannie looked up. In her eyes was a sadness that ran as deep as her lifelong love for Edwin.

"There is nothing to forgive, dearling. You are their daughter. What were you to think?"

Emily's eyes stung. "I want you to know, Mother's last wish was that you marry Papa and that I give you both my blessing. I intend to."

Fannie made no reply. She studied Emily a long time, and finally reached down to collect the buffer, washcloth, and towel from the tabletop. "We must make a satin pillow for the casket, and prepare the front parlor and make black wreaths and armbands and press our black dresses and . . ."

"Fannie . . ." Emily came around the table and touched Fannie's arm. The two women stared at each other through a blur of tears, then pitched together and clung.

"I don't know what I'd have done without you this morning," Emily whispered. "What any of us would have done without you."

Fannie lifted her eyes to the ceiling as her tears spilled. "Yes, you do. You would have persevered, because you're very much like me."

Edwin came home with Reverend Vasseler to find Fannie and Emily sitting side by side in the kitchen beside Josie, forming roses of black crape: cutting circlets, stretching them over their thumbs, then stitching the tiny petals together to shape the flowers.

Reverend Vasseler stood beside the table, said a prayer for the departed and another for the living, resting his hands on Emily's and Fannie's heads, offering special condolences to the younger woman, whose wedding was to have been today. Edwin stood transfixed by the sight of his wife all laid out, grateful he had been spared the agony of having to perform undertaking duties. *Fannie, bless you, dear Fannie.* His eyes remained dry and unblinking and he forgot about Reverend Vasseler's presence until the minister spoke softly and touched his arm consolingly. "She's in the Lord's hands now, Edwin, and He is all good."

The day evolved into a series of vignettes: good Christian women coming to help sew black crape roses, to carry away the soiled bedding, to bring custard pies and chocolate cakes and hamburg casseroles; Edwin carrying the copper hip-tub upstairs and emerging after his bath wearing his black Sunday suit on a Thursday; Frankie returning from Earl's to take his turn in the bath; then the women doing the same; Tarsy, arriving owl-eyed and uncharacteristically silent, volunteering to press Emily's black dress, then remaining at her side throughout the afternoon; the family standing motionless while Fannie stitched mourning bands onto their sleeves; the sound of the church bell announcing the death hourly; and late in the day, Charles arriving with a buckboard, bringing a pungent-smelling cedar coffin, as lovingly and meticulously joined as the cupboard he'd made for Tom Jeffcoat.

He entered the kitchen, hat in hand, encountering the ladies still sitting in a circle, within a dozen roses of completing the second impressive black crape wreath, which lay on their laps. Emily glanced up at Charles's long face and laid aside her needle. The ladies murmured, lifting the wreath from Emily's knees so that she might rise and go to him. One of them reached back to squeeze Charles's wrist, offering a low word of consolation. But Charles's eyes remained fixed upon Emily as she rose and left the group with a slow-moving dignity.

"Hello, Charles," she said, a subdued stranger in a black tight-necked dress and skinned-back hair parted down the center.

"Emily, I'm so sorry," he offered sincerely.

"Come," she whispered and, without touching him, led the way into the dining room, around the corner from the black-garbed women whose needles continued flashing. In the empty room she faced him.

Sadness lined her face but she stood before him with all other emotions hidden. Reaching down, he scooped her gently against him. A sound came from her throat as her cheek met his jacket—a sob, swallowed; gratitude, unspoken. He felt solid and comforting, and smelled of wood and winter.

"I've brought the coffin," he said against her hair.

She drew back and reached into his eyes with her own. "Thank you for making it, Charles. Papa appreciates it so. So do I."

"It's cedar. It'll last a hundred years."

She wiped her eyes, smiled dolefully, and rested her hands on his arms. "I'm sorry about the wedding, Charles," she told him.

"The wedding—awk, what does that matter?" For her benefit he assumed a note of false bravado. "We can do that any old time."

She experienced a sharp sting of guilt for feeling reprieved when it took such an obvious effort for Charles to mask his deep disappointment. Unable to hide it from her, he dropped his gaze and fiddled with the crease in his black Stetson. He was dressed in proper mourning garb—a black suit and stringtie over a starched white shirt. She stared at his chest while her mind absorbed the fact that the customary period of mourning measured one full year—surely he was aware of that, too.

"Charles," she whispered, covering his wrist, stilling his hands. "I am sorry."

He swallowed thickly, still staring at his hat, then made a visible effort to put secondary concerns aside until a more appropriate time.

"You doing all right, Em?" he asked throatily, as always more concerned for her than for himself.

"Yes. Are you?"

"I was glad to have the coffin to work on, to keep my hands busy today."

With both of her hands she squeezed one of his, then drew a deep breath and squared her shoulders. "And I was glad to have the wreaths."

"Well." Charles lifted his bereaved eyes, fingering the hat crease unnecessarily. "I'd better go find Edwin to help me carry it in. You go sit down, Emily. It's going to be a long night."

And so it was Charles who helped Edwin lay Josephine in the aromatic cedar box, who moved her broken bones for the last time and arranged them on white muslin, and centered her head on the white satin pillow, and handed Edwin her prayer book and waited nearby as Edwin placed it in Josephine's crossed hands. Then, together they carried the coffin to the parlor, placed it in the bay window upon two wooden chairs, and propped the lid on the floor before it.

In the kitchen the ladies formed the last black rose and affixed it to the wreath. Emily respectfully placed it against the coffin lid, then stood in a circle of loved ones, gripping Tarsy's hand on her left and Charles's on her right.

"It's a beautiful coffin, Charles."

It was. And by his making it, and helping Papa lay Mother in it, and standing beside all of them through this difficult ordeal, Charles had endeared himself to the family more than ever.

Chapter 16

The hard kitchen chairs were arranged in an arc facing the coffin. Sitting on one, Emily experienced some wholly profane thoughts about wakes. What possible good could they do either the loved ones or those who kept their all-night vigils over the corpse? Comfort for the living and prayers for the dead, she supposed, though she found herself praying little and comforted less. The townsfolk were kind to come and pay their last respects, but it put a tremendous strain on the family. How many times could one repeat the same trite phrase? Yes, Mother was better off now; yes, she'd lived a good Christian life; yes, she'd been a good woman. But Emily found Fannie's story about the hair dye a more proper elegy than the doleful study of those who came to gaze down into the casket and shed tears.

Guiltily she put such thoughts from her mind, but as she glanced at her brother, the irreverence persisted.

Poor Frankie. He sat dutifully between Papa and Fannie, squirming on his chair, being touched on the knee and reminded of propriety if he slouched or slipped too far forward or perched on the edge of his seat. Frankie was too young to be here. Why burden him with this depressing memory? Tomorrow's funeral would be enough. He slouched, toyed with a button on his suit for two full minutes, and sighed, slumping back. Fannie touched his knee again and he straightened obediently. Emily caught his eye, mimed a kiss, and felt better.

Her gaze moved on to Papa. Each time she'd looked at him today a knot of tears had formed in her throat and she'd wanted to lunge into his arms and pour out her apologies and tell him about her last talk with Mother. Why was it that the one to whom she most needed to offer an olive branch was the one to whom she had scarcely spoken? There had been people around them all day, lending no chance to speak privately. But that was only an excuse, Emily admitted. It was hardest to go to Papa because she loved him most.

She closed her eyes and prayed for strength and made a silent promise to put things right between herself and her father.

She opened her eyes again and watched Tarsy quietly open the door to admit another friend of the family. What a surprise Tarsy was turning out to be, loyal to a fault, quietly greeting mourners and taking their coats, thanking them for coming. And Charles was equally as helpful, greeting neighbors as if he were already one of the family, drawing up chairs for the older women who wanted to pause longer and pray, making sure the stoves were kept stoked with coal.

Reverend Vasseler began another mournful incantation. Emily attempted devoutness but when she closed her eyes the oak seemed harder, the smell of the black dye in her dress seemed poisonous, and she kept wishing she had a watch.

Dear Lord, make me properly mournful about my mother's death. Make me consider it the loss it truly is instead of the fortuity that saved me from marrying Charles today.

At the end of the prayer she opened her eyes to find Tom Jeffcoat standing just inside the parlor door dressed in his sheepskin jacket, doffing his Stetson, gazing at her. Within Emily, alarm and glory set up opposing forces. The emotion she'd been unable to dredge up for lamentation swelled abundantly at the sight of him.

You came.

I wanted to come as soon as I heard.

You mustn't look at me that way.

Your wedding is canceled.

My wedding is canceled.

Tarsy came forward to greet Tom, whispering a thank-you on behalf of the family, taking his jacket and hat. They spoke together, low, and Tarsy touched his hand before slipping away. Charles formally escorted him through the candlelit room to the front tier of chairs, where Papa was the only one to rise.

"Edwin, I'm so sorry," Tom offered, squeezing Papa's hand protractedly.

"Thank you, Tom. We all are."

"I feel like an outsider here. I didn't know her well."

"Nonsense, Tom, we're all happy you came. Mrs. Walcott was fond of you."

"Don't worry about your horses tomorrow. I'll see to them if you like."

"Why, thank you, Tom. I appreciate that."

"And my rigs are yours for anyone who needs a ride to the graveyard. I'll have them ready to go."

Edwin squeezed Tom's arm.

Tom moved on to Frankie, extending a hand as he would to an adult. "Frankie, I'm awfully sorry about your ma."

"Me too . . . sorta."

"If she's in heaven, you know what they say about heaven." Tom leaned near Frankie, daring a brief note of lightness for the boy's benefit. "You got to keep on behaving or she'll know about it."

"Yessir," Frankie replied respectfully.

Tom's eyes softened as he moved on. "Fannie." He took her hand in both of his and kissed her cheek. "My condolences, Fannie. If there's anything I can do—anything—all you have to do is say so."

"Thank you, Tom."

He straightened and moved to the last family member, standing above her for some seconds before speaking. "And Emily," he said somberly, extending his two hands. She placed hers in them and felt the contact warm a path straight to her heart. His eyes, dark with concern and love, fixed upon hers, bringing a momentary suspension of grief, a delight in the memory of kissing him only a short time ago. Her heart swelled, and she felt healed. *I needed this so badly, just to see your face, to touch you.* The pressure on her knuckles threatened to change their shape. Her mother's admonition came back, granting sanction to the intense feelings she had for him, but Charles and Tarsy looked on so she repressed all outward displays and sat gazing up at him formally.

"Tom," she said quietly, the mere pronunciation of his name easing a deep need to rise into his arms.

"I'm sorry," he whispered fervently, and she understood that he spoke not merely of her mother's death, but of the fact that he could not embrace her as he wished, and that in the days ahead he would force a painful break between herself and Charles, that even her friendship with Tarsy would be threatened. There would be difficult confrontations for both of them. But in that moment as they held hands before Josephine Walcott's coffin, the decision was sealed. As if Josephine's death had been a sign for them, they realized nobody but they could correct the course of their lives, and they would. It was only a matter of waiting for the proper time.

Throughout the night neighbors stayed in shifts, sitting beside whichever family members remained in the parlor while others broke to rest. But little sleep came to Emily during the one- or two-hour respites. When she closed her eyes she saw Papa, hurt and mournful; or Charles, true and trusting; or Tarsy, noble and supportive; or Tom, offering with his eyes what he dared not speak aloud.

By dawn everyone looked haggard and drawn. The last of the neighbors went home, leaving the family members to tiptoe about the silent rooms and dress for the funeral.

At the funeral itself Emily and Tom remained decorous when they met. They encountered one another at the graveyard, across a snowswept knoll separated by most of the residents of Sheridan. He gave her a slight, formal bow, which she returned, but he remained carefully expressionless when, during the dropping of the symbolic spadeful of dirt, she gave way to weeping and Charles bolstered her with a supportive arm.

Back at the house, where mourners gathered for a repast, they bumped into each other in the dining room archway, he with a plate in his hand, she with a guest's coat in hers.

"Tom," she said simply.

His gaze took in the purple shadows beneath her eyes, but he remained properly formal. "Emily."

"Thank you for lending your carriages for the funeral."

"No thanks are necessary, you know that."

"And for taking care of Papa's stock today."

With a finlike motion of his palm he made the help seem of little consequence.

"How are you?" he asked.

"Terrible. Relieved and feeling guilty about it."

"I know the feeling."

"Tom, I have to go greet people at the door."

"Sure, I understand. Is that someone's coat? I'll take it if you like."

"Oh, thank you. You can put it upstairs on any of the beds."

He took it from her and headed away, but she called, "Tom?"

He turned back to find the doleful expression softened in her eyes. "I love you," she said quietly.

His decorum suffered a near-collapse. His Adam's apple bobbled and his lips dropped open. His eyes widened with a smitten expression as unmistakable as the tinge of pink that painted his cheeks. But he only nodded formally and turned away with the feelings still churning in his blood. As he mounted the stairs with a stranger's coat, he pondered 365 days of mourning and damned every one of them.

The house had emptied of all but the family. Dusk had fallen and a pale paring of a moon hovered above the southeast horizon. The parlor was back in order, the dining room neat, the lanterns lit. Footsteps sounded unnaturally loud in the empty house, so nobody moved much. Speaking felt disrespectful so nobody said much. Eating seemed decadent so nobody ate much. The four who had laid their loved one to rest clustered in the kitchen, experiencing a disquieting reluctance to be alone.

Fannie sat in a hard chair, silently reading a book of poems. Frankie sprawled in the rocker, chin to chest, thoughtlessly enlarging a hole in the knee of his everyday pants. Emily spiritlessly shifted a salt shaker back and forth across the tabletop. Edwin stood at the window, staring out with melancholy listlessness. He sighed—a deep, burdened sigh—and reached toward the coat peg for his jacket.

"I think I'll go down to the stable, look in on the horses," he told the others. "I won't be gone long." The door opened and closed, sending a cold puff of winter air into the room.

Emily stared after him.

Fannie raised her eyes from the page. "Why don't you go with him?" she suggested.

The salt shaker tipped over as Emily thrust herself from her chair, grabbed a jacket, and ran into the crisp dusk, calling, "Papa, wait!"

Edwin turned, surprised, and watched her jog down the snowy path toward him. Reaching him, she came up short, closing her throat button, then stuffing her hands into her pockets. "I'll walk with you," she offered quietly. The moment lengthened while they studied each other uncertainly.

"All right," he answered, turning toward town as she joined him. They walked without touching, Edwin studying the horizon, Emily watching her feet. They had mourned together, had hugged and held and consoled one another. But the subject of Fannie remained unsettled between them. How difficult it was to unravel a lifetime's snarls.

At last Emily took Edwin's arm and pressed close against it. Silently, he glanced down at her while they continued walking. Edwin drew a deep, ragged sigh. "Should have a nice clear day tomorrow," he predicted in a conspicuously gruff voice.

"Yes . . ." She looked up, too. "Cold but clear."

Tomorrow's weather was the last thing on their minds. They walked on with arms linked as it used to be.

In time she took the plunge. "Papa?"

"Yes?"

"I think I've grown up a fair bit through all this."

"Yes, I imagine you have. Sometimes growing up can hurt a lot, can't it?"

"Yes, it can."

Any tears that slipped from Edwin's and Emily's eyes did so without the other seeing. They moved on in silence for some time before Edwin remarked as if in summation, "I did love your mother, you know. And I suppose she loved me, too, in her own way. But we had trouble feeling close to one another."

"I know. She told me."

"I assumed she had, that day you came downstairs and offered to help Fannie get supper on the table."

"Yes, that was the day."

"What else did your mother tell you?"

"Everything. About you and Fannie, and how you loved her before you married Mother. And how angry you got when Mother wanted to bring Fannie here." Emily paused before finishing more quietly, "And that I must accept Fannie when you marry her."

Edwin covered Emily's hand on his elbow, and squeezed it with his wide, gloved hand. He fixed his attention on the street ahead while asking, "Would you mind?"

Their gazes met. They stopped walking. "Not at all. I love her, too."

"And would you mind if an old man gives you a hug right here in the middle of Loucks Street?"

"Oh, Papa . . ." They moved as one against each other, Emily seizing his sturdy neck and pressing her cheek against his graying beard. "I love you so much."

Smiling, he crushed her in a powerful hug and kissed her temple. "I love you, too, honey." They rocked from side to side until the brunt of their emotions had passed, then Edwin suggested, "Now what do you say we go poke around that livery barn? There's nothing that makes us feel better than the smell of horses and the feel of hay under our feet."

Renewed, they walked on, arm in arm, through the gathering night.

During the days that followed, the Walcott home took on a sense of disburdening so quick and facile it sometimes left the family members feeling guilty for not missing Josephine more. They wore black armbands but felt less aggrieved than during the months of her suffering. They hung the black crape wreath on the door, but within the house contentment settled. Emily and Fannie penned appreciation notes to all who had sat vigil or brought foods, but the delivery of the notes seemed to signal the end of repining.

The house became tranquil as it had never been during its two years as a hospice. Daytime, it thrived under a routine relieved of the strains imposed by one ailing. At night it was blessedly silent without her coughing, allowing everyone the bliss of uninterrupted sleep. Mealtimes became especially pleasant, with the entire household gathered around the kitchen table, sharing tidbits about their days and exchanging bits of town gossip. Evenings held a sense of leisure with all of them clustered in the kitchen for popcorn, or in the parlor for Parcheesi. Sometimes Fannie would play the piano, and Frankie would lie on the floor, leaning on one elbow, and Emily would hum, and Edwin would doze with his head dropped back against his chair.

Charles was conspicuously absent during this time, for, after the funeral, the first time he had suggested coming over in the evening Emily had used as an excuse the responses she and Fannie had to write. The second time he suggested it she told him she needed some time alone with her family, and that when she was ready to spend more time with him she'd let him know.

Charles looked hurt, but complied.

Two weeks went by, and he stayed his distance. Three weeks passed while she felt underhanded and small for not making a clean break with him. But it seemed untimely to do so before she and Tom had the opportunity to cement their own plans. That opportunity had not arisen because he was keeping his formal distance—that distance dictated by the strict rules of Victorian mourning. The situation was stultifying and—in Emily's mind—silly, but shunning those rules was unheard of.

One night, a month after the funeral, the Walcotts were all gathered in the kitchen when Emily glanced up to find Edwin watching Fannie over the top of his newspaper. Fannie was writing a letter, unaware of Edwin's intense regard. She signed her name, laid down the pen, and glanced up. Heat lightning seemed to flash between the two while Emily observed, feeling like a voyeur. Papa's eyes appeared dark with leashed ardor, while Fannie's became polarized in return. For a full ten seconds their feelings were as readable as the signature Fannie had just penned upon the paper.

Fannie recovered first, dropped her flushed gaze, and slipped the letter into an envelope. Giving her attention to waxing it, she inquired, "Would you like me to see after Joey's personal things, Edwin?"

Edwin cleared his throat and raised the newspaper between them once more. "What had you intended to do with them?"

"Whatever you like. I'm sure there will be keepsakes Emily will want, but the rest we could give to the church. There are always needy people."

"Fine. Give them to the church."

When Fannie turned to discuss the sorting of clothes with Emily, the younger woman found herself absorbed by the impact of what she'd just witnessed. Why, it was no easier for Papa and Fannie to pretend indifference to one another than it would have been for herself and Tom, had he, too, been sitting across the table. Apparently Mama had been right: Papa and Fannie smoldered with an intense attraction for one another, and the only things that kept it dampered was the awesome stringency of propriety.

But as long as they observed the rules of mourning, how could Emily herself hope to forgo them?

Emily was one hundred percent correct about her father. Edwin walked around feeling like a volcano ready to erupt, remaining aloof from Fannie by the sheer dint of will. But he gave himself one consolation—since Josephine's death, he had developed the habit of running home for coffee and a sweet at mid-morning, simply to get a glimpse of Fannie. He never stayed more than ten minutes, and he never touched her. But he thought about it. And so did she. In the clean, quiet privacy of the house they shared, where she performed all the duties of a wife, save one, they both thought about it.

On the day following their exchange of glances over the newspaper Edwin indulged himself his ten A.M. Fannie-break.

He entered the kitchen to find it empty. On the sideboard a cake cooled—his favorite: brownstone front. He crossed the room and plucked a raisin from it, marring its smooth top, something he wouldn't have dreamed of doing to one of Josie's cakes. He smiled and filched another one, plus a walnut, warm and flavored of cinnamon and cloves from the cake.

Above, he heard sounds from his bedroom and went upstairs to find Fannie kneeling on the floor before the open chifforobe, folding one of Josie's shirtwaists on her lap. He hadn't made any secret of his arrival, clunking up the stairs as noisily as Frankie might. But when he came to a halt in the bedroom doorway, Fannie refrained from acknowledging his presence. She placed the garment aside and began folding another as he circled the foot of the bed and shuffled to a halt behind her, gazing down at her head.

"There's coffee on the back of the stove," she told him, forbidding herself even a backward glance. "And a brownstone front cake."

"I know. I already sampled it. Thank you."

They had never been alone in this room before. Always, Josie had been in it with them. But Josie was gone now.

Edwin dropped a hand to Fannie's pale hair and idly caressed it. For the space of two heartbeats her hands stopped their task, then sensibly continued.

"Am I expected to wait a whole year before making you my wife?"

"I believe so."

"I'll never make it, Fannie."

She drew an unsteady breath and said what had been on her mind for four weeks. "Which is why I feel it would be best if I leave soon."

He answered by closing his hand around her neck possessively, kneading it, sending shivers down her spine.

"It doesn't look good, Edwin, my staying on."

"Since when have you been concerned about how things look, you who ride bicycles and wear knickerbockers?"

"If it were only for myself I wouldn't be concerned, but you have two children. We must consider them."

"You think they'd be happier if you leave?"

She spun on her knees, knocking his hand aside, and lifted her face in appeal. "You're intentionally distorting my meaning."

"If you think I'm going to let you go, you're crazy, Fannie," he warned vehemently.

"And if you think I'm going to allow any improprieties between us as long as I'm single and living in your house with your children, you're crazy, too!"

"I already have Emily's approval to marry you, and I'm sure Frankie won't mind a bit. You've been as good a mother to him as his own was. Maybe better."

"This is not the time or the place, Edwin."

"I only want to know how long I have to wait."

"A year is customary."

"A year!" He snorted. "Christ."

She considered him with gentle reproof in her gaze. "Edwin, I'm only now packing up Joey's clothes. And I didn't want to repeat the graceless old saying about not letting the body cool, but perhaps you need to hear it today."

He stared at her for five tense seconds, then spun about and clumped from the room with frustration in every footstep.

Fannie was right, of course, but her clinging to gentilities did little to relieve the overburdening sexual suppression Edwin practiced in the days that followed. He gave up the habit of going home for coffee, making sure he was there only when one of the children was also present. He carefully guarded his watchfulness, and kept a proper distance, and to his immense relief Fannie mentioned no more about leaving.

Meanwhile, Emily, too, suppressed her need to see Tom Jeffcoat until the proper time could come for her to make the break with Charles. She had chosen not to tell her family until after the deed was done, so when they asked what had happened to Charles lately, she said he was busy in the evening building furniture on speculation, stockpiling it for sale to the preempters who'd begin rolling through again in the spring.

During the first two weeks following the funeral she saw Tom only from a distance, across the length of the block dividing their livery stables. The first time they stood and stared. The second time he raised a hand in silent hello and she raised hers back, then they stared again, lovelorn, bound by the same strict rules that held Fannie and Edwin apart.

Not until a full month after the funeral did they bump into each other accidentally. It happened as Emily left Loucks's store with a basket of drygoods she'd picked up for Fanny. Tom was coming in just as she was going out, and they nearly ran each other down on the boardwalk.

He steadied her by both arms—a lingering excuse to touch—while their blood rushed and they stared into one another's eyes with thwarted longing seeming to flush their entire bodies.

Finally releasing her arms, Tom touched his hat brim. "Miss Walcott."

How obvious. He had not called her Miss Walcott since the first week he'd come to town.

"Hello, Tom."

"How are you?"

"Better. Everyone's adjusting at home."

His Adam's apple bobbed like a fishing cork and his voice dropped to a whisper. "Emily . . . oh, God . . . I wish I were." He sounded miserable.

"Is something wrong?"

"Wrong?" He glanced furtively up and down the boardwalk. Though it was empty, he made fists to keep from touching her. "That was a hell of a thing you said to me the day of the funeral. You can't just say a thing like that and walk away."

She felt suddenly buoyed and optimistic, realizing he'd felt as lonely and denied as she. "You did the same thing to me one day on the street. Remember?"

They both remembered, and smiled and basked in each other while they could.

"Charles tells me you haven't been seeing him much."

"I asked him for some time to myself. I've been trying to ease away from him."

"I want to see you. How long do I have to wait?"

"It's only been a month."

"I'm losing my mind."

"So am I."

"Emily, if I—"

"Howdy!" Old Abner Winstad came out of the store just then, stepping between the two without bothering to apologize for interrupting.

"Hello, Mr. Winstad," Emily said.

"Well, give your family my best," Tom improvised, tipping his hat to her before adding, "How're you, Mr. Winstad?"

"Well, to tell the truth, sonny, my lumbago's been acting up lately and I went to see Doc Steele, but I swear that man's got no more compassion than a—"

Abner found himself talking to thin air as Tom headed down the boardwalk, forgetting whatever it was he'd been heading into Loucks's Store for.

Abner scowled after him and groused, "Young whippersnappers . . . got no respect for their elders anymore."

Another two weeks went by during which Emily saw little more than a glimpse of Tom down the street. It was late February and dreary outside, and the snow had turned dirty, and she missed Tom so much she could scarcely bear it. She had decided she'd give herself two more days, and if she hadn't run into him she was going to make a clandestine late-night trip to his house, and the devil pay the consequences!

Who made up these damned rules of mourning anyway?

She applied more oil to her rag and began working it into another piece of harness while Edwin crouched beneath Pinky. He let the forefoot clack to the floor and straightened, announcing, "Pinky's thrown a shoe. Will you take her across the street?"

Emily's heart suddenly burst into quick-time, and she stared at her father's back. Did he know? Or didn't he? Was he intentionally giving them time alone or didn't he realize he'd just answered her prayers? She stared at his crossed suspenders and squelched the urge to press her cheek to his back, slip her arms around his trunk, and cry, "Oh, thank you, Papa, thank you."

Instead, she dropped her oiling rag, wiped her palms on her thighs and replied tepidly, "I suppose."

Turn around, Papa, so I can see your face. But he left Pinky tied in the aisle and moved off toward the next stall without giving his daughter a clue about his suspicions or lack of them.

With her heart racing, Emily plucked an ancient, misshapen wool jacket off a peg and gratefully led Pinky away. Out on the street, walking toward Tom's stable, she became flustered by an uncharacteristic rash of feminine concerns.

I-forgot-to-check-my-hair-I-wish-I-were-wearing-a-dress-I-probably-smell-like-harness-oil!

But she'd run from their own barn thinking of only one thing: getting to Tom Jeffcoat without wasting a solitary second, relieving this immense, insoluble lump of longing that she had carried in her chest day and night since the last time she'd been in his arms.

She led Pinky into Tom's livery stable through the "weather door," a smaller hinged access set within the great rolling door. Inside, she heard his voice and stood listening, entranced by each inflection and tone merely because it came from him. Little matter that he spoke in the distance, to a stranger, about fire insurance. The voice with its own distinctive lilt and lyricism was his, unlike any other, to be savored just as she savored each glimpse of him, each precious stole touch.

She closed the weather door and waited with anticipation pushing against her throat. He appeared in the office doorway and she experienced the giddy joy of watching pleasant surprise flatten his face and color his cheeks.

"Emily . . . hello!"

"Pinky needs a reshoe. Papa sent me." She saw him bank his urge to come to her, saw him tense with impatience over the unconcluded business still waiting in his office. "Take her down to the other end. I'll be there in a minute."

She felt as if she had stepped into someone else's body, for the sensations aroused by him were foreign to her. There was impatience, welling high, counteracted by as great a sense of unrush now that she was here in this realm, where everything around her was his, had been built and touched and tended by him. *Take your time coming back to me. Let me bask in the knowledge that you will. Let me steep in this place that is yours, where you have slept and labored and thought of me.*

She walked Pinky to the smithy at the far end of the barn, tethered her outside the door, then wandered inside where it was warm and smelled of hot metal and charcoal and—was she only imagining it?—the sweat of Tom Jeffcoat. She unbuttoned her heavy jacket and stuffed her gloves into the pockets, wandered past his tool table, touched the worn, smooth handles of hammers that had collected the oils from his hands and maybe those from his father's and grandfather's hands as well. Wood . . . only wood . . . but precious and coveted for having been closer to him than she. She stroked the anvil, scarred at the blunt end and worn brilliant as a silver bullet at its point; beside it he had stood as a boy, watching his grandfa-

ther at work. Upon it he had learned as a man. Steel . . . only steel . . . but the anvil seemed as much a part of him as his own muscle and bone.

Pinky nickered at being left on a short line and Emily sauntered back to her,
glancing down the corridor to where Tom and the salesman now stood near the
weather door, exchanging final comments.

"Maybe in the spring then, Mr. Barstow, after the first cattle drive comes
through and the homesteaders start showing up again."

"Very good, Mr. Jeffcoat, I'll pay you a call then. In the meantime, if you want
to reach me you can write to the address I gave you in Cheyenne." The two men
shook hands. "You've got a mighty nice setup here. Well, I'd better let you get
back to your customer."

"Appreciate your stopping, Mr. Barstow." Tom opened the door and saw the
man out.

When the door closed he turned to find Emily watching him from the opposite
end of the corridor. For moments neither of them moved, but stood transfixed by
one another, marking time to the beat of their own leaping hearts, experiencing the
same ebb and rush of protracted yearning that she had felt earlier. He started moving toward her, slowly at first . . . and disciplined. But he hadn't taken four steps
before she was moving, too, with much less discipline than he, striding long and
purposeful.

Then they were running.

Then kissing, wrapped together openmouthed and urgent after weeks of deprivation, feeling one agony end while another began. They kissed as if starved—
deep, engulfing, whole-mouthed kisses that knew no limit of possession.

Tearing his mouth from hers Tom demanded breathlessly, "Tell me now . . . tell
me again."

"I love you."

He held her head, smattered her with hard, impatient, celebratory kisses. "You
really do. Oh, Emily, you really do!" He clutched her possessively, swiveling them
both in a circle, dropping his head over her shoulder. "I missed you. I love
you . . ." And realizing his tardiness in saying so, chastised himself, "Oh, damn
me, I should have said that first. *I love you.* It's been the longest six weeks of my
life." Again they kissed, futilely trying to make up for lost time—wet, wide kisses
during which they caressed each other's backs, ribs, waists, shoulders.

"Just stand still for a minute," he breathed, clasping her near, ". . . and let me
feel you . . . just feel you."

They pressed together like leaves of a book left out in the rain, with Tom's
aroused body pocketed against her stomach, both of them shaken and wanting so
much more than allowed.

"You feel so good," she whispered. "I think about you all the time. I imagine
being close to you like this."

"I think about you, too. Sometimes during the day I stand and stare out the window at your dad's livery stable, at the office window, and I know you're in there
studying, and it's all I can do to keep from marching up there and hauling you
back here."

"I know. I do the same thing. I stand in the window and read the sign above
your door and tell myself it won't be long. It won't be long. But it is. The days
never seem to end. When I bumped into you in front of Loucks's store it was terrible. I wanted to follow you back here so badly."

"You should have."

"Afterwards I went home and curled up on my bed and stared at the wall."

He chuckled—a sound life rife with suppressed desires. "I'm glad."

"It scares me sometimes. I never used to be this way but lately I grow listless and I can't seem to concentrate on anything and I miss you so much I actually feel sick."

"Me, too. Sometimes I find myself banging away on a piece of iron that's too cool to shape."

They laughed tightly, falling silent at the same moment, overwhelmed to learn that they'd suffered the same agonies. They hugged again, straining together, rocking from side to side while his hands stroked her ribs, narrowly avoiding her breasts. With her upraised arms overlapped upon his shoulders she waited breathlessly for the touch she had no intention of fighting.

Please, she thought, *touch me just once. Give me something to survive on.*

And as if he heard, he found her breasts, but finding them, realized they stood in the main corridor where anyone might enter and discover them.

"Come here . . ." he whispered, and hastily drew her through the smithy door into the warm, shadowed room where he backed her against a rough wood beam. Slipping his hands inside her coat, he captured her breasts straightaway, cupping and caressing them, pushing her suspenders aside, dropping his open mouth over her uplifted one. From her throat came a muffled sound of accession as she rested her arms upon his shoulders.

"Em . . ." he breathed against her face as the kiss ended.

She'd brook no endings, but picked up where he left off, keeping his mouth, and curling her hands over his upon her breasts when they would have slipped away. He emitted a muffled groan and dipped at his knees, matching their hips, marking her with a controlled ascent that drove her against her leaning post. His caresses became reckless, splendid, rhythmic.

When the effort of breathing seemed to crush his chest, he reluctantly dropped his hands to her waist and his forehead against the post. Resting lightly against each other, they regrouped. For moments their minds emptied of all but the welcome truth—they loved with equal passion; it had not been imagined or embroidered during their weeks apart into something it wasn't. What they had felt then, they felt now, mutually and intensely.

"Em?" The name came out muffled against her shoulder.

"What, Thomas?"

"Please marry me."

She closed her eyes and whispered simply, "Yes."

He reared back. Even in the dimness she saw the grand shock possess his face. "Really? You mean it?"

"Of course I mean it. I really have no choice in the matter." She hugged him rapturously, taking a moment to envision herself as his wife, in his bed, at his table, in this livery barn with a half dozen black-haired stairsteps fighting over who was going to hand Daddy the next horseshoe nail. It surprised her not in the least to be imagining herself with his children after purporting to be in no hurry to have them. She savored the image, breathing the scent of his neck while her breasts lifted against him. "Oh, Thomas, this is how it should be, isn't it? It's what my mother meant."

He leaned back to search her face. In the meager light from the forge her eyes appeared as black jets.

"I have so much to tell you," she said. "Could we sit down? Close, where we can hold hands, but not this close. I can't think too clearly when you're touching me this way."

They sat side by side on a pair of short nail kegs, their finger linked on his left knee. When they were settled Emily began in an evenly modulated voice.

"The day before my mother died she enjoyed a remarkable spurt of vigor. She felt strong and could breathe well, so she talked a lot. We all took it as a good sign, and we were so happy. Papa even carried Mother down to the supper table, and she hadn't been strong enough to sit through a meal for months. I've thought about it often since, how we all thought it meant a real turnaround, but it ended up being quite the opposite. It seemed almost as if she was fortified for a very good reason—to tell me the truth about herself and Papa and Fannie."

Staring at their joined hands, Emily told Tom the entire story. He sat quietly, moving only his thumb across the creases in her palm. Minutes later she finished, ". . . and so I'm reasonably certain Papa and Fannie intend to get married as soon as it's decent. But Mama wouldn't have had to tell me, would she? She could have let me go on believing that her marriage to Papa was all a bed of roses. When she died it seemed—this is hard to say because sometimes it sounds absurd even to me—but it seemed as if her death was deliberately timed to prevent my marrying the wrong man."

They stared at their hands, thinking of Charles. When their eyes met their gazes held underlying regret for having to hurt him.

"If I could only be taking you away from somebody beside Charles. Why does it have to be him?"

"I don't know." She pictured Charles and added, "If he were unscrupulous or unlikable this would be so much easier, wouldn't it?"

"Emily?" Their gazes remained rapt. "We have to tell him. Now . . . today. We can't sneak around behind his back anymore."

"I know. I knew it at the wake when you came and took my hands."

"Would you like me to tell him?" Tom asked.

"I feel like I should."

"Funny . . . I feel the same way." They thought about it for a moment before he suggested, "We could tell him together."

"Either way, it won't be any easier . . . for him or for us."

Abruptly Tom dropped her hand and covered his face, heaving a deep sigh into his palms. For minutes he sat thus, knees cemented to elbows, the picture of gloom. She felt dejected for him, wishing she could ease his sense of traitorousness, yet it was no greater than her own. Her eyes stung and she touched his forearm, fanning a thumb over the coarse black hair that reached well past his wrist into the back of his hand.

"I didn't think love was supposed to hurt this much," she venured at length.

He laughed once, mirthlessly, scrubbed both hands down his cheeks, then flattened his lower lip with two fists, staring at his anvil. Minutes passed, bringing no solution to the anguish both felt.

"You want to know something ironic," he mused at length. "While you've been keeping him away, he's been spending more time with me. Every night I've been listening to him wail about how much he loves you and how he's losing you, but he doesn't understand why. Christ, it's been torture. I was on the verge of telling him so many times."

She searched her mind for consolation and found only one. "But Thomas," she told him honestly, "I've never loved him the way I love you. It would have been wrong to marry him."

"Yeah," he mumbled, only half-convinced, and they sat silently until their backsides began feeling the raised rims of the nail kegs.

Finally Emily sighed and pushed to her feet. "I should go so you can shoe Pinky. Papa is probably wondering where I am."

Tom withdrew from his moroseness and stretched to his feet. "I'm sorry I got so moody. It's just hard, that's all."

"If you took it lightly, I wouldn't love you as much, would I?"

He wrapped both arms loosely around her shoulders and rocked her from side to side. "This might very well be one of the hardest things we'll ever do, but afterwards we'll feel better." He stopped rocking and asked, "Together then? Tonight?"

She nodded against his chin.

"Emily?"

"What?"

"Could I pick you up at your house?"

Her stillness warned him that she'd guarded their secret well. Again he drew back to search her face. "There's been enough cat and mouse. If we're going to do this, let's do it right. Your father was honest with you, isn't it time you're honest with him?"

"You're right. Seven o'clock?"

"I'll be there."

Chapter 17

How does a woman dress for the breaking of her engagement? In her bedroom that evening, with the lamp at her elbow, Emily studied her reflection in the mirror. She saw a worried face framed by coal-black hair, troubled sapphire eyes, a frowning mouth, and a scoop of bare throat above a white shift. She had little choice of dress—not for a full year—yet mourning garb seemed appropriate for tonight's mission.

The dress was plain, trim above, full below, constructed of unadorned black muslin. As she buttoned it up the front she saw her body shape it, rounded here, concave there, until the high cleric collar drew the last inch tight and she studied herself as a woman. She had rarely thought of herself in the feminine sense, but since she'd fallen in love with Tom she saw herself through his eyes—thin, trim, not unpleasantly curved. She touched her hips, her breasts, closing her eyes, recalling the swell of feelings aroused by Tom. A year . . . dear Lord, a year . . .

Guiltily she opened her eyes, plucked up a brush, and began punishing her hair, currying it mercilessly before winding it up in a severe figure eight and ramming the celluloid pins against her scalp.

There. I look like a woman filled with remorse for what I have to do.

But minutes later she felt more like an anxious schoolgirl as she waited in the dark at the top of the stairs for the sound of Tom Jeffcoat's knock. From the parlor below, beyond her range of vision, she heard Fannie playing the piano while Papa, she knew, read his newspaper. Earl had come over tonight; he and Frankie more than likely lay on their bellies on the floor, building card houses.

When a knock sounded Frankie exclaimed "I'll get it! Maybe it's Charles!" He shot across Emily's range of view while she clattered downstairs in an effort to cut him off.

"I'll get it!"

"But it might be Charles!"

"I *said* . . ." She skidded to a halt in the entry and forced his hand off the knob. ". . . *I'll get it, Frank!"*

He backed off, looking maligned. "Well, get it then. What're you standin' there for?"

"I will," she whispered through clamped teeth. "Go back to your cards." Instead, he sat down on the second step to be a thorn in her side. Peering through the lace curtains she saw the outline of Tom's shoulders and felt a twinge of desperation. Fannie stopped playing the piano. Papa's paper rustled as he lowered it to his knee, waiting to see who appeared around the stub wall. Earl was probably gawking, too, and he'd certainly spread the news as soon as he got home.

"Well, for pity's sake," Edwin called exasperatedly, "will one of you open the door!"

"Open the door, Emileeee," her little brother repeated in a sing-song.

She drew a fortifying breath and did the honors.

"Hello, Emily."

He looked incredible! Ruggedly attractive in his sheepskin jacket, with cheeks freshly shaved and ruddy from the cold, hat in hand, and hair flopping attractively over his forehead. Emily stared, tongue-tied.

"Emily, who is it?" Papa called from the parlor.

He stepped inside, closing the door. "It's Tom, sir."

"Tom!" Dropping his paper, Edwin hustled to the foyer, followed by Fannie. "Well, this is a surprise." He reached for Tom's hand, inviting enthusiastically, "Come in! Come in!"

"Thank you, Edwin, but I've come to take Emily out."

Nonplussed, Edwin glanced between the two. "Emily?" he repeated disbelievingly. Fannie smiled vacuously. Frankie thumped from one step to the next on his butt. Five full seconds passed in utter silence, then from the parlor Earl complained, "Aw shucks, the wind knocked my cards down!"

Fannie recovered first. "Well . . . that's nice. Are you going for a walk?"

"Yes, to Charles's," Emily replied hastily.

"Oh, to Charles's." Edwin looked relieved. "We haven't seen him around for a couple weeks. Tell him hello."

"Can I come along?" Frankie asked, popping off the step.

"Not tonight," Emily answered.

"Why not? There's no school tomorrow and Charles says—"

"Frank Allen!" Emily demanded, "Enough!"

"Tom doesn't care, do you Tom?" The boy appropriated Tom's wrist and suspended himself from it. "Tell her I can go, pleeeease?"

"Afraid not, Frankie. Maybe some other time."

"Aw, jeez," he mumbled and clunked to the parlor to fling himself down petulantly.

Fannie advised, "It's a chilly night, Emily, be sure to wear a scarf."

Emily caught her coat from the hall tree and began stuffing her arms into it, unaided, but Tom stepped behind and held it while the others watched and assessed his gallantry with undisguised fascination.

"We shouldn't be gone more than an hour or so," Tom remarked, opening the door for Emily.

She flashed Edwin and Fannie a tight smile. "Good night, everyone."

"Good night," Fannie responded.

Edwin said nothing.

The porch steps might have led down from a gallows as Tom and Emily descended them with their gazes trained straight ahead. Not until they reached the street did Tom release the tension from his shoulders.

"Whew!"

"Fannie knows."

"You mean you've told her?"

"No, she's guessed, I can tell. She guessed that I had a yen for you from the first week you came to town."

"Oh, really?" His voice held a teasing note. He glanced back over his shoulder, gauging their distance from the house, and took her hand. "This is news."

She turned a spare grin his way to find a similar one aimed at her. They walked in silence, fingers linked, enjoying the momentary lift of spirits.

Eventually he asked, "What about your father?"

"I think he's putting off admitting what's right before his eyes."

"I thought it would be best to get this thing over with, with Charles first, before we told him."

"I agree. Charles deserves to be the first one who knows, and until he does, I can't draw an easy breath."

On Charles's porch they no longer held hands. They no longer teased. They avoided glancing at each other. "Everything's dark. It doesn't look like he's home." Tom knocked, then backed off to stand a proper distance from Emily.

They waited. And waited.

Tom glanced briefly at Emily, then knocked again, but still no answer came. The windows remained dark.

"Where could he be?" Emily raised distraught eyes to Tom.

"I don't know. What should we do, try to find him?"

"What do you want to do?"

"I want this over with. Let's go see if we can dig him up." He tugged her hand and they set off toward town. Loucks was closed up for the night. The saloons were open so Tom went into the first alone—women wearing mourning bands wouldn't dream of entering a saloon—leaving Emily to wait on the boardwalk. Inside the Mint he drew a drunken slur from Walter Pinnick, an invitation to a poker game from a trio of Circle T ranch hands, and a suggestive glance from a powdered whore named Nadine. He ignored them all and questioned the bartender, came out a minute later, reporting to Emily, "He's been here but he left and said he was going to my place."

"But we passed your place and he wasn't there."

"Do you suppose he went to the livery after he found out I wasn't home?"

"I don't know. We can try."

They ran Charles to ground midway between Walcott's and Jeffcoat's Livery Stables, where he'd obviously been searching for Tom. From twenty yards away he spied them and waved, hurrying toward them.

"Hello, Emily! Hey, Tom, where have you been? I've been looking all over for you!"

Tom called, "We've been looking for you, too."

They met in the middle of Grinnell Street, shifting their feet for warmth, sending puffs of white breath into the air as they spoke.

"Oh yeah? Something up for tonight? Lord, I hope so. This town dies after six o'clock. I went down to the Mint and had a beer, but there's only so much of that a man can stand, so I came looking for you." He appropriated Emily's arm. "I didn't expect to find you, too, what with the mourning and all." He dropped his eyes to her coat sleeve, still with its broad black band sewed in place, while she averted her gaze to the rutted street.

"We'd like to talk to you, Charles," Tom said.

"Talk? Well, talk away."

"Not here. Inside. Why don't we go down to my stable?"

For the first time Charles grew wary, flashing assessing glances from Tom to Emily, who carefully avoided all eye contact. "About what?" He fixed a questioning gaze on Emily but she dropped her eyes guiltily.

"Come on, let's get out of the cold," Tom suggested sensibly.

Charles spent another worried glance on his two best friends, then forcibly lightened his attitude. "Sure . . . let's go."

They walked the frozen street three abreast, with Emily between the two men and not an elbow touching. Tom opened the weather door and led the way into the dark barn. Inside, they stood in dense blackness surrounded by the smell of horses until Tom found and struck a match, and reached overhead for a coal-oil lantern. Squatting, he set it on the concrete floor. Watched by the other two, he opened its door with a metallic *tink,* lit the wick, rose, and replaced the lantern on the nail overhead. During the process the tension in the barn multiplied tenfold.

The lantern shed an eerie light on Tom's unsmiling face as he dropped his arm and confronted Charles. The sheer somberness of his expression lent additional gravity to the scene. For moments he remained silent, as if searching for the proper words.

"So what is it?" Charles demanded, glancing from Tom to Emily and back again.

"It's not good," Tom replied honestly.

"And it's not easy," Emily added.

Charles snapped his regard to her, suddenly angry, as if he already knew. "Well, whatever it is, say it!"

A spur of dread gripped her, shutting her throat. Dry-eyed, she stared at him and began, "Charles, we've been friends for so long that I don't know how to begin or how to—"

Tom interrupted. "This is the hardest thing I've ever had to say in my life, Charles. You're a true friend and you deserve better."

"Better than what?" Charles remained silent, stiff-faced, waiting.

"Neither one of us wanted to hurt you, Charles, but we can't put off telling you the truth any longer. Emily and I have fallen in love."

"Son-of-a-*bitch!*" Charles' reaction was immediate and forceful. His fists bunched. "I knew that was it! One look at your faces and a blind man could see you're both guilty as hell!"

"Charles." Emily reached for his arm. "We tried not to—"

"Don't touch me!" He twisted sharply, elbowing free. "Don't, by God, touch me!"

"But I want to explain how—"

"Explain to somebody else! I don't want to hear it!"

Tom tried to reach out. "Give her a chance to—"

"You!" Charles lunged and slammed Tom in the chest, sending him quickstepping backward. "You sonofabitch!" The attack was so unexpected it temporarily stunned Tom. "You underhanded, sneaking sonofabitch!"

Recovering, Tom cajoled. "Come on, Charles, we don't want to make this any hard-*ergh!*" A second shove ended the word on a grunt and set Tom back another step.

"My *friend!*" Charles sneered, pushing Tom again, just hard enough to force him backward. "My two-timing, back-stabbing, double-crossing sonofabitch friend!"

Tom went lax, letting himself be manhandled. "All right, get it off your chest."

"Y' goddamn right I will, you sneaky bastard! And you're gonna be mighty sorry when it's over!"

Tom let himself be thumped again, and again, arms hanging loose, until his shoulders struck a buckboard on the turntable and his hat tipped askew. He reached up slowly to right it, then took a spraddled stance and raised his palms. "I don't want to fight you, Charles."

"Well, you're going to, and it's not gonna be pretty! If you think I'm going to let you steal my woman and walk away untouched, you're wrong, Jeffcoat! Not after I had a claim on her since I was thirteen years old!"

Horrified, Emily came out of her stupor. "Stop this, Charles!" She grabbed Charles's arm. "I won't let you fight!"

"Back off!" With a thrust of his elbow he tossed her aside, then glared at her. "You want to play Jezebel and pit one friend against another, well, fine, now you can just stand there and watch the results! You're going to see some blood before this is over so you better take a last look at his pretty face before I mess it up!"

Pivoting unexpectedly, Charles threw his full weight into a violent punch that snapped Tom's head back and cracked his shoulders against the buckboard. His hat flew. He grunted and doubled over, holding his belly.

Emily screamed and came at Charles with both hands. She dragged him back no more than two feet before he swung and pinned her arms at her sides, slamming her against a stall door with enough force to clack her teeth together. "Keep off or by God, I'll lay one on you, too, woman or not! And believe me it wouldn't take much right now, the way I feel!"

Incensed, Tom came at Charles from behind. He spun him, gripping his coat front, raising him to tiptoe. "You try it and it'll be the last move you ever make, Bliss! All right, you want to fight ... you think it'll settle anything ..." He backed off, crouched, beckoning with eight fingers. "Come on ... let's get it over with!"

This time when Charles lunged, Tom was prepared. He took a shoulder in the chest, but dug in and braced, throwing Charles upright and catching him beneath the chin with both forearms, following with an immediate left to Charles's jaw. The crack sounded like a rake handle breaking. Charles landed on his ass on the concrete and sat for a moment, stunned.

"Come on," Tom challenged again, his face pinched with intensity, "You want a fight, you've got it!"

Charles rose slowly, grinning, wiping his bloody lip with a knuckle. "Hoo-ey!" he goaded, centering his weight in a crouch. "So he's in love." His face turned hard. His voice became threatening. "Come on, bastard, I'll show you what I think of your—"

A solid right shut Charles up and bounced him off the buckboard. Rebounding, he threw his momentum into a volley that dented Tom three times below the waist. Before Tom could straighten, Charles caught him by the throat, forcing him backward across the corridor until they crashed into a stall door. Inside a bay gelding whinnied and danced, rolling his eyes. Emily leapt to life, screamed, and attacked from the rear, pulling at Charles's jacket collar while he gripped Tom's windpipe. She hung on until the neck opening wedged above Charles's Adam's apple and cut off his own air supply.

"How long, Jeffcoat?" Charles demanded in a raspy, constricted voice. "How long have you been after my woman? I'll make you pay for every goddamned day!"

"Charles, stop it! You're choking him!" Emily drew rein on Charles's collar but a button popped off, dropping her to her rump. Shooting up, she collared Charles again, this time with an arm, leaping like a money onto its back.

"Get off me and let us fight!" With a flying elbow Charles knocked her off and she stumbled backward, cradling one breast, wincing with pain.

"You sonofabitch, you hurt Emily!" Tom roared, enraged. The rage felt wonderful! Hot and healing and revitalizing! His knee came up and thrust Charles off, sent him pedaling backward, followed by Tom, who propelled himself through the air with an intensity outdistancing any he'd ever known. Two well-aimed clouts knocked Charles to his back, but he was up in a split second, and Tom took as good as he gave. Both men were powerful, with chests like drafthorses, forearms thick as battering rams—a blacksmith and a carpenter, conditioned by years of swinging weighty hammers. Augmented by sudden enmity, their strength became immense. When they set out to punish, they did.

Flatfooted, they bare-knuckled one another—faces, stomachs, shoulders—exchanging a flurry of punishing blows and grunts that carried them from one side of the stable aisle to the other. Against a stall door, onto the floor, then up, riding the splintery wood with their shoulderblades, accidentally opening the latch, further adding to the confusion as the horse inside whinnied and pawed in terror. Neither man heard. When Tom upended Charles with a punishing uppercut, Charles picked himself up and returned the favor.

In minutes their faces bled. The skin on their knuckles split. Still they fought, growing weaker with each punch.

A dying blow caught Charles and sent him stumbling backward, tripping over a buckboard trace. He plopped onto the turntable, setting it in motion, carrying him several feet away from Tom, who followed unsteadily, weaving on his feet. Panting, the two rested for ten seconds before obliging one another again, this time on the floor, rolling, too close for effective swings.

Still they tried, cursing, clouting each other with ineffectual close-range shots until they struck the far wall, where they lay in a tangle of arms and legs. Nose to nose, they panted, gripping each other's jacket fronts.

Charles scarcely had the breath to speak. Still, he taunted brokenly, "How far ... did you ... go with her, huh, f—friend?"

Tom was in no better shape. "You got a d—dirty mind, B—Bliss!"

Dizzy and stumbling, Tom struggled to his feet, hauling Charles with him. He pulled back for another swing but inertia nearly tumbled him backwards. Charles was equally as sapped. He reeled onto his heels with his fists clenched weakly. "Come on ... you bastard ... I'm not through!"

Tom faced off, quarter-bent, swaying, his arms hanging like bell clappers. "Yes you are ... I'm m—marrying her," he managed between strident breaths. Talking hurt nearly as much as slugging. Still they hung before one another, close to exhaustion.

"You wanna ... call it quits?" Tom got out, wobbling on his feet.

"Not by a ... damn sight."

"Awright then ..." He hadn't the strength to throw a punch, but came at

Charles with his entire body. Backwards they went, stumbling into the opened stall, against the withers of the frightened bay gelding, smashing him against the stable wall as they fell in a loose tangle of diminished force.

On her knees near the turntable Emily wept, covering her mouth with both hands, afraid to interfere again.

"Please ... please ..." she prayed behind cold fingers, hunkered forward over her knees.

The men crashed out of the stall, falling apart, swaying on their feet, sidestepping like drunks, trying to focus through swollen eyes. Their jackets looked as though they'd been worn in a slaughterhouse.

"You ... had ... enough?" Tom managed through battered lips.

"So ... help ... me ... God ..." Charles never finished. He collapsed to his knees, buckling at the waist.

Tom followed suit, falling forward onto all fours, his head dangling as if connected to his body by a mere string. For seconds the stable was filled with the sound of their harsh breathing. Then came Tom's voice, pitiful with emotion, very near tears.

"G—Goddamn you ... why'd you hafta ... b—bring her to my h—house for that shivaree?"

Charles wobbled on his knees, barely upright. He tried to point a bloody finger at his foe but his arm kept falling. "You k—kissed her in that g—goddamn cl—closet ... didn't you!"

Winded, Tom nodded, unable to lift his head.

Charles fell off his knees with a loose-jointed thump, dropping to his side and catching himself on an elbow.

"What a s—sucker I was, b—building you furniture ..."

"Yeah ... stupid sonofabitch ... I'm gonna ... take an axe ... and b—bust that thing ... to smithereens ..."

"Do it! ... g'wan ... do it ..." Charles let his head flop back against his shoulder. "I don't give a d—damn."

Emily stared at them, dumbfounded, crying, with her hands clapped to her mouth.

Still on all fours with his head hanging, Tom spoke as if to the floor. "I didn't mean ... to fall in ... love with 'er, man ..."

The two men breathed like engines running out of steam, their enmity gone as suddenly as it had appeared, both of them pitiable now as truth came to take its place between them. After a full thirty seconds Charles collapsed onto his back, eyes closed. He groaned. "Christ, I hurt ..." His right knee, upraised, undulated from side to side.

"I think ... my ribs're broke." Tom remained on all fours, his forehead hanging inches above the floor, as if unable to rise.

"Good. So's my ... goddamn heart."

On hands and knees, Tom crawled painfully across the aisle until he knelt above Charles and peered down blearily into his friend's face. There he hung, with the breath catching in his throat, until he finally whispered gutturally, "I'm sorry, man."

Charles closed his fingers over a puny lump of hay and flung it at Tom's face, missing. His hands dropped to the concrete, palm-up.

"Yeah, well, go to hell, you bastard." He lay exhausted, eyes closed.

Emily watched their breakdown through a blur of tears. In her many years of friendship with Charles, Emily had never heard him curse so much, nor had she ever seen him strike a soul. Neither had she suspected Tom would engage in violence. She had witnessed the past five minutes with horror and fear and a heart that broke for both of them. It was obvious their real pain was not that inflicted by fists. Those wounds would heal.

But now that it was over her stomach trembled and reason rushed in, bringing with it justifiable anger. How horrible that two human beings would hurt each other so.

"You're both crazy," she whispered, wide-eyed. "What good did this do?"

"Tell 'er, Jeffcoat."

"I would, but I dunno. I feel like a chunk of beef that's been put through the meat grinder . . . both ways." Tom sucked in his belly and tested it tenderly with one limp hand.

"Good."

"I think I have to puke."

"Good."

Still staring at the floor, Tom spit out a mouthful of blood and the nausea passed. "Ohhh, gawwwwwwd!" he groaned, settling back gingerly onto his heels. "Oh, holy . . . jumpin' . . . Judas." He closed his eyes and cradled his ribs with an arm.

Charles opened his eyes and rolled his head. "They broke?"

The pain became so intense that Tom could only shake his head and mouth the words, *I don't know.*

"Emily?" Charles said thickly, the word distorted by his bruised lips as he blearily searched for her.

She sat above and behind him. "What?"

He skewed his head and peered at her backwards. "Maybe you better go get the doc. I think I busted his ribs."

Instead, she sat where she was, appalled by what they'd done to one another. "Oh, look at your faces, you fools, just look at them," she cried plaintively.

They did. Surprised by her vehemence, Tom and Charles took a good look at the carnage they had reaped and it mellowed them further. Emily's outburst seemed to snap belated common sense back into both men's heads and make them realize they'd fought first without discussing anything—just slammed each other with fists, as if that would fix everything. But it wouldn't. They'd have to talk, and as they rested on the bricks, emotionally as well as physically exhausted, the realization came slowly, bringing with it a pathos magnified by Charles's first question.

"All right . . . so how did it happen?"

Tom shook his head, studying his soiled knees despondently. "Hell, I don't know. How did it happen, Emily? Working with the horses together, playing those stupid damn parlor games, I don't know. How does it ever happen? It just does, that's all."

"Emily, is he telling it straight? Did you tell him you'd marry him already?"

"Yes, Charles," she replied, studying the top of Charles's head as he remained on his back on the floor.

"He's an asshole, you know." Charles's voice held a trembling note of affection. "You want to marry an asshole who'd steal his best friend's fiancée?"

She swallowed and felt tears forming afresh, watching the two men stare at one another.

Tom's voice softened and became as emotional as his friend's. "I wish it could've been another woman. I tried Tarsy. I wish to hell it could have been

Tarsy. But she was like . . . like too much divinity . . . you know what I mean?" His voice dropped to a near-whisper. "I tried, Charles, but it just didn't work." After a long pause he touched Charles on the hand. "I'm sorry," he whispered.

Charles shook him off and flung an arm over his eyes. "Aw, get out of here. Go on, get out of here and take her with you!" Horrified, Emily watched Charles's Adam's apple bob and realized that beneath his bloody jacket sleeve he was battling tears.

She struggled to her feet, her skirt wrinkled and strewn with straw.

"Come on, Tom . . ." She took his arm. "See if you can get up."

He drew his sad eyes away from Charles and straightened like an arthritic old man, accepting her aid. He hobbled as far as the open stall door and clung to it for support. When he'd caught his breath he remembered.

"You all right, Em?"

"Yes."

"But you caught an elbow, I saw it."

"I'm not hurt. Come on," she whispered. "I think Charles is right. I think we ought to find Doc Steele and have him take a look at you."

"Doc Steele is a quack, and cranky to boot. Everybody says so."

"But he's the only doctor we have."

"I don't need any doctor." Walking half the length of the barn proved too much for Tom, however.

"Stop," he pleaded, slamming his eyes shut. "Maybe you're right. Maybe you'd better go get Doc and bring him back here. That way he can check both of us."

She lowered Tom where he stood, and left him sitting propped against a wooden half door on the cold brick floor.

Three minutes later, when she beat on the front door of Doc Steel's house, Hilda Steele answered, wrapped in a robe with her hair in a frowsy braid.

"Yes?"

"It's Emily Walcott, Mrs. Steele. Is the doctor here?"

"No, he's not. He's out on circuit till the end of the week."

"Till the end of the week?"

"What is it? Is it something serious?"

"Would you . . . I . . . no . . . I'm not sure . . . I'll get my father."

She ran home instinctively, her mind empty of all but worry for Tom and Charles. When she burst in the front door Edwin and Fannie were seated side by side on a sofa. Earl had gone home and Frankie was nowhere in sight.

"Papa, I need your help!" Emily announced, wild-eyed and breathless from running.

"What's wrong?" He met her halfway across the parlor, taking her icy bare hands.

"It's Tom and Charles. They've had a fight and I think Tom has some broken ribs. I'm not sure about Charles. He's lying flat on his back at Tom's livery stable."

"Unconscious?"

"No. But his face is a mess and I can't move either one of them. I left them there and ran to get Doc Steele but he's gone somewhere and Tom can't walk and . . . oh, please, help me, Papa. I don't know what to do." Her face crumpled. "I'm so scared."

"Fannie, get my jacket!" Edwin sat down and began pulling on his boots. Fannie—a bundle of efficiency in an emergency—came running with his jacket, already thinking ahead. "What do you have in your medicine case for setting bones, Emily?"

"Adhesive plaster."

"A styptic?"

"Yes, crowfoot salve."

"We'll need some sheets for binding. Edwin, go along while I get them. I'll follow as soon as I can."

Hurrying down the snowy streets, Edwin asked, "What were they fighting over?"

"Me."

"I thought as much. Fannie and I spent the evening speculating about what was going on. You want to fill me in?"

"Papa, I know you're not going to like it, but I'm going to marry Tom. I love him, Papa. That's what we went to tell Charles tonight."

Jogging, Edwin spoke breathlessly. "That's a hell of a thing to do to friends."

"I know." Tears leaked from Emily's eyes as she added, "But you should know how it is, Papa."

He jogged on. "Yes, d—damned if I don't."

"Are you angry?"

"I might be tomorrow, but right now I'm chiefly concerned about those two you left bleeding down there."

On their way past Walcott's Livery Emily tore inside, snatched her bag, and joined her father on the run. They entered Tom's place like a train of two, bumping nose to shoulder blade. The scene inside was ironically peaceful. The single coal-oil lantern cast murky light over the near end of the corridor where Tom sat propped against the right wall; farther down, Charles sat against the left. Beside the turntable one stall door gaped open. The bay gelding had roamed out and stood peering inquisitively into the dark smithy at the far end of the building.

Edwin hurried to Tom first and dropped to a knee beside him. "So you've got a messed up rib or two," the older man observed.

"I think so . . . hurts like hell."

"Fannie's bringing something to bind them up with."

Emily explained, "Doc Steele wasn't home. I had to get Papa."

Edwin moved on to Charles. "I'm glad to see you propped up. She said she left you laying flat on your back and not moving. Scared the daylights out of us."

Through swollen lips Charles said, "Unfortunately, Edwin, I'm not dead or even close to it."

"That face is a mess though. Anything else hurt?"

Staring morosely beyond the turntable at Emily and Tom, Charles wondered aloud, "Does pride count, Edwin?" Then he glanced away.

On her knees beside Tom, Emily wailed, "Oh, Thomas, just look what you've done to yourself. Who asked you to fight over me?"

"I guess you're not too pleased."

"I should put another lump on your head, that's what I should do." She touched his cheek tenderly, whispering, "Don't you know I love this face? How dare you mutilate it?" They spent a moment delving into each other's eyes—hers troubled, his bloodshot and swollen—then she rose from her knees. "I'll get some water to clean you up." She found a chipped enamel pail in one of the stalls and returned with it full of water, knelt and retrieved gauze from her veterinary bag. When she dabbed at the first cut, Tom winced.

"Good enough for you," she declared unsympathetically.

"You're a hard woman, tomboy, I can see that. I'm gonna have to work on softening—*ow!*"

"Be still. This will stop the bleeding."

"What is it?"

"Crowfoot weed—old Indian cure—modernized some."

"Humph."

Fannie bustled in, hatless, toting a striped canvas bag with handles. "Whom should I see to first?"

Emily answered. "Get Tom's shirt off while I see after Charles's cuts."

While Edwin and Fannie stood Tom on his feet, Emily slipped across the aisle and knelt uncertainly beside Charles. How awkward, looking into his bruised face, meeting his hurt, reproachful eyes.

"I should get rid of some of that blood so we can see how bad the cuts are."

His reproof continued as he silently stared at her. Finally he demanded in a grieved whisper, "Why, Emily?"

"Oh, Charles . . ." She swung her gaze high, trying not to cry again.

"Why?" he entreated earnestly. "What did I do wrong? Or what didn't I do right?"

"You did everything right," she replied, abashed, "it's just that I've known you too long."

"Then you should know how good I'd be to you." His eyes, already bruised, looked even sadder as he spoke.

"I do . . . I know . . . but something was . . . was missing. Something . . ." Searching for graceful words, Emily studied her thumbs, which were needlessly flattening a wad of wet gauze.

"Something what?" he insisted.

She lifted dismayed eyes and whispered simply, "I've known you too long, Charles. When I kissed you it felt like kissing a brother."

Above his beard a pink tinge appeared between the bruises on his cheeks. He sat in silence, digesting her words for moments before replying with hard-won approbation, "Well, that's a damned hard one to argue with."

"Please, could we talk about it some other time?"

Again he fell silent, his mood deteriorating before he agreed dully, "Yeah, some other time . . ."

When she washed his face and knuckles he remained stoic, studying a wheel hub on the wagon. She swabbed his bruises with damp gauze, then applied the styptic salve, touching his face, his eyebrows, his beard, his lips for the last time. She discovered in a hidden corner of her heart an undeniable ache because it *was* the last time, and because she had hurt him so terribly, and because he loved her so much. She wrapped his bruised knuckles, tied the last knot, and sat back dropping her hands primly into her lap.

"Is there anything else?" she asked.

"No." He stared at the wheel, stubbornly refusing to look at her. Oddly, she needed him to look at her just then.

"Nothing feels broken?"

"No. Go on. Go bandage him up," he ordered gruffly.

She remained on her knees, studying him, waiting for some sign of exoneration, but none came. No glance, no touch, no word. Just before rising, she gently touched his wrist while whispering, "I'm so sorry, Charles."

A muscle contracted in his jaw but he remained taciturn, distant.

She crossed the corridor to tend Thomas, aware all the time that she had at last attracted Charles's attention. His hard eyes followed every move she made, like ice picks in her back.

Edwin and Fannie had rolled down the top of Tom's underwear and had implemented an uneducated fingertip examination.

"Fannie and I think something's broken."

Having touched Tom so few times before and never this intimately, Emily was naturally reluctant to do so now before three pairs of watchful eyes. She swallowed her misgivings and traced his ribs, submerging personal feelings and watching his face for reactions. His wince came on the fourth rib she tested.

"Probably fractured."

"Probably?" Tom asked.

"Probably," she repeated. "A green-stick fracture, I'd guess."

"What's a green-stick fracture?"

"It breaks like a green stick—curled on the ends, you know? Sometimes they're harder to mend than a clean break. I can plaster it or you can wait till the end of the week until Doc Steel gets back," Emily told him.

He glanced from Edwin to Fannie to Emily before inquiring dubiously. "Do you know what you're doing?"

"I would if you were a horse or a cow . . . or even a dog. Being a man, you'll just have to take your chances on me."

Sighing, he decided. "All right, go ahead."

"When I plaster an animal I shave the area so it doesn't hurt when the plaster comes off. We'll bind you first in sheeting, but sometimes the plaster soaks through."

Tom dropped a baleful glance at the wedge of black hair on his chest. Emily averted her eyes out of self-consciousness, feeling Charles's watchful stare as well as Fannie and Papa's closer regard.

"Oh, hell . . . all right. But don't take off any more than you have to."

She shaved the point of his hirsute arrow from waist to midway up his pectoral arch—an unnerving personal area made the more distracting by the fact that he kept jumping and flinching from the cold soap and blade, and because it was, after all, the naked stomach of the man she was going to marry.

Once he twitched and complained, irritably, "Hurry up, I'm freezing." She bit back a smile: so he would have his grouchy moments, as a husband. Maybe, as a wife, she could find ways to sweeten him at those times.

While Fannie wrapped his ribs with cotton, Emily measured, cut, and wet the adhesive plaster strips. She ordered Tom to drop his hands to his sides and expel his breath, and while he stood so, she wrapped him from back to breastbone with overlapped pieces until his trunk resembled the armor on a gila monster.

"There. It's not fancy, but it'll help."

He glanced down, cursed softly in self-disgust, and asked, "How long do you think I'll have to keep this on?"

"Four weeks, I'd guess, wouldn't you, Papa?"

"Don't ask me! I don't even know what you came to get me for. I haven't done a thing but watch."

It was true. Under stress, Emily had performed with proficiency and calm, as she had that day at Jagush's. Though Tom admired the fact, she made light of it, telling Edwin, "You were my moral support. Besides, I wasn't sure if I'd have to lift them. Thank you for coming, Papa. You too, Fannie."

"Well," Edwin announced, "I guess I'd better hitch up a rig and haul these two home." First he moved back to Charles. "Charles, how're you doing, son?"

Edwin had called Charles *son* for so long, doing so seemed second nature to him. But the word caused an uncomfortable lull as he helped Charles to his feet. Until now there'd been distractions to override much of the tension between the two suitors. But as they faced each other across the dim corridor, polarity surfaced between them, at once repellent and attractive. Broken engagements and broken bones and broken hearts. All were present in their silent exchange of glances.

Then Charles shuffled toward the door. "I'll walk home," he said glumly. "I feel like I need the fresh air."

"Nonsense, Charles—" Edwin began, but Charles pushed past him and left the livery stable without a backward glance.

In his wake Edwin exhaled a heavy breath. "I guess you can't expect him to be overjoyed, can you?"

Tom spoke up. "I know Charles means a lot to you, sir. I meant to plan a better time to tell you about Emily and me. I meant to ask you for her hand properly. I'm sorry you had to find out this way."

"Yes, well . . ." Edwin blustered, searching for words to hide his own dismay at losing Charles as a son-in-law. While playing the part of humanitarian Edwin had set aside his own consternation at the turn of events, but it surfaced now in an unexpected and tactless outburst. "Now I know about it, and she tells me she loves you, but young man, let me warn you . . ." Edwin shook a finger at Tom. "The period of mourning is a year long, so if you have any other ideas you'd better put them out of your head!"

Chapter 18

Emily rode behind her father, smoldering with mortification while they took Tom home in a four-seater buggy. She could not believe Edwin's crassness!

Edwin drove—mulling events silently, feeling ambivalent, even a little sheepish after reconsidering his outburst. At Tom's house he cast a reproving eye upon Emily as she anxiously watched her injured swain alight. Tom moved by increments, guarding his ribs as she stepped onto the foot bracket and over the side. When he reached the ground Emily stood as if to follow, but Edwin ordered, "Stay where you are. You're coming home with us."

"But, Papa, Tom needs—"

"He'll make out just fine."

Anger flared and Emily retorted acidly, "I can make my own decision, Papa, thank you!" She propped her fists on her hips and glared at her father.

Tom looked up and advised diplomatically, "He's right, Emily. You go home. I'll be all right. Thank you for your help, Edwin . . . Fannie."

"Yeah," Edwin replied ungraciously to cover his own growing discomposure over his lack of discretion. "Giddap!" He slapped the rains so suddenly Emily sat down with a plop.

"Papa!" she railed, outraged, gripping the edge of the seat.

He drove on without turning around. "Don't Papa me! I know what's best for you!"

"You're being unspeakably rude! And I never thought I'd live to see the day when you became domineering!"

"You're in mourning," Edwin declared with stubborn finality.

"Oh, *I'm* in mourning, so that means I'll have to put up with *your* surliness for a year?"

"Emily, I'm your father! And I'm not surly!"

"You're surly! Is he surly, Fannie? Tell him!"

Fannie had opinions but decided it best to withhold them until she and Edwin were alone. She had no intention of playing devil's advocate with Edwin's daughter as witness. A flourish of her hands ordered clearly, *Leave me out of this.*

"Not only is he surly but he's rude to my fiancé!"

"Your fiancé—hmph!" Edwin scowled at the rumps of the trotting horses.

"You found him totally likable when he knocked on the door earlier tonight. Why, your face lit up like a rainbow when you saw him coming in."

"You have damn near a full year of courtship ahead of you, young lady, and I won't have you tucking him into bed!"

"Tucking him into ... oh, Papa!" Abashed, Emily fought the sting of tears.

"Edwin," Fannie unbraided, abandoning her vow to remain silent. "That was uncalled for."

"Well, dammit, Fannie," he blustered, "Charles is like a son to me!"

"We know that, Edwin, so perhaps you need not reiterate the fact quite so often. There is a new fiancé to be considered, and he has feelings, too."

In strained silence they rode the remainder of the way home. Pulling up, Edwin stared straight ahead while Emily leapt from the wagon and stormed into the house in a state of dudgeon. Fannie silently squeezed Edwin's hand before following.

Inside Emily paced turbulently, spinning to Fannie the moment she entered. "How could he say such a thing?"

Fannie calmly lit a lamp and drew off her coat. "Give him a day or two to get used to the idea of you and Tom. He'll come around."

"But to point his finger at Tom and give him orders as if he were ... as if he were anything less than a gentleman! I was absolutely mortified! And his remark about my tucking Tom into bed was absolutely inexcusable! I wanted to die on the spot!" Indignant tears spurted into Emily's eyes. "We've done nothing to be ashamed of, Fannie, nothing!"

"I know, darling, I know." Fannie hooked Emily in her arms and tucked her close. "But you have to remember it hasn't been an easy time for your father. His whole world is in a state of flux. He's lost your mother, now he feels like he's losing Charles. You're making plans to marry and move away from the nest. It's natural that he's upset, and if he displays it in ways that could sometimes be more tactful, we must be patient with him."

"But I don't understand, Fannie." Emily pulled back, too agitated to be held immobile. "He's always been on my side, and he always said that the most important thing in life is to be happy. Now I am ... I ... I'm going to be, when Tom and I are married. You'd think Papa would think about that, would want that for me, instead of wanting me to marry somebody I don't love. The remarks he made tonight were totally unlike him. I'd expect Mother to say something like that, but not Papa. Never Papa."

Fannie studied the younger woman, smiling benignly. For seconds she pondered whether or not it was prudent to speak what was on her mind. Would it be fair to Edwin to speculate on the underlying reason for his outburst? Perhaps not, but it might at least help Emily understand some of the stresses that had come to bear on her father. "Come here. Sit down." Fannie took Emily by the hands and drew her down onto a kitchen chair, taking another herself, clasping Emily's hands across the corner of the kitchen table. She chose her words carefully. "You're nineteen years old, Emily, a full-grown woman." She spoke placidly, in a voice eloquent with understanding and wisdom. "Certainly you're old enough to have been exposed to the temptations that come along with falling in love. They're natural, those temptations. We fall in love and we want that love consummated. Well, it's no different for your father . . . and me. Perhaps now you can understand that the warning Edwin inadvisedly issued to Tom was really directed at himself."

The anger fell from Emily like a stripped garment, replaced by a wide-eyed stare of incredulity.

"Oh, you mean . . ." she stammered to a halt, her face still and open. And again, quieter, she breathed, "Oh."

"Have I shocked you, dear? I didn't mean to." Still smiling, Fannie dropped Emily's hands. "But we're both women, both in love, both trapped in this execrably *stupid* convention they call mourning. Perhaps we just handle it better than men do. Perhaps that's our strength, after all."

Emily stared at Fannie, too amazed for words.

"Now, dearling, it's late," Fannie observed, ending the intimate revelation with her usual grace. "Hadn't you better get ready for bed?"

Two hours later Emily lay in bed wide awake, still pondering the unexpected and startling disclosure made by Fannie in the kitchen. Even at their age, Papa and Fannie still experienced carnality! The realization relaxed much of Emily's rancor for Edwin.

How often she had wondered, but it wasn't a subject about which one inquired, certainly not of a parent. Certainly not of *her* parents! Lying beside the sleeping Fannie, listening to her measured breathing, Emily absorbed the truth that the other woman had so honestly revealed, truth that Fannie undoubtedly understood every bride-to-be would be wondering about: these feelings that she and Tom felt for one another could and very likely *would* preserve through much more of their lives than she had ever guessed.

In recent days, since Tom's first kisses and caresses, Emily had devoted many long insomniac hours to speculation about that very subject. Carnality. It was awesome and overpowering and intimidating. And, before marriage, a woman's responsibility seemed to be to combat it for both herself and the man.

Contemplating it, Emily conjured up the image of Tom, his lazy blue eyes, his smile, his lips, kisses, hands. She lay with the quilts caught tightly beneath her arms, her own hands flattened over her pelvis where the restive throb beat, deep inside. Warmth came with it, and nubilous images sprawled by memories of the few times Tom had held and petted her.

It brought speculation on the marriage act. There were words for it—copulation, conjugation, consummation, coupling, intercourse, sowing oats (Emily smiled) . . . making love (she sobered).

Yes, making love. She liked that phrase best.

What would it be like? How would it begin? Would it be dark? Light? Between sheets or on top of quilts like that one night at Tom's house? Would it be halting or spontaneous? What would he say? Do? And herself, how was she expected to react? Or *act?* And afterwards, would they feel awkward and self-conscious? Or would the marriage act create a magical lingering intimacy?

The marriage act. Another phrase, though sometimes untrue. Sometimes it happened outside the marriage—Tarsy had educated Emily on that point. Perhaps Tom had done it with someone already, someone he knew before, someone experienced in the proper ways. His former fiancé? Tarsy, even?

Emily opened her eyes and stared at a streak of moonlight bending around the corner of the room. She gulped at the stone lying in her throat. Suppose he had done it with Tarsy after all. Emily had tried to believe otherwise, but sometimes she wondered.

Tarsy, who had admitted how close they'd come.

Tarsy, who had also admitted that she sometimes thought of "trapping" Tom into marriage.

Tarsy, who had changed so much in the past several months because she loved Thomas Jeffcoat.

Tomorrow I must tell Tarsy. Tomorrow, before word reaches her from any other source.

At 5:30 the following morning Emily left a note on the kitchen table: *Going to feed Tom's horses. Back in an hour. Emily.*

She went first to his house. All was dark, so she circled around and knocked on his bedroom window, backed off and waited, but no response came. She banged again, harder, and pictured him rolling from bed, groaning, wrapped in plaster. It took a full minute before the shade flicked aside and his face appeared as a white blur in the shadows beyond the distorting window glass.

"Tom?" On tiptoe, she put her mouth closer to the window. "It's Emily."

"Em?" His voice came faintly through the wall. "What's wrong?"

"Nothing. Stay in bed. I'm going to take care of your stock today. You just rest."

"No, you . . . to . . . up . . . ."

Emily lost most of his reply to the buffering wall.

"Go back to bed!"

"No, Emily, wait!" He flattened a palm on the window. "Come to the door!"

The shade dropped and she stared at it, hearing again her father's admonition about tucking him into bed. Before she gathered the intelligence to walk away the shade turned golden as he lit a lamp, then faded as he carried it out of the room toward the front of the house.

5:30 A.M. The very hour created intimacy, the very fact that he'd been asleep. Emily paused, staring at the shade, fully intending to leave without putting a foot on his porch.

From around the house she heard him calling. "Em?" Faintly, in a half whisper.

Firming her resolve, she rounded the front corner and mounted two porch steps, then stopped dead in her tracks.

His head and one naked shoulder poked through the door. "Come on in here, it's cold!" His breath made a white cloud in the chill predawn air.

"I'd better not."

"Dammit, Emily, get in here! It's freezing!"

She thumped up the steps and inside, keeping her hands in her pockets and her eyes on the floor. He closed the door and rubbed his arms to warm them. She knew without looking, that his feet and chest were bare, and he wore only trousers and the white bindings around his ribs. Again, Emily wondered what her father would say.

"I'm sorry I woke you up."

"It's all right."

"I didn't want you to get out of bed. I thought if I just knocked on the window I could tell you and leave." Her glance flickered up to his shoulders, then quickly down.

"What time is it?"

"Five-thirty."

"Is that all?" He groaned and flexed gingerly. "Lordy, I couldn't get to sleep last night. My ribs hurt."

"How do you feel this morning?"

"Like I've been pulled through a keyhole." He spread a hand over the bandages, then reached up and tested his incisors, adding, "I think some of my teeth are loose."

"To say nothing of your bones. You've got no business throwing hay with cracked ribs. I'll take care of your livery stable today."

"I want to say no, but the way I feel I think I'd be wiser to say thank you. I really appreciate it, Emily."

She shrugged. "I don't mind, and I know your horses by name."

His eyes drifted fondly over her face and her boyish attire. "Besides," he said softly, "someday they'll be yours, too."

She swallowed, feeling herself blushing, realizing once again that they were in his home, in total privacy, and he was far from decently dressed. To remind him of the same thing, she broached the subject that could not be avoided forever.

"I'm sorry about what my father said last night."

She felt his eyes probing and studied his bare toes, imagining them beneath her own as the two of them curled together like spoons beneath the quilts.

"Is that why you're scared to look at me, Emily, because of what he said?"

She felt herself color, and gulped. "Yes."

"I'd sure like it if you would."

"I'm dressed in my barn clothes."

"And I'm not complaining."

She lifted her head slowly and her lips dropped open, her eyes grew dismayed. "Oh, Thomas . . ." His face was swollen and discolored. His hair stood in tufts like that of an old buffalo after a hard winter. His left eye was opened less than a quarter inch and the right one squinted without his intending it to. Beneath it a pillow of skin had turned magenta, tinged with blue. His beautiful mouth and jawline were those of a mutilated stranger. "Look at you."

"I suppose I'm a mess."

"You must hurt terribly."

"Bad enough to keep from kissing you the way I'd like to," he admitted, taking her elbows anyway, and drawing her off-balance.

She resisted discreetly and said, "Tom, I need to talk to you." There were things that needed airing and they were best said with a minimum of intimacy involved.

"So serious," he chided gently.

"Yes, it is."

He dropped his playful mood. "Very well . . . talk."

She drew a deep breath and told him, "I hated it, your fighting over me. I felt helpless and . . . angry."

His eyes probed hers with a hint of rebelliousness in the brows. But after a moment's silence he offered, "I'm sorry."

"I hate seeing you disfigured this way."

"I know."

"I would never have taken you for a fighter."

"I never was . . . before."

"I wouldn't like it much if you did it after we were married."

They both recognized the moment for what it was; not a squaring-off but a structuring for their future. His answer—the one she'd hoped for—spoke of the deference with which he would hold her wishes when she became his wife.

"I won't. That's a promise. I didn't *want* to fight him, you know."

"Yes, I know."

She stood with her gaze pinned on his black-and-blue eyes, wrapped in a queer combination of emotions—regret for having had to take him to task; pity for his poor, abused body; desire for that same body, no matter how unsightly it looked. She wanted badly to reach, soothe, press her face to his naked neck and touch his warm shoulders. A startling thought surfaced: *I love him so much that Papa is right. I have no business here in his house, not even in barn clothes.*

Instinctively she moved to leave, but reaching the door she turned. "I'm going to tell Tarsy about us this morning. As soon as I feed your horses I'm going over to her house and get it over with. I just wanted you to know."

"Do you want me with you?"

"No, I think it's best if I go alone. She's probably not going to be any more understanding than Charles was. The two of you will want to talk privately once she knows. I'll understand that and I promise I won't be jealous."

"Emily . . ." He moved toward her.

"I've got to go." She opened the door quickly.

"Wait."

"You know what Papa said."

"Yes, I know what Papa said but Papa isn't here now."

Advancing, he thumped the door closed and positioned himself between it and her. He hooked an elbow around her neck and drew her lightly against him, resting one bruised cheek against her floppy wool cap. In a husky voice he said, "I think it's a damn good thing I'm so bruised up or we'd be in a peck of trouble here."

Oh, his smell. A little musky, a little mussed, a little male, the natural scent of skin and hair aged by one night. Thank God for gloves, she thought, with her own resting against his hard white bindings, inches from his bare chest. She wanted nothing more than to touch all of him that was naked, to learn his texture with her bare fingertips. While she steadfastly refrained, he slipped his hand up inside the back of her jacket and pulled her lightly against him, lazily rubbing her spinal column through a rough flannel shirt. He explored her slowly, his hand moving up, as if counting each vertebra, gently urging her closer. A warm hard hand, a warm hard man—how easy it would be to succumb to both.

Her heartbeat hearkened and her breasts felt heavy.

"Thomas . . ." she whispered in warning.

"Don't go," he begged softly. "It's the first time without Charles between us. Don't go."

She felt it, too, the easing of constraint upon their consciences since her engagement was formally broken. But constraints took other forms, and she drew back reluctantly. "I can't come here anymore, not to your house. We have almost ten months to wait, and that's too long. I have to go," she repeated, backing away from him.

He watched her walk backward till her shoulders bumped the door. They gazed at each other with frustrated desire drawing long lines upon their faces.

He moved toward her slowly, and her heartbeats seemed to fill her throat. But he only reached behind her for the doorknob. Opening the door for her he said softly, "Let me know how it goes with Tarsy."

"I will."

At ten o'clock that morning Tarsy answered the door herself, wearing a trim-bodiced dress of candy-pink stripes with flattering shoulder-to-navel tucks that minimized her dainty waist, and a generous gathered skirt that exaggerated her rounded hips.

Emily wore the same clothes in which she'd fed Tom's horses and cleaned his stalls—a wool jacket, trousers, and soiled leather boots.

Tarsy's hair was freshly curled and caught up on the back of her head with a matching pink ribbon.

Emily's was jammed up inside her brother's floppy wool cap.

Tarsy smelled of lavender soap.

Emily smelled of horse dung.

Tarsy turned up her pretty nose. "Phew!"

Apologetically, Emily left her boots outside the door and stepped into the front entry stocking-footed. Mrs. Fields arrived from the kitchen, her hands coated with flour. "Well, Emily, for goodness sake, this is a surprise. We hardly ever see you this early in the day." She was a buxom woman with wavy blond hair done up in a French twist, the only woman Emily had ever known who wore cheek paint in her kitchen and scented herself at this hour of the day. The smell of honeysuckle toilet water wafted in with her, covering that of yeast from the dough on her fingers.

"Hello, Mrs. Fields."

"How is your father?"

"Fine."

"And Miss Cooper?"

"Fine."

"Will she be leaving soon, going back East?"

Emily detected a bit of nosiness and took pleasure in replying, "No, ma'am. She's staying."

"Oh." Mrs. Fields's left eyebrow elevated.

"She has no family back there. Why should she?"

Mrs. Fields allowed her eyebrow to settle to its normal level and blinked twice, as if taken aback by Emily's quick defense of Fannie.

"Well ... I thought that since your mother is gone—may she rest in peace—Miss Cooper's services would no longer be needed."

"On the contrary, we all need her very badly and begged her to stay. You see, I've decided to continue my veterinary studies after all, and to work at ... at the stables indefinitely, so I'm abandoning most of the domestic duties to Fannie. I just don't know what we'd do without her anymore."

Mrs. Field's mouth drew up as if she were attempting to pick up a coin with her lips. "I see." She flashed a glance at Tarsy, then added, "Well, give your family my best," and returned to the kitchen.

When she was gone, Tarsy took Emily's arm and turned her toward the steps. "Come upstairs and see the new piece of organdy that Mama's going to make into a spring gown for me. It's called pistachio—whatever that means!—and we've decided on the most absolutely smashing design from the latest issue of *Graham's*. Mama has agreed to let me have a soiree here—don't you just *love* the word?—soiree ..." Reaching the top of the steps, Tarsy lifted her skirt in two fingers and performed a dipping swirl toward her bedroom door. Whisking through it, she caught up a piece of green fabric from the tufted stool before her vanity. Petting it, she swung back to Emily. "Isn't it de-*lusc*ious?"

Emily dutifully touched the organdy with a knuckle that hadn't been washed since she'd been handling a pitchfork, gazing down absently in a way that Tarsy took for longing.

"Oh, poor Emily, I just don't know *how* you'll tolerate wearing black for a *whole year.* I would simply wither away and die if it were me. Maybe someday you can sneak up here and try on my pistachio gown after it's made up!"

Emily remained stone sober. "It's very nice, Tarsy, but I have to talk to you about something important."

"Important?" Tarsy's brow wrinkled delicately: what could be more important than a new gown of pistachio organdy for a soiree?

"Yes."

"Very well." Tarsy obediently laid the cloth aside and plunked onto the foot of the bed in a billow of pink skirts, her folded hands lost in her lap.

Emily dropped onto the tufted stool facing her friend, wondering how to begin.

"Well?" Tarsy's hands flashed, then disappeared once more into the folds of her skirt.

"I've decided not to marry Charles."

"Not to . . ." Tarsy's jaw dropped. Her eyes widened. "But, Emily, you and Charles are . . . are . . . well, heavens! You two simply go together . . . ham and eggs! Peaches and cream!"

"Not really."

"He's absolutely going to *die* when you tell him."

"He already knows."

"He does?"

"Yes."

"Well, what did he say?"

"He was very angry . . . and hurt."

"Well, I imagine so." Tarsy plucked fussily at the peaks of her skirt. "My goodness, you two have known each other forever. What reason did you give?"

"The true one, that I love him more as a brother than as a husband."

Tarsy considered, then lowered her voice to a conspiratorial whisper. "But how do you know, Emily, when you've never . . . I mean . . ." Tarsy shrugged and gave Emily an ingenuous gaze. "You never have . . ." Her head jutted forward. ". . . have you?"

Emily colored, but answered, "No."

"Well then, maybe you'd feel different." Hurriedly she added, "After you're married, I mean."

"No, I won't. I'm sure of it."

"But how do you know?"

"Because . . ." Emily clamped her palms between her knees and forged on. "I know now what it feels like when you really love somebody."

Tarsy's face lit like a gas jet. Her eyebrows shot up and her expression turned avid as she bent forward. "Oh, Emily . . . who?"

How ironic it felt to be confronting a woman of Tarsy's pulchritude: the ugly duckling telling the swan she had won the drake. Ironic and frightening. Emily's heart felt as if it would flop clear out of her body as she answered steadily, "Tom."

"Tom?" Tarsy repeated in a faint, colorless vice. Her face flattened and she straightened cautiously, reluctant to assimilate the truth.

"Yes, Tom."

"Tom Jeffcoat?" Tarsy's pretty mouth distorted.

"Yes."

"But he's—" She stopped herself just short of adding, *mine.* Nevertheless it reverberated in the air between the two women. Tension suddenly buzzed as Emily watched Tarsy struggle to understand. A gamut of reactions fleeted across her face—disbelief, doubt, and finally amusement. Flinging her arms high, Tarsy fell back onto the bed, throwing her breasts into prominence—a woman who believed she had no competition from this unfeminine, board-chested veterinarian who didn't know diddly-squat about charm, enticement, or flirting. What man would prefer a woman who boldly admitted hating housework and disdaining babies? Not that Tarsy herself was any too anxious to embrace either, but Tom would never guess the truth until she was comfortably sleeping in his bed nights.

"You? Oh, Emily . . ." Supine, Tarsy laughed at the ceiling till the mattress bounced. Then she braced up on an elbow, catching a jaw on one shoulder. Her blond hair cascaded over one arm and her bewitching eyes took on a gleam of confidence. "Emily, if you want a man like Tom Jeffcoat to notice you you'll have to trade your smelly boots for button-top shoes and learn to curl your hair and wear dresses instead of those wretched pants." Tarsy fell back onto both elbows, once again throwing her breasts into relief. She set her legs swinging and decided to be generous with her advice. "And it wouldn't hurt you to wear a corset that . . . well, you know . . . sort of helps you out a little up here. And as for admitting that you don't like housework and you don't want b—"

"I'm going to marry him, Tarsy."

Tarsy's legs stopped swinging. Her lips clamped shut and her face blanched. The room held a knotty silence before Emily continued as kindly as possible.

"I wanted to be the one to tell you before you found out from someone else, and chances are you would have the minute you left the house."

"You . . . marry Tom!" Tarsy snapped erect, her face pale. "Don't be absurd! Why the two of you couldn't recite the Pledge of Allegiance without fighting over it!"

"He asked me and I said yes. We told Charles together last night and the two of them had a terrible fistfight, which you're also bound to find out. I'm really sorry, Tarsy. We didn't mean to—"

"Why you two-faced, conniving bitch!" Tarsy shrieked, leaping off the bed. "How dare you!" She swung full-force, slapping Emily's face so hard it knocked her sideways, teetering the vanity stool.

Emily's heart contracted with shock and fright. Stunned, she righted herself on the seat and stared while Tarsy's face turned unattractively rubicund. "I wanted him and you knew it! You knew I planned to marry him and you plotted to get him from me all the while, didn't you! You *milked* me for *personal privileged* information!" Enraged, Tarsy threw herself around the bedroom while Emily, who never witnessed female anger of such magnitude, sat too stupefied to move. Gripping her temples, Tarsy raved, *"Urrrr! You low . . . cunning . . ."* She swung about abruptly, nosing Emily backward on the bench. "You let me tell you things I *never* would have told anyone else. *Never!"* Suddenly she backed off with a malevolent sneer, dropping her hands onto her hips. "Well, how's this for privileged information, Miss Judas Walcott! What I convinced you of a few months ago was nothing but a convenient lie. *You* may be a virgin, but I'm not! *I did it!* With your precious Tom Jeffcoat, who wouldn't take no for an answer! Take *that* to your wedding bed and sleep with it!" Reveling in her malevolence, Tarsy tossed her head and gave a spiteful laugh. "Go on, marry him and see if I care! If Tom Jeffcoat wants a freak who dresses like a man and smells like horse apples, he can have you! You're exactly what he deserves! Huh! You probably haven't got the right equipment to make him babies anyway!" Tarsy's expression turned hateful. "Now get out! . . . *Get out!"* She grabbed Emily's jacket and jerked her roughly to her feet, then thrust her through the doorway.

"Girls, girls, girls!" Mrs. Fields arrived, puffing, at the top of the stairs. "What's all this shouting about?"

"Out!" Tarsy screeched, shoving Emily past her mother, bumping her against the handrail and down two steps.

Emily grasped the rail to keep from tumbling to the bottom. "Tarsy, you're not being fair. I wanted us to talk about it and—"

"Don't you ever speak to me again! And you can tell that toad-sucking swine Tom Jeffcoat that I wouldn't cast him so much as a moldy crumb if he was starving to death at your kitchen table, which he'll be soon enough, since you don't know the first pathetic thing about cooking! But he'll learn that, too, won't he, along with the fact that all you care about is stupid animals! Well, go! What are you waiting for, standing there like a moron with your mouth hanging open. Get out of my house!"

Demoralized, Emily fled. Racing from Tarsy's yard, she gulped back tears and bit back tardy rejoinders, holding her hurt inside until she could find privacy to do her crying alone. But where? Fannie was at home. Papa was at their own livery.

She went to Tom's livery barn, inside the building with the sign on the door saying, "Closed for the day," into the familiar scent of hay and horses and liniment and leather, where she mounted the stairs to his loft and sank down into the hay. At first she sat as stoically as an Indian before a council fire, doubling her knees up tightly against her chest and hugging them hard in an effort to relieve the tight band of misery that seemed as if it would crack her ribs. She rocked in slight short thrusts, staring dry-eyed while the hurt pinched her vocal cords and stung her nose and throat. Deep within, minute trembles shook her belly and tensed her thighs. She pulled them tighter to her chest and, as the avalanche of misery descended, dropped her forehead to her knees.

She wept bitterly—hurt, degraded, demoralized.

I thought you were my friend, Tarsy. But friends don't hurt each other this way, not on purpose.

While racking sobs filled the hayloft and shook Emily's shoulders, she heard again and again Tarsy's abasing evaluation. A flat-chested freak who dresses like a man and smells like horse apples and probably hasn't got the right equipment to make babies anyway. A moron.

Hurt piled upon hurt as Emily realized Tarsy's friendship had been false all along. Today she had revealed her true feelings, but how many times had Tarsy secretly laughed behind her back, ridiculed, derided, probably even among their crowd of mutual friends?

But as if the vindictive assessment were not enough, Tarsy had exacted her revenge by imparting one last pernicious arrow, and this one aimed straight at Emily's heart.

She and Tom had been lovers after all.

Emily wept till her entire body hurt, until she fell to one side, clutched her belly, and curled into a tight, wretched ball. *Tarsy and Tom, together.* Why should it hurt so much to know? But it did. It did! Knowing was different from speculating. Oh, Tarsy, why did you tell me?

She wept until her entire frame ached from recoiling, until her face was swollen, her cheek raw from rubbing against the scratchy hay, and her stomach muscles hurt to be touched. When the worst was over she lay listless, shaken by leftover sobs, staring at her own limp hand lying knuckles-down in the hay. She closed her eyes, opened them again because, closed, they stung. How long had she been here? Long enough to be missed. But she remained, weighted by an apathy more immense than any she had experienced before, studying her hand, dully opening and closing her fingers for no reason that came to mind.

In time her thoughts clarified.

Perhaps the men's way was more civilized after all. A swift, clean fistfight would have been preferable to this insidious, long-term venom inflicted by Tarsy's words. Emily understood now why the men had fought. If it were possible she would do it herself, go back to Tarsy's and take ten smacks on the chin and crack a couple ribs, then go home and lick her wounds as the men were doing today. Instead, she would live for years festering with the knowledge of her own short-comings as a woman, and of Tom's sexual predilection for another. Emily sighed, closed her eyes, and rolled to her back, hands lax near her ears.

Tarsy, and Tom had been lovers.

Forget it.

How?

I don't know, but you must, or Tarsy will have won.

She has won and both us will know it on my wedding night.

She took her heartache to Fannie, whom she found in the kitchen, making chicken noodle soup.

"F—Fannie, can I talk to you?"

Fannie turned from the stove where she was dropping noodles into a pot of boiling broth.

Try though she might, Emily could not hold her tears back. They began falling as her face crumpled.

"Dearling, what is it?" Dusting off her hands, Fannie hurried toward Emily.

"Oh, Fannie ..." Emily went gratefully into the older woman's arms. "It's Tarsy." Some moments passed before Emily could continue. "I just came from her house. I told her I'm going to marry Tom and she ... she turned so hateful. Oh, Fannie, she sl—slapped me and c—called me the most awful names. I thought she was my f—friend."

"She was. She is."

Emily shook her head. "Not anymore. She said t—terrible things to me, things to deliberately hurt me."

Fannie's own heart ached for Emily. Holding her, she loved her with a maternal intensity, simply because she was Edwin's flesh and blood. She felt privileged to be able to share Edwin's children, even through such a painful ordeal as this.

"What did she say?"

Emily poured out her hurt, eliminating nothing. By the time she ended, her face and eyes were freshly swollen from weeping. "I just don't understand how she could have t—turned on me so. I know she loves Tom. I *know* that, and I was sorry to have to ... to hurt her, but the things she said to me were malicious, meant to inflict as much pain as they could."

"Ah, dearling, growing up is hard, isn't it?" Fannie cradled and rocked the young woman who, given other circumstances, might have been her own daughter. "So you've paid a price already for your love and you're asking yourself if he's worth it." She gently pushed Emily back to look into her streaming eyes. "Is he?" she inquired softly.

"I thought so ... before today."

"What you must do, dearling, is weigh the gain of him against the loss of Tarsy. You knew she would be hurt, didn't you, even before you told her?"

"Yes, but she had changed so much. I thought she'd grown up and become ... become ..." Emily found it hard to delineate the recent changes in Tarsy. "The way she helped at the funeral, the way she'd stopped dramatizing everything. I liked the new Tarsy. I thought I had a friend for life."

Fannie found a handkerchief and dried Emily's cheeks. "She's a woman spurned. Spurned women are dangerous creatures. And oddly enough, though you thought she had changed, I find her reaction quite in character. So she has unleashed her wrath on you, and called you names and hurt you with insinuations about herself and the man you love. The question is, what are you going to do about it?"

"Do?"

"You can believe her and let it eat inside you like a bad worm in a good apple. Or you can reason it through and come to grips with the fact that though Tom may have liked, even loved, Tarsy at one time, if he truly loves you now, it takes nothing away from that love. Nothing."

As the eyes of the two women locked, Fannie's words resounded in Emily's heart. Who should know better than Fannie about a man who had genuinely loved two women?

"I want you to do something for me," Fannie said, taking Emily's hand. "I want you to promise that the next time you're with Tom you won't confront him with this, that you'll give yourself at least a full day, maybe two, to decide if you even should. Will you do that for me?"

In a near-whisper Emily agreed, "Yes."

"And I want you to do one other thing."

"What?"

"Saddle a horse and go for a ride. You need it far more than you need chicken noodle soup right now."

Wishing to avoid her father and the questions her red eyes were sure to raise, Emily went back to Jeffcoat's Livery Stable and saddled Tom's buckskin, Buck. She led him outside into a noonish day that couldn't decide between sun and cloud. She buttoned her jacket high, stuffed her hair into Frankie's cap, drew on her soiled leather gloves, and mounted. Heading in the opposite direction of Edwin's livery stable, she circled through town and headed upland, walking Buck, which suited her mood.

Think of other things. Look around you—life goes on.

Ravens wheeled and cawed overhead, scolding the horse and rider while accompanying them up-mountain. A pair of unwary ermine came swiveling out of a deadfall, then scampered back beneath. Upon a frozen cactus paddle two black-capped chickadees whistled, perkily tilting their heads. The sound of Buck's hooves breaking the crust of snow cracked like pistol shots in the still cold day. The winter air felt cool upon Emily's hot face while the sun on her shoulders felt cool upon Emily's hot face while the sun on her shoulders felt warm. The greasewood trees hunkered close to the earth, tangles of black lace against the white, white snow. Beneath them deer had pawed away the snow, leaving great patches of exposed grass. Spires of brown grasstips speared up, connected by a network of mice tracks that looked like hieroglyphics on the snow. The ravens grew brazen and flapped nearer, their wings as black as Tom Jeffcoat's hair.

Undoubtedly Tarsy had run her fingers through it more than once.

Remember her rubbing against his pant leg while they played Poor Pussy? Remember them kissing during a forfeit and how his hands caressed her back? How long were they lovers? How often? If I'm not as good as she—and how can I be?—will he be disappointed and seek her out again?

Emily rode with her head hanging until her abstraction was interrupted by the sound of wind chimes.

Wind chimes?

She lifted her head at the same moment Buck stopped moving, and found herself at the edge of an upcountry meadow, and there before her grazed the straggling remnants of a buffalo herd. Few of the great beasts remained, and those that did were considered precious relics of the past. She'd never seen any this close and sat motionless, afraid of scaring them off. Pawing the snow, foraging beneath it, they presented their rumps until one old bull raised his head and assessed her with a wary black eye, warning the others. As one, they poised to run, ugly beasts, humped and hairy, their faces unlovable, their coats matted and tangled. But suddenly they moved in concert, trotting away, setting into motion hundreds of sparkling icicles that hung from their shaggy undersides and tinkled like an orchestra of wind chimes. The sun glanced off them, creating prisms while the sound drifted across the snowy meadow in a sweet glissando.

Emily heard it and her cares seemed momentarily lifted by finding the unexpected beauty in such an unlikely place.

She sat watching the buffalo until the chiming grew distant, then faded into silence.

Sighing heavily, unsure of what she faced the next time she saw Tom, Emily touched her heels to the warm flank beneath her and said, "Come on, Buck, let's go home."

Chapter 19

Tom waited all that day to hear from Emily, but he heard nothing. At three in the afternoon he rolled from his bed with all the speed and agility of an iceberg. Ohhh, sweet Savior, did it hurt. He sat on the edge of the mattress, eyes closed, breathing shallowly, trying to work up the courage to rise to his feet.

Next time you fight a man, make it someone punier than Charles Bliss.

Cautiously he creaked to his feet, standing with knees crooked, clutching the footrail of the bed while waiting for the meatgrinder to stop tenderizing his pectorals.

Damn you, Bliss, I hope you hurt as much as I do.

A shirt. Reach slow . . . one arm . . . second arm—Lord Almighty, something's tearing apart in there!

Eventually he got the shirt over his shoulders to find that, buttoning it, his hands ached. He glanced down: what pitiful knuckles—black and blue and swollen as dumplings. Donning his trousers and boots, he swore off fighting forever, but by the time he was halfway to his livery stable he'd begun to move easier.

Emily's note hung on the door: *Closed for the day.* He glanced back at Edwin's to find Charles standing out front, motionless, staring at him. Yesterday Tom would have raised a hand in greeting; today he forcibly tempered the urge. Seconds ticked past while the two men assessed one another, then Tom turned and went inside.

"Emily?" he called.

Only silence answered.

Was she at Edwin's stable? Had Charles been there with her only minutes ago? So what if he was? It was bound to happen if they all expected to live in this town together.

He glanced at the turntable, the stall whose door had been knocked open during the fight, the spot where Charles had sat, propped against the wall. A wave of regret struck Tom. Friends were precious commodities; it hurt like hell to lose one.

He did what paltry work he could, passing time until evening, but Emily remained strangely absent. He fed the horses their supper—slow as he was, it took twice as long as usual—and puttered around until well after nightfall, but still she hadn't shown her face. He considered the inevitable questions that would be raised by his bruised, swollen face. Finally, he went home, ate some bread and sausage, and went to bed.

He expected her to show up all the next day, but once again he was disappointed. In the evening on his way home from work he detoured by her house, stared at the lighted windows, and cursed under his breath for no reason he could name. Upon second thought, the reasons became very clear: he'd lost his best friend; the girl he loved was showing signs of withdrawal; and her father was openly displeased about their announced plans to marry.

Well, Edwin, you'd better get used to it, Tom thought defiantly, mounting the porch steps and knocking on the door.

Frankie answered, his mouth smeared with grease.

"Is Emily here?"

"She's eatin' supper."

"Would you call her, please?"

"Emileeeeee! Tom's here!" the boy bellowed, then inquired, "Are you really gonna marry her instead of Charles?"

"That's right."

"Then who's Charles gonna marry?"

Tom forced back a smile at the boy's simplistic inquiry: as if that were the full depth of the problem.

"I don't know, Frankie. I hope he finds somebody just as nice as your sister."

"You think she's *nice?*" The boy turned up his nose.

"Give yourself about three or four years and you'll discover she's not the only nice girl around here. You'll probably discover a dozen that'll turn your head."

"Hello, Tom," Emily greeted quietly, appearing silently and standing with her hands crossed upon her spine. She wore a simple, high-necked dress of unadorned black that emphasized the wan color of her face and the constrasting blackness of her lashes and eyebrows. Her hair was prettier than he ever recalled seeing it, caught back with combs—like curled midnight falling to her simple round collar. She appeared the quintessential woman in mourning, for she neither smiled nor fidgeted, but stood studying Tom with polite reticence.

"Hello, Emily." They stared at each other, Tom with the gut feeling that something was terribly amiss, not knowing what. "Sorry to interrupt your supper."

"That's all right." She glanced down at her brother. "Frankie, tell Papa and Fannie I won't be a minute."

"You're really gonna marry him instead of Charles?"

"Frankie, you're excused!"

The boy disappeared and Emily invited, "Come in," but her voice and eyes held cordiality in reserve.

Tom stepped inside and closed the door more carefully than necessary, taking the extra seconds to gather his own emotional equilibrium. He'd realized the moment she'd come around the corner that her displeasure with him was real. When he turned to face her again he knew that whatever was wrong went deep and strong in her. He felt a flash of apprehension that heated quickly into outright fore-boding as she stood prim and withdrawn and somber, with her hands folded demurely behind her back.

"How are you?" she inquired politely.

"Why didn't you come over after you talked to Tarsy?"

"I've been busy."

"All day yesterday and all day today?"

"I've been studying. I have to take a test on diseases of the nervous system in horses and it's hard to remember all the terms."

His troubled eyes sought and held hers. "Emily, what's wrong?"

"Nothing's wrong." But her glance fell and her lips drooped.

"What did Tarsy say?"

Emily brushed the top of the wainscot on the stub wall beside the door, studying her fingertips as she spoke. "What you'd expect. She was angry."

Tom reached out and took Emily's hand. "What did she say?"

"She showed me the door."

"I'm sorry."

Emily retrieved her hand, still with eyes averted. "I guess I should have expected it. She's not exactly the most tactful girl in the world, or the most mannerly."

"Emily, you haven't answered me. I want to know what she *said*. When you left me yesterday morning you were reasonably happy, and you said I'd see you after you talked to her. Now, two days later, I come to your door and you ask me 'how are you,' as politely as you'd ask Reverend Vasseler. And you won't look at me or let me hold your hand. Tarsy said something, I know she did. Now what was it?"

Emily's eyes, when they lifted to Tom, were filled with grave disappointment. "What would you think she'd say, Tom?"

He stared at her, frowning and puzzling for several seconds until he realized that whatever had passed between the two women would not be divulged by Emily. He straightened and announced stubbornly, "All right, I'll ask her myself."

"As you wish," Emily replied coolly.

Dread seized him. What had he done? What could have changed Emily so drastically in less than forty-eight hours? Relenting, he took her hand and stepped close, but she refused to raise her eyes. "Emily, don't be this way. Talk to me, tell me what's bothering you."

"I'd better get back to supper." Again she freed her hand and put distance between them.

"Will I see you tomorrow?"

"Probably."

"When? Where?"

"Well, I don't know, I—"

"Can I come here after supper? We could maybe go for a walk, or a ride."

"Fine," she agreed unenthusiastically.

"Emily . . ." But he was lost, forlorn, without a clue as to his wrongdoing. He approached her once more and took her shoulders as if to lean down and kiss her, but at that moment Edwin spoke from the far end of the parlor. "Your supper is getting cold, Emily."

Tom sighed, put-upon, and dropped his hands from Emily. He set the edges of his teeth together and studied his fiancée with growing dissatisfaction, then stepped forward where Edwin could see him.

"Good evening, sir," he said, formally.

"Tom."

"I just stopped by to say hello to Emily."

"Yes—well, it's suppertime." Edwin flapped a white napkin toward the dining room behind him and admonished his daughter, "Emily, don't be long."

When he had returned to his meal Emily whispered, "You'd better go, Tom."

His patience suddenly snapped and he made little effort to hide the fact. Stepping back, he gave his hat brim an irritated jerk and said, "All right, goddammit, I'm going!" The porch door opened with enough force to suck dustballs outside, then slammed behind him with equal force. His footsteps pounded across the porch floor as he clunked away, unkissed, unwelcomed, royally pissed off and scared to boot.

What had happened? What the hell had happened? Stalking down the snow-packed path Tom felt his irritation mount. Women! Emily was the last one he'd expect to act like a sulky brat without explaining why. Two days ago he'd fought for her and he thought he'd won her, but she had grown as tepid as second-round bathwater. Something had happened to change her, and if not Tarsy, what else?

Goddamn that Tarsy! Tom took a decisive right-face at the street. She'd said *something* and he aimed to find out what!

Several minutes later, when he knocked on Tarsy's door, the reverberations shook the entire wall. Tarsy herself answered, but she hadn't opened the door two feet before she saw who stood on the porch and tried to slam it again. Tom wedged his foot inside and grabbed Tarsy's wrist.

"I want to talk to you," he informed her in a voice harsh and flat with warning. "Get your coat and get out here."

"You can go straight to hell on a saw blade!"

"Get your coat, I said!"

"Let go of my wrist, you're hurting me!"

"So help me God, I'll break it if you don't get out here!"

"Let go!"

He yanked her so hard her head snapped. "All right, you can freeze!" Effortlessly he whirled her out onto the dark porch and slammed the door, planting himself before it.

"Now, talk," he ordered threateningly.

"You bastard!" She slapped him so hard his head hit the doorframe and his ears rang. "You scum-sucking, two-timing peckerwood!" She kicked his shin.

Recovering from surprise he caught her by both forearms and crossed them on her chest as he threw her against the cold wall. "You're some lady, you know that, Tarsy?" he sneered, nose to nose with her.

"You don't want a lady, and you know it, Jeffcoat. You want something that dresses like a muleskinner and smell like horse shit! Well, you've got her and you can have her! She's the saddest excuse for a female this town's ever seen and I hope the two of you dry up and wither away together!"

"Watch it, Tarsy, 'cause I'm just one step away from giving you a sample of what I gave Charles the other night. Now, what did you say to Emily?"

Tarsy bared her lips in a parody of a smile. She lifted her chin and her eyes glittered with vindictiveness. "What's the matter, lover boy, isn't she so eager to let you paw her anymore? Won't she unbutton her pantaloons, or does she wear a union suit like the boys?"

He thrust her arms so tightly against her that stitches popped in her sleeves. "You're taking about the woman I'm going to marry, and you'd do well to remember that men don't marry the ones who let men paw them."

Tarsy's nostrils flared. "And maybe you'll find out women don't marry men who sample others."

"You told her that!"

"Why not? It might as well be true. There were plenty of times you wanted to."

"Why, you lying little bitch," he ground out through clenched teeth.

"You wanted to, Jeffcoat," she goaded with malicious satisfaction. "A dozen times you touched me like I never let any other man touch me, and you loved it. You got so hot I could see steam rising from your pants—so what's the difference? You know my body better than you'll ever know hers, and I'm not about to let her forget it, not after she stabbed me in the back. I wanted to marry you, you philanderer! Marry you, you hear!" Tarsy shouted, her eyes fiery with rage. "Well, if I can't have you nobody else can either. Just wait and see what you get out of her on your wedding night!"

Tom had never hated any living being with such pagan intensity. It built within him like lava heating, boiling toward the surface, bringing the overwhelming wish to punish. But she was dirt—not worth bruising his knuckles upon. He dropped his hands, unable to bear touching her a moment longer.

"You know," he remarked quietly, "I pity the poor sap who gets snagged by you. That won't be a marriage, it'll be a life sentence."

"Ha!" she barked. "At least he'll know he's in bed with a woman!"

"Quiet!" Tom's mood changed abruptly from belligerent to wary as he cocked an ear toward town, listening.

"Can't you take—"

"Quiet, I said!" His fight with Tarsy ended as swiftly as it had begun. "Listen!" He turned toward the porch steps and peered into the darkness. "Did you hear that?"

"Hear what?"

"There it is again . . . bells. And shouting."

The sounds drifted up from the town below, a churchbell, ringing clamorously, and the faint faraway accompaniment of distraught shouting. Tom moved to the top of the porch steps and waited, tense, staring out into the sky over the town below.

"Oh, my God," he whispered. "Fire."

"Fire?"

He launched himself into thin air, sailed above five porch steps, and hit the yard running. "Tell your father! Hurry!"

He neither waited nor cared if Tarsy followed. Instincts took over and he hurtled pell-mell across the yard toward the street, and on toward the business section of town where already a telltale orange glow had begun lighting the sky. *Whose place? Whose place?* If it wasn't on Grinnell Street, it was damned close. Propelled by adrenaline, he raced, ignoring the pain that jarred his ribs with each thud of his heels on the frozen roads. His heart hammered. His throat hurt. He plummeted downhill, feeling the street drop beneath him until the houses cut off his view of the horizon and he lost sight of the pale golden dome blooming in the nighttime sky.

Ahead, panicked voices shrilled. *"Fire! Fire!"* The frantic ringing of a second bell joined the first. Around Tom, house doors opened and people spilled into yards and began running almost as if mesmerized, without stopping for coats. "Whose is it?" everyone asked, their voices jarred by the impact of barreling downhill.

I don't know. Tom didn't know if he answered aloud or only in his thoughts. His legs churned like steel drivers. His eyeballs dried. His lungs burned.

The man behind him fell off to begin throwing open doors along Burkitt Street, shouting into houses. Somewhere the faint *ting* of a dinner triangle joined the *clong* of the churchbells, but Tom scarcely heard. Nearing the foot of Burkitt Street, he joined a mass of others who had been galvanized into motion with the same abruptness as himself. Footsteps thundered louder, growing in number as the crowd approached Main Street, where runners funneled together and bumped one another like a stampeding herd.

Whose place? Whose place?

The throng sailed past the Windsor Hotel, joined by a quintet of men running out the door with their arms full of blankets, and a contingent of women carrying buckets. "Looks like one of the liveries."

Some ran too hard to voice speculation. Others puffed along, trailing the word that seemed to taint the very air Tom sucked in as he raced.

Liveries!

Through a haze of fear and the roaring of his own pulse he caught other scraps of words . . . she's a big one . . . it's got to be hay . . .

From three blocks away he smelled it. From two blocks away he knew it wasn't Edwin's place. From the corner of Grinnell Street he saw the flames already eating the sides of his own livery stable.

Oh Jesus, no!

"Get the horses!" he screamed from a hundred yards away, racing wildly. *"I got a pregnant mare in there!"* Ahead, figures appeared like charred stick-men as they scurried before the burning building, filling buckets, forming a brigade, pumping at the cistern out front. The red fire wagon, with its trio of bells clanging, bounced along the frozen ruts ahead of Tom, pulled by running men because it would have taken more time to hitch the horses than to tow it manually the two blocks from its storage shed. He passed it and arrived in the tumult just as someone led Buck out. The stallion reared in fright while the man fought to calm him and lead him to safety.

Tom screamed frantically, "My mare! Did anybody get my mare out!"

"No! No mares! Only this stallion so far!"

Another voice yelled, "Man the pumps! Stretch that hose out!" A dozen volunteers gripped the handles of the old Union fire rig, but she was an ancient side-stroke pumper, built in 1853, and scarcely up to the day's standards. As the paltry jet of water fell from her hose Tom shouted at the fire crew, "Aim the water to the right. The mare is in the third stall!"

Another voice bellowed, "Pump, boys, pump!"

On either side of the fire wagon men worked furiously on the wooden handles. Horses whinnied in terror. Men shouted orders. Dogs barked. Women formed a bucket brigade to refill the tank on the old Union pump while others held their children back to watch from a distance.

"Who's getting my horses! Is anybody getting my horses!"

"Easy, boy . . . it's gotten too—"

"Get your hands off me!" Tom tore a blanket from one of the hotel contingent and ran toward the hose men, yelling, "Wet me down! I'm going in!"

The pump had gathered enough force to set him back a step as the stream of water hit him in the chest. A man grabbed his arm, momentarily blocking the spray. It was Charles.

"Tom, you can't!"

For a split second Tom's eyes flashed hatred. "Goddamn you, Charles, you didn't need to do this! Goddamn you to hell!" Tom shouldered past him, roughly bumping him aside. "Get out of my way!"

"Tom, wait!"

Emily and Edwin appeared in the confusion, grasping Tom's elbows, pleading and warning, but he knocked all hands aside and dashed into the flaming barn.

Behind him, Charles ordered, "Give me one of those blankets!"

"Don't be foolish, boy—"

"Edwin, you do what you want, but I can't let those animals die without trying to help them! Gimme some water, Murphy!"

"Papa, let me go!" Emily screamed, fighting Edwin's hands as she, to, struggled to get a blanket.

"Get to the pump!" he ordered her. "You'll be no help to him dead! Get to the pump and help the women!"

"But Buck is in there and—"

"They got Buck out!"

"—and Patty. Papa, she's in foal!"

"Emily, use some sense! Go get your medicine bag. If they get any more horses out, they'll need it. Then get to the pump with Fannie and keep that water running! Wet down more blankets! I'm going in, too!"

"Papa!" She caught his hand. In the midst of the chaos they exchanged frightened glances. "Be careful."

He squeezed her hand and ran.

Inside, Tom hunkered beneath the wet blanket, running through a sea of smoke. Immediately his eyes smarted and teared, blinding him further. Water splattered around him, sizzling as it struck flaming wood. Sweet Jesus, the beams were already burning and spreading along the loft floor. The stench of scorched leather, wood, and dung stung his nose. He swabbed his eyes with a corner of the sopped blanket, then plastered it over his face. Squinting, he made out the outline of his pride and joy, a new Studebaker carriage standing on the turntable as he'd left it. A chunk of flaming debris fell from above onto its leather bonnet. Surrounded by the terrified shrieks of horses and the thumps of their hooves he forgot about everything that was not flesh and blood. Down one bank of stalls he ran, throwing doors open, yelling. "Git! Git! Hyah! Hyah!" Back up the other side, forgetting about singling out any particular animal. Behind him some of the terrified horses balked at leaving their stalls or milled about, afraid of moving toward the fire surrounding the exits. He threw open the last stall door and charged inside only to be flattened against the wall by a muddled, wild-eyed mare named Bess who tried to turn around in the narrow space. He flung the blanket over Bess's head and, clutching it in a clump beneath her jaw, dragged the animal forward. Terrified, Bess braced her forelegs and whinnied.

"Goddamn it, Bess, you're comin' if I have to drag you!"

An immense roar rose—hay igniting somewhere, filling his ears like a hurricane. He stretched out a leg and kicked Bess hard in the groin. She fishtailed violently, then reared high, swinging Tom clear off his feet as he gripped the blanket. His ankles slammed against the wall. But when he landed, still clutching the wet wool, Bess followed at a frenzied trot.

He burst from the burning building already tearing the blanket off the horse. "Water!" he shouted. "More water here!" As the spray fanned over him he removed his leather hat and doused his hair, then slammed the hat back on and lowered his hands to fill his gloves. Turning, shrouded again by the blanket, he headed back into the barn with the jet pelting his back, running in an icy river down his plaster cast.

Ten feet inside the barn, he collided with Charles coming out. "I got Hank!"

Charles shouted above the roar, leading a dun saddlehorse. "You've got time to get one more but that's all!"

Tom plunged into the wall of heat and light. Running, he sucked hard against the blanket, but even through it he breathed and tasted acrid smoke and singed wool. It burned all the way to his lungs until they felt as if they would explode. Through stinging, watering eyes, he searched and found a frantic Rex who, thankfully, followed him without resisting. But by the time he got Rex outside he turned back to watch a rafter at the far end of the building collapse in a roaring golden rain of sparks that changed swiftly to a white sheet of flame. Emily rushed forward to take Rex.

"Don't go back in, Tom, please!"

"Patty!"

"Leave her! You won't make it!"

"One more trip!"

"No!" She grabbed his arm but he lurched free, heading back inside.

"Water!" she shrieked maniacally, watching him go. "Give him water!"

Sucking in his last clear air Tom flung the blanket over his head and bent low, heading inside. Five feet from the door someone tackled him from behind. He rolled through the dirt and came up kneeling, incensed, facing Charles, who was picking himself up from the ground.

"Sonofabitch, Bliss, what're you doing!"

"You're not going back in!"

"The hell I'm not."

"You do and she'll be a widow before she's a bride!"

"Then take good care of her for me!" Tom shouted, bolting into the conflagration before Charles could stop him. Emily witnessed the exchange biting back tears. She watched helplessly as Tom disappeared into the flames; then to her horror, Charles turned and yelled back at the hose men, "Train 'er right on my back!"

His call jolted Emily out of her stupor. "Charles! No!" she called, straining forward only to be dragged back by Andrew Dehart, who'd appeared with his waterwagon to help fight the fire.

"Don't be foolish, girl!"

"Oh God, not Charles, too," Emily despaired, flattening her mouth with the palms of both dirty hands. But Charles ran into the inferno trailed by a puny jet of water.

"You got a horse who could use a little attention," Dehart reminded her, and she grimly forced herself to turn back to Rex, who had a gash on his withers and a raw burned patch on his rump. Someone called from nearby, "Got one over here that needs your help, too, Emily!" Suddenly it seemed that everyone needed her at once. With fear gripping her throat, she immersed herself in duty, substituting efficiency for tears, dusting burns with boric acid, applying pineoleum to others, even slapping a quick bandage on a burned arm in between animals. The pregnant mare showed up, led by Patrick Haberkorn, but she was burned badly, demented with pain, wild-eyed and sidestepping in terror.

"Get Tom!" Emily ordered, grabbing Patty's bridle, already realizing she'd have to be put down.

"I don't know where he is."

"But he went in after her!"

"She ran out on her own."

Patty shrieked in pain, rearing back and yanking Emily off-balance. She stared at Patrick's soot-streaked face, feeling hysteria threaten. The fire leapt and licked the sky fifty feet above the barn. It lit the night to a blinding brilliance. It burned the skin and dried the eyes and turned faces into orange caricatures of gaping awe. The mare whinnied again, reminding Emily of her responsibility.

"Get me a gun," she ordered dully.

Fannie cane running up just then, frantic. "Your father—have you seen him?"

Emily turned to Fannie, feeling as if a winch had tightened about her throat. "Papa?"

"Didn't he come back out?"

"I don't know."

Patrick was handing her a pistol and she could only handle one emergency at a time. Emily took the gun, put it to the mare's head, and pulled the trigger. She closed her eyes even before the dull thud sounded, and turned away from the sickening sound of the mare's last reedy breath. Opening her eyes, she saw Fannie facing the inferno and moved to take her hand and watch it, too. Flames erupted through the roof, sending a section of it dropping into the hayloft. An explosion of sound lifted into the night as another section of hay ignited. In a shocked, disbelieving voice, she said, "Oh God, Fannie, Tom's in there, too."

Watching tragedy occur before their very eyes, the two women stood helplessly, gripping one another's hands. The heat scorched their faces. Tears and heat waves distorted their view of the awesome, shimmering spectacle, which danced and wavered against the night sky.

Men formed a cordon, pressing the crowd a safe distance away. "Get back . . . get back!" Emily and Fannie stumbled backward dumbly. At some time during their vigil Frankie appeared, his eyes immense with fright. "Where's Pa?" he asked dubiously, slipping his small hand into his sister's, staring at the inferno.

"Oh, Frankie," she despaired, dropping to her knees and wrapping both arms around him. She pressed her cheek to his and held him hard, their faces lit by the blaze. She felt him swallow, felt his jaw slacken as he stared at the awesome spectacle before them.

"Pa?" the boy appealed quietly, his body absolutely still.

Emily's throat filled, her eyes smarted, and she hugged Frank harder. Hot tears rolled from her eyes, evaporated by the intense heat before they reached her chin. Beside her, Fannie stared dully at the flames, crying without moving a muscle.

In the chaos around them none of the three heard Edwin until he called breathlessly behind them.

"Fannie? Emily?"

As one, they spun.

"Pa!"

"Papa!"

"Edwin!"

Frankie catapulted into his father's arms, bawling. Emily flung a stranglehold about his neck while Fannie took two halting steps toward him, covered her mouth, and began sobbing as she had not when she'd thought Edwin lost.

"Pa! Pa! We thought you was in there," Frankie cried while he and his sister clutched Edwin's filthy neck.

He gave a choked, emotional laugh. "I led two horses out the rear door and took them down to our own paddock."

"Oh, Papa!" Emily couldn't quit saying the word.

Still holding Frankie on one arm, he circled her with the other.

"I'm all right," he whispered thickly. "I'm all right." He looked beyond his clinging children to find Fannie still standing with eyes streaming, mouth covered tightly.

"You thought so, too?" he asked, fading out of his children's embraces. He opened his arms and Fannie came into them.

"Thank God," she whispered, closing her eyes against his soot-covered cheek. "Oh, Edwin, I thought I had lost you."

His hand covered her hair and he held her fast against him, little caring that a circle of curious gazes were directed their way as dozens of townspeople witnessed their unguarded embrace. Fannie was the first to pull back, with concern furrowing her brow. "Edwin, did you see Tom or Charles come out the other side?"

Edwin's attention swerved to the structure, which by now had begun to crumble in upon itself. Even the pump men had stopped their helpless firefighting. Those manning the hose held it lifelessly while mere drips of water fell from its nozzle. At the cistern the women's hands rested inertly upon the steel pumphandle, which had turned lukewarm from the intense heat. At their feet pails sat, filled but unused.

Edwin gulped and murmured, "Dear God."

Emily and Frank stood motionless at his side, holding hands tenaciously, staring at the fire.

At that instant someone called, "Emily, come quick!" It was the hotel owner, Helstrom, gesturing frantically, then taking Emily's arm and dragging her with him. "Around back. Those two men o' yours are out there in a pile!"

Everybody ran—Emily, Edwin, Fannie, and Frank, trailed by a string of others, following Helstrom through the pole gate, around the paddock, to the rear of the building where a knot of men knelt over a sodden heap containing the inert bodies of Tom and Charles. Tangled in wet blankets, the pair lay sprawled on the ground, their eyes closed, their faces streaked and filthy. Doc Steele was already there kneeling beside Tom, opening his bag. Emily skidded to her knees beside him.

"Are they alive?"

Steele pulled up one of Tom's eyelids, popped a stethescope in his ears, and listened intently. "Jeffcoat is. His breathing is bad though. Must've taken in a lot of smoke. Bring snow!" he called, already beginning a cursory inspection—from Tom's tangled wet hair, which had been protected by a wide leather Stetson; to his midsection, wrapped in wet plaster as effective as asbestos; down his trunk and thighs, which had been covered by heavy sheepskin whose natural fur lining had absorbed a protective barrier of water. Even the narrow space between it and his calf-high leather boots had come through unscathed. Steele assessed it all, then pulled off Tom's gloves, inspected his hands, and pronounced, "I'll be damned. Not a burn on him, nothing but singed eyebrows."

While Steele shifted his attention to Charles, Emily knelt over Tom, still overtly concerned about his breathing. Even without the benefit of a stethoscope she heard the strident hiss accompanying each breath, and saw with what effort his lungs labored.

Don't die . . . don't die . . . keep breathing . . . I'm sorry . . . I love you . . .

Behind her, Doc Steel's voice announced, "Bliss is in no grave danger. His hands got burned, though. Where's that snow?"

Charles! How could Emily have forgotten Charles? She turned to find him lying on his back, staring at the stars with his hands being submerged in two overturned pails of snow. When she leaned over his face he smiled weakly.

"Hiya, Em," he whispered.

"Hiya, Charles," she returned chokily, gulping back a knot of emotion. "How're you doing?"

"I'm not too sure." He lifted one limp hand to test his face, dropping clumps of snow onto it. "Think I'm still alive."

She gently pushed his arm down. "Your hands are burned. You'd best keep them in the snow until Dr. Steele can dress them." She tenderly brushed the snow from his cheek and, in a voice that trembled on the brink of tears, scolded affectionately, "You dear, foolish man—where were your gloves?"

"I didn't stop to think."

"You two are getting to be a lot of trouble, you know, always needing patching up in the middle of the night."

He smiled wanly and let his eyes drift closed. "Yeah, I know. How is he?"

"He's still breathing, no burns, but he's unconscious. Who brought who out?"

He opened his eyes again, wearily. "Does it matter?"

So she knew it was Charles who had carried Tom out. She struggled with a heartful of gratitude and lost the battle to contain her tears. "Thank you, Charles," she whispered, bending low, kissing his forehead.

As she straightened he said in a cracky voice, "Em?"

She couldn't speak through the lump in her throat, could only gaze at him through the tears that distorted his beloved, sooty face with its singed beard and red-rimmed eyes.

"He thinks I set the fire. Tell him I didn't. Will you tell him—"

"Shh." She touched his lips.

"But you've got to tell him."

"I will as soon as he wakes up."

"He's going to, isn't he, Em? He isn't going to die." Tears leaked from the corners of Charles's eyes, washing a pair of white paths as they fell down his temples. Suddenly Charles rolled to one side and grabbed Tom's thick jacket sleeve, dragging himself closer to the unconscious man. "Tom, I didn't do it, you hear me? Don't you die without listening to me! Jeffcoat, damn you, d—don't you dare d—die!"

As Charles's strength gave out he fell back, sobbing, with an arm thrown over his eyes. His chest heaved pitifully. Snow dripped from his fingertips.

Fresh tears stung Emily's eyes as she leaned over, shielding him from the curious stares of others.

Oh, Charles, my dear, dear Charles. I don't think I've ever loved you more than I do at this moment.

Doc's voice intruded. "Let me at that man's hands and somebody get Jeffcoat inside under some warm blankets."

Within minutes Charles's hands were dressed—the worst burns on their backs—and the two men were loaded on wagons. Watching the rig take Charles away, Emily felt heartsick, but Tom lay stretched on the second wagon bed, unconscious, and his fate still hung in the balance.

As the wagon rolled through the night, its riders remained respectfully silent. The stench of smoke hung over the town and children were being slowly herded home by their mothers.

At Tom's house a group of somber volunteers carried him inside, laid him on his bed, and nodded to Emily as they filed out. Her father came last.

"I'll be staying," she told him quietly, "to see after him until he's better."

Edwin's sad, loving eyes rested on Emily's.

"Yes, I know," he said, accepting her decision without dissent.

"And I'll be marrying him as soon as he's strong enough to stand on two feet."

"Yes, I know."

"Papa—"

"Sweetheart—" She was in his arms before the endearment had cleared his lips. More tears—hot, and healing—wrinkled the world she saw beyond Edwin's shoulder.

"I'm so damned sorry," he managed in a broken voice.

"Oh, Papa, I love him so much. He's just got to live."

"He will."

She sniffled and clung to his familiar bulk. His arms—oh, his wonderful reassuring father's arms—how substantial they felt and how badly she needed them at this moment. She may have defied him, but she had never stopped needing his comfort, friendship, and approval. Without them she had been miserable. "I thought I was going to have to chose between you and I didn't know what I was g—going to do without you."

"You won't have to worry about it anymore. I'm a stubborn old fool—Fannie made me see that. But you won't hear another word out of me. You're getting a good man. I knew it all the time, but I was too ornery to say so. I'm sorry I said those things the other night."

She squeezed him harder, feeling as if she had just emerged from shadow into sun.

"You're the best father there ever was."

He crushed her against him, then drew back, clearing his throat self-consciously while she wiped her eyes with a sleeve.

"Well ..." Edwin said.

"Yes ... well ..."

Neither of them knew how to end the delicate moment.

Finally Emily asked, "Will you send Frankie back with some clean things for me?"

"I'll do better than that. I'll bring them myself as soon as I make sure Charles is settled. They took him to our place, you know. Fannie insisted."

"Good. He deserves the best."

Edwin caught one of her dirty hands and raised it to his lips. "I'm afraid the best has been taken by someone else, though."

"Oh, Papa."

"You'd better go see after your young man," Edwin said, dangerously close to getting emotional again.

She pecked him on the cheek in a fond farewell. "And you'd better take a bath. You stink."

Chapter 20

Closing the door behind Edwin, Emily stared at it exhaustedly. The bedroom seemed miles away. Her shoulders ached, her eyes burned, her throat felt parched and raw, but she forced her feet to move. In Tom's bedroom doorway she paused, studying his still form on the bed, holding her breath and listening to his. It sounded grainy and labored, no better than before. When he inhaled, an invisible wind whistle seemed to play in his throat. When he exhaled, his breath was accompanied by a rattling wheeze.

She stood at his bedside and studied him despondently, tempted to cry, realizing that to do so would serve no purpose. If only there were some way she could help. But Doc Steele had said, "There's nothing we can do for his lungs—either they'll make it or they won't. Clean him up some. Keep him warm. Keep the windows closed because the town is full of smoke. If he wakes up, feed him lightly. A resting body doesn't need much nourishment, it lives off its own fat."

Clean him up some, keep him warm. It seemed too little to do when you loved someone this much and had rebuffed him the last time the two of you had spoken.

She knelt and touched her lips to his dirty right hand. *Don't you die, Tom Jeffcoat, do you hear me? If you die, I'll never forgive you.*

When she'd spent another bout of useless emotionalism, she pushed herself heavily to her feet and went to the kitchen, built up the fire, and drew warm water from the reservoir. Carrying a basin, she returned to the bedroom to bathe Tom.

She did so lovingly, with no burdening sense of impropriety. Instead, she felt entitled, for she loved him wholly and would—if he lived—see after his welfare for the remainder of their lives. She washed his face, with its motionless eyelids and its poor bruised features, cataloging each, praying that she might see that face on the adjacent pillow each morning for the rest of her life, that she might watch it take on years and creases and character as the two of them aged together.

She washed his long-fingered, calloused, limp hands, which would know all of her in all ways, would stroke her skin in passion and rub her tired back when she grew weary, would hold their children someday, and, with his forefathers' anvil and eight surviving horses, would provide for them all through years to come.

She washed his arms and chest—broad chest, sturdy arms—above a fringe of dirty white plaster, and paused with her hand upon his slow and regular heartbeat, then kissed him there for the first time ever.

She washed his long legs and feet, which would carry him down an aisle with her, and over a threshold, and into this room one fine, wondrous wedding day soon.

They would, oh, they would.

And when he was clean, she covered him to the neck, then dragged his oversized kitchen rocker into the room, dropped heavily upon it, and slumped forward across the bed near his hip.

Edwin found her that way when he returned with her clean clothes—exhausted and haggard and dirty, but he hadn't the heart to awaken her. Leaving her clothes nearby, he tiptoed from the house with a heavy heart and a prayer for Tom Jeffcoat's safe delivery back to consciousness.

Emily awakened later at the sound of Tom stirring. She leapt to her feet and leaned above him, gazing into his unfocused eyes. "You're going to be all right, Tom," she whispered, taking his hand.

"Em'ly?" he croaked. His heels shifted restlessly against the sheets and he seemed to be searching for the source of her voice.

"Yes, Tom, I'm here."

His bleary eyes found her. His left index finger crooked against his soiled white plaster wrap as if trying to coax the rest of the unwilling hand to lift. He managed only two words in the same pathetic croak as before: "She lied."

"Tom?" Emily called anxiously, bending even closer. "Tom?"

But he had already slipped back into oblivion, leaving her with no opportunity to apologize or reassure. Disappointed and worried, she perched on the chair, holding his unresponsive hand. He had been through such hell. He had fought a fire that he believed was set by his best friend. He had lost his barn, some of his stock, and his livelihood. He had suffered shock and physical damage enough to put him in a state of unconsciousness. Yet through it all his chief worry was that he might lose her because of Tarsy's lies.

Emily's unwanted tears started again, stinging like a douse of kerosene in her poor maltreated eyes.

I'm sorry, I believed her, Tom. I should have known Tarsy would use any means available to get satisfaction—honest or dishonest. Please get well so I can marry you and we can put all this strife behind us.

In Edwin Walcott's home the baths were done, the invalid bedded down, the boy long asleep, and the place blissfully quiet. Dressed in a nightshirt, Edwin stepped from his bedroom and crossed the hall to rap quietly on his daughter's bedroom door.

"Come in," Fannie called softly.

He opened the door and stood framed within it, motionless. Fannie sat at a vanity table glancing back over her shoulder. She wore a dressing gown of pale blue scattered with violets, belted at the waist. Her hair—wet—trailed down her back; her hand—poised—held a tortoiseshell comb.

"Come in, Edwin," she repeated, swiveling to face him, dropping the hand to her lap.

"I just came to say good night and to thank you for having the bath water all hot. It felt wonderful."

"Yes, it did, didn't it? But there's no need to thank me." She smiled serenely, her eyes lingering on his wet hair, rilled with fresh comb tracks, his shiny forehead and the brushed beard, whose attractiveness still took her by surprise each time she saw it. It created the perfect frame for his lips, making him appear the more highly colored when contrasted against the dark facial hair, more soft for the beard's crisp outline. It complemented, too, his dark, dear eyes.

"You must be very tired."

"I am." He smiled softly. "You?"

"No. Just thinking."

"About what?"

"About the children—Tom and Emily. You gave Emily your consent to stay there, didn't you?"

Leaving the door discreetly open, Edwin wandered in and, while he spoke, touched things—incidental things—a picture on the wall, the back of a chair, the knob on a bureau. "It seemed ridiculous not to. She would have stayed in any case."

"She's very much in love with him, Edwin."

"Yes, I know. She says she'll marry him as soon as he can stand on two legs."

"And you gave her your consent for that, too?"

"She didn't ask for it. She's a grown woman. I guess it's time I treated her like one."

"Yes, of course you're right. And after what they've been through who in Sheridan would dare point a finger?"

Edwin gave up his distractions to study Fannie across the room, hoping the same thing was true regarding the two of them. In the lamplight her wet hair gleamed like liquid copper. Edwin thought he could smell it clear across the room, it and the lilac soap with which she'd bathed. The bodice of her dressing gown revealed a narrow wedge of bare throat, and as she dragged a fallen tress behind her ear her sleeve fell back, baring one fine white arm, lightly peppered with freckles. She was lovely and warm and all the things he had ever desired. But Edwin repressed the urge to cross to her, though he could not resist talking, staying—just a while longer.

"You were thinking about us, too, weren't you?"

"Yes."

"What about us?"

She considered momentarily, dropping her gaze as she placed the comb on the vanity behind her, then returning her uplifted eyes to him and tucking her hands between her knees. "About what I'd have done if I'd lost you."

"But you didn't. I'm still very much alive and unharmed."

"Yes," she replied in the most dulcet of tones, letting the word drift winsomely before adding, "I see."

She studied him unwaveringly, this man she loved: scrubbed, shiny, masculine, and decidedly less than decent in only a nightshirt and bare feet. If he had come here to test her he was succeeding with little effort. She could no more turn him away than she could have stopped tonight's fire. "Is that what you always sleep in?"

"No. Not always." The striped garment reached Edwin's mid-calf. "My underware got sooty and wet. I left it in the tub downstairs."

"I didn't think I remembered ever washing that before." She let her eyes trail down to his naked toes and back up. From across the room she thought she saw his cheeks take on color above the crisp, dark border of his beard.

When she spoke again, her tranquil voice held no coquetry, only an abiding certainty that what she was suggesting was right and deserved. "Why don't you close the door, Edwin?"

She saw him carefully bank his surprise. Their gazes locked and the universe seemed devoid of all creatures save them. Then he closed the door—without haste, without sound—and turned, lifting his gaze to her as he crossed the room. She followed with her eyes, lifting her face as he neared and paused before her. For moments he stood motionless, his eyes delving into hers. At length he reached out to stroke her damp hair back from her face, which he tipped to a sharp angle.

"It'll be tonight then?" he asked simply.

"Yes, darling, tonight."

Leaning low, he kissed her dear mouth, a tender, fleeting touch; likewise, her left eyelid, her right, and each cheek. His heart repeated a cadence it had known only years ago, when they were both young and raring but had banked their urges as all properly raised children were taught to do. So many years ago. So many mistakes ago. He drew back to question softly, "Because you almost lost me?"

"Because I almost lost you. And because life is precious and we've squandered too much of ours."

Again he covered her mouth with his own and drew her up by the jaws, the kiss a gentle thing of rediscovery. In time he urged her lips apart and tasted her fully, still holding her jaws, for to touch her anywhere else would be to rush his sweet reunion for which they had waited so long. Scarcely lifting his head, he murmured, "We have a houseguest."

"He's asleep."

"And Frankie."

"He's asleep, too, though I believe I should not care if either of them opened the door this moment and walked in. Oh, Edwin, my heart has been yours too long without making it official."

"I love you, Fannie Cooper. I've loved you longer than I've loved any other human being on this earth."

"And I love you, Edwin Walcott . . . as much as I might have loved any husband, any father of my children, which in my heart you always were. I love you unconditionally . . . shamelessly."

"Oh, Fanny, Fannie." His voice grew ardent with passion and he strewed fevered kisses across her face and throat. "We should have done this years ago."

"I know."

He bracketed her breasts; their swells filled his hands as he kissed her again with a lifetime's restraints at last abandoned. As their tongues joined, he found the twist of her belt and freed it straightaway, slipping both hands inside and caressing her through a thin muslin nightgown—breasts, buttocks, spine—then settling her against his hips to discover that their bodies blended as he remembered. Abruptly he drew back. "Let me take this off." As his hands rose, so did hers, and he removed her garments in one clean sweep, relegating them to a puddle at her ankles. "Ohh . . . Fannie." His eyes dropped from her pleased smile to the sight of his own great hands lifting her breasts, his thumbs sweeping up lightly to brush their crests. He flattened a palm upon her soft abdomen, examined with his fingertips the nest of feminine curls the color of sunset. "I knew you'd look this way. Small . . . pale . . . freckled . . . I love your freckles."

"Oh, Edwin, nobody loves freckles."

"I do, because they're yours." He kissed some that tinted her most intimate places while she watched his head from above, loving the sight of him bowed low to her. In time she urged him upright.

"I'm impatient . . . let me see you, too, Edwin." He stood and lifted his arms, and she took his nightshirt the route hers had gone, up and away until it landed with as much forethought as a seed borne upon wind. "Oh, my . . ." she praised, spreading a hand upon his hirsute chest, riding it down his belly and lower, touching him first with the backs of her knuckles. "Aren't you magnificent," she breathed, watching her fingers skim over his hot flesh.

He chuckled once, deeply and affectionately. "You *are* shameless, Fannie, aren't you?"

"Absolutely." She smiled, lifting her face for his kiss as she took him in hand without a trace of diffidence.

A shock rippled through him at her first stroke.

"Fannie—" he whispered, the word throaty and broken.

He touched her likewise, without compunction, inside her warmth and wetness, bringing a shudder to her frame as she hunched slightly and sucked in a swift breath. He stirred her until she arched, whispering, "Oh, Edwin . . . at last . . . and so good . . ."

Within seconds impatience bore down upon them and weighted their limbs. He swept her up and onto the bed, dropping down beside her, kissing her breasts and belly, murmuring praises against her skin while her hands threaded his hair.

She was wholly unencumbered by false modesty, giving access where he would seek, touch, explore. She had always been a woman who knew her own mind, and when that mind was decided, as it was now, she flew free.

"My turn," she whispered, rolling him to his back, taking the same liberties she had allowed. Where he'd touched her, she, too, touched him. Where he'd kissed, she, too, kissed, until both had learned the long-denied flavors and textures of the other. Only when she had taken her fill did she allow him dominance again.

Once more upon her back, Fannie stretched, catlike, smiling first for herself and secondly for him as he stroked her and watched her arch in unrestrained satisfaction. There, stretched supine, with her arms upthrown, she experienced a grand, racking climax, lifting and shuddering with unexpected swiftness beneath Edwin's hands. Upon its dying ebbs he kissed her beaded breast and said against her skin, "I knew you'd be like this, too. I just knew it. Fannie, you're wonderful."

"Mmm . . ." she murmured, eyes closed, lips tipped up in plain delight. "Come . . ." and with her small hands she steered him, stirred him, settled him where he should have been since they were seventeen, full upon her waiting, welcoming body.

When he entered her Fannie's eyes remained open, feet flat on the bed, hips raised in welcome. He settled himself deep—the first time, deep.

"Ahh . . ." he breathed as they took their due.

She smiled, watching the meshing of his black locks with hers of apricot hue. "We're beautiful together, aren't we?"

"Beautiful," he agreed.

When he moved, she moved in counterpoint, spellbound by the wonder of their bodies expressing what they had felt for so long. In time she threw her head back, chin high, rocking against him. When he shuddered, she watched, thinking how beautiful his face, gone lax in the throes of fulfillment. She watched to the end, savoring the sight of his closed eyes, his trembling arms as he waited out the last ripple of feeling.

With its passing, his eyes opened.

They smiled with newfound tenderness. Having believed for so many years that they could not love more, they found themselves awed by the force of their feelings now that they had shared each other physically.

"Edwin . . ." She cupped and stroked his silken jaw. "My beloved Edwin. Come closer. Let me hold you the way I've always dreamed of holding you . . . afterwards."

He rested upon her, warming her collarbone with his breath, wetting it with a faint, suckling kiss. A very weary kiss.

"I'm so tired," he admitted, the words nearly indistinguishable against her flesh.

"And so beautiful."

He smiled, near exhaustion. "You will marry me, Fannie . . ." he murmured as he drifted off to sleep. ". . . . soon, won't you?"

She smiled at the ceiling, combing his clean, damp hair with her fingers. "Absolutely, Edwin," she replied serenely. "Soon."

Dawn came, and crossed their bed, and another across town.

* * *

Tom Jeffcoat flexed his legs and winced behind closed eyes. He opened them and saw sunstreaks on the ceiling, angled, oblique—the heavy gold of earliest morning. Outside a dog barked, faraway. Sparrows chirped in the eaves. His bare shoulders were cold, and in the room he caught a scent reminiscent of charcoal. He swallowed with a dry, parched throat and remembered: the fire . . . the stable . . . the horses . . . Emily . . . Charles . . .

Disconsolate, he let his eyes fall closed.

Oh God, nothing's left.

The mattress jiggled—barely a flutter. He rolled his head and there sat Emily—dirty, drooping, asleep on his kitchen rocker, with her feet—in soiled stockings—sprawled on the mattress.

Emily, you poor bedraggled girl, how long have you been there?

He studied her without moving, feeling the weight of depression descend, wondering how he was going to support her, how many horses he'd lost, if they'd gotten the mare out, who else was in the house, if they'd apprehended Charles yet, how he was going to repay his grandmother, how long he'd have to wait now to get married.

He let his eyes drift closed and gave way to despair. I'm so thirsty . . . and tired . . . and broke . . . and burned out. Charles, damn you—why did you have to do a thing like this? And you, too, Tarsy. I thought you were both my friends.

He opened his eyes and willed them to remain dry. But it hurt, dammit, it hurt to think they'd turn on him this way! His throat felt as if he'd swallowed a piece of his own burning building. While he was still trying to gulp it down, Emily sighed in her sleep, rolled her head, and opened her eyes. He watched awareness dawn across her face, then a quick succession of emotions—fear, relief, pity—before she lunged to her knees beside the bed, capturing his hand and pressing it to her mouth.

"I love you," she said immediately, lifting brimming eyes. "And I'm sorry I believed Tarsy."

His thumb moved forgivingly across her knuckles. Their gazes lingered while his thoughts became laced with a jumble of emotions too profound to voice. He rolled slightly and drew her close by the back of her uncombed head and put his face against it. He held her thus, breathing the scent of smoke from her hair, feeling tears gather in his throat, segregating matters of superficial importance from those of real consequence. Life. Happiness. Loving. These were what really mattered. As he sorted and logged these realizations, Emily spoke, her voice muffled against the bedding.

"I was so afraid you wouldn't wake up so I could tell you. I thought you might die." At the hollow of her breast she clutched his hand, gripping it so hard her nails dug into his flesh. "Oh, Tom, I was so scared."

"I'm all right," he managed in a scraping whisper. "And it doesn't matter about Tarsy."

"Yes it does. I should have trusted you. I should have believed you."

"Shh."

"But—"

"Let's forget about Tarsy."

"I love you." She lifted her face, revealing streaming eyes. "I love you," she repeated, as if afraid he would not believe her.

"I love you, too, Emily." He touched her dirty face with a cluster of bruised knuckles and dredged up a weak smile. "But do you think I could have some water? My throat feels like my barn must look."

"Oh, Tom, I'm sorry . . ." She popped up and ran out to the kitchen, returning with a big glass of wonderful-looking water. "Here."

He struggled up, with her ineffectually trying to help, and, propped on one hand, downed the entire glassful while she watched.

"Another, please."

He drank a second in the same fashion, then leaned back as she adjusted the pillows behind him.

"How do you feel? Does it hurt to breathe?"

Rather than reply he asked a question of his own. "The mare—did she get out?" Emily's sorrowful expression answered, even before her words. "I'm sorry, Tom."

"How many did I lose?"

"Only two—Patty and Liza."

"Liza, too," he repeated—one of the pair who'd brought him here from Rock Springs, his first pair. "Is anything left?"

"No," she answered in a near-whisper, "it burned to the ground."

He closed his eyes, let his head fall back, and swallowed.

The sunny room suddenly seemed gloomy as Emily watched him battle despair, willing herself to keep dry-eyed while she searched for words of consolation. But there were none, so she simply sat down and took his hand.

"What about Charles?" he asked, still with his eyes closed.

"Charles is at my house. He's got burns on the backs of his hands, but otherwise he's all right."

Tom lay motionless, giving no clue to his reaction, but she knew what he was thinking.

"Charles didn't set fire to your barn, Tom."

He lifted his head and fixed her with judgmental eyes. "Oh, didn't he?"

"No."

"Then who did?"

"I don't know. Maybe it was lightning."

"In February?"

Of course, he was right, and they both knew it. Though she hated to suggest it, she ventured, "Maybe it was Tarsy."

"No. I was standing on her porch steps exchanging insults when we heard the firebells start."

"Then who's to say it was *started* at all? It could have been an accident."

But he was a careful man who put out lanterns before he closed up for the night. And a forge, contrary to popular belief, was one of the most fire-safe structures built, by virtue of its being a constant threat if improperly constructed and insulated.

He heaved a deep sigh. "God, I don't know." His head fell back and she sat uselessly, feeling so sorry for him. He looked defeated and weary and worried.

"Are you hungry?" she asked, a paltry offering, but the only one at her disposal.

"No."

"Your lips are dry. Would you like me to put some petroleum jelly on them?"

He lifted his head and studied her for a long, silent moment, then answered softly, "Yes."

She produced a squatty jar of the ointment and sat down on the edge of the mattress to apply it. Her touch upon his mouth healed more than his chapped lips. It began easing the infinite ache in his heart.

"You stayed here all night." He spoke quietly.

"Yes." She capped the jar and dejectedly studied it in her lap.

"Your father will come in here and have the rest of my hide," he speculated gently.

"No, he won't. Father and I have come to an understanding."

"About what?"

She set the jar aside and said to the sunny wall. "I told him I intended to stay here and take care of you until you're back on your feet again." Glancing over her shoulder she met his gaze foursquare. "I also told him that the moment you are I intend to become your wife."

He remained expressionless, watching her for a long time before she saw hopelessness overtake him again. He drew a shallow sigh and puffed it out as if holding his pessimism to himself.

"What's wrong?" she asked.

"Everything."

"What?"

"Listen to me, Emily." He took her hand and rubbed his thumb over her knuckles, concentrating on it as he detailed his disastrous situation. "I've got two cracked ribs. Who knows how long it'll be before I can work again? My livery stable is burned to the ground and I have no money to pay for the one that's lying in ashes, much less to rebuild. You've just told me my carriages are gone, and two of my horses died, and you want to marry me?"

"You'll heal and we'll rebuild," she announced stubbornly, leaving the bed and lugging the rocker to the corner of the room, where she clunked it down with a note of finality.

"With what?" he said to her back. "I've got no fire insurance, no hay, nothing."

"Nothing?" She turned and accosted him with common sense. "Why, of course you've got something. You've got this house, and a great big lot in a prime location in a town that's growing every year, and an anvil that belonged to your grandfather, and eight healthy horses in my father's paddock." She joined her hands stubbornly over her stomach. "And you've got me—the best veterinarian and stablehand in Johnson County. How can you call that nothing?"

He hated playing devil's advocate, but believed he had little choice. "Emily, be sensible."

She approached the bed and fixed him with a look of determination. "I am being sensible. I did all my being stupid last night while I sat in that chair and worried and bawled and acted like a perfect ninny. Then I made up my mind that worrying is idiotic. Nobody ever succeeded by worrying. It's a waste of energy. Hard work is what succeeds, and I'm willing to do plenty of it if you are, but I think the first step is to get ourselves legally married so we'll have that hurdle out of the way."

"And what about the period of mourning?"

"The period of mourning be damned," she decreed, dropping to the bed and taking his hand again while her voice softened with sincerity. "If you had died in that fire I would never have forgiven myself for mourning away the few happy weeks I might have had with you. I love you, Thomas Jeffcoat, and I want to be your wife. Conventions and burned barns don't matter as much as our happiness."

He sat studying her, comparing her to Tarsy and Julia and the other women he'd known. None had her spirit, drive, or optimism. None would have stood beside him staunchly in the face of the defeats he'd just suffered. Emily was ready to plow ahead, undaunted, and take him and his dismal financial prospects and a future whose only certainty seemed to be a lot of hard work and worry. And he had no doubt that if anyone raised an eyebrow over her nursing him overnight in the privacy of his own home *before* they were married, she'd take them on over that issue, too.

"Come here," he ordered quietly.

She came, and lay in the crook of his arm with her head tucked in the hollow of his shoulder. The golden sun poured across the bed, gilding their faces. They listened to the sparrows in the eaves. They listened to their own breathing and the sounds of the town awakening on a Saturday morning. They linked fingers atop his bandaged ribs and watched the sun streaks slant down the walls.

Emily fit the pad of her thumb against Tom's and said thoughtfully, "Thomas?"

"Hm?"

"Charles didn't set fire to the barn. He wouldn't do such a thing. He's the one who pulled you out of it and saved your life. I was there, so I know. When he thought you might die . . ." Emily paused before admitting, ". . . he cried. Please believe me, Tom."

He pressed his lips to her hair and closed his eyes for a long moment, telling himself to believe it. Wanting to believe it.

"You still love him, don't you?" he asked against her hair.

She sat up and studied Tom, unruffled. "Of course I do," she admitted. "But not the way I love you. If I felt that way about him I'd have married him when I had the chance. If I can believe you about Tarsy, you must believe me about Charles. Please, Tom. He would never destroy what was yours, because in hurting you he'd hurt me, too, don't you see?"

He considered the three of them and their incredible triangular love. "Do you honestly think we can survive in this town—all three of us?" Tom asked.

"I don't know," Emily answered honestly.

They sat thinking, troubled, for long minutes before he asked, "Would you go back East with me?"

She felt the grip of loneliness at the thought of leaving her father, Fannie, and Frankie, but there was only one answer she could give.

"Yes, if that was your choice."

His respect and love for her increased tenfold as he recognized the emotional strife that had accompanied her answer. They were still sitting, holding hands, with tens of questions unanswered, when someone knocked on the front door. Emily stirred and went to answer.

At the sight of the two familiar faces on Tom's porch, her spirits lifted. "Hello, Papa. And Fannie . . . I didn't expect to see you both here."

"How is he?" Fannie asked, stepping into the house.

"Awake, tired, feeling like a piece of oversmoked jerky, but quite alive, and he's going to stay that way. Oh, Fannie, I'm so relieved."

They exchanged hugs and Edwin said, "We want to talk to both of you."

"Papa, I'm not sure he should talk a lot. His voice is raspy and his throat hurts."

"This won't take long." Edwin brushed past his daughter and led the parade into the bedroom, observing jovially as he entered. "So you made it, Jeffcoat!"

"Seems that way."

"Looking a little the worse for wear."

Tom chuckled and boosted himself up higher against the pillows. "I'm sure I do."

Edwin, in an unusually expansive mood, laughed and took Fannie's hand, drawing her along with him to the bed. He ordered his daughter, "Here, Emily, sit down. We have some news you'll both want to hear."

Emily and Tom exchanged curious glances while she perched at his shoulder with Fannie at his knee and Edwin standing beside the bed.

"First of all, they've arrested Pinnick for setting fire to your barn. He tied on a good one down at the Mint Bar last night and when they found him this morning, curled up on the boardwalk, still half-pickled, he was holding on to a bottle of whiskey and blubbering about how sorry he was, he didn't mean to burn the whole thing down, he only meant to set you back a spell so he'd get back the business he lost when you moved into town."

"Pinnick?" Tom repeated, flabbergasted.

"Pinnick!" Emily rejoiced, clapping her hands, then reaching for one of Tom's.

Edwin continued: "And I was barely into my britches this morning when Charles comes stomping downstairs and through the kitchen buttoning his jacket and cussing a blue streak about that damned Jeffcoat and what a nuisance he was. The way I remember it, he said, *How many buildings does a man have to put up for him, anyway?* Then he bellers that he's heading off to see Vasseler about a barn-raising and that it's by God the last one he's going to do for Tom Jeffcoat. So they're out there right now, Vasseler and Charles, rounding up a work crew to get started the minute the ashes cool. And on top of that, Fannie and I—"

"I get to tell this part," Fannie interrupted, hushing Edwin with a squeeze on his arm.

Edwin paused in mid-word, glancing at his future wife, clapped his jaws shut, and gave her the floor with a wave of a hand.

Fannie looked bright and happy as she continued, "It seems I was quite indiscreet last night when I threw my arms around your father and kissed him in the middle of all that hubbub with almost everyone in town watching. Since they all know the truth by now, Edwin and I have decided it would be most expedient if we got married posthaste. We were wondering if the two of you would like to plan a double wedding, perhaps at the end of next week?"

Before Tom and Emily could wipe the shock from their faces, Fannie added, "Unless, of course, you'd prefer separate ones, in which case we'll certainly understand."

In the resulting outburst everyone talked and hugged and shook hands at once, and laughter filled the room. Felicitations rebounded from the walls and the sense of goodwill multiplied among all four. Like conspirators in an innocent prank, they agreed with Fannie, who said, "What's good enough for a father is certainly good enough for a daughter! Just let anyone wag a tongue now!"

When Fannie and Edwin had gone, Emily and Tom stared at each other in renewed amazement, then burst out laughing.

"Can you believe it! In two weeks!"

"Come here," he ordered as he had earlier, this time with a much brighter outlook.

She slipped beside him, doubled her knees up against his hip, and hugged him voraciously around the neck. They kissed in celebration and he said against her ear, "Now, I won't take any back talk from you. You're picking up your bundle of clothes and going home where you belong."

"But—" She pulled back.

"No buts. I can take care of myself, and one night in my house is all the tarnish I want to put on your halo. The next time you come into this room it'll be as my wife. Now, git, so I can get up. There's a carpenter I've got to see."

"But, Tom!"

"Out, I said! But if it would make you feel any better, you can pump me some water and put it on to heat before you leave. Then I'd suggest you go home and do the same for yourself. You smell like a chimney sweep." She laughed and shimmied off the bed while he pulled himself to the edge of the mattress and sat with the sheet across his lap. Happy, and hopeful, and suddenly gay, she swung back to him and looped her arms around his neck.

"Know what?" she inquired teasingly.

"What?" he repeated, nose to nose with her.

"I gave you a bath last night."

"You did!"

"And you've got ugly knees."

He laughed and spread his hands near the sides of her breasts. "Miss Walcott, if you don't get out of here I'm going to be on them and I'll probably overwork my poor scorched lungs and die in the process, and how would you feel then?"

"Thomas Jeffcoat, for shame!" she scolded.

"Good-bye, Emily," he returned with a note of warning.

"Good-bye, Thomas," she whispered, kissing the end of his nose. "You're going to miss me when I'm gone."

"Yes I will, if you give me half a chance."

"I love you, knees and all."

"I love you, smoke and all. Now will you get out of here?"

"What are you going to say to Charles?"

"None of your business."

"After we're married, I might invite him to supper sometime."

"I'll tell him you said so."

"Fine."

"Fine."

"And I might invite Tarsy, too."

He scowled menacingly.

"All right, all right, I'm going. Are you coming courting tonight?" she asked blithely from the doorway.

He rose from the bed, giving her a flash of ugly knees and bare calves as he said, "Always keep 'em guessin', that's my motto," and closed the bedroom door in her face.

Thirty minutes later Tom found Charles down at Edwin's livery stable. When he stepped inside, there was the man he sought, hitching up a pair of Tom's own horses to a buckboard, with bandaged hands.

Tom closed the door and the two stood staring at each other, then Charles returned to his task, bending to connect a tug strap to the doubletree. Tom approached slowly, his bootsteps sounding clearly through the cavernous barn. Near Charles, he stopped.

"Hello," Tom said, looking down at Charles's worn Stetson.

"Hello."

"Where are you taking my horses?"

"Out to the mill for a load of wood to put up the last goddamned stable I'm ever gonna build for you."

"Need some help?"

Charles peered up past his hat brim with a sarcastic gleam in his eye. "Not from any broken-down cripple with two cracked ribs."

"Yeah, well, look who cracked 'em."

Charles walked around to the other side of the team and continued buckling harness parts.

"I hear your hands got burned."

"Just the backs. The palms're still working. What do you want?"

"I came to thank you for hauling my carcass out of that building last night."

"You're one hell of a lot of trouble, you know that, Jeffcoat? This morning I'm wishing I would've left you in it."

"Bullshit," Tom replied affectionately.

From the far side of the horses came a rueful chuckle, then, like an echo, "Yeah, bullshit."

Charles squatted and Tom stared at his boots, visible beneath the team's bellies. "I'm marrying her at the end of next week."

"What day?"

"I don't know."

"Saturday?"

"I don't know."

"You marry her Saturday, I'll have the damn barn done by Friday. You marry her Friday and I'll have it done by Thursday."

"What does that mean?" Tom stepped around the horses just as Charles stretched to his feet. Their eyes met directly.

"You didn't expect me to hang around and be your best man, did you?" Charles nudged past Tom and kept a shoulder intruding as he threaded the reins through the guides. "I'll be cracking a whip over that building crew, then I'm gone."

"You're leaving?"

"Yup." Charles folded his lips tightly to his teeth as he moved to the other side of the team.

"Where to?"

"Montana, I think. Yeah, Montana. There's a lot of open land up there, and the big drives are winding up there. Plenty of rich ranchers settling in Montana and all of them needing barns and houses ... buildings'll be going up all over hell. I'll be rich in no time."

"Have you told Emily?"

"You tell her."

"I think you should."

Charles laughed mirthlessly and threw the other man a cutting glance. "Take a leap, Jeffcoat!"

"You don't have to go, you know."

"Like hell, I don't. I'd hang around here and I'd have her one day, come hell or high water, but it might not be till after both of us were old married folks raising a batch of kids. Wouldn't that be just fine and dandy?"

"Charles, I'm sorry."

"Don't make me laugh."

"For what I said last night at the fire."

"Yeah, well, don't be. Pinnick just thought a little faster than me, that's all. Damned old drunk ... if I'd've lit the fire myself I'd be on my way to Montana already instead of wasting another week puttin' up your goddamned barn." The horses were hitched. Charles clambered onto the wagon and took the reins. "Now open the door so I can roll, you two-bit iron twanger."

Tom slid back the great rolling doors, then stood outside with his hands in the pockets of his jacket, his hat pulled low over his eyes as he watched Charles pass him with the rig.

To his back Tom shouted, "You take care of my horses, Bliss! You can't put 'em away dry like a darned old piece of oak, you know!"

"And you take care of my woman, 'cause if I hear you didn't I'll come back and kick your ass clear to the other end of the Bozeman Trail!"

"Shee-it," Tom muttered, watching the wagon roll away. But when it was gone, he remained beside the open doors, feeling bereft and heavyhearted, and missing Charles even before he was gone.

Chapter 21

The marriages took place on a day in early March when the chinook winds descended the eastern slope of the Rockies, fanning the earth with a breath warm as summer. A real snoweater, the townsfolk observed, stepping out their doors at midmorning, recognizing the warm, dry current that came each year unannounced. It brought the smell of the sea, from which it originated, and of the earth, which it bared along its way, and of spruce and sprouts and spring. Billowing down from the Big Horns across the wide Sheridan Valley, the chinooks flattened an entire winter's snow in a single day, sipped half of it up and sent the other half glistening in runnels that caught chips of sun and scattered them back toward the cobalt sky. They breathed on brooks and streams, which chimed with a tinkle of breaking ice to the unending background sigh of rushing water. They brought an unmistakable message—rejoice, winter's over!

By high noon the transformation was well underway, and when the bells of the Sheridan Episcopalian Church pealed, they drew a congregation whose winter spirits had been magically lifted.

They came in open carriages, breathing deep of the warm air and turning their faces to the sun. They came smiling, happy, dressed in lighter clothes and lingering outside to soak up the miraculous day until the last possible moment.

That's where they all were, outside in the chinook and the sun, when Edwin Walcott's finest Studebaker landau came briskly down the street with its twin tops down, making no excuses for shunning Victorian mourning in honor of this glorious occasion. The landau itself gleamed in yellow paint with black trim, and Edwin had chosen his blackest black gelding, Jet, to do the wedding day honors. Along Jet's shiny black flanks the harness was studded with cockades of white ribbon trailing streamers that undulated gracefully as the gelding, enlivened, too, by the chinooks, pranced smartly. In his mane more ribbon was braided and on each of his blinders and between his ears perched a crepe-paper rosette. The wagon traces looked like maypoles, twined with ribbons and rosettes and wands of pussy willows. The landau itself was nothing short of a bower. Cockades, streamers, and more pussy willows circled its seats, nestled in bunting of pale green net that had been fixed in the downturned bonnet.

In the front seat sat Fannie Cooper, in ivory, holding an enormous net-swathed hat on her head while beside her Edwin Walcott perched proud-chested and beaming, wearing a dapper beaver top hat and cutaway coat of cinnamon brown, holding a buggy whip trimmed with yet another paper rose and streamers.

Behind them rode Emily Walcott, wearing her mother's elegant silver-gray wedding dress, with a sprig of dried baby's breath in her hair, beside Thomas Jeffcoat, dashing in dove gray—top hat, gloves, Prince Albert coat, and striped trousers. Squashed between their knees on the edge of the seat rode Frank Allen Walcott, sporting a new brown suit with his first winged collar and ascot, beaming fit to kill, standing up well before his father drew rein, waving and hollering at the top of his lungs, "Hi, Earl, look at this! Ain't this something!"

So the wedding guests were laughing when Edwin drew Jet to a halt before the Sheridan Episcopal. Frankie clambered excitedly over Tom's legs and leapt down to show Earl his new duds and to exclaim over the decorated landau. Edwin slipped the buggy whip into its bracket and vaulted from the wagon like a man of twenty, unable to dim his smile as he swung Fannie down. Tom alighted less agilely, hiding a clumsy plaster cast beneath his wedding finery, but when he reached up a helping hand to his bride-to-be the eagerness on his face was unmistakable. With his gray-gloved hand he took her bare one, squeezing it much harder than necessary, sending her a silent message of joy.

"They're smiling," he whispered, with his back to the church.

"I know," she replied secretly while stepping down. "Isn't it wonderful?"

They were smiling—the entire waiting crowd—infected by the obvious happiness that shone from the faces of the nuptial couples as they alighted from the carriage with not a garment of black in sight.

Emily and Tom faced the crowd, watching Edwin and Fannie move before them up a pair of wooden planks that Reverend Vasseler had provided as a moat across the streaming ditch, Edwin keeping a possessive grip on Fannie's elbow. Tom claimed Emily's elbow, too, as they followed the older couple, who were receiving felicitations, left and right, even before the vows were spoken.

Reverend Vasseler waited on the church steps, with Bible in hand, smiling down on the new arrivals, shaking hands with each of them as they stopped on the step below him.

"Good morning, Edwin, Fannie, Thomas, Emily . . . and Master Frank."

"It's a beautiful day, isn't it?" Edwin spoke for all of them.

"Yes, it is." Reverend Vasseler scanned the flawless sky as a wayward chinook breeze lifted his thinning hair from his forehead and set it back down. "One would think the Lord was sending a message, wouldn't one?"

Upon the heels of the minister's benign postulation they entered the church in procession, with Vasseler himself in the lead, followed by the resplendent couples and Frankie, then the entire fold.

The organ played and the wind came in the open windows. The church was trimmed with more pussy willows and white cockades on every pew. Frankie sat up front between Earl and his parents, and when the sound of settling bodies silenced, Reverend Vasseler lifted his chin and let his voice ring out clear and loud.

"Dearly beloved . . . we are gathered here today, in the sight of God, to join this man and woman . . ." The minister paused and shifted his gaze from one couple to the next. ". . . and this man and woman . . . in the state of holy matrimony." Smiles broke out everywhere, even a small one on the face of the man officiating.

The smiles disappeared, however, at the speaking of the vows, for when Edwin took Fannie's hands and gazed into her eyes, the love that radiated between them shone as unmistakably as the silver in their hair.

"I, Edwin, take thee, Fannie . . ."

"I, Fannie, take thee, Edwin . . ."

There was a special radiance in the older couple that sparked tears in the eyes of many looking on and held them in thrall as Edwin, upon the last words, placed Fannie's right hand over his heart and covered it with his own for all to see.

Then Tom and Emily faced each other and once again hearts went out to them as they clasped hands and exchanged vows with their eyes even before doing so with their lips. They emanated a serenity surpassing their years as they stood before God and man, conscious only of each other, and spoke their vows in voices that could be heard clearly in the rearmost pew.

"I, Thomas, take thee, Emily . . ."

"I, Emily, take thee, Thomas . . ."

When their last words were spoken and a blessing called down, Reverend Vasseler opened his arms wide as if in a blessing of his own, and said. "Now you may kiss your brides."

As the two couples exchanged their first married kisses, the women looking on drew handkerchiefs from their sleeves while the men stiffened their spines and stared straight-on to keep from divulging the fact that their eyes, too, held a conspicuous glint of moisture. Emotions billowed even more as, upon the heels of the first kisses, the newlywed couples broke apart and exchanged partners. Edwin kissed his daughter, and Tom his new mother-in-law, followed by a heartfelt embrace between the two women and a congenial handshake between the two men. The organ burst forth with recessional tidings, and four smiling faces turned toward the open rear doors, poising for a moment with arms linked, four-abreast, as if to tell the world that love, honor, and respect went four ways among them.

Arm in arm, Emily and Tom led the exit, followed by Edwin and Fannie, who, while passing the first pew, collected a smiling Frankie and left the church holding his hands between them.

Outside, rice flew, and the brides ran across the bouncing wooden moat and boarded the ribbon-bedecked landau and drew their skirts aside while two happy husbands stepped up behind them. Frankie scrambled into the front seat and begged to take the reins, beaming like a full moon when Edwin said yes and handed him the supple buggy whip with the streamers trailing from its handle.

They rode through town with the brides crooked in their husband's arms, nestled in a bower of pussy willows and white roses, followed by the splash of shoes and kettles trailing through the swimming streets behind the Studebaker.

At Coffeen Hall they were feted with a wedding feast provided by their friends, customers, and fellow church members. The celebration lasted into the late afternoon and by the time it ended the chinooks had stolen the last of the snow and left behind a naked valley waiting for its spring raiments.

An hour before sunset, two brides and grooms boarded the landau once more. Frankie stayed behind, waving them goodbye in his bedraggled, food-stained wedding suit. He would spend the night at Earl's, and tomorrow, he promised his father, he and Earl would wash down the landau as a wedding gift of their own.

But now, it wheeled through the March mud as spattered and bedraggled as the two boys had looked, its streamers soiled and its rosettes crushed. No matter. Soiling it had been joyous and memorable.

The evening was mellow, the sound of the wheels a susurrus. Edwin drove while Fannie pressed her cheek against his sleeve. In the backseat Emily sat holding hands with Tom in the folds of her pearl-gray skirt. Her cheek lay not against his sleeve, however, but straight toward the wind, for it was warm with expectation while Tom squeezed her hand fiercely and their thumbs played games of pursuit and capture.

At Tom's house Edwin brought Jet to a halt. He turned, resting one arm along the top of his seat, looking back at his daughter and her new husband.

"Well . . ." His smile passed affectionately between both of them. "Happy wedding day," he said with soft sincerity. "I know it's been for us." On the seat he took Fannie's hand and momentarily shifted his smile to her.

"For us, too," Emily returned. "Thank you, Papa." Over the back of the seat she kissed him, then Fannie. "Thank you both. It was a wonderful day, and the landau was a grand surprise."

"We thought so," Fannie agreed. "And it was certainly fun picking those pussy willows, wasn't it, Edwin?"

They laughed, momentarily relieving the heart-tug that accompanied the moment of good-bye as a daughter left her father's abode forever. Tom alighted and helped Emily down, then stood beside the carriage looking up at the couple above him. He reached and took two hands—one of Edwin's, one of Fannie's, squeezing them earnestly. "Don't worry about her. I'll make sure she's as happy as the two of you are going to be, for the rest of her life."

Edwin nodded, uncertain of his voice, should he try to speak. Tom released his hand and leaned forward to kiss Fannie. "Be happy," she whispered, holding his cheeks. "Happiness is everything."

"We are," he replied, and stepped back.

"Fannie . . ." Emily, too, accepted a kiss while fresh emotions welled up.

As usual, Fannie knew how to end the delicate moment with the proper mixture of affection and finality. "We'll see you tomorrow. Congratulations, dearling."

"You, too, Fannie."

"Good-bye, Papa. See you tomorrow."

"Good-bye, honey."

The landau pulled away, trailing bedraggled streamers. A bride and groom watched it go, but even before it reached a corner they had turned their regard to one another.

He smiled.

She smiled.

He took her hand.

She gave hers gladly.

They walked to his house together. At the porch steps he said, "I'm sorry I can't carry you in, Mrs. Jeffcoat."

"You can do it on our silver wedding anniversary," she told him while they mounted the steps shoulder to shoulder. He opened the door and the two of them entered his kitchen, where all was silent and serene and bathed in sunwash. They locked palms, standing close, toe to toe, projecting ahead not twenty-five years, but a single night.

"It was a wonderful wedding day, wasn't it?" he said.

"Yes, it was. It is."

"Are you tired?"

"No, but my feet are wet."

"Your feet?"

"From crossing the yard."

"You're home now. You can take your shoes off anytime." His grin, unformed, remained a mere suggestion in his eyes.

"All right, I will, but will you kiss me first? It takes a long time to take shoes off."

He smiled wide, overjoyed at her lack of guile. "Oh, Emily . . . there's nobody like you. I'm going to love being your husband." They stood so close he had only to bend his arms to tip her against him. He kissed her obligingly, averting his face to meet her upraised one, gathering her into the curve of his shoulder while they stood almost stock-still against one another, twisted slightly at the waist. It was a sweet beginning, tasting each other with unhurried ease, letting their mouths form and fit and feast while remaining still everywhere else.

When their mouths parted—a hairsbreadth only—she seemed to have forgotten how to move.

"Your shoes," he whispered, his breath brushing her lips.

"Oh . . . my shoes," she said dreamily. "What shoes?"

He smiled and delicately kissed her upper lip . . . then her lower one . . . then the corner of her mouth where he probed inquisitively with the tip of his tongue before riding it, as if crossing a rainbow, to the opposite corner. "You were going to take your shoes off," he reminded her in a velvet voice.

"Oh, yes . . . where are they?"

"They're down there someplace."

"Down where?"

"Someplace on your damp feet."

"Mmmm . . ."

"Should I take them off for you?"

"Mmmm . . ."

He tipped his head farther and fit his mouth upon hers with incredible perfection. As their tongues dipped deep for second tastes his hand played idly over the small of her back. They took third tastes, and fourth, still resting against each other with only the faintest contact, his fingers drawing circular patterns along her waistline, where fasteners and ties and boning formed lumps within her silver dress. In time she freed her lips reluctantly and whispered against his chin, "Thomas?"

"Hm?"

"My shoes."

"Oh yes." He cleared his throat and drew her by the hand to one of his kitchen benches, where she sat gazing up at him, her cheeks colored by a becoming blush. He went down on one knee before her and searched beneath her skirts to find one delicate ankle, which he drew forth and studied silently. Her shoes were high and buttoned, made of pearl-gray leather and silk vesting, which encased her foot tightly well past the ankle.

"I see this won't be as easy as the time I pulled your boot off. Did you bring a buttonhook?"

"It's in the bedroom with my things."

He looked up and neither of them spoke while his thumb stroked her anklebone through the silk vesting, heating a spot that shimmied straight up her leg. At length he said quietly, "I guess I'll have to go get it. Would you like to come with me?"

Sitting in his gold-streaked kitchen with an hour yet to go before sunset, she nodded with virginal uncertainty.

He dropped her foot and rose. Her eyes lifted to him and he read that uncertainty, drew her up by the hand, and ended her misgivings by leading her through the long spears of light slicing across his kitchen floor, past the foot of his staircase and into the bedroom where now the windows were trimmed with curtains and shades and her own bureau stood against one plastered wall.

"Get it," he ordered quietly, with all traces of teasing gone, "and take them off."

He removed his top hat and put it in the closet, where her clothing now hung beside his. She found the buttonhook and sat on the edge of his bed, which was spread with Fannie's homemade quilt, the quilt she'd been standing behind the night he'd chosen her bare feet from among all the others. She bent forward, concentrating on her shoe buttons, while he removed his gloves from his pocket and lay them on her bureau, then shrugged from his jacket and hung it neatly in the closet. He went to the north window and pulled it up but left the shade at half-mast, letting the remnants of the chinooks drift into the room from the uninterrupted grassland beyond. He went to the east window—the one facing the street—opened it, too, but drew that shade to the sill.

She slipped off one shoe and began unhooking the buttons on the other while he took off his boots, standing first on one leg, then on the other, and set them in the closet.

When her second shoe was removed, Emily crossed her toes and looked up uncertainly. Tom stood watching her, drawing the tails of his shirt from his trousers while his suspenders trailed down beside his knees.

"You can put them in the closet beside mine," he invited.

She crossed before him, feeling doubtful and ignorant and taken unawares because it seemed that what she thought would not happen until well after sundown would happen well before. She bent to set her shoes beside her husband's and as she straightened his arms came around her from behind. His warm, soft lips kissed her neck.

"Are you scared, Emily?" His breath made dew upon her skin and fluttered the flossy hair upon her nape.

"A little."

"Don't be scared . . . don't be." He kissed her hair, her ear, the ruching of her high collar while she covered his arms with her own and tipped her head aside acquiescingly.

"Thomas?"

"Hm?"

"It's just that I don't know what to do."

"Just lean your head back and let me show you."

She dropped her head back onto his shoulder and his hands skimmed up her ribs . . . up, up. She closed her eyes and leaned against him, breathing with increasing difficulty as he taught her the myriad shapes of pleasure; moving his hands in synchronization over her firm breasts, lifting, molding, flattening; then lifting once again. He kneaded circles upon them with the flat of his hand before the pressure disappeared and only his fingertips explored the hardened cores, as if picking up stacked coins. She grew heavy and drugged by arousal, warm within her clothing, and confined by it. Her breath became hard-beating. His right hand slid down and covered the back of hers, his fingers closing tightly in her palm, which he lifted to his mouth and kissed hard before releasing her completely and stepping back to search through her hair for pins.

One by one he plucked them out and dropped them to the floor at their feet. They fell like ticks of a clock marking off the last minutes of waiting. When all were heedlessly strewn, he combed her hair with his calloused fingers, spilling it in a black waterfall down her back. He plunged his face into its waves and breathed deep. He kissed it, gripping her arms from behind, working them almost as he'd worked her breasts, in hard, compact circles. He made of her hair a sheaf, and drew it over her left shoulder, then stood away, touching her only with his fingertip while opening the long line of pearl buttons down her back, to her hips. He found, within, the string-ties at the base of her spine, and tugged them free, loosening them to her shoulder blades. He unbuttoned the petticoat at her waist, then skimmed it all down—dress, corset, garters, petticoat, and stockings—in one grand sweep, leaving her clothed in only two white brief undergarments. Caressing her arms, he dropped his head and kissed her shoulder, then her nape, then turned her—still standing in a billow of abandoned clothing—to face him.

"Could you do that to me?" he asked in a soft, throaty voice. "Mine is much simpler."

Feeling herself blushing, she dropped her eyes from his face to his throat, from his throat to his wrinkled shirt.

"If you want to," he added in a whisper.

"I want to," she whispered back, and caught up one of his hands to free first a cuff button, then its mate, while he held his wrists at an obliging angle. She had just turned her attention to his collar button when he reached out and, with the backs of four knuckles, brushed the peak of her left breast through its white cotton covering.

"I love you, Mrs. Jeffcoat," he whispered, bringing an added glow to her cheeks while continuing his seemingly idle caress, watching as she shyly avoided his eyes. With each successive button she moved slower, until, reaching the bottom one, she gave up her task and closed her eyes while his knuckles went on fluttering over her nipple.

"I ..." she began, but her whisper faded as she leaned both forearms against his hard plaster cast. For seconds she stood thus, balancing against him, absorbing the grand rush of sensation created by so faint a touch it might have been only the warm chinook fluttering her chemise against her skin. The fluttering stopped and his hands brushed upward between her elbows to free four tiny buttons between her breasts.

"You ... ?" he whispered, studying her closed eyes, reminding her of her unfinished thought.

"I ..."

He spread her chemise wide and slipped both hands inside, laying them flat upon her naked breasts for the first time.

She lifted languorous eyes to his and let her body be rocked gently by his caresses, drowning in the deep blue of his eyes, then closing her own as his open mouth descended to hers. With warm tongue and warm hands he stroked her, teaching her open mouth and naked breasts how rapture begins and builds. When she was taut and ruched he removed her chemise and pantaloons, slipped his hands to her back, and caressed it with widespread fingers. He drew her firmly against him, against cold, hard plaster above, and warm, hard man below. Barefoot, she lifted on tiptoe and wrapped her arms about his sturdy neck, lavishing in the play of his hands over her naked skin.

Still caressing her back, he leaned away, and searching her eyes, freed his last shirt button with one hand. Following his lead, she divested him of the garment, reaching up to push it from his shoulders with polite decorum that oddly suited the moment—one of her last as an innocent. When she had laid his shirt with great care atop her own fallen dress he captured her wrists, gripping them firmly and skewering a thumb into each of her palms. He kissed the butt of the left ... and the right ... then laid them on his chest, above the white plaster, teaching her the ways a man likes first.

"We're married now ... you can do what you like ... here ..." He played her palms across his firm pectoral muscles. "Or here ..." He took them to his waist. "Or here ..." He left them at his trouser buttons.

These, too, she freed, slipping her fingers between his waistband and the worn edge of plaster. She did it all, all he bid, self-conscious but willing until both of them were naked, and they walked that way to the side of their bed where he threw back the covers, piled the pillows one atop the other, and lay down first, then reached a hand to her in invitation.

She lay down beside him and suddenly everything was natural—to twine her arms around him and be taken flush against his body, to feel the sole of his foot ride up the back of her calf and follow his lead with her own, to make a place for his knee, which cradled high against her, to feel his hand on her hip, then on her stomach, and his tongue in her mouth while he touched her within for the first time and groaned into her mouth. To feel her own hand guided to his distended flesh and taught a love lesson which she was more than eager to learn. To feel the rivers of her body flood their banks as if the chinooks had melted a winter's snowfall there inside her as it had outside their open window.

He touched her in all ways—wondrous, deep strokes, and tender surface petting. He wet her breasts with kisses, and suckled them, and fired her body with befitting want, along with his own. He made her quiver and seek and damn the wrappings around his ribs that robbed her of the flesh that was rightfully hers.

"I love you," he told her.

"Do," she said when desire had bent her to his every whim but one.

"I'm sorry about this damn cast," he said in a gruff, breathless voice.

But the cast created no barrier whatsoever as he arched above her and entered her in a long, slow stroke. She closed her eyes and received him, becoming his for life—wife and consort, inseparable. She opened her eyes and looked up into his face as he poised above her, still for the moment, waiting.

She whispered three words. "Heart, soul, and senses."

And as he began moving they sealed the vow forever.

It was a splendid thing, of thrumming hearts, and souls in one accord. And senses—ah, the senses, how they reveled. She closed her eyes and loved the feel of him filling her body, and the sound of his harsh breathing matching her own, and the smell of his hair and skin when he closed the space between them, and as the beat accelerated, his soft throaty grunts and sheer, swift thrusts. Then at her own unexpected spill, a rasping cry—hers—followed in short succession by his deeper, throatier one as he shuddered upon her.

Then silence, broken only by their own tired breathing and the caressing scrape of his thumb against her skull going on . . . and on . . . and on.

She lay upon her side with her mouth at his throat and his heavy hand on her head, the thumb still in motion. She felt beneath her ear his relaxed arm, and upon her knee his heavy enervated leg. She experienced her first total repletion—a wholly unexpected gift—lying there surrounded by his tired limbs.

"Mmmmm . . ." She felt the sleepy syllable vibrate against her lips and pictured his cheek against the pillow above her, his eyes closed, his hair disheveled.

She stroked his naked hip—only once; she hadn't the further energy. Her hand fell still and they lay on, drifting in the realm of the blessed. She had not expected the satisfaction. It was a gift as precious and unforeseen as the arrival of the spring winds.

When she'd thought him asleep, he spoke in a soft rumble, the words resounding through his arm to her ear. "Heart, soul, and senses."

"Yes." She kissed his Adam's apple.

He pulled himself from his lethargy to tip his face on the pillow and look down into her eyes.

"How are your heart, soul, and senses now?"

"Happy."

"Mine, too." He touched her nose lovingly and they basked awhile, appreciating each other silently, recounting the last half hour. "Did I bang you up with my cast?"

"Only a little."

"I'm sorry, tomboy."

"Say that again."

"Tomboy." He grinned.

"The first name you ever called me, and the last before you kissed me."

"Did I?"

"In the closet. 'Come here, tomboy,' you said."

"You remember it very well."

"Very well."

"Come here, tomboy." He grinned and drew her close to renew old memories.

Sunset had come and gone, and he had taught her a few ways to avoid being bruised by his cast. She slipped from bed and found in her bureau drawer the post-card with the floral heart and verse and propped it up against the base of the lamp where they could both see it first thing upon waking in the morning.

The town was still and the wind had died. At the sill the curtains hung motionless. Emily stood looking through the lace, feeling the air cool toward nighttime. Tom came up behind her and doubled his forearms across her chest. They rocked peacefully.

She hooked her hands over his arm and spoke for the first time of those who'd been absent from their wedding ceremony.

"I missed them," she said.

"So did I," he replied against her hair.

"Even Tarsy. I didn't think I had any feelings left for her, but I do."

"I don't think she'll come around too quickly, probably never."

They ruminated for minutes, staring out the window toward the north, rocking still, before she asked, "Do you think Charles is in Montana by now?"

"No, not yet."

"Do you think he'll ever come back?"

Tom sighed and closed the window, then put an arm around her shoulders and walked her toward the bed. "The world's not perfect, tomboy. Sometimes we have fires and fistfights and lose friends."

"I know."

They got beneath the covers and snuggled, back to belly, facing her valentine.

She found his hand and cupped it upon her breast. She felt his warm breath on the back of her head and asked winsomely, "Is it all right if I keep loving him, just a little?"

He kissed the crown of her head and said, "He'll come back someday. With both of us here waiting, he'll come back."

THE
GAMBLE

Chapter 1

1880

Agatha Downing looked out the window of her millinery shop and saw a life-sized oil painting of a naked woman crossing the street. She gasped and clenched her fists. *That man again!* What would he think of next? It wasn't enough that he'd set up business right next door selling spirits and encouraging honest men to squander their hard-earned money at gambling. Now it was pictures of naked women!

Aghast, she pressed a hand to her boned corsets and watched the jovial band of ne'er-do-wells coming her way. Shouting ribald accolades, they jostled their way toward the Gilded Cage Saloon, bearing the framed canvas on their shoulders. The street was wide and muddy; it took them some time to cross. Before they were halfway, all the men on the boardwalk had joined them, hooting, doffing their hats, paying lewd homage to the Rubenesque nude. The closer they got, the tighter Agatha pressed her corsets to herself.

The disgraceful figure stood a good six feet high with arms raised to heaven as if waiting to ascend—full front, voluptuous, and naked as a fresh-hatched jaybird.

Agatha dropped her glance from the disgusting spectacle.

Heaven, indeed! The entire lot of them were bound in the other direction. And, it appeared, they were aiming to take the children down with them!

Two young boys had spotted the revelers and came running down the middle of the muddy street to get a closer look.

Agatha flung her door open and limped onto the boardwalk.

"Perry! Clydell!" she shouted at the ten-year-olds. "Go home at once! Do you hear?"

The pair came up short. They looked up to see Miss Downing pointing a finger toward the end of the street.

"At once, I said, or I'll tell your mothers!"

Perry White turned to his friend Clydell Hottle with a sickly expression on his freckled face. "It's old lady Downing."

"Aw, shoot!"

"My ma buys hats from her."

"Yeah, mine, too," Clydell despaired. They gave a last inquisitive glance at the naked lady on the painting, turned reluctantly and shuffled back toward home.

Mooney Straub, one of the town's drunks, raised his voice from the mob in the street and called after them, "Wait'll you're a little older, boys!" Coarse laughter followed and Agatha's outrage burned even hotter.

They were nothing but riff-raff. Though it was only ten o'clock in the morning, Mooney Straub could scarcely stand on his feet. And there was Charlie Yaeger, whose wife and six children lived in a hovel fit for pigs; and Cornelia Loretto's young son Dan, who'd been hired on next door as a keno dealer, shaming his poor mother terribly; and the fearsome-looking bartender with thick white hair growing over only the left half of his skull and a livid red scar covering most of his face; and the tall skinny Negro piano player whose eyes never seemed to miss a thing; and George Sowers, who years ago had struck it rich in the Colorado gold fields but had drunk and gambled away his entire fortune. And leading the troop, the one responsible for delivering this plague upon her doorstep: that man they all called Scotty.

Agatha stationed herself on the steps before the saloon and waited as the brigade of Satan's army splashed its way through the spring mud. When they reached the hitching rails, Agatha spread her arms wide.

"Mr. Gandy, I must protest!"

LeMaster Scott Gandy lifted a hand to halt his followers.

"Rein in there, boys. Seems we've got company." He turned slowly and raised his gaze to the woman standing above him like an avenging angel. She was dressed in dull gray. Her Austrian-draped tie-back skirt was cinched tightly, front to back. Her bustle jutted high like the spine of a spitting cat. Her hair was drawn back into so severe a knot it looked as if it gave her a perennial headache. The only spots of color she possessed were the twin blotches of pink on her stiff white cheeks.

Letting a grin lift one corner of his lips, Gandy lazily doffed his low-crowned black Stetson.

"Mornin', Miz Downin'," he drawled in an accent fairly oozing dogwood and magnolia blossoms.

Her fists clenched at her hips. "This is an outrage, Mr. Gandy!"

He continued holding the hat aloft, grinning lopsidedly. "I said, Mornin', Miz Downin'."

A fly buzzed past her nose but she didn't bat an eye. "It is *not* a good morning, sir, and I won't pretend it is."

He settled the flat-crowned Stetson on his coal-black hair, pulled one boot out of the mud, gave it a shake, and settled it on the lowest step. "Well, now," he drawled, reaching into his waistcoat pocket and extracting a cheroot. He squinted at the blue Kansas sky. He squinted at her. "Sun's out. Rain's stopped. Cattle're bound t' be comin' through soon." He bit the end off the cheroot and spit it into the mud. "I'd call that a middlin' good day, ma'am. How 'bout you?"

"You can't mean to place that . . ."—she pointed indignantly at the picture— ". . . that sister of Sodom on the walls of your establishment for any and all to see!"

He laughed, the sun glinting off his straight, white teeth. "Sister of Sodom?" He reached inside his close-fitted black sack coat, patted his vest pockets, and came up with a wooden match. "If y'all find it offensive, no need t' worry. Once I get it inside, y' won't have t' see it again."

"Those innocent children have already seen it. Their poor mothers will be horrified. And what's more, anyone, young or old, can peek beneath those ridiculous swinging doors any time." She shook a finger at his nose. "And you know perfectly well the children will!"

"Shall I post a guard, Miz Downin'?" His drawl was so pronounced, *guard* sounded like *god*. "Would that satisfy y'all?" He struck the match on the hitching post, lit the cheroot, tossed the match over his shoulder, and grinned up at her through the smoke.

The slow, nonchalant drawl aggravated her as badly as his cavalier attitude and the stench of his cigar.

"What would satisfy me is to see you send that sinful painting back where it came from. Or, better yet, use it for firewood."

He glanced over his shoulder and appreciatively scanned the naked image from heat to foot. "She's here . . ."—he turned back to Agatha—". . . and she stays."

"But you simply can't hang such a picture!"

"Oh, but I can," he replied coolly, "and I will."

"I cannot allow it."

He smiled rakishly, took a deep drag of the cheroot, and said invitingly, "Then stop me." With the cigar he gestured over his shoulder. "Come on, boys, let's take the li'l lady inside."

A roar rose behind him and his henchmen lunged forward. Gandy took one step up only to find that Miss Downing had taken one step down. His knee came against her stiff gray skirt, sending her bustle higher up in back. His grin remained fixed, but he raised one eyebrow. "If y'all will excuse us, Miz Downin'."

"I'll do nothing of the sort." It took great fortitude for Agatha to hold her ground with his knee-high boot touching her skirt. But she stared him down. "If the respectable businessmen of this town are too timid to speak up against these dens of vice and corruption you and your ilk have brought upon us, the women are not!"

Gandy pressed both palms to his knee and leaned forward till his hat brim nearly touched her nose. He spoke quietly, the drawl more pronounced, but with an unmistakable note of menace. "I wouldn't like t' manhandle a woman in front of the townsfolk, ma'am, but if y'all don't step aside you'll leave me no choice."

Her nostrils narrowed. She drew herself up more erect. "Those who step aside to allow indecencies of this sort are as guilty as if they'd committed them themselves."

Their eyes clashed and held: his piercing black, hers defiant green. Behind Gandy the men waited in ankle-deep mud, their snickers having subsided into expectant silence. Down the street Perry White and Clydell Hottle shaded their eyes with their hands, waiting to see who won. On the opposite side of the street, a saloonkeeper and his bartender stepped to their own swinging doors, observing the confrontation with great amusement on their faces.

Gandy stared into Agatha Downing's determined eyes, realizing his steadiest customers and best friends waited to see if he'd back down to a female. To do so would make him the laughingstock of Proffitt, Kansas. He wasn't raised to be disrespectful to the weaker sex, but she left him no choice.

"As y' wish, ma'am," Gandy drawled, then nonchalantly anchored the cigar between his teeth, clamped his hands around Agatha's arms, whisked her off the step, and planted her eight inches deep in the mud. The men roared with approval, Agatha yelped, flailed her arms, and tried to pull her shoes out of the quagmire. But the mud only sucked her in deeper, and with an ignominious splat, she landed on her bustle in the ooze.

"Attaway, Gandy!"

"Don't take no guff offa no skirts!"

While Agatha glared at Gandy, his henchmen carried the naked lady up the wooden steps through the swinging doors of the Gilded Cage Saloon. When they'd disappeared, he tipped his hat and offered a dazzling smile. "G'day, Miz Downin'. It's been a pleasure." He made his way up the steps, cleaned his boots on the boot scraper outside the door, then followed the rowdy rabble inside, leaving the half doors swinging behind him.

From the opposite boardwalk the entire confrontation had been observed by a woman dressed in unrelieved black. Drusilla Wilson paused with valise in hand.

She had the build and rigidity of a railroad tie, a nose like a scythe blade, and eyes that looked as if they could drill through granite. Her thin mouth was downturned, the upper lip almost obscured by the lower. Her jaw was undershot, reminiscent of a grouper's. Beneath the undecorated brim of a stark black Quaker bonnet, a thin band of hair showed, and an inch of its center part. That hair—black, too, as if nature approved her bid to appear formidable—was drawn flat down over her temples and pinned her ears against her skull. She radiated the kind of sternness that caused people, when introduced to her, to step back instead of forward.

After witnessing the altercation across the street, Miss Wilson turned to a red-bearded man with a waxed handlebar moustache who stood just outside the swinging doors of the Hoof and Horn Saloon. He was clad in a red-and-white striped shirt with elastic sleeve bands cinched around a pair of enormous arms. Those arms were crossed over a massive chest that bounced each time he chuckled. On his fiery hair sat a black felt bowler. The stub of a dead cigar protruded from the red brush surrounding his mouth.

"That woman's name—what is it, please?" Drusilla Wilson demanded officiously.

"Who? Her?" He nodded toward Agatha and chuckled again.

Drusilla nodded, unamused.

"That's Agatha Downing."

"And where does she live?"

"Right there." He removed the stogie and pointed with its sodden end. "Above her hat shop."

"She owns it?"

"Yup."

Drusilla glanced at the pitiful figure on the far side of the street and murmured, "Perfect." Lifting her valise in one hand, her skirts in the other, she started toward the stepping stones that crossed the muddy thoroughfare. But she turned back toward the red-bearded man, who still smiled as he watched Agatha trying to extricate herself from the mud.

"And your name, sir?" she demanded.

He gave her his brown-toothed smile, then plugged his tiny mouth with the cigar once more. "Heustis Dyar."

She cocked one eyebrow at the scarlet lettering on the false-fronted building above his head. "And you own the Hoof and Horn?"

"That's right," he announced proudly, slipping his thumbs behind his suspenders, jutting out his chest. "Who wants t' know?"

She gave a smug half nod. "Drusilla Wilson."

"Drus—" He yanked the cigar from his mouth and took one step toward her. "Hey, wait a minute! What're you doin' here?" Scowling, he whirled toward his bartender, whose forearms rested on the tops of the swinging doors. "What's *she* doin' here?"

Tom Reese shrugged. "How should I know what she's doin' here? Startin' trouble, I reckon. Ain't that what she does everyplace she goes?"

Starting trouble was exactly what Drusilla Wilson was doing there, and as she turned toward her "sister" in the mud, she vowed that Heustis Dyar and the owner of the Gilded Cage would be the first to feel its impact.

Agatha was having great difficulty getting up. Her hip again. At the best of times it was unreliable; at the worst, unusable. Mired in the cold, sucking muck, it ached and refused to pull her weight up. She rocked forward but failed to gain her feet. Falling back, her hands buried to their wrists, she wished she were a cursing woman.

A black-gloved hand was extended her way.

"May I help you, Miss Downing?"

Agatha looked up into cold gray eyes that somehow managed to look sympathetic.

"Drusilla Wilson," the woman announced tersely, by way of introduction.

"Drus—?" Dumbstruck, Agatha stared up at the woman in awe.

"Come, let's get you up."

"But—"

"Take my hand."

"Oh . . . why . . . why, thank you."

Drusilla grasped Agatha's hand and hauled her to her feet. Agatha winced and pressed one hand to her left hip.

"Are you hurt?"

"Not really. Only my pride."

"But you're limping," Drusilla noted, helping her up the steps.

"It's nothing. Please, you'll soil your dress."

"I've been soiled by worse than mud, Miss Downing, believe me. I've had everything from beer to horse dung flung at me. A little of God's good clean mud will come as a welcome relief."

Together they passed the door of the Gilded Cage. Already the piano had started up inside and loud laughter billowed out into the otherwise peaceful April morning. The two women made their way to the adjacent shop, whose window announced in bright, gilded letters: AGATHA N. DOWNING, MILLINER.

Inside, Agatha forgot her soiled condition and said emotionally, "Miss Wilson, I'm so honored to meet you. I . . . why . . . I . . . I can't believe you're actually here in my humble shop."

"You know who I am, then?"

"Most certainly. Doesn't everybody?"

Miss Wilson allowed a dry chuckle. "Hardly everybody."

"Well, everyone across the state of Kansas, anyway—and I dare say across the United States—and most certainly everyone who's heard of the word *temperance.*" Agatha's heart beat fast in excitement.

"I should like to talk with you awhile. Might I wait while you change clothes?"

"Oh, most certainly!" Agatha gestured toward a pair of chairs at the front of the shop. "Please, make yourself comfortable while I'm gone. I live upstairs, so it won't be a minute. If you'll excuse me . . ."

Agatha moved through the workroom and out a rear door. Crude, wooden steps slanted along the back wall of the building to the apartments above. She took the stairs as she always did: two feet on each step, with a white-knuckled grip on the rail. Stairs were the worst. Standing and walking on a flat surface were tolerable, but hitching her left leg up each riser was awkward and painful. Her tie-back skirt made the going more difficult, severely restricting movement. Halfway up, she bent and reached beneath her hem to free the lowest set of ties. By the time she reached the landing at the top, she was slightly breathless. She paused, still gripping the rail. The common landing was shared by the residents of both apartments. She glanced at the door leading to Gandy's lodgings.

Another woman might have allowed herself tears in the aftermath of an ordeal such as he'd put her through. Not Agatha. Agatha only puffed out her chest with justifiable anger and knew an immense zeal to see the man brought to heel. As she turned toward her own door, she smiled at the thought that help had arrived at last.

It took her some time to remove her dress. It had twenty-eight buttons running up the front, eight tape ties caught up inside to form the rear bustle, and half that number lashing the apron-style skirt around her legs. As each tape was freed, the dress lost shape. By the time the last was untied, the bustle had given up all its bulges and grown as flat as the Kansas prairie. She held it aloft and her heart sank.

That man! That wretched, infuriating man! He had no idea what this would cost her in time and money and inconvenience. All her thousands of hand stitches, coated with mud. And no place to wash it. She glanced at the dry sink and the water pail beside it. The water wagon had come early this morning to fill the barrel, but it was on its wooden cradle beneath those long, long stairs. Besides, the dry sink wasn't large enough to accommodate a wash job like this. She should run it down to the Finn's laundry immediately, but considering who was waiting downstairs, that was out of the question.

Her ire increased when she removed her cotton bustle and petticoats. At least the dress was gray; these were white—or had been. She feared not even the Finn's homemade lye soap could remove mud stains as heavy as these.

Later. Worry about it later. Drusilla Wilson herself is waiting!

Downstairs, the visitor watched Miss Downing limp to the rear of the store and realized that limp had not been caused by her fall today. It appeared to be the sort of disability to which Agatha N. Downing had inured herself a long time ago.

As Agatha disappeared through a curtained doorway, Drusilla Wilson looked around. The shop was deep and narrow. Near the lace-curtained front window was a pair of oval-backed Victorian chairs tufted in pale orchid to match the curtains. The chairs flanked a tripod pie-crust table holding the latest issues of *Graham's, Godey's,* and *Peterson's* magazines. Wilson disregarded these in favor of a tour of the premises.

An assortment of hats in both felt and leghorn straw were displayed on *papier mâché* forms. Some were trimmed, some plain. The walls were lined with tidy cubbyholes holding ribbons, buttons, lace, and jets. An assortment of folded gauzes and jaconets lay fanned across a mahogany tabletop, representing the full prism of colors. In a wicker basket a selection of paste fruit looked nearly real enough to eat. Finely crafted artificial silk daisies and roses lay upon a flat basket. Upon another counter was displayed a selection of fur tippets and pheasant feather fans. Ostrich plumes hung on a cord near the rear wall. One glass cabinet appeared to contain an entire aviary of birds, nests, and eggs. Butterflies, dragonflies, and even cockchafers added to the collection. Set off by a pair of stuffed fox heads, the case looked as much like a scientific exhibit as a ladies' millinery display.

It took little more than two minutes for Drusilla Wilson to ascertain that Miss Downing ran a well-established business—*and,* she surmised, a line of communication with the women of Proffitt, Kansas.

She heard the shopkeeper's irregular footsteps and turned just as Agatha parted the lavender velvet curtains.

"Ah, a wonderful shop, wonderful."

"Thank you."

"How long have you been a milliner?"

"I learned the trade from my mother. When I was a girl I helped her do seamwork in our home. Then later, when she became a milliner and moved here to Proffitt, I came along with her. When she died, I stayed on."

Miss Wilson scanned Agatha's clean clothing. She found the periwinkle-blue a little too colorful for her taste and slightly too modern, with its fussy tie-ups at the rear and row upon row of tucks down the front. And she didn't hold with those tight apron skirts that showed the shape of a woman's hips all too clearly, nor with the form-fitting bodice that displayed the breadth of a woman's chest too specifically. Miss Downing didn't seem in the least concerned that she showed off both sets of contours with shocking clarity. But at least the tight, cleric collar was modest, though its lace edging was sinful, and the sleeves were wrist-length.

"So, Miss Downing, feeling better?"

"Much."

"One gets used to it when fighting for our cause. Whatever you do, don't discard the soiled dress. If the mud stains don't come out, you may want to wear it when standing up to the enemy in the next battle." Without warning, Miss Wilson briskly crossed the room and captured both of Agatha's hands. "My dear, I was so proud of you. So utterly proud." She squeezed Agatha's fingers very firmly. "I said to myself: *There* is a woman of stalwart mores. *There* is a woman who backs down at nothing. *There* is a woman I want fighting on my side!"

"Oh, nonsense. I only did what any woman would do in the same situation. Why, those two children—"

"But no other woman did it, did she? You were the only one who stood up for virtue." Again she gave Agatha's hands an emphatic squeeze, then released them and stepped back.

Agatha became flushed with pleasure at such high praise from a woman of Drusilla Wilson's renown. "Miss Wilson," she declared honestly, "I mean it when I say it's an honor to have you here. I've read so much about you in the newspapers. My goodness, they are calling you the most powerful scepter ever wielded for the temperance cause."

"What they say about me matters little. What matters most is that we're making headway."

"So I've been reading."

"Twenty-six locals of the national Women's Christian Temperance Union formed, statewide, in '78 alone. More last year. But we're not through yet!" She raised one fist, then dropped it as her lips formed a thin smile. "That's why I'm here, of course. News of your town has reached me. I'm told it's getting out of hand."

Agatha sighed, limped toward her rolltop desk set against the rear right wall, and sank to a chair before it. "You saw firsthand exactly how much. And you can hear for yourself what's going on next door." She nodded toward the common wall between her shop and the saloon. Through it came the muffled strains of "Fallen Angel, Fall into My Arms."

Miss Wilson pursed her lips and cracks appeared around them as upon a two-day-old pudding. "It must be trying."

Agatha touched her temples briefly. "To say the least." She shook her head woefully. "Ever since that man came a month ago, it's gotten worse and worse. I have a confession to make, Miss Wilson, I . . ."

"Please, call me Drusilla."

"Drusilla . . . yes. Well, as I began to say, my motives in confronting Mr. Gandy were not strictly altruistic. I fear you praised me a little too precipitously. You see, since that saloon opened next door, my business has begun to suffer. The ladies are reluctant to walk the boardwalk for fear of being accosted by some inebriate before they reach my door." Agatha's brow furrowed. "It's most distressing. There are horrible fights at all hours of the day and night, and since that man Gandy won't allow fisticuffs on the premises, his bartender throws the fighters out into the street."

"I'm not surprised, given the price of mirrors and glassware out here. But, go on."

"The fights aren't the only thing. The language. Oh, Miss Wilson, it's shocking. Absolutely shocking. And with those half doors the sound drifts out into the street so that there's no telling what my ladies might hear as they pass by. I . . . I really can't say I blame them for hesitating to patronize my shop. Why, I might feel the same, were I in their place." Agatha knit her fingers and studied her lap. "And, of course, there's the most humiliating reason of all for them to avoid the general area." She looked up with genuine regret in her eyes. "There are those of my customers whose husbands frequent the saloon more than they do their own homes. Several of the women are so abashed at the idea of running into their husbands on the street—in *that* condition—that they shy away at the mere thought."

"Unfortunate, yet your shop looks prosperous."

"I make a fairly decent living, but—"

"No." Miss Wilson presented her gloved palms. "I didn't mean to inquire as to your financial status. I only meant it as an observation that you're well established here and undoubtedly have most of the women in town on your list of clientele."

"Well, I suppose that's true—or was, until a month ago."

"Tell me, Miss Downing, are there any other millinery shops in Proffitt?"

"Why, no. Mine is the only one. Mr. Halorhan, down at the Mercantile, and Mr. McDonnell, at the Longhorn Store, sell the ready-mades now. But," she added with a touch of superiority, "of course they're not trimmed to match."

"And if I may be so forward, might I inquire if you're a churchgoing woman?"

Agatha scarcely managed to keep from bristling. "Why, most certainly!"

"I thought as much. Methodist?"

"Presbyterian."

"Ah, Presbyterian." Miss Wilson cocked her head toward the saloon. "And Presbyterians do love their music, don't they?" Nothing could bring tears to a drunken man's eyes like a chorus of voices raised in heavenly praise.

Agatha gave the wall a malevolent glance. "*Most* music," she replied. The song had changed to "Buffalo Gals Won't You Come Out Tonight?"

"How many saloons are currently—shall we say—*prospering* in Proffitt?"

"Eleven."

"Eleven! Ach!" Drusilla threw back her head in vexation. She marched around with both hands on her hips. "They chased them out of Abilene years ago. But they just kept moving farther down the line, didn't they? Ellsworth, Wichita, Newton, Hays, and now Proffitt."

"This was such a peaceful little town before they came here."

Wilson whipped around, jabbed a finger into the air. "And it can be again." She strode to the desk, her face purposeful. "I'll come straight to the point, Agatha. I may call you Agatha, may I not?" She didn't wait for an answer. "When I saw you stand up to that man, I not only thought: There's a woman who'll stand up to a man. I also thought: There's a woman worthy of being a general in the army against the Devil's Brew."

Agatha touched her chest, surprised. "A general? Me?" She would have arisen from her chair, but Drusilla blocked the way. "I'm afraid you're wrong, Miss Wi—"

"I'm not wrong. You're perfect!" She braced herself against the desktop and leaned close. "You know every woman in this town. You're a practicing Christian. You have additional incentive to fight for temperance, since your business is being threatened. And, furthermore, you have the advantage of juxtaposition to one of the corrupted. Close him down and the others will follow, I assure you. It happened in Abilene; it can happen here. Now what do you say?"

Drusilla's nose was so close, Agatha pressed against the back of her chair. "Why, I . . . I . . ."

"On Sunday I intend to ask your minister for a few moments in the pulpit. Believe me, that's all it'll take, and you'll have a regular army at your command!"

Agatha wasn't sure she wanted an army, but Drusilla rushed on. "You'll not only have the backing of the national Women's Christian Temperance Union, but of Governor St. John himself."

Though Agatha was aware that John P. St. John had been elected on a strong prohibition platform two years ago, beyond that she knew nothing whatever of politics, and little more of organization on such a scale.

"Please, I . . ." She released a fluttery breath and inched herself up to her feet. Turning away, she clasped her hands tightly. "I wouldn't know the first thing about organizing such a group."

"I'll help. The national organization will help. *The Temperance Banner* will help." Wilson named the statewide newspaper inaugurated two years before to support temperance activities and prohibition legislation. "And I know what I'm talking about when I say the women of this town will help. I've traveled well over three thousand miles. I've crossed and recrossed this state and have even been to Washington. I've attended hundreds of public meetings in schoolhouses and churches all across Kansas. In every one I've seen a rousing group of supporters formed almost immediately for The Cause."

"Legislation?" The word scared the wits out of Agatha. "I'm ignorant of politics, Miss Wilson, nor do I wish to be involved in them. Running my business is quite enough for me to handle. I will, however, be happy to introduce you to the women from Christ Presbyterian if you wish to invite them to an organizational meeting."

"Very well. That's a start. And could we hold it here?"

"Here?" Agatha's eyes widened. "In my shop?"

"Yes." There was nothing timid about Drusilla Wilson.

"But I haven't enough chairs and . . ."

"We'll stand, as we often must at the doors of barrooms, for hours at a time."

It was easy to see how Wilson had managed to organize an entire network of U.C.T.U. locals. Her eyes pinned Agatha as successfully as a lepidoterist's pin holds a butterfly. Though Agatha was unsure of many things, she was certain of one. She wanted to get even with that man for what he'd done to her this morning. And she wanted to be rid of the noise and revelry reverberating through the wall. She wanted her business to thrive again. If she didn't take this first step, who would?"

"My door will be open."

"Good." Drusilla clasped Agatha's hands and gave them one firm pump. "Good. That's all it will take, I'm confident. Once the women gather and see that they're not alone in their fight against alcohol, they'll surprise you with their staunchness and support." She stepped back and drew on her gloves. "Well." She picked up her valise. "I must find the hotel, then take a walk through town and pinpoint the objects of our crusade, all eleven of them. Then I must visit your minister, Reverend—?"

"Clarksdale," Agatha supplied. "Samuel Clarksdale. You'll find him in the small frame house just north of the church. You can't miss it."

"Thank you, Agatha. Until Sunday, then."

With a whisk and a flourish, she was gone.

Agatha stood rooted. It felt as though an August tornado had just blown through. But when she looked around, things remained magically unchanged. The piano tinkled on the other side of the wall. Outside a dog barked in the street. A horse and rider passed beyond the lace curtains. Agatha pressed a hand to her heart, released a deep breath, and dropped to her chair. A member, yes. But an organizer, no. She hadn't the time nor the vitality to be the head of the town's temperance organization. While she was still pondering the issue, Violet Parsons arrived for work.

"Agatha, I heard! *Tt-tt!*" Violet was a titterer. It was the only thing about her that Agatha disliked. A woman with hair as white as snow and a mouth with more wrinkles than a Spanish fan should have outgrown tittering long ago. But Violet tittered constantly, like an organ grinder's monkey. "*Tt-tt-tt.* I heard you came face to face with our proprietor right on the saloon steps. How ever did you get up the nerve to try to stop him?"

"What would you have done, Violet? Perry White and Clydell Hottle were already hurrying down the street, hoping for a better look at that heathen painting."

Violet placed four fingertips over her lips. "Is it really a painting of a . . . *tt-tt-tt* . . ."—the titter changed to a whisper—". . . naked lady?"

"Lady? Why, Violet, if she's naked, how can she be a lady?"

Violet's eyes brightened mischievously. "Then she really is . . ."—again, the whisper—". . . naked?"

"As a jaybird. Which is precisely why I interfered."

"And Mr. Gandy . . . *tt-tt-tt* . . . Did he really set you in the mud?" Violet couldn't help it; her eyes—the exact shade of Agatha's dress—sparkled as they always did when Gandy's name came up. Violet had never been married, but she'd never stopped wishing. From the first time she'd seen Gandy sauntering down the street with a flirtatious grin on his face, she'd started acting like an idiot. She still did, every time she caught a glimpse of him. The fact never failed to sour Agatha.

"News travels fast."

Violet blushed. "I stopped down at Halorhan's for a new thimble. I lost mine yesterday, you know."

Already the incident on the street was being discussed at Halorhan's Mercantile? How disquieting. Agatha produced the thimble and clapped it down on a glass countertop. "I found it. Underneath the leghorn straw you were working on. And what else did you learn at Halorhan's?"

"That Drusilla Wilson is in town and spent close to an hour in this very shop! Are you going to?"

"Am I going to what?" Agatha grew vexed at Violet's assumption that she knew everything being discussed at Halorhan's on any given morning. Violet thrived on gossip.

"Hold a temperance meeting here?"

Agatha's torso snapped erect. "Heavens! The woman walked out of here less than fifteen minutes ago, and already you heard that at Halorhan's?"

"Well, are you?"

"No, not exactly."

"But that's what they're saying."

"I agreed to let Miss Wilson hold one here, that's all."

Violet looked petrified. Her eyes grew round and blue as two balls. "Gracious, that's enough."

Agatha moved to her desk and sat down, discomfited. "He won't do anything."

"But he's our new landlord. What if he evicts us?"

Agatha's chin rose defiantly. "He wouldn't dare."

But the thought had already occurred to LeMaster Scott Gandy.

He stood at the bar with one boot on the brass rail, listening to the men make ribald comments about the painting. Business was brisk already, considering the hour. Word traveled fast in a town this size. The place was crowded with curious males who'd come to get a look at the nude. When Jubilee and the girls arrived, business would thrive even more.

Unless that persimmon-mouthed milliner continued harrassing him. Gandy frowned. That woman could develop into one bodacious, infernal nuisance if she put her mind to it. It took only one like her to rile up a whole townful of females and start them nagging at their husbands about the hours they spent at the saloon. If she was upset about the painting, she'd be incensed about the girls.

Gandy tipped the brim of his Stetson low over his eyes and rested both elbows on the bar behind him. He stared thoughtfully across the quiet street at Heustis Dyar's place, wondering when the first beefs would come. That's when the fun would really start. When those rowdy, thirsty cowpunchers hit town, that little do-gooder next door would more than likely pack up and light out for other parts and his worries would be over.

He smiled to himself, extracted a cheroot from the pocket of his vest, and struck a match on his boot heel. But before he applied it, the object of his thoughts—Goody Two-Shoes herself—materialized from next door and moved past the saloon. For no more than five seconds her head and feet were clearly visible above and below the swinging doors. But that's all it took for Gandy to realize she wasn't walking normally. The match burned his fingers. He cursed and dropped it, then hurried toward the swinging door, standing in the shadows to one side. He watched her make her way along the boardwalk. He listened to the shuffling sound made by her shoes. He began to grow warm around the collar. Five doors down, she descended a set of steps, gripping the rail tightly. But instead of using the stepping-stones to cross the street as all the ladies did, she lifted her skirts and trudged laboriously through the mud to the other side.

"Dan?" Gandy called.

"Something wrong?" Loretto didn't look up. He fanned the deck of cards into a peacock's tail, then snapped it together. It was too early in the day for gamblers, but Gandy had taught him to keep his fingers nimble at all times.

"Come here."

Loretto squared the deck and rose from the chair with the same unjointed motion he so admired in the boss.

He came up behind Gandy at the swinging doors. "Yes, boss?"

"That woman." Agatha Downing had reached the far side of the street and was struggling up the steps to the boardwalk, clutching an armful of clothing that looked suspiciously much like the gray dress she'd been wearing earlier. Gandy scowled at her clean skirts—blue now. They churned unnaturally with each step. "Is she limping?"

"Yessir, she sure is."

"Good God! Did I do that t' her?" Gandy looked horrified.

"Not hardly. She's limped ever since I knew her."

Gandy's head snapped around. "Ever since you knew her?" This was getting worse.

"Yup. She's got a gimp leg."

Gandy felt himself blush for the first time in years.

"A gimp leg?"

"That's right."

"And I set her in the mud." He watched Agatha disappear with her dirty clothing into the Finn's laundry down the block. He felt like a heel.

"You didn't exactly set her in the mud, Scotty. She fell."

"She fell *after* I set her in the mud!"

"Whatever you say, boss."

"Well, why didn't somebody say somethin'? How in tarnation was I supposed t' know?"

"Just figured you did. You been doin' business next door to her for a month now. You collected rent from her. She walks down to Paulie's twice a day so regular you could set your clock by her. Breakfast and supper. Never fails."

But Gandy had never looked twice at the woman. She was the kind who blended into the weatherbeaten boardwalk. A dull, gray moth upon a dull, gray rock. When he'd gone next door to introduce himself as the new owner of the building, she'd been sitting at her rolltop desk and hadn't risen from her chair. Instead of bringing the rent over herself, she'd sent it with a timid, twittering old woman who looked as if she'd just swallowed a frog. The few times he'd eaten at Paulie's he didn't recall seeing her there.

Sweet Jesus! What would the women of Proffitt say? If it was true that there was an "organizer" in town, he'd have them all on his head. And they'd have plenty to say in that nuisance of a rag they printed. He could see the headline now: SALOON OWNER TOPPLES CRIPPLED TEMPERANCE WORKER IN THE MUD.

Chapter 2

At five-thirty that afternoon Scott Gandy left the rear of the saloon and walked up the same steps to the same landing Agatha had ascended earlier. He glanced at the two long windows, one on either side of her door, but as usual they were shrouded by thick lace. He tossed his cheroot over the railing and entered his own door. The saloon and its overhead apartments occupied three-fourths of the building, the millinery shop and corresponding apartment, one fourth. Upstairs, his portion was bisected by a hall with the door at its west end and a window at its east. To the left were four rooms of equal size. To the right were Gandy's living quarters and his private office. He entered the office, a small, spare room with wainscoted walls, a single west window, and only the necessary furnishings: a desk, two chairs, coat-tree, safe, and a small cast-iron stove.

It was a cold room, the window curtainless, the wall above the waist-high wainscot painted a drab sage-green, the oak floor raw, bare. He moved to the safe, knelt, and spun the dial, locked away a packet of bills, then, with a sigh, stood and rubbed the back of his neck. Lord, it was quiet. Getting close to suppertime. Ivory had deserted the piano downstairs and Jack had gone to eat. Gandy glanced out the window, hooked his thumbs in his waistcoat pockets, and absently drummed a rhythm on the silk. The view outside offered little to buoy him. Unpainted

frame buildings, muddy streets, and prairie. Nothing but prairie. No spreading water oak trees festooned with Spanish moss, no scent of magnolia drifting in on the
spring breeze, no mockingbirds. He missed the mockingbirds.

This time of day at Waverley, the family used to gather on the wide back veranda and sip glasses of minted iced tea, and Delia would toss cracked corn to the
mockingbirds, trying to entice them to eat from her hand. He could see her yet,
squatting in a billow of hooped skirts, cupping the corn in her palm. Golden head
with ringlets down to her shoulders. Skin as white as milk. Fiddle-waisted. And
her eyes, as dark and arresting as the notches on a dogwood petal, forever allur-
ing.

"Why don't you feed the peacocks?" his father would call to her.

But Delia would kneel patiently, cupped hand extended. "Because the peacocks
are too audacious. And besides"—Delia would rest her chin on one shoulder and
look back at her husband—"no fun tryin' to get a tame bird to eat from your hand,
is there, Scotty?" she would say teasingly.

And his mother would glance his way and smile at the look she saw on her
son's face. But he never cared who knew it. He was as smitten with Delia as he'd
been the first time he'd kissed her when they were fourteen years old.

Then Leatrice would waddle to the door—good old Leatrice, with her skin as
dark as sorghum syrup and breasts the size of watermelons. He wondered where
she was now. "Suppuh, suh," she'd announce. "Pipin'."

And Dorian Gandy would take his wife's arm, and Scott himself would rise
from his chair and slowly extend a hand to Delia. And she'd smile up at him with
a promise for later and let herself be tugged to her feet. Then, hand in hand, they
would follow his parents inside beneath the high, cool ceilings.

But those days were gone forever.

Gandy stared at the prairie. He blinked once, hard. His stomach rumbled, reminding him it was suppertime now. With a deep sigh, he turned from the window
toward the desk and glanced at the calendar. Nearly four weeks he'd been here.
Jubilee and the girls would arrive any day. They couldn't get here fast enough to
suit him. Things were dull without Jube.

Leaving his office by a second door, he entered the adjoining sitting room of
his private apartment. It was much cheerier, with burgundy draperies, a factory-
made rug, and sturdy, masculine furniture. It held a leather settee with matching
chairs, heavy mahogany tables, and two banquet lamps. To his left a door led directly to the hall; to his right a dresser held his humidor and hat block. On the
wall above it hung a watercolor behind which was stuck a branch from a cotton
plant, its three bolls grayed in their brown clawlike husks. The painting was that
of a pillared mansion with a wide front veranda, flanked by lush greenery and
sprawling lawns on which stood two poised peacocks.

Waverley.

His gaze lingered on the picture while he placed his hat on the block. Nostalgia
hit him with the force of a blow. From the humidor he took a cheroot, as rich and
brown as the soil from which that cotton boll had sprung, the rich Mississippi bot-
tomlands of the great Tombigbee River. Lost in thought, he forgot to light his cigar, but absently stroked its length. He thought about Waverley for so long that
he eventually laid the cheroot on the dresser, unused.

He wandered into the adjoining bedroom and tossed his jacket onto a double
bed. He recalled the rosewood four-poster at Waverley where he'd brought his
bride and bedded her for the first time. The gauzy netting hanging all around, circling them in a private haven of their own. The flickering gas lantern sending trellised shadows through the mesh against her skin.

Again he blinked. What was it that had triggered all these thoughts of Waverley? It wasn't good to pine for the old days. He stripped off his vest and shirt and tossed them across the hobnail bedspread. At the washstand he used the pitcher and bowl. Delia had taught him that. She liked her man clean, she'd always said. Since Delia he'd learned that a lot of women liked a clean man, and clean men were so rare they could get a woman to do almost anything for them. It was only one of the sad things he'd learned since he'd lost Delia.

Stop it, Gandy! There's no goin' back, so why do you punish yourself?

Toweling his face, he ambled to the front window. It overlooked main street, giving him a view of something that at last took his mind off Delia and Waverley: Miss Agatha Downing limping toward Paulie's Restaurant to have her supper. The towel stilled against his chin. Her limp was very real, very pronounced. How could he have missed it before? He frowned, recalling her plopping backward in the mud. Again, he almost blushed.

She entered Paulie's and disappeared. He lunged to the bed and pulled the watch from his vest pocket. Six o'clock exactly.

He glanced toward the street, flung the towel aside, yanked a clean shirt from the chifforobe, and threw it on. There was no logical reason for him to hurry, yet he did. Holding the vest in his teeth, he grabbed up his jacket and hat and hit the stairs at a run, still stuffing his shirttails in. By the time he reached Paulie's, everything was buttoned and tucked into place.

He saw her immediately upon entering. Her dress was the color of an evening sky and the top of her bustle poked through the back of her chair as Cyrus Paulie stood taking her order. Her shoulders were narrow, her neck long. She was small-ribbed and thin-armed and her dress fit with remarkable snugness. She wore a mountainous hat decorated with butterflies and bows beneath which little of her hair showed.

Gandy moved inside and took a seat behind her, heard her order chicken.

So why was he here, staring at the back of an old, lame woman? All those remembrances of home, he thought. Mississippi gentlemen were raised to have better manners than those he'd displayed today. If his mother were alive, she'd take him to task for his rudeness. And if Delia were alive—but if Delia were alive, he wouldn't be living out here in this godforsaken cowtown in the first place.

Cy delivered a plate of chicken dinner to Miss Downing, and Gandy ordered the same, studying her back while they both ate. When Cy came to deliver her apple cobbler and pick up her dirty plate, Scott signaled him over.

"How was the meal, Scotty?" Cyrus Paulie was a jovial fellow with a ready smile. Unfortunately, his teeth looked as if someone had opened his mouth and thrown them in without caring where or in which direction they landed. He piled Scott's dirty plate atop Agatha's and displayed his sorry collection of snags.

"Meal was fine, Cy."

"Get you some apple cobbler? Made fresh this afternoon."

"No, thanks, Cy. I'll just settle up." Scot drew a silver dollar from his waistcoat pocket and dropped it into Cy's palm. "And take out the price of Miz Downin's supper, too."

"Miss Downing?" Cy's eyebrows nearly touched his hairline. "You mean Agatha?"

"I do."

Cy glanced at the woman, then back at the saloon owner. No sense reminding Gandy he'd set the woman on her rump in the mud that very morning. A man didn't forget a thing like that.

"Sure thing, Scotty. Coffee?"

Gandy patted his flat belly. "No, thanks. Full up."

"Well, then . . ." Cy gestured with the dirty plate. "Stop in again soon."

At the same time, Agatha took the proper coins from her handbag and caught Cyrus Paulie as he passed her table.

"Well, how was everything, Miss Downin'?" he inquired as he stood beside her, resting the plates against the long white apron lashed around his middle.

"Delicious, as usual. Give Emma my compliments."

"Sure will, ma'am, sure will."

She extended her coins. He ignored them and picked up her cobbler bowl. "No need for that. You meal's already paid for."

Agatha's eyes widened. Her head snapped up, her hat teetered. "Paid for? But—"

"By Mr. Gandy." Cyrus nodded to a table behind her.

She spun in her chair to find the bane of her morning seated at a nearby table watching every move she made. Apparently, he'd been doing so for some time; there was a soiled napkin on his table and he was enjoying an after-dinner cigar. His dark eyes were riveted upon her. While they stared at each other, the only thing that moved was the smoke coiling about his black hair. Until he politely nodded his head.

The color leaped to her face. Her mouth tightened. "I can very well pay for my own, Mr. Paulie," she declared, loudly enough that Gandy could hear. "And even if I couldn't, I would not accept a meal from a lowlife like him. Tell Mr. Gandy I would cheerfully starve first."

She threw two coins on the table. One hit a sugar bowl and ricocheted to the floor, where it rolled for a full five seconds, then circled to a halt. In the silence it sounded like thunder.

Agatha rose from her chair with all the dignity she could muster, feeling the curious eyes of other diners watching as she shuffled past Gandy to the door. He watched her all the way, but she lifted her chin high and glared at the brass doorknob.

Outside, her eyes stung with humiliation. Some people got their satisfactions in cruel ways. She supposed he was chuckling.

At home she struggled up the stairs, wishing once—just once!—she could stomp up the steps with all the outrage she felt. Instead, she was forced to stump up like an old woman. Well, she wasn't an old woman. She wasn't! And to prove it, when she got to the top she slammed the door so hard a picture fell off her parlor wall.

She tore her hat off and paced the length of her apartment, rubbing her left hip. How humiliating! With a whole room full of people looking on he chose to do a thing like that. But why? To taunt her? She'd put up with taunting since she was nine years old and had gone bouncing down a flight of stairs. Forever after, children had giggled, teased, and found disparaging names for "the gimp." And even adults couldn't resist a second glance. But this—this was debasing.

In time her anger subsided, leaving her empty and forlorn. She put her hat in a bandbox, stowed it on the chifforobe shelf, wandered to the front window, and looked down on the street. Dusk had fallen. Across the way the lights from the Hoof and Horn splashed onto the boardwalk from behind the swinging doors. Below, they most likely did the same, though she could see no more than the railed roof of the boardwalk, just outside her floor-length window. The piano had started up. Its faraway tinkling, coupled with the sound of laughter, made her sad. She turned, studying the apartment: the perimeter of her world. One long, stuffy shotgun room filled with her old maid's furnishings. Her prized Hepplewhite bed and matching chest with its inlay of white holly, the maroon horsehair settee with ivory crocheted antimacassars, the gateleg table, the lowboy, corner curio cabinet, the six-plate stove, the banjo clock, the sampler she'd knocked off the wall.

With a sigh she went to pick it up. Hanging it on the nail, she read the familiar lines:

> *Needle, thread, embroidery hoop;*
> *Satin stitch, French knot, and loop;*
> *Patience, care, and fortitude;*
> *Practice makes my stitching good.*

As she gazed at the sampler, a sad expression covered her face. How old had she been when her mother taught her to stitch? Seven? Eight? Before the accident, most certainly, because one of her earliest recollections was of standing beside her mother's chair in the shabby house in Sedalia, Colorado, where her father had staked his claim in the gold fields, certain that *this time* he'd strike it rich. She remembered the house clearly, out of all the rest they'd lived in, because it was the one where *it* had happened. The one with the steep steps and the dark, narrow stairwell. Her mother had gotten an ivy plant from somewhere and had hung it in the kitchen window. The ivy had been the only cheerful note in the otherwise pitiful place. There was a worn wooden rocking chair below the plant. It was beside this chair Agatha had been standing, watching her mother demonstrate a perfect petal stitch, when she had piped up in her childish voice, "When I grow up I'm going to have little girls and I'll do embroidery on all their fancy dresses."

Regina Downing had laid down her handiwork, drawn Agatha against the arm of the rocker, and kissed her cheek. "Then you be sure to get you a man who doesn't drink up all the money for those pretty little dresses. Promise me that, will you, Gussie?"

"I promise, Mommy."

"Good. Then sit down here on the stool and I'll teach you the petal stitch. Got to know that one for making daisies."

The memory had lost none of its clarity over the years. Not the warm autumn sun cascading through the window. Not the sound of steam hissing from a kettle on the cookstove. Not the smell of barley soup and onions stewing for their supper. Why it had remained so clear, Agatha didn't know. Perhaps it was the promise she'd made her mother, the only one she ever recalled her mother asking of her. Perhaps it was the first time she'd voiced her wishes about having little girls of her own. Perhaps it was nothing more complex than the fact that she had learned the petal stitch that day, and she'd been stitching ever since.

For whatever reason, the memory persevered. In it she was a hale and healthy little girl, leaning her belly against the arm of her mother's rocker, standing on two sturdy legs. Her only other memory of that house was the night she made that fateful trip down the stairs, pushed by her own drunken father, ending forever the possibility of acquiring daughters or a husband to give them to her. For what man wanted a cripple?

In the gloom of her lonely apartment, Agatha turned from the sampler and prepared for bed. She locked her door, hung up her clothing, including the cotton pad she wore over her left hip to make it match the right. She donned her nightdress and gave the weights of the banjo clock their nightly pull. Then she lay in the dark and listened to it.

Tick. Tock. Tick. Tock.

Lord, she hated the sound. Night after lonely night she went to bed and heard it marking off the days of her life. There were things she wanted, so many things. A real house, with a yard where she could plant flowers and vegetables, and where she could hang a swing in a tall cottonwood tree. A kitchen where she could cook suppers, a kitchen with a big oak table set for four, or six, or even eight. A clothesline where she could hang washing: snow-white socks from short to long, the longest hanging beside a man's oversized chambray shirt. Someone who'd toiled all day and came home hungry and shared the supper table, laughing with his children. Those children, scrubbed shiny, wearing the beautiful hand-stitched nightdresses she would make herself, tucked into beds down the hall at this time of day. And someone there beside her at bedtime. Another human being telling her how his day had been, asking about hers, then holding her hand as he sighed off to sleep. Another's even breathing in the same room with hers. He need not be handsome, or rich, or doting. Only sober, and honest, and kind.

But none of it would happen. She was thirty-five already; her child-bearing years were nearly gone. And she worked at a business whose customers were only women.

Tick. Tock.

Foolishness, Agatha. Nothing but an old maid's muse. Even if by some miracle you met a man, a widower, perhaps, who needed someone to look after his children, he'd take one look at you and realize you wouldn't last long kneeling in gardens, or standing at washboards, or chasing nimble-footed children. And, besides, men don't want women who have to pad their bodies to be symmetrical. They want the uncrooked ones.

Tick. Tock.

She thought of all the thousands of women who had men such as she imagined, yet complained about having to weed the garden, toil over a hot stove, scrub socks, and listen to children quarrel. They didn't appreciate what they had.

I would be such a good mother, she thought. It was a conviction she'd had for as long as she could remember. If her legs were strong enough to birth a baby, the rest would be easy. *And I'd be a good wife, too. For if I were ever blessed with the opportunity, I would never take it for granted. I would protect what I had by giving my best.*

From below came the tinkle of the piano, and instead of a man's steady breathing at her side, the last thing she heard was a gambler shouting, "Keno!"

When Violet Parsons came in for work at eleven the next morning, she burst into the workroom babbling.

"Is it true? Did Mr. Gandy really take you out for supper last night?"

Agatha sat at the worktable near the window, stitching a raspberry-silk lining into a Dolly Varden hat. Her needle kept moving, but she glanced up irritatedly.

"Who told you that?" Violet lived in Mrs. Gill's boardinghouse with six other old ladies. They carried news faster than Western Union, though it was a mystery how.

"Did he?" Violet's eyes grew as bright as periwinkles.

Agatha felt her neck grow warm. "When you left here yesterday, you went straight to Mrs. Gill's for supper. This morning you walked a mere four blocks to get here. How in heaven's name could you have heard such a thing so fast?"

"He did! I can tell he did!" Violet covered her lips. *"Tt-tt.* I'd give my mother's pearl brooch if a man like that would take *me* out to supper. *Tt-tt."*

"Violet, shame on you!" Agatha formed a knot, snipped a thread, and began to rethread the needle. "Your mother would be horrified if she could hear you say such a thing, may she rest in peace."

"No, she wouldn't. My mother liked handsome men. Did I ever show you the daguerreotype of my father? Come to think of it, Mr. Gandy looks rather like Papa, but Mr. Gandy is even handsomer. His hair is darker and his eyes are . . ."

"Violet, I've heard quite enough! I swear people will begin to snicker if you don't stop rhapsodizing over that man."

"They say he bought you a roast-chicken dinner last night at Cyrus and Emma's."

"Well, they're wrong. After what he did to me yesterday morning, do you think I'd accept dinner from him? Why, the food would stick in my throat."

"Then, what *did* happen?"

Agatha sighed and gave up. If she didn't answer, she'd get no work out of Violet all day. "He offered to pay for my meal, but I told him in no uncertain terms I'd starve first. I paid for my own."

"He offered . . ." Violet's eyes glittered like sapphires. "Oh, wait till I tell the girls." She pressed a hand to her heart and closed her wrinkled eyelids. They twitched while she sighed.

Senile, though Agatha. *I love you dearly, Violet, but you're going senile living with all those old women.* Not one of the "the girls" would ever see sixty again.

"Aren't you a little old to be getting spoony over a forty-year-old man?"

"He's not forty. He's only thirty-eight."

Agatha was abashed that Violet knew, precisely. "And you're sixty-three."

"Not yet I'm not."

"Well, you will be next month."

Violet ignored the fact. "Five different times I've passed him on the boardwalk, and every time he's smiled and doffed his hat and called me ma'am."

"Then gone down the street and hired one of the soiled doves, no doubt."

"Well, at least he doesn't have any of them working in his place—you have to say that for him."

"Not yet he hasn't. But the punchers haven't arrived yet either."

Violet's eyes grew troubled. "Oh, Agatha, do you think he will?"

Agatha lifted one eyebrow. Her needle poised eloquently. "After what he carried in there yesterday, I wouldn't put anything past him."

"The girls said Mr. Gandy was a . . ." Violet's words halted as the shop door opened in the front room. "Just a minute. I'll see who it is."

Agatha continued stitching. Violet parted the lavender curtains and stepped through. "Oh!" Agatha heard. Breathless and girlish.

"Mornin', Miz Parsons. Fine mornin', isn't it?" drawled a deep baritone voice.

Agatha's spine stiffened. She gaped at the swaying curtains.

"Why, Mr. Gandy, what a surprise." Violet sounded as if she'd just run full tilt against a fence post and knocked herself stupid.

Scott Gandy doffed his hat and bestowed his most charming smile. "I dare say it is. I reckon y'all don't get a lot o' gentlemen customers comin' round."

"None at all."

"And I suspect I'm not any too welcome after what happened out front yesterday mornin'."

Loving Savior, he has dimples! thought Violet. And he's carrying Agatha's dress! The gray frock and a white petticoat were folded neatly over his arm. It reminded Violet that she must not excuse his rudeness too readily. She bent closer and whispered, "Agatha was very upset, I'll grant you that."

He bent, too, and whispered back, "I'm sure she was."

"She still is."

"It was a most ungentlemanly thing for me to do. Most ungentlemanly." Their noses were so close Violet could see herself reflected in his back irises. She caught a whiff of fine tobacco and bay rum, scents she rarely smelled working in a millinery shop and living with the girls. Still, she couldn't let the scoundrel get off without a scolding.

"See to it that it doesn't happen again, Mr. Gandy," she chided, still in an undertone.

"It's a promise." He looked properly contrite, the smile gone, the dimples erased. Violet's heart melted. Suddenly, she realized they were still nose to nose, and she straightened with a snap, blushing.

"Can I help you, Mr. Gandy?" she inquired in a normal tone of voice.

"I was hopin' Miz Downin' would be in. Is she here, Miz Parsons?"

In the back room Agatha clasped the edge of the worktable, wishing she were nimble enough to leap to her feet and streak out the back door.

"She's in the back. Just follow me."

Don't you dare, Violet! thought Agatha. But it was too late. The curtains parted and Violet led the way into the workroom, followed by their landlord.

"Mr. Gandy is here to see you, Agatha." Violet stood aside and let Gandy pass into the room. He moved with the unhurried pace of those accustomed to surviving in the humidity and heat of the Deep South, crossing slowly to the woman at the worktable beside the west windows. She sat stiff-backed, tight-mouthed, pouring her attention solely on the stitches she was furiously applying to the lining of a felt hat. Her face was as bright as the silk on which she sewed.

Gandy stopped beside her chair and removed his hat.

"Mornin', Miz Downin'," he said quietly.

She refused to answer or look up.

"Can't say I blame you for not wantin' t' talk t' me."

"If there's something you need from the shop, Miss Parsons can help you."

"I've come t' see you, not Miz Parsons."

"I've already had my breakfast. And paid for it myself." She jabbed the needle through the felt as if it were his hide.

"Yes, ma'am. I saw you goin' down t' Paulie's this mornin'." Her head snapped up and their gazes collided. For the first time she saw that he held her gray dress and white petticoat over one arm. Her face turned a shade brighter. "Thought about tryin' t' talk t' you there, but decided it'd be best t' do so in private."

The needle seemed to grow slick in her fingers. What possible reason could he have for observing her comings and goings?

"Last night at Paulie's, I want t' say that—" He cleared his throat nervously.

She gave up all pretense of sewing and glared up at him. "Last night at Paulie's you should have had the good grace to leave when you saw I was there. Was it amusing, Mr. Gandy? Did you enjoy humiliating me in front of people I know? Did your . . ." She paused disdainfully. "Did you *friends* in the saloon get a good laugh when you told them how you offered to buy supper for that old-maid milliner with the game leg?" She threw down her work. "And what, pray tell, are you doing with my personal belongings?"

Scott Gandy had the grace to blush effusively.

"Is that what you all think? That I offered t' buy your supper to make fun of you?" His black eyebrows curled. A wedge of creases appeared between them.

She picked up the hat and stabbed it again, too upset to meet his eyes. "Isn't it?"

"Not at all, ma'am, I assure you. I'm from Miz'sippi, Miz Downin'. My mama taught me early t' respect womenfolk. Whatever it might look like, I had no intention of setting you in the mud yesterday or of embarrassing you last night in the eatin' saloon. I wanted to pay for your supper by way of apology, that's all."

Agatha didn't know whether to believe him or not. She was making hash of her stitches, but she kept pushing the needle because she didn't know what else to do, and she was too embarrassed to look up at him.

"I truly am sorry, Miz Downin'."

His voice sounded contrite. She looked up to see if his eyes were the same. They were; and his mouth was somber. Rarely in her life had she seen a face more handsome. It was easy to see why featherheads like Violet became unhinged over him. But she was not Violet, nor was she a featherhead.

"You think a mere apology excuses such gross behavior?"

"Not at all. It was inexcusable. However, I didn't know at the time you had difficulty walking. Later I saw you goin' on down to the Finn's with your dirty clothes and I thought I'd injured you when I knocked you down. Dan Loretto set me straight. However, when he did, I felt even worse."

Agatha dropped her chin, squirming under his direct gaze.

"I know I can't do anythin' about the embarrassment I caused, but I figured the least I could do was take care o' the laundry bill." He laid her dress and petticoat carefully across the worktable. "So, here. All clean and paid for. If anythin's damaged beyond repair, ya'll be sure t' let me know and I'll make it right."

No man had ever touched Agatha's petticoats. To have a man like him do so was rattling. His hands were very dark against the white cotton. She glanced aside, distraught. Her eyes fell on the hand that held his black hat against his thigh. On his little finger glittered a pea-sized diamond ring set in gold. The hat was a good one—if there was one thing she knew, it was hats. This one was a Stetson, by the look of it, a "wide-awake" beaver felt with low crown and wide brim, the newest profile for men. He had money enough for diamonds and new Stetsons and sheet-sized oil paintings—let him pay her laundry bill. She deserved it.

She braved meeting his eyes directly, her own cold and accusing. "I suspect, Mr. Gandy, that you've gotten wind of the battle about to be waged in this town over the sale of spirits, and you're here seeking to protect your interests by placating me with a few hollow apologies. Some women . . ."—it was all Agatha could do to keep from glaring at Violet—". . . might have their heads turned by your smooth talk. I, however, know when I'm being hogwashed by a stream of self-interested ooze. And if you think I'll back down on the issue of the lewd painting, you're mistaken. Violet is afraid you'll evict us if I cross you; however, *I'm* not."

In her zealousness, Agatha did something she rarely did before strangers—she got to her feet. Though Gandy still topped her by a good ten inches, she felt seven feet tall. "I intend not only to cross you, but to find others who'll do the same."

Near the curtain Violet was waving like a windmill in a gale, trying to shut her up. Agatha went on, all the more aroused. "I may as well tell you—you'll find out soon if you haven't already—I've given approval for Proffitt's first temperance meeting to be held here in my millinery shop this Sunday evening." She paused, folded her hands over her stomach, and retreated with one dragging step. "Now, if you feel within your rights to evict us, go ahead. Right is right and wrong is wrong, and selling spirits is wrong, Mr. Gandy; so is hanging filth like that on a public wall."

"I have no intention of evicting you, Miz Downin', and bringin' every temperance worker and that newspaper o' yours down on my head. Neither do I intend t' quit sellin' liquor. Furthermore, the picture is hung, and that's where it'll stay."

"We'll see about that."

Gandy paused, thought, and then his face took on the expression of a poacher watching a doe approach a snare. He absently reached into his vest pocket for a cigar.

"Oh, you will?"

The cigar had scarcely touched his lips before she exploded. "Put that thing away! You may smoke your devil's weed in your own filthy brothel, but not in my millinery shop!"

As if suddenly realizing what he held, he looked down and stuck it back in his pocket. But he did so grinning, dimpling only one cheek.

"Yes, ma'am," he drawled. He glanced over his shoulder, turned slowly, and confronted Violet. "And what are your views on all this, Miz Parsons?"

Violet acted like a perfect ninny, touching her lips and blushing like a scalded pig. Disgusted, Agatha watched Gandy work his wiles on her. "Men've been drinkin' and gamblin' and likin' their ladies for as long as this country's been here. Let the men have a little fun, we thought. No harm in that now, is there?"

Violet answered. "Tt-tt."

"It's indecent!" Agatha reproved, incensed.

Gandy turned back to her. "It's free enterprise. I try to make an honest livin', ma'am, and to do that I have to keep one step ahead o' those other enterprisin' chaps along the street."

"Honest? You call it honest, taking men's hard-earned money at gambling tables and a brass rail?"

"I don't force 'em to come to the Gilded Cage, Miz Downin'. They come o' their own free will."

"But it's ruining my business, Mr. Gandy. All that drinking and revelry—the ladies don't want to come anywhere near the place."

"I'm sorry about that, truly I am, but that's free enterprise, too."

Agatha became outraged at his blithe claim of irresponsibility. Her voice grew sharper. "I'll say it once more. Evict us if you will, but I intend to do everything in my power to shut you down."

To her utter consternation, he grinned. Matched dimples appeared this time in his swarthy cheeks and a twinkle came into his onyx eyes.

"It that a challenge, Miz Downin'?"

"It's a fact!" she spat. Agatha found she detested his Southern drawl. She detested even more the cocky way he settled the Stetson on his head and fixed his lazy grinning eyes on her, taking his sweet time about leaving.

Gandy had come into the dress shop contrite. He was now amused. He studied the bridling female in the subdued blue dress with its high, tight collar and its stern, tied-back skirts. He'd taken her for an old woman when he'd first seen her. Upon closer scrutiny, he discovered she wasn't really old at all. Younger than himself, probably. Slim, well shaped, and with a spark of conviction he grudgingly admired. Her hair held a surprising glint of red, with the window light behind it. She had a magnificent jawline. Clear, clear skin. Unyielding green eyes as pale as sea spray. A damned pretty set of lips. And a lot of old-lady ways.

But she certainly wasn't old. Put a feather in her hair, paint a little crimson on those lips, loosen up a few springy ringlets in that hair, teach her to sing a bawdy drinking song, and she'd look as good in the saloon as Jube or Pearl or Ruby. He withheld a silent chuckle, imagining how aghast she'd be if she knew how he was picturing her.

"I'll take it as a challenge. Y'all do everythin' in your power t' shut me down.

March, make banners, sing—whatever it is you temperance workers take it into your heads t' do. And I'll do whatever is necessary to attract customers to the Gilded Cage."

"You think it's a game, don't you? Well, it's not. Miss Wilson doesn't play games. She's here on a mission."

"I know, I know." He held up both palms and acknowledged blithely, "She's aimin' t' clean me out, too."

"She most certainly is."

"Well, then, I'd best get back to work and prepare for the war, hadn't I, ladies?" He touched the brim of his hat and bowed. "G'day, Miz Downin'." He turned and approached Violet, who remained by the curtained doorway, looking as if he'd just complimented her on her underwear. "Miz Parsons," he said softly, taking one of her blue-veined hands and raising it slowly to his lips. "It's been a pleasure."

Violet's eyeballs threatened to roll in their sockets. Looking on, Agatha's did.

"Violet, see the landlord out, will you!" she snapped. "Then leave the front door propped open. The place suddenly reeks of stale cigar smoke."

Gandy turned, grinned, nodded, and left.

When Violet reappeared, she flopped into her work chair, fanning her face with a handkerchief. "Did you see that, Agatha? He kissed my hand!"

"Perhaps you'd best check it for twin punctures."

Violet's euphoria would not be dampened. "He actually kissed my hand!" she repeated breathily.

"Oh, Violet, will you act your age!"

"I am. I have a weak heart, and I'm having terrible palpitations."

Agatha seethed. Oh, that Gandy was a shrewd manipulator. He knew a besotted old hen when he saw one, and he didn't pass up any advantage.

Violet half lay against the edge of the worktable, exaggerating his Southern accent. " 'Y'all do everuhthin' in yoah powuh tuh shut me down . . . Have you ever heard anything so wonderful in your life? When Mr. Gandy talks, I swear I can smell magnolia blossoms right here in Proffitt, Kansas."

"All I smelled was stale tobacco."

Violet popped up. "Oh, Agatha, you have no romanticism in you. He smelled like bay rum, too. I remember my papa used to wear bay rum."

"Your papa didn't operate a saloon, nor was he kicked off the riverboats for having cards up his sleeve."

"Nobody knows that for sure about Mr. Gandy."

"Oh?" Agatha inquired with asperity. "You mean there's something *the girls* haven't been able to verify?"

Suddenly, Violet spied Agatha's dress and petticoat on the worktable. She laid her hand on them almost reverently. "He paid to have these washed. Imagine that."

Agatha sniffed.

"And he offered to buy you supper."

Agatha sniffed louder.

"And he came in here especially to apologize for everything."

Had she sniffed any harder, Agatha might have sucked in some stray threads and choked herself. So she preached instead. "Oh, he's an oily-tongued dandy, all right. But with the help of Drusilla Wilson and the women of Proffitt, Kansas"— Agatha raised one hand and pointed toward heaven—"I'll wipe that insufferable grin off his brown hide!"

On the other side of the wall, LeMaster Scott Gandy stalked into the saloon, sending the doors flapping widely behind him. "Jack, make up a sign!" he bellowed.

He bit the end off a cigar, spit it into the cuspidor with deadly accuracy, and blew the first smoke ring with equally deadly accuracy; it appeared to wreath a florid nipple on the nude behind the bar. He narrowed one eye on the nipple and the ring, as if taking a bead down the bore of a Winchester. "We're goin' t' have a picture-namin' contest. The man who tags our rosy-breasted li'l lady here gets the first dance with Jubilee when she arrives!"

And so the battle lines were drawn.

Chapter 3

🍒

On Sunday, Reverend Samuel Clarksdale of Christ Presbyterian Church was upstaged in the pulpit by Drusilla Wilson whose message was concise and inspiring: Those who stood by and watched a loved one chained to the evils of alcohol without helping when they could were equally as guilty as if they themselves had placed the bottle in the loved one's hands.

When Sunday services ended, Miss Wilson was greeted effusively by the women in the congregation. Many squeezed her hand heartily, some with tears in their eyes. Many did the same to Agatha Downing, thanking her in advance for providing them with a gathering place.

Agatha outfitted herself for the meeting in a stiff-necked dress of somber brown, her bustles lashed firmly behind her, skirts tied back so tightly her steps were considerably shortened. She was ready well before seven, so she went downstairs and dusted the countertops and lit the lanterns. Dusk had not quite fallen when she opened the shop door to greet Drusilla Wilson. As usual, the woman was ready with a firm handclasp.

"Agatha, how nice to see you again."

"Come in, Miss Wilson."

But before stepping inside, Drusilla glanced toward the door of the saloon. "You've seen what we're up against, I imagine?"

Agatha appeared puzzled, then stepped onto the boardwalk herself.

The swinging doors were thrown back. The painting behind the bar could be viewed from an oblique angle along the left wall. On the boardwalk out front stood that wretched Southerner, dressed to the nines, with a smoking cheroot in his mouth and one eyebrow draped on a double-sided billboard announcing:

NEW LADIES IN TOWN
NAME THE PAINTING BEHIND THE BAR
AND WIN THE FIRST DANCE WITH
MISS JUBILEE BRIGHT
THE BRIGHTEST GEM OF THE PRAIRIE
SOON TO APPEAR AT THE GILDED CAGE
WITH HER JEWELS
PEARL AND RUBY

He thoughtfully allowed Agatha time to read it before tipping his hat and grinning slowly. "Evenin', Miz Downin'."

Oh, he had gall. Standing there smirking and drawling. She'd like to knock that sign out from under him and send him sprawling!

"Y'all expectin' a pretty good turnout, are ya?"

"Most certainly."

"Not as good as mine, I'll wager."

"Have you no decency? It's the Lord's day!"

"None whatsoever, ma'am. Got t' have the welcome mat out when that first herd hits town. Could be any minute now, for all we know."

She lifted one eyebrow toward the sign. "Jubilee, Pearl, and Ruby? Polished gems, I'm sure." She could see them already—lice-carrying, diseased whores with singed hair and fake moles.

"Genuine, all three."

She snorted softly.

He puffed on his cigar.

At that moment a tall lanky mulatto with deepset eyes and kinky black hair rolled the piano near the door. He was so thin he looked as if a gust of wind would blow him over. "Time to make some music, Ivory?"

"Yessuh."

"Ivory, I don't believe you've met Miz Downin', our next-door neighbor. Miz Downin', my piano man, Ivory Culhane."

"Miz Downin'." He removed a black bowler, centering it on his chest as he bowed. Replacing the hat at a rakish angle, he inquired, "What can I play for ya, ma'am?"

How dare these two act as if this was nothing more than an afternoon ice-cream social! Agatha had no wish whatever to exchange pleasantries with the pimp saloon owner, nor with the man whose infernal plunking kept her awake night after night. She gave the latter a sour look and replied tartly, "How about 'A Mighty Fortress Is Our God'?"

His teeth flashed white in a tea-brown face as he smiled widely. "'Fraid I don't know that one. But how 'bout this?" With one fluid motion Ivory seated himself on a clawfooted stool, revolved it to face the keys, and struck up the opening chords of "Little Brown Jug," a song recently composed by the "wets" to rile the "drys." Agatha drew herself up and swung away.

When the ladies began arriving the two were still there, Ivory's songs filling the street with his musical invitation, Gandy with his nonchalance and grin intact, excreting Southern charm like so much musk from a muskrat. He greeted each lady who came along.

"Evenin', ma'am," he said time after time, touching his hat brim. "Y'all enjoy your meetin', now." His grin was especially dashing for Violet and the delegation from Mrs. Gill's boardinghouse. "Evenin', Miz Parsons. Nice t' see y'all again, and your friends, too. Evenin', ladies."

Violet tittered, blushing, and led the way next door. She was followed by Evelyn Sowers, Susan White, Bessie Hottle, and Florence Loretto, all of whom had a personal stake in the goings-on at the Gilded Cage Saloon. There were others, too. Annie MacIntosh, sporting a bruise on her left cheek. Minnie Butler, whose huband had a yen for the gaming tables. Jennie Yoast, whose husband made the rounds of all the saloons every Saturday night and sometimes was found sleeping on the boardwalk on Sunday mornings. Anna Brewster, Addie Anderson, Carolyn Hawes, and many others whose men were known to have exceedingly limber elbows.

Attending the meeting were thirty-six women, most of them eager to stamp out the evils of the ardent spirits; a few were merely curious about what "those fanatics" did when they got together.

Drusilla Wilson personally greeted each arrival at the door with her hostess as her side. The meeting began with a prayer, followed by Miss Wilson's opening statement.

"There are four thousand rum holes spreading death and disease through all ranks of American society, vile dens that respectable people abhor from a distance. Your own fair city has become blemished by eleven such chancres. Many of your husbands are wooed away from home night after night, robbing your families of their protectors and providers. The human wreckage caused by alcohol can come only to tragic ends—in hospitals, where victims die of delirium tremens, or in reformatories such as Ward Island, or even asylums such as that on Blackwell Island. I've visited these institutions myself. I've seen the creeping death that preys upon those who've begun with a single innocent drink, then another and another, until the victim is abysmally lost. And who is left to suffer the effects of intemperance? The women and children—that's who! From half a million American women a wail of anguish is sounded over an otherwise happy land. Over the graves of forty thousand drunkards goes up the mourning cry of widow and orphan. The chief evils of spirits have fallen on women. It is eminently fitting that women should inaugurate the work for its destruction!"

As Wilson spoke, the faces in the audience grew rapt. She was earnest, spellbinding. Even those who'd come only out of curiosity were becoming mesmerized.

"And the saloons themselves are breeding places for the vermin of this earth—gamblers, confidence men, and *nymphs du prairie.* Let us not forget that Wichita, at its most decadent, sported houses of ill repute with no less than three hundred painted cats! Three hundred in a single city! But we cleaned up Wichita, and we'll clean up Proffitt! Together!"

When her speech ended, the crowd voiced a single question: How?

The answer was concise: by educating, and advocating prayer and willpower. "The W.C.T.U. is not militant. What we achieve, we shall achieve by peaceful means. Yet, let us not shirk our duty when it comes to making that destroyer of men's souls—the barkeeper—aware of his guilt. We shall not destroy the vile compound he sells. Instead, we will give his clientele something more powerful to lean on—faith in his God, his family, and hope for his future."

Miss Wilson knew when to evangelize and when to cease. She had them aroused now. To bag them for the cause, all she needed were three or four gut-wrenching stories from their own lips.

"You've all been at home growing impatient for this day. Now is the time. Bare your hearts to your sisters who understand. They've suffered what you've suffered. Who would like to rid themselves of their grief first?"

The women exchanged furtive glances, but none came forward.

Wilson pressed on. "Remember, we, your sisters, are not here to judge, but to support."

Through the saloon wall came the cry of "Keno!" And from the piano, "Over the Waves." Thirty-six self-conscious women all waited for someone else to start.

Agatha's teeth and hands clenched. Her own agonizing memories came back from her past. She considered telling her story at last, but she had held it inside for so long she was unable to bring it forth. Already an object of a certain amount of pity, she had no desire to be pitied further, so she held her silence.

The first to speak was Florence Loretto. "My son . . ." she began. Every eye settled on her. All was silent. "My son, Dan. He was always a good boy when he was young. But when my husband was alive, he used to send the boy down to the saloon to fetch his whiskey. Claimed he had a touch of the rheumatism and hot toddies took the pain out of his joints. That's how it started. But by the time he died, he was liquored up more than he was sober. He was a grown man, but Dan . . . Dan was young, and he'd found out he liked the atmosphere at the saloon. Now he's dealing cards right next door, and I . . . I . . ." Florence covered her face with one hand. "I'm so ashamed, I can't face my friends."

Addie Anderson rubbed Florence's shoulder and offered, quietly, "It's all right, Florence. We all understand. You did what you thought best when you were bringing him up." She faced Miss Wilson as she went on forthrightly. "My husband, Floyd, he used to be sober as a judge, except for maybe when somebody got married or on the Fourth of July. But he got sickly a couple years back and had to take on somebody to look after the shop while he was down. Jenks, his name was, fine-lookin' young man from St. Louis, with letters to recommend him. But they was all phony. Jenks got his fingers in the books and rigged 'em so's he could swindle us without Floyd ever knowin' what he was up to. By the time Floyd discovered it, it was too late. Jenks was gone, and so was the nice nest egg we'd saved up. That's when Floyd started takin' to drink. I try to tell him, 'Floyd,' I says, 'what good does it do to spend what little money we got gettin' drunk every night?' But he don't listen to nothin' I say. We lost the store and Floyd went to clerk for Halorhan, but it's a big come-down to him, clerkin', after he was his own boss all those years. The money Halorhan pays him goes nearly all for whiskey, and we're behind six months on our account at the store. Halorhan's been good, but lately he's been warnin' Floyd, if he don't pay some on what we been chargin', he's gonna have to let him go. Then . . ." Suddenly Addie broke into tears. "Ohh . . ." she wailed.

It made Florence Loretto's plight seem less drastic, and she, in turn, comforted Addie.

After that the women opened up, one by one. Their plights were all similar, though some stories were more pitiful then others. Agatha waited for Annie MacIntosh to admit where she got the bruise on her cheek. But Annie, like Agatha, remained silent.

When a lull fell, Drusilla Wilson took the meeting in hand once again. "Sisters, you have our love and support. But to be effective, we must organize. And organization means becoming a recognized local of the national Women's Christian Temperance Union. To do so you must elect officers. I'll work together with them to draft a constitution. Once that is accomplished, committees will be formed to draw up temperance pledges." She displayed several varieties, all of which could be pinned on a reformed man's sleeve. "One of your first goals will be to get as many pledge signatures as possible, and also to solicit new members for your local."

Within a quarter hour, Agatha found herself—over her own protests—voted the first president of the Women's Christian Temperance Union of Proffitt, Kansas. Florence Loretto became vice-president, over her own protests. Annie MacIntosh surprised everyone by speaking for the first time that evening, volunteering to be secretary. Agatha nominated Violet for treasurer, observing that it would be easy for the two of them to work together, since they saw each other every day anyway. Violet also objected, to no avail.

Dues were set at twenty-five cents—the price of one shot of whiskey—per week. A pledge committee of four was formed for the purpose of hand-lettering pledges until some could be professionally printed. A committee of three was delegated to query Joseph Zeller, editor of the *Proffitt Gazette,* on the cost of printing pamphlets and advertisements and pledges. A rally was scheduled for the following night for the purpose of soliciting signatures on temperance pledges, starting in the closest saloon.

The meeting closed with Miss Wilson teaching the ladies their first temperance song:

> *Cold water is king*
> *Cold water is lord! And a thousand bright faces*
> *Now smile at his board.*

They sang it several times, in rousing harmony, until their voices drowned out the sound of "Camptown Races" coming from the other side of the wall.

As the meeting closed, everyone agreed it had been an exhilarating evening. As Drusilla Wilson left, she assured Agatha that help and directives would come from the national organization as well as through *The Temperance Banner.* And Miss Wilson herself would remain in town until the organizational wrinkles had been ironed out.

Agatha closed the door behind the last woman, leaned back against it, and sighed. What had she gotten into? More than she'd bargained for, most certainly. Not only organizer, but president. Why ever had she agreed to hold the meeting here in the first place?

With another sigh she pushed away from the door and turned out the lanterns. In the darkness she left the workroom by the back door. The rear of the building gave on to a path leading to a storage shed and the smaller building she genteelly referred to as "the necessary." After visiting it, she made her way upstairs, head down, as usual, watching her feet. She was two steps from the top when a voice brought her head snapping up.

"So how did the meetin' go?"

She couldn't see him, only the glow of his cigar in the dark on his half of the landing.

"What are you doing here?"

"Inquirin' about the meetin', Miz Downin'. No need t' jump so."

"I did not jump!" But she had. How awkward to think he'd been sitting up here watching her walk out to "the necessary" and back, equally awkward to realize he'd observed her struggling up the stairs in her shuffling, one-two fashion.

"Pretty good turnout y' had there."

"Thirty-four. Thirty six, counting Miss Wilson and myself."

"Ahh, commendable."

"And I've been elected president." It was the first time she'd taken any joy in the fact.

"President. Well, well . . ."

Her pupils had dilated enough to see that he was sitting on a chair tipped back against the wall with his boots crossed on the railing. The acrid scent of his cigar smoke reached her as the tip glowed orange once more.

"We had such a rousing meeting that none of us even minded the sound of Mr. Culhane's piano coming through the wall. As a matter of fact, we sang so loud, we drowned it out."

"Sounds inspirin'."

She could hear the grin in his voice.

"I dare say it was."

"And what did y'all sing?"

"You'll know, soon enough. We'll come in and do it for your patrons. How would that be?"

He laughed, the cigar still clamped in his teeth.

"T' tell the truth, we won't be needin' you. Jubilee and the girls'll be here any day, and we'll have all the singin' we'll need."

"Ohhh, yes. Jubilee and the girls—from the billboard? My, they sound wonderful," she intoned sarcastically.

"They are. You'll have t' come over and take in a show."

His cigar smoke irritated her. She coughed and struggled up the last two steps. "How can you smoke those disgusting things?"

"Habit I learned on the riverboats. Kept my hands filled when I wasn't playin' cards."

"So you *were* thrown off the riverboats!"

He laughed and his chair clunked down on all fours. "The ladies o' your club been speculatin' 'bout me, have they?" He rose and his boot heels resounded with calculated laziness across the narrow landing until he stood before her at the top of the stairs.

"Hardly. We have bigger fish to fry."

"Supposin' I was, though. Supposin' I was a big, bad gambler who knew every trick in the book. Man like that'd know how t' handle a few old squawkin' hens who set out t' shut down his saloon, don't ya think?"

Fear quickened her blood. He stood ominously close, backing her up to the stairs. She had a dizzying sense of déjà vu, certain that in an instant she'd go tumbling down as she had long ago. Her muscles tensed as she anticipated the sharp blows, the scraped skin, the sickening disorientation of somersaulting from tread to tread. With one trembling hand she grasped the railing, knowing it would do little good should he decide to give her a shove. His eyes became red sparks as he drew on the cigar once more. The smell grew sickening, and her palms began to sweat.

"Please," she choked in a whisper, "don't."

Immediately, he stepped back and took the cigar from his mouth. "Now wait a minute, Miz Downin', you do me an injustice if you think I was entertainin' thoughts of pushin' you down those stairs. Why, I . . ."

"You pushed me down once before."

"In the mud? I told you, *that* was an accident!"

"So would this be, I'm sure. Anybody who's seen me climb stairs knows I'm not too steady on them. But if you think threats will stop me, you're dead wrong, Mr. Gandy. They only serve to refresh my zeal. Now, if you will kindly let me pass, sir, I'll say good-night."

She sensed his reluctance to let her go thinking ill of him. Yet his belligerence radiated palpably. They stood nose to chest for ten crackling seconds. Then he stepped back. The sound of her solid step followed by the dragging one alternated across the landing. All the way to her door she kept expecting to be lifted by the scruff of her neck and thrown bodily down the stairs. When it didn't happen she was surprised. She reached her door, slithered inside, closed and locked it. The shakes started immediately. She pressed her palms and forehead against the cool wood, wondering what she'd gotten into by allowing herself to be buffaloed into the presidency of an organization setting out to close down not only Scott Gandy, but ten others like him.

Jubilee and her Gems arrived the following morning on the eleven-oh-five train. Three women with their looks couldn't step off a coach without causing a stir.

The one known as Pearl appeared to have been named for her skin. It was as pale and luminous as a perfect ocean pearl. Against it, her brown eyes appeared to take up a good quarter of her face. They were darkened with kohl, adding to their size. Her lips were tinted scarlet and flashed like a wine spill on white linen. But her delicate features were shown off to best advantage by the stand-up collar of her fuchsia traveling costume, which bared a goodly amount of her throat and fit like a banana skin. Her hair was the glossy brown of caramelized sugar, piled into a nosegay of curls high on her head, pitching her shepherdess hat provocatively forward.

"Hiya, fellas!" she called from the train steps, and old Wilton Spivey set sparks off the trackside ballast churning to reach her first. He dropped the tongue of the baggage dray and leaped over two tracks, beat out Joe Jessup, who'd started from the opposite direction, and reached the foot of the train steps, panting. Wilton was toothless as a frog and balder than a brass doorknob, but Pearl didn't care. She smiled down, cocked one wrist, and extended a hand.

"Just what I was needin'. A big handsome man with lots of muscles. My name's Pearl. What's yours?"

"Wiwton Thpivey, at your thervith, ma'am." Wilt didn't talk so good with those bare gums, but his eyes sparkled with lecherous delight.

"Well, Wiwton, come on, honey. Don't be shy."

Wilton lifted her down, revealing Ruby, behind her.

Ruby was a shapely young Negress with skin the color of creamed coffee. Her hair was straighter than any black woman's hair Wilton Spivey had ever seen. It swept back from her left ear, straight up from her right, sleek as fast water on a black rock, ending in a curl like an inverted ocean breaker looping the edge of her high canary-yellow hat. She had magnificent upsweeping eyebrows, heavy-lidded black eyes, and lips as puffy as a pair of bee stings, painted a violent magenta. She rested eight knuckles on her cocked hips, gave a little jiggle that shimmied her tight yellow dress, and announced in a deep, rich contralto, "And I'm Ruby."

Joe Jessup gulped and uttered, "Holy smokes, if you ain't!"

When Ruby laughed it sounded like thunder building on a mountainside—deep, chesty, voluptuous.

"What I s'posed t' call you, honey?"

"J . . . Joe J . . . Jessup."

"Well, J . . . Joe J . . . Jessup." Ruby sidled down one step, leaned over till her breasts hovered only inches before his face. With one unearthly long nail she left a pale white line all the way from Joe's ear to the center of his chin. "How 'bout I call you J.J.?"

"F . . . fine. R . . . ride to wherever you're goin', Miss Ruby?"

"'Preciate it, J.J. That'd be the Gilded Cage Saloon. Y'all know where that is?"

"Sure do. Right th . . . this way."

By this time there were four others in queue, waiting their turns at the foot of the train steps.

Above them, like an angel straight from the pearly gates, appeared Miss Jubilee Bright—as promised, the brightest gem of the prairie. If the others seemed suited to their names, Miss Jubilee seemed born to hers. She was—incredibly—white all over! Her hair was white, not the blue-white of Violet Parsons's, but the blinding white of spun glass. It frothed high upon her head like a tempting ten-egg meringue. She was dressed, too, in unadulterated white, from the tip of her tall velvet hat with its trimming of egret feathers to the toes of her ankle-high kid boots. Her dress, like that of Pearl's and Ruby's, sported no bustle out back, but clung to her generous curves from shoulder to knee before flaring into walking pleats. It sported a diamond-shaped neckline revealing a tempting glimpse of cleavage, with a fake black mole placed low enough to draw any man's eyes in its direction. Another mole dotted the left cheek of a face lovely enough to need no beauty marks. The startling almond eyes, the pouting lips, the pretty little nose could hold their own in any company. It truly was an angel's face.

She raised both arms and called, "Just call me Jube, boys!" And she leaned out with her arms still extended, allowing two cavaliers to grasp them and lower her to the ground. When she got there she left her arms around their shoulders, rubbing their muscles approvingly.

"My, my, I do love my men strong . . . and polite," she purred in a naturally kittenish voice. "I can tell we're goin' to get along ju-u-ust fine." Simultaneously, she gave them each a clap. "So, who'm I hangin' on to here?"

"Mort Pokenny," answered the man on her left.

"Virgil Murray," answered the man on her right.

"Well, Mort, Virgil, I want you to meet our friend, Marcus Delahunt. Marcus plays the banjo for us. Meanest picker this side of N'awleans."

The last man off the train carried a banjo case and wore a straw panama with a wide black band. His boyish face wore a happy smile revealing one crooked tooth, which only added to his appeal. His blue eyes were set wide in a fair face framed by collie-blond hair. Not a particularly manly face, with its pink complexion and sparse blond whiskers, but one forgot that when viewing his open expression of apparent pleasure with the world. Standing with one long-fingered hand on the rail, the other gripping the banjo case, he smiled and nodded silently.

"Marcus here can't say a word, but he can hear better than a sleeping dog, and he's smarter than the rest of us all put together, so don't ever let me catch you treating him like a dummy."

The men offered hellos, but immediately returned their interest to the women. "So what do you boys do for excitement around here?" asked Ruby.

"No much, ma'am. Been a little dull lately."

She laughed throatily. "Well, we're gonna fix that, aren't we, girls?"

Jubilee scanned the train platform and inquired of Mort and Virgil, "You seen that rascal Gandy around these parts?"

"Yes, ma'am, he's—"

"Enough of that ma'aming now, Virgil. Just call me Jubilee."

"Yes, ma'am, Miss Jubilee. Scotty, he's over't the Gilded Cage."

She flapped one hand, affected a winning pout. "Isn't that the way with a man—never there when you need him! Well, we're going to need some strong arms. Got a little something that needs hauling over to Gandy's saloon. You boys willing to give us a hand with it?"

Six males tripped all over themselves, shouldering forward.

"Where's that wagon of yours, Mr. Jessup?"

"Comin' right up!"

Jubilee gave a "come on" with one shoulder and led the troop toward the freight cars at the rear of the train. Already the doors were being rolled back. The freight master stood beside one, looking in, scratching his head.

"Durnedest thing I ever seen," he remarked. "What in tarnation they gonna do with a hunk of junk like that?"

"Yoo-hoo!" Jubilee called, waving.

The freight master glanced up and saw the crowd advancing.

"Did it make it all right?"

"It did," he called back. "But what in tarnation you gonna do with it?"

Jubilee, Pearl, Ruby, and all their eager escorts reached the open freight car.

Jessup arrived with his wagon. Jube rested her hands on her hips and winked at the aging freight master. "Come on over to the Gilded Cage some night and find out, honey!" She turned to the others. "Gentlemen, let's load this thing and get it over to Gandy's!"

Violet was minding the front of the store several minutes later when she looked out the window and shrieked. "Agatha! Agatha, come here!"

Agatha lifted her head and called, "What is it, Violet?"

"Come here!"

Even before reaching the front room, Agatha heard banjo music from outside. It was a warm spring day; the shop door was propped open with a brick. "Look!" Violet gaped and pointed to the street beyond. Agatha came up quietly into the shadows behind her.

Another delivery for the saloon next door. One glimpse told Agatha she should order Violet to close the door, but there was too much that appealed to her in the scene outside.

Joe Jessup's buckboard came up the street piled with a crowd of exuberant men, three gaudy ladies, and the most enormous birdcage Agatha had ever seen. Six feet high it stood, made of bright, shining gold that caught the noon sun and sent it shimmering. Suspended from its onion-shaped roof was a golden swing, and upon it perched a fancy lady dressed in pure white. Another, wearing heliotrope pink, sat on the tail of the wagon between Wilton Spivey and Virgil Murray, the three of them swinging their legs and swaying to the music. The third woman, looking like a bumblebee in her black skin and yellow clothes, sat on Joe Jessup's lap as he drove the wagon. The banjo player stood just behind them, nodding from side to side in rhythm with the song. The wagon was packed with people crowded around the birdcage, and, like the Pied Piper of Hamelin, the wagon had attracted a trail of children and bright-eyed young fellows who'd left their desks and clerking stations to be part of the music and to ogle the women in the startling costumes. As they came down the street, the entire troupe was singing lustily.

> *Buffalo gals, won't you come out tonight,*
> *Come out tonight, come out tonight,*
> *Buffalo gals, won't you come out tonight*
> *And dance by the light of the moon.*

Agatha tried very hard to be critical. But she couldn't. She was gripped instead by envy. Oh, to be young and attractive and unfettered by self-consciousness. To be able to ride down the street on a wagon at high noon, singing one's heart out to the sky and laughing. Shouldn't there be, in everyone's life, at least one such reckless memory? But there was none in Agatha's.

This was as close as she'd ever come: tapping her hand against her thigh in rhythm with the music. When she realized what she was doing, she stopped.

As the wagon drew abreast of her store, she got a closer look at the woman in white. She was the prettiest thing Agatha had ever seen. Delicate face with slanting eyes and cupid's own smile. And she knew how to choose a good hat. She wore one of fashion's current entries in the war between the high- and flat-crowned hats, the kind called "three stories and a basement." It was exquisite: towering, but well balanced, and trimmed with expensive egret feathers. Even when the woman swung on her perch, the hat sat securely.

"Look at that white hat," she whispered.

"Look at all of them," replied Violet.

"Good hats."

"The best."

"Their dresses, too."

"But look—no bustles, Agatha."

"No." Agatha envied them for not having to hang fifteen pounds of metal on their rumps every morning.

"But so much chest. *Tt-tt.*"

"They're fancy ladies, I'm sure." The thought saddened Agatha. All that bright promise would grow to nothing. All their young beauty would grow faded before its time.

The wagon came to a stop before the saloon. Mort Pokenny opened the cage door and the woman in white stepped out. She stood with hands akimbo and shouted at the swinging doors. "Hey, Gandy, didn't you send for three dancing girls from Natchez?"

Gandy himself materialized, surrounded by his employees, all calling out greetings, reaching for the ladies, shaking hands over the side of the wagon with the banjo player. But Agatha watched only the woman in white, high on the wagon, and the man in black, below her. He hooked one boot on a wheel spoke and tilted his hat to the back of his head. In the middle of the melee they had eyes only for each other.

"'Bout time you were gettin' here, Jube."

"Got here as fast as I could. Took 'em a month to build the damned cage, though."

"That all it's been?" His dimples formed as he grinned.

"You wouldn't've missed old Jube, now, would y'?"

Gandy threw back his head and laughed.

"Never. Been too busy gettin' the place set up."

Jubilee scanned the boardwalk. "Where's that town full o' cowboys you promised I could pick from?"

"They're comin,' Jube, they're comin'."

Her gaze returned to Gandy and her eyes glittered with teasing and impatience. "You gonna stand there flappin' all day, or help a lady dismount?" Without warning she launched herself over the side, flying through the air with feet and arms up, never doubting for a moment that a pair of strong arms would be there to catch her. They were. No sooner had Gandy caught her than they were kissing boldly, mindless of the hoots and whistles around them. She twined her arms around his shoulders and returned his kiss with total unconcern for the spectacle they were making. The kiss ended when his hat started slipping off. She snatched it off his head and they laughed into each other's faces. She plopped the hat on his thick black hair and tilted it well forward.

"Now put me down, you rebel dandy. I got others to greet, you know."

Looking on, Agatha felt a curious flutter within her stomach as Gandy's black eyes lingered on the woman's beautiful kohled ones and he held her a moment longer. Watching them, one could almost guess what fun they had alone together. Pleasant mischief radiated between them. Even their vocal exchange had been filled with it. How did women learn to act that way around men? In her whole life Agatha had never been in the same room with a man without feeling ill at ease. Nor had she carried on a conversation with one without groping for a topic. And, of course, to leap off the side of a wagon would be, for her, nothing short of a miracle.

Gandy set Jubilee down and greeted the others.

"Ruby, sweetheart, y' knock my eyes out." He gave her a kiss on the cheek.

"And Pearl, you're bound t' break a few hearts in Proffitt, Kansas, before the season's over." She, too, got a kiss on the cheek. Next he clamped both hands on the banjo player's shoulders and looked him square in the face. "Hello, Marcus. Good t' see you again." The man smiled. He made a strumming motion across his banjo and raised his eyebrows. "That's right," Gandy answered, "good for business. Y'all got the town stirred up already. They'll be mashin' the door down tonight."

Gandy turned back toward Jubilee, shrugging out of his jacket. "Here. Hang on to this for a minute." He gave her a wink and Agatha watched the woman clasp the jacket to her breast and bury her nose in its collar. It seemed so intimate a motion that Agatha felt guilty witnessing it. She wondered how any woman could look so entranced by the smell of cigar smoke.

"Let's get it inside, boys." Gandy leaped onto the wagon and with five others hefted the cage. She watched his black satin waistcoat pull taut across his shoulder blades, his forearms knot as he lifted the contraption. He wasn't overly brawny, yet neither was he flimsy. But he had muscles in all the places a man was supposed to; enough to deal with an impulsive woman who came flying through the air into his arms, or a nettlesome one who organized a local temperance union. She recalled last night at the top of the stairs—had he thought about pushing her or not? Now in broad daylight, watching him work in the sun, he hardly seemed capable of malevolence. Perhaps it had been her imagination after all.

The work gang inched the heavy cage off the wagon, up the boardwalk steps, and inside the saloon. The ladies and the loiterers followed, leaving the street to the children. Violet and Agatha retreated into the shop but could still hear the sound of happy chatter and occasional laughter.

"So that was Jubilee and the Gems."

"Such lovely names . . . Jubilee. Ruby. Pearl."

Agatha thought all three names sounded concocted, but she reserved her opinion. "So, he's brought in calico queens after all."

"We don't know that for sure."

"Violet, they were wearing kohl on their eyes, and carmine on their lips, and their chests were showing."

"Yes," Violet uttered disappointedly, "I suppose you're right." Suddenly, she brightened. "But, oh, my!" She sighed, a rapt expression on her face. "Wasn't that something the way Mr. Gandy kissed the one named Jubilee?"

"Doesn't it seem a bit shameless to you, right out there on the street?"

"Well, perhaps a bit. But I'm still jealous."

Agatha laughed and experienced a shaft of appreciation for Violet. The woman was so forthright. And earthy in her own way. How was it she'd never found a young swain to kiss her in the middle of a street in springtime? "Come." Agatha held out an arm in invitation. "Let's get to work. That'll take our minds off it."

But within five minutes the sound of hammering and sawing became so distracting they found themselves gazing time and again at the wall.

"Now what do you suppose they're doing that's making all that racket?"

"I don't know." Violet's eyes sparkled. "Would you like me to go take a peek?"

"Certainly not!"

"But aren't you curious?"

"Maybe I am, but you know what curiosity got the cat."

Violet drooped in resignation. "Honestly, Agatha, sometimes you're no fun at all."

Their thimbles pushed in unison.

Push, pull. Push, pull.

It was as bad as the clock at bedtime, Agatha thought.

Push, pull. Two old maids, stitching their lives away. No! One old maid and one not-so-old maid!

The sound of footsteps in the front room interrupted her musings.

"Hullo?" It was Gandy again.

Violet dropped her thimble, pressed a hand to her heart, and went pink as a baby shoat. "Oh, my sakes!" she whispered.

"Go see what he wants this time."

But before Violet could move, Gandy stepped through the lavender curtains, hatless, jacketless, and slightly breathless, with his sleeves rolled up to the elbows. He stood before them with feet widespread, his hands on his waist. "Got a rush job for you, Miz Downin'."

Agatha raised one eyebrow and let her gaze drop from his black tumbled hair to the toes of his polished boots.

"Something in a rose bengaline, perhaps? Should go well with your dark hair."

He laughed and ran eight fingers through his hair, leaving it standing in attractive rills. "We'll save that for Jube. What I need is much simpler. A big drawstring sack—doesn't matter what color or what material. Somethin' big enough to cover up a six-foot birdcage. But I need it by tonight."

Agatha lay aside her work with strained patience. "I'm a milliner, Mr. Gandy, not a dressmaker."

"But you have all those bolts o' cloth out there." He thumbed toward the front. "They're for sale, aren't they?"

"Not for birdcage covers."

"Why not?"

"And not to saloon owners."

"My money's good. And I pay well."

"I'm sorry, Mr. Gandy. Try Mr. Halorhan. He handles yard goods."

"The cloth won't do me any good without someone t' sew it."

"Even if I were willing, it could never be done by evening."

"Why not? It's a simple enough job."

"It would be if I had a sewing machine, but, as you see, I don't."

She glanced to the advertisement for a Singer hanging on the wall. His eyes followed.

"How many hands would it take to have it done in . . ."—he withdrew a gold stem-winder from his vest pocket—"five hours?"

"I told you, I don't do work for saloon owners."

He put the watch away and frowned at her. "You're one stubborn wench, Miz Downin'."

Wench? The word brought a swift flag of color to her cheeks and she supposed she, too, now looked like a shoat. Never in her life had she been called a wench. It was disconcerting to find that it made her feel giddy. But she quickly picked up her work again. He studied her for a full ten seconds, scowled a while, then pivoted and shouldered through the velvet curtains, leaving them swaying.

Agatha and Violet gaped at the doorway, then at each other.

"Tt-tt."

"Violet, you must stop tittering every time you see that man. And you're blushing, for heaven's sake."

"So are you."

"I am not!"

"You are, too! Why, Agatha, he called you a wench! Tt-tt."

"I've never been so humiliated. The man has no manners at all."

"I think he's adorable."

Agatha sniffed. But inside, she was beginning to agree with Violet.

Violet fanned her warm face. "My, my, my." She studied the curtains that had brushed his shapely shoulders. "A cover for that birdcage?"

"Saloon people are crazy. Don't try to figure them out."

"But why would he want such a thing?"

"I'm sure I have no idea."

They hadn't time for speculation before they were surprised by the reappearance of Gandy, this time bursting in through the back door, towing Miss Jubilee by a wrist. She was followed by Ruby and Pearl.

Again both milliners blushed highly. And Agatha became so incensed, she got to her feet. How dare he bring those painted women in here!

"Girls, I want y'all t' meet Miz Downin' and Miz Parsons, our closest neighbors. Ladies, these three delightful creatures are Jubilee, Pearl, and Ruby, the gems of the prairie."

Jubilee dipped her knees. "Charmed."

"Pleased to meetcha," said Pearl.

"Miz Downin', Miz Parsons," Ruby greeted.

Agatha and Violet stared. Gandy stalked out to the showroom and returned immediately with a bolt of red satin. He flopped it onto the worktable and clinked down a stack of gold coins beside it.

"Ten of 'em. Count 'em. They're yours if you can have a drawstring cover made for that birdcage by seven o'clock tonight. Jube, Pearl, and Ruby'll help you stitch it."

"Aw, Scotty, come on . . ."

"Now, Jube, honey, you're a female, aren't you? All females know how t' sew."

"Not this one!"

Agatha's gaze flashed between the two brightest things in the room: Miss Jubilee and the stack of gold coins. One hundred dollars. Her mouth watered. Her eyes flickered to the drawing of Mr. Singer's masterpiece with the price printed in bold numbers beside the flywheel. Forty-nine dollars. When would she ever again see enough money to cover the price of the only thing in the world she coveted?

Her lips opened but no sound came out. What would Miss Wilson say? What would her fellow union members say? The president of the local W.C.T.U. sewing accoutrements for the Gilded Cage Saloon. But, oh, all that money!

Pearl was complaining. "I never sewed anything in my life!"

"I did. And plenty," put in Ruby. "Nothin' to it."

"But, Ruby—"

"Quit your frettin', Pearl. If the boss say stitch, we stitch."

"I'm with Pearl," Jubilee said. "I'm no seamstress."

Agatha found her voice at last. "Neither am I. I'm a milliner. And at seven o'clock tonight I will be in the Gilded Cage soliciting signatures on temperance pledges from the customers at the bar. What would my co-workers think if they knew I'd made the red cover for your birdcage?"

"Nobody has t' know," Gandy interjected, stepping closer to Agatha. "That's why I brought the girls in the back door, so nobody'd see them." He stood so near she smelled tobacco smoke on his clothing again. She dropped her gaze to the floor. Her chin snapped up again when he lightly grasped her upper arms.

"Please, Miz Downin'?"

How disconcerting to be taken so by a man. "It would be a conflict of interests, don't you see?"

"Then perhaps a little added incentive . . ." He turned and she thought he was going to add another coin to the stack. Instead, he took one away and slipped it into his waistcoat pocket.

"We've wasted five minutes already. In another minute the price goes down ten dollars. The sooner you say yes, the better."

"But you . . . I . . ." Agatha clasped her hands and glanced helplessly from Gandy to his ladies to the stack of coins.

"Agatha," Violet warned, "don't be foolish."

"Violet, shush!" She would not be coerced this way, especially by a woman without enough sense to see they were being bribed.

"Your money undoubtedly came from the poor unfortunate souls of this town who frequent your estab—"

"Eighty," he interrupted calmly, removing another coin and dropping it in his pocket.

"Mr. Gandy, you're despicable."

He glanced in a circle. "Don't see any overabundance o' customers in here today."

He directed his next question to Violet. "How's business been lately, Miz Parsons?"

"Not too—"

"Violet, I'll thank you to take a lock!"

"Well, he can see it's true, Agatha. All he has to do is look around. And weren't you just saying the other day—"

"Violet!"

Violet ignored her boss and leaned confidentially close to Gandy. "Things aren't going so well in the hat business. Seems with all this talk about women's suffrage the hat is becoming the symbol of emancipation. Tsk, tsk." She shook her head sadly. "Some women are actually giving up wearing them altogether. It's bound to get worse, too, now that we've started our own temperance union."

Gandy's dimples appeared. He stretched out a hand and plucked up another coin. Then he grinned askance at Agatha.

"Seventy."

Agatha's throat went dry. She stared at the remaining coins, wishing she could gag Violet.

"I haven't the foggiest notion of what it is you want in the first place," she said, less forcefully. "All I know is hats."

"Something t' cover the birdcage. Use your imagination. Tied at the top, loose at the bottom, split up the side so the door can open. Jube can show you."

"I sure can, Miss Downing."

Agatha looked into the stunningly beautiful slanted eyes of Miss Jubilee and recalled her sitting perched like a snow-white dove on the swing as the wagon rolled down the street.

"Sixty," Gandy said in the softest tone yet.

Agatha's head snapped around. Her glance dropped to the dwindling stack of coins, then lifted to the picture of the sewing machine. Greed buoyed her heart. Despair weighted it. Two more coins and the sewing machine would be beyond her means. Gandy's hand moved again.

"Stop!" she called.

He hung the hand by one thumb from his waist and waited.

She dropped her head guiltily. "I'll do it," she agreed quietly.

"Good, Jube, Pearl, Ruby, y'all do whatever she says. Just be ready t' greet the customers at seven o'clock sharp." His hand moved to the coins again. *King-k-k-*

king! The four rescinded gold pieces joined the others. "A deal's a deal," he said, then stepped close to Agatha, extending his hand. "By seven, then, Miz Downin'?"

She stared at his hand. Long, dark fingers peppered with wispy black hair. Clean nails. Thin wrist. The conspicuous diamond glittering from his little finger. She removed her thimble and placed her palm in his very warm one. He squeezed firmly and shook hands with the solidity he'd afford any man. Somehow, she felt flattered. Against her will, she looked up. His dimples were deep. His eyes were unduly attractive. He had disarmingly perfect lips. Why did it seem that only the scoundrels were so blessed?

"By seven," she agreed.

But it felt as if she'd made a pact with the devil.

Chapter 4

Agatha sent Pearl over to measure the height and circumference of the cage. Then the five women set about making the cover. It was a simple enough design, like a flat window curtain with a drawstring at the top. She lit a fire in the stove and warmed the irons to press a one-inch hem around the perimeter. She handled the irons herself, while Violet and Ruby worked just ahead of her, marking the width with chalk, and Pearl kept the silk flowing wrinkle-free from the pressing board. Jubilee, meanwhile, took the cool irons to the stove and brought the hot ones back. Then the women sat in a rough circle and began stitching the hems into place.

It was immediately evident that Jubilee and Pearl had told the truth; they were hopeless with a needle. Ruby, on the other hand, was nimble-fingered and careful to make her stitches uniform and invisible. It wasn't long before Jubilee jabbed her finger. "Ouch!" She stuck it in her mouth and sucked. "Damn and double damn anyway! I can't sew! I'm making a regular mess of it, and now I'll get blood on the silk."

"Why don't you just sit back?" Agatha suggested. "Actually, with Ruby being as adept as she is, we'll finish with time to spare."

"Can I quit, too?" Pearl pleaded. "I'm no better at this than Jube is."

Agatha glanced at Pearl's pitiful handiwork. "You, too. If you'll just hold the satin on your lap and help guide it around to keep it from wrinkling, that will be sufficient."

Three thimbles clicked against three needles and the shimmering cloth shifted slowly across their laps.

"Would you look at Ruby!" Jubilee exclaimed after some time. "Where did you learn to stitch like that, Ruby?"

"Where you think? Waverley, o'course. My mama work in the big house for Miz Gandy and she teach my mama t' do fine stitches, and my mama teach me."

"You mean the young Mrs. Gandy or the old Mrs. Gandy?"

"Old one. Young one too flighty for stitchin'." The black woman gave the white one a meaningful grin. "She jus' like you, Jube."

The three laughed good-naturedly.

Violet missed a stitch at the mention of the young Mrs. Gandy. "Waverley?" she probed.

"Waverley Plantation, down in Columbus, Miz'sippi, where Mr. Gandy grew up."

"You mean our landlord grew up on a plantation?" Violet's romantic visions became evident in her eyes.

Ruby's husky voice reminisced. "Prettiest one you ever seen. Big white columns out front and back, big wide verandas. And cotton fields all around, reachin' farther than a fox can run on a cool mornin'. And the Tombigbee River shuggin' through the middle of 'em. It a glory sight, that place."

Agatha's interest had been aroused, but she let Violet ask the questions.

"You mean he owned it?"

"His daddy did. That was the old Mr. Gandy. He dead now and so's his missus. But they was as fine a white folks as you'll find. My mama and daddy was slaves for old Mr. Gandy. Me, too, before the war come. Me and Ivory and the boss, we all born on Waverley. Runned barefoot together and shucked pecans and swum in the river in our nothin'-ons. Whoo-ee, that was a time! 'Course, that was before the war."

Agatha tried to picture Gandy as a young boy running barefoot with a pair of black children but the picture wouldn't gel. She saw him instead with a cigar in his mouth and a glass of whiskey in his hand.

Violet was so curious she sat on the edge of her chair. "What happened to Waverley?" she prompted.

"Still there. War missed Columbus. They fight in a big circle all around it, but not there. All the big houses still standin'."

"Waverley," Violet repeated dreamily. "What a romantic name."

"Yes, ma'am."

Try though she might, Agatha could not keep her curiosity at bay. "Who owns it?"

"He does, the boss. Only went back once since the war, though. Found too many ghosts, I reckon."

"Ghosts?" Violet's eyes rounded.

"The young Miz Gandy—she and the little girl."

Agatha's needle stilled. She looked across the red satin at Ruby. "He had a wife . . . and a daughter?"

Ruby nodded, never taking her eyes off her stitching. "Dead. Both of 'em, and after the war ended, too. But he never made it home in time t' see 'em again."

It flashed through Agatha's mind that other men had turned dissolute for far less reason. Still, it was a shame. He was young, after all.

Violet had become so engrossed in the story she had to be reminded to keep sewing. Still, she asked more questions.

"How did they die?"

Ruby's glance lifted briefly, but her fingers kept moving. "If he know, he might go back, but nobody know for sure. Found 'em on the road, halfway to town, layin' upside the wagon, and the mule standin' there between the hitches, waitin' to be drove on. Young Mr. Gandy, he gits back and they's already buried inside the black iron fence 'cross the road beside his mama and daddy."

"Oh, my, that poor man," sympathized Violet.

Ruby nodded. "Lef' to fight them Yankees an' come back to nothin' but a few

niggers trying to scratch some collard greens outta them used-up cotton fields."
She shook her head sadly. "Second time he lef' he never go back."

"And he took you with him?"

"Me?" Ruby looked up, surprised. She laughed in her throaty contralto. "No,
not me. I one uppity nigger. When they tell me I free, I go off to the city. Natchez.
Figure to live fancy an' have me easy days till I see my chariot comin'." She
chuckled again, ruefully. "Ended up on my back on the rivuhboats, pleasurin' the
gennulmen. No chariot comin' for me no more," she finished realistically.

To Agatha's surprise, Jubilee leaned and pressed her white cheek to Ruby's
black one. "Now, Ruby, that's not true. You're a good woman. The best. Why,
look what you did for me. And for Pearl, too. Right, Pearl?"

Pearl said, "You listen to Jube, Ruby."

Ruby kept stitching, her winged brows lifted as if with superior knowledge.
"Wasn't me did it. It was him."

"Him?" Violet's eyes glittered with interest. "Who?"

"Young Mr. Gandy, that who." While she continued her story, Ruby stitched
steadily, her eyes on her work. "Took to gamblin' on the riverboats, an' he git
wind Ivory an' me workin' the *Delta Star* outta Natchez. I was doin' what I was
doin', and Ivory, he was a roustabout—roosters, they called 'em. 'Hey, rooster, we
got to double trip this load,' they'd call, and them poor deckhands has to unload
a hunnerd tons o' cargo to lighten the load when the river she's low, then load it
all again when the captain come back after leavin' off the first half upstream.
They got to cut firewood an' dive under when we hit snags—don't mattuh how
many snakes in that watuh! Cap'n say dive, roosters they dive. Poor Ivory, he
never been whupped before, not while he work for old mastuh Gandy. And me,
I nevuh know how good Waverley is till I go 'way on my own.

"So after the war is over, young boss he find Ivory workin' deckhand, bein'
whupped by dat bastuhd mate, Gilroy, whenever he took a mind to whup 'im. An'
me and the girls here, workin' that floatin' crib, hatin' every minute of it. Hogg,
too—Gandy's bartender?—he a fireman, workin' in that stinkin' engine room,
standin' in river water to his knees. An' Marcus, playin' banjo but gittin' laughed
at 'cause his tongue ain't right an' he can't mutter nuthin'. We all on board one
day when the cap'n send down the order t' tie down the valve—ice jam ahead.
Jack Hogg, he says, 'Can't do it, suh. She ready to blow now, suh.' Cap'n holluh,
'Tie de son-bitch down and stroke 'er good, fireman. I got apples and lemons'll
be worth half as much, that suckuh Rasmussen beat me to Omaha!'

"So Jack Hogg, he ties 'er down. Next thing you know, Jack Hogg an' most
the res' o' us flyin' th'ough the air like we on our way to glory land. But we all
live. Marcus, he up front plink-a-plinkin' in the gamblin' saloon, where Mistuh
Gandy sit gamblin' and jus' win hisself a pot o' money, so them all right. Me an'
the girls, we strollin' the decks, lookin' for our nex' lay, so we fly straight into
the water. Ivory, he lucky, too. He up by d' woodpile, gittin' set to load some
down. But Jack, he down by the boiler. He scarred bad.

"Young Mr. Gandy, he take care of us all, though. 'Riverboat days endin', he
says. 'Got to git out while there's someplace else to git to.' He say he got
friends—us. 'Nuff poke to start a saloon. Got Marcus to play the banjo. Ivory—
shoot, Ivory ain't cut out to be no rooster nohow. Ivory, he a piano man, an' the
boss know it. And Jack Hogg, he never want to be near no boiler again, but
he tend bar, soon as he heal. An' Pearl an' Jube an' me—no more entuhtainin' the
gennulmen, huh, girls? We young. We pretty. We gonna be dancin' girls, the boss
say. And what we think 'bout that?

"We say, whatever you say, boss."

"He say only one place t' make money quick. Head o' the Chisholm Trail, where the railroads is. So we come, an' the cowboys come. An' things is better than they been since before the war. We ain't fam'ly, but we 'bout as close as can be without bein' kin blood. That why when Mr. Gandy say sew, we sew, right, girls?"

The girls agreed.

Agatha sat through Ruby's recital with growing surprise. Gandy was their benefactor? He had taken these three women *away* from a life of iniquity? "You mean, you don't . . ." Her glance took in Ruby, Pearl, and Jubilee. "You're not . . ."

Jubilee laughed. Unlike Ruby's laugh, hers was light and lilting and seemed to match her wonderful uptilted eyes. "Prostitutes? Not anymore. Like Ruby said, just dancers now. And it's a welcome change. No more whiskey tongues choking us. No more greasy hands pawing us. No more . . . oh!" Jubilee noted Agatha's dropped gaze, her florid cheeks. "I'm sorry, Miss Downing. Never learned my manners proper."

"Like Jube says," added Pearl, "it's a sight better, just dancin'. And we're good dancers, too, aren't we, girls? And pretty fair singers, though Jube outshines Ruby and me in that department. Wait'll you hear her, Miss Downing, you won't believe it. Scotty says she's got a voice that'd shame a mockingbird."

"Oh, Pearl, you're always saying that." Jubilee turned bright eyes on the pair of milliners. "But wait till you see Pearl's high kick. Why, when Pearl starts kicking, you'd better hang your lantern someplace else, or she'll put it out! Isn't that right, Ruby?"

Ruby laughed her throat rumble. "Tha's right. Pearl got a li'l specialty she perfec'ed. She can kick the hat off any man 'thout rearrangin' one hair on his head, can't ya, honey?"

Now it was Pearl's turn to laugh. "But it was Ruby's idea. Ruby's always the one with the best ideas. Tell 'em about your disappearing trick, Ruby."

"Aw, go on." Ruby flapped a pink palm.

"Well, the men sure love it."

"The men—humph!—what them men know anyhow?"

"Tell 'em, Ruby," they both cajoled.

"Tell us, *tt-tt.*"

"Tell 'em yourself, if you think it's anythin' two ladies like them'd wanna hear."

Pearl told it. "Scotty's gone straight now, but that doesn't mean he couldn't palm a card if he wanted to. Well, back on the riverboat, he showed Ruby a little sleight of hand and Ruby put it to work in our act. She can get any man's watch and chain without him knowin' what she's up to. And by the time he finds out it's missing—where do you suppose it turns up?"

Against her will, Agatha was captivated. "Where?" she asked.

"Yes, where?" Violet repeated eagerly.

Pearl cupped a hand around her mouth and answered in a stage whisper, "Between her bosoms, that's where!"

Violet covered her mouth. *"Tt-tt."*

Agatha pinkened. "Oh . . . oh my!" Yet she was less horrified than she'd have been a week ago. There was something infectious about this trio. Perhaps it was their great camaraderie or their unselfish pride in one another. It seemed unusual that three women in their line of work could harbor so little jealousy among themselves.

"It's surprising," Pearl went on. "A man'll do near anything when you're alone with him behind a locked door, but put him in public and he'll blush like a fool at the least teasing. Now, when Ruby lets a man's watch chain dangle out of her bodice—and he has to pull it all the way out if he wants it back—why, you've never seen a funnier sight. Especially if the watch is made of gold. Gold warms up faster than silver, just bein' against your skin. And when they feel that warm gold . . ."

"Now, Pearl," interrupted Jubilee, "you're forgetting these are ladies we're visiting with. You can't talk to them like we talk to one another."

"Oh! Oh, you're right." Pearl colored becomingly. "Didn't mean to make you uneasy, Miss Downing, or you either, Miss Parsons. Sometimes my tongue runs away with me."

"It's quite all right. You see, Violet and I had the mistaken impression that you were going to do much more than dance at the Gilded Cage. Since you aren't, we're quite relieved. Well!" Agatha snipped a thread and tended to business because she didn't quite know how to respond to the subject under discussion. "All we have to do is string the cord through the top and we're finished."

"How're we going to do that?" Jubilee asked, staring at the casing.

Agatha got up and limped toward the supply cabinet. "It's quite simp—"

"Why, Miss Downing, you're limping!" Jubilee exclaimed.

Agatha felt a rush of blood, a moment of awkwardness as she wondered how to respond to such a blatant observation. Thank heavens she was reaching into the honeycombed case for a hank of cord and a thick darning needle. By the time she faced the group again, she'd regained her poise. "It's nothing."

"Nothing? But—"

"I've had it for years. I'm used to it by now." But Jubilee's beautiful almond eyes were wide with concern.

"You mean you weren't born that way?"

Oh, dear, how dreadfully acute she is, thought Agatha. *Isn't she bright enough to know she's being tactless?* Rattled, Agatha nevertheless answered truthfully, "No."

"Then how did it happen?"

"I fell down some stairs when I was a young girl."

Agatha could tell Violet was curious, too. Oddly enough, in the years they'd known each other Violet had never ventured to ask these questions.

Jubilee looked smack down at Agatha's skirts. "Oh, gosh, you poor girl. How awful!" Several thoughts struck Agatha at once: it had been years since anyone had called her a girl; Jubilee was not being nosy, but, in her naïve way, compassionate; because of this, Agatha could no longer be annoyed.

Jubilee followed her first impulse. "Here, let me help you with that." She approached Agatha, closed the door of the cabinet for her, and took the items from her hands. Chattering, she carried them back to their chairs. "And here we are talking about high kicks. We should have known better, but how could we? Still, it doesn't seem fair, does it?"

Agatha found it disconcerting to have her recurring thoughts spoken by a woman who was supposed to be "wicked." She couldn't help warming to the impetuous Jubilee.

"I'm not an invalid, Miss Jubilee," she advised her with a wry smile. "I can carry my own needle and cord."

"Oh!" Jubilee glanced at the things in her hands and gave a fluttery laugh. "Oh, of course you're not! What's the matter with me?" She stuffed the cording back into Agatha's hand and passed her the needle.

How could anyone help but be charmed by Jubilee Bright? Nobody ever confronted Agatha's lameness head-on. Now that she'd adjusted to the direct questioning, it became a welcome change from the sidelong glances of curiosity she usually received. And Jubilee did it with such refreshing lack of embarrassment Agatha felt her own tongue loosening.

"I do quite well, actually. Stairs are the worst, and I live upstairs." She pointed up.

"Upstairs? You mean above the store?" Jubilee peered at the stamped-tin ceiling.

"Yes."

"Then we're going to be neighbors!" When Jubilee smiled she was a breathtaking sight, all sparkle and animation. The tilt of her wide eyes matched that of her open lips, giving her a look of youthful eagerness. She must have been greedily sought after in her former profession, Agatha thought. "We're going to be living upstairs, too, so listen, if there's ever anything we can do to help you— haul things up and down, or run and fetch—you be sure to call on us." Jubilee turned to her friends. "Isn't that right, girls?"

"Sure thing," Pearl agreed. "We sleep late in the mornings, but we always have afternoons free."

"Me, I'm strong as a horse, and I was born takin' orders," claimed Ruby. "Any way I can he'p, just beller."

How was Agatha supposed to dislike these three? Whatever their pasts, Ruby, Pearl, and Jubilee appeared to have intrinsic generosity that ran deeper than that in some of the Presbyterians she knew.

"Thank you all, but for now, just stretch the top of the curtain flat so I can get the cord through the casing."

"How you going to do that?" Jubilee inquired.

"Easily. Tie the cord through the eye of the needle and run it through backward." Jubilee's eyes grew bigger and bigger as she held the edge of the red satin and watched Agatha work. "Balls o' fire, would you look at that!"

A spurt of laughter escaped Agatha. "You girls certainly have colorful language."

"Sorry, ma'am. It's where we've worked. But that's amazing."

"What?" Agatha busied herself pursing the fabric on the cord.

"That! What you're doing! How'd you learn such tricks?"

"My mother taught me."

"Why, I never would've thought of a thing like that. I'm lucky I can tie my own boot strings."

Agatha had known how to thread a casing for so long she took it for granted. She looked up at Jubilee's entranced almond eyes and felt a flicker of pride in her work.

"I've been doing it so long it's second nature to me."

"You sure are lucky, knowing a trade like you do."

"Lucky?" When was the last time Agatha had thought of herself as lucky?

"And having a mother to teach you. I didn't have a mother. I mean, she died when I was born, they tell me. Lived in St. Luke's Orphanage when I was little." Suddenly she flashed a mischievous smile. "Wonder what those nuns would say if they could see me now?" There wasn't the faintest note of self-pity in Jubilee's revelation. With a quicksilver shift of expression, she became engrossed in Agatha's occupation again. "Your mother, did she teach you lots of sewing tricks? I mean, like how to make dresses and petticoats and other things besides hats?"

"Well, actually, yes, I make all my own clothing."

"All your own! You mean you made that?" She took Agatha by an elbow and inspected the intricate shaping of her bodice—welts, gussets, flutes, and tucks. She turned to her and exclaimed, "Would you look at this, girls!" The three of them examined the details of Agatha's Austrian draped tie-back, and her even more elaborate cascading bustle. "That's some fancy work!"

They oohed and ahhed, even Ruby, who was handy with a needle herself.

"Petticoats, too?" Before Agatha could object, they lifted her rear hem to inspect the cagelike bustle, which fell from waist to heels in a set of horizontal ribs securely set in white cotton. Agatha was so surprised, she forgot to object.

"She could do it, couldn't she?" Jubilee asked Ruby.

"Do what?" Agatha demanded.

"Do what?" repeated Violet.

The girls ignored them. Jube was waiting for an answer. "Couldn't she?"

Ruby closely studied the construction of Agatha's clothing. "I b'lieve she could."

"Do what?" Violet insisted.

"Make those new skirts we been wanting for that French dance."

"New skirts?"

"French dance?"

"The cancan," Pearl informed them. "No offense, Miss Agatha, but I've been practicing my high kick especially for it. But I can't do the cancan without one of those ruffled skirts."

"Ruffles run clear around in layers," Ruby added, gesturing. "Like the old crinolines, only *inside* the skirt."

"You could do it!" Jubilee said enthusiastically. "I know you could, and I'll talk to Gandy about paying—"

"Please, ladies, please!" Agatha held up both palms. "I'm sorry. I can't."

They all talked at once.

"What you mean . . ."

"Oh, please say you will . . ."

"But where else are we going to . . ."

Agatha chuckled, beleaguered but flattered by their enthusiasm. "I can't. How would it look if the president of the local W.C.T.U. sewed costumes for the saloon dancers? The cover of the cage was bad enough, but if I do any more somebody is sure to find out. And furthermore, I have no sewing machine."

Three dejected dancers looked around to find it was true.

"Oh, damn," Pearl said, plopping down on a chair, "that's right."

"Pearl, you mustn't use such words," Agatha reprimanded gently, touching her shoulder.

With her chin in her palm, Pearl sulked. "I suppose not. But I'm disappointed."

"You know . . ." Agatha struggled a moment. Finally, she admitted, "So am I. I could have used the business, but I guess you can see it is neither possible nor advisable."

Violet began, "But, Agatha, couldn't we—"

"No, Violet, it's out of the question. Girls, you saw how long it took five of us to hem this. Ruffles require yards and yards of hemming. And to do it by hand . . . well, I doubt Mr. Gandy would be willing to pay for my time."

"You let us handle Mr. Gandy."

"I'm sorry, Jubilee, really I must say no."

The girls continued looking glum. Finally Jubilee sighed. "I guess we might as well go, then. Should we take this with us now?" She lifted the red silk between two fingers.

"You may as well. It'll save me taking it over, and Mr. Gandy's already paid me for it."

"Well, thanks for the rush job, Miss Downing. You, too, Miss Parsons. If you change your minds, let us know."

As Pearl opened the back door, Agatha suggested, "Perhaps you can order the dresses from St. Louis or . . . or . . ." It suddenly struck Agatha how absurd her suggestion was. Cancan dresses weren't exactly advertised in the ready-made catalogues.

"Sure," Jubilee said. Then they filed out despondently.

When they were gone, Violet gazed at the door. "Well, my stars," she said breathily, touching her temples.

"My sentiments exactly," Agatha rejoined, dropping into her chair. "That's the most zest this old shop has seen since it opened."

"They're wonderful!" Violet exclaimed.

Yes, thought Agatha sadly, *they are.* "But we cannot befriend them, Violet, you know that. Not when we've just been voted officers of the temperance union."

"Oh, bosh! They don't sell spirits. And they're not ladies of the evening anymore. They just dance. Didn't you hear them?"

"But their dancing promotes the sale of spirits. It's all the same."

Violet's mouth pursed. For the second time in several hours she declared in a piqued voice, "Sometimes, Agatha, you're no fun at all!" Then, leading with her chin, she left the shop for the day.

Alone, Agatha pondered the strange afternoon. She'd felt more alive than she had in years. She'd laughed and for a time completely forgotten that the young women were unsuitable clientele for her millinery shop. She had simply enjoyed them instead. But most amazing of all was that she'd actually told them about her accident. It had felt wonderful. And the girls had been amusing. But now that the hubbub had died down, she felt depressed. She wondered what it felt like to be part of a sorority such as that shared by Jubilee, Pearl, and Ruby, to be true friends as they were. Violet was her friend, but not in the sense that the three young dancers were friends. They radiated a real understanding and acceptance of one another, a pride in their limited accomplishments, and an amazing lack of competition. Also, they had the group they called their "family"—not a real family, but better, perhaps, because they were related by choice, not by blood. And that "family" was headed by a riverboat gambler they followed as if he were the Messiah. Curious. Enviable.

Enviable? The notion jolted Agatha. Women who'd pleasured men for money, who'd learned how to lift pocket watches from unsuspecting dandies, who danced in saloons with pictures of naked women on the wall and kicked hats from men's heads. How was it possible she could believe for an instant she envied them?

But if she didn't, why was she suddenly so sad?

It was getting late. Soon it would be time to get ready for the seven o'clock gathering.

Agatha rose from her chair and saw the gold coins winking at her from the worktable, right where Gandy had left them. She wondered how long it would take to get a sewing machine shipped in from Boston.

Agatha, don't be silly!

But the girls are so lively, so much fun to be around.

Agatha, you're getting as senile as Violet!

And imagine what you could earn, making three cancan outfits.

It would be tainted money.

But so much of it. And he pays so well.

Agatha, don't even think it! –

Well, he does. A hundred dollars for less than three hours' work. And three helping hands thrown in!

It was a bribe and you know it.

Bribery money buys sewing machines the same as other money.

Listen to yourself. Soon you'll be stitching cancans!

I've a mind to try it, with or without a sewing machine.

Since when did you become mercenary?

Oh, all right, so he paid me too much!

And what do you intend to do about it?

She picked up the ten gold coins and feathered them onto her palm. They were so heavy! She'd never known before how heavy ten ten-dollar gold pieces were. And they warmed fast, as the girls had said. She peeled off six and set them aside, then layered the remaining four like dominoes along her palm. Forty dollars was a lot of money. Warm, heavy money.

In the end she listened to her conscience, resolutely clamped her palm shut, and headed for the back door. Even as she did she wished she were as uninhibited as Pearl so she could curse at herself for what she was about to do.

The back door of the Gilded Cage opened on to a short corridor between a pair of storage rooms. Standing in the shadows, Agatha went unnoticed at first. There was neither piano nor banjo music, only the sound of happy chatter. A gay band of saloon regulars, and all the establishment's employees, clustered around the gilded cage as Gandy and the girls settled the cover over it and arranged its folds. Momentarily, Agatha envied them again. The camaraderie. The way they laughed and teased one another.

She saw immediately what all the hammering had been about. A rope led from the tip of the cage to a pulley mounted in the ceiling, where a trapdoor had been installed. They were bantering about it, pointing, looking up. Jubilee said something and they all laughed. Then Gandy looped an arm around her shoulders. They looked into one another's faces and shared a private chuckle. Then his hand swept down the hollow of her back and lingeringly squeezed her buttock.

Agatha's mouth went dry. Her neck felt hot.

She had no idea people did things like that out of their bedrooms.

She gathered her equilibrium and moved down the hall toward them. The scarfaced bartender saw her and left the group to greet her.

"Evenin', Miss Downing," He tipped his bowler.

She was surprised that he knew her name. But he treated her politely, which demanded politeness in return. "Good evening, Mr. Hogg."

Immediately, she could tell he was surprised that she knew his name as well. The unscarred half of Jack Hogg's face smiled. It was grotesque but she forced herself not to look away, as people sometimes looked away from her.

"Cover looks wonderful, ma'am. Just what Scotty wanted." When he spoke, the right corner of his mouth drew down; the left corner didn't move at all.

It struck Agatha how ironic it was that she was standing in the saloon with the picture of the naked woman on the wall, receiving compliments on the red cover she'd sewn. Heaven help her if anyone should walk past the door and glance inside.

"I didn't come to chitchat. May I speak with Mr. Gandy, please?"

"Sure thing, ma'am." He raised his voice. "Hey, Scotty! Lady here to see ya."

Gandy turned from the talkative group near the cage. When he saw Agatha, his dimples appeared and he dropped his arm from Jubilee. He flicked down his shirtsleeves, reached automatically for his jacket from the back of a chair, and shrugged it on while crossing to her.

"Miz Downin'," he greeted her simply, coming to a halt before her. He thrust his head forward, still adjusting his lapels, a simple enough motion, yet masculine. She was unaccustomed to witnessing men don their clothes. It did something restive to her stomach.

"Mr. Gandy," she returned civilly, fixing her gaze on his chest.

"Y'all did a fine job. 'Preciate your hurryin' like y' did."

"You overpaid me." She held out the four gold pieces. "I cannot in good conscience accept all this money."

Still holding his lapels, he glanced at the coins. "Deal's a deal."

"Exactly. Sixty, I believe it was. I'll accept that much, even though it's still more than equitable."

He remained silent for so long that she glanced up. He was considering her with his head tilted to one side. His hair touched his white collar. His necktie hung loose. His dimples were gone.

"You're an amazin' woman, y'know that, Miz Downin'?"

Her gaze dropped beneath his disconcerting perusal.

"Please, just take the money."

"You're plannin' t' come back here in . . ." He pulled his watch out and she concentrated on his dark thumb as it released the catch. The cover flipped open. It was made of bright, shiny gold. She wondered if he'd ever extracted it— warm—from between Ruby's breasts. Or was it only Jubilee he touched intimately?

She returned from her woolgathering to hear him asking, "Why?"

"I . . . I'm sorry. What were you saying?"

One of his eyebrows curled like a question mark fallen sideways. "In less than an hour you're plannin' t' come back here and begin the ruination of my business. Yet you come in here with forty dollars sayin' I overpaid you for a sewin' job you didn't wanna do in the first place. Why?"

She glanced up again. More quickly down. He was too ungodly handsome. "I told you, my conscience would bother me if I kept it all."

She'd never met a man so adept at insouciance. His voice became so soft it alone triggered her blush. "It'll take some money t' shut me down. Why don't y'all add it t' your temperance fund?"

Her head snapped up. He was grinning like a stroked cat, laughing at her.

"Take it!" she demanded, grabbing his wrist and slapping the coins into his palm.

His dimples deepened and she turned to leave. He grabbed her arm to stop her. She pierced his hand with a malevolent look and he immediately released her. "Sorry."

"Was there something else, Mr. Gandy?" she inquired sharply.

"The girls tell me they asked you t' make some costumes for them but you refused."

"That's right. I'm all through doing business with you. From here on out I fight you."

"Ah, commendable." He raised one long index finger. "But don't forget free enterprise. You know now that I really do pay well."

"I explained to the girls that I have no sewing machine. It would take an impossible length of time and it wouldn't look good to the ladies of the temperance union. Besides, I'm a milliner, not a seamstress."

"That's not what they said after watchin' you put together that cover."

"The answer is no, Mr. Gandy."

"Very well," he conceded with a half bow. "Thank you for returnin' my money. Maybe I can buy a nude for the other wall."

She realized as she stood there sparring with him that her heart was beating a little too earnestly. Her face, however, remained stern.

"Until seven o'clock, then," she said, repeating his earlier words, offering the faintest bow.

He raised his chin and laughed. "We'll be expectin' y'all. And the doors'll be open."

As she left, he withdrew a cigar from his pocket and studied the rear of her skirts—poufs and froufrous. And enough cloth to make a revival tent! He wondered how in tarnation the woman put together such a rig. Nimble-fingered little thing, he thought. And living on a shoestring, if his guess was right. He'd be willing to bet that ten-dollar gold pieces weren't the only things that spoke louder than words . . . in her case, so did sewing machines.

He was a gambler. He'd put money on it.

Chapter 5

The ladies of the Proffitt Women's Christian Temperance Union met on the boardwalk shortly before seven P.M., bringing their temperance pledges with them. At the top was the organization's name and motto, coined by Frances Willard, the founder and president of the national W.C.T.U.: For God and Home and Native Land. The pledge contained the promise that he who signed, "with God being his helper, would never touch, taste, or handle, for beverage purposes, any intoxicating liquor, including wine, beer, and cider," and that he would "use all honorable means to encourage others to abstain." Below were blanks for name and date.

When the ladies arrived, Gandy, wearing a convivial smile, came out to the boardwalk to greet them. From the shadows Agatha studied him. The saloon lanterns threw a cone of light through the open doors as he stood pressing them open. The orange glow highlighted only parts of his face. It appeared freshly shaven for the occasion. From the low crown of his black hat to the tips of his shiny black boots, he was indecently attractive. Freshly brushed black suit, ice-blue waistcoat, immaculate white collar, and black string tie. Even the malodorous cheroot was absent from his fingers.

He took his time, letting his glance pass from one female face to the next until he'd met each pair of eyes. Only then did he leisurely tip his black Stetson.

"Evenin', ladies."

Some shifted nervously under his indolent perusal. Several nodded silently. Others glanced uncertainly at Drusilla Wilson. Agatha stood stiffly, watching. How confident he was of his charm, of his effect on those of the opposite sex. His very pose seemed calculated to enhance his striking appearance—weight on one hip, jacket gaping open, hands draped lazily over the tops of the swinging doors, the diamond ring winking even in the twilight.

Gandy's dark, amused eyes picked out Agatha.

"Miz Downin'," he drawled, "you're lookin' exceptionally fine this evenin'."

Agatha wished she could slip between the cracks in the boardwalk. Momentarily, she feared he would mention the job she'd done for him—she wouldn't put it past him to thank her drolly. To her relief his attention moved on.

"Miz Parsons. My, my." His dimples proved more effective than flowery words. Violet tittered.

Stepping farther onto the boardwalk, Gandy turned to Drusilla.

"Miz Wilson, I don't b'lieve I've had the pleasure."

She glanced at his extended hand, clasping her own together. "Mr. Gandy, I presume."

He nodded.

"I'll shake your hand when it has put your signature on this." She thrust forward the pledge and a pen. Gandy scanned them coolly, then threw back his head and laughed.

"Not today, Miz Wilson. With three dancin' girls and that white-limbed beauty on the wall in there, I b'lieve I have the winnin' hand." He pressed both swinging doors back against the wall. "But y'all do what y' can t' reverse the odds."

With a half bow he turned and left them.

It became obvious with the arrival of the saloon's first patrons that its attractions far outweighed those of any temperance pledge. The swinging doors remained folded back. From inside came the welcoming sound of the piano and banjo. The oil painting beckoned from the wall. The green baize of the gambling tables welcomed like oases in a desert. Gandy himself greeted his customers. And everyone awaited the appearance of Jubilee and the Gems.

Outside, the ladies took up a chorus of "Cold Water Is King," singing at the top of their lungs, only to inspire Gandy to send Marcus Delahunt onto the boardwalk to play his banjo and muddle their song. When Mooney Straub, Wilton Spivey, and Joe Jessup approached, the music grew louder from both factions.

Drusilla Wilson herself approached the trio, shouting to be heard above the din.

"Friends, before you set foot inside to support this ally of Satan, consider how you might better work toward your final salvation. Beyond these doors is the twisting road to ruin, while on this paper is the . . ."

Their laughter covered the remainder of her plea.

"Lady, you gotta have a wheel loose if ya think I'm signin' that thing. Ain't ya heard? There's dancin' women here!"

"And that pitcher o' the naked lady," added Mooney.

"And we aim to name 'er!"

Guffawing, they jostled three abreast through the open door. The place began to fill fast. Things were much the same with Drusilla's next three attempts to waylay Gandy's customers. They laughed in her face and hurried inside, already reaching for their coins.

Then came a ne'er-do-well named Alvis Collinson who'd lost his wife to pneumonia two years earlier. A surly man with a nose like a mushroom, Collinson was known around town for his hair-trigger temper. He worked at the stockyards when he worked. When he didn't, he spent most of his time drinking, gambling, and starting fights. Countless knuckles had rearranged his face. The left eyelid drooped. The nose bulged hideously. The cheeks, with their broken capillaries, had the appearance of a red cauliflower. His filthy clothing appeared oily from body excretions. When he passed Agatha the air turned sour in his wake.

Evelyn Sowers surprised everyone by stepping forward and accosting him.

"Mr. Collinson, where is your son?"

Collinson stopped. His head jutted and his fists clenched.

"What business is it o' yours, Evelyn Sowers?"

"Have you left him home alone while you sit here night after night pickling your innards?"

"What the hell ya doin' here anyway, all you old biddies?" Alvis cast a hateful glare across the entire group.

"Trying to save your soul, Alvis Collinson, and give your son back his father."

He swung back to Evelyn. "Leave my boy outta this!"

Evelyn stepped directly in front of him. "Who's taken care of him since your wife died, Alvis? Has he had his supper? Who'll tuck him into bed tonight? A five-year-old-boy—"

"Get outta my way, hag!" He gave her a push that sent her stumbling backward. Her head struck a post and several ladies gasped. Their song faded into silence. But Evelyn bounced off and grabbed Collinson's arm.

"That boy needs a father, Alvis Collinson. Ask the Lord where he'll get one!" she shouted.

He shook her off. "Haul your bustles back to your kitchens if ya know what's good for ya!" he roared, stamping inside.

By now Marcus Delahunt's fingers had stopped moving on the banjo strings. In the sudden silence Agatha's heart hammered with fear. She glanced inside to find a frowning Gandy observing the altercation. With a jerk of his head he motioned Delahunt inside, calling, "Close the doors."

The musician went in, leaving the doors flapping.

"Ladies, let us sing," Drusilla interjected. "A new song."

While they sang "Lips That Touch Whiskey Shall Never Touch Mine," the saloon filled to capacity and not a man had signed a pledge. As the last verse began outside, a roar went up inside. Over the tops of the swinging doors Agatha saw Elias Potts being clapped on the shoulder and congratulated for winning the picture-naming contest. The portly druggist was hoisted to a tabletop and seated in a spindle-backed chair. Then they lifted their drinks in a toast to the nude, shouting, "To Dierdre and her garden of delights!"

Overhead, the new trapdoor opened and the red-shrouded cage began descending on a thick red satin rope. The men roared, and clapped, and whistled. The background music of the banjo and piano was scarcely audible above the uproar. Potts, scarlet to the fringe of his near-bald head, grinned and dried the corners of his mouth as the cage hovered before him.

The piano player struck one fortissimo chord.

A long leg jutted out from between the folds of red.

The banjo and piano hit and sustained another chord.

The high-heeled white boot rotated on a shapely ankle.

A glissando rolled.

The leg shot out and the toe of the boot braced on Elias Potts's left knee.

The music stilled.

"Gentlemen, I give you the jewel of the prairie, *Miss Jubilee Bright!*"

The music swelled and the red drapes swooshed to the ceiling! The men went crazy. There stood Jubilee, dazzling in unrelieved white.

The words about whiskey faded from Agatha's lips as she stared. Jubilee leaned from the cage in a dress slit from hem to hip, its strapless bodice covered in glittering white sequins. In her incredible white hair bobbed an even whiter curved feather whose tips, too, flashed with sequins. She braced her toe on Potts's knee and leaned forward to stroke his jaw with a fluffy white boa. Her voice was sultry, the words slow and ripe with innuendo.

> *"It's not because I wouldn't . . ."*

Never had Agatha seen a more beautiful leg than the one braced on Potts's knee, never a more enviable face than the one leaning close to his. She could not tear her eyes away.

> *"And it's not because I shouldn't . . ."*

Jubilee sidled in a full circle around Potts's chair, letting her shoulder blades graze him.

> *"Lord knows it's not because I couldn't . . ."*

She flipped the boa around Potts's neck and sat on his lap with the heel of one white boot crossing her opposite knee. She slid the boa back and forth in time to the music.

> *"It's simply because I'm the laziest girl in town."*

The men whooped and hollered while Potts grew ripe as an August watermelon. Ivory Culhane raised his voice. "Gentlemen, the gems of the prairie, Miss Pearl DeVine and Miss Ruby Waters!"

From above, two vampish bodies slithered down the red satin rope. It twined around and between their legs—black fishnet stockings, high-heeled black boots— and along their skimpy costumes—black satin and sequins and scarcely enough material to make a corset. Hand below hand, Pearl and Ruby came down the rope while whistles and wolf calls drowned out their song. The nearest hands plucked them from the roof of the cage and deposited them on the edge of the green-topped table where they sat, leaning back against Potts's legs, peering up at him provocatively. Behind him, Jubilee cradled the back of his head against her bosom and tickled his nose with the boa.

> *"It's not because we wouldn't.*
> *It's not because we shouldn't.*
> *Lord knows it's not because we couldn't.*
> *It's simply because we're the laziest girls in town."*

Watching, listening, Agatha was both repelled and mesmerized. So much skin! But so healthy and beautiful.

"We'll accomplish no more here tonight," Drusilla Wilson announced, bringing Agatha to her senses. "We'll move on to the next saloon."

Resisting the urge to look back over her shoulder, Agatha followed the others. At the Branding Iron Saloon they marched directly inside and signed up their first reformer, Jed Hull, who became frightened by the newspaper drawing of the Blackwell Island Asylum for Inebriates that Drusilla Wilson passed around.

Angus Reed, the Scot who owned the Branding Iron, couldn't believe his eyes when he saw Hull being shepherded out the door. He leaped over the bar and shouted, "Where the hell you going, Hull? Haven't you got enough guts to stand up to a bunch of female do-gooders who belong at home breeding babies?" But he was too late. With a violent curse he swatted the bar with a wet towel.

Inspired by their first success, the reformers marched on to the Cattlemen's

Crossing, where the price of drinks had been cut to twenty cents and had lured several hard-core imbibers away from the show being staged down at the Gilded Cage. The owner, an irascible former cowpuncher who went by the name of Dingo, suffered inflammatory rheumatism from drinking too much gyp water in his trail days. Though his stiff joints kept him from leaping over the bar as Reed had, they lent him a perpetual orneriness. He hobbled from behind his kegs and kicked Bessie Hottle smack in her bustle. "Git your ass outta my saloon and don't come back!"

Red to the ears, Bessie led the quick retreat.

Next they invaded the Alamo, where Jennie Yoast and Addie Anderson encountered their husbands and more wrath from the owner, a half-breed Mexican named Jesus Garcia who cursed a string of Spanish epithets when he saw two of his best customers shamed in public and chased home by their wives.

The next three saloon owners were too amused to object when the band of women descended upon them, singing "Lips That Touch Whiskey." Slim Tucker laughed his guts out. Jim Starr offered each of the ladies a drink on the house. And Jeff Diddier swigged down a double shot of bourbon, backhanded his mouth dry, and joined in singing the last chorus of their song.

At The Sugar Loaf Saloon, the owner, Mustard Smith, pulled a shotgun from behind the bar and gave them thirty seconds to clear out. It was rumored that Smith wore his full black beard to cover a scar that ran from ear to ear. The ladies didn't stop to inquire if it were true. Everyone knew he'd ridden with B. B. Harlin's gang, and three of them had been hanged from a railroad trestle. When Mustard ordered, "Clear out," they cleared.

At the Hoof and Horn they had little luck. The place was empty, having lost its few customers to the lively show across the street. The ladies said a simple prayer for the salvation of Heustis Dyar's soul, then left peaceably. Behind them, Dyar stood with hands akimbo, eyes burning, chewing his cigar stub as if it were a piece of raw meat.

At Ernst Bostmeier's Saloon they signed up their second reformer of the night, one of the customers who frequented Ernst's place because he served a free pickled egg with each glass of beer. As the ladies walked out the door with their saved soul in tow, the grumpy old German proprietor threw a pickled egg that missed Josephine Gill's shoulder by a mere inch. "Dere's more vere dat come from!" he bellowed in his thick German accent, shaking his fist. "Ent I only miss ven I vant to!"

The remainder of the saloon visits proved uneventful. In each, the owners, bartenders, and clientele were merely amused by what they considered a pack of distempered old maids and errant housewives with not enough dirty socks to keep them at their scrub boards.

It was well after eleven o'clock when Agatha climbed the stairs to her apartment. Downstairs the laughter and music still poured into the night. On the landing it was dark. Before she could unlock her door her fingertips brushed a paper hanging on it.

Her heart lurched and she spun about, backing up against the door.

Nobody was there.

Chills crept up the backs of her arms. She held her breath, listening. The only sound came from the continuing revelry in the Gilded Cage.

Quickly, she jerked the note free. A tack dropped to the landing floor and rolled away. She spared not even a moment to pick it up, but hurriedly unlocked the door and slipped inside.

Somehow she knew even before the lamp was lit what she'd find.

STAY OUT OF THE SALOONS
IF YOU KNOW WHAT'S GOOD FOR YOU!

It was printed in capital letters on a clean sheet of white paper. She hurried back to the door and locked it, tested the knob, then leaned against it with a sigh of relief. She scanned the narrow apartment—the bed and chifforobe were the only two places large enough to conceal a man. She stood stock-still, listening for breathing, rustling—any sound at all. The faraway chords from the piano and banjo covered any faint sounds the room might have held. She struggled to her knees, peered beneath the bed from across the room.

Black shadows.

Don't be silly, Gussie, your door was locked.

Nevertheless, her heart pounded. She inched closer until the lamplight revealed nothing but dust balls hiding under the bed. On her feet once more, she tiptoed to the chifforobe, paused with her fingers on the handle. Abruptly, she flung its doors wide, then wilted with relief.

Only clothing.

Who were you expecting, silly goose?

She pulled down her window shades, both front and back, but the creepy feeling persisted while she undressed and retired.

It could have been any of them. Angus Reed, who'd jumped over the bar and shouted angrily when they took away one of his customers. That rheumatic old cowboy, Dingo—people said his rheumatism made him ornery as a rabid skunk when it acted up. And how about Garcia? He was visibly upset to have two of his regulars carted home by their wives. Bostmeier, the German? Somehow she doubted it; in the dark she smiled at the memory of that pickled egg flying through the air. If Bostmeier wanted to threaten anyone, he'd do it in person. But what about Mustard Smith? Agatha shivered and pulled the covers tightly beneath her chin. She saw again the drooping batwing moustache, the full beard, the hooded eyes, and the crooked mouth. *The shotgun.* If it were true, if Smith *had* ridden with B. B. Harlin's gang, if they *had* all been hanged, if he *was* the only one to have lived through it, what kind of malevolence might lurk in such a man?

She considered all the others—Dyar, Tucker, Starr, Diddier, and the rest. She didn't think any of them had taken the W.C.T.U. seriously.

So what about Gandy? Lying on her back, she crossed her arms tightly over her breasts.

Gandy?

Yes, Gandy.

Gandy, with his dimples and his "Evenin', ladies"?

Exactly.

But Gandy has no reason.

He owns a saloon.

The busiest one in town.

For the moment.

He's too cocksure to resort to threats.

What about at the top of the stairs last night?

You don't really think . . . he wasn't going to . . .

You thought so, didn't you?

But tonight he was so charming to all of us, and I could see he was upset when Alvis Collinson shoved Evelyn.

A clever man.

What are you saying?

What are you saying?
No. I refuse to believe it of Gandy.
See, Agatha? See what ten gold pieces will do?

The Gilded Cage closed at midnight. Dan Loretto went home. Marcus Delahunt polished the neck of his banjo, then tucked it away in its velvet-lined case. Ivory Culhane closed the key cover on the piano and Jack Hogg washed glasses. Pearl stretched, Ruby yawned, and Jubilee watched Gandy close and lock the full outer doors. When he turned, she smiled.

Smiling, too, he weaved his way through the tables to her. "So what's the smile for?"

She shrugged and walked toward the bar with him. "It's good to be back, that's all. Hey, fellas, isn't it good to be back together again?" Reaching Ivory, she gave him an impulsive hug. "Gosh, I never thought I'd miss everybody so much."

"Hey, how 'bout me?" Jack Hogg put in.

Jubilee leaned across the bar and hugged him, then gave him a peck on his cheek. "You, too, Jack." She leaned both elbows on the varnished mahogany surface and propped up her chin. "So, how's business been around here?"

Gandy watched her and the others as they gathered around. Jack, Marcus, Ivory, Pearl, Ruby, and Jubilee—the only family he had. A bunch of loners who'd all been scarred in one way or another. Not all their scars showed, as Jack's did, but they were there just the same. When he'd gathered them together after the explosion on the riverboat two years ago, something magical had happened; he had felt a oneness of spirit, a bond of friendship that filled the voids in all their lives. Superficialities mattered not a whit—skin color, relative facial beauty, or lack of it. What mattered was what each brought to the group as a whole. They'd been split up for a month while he got the Gilded Cage set up and operable. It had seemed twice that long.

"I went down to New Orleans to visit the girls in a crib I used to work," Pearl was saying.

"As long as you weren't tempted to stay," Ivory remarked.

"Uh-uh! Never again." Everyone laughed. "You see the doc in Louisville, Jack?"

"Sure did." Jack removed his white apron and laid it across the bar. "Doc says it won't be long I'll be lookin' as pretty as Scotty here."

Again they laughed. Ruby turned and looped an arm through Scotty's. "What you want a face like that for? Look a little coluhless t' me."

Jack's scar grew brighter as he laughed again with the others.

"So, where'd you go, Ruby?"

"Went down t' Waverley. Visit my mama's grave."

Every glance shifted to Scotty. He revealed none of the emotions he felt. "How is it?"

"Looks seedy. A few o' the old ones still there, shiftin' for theirselves, growin' greens an' livin' in the cabins. Leatrice"—the strange name rhymed with mattress—"she still there, waitin' for Lord knows what."

At the news, Gandy felt a stab of nostalgia, but he only inquired, "You give her a kiss for me?"

"Mos' suttenly did not. Y'all wanna kiss Leatrice, ya'll go down an' do it yourself."

He pondered momentarily, then replied, "Someday, maybe."

Jubilee stood near Marcus, half leaning against him. "Marcus and I saw about getting the cage made and picked up a couple jobs here and there playing and singing before we met the girls in Natchez. We did one place called the Silver Slipper." She draped an elbow over Marcus's shoulder and looked smug. "They wanted us to stay awful bad, didn't they, Marcus? We drew crowds that filled the hat every night."

Marcus smiled, nodded, and made motions, as if counting out dollar bills. Everybody laughed.

"Is this a bribe, you two?" Scotty inquired. "I already pay you more than you're worth."

"What do you think, Marcus?" Jubilee lounged on Marcus's shoulder while looking teasingly at Scott. "Should we go across the street and offer our talents to one of the saloons over there?"

"Just try it," Scotty replied, taking aim with a forefinger as if it were a gun, pointing it straight at Jubilee's pretty pink nose.

"What about you, Ivory?" Pearl asked.

"I stuck with the boss. Had to get the piano hauled in here and tuned up, and plenty to do gettin' the whole place set up. Had to help him pick out the picture for the wall." Ivory raised one eyebrow and half turned toward the nude. "So what do you think of her?"

The men smiled appreciatively. The women looked away and arched their eyebrows with a superior air.

Pearl said, "With those thighs she doesn't look like she could kick a hat off a kitchen chair, much less a man's head, does she, Ruby?"

"Pro'bly couldn't sing a note, eithuh," Ruby added.

"Tsk-tsk," Jubilee added. "And the poor thing certainly is running to fat."

When they trooped upstairs they were all in good spirits. Ivory and Jack retired to the first room on the left. Marcus took the next. Pearl and Ruby shared the one just beyond the gilded cage, which now occupied the dead center of the hall, where the new trapdoor had been cut. That left Jubilee and Scotty.

She stepped into her room and lit a lamp, while he lounged against the doorframe.

"It's a nice room, Scotty. Thanks."

He only shrugged.

She flung her white boa over a pink oval-backed settee. "A window. A view of the street." She moved to the front of the room, leaned both palms on the sill, and looked down at the row of coal-oil lights. Then she glanced over her shoulder at the man in the doorway. "I like it."

He nodded. It was good just looking at her. She was a strikingly beautiful woman and he'd missed her.

"Whew!" She swung around, hands to the ceiling, flexing her shoulders. "What a long day." She plucked the feather from her hair, discarded it, and picked up a buttonhook. Dropping to the pink settee, she held it out to him. "Help me with my shoes, Scotty?" Her voice was quiet.

For several seconds he didn't move. Their eyes exchanged messages. Unhurriedly, he pulled his shoulder away from the doorframe and crossed the room to go down on one knee before her. He cradled her white boot against his groin and unhurriedly freed the buttons. Without looking up, he asked, "So how'd things go in Natchez? You meet anybody who struck your fancy?"

She studied his thick black hair. "No. Did you?"

"Uh-uh."

"No sweet young Kansas thing, fresh from her mama's arms?"

He pulled off one boot, dropped it, and looked up, grinning. "Nope."

He took her other boot against him and began applying the hook. She watched his familiar dark hands perform the personal task. In the lamplight the ring flashed brightly against his dusky skin.

"No pining Kansas widow who's been alone since the war?"

His dimples formed as he looked up into her familiar almond eyes and spoke lazily.

"Kansas widows don't cotton to Johnny-reb gamblin' men who open up saloons in their towns."

She threaded her fingers through the hair over his right ear. "Well, gosh-a-mighty, if we aren't two of a kind. Natchez mamas don't turn their sons loose to no soiled doves-turned-dancer, either."

He dropped the second boot, kissed her toes, and rubbed them with his thumb. "I missed you, Jube."

"I missed you, too, you no-count gamblin' man."

"Wanna come t' my room?"

"Just try to keep me away."

Rising, he held out a hand. He led her past a tapestried screen, snagging her turquoise dressing gown from over the top of it and flinging it over his shoulder. "Bring the lantern. You won't be needin' it in here tonight."

In the blackness at the other end of the hall a door remained slightly ajar. From his own dark room Marcus watched the lantern light splash the hall. Through the bars of the gilded cage he saw Scotty lead Jube by the hand to his doorway. Her hair shone so brightly it seemed as if it alone could have lit their way. Her white dress and bare arms appeared ethereal as she padded silently behind Scotty. What would it be like to take her hand? Walk her barefoot to bed? Remove the pins from that snow-bright hair and feel it spill into his hands?

Since the first time he'd seen her, Marcus had wondered. During the past month, while they'd traveled alone together, there were times when Jubilee had touched him. But she touched anyone and everyone without compunction. A touch didn't mean to Jube what it meant to Marcus. Tonight by the bar she'd draped her arm over his shoulder. But she never suspected what happened inside him when her hand took his elbow or she adjusted his lapel, or—most of all—when she kissed his cheek.

She kissed all their cheeks whenever the spirit moved her. She'd kissed Jack's only thirty minutes ago. They all knew it was Jube's way.

But nobody knew the hidden torment of Marcus Delahunt.

Often he had to touch her to get her attention, so he knew what her skin felt like. Sometimes when she'd turn to watch him communicate some silent message, he'd have to remind himself to make the motions. To look into Jube's eyes, those stunning pale brown windows of her soul, was to lose his own. How often he'd longed to tell her how beautiful he thought she was. Locked in perpetual voicelessness, he could only think it. Often he played it to her on his banjo. But all she heard were musical notes.

Down the hall Scotty's door closed. Marcus pictured him taking the white dress from Jube's body, laying her across his bed, murmuring love words to her, telling her the thousand things Marcus himself wanted to say. He wondered if sound made a feeling when it rose from one's throat. He wondered what laughter felt like when it was more than the shaking of one's chest, and what it was like to whisper.

To love a woman, a man had to be able to do all those things. He pictured

Scotty doing them now. Nobody else Marcus knew was good enough for her. Her pale beauty deserved Scotty's dark good looks. Her bright laughter deserved his teasing grin. Her perfect body deserved another equally as perfect.

What would a man say first?

You're beautiful.

Do first?

Touch—her cheek, her lips, her angel hair.

Feel like?

As if the world and all its glory were in his hand.

Jube ... Jube ...

"Jube, let me do that," Scotty was saying in the room across the hall. He did all the things Marcus Delahunt could only dream of doing. One by one he pulled the pins from Jube's fluffy, white hair. He felt it tumble into his hands and smoothed it over her milk-white shoulders. He unbuttoned her dress, then freed her corset stays and watched her long-legged body emerge as she kicked free of garters and stockings. When she turned and looped her arms around his neck, he placed his hands on the sides of her breasts and kissed the black mole between them, the one the rest of the world thought she glued to her skin each morning. He kissed her willing mouth, touched her in ways that temporarily held loneliness at bay. He laid her on the bed and murmured endearments and told her how he'd missed her and how glad he was to have her back. He linked their bodies with the most intimate of caresses and found within her a surcease for emptiness. He even cleansed her and himself when it was over. And wrapped her close in the big, soft bed and slept naked with her breast within his palm.

But between them the word *love* was never spoken.

Chapter 6

The first herd of Texas longhorns arrived the following day. Bawling and bull-headed they came, driven by men who'd been three months in the saddle on a dusty, dry trail. Both the cattle and the men were dirty, thirsty, hungry, and tired. Proffitt was ready to accommodate them all.

Its inordinately wide streets were designed first to handle the unlovable beasts with horns twice the width of their bodies; next, to assuage the frustrations of the weary Texas cowboys who drove them.

Agatha looked out the window of her millinery shop and watched two boys race across the street—their last chance to do so for some time. From the far end of town the rumble of hooves could already be felt. Resignedly, she said, "Here they come."

The herd passed through Proffitt from west to east, a shifting, drifting, sometimes unmanageable mass of beef flesh that created a stream of red, brown, white, and gray cowhide for as far as the eye could see. Beside them rode the hardscrabble cowpunchers as tough as the hundreds of miles of mesas they'd crossed.

Saddle-weary and lonely, they wanted three things: a drink, a bath, and a woman, usually in that order.

The prostitutes had already returned to the cat houses on the far west edge of town after wintering in the bagnios of Memphis, St. Louis, and New Orleans. Garbed in dressing gowns and scanty corsets, they stood on the railed roofs and hung from the windows, waving and beckoning.

"Hiya, cowboy! Don't forget to ask for Crystal!"

"Tired of that saddle, cowboy? Li'l ole Delilah's gt somethin' softer ya can ride."

"Up here, big boy! Hoo-ee! Would you look at that beard, Betsy?" Then cupping her hands to her mouth, she called, "Don't' shave off that beard, honey. I *lo-o-ove* beards!"

The trail-worn cowboys stood in their saddles and waved their battered John B's, white teeth flashing in their grimy faces. "What's your name, honey?"

"Lucy! Just ask for Lucy!"

"Keep it hot, Lucy! Big Luke'll be back!"

The cattle flooded the street from hitching rail to hitching rail, sometimes even clattering into the boardwalks themselves. Unruly and stupid, they often reverted to their wild, untamed nature, charging into the open doorways of saloons, breaking windows with their horns, rolling their eyes and charging anything that got in their way.

"Here goes the last of our peace for the summer," lamented Agatha as the lead bull led the herd past her door.

"I think it's exciting." Violet's eyes glittered.

"Exciting? All that dust and noise and smell?"

"It isn't dusty."

"It will be. As soon as this mud dries."

"Honestly, Agatha, sometimes I don't know what it is that tips your damper."

At that moment Scott Gandy and Jack Hogg stepped onto the boardwalk and stood watching the mass of moving beef. Hogg wore a starched white apron tied around his belly. Gandy wore his usual black trousers but had left his sack coat behind. Today his vest was coral. His sleeves were rolled up to the elbow. He braced one boot on the rail and leaned on his knee.

Violet poked her head outside and shouted above the sound of the herd, "Hello, Mr. Gandy!"

He swung around and dropped his foot. "Miz Parsons, how are you?"

"Better be careful. Sometimes those creatures take a mind to visit the saloons."

He grinned. "I will. Much obliged." The late morning sun lit his boots and trousers, but the shadow of the roof fell across his head and shoulders. His eyes moved to Agatha, hovering behind Violet. His voice cooled.

"Miz Downin'." He tipped his hat.

For a moment their eyes clashed. Was he the one? Certainly he lived closest, could easily have left the saloon and run upstairs to tack a note to her door anytime while she was gone last night. Was he capable of such duplicity? Standing in the morning sun with the dimples decorating his face and the reflection from his coral-colored vest lighting his chin from below, he certainly didn't look ominous. Still, her heart tripped with uncertainty. She nodded curtly.

"Close the door, Violet."

"But, Agatha—"

"Close it. All that noise gives me a headache. And the stench is unbearable."

When the door closed, Jack Hogg observed, "I don't think Miss Downing likes us."

"That's puttin' it mildly."

"You think she and that temperance union of hers can do us any harm?"

Gandy propped his foot on the handrail again and reached into his vest pocket for a cheroot. "Not with Jube and the girls here." His eyes followed a driver who rode higher than the herd, flapping his hat and cursing at the beasts. "We'll have those cowpokes fightin' for a place t' stand in the Gilded Cage."

Hogg's eyes lit with amusement. The unscarred corner of his mouth lifted. "Think Jube and the girls opened a few eyes last night, huh? Did you see that Downing woman gawk when Jube came out of the cage?"

Gandy lit his cigar and chuckled. "Can't say's I noticed."

"Like hell you didn't. You were enjoying it as much as I was."

"Seems t' me I do recall seein' her face over the top of the swingin' doors, lookin' a little interested."

"Shocked, you mean."

Gandy laughed.

"That's probably more skin than she ever saw on her own body."

Gandy drew deep and expelled a cloud of smoke. "Probably."

"A woman like that, heading up a group of females with reform on their minds, they get up a head of steam and they can cause plenty of grumbles."

Gandy's boot hit the worn floor of the boardwalk. He tugged his vest down, crooked the cheroot in one finger, and turned to Jack Hogg.

"Y'all just leave Miz Agatha Downin' t' me."

The cattle milled and mooed all that day—and the next and the next—bisecting Proffitt in an ever-shifting mass of hooves, hides, and horns. Tucked up beside the railroad tracks on the east edge of town, the stock pens stretched across the prairie like an endless crazy quilt. Trains clanged in empty and went out full, headed for the packing houses of Kansas City. The drumming of hooves on the loading ramps rolled steadily from sunup to sundown. Cowpunchers with long poles walked or straddled the wooden rails, earning their trade name by prodding and poking the cattle to keep them moving. Only when the last brand had been counted, and their tally books were folded away inside their vest pockets, did the "punchers" get paid by their foremen.

Sporting a hundred dollars' trail wages in their pockets, raring to spend every last cent, they took Proffitt by storm. They hit the saloons first, then the clothing stores. But the busiest place in town was the Cowboy's Rest, where for two bits they leaped into a tub of hot bathwater—some fully clothed. They shucked off and threw away their filthy, rawhide-patched britches, emerging from the bathhouse in stiff new Levi Strauss blue denims and crisp yoked shirts with pearl buttons running down their chests. At Stuben's Tonsorial Parlor they lay back in comfort and received their first haircuts and hot shaves in three months. They tied new silk bandannas around their throats and hit for the women and whiskey. Smelling of blue dye and hair pomade, some with new Stetsons that had cost them a third of their poke, or new boots that had cost them half, they visited the likes of Delilah, Crystal, and Lucy, whose yard signs warned: NO ADMITTANCE TO UNBATHED MEN.

As the town's population swelled from a modest two hundred to fifteen hundred, merchants' tills rang as incessantly as the hammer from Gottheim's Blacksmith Shop. Proffitt's three livery barns were busier than anthills. The Kansas outfitters sold enough harness to reach across the entire state. At the Drover's Cottage—offering *real* mattresses and pillows—all one hundred rooms were filled. Halorhan's and the Longhorn Store sold enough Bull Durham tobacco to fill a hayloft. Union suits practically walked out on their own legs. But of all the establishments in town, eleven did better than the rest. Eleven proprietors of eleven saloons stood back and watched themselves get rich overnight selling Newton's whiskey at twenty-five cents a glass, keno cards at twenty-five cents a game, and Lazo Victoria cigars at a nickel a smoke.

Prosperity was a difficult thing to fight, the ladies of the W.C.T.U. found out. The night after the first herd arrived, they broke up into small groups and dispersed to all eleven saloons to solicit pledge signatures. Agatha's group took the Gilded Cage. Though they tried to get the cowboys' attention, it was impossible. Their interest in throwing whiskey down their throats was too intense. When the bar became so crowded that it could not accommodate all the drinkers at once, they formed a double flank. Someone cried, "Fire and fall back!" And every glass went bottoms-up. Then the second contingent took its turn bellying up to the bar. Once Jubilee and the girls appeared, the noise inside grew so horrendous, the clientele so unruly, that Agatha declared it was useless and sent the women home.

In her apartment she settled down to read the book Drusilla Wilson had given her, T. S. Arthur's *Ten Nights in a Barroom.* It told the story of Joe Morgan, a likable but weak-willed man who frequented a saloon run by the hardhearted, money-grubbing Simon Slade. Gradually, Joe became addicted to alcohol and lost whatever will he'd once possessed. Devoid of ambition, he became increasingly irresponsible and spent all his time in the bar, where his daughter Mary came to beg him to return home. One day poor Mary was struck in the head by a beer mug, thrown at her father by Slade. Poor Mary died. Within a few days, Joe had died as well, a victim of delirium tremens. Joe's wife was left a widow, childless and impoverished.

The story left Agatha depressed. Listening to the music and revelry from downstairs, she tried to think of Gandy as another Simon Slade. The picture wouldn't gel. When she was reading the book, Slade came across as a whiskered, crude oaf of rough-spoken ways and greedy bent. Gandy was none of these. He was mild-mannered, neat to a fault, and apparently generous. Though it would be difficult to fight such a charming man, fight him she must.

But not without proper ammunition. During the next few days temperance activities were suspended until Joseph Zeller could get their pamphlets printed. When he did, Agatha sent Violet, as the official W.C.T.U. treasurer, to the *Gazette* office to pick them up. She also wired away for additional copies of *Ten Nights in a Barroom* from the publisher. She read her latest issue of *The Temperance Banner,* taking notes, gathering ideas for her local. And she wrote two letters: one to Governor John P. St. John, supporting his introduction of a prohibition bill before the Kansas State Legislature; the other to the First Lady of the United States of America, Lucy Hayes, thanking her for her staunch support of the temperance movement, and for forbidding the serving of alcoholic beverages in the White House so long as her husband, Rutherford, was in office.

Agatha felt much better then. It seemed as if she'd been powerless against the many attractions innovated by the proprietor of the Gilded Cage Saloon. But the pamphlets would help. And anyone who read a copy of *Ten Nights* couldn't help but be moved by it. The letters, too, gave her a great sense of power: the voice of the American people at work.

It had been three days since she'd seen Gandy. Business at the millinery shop had picked up somewhat, too. A couple of cowpunchers had ordered wide-brimmed leghorns to be decorated for their "mothers"—Agatha smirked, recalling how serious the pair had looked when explaining who the hats were for. How gullible did they think she was? No "mother" would wear a leghorn hat decorated with grosgrain "follow-me-lads" trailing off the back brim to the center of her back. She had no doubt she'd see her creations sashaying down the street on the heads of two soiled doves one day soon.

Agatha's thoughts were interrupted when someone pounded on her back door. Before she could reach it, Calvin Looby, the station boy, stuck his head inside. He wore a white-and-navy-blue-striped railroad cap and small, round, wire-rimmed spectacles. His chin looked as if he'd rammed it into the point of an anvil and set it back a good two inches. He had teeth like needles and nearly nonexistent lips. She'd always pitied poor Calvin his bad looks.

"Delivery for you, Miss Downing."

"A delivery?"

"Yup." He checked his railroad bill of lading. "From Philadelphia."

"But I didn't order anything from Philadelphia."

Calvin removed his railroad cap and scratched his pate. "Funny. Says here plain as a windmill on a Kansas prairie: Agatha Downing. See?"

She peered at the paper Calvin extended.

"So it does. But there must be some mistake."

"Well, what you want I should do with it? Railroad delivered it to its destination. That's all we're responsible for. I'd have to charge you to haul it back to the depot again."

"Charge me? But . . ."

"'Fraid so. Regulations, ya see."

"But I didn't order it."

"How 'bout Miss Violet? Think she could've ordered it?"

"Most certainly not. Violet doesn't do my ordering for me."

"Well, it's a mystery." Calvin looked back over his shoulder into the yard. "What do you want me to do with it, then?"

"Do you know what it is?" Agatha went to the back door.

"Carton says: Isaac Singer Patented Treadle Sewing Machine."

"Sew—" Agatha's heart began to thud. She stepped outside anxiously. There stood a sleepy old piebald mare hitched to a parsley-green railroad dray. On the dray a huge wooden crate stood out against the backdrop of her shed and "the necessary."

"But how . . . who . . . ?"

Suddenly, she knew. She looked up at the rear of the building. The landing was empty but she had the feeling he was somewhere chuckling over her confusion. She glanced at the single window facing the backyard from his office. It was vacant. She turned back to Calvin.

"But if you take it back, what will happen to it?" She moved closer to the carton, drawn against her will.

"We'll put it on the next train heading back to Philadelphia. Can't let a thing that big lay around the depot takin' up space."

She walked to the wagon and reached up to lay her palm on the side of the carton. It was warm from the midday sun. She experienced a sharp stab of greed. She wanted this piece of machinery with a pagan intensity that yesterday she'd have thought it impossible to feel. She had the money, thanks to Gandy. But spending it seemed so final. Consorting with the enemy. But heaven knew her failing business would be miraculously revived by such a machine.

She turned to Calvin, wringing her hands. "What are the shipping costs, exactly?"

Calvin studied his paper once more. "Doesn't say here. It just says where t' deliver it to."

She'd had that catalogue clipping on her wall for so long—suppose the price had gone up appreciably?

She made a quick decision. "Could you bring it into the shop, Mr. Looby? Perhaps if we open the crate I can find the papers inside."

"Sure thing, Miss Downin'."

Calvin clambered onto the dray, pushed and shoved and unloaded the cumbersome crate onto a flat, wheeled conveyance, which he rolled through the back door of the hat shop. In the workroom, he removed the wooden cap with a claw hammer. Atop the packaging material was the bill. Stamped across it in neat black ink were the words PAID IN FULL.

Confused, Agatha looked from the bill to Calvin. "But I don't understand."

"Looks to me like somebody give you a gift, Miss Downin'. Well, what d'you know about that!"

She stared at the paper.

Gandy? But what was his motive? Three cancan dresses? Perhaps. But there could be several other motives in that shrewd mind of his. Bribery. Whitewash. Subversion.

If it was bribery, she wanted no part of it. She already felt uneasy about accepting the generous amount he'd paid her for making the red birdcage cover.

And if he were seeking to throw a red herring over his secret nighttime counterplays, it seemed odd he'd spend so much money to do so.

Subversion? Would he be devious enough to undermine her W.C.T.U. efforts by suggesting to the officials that she was doing business with the enemy? Oddly enough, she didn't want to believe it of him.

Perhaps he was still feeling guilty for pushing her in the mud. *Don't be silly, Agatha.* Yes, he had looked somewhat remorseful that day, but he was a gambler, well versed in assuming whatever face he thought it advantageous to assume.

There was, of course, one other possibility. Free enterprise. Jubilee and the girls most certainly would keep the edge of the mahogany bar belly-shined, especially in red cancan skirts. Perhaps Gandy's spirit of competition was aroused by the thought of doing all in his power to crowd his saloon with more men than it could comfortably hold. To lord it over the other ten saloon owners in town out of sheer contrariness.

The thought made her smile. She sobered abruptly. Whatever his motives, Agatha realized she could not be a party to them.

"Put the cover back on, Mr. Looby. Take it back to the station."

"As you say."

"I think I know who ordered it, and he can pay the return charges."

"Yes, ma'am." He matched the nail holes, lifted his hammer.

"Wait! Just a minute!"

Looby scowled impatiently. "Well, what's it to be?"

"I just want to see it. One peek. Then you can pack it off."

That one peek was fatal. No one who'd worked with stitches as long as Agatha had could possibly glimpse that wondrous piece of American ingenuity without coveting it in a wholly gripping way. The black paint shone. The gilt logo gleamed. The silver flywheel tempted.

"On second thought, leave it."

"Leave it?"

"Yes."

"But I thought you said—"

"Thank you so much for delivering it, Mr. Looby." She led the way to the door.

"My, haven't we been having some ideal weather? If this keeps up, the streets should dry in no time."

Looby glanced from her to the crate and back again. He took off his railroad cap and scratched his head. But it was beyond him to try to figure out the workings of the female mind.

When Looby was gone, Agatha checked the time—nearly eleven o'clock. Violet would arrive any minute. Hurry, Violet!

When the little white-haired woman stepped into the millinery shop, she found Agatha standing just inside the curtained doorway, her hands clasped excitedly beneath her chin.

"Oh, Violet, I thought you'd never get here!"

"Is something wrong?"

"Wrong? No!" Agatha flung out her hands and flashed a beaming smile toward the heavens. "Nothing could be more right! Come!" She turned toward the workroom. "Let me show you." She led Violet directly to the packing crate. "Look!"

Violet's eyelids sprang open. "Gracious sakes alive, if it isn't a sewing machine! Where did it come from?"

"From Philadelphia."

"You mean it's yours?"

"Yes."

Violet didn't remember ever seeing Agatha this happy. Why, she was actually pretty! Funny thing, Violet had never realized it before. Her pale green eyes were alight with excitement. And her smile—gracious sakes alive, what that smile did for her face. Took off a good five years from it and made her look the age she actually was.

"But why didn't you tell me?"

"It's a surprise."

Violet walked in a circle around the crate. Agatha's excitement was infectious. "But . . . but where did you get the mon—" She stopped, looked up. "The ten gold pieces from Mr. Gandy."

"Six. I gave four of them back."

Violet's eyes glittered with shrewd speculation. "We're going to make the can-can dresses, aren't we, Agatha?"

"My stars, Violet! I haven't had time to give it a thought. Come, help me get it out of the crate." Agatha lost all her usual reserve, hustling about like a carefree girl in search of a hammer and screwdriver. She looked so radiant Violet couldn't quit studying her and smiling. When she'd found the tools she set to work. "We'll just knock the front off the packing crate and pull the machine straight out. The two of us should be able to handle it."

Violet couldn't believe the sudden change in the woman she'd seen somber for so many years. "Do you realize what you're doing, Agatha?"

Agatha looked up. "Doing?"

"You're kneeling."

Agatha glanced down. Glorious day! She was! But she was too excited to stop wedging the screwdriver between two slabs of wood. "So I am. Hurts a little bit, but I don't care. Come on, Violet, get your fingers in there and pull."

Instead, Violet's fingers gently touched Agatha's shoulder.

Agatha lifted her face.

"You know, dear, you should do this more often."

"What?"

"Smile. Act young and coltish. What a pretty, pretty young thing you are this way."

Agatha's hands fell still. "P . . . pretty?"

"Most certainly. Why, if you could see your eyes right now, they're as bright as spring clover in the morning dew. And you have roses in your cheeks that I've never seen there before."

Agatha was stunned. *Pretty? Me?*

Not since her mother's death had anyone called her pretty. The roses in her cheeks grew brighter from self-consciousness. Uncomfortable with the unaccustomed praise, she turned to her work again.

"You know, Violet, I think you've been out in the noon sun too long. Now help me with this thing."

Together they worked to free the sewing machine and pull it onto the workroom floor. Agatha touched it reverently, her eyes still gleaming.

"Imagine what a difference it's going to make in the business. I *have* been worried lately, though I didn't want to admit it. Ends have scarcely been meeting. But now . . ." She tested the sleek steel flywheel, brushed her hand appreciatively along the smooth oak cabinet. "Let the hat business dwindle. We can make dresses, can't we, Violet?"

Violet smiled lovingly at the changed young woman before her. "Yes, we can. As fancy as anyone wants them."

Suddenly Agatha sobered. Her face turned worried. "I am doing the right thing, aren't I?"

"The right thing?"

"It really is Mr. Gandy's money that's buying this."

Violet turned realistic, pursing her lips. "You earned that money, didn't you?"

"I don't know. Did I?"

"You most certainly did, young lady. You did a rush job for him that nobody else in town could have done. And you did it with some of the best red satin he could have found. There should be a markup on the satin, shouldn't there?"

"You really think so, Violet?"

"I know so. Now, are you going to stand there all afternoon, or are you going to thread that thing and give it a whirl?"

With the help of the instruction book they loaded the bobbin, dropped it into the bullet-shaped shuttle, followed the diagram, and guided the upper thread into place. When the needle was threaded and a piece of cloth had been secured beneath the presser foot, their eyes met in anticipation.

"Well, here goes." Agatha placed both feet on the treadle, gave one pump, and jerked her feet and hands back. "Awk! It went backward!"

She looked up to Violet for guidance. Violet shrugged. "I don't know. Try it again."

Agatha tried it again. Once more the cloth moved backward. She got up from her chair. "Here, you try it."

Violet took her place and gingerly tested the foot treadle. Backward again. They looked at each other and giggled. "Forty-nine dollars for a sewing machine that only sews backward." The longer they giggled, the funnier it got. With their next attempt the machine took one stitch forward, one back, and another forward. The two women laughed themselves breathless.

Finally, Agatha exclaimed, "The book! Let's read the book."

Eventually, they figured out that the flywheel needed a boost in the right direction to get it along. Agatha sat with the long swatch of cotton flowing smoothly beneath the needle. The belt made a soft hum as it drove the mechanism. The needle arm created a rhythmic cadence. Beautiful, tight stitches appeared magically, at an almost dizzying pace. Agatha's hip hurt as her feet pumped, but she was too excited to notice. It was all she could do to give up her seat to Violet and let her give the machine a second try.

"Isn't it miraculous?" She leaned over Violet's shoulder, watching the blue cotton move smoothly, listening to the wondrous sound of well-oiled machinery working at an unbelievable pace.

Oh, Gandy! she thought. *How ever can I thank you?*

At five o'clock Agatha gave the sewing machine one last appreciative touch, carefully placed the boxy wooden cover over it, then closed the shop. She paused to glance at the rear door of the salon. It was closed, but still she could hear the place was busy. Undoubtedly, it would get busier tonight. Now would be a far better time to speak to him. Perhaps she could slip in unobtrusively and signal him to the back hall for a moment.

She opened the door and stepped in. The music was absent, but the cowhands' voices created a steady chatter. Laughter and clinking glasses filled the place. Straight ahead she saw Dan Loretto at a crowded table, dealing cards. The smell of stale smoke and old liquor stopped her momentarily. But she gripped her hands and inched her way to the end of the short corridor, searching the main room for Gandy. The moment she came into view, Jack Hogg noticed her. She crooked a finger. He dried his hands and immediately left his post.

"Why, Miss Downing, this is a surprise."

"Mr. Hogg." She nodded in greeting. "I'd like to talk to Mr. Gandy."

"He's in his office. Top of the landing, first door on your right."

"Thank you."

Outside the air wasn't much fresher. Already the smell from the stock pens drifted over the town. The incessant sounds of lowing cattle and clattering trains carried through the late afternoon as Agatha took the stairs. Reaching the landing, she glanced at his window, but the rippled glass gave no more than a reflection of the blue-washed sky. The door squeaked as she opened it and peered along the shadowed hall.

So this was where the gilded cage rested during the day! She smiled at Gandy's ingenuity.

She'd never been upstairs in this half of the building before. Four doors on the left. Two on the right. A window at the far end of the hall overlooking the street. Everything quiet. She felt like a window peeper—why, she wasn't certain. Perhaps because people might be sleeping behind those closed doors at this very moment.

Gandy's office door was closed. She knocked lightly.

"Yes?"

She turned the knob and peeked timidly inside. Gandy sat at an ordinary oak desk in an austere office. He leaned forward, writing, a smoking cigar in an ashtray at his elbow.

"Hello."

He looked up. His face registered surprise before he poked the pen into its holder and leaned back on his well-sprung swivel chair.

"Well, bowl me over," he said softly.

"May I come in?"

Only her head showed around the door. The childlike entry was so untypical of her, he couldn't help grinning. "By all means." He half rose as she slipped inside and glanced around with frank curiosity.

"So this is where you do business."

He dropped back into his chair, pushed away from the desk, crossed a knee with an ankle, and interlaced his fingers across his stomach.

"Not too fancy, but it serves the purpose."

Her gaze moved across the dull wainscoting, the drab green walls, the tiny stove, the unadorned window with its uninteresting view of the back alley and the prairie beyond.

"Somehow I expected to find you in more lavish surroundings."

"Why?"

"Oh, I don't know. The way you dress, maybe. Those bright vests." Today his vest was celery-green. His black string tie was loosened, his throat button freed, and his shirt-sleeves rolled to mid-arm. His black sack coat hung on the back of his chair. It was five in the afternoon and he needed a shave. She took a moment to appreciate his semitidiness. Heavens above, he *was* one handsome man!

"Funny, I never thought you noticed."

She met his eyes directly. "I work with clothing, Mr. Gandy. I notice everything about it." She continued scanning the room—the safe, the coat-tree. . . . an open doorway? Her eyes fixed upon it, her interest piqued. In his sitting room were the lavish surroundings she'd expected. And a lady's turquoise-green dressing gown flung across the settee.

He studied her, amused by the interest she suddenly showed in his sitting room and the bedroom beyond. From behind, he catalogued her with a more critical eye than ever before. The elegant rear draperies of her garnet taffeta dress. The shapely "Grecian bend" lent to her lumbar region by unseen corsets. The attractive puff of her bustle, her narrow shoulders, neat hair, and graceful arms accentuated by tight, tight sleeves and a high clerical collar. She dressed with magnificent taste in genteelly elegant clothes. Forever proper.

But something was different about her today. He couldn't pinpoint exactly what.

Agatha realized her mistake only after staring too long into his private apartment. She turned to catch him watching her carefully.

"I . . . I'm sorry."

"It's quite all right. A little more roomy than yours, I take it."

"Yes, quite."

"Have a chair, Miz Downin'."

"Thank you."

"What can I do for you?"

"I believe you've already done it."

He cocked one eyebrow. One dimple pocked his cheek. "Oh?"

"You saw the advertisement for the sewing machine on my workroom wall, didn't you?"

"Did I?"

"Don't spar with me, Mr. Gandy. You saw it and you read my mind."

He chuckled. "Come to the point, Miz Downin'."

"The point is—there's a brand-new patented Isaac Singer sewing machine downstairs, and the packing slip claims it's already paid for."

His smile grew cheeky. "Congratulations."

"Don't be obtuse. I came to thank you for taking it upon yourself to order it, and to pay what I owe you."

"Did I say you owed me anything?"

She produced five gold coins and stacked them on the corner of his desk. "Fifty dollars, I believe, is the correct amount, isn't it?"

"I forget."

She tried to be harsh but her eyes sparkled too brightly, her lips refused to obey. "If you think I'm going to accept an expensive sewing machine from a saloon owner, you . . ."—How had Joe Jessup said it, again?—". . . you have a wheel loose, Mr. Gandy."

He laughed, then tipped his chair farther back and linked his fingers behind his head. "But it's a bribe."

Her return laugh caught them both by surprise. Then they were laughing together. Gandy noted how her face had changed. That's what was different about her today! It wasn't her hair or her clothing; it was her mood. For once she was happy and it transformed her. The plain gray moth had become a bright, gay finch.

"You admit it?"

Grinning amiably, he shrugged, still with his elbows in the air. "Why not? We both know it's true."

He was an enigma. Dishonest and truthful at once. She found it increasingly difficult to rationalize him. "And what do you hope to gain by it?"

"For starters, three bright red cancan dresses."

A disquieting awareness of his masculine pose hit her like a fist in the stomach. The paler color of his bared wrists and forearms, the tendons running taut from the hands clasped behind his head, the crinkles on the armpits of his white shirt, the black boot resting casually across his knee, the smoke ascending from the ashtray between them.

"Ah," she crooned knowingly, "three bright red cancan dresses." She cocked one eyebrow. "And after that?"

"Who knows?"

She dropped the game-playing. Her voice turned serious. "I'm committed to my temperance work. You know that, don't you?"

He dropped his arms and studied her silently for several seconds. "Yes, I know."

"No amount of bribery can change my mind."

"I hadn't thought it could."

"Tomorrow night we'll be downstairs when your customers arrive, handing out pamphlets that we've had printed, passing out literature detailing the hazards of the fare in which you deal."

"Then I'll have t' think of a new way t' woo my customers, won't I?"

"Yes, I suppose you will."

"You haven't been around for a couple o' days."

"I've been busy. I wrote a letter to the First Lady, thanking her for keeping the White House dry."

"Old Lemonade Lucy?"

Agatha burst out laughing, then smothered the sound with a finger. "So disrespectful, Mr. Gandy."

Half the country called the First Lady that, but it had never seemed quite so funny before.

"Me and plenty of others. She keeps that place drier than the great Sahara."

"At any rate, I wrote to her. *The Temperance Banner* encourages its members to do so. I also wrote to Governor St. John."

"St. John!" Gandy wasn't so blithe about this news. Murmurings about the proposed amendment to the state constitution had more than one Kansas saloon owner nervous. "My, my. We are busy little beavers, aren't we?"

Studying her, he reached for his cheroot and took a deep draw on it. The smoke rose between them before he seemed to realize he'd exhaled it. "Oh, pardon me. I forgot—you hate these things, don't you?"

"After the sewing machine, how could I possibly deny you your pleasure, especially when we're on your battleground?"

He rose and went to the window, anchored the cigar between his teeth, and lifted the sash. She watched his satin waistcoat stretch across his back, wondering which of them would win in the final outcome. He stood looking out, smoking the cheroot, wondering the same thing. After some moments he braced one boot on the sill, leaned an elbow on his knee, and turned to study her over his shoulder.

"You're different than I thought at first."

"So are you."

"This . . . this war we're engaged in, you find it rather amusin', don't you?"

"Me?" She spread a hand on her chest. "I thought you were the one who found it amusing."

"Maybe. In a way. It isn't turnin' out anything like I thought it would. I mean—what general reveals his battle plan to the enemy?"

She smiled. Her face became transformed into the younger, pretty countenance Violet had remarked upon earlier. Her pale eyes softened. Her austerity dissolved.

"So tell me—what name did Mr. Potts give your 'Lady of the Oils'?"

"I'm surprised you didn't hear the other night when you swept in with your invadin' host." Again he made her laugh.

"There were only four of us."

"Is that all?"

"And, anyway, how was it possible to hear anything in that din?"

"Her full name is Dierdre in the Garden of Delight, but the men have nick-named her Delight."

"Delight. Mmm . . . I'm sure Mrs. Potts is thrilled that Elias won your contest. Next time I see her, I must be sure to say congratulations."

Gandy replied with a full-throated laugh. "Ah, Miz Downin', you're a worthy opponent. I must say I'm comin' to admire you. However, y'all didn't last too long in the saloon the other night."

"We were crowded out."

"Tsk-tsk." He shook his head slowly. "Too bad."

She decided it was time to stop playing cat-and-mouse with him.

"You *are* my enemy," she stated quietly. "And in spite of how my personal opinion of you may be slowly altering, I must never lose sight of that fact."

"Because I sell alcohol?"

"Among other things." It was difficult to believe those other things when he leaned on the windowsill that way—all charm and humor and enticing looks. But she understood quite clearly how he shamelessly used his charm and humor and enticing looks to sway her from her good intentions.

"What else?"

Her heart thudded harder than normal. She didn't stop to question the wisdom or the consequences of what she was about to ask.

"Tell me, Mr. Gandy, was it you who pinned the threatening note to my door the other night?"

Amusement fled his face. His forehead beetled and his foot hit the floor. "What?"

Her heart thumped harder. "Was it?"

"How the hell can you ask such a thing?" he demanded angrily.

It thumped harder still. But she rose to her feet, plucked his pen from its holder, and held it out to him. "Will you do something for me? Will you print the words *good, stay,* and *what* on a piece of paper in capital letters while I watch you?"

He glared at the pen, then back up at her. He clamped the cheroot between his teeth and yanked the pen from her fingers. Leaning from the waist, he slashed the letters across a piece of scrap paper. When he straightened, his eyes bored silently into hers. He neither offered to hand her the paper nor backed away, but stood so close to the desk she'd have to brush him aside to reach it.

"Excuse me." She nearly bumped him, but he stood his ground rigidly.

"Don't push your luck," he warned through gritted teeth, just above her ear.

She picked up the paper and retreated. The smoke from his cigar burned her nostrils as she studied his printing.

"Satisfied?"

Relief closed her eyelids, brought a light rush of breath from her nostrils.

He stood before her seething with anger. What the hell did this woman want from him?

She opened her eyes to confront him directly. "I'm sorry. I had to be sure."

"And are you?" he snapped.

She felt her face color but stood her ground. "Yes."

He swung toward the desk, stubbed out his cigar in two angry twists of the wrist, and refused to glance her way again. "If you'll excuse me, I have a lot o' work to do. I was orderin' a shipment o' rum when you interrupted me." He sat down and began writing again.

Her heart turned traitor and flooded with remorse. "Mr. Gandy, I said I was sorry."

"G'day, Miz Downin'!"

Her face burning, she turned and shuffled to the door, opened it, and paused with her back to him. "Thank you for the sewing machine," she said quietly.

Gandy's head snapped up. He stared at her back. Damned infernal harpy! What was it about her that got beneath his skin? She took anther shuffling step before his bark stopped her.

"Agatha!"

She hadn't thought he remembered her name. Why should it matter that he did?

"I'd like t' see that note if you've still got it."

"Why?"

His face tightened even further. "I don't know why in blue blazes I should feel responsible for you, but I do, goddammit!"

She didn't hold with profanity. Why, then, didn't she take him to task for it?

"I can take care of myself, Mr. Gandy," she declared, then closed the door behind her.

He stared at it, unblinking while he heard the outer door open and close. With a vile curse he flung down his pen. It left a splatter of ink on the order he'd been writing. He cursed again, ripping the paper in half, and threw it away. Then he balled his fists one around the other, pressed them against his chin, and glared at the office wall until her shuffling footsteps finally stopped sounding through his open window.

Chapter 7

The W.C.T.U. ladies learned a new song. They sang it with rousing enthusiasm at four saloons the following night.

> *Who hath sorrow? Who hath woe?*
> *They who dare not answer no.*
> *They whose feet to sin decline*
> *While they tarry at the wine.*

They handed out pamphlets to the men and continued soliciting signatures on pledges. To everyone's surprise, Evelyn Sowers stepped forward several times, boldly accosting saloon goers. With her intense eyes, her sometimes dramatic gesturing, she displayed an amazing oratory flair none had known she possessed.

"Brother, take care of your future now." She seized upon an unsuspecting cowboy who scarcely looked old enough to shave. "Don't you know Satan assumes the shape of a bottle of spirits? Beware that he does not trick you into believing otherwise. Have you thought about tomorrow . . . and tomorrow . . . and the tomorrow after that, when your hands begin trembling and your wife and children suffer without—"

"Lady, I ain't got no wife and children," the young cowpoke interrupted. With wary eyes he sidestepped Evelyn, as if she were a coiled rattler. As he made for the door of the saloon, Evelyn fell to her knees, hands lifted in supplication.

"I beg you, young man, stay out of that male refuge! The saloonkeeper is the destroyer of men's souls!"

The shiny-faced youth glanced over his shoulder and scuttled inside with a look that said he feared Evelyn far more than the dangers to be found behind the swinging doors.

Four more cowboys came along the boardwalk spiffed to the nines, their spurs shining, their jinglebobs ringing. Evelyn stopped them in their tracks with her emotional appeal.

"Do you recognize the evils of the vile compound you've come here to consume? It robs men of their faculties, their honor, and their health. Before you step through that door—"

But they'd already stepped through, looking back at Evelyn with the same trepidation of the young cowpoke.

Evelyn seemed to have found her true calling. During the remainder of the evening as the ladies made a sweep of four saloons, she embraced her newfound ministry with growing fervor.

"Abstinence is virtue; indulgence is sin!" she shouted above the noise from the Lucky Horseshoe Saloon. And when she couldn't outshout the noise, she led her troops inside, walked straight up to Jeff Diddier, and stated, "We've come on a mission of morality—to awaken your conscience." When Evelyn produced a temperance pledge and demanded that Diddier sign it, the ruddy-faced bartender answered by pouring himself a double shot of rye and gulping it down before Evelyn's eyes.

Though Agatha personally didn't hold with Evelyn's histrionics, the woman succeeded in shaming two of Jim Starr's customers into signing the pledge. This success prompted four of Evelyn's "sisters" to drop to their knees with her and begin singing at the top of their lungs. Agatha tried it. But she felt like a fool, kneeling in the saloon. Thankfully, after several painful minutes on the hard wooden floor, she was forced to stand again.

At The Alamo Saloon, Jack Butler and Floyd Anderson appeared to be so embarrassed by seeing their wives in the company of the fanatic Evelyn that they shamefacedly slipped out the door and disappeared. Spurred on by yet another victory, Evelyn grew increasingly flamboyant in both speech and gestures.

By the time the W.C.T.U. contingent reached the Gilded Cage, the place was going strong, and so was Evelyn. She elbowed her way into the crush of men, raised both hands to heaven, and bellowed, "What an army of drunkards shall reel into hell!"

The dancing and singing stopped. Ivory turned from the piano. The card games halted. Evelyn looked manic. Her eyes blazed with unnatural fervor; her fists came down on tabletop after tabletop. "Go home, Miles Wendt! Go home, Wilton Spivey! Go home, Tom Ruggles! Go home, all of you, back to your families, you sinful wretches!" Evelyn grabbed a mug of beer and upended it at Ruggles's feet."

"Hey, watch it!" He came out of his chair.

"Filth! *Nux vomica!* Swill a man wouldn't feed to his swine!"

Agatha felt her face coloring. The W.C.T.U. members prided themselves on nonmilitancy and grace. She looked up, found Gandy's eyes leveled on her, and glanced away quickly, only to confront three other pairs of dismayed eyes— Jubilee's, Pearl's, and Ruby's.

Into the sudden lull Gandy spoke with his usual *savoir vivre*. "Welcome, ladies." He stood behind the bar, hatless, dressed totally in black and white.

Evelyn swung on him. "Ah, the rum-soaked ally of Lucifer! The trafficker in ardent spirits! Beg the Lord's forgiveness for the negligence and bestiality you cause to be visited upon innocent families, Mr. Gandy!" Two cowboys who'd had enough scraped back their chairs and headed for the door.

Gandy ignored Evelyn's tirade.

"You're just in time." He raised his voice and called, "Drinks're on the house, everyone!"

The pair of cowboys spun in their tracks. The roar that rose nearly deafened Agatha. While it boomed around her ears, she met Gandy's eyes again. Though the others might be unable to read beyond his surface charm, she had seen him grin too many times not to recognize the absence of mirth in his expression tonight. His eyes pierced her like two icicles. Gone was the amusing glitter she'd come to expect. What passed for a smile was really a baring of teeth.

While their gazes locked, he found the neck of a bottle, filled his glass with amber liquid, and lifted it.

Don't, Gandy, don't.

He gave her a salute so slight nobody else noticed. Then he tipped his head back and changed the salute to an insult.

She had never seen him drink before.

It hurt.

She turned away, feeling empty for no reason she could explain. All around men pushed their way to the bar and raised their glasses for free drinks. Behind her the piano and banjo started up again. Jubilee and the Gems struck into a chorus of "Champagne Charlie," ending with the words, "Come join me in a spree." Evelyn knelt in the middle of the rowdydow praying for the depraved. With her hands crossed over her chest and her eyeballs rolled back, she looked as if she'd been bitten by a rapid dog. At the keno table, men jeered. From the wall, Delight smiled down benevolently on the chaos.

There simply had to be a better way.

Agatha signaled the others to follow her to the door, but only Addie Anderson and Minnie Butler did. As they reached the exit, Agatha turned for one last look. Gandy's obsidian eyes impaled her. She wheeled and pushed through the swinging doors.

And that's when she met Willy Collinson for the first time.

He'd been squatting down, peering beneath the shuttered panel into the saloon, when the door hit him in the forehead and rolled him over like a ninepins ball.

"Ooooowwww!" he howled, holding his head and bawling. "Oww-www-weee."

Agatha struggled to one knee to help him up. Addie and Minnie hovered, clucking with concern.

"I'll see to him. You two go home to your husbands."

When they'd gone, Agatha righted the boy. Standing, he was the same height as she was, kneeling.

"My goodness, child, what were you doing so close to that door? Are you all right?"

"My h . . . head," he sobbed. "You h . . . hit my h . . . head. Owww! It h . . . hurrrrts!"

"I'm sorry." She tried to see how much damage she'd done, but he clutched his head and pulled away. "Let me see."

"Nooo, I w . . . want my p . . . pa."

"Well, your pa's not here, so why not let me see if I can repair the damages?"

"Leave m . . . me al . . . alone."

In spite of his stubbornness, she forced his hands down and turned him toward the pale light coming from the saloon door. His blond hair could have been a sight cleaner. His overalls were soiled and too short. A trickle of blood ran toward his eyebrow.

"My heavens, child, you're bleeding. Come and we'll wash it off."

She struggled to her feet, but he jerked free of her.

"No!"

"But I live right next door. See? This is my hat shop, and my apartment is right above it. We should take care of that head right away."

"Pa says I ain't supposed to go with strangers."

She dropped her hands to her sides. He was calmer now. "But what did he say about emergencies?"

"I don't know what them are."

"Getting bumped in the head by a swinging door—*that's* an emergency. It truly is. Your forehead needs washing and a touch of iodine."

He backed away, shaking his head no. His eyes grew round as horse chestnuts.

"Look out. Someone will come out and smack you again. Come along." She reached out a hand with a businesslike air. "At least move away from the door while we talk."

Instead, he knelt down and peered beneath it.

"You're too young to be peeking in there!"

"Gotta find Pa."

"Not that way, you won't." She stood him on his feet none too gently. He began to sniffle again. "There are things going on in there that a boy your age shouldn't see. How old are you, anyway?"

"None o' your business!" he said defiantly.

"Well, I'll make it my business, young man. I'll march you straight home to your mother and tell her what I found you doing."

"I ain't got no mother. She died."

For the second time that night, Agatha's heart felt pierced. "Oh," she said softly, "I ... I'm sorry. I didn't know. Then we *must* find your father, mustn't we?"

He dropped his chin to his chest. "He ain't been home since after work." His chin began to tremble and he rubbed one eye with his dirty knuckles. "He said he'd come home tonight ... b ... but ... he n ... never come."

His voice quavered. Agatha felt sick with pity. Awkwardly, she touched his blond hair. She'd been around so few children in her life. How did one speak to a five-year-old? Six-year-old? Whatever his age, he wasn't old enough to be wandering in the street after dark. He should be in a warm bed after a warm bath and a hot supper. "If you'll tell me your name," she encouraged softly, "I'll try to help you find him."

Still scrubbing his eyes, he glanced up uncertainly, revealing wide glimmering eyes, a pug nose, and a trembling mouth. She watched him struggle with indecision.

"I'm really a very nice lady." She gave him a kind smile. "I have no little boys of my own, but if I did I'd never bump them over with swinging doors." She tipped her head to one side. "The lucky thing was, you rolled up just like a porcupine."

He tried not to laugh but couldn't stop himself. It came out as a reluctant snuffle.

"That's better. Now, are you going to make me guess what your name is?"

"Willy."

"Willy what?"

"Collinson."

Suddenly, she understood. *Take it slow, Gussie. Don't lose his trust now.*

"Well, Willy Collinson, if you'll sit down there on the step, I'll go back inside and see if I can spot your father and tell him you're waiting to walk him home. How's that?"

"Would you? He gets awful mad when I go in after 'im."

"Of course I would. You sit here and I'll be right back."

She paused at the swinging doors, looking over them at the revelry inside. Evelyn was gone. Behind the bar Gandy and Jack Hogg served drinks. Jubilee and the girls circulated, talking to the customers. In the near corner Dan Loretto dealt a game of blackjack. Agatha pushed the doors open and eased through the mob, searching for Collinson, unable to spot him. She tried to recall if she'd seen him earlier tonight but didn't remember. Passing a round table crowded with men, she felt a hand brush her thigh. Another reached out and clutched her arm. She jerked free, panicked, and advanced toward the bar. Gandy was laughing at something one of the customers said, looking down as he poured amber whiskey into a shot glass.

"Mr. Gandy?"

His head snapped up. The laughter fell from his face.

"I thought you were gone."

"I'm looking for Mr. Collinson. Is he in here?"

"Alvis Collinson?"

"Yes."

"What do you want with him?"

"Is he in here?"

"You've lived in Proffitt longer than I have—find him." His jaw tensed and his eyes remained hard with challenge.

Someone bumped her from behind. She lost her balance and caught at the back of a leather-covered shoulder to keep on her feet.

"Hey, what's this?" The cowboy turned lazily, slipped an arm around her hips, and flattened her to his side. His breath reeked as he leaned close. "Where ya been hidin', li'l lady?"

She pushed against him, straining away.

"Let her go, fella," Gandy ordered.

The stranger ran his hand up Agatha's ribs, squeezing. "Feels too good to let it go."

Gandy was over the bar so fast he kicked two glasses off and beat them to the floor.

"I said let her go." He grabbed the wandering hand from Agatha and flung it back. "She's not one of the girls."

"All right, all right." The cowboy raised both palms, as if Gandy had pulled a derringer. "If she's your own personal property, ya shoulda said so, buddy."

A nerve jumped in Gandy's cheek. Agatha's stomach trembled and she blinked at the floor.

Gandy plucked a bone-colored Stetson off the bar and shoved it against the cowpoke's belly. "There're plenty o' whorehouses down the street, if that's what you're lookin' for. Now, git!"

"Jesus, man, you're touchy."

"That's right. I run a clean saloon."

The cowpoke slapped his hat on, pocketed some change, and flashed Agatha an angry glare. She felt other eyes probing her from all directions and turned away so Gandy couldn't see the tears of mortification in her eyes.

"Agatha."

She stopped, squared her shoulders.

"What do you want with Collinson?"

She glanced back at him. "His little boy's outside waiting for him to come home."

Gandy's resolution faltered for an instant. A vein stood out on his forehead as his eyes locked on hers. He nodded toward a table in the rear corner. "Collinson's over there."

She turned away.

His hand caught her elbow again. She looked up into his displeased eyes. "Don't rile him. He's got the temper of a wild boar."

"I know."

This time Gandy let her go. But he kept a close eye on her all the while she worked her way through the throng past a surprised Ruby, who stopped her to say something. She nodded, touched Ruby's hand, then moved on. Collinson glanced up in surprise when she stepped to his elbow. He listened to what she had to say, glanced toward the swinging doors, scowled, then threw down his cards angrily. He nudged her aside rudely when he lurched from his chair. She wobbled and, across the room, Gandy took one quick step toward her. She caught her balance against the side of the table and he relaxed. Collinson elbowed his way through the crowd, leaving her to fend for herself.

When she started working her way toward the door, Gandy did the same. He wouldn't put anything past Collinson.

Outside, the son-of-a-bitch was laying into his kid. "What the hell ya mean comin' up here when I tole ya to keep outta the saloon?" He pulled the boy off the step by one arm. Agatha's hands closed over the tops of the swinging doors. Her body strained toward the boy, tensed with uncertainty. Gandy silently came up behind her and gripped her shoulder. Her head snapped around. Without a word he moved in front of her and led the way onto the boardwalk, already reaching for a cheroot.

"You winnin' tonight, Collinson?" he inquired, forcing a bantering tone. He lit the cigar with deceptive calmness.

"I was till the twerp comes badgerin' me t' git home."

"Who's this . . . ? Well, howdy, son. Kinda late for y'all t' be out, isn't it?"

"I came to git Pa."

"Boy, I tole you, I come home when I'm good and ready. Now, I left a winnin' hand layin' on that table. How come you ain't at your Aunt Hattie's?"

She ain't my aunt, and I don't like it at her place."

"Then git on home to bed."

"I don't like it there, neither. It's scary there alone."

"I told you, boy, that's bullshit. Chickens is scared o' the dark."

Gandy stepped forward and spoke to the boy. "Oh, I don't know. I recall times when I was a lad, I used t' think I heard voices behind me in the dark."

"Butt out, Gandy!"

The two men stood nose to nose in the deep shadows. The little boy looked up at them. Agatha moved beside him and put her hand on his shoulder.

"Take the boy home, Collinson," Gandy advised in an undertone.

"Not while I got me a winnin' hand."

"I'll cover your bet. Take him." Gandy reached for Collinson's arm.

The larger man shook it off and pushed Gandy back a step. "I cover my own bets, Gandy. And the brat lays off me when I'm having' a good time!" He took a threatening step toward Willy. "Got that, kid?"

Willy huddled against Agatha's skirt.

Gandy answered for him. "He's got it, Collinson. Go on back inside. Enjoy your game."

"Damned right I will." He plucked Willy away from Agatha and aimed him toward the street. "Now quit snivelin' and git home where ya belong." He gave Willy a shove that sent him scuttling down the steps.

Willy ran a short distance, then turned to look back at his father. Agatha heard his soft, muffled crying.

Collinson spun and stomped back inside, muttering, "God-damned kid could give a man liver trouble . . ."

Willy turned and ran.

"Willy, wait!" Agatha struggled down the three steps, but she was no runner. She hobbled after him but made it only the length of the hitching rail before she gave up the hopeless pursuit. "Willy!" Her anguished cry blended with the noise drifting out of the saloon as she gripped her aching hip.

Gandy watched her struggle, heard the boy running off, crying in the dark.

Agatha spun around and appealed, "Do something, Gandy!"

In that instant he began to see too clearly what it was this woman wanted of him and he wanted no part of it. But he answered the tug of his own unwilling heart.

"Willy!" He tossed aside his cheroot, leaped to the street, and took off at a run, his heart already pounding. A five-year-old's legs were no match for Gandy's long limbs. He caught up with Willy in less than a dozen strides and plucked him from the middle of the street into his arms.

The child clung to Gandy and buried his face in his neck.

"Willy. Don't cry . . . hey, hey . . . it's all right." Gandy had no experience with comforting children. He felt awkward and slightly terrified. The child weighed next to nothing, but the skinny arms clung to Gandy as if he himself were the boy's father. Gandy swallowed hard, twice. The lump in his throat refused to budge. He carried Willy back to Agatha and stood before her, feeling out of his depth.

She touched Willy's shuddering back, rubbed it reassuringly. "Shh! Shh!" Her voice was low and soothing. "You're not alone, little one." She smoothed the cowlick on top of Willy's head. Gandy's hand spread on the child's rumpled shirt, over the thin ribs that heaved in rhythm with his sobs. Her hand moved down. Their fingers touched briefly. A spark of good intentions bound them in that instant and they each fought the urge to link fingers in their joint effort to help the boy. Together, they turned toward the steps and sat side by side, with Willy on Gandy's lap.

"Willy, don't cry anymore."

But the little boy could not be silenced. He burrowed into Gandy, who helplessly looked over the blond head at Agatha. He saw the glint of tears in her eyes as her hand rubbed Willy's thin arm.

"I'd take him myself if I could, but . . ." During her brief pause he remembered the pitiful sight of her trying to run after the boy. "Could you carry him up to my place?"

He nodded.

They went through the dark millinery shop, out the back door, and up the back stairs. It had never taken Gandy so long to make the climb. With Willy in his arms he adjusted his pace to Agatha's, watching her shuffling two-step as she clung to the rail. All the way up, he found himself recalling his youth at Waverley— healthy, hale, and surrounded by all the love and security a little boy could want to allow him to grow up happy.

At the landing Agatha unlocked her door and led the way into total blackness. "Wait here. I'll light a lamp."

Gandy stood still, listening to the two of them—Agatha, shuffling away; Willy, sobbing against his neck.

A lantern flared halfway down a room with the proportions of a stick match. Gandy barely had time to form the quick impression before she spoke again.

"Bring him over here."

He set the boy on the tiniest gateleg table he'd ever seen.

"If I could impose upon you one more time, it will be the last." She handed him a white enamel pail. "Could you fill this for me?"

He hurried back downstairs and filled her water bucket from the barrel beneath the steps. As he headed back up with the weighty pail, he thought of Agatha instead of the boy. If it was that difficult for her to climb the stairs empty-handed, how did she manage it with a bucket of water?

When he returned Willy was calmer. The two of them were quietly talking. He set the bucket on a low stool beside her dry sink and turned to find Agatha wiping the boy's lower eyelids with her thumbs. Gandy moved to stand beside them, looking down on the blond head and narrow shoulders. Willy was undeniably dirty. Hair, clothing, fingernails, neck—all could stand more than a bucket of cold water. Gandy's eyes met Agatha's and he saw she was thinking the same thing.

"Now, let's take care of that bump on your head." She turned and grabbed a cloth from a towel holder on the wall, slung it over her shoulder, and scooped a dipperful of water into a basin. The water sloshed close to the brim of the basin as she bought it to the table. Gandy stood by, feeling oversized and useless as she dipped and wrung and applied the cloth to Willy's forehead.

The boy pulled back, whimpering.

"I know it hurts. I'll be gentle."

Gandy braced one palm on the table beside Willy and talked. "I remember once when I was about your size, maybe a little older. We had this river where I lived. The Tombigbee, it was called. My friend and I used to swim there durin' the summer. That was down in Miz'sippi, and it gets mighty hot in Miz'sippi 'round about July." He accented the "Ju" in July. Agatha glanced up and smiled. "So hot, in fact, that sometimes we wouldn't wait t' shuck off our britches. We'd jump in clothes and all. Time I'm talkin' about, Cleavon and me—" He glanced at Agatha and told her, "Cleavon is Ivory's real name." He returned his attention to the boy. "Well, anyway, Cleavon and me went runnin' down to that river full tilt. Head first in the water we goes, and sure enough, I hit a rock and put a goose egg on my forehead the size o' your fist. Y' got a fist, don't y'?"

Willy proudly displayed one puny fist. He had stopped resisting Agatha and sat entranced. From the corner of his eye, Gandy saw her pick up the iodine. He rambled on.

"Knocked me out colder'n a clam, too. My friend Cleavon fished me out and went yellin' for help. My father came down to the river himself and carried me back up to the house. We had this old dictator called Leatrice . . ." Agatha smiled at the name: Lee-att-riss. "She was black as an eight ball and shaped about the same, only much, much bigger. Leatrice scolded me. Told me I didn't have a lick o' sense in my head.

"Well, now, Willy, I figured I was smarter than her." Agatha applied the iodine and Willy scarcely flinched. "After all, I went down to the river swimmin' when it got up to a hundred degrees in July. Leatrice, she stayed in the hot kitchen."

"How come?" Willy asked.

"How come Leatrice stayed in the kitchen?"

Willy nodded vigorously. Gandy's eyes met Agatha's briefly. Had she been for the North or South? he wondered. And fifteen years after the war, did it still matter to her, as it did to some?

"B'cause she worked for us. She was our cook."

"Oh." Willy was blessed with a child's ignorance of overtones. He went on with undisguised interest. "What happened to your goose egg?"

Gandy laughed. "Leatrice put a foul-smellin' marigold poultice on it and made me drink basswood tea for my headache."

"Did it go away?"

Gandy laughed. "Most of it." He leaned forward, touching a finger to his hairline. "Still carry a little scar right here to remind me never to dive into rivers without knowin' what's beneath the water. And my father had a swimmin' pool dug after that, and that's where I did my swimmin' from then on."

When he straightened, Agatha studied his hairline, searching for the scar.

His eyes roved in her direction. She dropped her glance.

In the lull, Willy asked, "It still hurt?"

"Nah. Don't even remember it's there most times. Yours'll go away, too."

Willy gingerly tested the bruise on his forehead and declared, "I'm hungry."

If Agatha had had her way, she'd have had a pantry that was a child's delight, filled with tasty treats to make him forget his bumps and scrapes. If she'd had her way, she'd have stuffed Willy until his belly popped. As it was, all she could offer was, "How about some rusks?"

Willy nodded enthusiastically.

She found the dry cinnamon toast and left Willy sitting on the table edge with the entire tin.

"I wish I had a kitchen," she told Gandy. "I've always wanted one."

For the first time he took a good look at her lodgings. The apartment was half the size of his—and his seemed cramped. There was a stove, the dry sink, but no other signs of the domestic trappings necessary for cooking. Her furnishings were old and sturdy. A sampler hung on the wall, lace curtains on the windows. It was almost painfully neat.

"How long have you lived here?"

"Thirteen years. Since my father died. We lived in Colorado when he was alive. After he was gone, Mother wanted to make a new start, get away from bad memories. So we came here and she opened up the millinery shop. I've lived here ever since."

"But you don't like it?"

Her eyes met his. "Does anybody like what life doles out to them? It's where I live. It's where my work is. I stay, just like hundreds of others."

He'd always felt so free to come and go where he pleased, to pull up roots and plant them somewhere new. He couldn't imagine staying in a place he disliked for so long. He himself didn't think Proffitt was the Garden of Eden, but he intended to stay only long enough to make a killing. Then he'd move on.

While his gaze roved around her dwelling, hers rested on him. "Your collar is soiled."

Gandy came away from his musings to realize she'd spoken to him.

"What?"

"I said, your collar is soiled." He dropped his chin but he couldn't see. "A little of Willy's blood," she clarified.

Gandy spied a tiny oval mirror above the dry sink and went to peer into it. He had to dip his knees to do so. He rubbed the collar.

"I could try to get it out with a little cold water."

He turned. "Would you?"

No, she wanted to reply, sorry now that she'd made the offer. Whatever was she trying to prove, fussing over Gandy's clothing? It was having the little boy here, and the man—almost as if the three of them were a family. She'd best not carry the pretext too far.

But she'd offered, and he was waiting. "Let me get some fresh water." She took the washbasin to the dry sink and stopped before him. He stood directly in front of the doors. "Excuse me." She glanced down.

"Oh . . . sorry." He jumped and stepped back.

She poured the dirty water into a slop pail, closed the doors, and refilled the basin. When she turned to him with a damp cloth, their eyes met briefly, then flashed apart.

"Perhaps you should loosen your tie."

"Oh . . . sure." He gave it a yank, worked it free with a finger, whipped it off, then stood waiting.

"And the collar button."

He freed it.

Her hands lifted and his chin shot up. Oddly enough, she sensed that he was as uncomfortable as she. She inserted the corner of a clean towel behind the collar and soaked it from the front with a wet one. It was the first time in her life she had ever touched a man's neck. It was warm and soft. The whiskers on the underside of his jaw grazed the back of her hand, sharp but not unpleasant—another first. His beard was inordinately heavy and black. He nearly always appeared to need a shave. The scent of his tobacco clung to his clothes. In lighter doses it became distinctly pleasant.

Gandy studied her stamped-tin ceiling. *What in hell's name're you doin' here, boy? This woman is trouble. An hour ago she and her infernal "drys" were harassin' your customers and tryin' to get them to go home! Now you're standing' with your chin in the air, lettin' her mollycoddle you.*

"You know, it's funny," he commented, still studying her ceiling.

"What?"

"What we're doin' now, and what we were doin' an hour ago."

"I know."

"I have mixed feelin's about it."

Her hands dropped and so did his chin. Their eyes met. Hers wavered away.

"So do I," she admitted softly. Again she lifted her face and met his gaze. "This wasn't exactly our choice, though, was it?"

He glanced at Willy, then back at her. "Not exactly."

"And just because I've sponged your soiled collar doesn't mean I've joined your camp."

"You'll be back with more ammunition."

A tiny sting of regret coiled within Agatha as she answered, "Yes."

"And I'll keep sellin' whiskey."

"I know."

While Willy sat on the table eating rusks, Agatha and Gandy stood looking at each other. They were enemies. Or were they? Most certainly they were not allies! Yet neither could deny, through some mysterious means, that they had become friends.

There was something on her mind that she simply had to say. She lay the wet cloths over the edge of the dry sink, half turning from him. "I want you to know, I was embarrassed by what Evelyn Sowers did in your saloon tonight. She's turning into a radical, and I'm not certain if I can stop her." She swung around, revealing a troubled expression. "I'm not even sure if it's my job to try to stop her. I didn't ask to lead the W.C.T.U., you know. Drusilla Wilson finessed me into it."

In the narrow, quiet, lonesome-looking room, Gandy suddenly became aware of how clearly the sounds of the music and voices filtered through the walls into her apartment. She opened her shop early in the morning. He supposed many mornings she opened it tired and grouchy, while he and the gang slept soundly on the other side of the wall.

"Listen, I'm sorry about the noise."

She hadn't expected him to say such a thing. Neither had she expected to hear herself answer as she did.

"And I'm sorry about Evelyn Sowers."

It struck them both at once—they were smiling at each other.

Gandy recovered first. "I'd better get back. It's busy down there and they need me."

She glanced at the shadows thrown by the lantern light into the open neck of his shirt. "I couldn't get all the blood out of your collar."

He touched it and glanced down. "That's all right. I'll stop by my apartment and put on a clean one."

Gandy glanced at the table. Willy was munching, scratching his head and swinging his crossed feet. Gandy spoke to Agatha in an undertone. "What are you goin' t' do with him? You can't very well keep him here."

"I'll walk him home. I wish I didn't have to, but . . ." She glanced at the boy, then back at Gandy. Her face saddened. "Oh, Gandy, he's so little to be left alone that way."

He reached out and squeezed her upper arm. "I know. It's not our problem, though."

"Isn't it?"

Their eyes communicated for several long, intense seconds. He dropped his hand.

"I intend to ask Reverend Clarksdale to talk to Alvis Collinson," she said.

"Do you think it'll do any good?"

"I don't know. Do you have a better idea?"

He didn't. Furthermore, he didn't want to become embroiled in Willy's problems. He was no crusader. That was her forte. But he crossed to stand before the boy.

"You about full yet?"

Willy beamed and wagged his head no.

"Well bring one for the road. Agatha's goin' t' walk you home."

Willy stopped chewing. His face fell. He talked through a mouth full of rusks. "But I don't wanna go home. I like it here."

Gandy hardened his heart, handed Willy one rusk, put the cover on the tin, and lifted him from the edge of the table. "Maybe your pa is home by now. If he is, he's probably worried about you."

Fat chance, he thought, meeting Agatha's eyes, which reflected a similar thought.

They left the lantern glowing and walked out to the landing, all holding hands, with Willy forming a living link between Agatha and Gandy. She expected Gandy to leave them there and enter his apartment. Instead, he put his hands under Willy's armpits. "Up you go!" He carried him down the stairs, patiently keeping pace beside Agatha. At the bottom he set Willy down and squatted before him. "Tell y' what. Y'all come by and visit me some afternoon." He swiveled on the balls of his feet and pointed with a long index finger. "See that window up there? That's my office."

Willy looked up and smiled. "Really?"

"Really. You ever seen cotton—I mean real cotton just the way it grows?"

"Uh-uh."

"Well, I got some up there. Y'all come visit and I'll show it to y'."

Impulsively, Willy flung his arms around Gandy's neck and gave him an enormous hug. "I'm comin' tomorrow!"

Gandy laughed and turned the boy toward Agatha. "Go on home now, and sleep tight."

When Willy returned to Agatha, his hand reached for hers without hesitation. As she took it, her heart contracted, then felt an upsurge of happiness.

"Say good-night to Mr. Gandy."

Willy turned, still holding her hand, and waved over his shoulder. " 'Night, Mr. Gandy."

" 'Night, Willy."

Gandy had a sudden thought. "Agatha, wait!"

She stopped. He held up a finger. "Just a minute." He disappeared into the shadows beneath the steps and entered the rear door of the saloon. In only a moment he returned, stepping out into the moonlight. "All right," he said quietly.

So Alvis Collinson was still inside. Instinctively, she tightened his fingers around the small hand she held.

"Good night, Gandy," she said softly.

"G'night, Agatha."

Wearing a troubled frown, the tall man with the black whiskers watched them walk away into the dark, holding hands.

Collinson's house was a pigsty. It had a dirt floor and a rusting stove. Filthy dishes with spoiled food tainted the air. Soiled clothing lay wherever it had been dropped. Agatha had to close her mind to the condition of the bed into which she tucked Willy.

"You'll be all right now."

His luminous brown eyes told her his bravery was slipping, now that she was about to leave him.

"You goin', Agatha?"

"Yes, Willy. I have to."

His chin quivered. She knelt beside the bed and brushed the hair back from his temple. "When you visit Mr. Gandy, be sure to drop by my shop and say hello to me."

He didn't answer. His lips compressed. Tears formed in the corners of his eyes. *May your soul burn in hell, Alvis Collinson, for treating this beautiful child as if you wished he weren't alive, while I would give my one good hip to have one like him.* It was all she could do to keep her eyes dry.

"You'll do that, won't you?"

He swallowed and nodded. A tear slipped down his cheek.

She bent and kissed it, feeling as if her heart would burst its bounds.

The stench of the bedclothes seemed to linger in her nostrils all the way home.

Chapter 8

Within a week Willy became a fixture at Agatha's millinery shop. She'd hear the back door open and a moment later he'd be standing at her elbow asking, "What's that?" "Why're ya doin' that?" "What's this for?" He had been unfairly slighted in the education department. Though he was curious about everything, he had basic understanding of little. She answered each of his questions patiently, pleased by the way his eyes lit up at each new tidbit he learned.

"That's a thimble."

"What's it for?"

"Pushing a needle, see?"

"What's them?"

"What are they?" she corrected. Then she answered, "Stones, just plain old stones."

"What y' gonna do with 'em?"

"Hold down the pattern while I cut around it . . . see?" Since she'd acquired the sewing machine, she'd subscribed to Ebenezer Butterick's fashion journal and had ordered twenty of his tissue patterns, which had excited her customers and already brought in several dress orders. Today, however, she was cutting out the first of three scarlet-and-black cancan dresses. She selected stone after stone from a tin washbasin, weighting the tissue into place. With his chin on the edge of the high worktable, Willy watched intently while she cut out the skirt. His eyes documented how carefully she pushed aside each severed piece with the pattern and stones still in place. He checked the washbasin, then the remaining pattern pieces.

"You're gonna need more stones, Agatha."

She peered into the basin. "So I am, Willy." She affected a frown. "Oh, bother, how I hate to stop working to go out and get them."

"I'll go!" He was heading toward the door before the smile lifted her cheeks. "Willy?"

He spun, brown eyes eager, hair sticking up on end. "Huh?"

"Take the basin to collect them in." After dumping the remaining stones onto her worktable, she handed it to him. As she continued working, she looked up often and gazed out the back door to see him squatting in the dirt, his curved backside almost touching the ground, chin to knees, digging with a stick. He came inside five minutes later, proudly bearing a basin full of dirty rocks.

"Take them out back and wash them first or they'll soil the cloth."

He bounded outside but returned in seconds. "I can't reach."

She laughed and felt happier than she ever remembered feeling as she went outside to help him. While she bent to scoop water from the deep wooden barrel, she commented, "We'll have to get you a little stool to stand on, won't we?" Before she went back inside, she added sternly, "And make sure you get those hands clean at the same time."

When he came back in, his soiled clothes were covered with damp sports where he'd dried the rocks. He huffed and puffed, carrying the heavy basin, but set it down proudly at her feet.

"There! I done it!"

"I did it," she corrected.

"I did it," he parroted.

She made a great show of examining the rocks. "And a fine job, too. All clean and—my goodness!—even dried. Go out front and ask Violet for a penny. Tell her I said you earned it."

His face grew radiant, the cheeks rounded like October apples. Then he spun and darted through the curtain. Agatha smiled at the sound of his giddy, high voice.

"Hey, Vy-let, Agatha says to ast you for a penny. She says t' tell you I urnt it."

"She did?" came Violet's reply. "Well, now, just what did you do to earn it?"

"Picked 'er some rocks and washed 'em and dried 'em."

"She's right. That's hard work. I don't know what we did before we had you around here." Agatha imagined Willy's shining eyes following Violet's hands as she fetched a penny from the cash drawer of the desk. A moment later the front door slammed.

He was back in less than five minutes with a sarsaparilla stick. Sucking it, he took up his stand beside the worktable again.

"Wanna suck?" He pointed the stick in Agatha's direction. Knowing how rarely he got candy, Agatha realized the value of a lick. She hadn't the heart to say no.

"Mmm . . ."

"Sassparilly." He rammed it back into his mouth. A minute later he inquired, "What's that?" One stubby finger pointed.

"That's powdered chalk."

"What's it for?"

"Pricking."

"What's pricking?"

"That's what it's called when I mark the places where I must stitch this dart together."

"What's a dart?"

"A dart is a row of stitching that holds the cloth together and gives the dress shape."

"Oh." He scratched his head vigorously, working the sarsaparilla stick on his tongue as if it were the plunger on a butter churn. He watched her hands intently. "You gotta get that chalk through them tiny holes?"

"That's right." The only markings on the thin paper were holes of graduated sizes, each size having its own meaning. She carefully sprinkled fine powdered chalk across them and rubbed it in before fastidiously removing the pattern piece, leaving a series of clearly marked white dots. "See?"

"Garsh!"

"Isn't it remarkable?" She, too, was still awed by the new patterns and her sewing machine. Work had become exciting.

She curled the pattern piece and tapped the chalk back into the glass pot. Willy scratched his head and chewed up the last of his sarsaparilla. "Could I try doin' that sometime?"

"Not today. And most certainly not until you wash those sticky hands. *And* the edge of the table!" She looked pointedly at the smudged spots where his fingers had been resting.

After that day he began showing up with cleaner hands. But the rest of him was still a mess. He scratched his head constantly. He wore the same clothing day after day. He smelled abominable. Agatha spoke to Reverend Clarksdale, but it seemed to make no difference. Alvis Collinson paid no more attention to his son than before. But the attention Willy lacked at home he got in Agatha's workroom. The hours he spent there became the brightest of her day, and of his, too, she suspected.

At nighttime her W.C.T.U. work continued. She made it a practice to attach herself to any of the groups except that including Evelyn Sowers. She set up a routine of visiting four saloons each night, ending, regularly as clockwork, at the Gilded Cage. As time went on, more and more local men signed temperance pledges. Few of them, however, were Gandy's regular customers.

He was too innovative to lose any.

The night Agatha stationed herself outside his door and read aloud from *Seven Nights in a Barroom,* he hung out a shingle advertising free popcorn.

The night she distributed pamphlets entitled "Help the Heathen Cowboy of the West," he offered a token good for one free bath at the Cowboy's Rest in exchange for each pamphlet handed in at the bar.

The night she led the ladies in the song, "Lips That Touch Whiskey Shall Never Touch Mine," he posted a list of the newest drinks available at the Gilded Cage—concoctions with such intriguing names as gin slings, mint juleps, sangarees, sherry cobblers, timber doodles, and blue blazers.

The night she led the ladies in the old Christian standard, "Faith of Our Fathers," he nodded at Ivory, who immediately chimed in with a piano accompaniment. Then Gandy stood behind the bar and directed his entire clientele in the most rousing rendition of the song Proffitt had ever heard . . . in or out of church! When the "amen" faded, he grinned at Agatha and announced, "Free sardines at the bar! Come and get 'em, everybody!"

When she passed around a collection bowl seeking donations for the movement, he announced the keno pot would double that night.

Yes, Gandy most certainly was innovative. But Agatha had come to enjoy the challenge of trying to best him.

One evening, before his crowd arrived and before her constituents gathered, she walked into the Gilded Cage and headed directly for the bar. Gandy was on its near side, leaning back with his elbows resting on its well-polished edge, watching her approach. His Stetson was pulled low. He puffed on a cheroot without touching a finger to it. His ginger-brown waistcoat was immaculate. And his dimples were intact.

"Well, what brings you in so early, Miz Downin'?" He always called her "Miss Downing" when others were around.

She handed him a copy of "Help the Heathen Cowboy of the West."

"My free bath token, if you please, Mr. Gandy."

He glanced down at the pamphlet, removed the cheroot, and broadened his grin. "I have t' presume you're serious."

She nodded. "Most certainly. A pamphlet for a token, I believe the sign says."

He took the pamphlet and flicked through the pages. "I hope y'all don't expect me t' read it."

"Do as you like, Mr. Gandy. My token, please?" she repeated amiably, holding out a palm. She and Gandy hadn't the slightest problem confronting each other with the utmost civility even while issuing challenges back and forth.

Again he leaned back against the bar, elbows caught up as before. Over his shoulder he instructed, "Give the lady a bath token, Jack."

The cash register rang and Jack Hogg extended a round wooden slug. "Here ya go, Miss Downing."

"Thank you, Mr. Hogg."

"Best time to go down to the Rest is probably early in the morning before the cowboys are up."

Her neck grew pink; no respectable woman in the state of Kansas would be caught mummified in a place like the Cowboys' Rest. Still, she returned politely, "I'll remember that."

She turned to leave.

"Oh, Miss Downing?" She turned back to Jack. "I got a shirt ripped out under the arm that could use a little stitching up on that sewing machine of yours."

"Bring it over any time. If I'm not there, Miss Parsons is."

"I'll do that." He tipped his bowler and smiled. She no longer thought of the livid half of his face but imagined how handsome he'd been before it became scarred.

As she passed Gandy, he picked up a platter from the bar. "Have a sardine, Miz Downin'?"

She glanced at the platter, then up at him. His dimples, declared very plainly that he expected her to decline.

"Why, thank you, Mr. Gandy. I don't mind if I do." She detested fish, but she plucked one from the platter and popped it into her mouth without hesitation. She chewed. Stopped. Chewed again and swallowed, then shivered violently and squinted hard.

"What's wrong? Don't like sardines?"

"Shame on you, Mr. Gandy! Have you no conscience at all, feeding your customers fish that are as salty as the seven seas?"

"None whatsoever."

"And popcorn, which I'm sure is the same."

"Next week we're bringin' in fresh oysters. Not as salty, but a delicacy nevertheless." He cocked one eyebrow and hefted the platter. "Have another?"

She glanced wryly at the lineup of slick fish. "Free enterprise, I suppose you call it." He set the platter down and laughed. She licked the oil off her finger and thumb. "What will you think of next, Mr. Gandy?"

"I don't know." His gaze was totally friendly and winning. "I'm runnin' out o' ideas. How about you?"

She didn't laugh. But it took great self control not to.

Agatha decided it was best to be frank with her fellow W.C.T.U. members and tell them she was doing work for Mr. Gandy and his employees.

Evelyn Sowers puckered up and snorted. "Consorting with the enemy!"

Agatha had expected this. "Perhaps it is, but to a good end. Ten percent of all the profits I earn from Mr. Gandy will be donated to the cause. As you all know, our coffers are very slim."

Evelyn's mouth remained sour, but she offered no further argument.

Jubilee, Pearl, and Ruby came for a fitting. They sashayed through the back door in lazy fashion, chattering and laughing, wearing their dressing gowns. Pearl's was pink. Ruby's was purple.

Jubilee's was turquoise-green.

Agatha tried hard not to stare at it.

The three laughed and came inside the shop proper. "Hello, Agatha. Hello, Violet. Howdy, Willy."

Willy left Agatha's side to run and meet them. "You gonna try on your new dancin' dresses?"

Ruby tweaked Willy's nose. "Sho' nuff."

"I'm gonna peek under the door and watch you dance in 'em."

Jubilee affectionately turned him by a shoulder. "Oh, no, you're not, young man."

"Am, too."

"If I catch you, I'll paddle your backside."

Willy wasn't threatened. He smiled and shook his head confidently. "Uh-uhhhh."

"How do you know I won't?"

"'Cause I'll run and tell Scotty and Agatha and they won't letcha."

With her hands on her hips, Jube leaned down and rested her forehead against Willy's. "Pretty smart little scalawag, aren't you, Willy Collinson?"

"Agatha says I am."

Everyone laughed. Pearl tousled Willy's hair.

He lifted brown eyes to her. "I been helpin' Agatha make your dresses, Pearl."

"You have!"

"Ain't I, Agatha?" He turned excitedly to her.

"Haven't I?" she corrected, beaming down at him. "He most certainly has. He puts the weights on the patterns after I lay them on the fabric."

Violet added, "And he helps keep the ruffles from curling while Agatha and I do the gathering."

Ruby rested a fist on one hip and assumed a falsely supercilious pose. "Well, would y' feature that now!"

"And Agatha says she's gonna get me a stool so I can see up on the table better and reach into the water barrel."

Another laugh.

Then Agatha got down to business. "The dresses are ready for fitting." She brought them out and hung them on a high rod. "They're going to be quite, quite stunning."

They were. Especially on three such exquisite bodies. Agatha couldn't help envying the girls as they slipped from their robes, displaying wasp waists shaped by flattering corsets with spoon busks running down the center fronts. Upon Agatha's request, all three had worn their high-heeled boots so the hem lengths could be properly adjusted. Agatha had never been able to wear high-heeled shoes. How shapely the women's ankles and legs looked in them. Watching was almost as much fun as wearing them herself.

Juiblee and Ruby stood atop the worktable while Agatha and Violet marked their hems with chalk. Pearl lounged on a chair, waiting her turn.

"You know that cowpoke named Slim McCord?" Jubilee inquired.

"That tall, skinny one with the nose like a carrot?"

"He's the one."

"What about him?"

"He tried to tell me it gets so hot on the trail sometimes that they have to dip the horses' bits in the water bucket to keep 'em from burning their tongues."

From the corner of her eye, Pearl flashed a glance to make sure Willy was listening. "You believe that?"

"Hmm . . ." Ruby appeared thoughtful. "I dunno. But what about old Four Fingers Thompson, who claims whenever the chuck wagon runs out of salt he licks the horse's sweat from his saddle?"

Willy listened to every word, enthralled.

"Listen to this one, everybody!" Pearl said excitedly. "Old Duffield asks me, 'Ya know how t' tell when the wind's pickin' up in Texas?' " Pearl let the mystery build, then angled a glance at Willy. "You know how, Willy?"

He shook his head, then scratched it.

"Well, accordin' to Duffield, you nail a log chain on top of a post, and when the wind blows it straight out—that's calm. When the last link snaps off, you can expect rough weather."

Everyone laughed and Willy plunged gaily against Pearl's lap. "Aw, you're just funnin' me, ain't you, Pearl?"

She tousled his hair and smiled.

The girls always brought an air of festivity, and they, along with all the other employees of the Gilded Cage, had taken an interest in Willy. Agatha loved having them in the shop. When the fitting was done and they left, it seemed dull.

Willy sat on the threshold of the back door, playing with a green worm and scratching himself. He bent at the waist, watched the worm crawl across his boot, and scratched his neck. He sat straight and watched the worm crawl from index finger to index finger, then gave his armpit a good workover. He put the worm on his knee and scratched his crotch. He set the worm on the ground and scratched his head.

"How would you like a bath, Willy?"

He pivoted on his backside. "A bath! I ain't takin' no bath!"

Agatha and Violet exchanged wry glances. "Why not?"

"Pa never makes me take none."

"Take *any,*" she corrected, then hurried on. "Well, he should. Baths are important."

"I hate baths!" Willy declared emphatically.

"Nevertheless, I think you need one. I have a token. All you have to do is give it to Mr. Kendall at the Cowboys' Rest and you can have one free."

Willy jumped up as if he'd suddenly remembered something. "I gotta go down and watch 'em load the cows on the cattle cars. See ya, Vy-let. 'Bye, Agatha." He scuttled off without a thought for the worm, which by now was crawling up the doorframe.

At four-fifteen that afternoon, Agatha knocked on Gandy's office door.

"Come in."

"It's me." She entered to find him squatting before the safe counting a stack of bills. Immediately, he stretched to his feet.

"I thought you were fittin' the girls' dresses this afternoon."

"We're finished already."

"When will they be ready to wear?"

"Another day or so."

Everything looked the same, except for a tall glass jar of black licorice whips that hadn't been on the corner of his desk before.

"Is there some problem?" He nonchalantly flung the stack of bills onto his desk.

"Not with the dresses, no."

"Well, sit down. What is it?"

She perched on the edge of an oak armchair. He dropped into his swivel chair and unconsciously reached for his vest pocket. The cheroot was half withdrawn before he realized what he was doing and tucked it away.

"It's Willy I've come about."

A crooked smile captured Gandy's lips and his eyes dropped to the apothecary jar.

"Oh, that Willy, he's somethin', isn't he?"

Her eyes followed the path of his. "He's an angel. It appears he's been coming to visit you quite regularly."

Gandy nodded and chuckled. He cupped his fists loosely and rested his chin on them. "You, too?"

"Yes, every day."

He noticed her staring at the licorice and explained hastily, "They're not just for him. I like 'em, too."

She smiled, sensing his reluctance to seem too taken with the boy. "Yes, I'm sure you do."

As if to prove it, he lifted the glass cover and helped himself to one, then angled the jar her way. "Have one."

It was on the tip of her tongue to decline, but her mouth began watering. How long had it been since she'd had a licorice whip? "Thank you."

Gandy clinked the cover back on, took a bite of his candy, and sat back, chewing. Agatha nibbled hers, then absently studied the limp black licorice stick in her fingers. She glanced up and placed the wooden token on his desk. "I'd like to trade this in."

He gave it a cursory glance, then rested his gaze on her. His dimples appeared, along with a teasing grin. "I'm afraid you'll have t' go down t' the Cowboys' Rest for that. We don't give baths here."

"For Willy," she explained.

"Willy?"

"He smells." She paused eloquently. "And he needs a bath worse than any human being I've ever met."

"So send him down there."

"He won't go."

"Tell him—"

"I'm not his mother, Mr. Gandy, nor his father. Willy says his father doesn't make him take baths, which is altogether too obvious. When I suggested his going alone, he took off like a shot to watch the cowpokes load cattle."

Gandy took another chaw of licorice. "So what do you want me t' do about it?"

"He'd go with you."

"Me!" Gandy's eyebrows flew up.

"He worships the ground you walk on."

"Now wait a minute." Gandy rose from his chair and moved as far away from Agatha as he could get. In the corner near the window he turned and pointed at her with the floppy candy stick. "I'm not the boy's father either. If he needs a bath, let Collinson see to it."

Agatha spoke calmly. "That would be ideal, wouldn't it?"

She took another dainty nibble of licorice. He threw his on the desk.

"Why should *I* do it?" he asked in exasperation.

She continued reasonably. "I'd take him there myself, but it wouldn't be proper. Women don't go to public baths. You go there anyway on a regular basis, don't you?"

Gandy looked thunderous. "I don't mind havin' him come up here now and then, but I'm not goin' t' start squirin' that ragamuffin around as if he were my own. He could get to be an infernal nuisance. And I'm not goin' to be around this town forever, you know. It wouldn't be good if he grew attached to me."

Agatha brushed a nonexistent piece of lint off her skirt and said succinctly, "I think he has lice."

"Lice!" Gandy stared at Agatha, aghast.

"He scratches incessantly. Haven't you ever noticed?"

"I . . ." Damn the woman! Why didn't she leave him alone? Gandy took up pacing, running his fingers through his hair.

"Have you ever had lice, Mr. Gandy?"

"Most certainly not."

"Been bitten by a flea, then?"

She had the aggravating power to make him answer when he didn't want to. "Who hasn't? We had dogs and cats when I was young."

"Then you know it's not the most pleasant thing in the world to be infested. Fleas bite and jump away. Lice stay and suck. They're constantly on the move in a person's—"

"All right! All right!" Gandy's eyes slammed shut. He held up both palms in surrender. "I'll do it!" He opened his eyes, scowled at a corner of the ceiling, and cursed softly under his breath.

Agatha smiled. "His head will need scrubbing with kerosene first."

"Jesus!" Gandy mumbled disgustedly.

"And his clothes will need washing. I'll see to that."

"Don't put yourself out, Agatha," Gandy advised sarcastically.

"I've left the token to pay for his bath." It looked ridiculous lying on the desk next to his stacks of money. "Well . . ." She rose to leave. "Thank you for the licorice stick. It was a wonderful treat. I haven't had one in years."

"Humph!"

Amusement got the better of her and she smiled cajolingly. "Oh, come on, Gandy, it's not so bad. Just pretend the kerosene is that atrocious Kansas sheep dip you sell downstairs."

He stood with both fists on his hips. His dark eyes lost none of their attractiveness when his expression grew fierce.

"Agatha, *you're* the damned infernal nuisance, you know that?"

She looked at his mouth and burst out laughing.

His scowling lips were ringed with black, like the raccoon's eye. He bristled and tried to look mean. *Damned interferin' woman! Comin' in here with those unsettlin' pale green eyes and her maneuverin' ways, makin' my conscience act up, then laughin' at me t' boot.* "What in tarnation's so funny?"

She opened the door, still laughing, and suggested over her shoulder, "Wipe your mouth, Gandy."

When the tail of her bustle disappeared, he stomped into his apartment and peered at himself in the mirror above the washbowl. Angrily, he wiped the licorice from his mouth. But in a moment a willful chuckle threatened. He pondered silently for some moments. The damned woman was starting to grow on him.

He tallied up her physical attributes, one by one: the attractive mouth; the flawless skin; the determined jawline; the arresting opacity of her sea-green eyes; the surprising glint of mahogany-red in her artfully arranged hair; her mode of dress, always formal and superbly tailored, but somehow right for her; her high-riding bustles. He'd never much cared for bustles before, but on Agatha they took on a certain undeniable sense of class.

He studied his reflection in the mirror.

Be careful boy, you could fall for that woman, and she's not exactly the triflin' kind.

The skinny little boy, smelling of kerosene, and the tall sturdy man, smelling of cigar smoke, stood in a room redolent of wet wood. Two wooden tubs of steaming-hot water waited in the middle of the damp pine floor. In one corner a scarred hoop-back chair held two dingy Turkish towels, a bowl of unrefined soft yellow lye soap, and a stack of clean clothing.

"Well, shuck down, boy. What're you waitin' for?" Gandy removed his jacket and draped it on the back of the chair.

Willy's lower lip protruded. "You tricked me."

"I did not. You lost that game of five-card stud fair and square."

"But I ain't never played before. How was I s'posed t' win?"

"That's luck, Willy. It just happened t' be with me durin' that particular hand. And I thought Agatha told you not t' say 'ain't' anymore." Gandy's vest joined the jacket. He pulled his shirttails out, unbuttoned the garment, and still Willy hadn't lifted a finger to undress. Gandy put the crock of soap on the floor and sat down to remove his boots.

"Boy, I been without a cheroot now for nigh on an hour, and if you don't want t' go up like a firecracker, you'd better get yourself in that tub and get rid of the kerosene."

Pouting, Willie dropped to the floor and began tugging at his curled-toe boots. Gandy watched from the corner of his eye and grinned. The boy's lip looked twice as large as usual. His chin was flattened with disgust. His disheveled hair made him look like an old blond hen that had taken more than her share of pecking from her coop mates.

"I gots a knot." Willie refused to look up as he grumbled.

"Well, untie it."

"I can't. It's too tight."

Dressed in nothing but a knee-length cotton union suit, Gandy went down on one knee before the boy. "Here, let's see . . ."

Willie had a knot, all right. All he had were knots. His boot strings were a series of them. The boots themselves looked as if they should have been scrapped months ago. When they came off, the smell nearly knocked Gandy on his prat.

"Lord o' mercy, boy, you smell like a boar's nest!"

Willie snickered, burying his chin against his chest, and sheepishly tried to cover his mouth with a wrist. Then he reached out blindly and punched Gandy on the knee.

"Do not," he mumbled.

"Well, at least like a polecat, then."

Another punch.

"Don't neither!"

"Whoo-eee! Takes my breath away! If it's not you, who could it be?"

Willie's face hurt from holding in the laughter, so he punched Gandy again and knocked him off balance.

Gandy smirked at him, dimpling. "Yessuh, I think I see four she-polecats waddlin' toward the door right now."

This time Willy's laugh burst free before he could stifle it. His head came up and he thumped himself full-body against Gandy's chest. "I don't care. You still tricked me, Scotty."

It was the second time Gandy had had Willy in his arms. Even smelling of kerosene and sour feet, the boy made his heart melt. With their faces separated by only inches, Gandy grinned and inquired, "You ready t' get in that water now?"

"If I hafta." The angelic expression returned to Willy's face. "My head stings."

They stood side by side, stripping. When they were both naked they faced each other, man to man, Gandy looking down, Willy up. Willy, with a penis like a tiny pink acorn; Gandy's nothing whatever like a tiny pink acorn. Willy, with legs like white matchsticks; Gandy's long and hard and sprinkled with coarse black hair. Willy, with ribs like a marimba; Gandy, with a torso like a full bag of oats.

Their eyes—deep brown and long-lashed—were very much alike as Willy looked up appealingly. "When I get big, will I look like you?"

"Probably."

"Will I have me a big tallywhacker?"

Gandy laughed, arching backward, hands on hips. He grinned on down at the face that was eye level with his navel.

"Willy, my boy, where did you learn a word like that?"

"Heard Ruby talkin'."

"Ruby? What'd she say?"

"She said she liked a man with a big tallywhacker, and Ruby's my friend, so I want her t' like me."

Gandy touched Willy's nose. "If you want the ladies t' like you, take a bath at least once a week. Now, come on . . ." Gandy dropped to one knee beside a tub. "Head first."

Willie knelt down, clutched the lip of the tub, and leaned over. His dirty gray ankles cradled a bare backside with buttocks as white and miniature as loaves of unrisen bread. Each vertebra stuck out like a pebble on a washed shore. And that hair—ye gods!

What a sight, thought Gandy, all skin and bones held together by goose bumps and dirt. Reaching for a handful of soap, he smiled, braced an elbow on one updrawn knee, and set to work.

There was something eminently satisfying about scrubbing the small head. Gandy's wide hands looked so dark against Willy's paleness, his forearms so powerful beside the skinny neck. He thought of his own child, wondered if he'd have done this for her, had she lived.

Forget it, Gandy, it's past.

He folded one of Willy's ears back, then stretched it to peer inside. "Boy, what you been growin' in here? Time t' harvest it, don't you think?"

Willy gurgled, his bony elbows pointed at the ceiling.

"Hurry up!"

"I'm hurryin'. But I shoulda brought a shovel."

Again the boy giggled. "You're funny, Scotty," came his muffled words.

Odd, how such insignificant praise from a small boy made him feel profoundly happy. When Willy's hair was clean, Gandy ordered the tub removed and another of fresh water brought in.

"Jump in and warm up."

He himself shuddered with appreciation as he folded his long limbs into one tub, while Willy sank Indian fashion into the other. Soaping and rinsing, raising his arms and curving his shoulders, Gandy showed the boy how a real bath was handled.

"Ream those ears out good now, ya hear?"

"I will," the boy replied disgustedly, following Gandy's lead.

"And not only inside, behind 'em, too."

"What if I go deef? It ain't no good t' git water in your ears."

"I promise y' won't go *deef.*"

"That's what Gussie says, but—"

"Gussie?" Gandy's palms stopped scouring his chest.

"Yeah, she checked my ears and—"

"Who's Gussie?"

"Agatha. She says when she was little her ma always called her Gussie, an' she said I could call her it, too. Anyway, Gussie, she checked my ears an' said . . ."

Gandy heard only bits and pieces of what Agatha said. *Gussie?* He sat back, thoughtfully ladling water over his chest, fitting the nickname to her face. His hands stopped moving. Why, of course . . . Gussie. He smiled and reached out one long arm, dried his fingers, then plucked a cheroot from his vest pocket. When it was lit, he lazed back contentedly with his knees sticking up like mountains, arms cradling the top of the tub, thinking of her.

A curious woman. Moralistic to a fault, but with an underlying respect for everyone and everything that won his respect in return. She had an amusing way of challenging him where temperance matters were concerned. He'd come to almost look forward to her appearance in the Gilded Cage each night. Yes, she crusaded beside all the others. But her campaign was tempered by an abiding belief in man's basic rights to live his life as he saw fit. When he thought about it, it became downright admirable; on the one hand, she could sing and hand out pamphlets and solicit signatures on a temperance pledge; on the other, she could allow that Gandy had a perfect right to run his business along with the other saloon owners in town.

Another of Agatha's dichotomies absorbed his thoughts. She was fascinated by Jubilee and the girls. Though she tried to pretend she wasn't, there were times when he caught her studying them as if she found them the most entrancing creatures on earth.

And the boy. She was particularly good with the boy. Too bad she never had any children of her own. She'd have done a much better job at raising them than would a reprobate like Collinson.

Gandy glanced over at Willy and chuckled. The lad was doubled forward with his chin and lips just below the water's surface looking as if he enjoyed every minute in the tub.

Gandy blew a puff of smoke toward the ceiling. "Agatha made you some new duds."

Willy's head popped up. His eyes rounded in disbelief. "She did?"

"Britches and a shirt." Gandy nodded sideways. "Over on the chair with mine."

"Garsh . . ." The water dripped off Willy's chin as he became transfixed by the stack of folded clothing. "She din't tell me."

"Reckon she wanted it t' be a surprise."

Willy's eyes remained riveted on the chair while he stood up. "Can I git out now?"

"You sure you're scrubbed clean?"

Willy raised both elbows and gave each armpit a cursory check. "Yup."

"All right."

A glistening backside pointed Gandy's way as two wet heels thumped on the floor. Gandy reached for the towels, tossed one to Willy, and stood to use the other. Willy gave his body no more than a quick hit with the wadded-up towel before he dropped it in the puddle and headed for the clothing.

"Hey, not so fast there, sprout. You're still drippin'. Come here." Gandy slung his own towel over one shoulder and hunkered down with Willy between his knees. He grinned at the way the boy shivered and huddled. But Willie seemed unaware of anything except the fact that new clothing waited on the chair. While Gandy swung him this way and that, drying his back, armpits, ears, the boy craned toward the chair as if his head were mounted on a spring.

"Hurry up, Scotty."

Gandy smiled and released Willy with a pat on his backside. "All right, go."

The britches were blue muslin. Willy gave no thought to underwear. He hitched his buttocks on the edge of the chair seat and slipped impatiently into the new pants. Agatha had put a drawstring at the waist. Willy cinched it up and crossed to Gandy, staring down his belly. "Tie me up."

"Put your shirt on first and we'll tuck it in."

The shirt closed up the front with white mother-of-pearl buttons. It was made of blue-striped gingham and the sleeves were several inches too long. "Button me."

Gandy smiled secretly and did as ordered. The buttons held the cuffs from slipping over Willy's small hands. He tied the drawstring at Willy's waist and tucked the strings inside, then held him by both hips.

"You look pretty spiffy, boy."

Willy pressed the shirt against his chest with both palms. "Ain't they pretty?" He gazed down in wonder but suddenly spun from Gandy's hands. "Hey, I gotta go show Gussie!"

"Not so fast. What about your shoes?"

"Oh . . . them." Willy plunked backward onto the floor and slipped on his boots over bare feet—he'd come with no socks.

"And hadn't we better comb your hair?"

"I ain't got no comb."

"I do. Just a minute."

When Gandy was dressed, he sat on the hoop-back chair with an impatient Willy between his thighs. He parted his clean blond hair carefully and swished it into a perfect windrow above his brow, combed it back above his ears, and made a neat tail at his nape. When he was done he held Willy by both arms for inspection. "Agatha won't know you."

"Yes, she will—lemme go!"

"All right. But wait for me."

Outside, the man had to lengthen his stride to keep up with the boy.

"C'mon, Scotty, hurry up!"

Gandy grinned and hurried. The day was balmy. Agatha's front door was open. Had it not been, Willy might have broken the window throwing the door out of his way.

"Hey, Gussie, Gussie! Where are you?"

He ran through the lavender curtains as she called, "Back here!"

Gandy followed just in time to see Willy standing beside Agatha's chair, chest puffed while he inspected himself and boasted, ''Lookit me, Gussie! Ain't I pretty?"

Agatha clapped once and rested her folded hands beneath her chin. "Why, for the love of Pete, who do we have here?"

"It's me, Willy!" He patted his chest convincingly.

"Willy?" She studied him dubiously, then shook her head. "The only Willie I know is Willy Collinson, but he doesn't look all shiny like you. He doesn't smell like fresh soap either."

Willy's breathless words tumbled out one atop the other. "Scotty an' me, we took a bath and washed our hair an' he brung me my new clothes you made an' he tied my string an' ... well ... but I couldn't button an' he helped me an' I love 'em, Gussie!" He catapulted himself into her arms and hugged her tenaciously.

Gandy stood just inside the doorway watching. Willy kissed Agatha flush on the mouth. She laughed self-consciously and flushed with happiness.

"My goodness, had I know I'd get all this attention, I'd have made them days ago."

"An' I cleaned my ears real good, just like Scotty said, an' I scrubbed everythin' an' he combed my hair. See?" Willy raced back to Gandy, caught him by a hand, and tugged him forward. "Din't we?"

Agatha raised her eyes to Scott Gandy, standing above her. It was close to being a wife and mother as she had ever felt. Within her heart fullness abided. At her knee the child leaned, touching her, smelling soapy, his shirt—with room for growth—standing out from his slight body in starched peaks. Close before her stood a man who, along with her, had made one small neglected soul feel happier and more cared about then he'd perhaps ever felt in his life.

She reached up a hand, unable to say all that flooded her heart. Scott Gandy took it, held it tightly, and smiled down at her.

Thank you, she mouthed silently above Willy's head.

He nodded and squeezed her fingers so hard the touch ricocheted off her heart.

Suddenly, they both became self-conscious. Gandy dropped her hand and stepped back. "He'll need new socks and underwear. I thought we'd go over to Halorhan's and pick some out."

As Agatha watched the two walk away, hand in hand, her eyes stung with joy.

At the curtains, the boy swung around and flashed a quick wave. "See y' later, Gussie!"

Gandy's brown eyes settled on her pale green ones. His wore an expression somewhere between a tease and a caress. "Yeah, see y' later, Gussie," he said.

She blushed and dropped her gaze. Her heart fluttered like a cloud of butterflies lifting into the air. When she looked up, the doorway was empty of all but the swinging lavender curtains.

Chapter 9

Alvis Collinson suffered from a perennial case of gout. On the morning following Willy's bath, he awakened with both big toes throbbing. He tended to blame everything on Cora's dying, his gout included.

Damn you, Cora, for goin' and leavin' me without no woman t' do for me! Toes throbbin' like a pair o' bitches in heat, and I have t' git up and fend for m'self. No hot breakfast waitin'. No clean shirts t' put on. No woman t' fetch the coal and heat the water. Goddamn women, anyway—no good when ya got 'em and no good when ya ain't. And goddamn Cora the most, always harpin' at me t' be somethin' better, do somethin' more refined than pokin' cows. Refined meanin' somethin' fancy like Brother Jim, who gits hisself a pantywaist job as Registrar of Deeds just about the time the land agents started blowin' up this part o' the country t' strangers. Brother Jim who dudes hisself up in fancy suits ev'ry mornin' and walks down the boardwalk t' his prissy office doffin' his hat to' the ladies as if his farts don't stink. Why, hell, Cora couldn't look at Jim without her eyes buggin' outta her head and her tits swellin' up.

And nobody was gonna convince Alvis Collinson that miserable brat wasn't Jim's bastard. More than once Alvis had come home unexpected and caught Jim sniffin' around Cora. And her nose was twitchin' too, goddammit to hell if it wasn't!

Not tonight, Alvis, I'm too tired. As if once she got a sample of Brother Jim her own husband wasn't good enough anymore. Then she had the nerve to drop her whelp and check out for good.

Come on, Brother Jim, show your face around this town once more—just once!—so I can whip the piss outta you and dump your brat on you, where he belongs. I'm gettin' tired o' bein' tied down by that little thorn in the side when he ain't even mine.

In the kitchen, Willy stood on a chair, on tiptoes, peering into a small milky mirror hung high on the wall. His fine yellow hair gleamed with water. Painstakingly, he ran the comb through it, parted it on one side, then sliced it flat over the crown of his head from left to right. He tried to swish it back just like Scotty had done, but it wouldn't stand up in the sideways peak. He tried again and failed. He clamped the comb between his knees and used his palms this time, shaping the crest as if it were made of piecrust dough. After several attempts, he had finally done it fairly well. *Boy, is Pa ever gonna be surprised!*

He clambered off the chair, dropped the comb on the table, and went to the bedroom doorway, beaming with pride.

"Pa, look! Lookit what I got!"

Alvis scowled at the doorway, nursing one aching toe. It was the brat, already up and dressed. "Lookit what?" he growled.

"These!" Willy rubbed his breast pockets. "They're from Gussie and Scotty. Gussie, she made me the britches and shirt, and Scotty, he bought me the new boots after him an' me took a bath together down at the Cowboys' Rest."

Collinson's eyes narrowed on the boy. "Scotty? Ya mean Gandy? The one from the saloon?"

"Yeah. First he give me a goin'-over with kerosene. Then we took our bath and—"

"And who the hell's this Gussie?"

"Agatha, down at the millinery shop. She gots this new sewin' machine Scotty bought for her, and she made me new britches and this new shirt, too."

The gout seemed to spread from Alvis's toes to the rest of his body.

"Oh, she did, huh? And what right's she got takin' over my kid, huh? Wasn't ya dressed good enough t' suit her?" Alvis struggled to his feet. "She the one behind that damned snoopin' preacher man come pokin' his nose 'round here? Is she, huh?"

"I don't know, Pa." The light went out of Willy's face. "Don't you like my new things?"

"Git 'em off!" Alvis hissed. Then he rummaged through the clothes he'd dropped beside the bed last night, searching for his socks. "Just like Brother Jim, ain't ya?" he mumbled, while the confused child tried not to let his disappointment show.

"But they're . . ."

"Git 'em off, I said!" Barefoot, Alvis lunged to his feet. He stood before the boy with his fists clenched, dressed in a filthy union suit with the legs cut off at mid-thigh, the back hatch sagging. His whiskered face contorted with rage. "Ain't nobody tellin' me I ain't dressin' my own brat good enough, ya understand?" Willy's lower lip trembled and two tears formed in his eyes. "And quit that snivelin'!"

"I ain't takin' 'em off. They're mine!"

"Like hell ya ain't!" Collinson caught the boy by the back of the collar and tossed him onto a scarred wooden chair. It screeched, tilted back on two legs, then clattered onto all fours. "Where's your old boots? Git 'em on, and your britches and shirt, too. I'll show them uppity sons-a-bitches t' keep outta my bus'ness! Now, where's them boots? I told ya, boy, t' quit your snivelin'!"

"But I like the . . . these. They're a pre . . . present from Sc . . . Scotty."

Collinson dropped to one knee and jerked the boots roughly from Willy's feet. The angle of his big toe against the floor caused a shard of pain to shoot up his leg, incensing him further. "When I decide you need new boots, *I'll* buy you new boots, ya got that, boy?"

Willy's eyes streamed and his chest jerked as he tried not to sob.

"Now git on your old ones!"

"I ain't g . . . got 'em."

"What d' you mean, you ain't got em?"

"I j . . . just ain't."

"Where are they?"

"I d . . . don't kn . . . know."

"Goddammit to hell! How can ya lose your own boots?"

Willy peered up fearfully, his thin chest palpitating as he held in the sobs. Collinson's fists clenched and he yanked the boy roughly off the chair onto his feet.

"Ya lose your boots, ya go barefoot. Now gimme the rest."

Minutes later, when Collinson limped angrily out of the house, Willy threw himself on his bed and let the pent-up weeping escape. His hot tears wet the tender white skin of his freckled arm as he cried against it. One skinny bare foot curled around the opposite ankle as he rolled up in a ball. The crest in his gleaming gold hair, which Alvis hadn't even noticed, became disheveled by the sour bedclothes.

Agatha's heart slammed into her throat when the voice roared from the front room.

"Where the hell is ev'rybody!"

Violet hadn't arrived yet. Agatha had no choice but to answer the call herself. She shuffled to the curtains and parted them. Immediately, the gruff voice shouted again.

"You the one they call Gussie?"

She composed herself forcibly. "Agatha Downing is my name, yes."

Collinson squinted, recognizing her as that "temperance bitch" who was always stirring up trouble lately, the same one who had stuck her nose into his business once before when Willy had come looking for him at the saloon.

"You're outta line, missus." He flung down the shirt and pants on top of the aviary display case.

"Miss," Agatha retorted tightly.

"Aw, well, that explains it, then. Ain't got no whelps o' your own, so ya take over other people's." Holding Willy's new boots in one hand, he brandished them at her nose. "Well, git yourself some o' your own. My boy don't need your charity. He's got an old man, and I'll see after my own. Is that understood?"

"Perfectly."

Collinson glared at her hard, then headed for the open door. Before reaching it he turned back. "And one more thing. Next time ya go whisperin' things t' the preacher, tell him t' mind his own goddamned business." He started for the door again and once more stopped to demand, "Where the hell's Gandy? I got words for him, too."

"More than likely still asleep upstairs."

He threw her one last glare, shouldered around toward the door, then disappeared. Agatha's heart was still thudding sharply when she heard the sound of shattering glass. She hurried to the front door just in time to see Collinson fling the second boot through a window overhead. "Gandy, wake up, ya son-of-a-bitch! I'll buy my own boy's boots, so stop interfering! The next time ya take him to the Rest for a bath, you'll need one yourself t' wash off the blood—ya hear me, Gandy?"

Curious heads poked out of doorways all along the boardwalk. As Collinson limped down the middle of main street, he glared at Yancy Sales, leaning out the door of his Bitters Shop, "Whaddaya gawkin' at, Sales? Ya want a boot through your window, too!"

Every head withdrew.

* * *

Upstairs, Gandy awakened with the first crash. He braced himself up on his elbows and squinted into the morning sun beaming in the window on the far side of Jube.

"What the hell . . ."

Jube lifted her head like a prairie dog peeping from its hole. "Mmm . . . mmm . . ." Her face fell into the pillow and Gandy rolled across her to look at the boot lying beside the bed.

He flopped onto his back and uttered, "Oh, Jesus!"

"Wh . . . zz . . . tt?" came Jube's muffled voice.

"The new boots I bought yesterday for Willy." He closed his eyes and thought how long it had been since he'd gotten into a rip-roaring fistfight. It would feel mighty good again.

A quiet knock sounded on his door. He rolled from the bed, naked, and stepped into his black trousers. Barefoot, he padded to the sitting room and opened the door.

Agatha stood in the hall, hands clasping and unclasping nervously.

"I'm sorry to disturb you so early." Her glance flitted from his stubbled cheeks to his naked chest, then down to his bare feet, and finally to the end of the hall. She'd never seen him any way other than impeccably dressed. She was unsure of the rules of propriety when faced with a man's hairy chest and toes. Her face turned pink.

"Believe it or not, I was already awake." He combed his hair back with his fingers, giving her a flash of dark hair under his arms. "Collinson's a real sweetheart, isn't he?"

She met his eyes squarely, her brow wrinkled in concern. "Do you think Willy is all right?"

"I don't know." He, too, frowned.

"What should we do?"

"Do?" Dammit! He hadn't wanted to get mixed up with Willy in the first place. "What would you suggest we do? March down to Collinson's house and ask him if he's mistreated the boy?"

Agatha's irritation sprouted. "Well, we can't stand by and do nothing."

"Why not? Look what happens when we try to play the good Samaritan." Even as Gandy replied, he remembered Willy, naked as the day he was born, looking up with his liquid brown eyes, asking him, "When I grow up, will I be like you?"

Just then Jubilee shuffled up behind Gandy, yawning, her white hair bunched in disarray. "Who is it, Scotty . . . ? Oh, it's you, Agatha. Mornin'." She was wearing the turquoise dressing gown. It buckled open as Jubilee balled her fists and stretched both arms sleepily, tilting her head to one side. Agatha caught a glimpse of enough cleavage and flank to guess that Jubilee slept in the altogether. Her voice became sharp.

"As soon as you wake up, you can tell Mr. Gandy I'm sorry I got him out of bed."

Picking up her skirts, she turned and made an exit with as much dignity as she could muster.

Not five minutes later everybody arrived at the millinery shop at once: Mrs. Alphonse Anderton, for a fitting on her new dress; Violet, for work; Willy, bawling; and Gandy, still barefoot, buttoning a wrinkled shirt with its tails flapping.

"Listen here, Agatha, I resent your—" Gandy pointed a finger angrily.

"Well ..." Mrs. Anderton pompously scrutinized them, ending with Gandy's bare feet. "Good morning, Agatha."

"Tt-tt."

"My p ... pa ... he s ... says I c ... can't c ... come here no more t' s ... see youuuuuu ..."

Agatha stood behind a glass counter, so Willy ran straight to Gandy. Gandy went down on one knee and hauled the sobbing boy tightly against him. Willy clung to Gandy's neck. Gandy forgot his anger and Agatha's chest felt as if it would crack as she listened to Willy's sobs. "He t ... took away m ... my new b ... boots."

"Please take care of Mrs. Anderton, Violet," Agatha ordered quietly, then moved to Gandy, and he straightened with Willy in his arms.

"Bring him into the back room," Agatha said.

Even after they were alone the boy sobbed and sobbed and spoke in broken snatches. "M ... my n ... new sh ... shirt and br ... britches ... he ... t ... told ... m ... me ..."

"Shh!" Gandy whispered going down on one knee again. Willy burrowed his blond head against the man's sturdy dark chest and half-buttoned white shirt.

Agatha felt as if she were choking. She sat down on Willy's little stool beside them, petting his head, smoothing his hair, feeling helpless and woeful. Over Willy's shaking shoulder her gaze met Gandy's. He looked shaken. She reached out and touched the back of his hand. He lifted two fingers, hooked two of hers, and pulled them against Willy's neck.

Why couldn't this child have been ours? We would have been so good to him, so good for him. It was a fleeting thought, but it brought to Agatha a bitter realization of the injustices of this world.

In time Willy calmed. Agatha withdrew her fingers from Gandy's and pulled a scented handkerchief from a pocket concealed within the back drapes of her dress.

"Here, Willy, let me clean up your face."

He turned, dripping, eyes and lips puffy. As she mopped his cheeks and made him blow, she wondered what either she or Gandy could say to restore Willy's broken heart.

"You mustn't blame your father," she began. "It was our fault, Scotty's and mine." She had never called Gandy by his first name before. Doing so gave her strength and a feeling of communion with both him and Willy. "We hurt your father's pride, you see, by giving you new clothes, taking you for a bath. Do you know what that means—pride?"

Willy shrugged, trying not to cry again.

Agatha didn't think she could speak one more word without breaking into tears herself. She looked to Gandy for help and he came through.

"Pride means feelin' good about yourself." His long, dark fingers combed back the blond strands above Willy's ears. "Your father wants t' buy you things himself. When we bought them instead, he thought we were tellin' him that he wasn't seein' after you properly."

"Oh." Willy said the word so softly it was scarcely audible.

"And as for you comin' t' visit us—I don't see why you shouldn't. We're still your friends, aren't we?"

Willy gave the expected smile, though it was tentative.

"But it might be a good idea t' slip in the back door and make sure you don't come when your pa's in the saloon, all right? Now, how about a licorice stick?"

Willy's face remained downcast as he answered unenthusiastically, "I guess so."

Gandy got to his feet, lifting the boy on his arm. He waited until Agatha, too, rose, then hooked an arm loosely about her shoulders as the three of them ambled toward the back door. She felt awkward, bumping against his chest and hip with each clumsy step she took. But he didn't seem to mind. At the door he dropped his arm and told her, "Willy 'll be down later, but send him back up at dinner time and I'll have Ivory go over to Paulie's and pick up some picnic food."

Perhaps that was the moment when Agatha first realized she was falling in love with Gandy. She looked up at him, his hair still tousled, his cheeks still shaded with a night's growth of whiskers, his shoulders and arms looking as if they could handle all the Alvis Collinsons of this world as they held Willy.

"Thank you," she said softly. "And I'm sorry I was short with you upstairs. I understand. I feel the same way at times."

For a moment his eyes lingered on hers, bearing a soft expression, while Willy glanced back and forth between the two of them, his freckled arm resting on the back of Gandy's neck.

"Ain't you comin', Gussie?" the child asked plaintively.

"No, Willy." She dried a lingering tear with her thumb. "I'll see you later." She raised up and kissed his shiny cheek. As they left she realized she had placed herself in double jeopardy. She was falling in love not only with the man, but with the boy as well.

Later that day the girls came to try on their finished cancan dresses and Agatha seized the opportunity to apologize to Jubilee for her snappishness that morning.

Jube passed it off with a wave of her hand. "I was still so sleepy I didn't even know what you were saying."

All the while Agatha buttoned Jubilee into the sleek-fitting bodice she couldn't forget the way Jube had padded to Gandy's door, all warm and tumbled from sleep, looking more beautiful in disarray than most women looked after an hour at their dressing tables. She recalled Gandy's bare chest and mussed hair, his trousers with the waist button still freed, his bare feet.

Then she glanced at Jubilee, twirling before the wall mirror. Radiant, beautiful Jubilee.

Gandy is spoken for, Agatha, she told herself. *Besides, what would he want with someone like you when he has a stunning gem like her?* "Will you dance the cancan tonight?"

"Tonight's the night," Jube answered. "Second show, though. We're going to make them wait till eleven so they'll be good and anxious."

"Will you be there?" Pearl asked Agatha. Nobody found the question the least bit odd. The girls had grown used to seeing Agatha and her troops in the Gilded Cage at one time or another each night.

"I'll be there earlier," Agatha replied, squelching her disappointment. After all the work she'd done on the dresses, she wanted to see them flashing to the music.

But that night, true to their word, the girls saved the best for last, and Agatha bade good-night to the W.C.T.U. ladies on the boardwalk without seeing a solitary flash of red or a single high kick. It was a warm, sultry night for mid-June. The saloons had been stuffier than usual. No wind blew under the doors. The odor of dung from the hitching rails seemed to permeate everything. She took the shortcut through her store, made her last trip to the necessary, then mounted the stairs.

Her tiny apartment seemed stifling. She carried a hard wooden chair onto the landing and sat listening to the music from below, fanning herself with a lace handkerchief. From the opened back door of the Gilded Cage came a lively new song she'd never heard before. The cancan, most likely. Her fingertips kept rhythm against her thigh and she tried to imagine Pearl doing her notorious high kick with the red taffeta ruffles rustling and frothing about her.

A coyote howled in the distance.

Yes, I feel the same, she thought. *Howlingly lonely.*

She thought of Gandy and Willy—it was insanity to become embroiled in the lives of two such unlikely candidates, yet she feared it was too late to extricate them from her affections. She was doomed to heartache on two counts, for Collinson had made it clear Willy was his, and Jube had made it clear Gandy was hers.

She thought of Jube, pretty Jube, dancing the cancan downstairs right now with Ruby and Pearl. She pictured their legs flashing through the air, and it made her feel weighted and unwieldy. She wondered what it felt like to kick a man's hat from his head. She wondered what the cancan looked like and had a sudden idea that left her feeling nervous but determined.

She took her chair back inside, but instead of getting ready for bed, she found one of her voluminous outdated petticoats and laid it on the table. Into it she put the items she needed, then lay down on the bed fully clothed to wait.

It seemed to take forever for the noise below to stop and for the bar to close down. Then again forever before Agatha heard everybody from next door make their way to their rooms and retire for the night. She lay stiff and flat, as if any movement would betray her plans.

She allowed a full hour to pass after all was quiet before she cautiously sat up and slipped from her bed. In total darkness she found the bundle she'd prepared beforehand, plus a single candle in a holder and her sampler from the wall. She moved down the outside stairs barefoot, making no more noise than a shadow.

The dress shop was silent and dark. She felt her way into the workroom, lay her bundle on the table and lit the candle. She lifted it to check the shadowed corners of the room, breathing shallowly.

Don't be silly Agatha, it's only your own conscience you're scared of.

Turning her attention to the bundle, she felt like a burglar. She folded back the white petticoat to reveal a hammer, nail, brace, and bit. She picked up the brace and bit and Willy's stool and shuffled to the common wall between the millinery shop and the saloon. From the corner she measured off four paces, picturing the pine boards on the other side of the wall, the places where occasional knots had fallen out. She set the stool down and struggled up onto it. Guiltily, she glanced behind herself—but of course no one was there. Again it was only her conscience that seemed to be watching from the shadows on the far side of the room.

Determinedly, she braced the bit against the wall and slowly, slowly began boring. She stopped often and lifted the candle to check the depth of the hole. At last the far end of the drill slipped through. She closed her eyes and sagged, resting a palm against the wall. Her heart hammered crazily.

Please don't let there be any wood shavings on the saloon floor.

Agatha, you should be ashamed of yourself.

But I only want to watch the girls dance.

It's still eavesdropping.

It's a public place. If I were a man I could sit at a table and watch everything I'll see through this hole and nobody would think a thing of it.

But you're not a man. You're a lady, and this is certainly beneath your dignity. Who will it hurt?

How would you like it if somebody looked the other way through the hole?

Agatha shivered at the thought. Perhaps she wouldn't use it after all.

The wood shavings all seemed to come her way when she withdrew the drill bit. She pressed her face against the wall and peered into the hole. Solid black. The wainscot felt cool against her hot, flushed cheeks and again she experienced the queer sensation that those upstairs knew what she was doing.

She set the drill down and with three sharp raps drove the nail into the wall. Holding her breath, she paused, looking up at the ceiling, listening for the slightest movement. All remained silent. Releasing her breath, she hung the sampler over the hole and put Willy's stool where he'd left it. Then she carefully swept up the wood shavings and hid them beneath some fabric scraps in her wastebasket, blew out the candle, and returned to her apartment.

But she could not sleep for the remainder of the night. Clandestine activities at three A.M. did not set well with Agatha. Her nerves jittered and she felt as if she had a touch of dyspepsia. She heard a train rumble through town. And near dawn the distant coyotes yapped in chorus. She saw the sky lighten from black to indigo to chambray-blue. She heard the lamplighter move down the street, snuffing the lanterns, closing their doors, growing closer and closer, until he passed beneath her window and then faded off in the opposite direction. She heard the town cowherd gather the local cows from backyard sheds and herd them down the main street toward the prairie to spend the day. The dull clong of the lead cow's bell became fainter and fainter and fainter . . . and at last Agatha slept.

She was awakened by her first customer of the morning rattling the shop door downstairs. After that the day was disastrous. She snapped at poor Violet and became impatient with Willy's questions. A fight broke out in the Gilded Cage in the late forenoon, and when Jack Hogg threw the two hotheads out onto the boardwalk their momentum carried them in the direction of the hat shop and a flying elbow broke one of the small panes of her front window. When Gandy came to apologize and offer to pay for the damages, she treated him abominably and he stomped out angrily with a scowl on his face. The mute man, Marcus Delahunt, brought over a shirt with a simple torn seam, but the bobbin jammed on her sewing machine and the thread formed a bird's nest of knots on the underside of her stitching. Delahunt watched her slam things around in frustration, touched her calmingly on the shoulders, then sat down himself to find the problem: two coarse blue frayed yarns caught in the bobbin race. He mimed a question: Did she have any oil? She produced a tin can with a long, skinny spout and he squirted oil into twenty places, worked the flywheel back and forth, rose from the stool, and flourished a palm toward the machine as if introducing it to Agatha.

It ran as if new. In no time she had his shirt mended.

She looked up square into Marcus's face, feeling small for her churlish behavior, not only to him, but to everyone all day long. "Thank you, Marcus."

He nodded and smiled and mimed something she could not understand.

"I'm sorry. Say it again?"

He glanced around the shop searchingly, spotted the calendar hanging beside the back door, the oil can, and measured out seven days on the calendar.

"Every week. I should oil it once a week?"

He nodded, smiling, making a smooth-running driver of his elbow, illustrating how the machine would run if she'd follow his advice.

"I will, Marcus." She squeezed the backs of his hands. "And thank you."

He reached for his pocket, as if to extract money. She stopped his hands.

"No. It was nothing. Thank you again for fixing the machine."

He smiled, doffed his hat, and left.

After that Agatha's temper mellowed, but at suppertime, instead of eating, she napped, overslept, and was late joining the other W.C.T.U. members for their evening circuit.

By the time ten o'clock came she was in a state of intense anxiety.

Her conscience would not relent.

You were surly and short with everyone all day long, and you know why. It's because of that blame hole you drilled in the wall. If you can't live with it, patch it up!

But it drew her like an Aladdin's lamp.

In the dark of night she shuffled through the blackness of her familiar back room, then ran her fingers along the stamped wainscoting. Against her fingertips she felt the beat of the music sending tremors through the wall. The rhythm pulsed up faintly through her shoes. Carefully, she lifted the sampler away. Into her silent, lonely world streamed a tiny pinpoint of light. She leaned close and put her eye to the hole. There were Jubilee, Ruby, and Pearl doing the cancan.

Their magnificent skirts—shining black on the outside, ruffled red on the inside—flashed left and right. Their long legs created shots of black fishnet in triplicate. In ebony ankle-length high-heeled boots they pranced and strutted, wagged their calves and kicked. Their feet shot to the heavens. Their torsos leaned forward, then back, before they circled and shouted and tossed their heads until their red hair feathers trembled.

It was a bawdy dance, but Agatha looked beyond its lustiness to find in their leggy bodies the symmetry, grace, and agility she herself had not possessed since she was nine years old.

The music hushed and Jack Hogg was pressed into work as an announcer, calling out above the noisy crowd. Though Agatha couldn't make out the words, she watched everything. The girls circulated through the saloon, capturing the hands of six bright-faced, eager men whom they tugged along to the front of the bar. Ruby and Jube arranged the cowpokes in an evenly spaced line and flirtatiously squared the men's Stetsons on their heads. Jack produced a pair of cymbals and called out a verbal fanfare joined by that from the instruments.

Then up strutted Pearl, skirt caught up to her waist, her long legs supple and strong as she twirled like a top along the line of erectly postured men.

The cymbals crashed. Pearl's toe shot up in a swinging arc. The first hat tumbled to the floor.

She whirled, kicked, and another hat flew to the floor.

Down the line she went until six Stetsons lay strewn at the men's feet.

Agatha's heart pounded. Exhilaration made her double her fist and she punched the air along with the last two incredibly high kicks. Through the wall she heard the rumble of applause, men's sharp wolf whistles, and the stomping of feet.

Jubilee and Ruby joined Pearl for a final chorus, including a totally immodest pose in which the three of them spread their legs, flung their skirts up over their derrieres, and peered at the audience from between their knees. A last volley of breathtaking contortions, a final flourish of red ruffles, and the three of them fell to the floor with their legs split and their arms raised.

Agatha found herself as breathless as the dancers. She watched their bare chests heave beneath their brief silk bodices and saw beads of perspiration trickle down their temples. She felt as if she'd danced right along with them. Her body wilted against the wall. She slid down and slumped onto Willy's stool.

It was a wicked dance, suggestive and brazen. But spirited and filled with the zest of life. Agatha closed her eyes and tried to imagine kicking the hat off a man's head. It suddenly seemed a most desirable talent. Why, if she could do it— just once—she'd feel blessed. She rubbed her left hip and thigh, wondering what it felt like to be beautiful, and whole, and uninhibited . . . what it felt like to laugh and whoop and raise a ruckus in flashing red-and-black skirts.

She sighed and opened her eyes to darkness.

Agatha, you're getting dotty, watching cancan dancers through a hole in the wall.

But for a while, watching them, she had become vicariously young and resilient and happy and filled with a joie de vivre. For a while, watching them, she had done what she had never done before. For a while, she, too, had danced.

Chapter 10

The summer moved on. Across the prairie the gama and buffalo grass grew tinder-dry. At night, heat lightning flashed, bringing only empty promises. Around the perimeter of Proffitt, the townsmen burned a wide firebreak. The dust created by the incoming cattle infiltrated everything: shelter, clothing, even food. The only damp spot for miles around seemed to be at the base of the windmill in the center of main street, where a pump kept the public watering tank full for thirsty stock. The flies increased; with so much manure everywhere, they thrived. So did a colony of prairie dogs that decided to make their village in the middle of main street. Occasionally, a cow broke its leg stepping into one of their holes and had to be shot on the spot and butchered. If this happened between Tuesday and Thursday, it became cause for celebration: Friday was the regular butchering day at Huffman's Meat Market, and with temperatures in the high eighties, nobody risked buying meat after Monday.

A band of Oto Indians came and camped on the south edge of town. To the north the prairie became dotted by the wagons of immigrants waiting to file claims on government land. Every day the land agents rented a steady stream of rigs from the livery stables and rode out to show the unclaimed sections to the eager-eyed immigrants. Drummers came in on the train, selling everything from patent medicine to ladies' corsets.

Gandy and Agatha saw less of Willy. He ran barefoot with a gang of boys who hung around the depot selling cookies, hard-boiled eggs, and milk to the passengers while trains stopped for thirty minutes to take on water. Occasionally, he ate with Gandy, but Agatha suspected most of his nourishment came from filched cookies, milk, and hard-boiled eggs. Agatha's only consolation was that it wasn't really a badly balanced diet.

On the Fourth of July the "drys" had one parade. The "wets" had another.

On one street corner the editor of the *Wichita Tribune* spoke out in favor of ratification of the prohibition amendment introduced by Senator George F. Hamlin in February of '79 and signed by the governor the following March.

On another corner a liquor advocate bellowed, "The saloon is an indispensable fixture in a frontier town, and liquor itself proves as powerful an aid to communication as printer's ink!"

A white-ribboned temperance stalwart cried out, "The chains of intoxication are heavier than those which the sons of Africa have ever worn."

From the wet camp came: "Drinking symbolizes equality. In the bar, all men are equal."

As July progressed the issue of prohibition became hotter along with the weather. From the pulpit of Christ Presbyterian, Reverend Clarksdale called down blessings upon "all the noble actors upon the human platform of temperance."

The town assembly staged a late July debate between the temperance and liquor forces. Distinguished orator and Methodist-Quaker preacher Amanda Way came to town to speak for the drys. Miss Way proved so convincing that before the evening was over, the ladies of the Proffitt chapter of the W.C.T.U. had additional reason to celebrate: George Sowers signed the temperance pledge.

There was only one way he could possibly keep his promise, and that was to remove himself from temptation: George took to collecting buffalo bones. With seventy-five thousand of the creatures having been slaughtered in the fifteen years since the Civil War, the prairie now seemed like an immense boneyard waiting to be harvested. On the morning following the signing of the pledge, George was seen driving west with a swayback nag hitched to a weatherbeaten wagon. The next day he was seen heading east to sell his chalky pickings to the fertilizer and bone-china producers in Kansas City. Though the bone trade left George a far cry from the gold baron he'd once been, Evelyn seemed satisfied. For a while she mellowed.

During that summer the ranks of the W.C.T.U. local swelled. They outgrew Agatha's back room and began having their regular Monday evening meetings in the schoolhouse. Then in early August Annie MacIntosh showed up at a meeting with a black eye, a cut lip, and two cracked ribs. She fell into the arms of her "sisters" and sobbed out the truth: her husband, Jase, beat her whenever he hit the bottle.

That was the end of Evelyn Sowers's mellow period. That very evening she led the march on the Sugar Loaf Saloon, bearing Annie along, surrounded by a protective wall of frenzied, angry women. She marched up to Jase MacIntosh, made a powerful fist, and put every ounce of her two hundred fifteen pounds into a swing that caught Jase on the jaw and flipped him backward off his chair. She stood above him, planted one thick-heeled black shoe in the middle of his chest, and hissed, "That's for Annie, you rum-soaked ally of Satan! You're a gangrenous excretion poisoning the life of this community!" She pointed to Annie and bellowed to the customers at large, "See what this has done to a good wife who's done nothing to deserve it except raise his children, wash his clothes, and clean his house?" She glared down at Jase. "Well, no more. Annie will live with George and me now, and you'll never lay a hand on her again." On her way to the bar she planted her full weight on MacIntosh's chest, nearly breaking his ribs. "And as for you"—she confronted Mustard Smith with both fists on her beefy hips— "you swine! You destroyer of the home! You're the cause of the human wreckage you see before you day in and day out. It's a wonder you can look at yourself in the mirror every morning!"

Mustard Smith drew a Colt .45 and pressed the barrel to the end of Evelyn's nose. "Git out, bitch," he growled low in his throat.

Evelyn didn't bat an eye. She pressed forward until the gun barrel flattened her nose grotesquely. When she spoke no air came through her nostrils.

"Shoot me, go ahead, you slimy lizard. I ain't scared of you or any of the other saloon owners in this burg. Shoot me and you'll see a thousand others like me crawlin' over you like vermin over a dead skunk."

Smith calmly pulled the trigger.

The chamber was empty.

Though Evelyn stood foursquare to the fearsome saloon owner, her union members sent up a gasp.

"Next one'll be loaded," Smith warned.

"You can kill one W.C.T.U. member, or a dozen of us, but you can't kill the whole legislature, Smith." With a satisfied smile, Evelyn turned away, the tip of her nose imprinted with a tiny red doughnutlike circle. "Let's go, sisters. On to the next dispenser of strychnine!"

When Agatha returned to her apartment at ten o'clock that night, she was weak from emotion and fright. Evelyn might be fearless in the face of enemies such as Mustard Smith and Jase MacIntosh, but Agatha wasn't.

As she climbed the back stairs she felt each tense minute of the past three hours in her aching limbs. It required a supreme effort to drag herself up the stairs. There were times when she grew unutterably weary of fighting the temperance battle. Tonight was one of them. She approached her door eagerly and reached out with the key in her hand.

The door was ajar.

In the dark her toe struck something that rolled in a circle. She reached down for it. It was her doorknob.

A brief cry of fright escaped her throat. She pressed a hand to her hammering heart and felt the sickening clench of fear grab her chest. Hesitantly, she reached out and pushed the door wider. It struck something and halted. A man? She didn't think, only reacted: whacked the door back as hard as she could with the full force of her body! Instead of hurting anybody inside, she missed a step and fell, injuring herself. She lay on the floor with pain shooting up her hip, fear exploding everywhere inside her body. Waiting for somebody to kick her, hack her, kill her.

Nothing happened.

From downstairs came the sound of "Pop Goes the Weasel." From inside her chest came the pop of her own thudding heart. She pushed herself up and made her way to the table, her feet shuffling through objects of soft and hard texture. With trembling hands she struck a match and held it above her head.

God in heaven, what a mess!

Everything had been ransacked. Clothing, knickknacks, bedding, papers. Broken glass and upset chairs lay strewn like flotsam behind a tornado.

The match burned her fingers and she dropped it. With the next one she lit the lantern. But she remained rooted, too stunned to cry, too petrified to move. Within thirty seconds shock overpowered her body. Chattering teeth, jolting limbs, glassy eyes. When she moved, she did so without conscious thought, radiating toward help not because it was the wisest thing to do, but because she'd lost the power to reason another course.

Dan Loretto was calling out keno numbers at the table nearest the back door as she shuffled in. He glanced up and immediately leaped to his feet.

"Miss Downing, what's wrong?"

"Somebody br . . . broke into my ap . . . partment."

He put his arm around her shaking shoulders. "When?"

"I don't know."

"Are you all right?" It felt as if she'd rattle her bones loose, she shook so hard.

"I . . . I . . . yes . . . I was out . . . I . . . I didn't know what to do."

"Wait here. I'll get Scotty."

Gandy was playing poker near the front, facing the swinging doors. Dan slipped up behind him and whispered in his ear. "Miss Downing is here. Somebody broke into her apartment."

Gandy's cards hit the table before the last word left Dan's lips. "Deal me out."

His chair screeched back and he rose, ignoring the fact that he left money in the pot on the green baize tabletop. He took one look at Agatha, waiting near the rear hall, and swerved to the bar. Without breaking stride he ordered Jack Hogg, "Bring the shotgun and come with me." On his way past the piano, he commanded quietly, "Keep playin', Ivory . . . you, too, Marc. Keep the girls dancin'."

Agatha looked like a ghost, glassy-eyed and pasty.

"Agatha," he said, even before he reached her, "are you hurt?"

"No."

With an arm around her shoulders, he swept her along toward the back door, followed by Jack and Dan. "Is somebody up there?"

"Not any . . . m . . . more." Why wouldn't her teeth stop chattering?

"You sure?"

She nodded, breathless, struggling to keep up with his long-legged strides. "I'm sure. But everything's t . . . torn up."

He charged out the back door, tugging her along by the hand, agitated at holding back to accommodate her. He'd seen her walk up steps before; there wasn't that much time to waste.

"Hang on," he warned, then unceremoniously plucked her off her feet into his arms. "Boys, go on ahead." She hung onto Gandy's neck with both hands, while Dan and Jack took the stairs two at a time. They flattened themselves against the wall on either side of her door. The barrel of the shotgun went through first.

"We got a loaded gun out here!" shouted Jack. "If you're in there, you better be spread-eagled on your belly!"

Riding in Gandy's arms, Agatha told him, "I've been in . . . side. They're gone already."

"You've been inside! All alone?" He mumbled a curse and plunked her none too gently on the top step. "Now sit there and don't move!"

Gandy came up short in her doorway. *Lord o' mercy!* he thought. *Somebody's really done a job on this place.* Dan and Jack had already made their way inside and turned, looking back at him.

"It's a real mess."

"Jesus!" exclaimed Jack.

Gandy stepped over a broken teapot, leaned to pick up a music box with the cover twisted and one hinge broken. In the silence it began tinkling out a soft song.

"What do you suppose they were lookin' for?" Dan asked, turning toward the bedroom, where a torn pillow had caused feathers to scatter like fresh snow over everything.

Agatha spoke from the doorway. "My cash from the millinery shop, I imagine."

Gandy spun to face her. "I thought I told you to wait out there."

She hugged herself and raised her green eyes appealingly. "I'd feel safer in here with you."

The music box still tinkled:

> *Beautiful dreamer, wake unto me,*
> *Starlight and dewdrops are waiting for thee . . .*

She came toward him with her broken gait, staring at the delicate metal box in his long, dark hands. On its cover was painted a white-wigged lady with one wrist draped over the back of a garden bench, her skirts swagging delicately, while willows wept in the background.

"It was my mother's," she told him softly, taking it, listening a moment, then closing the cover. She glanced away. Tears came to her eyes for the first time. She pressed the music box just below her breasts, covered her lips with trembling fingers, and said softly, "Oh, dear."

Gandy stepped over the teapot again and took her in his arms with the music box pressed between them. "Easy, Agatha," he soothed. She seemed unaware of his presence. He righted an overturned chair and forced her to sit, then stood with both hands gripping her shoulders. "Agatha, listen to me." She raised tear-filled eyes. "Where do you keep your cash box?"

"Downstairs . . . in a desk drawer. I just lock it up at night. I don't bring it up here."

"Where's the key?"

"With the rest of . . ." She looked around vacantly, as if expecting them to appear out of thin air. "Oh, dear," she said again. Her eyes grew wide and frightened as she looked back up at Gandy. "I don't know . . . oh, dear . . . where could they be?"

"Did you have them tonight?"

"Yes. I . . . I remember coming to the top of the steps and reaching toward the door to unlock it, only the knob was lying at my feet."

Gandy shot a glance at Dan. "Check the landin'. Jack, you'd better go for the sheriff." When they were both gone, Gandy returned his attention to Agatha. In the harsh lantern light her face appeared milk-white. She held herself unnaturally stiff. He kneaded both her shoulders, rubbing his thumbs hard along her tense neck. "We'll find out who did this . . . don't you worry." And a minute later: "You doin' all right?"

She raised her translucent green eyes and nodded.

Dan came in with the keys. "I found 'em. Want me to check downstairs, Scotty?"

"Do that, would you, Dan?"

When he was gone, Scotty picked his way about the apartment, stepping over Agatha's private possessions. He felt a lonely desolation looking at her clothing, her papers, her bedding—all the things that nobody but she should have access to. It made him feel as if he himself were guilty in some small way for laying siege to her private life. He turned and came back to her. "I don't think they were after money."

Startled, she gaped at him. "But what else?"

"I don't know. Did you find any note? Any clue at all?"

"I went only as far as the table." They both glanced around but spotted nothing except the rubble left by the ransacker.

"Do you think it could be Collinson?" he asked.

"Collinson?" The idea terrified her more than the notion that robbery had been the motive.

Dan clumped up the stairs and burst through the doorway, breathless. "Nothin' down there. Everything's locked up tight." He handed the keys to Agatha, then dropped back a step. "What do you think, Scotty?"

"Hell, I don't know. But I *do* know she can't stay here tonight. We'll take her next door."

Agatha couldn't believe her ears. "Next door?"

"You can bunk in with Jube."

"With Jube?" But Jube slept with him.

"It's not safe in here with that doorknob broken off. And, besides, you're in no emotional state to be alone."

At that moment Sheriff Ben Cowdry stepped to the open door. A singularly dour man who wasted little time on civilities, he surveyed the scene with both hands hooked on his hipbones, eyes narrowed, missing little.

"Hogg told me what happened here." He picked his way inside, raising his boot heels high to step over the articles on the floor. His eyes moved carefully from one spot to the next. He glanced at Agatha. "You're all right, Miss Downing?"

"Yes."

"Her money's still downstairs, locked up in a desk drawer," interjected Loretto.

"Hmm ..." The sheriff stood with feet planted wide, swiveling slowly, his small black eyes searching from beneath the brim of his brown Stetson.

"Any ideas?"

"One," said Gandy. "Miz Downin' and I have taken Willy Collinson under our wing, and his old man doesn't like it much. He paid us each a visit, which I'm sure you heard about."

"The boot through the window?"

"That's right."

"What'd he say?"

Gandy related the story of what had transpired that day, while the sheriff surveyed the apartment, touching little, missing nothing. When he came to stand again before Agatha's chair, he minced no words. "It strikes me that you've got plenty of folks riled up around this town over that temperance group you started. Do you think it could be one of them?"

"I ... I don't know."

Gandy spoke up. "Once before one of them paid her a call." He swung toward her. "Have you still got the note, Agatha?"

"Yes, it's in my top bureau door." She rose and got it, then brought it back to the sheriff. Her fingers trembled as she handed it to him. "I found it tacked to my back door one night after a temperance meeting."

He took his time reading it, studying the paper long after he must have understood the brief warning it contained.

"Do you mind if I take this?" he asked at last.

"No, of course not."

He folded it, slipped it into his shirt pocket, and once more went on the prowl around the perimeter of the apartment, glancing closely at the mop boards, the furniture, the bedclothes, then checking behind her small heater stove. When he reached the door, he hooked it with a single finger and slowly swung it away from the wall.

"I think I've found it."

Agatha's pulse quickened. Gandy squeezed her shoulder. "What?" Gandy asked.

With a jerk of his head, Cowdry advised Jack to move out of the way. Jack stepped in off the threshold and the sheriff closed the door without uttering a word. Into the dun paint on its backside was scratched:

TEMPERUNCE BEWARE

The sheriff appeared deceptively cool. Agatha and Gandy both knew that beneath his unruffled exterior a shrewd mind clicked.

"Got any ideas?" he inquired.

It could have been anyone—Mustard Smith, Angus Reed ... any of the saloon owners of Proffitt. Or any of their libating regulars. The list was so long it dizzied Agatha to ponder it.

Gandy stood close beside her. He saw her eyebrows take on an expression of

dismay. She was shaken, he could tell. A woman alone with a dangerous enemy—
she had good reason to be frightened. He was surprised at the burst of protectiveness he felt toward her.

"Agatha?"

She raised her pale green eyes. They still expressed fright.

"It could be anybody," she admitted in a reedy, trembling voice.

Gandy turned to Cowdry. "She's right. It could be Mustard Smith, Diddier,
Reed, Dingo—any of them. About the only one it wouldn't be is Jesus Garcia. I
don't think he can write English."

"I'll have my deputy pass through the alley a time or two each night. Beyond
that, there's little I can do until I get some positive proof. So keep me informed
of any peculiar doings, if you will."

Agatha assured him she would, and he bade them good-night. When he was
gone, Gandy sent Jack and Dan downstairs with instructions to send Jubilee back
up. Then he turned to Agatha.

"Get whatever you'll need for the night. You're comin' with me."

"Please, Scott, I . . . I wouldn't feel right, intruding on Jubilee."

"I'm not leaving you here alone. Now do as I say."

"But there's nothing wrong with my bed. I have one pillow left and—"

"Very well. If you won't fetch your things, I will." He made a move toward her
chifforobe. "Are they in here?" He began opening a door.

"All right, if you insist. But if I think Jubilee has the slightest objection, I'm
coming straight back here."

He grinned and stepped aside to let her fetch her nightgown and dressing gown.
His eyes followed as she moved toward her bureau. But its top had been razed,
and she searched sadly through the mess on the floor for her hairbrush and picked
up a hairpin dish. The latter was broken. She fit the two pieces together and held
them for a moment. Her face was sad.

She looked up and their eyes met.

"I'm sorry, Gussie." She looked as if she might cry again, so he said, "Let's
go," and took her elbow. She stopped beside the lantern on the table and turned
to scan the room that she always kept so fastidiously neat.

"Who would do such a thing?"

"I don't know. But I don't want you worryin' about it tonight." He tugged at
her arm. "We'll come over and help you clean it in the mornin'. Now douse the
light."

She did, and darkness fell around them. They picked their way to the door,
which Gandy closed as best he could before opening his hall door and letting her
pass before him. "Jube's is the last on the left." The gilded cage was lowered and
the trapdoor was open halfway down the hall. Through the hatch a cone of light
lit the ceiling, bringing with it slow-moving curls of cigar smoke. The sound of
the piano and banjo drifted up clearly. Agatha glimpsed the bar below as she
shimmied past the opening. At Jube's door she waited. Gandy opened it and
stepped inside without any apparent compunction. He knew precisely where to
find the lantern. Agatha heard the match strike. Then his face burst into view
above the flaring wick. He replaced the chimney and came back to her.

"Jube'll be up in a minute. Will you be all right?"

"Yes."

"Well . . ." For the first time that night Agatha felt awkward with him. Neither
of them knew quite what to say. She had never been escorted to a bedroom door
before. He had never escorted a lady there and left her. "I'll shut down a little
early so the noise won't keep you awake."

"Oh, no . . . please. Not on my account."

"Jube will be up as soon as she finishes this song." He turned and disappeared before she could thank him.

Jube's room overlooked the street. The double front windows were open and the summer breeze billowed the white curtains inward like filled sails. Nothing was orderly, yet the disarray was soothing. Dancing costumes were draped over the edge of a brocaded dressing screen along with black net stockings and garters. The doors to the armoire were wide open. Inside hung Jube's many white dresses. Beside it a dressing table was strewn with hair feathers, creams, lotions, and face paint of various kinds. Agatha couldn't help smiling at the ashtray and a tin box of cigars, which looked so out of place among the otherwise feminine clutter. The bed was made of brass and had not been made up that morning.

The door opened and Jube bustled in. "Agatha, Scotty just told me! My goodness, you must be in a state of nerves. Imagine someone breaking into your place that way. But don't you worry about a thing. You'll be sleeping right here with me tonight." Her hug was swift and reassuring. Agatha suddenly found herself extremely happy to have Jube's talkative company. It would have been terribly unnerving to spend the night in the mess next door, listening to each creak of the building, wondering if it were a footstep in the dark.

"I really appreciate this, Jubilee."

"Oh, phooey! What're friends for?" She dropped to the chaise and began releasing her shoe buttons with a hook. "Besides, my feet hurt tonight. I was glad to get off a little early. Scotty says he'll kick the last customer out by midnight."

"I told him he didn't have to do that."

"I know, but you can't change Scotty's mind when it's made up. Might as well get ready for bed."

Agatha glanced around diffidently. Jube was already pulling the feathers from her hair, so Agatha followed suit with her hairpins. To Agatha's chagrin, Jubilee stood beside the chaise and stripped off her brief dancing costume, then glanced up to find Agatha standing uncertainly beside the bed.

"You can use the screen if you'd like."

While Agatha undressed she heard Jubilee humming "A Bird in a Gilded Cage," then lighting a cigar and clattering things around on her dressing table. The scent smoke drifted behind the screen and Agatha couldn't help smiling. She recalled the day she'd first seen Jubilee arriving on the wagon. If someone had told her then that she'd end up spending the night sharing Jubilee's room, she would have called him insane. Yet here she was.

She stepped from behind the screen dressed in a high-necked nightgown and wrapper trimmed in plain white eyelet.

And there was Jubilee. Standing before her dressing table mirror scratching her bare white belly and breasts, clad in nothing more than her pantaloons. The cigar was clamped between her teeth and she talked around it. "Damned corsets." She scratched harder, leaving red tracks in her pale skin. "Isn't it aggravating how they itch when you take 'em off? While you ladies are campaigning for women's rights, why don't you campaign to get rid of corsets forever." She held both plump breasts in her hands and pushed them high until the mole between them disappeared in her cleavage. "Imagine that." She chuckled, as if she were in the room alone. "Walking down the street in a dress without boned corsets. Wouldn't that be something now?"

She swung around and Agatha dropped her gaze. She had never seen a naked woman before, much less one who unabashedly displayed her breasts before another. Jube puffed on her cigar and crossed the room to the chaise. She leaned over, breasts hanging, and rifled through the accumulation of garments until she came up with her turquoise dressing gown. When she straightened to thread her arms through the sleeves, her rosy nipples seemed to flash like beacons in the room.

Nonplussed, Agatha didn't know where to look.

Jube didn't seem to notice. She carelessly looped her belt and exclaimed enthusiastically, "Why, Agatha, what marvelous hair you have! Could I brush it?"

"B . . . brush it?" No woman had brushed Agatha's hair since her mother died.

"I'd love to. And it'll relax you. Come on." Jube set her cigar in the ashtray, snatched a brush from her dressing table, and patted the seat of the low bench before it. "Sit down."

Agatha couldn't resist. She sat at Jubilee's dressing table and allowed herself to be pampered. It felt wonderful. At the first sensation of the bristles massaging against her scalp, shivers crept up the back of her neck and arms. Her eyes closed.

"Nobody's combed my hair since my mother was alive. And I was a child then."

"It's so nice and thick," she praised. "Mine is too fine and straight. I always wished I had heavy hair like this. And you're so lucky to have waves. I have to put mine in with the curling tongs."

"Isn't it funny?" Agatha opened her eyes. "I always wished mine were lighter and straighter and blonder."

Jube stroked the full length of the tresses, from crown to shoulder blade. "Do you think anybody's happy with what they got?"

Agatha thought it a curious question, coming from a beautiful woman like Jubilee. Their eyes met in the mirror.

"I don't know. But everybody makes wishes, I suppose."

"What would you wish for it you could have anything in the world?"

It had always seemed the most obvious thing in the world to Agatha. It stunned her to think Jubilee didn't find it obvious at all. Her blond head was tipped to one side as she idly wielded the brush.

"Two healthy hips and legs."

Jubilee's response was not what Agatha had expected—no big-eyed look of dismay at having overlooked the obvious. Instead she seemed dreamy as she continued shaping and reshaping Agatha's hair, observing, "Yes, I suppose so. But isn't it funny? I never think of you as lame."

Jube's words were such a surprise! Agatha had always been so sure everyone looked upon her with pity, yet somehow she truly believed Jube. There had never been anyone with whom she could share her intimate feelings, anyone who'd share theirs, so Agatha asked, "What would you wish for?"

Jube set the brush down, drew the hair tight and high to the crown of Agatha's head, and shaped it like a bird's nest, holding it up with her hands. Only then did her gaze lift to Agatha's again. Very softly she answered, "A mother to comb my hair sometimes. And a father who was married to her."

For a long moment the two women communicated with only their eyes. Then Agatha swung around. "Oh, Jubilee." She took both of Jube's hands and held them fondly. "Are we foolish, do you think, sitting here wishing for what we can never have?"

"I don't think so. What's the harm in wishing?"

"None, I suppose." Agatha blinked rapidly, then made a soft sound in her throat—not quite a laugh. "It just occurred to me that a year ago one of my wishes might have been for a friend. And now I believe I've found several where I least expected to. Jubilee, I . . ." Agatha's voice choked with emotion as she searched for the proper words to say how much she'd come to value the friendship of Jubilee, Scott, and the others. Her feelings for them had sneaked up on her unaware. Only now, when she needed them and they were there with helping hands extended, did she recognize the depth of their friendship. "I mean it when I say thank you for taking me in tonight. I'm so glad you're here. I was very upset about what happened in my apartment, but I feel so much better now."

Jube leaned down and pressed her cheek to Agatha's. "Good. Then why not jump into bed? It sounds like the rest are coming up now, so you should be able to get some sleep. Then Scotty says in the morning we'll all pitch in and clean up your place." Jube flicked the coverlet back, then patted the sheets with her palm. "Come on, now."

Agatha complied willingly. She plumped the pillow, then sat against it, raising her arms to do her last routine chore of the day.

"What are you doing now?"

"Braiding my hair."

"Why?"

"I always braid it at bedtime."

"But why?"

Agatha tried to think of a good reason but could come up with none. "My mother taught me that's what a lady does with her hair at night."

"But then you have to lie on the lumpy braid. That doesn't make much sense to me."

Agatha laughed. She'd never analyzed it before, but Jube was right.

"That's the last thing I'd do with my hair at night—twist it up in kinks."

"Well, what would you do, then?"

"Do? Why, nothing. Sleep with it free." She ran the brush through her own hair, hung her head back, and shook it. "It's heavenly."

"Very well . . ." Agatha began combing out the half-formed braid with her fingers. "I will."

Still brushing her hair, Jubilee wandered to the dressing table and clamped her cigar between her teeth, puffing while she brushed. "Does the cigar bother you?"

"Not at all." Agatha found it was true. She had come to enjoy the aroma immensely from being around Gandy.

"It relaxes me . . . you know?" Jube explained. "After I finish dancin' I'm all keyed up. Sometimes it's hard to get to sleep right away." Jube crooked the thin, black cigar in her finger, walked around the foot of the bed and sat down, leaning against the brass footrail with the ashtray on her lap, still brushing her white-blond hair.

Somebody knocked on the door. "Hello. It's us." Pearl and Ruby came in without waiting for permission. "We heard the bad news. Don't you worry now. It'll probably never happen again."

They came in turns to press their cheeks to Agatha's and wish her good-night.

"If Jube get t' snortin', y'all come in with me."

When they were gone, another knock sounded.

"Yes?" Jube called.

"It's Jack and Ivory."

"Well, come on in—everybody else has."

Agatha scarcely had time to draw the bedclothes to her neck before the two appeared.

"You calmed down now, Miss Downing?" Jack asked.

"Yes, thank you. Jube brushed my hair and it made me forget all my troubles."

"Jube's good with a brush, that's for sure," remarked Ivory.

Jube had brushed *Ivory's* hair? Before she had time to imagine such a sight, he said, "Well, g'night, Miz Downin'. See y'all in the mornin'."

"Good night, Ivory."

"'Night, then," Jack added.

"Good night, Jack."

Just before the door closed Jack stuck his head back in. "Here comes somebody else."

He disappeared and Marcus came to take his place, bearing a steaming cup. His smile told Agatha it was for her.

"Oh, Marcus, how thoughtful." She reached for the cup. "Mmm . . . tea. Thank you, Marcus. It's exactly what I need."

He beamed, then made motions as if stirring in sugar and raised his eyebrows questioningly.

"No, thank you. Without is fine." She sipped and nodded approvingly. "Perfect."

He folded his hands beneath one ear and closed his eyes, as if sleeping.

"Yes, I'll sleep wonderfully after this. Thank you again, Marcus."

At the door he waved. She waved back. The door closed behind him.

Agatha's heart felt full to bursting, warmed by so much more than the tea. She wondered if perhaps she had stated her wish too quickly; perhaps what she wanted more than anything else was to keep this feeling forever, this wondrous familial feeling.

In companionable silence, she sipped and Jubilee smoked.

After some time Agatha remarked, "How thoughtful of Marcus."

Jube's face softened. She stopped puffing and watched the smoke rise. "He's sweet, isn't he? He's always doing something kind for someone. Marcus is about the kindest man I've ever known. Whenever I'm sick he brings me tea with honey and brandy. And once he gave me a back rub. That was heavenly."

"It bothered me at first that he couldn't talk," Agatha confided, "but I soon found out he can get his point across better than most people with voices."

"That's for sure. Sometimes I wish . . ." A wistful expression crossed Jube's face. Then she exhaled a cloud of smoke and murmured, "Oh, nothing."

"Tell me . . . you wish what?"

"Oh . . ." She shrugged and admitted sheepishly, "that he wasn't so shy."

"Why, Jubilee!" Agatha's eyebrows rose. "Do you have . . . feelings for Marcus? I mean, special feelings?"

"I guess I do. But how is a girl supposed to know when the man never makes a move toward her?"

"You're asking me?" Agatha spread a hand on her chest and laughed.

"Well, you're a girl, too, aren't you?"

"Hardly. I'm thirty-five years old. I no longer qualify."

"But you know what I mean. Sometimes Marcus looks at me . . . well, you know. Different. And just when I think he's going to—"

A knock sounded.

"Everybody decent?" came Gandy's voice.

Jube whispered to Agatha, "We'll talk more later." Then she raised her voice. "More than decent. Come in."

The door swung in slowly and Gandy leaned against the frame with his necktie loose and his jacket slung from one finger over a shoulder. He spoke to Jube but looked at Agatha.

"So, you got her all settled in, I see."

"Sure did. She's feeling much better now."

"She looks better." He brought his shoulder away from the doorframe and ambled inside, dropping his jacket across Agatha's feet. "You looked like a ghost when you came downstairs lookin' for me, did you know that?" He reached for her empty cup. "Here, I'll take that." He set it aside, then sat at her hip with one hand braced on her far side. "But your color is back."

She tried to tug the bedcovers higher, but his weight pinned them low. Her cheeks grew rosy-bright above the pristine white of her high-necked nightgown. And her hair was glorious, flowing free in rich, thick waves, catching the lantern light and tossing it back in highlights nearly the color of burgundy wine. He took a moment to let his eyes wander over it appreciatively before returning his gaze to her translucent green eyes. They were captivating eyes, unlike any he'd seen before, as pale as seawater. They had begun bothering him in bed at night, keeping him awake, as if she were in the room watching him. An unexpected stirring brought warmth to his chest as their gazes remained locked and his hip pulled the blankets down from her breasts.

"M . . . Marcus brought me the tea," she stammered, flustered by his nearness, by the fact that she was clad only in a nightgown, and could feel his body warmth against her hip. "And Jubilee brushed my hair." She touched it uncertainly, almost apologetically. "And all the others came in to wish me good-night."

"So, will you sleep now?"

"Oh, I'm sure I will." She tried to smile, but succeeded only in dropping her lips open and revealing the fact that her breathing was none too steady. Her fingertips fluttered to the buttons at her throat. Immediately, he captured the hand and drew it down. Then they sat with their fingers linked. Her heart beat like that of a captured bird, but there were so many things she wanted to say. "I don't know what I would have done without all of you tonight," she whispered. "Thank you, Scott."

"There's no need for thanks." He gave in to impulse and circled her with both arms, pulling her lightly against his chest. He held her that way, motionlessly, for several long, long seconds. "We're your friends. That's what friends are for."

Her heart slammed hard against him. She didn't know where to put her hands except against his shoulder blades. She was conscious of Jubilee watching them from the foot of the bed, and of the intensified scent of cigar smoke from Scotty's skin and clothing, and of the fact that her unbound breasts were flattened against his hard chest—the first time they'd ever found such a resting place.

"Good night, Gussie," he whispered, then kissed the tip of her ear. "See you in the mornin'."

"Good night, Scott," she managed to say in a whisper. While her heart still pounded within her breast, he rose, caught up his jacket, and moved around the bed. Standing behind Jubilee, he leaned over the brass footboard. Jubilee lifted her face and smiled upside down at him.

"G'night, Jube," he said.

They kissed upside down.

"'Night, Scotty. I'll take good care of her for you."

He winked at Jube and grinned at Agatha. "Y'all do that."

Then he, too, was gone.

When the lantern was extinguished and the building became silent, Agatha lay beside the sleeping Jubilee for a long, long time, as wide awake as she'd ever been in her life. She was confused and more aware of her own body than she ever recalled being. Not just the parts that usually hurt, but the parts that didn't. From head to foot she felt tingly. Within her breast her heart continued thudding as if it had been powered by some mystical force after lying dormant all these years.

How could Scott have done such a thing—nonchalantly sat down beside her and taken her into his arms without a thought for propriety? And she in her nightie! And Jubilee right there!

But when her hands had rested upon his shoulder blades and her heart lay against his, her own thoughts of propriety had fled. How good it had felt to be pressed to his solid bulk, held for a minute. How hot her face had felt, and how insistent her own pulsebeat. How full and heavy her breasts, when crushed. She remembered the smooth feeling of his cotton shirtback stretched taut as he held her. And his jaw against her temple. And his collarbone against her mouth. And the smell—ah, the smell—so different from her own violet water and starch.

In the wake of remembrance came embarrassment.

But he belongs to Jubilee—doesn't he?

Confused, Agatha tossed and turned to lie on her other hip. The same refrain kept spinning through her mind over and over again.

How can Jubilee belong to Scott if she has feelings for Marcus?

When she finally slept, it was fitfully, and without an answer.

Chapter 11

In the morning they all pitched in as promised. Marcus installed a new doorknob, and when Willy showed up they put him to work collecting feathers and stuffing them into a pillowcase. Agatha noticed he was scratching again and made a mental note to talk to Scott about it.

She'd awakened uncertain how to act around Scott this morning, but he treated her as platonically as always.

By ten-thirty Willy grew weary of chasing down feathers, so Agatha sent him off to Halorhan's to see if she'd received any mail.

He returned with the latest issue of *The Temperance Banner* and an envelope bearing a Topeka postmark and Governor John P. St. John's official return address.

"Why, it's from the governor!" she exclaimed.

"Oooo, the guv'nuh!" repeated Ruby. "My, ain't we in tall cotton!" She rolled her eyes and shook her fingers as if they'd been singed.

Agatha carefully slit the envelope and removed a letter engraved with the state seal, while they all gathered around: Marcus, with a screwdriver in his hand; Scott, with his elbow propped on a broom handle; the girls, perched on the edge of Agatha's tiny kitchen set; Ivory and Jack peeking over her shoulder; Dan with Willy climbing up on his boots to get a better look.

Agatha's eyes quickly scanned the sheet.

"Well, what's it say?" demanded Ruby.

"It's an invitation."

"Well, read it 'fore we git gallstones from frettin'!"

Agatha's glance flashed to Scott. Then she turned away nervously. Her mouth felt suddenly dry. She cleared her throat and moistened her lips.

Dear Miss Downing,

As an active member in the movement to prohibit the sale of intoxicants in the state of Kansas, your name has been mentioned to me by State Representative Alexander Kish, Miss Amanda Way, and Miss Drusilla Wilson. As you know, when I became elected governor of Kansas, I made a promise to my constituents to do all within my power to banish not only the consumption of alcohol, but its sale as well within the boundaries of our fair state.

To this end I heartily support the recent legislation passed by both houses of the legislature, proposing ratification of a prohibition amendment to our state constitution.

If those of us who in the past have worked with zeal toward this noble cause will clasp hands once again for more aggressive work than ever before, this amendment can and will be ratified by the voters of Kansas.

By way of expressing my appreciation for your work and encouraging your further support for the prohibition movement, I extend this invitation to afternoon tea in the rose garden of the governor's mansion on September fifteenth at two o'clock P.M.

The letter was signed by Governor John P. St. John himself.

When Agatha finished reading, nobody said a word. Her face and neck felt uncomfortably warm. She stared at the letter, afraid to look up and meet their eyes in the strained silence. The stiff paper crackled as she folded it slowly and then slipped it back into the envelope.

"What's wrong?" Willy's voice seemed to boom in the room as he glanced up from one face to another.

Finally, Agatha raised her eyes. She tried to think of an answer, but the only one that came to mind was, "Nothing," and it wasn't true. Scott still leaned on the broom, frowning at her. Marcus worked a thumbnail over a blob of dry paint on the screwdriver handle. Jack scratched the back of his neck, avoiding her eyes, while Ivory's long black fingers played a silent song against his thigh. The girls sat dejectedly, studying the floor they'd just helped clean.

One could have heard a snake breathe in the room.

"What's wrong, huh?" Willy repeated, confused.

Dan came to the rescue. "Whaddaya say, buddy?" He dropped a hand to Willy's head. "Wanna come downstairs and help me sweep up the place?"

Willy obediently turned to leave, but he craned his neck to look back at the dismal group as he and Dan walked away. "Well, sure, but what's wrong with everybody?"

"Things you don't understand, pup."

When they were gone the silence hung long and heavy. Finally, Ruby asked Agatha, "You goin'?"

With an effort, Agatha raised her eyes to Ruby's—black and inscrutable. It struck Agatha that Ruby was the descendant of a long line of slaves, and slaves learned early how to hide their deeper emotions. Not a glimmer of emotion showed upon Ruby's face at the moment.

"I don't know," Agatha answered heavily.

Ruby looked away, leaned over to pick up a dustpan. "Well, bes' be gittin'. Everythin's done 'round here."

They drifted away one by one until only Scott remained.

Through the open window came the distant mooing of cattle, the sound of wagon wheels and hooves passing on the street below, a ringing game of horsehoes in progress outside next to the hotel. But within Agatha's apartment all was silent.

Scott dropped his elbow from the broom, took two punishing swipes at the floor, then gave up to stare at the toe of his boot. He shifted his weight to the opposite hip and looked across the room at Agatha.

"Well . . ." He drew in a deep breath, then blew it out.

A small fissure formed in her heart. "Scott," she appealed, "what should I do?"

"You're askin' me?" He laughed once, hard and harsh.

"Who else can I ask?"

His voice grew angry, exasperated. He pointed toward the street. "Try those crazy women you march into the saloons with!"

"They're not crazy! They have good cause."

"They're a bunch o' dissatisfied wives who're lookin' for a way t' get their men back home when all it'd take is a little cuddlin' to' keep 'em from leavin' in the first place!"

She couldn't believe his willful blindness. "Oh, Scott, do you really believe that?"

"My father never hung around a saloon in his life. That's because his wife knew how t' please him at home."

"Your father lived on a plantation. There were probably no saloons for miles around."

He bristled visibly. His eyes hardened to black marble. "And just how do you know so much?"

"The girls told me long ago. The point is, there *were* no saloons, so your father acted as provider and stayed at home, which is where more men should stay."

Scott snorted disgustedly. "You've been hangin' around those fanatics too long, Agatha. You're gettin' t' sound just like 'em."

"The truth hurts, doesn't it, Scott? Yet you know it as well as I do—alcohol is addictive and debilitating. It impoverishes entire families by destroying a man's ability to work, and it turns gentle men into brutes."

Scott's scowl deepened. "What's worse is you're beginnin' to believe all those generalizations." He pointed a finger at her nose. "And that's just what they are! Half o' you women are kneelin' at every swingin' door in town singin' your damned self-righteous songs and you don't even have cause."

"What about Annie MacIntosh, with two cracked ribs and a black eye? Does she have cause?"

"Annie's a different story. Not every man who has a glass o' whiskey is like MacIntosh."

"And what about Alvis Collinson, who gambles away shoe money and grocery money and lets his own son sleep in a bed crawling with lice?"

Scott's teeth clenched. His jaw took on a stubborn jut. "You really don't fight fair, do y'?"

"What do you think is fair? To take Willy to the Cowboys' Rest once every month or so to assuage your guilt?"

"My guilt!" Scott's face darkened, his fist tightened on the broom handle, and his head jutted forward. "I don't have any guilt! I'm runnin' a business down there, tryin' to keep eight people alive!"

"I know. And I appreciate what you're doing for all of them. But don't you ever have doubts about the men you serve all that liquor to? About the families who desperately need the money they lose at your gambling tables?"

His expression turned smug. "It doesn't keep me awake nights, no. If they couldn't get whiskey from me, they'd get it somewhere else. Ratify that amendment and the saloons'll close—sure enough—but Yancy Sales'll be sellin' the same stuff I'm sellin', only he'll call it bitters, and every lawmaker in the country'll be in there buyin' it and claimin' it's for *medicinal* purposes."

"That may be. But if prohibition straightens up even one father like Alvis Collinson, it will have been worth the fight."

"Then go, Agatha!" He flapped one hand toward the depot. "Go t' the governor's shindig! Have afternoon tea in his rose garden!" He stomped across the room and slammed the broom into her hands. "Only don't expect me t' come runnin' to' save you the next time a fed-up saloon owner ransacks your bedroom!"

He stormed to the door and slammed it so hard she cringed. The new knob worked perfectly; the door closed and stayed closed, but she stared at it through a film of tears. She lowered herself to a chair and dropped her forehead to her hands. Her heart ached and her chest hurt. The familial closeness of last night had been shattered by her own choice. Yet it wasn't her choice at all. She felt torn and confused and grieved that she was falling in love with the wrong man—heaven help her, with the whole wrong "family." But one did not always choose—she was learning—for whom one cared. Sometimes life made that choice. But it was what one did with that choice after it was made that brought happiness or grief.

The day hadn't gone Collinson's way. In the morning a wild fat-bellied cow had mashed his leg against the fence before he could draw it out of the way. In the afternoon the kid showed up with feathers stuck on his shirt and admitted he'd been hanging around that interfering hat builder again—helping her clean house, no less. And tonight his luck had soured.

Eight hands in a row he'd lost, while the duded-up cowpoke beside him beat the house on the last three pots. Even Doc, with his muddled-up brain, had managed to win two out of the last six.

Loretto had it in for him, just like the rest of them around the saloon, and Collinson had a feeling he was pulling face cards out of his sleeve somehow. *Smart-aleck punk!* Collinson thought. *Half a year ago he was still pissin' in his bed, an' now he sits gussied up in a fancy black jacket and string tie, double-dealin' them that he used t' call friends.*

Collinson counted his money. He had enough for two more hands, and if he didn't win he'd be busted flat. He downed another shot of whiskey and nervously backhanded his mouth, then turned to nudge Doc's elbow.

"'Ey, ya got a spare cigar, Doc?"

"Doc" Adkins was no doc at all, but a self-proclaimed veterinarian who traveled around the country "pulling" calves and "worming" hogs by mixing wood ashes and turpentine with their feed. His business hadn't been too lively since he'd fed tincture of opium to one of Sam Brewster's sows, putting her to sleep permanently instead of curing her enteritis.

Some said Doc Adkins made a habit of sampling his own tincture of opium, which accounted for the distant expression in his yellow eyes and his torpid reaction to life in general.

But he was likable, nevertheless, and a faithful friend to the wretch Collinson. Doc found a cigar now and handed it to his drinking buddy. Lighting it, the florid-faced Collinson studied the dealer.

Loretto shuffled so slickly the cards hardly bent. He arched them in the opposite direction and they fell into line as if by magic.

"So your ma ain't too happy 'bout you dealin' cards here," Collinson remarked.

"I'm twenty-one," Loretto responded flatly.

"He's twenty-one." Collinson nudged Doc's arm with his cigar hand. "Ya hear that, Doc? Got hisself a moustache an' everythin'." Collinson chuckled derisively and glanced at the blond swatch beneath Dan's handsome nose. "Looks like a patch of durum the grasshoppers found tasty, don't it?"

Dan had sensed undercurrents building all night. Collinson was spoiling for a fight, and Dan had his orders. He squared the deck and raised two fingers to Jack at the bar, who immediately poured two double shots of whiskey. Jack nodded to Scotty, who caught the signal and turned from his conversation with a cowpoke to bring over the shot glasses.

"You gentlemen mind if I sit in for a few hands?" he inquired with practiced indifference.

"Why, shore." The young Texan beside Collinson looked relieved as Gandy caught a nearby chair with a boot and slid it up to the table.

"Your drink, Dan." Scotty stretched to place one shot glass before the dealer, then set the other at his own elbow.

"What's the game?" he inquired, reaching into his ticket pocket and extracting some bills.

"Blackjack," replied Loretto. "Who's in?"

Collinson shoved his next-to-last dollar into the center of the table.

Loretto smacked the deck down on his left and Collinson watched to make sure all hands stayed on top of the table during the cut. The punk was good, but he'd make a slip sooner or later, and when he did, Collinson would be watching. Meanwhile, he could be as cool as a frog on a lily pad.

While the first two rounds were dealt, he struck up a seemingly idle conversation with the cowpoke. "What they call ya, boy?"

"Who, me?"

Collinson nodded and squinted through his own cigar smoke.

"Slip." The boy swallowed. "Slip McQuaid."

Collinson checked his down cards—a pair of aces. That was more like it. He split them up and noticed the dealer, too, showed an ace along with his down card. Goddamned punk had to get it from up his sleeve—nobody could be that lucky that often—but it riled Collinson that he wasn't able to catch him at it. He wiped his mouth with the edge of a rough finger and pushed his last dollar in to cover the double wager. Loretto hit him twice—a nine and a four.

Collinson's eyes grew beadier. He shifted his soggy cigar to the opposite side of his mouth, riveting his eyes on the dealer while he spoke to McQuaid. "Hope that ain't got nothin' to' do with how ya play cards. Wouldn't wanna play with nobody had the reputation for bein' slippery." Collinson gave a tight laugh, watching Loretto check his down card without clearing the green baize tabletop.

"N . . . no, sir. I slipped off a wet saddle when I was first startin' to ride and busted my collarbone. My pa give me that name."

"Cards?" Loretto inquired of McQuaid, ignoring Collinson's innuendo.

Gandy noted the slight shift of Dan's hips beneath the table as he crossed his left ankle over his right knee, bringing the concealed derringer within reach.

McQuaid took a card and pondered, while Collinson questioned him further. "What outfit ya ridin' with?"

Gandy refrained from interfering, though Collinson broke a cardinal rule: disturbing McQuaid during play.

"Rockin' J, outta Galveston."

"That where ya learned t' play cards?"

McQuaid tensed but tried not to let it show. "I played some in the bunkhouse with the boys . . . One more," he told Loretto, then cursed when he tallied twenty-two.

Gandy waved a palm over his resting cards as a signal that he'd stand pat. His eyes met Collinson's belligerent stare and he forced each muscle to relax. *Loosen up, Gandy, be ready.*

"And where'd you learn, Loretto? I'll take a hit—over here." He knuckled the down four. Loretto upturned a seven. Collinson's brown teeth worked over the soaked end of his cigar while he considered and sweat broke beneath his arms. "Again." The king put him over. His temperature went up a notch. The god-damned punk couldn't be that lucky! Collinson still held twenty in his other set, but he'd been hoping to rake in double on this hand. "Yessir, I recall when Danny, there, was no taller'n an angleworm. Used t' wear *short* sleeves then." Collinson squinted pointedly at Dan's knuckle-length black sleeves. "You 'memeber, don't ya, Doc?"

"I remember," Doc replied vaguely, though it took him some time to do his rec-ollecting. "Hit me, Danny."

Loretto deftly whipped a card his way.

Doc took a long time pondering.

"Hurry up!" Snapped Collinson. "Don't see what the hell can take ya so long."

Again Gandy held his temper. When Collinson blew, he'd blow hard. Mean-while, Doc finally decided.

"Again," he mumbled.

With a snap of his wrist, Dan sent another card to its mark.

Doc peered at it myopically, sighed, and folded. "I'm out."

Collinson's face turned blood-red. "That leaves me against the house, don't it? Now just how lucky would a man have t' be t' win around here?"

"You got something to say, Alvis, say it." Dan kept one hand on the table but dropped the other to his thigh.

"Let's see your cards, boy," Collinson challenged, biting hard on his cigar.

Dan took another hit with the hand that had never been out of sight, then showed three cards totaling a perfect twenty-one.

"You crooked sons-o'-bitches!" Collinson's face turned ugly as he produced a knife. "Don't tell me you ain't got no cards up your sleeves!"

Gandy rose slowly, each muscle tense, prepared, but his voice came out like slow honey. "I don't allow fightin' in here, Collinson, you know that. Now put the knife away."

Collinson crouched with the blade flashing in his hand. Doc and McQuaid backed off.

"Put it away before somebody gets hurt," Gandy warned.

Collinson swung toward him. "You, too! I'd be doin' this town a favor gettin' rid of both o' ya! Which one o' you wants it first?"

"Be sensible and drop it," Dan said, bringing the gun into sight. "I don't want to have to shoot you, Alvis. Dammit! I've known you all my life."

"I ain't droppin' nothin' but one o' you!"

"Four dollars is hardly worth gettin' shot over," Gandy cajoled. "Put it away and we'll have a round on the house." He began to signal Jack.

"This ain't just about four dollars, Gandy, an' you know it. It ain't enough you bastards take my money with them cards you keep up your sleeves; you turn my own flesh an' blood against me, too."

The place had gone silent. Every eye in the room watched warily.

"Go home, Alvis. You're drunk," Dan said reasonably, rising to his feet. "I told you, I don't want to have to shoot you."

"I ain't drunk. I'm broke is what I am, ya crooked—"

"Give it t' me." Gandy moved in, palm up. "We'll talk outside."

"Like hell we will, you fancy, no-good son-of-a-bitch, stealin' everythin' I got—"

Alvis drew back his arm and all hell broke loose at once. The knife plunged into Gandy's upper arm. The derringer exploded and Collinson fell face down across the round, green tabletop. Customers dove to the floor. The girls screamed. In the sudden silence Gandy grimaced and grabbed his right arm.

"Damn! He got you anyway." Dan jumped forward to help and Jubilee came running, wild-eyed. But Gandy shrugged them both off and dropped to a chair.

"Check Collinson," he said quickly.

Dan rolled him over and felt for a pulse. He raised doubtful eyes to Gandy, who sat slumped and panting, still clutching his limp arm.

Dan raised his voice. "Somebody run and get Doc Johnson!" Then he turned to Adkins, who seemed to have come out of his stupor for the first time in years. His face was chalky, his eyes round with fright.

"Doc, get over here," Dan called. "He can use your help."

"Me?"

"You're a veterinarian, aren't you? See what you can do to keep him alive till Doc Johnson gets here."

"B . . . but I—"

"He's your friend, Adkins!" Dan bellowed impatiently. "For God's sake, quit sniveling and act like a man!" Then he turned to Scotty and went down on one knee beside him. He glanced up dubiously at Jubilee, swallowed hard, and fixed his eyes on the knife protruding from Gandy's arm. "What do you want me to do?"

Gandy was fading in and out from the pain. He lifted his head and stared dazedly into Dan's face. Sweat stood out in beads on his own. "Get . . . it . . . out . . ." he whispered, clutching his right biceps, where blood already had turned his black sleeve shiny.

At that moment, Agatha reached the back door after hearing the shot. She entered, puffing, and paused near the keno table to survey the scene before her. She saw someone lying on a gambling table with blood soaking his plaid shirt, and Scott was lying slumped on a chair with a knife protruding from his arm.

"Dear God!" she whispered, hurrying toward him.

Marcus tried to stop her, his hands strong on her arms, his eyes begging her to heed his silent plea and do as he indicated.

She met them squarely, understanding afresh that he cared enough to be concerned about her welfare as well as Scott's. "Let me go," she ordered gently. "He helped me; now it's my turn."

Marcus reluctantly released her and she hurried forward, already issuing orders to Jack and Ivory and all the girls, who hovered undecidedly around Gandy's slumping form. "Lay him down before he falls off the chair."

Dan and Jack reacted without a pause. Gandy groaned and his forehead grew shiny as they laid him on the raw pine floor. Agatha struggled to her knees beside him. She released his tight tie and collar button and touched his throat lovingly. "Oh, Scott," she whispered, her face drawn with concern, "oh, my dear."

He managed a faint smile. "Gussie . . ." he whispered weakly, fluttering the fingers of his bloody hand.

She clasped them tightly and pressed the back of his hand between her breasts, heedless of the fact that her own hand grew bloody.

Just then Doc Johnson burst through the swinging doors with his nightshirt tucked into his trousers, his suspenders trailing beside his knees, and his red hair standing up on end.

"Step aside!" It took him less than thirty seconds before he pronounced, "Collinson's dead."

The name penetrated Agatha's mind. Kneeling beside Scott, she fired a glance at Dan. "Collinson?" she repeated, shocked. "He shot Collinson?"

"No, I did," Dan corrected.

She looked down at Scott's blanched face, the knife protruding from his flesh. "Then how—"

"He tried to get Alvis to give over the knife . . . Alvis gave it over, all right."

"Move aside!" ordered Doc Johnson impatiently. He knelt down, took one look at the knife, and advised. "Better get this man drunk. And the drunker the better."

Jack fetched a full bottle of Newton's whiskey. Scott lay on the floor blearily smiling up at the bartender. "Make sure you got the ninety proof, Jack." He attempted a crooked smile, but it looked ghostly on his pale face.

Sheriff Cowdry arrived and made a silent inspection of Collinson's body, while Jack fed Scott more whiskey than Agatha thought one man could consume and still remain conscious. Jubilee sat on the floor with Scott's head in her lap while his blood dried on Agatha's palm.

Cowdry questioned the customers, then cleared them out. The undertaker came to haul away Collinson's body and two tables were pushed together to create an emergency operating room. Marcus, Dan, Ivory, and Jack lifted Scott gently and laid him down. He was grinning loosely, his lips wet, his face flushed. He beckoned Marcus with one finger.

"Listen . . ." he whispered mushily. "This stuff's damned good, but don't tell Agatha I said so." He chuckled drunkenly and craned his head to see Ivory, behind him. "And if I kick the bucket, none o' your Baptist dirges at my funerull, boy. I want the cancan, ya unnerstan'?"

Jack put the bottle to his boss's lips again. "One more, Scotty. That should do it." The liquor trailed down Scott's cheek and made a dark spot on the green baize. His eyes blinked slowly once, twice—but still didn't close.

"Gussie?" he whispered, his eyes suddenly searching. "Where's—"

"I'm here, Scott." She moved quietly beside the table and found his good hand. He clutched her desperately.

"Willy . . . you've got t' tell Willy." His eyes were rimmed with red. Against his black brows and hair his skin appeared waxy, except for the unnatural tinge of red brought to his cheeks by the liquor. "I'm sorry . . . tell 'im I'm sorry."

She touched the limp hair clinging to his perspiring brow, brushed it back. "I promise."

Doc opened his black case and began threading a needle with a piece of horsehair. "Bring a fresh bottle of whiskey," he ordered. "And anybody that's queasy, get out."

Agatha stayed long enough to watch Doc pull the knife blade out of the bone in Scott's arm, and to see his body convulse and to hear him cry out in agony. Long enough to hear Doc order, "Give him another shot!" long enough for her stomach to twist and her eyes to fill and her throat to thicken. But when Doc dipped the needle and horsehair into the whiskey, she slipped out the swinging doors to gulp the clean night air and sob alone.

Chapter 12

Agatha had not been back to the Collinson house since that first time. But the smell was the same: a combination of must, coal oil, sour linens, and unwashed bodies. Even before she lit a lamp she knew she'd find no improvement in her surroundings.

Groping at the kitchen table, she found stick matches and a lantern. When it was lit she avoided glancing around; instead, she headed straight for Willy.

He looked so small curled up in a ball with his chin on his chest. He didn't rouse, even when she brought the light near and set it on the floor. He was probably used to somebody stumbling around in the kitchen and lighting lanterns in the middle of the night. She stood a long time gazing down at him, swallowing the clot of emotion in her throat, wondering what would become of him. So young, so unloved, so alone. Tears burned her eyes. She clasped her hands beneath her chin and said a silent prayer for him. And for herself and the task she must perform.

Gingerly, she perched on the edge of his bed, forcing herself not to think of the other living things that shared it with him.

"Willy?" She touched his temple, the skull behind his ear. "Willy, dear."

He snuggled deeper into the caseless pillow and she spoke his name again. His eyes opened halfway and immediately she saw they were puffed from crying. When he was fully awake he bolted up, his eyes wide open.

"Gussie! What're you doin' here? If Pa sees you we'll both be in trouble!"

There were welts on the side of his neck and a red slash across his ear. Dried blood marked his dirty pillow.

"Willy, what happened to you?"

"Gussie, you gotta go!" His eyes grew frantic. "Pa'll—"

"It's all right. He's still uptown. Did he do this to you?"

When she tried to touch his ear, he shrugged away and dropped his eyes to his lap. "Naw. I slipped when I was climbin' on the cattle pens an' banged it on a rail."

She knew he was lying. He refused to meet her eyes, and he scratched at the bedclothes with one dirty index finger. She covered his hand and forced his chin up until she was looking squarely into his eyes. A child's eyes, she thought, should not have pillows of puffed skin beneath them.

"He did, didn't he?" she insisted quietly.

His eyes began filling. His lips tightened and his chin trembled in her palm. As his throat worked to repress the tears, she was torn between two fervid emotions: love for this forlorn orphan, and a heathen gratitude that his father was dead and could never hurt Willy again.

"He found some feathers stuck in my shirt and ast me where I got 'em, and when I told him he thrashed me good with his razor strop an' said I couldn't go t' your place or Scotty's no more. So you better git outta here, Gussie, or he'll take the belt t' me again." Though Willy managed the admission without breaking down, he came close. So did Agatha.

She drew a deep breath, squared her shoulders, and squeezed his hands hard.

"Willy, dear, I have some bad news for you."

He studied her blankly for a moment, then declared, "I ain't takin' no more baths."

"No ... no, it's not that. Darling, your father died tonight."

Willy's eyes widened with bewilderment. "Pa?"

"Yes. He was shot about an hour ago in Scotty's saloon."

"Shot?"

She nodded, allowing him a moment to accept that.

"You mean he ain't comin' home?"

Willy's brown eyes stared straight into Agatha's.

"He's really dead?"

Her thumbs rubbed the backs of his thin hands. "You know what that means, don't you?"

His gaze dropped and settled on a spot in the shadows beyond her shoulder. "I had a cat once and it died. Pa kicked it an' it flew against the wall and made a funny sound, and then my friend Joey an' me, we buried it outside by the toilet."

Agatha's tears could be held at bay no longer. Willy looked up with dry brown eyes to find hers swimming.

"That what they're gonna do with my Pa?"

"He'll be buried, yes, but in the graveyard where your mother is."

"Oh."

"Y ... you're coming home with me tonight. Would you like that?"

"Yes." The word came out flat, expressionless.

"Willy, your father was probably a ... a good man ... deep inside. But he'd had a lot of sadness in his life, with your mother dying when she was so young."

Willy's mouth thinned and he stared at the tucks on Agatha's bodice. Muscle by muscle tightened until a look of defiance was etched across his entire face. "I don't care if he's dead," he said stubbornly. But his chin quivered. "I don't care!" His voice grew louder and he punched the mattress. "I don't even care if they bury him outside by the toilet! I don't care ... I don't care ... I d ... don't ..."

By the time he plunged into Agatha's arms he was sobbing. His small fists clutched her dress and his scraggly head burrowed against her bosom. She spread her hand on his small back as it heaved.

"Oh, Willy." She cried with him, rocking him, cradling his head and pulling him against her aching heart. "Willy, darling ..." She understood him absolutely. She empathized totally. She rested her cheek against his head as time spun backward and she, too, became a defiant waif, making the same declaration Willy had just made, meaning exactly the opposite.

"Willy, it'll be all right," she said soothingly.

But how? she thought. *How?*

She put him to sleep in a shakedown on her floor but awakened in the morning to find him curled on his side in her bed with his warm little buttocks up against her lame hip. Her first waking thought was that he was the only male with whom she'd ever slept; her next was that having him there even for so short a time was worth all the work she'd have to go through to delouse her bed.

She took him down to Paulie's for breakfast and watched him pack away enough pancakes to shingle a schoolhouse roof. Then she left him at the Cowboys' Rest with instructions that Kendall was to scrub him everywhere, merci-lessly, then quietly dispose of his wretched clothes. She'd be back for him in thirty minutes with clean ones.

She found the britches and shirt she'd made for him still folded neatly in her bureau drawer. Carrying them, she went next to Gandy's apartment and tapped quietly on the door. Expecting it to be answered by Jubilee, she was surprised when Ruby appeared instead.

"How is he?" Agatha whispered.

"Middlin'. But he mule-strong, that one. He be fine."

"I've come for Willy's boots."

"Lemme have a look-see."

While Agatha waited outside she gazed at the picture of the white plantation house on the wall opposite the apartment door. Below, it, a dresser held Scott's humidor and a hat block with his black Stetson. It was odd how the sight of a man's personal possessions, in his personal domain, made a woman feel as if she'd shared something intimate with him.

Ruby appeared with Willy's boots. "How's that li'l guy doin'?"

"At the moment, not so well. He's at the Cowboys' Rest getting a bath, and you know how he hates baths."

"He know about his pa?"

"Yes. I told him."

"How he take it?"

"He claimed he didn't care." Agatha met Ruby's dark eyes while her voice soft-ened. "But all the while he cried his little heart out."

"Reckon you had the hardest job of all, tellin' him."

"It wasn't an easy night for any of us, was it?" The last time Agatha had talked to Ruby, the black woman had turned away with detached stoicism after Agatha had read the invitation to the governor's tea. How it had hurt. Agatha reached out to her now. "Ruby, I'm sorry I—"

"Lawd, I know it, woman. Ain't this a crazy mixed-up world, though?"

Ruby didn't take her hand. But it wasn't necessary. Agatha felt as if she had just shrugged out of a heavy yoke. She squared her shoulders and changed the subject.

"Willy wants to see Scott. Do you think it would be all right if I brought him up later today?"

"Don't see why not. Should take the boss's mind offa that throbbin' arm."

That afternoon at four o'clock, when Agatha knocked again on Gandy's door, she held the hand of a boy whose hair was neatly parted on the side and combed into a crisp gold wave above his brow. Along with a fresh barbershop haircut, he wore brand-new underwear and socks from Halorhan's Mercantile, shiny brown leather boots with unknotted strings, homemade blue britches, and a blue-striped shirt.

Ivory answered this time. He looked down at Willy and threw back his hands in feigned surprise.

"Well, what's this?"

"I had t' have another bath," the boy complained, putting on a sour expression.

"*Another* one?" Ivory looked properly shocked. "Tsk-tsk."

"We come t' see Scotty."

Agatha jiggled his hand. "We *came* to see Scotty."

"That's what I said, din't I?"

Ivory chuckled, then smiled at Agatha. "How're you, Miz Agatha?"

"How is Mr. Gandy?"

"O'nry. Doesn't much like bein' laid low."

She whispered conspiratorially, "We'll tread lightly, then."

His eyes were closed when they walked in. He lay in a curled-maple bed of masculine proportions, propped up against a bale of pillows with his arm bound in gauze. His chest was bare, the skin and black hair appearing dark in contrast to the white bedding. Agatha took one look at his face and recognized how much pain he'd suffered since last night.

Willy stood somberly at her side.

"Hi, Scotty," he said.

Scott's eyes opened and he smiled. "Sprout," he said affectionately, holding out a palm.

"Gussie says I can't hug you or jump on your bed or nothin'."

"She does, huh?" Gandy's brown eyes lifted to Agatha as she stood holding the boy's hand. The two of them looked right together. It felt right having them here. He had the insane urge to fold back the blankets and invite them both to lie down beside him and talk about foolish things and laugh with him.

"Hello, Agatha," he said quietly.

"Hello, Scott. How are you feeling?"

Confused, he thought. "I've had better days, but Ruby says, long as it's throbbin', y' know it ain't dead."

Willy looked up entreatingly, his hand still resting obediently in hers. "Can I go stand by him? I promise I won't jiggle nothin'."

"Of course you can." She released his hand and smiled as he crossed the room with uncharacteristic solemnity and inched as close to the bed as he could without touching it. Scott's good arm hooked him around the waist and pulled him against the edge of the mattress.

"You're lookin' mighty spit-shined there, sprout. Smellin' pretty, too."

"Gussie made me take another bath." His tone took on additional disgust. *"Then* she made me go to the barbershop!"

"She's a nasty one, isn't she?" Scott teased, flashing Agatha a dimpled grin.

Willy stuck out his stomach and rubbed it. "Got my new britches an' shirt back, though, an' my boots, too. An' Gussie bought me new underwear!"

"She did, huh?" Scott's eyes wandered to Agatha while his large hand roamed the small of Willy's back. A lazy smile tipped up the corners of his mouth.

Agatha spoke up briskly. "Yes, she did." She brought a side chair and placed it next to the bed for herself. "But Willy's already paying it off by sweeping the floor in the workroom and running to fetch my mail. We've had a busy day." She sat down and folded her hands in her lap.

"Did you know my pa is dead?" Willy inquired without preamble.

Scott's hand stopped rubbing and rested along the boy's ribs. "Yes, Willy, I did."

Willy went on. "Was you there when he got shot?"

"Yes."

"Did ... did *you* shoot 'im?"

"No, son, I didn't."

"Then who did?"

Again Scott flashed a glance at Agatha. Dan, too, was Willy's friend. Not wanting to disillusion the boy, Gandy answered evasively, "A man he was playin' cards with."

"Oh." Willy thought a moment, stared at Scott's bandage, and asked, "Did you get shot, too?"

"No, I had a little accident with a knife, that's all."

"Pa's knife?"

Scott cleared his throat and elbowed himself up a little straighter. "Listen, Willy, I'm really sorry about your pa, but I've got things worked out so you won't have t' worry." He patted the bed next to him. "Come on up here and I'll tell you about it."

Willy clambered up and sat beside Scott, his brown eyes intent on the dark face lying against the white pillows.

"I had Marcus clean out a corner o' the back room downstairs. You know—the one where we keep the extra bottles and the brooms and things? He set up a little bed down there for you and that's where you'll sleep from now on. How does that sound?"

Willy's face lit up. "Really?!"

Agatha experienced a stab of regret even as her heart swelled with gratitude toward Scott. Reason told her she couldn't take Willy in to bunk beside her permanently, but she'd rather hoped his situation would remain unsettled for a few more nights. However, if there was one place Willy liked to be, it was with Scott. He'd be utterly happy in a shakedown, even in the back room.

"But in the mornings you'll have t' get up and help Dan pile all the chairs on top of the tables while he sweeps. And you'll have t' help Jack wash glasses. And when the cuspidors need cleaning, that'll be your job, too. Agreed?"

"Gee, Scotty, really?"

"Yessir."

In his excitement Willy forgot himself and fell forward to give Scott a fierce hug. Scott winced and drew in a sharp breath.

"Willy!" Agatha hurriedly pulled him back. His expression immediately turned remorseful.

"Oh ... I ... I forgot."

"You'd better get down," she said quietly. "Another day when Scott is feeling better you can sit with him."

He clambered down and turned toward the bed with guilt drooping his boyish face. "I din't mean to hurt you, Scotty."

Scott forced himself to forget the sharp stabs of pain in his arm. "It's all right, sprout. You just gave me a twinge, but it's practically gone already."

Forgiven, Willy brightened immediately. "Can I tell Charlie an' the other guys where I'm gonna live?" he asked excitedly, referring to the boys who sold food at the depot.

"Don't see why not."

"An' can I tell 'em about the job you give me?"

"*Gave* me," Agatha corrected.

"Gave me."

Gandy managed a chuckle, though his arm still hurt like the devil.

"Go ahead, tell 'em."

"But, Scotty?" With quicksilver speed Willy's face became somber again.

"What now?"

"I can't help Dan with the sweepin' tomorrow, 'cause my pa is gittin' buried an I gotta go to the fune-rull."

Scott felt a lump form quickly in his throat. The boy's ingenuousness went to his heart like a hunter's arrow. "Come here," he requested softly, "but take it easy this time." Ignoring the pain in his arm, Scott stretched toward the edge of the bed and extended his healthy arm in welcome. Willy came carefully, as ordered, and when Scott's strong dark hand pulled the small body against his wide chest, when his coarse, unshaven cheek rested against Willy's blond hair, his voice grew low and unsteady.

"The day after tomorrow'll be fine, sprout. And I'll ask the doc if I can get up tomorrow so I can be at the funeral, too. How's that?"

"But Gussie's gonna take me."

Scott shifted his gaze to Agatha, still sitting beside the bed, watching Willy with a telltale tear in her eye and a sympathetic droop to her lips. At that moment her pale, pale eyes moved to Scott's very dark ones.

Gandy spoke softly, his bearded jaw catching strands of Willy's fair hair. "Gussie is a very dear lady. But I think I should be there, too."

The graveside of Alvis Collinson brought more mourners than he probably deserved. His friend, Doc Adkins, was there, and so was a fat, raw-boned woman named Hattie Twitchum, who wept noisily throughout the ceremony. Alvis had spent a lot of time at Hattie's since the death of his wife, and rumor had it that the last two of her seven children bore a remarkable resemblance to Collinson. Mooney Straub stood beside her, sober for the first time in memorable history. And every employee from the Gilded Cage was present: Jack, Ivory, Marcus, Dan, Ruby, Pearl, Jubilee. Standing in a tight little cluster of their own were Scott and Agatha, holding the hands of Willy between them. They looked very much like a mother, father, and son. Willy wore a brand-new store-bought suit, which was a miniature of Gandy's—white shirt, with everything else black. Agatha stood in a high-necked black bengaline dress with generous leg-of-mutton sleeves that narrowed sharply at the elbows, and a black shepherdess hat pitched forward on her head, crowned by a crisp black veil tied into a wide bow above the back brim. Gandy had one arm in his jacket sleeve, while the other hung against his ribs in a white sling.

Willy didn't shed a tear throughout the entire ceremony. When Reverend Clarksdale tossed a handful of soil on top of the coffin and quoted, "ashes to ashes, dust to dust," Agatha glanced down at him, expecting him to crumble. But though he clung tenaciously to her gloved hand, and to Scott's much larger one, his eyes remained dry.

As the ceremony progressed, she glanced more often at Scott's uncharacteristic paleness. Even through his tanned skin, the pallidity was evident. When the service had begun, he held his hat in his right hand, reserving his good left hand for Willy. But after some time he placed it on his head, as if even the effort of holding it in the weakened hand grew tiring.

When the final prayer ended and the noisy weeping of Hattie Twitchum faded away, Agatha thanked Reverend Clarksdale, who inquired after Willy's welfare.

"For the time being, we'll look after him," he replied.

"We?"

"Mr. Gandy and I."

Reverend Clarksdale's protuberant green eyes seemed to pop out farther, but Agatha decided she owed him no explanations. Furthermore, she could tell Scott had overtaxed himself.

"Thank you again, Reverend Clarksdale. Now, if you'll excuse us, Mr. Gandy needs to sit down."

By the time they'd climbed aboard one of the waiting black carriages, Scott's color had faded to that of tallow. He leaned back into the corner of the seat. Ivory saw him droop and came to take the ribbons. Marcus saw, too, and nudged Jube and made motions among himself, her, the boy, and his own wagon, then pointed to the prairie and rocked as if taking off for a ride.

Jube pointed to herself. "Me, too?"

Marcus nodded and Jube smiled.

She went to tell Willy, "Marcus has a carriage all paid for for the whole day. Shame to take it back to the livery stable and not get his money's worth. What about the three of us taking it out for a little ride?"

Willy shrugged and glanced up first at Scott, then at Agatha.

"I'll bet we could find some jackrabbits or some prairie dogs," Jube cajoled.

They were a remarkable group, Agatha realized again. Scott needed rest. Willy needed diversion. Marcus and Jube stepped right in to provide both.

But Willy wasn't as enthusiastic as they'd hoped. Obviously, he was anxious to get settled into his new lodgings instead.

Agatha put her arm around Willy's shoulders. "Scott needs to go home and lie down," she explained. "His arm is bothering him. Wouldn't you like to go out with Marcus and Jube for a while?"

"I s'pose," he answered unenthusiastically.

Shading her eyes, Jube looked up at Willy. "You haven't had your dinner yet. Maybe we could all take a picnic."

The suggestion brought the first spark of interest to Willy's brown eyes.

"A picnic?"

"Why not?"

"With lemonade?"

"If Emma Paulie made some today. And if Marcus agrees." She turned a fetching smile on him.

"Hey, Marcus," Willy called, "can we take a picnic?"

Marcus agreed and within ten minutes the three of them were pulling up in front of Paulie's Restaurant in a rented Studebaker buggy with shining yellow wheels and a bouncy black leather seat.

Emma Paulie had not made lemonade that day. But she had baked chicken, fresh bread, and pumpkin pie. She packed these in a peach crate, and along with it they took a jug of sarsaparilla and Marcus's banjo.

They turned the wagon northward, crossing the Union Pacific Railroad tracks and setting off across the prairie, leaving behind cattle trails, the town, and the graveyard.

It was a clear day, and the sun was warm on their backs. Overhead lambs'-tail clouds dotted a true blue sky. Around them Kansas stretched as flat as a stove lid. The undulant grasses sang a sibilant song, while from overhead a circling hawk watched them pass.

A killdeer scuttled away from the wagon path, trailing its tuneless note, and Willy asked what it was. Jube said she didn't know, but later she pointed out a meadowlark perched on a hackberry bush.

Marcus was content, listening to Jube and Willy chatter, glancing now and then at the boy's blond head at his elbow, and Jube's white one on the far side of the seat. Today was one of the rare times when she hadn't worn white. Against her dress of somber indigo blue, her fairness shone like a star in the midnight sky. She was the most beautiful creature God had ever created. And she certainly had a way with Willy. The lad had totally forgotten his original hesitation about coming and gazed up at her now, enthralled, as she gestured at the clouds and sang robustly:

> *Oh, he flies through the air with the greatest of ease,*
> *This daring young man on the flying trapeze.*

> *His movements are graceful, all girls he does please*
> *And my love he has purloined away . . .*

"Sing it again, Jube!" Willy piped up when the song ended.

She looked down at him from beneath the brim of a high blue hat. "I will, but I'll need a little help."

"But I don't know it."

"It's easy . . ." She taught him the words.

Oh, once I was happy, but now I'm forlorn . . .

Soon the two of them were singing loudly, their voices ringing across the boundless prairie, Jube's rich and true, Willy's off-key, missing words here and there. When they ended the last chorus, he crinkled up his nose and asked, "What's purloined?"

"Stolen."

"Oh. Then how come we don't just sing *stolen* away?"

Jube considered a moment, then turned toward the driver. "I don't know. Marcus, do you know?"

Marcus didn't know, but he loved smiling into her almond-shaped eyes. And he loved the tilt of her small, pretty nose, and the mole on the crest of her cheek, and her heart-shaped mouth that seemed always to be smiling. He tried to remember a time when Jubilee had grown snappish or pouting, but he could recall none. Her temperament was as bright as the rest of her. Their gazes held for some moments across the top of Willy's head, their smiles half formed, their bodies rocking with the motion of the rig. He wondered if he'd ever been happier in his life. He felt alive and vibrant, and he gloried in each precious moment of her company.

The only thing that marred his bliss was the fact that he could not tell her how he felt. How beautiful she looked. How he revered her, would do anything for her, give her anything it was in his power to give.

They picnicked in the middle of the prairie amid the abundant blooms of late summer. Wild aster in pale violet, blazing stars in heliotrope, goldenrod in rich yellow. But no wild-flower could ever match the beauty of Jubilee.

While she spread the blanket and knelt to unpack their food, Marcus sat cross-legged in the grass and took up his banjo. Immediately, Willy pranced over and hugged his neck from behind.

"Play somethin' fast, Marcus!"

He chose "Little Brown Jug," and soon Willy took up skipping in a circle around Marcus, in rhythm with the tune. Jube stopped unpacking and looked up. She smiled and began clapping. Willy giggled and lifted his new brown boots higher with each step.

She got up and stood close to Marcus, tapping one foot on the grass, dipping her shoulders as she clapped, laughing at Willy's antics.

"Hey, Willy, how 'bout a dance?" she teased.

Without missing a beat, he shouted, "Don't know how!"

"Aw, anybody can dance!"

"Not me!"

"You can, too—come on!"

She caught his elbow with hers and swung him in a circle, singing:

> *My wife and I lived all alone*
> *In a little log hut we called out own.*
> *She loved gin and I loved run*

I tell you we had lots of fun.
Ha! ha! ha! you and me,
Little brown jug how I love thee
Ha! ha! ha! you and me,
Little brown jug how I love thee.

Verse after verse she sang, with Willy joining in the chorus. Marcus picked up the tempo and laughed silently while the two joined hands and circled crazily until their heads hung back and Jube's hat fell off.

What a sight they made, carefree and exuberant, whirling and singing, then tumbling to the ground breathless and laughing. Willy fell to all fours, Jubilee to her back with an arm flung above her head.

"Hoo! What a time! Willy, you're some dancer!"

Willy popped up, grinning, swiping his brow with one small hand. "Wait'll I tell Gussie we was dancin' and singin'!"

Jube propped up on one palm, alarmed, "Willy, don't you *dare*—unless you want to get Marcus and me in trouble! A temperance worker like Agatha would be real mad if she knew we'd taught you such a song! Promise you won't tell!"

The words of the song hadn't fazed Willy. He was affected more by his thirst. "I want a sassparilly!" he demanded.

Marcus tucked away his banjo in its case and they all ate the main part of their picnic while lounging in the thick yellow Indian grass, after which Willy sat nearby eating too much pie and drinking too much sarsaparilla.

Braced on one elbow, Marcus gnawed on a drumstick and studied Jube at leisure. She sat so near that her skirts brushed his crossed ankles. She had let her hat lie where it fell, and its pin had pulled a piece of hair loose. The sun glanced off the drooping white strand as if it were spun of cobwebs. He imagined removing the remaining hairpins and letting it tumble to her shoulders, combing it with his fingers, burying his nose in it, then kissing her.

Willy brought Marcus back down to earth. "Feel my belly." He came waddling on his knees. "It's hard as a rock."

Marcus felt. Jube felt. "You're gonna get sick," she warned.

"Uh-uh." Willy waggled his head in big, wide sweeps. "I never git sick."

"But you'd better not have any more pie for a while. Or any more sarsaparilla, either."

Willy flopped on the grass, puffing, belly up. "Whew!" His mouth gleamed with grease. His shirt had worked itself out of his pants, leaving an inch of bare stomach showing. The strings of his new boots had come untied. He didn't care one bit. After several minutes a loud burp rumbled from him. Jube laughed, Marcus smiled, and Willy giggled.

"You're supposed to say 'Excuse me,'" Jube reminded him.

"'Scuse me." Then he burped again, louder than before, adding an additional crack to the sound by forcing it. While everyone shook with laughter, Jubilee packed away the picnic articles.

The saloon would remain closed till evening. There was no rush to get back, so they sat listening to the buzz and hum of life around them.

"Are clouds soft?" Willy inquired after a while, staring at the fluffy white patches overhead.

"I don't know." Jubilee leaned back on both elbows to study them, too. "They sure look soft, don't they?"

"See that one?" Willy pointed. "Don't it look like a white hen with a dirty belly?"

"Mmmm . . ." She pondered it, letting her head hang back and the sun heat her face. A hairpin slipped and fell to the grass. "Maybe. Maybe like a teapot with a broken handle."

"Nuh-uh. It don't, neither."

She lifted her head and nudged him with a toe. "Well, it does to me."

He giggled and scrambled onto all fours above her, clowning, looking for more attention, more teasing. "Looks like a hen."

"It's a teapot."

"A hen."

"A teapot." She flattened his nose with the tip of one finger. "To me it's a teapot, Willy Collinson."

He plunked down across her torso and knocked her to her back, her head thumping Marcus's hip. Instead of moving away, she lay back against him.

"How come you're so pretty an' other ladies ain't?" Willy inquired with a silly twist to his lips and eyebrows.

"What a little flatterer you are. But how can I trust a boy who thinks a hen looks like a teapot?"

Willy flipped over to stare at the sky again. He ended up with his head on her stomach. The proper cradle for her head seemed Marcus's stomach, and he raised no objections when she settled more comfortably against it.

They lay in the thick prairie grass squinting at the clouds, fit upon each other like three notched logs. The breeze fluttered above them, tipping fronds of wild side oats into and out of their range of vision. A monarch butterfly fluttered past and perched upon a brown-eyed Susan, where it sat fanning its wings. Somewhere in the hidden turf a prairie chicken added its staccato cluck to the buzz of katydids. The warm earth reached up to them from below; the hot sun baked them from above. Content, they lazed.

Willy's fingers relaxed; his palms opened. In time he began snoring softly.

Marcus lay with his fingers locked behind his head, glorying in the weight of Jubilee's head on his stomach, feeling his heart thumping steadily through his shoulder blades into the virgin soil, which seemed to return the beat in kind.

He thought about reaching down, finding her throat with his fingertips . . . touching . . . just touching . . . nothing more.

But before he could, he felt her head move. He lifted his own and found her watching him, flawless and peaceful, her cheek turned against his belly. Then she did the most incredible thing: she reached up and touched *his* throat with her fingertips, a touch as tentative as the fanning of the monarch's wings.

She smiled gently.

And filled him with wonderment.

And sent his heart rumbling like summer thunder.

And raised a wild, reckless hope within him.

Jube, he thought. *Aw, Jube, the things I'd say to you if only I could. The things I'd do.* But she was Scotty's, wasn't she? Marcus imagined a man like Scotty would know everything there was to know about how to kiss and please a woman. How ever would Jube find his own kiss appealing after knowing a man like that?

So instead of kissing Jube, Marcus contented himself with a single consolation. He touched her hair lightly, felt for the first time the sun captured in its bounty and the silken texture against his fingers.

Jube. Though his lips moved, no sound came forth.

But she saw her name and said his in response. And though he could hear perfectly clearly anything she chose to say, she, too, only mouthed the word.

Marcus.

And for today—for this one golden day—it was enough.

Chapter 13

The day had been insufferably warm for September, hot and humid after two days of rain. Not a breath of wind stirred through the apartment. The sheets felt clammy and no matter how many times Gandy nudged Jube over, she sprawled back onto his half of the bed and edged her warm leg against him. His arm hurt and the damnable coyotes wouldn't shut up. Yip-yip-yip. They'd been at it for more than an hour now.

He nudged Jube's leg away again. Face down, arms up, she crooked the knee and pressed it against him again. Agitated, he shifted over.

Things weren't good between himself and Jube. Something had gone sour, but he wasn't sure what. She slept in his room less often, and when they made love he had the feeling she didn't always want to. They'd done so earlier in the night, but when he'd asked her if something was wrong, she'd answered, "It's just the heat, and I'm tired."

"You wanna forget it, Jube? We don't have to."

"No . . . no, it's all right," she'd answered too quickly. Then when he'd reached for her, she'd gone on: "I just wish sometime we could do it when it wasn't one o'clock in the morning and I wasn't all tired out from dancing."

But it never used to matter whether it was one o'clock in the morning or one o'clock in the afternoon. Jube was ready. And enthusiastic.

Lying beside her now, Scott wondered if it was something he'd done. Something he hadn't done. Maybe she wanted to get married, was waiting for him to bring it up. He turned to study her in the dark. Her naked limbs were as pale as the sheets upon which she lay. Even her white-blond hair was indistinguishable from the bedding. She had blended into his life just as completely as her paleness blended with the sheets. It was a comfortable relationship, but not one he wanted permanently. Marry Jube? No, he didn't think so. The thought of marriage should bring a wild rush of eagerness, as when he'd been engaged to Delia. But it didn't. There were two different kinds of love, and the one he felt for Jube simply was not the marrying kind.

She rolled over and jostled his arm, sending a twinge of pain to his shoulder.

He sat up and found his trousers in the dark, slipped them on, buttoned all but the top fly button, then padded into the sitting room. Fumbling for his humidor in the dark, he found a cigar and a match, then left the apartment.

When he opened the landing door, a movement in the opposite corner startled him.

"Gussie, is that you?"

Agatha straightened in her chair and drew her wrapper together at her throat. "Yes. I . . . I couldn't sleep, it was so hot."

He came out and quietly closed the door. "I couldn't either."

She wrapped one bare foot around the other and tried to hide them beneath her robe.

"You mind if I join you?" he asked.

"No, of course not. It's your landing, too." She noted that he, too, was barefoot, and shirtless. He crossed to the top of the stairs and stood with his legs spread wide, gazing out across the prairie. His skin appeared pale against the dark night sky. Overhead, stars twinkled, but the moon was too new to add much brightness.

"Damned coyotes. Once they start in, they don't know when t' stop."

"I've rather been enjoying them. They've been keeping me company."

He looked back over his shoulder. She sat on a hard kitchen chair, angled in the corner, holding her wrapper at the throat, the picture of threatened propriety. He compared her to Jube, sprawled naked in the bed he'd left. The comparison was almost laughable, yet he didn't feel like laughing. He felt troubled.

"You look so different with your hair down." More approachable. He wondered what she'd do if he walked over and touched it. Her hair had always attracted him, rich and lustrous as it was. She dropped her chin and reached up self-consciously, as if to hide the unrestrained mass.

"I . . . I should have braided it. I usually—" She bit off the words, realizing she'd been about to reveal a very personal bedtime habit, and that it was hardly a proper subject for conversation between a barefoot man and woman at three o'clock in the morning. "When I stayed with Jubilee she told me hair needs to relax sometimes, so I . . . well . . ."

"There's no need t' get nervous, Agatha. It was only an observation." To Agatha's relief he dropped the subject and asked, "Do you mind if I smoke?"

"No, not at all."

He ambled to the opposite side of the landing and sat on the railing with his back against the wall, one knee drawn up, the other foot on the floor. He struck the match on the narrow board beneath him, and when he cupped it, his face flared orange for a moment. He shook out the match, tossed it to the ground below, then took a deep drag.

"Isn't it funny?" she commented. "I used to despise the smell of cigar smoke, but I've grown to enjoy it."

He chuckled, leaned his head back. "Yes, that's how it is with most wicked things—they rather grow on you." As he puffed on the cheroot the scent drifted to her—acrid but pleasingly masculine. The coyotes yapped in the distance and she forgot to be self-conscious with him.

"Willy tells me you taught him to play five-card stud."

Scott laughed and expelled another cloud of smoke. "Why, that little tattletale."

"Scott, really . . ." Her tone become indulgently scolding. "Five-card stud. To a five-year-old?"

"Hey, the sprout is smart for a five-year-old."

"And I'm sure he grows smarter by the day, taking up with you."

"He'll do all right, as long as he's got you t' keep him on the straight and narrow after I fill his impressionable young mind with all my nasty habits."

She had never met a man who could make her forgive his transgressions quite as readily as Scott Gandy could. She was smiling as she asked, "And how can you explain the fact that he's been breaking into choruses of 'Little Brown Jug' lately?"

"Oh, no you don't." He pointed at her with the coal of his cigar. "You're not gonna pin that one on me. Ask Jube and Marcus about that."

"I will," she promised, a touch of humor in her voice.

"And while you're at it, ask the sprout *why* I taught him five-card stud."

"Why don't you save me some time and tell me yourself?"

She watched the coal of his cigar brighten while he considered the matter silently. Then at length he confessed, "We had a single game for high stakes and he lost."

"And?"

He grinned. "And he had t' accompany me t' the Cowboys' Rest for a bath."

Now it was Agatha's turn to laugh. The sound was soft and feminine, and he realized how few times he'd heard it. Southern women laughed like that—his mother had laughed like that, with a breathy sigh at the end, and so had Delia.

"You're resourceful, Scott Gandy, I'll say that for you."

He removed the cigar from his mouth, draped an elbow over a knee, and drawled, "Why, thank you, Miz Downin'."

"And entertaining enough that I find myself grateful Alvis Collinson didn't manage to do you in."

He studied the coal of his cigar in the dark, then rolled his head toward her. "I remember something about that night. I remember openin' my eyes and you were kneelin' beside me, touchin' my face." The only movement on the balcony was the rising coil of smoke. Even the coyotes had stilled, and in the silence her eyes met his and held. "You called me 'dear.' "

Her heart tripped in a light, quick cadence. She felt her cheeks grow warm but was unable to turn away from his scrutiny. Did he know what happened inside her each time she looked at him? Did he know what a picture he made—lounging on that railing, his head angled her way, his arm draped lazily over the knee, his bare feet and chest compelling in the starlight, the line of his black trousers accenting his masculine pose? If he knew, he'd probably run as fast as he could, back inside to Jubilee.

"I was very frightened, Scott."

"It just struck me as curious—you bein' a temperance worker and me bein' a saloon owner."

"Don't oversimplify. You're much more than a saloon owner to me, and I believe I'm much more than a temperance worker to you. By some odd twist of fate I think we've become friends."

"I do, too," he replied quietly. "So how can you go off to the governor's tea and talk about prohibition?"

She felt as if he'd tossed cold water in her face. She'd known the time would come when they'd have to talk about it further, but she hadn't been prepared for it tonight.

"Scott, you don't really think I want to shut down the Gilded Cage, do you? It would mean I'd lose you and Jubilee and Pearl and Ruby and Marcus and . . . well, all of you. And you've *all* become my friends—I thought you understood that. It's an unfortunate circumstance that if prohibition closes down the others, it'll close you down, too. Please understand."

He jumped off the rail and started pacing agitatedly. "I don't! Dammit! I don't." Close to her chair he stopped, gesturing with the cigar. "Why you? I mean, why not let those other women fight for the cause?" He waved an arm at the rest of the world. "At least they have reason—some of 'em. Their lives have been affected by liquor."

She wasn't sure she could make herself tell it; after all, she'd held it inside since she was nine years old. Not even when Annie MacIntosh had wailed out her pitiful story had Agatha been able to force herself to follow suit. The hurt was too immense. She had carried it too long, guarded it too closely to share it easily.

Within her nightgown and wrapper her skin suddenly felt clammy. Her heart thrust so hard within her breast that she heard it in her ears.

"Sit down, Scott. It's very difficult for me to talk to you when you're stomping back and forth as if you wish there were still public dunking stools for recalcitrant women."

He drew up short, glared at her for a moment, then plunked himself down on the top step, presenting his back.

"There are times, Scott Gandy, when you act the age of Willy." He snorted but said nothing. "May I come over there and sit, or will you bite my head off?"

"Come!" he snapped belligerently.

"Are you sure?"

He glared over his shoulder. "I said come," he repeated with strained patience. "What else do you want—an engraved invitation like the governor sends?"

She rose from her chair, tightened her belt, and fidgeted with her neckline. He sat hunkered on the step, his pique so evident she was reluctant to approach him. Her bare feet shuffled across the raw boards of the landing and she perched on the top step, as far away from him as she could get. Looking askance, she noted his resistant pose: facing the opposite direction, knees wide, shoulders curled, the cheroot clamped in his teeth.

She drew a shaky breath, then began.

"When I was a child we lived in Colorado. Never in one house for long because my father had gold fever. He'd stake a claim and work it until it proved worthless. Then we'd pull up roots and move to the next town, the next house, the next worthless claim. He was always so sure that he'd strike it rich. When a claim was new, he was happy—and sober. But as it continued showing no color, he'd begin drinking. Lightly at first, then more heavily as his disappointment grew. When he was sober, he wasn't really a bad man, only filled with self-delusions. But when he was drunk . . ." She shivered and hugged herself.

Gandy's shoulders uncurled and he half turned, captivated by her mellifluous voice and her straightforward gaze. "He was one of four boys whose father had died, leaving them equal shares in a farm in Missouri. My father chose to sell out his shares to his brothers and make his way west instead of spending his entire life being a 'redneck dirt grubber'—as he put it." She laughed softly, sadly. "He only gave up one kind of grubbing for another. But he thought it preferable grubbing for gold instead of for rutabagas. That, he said, was woman's work, and he'd leave it to my mother.

"She was a hard worker, my mother. Wherever we moved she tried to make it a home, and at first the houses weren't so bad—we still had some of the money from the division of the farm to live on. But when it was gone the houses got older . . . colder . . . just as he did. And he got meaner."

Scott was studying her directly as she absently overlapped the panels of her wrapper upon her knees and smoothed them repeatedly. She lifted her face and stared at the invisible horizon.

"He began taking out his failures on my mother." She linked her hands and fitted them tightly around her knees. "When I was nine we moved to Sedalia to a pitiful little house with a drafty bedroom upstairs for them, and none for me. I slept in the kitchen on a cot." A winsome smile tipped up her lips. "At the foot of my bed, Mother had a rocking chair, right in front of a window, with an ivy hanging above it . . ." Her words trailed off and she turned her head away from him. She touched a wooden bar on the railing, picked at it absently with her fingernail. "I used to love that ivy."

He sensed there was more she wanted to say about her mother, but at present she kept the focus of her story on her father.

"He came home one night, drunk, angry, disappointed. It seemed he'd had the choice between two towns when we'd moved the previous time, and—typical of my father—he'd picked the wrong one. His friend Dennis, who'd staked a claim near Oro City, had struck gold, while my father's mine proved worthless again.

"He was so drunk that night. Cursing, throwing things. Mother was angry, too, accusing him of drinking up what little money we had when the house wasn't fit for mice and bats, and hadn't even a bedroom for me. She threatened to leave him, as she always did, only this time she headed upstairs to begin packing. I remember lying on my cot, listening to them fighting up there. The thumps on the floor, his cursing. I heard a muffled scream and ran upstairs with the childish wish to protect Mother. I know it was silly of me, but when you're that age you don't reason, you only react. They were at the top of the stairs, fighting. I don't remember much about those exact moments, except that I grabbed my father's arm, thinking to stop him from striking her, and when he shook me off I went backward down the stairs."

Gandy's heart began pounding as if he himself were tumbling down with her. *Oh, God, not that way,* he thought. Not by the hand of her own father. His cheroot suddenly tasted foul and he cast it aside. He wanted to tell her to hush, to halt the memories that must be excruciating for her to dredge up. But she went on in the same calm voice.

"Something . . ."—she clutched her knees and swallowed—". . . something happened to my hip. After that I had a . . ."

She could bring herself to say everything but the most painful word of all. Staring at her profile, so outwardly composed, Scott felt afresh the self-recrimination of the day he'd pushed her down in the mud. And contempt for the man who'd crippled her. And a choking sense of inadequacy because he could do nothing to reverse it. But he could say the word for her.

"Your limp?" he asked in a quiet, understanding tone.

She nodded, unable to look him in the eye. "My limp." She gazed off into the distance. "But the irony of it is that I did what I set out to do. I stopped their fighting—forever. She left him after that and we ended up here, where she opened the millinery shop. I never saw him again, but news came back to us when he died. I was in my late teens then. I remember the day Mother told me he was dead—he'd fallen off a mule and rolled down a mountainside. They hadn't found his body till some weeks later."

Scott's mind recaptured flashes of his own youth juxtaposed against hers. Secure, loved, knowing all the time he was both. He'd spent little time considering what it was like to grow up in any other kind of environment, until he moved to Proffitt and came up against Willy. And now Agatha.

"I told my mother I didn't care at all that he was dead." Her voice became lighthearted, but she rocked unconsciously, giving away the deeper emotions she concealed. "Not at all." He saw her struggling with tears for the first time since she had begun to relate her story. "Just like Willy the night his father died. He shouted it to me again and again, and ended up punching the mattress and sobbing in my arms."

"Oh, Gussie . . . Gussie . . . come here." He slid across the step and took her into his arms, stopping her pitiful rocking. She let herself be taken against him while she began to cry. But her weeping was silent and motionless. She acquiesced to his embrace but took no part in it. Her very stillness tore at his heart like a rusty blade. "Gussie, I'm sorry," he whispered brokenly.

"I don't want you to feel sorry for me. I never wanted that."

He pulled her face into the curve of his neck and felt her tears run down his bare collarbone onto his chest. "I didn't mean it that way."

"Yes, you did. That's why I never told you before. I've never told anyone before. Not even the women in the W.C.T.U. But I couldn't let you go on getting angry at me for what I must do. Please, Scott, don't be angry with me anymore."

She was small and narrow-shouldered, and fit perfectly beneath his chin. He stroked her hair, drawing it back from her face. There had been times lately when he'd wondered what it would feel like in his fingers. He scarcely noticed now, in light of his concern for her. "I'm not really angry at you. Maybe I'm angry at myself because half o' me agrees with you. Every time I took at Willy I know you're right. And I have t' force myself t' forget that there are thousands of other Willys in the world with nobody to help them out of a situation they don't deserve."

She closed her eyes and rested against him, absorbing the comfort he offered. His bare skin had grown sleek with her tears. He was hard and warm and smelled of the cheroots he smoked. And when his hand cradled her head and tucked her firmly against him, she went gratefully, her cheek pressed upon his chest with its coarse mat of hair.

He represented security, strength, and protection, and she'd had too little of all three in her life. She slipped her arms around his warm sides, spread her hands upon his naked back, and held fast.

And there in his arms, she began healing.

His fingers moved idly in her hair. His sure, steady heartbeat thrummed against her temple. The night shielded them. She wanted to stay that way forever.

But in time propriety interfered. She became aware that he was bare-chested and she wore only her nightclothes. She backed away to look up at him.

"Then you understand why I must go to Topeka?"

"Yes."

Meeting his direct gaze after crying in his arms became disconcerting. She groped for her lost sense of humor and told him, "I hate it when we fight."

She was rewarded with a small, sympathetic grin. "So did I."

She chuckled self-consciously and swiped her lower eyelids with the backs of her hands. "And I've never in my life dribbled all over a man's chest. I certainly don't intend to make a habit of it."

"Was I complainin'?"

"No, but it's not decent. You in practically nothing, and me in my night things. I've left you in a mess." She caught the edge of one sleeve, stretched it taut, and began drying his chest with it.

He caught her wrist. "Gussie, stop fussin' and listen."

His eyes were only dark shadows as she looked up into them. Her pulse suddenly drummed in her throat. She sensed that he'd become as discomposed as she by their brief intimacy, and the realization spurred her sexual awareness of him. He caught both her hands and held them loosely, dropping his gaze, then lifting it in a prolonged study of her shadowed features.

"Thank you for tellin' me. It means a lot t' me t' know I was the first one you trusted." Her chin dropped. She'd told him all that without blushing. Now, when there was nothing to be ashamed of, she felt herself get hot all over. He rubbed her knuckles with both thumbs. "And what I said before is true. When I say I'm sorry, I don't mean I go around feelin' sorry for you because you limp. You don't feel sorry for yourself, so others don't either. That's one of the things I admire about you. Long ago I stopped thinkin' of you as anything except Agatha, my spunky neighbor who's too much of a thorn in my side to be considered a cripple."

She couldn't help smiling sheepishly, still looking down at their joined hands.

"I don't mean to be a thorn in anybody's side, least of all yours." She withdrew her hands carefully before asking, "So what do you intend to do with me?"

He leaned against the far rail and studied her from beneath lowered brows for some time before asking, "What are the chances this law'll pass?"

She was relieved that once again, though still members of opposing factions, they could discuss the issue without rancor.

"The latest issue of *The Temperance Banner* gives it about a forty percent chance," she answered honestly. "But that margin is narrowing all the time." He drew in a deep breath and ran a hand through his hair, then sat gazing distractedly at a point somewhere beyond the rooftop of the necessary. "What would you do if it passed?"

"Do?" He rested both elbows on his knees and swung his face toward her. "I'd pack up and leave Kansas. What else *could* I do?"

The thought sent a bolt of dread through her. "Where would you go?"

"I don't know."

A coyote howled. The lonely sound seemed a proper accompaniment to their morose speculations.

"What about Waverley?"

"Waverley?" He bristled. "What do you know about Waverley?"

"Please, Scott, don't get belligerent again. I'm your friend. Can't you talk to me about it?"

She saw him struggle with some inner turmoil before finally admitting, "I don't know where t' begin."

"Let me help you," she suggested softly. "You lived there before the war with a wife and a daughter."

He scowled sharply at Agatha and she sensed his surprise that she knew this much. He remained silent for so long that she thought he would refuse to talk about it. After some time he shifted on the hard step, and pressed his thumb knuckles against his chin. She waited, listening to the coyotes, supposing that whatever he held inside was as difficult for him to reveal as her own story had been. At last he let out a deep sigh, dropped his hands between his knees, and said, "My wife's name was Delia. She was . . ." He paused, stared at the night sky, then finished emotionally, "all I ever wanted."

Agatha simply waited. In time he went on.

"Her daddy was a cotton buyer who came to our plantation periodically and often brought Delia and her mama along. So I'd known her nearly all my life. They sometimes stayed the night, and we had the run o' the place. Delia and I. And how we ran. We explored the river, and the gin, and the hen coops, played with the black children and picked wild scuppernongs, and dipped our hands in the melted wax in the dairy on cheese day and stole molasses cakes from the kitchen out back and ran wild as deer." His recollections had brought a soft grin to his face. "Her daddy stopped all that, though, 'long about the time she started tuckin' up her pigtails and my voice started changin'. Seemed like from that time on I knew I wanted t' marry Delia. Our mamas and daddies knew, too, and favored the idea.

"We were married in Waverley—she'd always loved it—in what my mama called the 'weddin' alcove.' Mama insisted on havin' it put in when the parlor was built—it was an arched alcove outlined with decorative plaster leaves where

mama declared all her children would be baptized and married before she herself
was laid out there in her casket."

He stopped and Agatha inquired, "How many of her children *were* baptized
there?"

"Three of us. All boys. But two of us never made it t' the alcove in our caskets."

"You had two brothers?"

"Rafael and Nash. They both died in the same battle durin' the war. They're
buried near Vicksburg instead of at Waverley beside the others." He mulled about
it for a moment, then seemed to pull himself to a happier train of thought.

"So after we were married Delia and I lived at Waverley. Ah, it was somethin'
then. I wish you could've seen it." He leaned back and gazed at the stars.

"I've seen the painting in your sitting room. It's beautiful."

"It was more than beautiful. It was . . ."—he paused, searching for words—
". . . majestic." He sat forward eagerly. "In its prime, Waverley supported twelve
hundred people and had every facility t' make it self-sufficient. We had an ice
house, a cotton gin, a tannery, a sawmill, a gristmill, a brick kiln, orchards, vineyards, stables, gardens, kennels, warehouses, a boathouse, and even a ferry."

"All that?" Agatha was awed.

"All that. And the house . . . everybody called it *the mansion* . . ." Again she
saw a ghost of a smile on his lips. "The paintin' doesn't do it justice. It always
reminded me of a proud eagle spreadin' its wings over its young ones with its
head straight up and watchful."

"Tell me," she encouraged. "Tell me everything."

"Well, you saw the picture."

"Not very closely."

"Next time you're in my apartment, take a closer look. Waverley's unique.
There's not another house like it in all the South. The eagle's wings, those are the
actual wings o' the house, the livin' quarters stretchin' out on either side o' the
center rotunda—or, as Mama liked t' call it, the cupola. And the eagle's head,
that's the rotunda itself—a massive entry shaped like an octagon with twin curved
stairwells that climb sixty-five feet to an observatory with windows on all eight
sides. I can still see my daddy strollin' the catwalk around those windows, every
mornin', surveyin' his holdin's. You know, Gussie, the cotton fields stretched as
far as the eye could see in all directions. We had three thousand acres in cotton,
food, and grain then. Fifteen acres of formal gardens, too."

In her imagination she could see Waverley, just as he described, proud and pillared and reigning above the lush green countryside.

"It was always cool in the house," Scott continued. "Every mornin' durin' the
hot weather, Leatrice—she was the bossy old despot who ran the place—would
climb those stairs and open all those windows, and the draft like t' tug the hair
out o' your skull. And if that wasn't cool enough, off the end o' the drive there
was a swimmin' pool made of brick and marble, with a roof t' keep the sun off
the ladies."

"The one you told Willy about the first night we met him."

"The only one in all of northern Miz'sippi. Delia loved it. She and I used t' go
down there and cool off at night sometime's when—" He suddenly halted and
cleared his throat, then sat up straighter.

"I've never been swimming. What's it like?"

"Never been swimmin'!"

She shook her head. "Or dancing or riding a horse."

"Would you like to?"

She looked away, embarrassed. But she couldn't lie. "Most of all I'd like to dance. Just once." She faced him again, her voice brighter, and enthusiastic. "But swimming sounds grand, too."

"I've have t' take you sometime. You'll love it. It's the freest feelin' in the world."

"I'd like that," she said softly. Then more loudly, she added, "But I interrupted you—you were telling me about Waverley."

"Waverley—oh, yes." He went on eagerly. "In the winter, when the fireplaces were lit, there was no place warmer. And we had gaslights, too, fueled by our own gasworks and piped into the house."

"Your own gasworks?"

"It burned pine lighter—that's what made the resin gas."

She'd never heard of such a thing and had difficulty imagining the luxury of gaslights that would flare at the touch of a finger.

"Oh, Scott, it sounds wonderful."

"There's a chandelier in the middle o' the entry hall that hangs all the way from the cupola roof above." He looked up at the stars as if they supported the chandelier. "And over seven hundred walnut spindles outlinin' the stairway and cantilevered balconies. And Venetian glass sidelights around the front door, and plaster moldings on the ceilings, and brass cornices on all the windows and mirrors in the ballroom."

"It has a ballroom?"

"The main floor o' the rotunda. It's made o' the heart o' virgin pine, and the twin stairs come sweepin' down on either side. Delia and I had our weddin' ball there, and I remember many others when I was growin' up."

"Tell me about Delia."

He pondered for several seconds, then began: "Delia was like Jube. Always happy, never askin' for more than what she had. I never quite understood what it was about me that made her so happy, but I was grateful that both of us felt the same way about each other. She had blond hair and hazel eyes and this teasin' lilt of a laugh that could lift a man's spirits faster than a chameleon slitherin' up a post. And when Justine was born, she looked exactly like Delia. Except she had my black hair." He swallowed and cleared his throat. "Justine was baptized in the weddin' alcove, just like my mama planned. That was right about the time Lincoln was sworn into office. I saw her and Delia one time after I joined the Columbus regiment and marched north. I made it back for my daddy's funeral in '64. But by the time I made it back for good, they were all gone."

Now it was Agatha's turn to console. She laid her hand on his arm. "Ruby told me about them shortly after she came here. You don't know how they died?"

"No. Robbers, probably. The South was so poor then, people were desperate. Soldiers returned to find poverty where there'd been wealth before. Who knows? It could've been one of our own soldiers. They said it appeared as if Delia's wagon had been waylaid on the road." He chuckled bitterly. "Whoever it was didn't get much, 'cause Delia was no richer than anybody else by that time." He swallowed hard. "But why they had t' kill the baby, too . . . What kinda person would do a thing like that?"

Agatha could only rub his arm while his grief brought bitter words he'd been holding in so long.

"Do you know what it's like to go back and find everything changed? The people you loved, gone. The house empty, but everything inside lookin' just like it did before, as if it were waitin' for ghosts t' come and inhabit it again. Everything else was there, too—the gin, the tannery, the gasworks, everything. But the slaves had scattered, some o' them killed in the war, maybe on the same battlefield like my brothers. Others were gone to who knows where. A handful stayed, hoeing collard greens and livin' in the old quarters."

She searched for consoling words, but the picture he'd drawn was too bleak to be erased by mere words, so she remained silent and merely stroked his arm.

"I stayed there three nights, but that's all I could take. You know what, Gussie?" He shook his head slowly. "I couldn't sleep in the bedroom Delia and I shared. I just couldn't make myself do it. So I slept in Justine's room, and I thought I heard her voice callin' for help durin' the night. Now how can that be when she's been dead all these years?"

Her heart ached for him and she wished once again for the right words to help him. "Perhaps it was your own voice you heard, Scott."

He shook his head as if to rid it of the memory. He drove his fingers through his hair and clasped his skull. "I couldn't stand it there. I had t' get out."

"And you haven't been back since?"

Again he shook his head.

"Do you think you should go?"

He stared straight ahead and after a long silence answered, "I don't know."

"Your wounds were fresh then. It might be easier now."

"I don't think it'll ever be easier."

"Perhaps not. But going back might lay your ghosts to rest. And Waverley is your heritage."

He gave a single harsh laugh. "Some heritage. With vines growin' up over the front porch and the fields lyin' empty. I'd rather not see it that way."

"Isn't anybody there you used to know?"

"Ruby says old Leatrice is still there."

"But the house—you said it's just as you left it. Vines can be trimmed away and fields can be replanted. Isn't there some way you could make it thrive again?"

"It'd take twelve hundred people t' make Waverley what it was."

Twelve hundred, she thought glumly. Yes, she saw his point.

They sat silent for a long time, going over all they'd shared tonight. The coyotes had given up their night chorus as dawn drew near. In the cattle pens east of town the first restless shifting and lowing could be heard. The big dipper began dimming overhead.

"Isn't it funny?" Agatha mused. "When I first saw you, I looked at you and thought: There's a man with no troubles, no conscience, no morals. You came to Proffitt wearing tailored clothes, with enough money to buy this building and open up a business that was destined to make you a rich man quickly, and I looked at your perfect, healthy body and your handsome face and thought how you had the world by the tail. And I hated you for it."

Her summary brought him back from the past. He turned to study her as she looked up at the brightening sky, her wrists crossed on her good knee, while the other leg stretched along the steps in front of her.

He'd never before realized that she saw him as handsome or perfect in any way. To hear her say so gave his heart a tiny surge of weightlessness.

"And now?" he asked.

She shrugged, held the pose, and turned her chin onto her shoulder. It was a motion he recalled Delia making countless times, only when Agatha did it, it was thoughtful instead of coy.

"Now," she said, meeting his gaze squarely, "I see I was wrong."

Abruptly, she dropped the pose, breaking the momentary sense of intimacy.

"You should think about going back, Scott. Whether or not the prohibition amendment is ratified you owe it to yourself. Waverley is your home. Nobody loves it as you do, and it seems to me it's waiting there for you. So many of the mansions like Waverley were burned in the war. It's a real treasure now. I think it deserves its rightful master back again."

She sighed and braced herself as if to rise. "Well!" She stretched, pressing her palms against the floor of the landing. "I've been sitting on this step until I'm not sure my one good hip will work anymore. I think it's time we go in and try to get some sleep before the sun comes up and catches us perched here like a pair of cats waiting for the morning cream."

She faltered, trying to rise, and he grasped her elbow to help her. Her limp was more pronounced as she crossed the landing toward her door. She stepped inside, then turned back.

"Scott?"

"Hmm?"

"Thank you, too, for telling me all that. I know it wasn't easy for you."

"It wasn't easy for you either, was it?"

"No."

He crossed his arms and tucked his hands against his ribs, then came toward her slowly, stopping only a foot away. Even in the shadows, she sensed his distraction.

"What do you suppose that means, Gussie?"

She was struck by the realization that more and more often lately he said things like that—leading questions intimating a change in his feelings toward her. But she caught, too, the hint of confusion each time those feelings surfaced, and she realized the hopelessness of their situation. They were nothing whatever alike. If, even for a fleeting hour, he thought he felt something more than friendship toward her, what could ever come of it? He ran a saloon and she wore a white temperance banner on her sleeve. He taught a little boy to play five-card stud on Saturday, while she took the same boy to church on Sunday. He slept with a woman to whom he wasn't even married, while her morals could not abide such an arrangement. He was as physically flawless a man as she had ever met, while her own body left much to be desired. And he was handsome enough to land any woman to whom he gave a second look, while she had never landed even a first one.

But most important, if the prohibition amendment was adopted by the people, he'd soon be leaving Kansas for good.

What end would it serve if she acceded to the hesitant invitation in his words? She was a woman with a broken body; she didn't need a broken heart, too.

"Good night, Scott," she said quietly, withdrawing into the shadows.

"Gussie, wait."

"Go to bed. Jube is probably wondering what happened to you."

When she had quietly closed the door, he stood staring at it, with his palms still tucked beneath his arms. What the hell was he trying to prove? She was right—Jube was sleeping in his bed right now, while he stood at Agatha's door thinking about kissing her.

He swung around angrily.

She's not the kind to take a kiss lightly, Gandy, so make damned sure before you do it that you mean it.

Chapter 14

If people thought it strange that one of the local saloon owners went to the railway station to see the local milliner off to a temperance tea at the governor's mansion, nobody said a word. After all, the newly orphaned Collinson boy was with them, and everyone knew they had taken him under their wing.

Willy was wearing his proudest possession: a pair of brand-new indigo-blue Levi Strauss britches with orange stitching and copper rivets—"just like the cowboys wear!"—as Willy had pointed out proudly when he came running into the store to model them for Agatha. "An', no suspenders, neither!"

"No suspenders!" She had turned him in a circle and duly admired him.

"Nope! Cuz they're choke-barreled."

Agatha and Violet had both laughed. "They're what?"

"Choke-barreled. That's what Scotty says the cowboys call 'em. Skinny-legged . . . see?"

He stood now at the station, seeing Agatha off in his choke-barreled blue denim pants, looking healthy and robust. His brown boots already had hundreds of scuffs, but his nails were clean, he had gained weight, and he no longer scratched.

Agatha, too, looked stunning. She had made herself a brand-new dress for the occasions, a gorgeous creation of tangerine faille. The jacket sported dolman sleeves, with a collar and trimmings of brown velvet. This summer's *Godey's* dictated that no dress should be made of only one material, so she'd chosen a deeper melon-colored taffeta for the underskirt, and a stiffer silk faille for the sheath-fronted overskirt: handkerchief-styled—pointed in the front, with cascading rear draperies. At her throat billowed an ivory lace jabot of silk stockinet. Her outfit was completed by a tilted gable bonnet of melon and russet, forming a pointed arch over her face.

Watching her bid good-bye to Willy, Scott Gandy admired not only her dress, but the way its colors complemented the red highlights of her hair, which was coiled into a French twist up the back of her head. He admired, too, her pale green eyes with their mink-dark lashes, her apricot skin, and her fine-turned jawline, which he had liked from the moment he saw it. And her attractive mouth, smiling gamely, though he suspected she wasn't so anxious to go, now that the last minute had come.

"How long'll you be gone, Gussie?" Willy held both her hands and looked up angelically. Scott had combed the boy's hair with extra care that morning—and, for the first time, used a tad of Macassar oil. It gleamed brightly in the sun.

"Just overnight. Now you do as I said and help Violet sweep up before closing."

"I will."

Gandy watched her gloved hands adjust Willy's shirt collar, then brush something off his cheek. "And teeth, nails, *and* ears tonight at bedtime—promise?"

Willy's face skewed in disgust and he scuffled his feet. "Aw ... I promise."

"I'll ask Scott when I get back." She touched the tip of Willy's nose to soften the warning. "Now you be a good boy and I'll see you tomorrow night."

" 'Bye, Gussie." He came at her with open arms.

"Good-bye, sweetheart." She bent forward in the constricting skirts and Willy kissed her flush on the mouth. She held him to her breast as best she could, while he balanced on tiptoes, stretched full length. For a moment her eyelashes fanned her cheeks and Gandy saw clearly how she'd grown to love the boy. He thought of where she was going, and for what reason, and admired her for the kind of commitment it took to go. If the law passed, one of them would eventually have to bid Willy a final good-bye. She realized that as well as he.

Agatha straightened. Willy backed up and slipped his hand into Scott's. She looked up into the man's dark eyes. They appeared momentarily troubled and she wondered what had brought on the disturbed look.

"Good-bye, Scott."

He summoned a quarter grin, as if consciously shaking off whatever had been bothering him. "Take care of yourself. And I'll take care of Willy." He looked down and waggled Willy's hand. "We're plannin' t' go over to Emma's for supper tonight, aren't we, sprout?"

"Yeah ... chicken and dumplin's."

Agatha watched the two of them smile at each other.

"Well, I'd best be boarding."

Scott reached down to pick up her small carpetbag and hand it to her.

"Don't worry about a thing back here."

"I won't."

For a moment his thumb pressed her gloved knuckles, then slipped away. They stood locked in a moment of uncertainty, a good-bye hug hovering on both their minds. Through her memory flashed the image of him greeting Jubilee on the day of her arrival—his bold caress on her buttocks, the kiss they'd shared while half the town looked on. But now he stepped back and Agatha realized how foolish she'd been even to think it. The hugging that night on the steps was one thing— that had been sympathetic sharing. To do it in broad daylight at the depot was quite another thing, she chided herself. She turned away quickly before either of them could give in to the urge.

From the window of her coach she watched Scott and Willy. Scott was wearing a trim suit of fawn-brown and a matching flat-crowned Stetson. His brown string tie lifted in the breeze, then settled back against his white shirt front. He said something to Willy and Willy nodded enthusiastically. Then Scott reached into his ticket pocket and withdrew a cheroot. He patted his jacket searchingly and she could tell he was teasing Willy about something. Willy began searching, too, and came up with a wooden match. Scott clamped the cheroot between his teeth and leaned over while Willy lifted one knee and struck the match against the thigh of his new stiff denim britches. Three times he tried it; three times he failed. Then Scott adjusted the match in Willy's fingers and demonstrated for him. The next time the match caught and Willy held it gingerly while Scott leaned down and lit his cheroot.

Next he'll have the boy smoking, she thought. But instead of frowning at the possibility, her lips tipped up in a melancholy smile. Watching them together—the tall, uncondescending man and the happy blond boy—she saw a growing love flourishing between them. The train began moving and they both lifted their heads, waving—the two most important people in her life. Yet she stood to lose one, and maybe both of them, soon. In less than two months the decision about prohibition would be put to the voters of Kansas.

She rested her head against the seat and let her eyes slowly close. Her eyelids stung and a lump came to her throat. She almost wished the prohibitionists would fail.

The formal garden of the gubernatorial mansion was laid out in a diamond parterre design. Meticulously pruned privet hedges outlined the graveled paths between the profusely blossoming roses. Red, salmon, white, and pink, they scented the air with their inimitable fragrance. Chrysanthemums formed cushions of yellow and bronze at the junctures of paths. Stately yews stood as erect and uniform as a green picket fence around the boundaries, while scattered horse chestnut trees provided lakes of shade at strategic points within the formal design. Upon white iron benches, bustled women sipped tea from demitasse cups while bearded dignitaries in formal attire crossed their hands behind their back and discussed the political situation in harrumphing voices, their moustaches bobbing.

It was all very pompous, very elite. Dressed in her crisp, up-to-date finery, carrying herself with regal bearing and impeccable manners, Agatha fit right in. But all the while she discussed the format adopted by her W.C.T.U. local in combating demon rum, all the while she learned new methods of reaching voters and spreading antialcohol propaganda, she felt traitorous to the two who'd waved her off at the depot.

The governor was especially decorous, cinched tightly into a winged white collar and black Oxford tie. He bowed over the hand of each lady present, huddling solicitously with Baptist ministers, conferring with well-known illuminaries of the temperance movement.

Drusilla Wilson was there, and Amanda Way, and other notable leaders whose photographs Agatha had seen in the *Banner*. Meeting and visiting with them, Agatha again felt misplaced. The ardor for the temperance cause ran hot in their veins, while hers had cooled considerably. Recalling her excitement the day she'd received the invitation to this event, Agatha wished some of it still bubbled within her. Instead, she thought about November 2 as the day the guillotine might very well fall—not on Scott Gandy, but on her.

She hired a carriage and driver to take her back to her hotel, ate dinner in the elegant dining room, and wished she were at Cyrus and Emma Paulie's restaurant eating chicken and dumplings with Willy and Scott. She settled into her tastefully decorated room with its screen-printed wallpaper and tasseled draperies and wished she were in her own narrow apartment with the piano and banjo thumping through the floor. She lay back in a bed lined with fat goose-down ticks and wished she were sitting on a hard wooden step looking up at the stars, listening to the coyotes howl and enjoying the scent of a man's cigar.

In the morning she shopped and found a harmonica for Willy and a carved ivory brooch for Violet. She passed a tobacconist's shop and paused.

No, Agatha, it won't do. You're a single woman and he's a single man. It simply wouldn't be proper.

Resolutely, she moved on, but a short distance beyond the shop she stopped and retraced her steps. She stood before the window, admiring cherrywood pipes, tulipwood humidors, and boxed cigars. She looked up and saw her reflection in the pane, lit by the early morning sun of the warm autumn day. She imagined Scott Gandy beside her, the two of them out for a stroll to the market, he in his flat-crowned Stetson and crisp fawn suit, she with her pert dress and gable bonnet, her hand caught in the crook of his elbow.

A horse and dray passed on the cobbles behind her. The clatter awoke her from her musing and she entered the shop.

Inside, it was dusky and aromatic, the smells heady, rich, and masculine. So different from the smell of dyes and starches and machine oil.

"Good morning, ma'am," the owner greeted her.

"Good morning."

"Something for your man today?" His handlebar moustache and rosy cheeks lifted as he smiled.

Your man. The thought was unduly provocative. Scott Gandy was not her man, nor would he ever be. But, for the moment, it was fun pretending. She knew nothing about brands, however, and realized she'd give herself away by questioning: What wife wouldn't know her husband's favorite brand?

"Yes. A pair of trimming scissors, perhaps."

"Ah, I have just the thing."

She left the store with a tiny gold blunt-nosed pair of scissors in a flat leather slipcase, wondering if when she reached home she'd have the nerve to give it to him after all.

How forward of you, Agatha. How unseemly.

But he has given me a Singer sewing machine. What is a tiny pair of scissors, compared to that?

You're rationalizing, Agatha.

Oh, go lick! I've been a prude all of my life, and what has it gotten me? For once I'm going to follow my heart.

Her heart led her home, hammering with expectation as the train pulled into the Proffitt depot late that day. Her heart told her she must not search the crowd for Gandy, must not expect him to be there. But she adjusted her hat and checked her hair and hoped her skirt wasn't too wrinkled and searched the depot for him in spite of herself.

He wasn't there. But Willy was—still in his stiff blue britches, standing on a bench of the depot veranda, exuberantly waving and jumping.

She stepped from the train and he came hurtling against her. "Gussie, guess what!"

"What?"

"I gots a cat!"

"A cat!" Her smile was radiant, though it took some effort not to search the platform in the hope that Scott might step out of the building belatedly. She told herself it was absolutely ridiculous to be disappointed at his absence.

Willy jabbered a mile a minute. "Vy-let, she said Miss Gill had a litter of 'em down at the boardin' house, and if she didn't git rid of 'em soon they was gonna have t' drown 'em, so I went over there and there was this one, he was purple and white—"

Agatha laughed. "Purple and wh—"

"And he was my fav-rite and I ast her if I could have it and she says yes, so I brung it to Scotty's and Scotty says I could keep it long as it slep' in my room nights so's it wouldn't get underfoot in the saloon, and during the day Moose can do mousin' in the storeroom."

"M ... Moose?" Agatha chuckled.

"That's what I named him, cuz he's bigger'n all the others."

"And Moose is purple?" Agatha wondered how she'd ever made it through a day without Willy to brighten it. He scratched his head now from excitement, not even realizing what he was doing, till his hair stuck up like hard-crack taffy.

"Well, sorta—Scotty says he's gray, but he looks purple t' me, with white specks where his whiskers come out, and he slep' with me last night and I din't roll over and squash 'im or nothin'! Wait'll you see 'im, Gussie! He's the most beautiful cat you ever seen!"

"*Saw.*"

"Yeah, well, come on. Hurry up! He's at the saloon and Jack's takin' care of 'im for me, but I hafta get back and watch 'im."

She had little choice but to "hurry up." Willy picked up her carpetbag and ran.

"Willy, wait! I can carry that."

"Nuh-uh! Scotty says I'm supposed t' carry it for you."

Oh, he does, does he? she thought as she hurried after him, chuckling.

What a sight Willy made. The bag was bigger than he. He clutched the handle with both hands, his scrawny shoulders arched high as he struggled along cheerfully. Once it reared back and caught him in the knees and he stumbled, falling over it. But he didn't stop jabbering. Just popped up again and ran on while Agatha limped along trying to keep up with him, falling more in love by the second.

He led her straight through the swinging doors at the Gilded Cage. It was mid-afternoon, early enough that there were only a few customers. They were all gathered around the bar—Mooney Straub, Virgil Murray, Doc Adkins, Marcus, Jube, Jack, and Scott—laughing and talking and leaning on their elbows with entranced expressions on their faces. Between them, across the top of the bar, paraded an adorable eight-week-old kitten. It stepped in a puddle, shook its paw, then crossed to Mooney's beer mug, nosed the foam, shook its head, and sneezed.

"Gussie's back! I brung her t' see Moose!"

Every head turned toward the door.

"Moose is up here, entertaining us," Jube told him.

Willy dropped the carpetbag and snatched Agatha's hand. "C'mon, Gussie!"

Her eyes locked on Scott's as Willy tugged her across the floor. He stood behind the bar with Jack, dressed in a black suit and amber waistcoat, looking excessively handsome, as usual. Behind him Dierdre displayed herself in her garden of delights, but Agatha scarcely noticed. She saw only Scott. It seemed as if she'd been away from him for a week. The fleeting expression on his face told her he, too, was glad she was back.

Then Marcus caught Willy beneath the arms and sat him on the edge of the bar.

"See him, Gussie?" Willy's eyes gleamed with pride. "Ain't he cute?"

She turned her attention to the gray-and-white fuzzball. "He's adorable."

Jube shifted over to make room for Agatha, and she found herself, for the first time in her life, elbowing up to a bar. They all watched Moose sniff the beer in Doc's mug and take a delicate lap. Everyone laughed, but Doc pulled the mug back. "Oh no, you don't. Enough of that stuff'll kill a little thing like you."

Marcus extracted a coin from his pocket and spun it on the bar. Immediately, Moose poised himself, his eyes intent on the spinning gold piece. It lost momentum and rolled across the kitten's toes. He skittered backward, arched his back, and hissed comically. Everyone laughed. Then Willy took several turns spinning the coin and finally the kitten advanced cautiously and batted it over with its paw. Marcus rested a hand on Jube's shoulder and watched from behind her. Willy got right up on the bar and sat cross-legged. Jack drew himself a beer and took idle sips while the cat entertained them all.

Agatha looked up and found Scott watching her. All the others' attention remained focused on the cat. The coin whirred as it spun. They all laughed again, but neither Scott nor Agatha heard. Nor did they smile. His gaze was steady, his eyes as dark as the level brim of his hat.

Her entire body seemed to pulse.

God help me, I love him.

As if he'd read her mind, his gaze dropped to her mouth. She grew warm with physical awareness such as she'd never experienced. When his eyes reclaimed hers, she felt a blush beginning and turned to Willy, tapping him on the knee.

"I have to go relieve Violet. Come over later. I have something for you."

He forgot the cat and snapped a bright-eyed look at her. "For me?"

"Yes, but it's packed in my carpetbag. Come over later after I've unpacked." As she withdrew from the bar, he called, "How long will it take you?"

She smiled indulgently. "Give me a half hour."

"But I can't tell time!"

Scott chuckled and dropped a hand on the boy's shoulder. "I'll tell you when a half hour is up, sprout."

As Agatha picked up her carpetbag and left, she realized she and Scott had not spoken a word to each other. Not verbally, anyway. But something had passed between them that seemed more powerful than audible phrases. He had missed her—she was sure of it. He had feelings for her—his eyes seemed to say so. Yet how could that be? It seemed too incredible to believe. But if it were true, might that not be the very reason he had refrained from meeting her at the depot? If he was as confused about those feelings as she, it would be natural for Scott to exercise extreme caution in exploring them.

Violet was thrilled with her ivory brooch and immediately fastened it at her throat. As Agatha had known he would, Willy came long before thirty minutes were up. He gave one blow on his harmonica and Moose arched. Violet, who claimed to be Moose's "godmother," took him in hand and stroked him while Willy tooted some more.

"I thought Marcus could teach you how to play it properly. He's very musical. I'm sure he can play more than just the banjo."

"Gee, thanks, Gussie!" It took very little to light Willy's eyes with wonder and bring on a hug and kiss. -

"I gotta go show Marcus!" He grabbed Moose and headed for the door.

Agatha made a snap decision. "Wait!"

Impatiently, he turned back. Violet looked on, but didn't that make it seem less ... less personal? And somehow, after the graphic looks Agatha had exchanged with Gandy, she'd lost her nerve to give him the gift herself.

"I've bought something for Scott, too. Would you take it to him?"

"Sure. What is it?"

"Nothing much. Just a pair of cigar snips."

She handed the packet to Willy and he hit for the door. "I won't tell 'im what's inside till he opens 'em."

She smiled and watched him disappear, the cat climbing on his shoulder. If she'd expected Violet to take her to task for giving Scott a gift, she was wrong. Violet was too smitten with the man to claim good reason where he was concerned.

Agatha thought back to the time when Violet's titters over Scott Gandy used to irritate her. How featherbrained she'd thought her. Now she herself felt quite the same each time she was in the same room with him. She imagined that if people knew, they'd think she, too, was featherbrained. And probably she was. Probably she only imagined those pulse-raising looks of probing intensity. And even if they were real, how could she possibly guess what thoughts moved inside his head?

Her introspection was interrupted when Joseph Zeller entered the shop through the front door.

"Miss Downing, Miss Parsons, how're you?"

They exchanged civilities and eventually Zeller got around to the reason for his visit.

"Miss Downing, I understand you've been to Topeka to meet the governor."

Oh, no, Agatha thought. But while she struggled for an insipid answer, Violet bubbled proudly. "She most certainly was. She received an engraved invitation to tea in the governor's rose garden, didn't you, Agatha?"

Impressed, Zeller smiled. "It's not every day a citizen of Proffitt rubs elbows with the governor, now, is it?"

He stayed for nearly thirty minutes, asking her question after question, and there was little Agatha could do except answer. But the feeling of betrayal intensified with each response she gave. He extracted from her every innovative move under way to enhance the public's awareness of the dangers of alcohol.

The article ran, front page, in the *Gazette,* and it brought about a flurry of propaganda from unexpected sources, all strongly favoring constitutional reform.

The *Gazette* itself ran an editorial recapping how temperance was emerging as the first issue to unite women all over the country. From the pulpit of Christ Presbyterian, Reverend Clarksdale encouraged his fold to vote for prohibition, reasoning that the dangers of cholera, which had first prompted people to mix ale with their water—thus beginning the alcoholic craze—no longer existed; thus, the need for the "purifying agent" was past. Teachers began lecturing in their classrooms on the danger of drinking intoxicants, and children, in turn, repeated the warnings at home, many of them badgering their fathers not only to stop drinking liquor, but to vote in November for ratification of the constitutional amendment banning it. The superintendent of schools announced an essay contest on the same subject, the winner in each school to receive a bronze medal and have his name engraved in a commemorative plaque to be sent to Lemonade Lucy herself. The Proffitt Literary Society announced a series of open debates at their weekly meetings, inviting members of both factions to participate.

Amid all this furor, Agatha and Scott avoided each other. Since her return from Topeka, she'd seen him only in passing, or through the hole in the wall late at night. It was from this vantage point that she first saw him use the gold cigar snips, though he sent no word of thanks, nor even acknowledged that he'd received them.

Agatha was chagrined. How humiliating to have given a man a gift for the first time in her life and not receive so much as a thank-you for it. Willy became their only link. As the boy bounced back and forth between them, he brought his usual enthusiastic reports on the everyday occurrences in the two halves of the Gandy building.

"Scotty says . . ."

"Gussie says . . ."

"Me and Scotty went . . ."

"On the way to church yesterday, Gussie an' me . . ."

"I lost Moose, so Marcus an' Scotty had t' move the piano . . ."

"Gussie an' Violet got this order for . . ."

"Pearl says if the probe-isshun law passes, she's goin' back t' . . ."

"Violet says Gussie's sulled up . . ."

"Scotty an' Jube had a fight . . ."

"Gussie's makin' me some warmer shirts for . . ."

"Scotty an' Jube made up again . . ."

* * *

It was October. Less than a month to go before Election Day. The weather had cooled. The flies rarely bothered anyone at night, the cattle drives had dwindled to a near halt, the saloon closed earlier, but still Agatha slept poorly. She didn't have nightmares, exactly. But it seemed as if the Proffitt Literary Society debates were happening inside her head while she slept.

In her dreams she listened to one in which Mustard Smith argued vociferously with Evelyn Sowers, and when he realized he was losing, he gave way to hard agitated breathing, staring at Eveyln like an enraged bull getting ready to charge. The air seemed to hiss between his teeth: in ... out ... in ... out ...

Agatha came awake in a single second.

The breathing was real. Coming from right beside her bed. Heavy, hissing, asthmatic. Fear shot through her. Her palms turned to sweat. Her muscles tightened. She lay corpse-still, staring, wondering who it was behind her shoulder. *Oh, God, what should I do? Where is the closest heavy object? Can I reach it faster than he can reach me? What should I do first, scream or jump?*

She did both at once, closing her fingers around a pillow and swinging backward as hard as she could. It never even touched him. He ripped it from her hand and pounced. Her scream was severed as his palm clapped over her mouth. His opposite arm caught her across her breast and ribs and hauled her backward till she was half off the bed.

"I warned you, but you wouldn't listen," he hissed in her ear. "You're gonna listen now, lady. I got somethin' here gonna make you listen real good."

The pressure moved up to both breasts. Something pricked her beneath the left jaw.

"I can't see too good in the dark. Is it cuttin' you yet?"

It was. She felt the tip of the knife enter her flesh and screamed behind his hand, clawing at his knife arm.

"Be careful, lady."

She stopped clawing. If she pulled on him and he flexed against her grip, the knife could go in clear up to her eye.

She heard her own voice whimpering. "Hmp-hmp-hmp," with each panicked breath. Scott, help me! Sheriff Cowdry ... Violet ... somebody! *Pleeeeeease!*

"You're the one who started all this prohibition bullshit around here. Organizin' and preachin' and prayin' on the saloon steps. Then goin' to whine to the governor until you got this goddamned state in an uproar. Well, there's eleven of us in this town don't like it. Understand?"

His grip tightened. Her teeth sliced her lip and she tasted blood.

She tried to beg, but the sound came out in muffled grunts against his sweating, salty hand.

"Now, you're gonna back off, sister, you understand? Tell them women to quit their goddamned debates. Tell that mealy-mouthed preacher to shut his yap. And break up that temperance society! You understand?"

She nodded in a crazed, frantic fashion and felt something warm trickle down her neck. The sharp pain from the knife tip made it feel as if the blade had actually pierced her eyeball. She screamed again. He squeezed her face until she feared her jaw had broken. Each heartbeat felt as if it would explode her veins.

The whimpering hastened as she went past panic to mindlessness. "Hmp ... hmp ... hmp!"

The smell of cigar smoke and sweat entered her dilated nostrils.

"You think I'm afraid to kill you, think again." Her eyes felt as if they'd pop from their sockets. "One dead organizer could do wonders as far as puttin' the dampers on all them self-righteous reformers out there. But I'll give you one last chance, 'cause I got a big heart, see?" He laughed maliciously.

"Hmp ... hmp ... hmp."

"Say there, sister, what's this I feel?" The knife blade left her flesh and his hand closed over her breast. "You know, for a gimp, you ain't half bad. Maybe I got a better way to keep you in line than killin' you, huh?" His hand slid down her belly and he laughed evilly as her thighs involuntarily tightened. A moment later she felt her own nightgown pushed inside her body. She stifled the urge to scream again, but her eyelids slid closed and tears trickled from their corners. "I'll bet you ain't never had it, have you, gimp Well, I ain't got time tonight, with that goddamned nosy sheriff walkin' the alley. But you better do right, or I'll be back. And it makes no difference to me whether you can wrap them legs around me or not. I'll make use of this."

He knocked her onto all fours on the bed, with her nightgown still inserted in her body, pushed her face hard against the mattress with one hand at the back of her neck.

"Now you stay just like that for five minutes—understand?"

She knelt on the bed like a Moslem facing Mecca, bleeding onto the sheets, her hip feeling as if it were breaking all over again. Five minutes or five hours, she was incapable of knowing which had passed. She only knew he'd thumped out the door and there was only one other way out of her apartment. She took it. Out the window, onto the narrow shelf behind the false storefront to the first window she found. She pounded, but Jube didn't come. Frantic, she groped her way to the next, pounded again, too dazed to realize it was still Jube's room. She groped to the next, banging on it with her fist, but it was the hall window. Crying, whimpering, she stumbled along the wall to the next window which was open several inches at the bottom. She pushed it up and went over the sill into Scott's bedroom.

She stood in the dark, chest heaving, hyperventilating, fighting for control of something more powerful than she'd ever faced before. "S ... S ... Scott ... h ... h ... h ... help ... me," she pleaded. "S ... S ... Scott ..."

Scott Gandy came out of a deep sleep at the sound of a whisper. He opened his eyes and wondered if Jube was mumbling in her sleep. No, she was crying. He rolled to look over his shoulder and saw a figure in white standing at the foot of the bed. His first instinct was to reach for his gun. But then the whimper came again, jagged, broken.

"S ... S ... Scott ... pl ... pl ... please ..."

Buck-naked, he leaped from the bed. "Agatha! What's the matter?"

"A m ... m ... m ... m ..."

In the grip of shock, she could only stammer. She quaked so violently he heard her teeth rattling. He took her by both shoulders, feeling his own heart jump with fear. "Easy, easy now, breathe deep, try it again."

"A m ... m ... man."

"What man?"

"A m ... m ... man ... c ... c ... c ..."

"Take your time, Gussie. A man ..."

"A man c ... c ... came int ... t ... to m ... my r ... room and he h ... had a kn ... kn ... kn ... kn ..." The longer she tried, the more the word stuck. "Kn ... kn ..." Tremors shook her entire body and she breathed as if she were thrashing in deep water.

He pulled her against him and held her steady, clasping her with hands and elbows, one palm on the back of her head. Still she panted in short, inadequate gusts, much like a winded dog. Against his chest he felt each sharp rise and fall of her ribs. "You're all right now. You're safe. Just take it a word at a time. A man came into your room and he had a—what did he have, Gussie?"

"Kn ... kn ..." She panted fast against his ear, as if summoning her vocal powers, then burst out, "Knife!"

"Sweet Jesus! Are you all right?" Each of his heartbeats felt like an explosion. He drew back but held her securely by her upper arms, bending close until he made out her wide, terrorized eyes.

"I d ... d ... don't kn ... kn ...".

Jube woke up and asked sleepily, "Honey? What's going on?"

Gandy paid no heed to her. "Did he hurt you?"

"I th ... think I'm bl ... bl ... Hmp ... Hmp ... bl ... bleeding."

He swung her into his arms just as her knees buckled. "Jube, get up! Agatha's hurt. Wake the men and run for the doctor!"

"Hmm?" she mumbled, still disoriented.

"Now, Jube!" he roared. "Get Doc Johnson!"

She pulled herself off the bed by her heels and found her robe on the way to the door.

"Send Jack in here!" he ordered as he laid Agatha on the warm bed. When he'd lit a lantern he immediately saw the blood on her white nightgown. Terror gripped him as he searched for its source and found the wound beneath her jaw. He scanned her body but found no tears in her nightgown.

She folded her arms up in the middle of her chest, closed her eyes and shuddered. "I'm s ... s ... so c ... cold."

He covered her to the neck and sat over her, feeling his own fear give way to rage. "Who did this?"

Still with her eyes closed she stammered, "I d ... d ... hmp ... hmp ... d ... don't kn ... know."

"What did he want?"

"S ... s ... saloons ... p ... prohib ..." She shook so hard the remainder of the word fell off into silence.

Gandy's words grew hard, clipped. "Did he hurt you in any other way?"

Her only answer was a tighter huddling and the tears that seeped from behind her closed lids as she ashamedly turned her head aside.

Through the covers he found her shoulder and squeezed it. "Gussie, did he?"

Biting her lips, squeezing her eyes closed, she shook her head violently.

Jack burst through the door dressed in nothing but his union suit.

"Somebody's attacked Agatha. Have a look out back." Marcus and Ivory arrived, too, dressed in nothing but trousers.

"Is she all right?"

"She's been stabbed. Maybe worse."

Jack's teeth grated, his jaw bulged. "Let's go!" he ordered, and took off at a run with the other men at his heels.

Gandy looked down at Agatha, tightened the covers beneath her chin, and demanded, "He put more in you than just a knife blade, didn't he?" He leaped to his feet. "Goddammit! I'll find out who the son-of-a-bitch is and he'll pay. I swear to God, he'll pay!"

Her eyes flew open and she sat up supplicatingly. "No ... please, he's d ... dangerous ... and strong!"

Gandy stormed across the room, swiped up his trousers, and stepped into them, turning to face her as he angrily closed the buttons up his belly. He swallowed the epithets that bubbled in his throat and crossed hurriedly to the bed, pressing her shoulders down. "Lie back, please, Gussie. You're still bleedin'."

Her fingertips slipped up to test her wound. He caught them before she could touch it.

"Please . . . don't."

"But your sh . . . sh . . . sheets."

"It doesn't matter. Please don't move till Doc Johnson gets here." He put her hand beneath the covers and covered her securely again. Then he sat beside her, silent, staring into her wide, dazed eyes, stroking the hair back from her forehead again, and again, and again.

"Scott," she whispered, tears pooling in her eyes, making them appear transparent, like deep green water.

"Shh! . . ."

"He didn't . . ."

"Later . . . we'll talk about it later."

The tears ran in silver paths down her temples. He dried them with his thumbs.

"Don't leave me."

"I won't," he promised.

Her eyes grew wild with fright when Doc Johnson arrived and took Scott's place on the edge of the bed. He cleansed the wound with boiled saltwater, then announced no stitches would be necessary. He liberally dampened a gauze patch with tincture of arnica, then applied it to the wound and fastened it in place with another strip leading around the top of her head. Meanwhile, Ruby, Pearl, and Jube hovered anxiously in the doorway. The men reported they'd found nobody in the alley, nor in Agatha's apartment. Doc Johnson washed his hands at Gandy's shaving stand, and, drying them, advised, "She's going to be in some pain tonight. A touch of whiskey might dull it. She'll be chilled until the shock wears off, but other than that, she should recover nicely."

"Jack, go down and get a bottle, would y'?" Gandy said, without removing his eyes from Agatha's pale face.

Jack disappeared without a word.

"Marcus, Ivory, thank y' for lookin'. If one of you would get the sheriff, I think it's best if I talk t' him tonight."

"I already told him. He should be here any minute."

"Good." Gandy turned to the women. "Girls, go back t' bed. I'll stay with her."

Jube hovered a moment after the others had left. He cupped her jaw tenderly. "Sorry, Jube. She asked me not t' leave her. Do you mind goin' t' your own room for the rest of the night?"

She kissed his jaw. "Of course not. I'll check in on her in the morning."

Scott was the only other one in the room while Ben Cowdry asked his question. Agatha had calmed down somewhat, and answered lucidly, repeating the threats her attacker made, recalling that he'd smelled of cigar smoke and seemed to have a big belly and a raspy voice. But when Cowdry asked if the man had harmed her in any other way besides the knife wound, her troubled eyes flashed to Scott's. He boosted himself away from the corner of the chifforobe and ambled forward.

"No, Ben, nothin' else. I already asked her."

Cowdry's eyes swerved from Gandy to Agatha, then back again. Rising, he adjusted his gun belt. "Good enough. I'll need to have you sign some papers regarding the attack when you're stronger. Don't worry, Miss Downing, we'll get him."

Gandy closed the sitting room door behind the sheriff and returned to the bedroom. Agatha's round, frightened eyes were trained on the doorway, waiting for him.

"I shouldn't be here, in your room."

He picked up the whiskey bottle and a glass on his way past the shaving stand. "Doctor's orders," he said softly, crossing to the bed, sitting on the edge of it with one knee updrawn. He uncapped the bottle, poured three fingers, then set the bottle on the bedside table. "Can you sit up?"

"Yes."

She struggled up, wincing as she strained her neck muscles, and he leaned close to stack the pillows behind her. She fell back with a sigh.

"Here." He held out the glass. She stared at it. "Have y' ever tasted it before?"

"No."

"Then be ready. It's fiery, but it'll help."

She reached out tentatively and took the glass into her delicate fingertips. She glanced up uncertainly.

He grinned. "What'd y' expect from a saloon owner?"

She braved a grin, but even that hurt her jaw. Clasping the glass firmly, she tipped it up and drained it dry in four gulps, squeezed her eyes shut, gave an all-over shiver, opened her eyes and mouth, and held out the glass for more.

"Whoa!" Gandy pushed her hand down to her lap. "Not so fast there. You'll be seein' pink prairie dogs if y' keep that up."

"I hurt. And my stomach is still jumping. And I'm not at all sure I still won't fall into a thousand pieces. If the whiskey will help, I'll take seconds."

She held up the glass and he eyed it dubiously, but reached for the bottle again. This time he gave her half as much. When she lifted it as if to swig it straight down, he stopped her. "Not so fast. Sip it."

She sipped, lowered the glass, and held it in both hands, then touched the bloody sheets and her bloody nightgown. "I've made a mess of your bed."

He smiled at her wan cheeks. "I don't mind if you don't."

"And I've chased Jubilee away."

Their eyes met directly and held. "It's all right. She doesn't sleep here all the time anyway."

She became aware of his knee flanking her thigh and lifted the drink as if in refuge. This sip drained the glass. Then she self-consciously backhanded the side of her mouth without looking up at him again.

"I feel better now. I can go to my own apartment."

"No. You'll stay here."

He reached for the empty glass but closed his fingers over both it and her hand. "What did he do to you, Gussie? I need t' know."

She raised her eyes and his were waiting, concerned, dark with emotion. She swallowed—it hurt terribly, all the way to the top of her skull. When she spoke, her voiced trembled and new tears balanced on her eyelids.

"He didn't do what you think. He only ... only t ... t ... t ..."

Gently, he took the glass from her death grip and set it aside. "Lie down," he ordered, lifting the covers, adjusting the pillows while she slid into the warm security of his bed once again. He covered her to the neck, then stretched out beside her and rolled her to her side, facing him. He spread a hand on her back, feeling through the bedding how the shudders had revived. He rubbed the hollow between her shoulder blades and stared at her flushing face.

"Open your eyes, Gussie."

She did, and she met his fixed gaze, saw at close range his black spiky lashes and intent brown eyes, his well-defined eyebrows and somber lips. The whiskey had begun to relax her, though she huddled beneath the covers with her arms crossed protectively over her breasts. His Adam's apple rose and fell as he swallowed.

"I care about you," he whispered hoarsely. "Do you understand that?"

He moved not a muscle for several long, intense seconds. He stared into her distraught, green eyes until she, too, swallowed.

"He touched me," she whispered, "In an awful way that made me feel dirty. And threatened to come back and do worse if I didn't begin to discourage the local interest in the ratification of the amendment."

"But it's too late for that t' do any good."

"I know."

With pillows cradling their cheeks, they lay and stared into each other's eyes.

"I'm sorry," he said softly, wishing he had the power to wipe away the violation she'd suffered. She blinked once, slowly, and he saw that the alcohol was beginning to take effect.

"That's enough," she whispered contentedly.

"Is it?" It didn't seem enough, to be angry, to send the men out searching, to fetch the sheriff and the doctor and feed her a few glasses of whiskey. She was a good woman, and pure, and she'd undeservedly suffered again at the hands of someone who worshipped alcohol.

Beneath his hand, her trembling had stopped. Her eyes, wide and so mesmerizingly pale, refused to waver. His eyes dropped to her lips—what raced through his mind had been a long time coming. There were times when he was certain she'd thought about it, just as he had.

He lifted his head only enough to miss her nose and kissed her—like the brushstroke of an artist who wished to bring a canvas to life in pastels. She lay as still as a drawing of herself, her eyes closed, holding her breath, her lips still.

He lay back down, watching. Her eyelids fluttered open. She breathed again, as if testing her ability to do so. He tried to read those eyes, searching for willingness, then realized she would be too timid to grant it knowingly. But he saw the pulse beat fast at her temple, and it was answer enough. He didn't know where it would ultimately lead, only that they'd both wondered for a long, long time, and that their curiosity needed satisfying.

He braced himself up on an elbow, clasped her shoulder, and gently rolled her to her back. Leaning above her, he searched her eyes for a long, ardent moment. Then, slowly, slowly, he lowered his mouth to hers. His tongue intuitively reached, but though she lifted her face, her lips remained closed. He stroked her lightly—once, only to touch the seam of her lips. It struck him fully: she didn't know what was expected of her. He hadn't realized she'd been holding her breath until the kiss lengthened and it rushed out against his cheek. His heart felt an odd catch—she was even more innocent than he'd guessed. He thought of asking her to open her lips, but it would startle her. So instead he told her with his lips, his tongue, with soft plucking bites, deft, damp strokes, the slow waggle of his head—*Gussie, Gussie, open up t' me.*

He sensed the moment when understanding swamped her. And lightened his hold—waiting, waiting—the kiss turned invitation now.

A first hesitant parting. Then he felt his way across her lips with his tongue tip—*Wider, don't be afraid.*

She heeded, opened her lips farther, and held her breath again, waiting for his first faint touch within.

At the moment of contact he sensed her pleasure and her shock at this first elementary intimacy. Her tongue was warm and tasted faintly of brandy as he stoked it with his own and drew small persuasive circles, encouraging her to explore him likewise.

She answered with a first shy response.

Like this?

He answered with another. *Like this—deeper, longer.*

She tried it, cautious, reserved, yet entranced and willing. He sensed her awe building at the warm, sleek sensations and kept the kiss gentle. He lifted his head by degrees, giving her a parting, openmouthed nudge before looking down into her face.

Her eyes opened. She was still covered to the neck, her hands caught on her breast between them.

"So that's how it's done, then," she whispered.

"You've never done it before?"

"Yes. Once. When I was about eight years old, in the backyard of a little neighbor boy who said if I let him kiss me I could play on his swing. He was ten. You're much better at it than he was."

He smiled, the dimples forming in his cheeks. "Did y' like it?"

"I have not liked anything so much since you gave me my new Singer."

He chuckled and kissed her once more, longer than before, but with no more urgency, letting her explore his mouth as she would. Beneath his chest he felt her hands fidget and gave her space enough to free them. They came from beneath the blanket and rested lightly on his bare skin, just beneath the shoulder blades, fanning lightly.

He lifted his mouth from hers and rested his lips against her forehead while her fingers continued brushing. "Gussie," he said, "wherever we end up, you and I, remember that I never mean t' hurt you by this."

She was suddenly very certain where they'd end up, and it would not be together in Proffitt, Kansas. The thought hurt worse than the tip of her assailant's knife.

"I must be slightly inebriated," she ventured, "to be lying in a man's bed drinking whiskey and kissing him."

He lifted his head, held her cheeks between his palms, and forced her to meet his gaze. "Did y' hear me?"

She swallowed and replied soberly, "I heard you."

"You're not a woman who'd take a thing like this lightly. I knew that before I kissed you."

"So did I, before I let you."

He looked down into her face as the lantern light fired the tips of her lashes to deep umber and drew becoming shadows beside her nose and mouth. With his thumbs he drew light circles on her temples. He saw even more clearly what he had seen before—compelling green eyes, a straight, fine nose, and soft, kissable lips, all arranged in an utterly beguiling fashion. He found it hard to believe no man had ever been enticed by them before.

"You must have found it strange that I never came t' thank you for the scissors." She swallowed but remained silent. "Did you?"

"Yes. You're the first man I ever gave a gift to."

He kissed her chin and told her softly, "Thank you."

"Why didn't you come to tell me before?"

"Because tonight isn't the first time I've considered doin' this. I considered it that day. But, Gussie, I don't want y' t' think I'm takin' advantage of y' when you've drunk your first whiskey, and when you've been taken by surprise once already tonight. That's not why I did it."

"Then why?"

"I don't know." His eyes grew troubled. "Do you?"

"To comfort me?"

He searched her eyes and took the easy way out. "Yes, t' comfort you. And t' tell you the scissors have been in my breast pocket ever since Willy brought them t' me. They're beautiful scissors." He watched her expression change to one of imminent shyness. "You're blushing," he told her.

"I know." Her gaze fluttered aside.

It had been so long since he'd seen a woman blush. With a finger he brushed the crest of her cheek where the soft skin had bloomed like a June rose. "Can I stay here? On top of the covers, beside you?"

Her eyes flashed to his. Pale green to stunning brown. She felt the weight of him pressing almost against her breasts. It would probably be as close as she'd ever get to the real thing.

"You can trust me, Gussie."

"Yes ... stay," she whispered, then watched as he rolled away to lower the wick on the lantern and turn the room into a secure black cocoon. She felt him roll toward her again and settle onto his side facing her. Then listened to his breathing and felt it stir the hair above her ear. And wondered what it would be like to be able to share his bed like this for the rest of her life.

Chapter 15

True to his word, Scott remained totally trustworthy throughout the night. Still, Agatha slept little. Lying beside a sleeping man did nothing to promote it. Not until a gray dawn was lighting the night sky did she finally slip into slumber.

A loud whisper awakened her.

"Hey, Gussie, you awake?"

She rolled her head and opened her eyes. Scott was gone. Willy stood in the sitting room doorway with Moose in his arms. Outside it was raining and thunder rumbled.

"Hello, you two."

He smiled. "I brung Moose t' see ya. Moose'll make ya happy."

"Oh, Willy. *You* make me happy. Come here."

He beamed and came at a run, threw Moose onto the bed, then clambered up and sat beside her in his familiar pose, ankles out on either side of him. His eyes immediately took in her bandage and the dried blood. When he spoke, his voice held horrified respect. "Gosh, Gussie, did that man do *that* to you?"

She curled on her side and petted his knee. "I'll be all right, Willy. It scared me more than it hurt me."

"But g-o-o-osh ..." He couldn't tear his eyes away from the sight.

Moose came pussy-footing across the blankets, nosed Agatha's lip, and tickled her with his whiskers. She giggled and rolled back, scrubbing at her nose. Willy giggled, too, watching. Then he offered, "Me an' Violet's gonna take care o' the store so you can rest today. Violet says t' tell you everything's under con ... con ..." He stopped, puzzled, and finally remembered the word. "Control."

"You tell Violet I'll be down shortly. I've never been a lazybones in my life, and I refuse to start now."

"So dat's where you are, you li'l rapscallion!" It was Ruby, swishing through the door with a covered plate in her hand. "Scotty know you got dat crittuh on his bed?"

"Yup. Moose is makin' Gussie happy again."

She chuckled in her dry, sarcastic way. "Moose is keepin' one young'un I know from helpin' with the sweepin' downstairs."

"Oh! I forgot!" Willy bounced off the bed and hit for the doorway. He caught himself on the doorframe and swung around, sending his feet flying. "Take care o' Moose for me, Gussie. He gets in the way when we sweep."

Ruby arched one eyebrow at the doorway when he was gone. "That chile evuh do anythin' slow?"

Agatha laughed. "You should see him on his way to the bathhouse."

"Eggs 'n' grits dis mornin'. Scotty says t' see ya eat 'em all. Emma says no rush returnin' the plate. I say, if I git my hands on dat no-count trash did this t' you, I'll pluck his balls bald, then grind 'em up for pig mash." She slapped the plate down unceremoniously. "Now eat."

Agatha couldn't help chuckling at Ruby's colorful language. There were times when she forgot about the girls' former lives, but reminders surfaced now and then in startling anecdotes or ribald language such as Ruby had just used. Eating her breakfast, after Ruby had exited, Agatha smiled to herself. *Oh, Ruby, I love you, too.*

Abruptly, Agatha turned thoughtful.

It was undeniably true. During the past six months she had grown to love all of Scott Gandy's "family." And they, in turn, loved her. They proved it in countless ways, by rallying around when she was in trouble, sheltering her while she feared, pampering her afterward. How miraculous. How sobering. Suddenly, she found herself toying with the grits, her appetite lacking. Supposing she lost them now, when she'd just found them?

Moose came sniffing. She set down the fork and fed him some scraps but found her eyes blurred by tears as she watched the kitten stand on her lap and lick the plate.

Petting Moose's tiny head, she prayed, *Dear God, don't let that amendment become law.*

The door between Scott's office and the sitting room was closed when Agatha rose. She paused in the nearer sitting room doorway, glancing at his sack coat tossed over an upholstered chair, a full ashtray beside it, a discarded newspaper, a discarded shirt collar beside his humidor. Once again she felt an unwarranted stab of intimacy, more poignant than before, as she realized their days together might be numbered.

The watercolor painting of Waverley drew her hypnotically. She shuffled across and stood studying it intently: a magnificent edifice any man would pine for, if forced to leave. Sweeping wings, Doric columns, and its crowning glory: the high, dominating rotunda studded by an eight-faceted peaked roof like a diamond in an elegant mounting.

She studied the broad entry door framed by top and sidelights, picturing Scott as a boy, charging through as Willy would. She pictured him as a young man marrying a beautiful blond woman somewhere inside, in a room with a wedding alcove. She pictured him as a new husband, reluctantly going away to war, galloping down the lane beneath the magnolia trees, turning for a last glimpse of his family, his tearful wife with their child on her arm, her hand raised above her head. She pictured him as a defeated "Johnny Reb," returning to hear the voice of his dead daughter haunting him in his sleep.

Agatha touched his rosewood humidor, let her fingertips linger upon the rich, polished wood he had smoothed so many times. She touched the worn collar that had circled his strong, dark neck.

You'll be going back, Scott. I know it. It's what you must do.

Leaving his apartment, she noted that the hall door to his office was open. She tried to hurry past, but he was sitting at his desk and glanced up.

"Agatha?" he called.

Reluctantly, she returned to the open doorway, standing well out in the hall, self-conscious in her bloody nightgown and bare feet.

"How are you this mornin'?" he asked.

The look of him stopped her heart. Rumpled, unshaven, uncombed, as she'd never seen him before. His white shirt, minus its collar, lay open at the throat, the sleeves rolled back to mid-arm. The lantern was lit on his desktop, throwing flame across the dark skin of his face, while beside him the rain slapped the bare windowpane and ran down in rivulets. Instead of a cheroot, he held a pen in the crook of his finger.

Everything had changed in the course of a single night. She could no longer look at that finger without recalling the touch of it tipping her chin up. She could not longer look at the wedge of skin at his throat without recalling the texture of crisp, masculine hair beneath her fingertips. She could no longer look at his full, sculptured lips without recalling the thrill of being passionately kissed for the first time. Nor could she look at him without coveting and wanting more of the same.

Possessiveness was something new to Agatha. So was cupidity. How swiftly they controlled once a woman had had a taste of a man.

"I feel much better." It was an outright lie. She felt sick at the thought of losing him.

"I had Pearl change your beddin' and take the soiled sheets t' the Finn's."

"Thank you. And thank you for the breakfast. I'll send Willy up with some money for it."

A pair of creases formed between his eyebrows. "You don't need t' pay me back."

"Very well, then. Thank you, Scott. You've been—you've all been very good to me. I . . . I . . ." She stammered to a halt as tears collected in her throat. She swallowed them and forged on. "I don't know what I would have done without you."

He stared at her, eyes dark with consternation, while she searched for equilibrium but found only heart-wrenching dread. Suddenly, he dropped the pen and shot from the chair, swinging toward the window as he'd done once before in this room when they'd had words. Staring out through the runnels of rain at a jagged spear of lightning, he said tightly, "Agatha, what happened last night—I never should have done it."

The drone of thunder sounded while she wondered how to respond. How did one respond when a heart was shattering? She drew upon some hidden store of strength she would not have suspected she owned.

"Why, don't be silly, Scott, it was only a kiss."

He turned his troubled face to her and went on reasoning as if she'd argued with him. "We're too different, you and I."

"Yes, we are."

"And after November 2, everything might change."

"Yes, I know."

"Then . . ." The thought went uncompleted. He drew a deep breath and spun away, then caught his palms on the shoulder-high ledge where the upper and lower windows met. Letting his head drop, he stared at the floor.

A choking, exhilarating, chilling shaft of hope shot through her body. *Why, Scott, what are you saying?* Too confused to remain any longer, she left him staring out the window.

But if he'd been intimating what she thought, that rainy morning brought an end to any talk of it. While October waned and they waited for Election Day, he avoided her whenever possible, and when he couldn't, he treated her with the same friendly deference as he did Ruby, Jack, or Pearl.

Willy learned to play "Oh! Susanna" on his mouth organ and Agatha suffered moments of regret over her poor judgment in choosing such a gift. Its shrill sound began to grate on her nerves.

Sheriff Cowdry asked every bartender in Proffitt to print the word *temperance* for him, in hopes of discovering who'd left the note on Agatha's door. But four of them replied that they didn't know how to write, and of those remaining, five misspelled the word exactly as it had appeared on the note.

The weather stayed gloomy and the streets turned into a quagmire. The stomach influenza went around and they all got it, one after another. Willy said Pearl called it the "Kansas quick-step," which he found tremendously funny until it was his turn to suffer the malady. He made the worst patient Agatha could imagine, and with Violet home from work with the flu, too, Agatha was left both to see after the store and nurse Willy.

She herself caught it next, and though she recovered in time to be able to go to the polling place to pass out last-minute literature with the other W.C.T.U. members, she stayed at home instead, using the flu as an excuse.

November 2 was a bleak day. The sky was the color of tarnished silver and a cold wind blew out of the northwest, bringing beads of snow so fine they could only be felt, not seen. The cowboys were gone, the cattle pens empty. The ruts on the street had frozen into uneven knots that nearly shook apart the buckboards that came into town in a steady stream as outlying settlers came to vote. The saloons were closed. The sheriff's office—acting as a voting poll—was the hub of activity.

Agatha avoided the windows, sitting in the lamplit recesses of her workroom shut away from the world. She tried not to think about the decision being made by the voters all across Kansas. She tried not to think of the four men from next door crossing the rutted street and walking along the opposite boardwalk to cast their votes, nor her longtime neighbor women, who even now stood in the stinging sleet encouraging the male voters—in their stead—to stamp out alcohol once and for all.

It was a long, restless night for many Kansans. Those in the apartments above Downing's Millinery Shop and the Gilded Cage Saloon were no exception

Nobody knew the exact time the news would tick along the telegraph wire the following day. Violet was back at work, but neither she nor Agatha could concentrate. They did little stitching and less talking. Mostly, they watched the clock and listened to the lonely sound of its pendulum ticking.

When Scott opened the front door shortly before noon, Agatha was seated at her pigeonhole desk and Violet was dusting the glass shelves inside the trimming display.

Gandy's eyes found Agatha immediately. Then he closed the door with deliberate slowness. But he remembered his manners and greeted Violet, who rose slowly to her feet.

"Mornin', Miz Violet."

For once she didn't titter. "Good morning, Mr. Gandy."

He crossed to stand beside Agatha, silent, grave, with his hat in one hand as if he were at a wake.

Her skin felt tight, even her scalp, and she found it difficult to breathe. She looked up into his solemn face and asked in a near whisper, "Which is it?"

"It passed," he said, his voice low but steady.

Agatha gasped and touched her lips. "Oh, no!" She felt as if the blood had suddenly drained from her body.

"Kansas is dry."

"It passed," Violet uttered, but neither the man nor the woman at the desk seemed aware of her presence. Their gazes remained locked while Agatha's face blanched.

"Oh, Scott." Unconsciously, she reached toward him, resting her hand near the edge of the desk.

His gaze fluttered to it, but instead of taking it, he tapped his hat brim upon his open palm. Their eyes met again, hers distraught, his expressionless. "We'll have some decisions to make ... about Willy."

She swallowed but felt as if a cork had plugged her throat. Yes, she tried to say, but the word refused to come out.

His eyes, with all expression carefully erased, leveled on hers. "Have you thought about it?"

She couldn't stand it, analytically discussing an eventuality that would rip one of their hearts out. Covering her mouth, she turned her face to the wall, trying to control the tears that sprang to her eyes. Her throat worked spastically.

He glanced away because he could not bear to watch, and because his own heart was hammering as wrenchingly as he knew hers was.

Violet moved to the front window, holding the lace curtains aside, staring out absently. Somewhere in the store Moose chased a wooden spool along the floor. Outside, the sound of an impromptu victory celebration had began. But at the pigeonhole desk a man and a woman agonized in silence.

"Well ..." Scott said, then cleared his throat. He fit his hat on his head and took an inordinate amount of time trimming the brim. "We can talk about it another day."

She nodded, facing the wall. He saw her chest palpitate, her shoulders begin to shake. Desolate himself, he wanted to reach out and comfort her, draw comfort in return. Ironic that he should be standing wishing such things about the woman who had fought actively to shut him down and had now succeeded. For a moment he strained toward her.

"Gussie ..." he began, but his voice broke.

"Does W ... Willy know?"

"Not yet," he answered throatily.

"You'd better g ... go tell him."

He watched her control her impending tears, feeling desolate. When he could stand it no longer, he swung away and hurried from the shop.

It was the first time ever that Violet recalled his leaving without saying a polite farewell to her. When the door closed, she dropped the curtain and stood in the gloom beside the window, feeling forlorn. That nice Mr. Gandy—how she hated to see him go. What excitement would be left in the miserable little town when the saloons closed?

She heard a sniffle and glanced around to see Agatha's face turned toward the wall, a handkerchief covering her mouth and nose. Her shoulders shook.

Immediately, Violet moved to the desk. "My dear." She touched her friend's shoulder.

The younger woman swiveled suddenly in her chair and clasped the older one tightly, burying her face against Violet's breast.

"Oh V . . . Violet," she sobbed.

Violet held her firmly, patting her shoulder blades, whispering, "There . . . there . . ." She had never been a mother, but she could not have felt more maternal had Agatha been her own daughter. "It will all work out."

Agatha only shook her head against Violet's lavender-scented dress. "N . . . no, it won't. I've d . . . done the m . . . most unforgivable thing."

"Why, don't be silly, girl. You've done nothing unforgivable in your whole life."

"Y . . . yes, I have. I've f . . . fallen in love w . . . with Scott G . . . Gandy."

Violet's eyes grew round and distressed as she looked down on Agatha's hair. "Oh, dear!" she proclaimed. Then, again: "Oh, dear." After some time she asked, "Does he know?"

Agatha shook her head. "Y . . . you heard wh . . . what he said about W . . . Willy. One of us w . . . will have to g . . . give him up."

"Oh, dear."

Violet's blue-veined hand spread wide upon Agatha's nutmeg-colored hair. But she didn't believe in platitudes, so there was little she could say to comfort the woman whose broken heart caused her own to break a little.

Heustis Dyar worked his cigar back and forth across his blunt, yellow teeth. Six hours since the news had come in, but it wasn't law yet! Not till they did the official paper work and made it into a law! Till then—by God—he, for one, was going to make use of his time.

He filled his glass again and tipped it up. It warmed a path all the way to his gullet.

"What right they got?" A drunk at the bar demanded sloppily. "Ain't we got rights, too?"

Dyar took another swallow and the question seemed to burn deep within him, along with the liquor. What right *did* they have to take away a man's livelihood? He was an honest businessman trying to make a decent living. Did they know how many shots a man had to sell to earn enough for a horse? A saddle? A Stetson? He'd been patient, watching that millinery shop across the street where the drys had started the whole mess last spring. He'd been more than patient. He'd even been considerate enough to warn that damned gimp milliner who was responsible for all this. Well, the warnings were done. She and her kind had howled and prayed and boo-hooed until they got their wish.

Jutting his jaw, Dyar bit the wax off the lower fringe of his red moustache. His eyes hardened and he stared out the small window at her darkened apartment. *What right, Agatha Downin', you interferin' bitch! What right!*

Dyar slammed his glass down, gave an enormous belch, and said loudly enough so everybody could hear, "I'd like drinkin' better if I didn't have t' stop t' piss so often."

Everyone at the bar chuckled, and Tom Reese refilled Heustis's glass as he headed for the back door. Outside, giving up the pretense of having to use the outhouse, he veered off the path and skirted the string of buildings between his back door and the corner. In less than three minutes he was mounting Agatha's back stairs.

* * *

Marcus had been the last one to get the flu, but when it hit him, it hit hard. Damned trots! He'd spent more time running out to the backyard privy than he did playing the banjo lately. And he hurt all over. Buttoning his britches and slipping his suspenders over his thin shoulders, he winced, then gingerly flattened a hand against his abdomen.

As he opened the privy door and stepped outside, he saw a movement at the top of the stairs. Quickly, he stopped the door from slamming, then flattened himself against the privy wall. Ignoring his painful stomach, he waited, gauging the exact moment when he'd make his move. He watched until the man at Agatha's door gave a furtive glance over his shoulder, then bent again to the lock.

When Marcus moved, he moved like a greyhound—full out, loping, taking the stairs two at a time, armed with nothing but anger. Dyar swung on the balls of his feet with the knife in his hand, but his reaction time was slowed by all the liquor he'd consumed, and his balance was precarious. Marcus flew across the landing, throwing his body into the attack. He kicked Dyar in the chest with both feet and heard the knife clatter to the decking. Never in his life had Marcus wished so badly for a voice. Not to yell for help, but to bellow in fury. *You bastard, Dyar! Lily-livered son-of-a-bitch! Preying on defenseless women in the middle of the night!*

Though Dyar outweighed Marcus by a good seventy-five pounds, Marcus had *right* on his side, and the advantages of surprise and sobriety. When Dyar got to his feet, Marcus threw a punch that snapped his red head back so hard the neck joints popped. Rebounding, Dyer caught Marcus in his sore gut, doubling him over, then followed with a solid clout on his skull. Rage burst inside the mute man. Glorious, undiluted rage. The roar he could not release transformed itself into tensile power. He picked himself up, lowered his head, and charged like a bull. He caught Dyar in the belly and neatly flipped him backward over the railing. The big man's scream was brief, silenced when he hit the hard-packed earth below.

Agatha's key grated in the lock at the same moment Ivory and Jack came running out their door. Marcus sat crosslegged in the center of the landing, rocking and cradling his right hand against his stomach, wishing he could moan. Everybody else babbled at once.

"Marcus, what happened?"

"Who screamed?"

"Are you hurt?"

Others came out the apartment door.

"What's going on out here?"

"Marcus! Oh, Marcus!"

"Who's that layin' down there?"

Scott and Ivory ran down the steps and called back up, "It's Heustis Dyar!"

"He must have been trying to break into my apartment," Agatha elaborated. "I heard the scuffle, then the scream, and by the time I got out here Marcus was sitting in the middle of the floor."

Willy awoke and came out the downstairs door to squat beside Scott.

"He the one who's been pesterin' Gussie?"

"Looks like it, sprout."

"Good enough for him," the boy pronounced.

"Is Agatha all right?" Scott asked Ivory.

"She seemed to be."

On the landing above, Jube bent over Marcus, sympathizing.

For a moment he forgot the pain in his hand and concentrated on the feel of her silky robe brushing his shoulder, the sleepy, warm smell of her. If the hand was broken, it was a small enough price to pay for the consolation of having Jube fussing over him.

Agatha, also in a dressing gown, knelt on his opposite side. "Marcus, You *caught* him!" The one she'd have thought least likely to take on a man the size of Dyar, yet he'd done it and come out the victor.

He tried for a shrug, but the pain reverberated down his arm and he drew in a hiss through clamped teeth.

"You've hurt your hand?"

He nodded.

Jack found the knife and held it up.

Jubilee's soft palm ran down Marcus's arm. "Oh, Marcus, you might have been killed."

Though he delighted in Jube's nearness and attention, he realized Dyar still lay in the alley. He swung his worried eyes to the railing, gesturing with his head—what about Dyar?"

Ruby called down, "How is Dyar?"

Scott answered from below, "Alive, but pretty well mashed up. We'll need t' call the doc again."

"And the sheriff, too," Jack added, still studying the knife.

"No-count redneck scum," muttered Ruby, then joined forces with the women who were lavishing Marcus with attention. They helped him to his feet, led him inside, lit lanterns, and checked the extent of the damage.

It turned out Marcus had broken a bone in his right hand. When Doc Johnson had secured a woodblock inside the palm and wrapped it in place with gauze, Marcus gamely displayed his agile left hand, fingering the frets of an invisible banjo—*At least it's not my chording hand,* his baleful expression said.

"Heustis Dyar will be wishing all he had was a broken picking hand," Doc Johnson noted wryly as Sheriff Cowdry carted Dyar off to jail.

As a thank-you, Agatha promised Marcus a free custom-made garment of his choice, as soon as he felt chipper enough to come downstairs and be fitted.

In his room, Marcus got a good-night kiss from Jube—a light brush on his lips that startled him, but before he could react, she said good-night and slipped out.

Scott, tucking Willy back into bed, had to bite his cheek to keep from smiling when Willy declared, "I heard most of it. Old Heustis sounded like fireworks comin' down before he went *splat!*"

"Go t' sleep, sprout. The excitement's over."

"Why would anyone wanna hurt Gussie?" he asked innocently, collaring Moose and falling back onto his pillow.

"I don't know."

The cat was so accustomed to sleeping with Willy that he flopped on his side with his head on the pillow as if he were human. Gandy half expected Moose to yawn and pat his mouth.

"It's b'cause o' the probe-isshun comin', ain't it?"

"I reckon it is, son."

"What're you gonna do when you can't sell whiskey no more?"

"Anymore," Gandy corrected absently, scarcely aware that he'd picked up Gussie's habit of correcting the boy. Briefly, he rested a hand on Willy's head. "Go back t' Miz'sippi, probably."

"But . . . well, couldn't you be a blacksmith or somethin'? Eddie's pa, he fixes harness. Maybe you could do that; then you could stay here."

Gandy covered Willy and tucked the blankets around his chin.

"We'll see. Don't fuss about it, y' hear? We've got time t' decide. The law won't take effect for a few months yet."

"All right."

Scott began to rise.

"But, Scotty?"

The tall, lanky man settled back down on the edge of the narrow cot. "You forgot t' kiss me good-night."

Leaning to touch his lips to Willy's, Scott tried to hold his emotions at bay, but the thought of kissing him good-bye for the last time tore at Gandy's innards. Suddenly, he clasped the boy tightly, holding him to his thrusting heart for a moment, pressing his lips to the top of the short-cropped blond head. He thought of Agatha, with her face turned sharply toward the wall, her throat working. He thought of taking Willy away from her and didn't believe he could do it. Yet, when he imagined leaving the boy behind, with Willy's bright brown eyes filled with tears, as he knew they would be, he wasn't sure he could do that either. He had to force himself to press Willy back down and cover him up again. He had to force his voice to remain calm. "Now go t' sleep."

"I will. But, Scotty?"

"What now?"

"I love you."

A giant fist seemed to squeeze Gandy's heart. Sweet Jesus! What a choice lay ahead. "I love you, too, sprout," he managed to say. Just barely.

Scott Gandy and his employees had a meeting one morning in mid-November to discuss when to close the Gilded Cage and where to go next. It was decided there was no point in delaying since the flourishing business of the drive months had already been reaped. Between now and the time the law took effect, business would be slow at best, with Proffitt's population diminished to its original two hundred. The question of where to go next left everyone staring at Gandy for an answer. He had none.

"I'll need a little time alone t' figure things out. Where I want t' go, what I want t' do. Maybe I'll go south, where the weather is warmer, and try t' get my thoughts together. What do y'all say to a little time off?"

They all said nothing. Seven glum faces stared blankly at him. He felt the weight of responsibility for them and momentarily resented it. Tarnation! Couldn't they think for themselves? Would they always look to him as their savior, the one to deliver them to the next safe, profitable port? But the fact was, he felt dejected, too. The Gilded Cage was scarcely taking in enough to support eight people, and it was important that he preserve a big enough lump of cash to start them out again in a new place. So why should he feel guilty about needing a little time away from them, asking them to fend for themselves awhile?

"Well, it'd only be until the first of the year or so. Then I'll pick a spot where y'all can wire me and I'll wire back and tell you where we'll be settlin' next and exactly when to come."

Still nobody said anything.

"Well, what do you think?"

"Sure, Scotty," Ivory answered flatly. "That sounds good." Then, hearing his own lack of enthusiasm, he put on a false brightness.

"Doesn't that sound good, y'all?"

They murmured agreement, but the moroseness remained. It was left to Scott to feign enthusiasm.

"All right, then." He slapped the green baize tabletop and stretched to his feet.

"No sense in hangin' around this dead little cow town any longer. Whenever you're packed and ready t' leave, y'all go ahead. I'll put the buildin' up for sale immediately."

"What about the sprout?" Jack inquired.

Scott did a good job of concealing his anxiety over the subject of Willy. "Agatha and I have t' talk about that yet. But don't worry. He won't be abandoned."

Quite the opposite. The sprout had two people who wanted him, and they'd put off discussing the subject as long as possible. But it could no longer be avoided.

For no good reason he could name, Gandy went upstairs to his office and penned a note to Agatha, then asked Willy to take it to her and wait for an answer.

Willy stared at the note as Scott held it out. "But that's dumb. Why don't you just go over there an' talk t' her?"

"Because I'm busy."

"You ain't busy'! Heck, you've been—"

"I thought Agatha taught you not to say *ain't!* Now, will y' take the note, or won't you?" he demanded more sharply than he'd intended.

Willy's expression dissolved into one of dismay over the unearned scolding from his hero.

"Sure, Scotty," he answered meekly and headed for the door.

"And put on your new jacket. How many times do I have t' tell you not t' run up and down the stairs in the cold without it?"

"But it's down in my room."

"Well, what's it doin' down there? It's winter, boy."

Mollified, yet further confused, Willy looked back at Scott with brown eyes that glistened. "I'll put it on before I come back up."

When he was gone, Scott fell heavily into his chair, then sat staring out the window at the snow, smitten by guilt for having been so curt with Willy. After all, it wasn't the boy's fault the saloon had to close, nor that he and Agatha were at this impasse.

Downstairs, Willy found Gussie in the workroom, pedaling on the sewing machine.

"Hi, Gussie. Scotty says t' give you this." He handed her the note.

The rhythmic rattle of the machinery slowed and the flywheel stopped spinning. Agatha's eyes dropped to the paper and a sense of foreboding flashed through her. *No, not yet,* she thought. *Please not yet.*

"Thank you, Willy."

Willy tipped onto the sides of his boots and jammed his fists into the pockets of the new warm winter jacket Scott had bought him. "He says t' wait for an answer." While she read the message, Willy grumbled, "Garsh, how come he's so grumpy lately?"

A flood of dread hit her as she completed reading the message. It was the eventuality she'd known was inescapable. Yet all the mental preparation in the world couldn't make it less painful. She came out of a lapse to hear Willy saying her name.

"I'm sorry. What, dear?"

"Why's Scotty so grumpy lately?"

"Grumpy? Is he?"

"Well, he talks like he's mad all the time when I never done nothin' wrong."

"Did anything wrong," she corrected. "And adults get that way sometimes. I'm sure Scott doesn't mean to be grumpy to you. He has a lot on his mind since the prohibition amendment passed."

"Yeah, well . . ."

She fondled the side of Willy's head, then ordered gently, "Tell Scott yes."

"Yes?"

"Yes."

"That all?"

"That's all. Just yes."

When he clumped out with none of his usual verve, she studied the back door and tried to imagine life without him bubbling in and out. She fully understood why Scott was grumpy lately. She herself was experiencing sleepless nights and worried days.

Drawing a deep, shaky breath, she reread the message:

> Dear Agatha,
>   We must talk. Would you come to the saloon just after closing tonight? We won't be disturbed there.
>
>   Scott

Willy advanced cautiously as far as Scott's office door, but no farther. His chin thrust out belligerently.

"Gussie says yes."

Scott turned in his swivel chair and felt a catch in his heart. "Come here, sprout," he ordered softly.

"Why?" Willy'd been burned once this morning. Once was enough.

Scott held out a hand. "Come here."

Willy came reluctantly, wearing a scowl. He moved around the corner of Scott's desk and stood just beyond reach, dropping his gaze to the hand that still waited, palm up.

"Closer," Scott said. "I can't reach y'."

Willy stood his ground stubbornly, but finally laid his stubby hand in Gandy's long one. "I'm sorry, Willy. I made y' feel bad, didn't I?" He pulled the boy close, then hauled him up onto his lap and tilted his chair back.

Willy snuggled against Scott's chest with obvious relief.

"I wasn't mad at you, y' know that, don't you?" Gandy asked in a husky voice.

"Then how come you yelled?" Willy asked plaintively, his cheek pressed against Scotty's vest.

"I've got no excuse. I was wrong, that's all. Can we be friends again?"

"I guess so."

Willy's blond head fit snugly beneath Scott's chin. His small body in the thick woolen jacket felt warm and welcome, with one hand pressed trustingly against Scott's chest. The pair of short legs dangled loosely against the long ones, and even that slight pressure felt welcome to Scott.

Peace settled over the two of them. Outside, snow fell. In the small iron stove a cozy fire burned. Scott propped a boot on an open drawer and indolently rocked the swivel chair until the spring set up a faint noise. He found Willy's fine hair with his fingers and combed it up from his nape again and again.

After a long time, when their hearts had eased, the man asked, "You ever think about livin' somewhere else?"

"Where?" Willy remained as before, savoring the feel of Scott's fingernails gently scraping his skull, sending goose bumps throughout his body.

"Someplace where there's no snow."

"I like snow," Willy returned sleepily.

"You know what a plantation is?"

"I'm not sure."

"It's like a farm. A big farm. Y' think you'd be happy livin' on a farm?"

"I dunno. Would you be there?"

"Yes."

"Would Gussie be there, too?"

Scott's fingers and the chair paused for only a second, then began their soothing rhythm again.

"No."

"Then I don't wanna go t' no farm. I want us t' stay here, together."

If only it were that simple, sprout. Scott closed his eyes for a moment, feeling the reassuring weight of Willy stretched along his trunk. He was loath to move, to break the sweet contentment they'd found together. But he felt a twinge of guilt for asking Willy about his wishes, as if asking the boy to make a choice against Agatha. He hadn't intended it that way at all. He realized it would be the perfect time to tell Willy the Gilded Cage would be closing soon and all of them would be leaving town. But he hadn't the heart at the moment, and he thought it best if he and Gussie broke the news to Willy together.

"Sprout?"

When Willy didn't answer, Scott pulled his chin back and looked down. Willy was sound asleep, his head sagging low against Scott's chest. Gently, he picked him up, carried him into the sitting room, and laid him on the settee, then stood studying him for a moment: the long dark lashes lying against the fair cheeks; the soft, vulnerable mouth; the skinny neck hidden within the scratchy wool jacket that had worked up nearly to Willy's ears.

Sprout, Gandy thought wistfully, *we both love you. Will you believe that when this is over?*

Chapter 16

Scott was the only one in the saloon when Agatha entered by the rear door shortly before midnight that night. He sat at one of the green-topped tables, slouched negligently in his chair with one boot crossed over a knee, one elbow hitched on the table edge beside a whiskey bottle and an empty glass. Mechanically, he flipped cards at his upturned Stetson on a nearby chair. Five in a row hit their mark.

The only lamp burning in the place was a single murky coal-oil lantern directly above the table. It threw a pale smudge of light onto the top of his head and gave his eyes an obsidian glitter. Agatha halted at the end of the short hall.

Between cards, his glance flicked to her. "Come in, Miz Downin'," he drawled in a voice so low it scarcely carried across the room. *Flip. Flip.* Two more in the hat. She threw a cautious glance at Willy's closed door. "Oh, don't worry about the sprout. He's asleep." *Flip. Flip.*

She advanced to the edge of the circle of light and paused with her hands on the back of the battered captain's chair like the one in which Gandy slouched.

"Sit down," he invited without rising.

She cast a glance at the cards still sailing toward the hat.

"Oh, sorry." With a cold grin he stretched to pick up the Stetson from the chair, scooped out the cards, then settled the familiar flat-crowned hat low over his eyes, casting them into complete shadow. His apology held not the slightest hint of contrition as he squared the deck and clapped it down beside the bottle.

She perched on the chair at his right, edgy because of his uncustomary arrogant manner.

"You wanted to talk to me."

"Wanted?" he bit out wryly. "Neither of us *wanted* t' have this conversation, did we?"

"Scott, you've been drinking."

He glanced ruefully at the bottle. "Looks like it, doesn't it?"

She grasped the bottle, sniffed its contents, made a disgusted face, and forcefully set it aside. "Rotgut!"

"Hardly. For this conversation I chose the best." He refilled his glass, then hefted the bottle her way. "Join me?"

"No, thank you," she replied tartly.

"Oh, of course not." He clunked the bottle down. "I forgot. Y'all don't touch the stuff, do y'?"

His drawl was very pronounced tonight. She'd thought at first he was drunk, but she realized now he was decidedly sober, which made his defiant attitude all the more distasteful. She stiffened and brought her chin up.

"If it's Willy you've brought me here to talk about, don't think you're going to cow me by brandishing your bottle in my face. I won't have it. Do you understand?" Her pale eyes snapped and her lips thinned with resolve. "We'll discuss it sensibly, without rancor, *and* without alcohol—or not at all."

His elbow was bent, but the glass stopped halfway to his lips.

"Put it down, Scott," she ordered, "or I'll go back upstairs right now. The answer to our dilemma won't be found in a bottle of fermented rye. I'm surprised you haven't learned that by now."

He considered downing it in one gulp, just to appease the unmitigated frustration she never ceased causing him, but in the end he set it down docilely, then slid it to the far side of the table, along with the bottle.

"Thank you," she rejoined calmly, holding his gaze firmly with hers. He felt suddenly childish, pulling such histrionics when she sat so unflinchingly, ready to meet him on equal terms. "Now," she added quietly, "about Willy."

He released a pent-up breath and informed her, "I'll be closin' the Gilded Cage by December first."

The starch left her in one second. "So soon," she said, mollified. Their animosity evaporated as if it had never existed. The rudeness with which he'd been arming himself, the obdurate primness with which she'd been doing the same, fled them both. As they sat in the dim circle of light they both became defenseless.

"Yes. There's no sense in us stayin' when we're not makin' any money. We have t' shut down eventually anyway, so why put it off?"

"But I'd hoped . . . I thought you might stay until after Christmas anyway."

"We've talked it over, all of us, and the others agree with me. The sooner we get out the better. We'll all be leavin' except Dan. He's decided t' stay here and live with his mother again."

"Where will you go?"

He picked up the glass he'd filled and took an idle sip; she made no objection this time. He rested both elbows on the table and drew circles on the green baize with the bottom of the glass. "I've thought a lot about what you said—about layin' ghosts t' rest, and I've decided you're right. I'm goin' back to Waverley, at least for the time bein'."

She reached across the table and gently squeezed his forearm. "Good."

"I don't know what I'll find there, what I'll do, but I have t' go back."

"It's the right thing for you to do. I'm convinced of it." His hat brim dipped slightly and she assumed he'd dropped his gaze to her hand. Immediately, she withdrew it and clasped it in her lap. The silence stretched long. "So . . ." she said at length, expelling a nervous breath. "We must make a decision about Willy. Do you want him?" She couldn't make out his eyes but felt them trained on her assessingly.

"Yes. Do you?"

"Yes." On her lap her fingers gripped harder.

Silence again, while they pondered where to go from there.

"So, what do you propose?" she asked.

He cleared his throat and sat up staighter, toying with the glass but not drinking. "I've thought and thought, but there doesn't seem to be any answer."

"We could ask Willy," Agatha suggested.

"I thought of that myself."

"But it doesn't seem fair to force him to make a choice, does it?"

He swirled the rye around and around. "This mornin' after I sent him down with the note, he came back up t' my office and we . . . well, we'd had a fight." He gave her a quick sheepish glance, then concentrated on the glass again. "Truth is, I snapped at him for no good reason. But we came t' terms and he sat on my lap a bit and we talked—about the plantation. I asked him if he thought he'd like t' live there. First he asked if I'd be there with him and I said yes. Then he asked if you'd be there, too, and I said no." Gandy looked up, but Agatha's gaze dropped to the green tabletop. "So Willy said no, in that case he didn't want t' go anyplace, just wanted us all t' stay here together."

She didn't move, just sat staring with her hands clasped in her lap. His gaze lingered on her eyelashes, and their elongated shadows reaching down her fair cheeks; her mouth, drooped in sad resignation; her fine jaw and stunning upswept hair, whose red highlights shone even in the murky light; her breasts, restricted by the stiff garnet taffeta of her prim, high-collared dress; and the arms she held militarily at her sides.

"No," she said faintly, "we cannot ask a boy of five to make a decision like that."

"No," he echoed. "It wouldn't be fair."

Still staring, she murmured, "What is fair?"

There was no answer, of course. Fairness was a thing neither of them had ever contemplated with such vulnerability before.

He loves Scott so much, she thought.

What would he do without his Gussie, he thought.

Every little boy needs a father.

A child needs a mother more than anything else, and she's the first one he's known.

He idolizes Scotty.

She teaches him constantly.

I'm too strict with him.

I'm too loose with him.

Waverley would be such a wonderful place for a little boy to grow up.

It wouldn't seem right t' take him away from everything familiar.

Around them, all was still. A winter chill crept along the floor. In the room at the rear a child slept, while Agatha and Scott decided his fate. The decision—either way—would be painful for all three of them.

Hesitantly, Agatha reached for the glass and took it from Scott's fingers. Her hand trembled and her eyes remained downcast as she raised it to her lips and sipped. Only then did her gaze meet Scott's.

"We must make an honest assessment about which home would be best for him."

He deliberated for a minute, his fingers linked loosely over his stomach, watching her. "There's no doubt in my mind. Yours. I don't even know where I'll be settlin' permanently."

"You'll settle at Waverley. I'm sure of it. You must—it's your birthright, and it would be a wonderful place for a boy to grow up. All that clean air and no rowdy cowpunchers around."

"But who'd see after him like you do? Who'd keep him on the straight and narrow?"

With a fey smile, she told him, "You underestimate yourself, Scott Gandy. You would. Underneath it all, you're a very honorable person."

"Not like you. And you could teach him. You've already started, with your constant correctin' and makin' him clean his nails and scrub his ears. I'm afraid I wouldn't have the patience for that."

"There are schools."

"Not nearby."

"And space. All that space. Why, Waverley has so many bedrooms he could sleep in a different one each day of the week. I have only a single room with no such thing as privacy for either of us."

"But you're the better influence on him. You make him go to church and mind his manners."

"Boys need masculine influence, too."

"Willy'll be all right. He's got a lot of spirit."

"Much of which he gets from you. Why, he's even affected a bit of a Southern drawl lately."

"But I have bad habits, too."

"Everybody has bad habits."

He didn't reply immediately, and she felt his eyes probing her. Unsettling. "Not you. Not that I've noticed."

"Fastidiousness can be a bad habit if it becomes fanatic. And sometimes I fear I get fanatic." She leaned forward eagerly. "Little boys need to . . . to . . . scuffle with one another in the dirt, and come home with bruised shins and climb trees and . . . and . . ." She ran out of ideas and spread her hands, then let them drop.

"If you understand all that, you won't be too fastidious with him."

It was her turn to study him, though she wished she could see his eyes. She had one last trump card. Playing it, her voice came out more softly, more intently. "I'm not certain I can afford to keep him, Scott. It's all I can do to keep myself and pay Violet's wages, even with the sewing machine."

"All you'd have t' do is wire me and there'd be any money you'd need."

His generosity moved her deeply. "He means that much to you."

"No more than he means to you."

For a moment they sat locked in the irony of the situation, two people who loved Willy so much they each tried to convince the other to take him.

"So," Agatha said at length, "we're right back where we started."

"It looks that way."

She sighed and her eyes drifted off to a dark corner of the room. When she spoke, it was wistfully. "A perfect mother, a perfect father—isn't it a shame one of us must live in Mississippi and the other in Kansas?" Suddenly, she realized what she'd said, and she feared he'd misinterpret it. She shot him a glance. "I didn't mean—" Her neck grew warm. Her eyes fluttered down.

"I know what y' meant"

Flustered, she searched for words to fill the awkward moment. "So how do we decide? We can't ask Willy, and we can't seem to agree who'd be better as a parent."

Zzzt! Zzzt! She heard the sound before she realized what it was: his thumbnail repeatedly riffling the edge of the cards upon the green baize tabletop.

"I have a suggestion," he said in a low voice that, at another time, under other circumstances, might have sounded seductive. *Zzzt! Zzzt!* "But I'm not sure how you'll take to it."

Her eyes dropped to the deck of cards.

"A single hand," he went on, "for the highest stakes ever."

She felt as she had the night she'd drilled the hole in the wall, as if she were contemplating something forbidden and would certainly get caught the moment she began. But who was there to catch her? She was a grown woman, an adult under no one's mandate except her own.

Not a muscle moved in his entire body, except for the thumb that kept flicking the edge of the deck. Sitting back easily, he watched her battle with her own stern code of ethics. "What do you say, Gussie?"

Her heart seemed to lodge in her throat. "W . . . Willy's future, decided by a game of cards?"

"Why not?"

"But I . . . I've never played before."

"Five-card stud. No draw. Read 'em and weep."

A faint line of confusion appeared between her eyes as they raised to his. "I . . . I don't understand."

"I'll explain the rules of the game. They're simple. What do you say?"

She swallowed and tried to probe the deep shadow cast by his hat brim. "Take off your hat."

His shoulders flinched. "What?"

"Take off your hat so I can see your eyes."

After a long pause he removed it slowly and laid it on the table. Her clear, true eyes pinned his cool brown ones with an unwavering look.

"When you and Willy played and the stakes were a trip to the Cowboys' Rest, did you cheat?"

His brows curled. Then he forcibly smoothed them and eased his shoulders back against the chair. "No."

"Very well." She turned all businesslike. "Explain the rules."

"Are you sure, Gussie?"

"I've done everything else this saloon encourages—watched women dance the cancan, drunk rye whiskey, even learned to like the smell of your cigar smoke. Why not poker, too?"

A lopsided grin tipped his mouth. A dimple appeared in his left cheek. Tarnation! She was some game woman! He turned the deck face up. The cards were numberless, difficult to read, but she concentrated hard as he explained the rank of poker hands from highest to lowest, rearranging the cards to illustrate each: straight flush, four of a kind, full house, flush, straight, three of a kind, two pair, one pair.

"Do you want me t' write them down?"

"No, I can remember." She recited the rank, perfectly. His eyes settled on her with undisguised admiration. Had the stakes been lower, he might have made a teasing comment. Instead, he scooped up the cards and began shuffling.

She watched his long, strong fingers manipulate the cards with economical movements. She listened to the crisp snap of the edges meshing before he scraped them together neatly and tapped them into line. The ring flashed on his finger and she recalled the day he'd first come to town—how little she'd suspected his coming would bring her to share a poker table in a dimly lit saloon with him at midnight.

He slapped the cards down before her and she jumped.

"What?" Her eyes flew up.

"You can deal."

"But I . . ." Her eyes dropped to the blue-and-white deck. *Samuel Hart,* she read on the top card.

"Shuffle, too, if y' still don't trust me."

"I do."

"Then deal. Five cards—one to me, the next t' you, face up."

She stared at him as if he'd suggested they remove their clothing alternately. He sat back and drew a cheroot from the pocket of his ice-blue vest, then the gold scissors with which he snipped the end. She watched, mesmerized, while he tucked the scissors away and lit the cigar.

"I never gamble without one of these in my hand," he enlightened her.

"Oh."

Silence fell and his smoke drifted to her nostrils.

"Go ahead, Gussie," he said quietly. "Deal."

She reached for the cards as if expecting a scorpion to appear from beneath the deck. They felt alien in her hands, slippery and new, yet oddly unthreatening, considering the potential havoc they might bring on her.

She dealt him his first card, without shuffling.

He withdrew the cigar from his lips and reminded her, "Face up."

Obediently, she turned it over. It bore three black clovers.

"Trey," he said. She glanced up in confusion and he added softly, "Three."

Her own card showed a crowned lady and a red heart.

"Queen of hearts," he explained. "Beats my trey."

His third card proved to be another three, but by the time she'd dealt four cards each, nothing else on the board showed promise. With trembling hands she turned up his last card: a seven of spades matching nothing. Before turning over her own last card, she stared at the figure on its back. It seemed to shimmy before her eyes. Her heart knocked in her throat. Her pale eyes met Gandy's dark ones across the table, while the smoke from his cigar rose between them. He sat as calmly as if waiting for dessert, while she trembled as if with the ague.

"No hard feelin's, whatever it is," he said.

She agreed with a silent nod of the head, not trusting her voice to come out steadily

She took a deep breath, held it, and slapped the last card over.

It was a two. His pair of threes beat her pair of deuces.

She stared at it and swallowed. He let his eyes slide closed and expelled a soft breath through his nostrils, struck by the irony of winning Willy with one of the worst hands he'd ever been dealt. He opened his eyes to find Agatha looking gray and stunned. His strong hand flashed across the table, covering the back of hers and squeezing hard . . . hard.

The future of three people, decided on the turn of a card. What was it men found so God Almighty exciting about gambling? She felt sick, hollow, afraid to raise her eyes and see in Scott's the glitter of victory.

But no sign of victory glittered in Gandy's eyes. Instead, they looked bereaved.

"Gussie, I—"

"Don't!" She jerked her hand away. "Don't say anything noble. I lost fair and square. Willy's yours!"

She jerked to her feet. The chair squealed back, but she moved too quickly and rocked against the edge of the table. The liquor sloshed over the rim of the glass and made a black blot on the green cloth, but neither noticed as Gandy, too, lurched to his feet.

"Gussie, wait!"

She picked up her skirts and limped quickly for the back door before she disgraced herself by crying in front of him.

When she was gone he stood in the silent murkiness of the cold saloon, telling himself it had been a fair hand; she had even dealt it. Fate had made the choice.

Then he grabbed the table and with a vile curse overturned it, sending chairs reeling and cards flying across the room. The glass shattered. The bottle rolled against a table leg, where it lay, gurgling its contents onto the raw floorboards.

Listening to it, he felt worse.

He sank to a chair, slumped forward, and clasped his skull. Lord Almighty! How could he take that boy away from her? She had nobody in the world. Nobody! And he had so many. He sat that way until somebody touched him lightly on the wrist. He straightened as if he'd been shot.

"What're you doin' up?" he demanded, none too gently.

"I heard a noise," Willy replied. "You all right, Scotty? You got the trots again or somethin'?"

"No, I'm all right."

"You don't look all right. You look kinda sick. What happened to the table?"

"Forget it, sprout. Listen . . . come here."

Willy padded toward Scott's outstretched hands, then found himself swung up onto his lap.

"I've got somethin' t' tell you." Scott's long hand ran up and down Willy's back, over the scratchy long underwear he wore now that cold weather was here. "Remember I asked you about the plantation—whether you'd like t' live there? Well, you're goin' to. It's called Waverley, and it's where I lived when I was a boy your age. I'll be closin' up the saloon any day now and movin' back there, but I'm takin' you with me, Willy. Would you like that?"

"You mean I'll live with you for ever and ever?"

"That's right. For ever and ever."

"Wow!" Willy cried, awed.

"Y' think you'd like that?"

"Sure—gee!" His face lit up.

"We'll ride on the train. It's a long way to Miz'sippi."

"A train—golly!" His delighted eyes grew as bright as a pair of Southern pecans. "I ain't never ridden on the train before." Then he tipped his head, closed his hand around one of Scott's lapels, and looked straight into his eyes. "Will Gussie be goin' with us?"

Scott had expected the question. Still, it hit him with the force of a fist in the solar plexus. "No, son, she won't. Gussie lives here. Her business is here, so she'll be stayin'."

"But I want her t' come along with us."

Scott wrapped both arms around Willy and tucked him against his chest. "I know y' do, but it just isn't possible."

Willy pushed himself away and glared into Scott's eyes again. "But she's our friend. She'll feel bad if we go away without her."

A lump formed in Scott's throat. He cleared his throat and clumsily closed the top button on Willy's underwear. "I know she will. But maybe y'all can come back sometimes on the train t' visit her. Would y' like that?"

Willy shrugged and stared disconsolately at his lap. "I guess so," he mumbled. His mood so reflected Scott's that when the man took the boy by the shoulders he spoke to soothe both their withered spirits.

"Listen, son, sometimes we love people, but we have t' leave 'em behind. It doesn't mean we forget 'em, or that we won't ever see 'em again. And Agatha loves you—you can't forget that. She'd keep you here if she could, but it would be very hard for her with such a tiny place to live in. At Waverley there'll be plenty o' space, and you'll have a room of your own in the big house—you know, the one on the picture in my sittin' room? You won't be sleepin' in the storeroom anymore. And there'll be lots t' see and do. We'll get you a horse and you can learn to ride. And there's a river where you can fish." Scott forcibly brightened his voice. "And wait till I show you the scuppernong vines you can swing on in the woods. Why, they climb up in the water oak trees so high y' can't see the tops of 'em!"

"Really?" Some of Willy's enthusiasm returned, but it was still underscored by a note of unhappiness.

"Really."

"But I could come back an' see Gussie?"

"Yes—that's a promise."

Willy thought for a moment, then decided, "She'll feel better when I tell 'er that."

Scott rested a hand on the boy's fair head. "Yes, I'm sure she will."

"I'm takin' Moose, ain't I?"

This one was tough. Scott had been anticipating it, too, but hadn't known how to answer.

Mistaking the reason for Scott's hesitation, Willy amended, "I mean *aren't* I?"

Agatha's influence. The boy still needed it badly, and Scott was hit afresh by guilt for having held the winning hand. He took Willy lightly by both arms, running his hands up and down. "It would be hard on the train, son. We'll be beddin' down in a sleepin' car, and animals can't sleep there. But I was thinkin'. You're right—Agatha's gonna miss us. Maybe she'd like t' keep Moose for company."

"But . . ." Willy's eyes began to fill with tears, but he struggled to repress them.

He'd lost so much in the last half year. First his father, now Agatha, and even his cat. It was expecting a lot of a five-year-old to accept these losses stoically.

"As soon as we get t' Waverley, we'll get you another cat," Scott promised. "Deal?"

Willy shrugged and dropped his chin. Scott took him against his chest once more.

"Oh, Willy . . ." He ran out of false enthusiasm and sat a long time with his cheek against Willy's hair, staring at the floor. He realized the best thing for all concerned was to make the break clean, fast. He'd order everybody to pack tomorrow and by the following day they should be ready to go.

"It's late. Reckon we oughta catch some sleep?"

"I reckon," Willy answered glumly. Scott stretched to his feet with Willy riding his arm and reached overhead for the lantern. "Can I come up with you?" the boy requested.

Scott stopped in the doorway to the storeroom. "I think Jube is sleepin' with me tonight," he answered truthfully.

"Oh." Willy's disappointment was evident before he inquired, "How come she sleeps with you an' she kisses Marcus?"

"She what?" A line of consternation bisected Gandy's eyebrows.

"She kisses Marcus. I saw her the night he hurt his hand. An' the day we went for the picnic they almost did. I could tell."

"Marcus?" So that's what was wrong!

"Is Jube an' Marcus an' everybody else gonna come to Waverley with us?" Distracted, Scott took some time in answering. "Are they?" Willy repeated.

"I don't know, sprout." He entered Willy's room and tucked him in, still with his thoughts elsewhere. "Now, y'all go to sleep and before you know it morning will be here. We'll have plenty t' do t' get ready."

"All right."

Scott leaned to kiss him. Halfway to the door, Willy's voice stopped him. "Hey, Scotty?"

"What?"

"Are there cows in Miz'sippi?"

"You mean like here, durin' the drives?"

"Yeah."

"No. Only the ones we'll keep for milkin'. Now go to sleep."

Scott felt somewhat better as he left Willy, realizing the boy's thoughts were turning inquisitive. It was the first solid sign of enthusiasm since Willy had learned Agatha wouldn't be accompanying them. But by the time he'd reached his room, he'd traded thoughts of Willy for those of Jube.

She wasn't in his bed as he'd expected. It made sense, though. Now it all made sense.

Willy was on his stool beside Agatha's sewing machine early the next morning, holding Moose in his arms. With typical childish directness he told her, "I have to go away with Scotty on the train an' live with him in Miz'sippi an' he says you can't go with us."

She intentionally kept sewing. Somehow, fingering the moving fabric kept her from breaking down. "That's right. The prohibition law is closing the saloon, but I still have to make dresses and hats for the ladies of Proffitt, don't I?"

"But I told him you're gonna feel bad. Ain't you gonna feel bad, Gussie?"

She pedaled as if her very body drew life from the flashing needle. "Of course I will, but I'm sure I'll see you again."

"Scotty says I can come back on the train."

The pedaling stopped abruptly. Agatha reached for Willy's hand, unable to help herself. "He did? Oh, that's so nice to know." Her consolation prize. But it was of little value at the moment. So she forced herself to begin working again. "I'm making you a pair of warm woolen britches to send with you."

"But, it's warm there," he reasoned.

"You'll still need them."

"Scotty says there's vines to swing on an' he's gonna buy me a horse so I can ride."

"My, won't that be something?" *Yes, all the things this child deserves.*

"But, Gussie?"

"Hmm?"

"He says I can't take Moose. Will you keep 'im?"

Please, God, make Willy dash off to some other pursuit. Make this day rush past on wings. Let me get through it without breaking down in front of him.

But she had to stop sewing again because she couldn't see the needle through her tears. She bent to pick up a scrap from the floor, secretly drying her eyes before facing Willy and giving Moose a quick scratch beneath his chin.

"Why, of course. I'd love to have Moose. Who else would do the mousing around here if you took him?"

"Scott says I can get a new cat when we get there. I'm gonna name him Moose, too, prob'ly."

"Ah, a good choice." She cleared her throat and turned back to her work. "Listen, dear, I have a lot to do. I wanted to try to get a shirt cut out and stitched up for you, too."

"Could you make it white, with a collar that comes off, like Scotty's?"

Please, Willy, don't do this to me! "Wh . . . white—wh . . . why, of course."

"I never had one with a collar that comes off."

"By tomorrow you w . . . will, dear."

"I gotta go tell Scotty!" He jumped off his stool and tore off. When the door slammed, Agatha leaned her elbows on the machine and covered her face with both hands. Everything inside her trembled. How long would the pain continue to intensify before finally leaving her numb?

Shortly after noon Willy came down with a note for Agatha, but she was busy out front with a customer, so he gave it to Violet instead.

"I'm not s'posed t' bother her when she's busy," he confided earnestly.

Violet smiled shakily and produced a nickel from her pocket. "Very good, sir. I'll deliver the message when the customer leaves. Now you run along and buy yourself a sarsaparilla stick."

He looked from his palm up to Violet's watery blue eyes. "A whole nickel! Thanks!"

"Hurry along now. I've got things to do." She had very little to do, but it was a relief when Willy dashed out again and she could blot her tears in private.

When the customer left, Violet parted the lavender curtains and entered the front room.

"Willy delivered this for you a while ago."

Her eyes dropped to the envelope. She recognized Scott's writing by the single word: Gussie.

Violet stood smack before her, squeezing four fingers tightly with the opposite hand, watching Agatha's eyes as she read the message aloud:

> Dear Gussie,
>   Willy and I request the pleasure of your company at Paulie's for supper tonight. We'll pick you up at your door at six o'clock.
>
> > > > Affectionately,
> > > > Willy and Scott

Violet was blinking hard. "Well . . . my . . . isn't that nice?"

Agatha serenely folded the note and slipped it back into the envelope. "Yes," she said quietly.

Violet fluttered a hand. "Well, you must . . . you must let me close up tonight, and go upstairs early to get dressed."

Agatha lifted sad eyes, and as they met Violet's the two women stood locked in a gaze that dropped all pretensions. They were both miserable and heartsore, and neither tried to hide it. Agatha pressed her firm cheek against Violet's soft, wrinkled one. "Thank you," she said softly. Violet hugged her hard for a brief moment. Then Agatha backed away and dashed the moisture from beneath both eyes as if irritated that it was there so often lately. "If I don't tend to business," she said brusquely, "I'll never get that shirt done for Willy in time."

They were all dressed in their best finery when Agatha answered her door at six that night: Scott in his fawn-colored suit and a thick brown greatcoat she'd never seen before; Willy in the Sunday suit he'd gotten for his father's funeral, and his new wool winter jacket; Agatha in the rust-and-melon dress she'd worn for the governor's tea, though she'd left the bonnet behind, which pleased Scott. Her hair was too beautiful to cover with birds' nests and plumes. He'd always meant to tell her that, but somehow he had never found the proper time.

"Good evenin'," he said when she opened the door. Their eyes met and held until Willy piped up.

"Hi, Gussie. I'm here, too."

Immediately, she bent to hold his cheeks and kiss him. "Of course you are. And, my stars, don't you look handsome!"

He smiled proudly and looked up. "Just as handsome as Scotty?"

She looked into the face of the man she would never forget as long as she drew breath. Her answer came out much more quietly than the question. "Yes. Just as handsome as Scotty."

She had always wanted to tell him that, but she had been bound by the proprieties of the single woman. However, with Willy putting the question to her, what else could she do but answer truthfully? It wasn't the way she'd have said it, had she been granted the choice of time, place, and situation, but at least he knew now.

His lips opened, then closed on a faint gust of breath.

She turned away. "I must get my pelisse." She hadn't expected him to be so near when she turned from the chifforobe with the garment in her hands. She swung around and bumped his arm. Her heart caromed at his nearness, his scent, his broadness in the heavy winter coat, the striking appeal of his face.

"Here, let me," he demanded softly, taking the pelisse from her hands.

"Thank you." She turned and he placed the brown velvet cape over her shoulders, then squeezed her arms tightly and pulled her back against him.

"Please don't put the hood up," he requested in a whisper, his lips brushing her ear. "Your hair is too lovely t' spoil."

The rush of her pulses seemed to flutter the very air around her. "Scott . . ." she whispered, closing her eyes, drowning in bittersweet emotions.

"Hey, I'm hungry!" Willy called from the doorway. "Come on."

Reluctantly, Scott released Agatha and stepped back, allowing her to lead the way out. Willy thundered down the stairs at breakneck pace. Agatha clutched the rail but found her free elbow held tightly by Scott. She could think of nothing to say as they reached the bottom and he let his hand slip all the way down to clasp hers. He held it tightly until they reached the end of the alley. On the boardwalk, he again took her elbow.

The meal was a farce she'd never thereafter recall clearly. She and Scott talked, but of what remained vague. Willy chattered with boyish enthusiasm and asked endless questions of Scott: "Where will my new cat sleep?" "What's a scuppernong?" "Are there snakes there?"

Scott answered succinctly—in the kitchen; a wild grape; yes—but rarely gave his undivided attention to Willy. He stared at Agatha instead, feeling restive and agitated, semiaroused and guilty. She was lovely. Why hadn't he *really* seen it before? What had taken him so long? And she was more of a lady than any woman he'd ever known.

She ate little, but with such incredible delicacy that each movement of her hands and jaws appeared more a dance than the banal acts of lifting food and masticating. He sensed how close to the breaking point she hovered, her tears so near the surface her eyes appeared the deep hue of a magnolia leaf in the spring rain. She was breathless, too, and flushed from trying to contain the emotions so close to welling over. Her fingers trembled and her voice shook, but she forced fleeting laughter for Willy's sake, whenever the child's comments demanded it. She seemed unable to meet Gandy's eyes, though he longed for her to do so throughout the meal. Not until their coffee arrived and he reached for the cheroot and gold scissors did she at last lift her luminous green eyes to his. And once, while he smoked, she closed those eyes and drew a deep breath through distended nostrils, as if savoring the scent for the last, last time. His eyes dropped to the hand she rested on her heart and he wondered if it raced like his. Then she opened her eyes and caught him watching her and hid her face behind her coffee cup.

He pulled out his pocket watch. "It's late," he noted.

"Yes." Still she refused to look at him. But she wore her hood down as they made their way slowly back to their lodgings. Approaching the stairs, she veered toward them, but he drew her back with a tight grip on her elbow.

"Come with me. We'll tuck Willy in together."

Her throat filled. Her heart hammered. But she couldn't say no. "All right."

The saloon was silent, dark, a bleak reminder of its former gaiety. Agatha was glad she didn't have to see into it in the dim glow of the lantern. Willy's wretched little cubicle was enough. She'd never been into it before and compared the stained wooden floor, the yeasty scents that permeated the room, to what it must be like at Waverley—bright windows and a high bed and more than likely a fireplace in each bedroom.

He shucked down to his woolen underwear and handed her each piece of clothing. She carefully hung them up for morning and smiled as she watched him leap onto his cot, shivering, the trapdoor of his underwear momentarily flashing into view as Moose appeared and leaped up, too. The room was drafty and far from warm. She felt the cold in the marrow of her bones, especially in her left hip, when she knelt down to Willy's outstretched arms.

"G'night, Gussie."

"Good night, sweetheart."

Oh . . . oh . . . the smell of him. She would never forget the smell of him, the little-boy smell she'd come to love. And the fleeting touch of his precious lips.

"You're coming t' the train with us in the mornin', ain't . . . aren't you?"

She smoothed the hair back from his temple with one thumb and took a long, loving look into his heartbreaking brown eyes. "No, sweetheart. I've decided it would be best not to. The store will be open and—"

"But I want you to come."

Agatha felt Scott go down on one knee beside her, his thigh pressing against the thick draperies of her skirt. He rested one arm around her waist and the other on Willy's stomach, looking directly into the child's eyes.

Beneath his left arm he felt the trembling disguised by Agatha's loose pelisse.

"Listen, sprout," he said, forcing a grin, "y' didn't forget about Moose, did y'? She'll have t' be takin' care of Moose now, won't she?"

"Oh, yeah, that's right." Willy dragged the cat close. "I'll bring Moose down just before we leave, all right?"

She couldn't speak, could only nod her head.

"Well, g'night," he chirped, too young to realize the full import of last times, finalities.

She kissed him, letting her lips linger against his warm cheek. Scott kissed him, bending his dark head so close his shoulder brushed her breast.

"Sleep tight, sprout," he said throatily, then stood and reached for Agatha's elbow. Her heel caught in her bustle as she rose, and her hip sent out a shot of pain as she struggled clumsily to her feet. His hand tightened securely and guided her up.

When the lantern was out they moved through the dark to the rear door of the saloon. Scott's hand still clutching her arm. Up the stairs . . . slowly, reluctantly, counting the fleeting seconds until they reached the rough wooden landing. She moved to her door and stared at the knob unseeingly.

"Thank you for the supper, Scott."

He stood close behind her, uncertain of his ability to speak if he tried. His words came out deep and throaty. "May I come in for a while?"

She lifted her face. "No, I think not."

"Please, Gussie," he begged, this time in a racked whisper.

"What purpose would it serve?"

"I don't know. I just . . . God, turn around and look at me." He turned her by an elbow, but she refused to lift her eyes. "Don't cry," he pleaded. "Oh Gussie, don't cry." He squeezed her elbows fiercely.

She sniffed once and swiped beneath her eyes. "I'm sorry. I can't seem to help it lately."

"Aren't you really comin' t' the station tomorrow?"

"I can't. Don't ask it of me, Scott. This is bad enough."

"But—"

"No, I'll say my good-byes here. I won't make a fool of myself in public!"

He dredged up the words that had been haunting him all through the painful good-night downstairs. "Willy should be stayin' here, with you."

She pulled free of his touch and half turned away. "It isn't only him, Scott, and you know it."

She felt his surprise in the tense moment of silence before he swung her back to face him so abruptly the hood of her pelisse struck her ear. "But why didn't you . . ." He glowered down at her, holding her again by both arms. "You've never said anything."

"It wasn't my place. I'm the woman. Oh . . . I'm sorry, Scott." She turned her head sharply aside. "I shouldn't have now. It's just . . . I'll m . . . miss you so much."

"Will you, Gussie?" he asked with wonder in his voice, holding her in place and letting his gaze roam from her hair to her chin, then from ear to delicate ear. "Will you really?"

"Let me go," she entreated.

He drew her a fraction closer. "Let me stay."

She shook her head wildly. "No."

"Why?"

"Let me go!" she cried, whirling from him, stumbling toward the door.

"Gussie, wait!" Just as her hand reached the knob she was spun around and lifted bodily. Her pelisse twisted, binding her feet, catching one arm within its folds. The other groped for something solid and found his neck. Her feet hung a foot off the floor. Her trapped elbow dug into his ribs. They stared into each other's eyes while denial and arousal warred within them, colored by the awareness that in the morning a train would bear him away from her forever, along with the child she loved.

"Please, don't," she begged in a jagged whisper.

"I'm sorry," he said just before his lips covered hers. The shock of his open mouth sent a current straight to her core. Her own opened and their tongues meshed—glorious, succulent, shattering. It was nothing like the other kiss they'd shared. This one was greedy and fated, desperate and clinging. He washed the interior of her mouth with his tongue, then, turning, made a soft noise in his throat as he pressed her against the wall. Even while he awakened a deeper yearning than any she'd imagined, she begged him silently to stop. Even while her own throat emitted a sound of passion, she willed him to relieve her of this torture before her heart burst.

She tore her mouth free. "Scott, if I—"

His mouth stopped her protest, stopped the soft open lips that threatened reason. She felt the flowering of passion as a gentle tug at her innards, an involuntary response plucked to the surface by the insistence of his tongue. Hers could do no less than answer, twine, explore, excite. New, delightful things happened in her body until she jerked her head back sharply and gasped for breath.

Her head hit the wall. Her captured arm ached. She couldn't reach the floor.

"Put me down," she begged.

He let her slip, freeing his hands. They threaded about her waist, inside the pelisse, learning the feel of her ribs inside their cage of steel and laces. His lips chased hers, but she rolled her head, avoiding further kisses that robbed her of ordinary sense. "If you have any feeling for me at all you'll stop." Her arm worked free and she captured his face in both hands, holding his head still. "You're making it harder," she whispered fiercely.

With his body bracing hers, he suddenly fell still. His eyes, only deep shadows, raked her face. A shudder of remorse quaked in him and he sagged against her. "I'm sorry, Gussie. I wasn't goin' t' do this. I was only goin' t' walk you t' your door." His hands left her ribs and, outside her cape, drew her lightly against his chest. With a sudden slump he spun them both about, leaning back weakly against the wall, bearing her weight.

"I don't want to go," he said thickly, looking up at the starless sky, with her head nestled just beneath his chin.

"Shh!"

"I don't want to take Willy away from you."

"I know."

"Jesus, I'm goin' t' miss you."

She rested her temple against his chest and tried to swallow the knot of love in her throat.

"S . . . Scott . . ." She pushed away, stood on her own again, and lay both palms on his vest. "It's still not proper, I'm still the . . . the woman. But there's something I must say or forever regret not doing so." She lifted a gloved hand to his jaw and looked at his lips as she said it. "I love you. No . . ." She waylaid his response by touching his lips. "It isn't necessary. It would only make life more unbearable without you. Just take care of Willy for me, and send him back whenever you can. Promise?"

He clasped the back of her hand and removed it from his mouth. "Why won't you let me say it?"

"You would only do so because you feel sorry for me. It's not reason enough. Promise me," she reiterated, "you'll send Willy back."

"I promise. And I'll come wi—"

This time it was her lips that silenced his before he could speak the lie. Once he left her he'd forget all about this night, when parting seemed so terrible. She flung her arms around his neck and kissed him once—just once as she'd dreamed of doing, holding his head, pressing her breasts against him, and feeling his arms take her—full length, nothing disguised.

"Good-bye, Scott," she whispered, pulling away. And in a flash she was gone, leaving him bereft and confused.

Inside, she turned the key in the lock, then fell back against it, listening.

"Gussie?" he called softly.

She clamped her upper lip between her teeth.

He rapped softly. "Gussie?"

After the third appeal went unanswered, she finally heard his footsteps cross to his own door.

That night was like a dress rehearsal for the ordeal of saying good-bye to everybody the following day. They came down, one by one, and each parting was harder than the previous one, until finally the one who poked his head around the door was Willy. He came last, after all the clunking and thumping of suitcases and packing crates had stopped next door. He was dressed in his Sunday suit again and clutched Moose against his shoulder.

"Gussie, we gotta go. We're nearly late."

"Come here, darling." She turned on her swivel seat before the sewing machine. He came into her arms, throwing one arm around her neck, the other maintaining a death grip on the cat.

"Scotty says t' tell you he'll write."

"You must write, too, as soon as you know how. I'm sorry I can't keep you."

"I know. Scotty says I hafta remember that you love me."

"I do . . ." She held his face in both hands. They were both crying. "Oh, I do. I'll miss you terribly."

"I w . . . wish you was m . . . my mother," he choked out.

Clasping him tightly to her breasts, she vowed, "So do I. I couldn't love you more if I were."

"I love you too, Gussie. Take good care o' Moose for me and don't feed him no milk. It gives him the trots."

"I won't." She laughed pitifully, taking the cat from his shoulder as he pulled away.

He paused uncertainly, clasped his hands behind his back, and shrugged. "Well . . . see ya."

She rested her face against the cat's warm fur but couldn't force a sound from her throat. Willy spun to Violet, waiting with tears running down her cheeks. " 'Bye, Vy'let." She bent down for a swift kiss. Then he sprinted toward the door, paused, and turned, holding the knob. " 'Bye, Moose," he said, then ran.

In their compartment on the train, while Scott stowed their carry-on luggage, Willy demanded, "But why wouldn't she come?"

"She didn't want t' cry where everyone could see her."

"Oh." Still feeling blue, Willy continued studying the busy train depot, hoping Agatha would change her mind after all. "She cried when I gave her Moose."

Scott settled into a seat, steeling himself against emotions he couldn't afford to feel. "I know." Though he knew it was useless, he found himself scanning the people seeing passengers off, and there were many, most of them former customers who came to wave a last good-bye to Jube and the girls.

He hated leaving Agatha this way, taking with him the memory of her tears as she ran into her lonely apartment. Outside, the wind buffeted the sides of the train, shredding the smoke from the engine, lifting the steam whistle's lonely shriek and throwing it back along the line, an eerie accompaniment to their departure from the place he'd always called a dreary little cow town. He'd never expected to ache so when he left it. But Proffitt had brought him Agatha, and leaving her did, indeed, make him ache. A deep furrow marred his brow as he stared out the window in silence. He saw the conductor draw the portable step, then disappear inside the train. He scanned the crowd hopefully. Just as the train lurched to life he saw her.

"There she is!" he exclaimed, grabbing Willy onto his knee and pointing. "There, behind all the others! See? In her brown cape."

She stood apart from the others, her gloved hands crossed over her breast. She wore the brown velvet pelisse with the hood up. He'd never seen a lonelier-looking picture in his life. "Gussie!" Willy flattened one hand against the cold glass and waved exuberantly with the other. " 'Bye, Gussie, 'bye!" She couldn't have seen them board; she'd only appeared moments before the train began moving. And it was apparent as she scanned the flashing windows that she had no idea behind which they were. But as the wild wind caught at the hem of her pelisse and tossed it aloft, she lowered its hood and waved . . . and waved . . . and waved . . . until all the windows had streamed past and they lost her from sight.

Then Willy was crying quietly.

And Gandy lay his head back, closed his eyes, and swallowed thickly to keep from doing the same.

Chapter 17

None of Gandy's extended family seemed any less orphaned than Willy. Without loved ones or homes, and with Christmas coming on, anywhere they'd have gone would have been chosen against their will. By tacit agreement, they all went to Waverley together.

During the trip, they broke into smaller groups to share seats and berths, so Scott saw little of Jube. He spent much time wondering about her and Marcus, recalling what Willy had said. They didn't sit together much; Jube spent most of the time with Ruby and Pearl. But in the evening, after they'd been traveling several hours, Gandy needed to stretch his legs and, strolling down the aisle, he passed them sitting side by side. Marcus appeared to be asleep. Jube's head lay back against the seat but her face was turned toward him, and upon it Scott saw a winsome expression she'd never turned upon himself. She caught sight of Scott in the aisle and flashed him a quick self-conscious smile. Then her cheeks turned a becoming pink. To the best of his recollection, it was the first time he'd ever seen Jube blush.

Later, when he and Willy had retired to their bunks, he lay on his back behind the drawn curtains, one wrist behind his head, pondering the sleeping arrangements at Waverley. It was the perfect time to make the break. Whether or not Marcus and Jube had declared their feelings for each other, it would no longer be right for Jube to share Scott's bed.

How was it he and Jube hadn't talked about their deteriorating love affair? Because it had never really been a *love* affair. It had been a convenient arrangement that temporarily suited them both. Had it been anything more, he'd be jealous now, angry, hurt. Instead, he felt only relief. He hoped that Jube and Marcus would find in each other the perfect mate.

Wouldn't that be something? He smiled in the dark, thinking of it. Jube and Marcus, married. Maybe they could hold the service in the wedding alcove: Wouldn't that grand old house love to see life revived within its walls?

You're dreamin', Gandy. You can't keep the group there. How will they live? What will they do? Where will the money come from? You're a fool t' be goin' there in the first place. All it'll do is revive dreams of how it was, how it can never be again. And what about Willy? You promised him things you aren't sure you can give him. What'll he think if you inform him that he won't be livin' at Waverley after all? And what kind of life will he have traipsin' along after you and your troop, openin' saloon after saloon across the country?

Restive, he shifted, trying to get more comfortable. But the clatter and sway of the train kept him wide awake. He raised the heavy felt shade and tied it into place with its braided silk cords, then watched the countryside shimmy away beneath the glow of a winter moon. The train traveled southwest now. All traces of snow had vanished. Beside the tracks black snakes of water reflected the moon, while trees studded the landscape. Missouri? Arkansas? He wasn't sure. But already the flatness of the prairie had given way to gentle hills that swelled and rolled like a midnight sea.

He thought of Proffitt, the abandoned saloon, Agatha alone upstairs. *She cried when I gave her Moose.* A thick knot seemed to lodge in his chest as he pictured her curling up with Willy's cat, waking up tomorrow morning and going downstairs with no Willy to barge through the door and break the monotony of her humdrum life.

You did what you had to, Gandy. Forget her. You have enough t' worry about gettin' your own life in order, facin' the ghosts of Waverley again, deciding how to provide for a family of eight. Agatha's been on her own a long time. She'll make out fine.

But no matter how many times he reiterated these thoughts, he could not evict her from his memory.

On the afternoon of the second day the train carried Gandy and company into the town of Columbus, Mississippi, which had been a bustling cotton-trading center on the Tombigbee River before the war. The old cotton chutes were still there, like curved tongues waiting to drop bales again from the empty warehouses along the river onto the riverboats that were dying a slow death beside the railroad tracks, which carried everything faster, cheaper, safer.

"When I was a boy," Scott told Willy, "I used t' like t' watch the slaves load cotton on the riverboats just like you watched the cowpokes load cows on the train."

"Here?"

"Sometimes here. More often at Waverley. We had our own warehouss and the riverboats pulled right up t' shore t' load."

The comment released a torrent of questions. "How far away is it? How long before we git there? Can I fish in the river right away? What color will my horse be?"

Scott chuckled at the boy's excitement, which mirrored his own, as his first glimpse of Waverley grew closer.

They bought supplies at Sheed's Mercantile store. Old Franklin Sheed looked like a dried apple doll with white whiskers. He squinted at Scott from behind corrugated eyelids, withdrew a pipe from his mouth, and drawled. "Well, blezz mah soul. LeMaster Gandy, i'n't it?"

He extended a hard hand and clasped Scott's.

"Sure is, though nobody's called me that in a long time."

"Good t' see ya again, boy. Y'all back for good?"

"Don't rightly know, Mr. Sheed." Realizing Willy listened, he added, "I hope so. Brought my friends here t' see the old place." He introduced them all around, ending with the boy, upon whose shoulders Scott rested his hands.

"Well, it's still there," Sheed said of Waverley. "Nobody messes with it, 'cept a few o' the old slaves used t' work for your daddy. They're still out there, keepin' trespassers off the place. Be s'prised t' see you after all these years."

Something good happened inside Scott, clasping Franklin's hand. His roots were here. Folks remembered him, his people, his heritage. He'd wandered for so long, lived among strangers who cared little about his past or his future, once he parted from them, that coming back to a place where his name was remembered gave him an immediate pang of nostalgia. And here was old Franklin Sheed, who'd sold Scott's father cigars and his mother cotton cloth for the very diapers she'd used for his brothers and himself.

"What's it been now, since your folks passed on?" Franklin wondered aloud. But before Gandy could answer, a pinched-up octogenarian in a tattered gray bonnet limped in with a black cypress cane.

"Miz Mae Ellen," the store owner greeted her, "y'all remember Dorian and Selena Gandy's boy, don't you?"

She lowered her head and peered at Scott for a full ten seconds, resting both hands on the head of the cane.

"LeMastuh, is it?"

"That's right, Miz Bayles." He grinned down at the withered woman, remembering how much taller she'd been the last time he'd seen her. Or had he only been shorter?

"Used t' feed you peaches when your mama came t' visit me at Oakleigh."

"I remember, Miz Bayles." His grin remained. His eyes teased. "And some o' the tastiest molasses cookies anywhere this side o' the Mason-Dixon line. But y'all never let me have more than two, and I used t' stare at the rest on the plate and swear I'd get even someday."

Her laugh filled the store like the gobble of an old hen turkey. She rapped her cane on the floor, then shot a sly glance at Jube, standing nearby. "And I used t' look at that face o' his and think t' myself, that boy's too handsome for his own good. He'll end up in trouble over it someday." Her shrewd eyes pinioned Scott again. "Did you?"

Scott's dimples deepened to disarming depths. "Not that I recall, Miz Bayles."

She glanced from Jube to Willy to Scott. "So you married up again, did you?"

"No, ma'am." Scott gestured toward Jube, then looked down at Willy. "These are my friends, Jubilee Bright and Willy Collinson." The others were browsing throughout the store so he didn't bother to introduce them.

"Willy, is it?" She studied him imperiously.

Scott waggled Willy's shoulder. " 'Member your manners, boy."

Willy extended a hand. "Pleased t' meet you, ma'am."

"Humph!" she snorted, shaking his hand. "Don't know why you should be— dried up prune like me, doesn't feed a boy more'n two molasses cookies at a time. But I have a grandson, A.J., and he's the one you'd like t' meet." She jerked a thumb at Scott. "You have this rascal bring you by someday and I'll introduce you two."

"Really?"

She poked Willy in the shoulder with the tip of her cane. "One thing you got to learn right up front, boy. Wrinkled-up old ladies don't say things they don't mean. They never know when they might drop over dead an' leave confusion behind."

Everyone laughed. Then Scott allowed Miss Bayles to make her purchases ahead of him. While she did, he inquired, "Y'all still live at Oakleigh, Miz Bayles?"

"Oakleigh is empty," she replied with stiff pride, carefully counting out her money from a leather pouch, then snapping it closed. "I live with my daughter, Leta, in town now."

For a moment Scott had been carried back into the past. Miss Bayles's revelation reminded him that Waverley wasn't the only grand mansion left derelict by the war. The turn of the conversation had put a damper on the subject, and when Miss Bayles turned with her purchases in hand, Scott politely tipped his hat.

"Greet Leta for me," he requested. "I remember her well."

"I'll do that, LeMaster. My best t' Leatrice. I remember her well, too."

Leatrice's name brought a resurgence of expectation to Scott. It remained within him as they bought ham and grits and flour and lard—enough food to feed a family of eight for several days. The good feeling stayed with him while they rented rigs at the livery—where again Scott was recognized and greeted enthusiastically by his given name—and while they set out for Waverley through the familiar Mississippi countryside.

Heading northwest, they rode through thick stands of oak, hickory, and post pine that opened into vast tracts of depleted cotton fields, few of which had been seeded in the last fifteen years. They passed Oakleigh, which appeared as only a faint white blur at the end of a long lane, half choked with underbrush and scuppernong vines.

The sky was clear but the breeze held a bite. The tips of the pines stroked the evening sky the way an artist's brush passed across a canvas, painting it the hue of a fading wisteria blossom. The carriages traveled upon a gravel road worn smooth by years of mule-drawn wagon wheels that had ground it down to fine silt. The scent of the earth was moist and fecund, unlike the dry, grainy scent of Kansas. Neither the sound nor odor of shifting cattle was anywhere to be heard or smelled. Instead, Gandy's senses thrilled to the sweet melodic trill of an occasional mockingbird rising from a thicket, and the scent of vegetation decaying now during the brief hiatus between growing seasons.

"Waverley land starts here," He said. Willy's eyes grew disbelieving as they rode on and on still father.

"All this?"

Scott only smiled and held the reins loosely between his knees. They entered the last mile, the last half mile. Then ahead, on the right, a black iron fence appeared. As they approached it, Scott slowed the rig. Beside him, Willy looked up. Then his eyes followed the path of Scott's.

"Somebody's buried way out here?" Willy asked.

"My family."

"Yours?" The boy glanced up again.

In the back seat Jube and Marcus turned to glimpse the cemetery.

"Who?" Willy asked, craning to watch the gray headstones slip past.

"My mama and my daddy. And my wife and our little girl."

"You had a little girl?"

"Her name was Justine."

"And what's that?" Willy asked, pointing to a wooden structure on their right.

"Why, that's the bathin' house. Inside is the swimmin' pool."

"Wow!" Willy raised up off the seat in excitement. Scott pressed him back down. "Y'all can see it later." He went on quietly, "And this . . ." Scott turned left into the drive directly opposite the pool house—". . . is Waverley."

The sight of it brought a leap to Gandy's heart, a thrill to his blood, even though, like Oakleigh, the house was glimpsed through snarls of vines and thickets of cedar and gum trees that had encroached upon the long lane, rendering it impassable. In its prime, the lane had been meticulously maintained. But today Gandy was forced to rein in after traveling less than a quarter of its length. In the early evening shadows the choking vegetation seemed to lend a menacing note to their reception. The overwhelming catlike smell of the gum trees seemed offensive, as if warning all mortals to keep away.

"Wait here," Gandy ordered, looping the reins around the whip bracket.

He went alone, picking his way through fifteen years' unchecked growth until he reached the massive magnolia—the one with the widest limb span in the state of Mississippi—that had dominated Waverley's front yard for as long as he could remember. But his disappointment redoubled at the sight of it, too, overrun by vines and hemmed in by his mother's precious boxwoods. She'd brought the boxwoods all the way from Georgia as a young bride and had nurtured them lovingly as long as she'd been alive. Their geometric perfection was long gone, for they'd been pruned by nothing but wild deer for years and years, leaving them grotesque and misshapen. Selena Gandy would have been appalled at their present disgraceful state.

Her son scratched his face on the unkempt bushes as he forced his way through them to the front entrance. The marble steps were intact, as was the iron grillework on the overhanging balcony and the ruby-red sidelights of Venetian glass surrounding the massive front door.

But the door itself wouldn't budge.

He cupped a hand over his eyes and tried to peer inside, but the door faced south, and now in the descending twilight little light came through the windows around the matching north door across the entry hall. All he could make out were the carved lyre-shaped inserts on the insides of the windows. Beyond these, images appeared vague, translucent, as if viewed through a glass of burgundy wine.

He pounded on the door and called, "Is anybody there? Leatrice, y'all in there?"

Only silence greeted him and the sudden rat-a-tat of a woodpecker somewhere in the dense growth behind him.

The back door proved no more hospitable than the front. The two entrances were identical, with twin Doric columns fronting recessed porches two stories high. The only differences were the second, shorter pair of columns guarding the front door and the pair of familiar black wooden benches on either side of the back door. The sight of them brought another stab of nostalgia to Scott. They were thick, heavy, made of bois d'arc wood from the cypress swamps down by the river, bent and looped into the modified fanback design by the hands of slaves long before he himself had been born. It was upon the bois d'arc benches he remembered his mother and father sitting while Delia fed the peacocks.

Leaving the house behind, he followed a track showing evidence of recent use, past the old kitchen, the octagonal ice house, the gardens, the tannery, the stables, toward the slave cabins out back. He smelled Leatrice's woodsmoke long before he reached her door.

Knocking, he called, "Leatrice?"

"Who dat?" she called in a voice like flatulent wind escaping a bloated horse.

"Open up and see for yourself." He smiled, his face close to the rough door as he waited.

"Sumbuddy full o' sass, fo' sure." The door swung open and there she stood, nearly as big around as the century-old magnolia out front, her skin as coarse and black as its bark, and, like the tree, looking every bit as if she were here to stay forever.

"What kind o' welcome is that?" he teased, leaning an elbow on the doorsill and letting a grin slide up his cheek.

"Who . . . Lawd o' mercy"—her eyes flew wide. "Dat you, Mastuh?" She had never added the *Le* to LeMaster, and had always scoffed at the familiar *Scott*. "Praise mah soul, chile! It's you!"

"It's me." He lunged inside and scooped her up, though his arms reached scarcely two-thirds of the way around her. She smelled of woodsmoke and cracklings and poke greens, and her hug was mighty enough to threaten his bones.

"Mah baby come home!" she rejoiced, shedding tears, praising the heavens. "Lawd, Lawd, he come home at lass." She backed off and held him by the ears. "Lemme have a look."

Her voice was like no other in humankind, a deep rumbling bass that could not come out softly, no matter how she tried. She had smoked a corncob pipe all her days, and it was anybody's guess what concoctions she'd stuffed into it. Something long ago had damaged her larynx and left it able to emit only the grating sound no one ever forgot once they'd heard it.

"Jiss like I thought," she pronounced, "skinny as a sparrow's kneecap. What they been feedin' ya, pot likker?" She turned Scott around by the shoulders, inspected him minutely, then swung him again to face her. "Well, ol' Leatrice fatten ya up in no time. Mose!" she called without looking back over her shoulder. "Come see who's heah."

"Mose is here?" Gandy's face registered happy surprise as he glanced beyond her shoulder.

"Sho' is," said the aged black man who emerged out of the shadows and crossed the wooden floor with an arthritic shuffle. "Nevuh goed. Stayed right heah where I belonged."

"Mose," Scott said affectionately, clasping one of the old man's bony hands in both of his own. Mose was as thin as Leatrice was fat. His silver hair topped his head like Spanish moss, and, standing, he listed slightly to the left and forward, as if his spine refused to straighten completely anymore.

"Fifteen years," the old man mused aloud in a thin, wispy voice. " 'Bout time ya was gittin' back heah.'

"I may not be stayin'," Scott clarified immediately. "Just came t' see the place again."

Mose released Scott's hand to brace his back. "Y'all be stayin'," he said, as if there were no question.

Scott let his eyes slide assessingly from Mose to Leatrice. "So you two finally took up together."

Leatrice cuffed him none too gently on the side of the head. "Watch yo' tongue, boy. Ain' I taught ya t' respec' yo' elduhs? Me and Mose kep' de place while y'all went gally-hooin' 'roun'." She turned away with an air of superiority. "'Sides, I wou'n't have 'im. He too lazy, dat one. But he company."

Scott rubbed the side of his head and smiled. "That any way t' treat the boy who used t' pick you wild blackberries and snitch roses for you from his mother's garden?"

When Leatrice laughed the rafters overhead threatened to split. "Set down, boy. I got warm cornbread an' black-eyed peas. Bes' get t' work hangin' some fat on dem bones."

Gandy stayed where he was. "I brought company. Think y'all could handle ham and biscuits for eight if I bring the ham and the fixin's?"

"Eight?" Leatrice humphed and turned away as if slighted by the question. "Like feedin' eight mosquitoes aftuh what I done feed in de good days. Y'all brung dat Ruby home, too?"

"I did. And Ivory, too."

"Ivory, too." Leatrice raised one eyebrow and added, sarcastically, "My, my, dat make four o' us. Soon we be raisin' cotton."

Gandy smiled. Being tongue-lashed by Leatrice was exactly what he needed to make him feel as if he were home at last.

"I left them stranded in the lane. Couldn't get into the big house."

"Key's right heah." Leatrice pulled it from between her ample breasts. "Been keepin' it in a safe spot. Mose, he open up." She drew the leather thong over her head and handed it to the old man.

But Mose gaped at it as if it had eight legs. "Me?"

"Yas, you. Now git!"

Mose backed off, shaking his head, eyes bugging as they fixed on the key. 'Ain't goin' in dere, nossir, not ol' Mose."

"What you talkin' 'bout. 'Cose you goin' in dere. Got t' open it up fo' young Mastuh an' his frien's."

Gandy watched the interchange with a puzzled frown.

"Git, now!" the black woman ordered imperiously.

Mose only shook his head fearfully and backed farther away.

"What is all this?" Scott demanded, frowning.

"Place got a hant."

"A hant!"

"Thass right. I heard her. Mose heard her. She in dere, whimperin'. Y'all go in, ya heah her soon 'nuff. What ya s'pose kep' folks out all dese years? Not jiss two old black folk goin' 'round checkin' de doors."

Gandy's neck stiffened even as he declared, "But that's ridiculous. A ghost?"

Leatrice picked up his palm and into it slapped the keys, still warm from her breasts. "Y'all open it up yo'self. Leatrice, she cook. Leatrice, she make biscuits, she make ham. Leatrice, she bring dem ham and biscuits far as de back door." She crossed her arms over her watermelon-sized breasts and gave one stubborn wag of the head. "But Leatrice don't go near no hants. Noooo, suh!"

As he picked his way back toward the house, armed with several tallow candles, Scott clearly recalled the child's voice he'd heard in the house after the war. Was it true, then? Was it Justine? Was she searching for her mother and father somewhere in the lofty, unoccupied rooms of Waverley? Or was it only the product of several overactive imaginations? He knew how superstitious black people were. Yet, he, too, had heard it, and he'd never had a superstitious bone in his body.

He shrugged aside the thought, rounded a corner of the house and bumped into something soft.

He gasped and let out a yelp.

But it was only Jack, prowling about the foundation of the old place, trailed by the others, who'd grown restless waiting in the carriages.

"She's a beauty," Jack declared, "and sound, too, from what I can see in this light."

"Let's go inside."

As he inserted the key into Waverley's front door, Scott found himself relieved to have the company of seven others, especially Willy, whose small hand he clasped tightly.

But once inside, all thoughts of ghosts fled. Even in the light of two candles, the massive rotunda welcomed him back. It smelled of disuse and dust, but nothing had changed. The Southern pine floors, the double staircase curving downward like two open arms, the giant pier mirrors reflecting the flickering candles, the hand-carved spindles lining the stairs, disappearing into the shadows overhead, the elegant brass chandelier dropping sixty feet from above—all waited to be polished and put to use again.

"Welcome to Waverley," he said softly, his voice echoing to the lookout four stories above his head, then dropping back down as if the mansion itself had spoken to him.

They lit a fire in the massive downstairs dining room and ate the supper Leatrice prepared, though only Ivory and Ruby caught a glimpse of her as she delivered the hot food to the back door. Afterward, discussing sleeping arrangements, both Ivory and Ruby said they'd be more comfortable away from the big house, which they'd scarcely seen before as slave children. Though Gandy tried to convince them they were welcome to sleep there, they prevailed upon Leatrice and Moses to put them up out back.

Gandy settled Marcus and Jack into one of the four massive second-story bedrooms, Peal and Jube in another, leaving himself and Willy. Of the two remaining rooms, there was the one he and Delia had shared and the northwest bedroom, which had forever been known as the children's room. After inspecting them both he left the choice to Willy.

"That one." Willy pointed. "It's got a rockin' horse."

Scott, relieved that he need not face sleeping in his familiar rosewood bed with Delia, led Willy into the children's room. Together they turned back the dust covers, shucked down to their underwear, and settled down beneath the dusty coverlets.

"Hey, Scotty?" Willy's voice sounded smaller than ever in the big room when the candle was blown out.

"Hm?'

"I'm cold.'

Gandy chuckled and rolled onto his side. "Then get over here."

Willy presented his back and burrowed his posterior into Scott's belly. Coiling an arm around him, Scott couldn't help thinking of Leatrice barking out the word "mosquito." It felt as if Willy had twice as many ribs as other people and half as much fat.

"This is nicer than the storeroom. Mmm . . ."

That was the last sound Scott heard from Willy. In minutes the boy was asleep.

But Scott lay in his childhood bed for hours, feeling Willy's heartbeat beneath his palm, listening to the regularity of his breathing, drawn back to Kansas by Willy's last remark.

He thought about Gussie, the empty town, the emptier saloon. He closed his eyes and pictured her at her sewing machine with Willy's empty stool beside her, limping down the street to eat alone at Paulie's, sitting on the top step in the winter wind, wrapped in her pelisse while snow fell on its hood. But the picture that burned brightest of all was none that he imagined, but one he recalled—Gussie with blood staining her nightgown as she lay in his bed and he kissed her.

He forced his eyes wide, as if attempting to transmute the memory into reality.

But around him pressed only unrelieved blackness. He tried to acclimate himself to its density, but it was difficult to do so. In Kansas there had been streetlamps. On the train the moon had lit the landscape. But here, at Waverley, beneath the giant magnolias and pines and creeping wisteria vines, the blackness was absolute. If there were a ghost, it could surely choose no better place. And if it wanted to make itself known, it could certainly choose no better time. After all, he already felt haunted by Agatha. What was one more ghost?

But none appeared. None spoke. And in the end, Gandy slept fitfully, warmed by Willy's small body.

He awakened early and lay for minutes recalling the past; remembering how his father had begun each day by surveying his domain from the very spot designed for it. That spot drew him irresistibly to follow in his father's footsteps. Quietly, he slipped from bed into his clothing and climbed up the stairs, up past the third floor, whose four closed doors led into the immense windowless attic beneath the main roof. The trunk room, they'd always called it, where Scott had often played with his brothers on rainy days and where members of the family had been isolated whenever they were ill.

He opened a door, unable to resist a peek into the dusky interior, cluttered with furniture, trunks, and flotsam from the past. Somewhere inside, Delia's clothing was stored, and his parents', too, he presumed. Someday he would explore it again, but now he closed the door and continued up the final sweep of stairs until he reached the railed catwalk that circled the octagonal rotunda, overlooking the entry below and the fields outside. Looking down the chain of the massive chandelier, he remembered nights when the doors of the twin parlors had been rolled back, transforming the area below into one vast, impressive ballroom. He and Rafe and Nash would creep from their beds after all the guests had arrived and from high in the shadows of the rotunda would look down upon the colorful hoop skirts of the ladies, while men in swallowtail coats guided them through the sweeping turns of the waltz.

He had a sudden vision of what Agatha's garnet dress would look like from above, with tier upon tier of rear draperies shot by gaslight as she glided across the pine floor below. He saw, too, her hair, neatly coiled up the back of her head, radiating the same red highlights as the taffeta she wore. Odd that he should envision her dancing when she herself had told him it was the one thing she'd always longed to do, but could not.

Whimsy, he chided himself. And useless at that. The problem at hand was figuring out how to make this place productive enough to support eight ... no, *ten*—he had to include Leatrice and Moses now, too. To bring one more would be sheer stupidity when he'd have difficulty supporting those he already had.

Sighing, he turned to the windows that had once been kept sparkling but were now filmed with dust, their corners mitered by cobwebs. He scraped one aside and it stuck to his finger, trailing the dry husk of a dead mud dauber. Shaking it free, he forced himself to look beyond the disconcerting evidence of neglect to the faded empire that was now his heritage.

He lifted his eyes and there, for as far as he could see, lay Waverley Plantation. But the land that had once been brought to abundance by a thousand black hands now lay lorn and gone to weed.

He walked slowly, sadly, around the eight sides of the rotunda, as his father had done every morning after breakfast, surveying the fiefdom, which in those days had been self-sufficient. To the east the trees opened, forming a great green meadow that dropped in an impressive sweep to the Tombigbee River, visible in the distance. Cattle and sheep used to grace between the house and the river, but none was there now. The solid sheet of green grass was dotted with brush, which in time would give way to solid forest if not cleared. And in the remaining three directions, woods and fields stretched away to infinity, their chief product nothing but a tangled crop of kudzu vine.

How could a mere ten people make it pay?

His morose reflection was interrupted by a small voice echoing softly from below.

"Scotty?"

It was the sprout, standing outside the bedroom door on the opposite side of the rotunda two stories below.

"So you're up." Their voices carried like bells across a valley, though they spoke scarcely above a whisper.

"Whatcha doin' up there?"

"Lookin'."

"Lookin' at what?"

"Come on up. I'll show y'."

He watched Willy climb the impressive staircase, his bare feet padding softly, the trapdoor of his union suit flashing between the banister spindles of the cantilevered balcony. By the time he reached the catwalk dust lined the edges of his toes.

"Whew!" he puffed, coming up the last step. "What's up here?"

Scott lifted Willy and perched him on an arm. "Waverley." He gestured, walking slowly from window to window. "All that."

"Wow ..."

"I don't know what t' do with it, though."

"If it's a farm, don't you gotta plant stuff on it?"

It sounded so simple, Gandy chuckled. "Takes a lot of hands t' plant all that."

Willy scratched his head and looked through the dirty window. "Gussie says I'm lucky t' see it. She says there ain't ... aren't many like it anymore, so I hafta learn t' up ... up ..."

"Appreciate?"

"Yeah—appreciate it. She says she wants t' see it someday 'cause she never saw no plantation before. She called it a ... a way of life. What's that mean, Scotty?"

But Scott wasn't listening to the question, rather to what came before. Almost to himself he murmured, "She wasn't talkin' about the land, she was talkin' about the house."

"The house?" Willy craned his neck to look at the peak of the cupola above them.

"The house ..." Scott threw a glance at the windows circling him, then at the ballroom floor below, the doors leading off the grandest staircase this side of the Mason-Dixon line.

"That's it!" he exploded.

"Where we goin'?" Willy bounced on Scott's arm as his black boots clattered down the stairs. "Hey, what're you smiling about?"

"The house. That's the answer, and it was so obvious, I overlooked it. Gussie told me the same thing she told you, last summer one night when I told her about Waverley. But I was too busy tryin' t' dream up a way t' raise cotton t' think about usin' the house t' make money."

"You mean you're gonna sell it, Scotty?" Willy asked, disappointed.

"Sell it?" As they reached the trunk-room level, where all those hoop skirts and swallowtail coats waited. Scott planted a loud, smacking kiss on Willy's cheek, but he was too excited to investigate now. "Never, sprout. We're gonna make it live again, and those Yankees who burned down damned near all the places like Waverley will pay a king's ransom t' see and experience one of 'em now. What you see around you, Willy, my boy, is nothin' short of a national treasure!"

They reached the sleeping level and, without breaking stride, Scott banged on doors, bellowing, "Wake up! Daylight in the swamp, everybody! Jack! Marcus! Jube! Pearl! Get up! We have t' get this place back in shape!"

His voice echoed through the rotunda, along with his footsteps, as he ran down the last curving section of stairs to the main entry. Sleepy heads began poking out from doors overhead as Scott, still with Willy on his arm, slammed out the back door.

"You're gonna meet Leatrice," Scott told Willy as they crossed the yard. "She believes in spooks, but other than that, she's all right. Y'all hear any spooks in the house last night?"

"Spooks?" Willy's eyes widened, but he grinned.

"Weren't any spooks, were there?"

"I didn't hear none.'

"*Any*. Then y'all tell Leatrice so, understand?"

"But why?"

"'Cause we need her to organize those slowpokes back there and make the dust fly. Nobody I know can do that better than Leatrice. Why, if we'd've had her commandin' the Confederate troops, the war would've turned out different!"

"But, Scotty, I'm still wearin' my underwear!"

"No matter. She's seen li'l boys in less."

Willy took to Leatrice like a tick to a warm hide. From the moment she ordered, "Come heah, chile, let Leatrice have a look at you," the bond was sealed. It made sense: she needed someone to fuss over, and he needed fussing. And being introduced to him while he wore only a scratchy woolen union suit endeared the sprout to her forever. The match seemed made in heaven.

But when it came to Scott's decree, she was far less enthusiastic.

"Ain't settin' foot in no house with no haunts."

"Tell her, Willy."

Willy told her, but still she pursed her lips and looked mean. "Nun-uh! Not Leatrice."

"But who's goin' to' get them movin'? The whole bunch is used t' sleepin' till noon. I need you, sweetheart."

At the word, her mouth loosened slightly. "Always was a sweet talkuh," she grumbled.

He went on while he saw her weakening. "And imagine the place full of people again, and music in the ballroom and every bedroom filled, and the old cookhouse fire stoked up and the smell o' sweet-potato pies comin' from the ovens."

She glared at him from the corner of her eye. "Who gonna cook?"

That took him aback. "Well, I . . . I don't know. But we'll think of somethin' when the time comes. First, though, we've got t' get the place waxed and polished again, and the grounds cleared and the outbuildin's cleaned up. What do you say, sweetheart? Will you help me?'

"Gotta think a spell," was all she would concede.

Leatrice thought for exactly four and a half hours. By that time Gandy's troops had arisen, eaten breakfast, and were desultorily following his inept orders. But the work they were producing, and the speed with which they produced it, was so disgraceful that when Leatrice glimpsed the clean-up crew carrying household items out into the yard for airing, she mumbled an imprecation about sweet talkers and threw up her hands.

Minutes later she appeared at the back door wearing an asafetida bag around her neck.

"Can't git dust outta rugs layin' 'em on d' ground," she announced imperiously, standing just inside the door with both hands on her hips. "Gotta git 'em in d' air an' whack 'em! Any fool knows ya don't start widda bottom layuh an' wuhk up. Time ya gits t' de top, d' bottom jiss as dirty as when ya commence."

Gandy came and gave her a grateful hug, but immediately backed off.

"Lord, woman, what've you got in that sack?" Gandy asked, almost gagging. "Smells like cat piss."

"None o' yer lip, boy. It's asafetida, keep de haunts off'n Leatrice. You want I teach dose sorry white folk how t' clean, you leave off sass 'bout how I smell."

Gandy grinned and gave a teasing salute. 'Yes, ma'am."

And from that moment on, Waverley's speedy, efficient revival was guaranteed.

Chapter 18

It was an immense undertaking, turning Waverley into a hotel retreat where Northerners would get the feel of a working plantation. But all the essential elements were there. They only needed dusting off and oiling and waxing and clearing and hoeing and mending.

Gandy's troop started with the rotunda and worked downward, as Leatrice dictated. And dictate she did, in a voice that carried like thunder and made the most dedicated sluggard straighten his spine and get his limbs a-flapping. Still, they could never have handled the massive job without the phenomenon that began the second morning. One by one familiar faces appeared at Waverley's back door—black, all of them, but with expressions telling how eager they were to lend a hand and see Waverley flourish again.

First came Zach, whose father had been a stable hand and had taught Scott all he knew. Zach set to work checking and mending harness, cleaning the old carriages and the stable itself. Then came Beau and his wife, Clarice, who smiled shyly when they greeted LeMaster Gandy, and obeyed without question when

Leatrice told them they could begin clearing a spot to make the old vegetable garden bigger. A pair of brothers named Andrew and Abraham headed up a crew that
cleared the long lane, and when it was passable, they went on to begin putting the
yard and grand front lawn in shape. They trimmed the boxwoods and pruned the
camellias and shaped the azalea bushes that had grown wild and rangy throughout
the formal gardens. There followed general repairs on all the outbuildings, and
thorough cleaning of their insides, where wild animals had nested, metal had
rusted, and wood had warped. A black woman named Bertrissa came along and
was put to work filling the black iron pot in the yard and beginning the massive
job of washing dust covers and bedding. Her man, Caleb, became part of the crew
that painted the mansion. Gandy himself headed it up, ordering four new ladders
built, then scaling one to do the highest spot—the rotunda—himself. As the men
swarmed over the outside of Waverley, the women swarmed inside.

Every drapery was aired and dusted, every inch of decorative brass cornice was
polished. Rugs were hung and beaten, some scrubbed by hand. Interior woodwork
was painted, floors waxed, windows polished, spindles washed and waxed, as
were the decorative lyre inserts on the front sidelights. Every piece of furniture
was either aired and beaten or scrubbed and polished. Every dish in the built-in
china cabinet was removed from its shelf, washed, and replaced on a freshly lined
surface. The closets were whitewashed, the chimneys swept, and the andirons polished until their brass knobs gleamed.

Scott himself checked out the old gasworks and got its burners working again.
Ivory took a contingent—including Willy—off into the woods to search out pine
lighter, and in the evening they lit the jets in the great, gleaming chandelier for
the first time they had a small celebration. Marcus played the banjo and Willy the
harmonica. The girls danced around the ballroom floor, while the others sat on the
stairs watching and teased them about soon having to give up the rowdy cancan
in favor of the sedate mazurka, which would be more fitting for entertaining
Northerners who would be paying a great deal of money to pretend they were elite
Southern planters for a week or two.

There was business to attend to also. While the work crews continued, Scott
drafted an advertisement to send to Northern newspapers, announcing the opening
of Waverley Plantation to the public in March, the month of camellias. He made
a trip to Memphis to secure a list of the country's one hundred most wealthy industrialists and sent personal letters of invitation to each. His idea bore quick results. Within two weeks he received reservation money from several who claimed
their wives would be exceedingly grateful to escape the rigorous Northern climate
and shorten the winter by spending its last weeks in the mellow atmosphere described by Gandy's advertisement.

It was a happy day when Scott purchased a reservations book bound in rich
green leather, and along with it a ledger in which he logged the first income
Waverley had made in well over eighteen years.

He'd taken as his office the same lower-level room his father had used for that
purpose, the one just behind the front parlor. It was a bright, cheerful room with
ceiling-to-floor jib windows that opened from the bottom up to provide a cool
draft during the hot weather when the rotunda windows were opened high above.
Now the jib windows remained closed, however, fronted by sea-green jacquard
tiebacks that brought the color of verdant things into the room during this season
when little grew. The walls were white plaster, as was the ceiling with its decorative sculptured work matching the moldings at the tops of the walls. No dominating bookshelves lined the wall; instead, the room was decorated with a set of
mahogany shell-carved furniture: blockfront highboy, secretary, and flattop desk,

and an assortment of upholstered wingchairs of rich taupe leather. The varnished pine floor held an Oriental rug with a pale pink dogwood design on a background of ice-green. The fireplace, with its decorative iron liner, kept the room cozy even when coals scarcely glowed.

Scott Gandy loved the office. He recalled his father sitting behind the mahogany desk, running the affairs of the plantation as he himself did now. Here, with pen and ledger in hand, he felt again a sense of continuity, but more—one of indomitable optimism.

The day he received the first advance deposits, he entered them in the books, stubbed out his cheroot, and went seeking Willy, determined to fulfill the promise he'd made to the boy before they'd left Kansas—to buy him a horse of his own. He charged through the house, calling, but it was a quiet afternoon, and if anybody was about, no one was answering. Scott took the stairs two at a time and charged into the children's room, which he still shared with Willy. But the boy wasn't napping, nor was he anywhere to be seen.

"Willy?" he called, stopping beside the bed with its ecru crocheted spread and matching tester.

It was then that he heard it—the soft whimpering of a child's voice and the single word, more a sigh than a cry: "Heeelp."

"Willy?" Scott spun about, but behind him the doorway was empty. The recently waxed floor gleamed, reflecting the unblinking eye of the rocking horse, the only one looking on.

"Heeelp." The word came again, soft, pleading, from behind him. He whirled and stared at the bed. The coverlet was rumpled, where a moment ago it had been smooth. He stared at the impression of a small body.

"Willy? Are you there?"

But it wasn't Willy's voice; it wasn't Willy's imprint. It was Justine's, Scott was certain. He waited, his eyes resting on the slight depression. The soft whimper sounded again, as if from the spot, but it brought no sense of fear or doom, only a strong wish to be able to ease whatever care it voiced.

The presence departed as suddenly as it had come, leaving Scott feeling certain he was again alone in the room. He felt helpless and guilty, as if he should have helped. But how?

He searched the other upstairs rooms, but all were empty, as were those on the lower level. At last he found Leatrice, out in the cookhouse in a rocking chair beside the fire with Clarice and Bertrissa, husking dried peas.

"Where's Willy?" he asked perfunctorily.

"Gone wid d' men."

"Where?"

"Out to d' woods someplace, puttin' up cordwood."

"How long have they been gone?"

"Lef' right aftuh breffus," she replied disinterestedly.

"Where are the women?"

"Down t' d' cabins, cleanin'."

Scott told no one about his encounter with the ghost, but the following day, when he took Zach and Willy to a stock auction, at which he hoped to bid on carriage horses and a pony for the boy, his mind was often distracted from the business at hand.

"Willy," he inquired in an offhanded manner while they strolled the barns, checking out horseflesh, "did y'all go out t' the woods yesterday right after breakfast?"

"Yup."

"And did ya come back t' the house before dinner?"

"Nope."

"Y' didn't take a nap in your room?"

"Nope."

"Had Leatrice made up your bed before y' left?"

"Nope."

So it hadn't been Willy's imprint on the coverlet. Then whose?

"Oh, lookit that one! That's the one I want. Can I have 'im, Scotty? Can I?" Willy's excitement and Zach's examination of a one-year-old strawberry roan gelding ended Gandy's speculation and forced him to turn his attention to the selection of Waverley's horseflesh.

He trusted Zach's judgment completely and when the day was over had bought the strawberry roan for the boy—"His name's gonna be Major," Willy declared—a team of skewbald carriage horses, and two full-grown riding horses—a stallion named Prince and a mare named Sheba.

It became a common sight after that to see Willy hanging around the stables, like a tick on Zach's pantleg, watering the horses, bombarding him with questions, bringing sweets from the house for Major, then turning circles in the middle of the corral as Zach taught him how to work the horse on a longe line.

Scott had almost forgotten the incident in the children's room until one day when he was heading up to the trunk room to check out the clothing he planned to disinter. As he passed the door of the bedroom, he heard Willy inside, talking to somebody. He backed up and glanced into the room. Willy sat on the floor, ankles out, building a tower of wood blocks, conversing with absolutely nobody.

". . . and Gussie, she lives in Kansas, where I used t' live. She gots my cat. His name is Moose. Gussie's gonna come for Christmas an' Zach says we're gonna shoot us a wild turkey for Christmas dinner."

"Willy, who are you talkin' to?" Scott peered inside curiously.

"Oh, hey, Scotty," Willy greeted, glancing over his shoulder before adding another block to his tower.,

"Who were y'all talking to just now?"

"Justine," the boy answered levelly, then hummed several notes of "Oh! Susanna."

"Justine?"

"Uh-huh. She comes an' plays with me sometimes when it's rainin' outside an' I hafta stay in."

Scott glanced at the windowpanes. A steady wash ran over them, obscuring everything beyond. He moved into the room and hunkered down beside Willy, bracing his elbows on his knees.

"My daughter, Justine?"

"Uh-huh. She's nice, Scotty."

Scott experienced his first moment of fear, not because the house might be haunted—after all, he was a reasonable man who didn't believe in ghosts, did he?—but because Willy seemed to believe this ghost was mortal.

"Justine's dead, Willy."

"I know. But she likes it here. Sometimes she comes back for a visit."

Scott glanced around uncertainly. Willy's tower toppled and he started rebuilding it, all the while humming happily. "Y' know the little cemetery across the road?" Scott inquired.

"Sure. I been there with Andrew and Abraham when they cut the grass and cleaned it up."

This was news to Scott, though he disguised his surprise and went on. "Then you know Justine is buried there."

"I know," Willy replied blithely.

"If she's buried there, she can't come back here t' play with you. It's just your imagination, Willy."

"She only comes t' this room. It used t' be hers."

Scott had never before disclosed the fact to Willy, though the sprout was certainly bright enough to associate a rocking chair with a nursery.

"Have you told Leatrice you've talked t' Justine?"

Willy laughed, a musical sound like the quick chatter of a tambourine. "Leatrice'd roll her eyes and run like a snake was loose, wouldn't she?"

Scott smiled and laughed, too. But then he turned thoughtful. "If y'all don't mind, son, let's not tell Leatrice about it. She's got enough on her mind, runnin' the place."

"All right," Willy returned, apparently unconcerned about the credibility of his experience.

"And one more thing." Scott stood and gazed at the top of Willy's head. "Who told you Gussie was comin' for Christmas?"

"You said I could see her sometime."

"But she's not comin' for Christmas, son."

"But, why not?" Willy lifted disappointed brown eyes and Scott groped for an answer.

"She just isn't, that's all."

"But, why not?"

"Because the house is crowded now until the cabins are ready. And we're all busy gettin' things ready for guests. There's a lot t' be done yet."

"But you said—"

"I'm sorry, Willy, the answer is no."

Willy leveled his tower with one angry sweep. "You lied! You said she could come!"

"Willy, that's enough!" Scott spun and stalked from the room, scowling, angered by the boy's insistence. Why not, indeed! Because Agatha was a complication Scott didn't need in his life right now. Because if he saw her again, saying good-bye would hurt worse than the first time. Because if Willy saw her again, there would be more tears and heartache when the two of them parted.

Besides, he had enough on his mind trying to reconcile himself to the fact that the house was being visited by a ghost. Common sense said it couldn't be Justine.

But three nights later, Scott was roused from a restless sleep by the impression of a voice echoing through the dark. His eyes seemed at first sealed, as if with wax, as he tried to open them. Someone was whimpering. Sad, childish whimpering. He must help . . . must help . . . must drag himself from this nether state . . . this drifting, misty cloud world . . .

The whimpering grew louder. His eyes opened. The room was pitch black.

"Heeelp . . ." a sorrowful voice beseeched.

Scott came awake as if thunder had struck. He braced up and leaned over Willy. But the child lay on his side with both hands softly curled in sleep, his breathing as regular as the beat of a metronome.

Again came the whimper, closer.

Scott braced up on both hands, peering into the dark.

"Who's there?"

The whimper approached and brought the soft brush of breath on his cheek while he sat stock-still. A scent filled the room, unidentifiable, floral.

He tried to pierce the darkness with his eyes. Nothing moved. No shadow or pale image. Only the sound, pitiful, pleading, a girlish whimper, and the plea again, "Heeelp."

"Justine?" he whispered, glancing left and right.

A movement on the blanket over his chest, as if someone was running a hand over it, searching for the binding, as if to turn it down and get beneath the covers.

"Justine, is that you?"

The sound quieted but the scent remained.

"We're in your bed . . . is that it?" The room grew hushed, the silence broken only by the sound of Willy's regular breathing. Again Scott sensed no dire intentions from the presence, only a restlessness he longed to calm.

"Justine?"

It was winter, the windows and veranda door were closed, yet a soft breeze seemed to sigh through the room, whisking away the scent and the presence.

Scott sat up straighter, reached out a hand, and touched . . . nothing.

"Justine?"

Willy stirred beside him, snuffled, then rolled over. The presence was gone.

Scott fell back, lifting the covers to his armpits, running a hand over them, staring at the ceiling in the ink-black night. Who else could it have been? And if she'd meant them any harm, wouldn't she have related it somehow? He closed his eyes, thinking of her as a beautiful, blond-haired baby. *Justine, my daughter, how we wanted and loved you. You remember, don't you?*

He closed his eyes, but opened them momentarily to find himself restless and mystified, but no longer disbelieving.

As Christmas approached, Scott temporarily forgot about the ghostly visitations, while Willy began pressuring harder and harder to have Agatha at Waverley for the holiday. "But I miss her," he whined, as if that was the only thing required to bring about the granting of his wishes.

"I know you do, Willy, but I don't have time t' take you t' Kansas on the train, and you're too young t' go alone."

"You said I could!" Willy became obstinate, stuck out his lip, and stamped his foot. "You said I'd be able t' go see her whenever I wanted to."

Scott grew impatient. "You're twistin' my words around, boy. I never said you could go whenever you wanted. Lord sakes, it's only been a little over a month since you saw her."

"I don't care. I wanna see Gussie!" Willy put on his most repugnant face and enormous tears rolled over his eyelids. Scott had the distinct impression Willy had conjured them up on command. The damned little nuisance had never acted so demanding before.

"I don't know what's come over you, boy, that you think you can go around stampin' your feet and pushin' out your lip t' try t' get your way, but it won't work with me, so let's have an end to it, y' hear?"

Willy stormed out of Scott's office and slammed the door so hard the overhead light danced on its chain.

"What the hell's got into him?" Scott muttered.

Four days before Christmas Willy received a gift from Gussie—a hand-made stuffed goose fashioned of soft white flannel with an orange felt beak and embroidered eyes. Willy again made demands, ending with another angry exchange between himself and Scott before the boy ran off crying. Scott glared at the door, then reached to the floor for Agatha's note, which Willy had dropped. He read it glumly. It was exclusively for Willy, with the exception of the brief closing in which she'd added:

> Tell everybody hello from me and wish them all the merriest Christmas. Scott, too.

Scott, too—as if he were nothing more to her than an afterthought. The idea raised a rage in him he didn't quite understand and could not seem to quell.

Christmas of 1880 should have been one of the happiest of his life. After all, he was back at Waverley. The mansion was festooned with holly and mistletoe and every fireplace was ablaze. The place gleamed with beeswax and bustled with life. Zach had shot a wild turkey and Leatrice was preparing it with chestnut stuffing and all the trimmings, just as she had in the old days.

But Scott spent the holidays listless and bitter, slouched in a leather chair in the front parlor, sipping eggnog and staring despondently at the wedding alcove. He had everyone he loved around him, didn't he? Yet his mind wandered back to a weatherbeaten clapboard building on a frozen mud street in Kansas where the wind howled and the snow flew and a woman without one soul to call her own spent the holiday alone in a narrow, dark, cheerless apartment.

In January, Willy grew more cantankerous and demanding each day. He cried almost every night for Agatha and spent more time talking to "Justine." Scott thought a friend might help, so he took Willy into town to meet Mae Ellen Bayles's grandson, A.J. But the two boys didn't get along at all, and Scott's impatience with Willy grew.

In February, Scott and the women finally got around to sorting out the collection of clothing in the attic. They unearthed a veritable gold mine of dresses that the girls could wear to lend an air of authenticity when dancing in the ballroom with the paying guests. But none was generous enough for Jube's breasts, and when she tried altering one, she ruined it completely.

Scott's caustic remarks made everyone lay low for days afterward.

The stables were spotless, the stalls filled with enough horses to provide transit to and from the train depot and enough for the guests' pleasure riding, too. The equipage had been oiled and, where necessary, replaced. The ice house was stocked with ice, which had been transported from town after arriving on a freight car packed in sawdust. The smokehouse spouted a slow stream of hickory smoke. Two dozen Rhode Island reds pecked about in a screened pen, and a pair of black-and-white cows kept the front meadow evenly groomed and the table supplied with milk and butter. Even the ancient, creaking ferry had been rejuvenated, the idea being to take the guests across the river to picnic on the other side. And, as a final touch, Scott had found a pair of peacocks to adorn the emerald lawn. Everything was perfect . . .

Everything but Scott. He was fractious and unbearable. Not a person in the house could look at him crosswise without getting snapped at. He stalked around with his heels clomping on the hardwood floors, as if to warn everybody to get out of his way. He snapped at the men and glared at the women and told Leatrice if she didn't get rid of that "stinkin' piss bag" her neck was going to rot off.

Scott blamed his sore temper on Willy.

Willy was turning into an obnoxious brat! Probably from hanging around Leatrice so much and picking up her officious ways. His grammar was deteriorating into a deplorable state and occasionally he let fly with an unconscious profanity, learned from the girls, who didn't always guard their tongues around him as they should. Everybody spoiled him abominably, and when Scott crossed him he grew surly or mouthy or both. He had turned six in January and belonged in school, but short of taking him into town every day, there was no way to facilitate lessons, and nobody around the place was inclined to take up tutoring him or even to teach him to pick up after himself. When Scott ordered him to do so, Willy charged away and declared Leatrice would make up his bed or pick up his clothes.

Then one day the girls ruined another dress. When Scott heard the news he stomped into the downstairs parlor, which doubled as a sewing room, and lashed out at them.

"Dammit! How many dresses do you think I can dig outta that attic! If Agatha were here *she* wouldn't have made mincemeat o' this one!'

It was Jube who hurled back what they'd all been thinking. "Well, if Agatha can do them better, get Agatha! It's what's been under your skin ever since you left Kansas anyway, isn't it?"

Gandy's face turned formidable. His cheekbones seemed to grow sharp, his mouth thin, and his eyes deadly as rapiers. He pointed a finger at Jube's nose.

"You'd better watch yourself, Jube," he growled.

"Well, isn't it?" She thrust her face toward him and put both of her hands on her hips.

Gandy's jaw locked and a muscle twitched in his left cheek. "Y' know, you can be put off this place," he warned in an ugly voice.

"Oh, sure, as if that would solve your problem!"

He spun toward the door. "I don't know what the hell you're talkin' about!"

"I'm talking about one Miss Agatha Downing." She caught his elbow and spun him back. "You've been like a bear ever since you left her and it's getting worse."

He threw back his head and let out a sharp barking laugh. "Agatha Downin'. Ha!" He glared at Jube and spat out, "You're crazy! Agatha Downin', that . . . that prissy little milliner?"

"But of course you'd be too bull-headed to admit it."

He jerked his arm from her grip. "Since when am I bullheaded, Jubilee Bright?"

"Since when am I a seamstress, LeMaster Scott Gandy?" She kicked the dress that lay puffed on the floor, then swung on him with combat in her eyes. "You know, we've been working our private skin off around her, scrubbing floors and waxing wood—you wanna know how many spindles are in that damned railing out there?" Jube pointed at the hall. "Seven hundred eighteen, that's how many! We know, because *we're* the ones who oiled them! Your old slaves come back to help—fine, we appreciate the help—and we do what we're told and go out to make the cabins livable again. And we peel onions when Leatrice says peel, and wash bedding when Leatrice says wash, and we polish brass when Leatrice says polish. And now Ivory's got some addle-pated idea about all of us planting a cotton crop in one of the near fields this spring, just to lend a little touch of the prewar South to this place. Well, I did all that, and I'll probably end up planting cotton, too. But I don't know possum-squat about sewing dressed, LeMaster Gandy!" She poked him in the chest. "And you'd best remember it!" Spinning away, she gave the dress a vicious kick, then fell to a nearby slipper sofa. Leaning back on both elbows, she caught one foot behind a knee, jutting out her breasts. "I'm an ex-prostitute, Gandy. Sometimes I think you forget that. I'm used to working in a reclinin' position in clothes that take a lot less upkeep than that." Her voice turned silky with challenge. "I'll wear it, honey, but you better get somebody else to make it fit me. And if that somebody is Agatha Downing, all the better. Maybe she'd have a sweetening influence on your sour temper."

Ruby sat in a nearby chair, knees crossed, one foot swinging, one magnificent eyebrow raised higher than the other. Pearl sat equally indolently, ignoring the dress she'd been working on when Scott entered.

He had never before seen three more ornery ex-prostitutes. They were harder than a ten-year drought. As his glance shot to the dress Pearl had discarded, he knew he'd be powerless against them as long as they all stuck together.

With a throaty curse he stalked from the room.

It was a day late in February with spring sending out feelers. Zach had turned out to be as adept a farrier as his father, and he was teaching not only Willy, but Marcus, too, all he knew about horses. Marcus had discovered he loved working with the animals. Like him, they were voiceless. But they conveyed messages just the same. Today the little two-year-old mare, Sheba, was anxious to get outside and kick up her heels. The staid pair of skewbald carriage horses blinked lazily in the sun that streamed through the window as he brought them water. And Scott's restless stallion, Prince ... well, he had other things in mind. His sap was up. His nostrils flared. His ears stood straight and his chestnut tail arched at the whinny of Cinnamon, the brand-new mare Scotty had just bought, who was prancing around the paddock outside and tossing her head in invitation.

Four o'clock, Zach had said, as soon as Scott came back from town, where he'd taken the boy visiting while he checked the price of cotton seed.

It won't be long now, Prince, Marcus thought and wished he could say it to the impatient stallion, whose phallus was already partially distended and hung beneath him thick as a man's arm.

"Marcus?"

He jumped and spun toward the door. Jube stood in the flood of light wearing a blue dress as plain as any housemaid would wear. Her white hair was caught up in a loose drooping fold. A knit shawl was looped around her shoulders.

He raised a hand in greeting and hurried toward her, hoping to detain her at the far end of the barn away from Prince with his glistening member exposed.

"I was looking for you." Her face was somber as he halted before her, blocking her path.

She looked beautiful, with loose hair at her temples and her mouth soft. His heart hastened as he silently adored her.

"Can we talk?" she asked.

He loved her for saying things like that—as if he were no different from other men. He nodded and she took his arm and began sauntering along the stalls, eyes downcast. "I had a fight with Scott yesterday." Marcus stopped, frowned in question, and waggled a hand, catching her eye. She went on quietly. "We've never had a fight before, but this one has been brewing for a long time. It was over a dress I ruined when I was trying to alter it. Only it wasn't really over that at all. It was over Agatha." At his surprised expression, she laughed softly, then took his arm and sauntered on. "Yes, *that* Agatha. I think he's in love with her but he won't admit it to himself, so he's driving the rest of us crazy. Haven't you noticed how grouchy he's been lately? And how he's driving us? Well, I, for one, have had enough of it. I told him in rather unladylike terms that I'm not used to working as hard as he's asked us to lately. I told him I think he should bring her here and maybe it would make him more bearable."

Marcus squeezed Jube's arm. He pointed to Kansas, then to the spot where they stood.

"Yes, here." She lifted her face and placed her hands on his elbows. "Marcus, you've never asked, but I'm going to tell you. It's over between Scott and me. It has been since before we left Kansas. Does that make a difference to you?"

He swallowed and felt his face flood with heat, and his heart started slamming.

"I think you're too honorable to make a move toward me as long as you think Scott has any prior claims." Once the words were spoken she became self-conscious. Her cheeks grew bright and she tossed her shoulders, moving unconsciously toward Prince's stall. "Oh, Marcus, I know it's not my place to say this, but if I wait until—

He lunged and grabbed her elbow before she could see into the stall. Her head swung around and their eyes clashed. Tightening his grip, he shook his head—an order.

"No?" she verbalized. "Don't say it? But, why? One of us has to."

His eyes darted from her to the stall and back. He shook his head more adamantly, unsure of how to make her understand it wasn't her words to which he objected.

"What?" She looked back over her shoulder and got a clear shot of the stall and the stallion within. "Oh!" she exclaimed, and her eyes widened.

Prince reared and pawed, his member bouncing lustily. Jube and Marcus stood locked in a moment of embarrassment so intense it seemed to stir the very air around them, lifting dust motes that drifted through the oblique shafts of light falling through the barn.

Then Zach spoke from the doorway and they leaped apart. "Better keep away from that stall. Horse like that's dangerous when he smells a mare in heat."

Suddenly, Scott followed Zach around the corner, entering the barn at a brisk clip, his mind obviously on the business at hand. "Better let him out, Zach. No sense gettin' the stall kicked apart. Marcus, Jube," he added, offhandedly, "if you're goin' to' watch y'all better get outside beyond the paddock fence. When he comes out he'll be in a hurry."

Marcus and Jube moved outside and stood at a whitewashed fence—apart from the others who'd come down from the house to watch, too. The aroused stallion, Prince, came trotting down the stone rampway into the paddock, his tail arched and streaming like a willow in the wind, his mighty head held high, the nostrils dilated. He halted a good distance from Cinnamon, forelegs locked, eyes turbulent. Mare and stallion stood face to face, unmoving, for what seemed like minutes. He snorted once. She turned away. As if enraged by her indifference, he raised his head and trumpeted long and loud, then shook his head until his mane flew.

The sound brought a question from Willy, who sat on the fence while Scott stood behind him, an arm loosely circling the boy. "Why'd he do that, Scotty?"

"He's callin' her. They're goin' t' mate now, you watch. It's how foals get started in the mare's womb."

At the moment it appeared as if nothing would get started anywhere. Cinnamon remained aloof. At the far end of the paddock she pranced back and forth, as far as the fence would allow. Each time she turned it was with a lunge and a dip that tossed her mane aloft. Haughty yet restless, she stood Prince off, racking back and forth along the fence.

He snorted, pawed the soft earth, bobbed his majestic head and, with it, his majestic phallus.

She turned her rump on him, her vaulted tail exposing her swollen genitals, already glistening. Her scent reached him, strong and hot, and his nostrils pulsated, his hide quivered.

Six steps he took before she swung on him in warning. As he halted, his distended organ dipped as if mounted upon strong springs. She shifted left. He shifted with her. She shifted right. He thwarted her once again. Imperiously, he came on, lord to lady, sire to dame.

She would have none of it and, with a quick snort and lunge, shot around him, biting his flank as she sprinted away.

At his grunt, she turned and they eyed each other from opposite ends of the enclosure, standing erect and well matched, their dark hides gleaming in the late-afternoon sun, tails now still. A pair of neon-blue dragonflies hovered in tandem over the paddock as if showing the horses what to do.

Again Prince advanced, one cautious step at a time. This time she whinnied, raising her nose to the air, waiting, waiting, until he neared, nosing her hindquarters. His head dropped and she stood her ground just long enough for Prince to fill his nostrils. Then she turned and nipped him again before dancing away.

Those who watched felt the tension, drawn to its peak. Every palm along the fence was damp, every spine tense. As in human nature, there was a point beyond which the female could taunt no longer without arousing the male beyond endurance. When he rounded on Cinnamon again, Prince was engorged to startling proportions as he moved in for the coup.

Enough of this high-flown loftiness, madame, his approach seemed to say. *The time is here.*

He stalked in, indomitable, masterful, and caught her in a corner. After all the evasiveness she'd displayed earlier, Cinnamon's surrender was surprisingly accommodating. She stood as still as the earth itself, only her eyes shifting to follow Prince as he made his final overture. Their velvet noses nearly touched. The coarse hairs on their nostrils fluttered as they blew upon each other like bellows. Then he trotted around behind her and reared only once while she stood docile, waiting. His root found its sleek target and his powerful forelegs circled her sides as he immersed himself to the groin.

She called out at the moment of impact, a high vaulting screech that seemed to quake the budding trees in the orchard and lift shivers on every human hide within range.

There was a wondrous elemental majesty to their mating. It was felt deeply by Marcus and Jube, leaving them exquisitely aroused. They stood with their forearms lining the top rail of the fence, elbows touching, watching the mounting stud and grunting mare before them. Never had they been so aware of each other.

In a life filled with many occasions when arousal had been demanded, Jubilee had experienced none so extreme as the one that gripped her now. In a life filled with few such occasions, Marcus found himself in a similar predicament. As Prince had caught the scent of Cinnamon, Marcus caught the scent of Jube. From the spot where their elbows touched, a current seemed to sizzle to their extremities. He wanted her with a force as primal as Prince's. But if he approached her now, would she think it was nothing more than lust aroused in him by the horses? If only he could say to her, *It's not just because of them, Jube, it's because I've loved you for longer than you'd ever guess.* If only he could say to her, *I want solace of heart as well as body, and I believe you're the only one I can find that with.* If only he could say, *Jube, Jube, I love you more than any man has ever loved you and I can overlook them all, all the ones who pleasured you first and undoubtedly better than I.*

But he could say none of these things. His heart was locked within a voiceless body and he could only stand beside the woman he loved and throb.

Prince's seed was sown. He emerged from Cinnamon glistening, wet, leaving vestiges of their intercourse on her sheeny rump.

Pearl left the fence and ambled toward the house with Leatrice. Jack wandered off toward the woodpile. Ivory and Ruby went in opposite directions. Zach moved off toward his cabin. Gandy lifted Willy off the fence and took him away, answering questions. One by one they left until only Jube and Marcus remained.

Their silence was strained.

"I'll help you with whatever you were doing in the barn." Jubilee offered.

She turned and he followed at her shoulder as she sauntered toward the barn, wondering if he'd make a move at last. She'd made it as plain as the blue sky above that she had feelings for him and wanted him in every sense of the word, but he was shy and, in all likelihood, put off by her debauched past. Walking with him, she rued it.

There were ways—blatant ways—to touch a man, to entice him. She knew them all. But because she did, she didn't want to use them on Marcus. When and if they came together, she wanted it to be because of love, not just lust. And she wanted *him* to be the one to make the first advance.

The barn was quiet. Only the lazy dust motes drifted in the aisle between the stalls. It smelled of leather and hay and the pleasant fecundity that permeated old wood even years after horses were gone.

Jube stopped in the aisle with Marcus behind her. He watched her chin drop, the fine strands of her angel hair caught on the collar of her blue dress, the distortion of her crocheted shawl as she tightened it with knotted fists. In the raters above their heads a pair of blue-winged swallows with apricot breasts fluttered about, building a mud nest.

"Marcus?" Her voice came, soft and pained. "Is it because I've been a prostitute?"

Is that what she thought? Oh, that she should have been laboring under the impression that it mattered to him.

He pivoted her by the shoulders and waved his hands before her eyes, shaking his head passionately. *No, Jube, no. It's because . . . because . . .* The ache in his body was nothing compared to his ache to put voice to all he felt. *Because I love you.*

When he told her, the motions were hard, muscular, tempered by a condensed anger at the slight that life had handed him. He touched his breast, thumped a fist on his own heart, and touched a fingertip to hers: *I love you.* He gestured wildly, as if to erase all they'd witnessed in the paddock—not that, this. Again he gestured: *I . . . love . . . you.*

She was in his arms so fast she knocked him a step backward. On tiptoe, she kissed him, flattening her body against his, even as his arms drew her close where he'd wanted her so long. And the tongue that could not speak spoke volumes as it learned the interior of her mouth. And the hands that had become the conveyor of his messages conveyed the most important one of all as they clasped her against his hammering heart, caressing her back, her waist, her head. She drew away and held his cheeks in both hands, her eyes intense and dark.

"Marcus, Marcus, I love you, too. Why did you wait so long to say it? I've loved you since that day of the picnic, maybe even before that."

He wished he could laugh, could know the heady release of the sound against her silky hair. Instead, he kissed her. Again and again and again—a league of impatient strokes that told her all he felt. And while they kissed, his hand fell to her breast, adoring, caressing. Hers stroked his hair, his back, his waist. He found buttons at her nape, freed them, and slipped a hand inside against her smooth skin. Her hands stroked his spine and, lower, until their bodies began moving against each other.

He loves me! she marveled. *Marcus really loves me.*

She loves me! he rejoiced. *Jube really loves me.*

But he wouldn't take her here in a stable, as if they, too, were merely animals in heat. She deserved better, and so did he, after all the time they'd waited.

Gripping her shoulders, he pushed her from him. Much like Prince's, his nostrils were dilated, his eyes turbulent. Much like Cinnamon, Jube stood docile, waiting, her lips open, the breath rushing between them in short, hard beats.

He pointed to a vacant stall and slashed the air with his hand—*not here, not like this.* He whipped her around and rebuttoned her dress, tucked two loose pins into her hair, then hauled her toward the door before she realized his intentions. With masterful footsteps and a firm grip on her hand, he led her across the beaten grass from the barn to the yard, along the worn wagon track past outbuildings, beside the formal gardens and the strutting peacocks, who lifted their heads to watch the couple pass. Up the back steps they went, across the deep veranda, and into the vast hall, where their footsteps echoed as they mounted the stairs.

Scotty stepped from his office, reading a letter. "Oh, Marcus, would you mind . . ."

The question died on his lips. His astounded eyes followed the pair, their footsteps reverberating from the magnificent staircase as Marcus tugged Jube along behind him. She glanced over her shoulder at Scotty—helplessly—and blushed to the roots of her hair. Then they disappeared above the turn of stairs and Gandy retreated quietly inside his office, closed the door, and smiled to himself.

Upstairs, Marcus took Jube straight to his room—the one he shared with Jack. He deposited her inside and without ado gripped an enormous armoire that appeared as if it would take Herculean strength to be budged. He slid it in front of the door as if it were a toy. But the screech echoed all through the house.

He turned, panting, and found a teasing smile on her face.

"You've scratched the freshly waxed floor," she said softly. "Leatrice will make us do it again."

His answer was to undo two shirt buttons, then jerk the tails from his pants before crossing the room to lift her off her feet. He carried her to the spooled bed and fell with her onto the soft coverlets. With his first kiss his hand found her breast, and before it ended he lay pressing her into the deep tick. As his body lay stretched upon hers, Jube learned that nothing had been lost between the barn and this room.

The only love Marcus had ever known had been bought. But this . . . this by some miracle had been won. With each caress he showed her how he prized her. His Jube, his beautiful, unattainable Jube, attainable, after all. She murmured in his ear, pouring out for both of them the words only one could say. He spoke with his roaming hands, his idolizing mouth, his eloquent eyes. When their clothing law strewn, he worshipped her duly. Other men had words at their disposal, words that they might employ at will to seduce and tantalize. Because he had none, Marcus used only his body.

But he used it so adroitly that Jube heard his voice in each lingering touch.

Jube, my beautiful Jube. How I love your hair, your skin, your eyes, your dark lashes, darling nose, beautiful lips, soft neck, your breasts, the mole between them, the shadow beneath them, your white, white stomach, and this . . . this, too, Jube . . . ahhh, Jube . . .

Many times in her past she had produced counterfeit ardor, but with Marcus, sham was not necessary. What she felt for him turned this act, for the first time ever, into one of love.

And when he rose above her and linked their bodies with a single smooth stroke, it was as foregone as the mating of the swallows in the rafters, the dragonflies in midair, the horses in the paddock.

When it was over and the tumult had been reached and moved beyond, they rested with their sweating brows touching. Jack tried the door and went away grumbling, and the smell of freshly fried hush puppies drifted up from the dining room below, and Leatrice's voice thundered out a warning that they were late for supper, and they laughed into each other's eyes and draped their spent arms over each other. Then Marcus knew they were not like Prince and Cinnamon. They could not separate and trot their individual ways as if this meant little more than the sating of animal drives.

Excited, he scrambled off the bed, leaving Jube so suddenly she shrieked and clutched herself. He had to ask her now, quickly, before they even went down to supper. He rummaged frantically for a pencil and paper—through the armoire, the pockets of his discarded jacket, two drawers, the top of a refectory table between the windows. Finally, impatiently, he thrust the fire screen aside and found a chunk of charcoal, pushed Jube off the far side of the bed, threw back the coverlets, and wrote on the rumpled bottom sheet:

Will you—

"Marcus, what are you doing! Leatrice will behead you!"

—marry me?

She stared at the question, so shocked her wide eyes seemed to tilt nearly to her hairline.

"Will I marry you?" she read, amazed.

He nodded, blue eyes bright, certain, blond hair mussed.

"When?"

He wrote on the sheet, underlining emphatically:

NOW!

"But what about a minister and a dress and a wedding feast and a—"

He landed on his knees in the middle of the bed, covering the word *marry,* grabbing her arms and tugging Jube to her knees before him. His eyes evoked a wondrous thump from her heart before he slammed his mouth down on hers and kissed her with the same authority he'd used when marching her up the stairs forty-five minutes ago.

He drew back, his unrelenting eyes holding her as forcefully as his grip upon her elbows.

"Yes!" she rejoiced, throwing her arms around his neck. "Yes, oh, yes, Marcus, I'll marry you. But in two weeks. Please, Marcus. I've never been courted before and I think I'm going to love it.

He kissed her again, starting hard, ending soft, wondering if joy this great could be fatal.

They were so late for dinner the hush puppies were all gone. Leatrice waddled around the table, collecting plates and scowling. She came to a halt at the sight of them careening to a breathless halt inside the dining room doorway, their faces shining with joy.

Scott looked up over his coffee cup and met Jube's eyes. Everyone else turned watermelon-pink and took a sudden interest in the crumbs on the tablecloth.

Where Marcus had towed Jube earlier, she now took the lead. Clutching his hand, she looked squarely at Gandy and announced, "Marcus and I are going to get married."

Six heads snapped up in surprise. Gandy set down his cup.

"In two weeks," Jube added quickly.

Every eye turned to Gandy, gauging his reaction.

A slow grin climbed his cheeks. When it reached his eyes and dimpled his face, the tension eased from the room.

"Well, it's about time," he drawled.

Jube catapulted into his arms. "Oh, Scotty, I'm so happy."

"And I'm happy for you."

He shook hands with Marcus and clapped him on the back, while Jube was passed around for hugs. When the congratulations ended, Scott stood with an arm around Jube's waist again. "I insist that the nuptials be spoken in the weddin' alcove," he told her.

Jube looked Gandy square in the eye and threw him into one of the major emotional upheavals of his life by declaring, "And I insist on inviting Agatha to the wedding."

Chapter 19

Oh, that winter, that endless unmitigated winter while Agatha's aloneness smote her daily. She had been alone before, but never as mercilessly as this. Before the advent of Scott, Willy, and Gandy's extended family into her life, her aloneness had been pacific. She had learned to accept the fact that her life would be a string of invariable days whose zeniths and nadirs fluctuated so minimally as to be almost indistinguishable, one from the other. She had learned to accept the blandness, the orderliness, the conformity. And the lovelessness.

Then *they* had come, bringing music and confusion and nonconformity and laughter. In terms of a lifetime, their presence had lasted but a brief heart flash, a few measly months out of years and years of solitariness. But in terms of living, she'd condensed more emotional vitality into those numbered days than she would experience in the remainder of her life, she was sure. Having lost it—and them— she was doomed to be forever aching.

Oh, the dullness after they were gone. The dullness had teeth and talons. It tore at her. She would never again be reconciled to it.

Sunset was the worst, that time of day between occupation and preoccupation, the time of long shadows and kindling lanterns when merchants drew their shades, women set their tables, and broods gathered in kitchens where warm fires glowed, fathers said grace, children spilled milk, and mothers scolded.

She watched the rest of the world end their days with these homely blessings and repined that they would never be hers. She bade Violet good-bye, went upstairs, lit her own lamp, and sometimes on a good day its shade would need washing. She sat down to read *The Temperance Banner* and sometimes on a good day one of its articles would interest her. She checked the clock after each article and sometimes on a good day she looked at it only five times before it was time to get ready to walk down to Paulie's. She touched up her already perfect hair and sometimes on a good day found enough strands out of place to justify taking it down and reshaping it. She limped down to Paulie's to eat her lonely supper and sometimes on a good day a child would sit at a nearby table and make eyes at her over the back of his chair. She drank her final cup of coffee with nobody to converse with and sometimes on a good day a man at a nearby table would light a cigar after his meal. And for a few moments she would gaze into the middle distance and pretend.

Then she went home with scraps for Moose and watched him eat, then wash himself, then curl into a contented ball and go to sleep. At bedtime she donned the nightgown she'd worn the night she slept in Scott's bed, then brushed her hair down, pulled the weights on the clock and, when she could avoid it no longer, climbed into bed—an old maid, getting older, sleeping with a spotted cat, while a pendulum ticked in the dark.

Most nights she lay awake listening for the tinkle of the piano and the ringing of the banjo, but the revelry was forever gone from below. She closed her eyes and saw long legs kicking toward the ceiling and red ruffles framing black fishnet stockings and a man with a cheroot between his teeth and a low-crowned black Stetson, and a little boy peeking under a swinging door.

One night when her restless recollections refused to desist, she rose from bed and crept downstairs with the key Scott had left her. She entered the back door of the saloon and stood motionless, holding the lantern aloft, watching light play along the short passage to the room where Willy had slept. Inside that room the cot was gone. The cradles that had held the kegs remained, along with the yeasty smell of old beer. But the boy was gone, and so were all reminders of his presence. She remembered the last night when she and Scott had tucked Willy into bed and he had kissed her. But the memory clawed at her heart and she left the storeroom.

In the main room of the saloon the chairs were upturned on the tables and the bar. But the piano was gone, and Dierdre, too, along with her Garden of Delights. The light from the single lantern created eerie shadows that crept along the walls and fell between the tables as Agatha moved among them. Here the scent of whiskey lingered, and perhaps the ineffable reminder of cigar smoke.

Something rustled and Agatha stopped, lifting the lantern high to peer into the murky corners. As if through a long tunnel came the distant tinkle of music, a lively song that wafted through the night with the tinny resonance of a harpsichord. Agatha cocked her head and listened. Now she recognized it—a piano and banjo together, and in the background the faint echo of laughter and feet tapping on a wooden floor.

> *Buffalo gals, won't you come out tonight,*
> *Come out tonight, come out tonight . . .*

She smiled and turned toward the spot where the piano was, where Jube and Pearl and Ruby were swishing their taffeta ruffles and lifting their heels in wondrous synchronization.

The sound stilled. The images vanished. It was only Agatha's imagination, the daft maundering of a melancholy and wishful woman standing alone in an abandoned saloon, shivering in a nightgown upon which a man had once pressed his body and a little boy had laid his head.

Go to bed, Agatha. There's nothing for you here, only heartache and the road to further unhappiness.

She never went into the saloon again after that, except once during daylight hours when she showed it to a party interested in renting it as a dry goods store. But when the man's wife lifted her nose and sniffed, she declared they would never get the whiskey smell out of the place. So they left without even checking out the back storeroom.

She wondered if others would come, new renters who'd spark her life with new friendships, new distractions. But who would come to this desolate little cow town anymore? Not even the cowboys now that the saloons were closed to them. Spring would arrive and the liveliness brought by the longhorns and their drivers would be absent. No noise, no commotion, no hubbub. How she would miss it, no matter what she'd said in the past. The cowboys and their disorderliness were as much a part of her life as the millinery shop. But without them and the prosperity they brought, the seasons would change and the town would wither, just as she and her business would, with nobody to care about either.

Christmas was an occasion to be suffered. Agatha's only delight—and it was a medicore one at that—was making a stuffed goose for Willy and sending it along with her first letter to him. She filled the missive with idle chitchat about how big Moose was getting and how he had snagged the hem of her garnet dress with his claws, and what she was giving Violet for Christmas, and how beautiful the roof of Christ Presbyterian looked with its mantle of snow. She included no clue of her overwhelming loneliness and was careful to refrain from asking how Scott was or sending him too personal a message.

Whenever she paid the rent, she made out the check and addressed the envelope with more care than she used on anything else these days, forming each flowing letter in intricate copperplate that looked as if it should be embroidered upon a pillowcase. But the enclosed letter stated only that she was sending the month's rent in the amount of twenty-five dollars, followed by a report on whether any prospective buyers had looked at the building. Except for the month of January, when the sniffing woman and her husband came, that portion of the letter was negligible.

There were outpourings she longed to express. But for fear of sounding like a desperate, love-starved spinster—which was exactly what she was—she bridled the urge.

She made it through the days by wearing a false cheerfulness that vanished the moment Violet's back was turned. But when she was in the shop alone she often found her hands idle while she stared at Willy's little stool and wondered if he'd grown tall enough that he wouldn't need it now; and wondered what it was like at Waverley, where he and Scott lived; and wondered if they missed her, too, sometimes; and wondered if she'd ever see either of them again. Then Moose would come and preen himself against her ankles and say, "Mrrr . . ."—the only sound in the otherwise silent shop—and Agatha would have to force herself out of a deep lassitude that seemed to pervade her more and more often as winter slogged along.

December, with its unendurable Christmas.

January, with its biting cold that made her hip ache worse.

February, with blizzards that blew down out of Nebraska and coated the snow with topsoil, making it as brown and forlorn as Agatha's life.

* * *

It was Violet who brought the telegram. Violet, with her blue eyes lit like a pair of gas jets and her blue-veined hands fluttering in the air and her blue hair trembling. And her titter was back.

"Agatha! Oh, my! Agatha, where are you? *Tt-tt.*"

"I'm here. At the desk."

"Oh, Agatha!" Violet slammed the front door. The shade snapped up and whirled on its roller but she took no notice. "You have a telegram! From *him! Tt-tt.*"

"A telegram? From whom?" Agatha's breath seemed to catch in her throat.

"*Tt-tt.* I was coming to work just as I usually do when somebody called from behind me and I turned around and there was that young man, Mr. Looby, the one from up at the depot, and he—"

"From whom, Violet?"

"—said, 'Miss Parsons, are you on your way to the millinery shop?' And I said, 'Yes, of course. Don't I go to the millinery shop every morning at eleven o'clock?' And Mr. Looby said—"

"*From whom, Violet!*" By this time Agatha's hands were trembling and her heart was making mincemeat of her chest.

"Well, you don't have to shout, Agatha. It isn't every day we get a telegram, you know. From Mr. Gandy, of course."

"Mist——" Agatha's voice refused to cooperate. "Mr. Gandy?" she managed on the second try.

"*Tt-tt.* Isn't it wonderful?"

Agatha stared at the piece of yellow paper in Violet's hand. "But how do you know?"

"Why, it says right here, plain as a barn fire on a dark night—L. Scott Gandy. *Tt-tt.* That's his name, isn't it? And he's asking if you'll—"

"Violet!" Agatha leaped to her feet and held out a palm. "Whose telegram is it?" Surprising, how calm that hand was when her body felt as if it contained a fault line that was separating.

Violet had the good grace to look contrite as she handed over the telegram. "Well, it was only folded in two. And, anyway, Mr. Looby told me what it said. Then he grinned and handed me this ticket made out for White Springs, Florida. *Tt-tt.*"

"A ticket—" Agatha's eyes dropped to the ticket and excitement made her body wilt into a chair as she began reading.

HAVE PROPOSITION FOR YOU STOP WILL DISCUSS ON NEUTRAL TERRITORY STOP MEET ME TELFORD HOTEL, WHITE SPRINGS, FLORIDA, MARCH 10 STOP TICKET INCLUDED STOP JUBE AND MARCUS ENGAGED STOP REGARDS STOP L SCOTT GANDY STOP

Each time Agatha read the word *stop,* her heart seemed to do just that. At the word *hotel,* her fingers covered her lips and she sucked in a quick breath. She was still staring, dumbfounded, when Violet tittered again.

"*Tt-tt.* That naughty Mr. Gandy. *Tt-tt.* He's sent a one-way ticket."

Agatha could scarcely breathe, much less speak. But she reached up woodenly and Violet placed the ticket into her trembling fingers—a stiff piece of white cardboard with black ink that seemed to dance before Agatha's confused eyes as she scanned the words *Proffitt* and *White Springs.*

"White Springs?" Shaken, she lifted her eyes to Violet. "But why White Springs?"

"Why, you just read it, didn't you? Neutral territory."

"But . . . but I've never even heard of White Springs, much less the Telford Hotel. Why would he ask me to go there?"

It was Violet's turn to cover her lips. Her blue eyes twinkled with illicit speculation. "Why, my stars, *tt-tt,* he's said it as clear as the Morse code can make it—to proposition you, my dear."

Agatha blushed and became flustered. "Oh, don't be silly, Violet. Having a . . . a proposition for me could mean anything."

"Then why is the ticket only one-way?"

Agatha's gaze fell to it. Within her body the fault line widened. "I . . . I don't know," she answered in a small voice.

"But, my goodness. Jubilee and Marcus engaged to be married—imagine that."

"Do you think you'll see Willy?"

"I don't know. Scott doesn't mention him."

"Well, what are you sitting there for, child? The tenth is the day after tomorrow."

The realization stunned Agatha. "Oh, gracious, so it is." Pressing a hand to her hammering heart, she glanced around the shop, as if trying to recall why she was there. "But . . ."—she raised distracted eyes to Violet—"but how can I get ready to go by then . . . and how can I leave the shop for an indefinite length of time . . . and . . . and there's that dress I've been working on for—"

"Bosh!" Violet spat. "Put that ticket down in a safe place and get upstairs this moment, Agatha Downing. Don't ask yourself how or why or for how long, not when a man like that is waiting in a hotel room in Florida for you. Just stuff as many gowns as you can into your trunk and be on that train when it pulls out tomorrow!"

"But—"

"One more word and I'll quit my job, Agatha!"

"But—"

"Agatha!" For an elderly woman, Violet could muster remarkable choler.

"Oh, Violet, can I really do such a thing?"

"Of course you can. Now, up with you." Violet reached for Agatha's hands and assisted her from the chair. "Check your gowns and your petticoats and make sure you take plenty of clean underwear, and if anything needs laundering we'd best get it down to the Finn's immediately. There's not a moment to waste."

"Oh, Violet." Agatha would have been appalled at her lack of coherence had she realized how many times she'd already said "Oh, Violet." But this time she embraced the birdlike woman and said fondly against her temple, "You have a magnificent rebellious streak in you that I've always admired. Thank you, dear heart."

Violet patted her shoulder, then shoved her away. "Upstairs with you now, and use a little vinegar in your rinse water. It brings out the red highlights in your hair. *Tt-tt.*"

He'd booked her a berth in a sleeping car, but sleep was out of the question. During the night she spent in it, her eyes scarcely closed. Such brimming anticipation could not be squandered in sleep. Hours like this were too precious, too rare, to let them slip through unconscious fingers.

She watched the land change from brown to white to green, a green more verdant than any she remembered in her entire life. She recalled the semiarid climate of Colorado with its piñon pines and poplars, but the earth itself was sere. And in Kansas, though a veritable ocean of blue-stemmed bunch grass filled every vista, it was green for only a short time each spring. Beyond the plains, Kansas offered little verdure but for an occasional copse of cottonwoods and hackberries. But the farther south and east Agatha traveled, the greener became the view out the train window.

They crossed the Tennessee River on a majestic trestle so high above a canyon it felt as if she were looking down on earth from heaven. Near Chattanooga the tracks twisted and turned through verdant ravines and several times she glimpsed waterfalls in the distance. With the foothills of the Appalachians behind, the land began flattening. Then there was Georgia with earth as red as ten-year-old rust, and more pines than she'd ever imagined, straight and thick and secret.

She changed trains in Atlanta and the rumbling wheels bore her ever closer to Scott and an assignation whose outcome she dared not contemplate for fear it might be one she must refuse. She shunted the thought to the recesses of her mind and immersed herself in the childlike joy of discovery. When she saw Spanish moss for the first time, she gasped in delight and looked around for someone to share it with, but everyone was either dozing or disinterested. The pines gave way to water oak and live oak and soon the tracks were bracketed by black water from which cypress knees projected, and the foliage became so thick it seemed no creature could live in it. But she saw a deer on an emerald knoll and before it quite registered upon her brain, it had turned tail and disappeared into the wall of growth behind it. Something flashed past, an impression of candy-pink tufts on a ball of green, too fast to absorb. She watched for another and saw one in time to inquire of the conductor.

"A tulip tree, ma'am. We're just about to pass over the Florida border. Tulip trees bloom early down here. Watch for white flowers, too, big white flowers on spreading green trees. Those'll be magnolias."

Magnolias. Tulip trees. Spanish moss. The very words accelerated her heartbeat. But what accelerated it even more was the realization that with each passing mile she was being borne closer and closer to Scott. Would he be there at the station? What would he be wearing? Would Willy be with him? Whatever would she say to him? What did a woman say to a man to whom she'd confessed her love but from whom she'd received no similar response?

The conductor weaved his way along the aisle, announcing, "Next stop, White Springs. White Springs, Florida." He paused a moment, touched the bill of his cap and said to Agatha, "Enjoy those tulip trees, ma'am."

"Yes, I . . . I will," she replied breathily, surprised to find that she could speak at all. As the train began slowing she was deluged with a mixture of silly concerns: *Is my hat on straight?* (But there was no hat; she'd come bareheaded in deference to his wishes.) *Is my dress wrinkled?* (Of course it was wrinkled; she'd been riding in it since she'd left home.) *Should I have worn the blue one?* (The blue one! The blue one was a dairy maid's dress compared to the one she'd made for the governor's tea.) *If he kisses me hello, where shall I put my hands?* (If he kissed her hello, she'd be doing well to remember she even had hands!) *Should I ask him immediately why he's brought me here?* (Oh, Agatha, you're such a priss! Why don't you try to be more like Violet?)

After all her concerns, she stepped from the train to discover Scott wasn't there to meet her. Disappointment turned to relief and relief back to disappointment. But there were hack and baggage lines to transfer passengers and their luggage from the depot to the hotels. So many hacks! So many hotels! So many people!

She signaled to a Negro driver who pulled up and tipped his wide straw hat.

"Aftuhnoon."

"Good afternoon."

He got down with a great lack of haste and stowed her trunk and bandbox in the boot, then shambled back to the side of the rig. He wore maroon felt carpet slippers on misshapen feet. His legs were bowed, and his lips were swollen.

"Where to?"

"The Telford Hotel."

"De Telfuhd. Sho' 'nuff."

She sat behind him on a cracked black leather seat, while a clip-clopping white mare moved over the sandy streets with no more hurry than his driver. Agatha's head swung left and right, trying to take it all in. An offensive odor pervaded the air but she seemed to be the only one aware of it. Well-dressed ladies and gentlemen strolled everywhere, crossing streets and hotel verandas, along shaded paths all seeming to lead in one direction. A bunch of mounted men with guns on their shoulders and quail hanging from their saddles followed a pack of hounds down the street. The carriage passed a sign that read, HUNT CLUB—HOUNDS FOR HIRE. A woman in a cane-backed wheelchair crossed the street behind them, pushed by a portly man in a beaver top hat. A band of laughing men with fishing equipment strode toward them with creels strapped over their shoulders. Everybody seemed to be playing.

"Sir?" she called her driver.

"Ma'am?" He half turned as if he could crane no farther around. His neck was crosshatched with furrows deep enough to plant seeds in, had it been made of earth instead of skin.

"I've . . . I've never been here before. What is this place?"

"Minnul springs, ma'am," he replied, the words so abbreviated her brow furrowed."

"I beg your pardon?"

"Minnul springs. Healin' watuh."

"Oh . . . mineral springs." So that was what smelled like rotten eggs.

" 'S'right, ma'am. Rich folk come, play some, res' some, soak in d' watuh some. Go 'way feelin' fine as a frog hair." He chuckled and returned to his driving. Within three minutes they drew up before an impressive three-story white edifice with a deep front veranda where ladies and gentlemen sat on wicker chairs and sipped from tall glasses.

"Telford, ma'am," the old man announced as he backed down from the driver's seat with arthritic slowness. With equal slowness he fetched her trunk and bandbox from the boot and delivered them inside the busy lobby.

"Be twen'-fi'e cen', ma'am," he said, returning, shifting his hat brim left and right, as if scratching his temples with it.

"I beg your pardon."

"Be twen'-fi'e cen'," he repeated.

"I . . . I'm sorry."

A familiar deep voice drawled near her ear. "I believe the fare is twenty-five cents, ma'am." She had never before experienced such a stirring reaction at the sound of a human voice. She snapped around and there he was, smiling down at her with familiar brown eyes, a pair of familiar dimples, a wonderfully familiar mouth . . . and a totally strange moustache.

"Scott," she could only think to say because her breath was short, her head light, and she felt curiously weak.

He looked tropical, in a nankeen suit as pale as bleached bone, a matching straw hat with a wide curved brim, and a black band that matched his collar-length hair, eyebrows, and the new moustache. His waistcoat was tight, molding his ribs above the twinkling gold watch chain that spanned its two pockets. At his throat he wore an ascot of striped silk—white on wheat, pierced by a single pearl stud.

"Hello, Gussie." He took both her gloved hands in his bare ones and squeezed hard while they smiled at each other with wide, bold gladness.

He realized in a flashing moment how much he'd missed her. And that she'd worn no hat, and that her hair was as beautiful as always, and her face as becoming, her smile as rare. And that her breasts appeared ripe, her breath harddriving within the boned, high-necked dress she'd made for the governor's tea. And that his heart was thudding to beat hell.

"Sorry I missed the train, but I wasn't sure which one you'd be on."

"It's all right. I've caught a hack."

Reminded that the driver waited, he released her hands to reach in his pocket. "Ah, the fare. Twenty-five cents, is it?"

"Yessuh."

He paid double that amount and the driver nodded twice while thanking him. Then Scott turned back to Agatha and retrieved both her hands. "Let me look at you." When he had, for so long her cheeks turned pink, he said, "No hat. Thank you."

She bobbed her head and laughed self-consciously, then lifted it to find his grin as delectable as ever and the scent of tobacco still marking him as the one she'd remembered out of thousands.

"Thank heavens nothin's changed," he said.

She assessed him in return. "I can't say the same for you."

"What? Oh, this?" He touched the moustache briefly, then took her hand again. "Got lazy and left off shavin' awhile."

It was an obvious lie. The remainder of his face was shiny from a fresh blading, and the precise black moustache was trimmed as if to military specifications. She loved it immediately.

"Very raffish," she approved.

"I was aimin' for refined." But he was pleased that she liked it.

"Possibly raffishly refined," she concluded, and they laughed lightheartedly, then stared at each other again, ignoring the hotel bustle that continued around them while their joined hands hung between them.

He squeezed her fingers, hard. "You look wonderful," he said.

"So do you."

They stared some more. Then Gandy laughed, as if his cup of joy had just run over.

She laughed, too—there was no controlling it when a heart was this happy. Then she found it impossible to look into his eyes any longer. "Is Willy here?" She glanced around.

"No, just us." Again their gazes locked. They stood among bellboys and hack drivers, women and men with children in tow, and a trio of the quail hunters making their way toward the kitchen with their unplucked supper in hand. Yet it seemed as if Scott had spoken the truth: just them. The flurry around them receded and they basked in their reunion. He changed the position of their hands, lifting hers until their palms matched, then meshing his fingers between hers and squeezing. Their absorption in each other continued inordinately until finally Scott seemed to realize it, freed her, and cleared his throat.

"Well ... uh ... I take it you haven't checked in yet."

"No."

"Let's do that."

Let's? His ambiguity left her with a feeling of palpitating uncertainty as he escorted her to the desk, watched her sign in, then took the key. But the room she was given was private, not even on the same floor as his.

"I arrived yesterday," he explained. "Mine is on the third, yours is on the second, so you only have t' climb one flight."

But what a flight—triple-wide steps with heavy oak railings; a landing with an enormous oval window bearing a leaded spider web design; a sprawling fern on a pedestal table, then more stairs with their rich scarlet runner overhung by double-bracketed gaslights.

"It's breathtaking, Scott. The most beautiful place I've ever been in."

"Wait till you see Waverley," he replied.

She seemed to float up the remainder of the stairs. But she didn't ask when. Not yet. The anticipation was too heady.

"You're still living there?"

"Yes." He leaned to put the key to the lock.

"And the others—Jube and all the rest?"

The door swung back. "They're there, too. We're turnin' Waverley into a resort hotel. Your room, ma'am." He ushered her inside with a light touch on her elbow. The moment her toes touched the thick Aubusson rug she forgot everything else.

"Ohhh, Scott!" She turned in a circle, looking up, then down. "Oh, my."

"You like it?"

"Like it? Why, it's magnificent!"

Scott draped an elbow on a high footpost of the brass bed, tossing the key, watching her scan the room a second time, enjoying her smile, her delight. She moved to one of the twin windows overlooking the street, touched the rose-colored overdraperies and the white Austrian drapes behind them, the silky wallpaper with its tiers of trellised rosebuds. Turning slowly, her gaze passed the lacy fern on its three-legged pedestal, the glass washbowl with its rose design in red on white, the matching water dispenser with its brass spigot, the drinking glass beside it, the bed with its woven counterpane of shell-pink and neatly folded quilt over the footrail, just in front of Scott.

Her eyes—green as the leaves of the fern with the sun glowing through them—stopped when they reached his. She clasped her hands, thumb knuckles pressing her breastbone. Her smile dissolved into an expression that made him want to leave his post at the foot of the bed and take her by both arms and feel his mouth moving over hers. Instead, he stood as he was.

"I cannot possibly allow you to pay for all this." She stood still and prim with her white gloves carefully placed.

"Why?"

"It wouldn't be seemly."

"Who will know?" Unspoken came the question: *Who will know anything we choose to do in this room?* For a moment it seduced them both.

Having completed her study of the room, she realized the most breathtaking thing in it was Scott Gandy in his tailored tropical suit with the vest that fit his chest much as her glove fit her trembling hand, and his intense dark eyes leveled upon her from beneath the brim of the finely woven planter's hat. And the new moustache that drew her attention time and again to his mouth.

"I will. You will," she replied, unsmiling.

Muscle by muscle, he drew himself away from the bedpost, unsmiling, too. "Sometimes you're too rigid with yourself, Agatha." He had taken a single step toward her when the bellboy spoke from the doorway.

"Trunks here."

Disappointed, Gandy turned, forcing a lightness to his tone. "Ah, good. Bring 'em in. Put 'em here." He tipped the bellboy, who left the door open as he went out. But the interruption had broken the spell. When Gandy turned back to Agatha she was strolling the perimeter of the room, carefully keeping her eyes on things other than him.

"The room's already been paid for, Gussie."

"I shall reimburse you, then."

"But it was my invitation."

"Why?" She stopped strolling, facing him from the diagonal corner of the bed. "I mean, why here? If Waverley is a hotel, then why the Telford in White Springs, Florida?"

He expelled a breath and consciously brought his grin back into place. "Because I remembered that you said you'd never been swimmin'. What better place t' learn than in a mineral spring of the first magnitude?"

"Swimming!" She pressed her chest. "You brought me all this distance so I could go swimming?"

"Don't look so surprised, Agatha. It's not just a pothole in a Kansas creek. *First magnitude* means the springs spout thirty-two thousand gallons of water an hour, and when you hit those bubbles you'll feel like you're floatin' in champagne."

As if she were doing so now, she laughed. "But I've never even seen champagne, much less floated in it."

"Looks exactly like spring water, but tastes much worse. Oh, by the way." He pointed to the spigoted dispenser and the drinking glass beside it. "Be sure you drink plenty of the water while you're here. They see to it y' have an ample supply in your room at all times. And they claim it does all kinds o' miraculous things t' your body. Cures gout, goiter, colic, constipation, cretinism, corns, catarrh, dandruff, and deafness. *And* makes the blind t' see and the lame t' walk."

She was smiling as he began, but when he'd finished, the last three words lingered as if they'd been repeated aloud.

"Does it really?" she commented quietly, dropping her gaze.

He came around the bed to stand before her. "Yes, really." He lifted her chin with the tip of the key and forced her to look at him. "I thought it would be good for you, Gussie. And I wanted a chance t' talk t' you . . . alone. There's no privacy around Waverley. People underfoot everywhere."

His dark eyes refused to waver from hers. The key was cold and sharp. Her heartbeat was unsteady. Gazing into his eyes, she felt the unwanted weight of propriety pressing hard upon her vitals and knew if he'd brought her here to seduce her, she would have to say no. Now that she was here, in this private bower where they answered to no one but themselves,. she realized she couldn't settle for an illicit liaison, no matter how strong her feelings for Gandy. When he reached for her wrist, her heartbeats swelled to the point where they caused an actual pain in her chest. But he only placed the key within her gloved palm, then folded her fingers over it and stepped back, dropping her hand.

"And, anyway, Waverley is my territory. It strikes me that wherever we've been, any time we've been together, we've been in somebody's territory. The millinery shop was yours. The saloon was mine. Waverley, too, would be mine. But White Springs is neutral, just as it was durin' the War Between the States. I thought it seemed like the perfect place for two scrappers like us t' meet."

"Scrappers—us?"

"Well, aren't we?"

"We used to be, but I thought we'd become friends."

He knew now he wanted to be much more than her friend, but he saw her nervousness reappear every time the notion transmitted itself to her. So he kept the mood light.

"Friends it is. So . . ." He stepped farther back. "As a friend, I wanted t' give you the waters of White Springs." He tugged his waistcoat into place as if preparatory to leaving. "I've already taken the waters earlier this afternoon, but I thought you might enjoy a bath before dinner. There's time yet and I'll walk you down t' the springhouse, or we can catch a hack if y' rather. Ladies bathe on the even hours, men on the odd, no mixed bathin' allowed, of course, except parents with children twice a day. Now, what do you say?"

"I have no bathing costume."

"Available at the springhouse."

She spread her palms, then joined them, her smile back in place. "Then what can I say?"

"Good. I'll give you time t' get unpacked, hang up your things. Then I'll be back for you." He checked his pocket watch. "Say in thirty minutes?"

"I'll be ready."

He crossed to the open door but stopped before leaving the room and turned to look back at her.

"It's good t' see you again, Gussie," he said simply.

"It's good to see you, too."

When he was gone she pressed both hands to her cheeks. They were warm as sun-baked stones. She sat on the edge of the bed, then fell back, placing her fingertips to the underside of her left breast, where her heart thrust with a mighty insistence that was becoming harder and harder to fight.

Closing her door, Scott remained with his fingers on the knob for long seconds, staring absently at the scarlet runner in the hall, asking himself again why he'd brought her here since he'd known all along it wouldn't work. A quick roll in a rented bed wasn't at all what he wanted from her, nor she from him. But if not that, what?

He drew in a deep breath, proceeded along the hall, and decided to let time answer the question for him.

Thirty minutes later they descended the grand staircase together, with her hand formally grasping his elbow.

"By foot or hack?" he asked when they reached the deep hotel veranda.

It was such a beautiful afternoon she said, "Let's walk. I've been riding for two days."

After the dismal winter in Kansas, the balmy temperature felt glorious. Birds sang and blossoms billowed, and once again she was struck by the lush greenness of everything.

"What are those?" she asked, pointing to a bush laden with pink blooms that looked much like roses.

"You mean you've never seen a camellia before?"

"I'm beginning to think I've never seen much of anything before. This place is wonderful. How ever did you find it?"

"I was wounded during the war and sent here t' recuperate."

She flashed him a startled glance. "Wounded?"

"Nothin' serious. A leg injury. But it got infected and the waters helped. There's a legend about the springs that goes back to the Seminole Indians. They recognized the medicinal value of the waters and it's said that the Indian wars were started when a papoose was shot off the back of a brave who was kneelin' at the spring t' drink. After that, Osceola declared that Indians from all tribes should be free t' use the springs without fear for their lives, and he banned all fightin' within a seven-mile radius. That tradition, as I said earlier, was carried on durin' the War Between the States. White Springs was declared neutral territory and soldiers from both sides were allowed t' come here t' recuperate from their battle wounds without fear o' retribution." He slanted a dimpled grin down at her. "Rather an appropriate spot for a whiskey peddler and a temperance fighter t' meet, wouldn't you say?"

She smiled and felt proud holding his arm, while strolling women gave him a second, then a third, glance. She pretended they were courting and even smiled sympathetically at the other women whose escorts, no matter how handsome, were eclipsed as Scott Gandy passed. Sometimes his elbow bumped the side of her breast. She loved the feeling. It reverberated down to her toes.

Within minutes they approached an impressive eight-sided structure. Agatha inquired admiringly, "Oh, my what's that?"

"That's the springhouse."

"But it looks like a grand hotel." The three-story pavilion of white clapboard with latticed foundation and black shingles rose majestically like an eight-sided doughnut whose hole held the bubbling white springs of the Suwannee River. Six facets of the octagon, three on each side, held changing rooms. These were connected by a promenade on the top level, where the continuous roof shaded white observation benches.

"One of the reasons I've always liked it," remarked Scott, "is because it's built in an octagon, like the rotunda at Waverley."

The approach was landscaped with more camellias, azaleas, and banana trees between which a wooden boardwalk led to the main door. Just inside, Scott turned Agatha over to an attendant, a young white woman with coal-black hair and a nose like a gravy ladle.

"It's her first time," he told the girl. "Give her the entire treatment."

"But—" Suddenly, Agatha hated being left in the hands of a stranger.

"I'll be back in an hour. Enjoy yourself."

Whatever she had expected, it wasn't the royal treatment that she received.

"My name is Betsy," the flat-nosed girl said when Scott was gone. "Follow me and I'll take you to your changing room." Betsy led her to the center of the building, where a wide opening gave a view of the actual waters within. But before Agatha had time for more than a glimpse, she was ushered in the opposite direction, into an elevator operated by a pulley and rope system to which Betsy applied herself. The way she strained upon the cables it appeared an enormous amount of work, but Agatha surmised that Betsy's biceps were even broader than her nose. She took Agatha to the third floor with no visible breathlessness. There they emerged from the elevator onto an outside railed veranda overhanging the springs, and along it Betsy led the way to the changing room. Inside, Agatha was given a pair of woolen knit drawers, a blousy top banded at the thighs, and a white cotton mobcap. When she emerged, barefoot, Betsy led her back to the elevator and lowered them to the ground level and finally the springs themselves. "It's icy year-round and it'll chill you to the marrow of your bones, but after several minutes you get used to it, and remember, when you're done here there'll be a hot bath waiting inside. Enjoy yourself, ma'am."

The smell was ghastly in the confines of the octagonal bathhouse. But the gurgling water sounded inviting.

"Cold" scarcely did credit to the first shock Agatha felt as she stepped into the water. Shivers raced up the backs of her legs and seemed to raise the hair off her skull. It felt awkward to be walking into a pool fully dressed, but she did it. To the knees (hugging her arms). To the thighs (stretching as tall as possible). To the waist (gasping). To the neck (chattering).

Sweet Savior, this was madness!

But other women bobbed in the water with only their heads showing. One nearby smiled at Agatha. Nonplussed, she returned the smile with a far less decisive one.

"It can be wonderful once you get used to it," the stranger remarked.

"I'm s . . . sure. B . . . but it's s . . . so c . . . cold."

"Revivifying," the woman returned and seemed to lie back in the water, suspended.

Agatha glanced down. Tiny bubbles rose all around her. A chuckle formed in her throat as the bubbles, like inquisitive minnows, played along her limbs and slipped beneath her bathing costume to work along her skin. They touched her in all her private places, popping along like a series of unending explosions that brought her flesh alive.

It tickled. It soothed. It came very close to arousing. But at the same time it relaxed. How could it create all these feelings at once?

She brought her arm just beneath the surface and watched the bubbles climb over it and erupt on the surface with a sound like meat frying in the other room. She spread her fingers and watched the air pockets rise between them. She need not have seen champagne firsthand to imagine she was floating in it. The continuous bubbles created an uninterrupted effervescence. She felt as if she herself had become champagne—airy, delectable, even drinkable.

She closed her eyes and steeped herself in the sensation of movement along the insides of her thighs, up the center of her spine, and between her breasts. She breathed deeply and let the feeling supplant all worldly cares.

And in those moments she came to understand sensuality in a natural, yearning way.

Later, when she became accustomed to the novelty of the bubbles, she experimented with a tiny bounce and was surprised by the unexpected buoyancy of her body. Never in her life had she felt buoyant; the sensation was infectious. She bobbed again, using her arms, feeling wondrously free and weightless. She followed the example of the friendly woman, resting on her back, lifting her feet, and for several seconds floated free of the restraints of gravity. How perfectly glorious!

When her feet drifted down to the bottom again, she glanced around to find no one paying particular attention to her and realized with a pleasant shock that here, in the water, she was no different from anybody else. Its buoyant properties made everyone equal. Suddenly, she realized, too, that her teeth were no longer chattering, the hairs on her arms no longer standing on end.

All too soon Betsy came to summon her from the water and escort her to the private bathing room where there waited a tin tub of hot water along with thick white Turkish towels. She was allowed to bask in the warm mineral bath for ten minutes before Betsy knocked and ordered her to dry in preparation for her massage. When Betsy reentered the room she told Agatha to lie face down on a slatted wood bench, with one Turkish towel beneath her, the other covering her from the waist down.

The mineral rubdown was more restorative than anything Agatha could imagine. She closed her eyes while deft hands worked her muscles in ways that made her feel as if she were floating on a magic carpet. Neck, shoulders, arms, buttocks, legs—all were attended with equal expertise.

When Agatha was dressed again and stepped off the elevator, some miracle seemed to have taken place in her body. She still limped—yes—but all vestiges of discomfort were gone. She felt limber, tensile, and utterly revivified. She felt as if she could walk miles and not tire, as if she could jump fences, race up stairs, skip rope! She couldn't, of course, but feeling as if she could was nearly as good.

Scott was waiting at the main entry, smiling.

"How was it?" he asked as she approached.

"Oh, Scott, it was extraordinary! I feel reborn!"

He took her arm and chuckled in deep satisfaction at her exhilaration. She was usually so reserved, it was fun to see her bubbling like the spring water itself.

"Nothing hurts! And look! I feel like I could walk back to Kansas. But in the water—oh, it was heavenly—I floated! I actually floated! There was a woman there who smiled at me and said something friendly and I watched what she did and tried it. I bounced! *I truly bounced!* All it took was a nudge with one foot and there I was, just like everybody else around me, bobbing like a cork. Oh, Scott, it was glorious. I've never felt so unencumbered in my life." She turned to look longingly over her shoulder at the bathhouse. "Can I come again tomorrow?"

He laughed and squeezed her elbow, then transferred her hand to the crook of his arm. "How can I refuse?"

"Oh, but . . ." Her brow curled in consternation. "Does it cost a lot?"

"You let me worry about that."

"But—"

"Hungry?"

"But—"

"I am. And White Springs is famed for some of the best cuisine in the Deep South. Quail is a specialty. I'm gonna take you back t' the hotel and stuff you with breast of quail sautéed in butter with black mushrooms and walnut sauce and steamin' saffron rice."

"But—"

"And afterward a wedge of Black Forest torte piled high with whipped cream. And plenty o' mineral water t' drink."

"But—"

"I don't mean t' sound critical, Gussie, but you're bein' terribly repetitive. Do you know how many times you've said *but?* Now, I invited y' here as my guest, and that's how it'll be. Not another word about it."

The dining room of the Telford was elegant, the linens starched to perfection, the service real silver. It was a far cry from Cryus and Emma Paulie's. Gandy was gratified to be able to treat Agatha to an elegant supper in such a place. He enjoyed watching her dine upon quail with black mushrooms and the other foods he'd suggested. She did so with great relish, as if her hour in the mineral baths had sharpened her appetite immensely. Somehow he'd expected her to eat with the picky affectation of most modern women. The fact that she didn't charmed him more than any silly dissemblance she might have practiced.

Her hair was wet around the edges, and as it dried, strands shrank from their restraints and formed miniature coils behind her ears. The gaslights lit them and formed shadows upon her neck and on the shoulder of her emerald-green dress. Likewise, her eyelashes upon her cheeks, shading her pale eyes.

He thought once more about kissing her. Her lips gleamed as she bit into the buttered quail, but each time she looked up and caught him watching her she carefully applied the napkin and glanced down.

He took up pondering his motives for bringing her here. Yes, he'd wanted to give her the waters themselves and all they could do for her physically. But if he were honest with himself, there were other physical experiences he wanted to give her. He took a bite of tender, succulent quail and let his eyes drift down her full breasts to her trim ribs. She wasn't the kind of woman a man compromised under the false pretenses of "taking the waters." When and if he ever touched her in an intimate way, he would feel compelled to do the honest thing.

She took a bite of meat, looked up, and caught him in a deep study of her feminine attributes. She stopped chewing. He took a gulp of mineral water. Tension buzzed around them for the remainder of the meal.

She wiped her lips for the last time and lay her napkin aside. He pushed his dessert plate back, ordered a cup of coffee, and lit a cheroot, after snipping it with the pair of miniature gold scissors.

"You're still carrying it, I see."

"Yes, ma'am."

As he lit the cigar, she watched his lips and moustache conform to the shape of it. Then she became immersed in the pungent aroma, relishing it again. A memory came back, clear as a reflection in still water.

"I remember the day that oil painting of Dierdre was delivered to Proffitt. You paid for my supper at Paulie's and I was so put out with you I wanted to . . . to ram your money down your throat."

"And you were so prim and proper and I was embarrassed as hell about pushin' you down in the mud."

"Embarrassed? You?" Her eyebrows rose.

"I was."

"I didn't think you were capable of being embarrassed about anything. You always appeared so . . . so cocksure. And so aggravatingly adept at teasing. Oh, how I hated you."

Scott leaned back casually in his chair and laughed. "I reckon y' had good cause."

"So tell me," she said, changing the subject abruptly, "how is Willy?"

Scott's eyebrows knit and he leaned forward, tapping the ashtray distractedly with his cheroot.

"Willy's not the boy he was when he left Proffitt."

Her happy mood vanished, replaced by concern. "What's wrong?"

"He's turnin' into a brat, that's what's wrong. He's hangin' around with too many of the wrong people, if y' ask me. A riverboat gambler, a bartender, a roustabout, three ex-prostitutes, and a black mammy with a mouth as sassy as a hissin' goose. The only one he doesn't seem to pick up bad habits from is Marcus. The girls spoil him terribly and he occasionally lapses into some of their gutter language. Leatrice gives him his way all the time, and when he goes off with the men into the woods it's hard t' tell what kind o' talk he's exposed to. He's even gotten demandin' with me. When I don't give him his way, he pouts or gets mouthy. I tell you, Gussie, sometimes when he talks back to me . . ."—he made a fist in the air—". . . I want t' turn him over my knee and tan his backside."

"Well, why don't you?"

The fist relaxed. Scott's expression softened. "I guess because he got enough o' that kind o' treatment from his old man."

"But Alvis Collinson never loved him, Scott. You do. He would surely know the difference."

He knew she was right and shook his head despairingly. "I can't do it, Gussie. I'll never be able t' raise my hand t' that boy."

In her chest she felt the lump of love expand, recognizing in those few words the kind of father he was; the kind she'd always wished for herself.

"But Willy must be reprimanded when the occasion calls for it or he'll only continue to get worse, and there's nothing more unlikable than a willful child."

"He's willful, all right. But it's not really his fault. Part of the problem is that he has nobody his own age t' play with. I've taken him into town a couple times t' spend an afternoon with a little boy his own age, named A. J. Bayles, but Willy is so insufferable t' A. J. that he hasn't been invited back again. And he's started talkin' to an imaginary friend."

Agatha didn't appeared to be fazed a bit. "That's not unusual. I did that a lot when I was a child. Didn't you?"

"I wouldn't be so concerned if it weren't this particular friend."

"Who?"

Gandy frowned at the ashtray and tamped out his cigar more times than necessary. "Gussie, you're goin' t' think I'm mad, but the bedroom where Willy and I sleep is ... well, that is ... it seems t' be haunted."

Instead of looking bemused, Agatha asked seriously, "By whom?"

"You believe me?" he asked, amazed.

"Why not? By whom?"

"I think it's Justine, my daughter."

"And she's the one Willy talks to?"

"Yes." Almost unconsciously, he reached across the table for her hand. His eyes were dark, worried. "Gussie, I've heard her, too. She calls for help. Never anywhere except in the northwest bedroom on the second floor, the one we call the children's room. But it's as clear as any human voice I've ever heard, and several times I've seen the imprint where she—or somebody—has lain on the bed, when nobody else has been in the room t' muss it."

"Does it frighten you?"

He considered a moment. "No."

"Is Willy frightened?"

"No. Quite the opposite."

"Then what harm can come of it? You seem to have a friendly ghost. And if you're her father, she surely wouldn't harm you or anyone close to you."

He looked at Gussie as if in a new light. "You're amazin'."

"My father was a miner. There are no more suspicious people in the world than miners. If they hear so much as a falling pebble in a deep shaft they attribute it to ghosts. And there are plenty who'll swear they were right, especially after cave-ins."

He was so relieved at her acceptance of his tale that he felt guilty for having tried to reason with Willy. "I told Willy it was impossible for him t' have seen and talked t' Justine. I suppose that was the wrong thing for me t' do."

"Maybe. If it were me, I'd allow him to talk to her all he wants. What harm can come of it? If she's just a figment of his imagination, he'll outgrow it in time. If not, he's no more deranged than you, is he?"

"Ah, Gussie, I'm so relieved. It's been on my mind so much lately, but I was afraid t' talk t' anybody at Waverley about it. I thought if I did, it might get back to Leatrice, and she's already wearin' a smelly asafetida bag around her neck t' ward off hants, as she calls 'em. If she finds out there really is one, we'll never get her inside the mansion again. And even though she's outrageously insubordinate, I need her there t' keep the place runnin' smoothly."

"This Leatrice sounds somewhat like Ruby."

"She is. But, as I said before, she's started to influence Willy. He's pickin' up her bossiness and her bad grammar. Which leads us to another point. Willy is six already. He should be goin' to school, but the closest one is in Columbus, and it's a ten-mile drive, one-way. I don't have the time t' make that trip twice a day, and there's certainly nobody on Waverley qualified t' tutor him."

Agatha's heartbeat accelerated even before Scott went on.

"Which is why I've brought you here, Gussie." He still held her hand, their fingers linked, palms down. "He needs you, Gussie, more than he needs anyone else right now. He cries for you at bedtime, and at Christmastime he raised a regular stink because I didn't bring you t' Waverley or send him t' Proffitt. I try t' do the right things for him, but after talkin' with you such a short time I realize my judgment isn't nearly as good as yours. He needs your steady, dependable sense of right and wrong. And someone who knows how to say no to him and make it stick. Somebody t' monitor what he picks up from the girls and Leatrice . . . and even me. He needs a teacher, daily lessons. You could do all those things, Gussie, if you came to Waverly."

So there it was—his proposition. So much for her foolish misconception that he'd brought her here with anything so tempting as seduction on his mind. She need not worry herself about it further. Neither need she waste even the briefest moments supposing that he'd brought her here to ask her to marry him. He didn't want her as a consort or a wife, only as a governess for Willy.

The picture of Willy crying for her at bedtime raised a surge of maternal caring within her breast. But it could not quite quell the disappointment she felt. She withdrew her fingers from Scott's and folded her hands in her lap.

"I would be a governess, then?"

"Why does that sound like such a cold word? You mean as much to Willy as any real mother could. That makes you so much more than a governess. Say you'll do it, Gussie."

And live in your house, longing for you for the remainder of my life?

"When would you want me to come?"

He sat forward eagerly. "Jube's taken that decision out of my hands by demandin' that I get you to Waverley with all due haste, t' start makin' her wedding gown. She and Marcus are plannin' t' be married on the last Saturday in March, and she said she wants you at the weddin'. Now what do you say?"

She felt obliged to put up some resistance, no matter how weak. "But I have a business. I can't just up and leave it."

"Why not? It's slowly dyin' anyway. Y' told me yourself hats will soon be a thing of the past. And with factories on the eastern seaboard turnin' out ready-made clothin', the seamstress's trade is sentenced to the same demise. It's only a matter of time."

"But what about Violet?"

"Ah, Violet." Gandy paused to recall the glinting blue eyes of the wrinkled little woman. "Yes, it would be hard for you t' leave Violet." He quirked one eyebrow. "Unless, of course, you left the entire business t' her."

"The whole business?"

"Well, what else are you goin' t' do with that . . . that aviary of birds' nests and butterflies, and those cubbyholes full of ribbons and lace, and that enormous roll-top desk? Why, you could even leave her the furniture in your apartment—that is, if you don't object. We certainly have all we need at Waverley. And wouldn't it be a nice change for Violet t' have a place of her own instead of only a tiny room at Mrs. Gill's boardin' house?"

The thought of Violet gave Agatha pause. Violet had become a true friend. Leaving her would be very sad, indeed.

"I think," Scott said, "that Violet would be the first one t' encourage you to say yes. Am I right?"

As if Violet were here, Agatha heard her titters at Scott's sudden appearance in the store, saw the little woman blushing as he leaned over her blue-veined hand and brushed it with his lips, heard her breathlessness as she sank to a chair and fanned her flushed face with a lavender-scented hankie.

"You never came within a country mile of Violet Parsons without her wishing she were forty years younger. How could I expect an unbiased opinion out of a woman like that?"

He laughed. "Then you'll do it?"

She might be a virgin, a virtual innocent. But there were vibrations between Scott Gandy and herself that could not be mistaken. She might vacillate between believing and disbelieving them, depending on her state of emotions. But in her saner moments she realized full well that within them both an undeniable physical attraction was being nurtured with each hour they spent together.

She should ask him—should she not?—what his intentions were on that score. Was she then, in time, meant to become his live-in mistress now that Jube was marrying Marcus? A man like Scott would not do without a woman for long, and though he hadn't said he loved her, love seemed unnecessary to him when considering consortium. After all, he hadn't loved Jube either. Yes, she should ask him, but how did a woman broach a subject like that with a man who hadn't even kissed her after a five-month separation? A woman like Agatha Downing didn't.

In the end she drew a quavering breath, held it a moment, then released it in a rush. "I will. On one condition."

"Which is?"

"That I leave Violet with everything except my Singer sewing machine. If she wants one, she'll have to buy her own. Mine was a gift from you and I think it's only fitting that I bring it to Waverley to make Jube's dress."

"Very well. Consider the freight paid."

When he saw her to the door, it was not with the good-night kiss for which she'd hoped, but with a firm handshake on the pact they'd made.

He took her to the springs twice each day for the next two days while they stayed to enjoy the spa, and though they grew friendlier than ever in terms of conversation and companionableness, not once during those two days at White Springs did he make the slightest advance toward her . . .

Until they were at the train depot and he was seeing her off again.

What was it about train depots that made hearts grow desolate even before good-byes were said?

Just before she boarded, he took her by both arms and kissed her squarely on the mouth. She sensed when he did it that he was determined to keep the kiss short and friendly. But when it ended and he looked into her eyes and her gloved fingertips rested against his breast, the temptation became too great and he drew her to him, more gently this time, and kissed her once—a moist, voluptuous kiss with his tongue saying good-bye inside her mouth—and made her knees go watery and her heart detonate like cannon shot.

When he set her back and looked again into her eyes, she had the awful feeling that men and women kissed this way all over the world, at moments such as these, and it was only her lack of experience that made her believe this was special between her and Scott, that it meant something more than it actually did.

Why did you wait three days to do that? she wanted to ask. But a woman of propriety didn't ask such things.

"Good-bye," she said instead. "And thank you for giving me swimming in White Springs. I'll never forget it."

"I didn't give you anything. White Springs was always here for you t' take."

But he had and they both knew it. He had given her more than any other human being had ever given. He had given her, if not his own love, then hers for him. And giving it, she discovered, was the next best thing to having it reciprocated.

Chapter 20

There was a mood created by rocking trains that lent itself to introspection—the landscape moving faster and faster until it became a smear of green in the distance; the incessant thunder of metal on metal shimmying up from below until its vibrations became as much a part of the rider as his own heartbeat; the keening whistle carried on the wind as a faint sigh; outside, the green turning to black, and a face looking back at the rider, and that face her own. It was like having one's subconscious staring back, demanding examination.

On her way back to Proffitt, Agatha spent the hours thinking about the gamble she was taking—and it was a gamble, wasn't it? Purgatory against heaven. For to live in Scott Gandy's house as nothing more than a governess was to deliver herself into eternal purgatory. She loved him, she wanted him, she wanted a life with him, but as his wife and nothing less. Yet he spoke of neither love nor marriage. Living in his house, keeping her feelings silent—would it truly be preferable to staying in Proffitt alone?

Yes. Because at Waverley there was Willy, too, and Willy's love meant almost as much to her as Scott's.

So what about the chances for heaven? Everything she'd ever wished for, that one day Scott would look her squarely in the eye and say he loved her, wanted to marry her and make Willy their own forever. That was really how it ought to be. Would he ever see that?

Ah, but that was the gamble, for she didn't know.

She had gambled once before with Scott Gandy and lost, and it had hurt. Hurt. But love was an infectious thing and a smart person would bet on it every time.

And Agatha Downing was one smart lady.

Leaving Violet turned out to be less painful than Agatha had anticipated, chiefly because Violet was thrilled with the new status of her life as a merchant businesswoman. And, as Scott had predicted, after having lived at Mrs. Gill's in a single room, Violet felt as if she were inheriting a villa in Agatha's apartment. Also, she maintained a breathless sense of awe at Agatha's having won a place in the household of LeMaster Scott Gandy, the man whose reckless smile had made her blush and titter so many times.

But at the last moment, when Agatha's things were packed, her sampler carefully tucked away between layers of clothing in a trunk, her older hats donated to Violet, her apartment ransacked of all meaningful personal possessions, the sewing machine carted off to the depot on a dray, the final instructions given regarding the status of the shop's books, Agatha looked around the building and her eyes met Violet's.

"We've spent a lot of hours here together, haven't we?"

"Most certainly have. We sewed plenty of stitches inside these walls. But then we did some laughing, too."

Agatha smiled sadly. "Yes, we did." Beside her, Moose let out an abused yowl from inside a poultry crate. "Are you sure you don't mind my taking the cat?"

"Of course I'm sure. That creature of Mrs. Gill's was gone for three days again last week and came home stinking to high heaven with her fur all matted down and limping, mind you! I'd like to have seen that. *Tt-ttt.* Anyway, in nine weeks there'll be a new batch of kittens at the boardinghouse, and Josephine won't know what to do with them when they start climbing the drapes and sharpening their claws on the furniture. No, you take Moose back to Willy. That's where he belongs." Violet paused and glanced around. "Well, now, we'd best get you two down to the depot just in case that train comes a bit early. Wouldn't want you to miss it, not with Mr. Gandy waiting at the other end. *Tt-tt.*"

Agatha closed the door of the dress shop behind her for the last time, turning to glance at the green shade she'd raised each morning and drawn each evening for more years than she cared to count. She glanced at the apartment windows overhead. The nostalgic remark she'd made inside had been voiced because of her affection for Violet. But not a twinge of regret troubled her as she turned her back on the building. It had been a lonely place all the years she'd lived there, and leaving it was a pleasure.

But when she and Violet said good-bye beside the steaming train, a sudden sharp stab hit both of them. Their eyes met and they both realized that it could in all likelihood be the last time they ever saw each other.

They hugged hard.

"You've been a dear friend, Violet."

"So have you. And I shan't give up hope that Mr. Gandy will see the light and take you for a lover, if not for a wife."

"Violet, you're outrageous." Agatha laughed with misty eyes.

"I'll tell you a secret, dear, one I've never told anyone before. I had a lover once when I was twenty-one. It was the most wonderful experience of my life. No woman should miss it." She shook a crooked index finger under Agatha's nose. "Now, you remember that if the chance comes up!"

Still chuckling tearfully, Agatha promised, "I will."

"And tell them all hello from me and give that handsome Gandy a kiss on the cheek and tell him that's from Violet, who wanted to do it every time he walked into the millinery shop. Now get on that train, girl. Hurry!"

And so parting was easy; Violet made it so with her unfailing spirit. It wasn't until Agatha was half a mile down the track that her tears fell freely. But they were happy tears, somehow. And Violet had certainly given her something to think about!

She thought about it during her brief waking hours on the long trip south, wondering about Violet and who her lover had been and if he was someone Violet had been running into all through the years. And how long had the affair lasted? And why hadn't they married? And what was it that made it the most wonderful experience in her life?

Agatha had always thought only wicked women coupled with men outside of marriage. But Violet was far from wicked. Violet was a good Christian woman.

The thought roiled around and around in Agatha's mind while the familiar transformation took place beyond the train window, while she gave up winter for spring, cool weather for warm, mud for blossoms. While the images of Scott and Willy danced before her eyes . . .

Then they became more than images. They were real, standing side by side on a red-cobbled depot yard, searching the windows that flashed past; Scott raising a finger and pointing—there she is!—and both of them waving, jubilant, smiling. Agatha's heart swelled at the brief glimpse of her two loves, and though she'd never before been in Columbus, Mississippi, the sense of homecoming was strong and sharp and sweet. They were at the foot of the steps when she emerged, Willy perched on Scott's arm.

"Gussie, Gussie!" he called, reaching.

He hugged her and knocked off the hat she'd worn only because she owned so many it was one less to carry in a bandbox. Scott caught it in his free hand while she and Willy hugged.

"Oh, Willy, I missed you." She closed her eyes to seal in tears of happiness. They kissed and he tasted of sarsaparilla. She brushed back his hair and held his face and couldn't get enough of looking at his beloved freckled cheeks and his precious brown eyes.

"Scotty says you're stayin' for good. Are you really, Gussie, are you?"

She smiled at Scott. "Well, I guess I am. I've packed up everything I own— even my sewing machine and Moose."

"Moose! Really?"

"Really. He's in a poultry crate in the baggage car and the porter has been feeding him."

Willy peppered her face with noisy kisses that landed anywhere and everywhere. "Garsh!" he rejoiced. "Moose! Did you hear that, Scotty? She brung Moose!"

"*Brought* Moose," Scott corrected. When Agatha would have smiled at him, Willy held her cheeks between both his hands, demanding her undivided attention. "Wait'll you see my horse. Her name is Cinnamon and she's pregnant!"

"She is!"

"Scotty let me watch her get bred."

"I see I'm just in time to get your education on the proper track for a boy of five."

"Six. I had a birthday."

"You did! I missed it?" She twisted her expression into one of exaggerated dismay.

"It's all right. I'm gonna have another one next year. Let's go get Moose. Zach is waitin' at the wagons."

Willy squiggled out of Scott's arms to the cobblestones and scampered off, leaving Gandy and Agatha facing each other. With no barriers between them their eyes met and held. The sense of rush dissipated.

"Hello, again," she said.

"Hello. How was the trip?"

"Fine. Rushed. Thank you for the fine accommodation. This time I actually slept."

"This time?"

"Last time I was too excited to sleep. This time I was too exhausted not to."

"No trouble gettin' things settled in Kansas?"

"Everything went fine." It was so hellishly tempting to touch him that she suddenly gave in to the urge. She went up on tiptoes, clipped an arm behind his neck, and kissed him on the cheek. "That's from Violet. She said I should tell you she wanted to do it every time you walked into the millinery shop." The hand holding her hat came around her back as he dropped his head obligingly.

When she would have backed away, his arm tightened. The dimples appeared in his cheeks, his voice softened. "That's from Violet. What about from yourself?"

She had the presence of mind to smack him blithely on the other cheek and make no more of it than a joke. "There. That's from me. Now give me my hat."

He placed it on her head. "I thought you gave up hats."

"That's asking a lot of a woman who's worn them all her life. I kept a few of my favorites, and this was the most convenient place to carry one of them." She reached to adjust it but he did it instead, studying the results critically.

"Uh-uh. I don't think so," he decided and removed it. "You always did look better without one."

"Hey, come on, you two," Willy interrupted. "Zach's waitin'."

Scott reluctantly shifted his attention to the boy. "All right, all right. Go tell Zach t' pull the wagon up t' the baggage car at the other end and we'll meet him there."

Gandy took Agatha's arm and they sauntered along the cobblestones toward the baggage car.

"You left the store in Violet's hands?"

"Yes. She was ecstatic. Who is Zach?"

"The son of one of our old slaves. He's very good with horses and is teachin' Marcus how t' be a ferrier. So y' brought the sewing machine."

"Of course. I wouldn't want to make a wedding dress without it. Did any of the others come to town with you?"

"No, but they're all at home waitin'. Do y' need anything from town before we head for Waverley? It's an hour's ride and we don't make it every day."

She needed nothing. She felt as though she had everything in the world she'd ever need or want as she watched the reunion between Willy and Moose—face to face, whiskers to freckles, the cat suspended as Willy held him beneath his front legs and kissed him, then squeezed him far too tightly, scrunched his eyes shut, and said, "Hey, Moose! Garsh, I missed you."

Agatha was introduced to Zach, who pulled up in a weatherbeaten wooden wagon upon which was loaded the empty poultry crate and the sewing machine and all of Agatha's gear, including the hat, which Gandy tossed through the air at the last minute.

Then she and Willy and Scott and Moose boarded a black well-sprung rig and headed for her new home. On the way Agatha saw her first redbud in bloom— clouds of rich heliotrope. And dogwood—clouds of cottony white. And wisteria— cascades of pure purple. In the ditches beside the road wild jonquils bloomed in patches so large it looked as though pieces of sun had dropped to the earth and shattered upon the grass. Here, as in Florida, the scent of the South prevailed— rich, moist, fecund. Already Agatha loved it.

They passed Oakleigh and Willy told Agatha that was where A.J.'s grandma and mother had lived before the war. They passed a little white church in a copse of pines and he told her that was where Leatrice went on Sundays. They passed the cemetery and he told her that was where Justine was buried.

They turned into the lane and Gandy told her, "This . . . is where I was born."

Waverley.

More grand, more majestic than Scott's watercolor had been able to depict. Waverley, with its towering pillars and magnificent rotunda and its wrought-iron lacework. Waverley, with its massive magnolia out front and the boxwoods trimmed to match their names. She looked up and her heart hammered—she was really here at last. She looked down and saw the peacocks on the lawn!

"Oh!" she exclaimed breathlessly.

Scott smiled, watching her, filled with pride at the appearance of the place, decked out in its floral finery, lustrous as a pearl on its emerald lawns.

"You like it?"

Her reply was all he could have hoped for. She sat speechless, with a hand pressed to her thrumming heart.

Jack saw the carriage and came hurtling across the grounds from the tannery, bellowing at the top of his lungs, "They're here, everybody! They're here!" And before the carriage stopped, the front door flew open and voices were whooping and people were barreling toward the rig with arms uplifted.

Agatha was passed from Pearl to Ivory to Ruby, getting hugs from all. Then came Jack, puffing from his run across the yard, sweeping her in a circle and making her laugh. Then Jube, radiant even in a cleaning dress of washed cotton.

"Jubilee, congratulations!"

The two women backed off and smiled at each other. Then Jube captured Marcus's arm to tug him forward. "Isn't it wonderful? If he says anything different, don't believe a word of it."

Marcus, always the perfect gentleman, smiled at Agatha but held back. She gave him an impulsive hug.

"Congratulations, Marcus! I'm so happy for you."

He made motions as if he were squirting oil and raised a questioning brow.

"Yes, it's all oiled and ready to go. We'll have her dress made in no time."

There was one other person waiting on the front steps with hands crossed over her bulging stomach and a leather pouch suspended from a thong around her neck, a woman shaped like a water buffalo, who could only be the indubitable Leatrice.

Everyone except Leatrice talked at once. Everyone except Leatrice hugged Agatha or kissed her on the cheek. Everyone except Leatrice smiled and laughed. Leatrice waited like a queen on a dais for her subject to be announced.

When the initial hubbub had died down, Scott took Agatha's elbow and escorted her up the marble steps.

"Leatrice," he said, "I'd like you t' met Agatha Downin'. Agatha, this is Leatrice. She's cantankerous and unreasonable and I don't know why I keep her. But I've been farther underwater than she's been away from Waverley, so I guess she's here to stay."

Leatrice spoke in a voice like an engine with gear trouble. "So you here at las', d' woman from Kansas. Maybe now we get sumpin' 'sides growlin' outta dis one heah." She curved a thumb toward Gandy. "Boy's been one bodacious bear t' live wid."

Gandy grew red around the collar and studied his feet. Agatha politely refrained from looking at him. "I've heard a lot about you, Leatrice."

"I jus' bet ya have, an' ain't none of it good, izzat right?"

Agatha laughed. The woman did, indeed, stink like a polecat, which Gandy had warned she would. "Well, I've heard that you rule with an iron hand, but I have a feeling there are times when *some*body needs it."

"Humph!" Leatrice readjusted her crossed hands over her barrel belly. "An' I know who."

Zach arrived with the baggage and the men began unloading it. Jack and Marcus came up the steps bearing the sewing machine. Zach and Ivory followed with a trunk, the latter with Agatha's pink-flowered hat perched on his head.

"Where you git dat hat, boy?" Leatrice demanded.

Agatha snatched it off. "It's mine, but the master of Waverley has issued his first order—no hats for me."

"Where to with these things?" Jack asked.

"The right parlor," Gandy answered, and the men moved inside.

Willy came by, lugging a hatbox nearly as big as he, while Jube and the girls followed with additional luggage. As they disappeared inside, Agatha plucked at the petals on the hat and peered up at Gandy with a teasing light in her eyes. "And where to with this thing?"

Gandy glanced wryly at the hat with its pink cabbage roses and whorl of net and its cluster of cherries in a sprig of green leaves.

"No offense, Agatha," he said, "but that is the singularly most ugly thing I've ever seen. Why any woman with hair like yours would want t' cover it with cabbage roses and cherries is a mystery t' me."

Agatha stopped plucking at the silk petals, sighed, and quite by chance won the black woman's heart forever by inquiring, "Would you have any use for one slightly used pink hat, Leatrice?"

Leatrice's eyes widened and fixed upon the gaudy creation. Her hands reached out slowly, reverently.

"Dis? Fo' me?"

"If you don't mind it being slightly worn."

"Lawdy . . ."

Gandy grinned at Agatha and said, "Come on. Let me show you the house."

They left Leatrice on the front steps, wearing the abominable-smelling asafetida bag around her neck and the pink hat on her head.

Scott took Agatha through a door wider and higher than any she'd ever seen into the grand rotunda, where she stood a moment to catch her breath. It was majestic. Spacious and bright with paneled doors rolled back revealing twin parlors on either side and the sweeping twin staircases twining down from overhead, forming a graceful frame for the matching back door across the shiny pine floor. She looked up and it was just as she'd imagined: the cupola roof overhead, the graceful brass chandelier, the catwalks and windows, the doors leading to the upper-level rooms, and the spindles—all seven hundred eighteen of them—like the ribs of a massive living thing.

She had that impression right from the start—that Waverley had a life of its own, apart from those who lived in it. It had dignity and a touching air of defiance, as if having survived the war gave it the right to feel superior. It dominated, too, its sheer scale dwarfing those who moved within its walls. But that dominance was tempered by an air of protectiveness. Agatha had the feeling that, should one need refuge, one had only to step between the twin staircases and they would embrace like powerful arms, holding any threat at bay.

"I love it," she declared. "How ever could you have stayed away all those years?"

"I don't know," Scott replied. "Now that I'm back, I really don't know."

"Show me the rest."

He took her into the front left parlor, a beautiful room with four high, dramatic windows, a large fireplace, and to the left of the doorway a graceful depression in the wall, surrounded by decorative plasterwork.

"The weddin' alcove," he announced.

"About to be used again," she noted. "How nice. I'm sure she'll be pleased."

"Jube is ecstatic."

"No. Not Jube. I meant the house." Agatha lifted her eyes to the high ceiling. "It has a . . . a presence, doesn't it?" She walked around a drake-footed Chippendale chair, trailed her fingers over the waxed surface of a Pembroke table, the back of a graceful sofa, then passed the piano, where she played a single note that hung in the air between them. "A personality."

"I thought I was the only one who believed that anymore. My mother did, too."

Through the low front windows they could see the boxwoods his mother had brought from Georgia.

"Perhaps she's looking over from her grave across the road and nodding in approval at how you've revived the place."

"Perhaps she is. Come, I'll show you my favorite room."

She, too, loved his office on sight. So much more personal than the front parlor, and bearing a more lived-in look, with his ledger left open on the desk, a crystal inkwell and a metal-nibbed pen waiting to be put to use again; his humidor undoubtedly stocked with cigars, the remains of one in a free-standing ash stand near his desk chair. The smell of him permeated the room, cheroots and leather and ink.

"It fits you very well," she told him.

She glanced up and found him watching her, not exactly smiling, but looking as pleased at having her here as she felt at being here at last.

"I'll show y' the dinin' room," he said, turning to lead the way across the hall. It, too, was huge, with a great built-in china closet and a massive rectangular table beneath another gas chandelier. The floor was bare and gleaming beneath the table and their footsteps echoed as they stepped farther into the room.

"Breakfast is at eight, dinner at noon, and supper at seven. Supper is always formal and all our guests share the meal with us."

"And Willy?" she asked.

"Willy, too."

So Scott Gandy would gift her with yet another thing—that ineffable sense of family that thrived around no place so heartily as around a supper table. Her sunsets need never be lonely again.

Her heart was full. She wanted to thank him, but he was already leading the way to the other front parlor.

"And this is your room," Gandy told her, stepping back to let her enter.

"Mine?" She stepped inside. "But . . . but it's so big! I mean, I wouldn't need half this space." Her sewing machine and trunks were already installed in the spacious room. Brightness everywhere—four gleaming windows—a south view of the front gardens, the drive, his mother's boxwoods, and, to the east, the river. Too much to take in without being overcome.

"I wanted you t' be on the main floor so you wouldn't have t' climb the stairs so much. If it's all right with you, we'll use a corner in here for Willy's classroom."

"Oh, it's more than all right."

This room was the twin of the first parlor, without the alcove, but with that rarity, a walk-in closet bigger than any two pantries she'd ever seen. There was a pretty bed with a white brocade tester, a chaise upholstered in multicolored floral, a small chest-on-chest, a five-foot freestanding cheval mirror on swivel brackets, and a library table holding a large bouquet of golden forsythia.

"I'm sorry, Gussie. You won't have much privacy, except at night. Durin' the day, to add to the feelin' of intimacy around the place, it would be nice if you kept the doors rolled back while you're workin' in here. That way our guests feel like they're one of the family."

She stood before the cheval mirror, catching his gaze in the glass. She turned slowly, wondering if he had the vaguest notion of what it meant to a woman like her to have a room like this in a house like this.

"I've had privacy, Scott. It's not all that desirable. All those years I lived in that dark, narrow apartment above the shop with nobody to come to my door and interrupt me or disturb me. You cannot guess how awful it was." She smiled, a smile of the heart as much as of the lips. "Of course I'll leave the doors rolled back while I work here. But I feel a little guilty about taking one of the loveliest rooms in the house that could be bringing in money from paying guests."

"Your job is seein' after Willy. I don't see how you can do that from one of the slave cabins. Besides, there are three guest rooms upstairs, equally as large as this one."

"But this is more than I'd hoped for. The nicest place I've ever lived."

He came several steps into the room and stopped beside the foot of the bed. "I'm glad you're here, Gussie. I've thought—"

Suddenly, Willy came charging through the doorway, claiming Agatha's hand. "Come and see my room, Gussie."

He tugged her along impatiently and Scott followed to stand at the bottom of the right stairway, watching them ascend. "Can you make the stairs all right?"

"Nothing could stop me," she replied, looking back over her shoulder.

On her way up Agatha was surprised to meet a middle-aged couple coming down. They were dressed for riding.

"Hello," the woman said.

"Hello."

Immediately, Gandy sprinted up the steps. "Ah, Mr. and Mrs. Van Hoef, off t' the stables?"

"Indeed," replied the man.

"A perfect day for a ride. Mr. and Mrs. Van Hoef, I'd like you t' meet Agatha Downin', the newest permanent resident of Waverley." To Agatha he explained, "Robert and his wife, Debra Sue, arrived yesterday from Massachusetts. They're our first official guests."

Agatha murmured a polite response. Then the Van Hoefs continued down the stairs.

"Guests already?" Agatha remarked.

"Van Hoef runs a successful milling operation and is reputed t' be one of the five most wealthy men in Massachusetts. Do y' know why he's here, Gussie?"

"No."

"Because of somethin' you said t' me one time when we were talkin' about Waverley. You called it a national treasure, do you remember?" She didn't. He went on. "I had no idea when I left Kansas how I was goin' t' make Waverley pay its way again. Then one day I was lookin' out the rotunda window"—he looked up to it, then back down at her—"and your words came back to me. I realized then what potential the place held. If it hadn't been for you, insistin' I come back here, I probably never would have. I just wanted to say thank you for badgerin' me into it."

"But I've done nothing. You and the others did it all."

Willy had gone ahead and was draped over the balcony railing, balancing on his belly. "Hurry up, Gussie!"

She lifted her head and caught her breath. "Willie! Get back!"

He cackled, the sound resonating through the great dome. "I ain't scared."

"I said get back—and I mean it!"

He thought he was funny, teetering on the banister, showing off.

"Scott, get him down from there."

It took Scott only seconds to pluck Willy off the rail and plant him on his feet. When Agatha reached him she was exceedingly angry. "Young man, if I ever catch you doing that again you'll be polishing these spindles all the way from the bottom to the top. Every one of them—is that understood?"

Willy grew sullen. "Well, golly, I don't know what you're so mad about. Nobody else gets mad. Heck, Pearl teached me how t' slide down the banister."

"She what!"

"She teached me—"

"*Taught* me. And you've done that for the last time, too. You can tell Pearl I said so. Now, how about showing me your room?"

Willy decided retaliation was a better course. "I don't wanna! You can look at my dumb room by yourself!"

"Willy, come back here!" Scott shouted.

Willy continued marching down the stairs. Scott began to head down after the boy but Agatha gripped his arm and shook her head. Her words carried clearly throughout the rotunda. "Why don't you show it to me instead, Scott? It's the room where Justine comes to visit Willy, isn't it? I'd like to hear all about it." She moved to the doorway. "Oh, isn't it lovely." They heard Willy's footsteps slow and pictured him gazing up longingly. They moved about the room, Scott giving a cursory tour, mentioning every item he was certain Willy had been eager to tell Gussie about—all his toys, the rocking horse, the view of the stables. When they emerged from the children's room and moved on to the guest room next door, they knew Willy had been listening and saw him dip out of sight beside the curved stair extension downstairs.

"When we first reopened Waverley we used all the rooms up here for ourselves, but one by one we improved the slave cabins so everybody has a house of their own. Jube and Marcus are fixin' up the old overseer's place and will move in there after they're married. The Van Hoefs are stayin' in here." He indicated the east front bedroom. "And tomorrow we have guests arrivin' from New York who'll take that room." He indicated the rear one opposite Willy's. "And this . . ."—he stopped in the doorway of the bedroom above the main parlor—". . . this is the master bedroom."

For some reason, Agatha hesitated to step over the threshold. "You were born here."

"Yes. My mother and father shared it, then Delia and I."

Delia, his lost Delia. Did he ever long for her?

"But you aren't using it for yourself?"

"No. I share Willy's room. That way we can rent this one out."

The master bedroom was done in the same ice-blue as the vest Gandy wore today. A tall rosewood tester bed with handcarved posts dominated the space. Incorporated into the intricate carving upon the center of its headboard was the convex oval that marked it as an original Prudent Mallard piece. Billows of white netting were tied back to its corner posts and beside it sat a set of three portable steps for climbing up to the mattress. A matching dresser took up nearly an entire wall. On the windows, tiebacks of ice-blue with an apricot bamboo design matched that of the heavy counterpane and tester. The design was picked up in a pair of Chinese Chippendale chairs that faced each other before the twin front windows with a low marble-topped table between them. The fireplace was done in Carrara marble with a decorative iron liner. The brass and-irons gleamed, matching the chandelier with its etched-glass globes overhead. A hand-tied rug of a deeper teal-blue with a rust border design covered the center of the virgin pine floor, leaving the varnished edges exposed.

"Will guests be coming soon to use this room?"

"Next week."

"Ah." She hated to see it happen. Somehow it felt as if the room would be desecrated by having strangers sleeping in the big Mallard bed where Waverley's heir had been conceived.

"Would you like t' see the view from the top?" he asked, to all outward appearances unruffled about giving his bed to strangers. "It's grand, but there are a lot of stairs."

"I want to see it anyway."

They climbed the single staircase leading from the second to the third floor, where they passed two closed doors. "This is the trunk room. I'll show it to y' some other time."

She saw his chin lift, his eyes drawn to the octagonal summit that topped the mansion like a gleaming crown on a monarch's head. She sensed his pride, his eagerness, to have her see all he owned. They mounted the last single stairway that brought them at last to the catwalk. And there below lay Scott's heritage. Agatha stood with her fingertips on the window ledge, staggered.

"It's breathtaking."

"See that field down there?" He pointed.

"Yes?"

"We've put in cotton. Just enough t' recapture the old days for the guests. And see the meadow leadin' down t' the river?" They gazed east now. "I plan t' fill it with more horses as I can afford them." They walked around until they were looking straight south along the driveway.

"And see that buildin' across the road?"

"Uh-huh."

"That's the swimmin' pool. Want t' see it?"

"I'd love to!"

When they reached the main floor they found Willy, pouting, on the bottom step.

"We're goin' t' see the swimmin' pool. Would y' like t' come with us?"

At Willy's continued sullenness, Gandy merely turned away and touched Agatha's elbow, indicating the front door.

"All right! I'll go!"

Scott and Gussie exchanged a secret grin.

They walked three abreast down the gravel drive, between the formal gardens and the spreading lawn. Gandy said, "Tomorrow, Willy, you'll be startin' lessons with Gussie."

"Lessons! But I was gonna—"

"And y'all be ready at whatever time she says and—"

"How can I be ready when I can't tell time yet?"

"Then that'll be one of your first lessons. Now stop makin' up excuses and listen t' me. I've made it clear to all the rest, there is one person and one person only who gives you orders around here—and that's Gussie. Understood?"

"What about you?"

"Me? Oh, well, sometimes maybe from me. But before you make plans t' go off with Zach in the stables, or out t' the woods with Jack, or into town with the girls, you make sure it's all right with Gussie. And if she gives you an order and you don't obey it—like up on the balcony today—there'll be trouble. If y' want t' grow up t' be a gentleman, and be smart and well liked by others, you have t' learn how. It doesn't just happen. And that's the reason Gussie is here."

They reached the pool area then, a white-painted wooden building beneath the oaks and hickories on the opposite side of the road. Inside, it was cool and shaded, lit by a few small windows. The pool itself was constructed of red brick and at one end a set of wide marble steps led into it.

"Not as fancy as White Springs, but in the middle of the summer it's a welcome relief at the end of a hot day."

"It smells much better than White Springs."

Scott laughed. Agatha recalled the feeling of weightlessness and marveled that she could experience it again any time she chose.

"Where does the water come from?"

"Artesian springs."

"Is it cold?"

"Like ice . . . touch it."

He was right.

"Ivory says he's gonna teach me how t' swim," Willy announced.

"Really swim?" inquired Agatha. "I mean, not just splash around, but really swim? In water over your head?"

Scott answered. "Ivory and I used t' swim in the river together when we were boys, before they built the pool. He's a strong swimmer. That's why he used t' get the job of checkin' underwater damage when he worked as a rooster on the riverboats."

"So it's all right with you if he teaches Willy?" Agatha asked.

"Absolutely. As long as Willy's with Ivory, he'll be in good hands."

"Very well, then. We'll set aside some time each day for the swimming lesson."

And so it was that an unconscious cooperation began between Agatha and Scott in matters concerning Willy. Though he had said she'd be solely in charge of Willy, it never turned out that way. As in the days when they all lived in Kansas, they consulted each other about anything that directly affected his upbringing or his welfare.

At supper that first night she sent Willy off to rewash his hands when they weren't clean enough the first time, and when he complained, Gandy reinforced her order by snapping a single word: "Willy!"

Willy grumbled his way from the room but returned with spotless knuckles. Agatha looked across the table at Gandy and thought, *We'll be better parents than most, married or not.* And she cherished the moment and the man and the little boy and being part of the camaraderie around a dining room table at sunset.

The following morning Agatha inquired if it would be all right to let Willy sleep later and begin his classes at ten A.M., since she had plenty of other work to keep her busy until then and there was no sense in rousing him inordinately early—she planned only three hours of schoolwork each day at the beginning.

"Three hours? That's all?" Scott responded.

"Three hours for a boy of six can seem like two days to an adult. I'll increase the time gradually."

"All right, Gussie, whatever you think is best."

On Saturday she approached him and asked, "What about church tomorrow?"

"Church?" he repeated, caught off guard.

"Yes, church. Willy has been going, hasn't he?"

Gandy cleared his throat. "Well . . . uh . . ."

"He hasn't." She looked disappointed in him and he chafed under her somber regard. "Oh, Scott, you can't neglect a boy's spiritual upbringing."

"Well, it's not that I didn't want him t' go, it's just that the nearest church is clear in Columbus."

"What about the little white one we passed on our way?"

"That's the black people's church."

"Black people's? Baptist, you mean?"

"Well, yes, Baptist, but it's for the blacks."

"Does Leatrice go? And Ruby?"

"Leatrice does, not Ruby."

"Then I'll see Leatrice about Willy and me going along."

"But, Gussie, y' don't understand."

"We all pray to the same God, don't we? What does it matter if it's Baptist or Presbyterian?"

"It doesn't. But it's *theirs!*"

"Will they throw me out?"

"No, they won't throw you out. It's just that the whites and blacks don't mix in church."

"How odd. Now wouldn't you think that would be the natural place for them to do so?"

And so she and Willy went to church with Leatrice and Mose and Zach and Bertrissa and Caleb. Leatrice, proudly wearing her bright pink hat, took charge of introducing them. "This heah's the master's li'l adopted boy, Willy, an' Miz Agatha Downin' from Kansas. She Presbyterian, but she willin' t' put up wit us."

It didn't really surprise Gandy that Agatha managed it. After all, it was women like Agatha who'd gotten the entire state of Kansas to change its mind about prohibition. He was waiting when they returned, sitting on one of the bois d'arc benches on the north veranda.

"Y'all enjoy yourself?" he inquired, rising as Agatha came up to the steps.

"It's a lovely little church. You must come with us next time."

And to Gandy's surprise, the idea became unexpectedly inviting.

He grew used to glancing up from the desk in his office and glimpsing Gussie at work in her room, diagonally across the rotunda from his. There was a satisfying feeling knowing she was there, steady, dependable. The guests loved her. She exuded an air of breeding of which the other girls fell just short. In her fine, rich gowns, with her hair always meticulously groomed, her nails buffed and trimmed into neat ovals, she was the picture of gentility the guests had all imagined when making their reservations for Waverley Mansion. She grew accustomed to greeting them when they arrived, coming out of her room to meet Gandy in the foyer, and together they'd open the front door and welcome whomever was stepping off the carriage. It was a logical mistake that more of them than not mistook her for his wife and greeted them as "Mr. and Mrs. Gandy." The first time this happened Gandy noted a blush color her cheeks and her eyes flashed briefly to his. But after that she took it in stride, allowing him to straighten out the misconception with a quick correction.

She assigned Willy the job of escorting each new arrival to the proper room, realizing that Willy's charm in itself would probably bring people back again. He could talk to anyone, familiar or strange, and much as he'd captivated her heart when she'd first met him, Willy won over wealthy industrialists and their wives within minutes after they set foot in the place. Realizing this, she broadened Willy's job to include giving a tour of the stables and the grounds for each incoming party. Afterward, he invariably received a tip. She had Marcus make him a little wooden bank shaped like a banjo with the strings stretched across the slot so whenever a coin was dropped the elastic strings twanged. Willy was so enchanted each time he dropped the money into it that he didn't mind saving. She made a miniature account book for him and taught him to enter each tip he made, including the date, the amount, and the name of the person who'd paid him. (Until he learned to write, she agreed to write the names for him, though he already knew numbers so could enter them himself.) She explained to him that when he grew up, undoubtedly he'd be running Waverley instead of Scott and he'd have to know how to keep books, just as Scott did. Also, simultaneously, she taught him to count dollars and cents, and to add. But more importantly, she taught him the value of a penny saved.

The three hours' formal work she did with Willy each day didn't begin to cover the time spent educating him. Manners were taught whenever and wherever the occasion called for it. How to use a measuring tape was taught when she cut out Jube's wedding dress; oiling the sewing machine was demonstrated when Marcus, at Gussie's request, allowed Willy to do the job, showing him how instead of just telling him. If some of the men went fishing, she sent Willy along to learn the sport. If Leatrice skinned catfish, Agatha had her show Willy how it was done. When Zach trimmed hooves or shod horses, Willy learned the names of the tools, the proper angle of the hoof, the fit of the shoe.

She taught him that play was the reward for work, making certain he had enough of each for him to grow up industrious, yet fun-loving.

He taught her, too. All about how Prince and Cinnamon had nipped at each other and played hard-to-get before Prince had mounted the mare with his long penis hanging nearly to the ground.

And all about how he'd come upon Jube and Marcus down by the old tannery one day and how Marcus had Jube's dress pulled up around her waist and Jube was giggling and bucking like a wild bronc.

And all about how the girls sneaked out to the brick pool at night sometimes and went swimming in nothing but their underwear.

Agatha was appalled at the earthy things Willy had witnessed around the place while he'd run roughshod with nobody monitoring him. She spoke to Scott about it. For the first time ever she failed to receive his support.

"Those things are natural, Gussie. I see nothin' wrong with him watchin' the horses mate."

"He's only six years old."

"And he's learned beside me that that's the way nature goes about propagatin'."

"And he's seen Jube and Marcus. What kind of lesson is that for a six-year-old?"

"They're in love. Isn't there a lesson in that, too?"

Too uncomfortable to face him any longer, she fled from his office. She lay awake nights wondering what Willy had seen when he'd watched the horses mate, and Jube and Marcus. The images in her mind made her restless and uncomfortably warm and she rose to open her window and saw lights flickering down in the pool house. She wondered what it would be like to experience that unearthly buoyancy wearing nothing but a thin piece of cotton. One day shortly before the wedding, when she was fitting Jube's dress, she asked her if it was true that the girls swam after dark. Jube said yes, and Agatha asked if they'd let her sneak out with them next time.

They went that very night, slipping down the driveway like four wraiths, their dressing gowns pale splotches of white beneath the giant magnolias. It was decidedly unladylike, walking barefoot at night with only a single thin garment underneath her gown, but Agatha had done so few forbidden things in her life, it was a pleasure to break the rules, just once.

They reached the pool house giggling, and they felt their way inside its black recesses—cool, damp dirt against their feet, then the colder, smoother marble at the edge of the pool. Jube teased, "Look out for water moccasins now." Two high-pitched squeals echoed eerily off the walls and the surface of the lightly gurgling water. Then a match caught and flared and the single lantern cast a thin orange light over one corner of the large enclosure. Jube turned, pulling the knot from her belt. "Anybody scared?" she inquired innocently.

Ruby pushed her in, robe and all. "Why, shucks, no, we not scared. Any snakes in dere, ya got 'em all out by now."

Though Jube came up gasping, she wasn't in the least angry. "Come on, you high-handed nigger woman. Get in here so I can get even with you!"

Ruby laughed, slipped from her robe, and walked down the marble steps like a naked ebony goddess, followed by Pearl. Jube splashed them and they gasped. Then the pair piled in to get revenge on Jube and soon the three of them were romping like children.

Agatha was much slower getting wet. She wore her cotton combination—a sleeveless garment that buttoned on one shoulder and at the crotch, combining pantaloons and chemise into one.

As Gandy had said, the water was icy. But once in it, she adjusted to the temperature just as she had at White Springs. The remembered weightlessness and grace returned—heavenly. The girls knew how to swim in a rudimentary fashion. They taught her to roll onto her back, flutter her feet, and use her hands like a fish's fins. And how to do a surface dive and come up nose first. And how to blow out through her nose to keep the water from getting into it. And how to rest in the water and pull in a deep lungful of air and hold it and feel herself lift, lift, lift to the surface and hang there as if floating upon a puffy cloud in the sky.

It ended altogether too soon. But Agatha promised herself she'd go again, soon.

Meanwhile, the plans for the wedding progressed. It took longer than expected before Jube's wedding dress was done and the overseer's cabin was livable. But finally everything was ready and the minister from Leatrice's Baptist church agreed to perform the ceremony.

They gathered in the front parlor on a late golden afternoon in early April—Gandy's family, and all the current guests at Waverley Mansion (all three rooms were filled now), and every former slave who'd returned to help the place thrive again. The room created a splendid setting for the bridal couple, with the sun slanting in through the tall west windows and the azalea bushes in profuse bloom, both outside and in. Enormous bouquets of pink ones had been placed on the piano and on tables throughout the room. In the wedding alcove, Jube, dressed totally in white—her color—stood beside Marcus, wearing elegant dove-gray. Jube held a cluster of white azaleas bound by a single white satin ribbon. Marcus held Jube's free hand.

Ivory played the piano while Ruby and Pearl harmonized on "Sweet Is the Budding Spring of Love."

The Reverend Clarence T. Oliver stepped forward and smiled benevolently at the bridal couple. He was a spindly man, with too much height and too little breadth, upon whose lanky frame clothing hung like a flag on a windless day. He wore round spectacles and couldn't seem to stand still, even when speaking. But the moment he opened his mouth one forgot about all this. His voice, a deep basso profundo, resonated like a jungle drum.

He opened his Bible and the ceremony began.

"Dearly beloved . . ."

Gandy stood nearby, recalling the day he and Delia had heard the same words in the same alcove. They'd been bright with happiness then, too, just as Jube and

Marcus were now. Their future had lain ahead of them, mapped out like a golden road upon which they had only to walk, hand in hand, to eternal happiness.

How brief that happiness had been and how relatively little he'd known in the years since. He envied Marcus and Jube, radiant with love, committing themselves to a future together. It was what he, too, wanted.

Between himself and Agatha, Willy fidgeted. She leaned over and whispered something to him and he settled down.

The minister asked who witnessed this union and Gandy spoke up. "I do."

Pearl and Ruby, together, said, "We do." (Jube had adamantly insisted on two female witnesses, declaring she could absolutely not choose one over the other, and the minister had finally given in.)

The minister asked, "Do you, Marcus Charles Delahunt, take this woman, Jubilee Ann Bright, to be your lawfully wedded wife, to have and to hold from this day forward, for better, for worse, for richer, for poorer, in sickness and in health and forsaking all others till death do you part? Signify by nodding yes."

Marcus nodded, and from the corner of his eye Scott saw Gussie pull a handkerchief from her sleeve.

The question was repeated to Jube.

"I do," she answered softly.

Scott watched Gussie dab the corners of her eyes.

"In the presence of these witnesses and with the power invested in me by God, I now pronounce you man and wife."

Willy looked up at Gussie and whispered, "What're you cryin' for?"

Gandy nudged the boy's shoulder.

Willy transferred his uplifted gaze to Scott. "Well, she's cryin'. What's she cryin' for?"

But the boy received no answer. Scott was engrossed in watching Agatha dry her eyes. Engrossed in the play of golden sun on the glossy red-tipped waves of her hair. And the curve of her jaw as she refused to turn and look at him. And the puffiness of her lips as she half covered them with the handkerchief. And the sudden crazy thumping of his own heart.

The conviction hit him as abruptly as if the ancient magnolia had suddenly toppled in the yard and crashed through the roof: *It should be us standin' in that alcove. It should be Gussie and Willy and me!*

Chapter 21

He pondered for two days, stunned by the realization that Agatha Downing had worked her way into his heart, a heart that had remained indifferent since Delia. Yet how could he remain indifferent to one who'd brought so much happiness into his life? Before Agatha there'd been no Willy, no Waverley. He'd been drifting, always drifting, searching for contentment in an unfulfilling affair with Jube, in the surrogate family with which he surrounded himself, in the string of riverboats and saloons where he gambled and sold whiskey and substituted the superficial gaiety of night life for the true contentment of family life. During those years he'd thought himself happy. Only in retrospect did he realize how shallow that happiness was. His "family" had been nothing more than a sad troupe of malcontents, searching for roots, for constancy, for purpose in their lives.

Jube and Marcus had found theirs in each other. And unless Gandy missed his guess, it wouldn't be long before Ivory and Ruby did the same. And what about himself and Gussie? When had he been happier than since she'd been at Waverly? Who had ever done more to lead him back to the values on which he'd been raised? When had he last felt the elemental familial security that he had since she'd arrived? Having her here, a mother to Willy, a hostess to their guests, a quiet influence on the girls, had completed the picture he'd had of Waverley revived. Only after she'd come had it been as he'd imagined. And now that she was here, he never wanted her to leave again.

He wanted to watch Willy grow to be a bright and honorable young man, guided always by the two of them; to watch their business prosper and share its success with her; to raise a batch of their own babies who would romp on the lawns with the peacocks and fill the rooms until he was forced to add a wing on to the house; he wanted the assurance that he'd retire with her and awaken with her and glance across the corner of the dining room table to find her sipping her soup with the impeccable manners he'd come to admire; he wanted to watch her magnificent mahogany hair fade to gray along with his own, and sit on the bois d'arc benches in their dotage, while their grandchildren fed corn to the peacocks.

LeMaster Scott Gandy wanted Agatha Downing for his wife.

Evenings were her favorite. Evenings, when the girls came across the lawn in their hoop skirts, gliding as if upon air. Evenings, when everyone gathered on the deep back veranda for mint juleps, while Willy fed the peacocks and the guests sat upon the bois d'arc benches and the smell of fresh-scythed grass filled the nostrils with green. Evenings, when they retired to the great dining room table and shared a meal amid happy chatter. Evenings, when the gas jets were lit and the house glowed with mellow light. Afterward, there was music in the parlor—Ivory on the piano, Marcus on the banjo, and the girls singing pastorale songs.

And sometimes they would dance gracefully with the guests on the polished pine floor of the great rotunda while the chandelier threw amber light upon their shoulders and their skirts swished with a sound like long grass soughing in summer wind. Then Scott and the other men would invite the lady guests to waltz, while Willy sat on the third step and played his harmonica and tapped his foot to Ivory's quiet renditions. And Agatha would look up from her embroidery and drop her hands to her lap and become lost in the enchantment of the graceful couples that never failed to raise a wellspring of longing in her breast.

Then one evening shortly after the wedding, Scott stood before her, bowing from the waist. "May I have this dance, Miz Downin'?"

Her heart fluttered and her neck grew hot.

"I . . ." To save face she chose to play it like a game, affecting a rich drawl, using her embroidery hoop as if it were a fan. "How kind, sir. Howevuh, Ah've danced til' mah feet ah simply fallin' off."

He laughed and captured her hand. "I refuse t' take no for an answer."

Her eyes flashed to the rotunda. Her cheeks flared. "No, Scott," she whispered anxiously, "you know I can't dance."

"How do you know? Have you ever tried it?"

"But you know—"

"We'll take it real slow." He plucked the hoop from her fingers and set it on the sofa. "I assure you it'll be totally painless. Come."

"Please, Scott . . ."

"Trust me."

He tugged her to her feet and linked their fingers firmly while escorting her to the rotunda, where three other couples circled slowly. How awkward she felt, facing him with her cheeks the color of ripe tomatoes and her hands unaccustomed to taking the waltz position.

"One here," he said, placing her left hand on his shoulder. "And the other here." He lifted her other palm on his own. "Now, relax. You're not expected t' prove anything, only enjoy yourself."

He began by swaying, smiling down at her, while she refused to lift her face. She didn't ever remember being so embarrassed in her life. But the others went about their dancing as if unaware that a lame woman groped in their midst.

He took a small side step and she moved too late, lurched, and was forced to grab his palm to keep from falling. His grip was sure and supportive. He stepped the other way and she preguessed him, finding that moving in that direction was much easier, much smoother. He took one step for every three the other dancers took. It was nowhere near a waltz, but he didn't seem to mind. She struggled along to his patient swaying—one awkward step left, one smooth step right. And when at last her face cooled she lifted her eyes. He was smiling down at her and she smiled back uncertainly. And suddenly it didn't matter that she really wasn't waltzing. It didn't matter that she had to clutch his hand and shoulder a little harder than the others. It only mattered that she was on a ballroom floor for the first time in her life. And that Scott looked beyond her clumsiness to her yearning and had given her a gift of more worth than all the crown jewels in the world.

Her heart filled with gratitude. Her eyes filled with love. She wished fervently that she could be graceful and unbroken for him, that she could whisk around the dance floor laughing, leaning back from the waist while she watched the chandelier go around and around above them. He was such a beautiful man, he deserved a perfect woman. It struck her that he was beautiful not only without, but within. He was one of those rare beings who measured people not by what he saw, but by what he learned of them. He was benevolent, generous, judicious, and honest. And he was all of these things to all people. He didn't put on one hat to please one person, and another to please the next. He expected people to accept him as he was, because that was his own way. He was the first person with whom she'd ever been able to relax fully, to whom she could admit her frailty and the extent of its emotional drain upon her. And knowing this, he had brought to her the gifts of swimming and dancing, two freedoms she had never hoped to know.

"Gussie, I didn't know you could dance!" Willy piped from his spot on the step.

She smiled at him with cheeks now lit from happiness instead of embarrassment. "Neither did I."

"Think I could do it?"

"If I can do it, anyone can."

He barreled off the step, brushing his way between two hoop skirts. Scott leaned over to pick him up. "Give Gussie your left hand," he ordered. "No. Palm up." Willy turned over his palm and Agatha placed hers on it. With Scott's left hand still around her waist, the three of them danced, Willy giggling, Agatha beaming, and Scott looking pleased.

This is how it should be, she thought, *the three of us together.* She savored the happy moments, storing them in her memory to take out and examine later—the warmth of Scott's hand on her back, the firmness of his shoulder beneath her palm, Willy's happy giggle, his small damp hand beneath hers, the play of amber light falling upon Scott's face from above, his dimples as he smiled, his dark, merry eyes.

When the dancing stopped she went upstairs with Willy. It was the only time each day she climbed the stairs, at his bedtime. He had come to expect it and she to enjoy it. She found his nightshirt and laid out a clean shirt and underwear for the next day, then watched as he folded his pants neatly, as she'd taught him. While he changed into his bedclothes she wandered to the dresser, glancing at Scott's things as she often did. Humming the song they'd danced to, tilting her head, she picked up his hairbrush, flicked her thumb over the bristles, then ran it through the hair just above her right ear as far as the French knot permitted.

"Need any help up here?"

She dropped the brush with a clatter and spun toward the doorway. Scott leaned against the frame with his weight on one hip. His eyes moved lazily from her flaming face to the hairbrush, then back again. His dimples looked as deep as the tufts on a chaise. He'd never come up before when she tucked Willy in. Willy generally scampered downstairs to find him in his office, give him a peck good-night, get a last drink of water, and delay bedtime as long as possible. She'd call over the rail, "What are you doing down there?" And he'd come trudging upstairs with an air of persecution. Then she'd plump his pillow, kiss him good-night, adjust the netting around his bed and extinguish the light. It was her custom to retire to her room immediately afterward. Scott would always be in his office as she passed his door. And when she'd turned to roll her own closed, she'd look up to find him watching her, smoking a cheroot or toying with a pen.

"Good night," she'd say.

"Good night," he'd answer.

Then the doors would roll and thump quietly between them.

But tonight he sauntered into Willy's room and adjusted the netting on the far side of the bed, then came around and sat down on the edge of it.

" 'Night, sprout," he said. Willy went pell-mell into his arms and gave him a reckless kiss.

"I like dancin'!"

Scott laughed and rumpled Willy's hair. "Y' do, huh?"

"Can we do it again tomorrow night?"

"If Gussie wants to."

"She will. You will, won't you, Gussie?"

Scott studied her, still wearing the grin. Tiny shocks of awareness buzzed up the backs of her legs.

"Of course." She busied herself with Willy. "Now, down with you, young man."

"Kiss first," he demanded, kneeling beside Scott, lifting his arms to Agatha.

She leaned down for the customary hug and kiss. Her leg bumped Scott's knee, her skirts buried his pant leg. The awareness trebled. Willy flopped back and the two of them stood up. Watching Scott close the netting, she was gripped by a fantasy as vital as air—that Willy was theirs, that as they exchanged good-nights with him, Scott would take her hand and lead her from the room, along the cantilevered balcony to the master bedroom. And there she would take down her hair and preen it with the brush they shared, and don a fine lawn nightgown with open lacework across the top, and look across the room and find his dark eyes following each movement, while he slowly unbuttoned his shirt and pulled it from his trousers. And they would meet on the big tester bed where he'd been conceived and he'd say "At last," and she would do with him the thing that Violet said no woman should miss.

But what happened was that they walked down the curving stairway with Scott adjusting his single step to her step and a half. And he turned into his office and she into her bedroom. But when the doors had rolled within a foot of each other, she paused and looked up to find him standing in his office doorway, watching her again.

"What?" she asked.

"Do you sleep when you go t' bed so early?"

"Sometimes. Not always."

"Then what do you do?"

"I read. Or work on my stitchery. The lighting is so good here, it's a pleasure, even after dark."

"I find it hard t' sleep if I go t' bed before eleven."

"Oh," she said, then stood there like a dummy, wondering if he could see her pulse race from clear across the rotunda.

"Are you sleepy?"

"Not in the least."

"Would you like t' come into my office for a while? We could talk."

Like they used to do on the steps, listening to the coyotes. How many times had she longed to do it again? "I'd like that."

He stepped back and allowed her to enter the office before him and she felt his eyes on her back as she circled the room, examining the furniture, the portrait of his parents on one wall, a set of clay pipes inside one of the glass-fronted cabinets. Behind her she heard the humidor close, a match strike. She smelled his tobacco even before she turned.

"Would you mind if I have a glass of brandy?" he asked.

"Not at all."

"Sit down, Gussie."

She chose a wingchair of sea-foam green, while he filled a tumbler and crossed to a leather chair no more than three feet away. As he settled down he freed the bow from his tie and unfastened his collar button.

"I see a lot of improvement in Willy since you've been here."

"I meant to thank you for giving me jurisdiction over him. I think it helps if he knows from whom to get his instructions."

"No need t' thank me. You were the natural one."

"He's very bright. He learns fast."

"Yes, he's come in here when I'm workin' and read things aloud over my shoulder."

She laughed softly. "He does like to show off, doesn't he?"

Gandy laughed, too. The subject seemed completely covered.

"Marcus and Jube seem happy," she said, voicing the first topic that came to mind.

"Yes, very."

"Does it bother you?"

"Bother me?"

Whatever had she been thinking to ask such a question? No matter how many times she'd wondered about it, she should have guarded her tongue.

"I mean ... well, the fact that Jube was ..." She came to an uncomfortable halt.

"My lover, and now she's Marcus's wife? Not at all. Does it bother you?"

"Me!" Her eyes snapped to his. He took a slow sip of brandy.

"Well, does it?"

"I . . . I'm not sure what you mean."

He studied her with distracting totality for several seconds, a half-puzzled expression about his eyebrows. Then he glanced aside and rolled his loose ashes against the ashtray. "Forget it, then. We'll talk about safe subjects. The cotton. Have y' seen the cotton? Why, it's up to my knees already."

"No. I . . . I haven't been out that way."

"You should take a walk out there. Or if you prefer, you could ride. Have you ridden yet since you've been here?"

"I've never ridden—in my life, I mean."

"You should try."

"I don't think I could."

"You didn't think you could dance either, but you did."

"I didn't really dance and we both know it. But it was so kind of you to let me pretend."

"Kind?" He studied her unwaveringly. "Did you ever stop t' think that maybe I *wanted* t' dance with you?"

No, she hadn't. She had thought of it only as something he gave, not something he enjoyed.

The front door opened and their guests, a railroad baron and his wife, Mr. and Mrs. DuFrayne of Colorado Springs, came in. As they passed Scott's office door, Jesse DuFrayne said, "We were out for a last walk. Beautiful night."

"Yes, it is," Gandy returned.

"And there's the sweetest smell in the air," Abigail DuFrayne added. "What is it?"

"Jasmine," Agatha replied. "It's new to me, too. Isn't it heavenly?"

"This whole place is heavenly," Mrs. DuFrayne returned. "I've told Jess we must come back every year." She smiled back over her shoulder at her husband and Gussie felt a pang of jealousy as he rested his hand on the back of her neck and smiled into her eyes as if the rest of the world had suddenly faded away. They were expecting their first child, yet they acted like newlyweds.

Agatha thought, *If Scott were mine, I'd treat him exactly the way Mrs. DuFrayne treats her husband.*

The couple in the doorway brought themselves forcibly from their absorption in each other and Abigail said, "Well, good night."

"Good night," Scott and Agatha said in unison as the couple linked hands and headed upstairs.

They were both aware that the DuFraynes were the last ones up. Nobody else would be coming through the foyer anymore tonight. When their footsteps disappeared overhead the office grew silent.

Scott finished his drink and tamped out his cigar.

"Well, I really should be going to bed, too." Agatha moved to the edge of her chair.

"Just a minute," he said, stopping her as she began to rise. "There's one more thing."

He rose casually, stepped before her chair, leaned forward, and rested both hands on its arms and kissed her indolently. She was so surprised that her eyes remained opened while his closed and he took his time, brushing her skin with his moustache, touching his smoky tongue to her lips. The only other place he touched her was at the knees, where his legs flattened her skirts. The kiss was lingering but soft, and it left her feeling stunned.

He locked his elbows and looked in her pale eyes.

"Sleep well, Gussie," he murmured, then straightened and saw her to the door.

All the way across the rotunda she resisted the urge to touch her lips, and the even greater one to turn back for more. Standing between the rolling doors, she turned, studied him with wonder, their expressions intent. Then, wordlessly, she backed into her room, rolled the doors closed, and let the shock waves build. She spun and leaned back against the doors and wondered what in the world had prompted him to do such a thing in such an offhanded way—*Just a minute . . . there's one more thing*—as if he were going to remind her to buy one last item of groceries as long as she was going to town anyway. She lifted her face to the ceiling, rested her fingers over her hammering heart, and let out a brief, silent laugh. Was this how courtships started? Or seductions? And did it matter to her anymore which it might possibly be?

She arose the next morning excited, expectant, and dressed with infinite care only to learn when she went to the dining room for breakfast that he'd left at dawn and wouldn't be back for two weeks. He was buying horses in Kentucky.

Two weeks! Kentucky!

Her world turned blue and empty.

Those fourteen days seemed endless. On the thirteenth evening she washed her hair and put vinegar in the rinse, and on the fourteenth day she styled it high, tight and becoming, and dressed in an ice-green day dress that made her eyes look paler, her lashes darker, her hair redder, and her skin fairer.

And every time the front door opened her heart seemed to slam into her throat and her pulse went crazy.

But he didn't come home.

On the fifteenth day she went through the same ritual again, only to go to bed deflated and worried.

On the sixteenth day she wore a plain gray plaid dress with a simple white collar because she and Willy were studying herbs in the garden while she gathered them for Leatrice. It had rained during the night and she had forgotten her hat. The sun was fierce, the humidity sapping, raising sweat on her brow that immediately brought flies buzzing. Slapping one away, she caught her wrist buttons on her hair and pulled the neat French twist askew, after which an irritating strand kept falling down across her jaw.

Of course, that's how he found her, sitting on a low "weeding chair" between the rows of basil and comfrey with sweat darkening her underarms and her hair untidy and a smear of dirt on her chin and a flat basket on her lap. The garden was on the opposite side of the house from the driveway, so she didn't know he'd returned until his shadow fell across her.

"Hello."

She looked up and felt the familiar earthquake in her chest at the sight of him standing above her with his hands on hips and one knee cocked.

"Hello," she managed to say, lifting a hand to shade her eyes. "You're back."

"I missed you," he said without prologue.

She flushed and felt sweat running down her sides and wished terribly that she could dip in the pool and not see him again until she looked as she had the day before yesterday in the cool green dress with her hair glossy and high.

"You're two days late."

"Have you been countin'?"

"Yes. I was worried."

"Hi, Scotty!" Willy interjected. "We're studyin' herbs."

The tall man rubbed the boy's head affectionately, but he gazed at Agatha all the while.

"Herbs, huh?"

"Uh-huh."

Scott dropped to one knee, curled a finger beneath Agatha's chin, and brushed the dirt with his thumb. Holding her so, he kissed her, a light, brief graze, while the scent of dill and angelica and saxifrage and spearmint lifted from the steaming earth and steeped like potpourri around them.

"I've brought you something'," he told her softly, while Willy watched and listened.

"Me?" It came out in a whisper.

"Yes. The calmest horse I could find. Her name is Pansy and you're goin' t' love her. Can the herbs wait?" She nodded dumbly while his thumb continued brushing her chin. "Then, come. You have t' meet her."

And so he gave her the third gift of the three unattainables she had mentioned so long ago on a landing in Kansas. Agatha was terrible at riding, stiff and tense and frightened. But he put her in the saddle and led Pansy around the paddock and taught Agatha to loosen up and enjoy the easy walk of the mare. In time she took the lines herself and guided the horse beside his, always at a sedate walk, beneath the shady trees in the pecan grove and along the grassy verges between the unused cotton fields and through the thick green shade of the wild magnolias that pressed close to the Tombigbee, where the horses dipped their heads to drink.

May turned to June and they rode each day, but the fleeting kisses were not repeated and she was left to wonder to what end he wooed her.

June came on torpid, sticky.

Gandy had spent one morning clearing the riding trails with a scythe. He'd forgotten how fast kudzu vines grew in the summer. They could strangle an entire garden in a matter of days. Out in the woods, where they were often forgotten, they could get a tenacious foothold if not discouraged regularly.

Riding in on Prince, with the scythe handle across his thighs, he pulled a handkerchief from his pocket and swabbed his neck. Sweat ran down the center of his back. His trousers stuck to his thighs. He wore a dusty broad-brimmed black hat with a sweat-soaked band. It was deadly hot for June. He left Prince at the watering trough and check the thermometer on his way to the ice house. Ninety-two degrees already and it wasn't even eleven o'clock. He descended five steps to a submerged stone building and from its wooden doorframe pulled an ice pick. Inside, it was dark and cool and smelled of wet sawdust. With a dusty boot he scraped some aside and gouged out a sharp wedge of ice, kicked the sawdust back into place, and emerged into the blinding midday light, sucking. He rammed the ice pick into the doorframe, left it twanging, and took the steps two at a time. At the top he almost knocked Agatha off her feet.

He grabbed her to keep her upright. "Gussie, I didn't see you."

"You didn't look."

He smiled down at her from beneath the brim of the dirtiest hat she'd ever seen him wear. She smiled up at him from beneath the brim of a simple wide sunbonnet of unadorned straw.

"Sorry. Y'all right?"

"I'm all right."

"You comin' out here for the same thing I just got?"

"I needed *some*thing. Gracious, but it's hot." She plucked at her dress as if to free it from her chest.

"You're in the South now. Gotta expect it to be hot." Suddenly, he slipped his ice into her hands. "Here, hold this while I get y' some." His hands were none too clean and she caught a whiff of sweat—half man, half horse—as he turned and headed back down the steps. As he yanked the ice pick from the doorframe, she noted the rings of dampness beneath the arms of his loose white shirt, and the long line of moisture running down its center back. In the year-plus since she'd known him, she'd never seen him so dirty. It felt intimate to see him so and did strange things to her insides. She heard the dull, rhythmic thud of the pick on the ice. Then he came back out, stabbed the doorframe, and closed the door.

"Here. Got you a nice pointed one, easy for suckin'."

They traded ice. His hands were no cleaner than before. Neither was his face. It was streaked with sweat, grimy in the cracks at the corners of his eyes. He made no apologies but sucked his own ice chip while it melted between his fingers and made rivulets of mud on his hands. She stood watching him with great fascination, her pale eyes fixed upon the springing black hair on his chest where the water dripped from his ice chip. She forgot that her own hands were freezing.

He pulled the ice from his mouth, backhanded his lips, and said, "Go ahead. It's good."

She took a lick and got some sawdust. When she spat, he laughed. "A little sawdust never hurt anyone."

She licked again and smiled.

"Well, listen," he said offhandedly, "I'm goin' t' see if Leatrice has some cold tea. See y'all at dinner time."

He dropped a kiss on her mouth with even less forethought than either of the two times before. His tongue took a single cold swipe at her lips. He backed up, stuck it out, and picked a piece of sawdust off it.

"Sorry," he said, grinning. And left her standing there, stunned.

Courtship or seduction? Either way, it matched none of her preconceived notions, but the chances of an unexpected kiss made her blood course each time she encountered him.

Gandy found Leatrice in the cookhouse with Mose, smoking her pipe and husking corn. It had to be one hundred five degrees inside.

"Lord, woman, you're goin' t' die of heatstroke."

"Heatstroke ain't nowhere neah as scary as what Mose just told me. Tell 'im, Mose."

Mose didn't say a word.

"Tell me what?"

"Hants is in de pool house now," Leatrice stated, too impatient to wait for Mose.

"In the pool house!"

"Mose seen 'em. Carryin' light, too, and lookin' for folks to pull unduh de watuh."

"What's she talkin' about?"

"I seen 'em. Lights flickerin' roun' down dere deep in de night when de res' o' de house asleep. Seen 'em floatin' in, like swamp mist, all white an' shiftin'. Ain't got no shape atall. Heard 'em laugh, too, high, like screech owls."

"That's ridiculous."

"Mose seen it."

"I seen it. Come up from de buryin' groun', dey did."

"You claimed there were ghosts in the house, too, but you haven't seen any since you've been in there, have you?"

"'Cause I wear my asafetida, dat's why."

"Mebbe dey move out. House too crowded, so dey tuk to de pool house instead."

Maybe they had. It had been some time since Gandy had experienced any manifestations of spirits in the big house.

It lay on his mind the following night when he couldn't sleep. Beside him, Willy was restless and he wished for a room of his own. But he and Willy doubled up to free more rooms for guests. The sultry weather continued. The sheets felt damp and the mosquito netting seemed to block out any moving air.

Scott rose, slipped on his trousers, and found a cheroot in his coat pocket. Barefoot, he padded out onto the upstairs veranda. He propped a foot on the rail, lit the cheroot, and thought about a night when he'd sat just like this on the sorry little landing he'd shared with Agatha in Proffitt. Lord, it seemed such a long time ago, yet it was less than a year. August, it had been. August or September with the coyotes howling.

An owl calling softly and he lifted his head.

At the far end of the driveway a tiny light flickered.

His foot dropped off the rail and he pulled the cigar from his mouth. Hants? Maybe Mose and Leatrice were right again.

He was downstairs in a trice. Not until he was reaching for the derringer in his desk drawer did he realize it would do little good against hants. He took it just the same—hard telling what he might run into at the pool house.

Outside it was no cooler than inside. The air was motionless, thick. Down by the river frogs sent up a full range of notes, from the shrill piping of tree frogs to the basso bark of bullfrogs. Walking barefoot through the damp grass, he stepped on a snail, cursed softly at the squish, and moved on soundlessly. The light was steady. He could see now that it came from a window of the poolhouse.

He approached the building stealthily, backing up against the outside wall— cold against his bare shoulder blades—holding the derringer in his right hand.

He listened. Sounded like someone was swimming. No voices, no movement of any other kind, only the soft lap of parted water.

He eased himself into the lighted door space. His gun hand relaxed and he breathed easy. Someone was swimming, all right. A woman, dressed in nothing but a white combination, and she had no idea he was here. She was on her stomach, heading for the far side of the pool with slow, easy strokes. A lantern sat on the marble steps. He moved beside it, curled his toes over the sleek stone edge, and waited. At the far end she dipped beneath the surface, came up nose first, smoothed the water from her face, then headed for him, on her back.

He waited until she had nearly reached him before speaking.

"So this is our ghost."

Agatha thrashed around, found her footing, and gaped up at him.

"Scott! What are you doing here?" She crossed her arms over her breasts and ducked below the surface. He stood stiffly, dressed in nothing but a pair of black trousers, his feet widespread, a gun in one hand, a scowl on his face. Lit from below, his expression appeared devilish.

"Me! What in tarnation are *you* doin' here in the middle of the night?"

She brought one hand from underwater to smooth her hair nervously. "Aren't I supposed to be here?"

"Hell's afire, Gussie, there could be snakes in that water!" He gestured impatiently with the gun. "Or you could get a cramp—and who'd hear you yell for help?"

"I didn't think you'd be angry."

"I'm not angry!"

"You're shouting."

He lowered his volume but propped both hands on his hips. "Well, it's a damned dumb idea. And I don't like you bein' here alone."

"I don't always come alone. Sometimes I come with the girls."

"The girls. I should've known they'd be behind it."

"They taught me to swim, Scott."

He softened somewhat. "So I saw."

"And it's been so hot, I've had trouble sleeping."

So had he—wasn't that what brought him onto the veranda in the first place? "Doesn't that icy water bother your hip?"

"Sometimes. When I first get in. But since I've been swimming regularly I think it's better."

"Regularly? How long has this been goin' on?"

"Since right after I first got here."

"But why do it at night? Why not durin' the day?"

She crossed her arms tighter, gripped her collarbone and looked away. Water dripped from her hair in magnified dribbles, while across the wooden ceiling shards of reflected lantern light danced like fireflies. Scott's glance dropped beneath the surface, but her bare legs were an indistinct blur.

"Well?"

"We . . ." She stopped guiltily.

"Gussie, I'm not upset about your usin' the pool, only about your usin' it at night when it's not safe."

"During the day the guests are around, and we don't have proper bathing costumes, so we . . ." Again she stopped, but her eyes came back to his.

A half grin touched his face.

"Ah, I see."

"Please, Scott. It's not proper for you to be here. I'll come out if you'll go back up to the house."

He dipped a bare toe into the water, wiggled it. "I have a better idea. Why don't I come in? It's a hot night and I couldn't sleep either. I could use a dip myself."

Before she could object, he laid the gun aside and splashed down the steps into the water.

"Scott!" she shrieked.

But he paid her no mind whatsoever. He made one clean dive and came up ten feet beyond her with a roar of shock.

"Waaaah!"

She laughed but stayed where she was while he headed for the far end in a powerful overhand crawl. He turned and came back her way, passing her without pause. On his third lap, he said, "Come on."

"I told you, I'm not properly dressed."

"Oh, hell, I've seen you in your nightgown." He struck out again and left her behind, absorbed in the physicality of the exercise. He was using one side of the pool. She decided it would be all right if she used the other.

But only her head showed above water while they shared the pool for the next ten minutes.

She was paddling idly on her stomach when his head popped up beside her like a turtle's.

"Had enough?" he inquired, smiling.

She backed off and clasped her collarbone again. "Yes. I'm cold now."

"Come on, then. I'll walk y' back t' the house."

He grabbed her by the wrist and began hauling her out of the pool.

"Scott!"

He just kept hauling.

"Do you know how many times you've said my name since I discovered you in here?"

"Let me go!"

Instead, he picked her up and climbed the marble steps and stood her on her feet at the top, where she shivered in a scrap of white that turned transparent the moment she left the water. He glanced once down her length and let her see the grin of appreciation before doing an about-face.

"I'll keep my back turned."

He did, while she executed a slapdash job of drying her face and arms, then slipped into her dressing gown with skin that was still damp and underwear that was soaked.

He smoothed the water off himself with his palms.

"Here, you can use this before I dry my hair with it."

He glanced over his shoulder and accepted the towel. "Thanks."

She watched covertly as he whisked it over his bare skin and gave his head a quick once-over, leaving the hair sticking up in spikes. Men were certainly more brusque about their toilette than women, she thought, amused.

He handed the towel back and combed his hair in a single swipe with both hands. Then he gave an all-over shake and grinned at her. "Never saw you with wet hair before."

She immediately grew self-conscious, bent at the waist, and wrapped the towel around her head. Straightening, she twisted it and secured the ends at her nape.

His eyes made another pass down her body before picking up the gun and the lantern. "Ready?"

She nodded and preceded him outside. On their way up to the house he said, "Leatrice thinks you're a ghost. Mose saw the lantern down in the pool house and must've heard y'all laughin' down there. He told Leatrice the place was haunted."

"Must I stop going down at night now?"

"I'm afraid so. But we can set aside a time durin' the day for you and the girls t' have the pool t' yourselves."

"Could we really?"

"Why not? It's much more sensible than in the dark. Would y' listen t' those frogs?"

They walked the remainder of the way to the house without talking, the chorus of frogs accompanying them. A thin sliver of moon lit the road to a dim ribbon of gray. From the gardens came the scent of night-blooming stocks. Beneath the spreading boughs of the magnolia tree Agatha looked up at the branches lit from below by lantern light. Stepping between the boxwoods, they moved into pale moonlight again. Their bare feet fell like soft drumbeats upon the hollow wooden floor of the veranda. The wide front door swung silently on oiled hinges.

Then they were inside, in the massive rotunda, which swallowed up all but a tiny circle of light from the inadequate lantern that Scott still held. One of her double doors was pushed back. They stopped beside it. She turned and lifted her face, with her arms crossed over her breasts.

"Well, good night," she said, unable to dream up an excuse to keep him a while longer.

"Good night," he answered.

Neither of them moved. She stood feeling her heart thump beneath one wrist, and warm water was dribbling down the insides of her legs, forming a puddle on the floor.

Her face was lovely and stark, framed by the white towel, wrapped turban fashion around her hair. He was conscious of the fact that her dressing gown had become soaked wherever there was underclothing beneath it, and that his own trousers clung and formed a puddle that crept along the waxed floor to pool with hers. He wanted to do the same thing himself—cling, pool himself with her.

His eyes dropped to the hollow of her throat, where a pulsebeat fluttered far faster than normal, as did his own.

"It was fun," she whispered.

"Was it?" he replied, holding the lantern high so it lit their faces to a rich apricot hue. He watched her eyes, wide, uncertain, realizing she was out of her depth in situations such as this, that her guarded posture had come from a life guided by stern moral codes.

Give me a sign, Gussie, he thought. *You stand like St. Joan, waitin' for the fire starter t' touch his flint.* But no sign came. She appeared scared to death, staring up at him with eyes as pale and clear as peridots. A droplet of water fell from his disheveled hair onto his naked collarbone. Her gaze snapped down to follow it, trailing lower and lingering on the wedge of coarse hair upon his chest. He saw her swallow, and the gravity that tugged him toward her became too powerful to fight.

He took her by both wrists and drew them away from her breasts.

Her eyes flew up. "I . . . should . . ." she whispered, but the rest went unsaid.

He lowered his head to kiss her, finding open lips, cool yet from the water. He touched them with his tongue and she responded timidly—a soft kiss of introduction and expectancy. He straightened and they studied each other's eyes, searching for and finding mutuality.

She twisted her wrists slowly until his grip relaxed, then with calculated deliberation curled her hands over his shoulders, looking at them there as if the sight awed her.

He stood stock-still, letting her adjust. "Are you afraid of me?" he whispered. "Don't be afraid."

"I'm not." To prove it, she raised up on tiptoes for a second, longer kiss. Her elbows rested on his chest. When the kiss ended she stood just so—eyes closed, forearms against him, breathing as if a fire had suddenly consumed all the oxygen around her.

She opened her eyes and met his. Her voice was uneven as she whispered, "What I told you the last night in Kansas was true."

"I know. It's true now for me, too."

She held his cheeks. "Then say it."

"I love you, Gussie."

Her eyes closed once more and her nostrils flared. "Please, oh, please, tell me once more so I'll know I'm not dreaming."

His hands closed tightly on her shoulders. "I love you, Gussie."

She opened her eyes and ran her fingertips over his lower lip, as if absorbing the wonder of his words. "Oh, Scott, I've waited so long to hear that. All my lonely life. But you must not say it unless you're certain."

"I am. I've known since the day of the wedding. Maybe even before that."

She looked pained. "Then why have you waited all this time to tell me?"

"I didn't know what you wanted first, t' be told or shown. And you're so different. You're fine and special and pure, the kind of woman a man woos for a while."

"Then put the lantern down, Scott . . . and the gun . . ." she begged softly. "And show me."

He stooped and in one fleet motion left them in the dark. When he came back up their embrace was immediate, their kiss intemperate, all seeking tongues and circling arms and driving breath—a clinging desire filled with impatience and a need to make up for lost time.

She threw her arms up and her head back, and the towel came loose from her head. He plunged one hand into her damp hair while hers spread upon his shoulder blades, running their width to learn the exquisite feel of his cool skin and taut muscle. He clamped an arm around her waist and drew their bodies so close the dampness from his trousers seeped through the dressing gown along her thighs.

One kiss followed another, growing more ardent, slanting this way, then that, while he found her breast with its cold, puckered nipple pressing against the wet garments. The moment he touched it she caught a breath in her throat and held it.

He fondled her until she began to breathe again . . . as if she were running uphill.

He reached for her belt and she thought of Violet's words and put up no resistance. The belt joined the towel on the floor and he parted the dressing gown, running his hand inside. She shivered.

"You're cold," he murmured against her forehead.

"Yes."

"I can warm you."

"Shall I let you?"

He kissed her and found the buttons at her shoulder. The wet undergarment folded beneath its own weight, exposing a single breast. Cupped, it filled his palm, the skin still cold, beaded, drawn. She shivered again from the transfer of heat as much as from the response that skittered down her stomach. Inside her wet clothing he found her other breast, puckered, too, with cold, and warmed it. Warmed her mouth with his tongue. Her wet stomach with his own. Her thighs with his thighs.

So fast, she thought, *so fierce the transition from want to wanton. So this is how it happens, not in a marriage bed, but in a hall, standing at a doorway while your knees turn to pudding and your skin to embers and you experience for the first time a man's turgid body impressing yours.*

Ignorant but eager, she lifted to him, took her fill of kisses, touched his damp hair as he'd touched hers, followed the tutelage of his tongue and lips, wondering if in a lifetime she would ever be able to make him understand what he meant to her. Words seemed paltry, yet she whispered, clasping his cheeks and letting her breath mingle with his.

"When you left Kansas I wanted to cry but I couldn't. My sorrow went too deep. But I grieved daily, and it could have been no harder had you died."

She kissed his chin, felt his jaw move as he spoke in a voice thick and gruff. "I asked myself over and over why I was leaving you. I didn't want to, but there was nothing else I could do."

"I thought about dying," she whispered. "Sometimes I wished I would."

"No, Gussie . . . no." He kissed her in quick hard motions, as if to force the memory from her head.

"It seemed preferable to living without you. I had always been lonely, but after

you were gone I thought I'd never before guessed the true meaning of the word.
I despaired of ever feeling this with you, and you were the first man I'd ever lain
beside and I knew there could be no other. Not for me. Not ever."

"Shh! Love, that's over."

Again they kissed while his hands moved over her with new urgency, as if to
reiterate the promise. Her breasts warmed, his caress grew gentler.

"That night we kissed on the landing it was hard for me to keep from doin'
this."

"I wouldn't have let you then."

"Why?"

"Because you were leaving."

"But I didn't want t' leave you. At the last minute I was sick at the thought."

"Sick? Were you really? I thought I was the only one who felt like that—sick,
from longing, from emptiness."

"No, you weren't the only one."

"But you had Jube. You didn't have to be alone."

"When you don't love someone, you still feel alone."

"You never loved her?"

"Never. We used t' talk about it, wish we felt more for each other. But we just
never did."

Inside her opened garment he ran his hand down her cool back, down her cold
buttocks. She pressed closer and found herself amazed at how little guilt she felt
at letting him fondle her so intimately.

"Scott?"

"Shh!" He kissed her and swept a hand around her hip, to the front, down her
stomach.

She drew back gently and halted it. "There's something I must say to you.
Please . . . please stop and listen."

He obeyed, holding her by both hips, while she rested her hands on his chest.

"When I was leaving Proffitt, Violet said something to me that has been on my
mind a lot since then. She confessed that when she was young she had a lover.
She called it the most wonderful experience of her life, one that no woman should
miss."

"Violet?"

She sensed his surprise, though she could see nothing of his face in the blackness. "Yes, Violet." With her fingertips she feathered the hair on his chest. "Then
she said she hoped Mr. Gandy would see the light and take me for his lover, if
not for his wife. I imagine that's where this is heading, and I want you to know,
Scott, that if you want me for only a lover, I'll agree. I'll invite you into my room
and . . . and . . . I would learn to . . . that is . . . I would do whatever . . ."

In the dark he tipped her chin up and kissed her, then folded both arms around
her and clasped his hands at the base of her spine.

"How brazen of you, Miz Downin'."

She knew the dimples had appeared, though she couldn't see them. Flustered,
she rushed on. "But if it's possible that you want me for something more than a
lover, I'd like to request respectfully that we put this off so that it can happen in
the master bedroom, in the bed where you were conceived and born, because I
should not want to conceive any of your babies anyplace else in this house." She
felt the chuckles building in his chest and her face became hotter and hotter, but
she drew a shaky breath and forged on. "And if there is not even the remotest possibility, well, then I respectfully request that we delay this until I have the opportunity to ask some personal and highly feminine questions to Leatrice, because

I'm quite sure she would know how I might prevent myself from getting with child."

Now she was certain she felt his chest shake with silent laughter.

"Why, Agatha, is this a proposal?"

She bridled slightly. "It most certainly is not. I'm simply stating my wishes before it's too late to do so."

"But you've even brought up conceivin' babies—it certainly sounds like a proposal t' me. Shouldn't we have the light on for this?"

"Don't you dare, Scott Gandy!"

She felt his hands enclose her upper arms and put her away from him. When he spoke again, all vestiges of teasing had left his voice. "Button up anything you want buttoned, and tie anything you want tied, because I'm goin' t' turn the lantern back on, Gussie."

"Please, don't, Scott." She would wither with self-consciousness when the lamp shone on her flushed face. But it flared to life and she had no choice but to cover herself hastily and confront the man who'd just caressed her wet, naked skin in the dark.

He held both her hands and looked her full in the face, utterly sober now.

"Agatha Downin', will you marry me?" he asked—just like that. Her mouth dropped open and not a word came out as he rushed on. "In the wedding alcove with everyone we know and love actin' as witnesses? Just the way my parents planned it, and with Willy there to put his stamp of approval on us, which is the way it oughta be since we're already a family, right?"

She covered her lips with three fingertips and her eyes flooded.

"Oh, Scott."

"Well, you didn't think I was goin' t' let you conceive my bastard babies in the downstairs bedroom just so Willy could have some playmates, did you? What kind of example would that be for the boy?"

"Oh, S . . . Scott," she blubbered again. But she was clinging to his neck and crying. "I love you so much." She kissed his neck, hard. "And I've wished for this, for Willy and you and me, for so long, but I never thought it would happen."

With his excitement growing, he held her far enough away to delve into her eyes with his own. "Say yes, Gussie. Then we'll wake up Willy and tell him."

"Yes. Oh, yes."

She hugged him once more. Then they kissed, standing in their mutual puddle, with her bare toes on top of his and her hair plastered to her head and his drying in spikes.

When she backed away, she laughed and covered her hair with both hands. "Scott Gandy, you're awful, asking a woman such a thing when she's wet and bedraggled. If you knew how many times I'd imagined this scene, and how many times I fussed with my hair and primped with my dresses because I knew I was going to be with you. Then you pick a time like this to ask me. I look awful!"

He grinned. "I was just goin' t' mention that, Agatha." Then he handed her the lantern—"Here, hold this"—and plucked her up in both arms. "You look fine t' me," he told her as he headed for the grand staircase. "However, if you're going to turn into a nag, I may decide t' change my mind."

She folded her free arm around his neck. "Just try it."

"Oh, and by the way, the weddin' night at Waverley is fine, but I intend for us t' honeymoon at White Springs, where we can have a little privacy."

"White Springs . . . mmm . . ." she murmured against his lips.

Climbing the stairs and kissing simultaneously made for uncertain progress. But they managed it beautifully.

Heedless of their damp clothes, they sat on the edge of Willy's bed and shook him awake.

"Hey, Willy, wake up."

Willy opened puffy eyes and screwed up his face. "Hmm?"

"We have somethin' t' tell you."

He sat up and rubbed both eyes with his knuckles. "What?" he demanded grumpily.

"Gussie and I are goin' t' get married."

Willy's eyes flew open. "You are?"

"How 'bout that?"

"Really married?"

Agatha beamed. "Really married."

"You mean so you could be my ma and pa then?"

"Exactly," she repeated, "so we could be your ma and pa then."

"Garsh!" he enthused. Full realization hit him and a crooked smile began to tilt his face. "Garsh ... really?" He lit up like the Willy they'd expected, and he popped up on his knees to hug Agatha, the closest one.

"A real ma and pa!" He backed off suddenly. "Hey, you're wet!"

"We've been swimmin'."

"Oh." He considered a moment, then said, "In the middle of the night?"

"We were hot," Scott added.

"Oh." Without missing a beat, he inquired, "Could we have some babies then?"

Agatha colored, laughed, and flashed a brief glance at the man behind her. "It's all right with me if it's all right with Scott."

"Could we, Scotty! I want a brother."

"A brother, huh? What about a sister?"

"I don't want no sister. Girls are dumb."

Scott and Agatha laughed. Then he agreed. "All right, one brother. But will you give us a while t' work on that, or do we have t' have him as soon as the knot's tied?"

Willy grinned and suddenly decided to act silly. He braced his hands on the bed and kicked twice like a donkey. "Right away! Right away!"

Agatha recognized wildness when she saw it coming on. "All right, Willy, you can celebrate in the morning. Now it's time to tuck back in again."

When they'd kissed him and received giant hugs and Willy had exuberantly beaten his heels against the mattress, and they'd laughed and settled him down once more, they slipped from his room, leaving the door ajar.

Scott picked up Agatha in his arms and started down the stairs.

"You don't have to carry me, you know."

"I know." He nipped her lips with his own, then licked her ear. "I like to."

She laid her head against the arch of his neck and savored the ride. Reaching her room, he pushed her door wider with a bare foot, carried her through sideways and laid her on the bed, then braced a hand on either side of her head.

His voice became an intimate murmur in the dark. "I want t' start workin' on that baby brother right now, y' know."

"I know. So do I."

"Are you sure you want one?"

"Maybe more than one. How about you?"

"If they all turn out like Willy, how about seventeen?"

She laughed and pressed her stomach with both hands. "Oh, please, no."

Their playfulness ended and he kissed her lingeringly. "I love you, Gussie. And, God, it feels so good."

"I love you, too, Scott, and I'll make the best wife you could ever wish for—just wait and see."

He kissed her again until they both felt their resolve dangerously weakened.

"See you in the mornin'," he whispered.

She held him to her with sudden fierceness, marveling that he was he, and she, she, and that fairy-tale endings happened after all.

"And for all the mornings for the rest of our lives."

He kissed her forehead and slipped from the room.

When he was gone she crossed her arms over her breasts, fists tight, guarding it all fiercely so none of it could escape, not a nuance, not an iota.

Mrs. LeMaster Scott Gandy! she rejoiced disbelievingly.

Chapter 22

They would be married the afternoon of July 15, a day that began with heavy morning rains. When the sun came out it blanketed Waverley with sweltering heat. Inside, the mansion was bearable, however, with the veranda doors and jib windows thrown open downstairs, the rotunda windows opened high above.

One of the wedding guests would be Violet Parsons. She'd come a week earlier to help Agatha make her wedding gown, and now, as Agatha donned it, the blue-haired woman tittered and beamed.

"I think it's the prettiest one we ever made. *Tt-tt.*" She held the gown while Agatha slipped it on, then secured the twenty-two covered buttons up the back. It was made of rich sleek silk the exact hue of a waxy magnolia flower, with high neck, form-fitting torso, and caterpillar sleeves ruched from shoulder to wrist. Its skirt was sleek at the front, flowing at the rear, with deep trailing scallops.

Violet joined her hands and sucked in a breath, pleased. "My, don't you look lovely."

They stood in the master bedroom before the cheval glass that had been brought up from downstairs. It reflected a bride with thick burnished hair twined high on her head, narrow shoulders, trim waist, and pale, dark-lashed eyes. Her air of total happiness gave her an almost ethereal glow.

"I *feel* lovely," Agatha admitted.

"Absolutely perfect, if I do say so myself."

Agatha turned to press her cheek to Violet's. "I'm so glad you're here."

"I am, too, though I must admit, I'm a tad jealous. Still, if I can't be the one marrying that handsome Mr. Gandy, I'm glad it's you. But I've told him ..." —she shook her finger at the bride—"... if it doesn't work out he only has to crook his little finger and I'll come running. *Tt-tt.*"

Agatha held Violet's cheeks and laughed. "Oh, Violet, you're priceless."

"I know. Now I must go pick the magnolias. I'll send Willy up with them."

When she was gone Agatha moved to the front window. The lane was lined with carriages, and blue awnings ornamented the great lawns. Below, the guests were entering, the food was being prepared, the minister had arrived, and the wedding alcove was flanked with bouquets of yellow day lilies and English ivy.

Agatha pressed a hand to her fast-tripping heart. It was still difficult for her to believe it was all happening, that she was standing in Waverley's master bedroom, where tonight she would share the high rosewood bed with the man she loved; that her clothing lay beside his in the bureau and hung beside his in the closet, where the scent of his tobacco mingled with that of her sachet; that it would be so for the rest of their lives. And there, outside, the carriages continued to roll in, bringing guests to honor the occasion.

It was as she looked down at them that she heard the sound behind her—the soft plaintive weeping of a child.

She turned. No one was there but the sound continued. Agatha remained remarkably calm, almost as if she'd been expecting the visitor on this auspicious day.

"Justine, is it you?" she asked.

Immediately, the weeping ceased.

"Justine?" She looked in a full circle but found herself alone in the room.

It began again, softer this time, but unmistakably real and distressed. Agatha reached out a hand.

"I'm here, Justine, and I'll help you if I can." The sound softened but continued. "Please don't cry. It's much too happy a day for tears."

The room grew silent, but as Agatha proffered her hand she felt a presence as clearly as if it were visible.

"Is it because I'm going to marry your father? Is that it?" She paused, looked around. "But you must believe that I'm not trying to take your mother's place in his heart. What she was to him will remain precious forever. You must believe that, Justine."

Agatha hushed, and all remained silent.

"I know you've met Willy already, and you've accepted him. I hope you'll accept me in the same way."

The change could not have been more evident had thunder suddenly ceased. The tension eased; peace settled over the room. Nothing touched Agatha's hand except a soft sighing wind, tinged with the scent of flowers. But as she dropped that hand to her side, she experienced a great sense of tranquility.

Then Willy burst in with two magnolias.

"Here, Gussie, Vy-let and me picked the best ones we could find."

She leaned down to kiss him. "Thank you, Willy." When she straightened, she glanced around the room, but the manifestation had vanished completely.

"Hey, you smell good!"

"Do I?" She laughed and accepted the flower.

"And you look so pretty! Wait'll Scotty sees you!"

Agatha cupped his cheeks and kissed his nose. "Have I told you lately that I love you?"

He giggled and scampered to the window. "Did you see all the carriages?"

"I did." As her thoughts turned back to the wedding, her exhilaration mounted. "Where did they all come from?"

"Columbus. Scotty knows everybody there."

Agatha turned to the mirror and secured one of the magnolia blossoms in the back of her hair.

"Vy-let says to tell you it's time now."

Agatha stepped back and pressed a hand to her heart. *It's time now. Time to step out and meet your groom and walk with him to the wedding alcove and join your life with his and never be alone again.* The realization put a serene radiance on Agatha's face. Willy came to stand beside her, looking up, his hair combed and oiled with Macassar into the familiar peak over his brow, undoubtedly done by Scott. She remembered clearly the first time Scott had combed it that way, after the two of them had taken baths, when Scott brought Willy back to her millinery shop wearing the new clothes she'd made for him. Looking at the boy both she and her future husband loved immensely, she felt infinitely blessed, certain that the fates had brought the three of them together with this in mind. Carrying a single magnolia—her bridal bouquet—she extended her free hand.

"Let's go."

He smiled and they walked to the door. Just before he opened it she smoothed his collar and asked, "Now, you remember what to do, don't you?"

"Yes, ma'am." He opened the door a crack and peeked out. "Come on. He's waitin'."

Agatha caught and held a deep, steadying breath, closed her eyes a moment, and listened to Ivory's piano music drifting up from below. But neither deep breaths nor music did anything to calm the nerves trembling within her stomach.

She stepped to the doorway and her eyes met those of her espoused.

He was indeed waiting, standing diagonally across the balcony, just outside the children's room door, dressed in unbroken ivory, waiting for the first glimpse of his bride. Their gazes locked across thirty feet of open space surrounded by nothing but spooled railings and a sense of heart-lifting anticipation. Below them their guests lifted anxious eyes, but in that first moment, bride and groom were conscious of nothing but each other.

She was radiant, in waxy white, with her dress trailing and the simple flower in her hair.

He was breathtaking, in a swallowtail jacket and tapered trousers that dramatically set off his black hair and moustache.

They stared at each other with hastened pulses and fluttering stomachs, compressing this moment to carry within their hearts always, until at last the murmur of voices from below intruded upon their absorption and Agatha smiled. Gandy's smile answered. Then it flashed to Willy, who cupped his fingers and gave a tiny, secret wave. Scotty answered with a broad wink. Then Willy gave his elbow to Gussie and escorted her to the head of the west stairway, while Scotty stepped to the head of the east.

Their descent would be talked about for years—bride and groom, resplendent in matching ivory, watching each other with dazzling smiles as the twin stairways led them down, down to where the stairwells curved toward each other like the interrupted arches of a heart; how they reached the bottom and met in the center of the rotunda floor, as if completing the heart's pattern; how the black minister, Reverend Oliver, from the tiny Baptist church up the road, was waiting there with the question, "Who gives this woman," and how Willy answered, "I do," then, with all due gravity, gave his future mother over to his future father, receiving a kiss from each of them; how the groom took the bride's hand and tucked it into the crook of his elbow, and escorted her across the grand rotunda to the wide parlor doors and a wedding alcove adorned with baskets of fragrant yellow day lilies and English ivy.

The room was crowded with guests but Agatha scarcely realized it as she dropped Scott's arm and stood formally beside him.

"Dearly beloved . . ."

Reverend Oliver offered a meaningful discourse on what it took to make a marriage thrive, on the importance of giving of oneself; the value of forgiving, the rewards of constancy, the virtue and scope of love. He spoke of the children with which this union might be blessed and Agatha felt Scott's elbow press firmly against hers. She glanced up from the corner of her eye to find his gaze fixed steadily on her face and thought about having his children and knew a burst of hope so profound it rocked her. His crossed hands parted, and in the folds of ivory satin at Agatha's hip he found her hand and squeezed it hard, doubling her joy.

Jube sang "Wondrous Love" in her faultless, crystal voice and the words filled Agatha's heart as richly as the scent of lilies filled her nostrils. And all the while Scott secretly held her hand, rubbing his thumb firmly along hers.

Then she was facing him and they were holding hands for all to see, and his cheeks were flushed, his palms damp, and she realized that she wasn't the only one shaken.

"I, LeMaster Scott Gandy, take thee, Agatha Downin' . . ." His voice, deeper than usual and carrying a slight tremor, betrayed a depth of emotion. But his dark, intense eyes never wavered from hers as he spoke his vows gravely.

Her heart swelled with love so intense it created a sweet hurt in her breast. *Scott, before you there was nothing, and now I have everything . . . everything. A lifetime hasn't enough days in which to lavish you with the love I feel.*

". . . till death do us part."

And then it was her turn.

"I, Agatha Noreen Downing, take thee, LeMaster Scott Gandy . . ." As Scott held Agatha's hand and listened to her soft, quavering voice, he realized she was very close to tears. He saw them glimmer on her eyelids and was touched in the secretmost corner of his heart. He squeezed her delicate fingers, thinking it a miracle that a woman like her had come into his listless life just when he needed her to make it whole and give it meaning again.

Gussie, he thought, *I intend t' keep these vows, t' spend the rest of my life thankin' you for what you've made of me.*

". . . till death do us part."

"The ring," said the minister in an undertone. Scott removed the glittering diamond from his little finger and slipped it onto Gussie's hand.

She watched it sliding over her knuckle with a sense of wonder, realizing it truly bound them forever. Then their gazes locked over their joined hands, and within their hearts the vow was sealed.

"I now pronounce you man and wife."

Scott's dark head bent over Gussie's burnished one, and their lips touched fleetingly. The kiss ended and he lifted only enough to look into her luminous green eyes while their breath mingled and the import of the moment settled within their souls. Husband and wife. Evermore.

He straightened, then squeezed her knuckles tightly, and his face broke into a flashing smile accompanied by deep dimples. Her glad smile blossomed in response, releasing the guests from the thrall in which they'd been held, many of the females misty-eyed.

The groom tucked the bride's hand into the crook of his arm and the two of them moved to a polished table where the family Bible lay open. There on a page already bearing many entries, Scott wrote:

July 15, 1881,
LeMaster Scott Gandy
married to
Agatha Noreen Downing

Then he kissed her again, this time hard, abrupt and exuberant, then wrapped his arms around her and dropped his lips to her ear.

"I love y'," he whispered.

"I love you, too!" She had to shout, for the piano had burst forth with a spate of exultant music and the murmur of their guests' voices rose to a considerable volume. Then Willy was there, demanding kisses again, as happy as the bride and groom.

In minutes they were separated by the congratulatory crowd and, strangely enough, saw each other only fleetingly during the remainder of the day. There were so many guests for Agatha to meet for the first time, so many old acquaintances for Scott to renew. A wedding feast was served buffet style and people scattered onto the lawns, wandered the gardens, or visited in the house. Some sat upon the rotunda steps, others on the bois d'arc benches. The heat was oppressive and champagne punch was served as a cooler. Children chased the peacocks and fed iced cakes to the horses. Dancing began in the rotunda and Scott captured Agatha briefly, beside one of the curving stairways, looped her arms around his neck, and lifted her free of the floor, then took her softly turning in his arms with their bodies pressed intimately close, their lips brushing. But they were discovered and separated by guests and the realization that they had more host and hostess duties to perform.

An hour later they bumped into each other in the doorway of the front parlor and scarcely had time to exchange a fond glance before they were interrupted by Mae Ellen Bayles and her daughter, Leta, and A.J., who by now had now become Willy's fast friend. Mae Ellen commanded Agatha's attention and when next she saw Scott he was standing under one of the blue awnings, smoking a cheroot, visiting with a thin man in a striped suit and another with great hairy ears. But a pair of young ladies of marriageable age came to *ooh!* and *ah!* over Agatha's diamond and ask questions about her wedding gown and she had to do the polite thing.

The day moved on toward evening and the heat intensified, the breeze stilled. Agatha grew hot and weary. Scott grew impatient. Violet drank too much champagne punch and flirted outrageously with a portly merchant named Monroe Hixby. Willy came tattling that he'd found the pair kissing in the grape arbor. Agatha wished she, too, could escape to the grape arbor for some stolen kisses and time alone with her groom. While visiting with one of Waverley's current paying guests, a Mr. Northgood from Boston, she restrained a sigh and searched furtively for Scott. She saw him across the lawn, tipping his head toward Mrs. Northgood. As if he felt Agatha's gaze, he looked up and this time when their eyes met they exchanged no smiles.

I want to be alone with you, his long-suffering look said.

And I with you, hers replied.

Mrs. Northgood rambled on about the cost of heating homes in Boston in the winter, but Scott heard little of her prattle. He watched Gussie straightening her spine and pressing her left hip as she turned to attend to something Northgood was saying. Scott frowned and touched his guest's elbow, interrupting her filibuster as she drew a breath. "Would you excuse me, Mrs. Northgood?" he asked, his concerned eyes fixed on his bride. Then he skirted the surprised woman and headed across the grass to give Gussie some needed relief.

Reaching her, he took her elbow proprietarily.

"I believe your wife is lookin' for you, Mr. Northgood."

Without apology, he led Gussie up the marble steps, across the crowded rotunda, and into his office, where a group of three men sat smoking cigars and talking commodities.

"Gentlemen, would you excuse us, please? We're expectin' Reverend Oliver with the marriage certificate for us t' sign."

The three moved off apologetically into the rotunda and he closed the door behind them.

"But we've already signed the marriage certificate," Gussie reminded him.

"I know." He turned to find her standing in the middle of the office floor wearing a weary grin, her weight on one foot—a sure sign that she was tiring. "I wish they'd all leave," he said baldly.

"How unkind of us to say so."

"You're tired."

"A little." He came toward her slowly, arms at his sides.

"I saw you rubbin' your hip, and now you're keepin' your weight off it."

"It's nothing. It always aches at the end of the day."

Without warning, he swept her up in his arms and dropped to a deep leather wing chair, draping her feet over its arm. Smiling, she looped her arms around his neck, while he settled them comfortably, slumping back, dropping an ankle over a knee. A teasing grin climbed his cheek, bringing one dimple into play.

"So. Agatha *Noreen,* is it?" He lazily pulled the bow from his tie.

"It is."

"Now why didn't I know that before?"

She playfully coiled a lock of his hair around her finger. "A woman without secrets is like an answered riddle. There's nothing to guess about."

"Oh, so I married a woman who'll keep secrets from me."

"Now and then, maybe."

"So tell me, Agatha Noreen Gandy, what else don't I know about you?"

"Mmm . . ." She tilted her head back and appeared thoughtful, threading her fingers together at the back of his neck. "Justine visited me today."

"Really?"

"Just before the wedding, in our room. I made my peace with her, I think."

"And so you believe me now."

"I always did, didn't I? I believe she was right there in the parlor, witnessing our exchange of vows. And I think she approved."

His absolute love for her became reflected in his eyes as they roved over her face. He ran a single fingertip from her hairline down her nose to her mouth, where it gently misshaped her lower lip while his dark eyes followed the movement.

When he spoke, he wore no smile. His voice was low. "Mrs. Gandy, I've been dyin' t' kiss you all day."

Her heart fluttered as he satisfied his urge, joining his mouth to hers while she tightened her arms around his neck. His shoulders came away from the back of the chair and pressed her across his lap. Their tongues joined in lush complement. Their blood and skin and muscle hearkened. Their hearts took up an impatient beat as his hand came from beneath her knees to caress her breast within its tight confines of ivory silk.

Her breathing hastened, rushed out against his cheek. Her flesh changed shape and he fondled it with this thumb, feeling its hard core pressing up to meet his touch.

"Shall I send them all away?" he whispered against her mouth, his hand still at her breast, shaping and reshaping her as this day had reshaped her life.

"I wish you could," she murmured.

He kissed her once more, wetting her lips, feeling his own washed by her tongue, letting his hand play down her ribs, along her hip, to her stomach, flat and hard and withheld from him by her tight, satin skirt. Down farther, to the suggestion of femininity between her legs where he was again thwarted by the stovepipe shape of the garment, which allowed no room for exploration.

She rolled close, freeing the rear of her dress in invitation. He slipped his hand between it and the free-hanging rear drapery, found a tape tie, and tugged, then slid his hand inside against her warm curves, down the back of one thigh.

Their kiss grew insatiable, brought the thump of impatience resounding through their bodies.

Someone knocked on the door. "Mr. and Mrs. Gandy?" Reverend Oliver opened it and stuck his head inside. "Somebody said you wanted me in here?"

Agatha and Scott started guiltily to their feet, their faces aflame.

"Oh . . . uh . . . yes!" Scott groped for a plausible explanation and suddenly remembered the gratuity. He leaned over the desk, opening its center drawer from the opposite side. "I wanted t' give you this." He withdrew an envelope. "It's not much, but we want you t' know we appreciate your performin' the service in our house, especially on a hot day like this." He shook Reverend Oliver's hand. "Thank you again."

"My pleasure." The minister pocketed the envelope. "It isn't often I get to perform the wedding service in a setting like this. Definitely my pleasure." He smiled benignly, adding, "And of course I wish you a lifetime of happiness. Looks to me like you're well on your way to that already."

"We are, sir," Scott agreed, then reached for Agatha's hand and drew her against his side, interweaving their fingers.

"Well . . ." The minister ran a finger around the inside of his clerical collar. "It is a hot one, isn't it? Believe the wife and I will bid our good-byes and head for home."

Scott left Agatha to see him out and she lost her husband once more to their guests, ending their brief escape and interlude.

It was well after eleven o'clock before they saw the last of the carriage lanterns flicker off down the road. Everyone was gone at last and the houseguests had disappeared to their rooms. Willy had finally collapsed and Scott had carried him upstairs. In the dining room the punch bowl was empty. The remnants of the celebration lay scattered in the front parlor and on the lowest steps of the double stairways, waiting for morning to be cleared away.

"Y'all wants I should put out d' gas jets in heah?" asked Leatrice, entering the rotunda, where Scott and Gussie sat on the bottom step.

"No, I'll do it. You go on t' bed, Leatrice."

"Reckon I will. Mah bunions is killin' me." But she waddled over and stood before them. "It wunt mah place t' say it befo', but now dat y'all took a missus agin . . . well, it's 'bout time ya come t' your senses. And ya sho' picked a good one, Master. Yo' mama an' daddy be pleased. Maybe now Waverley have some pickaninnies, like it ought to. Been too many yeahs since any babies born in dese walls. Yessuh, too many yeahs. Now come here and let Leatrice give y'all a hug 'fore she starts runnin' salt all ovuh de floors."

He rose and hugged her. Tall as he was, his arms wouldn't reach around her, but he rocked her lovingly and kissed her wiry hair.

"Thank y', sweetheart."

Immediately, she pushed him away and smacked him with mock severity. "Watch who you callin' sweethot, ya young pup." Next she swung to Agatha, motioning. "You next, girl. Come heah so I can git dis bawlin' ovuh wid an' res' mah bunions."

Then Agatha took her turn at being enfolded against Leatrice's spongy bulk.

"Ah loves dat boy," came her scraping voice at the bride's ear. "Y'all be good t' him, heah?"

"I will. That's a promise."

"An' have lots o' pickaninnies. He be good at daddyin'."

With that final word of advice, she set Agatha from her and waddled out the back door, grumbling once more about her bunions.

When she was gone, Scott and Agatha looked at each other and laughed. Then the laugh faded and they stood in silence, alone, with Leatrice's parting injunction and its underlying message drawing their thoughts to the big rosewood bed above.

"Wait here," Scott whispered, and left her standing while he extinguished the jets. In total darkness he found her once more, kissed her with a deep mingling of tongues, and lifted her into his arms to carry her upstairs. In their room the overhead flames flickered softly and the jets gave off a faint hiss. He took her inside and closed the door with a heel and still they kissed, savoring the realization that they were free to express their love in whatever way they desired. At last.

They lingered for long savory minutes of fully clothed delight, letting the wondrous sexual suppression build. He lifted his head and they gazed into each other's eyes. The flames from the overhead chandelier seemed to catch and flare within his dark irises and her pale ones. Their breathing had grown erratic and their pulses drummed in strange places within their bodies. He let her feet slip to the floor and still they stared, while his hands rested at the sides of her breasts . . . close, but still delaying.

"Mrs. Gandy," he said rejoicingly. "God, I can't believe it."

"Neither can I. Tell me I'm not dreaming."

"You're not dreamin'. You're mine."

"No, Mr. Gandy, I believe it's you who are mine."

He took both her hands and held them loosely. "And happy t' be."

"Can wives really kiss their husbands any time they choose?"

"Any time they choose."

She kissed him, simply to exercise her right—a chaste, light kiss on the mouth, but a miracle nonetheless to one who'd for so long had nobody. He let himself be kissed, standing docilely, and when it was over he smiled warmly into her uptilted face. "I used t' like the involved kisses, but the simple ones have their own sort of appeal, don't they?"

In answer she gave him a far wetter one, ending with a surprising amount of suction. "I like them all."

He laughed and slipped an arm around her shoulder, turning her toward the room. "Someone has been here and prepared a few surprises, it looks like."

"Violet," Agatha whispered fondly, her eyes sweeping the room.

Who but dear Violet? She had turned down the bed and freed the netting from the corner posts, sending crosschecked shadows over the crisp white sheets. She had brought up one of the baskets of sweet, sweet lilies from the front parlor and set it on the commode beside the bed, from where their heady perfume filled the entire room. And, irrepressible romantic that she was, she had carefully laid out Agatha's newly made white nightgown with its lovingly crafted open work across the bodice and its narrow blue ribbon waiting to be tied in a bow beneath a bride's virginal breasts.

The room glowed softly in the light of the gas lamps, the flowers bade a welcome, as did the soft shadows within the netting. The window sashes were lifted to the night air and into one a white moth flitted, moving to explore a woman's brush and hair receiver upon the bureau, then on toward the flowers and finally to the white net, where it beat its wings to no avail. Not even a moth would be allowed to disturb the two who'd lie there. All this from Violet.

"She insisted on making the nightgown herself," Agatha told Scott, "wishing all the time she could be here instead of me." He might have denied her claim, but her respect for him grew because he didn't. Because he understood love in its many guises more than any human being she had ever known.

"Would you like t' put it on now?" he asked simply.

Her cheeks flared but she lifted her face. "It's been so hot today. Could we . . . I mean . . ." She glanced at the pitcher and basin. "I thought I might like to wash up first."

"Would y' like t' take a swim?"

"A swim?" Her eyes flew to his.

"It wouldn't take long. We can be in and out like a flash."

She thought longingly of the cool, cleansing water and welcomed the temporary reprieve.

"Together?"

"Of course." He took her by both arms and turned her around, began freeing the buttons that held her rear draperies on. "We'll be settin' habits tonight, habits we'll probably keep for the rest of our life. A swim before bedtime might be one we'd never be sorry we started."

But she knew the habit he was concerned with was not the one of which he spoke, but the one he was initiating behind her at this very moment. Nonchalantly, he stepped around her and laid her outer skirt across one of the matched blue chairs. She watched with her heart hammering in her throat, thinking of the padding on her hip. As if it were most natural, he returned and set about freeing the buttons down the back of her dress. When it was open he kissed her shoulder, then circled her and skimmed the dress down her arms and held her hand as she stepped out of it. When it, too, lay on the chair, he removed his jacket and tossed it atop the dress, then returned to stand close before her. She was fully aware that her cotton combination revealed the vague image of nipples underneath. He let his eyes drift down to them briefly, then back up.

"Is there anything you'd like t' do?" he asked quietly, waiting. "There's no need t' ask, y' know."

She glanced up, then quickly down, and her fingers trembled as she reached for his vest buttons.

"I'm afraid I won't be very good at this." She laughed nervously.

He tipped up her chin. "You must promise never t' apologize at these times. And you must certainly know that nothin' pleases a man more than a blushin' woman."

His words only added rose to the pink already in her cheeks. When the vest was free she stood behind him and removed it—too formally, she realized too late, though he didn't seem to mind. He loosened his cuff buttons while she applied herself to those on his chest. When all were open to his waistband, she looked up and laughed nervously again, unconsciously gripping one hand with the other.

"Pull it out," he ordered softly. "Then the next move is mine."

His trousers were tight. When she tugged at his shirttails, his hips swayed toward her, but he only grinned and let her struggle. The tails were warm from his body, pressed into a network of wrinkles. Looking at them seemed as intimate as studying the flesh that had warmed them and made her heart canter. To show she had some spirit, she sailed the shirt across the room and let it fall near the chair.

But when he reached for the button on the waist of her petticoat, she grabbed his hand.

"Scott . . . I . . ."

His hands stilled but remained at the button. "Are you shy? Don't be shy, sweets," he said, touching her cheek.

"Be warned . . . I'm . . . I'm crooked."

His brows lowered. "You're what?"

"I'm crooked. My deformity . . . my hips . . . one is lower than the other and I . . . I pad one . . . and . . . and . . ." She had stammered only once in her life, after she had been attacked in Proffitt. How disconcerting, how embarrassing to be doing so again, half-undressed before her bridegroom.

But he attacked the problem directly. He put both hands on her hips and squeezed. "Is that what this is about? This puny wad of battin' I feel here? Let's see." In an instant her petticoat lay at her feet and her secret was exposed. He held her by the hips, dipped his knees and bent back, inspecting her. "I knew a woman once who put these in her bodice. Stuck my hand in there and came up with a bale o' cotton instead of a breast, and you can imagine what I . . . oh, damn my hide, I don't think I was supposed t' say that on my weddin' night, was I?"

Long before he finished she was laughing. She flung her arms about his neck. "Scott Gandy, I love you. I was so worried about it. So terribly worried."

"Well, worry no more, my lady. The point is, nobody's perfect, includin' me."

"Yes, you are."

"No, I'm not. Come here and sit down." He hauled her toward the portable steps beside the high bed. "You're not shy about your feet, are y'?"

"My feet?"

"Because I'm goin' t' take your shoes off."

He nabbed a buttonhook from the bureau and squatted before her wearing nothing but his wrinkled ivory trousers. Taking her heel in hand, he placed her foot flush against his crotch, and she couldn't help staring at the unexpected sight. Each time he wielded the hook, her foot bobbed against him. Heat rose in her body and her imagination ran wild. The shoe came off and he set it aside carefully, taking her silk-clad foot firmly in both hands, massaging it. She lifted her eyes to find his rising from the dark patches at her breasts to her own eyes.

"Anybody ever taken your shoes off before?"

"N . . . no." Her eyes skittered down again, drawn against her will to the seam of his trousers, then up his corded arms to the scar on the left one.

He kissed her instep. She felt her face grow hot, her insides liquify, as he regarded her with apparent calm. When he spoke, his voice was unnaturally silky.

"You have very pretty feet. Did y' know that?"

She stared at her white-stockinged foot in his dark, kneading fingers and couldn't think of a word to say. Feet? All this could happen inside a woman while a man fondled her *feet?* When her eyes flashed back up to his, he was grinning. Then he dropped his attention to her second foot, removed the shoe, and rested his elbows on his knees . . . still squatting as before.

"Take off your stockin's. Y' won't want t' get them wet."

He made no pretense about doing anything but enjoying the sight of her rolling the silk down her legs and plucking it off. But he waited until she had finished the task before rising and reaching for the button at his waist. "I like watchin' you do that," he mused, while she wondered what protocol demanded at a moment like this. Before she could decide if a woman watched or turned away, he shucked off his trousers and stood before her in thigh-length cotton-knit drawers. He reached for her hand, abruptly changing moods. "Come on. Let's go swimmin'."

They made the journey in haste beneath the black shadow of the magnolia, along the white ribbon of driveway, across the road, along the dew-laden grass to the swimming house.

"Scott, we forgot the lantern."

"Should I go back for it?"

Foolish question, after what he'd been doing to her in the bedroom. As if she wanted to waste time any more than he.

They swam in the dark, plunging in with scarcely a thought about the icy water or any dangers it might hide. They cleaned themselves secretly, thinking of the soft glow of the gaslights in the bedroom, the thick, high mattress, the filmy white netting, the rich scent of lemon lilies. She heard him go under and come up with a toss of the head that sent splatters across the water. He heard her strike out for the far end and followed. Then they turned together and swam a lap back to the marble steps, with him pulling ahead all the way. He was waiting when she got there, and caught one wet, slippery arm and hauled her against him, stealing a hot, wild, impatient kiss while pressing his turgid body full against hers.

She broke away, breathless, holding him by two handfuls of hair. "What were you doing back there in the bedroom, Scott Gandy?"

"You know. Don't tell me you don't know." She heard the seduction in his voice. "Tell me what it did t' y'."

She could no more have voiced it than she could have kept the color from leaping to her cheeks while he placed her hand on his intimate parts.

"Scott, you're wicked."

"Not wicked ... in love ... in rut ... doin' matin' dances with my wife, who loves them but is too shy t' admit it. I'll show you every step before I'm done."

He kissed her. Their lips were cold, their tongues hot. Her sleek arms caught him about the neck and their wet skins glided sinuously. And there, in blackness as absolute as space, he caressed her cold, shivering body through the wet cotton—breasts, hips, and, for the first time, the intimate spot between her legs. Water streamed down their noses, cheeks, through his moustache, into their mouths, along her back, and over his arm. Silken water that bonded them together like a liquid coil. His left arm caught her just below the shoulder blades, and she flattened her hands on his sleek back, while his free hand roved where it would.

"Gussie ... Gussie ... I want you. I'm goin' t' be so damned good for you."

It was good already, having his hands on her. Even through cold, wet cotton he made her gasp, and he covered the sound with his own mouth, then uttered, "Say it, Gussie ... say what you're feelin'."

"I love your hands ... on me ... I feel ... beautiful ... whole."

It struck her how coupling need not be reserved for rosewood beds with their counterpanes turned down and their meticulously laundered linens—how a body, when incited, might settle for a sleek, wet marble slab, if only this agony of waiting could be brought to an end.

Without a word, he led her from the pool. A cursory toweling, an impatient kiss, and they were hurrying through the ebony night to the great white house that took them in once again.

Their gaslights waited, casting a thin band of yellow across the balcony spindles as he carried her again up the curving staircase. When their bedroom door closed he stood her on her feet and caught her close in a single movement, their lips and arms clinging. The long, plodding hours of the day had served their purpose. Two aroused bodies, denied too long, strained together.

She had no time for shyness; he would allow none. When he stepped back it was without compunction, to free the buttons at her shoulders and roll her wet undergarment down to her hips, where it angled and clung. Cupping her breasts, he lifted them, looked down, adored.

"Look at you ... ah, Gussie." He dropped to one knee, took a cold puckered nipple into his mouth, and warmed it with his tongue, plucked it with his lips, caught it lightly between his teeth. Her eyes closed. Her breath caught. Tendrils of feeling coiled downward and a gamut of incredible sensations became hers. He warmed her other breast as he had the first, his moustache prickling faintly as he played the same arousing game with it—teeth and tongue, ebb and rush.

Her head fell back, her eyelids closed. The awkwardness she'd expected was nowhere to be found. To be a woman so loved took away all but the rightness of standing before a man while his lips ran over you.

He kissed the hollow between her ribs, caught the recalcitrant cotton undergarment, and rolled it past her hips until it dropped to the floor.

She lifted her head and her eyes came open. In them he saw that she was stunned by her own arousal, by each touch, each new plateau of passion he awakened in her. He touched her again, deliberately, while she looked down, a passing brush of his fingertips up her hair, stomach, breast. Then he stood and rolled his own wet drawers down and kicked them aside.

Her eyes locked on his face.

"Are you afraid?" he asked.

"No."

He waited, watching her pale eyes flicker with hesitation. "Would you tell me, if you were?"

"There's no reason to be. I love you." But her voice shook and her eyes refused to lower.

He lifted her hand and pressed his lips to her wedding ring. "Perhaps we shouldn't disappoint Violet. Would you like your new nightgown on? I'll only take it back off again, but that can be fun."

Without awaiting her answer, he crossed to the bed, brushed the netting aside, and picked up the nightgown. She watched him—naked and lean and unashamed—and thought, *I am twice blessed. Not only a beautiful man, but a gentle one. Gentle and patient with his ignorant virgin bride.*

He returned and she watched him, understanding that he was giving her time to acclimate, to study, to learn.

"Lift your arms," he ordered, and slid the nightgown down to cover her, then gathered the blue ribbon beneath her breasts and painstakingly tied it in a bow.

She touched his hands as they finished the task. "You're a very beautiful man, I think."

He took a long moment to study her face, slowly scanning the green eyes, the broad forehead, the mouth and jawline he'd first admired. "And you're a very beautiful woman, I think. We should do well together, shouldn't we?"

He picked her up and carried her to the bed, placed her on the high mattress, and joined her. Beneath the tester it was shadowed and private and the scent of the lilies drifted about their heads. Beyond the netting the moths continued their dance, while within it bright dark eyes held pale green ones.

He had a way about him—oh, indeed, a way. Easy and natural, taking her in his arms and lying full-length against her, kissing her languorously, while his hands began once more the magic they'd worked in the pool. She had expected moments of awkwardness, but how could one feel awkward with such a man? Ah, such a man.

He gave each part of her body its due—hair first—plucking the magnolia from it, laying it on her breast, while discarding hairpins until her tresses lay like a pool of copper beneath her. Lips next—warm, lush kisses in which his tongue invited hers to dance. Ears, neck, and breasts, brushing them first with the magnolia petals, then bestowing textured kisses through Violet's white cotton handiwork, biting her gently, wetting the cloth, and her, and bringing a murmur to her throat. He freed the blue ribbon he'd so recently tied and explored her flesh beneath the gown. Just the surface, skimming flat hands lightly over thighs, stomach, breasts, collarbone, as if memorizing the exterior before delving deeper.

"Mmm . . ."

"You like that?"

"Oh, yes . . . your hands. I know them so well. Behind my eyelids I'm seeing them while they touch me."

"Describe them for me."

"Beautiful hands with perfect long fingers, black hair—enough to make them incredibly masculine—reaching down from a narrow wrist, a wrist with a white cuff showing beneath your black jacket. That's how I pictured them while we were apart."

"You pictured my hands while we were apart?"

"Always. Lighting a cheroot, holding a poker hand, tousling Willy's hair. I used to go to bed at night in my apartment and think about your hands and wonder what it would be like if they did this."

"And this?" She held her breath and shifted in accommodation as he touched her intimately again.

"Ohhh, Scott . . ."

She felt the gown being jerked over her head with much greater impatience than it had been donned. They lay with nothing between them but time to explore.

"Touch me," he told her, "don't be afraid."

He was a revelation—firm, hot, and resilient. And when she reached he fell still. Still as the hand of a sundial while the world swirled on. He took her in hand to tutor her, and at her first stroke his breath grew labored in the quietness of the room. He rolled against her, and away, touching her with promise soon turned to fulfillment. Within her, spring arrived—a bud swelled, burgeoned, blossomed, and made her call out mindlessly as she reached the peak she'd been too ignorant to expect.

"Scott . . . oh, Scott . . ." she appealed afterward, wondering at the tears in her eyes and the slackening shudders that had claimed her.

"That's what it's all about, Gussie. It's wonderful, isn't it?"

She had no form of expression to convey all she felt—the wonder, the discovery, the newness. So she threw her arms about him and kissed him, squeezing her eyes shut. And before the kiss ended the miracle happened—she was at last filled, virgin no more. His body joined hers with the same ease and grace of all that had come before. He rested within her, unmoving, letting her adjust.

She felt his presence and spoke a single word, whispering it at his temple while he poised within her.

"Welcome."

"Gussie . . . my love . . ." he replied.

And all that followed was beautiful. His agile movements, his tensed muscles, the murmurs, the approval, the shift of position, the pause to appreciate and study each other at close range . . . then the beat again carrying them both on strokes of silk, restoring in her once more the wondrous charm of desire that burst its bounds a second time moments before he shuddered . . . and lunged . . . with teeth bared.

* * *

In the after minutes they fell to their sides, replete, touching each other's faces as if for the first time. They lay still as the shadows of the netting that textured their skin, giving the moment its due.

"Are you all right?" he whispered at length.

"Yes."

"Your hip?"

"Yes." She had forgotten all about her hip.

He took her to his breast, looped his leg over hers, and molded their bodies together like the wilted petals of the magnolia that lay crushed beneath them. He sighed, long and satisfied, and toyed with the fine mahogany hair at her nape, and she brushed her fingertips over his back. The moths beat against the netting, their shadows dancing over the entwined limbs of bride and groom.

"No one ever told me before," she said to him, awed.

"Told you what?"

She wasn't certain how to express all she felt—the wonder, the incredulity. "I thought it was ordained for procreation only."

He laughed—thunder beneath her ear. "Violet told you."

"Mmm . . . but not eloquently enough." She drew back to look into his face. "Scott . . ." she whispered, touching his eyebrow, his cheekbone, needing so badly to articulate her feelings. But words would sound paltry in the face of such immense emotions.

"Yes, I know."

"I don't think you do. Not about the years I lived alone and longed for the simplest things, like someone to share a table with at suppertime, and a clothesline where I could hang baby clothes, and something besides a ticking clock to listen to—another human voice, a kind word. But this . . ." She touched the wedge-shaped scar on his arm, recalling the night she'd seen the knife lodged there, thinking how close she'd come to losing him. "You've given me so much. Gifts that can't be bought and—"

"I haven't—"

"No." She touched his lips. "Let me finish. I want to say it." As she went on, her fingertips outlined his lips, then rested beside his mouth. "To swim, to ride, to dance—those are things I never thought I'd experience. They freed me, don't you see? I was earthbound until you gave them to me and made me feel no different from anyone else. But they were as nothing compared to Willy. I can't ever thank you enough for Willy, and at times when I realize he'll be ours forever, it still brings tears to my eyes."

"Gussie, you were—"

But her heart needed spilling, for it could not contain all it had been given. "And as if Willy weren't enough, you gave me a family, something I never had in my entire life. All these gifts you've given me . . . and now . . . tonight . . . this. Something more than I had ever imagined. Myself. Scott, you gave me myself." As she kissed his lips lightly, her own trembled. "I want to show my gratitude, to repay you, but there's nothing I can give. I feel . . . I . . . oh, Scott . . ."

Tears came to her eyes and she choked on the words.

He covered her lips with one forefinger. "And what about me? What do I get out of this marriage? Let me tell you somethin'. When I saw you step out of the bedroom door with Willy, it was like . . ." He rested his chin on her head, searching for the end of his thought.

"Like what?" she prompted.

"I don't know." He captured her eyes again, cradled her cheek in one palm. "It was too great t' describe. You, lookin' pretty as a magnolia blossom, dressed in that white dress. And Willy there with you, and everybody I love waitin' down-stairs, and the house full o' people again. I felt like I'd been reborn. Gussie, I've been at loose ends for so long. Wanderin', lookin' for my place in the world. All those years I gambled on the riverboats, then the saloons, one after the other. You can't know how empty I felt. I think, if I hadn't met you, I'd have kept right on wanderin', searchin', not knowin' for what. You're the one who made me see that I had t' come back here before I'd be happy again. You're the one who made Willy possible in my life and who made me take a second look at what I had with Jube, which was only an imitation of what you and I have. You talk about gifts—do you think you haven't given me any of your own?"

She burrowed against him again, pressing her cheek to his hard chest, closing her eyes, feeling as if another word would burst her full, full heart.

"I love you," one of them said.

"I love you," the other replied. It mattered not who spoke first, for the truth of it was absolute.

He kissed her, and when their lips parted, he looked solemnly into her eyes. "For always."

"For always," she repeated.

He rose to extinguish the lights. She watched the trellised shadows from the netting whisper across his skin and disappear as blackness stole him from her sight, but returned him to her in the flesh—firm, warm, and reaching.

In the dark his lips found hers. The yearning returned, and they welcomed it, nurtured it, and made love once more in the soft secret folds of night. And while about them Waverley spread its protective wings, and while the ghosts of its past mingled with the promises of its future, and while across the hall Willy slept, and outside the deer fed secretly on the boxwoods . . . L. Scott Gandy planted within his wife the greatest gift of all.